Anonymous

**Trübner's American And Oriental Literary Record**

Anonymous

**Trübner's American And Oriental Literary Record**

ISBN/EAN: 9783337223687

Printed in Europe, USA, Canada, Australia, Japan

Cover: Foto ©Andreas Hilbeck / pixelio.de

More available books at **www.hansebooks.com**

No. 243.

# TRÜBNER'S RECORD,

## A JOURNAL DEVOTED TO THE LITERATURE OF THE EAST.

WITH NOTES AND LISTS OF CURRENT

### American, European and Colonial Publications.

| MARCH, 1889. | THIRD SERIES. VOL. I. NO. 1. | PRICE 2s. |


## IMPORTANT ANNOUNCEMENT.

*In the twenty-four years since the late Mr. N. Trübner began to carry out under the title of "The American and Oriental Literary Record," the idea of supplying not only lists of books published in the various countries of the East, and throughout the whole of the American Continent, as well as of European works bearing upon those countries, but also literary information on books and their authors, the value and usefulness of the RECORD have been fully recognized throughout the literary world.*

*The growing importance and rapid spread of scientific research in the United States on the one hand, and the ever-increasing interest which literary men in this country take in the history, antiquities and civilization of the East on the other, have made it appear desirable to the publishers to expand the original design of the RECORD by assigning ample space to literary and scientific articles on subjects within its scope. They are making this departure with the greater confidence of success, as there is no other periodical in the English language which offers such a solid and comprehensive programme; and while they invite the co-operation of scholars in the special departments to which their studies are directed, they look forward for continued support to the literary public generally, who have for so many years accorded to the RECORD their signal approbation and patronage.*

*With a view to securing, as far as practicable, the indispensable superintendence, by a competent and experienced editor, of the Oriental section of the expanded issue, they have made arrangements with DR. ROST, of the India Office, to undertake the editorial management, and they are confident that in entrusting this department to his care they can rely upon its being directed with impartiality and independence of judgment.*

*In addition to personal notices, such as obituaries and literary notes of works projected or in progress, the publishers intend to devote more space to reviews, independent articles on Oriental subjects, and more especially to periodical statements as to the advance made in the various fields of Oriental research, so as to make the RECORD a depository of information concerning the current state of Eastern Literature in all its branches.*

*It is proposed as a first and tentative venture to issue six numbers annually, which will be published regularly in the middle of every alternate month, each issue to be a full "Record" of the events of the two preceding calendar months. But the publishers hope that they will soon be enabled to issue the RECORD monthly; this, of course, will depend upon the success of their venture.*

*The price of the New Series will be 10s. per annum payable in advance, or 2s. per number.*

# Flowers of the "Garden of Fragrance."

[*From the Persian of Sa'di's "Bostan," Chapter of Beneficence; couplet 15, et seq.*]

Of hearts uncomforted look to the state;
To bear a breaking heart may prove thy fate.

Help to live happy those thy help can bless;
Keeping in mind thy Day of Helplessness.

Since thou at others' doors needs't not to pine
In thanks to Allah turn no man from thine.

Over the orphan thy protection spread ;
Pluck forth his soul's grief; raise his sinking head.

When, with sad neck bent down, thou seest one,
Kiss not the lifted face of thine own Son !

Heed that such go not weeping ! Allah's Throne
Shakes to the sigh the outcast breathes alone.

With kindness wipe the tear-drop from his eye ;
Cleanse him from Dust of his Calamity !

There was a Merchant who, upon his way,
Marking one desolate and lamed, did stay

To draw the thorn which pricked his foot :—and
    passed :
And 'twas forgot ;—and the Man died at last :

But, in a dream, the Prince of Khojand spies
That man again, walking in Paradise ;—

Walking and talking in the Joyful Land—
And what he said the Prince could understand ;

For he spake thus, plucking the heavenly posies,
"*Ajab !—that one thorn grew me many Roses !*"

EDWIN ARNOLD.

*February,* 1889.

# The Remains of Pagan.

Some account of these is given by the late John Crawford in the narrative of his mission to Ava ; but he gives no impression of having appreciated their importance.

When accompanying Major (After Sir Arthur) Phayre to Ava in 1855, as secretary to the Mission, my feeling of the extent of these remains was very strong. We spent three and a half days at the place in going up the river, and two days again in descending ; and I devoted all the time that I could to making measurements and drawings of some of the larger or more remarkable buildings in the central part of the area ; a task in which I obtained valuable aid from the late Dr. Oldham of the Geological Survey, and Lieut. Heathcote of the Indian Navy.

After my return to Calcutta I worked up these measurements into a series of plans, elevations, and views on a tolerably large scale. But owing to circumstances which I cannot now trace neither my own copy of these drawings, nor a duplicate sheet which was furnished for transmission to the Court of Directors can be discovered, and but for the fact that the greater number of them was reproduced on a reduced scale by Day & Son, in excellent style, in the Narrative of Major Phayre's Mission (Smith and Elder, 1858), the result of our labours at Pagán would have been lost.

For more than 30 years I recurred to the desire that these remains should be thoroughly explored, surveyed, and investigated ; and this was often a subject of conversation with my lamented friend Sir Arthur Phayre. But whilst the Kingdom of Ava subsisted no opportunity presented itself. This came, however, at last with the annexation of 1885, and as soon as it seemed likely that Government could give ear to such a proposal, I proposed to Lord Cross that the Viceroy should be asked to move in the matter. Both Lord Cross and Lord Dufferin cordially acquiesced. A general survey of the Pagán area, on a scale of six inches to a mile, was made under Major Hobday's direction. And at the beginning of the present cold season, on a fresh application to Sir C. Crossthwaite, the Chief Commissioner of Burma, that officer despatched the most competent of all men for the task, Dr. E. Forchhammer, Archæologist for British Burma, to carry out a thorough examination of the remains.

These lines will suffice to introduce the notes on his work which Dr. Forchhammer has recently communicated.      H. YULE.

"Pagan, 2 January, 1889.

DEAR COL. YULE,

"I arrived in Pagan a month ago, my departure from Rangoon having been unavoidably delayed. With the old year I completed the survey of that portion of Pagan which appears to me the most ancient, and not the least important.

"My work begins three miles to the N.E. of the Shwè zi gòn Pagoda. Hidden amongst the hills and in deep ravines are found architectural structures, some of stupendous grandeur, others interesting as exhibiting on vaulted ceilings, walls, portals, and arches paintings, inscriptions, ornamental designs on plaster or cut in stone; lapidary representations of deities and personages from the Hindu, Buddhist and indigenous (pre-Buddhistic) pantheon. Walking along the edge of a ravine, I beheld a chasm of about 150 ft. depth which suddenly widened into a semicircular space; and before me rose from the bottom of the gorge to the full height of the perpendicular bank opposite a terraced, castellated structure, having more the appearance of a fortification in rocky Spain than of a temple, which once it was, while it is now the abode and hiding place of dacoits and wild beasts. The lowest and the central terrace are built entirely of blocks of a greyish-blue, fine-grained, hard sand-stone, having no geological connection in or about Pagan. The blocks are well hewn, and exhibit about the main portal, round the windows, and on the upper edge of the façade, ornamental stone carvings in relief of exquisite beauty and perfection. The interior has galleries, huge columns, and a central hall. The stone walls meet at a height of forty feet in an interwoven, complicated system of semicircular or pointed vaults and arches. A huge image of Buddha occupies the south side of the central chamber. Numerous niches contain stone sculptures of Buddha, Hindu deities, etc. The whole edifice leans on the south side against the precipice. Apertures from the galleries lead into artificial caves penetrating the hill in all directions. All the hills to the east of Pagan are similarly honey-combed with caves, the interior being in many places covered with plaster, showing paintings, decorative designs, and inscriptions. I take photos, prepare plans and drawings, and make careful measurements of all that is important. The interior of the Pagoda mentioned above has much in common with that of the Ananda: and it appears to me that nearly all the large and small Pagodas on the Pagan plain (as shown in Major Hobday's map) are imitations, frequently on a much enlarged scale, of the temples in the hills to the East of Pagan. The latter are certainly more ancient; one inscription bears the date Sakkaráj 550 (A.D. 1188); but there are older lithic records of which I have made careful prints pending their decipherment. I shall soon be able to send you some photos (they are being printed at Rangoon) and proof prints on bromide paper from drawings, plans, etc. I have succeeded in identifying the caves and temples in which the Chapter of five priests (pañcañga) resided on returning from their ten years' visit to Ceylon (A.D. 1171). On the Shwè zi gòn Pagoda are three indigenous Nat temples containing, cut in wood, the 37 pre-Buddhistic deities of the Burmans. There are also found a large bell with a trilingual (Talaing, Pali, Burmese) inscription, and two large stone pillars covered with writing which were brought from Thatòn when Manuha was defeated by Anauratha. The seven-armed Hindu deity protects the southern entrance. There are also rich etchings on gilded ground, and coloured or enamelled tiles with scenes of Godama's phases of existence pressed into them in relief. The enumeration of details, however, if not accompanied by illustrations, etc., would be tedious and of little use.

"My map of the ruins of Pagan is prepared on a scale of one mile to 12 inches. Ground-plans and sections will be made of all important buildings. Proofs will soon reach you. To Hobday's map I shall have to add three miles to the N.E. and one mile to the east side the whole length from North to South. The survey will then include the whole of Old Pagan, not only the temples within the present township of Pagan marked out as such by Government for administrative purposes. The details of the Shwè zi gòn Pagoda alone will claim my attention for about ten days. Inscriptions abound, and to print them off absorbs much time. Three months more will finish the work.

"I am carefully attending to all the points which you, in letters to Sir C. Crosthwaite and myself, have marked out as needing particular attention, and will send you reports from time to time.—Yours, etc.,

"E. FORCHHAMMER."

*Note by the Editor.*—To enable those of our readers who have no access to the magnificent volume in which the history of the "Mission to Ava" is recorded, to form some idea of the grandeur of the architectural remains of Pagán, we transcribe the following passage from the second chapter (p. 33):—

"Pagán surprised us all. None of the preceding travellers to Ava had prepared us for remains of such importance and interest. I do not find any mention of Pagán and its temples before the middle of the last century, when Captain George Baker and Lieutenant North were sent on a joint embassy to Alompra from the British settlement at Negrais. Lieutenant North died at Pagán, or rather at Nyoung-oo, a considerable trading town at the northern extremity of the ruins. On his way down, Capt. Baker seems to have stayed a week at "Pagang Youngoo." He mentions the great number of pagodas in the neighbourhood, and one in particular, "the biggest of any between Dagon [Rangoon] and Monchabue [Moutshobo, the residence of Alompra], kept in good repair, and celebrated by the people for having one of their god's teeth and a collar-bone buried under it." Colonel Symes visited some of the temples on his way both up and down the river, and gives a somewhat vague account of the Ananda, which was then undergoing repair at the expense of the Prince Royal. He was told that the prince had collected gold for the purpose of gilding it, an intention which the size of the building renders improbable, and which certainly was not fulfilled. Cox also describes the Ananda, and he took some measurements with the intention of making a plan of the building.

Among the ruins of the ancient city, on the 8th of February, 1826, the Burmese under the hapless Naweng-bhuyen, or "King of Sunset," made their last stand against Sir Archibald Campbell's army, which remained encamped there for some days afterwards. Havelock, in his History of the Campaign, notices the numerous monuments, but says : "The sensation of barren wonderment is the only one which Pagahm excites. There is little to admire, nothing to venerate, nothing to exalt the notion of the taste and invention of the people which the traveller might already have formed in Rangoon or Prome." It will be seen presently that we differ widely in opinion from Colonel Havelock.

The account that conveys the most truthful impression of Pagán is probably that contained in the travels of Mr. Howard Malcolm, an American missionary traveller.

Mr. Crawford, indeed, devotes several pages of his admirable book to the detailed description of some of these buildings, and gives an engraving of that which he considered the finest architectural work among them. From his selection in this instance I utterly dissent. The temple is altogether uncharacteristic of the peculiar Pagán architecture ; nor is it indeed well or accurately represented in the print. Mr. Crawford's descriptions too, accurate observer as he is, fail somehow to leave with his readers any just impression of these great and singular relics."

Sir A. Phayre, in his article 'On the History of the Burma Race' (*Journal of the Asiatic Society of Bengal* for 1868, p. 106), records his impressions as follows :—

"In the early part of the eleventh century of the Christian era, the great hero of the later Burmese history, A-nau-ra-htá, ascended the throne. That this king conquered Tha-htun and procured the Buddhist scriptures from thence cannot be doubted. His reform of religion is minutely and graphically described. He had intercourse with India and China. He appears to have established and maintained the influence of his government in the Upper Irrawaddy. In the reigns of his immediate successors, and during a period of little more than one hundred and fifty years, were built the magnificent temples which still remain uninjured at Pu-gán. They show a grandeur of design seen nowhere else from the Indus to the Cambodia river, and have rather the appearance of Gothic cathedrals than of Buddhist temples. It is remarkable that the most elaborate of these, in internal sculptured decoration, if not in general design, was the first erected. It is that called A-nan-da, which was built by Kyan-tsit-thá, supposed son of A-nau-ra-htá, who ascended the throne in the year 1064 A.D. Nearly the last of these great temples, called Dham-ma-yan-gyi, was built by King Na-ra-thú amidst general discontent at his tyranny and extortion, which were exercised apparently to provide funds for the building. It was unfinished at his death, and from its present appearance was probably never completed. The intercourse which at this period existed between Pu-gán and the countries of India and Ceylon will no doubt account for the beautiful architectural details of these buildings. But the designs for them appear not to have been derived from Indian examples, and the fervent revival of Buddhism may, for a short period, have called forth a talent which derived its existence from enthusiasm for religion."

Concerning the general bearing of those astounding memorials of mediæval architectural revival, Colonel Yule has these pertinent remarks in the Introduction of his "Marco Polo" (p. xliii; compare also his notes to Bk. II. ch. 54.):—

"In the Indo-Chinese Peninsula and the Eastern Islands a variety of kingdoms and dynasties were [in the days of Marco Polo] expanding and contracting, of which we have at best but dim and shifting glimpses. That they were advanced in wealth and art, far beyond what the present state of those regions would suggest, is attested by vast and magnificent remains of architecture, nearly all dating, so far as dates can be ascertained, from the twelfth to the fourteenth centuries (that epoch during which an architectural afflatus seems to have descended on the human race), and which are found at intervals over both the Indo-Chinese Continent and the Islands, as at Pagán in Burma, at Aynthia in Siam, at Ongkor in Kamboja, at Borobodor and Brambánan in Java. All these remains are deeply marked by Hindu influence, and at the same time by strong peculiarities, both generic and individual."

---

# Che Bernard Free Library, Rangoon.

The *Rangoon Gazette* of January 9th gives an interesting description of the ceremony attending the presentation to the Bernard Free Library of a large collection of palm-leaf manuscripts, in Pali and Burmese, by two wealthy Burmese gentlemen, Moung Hpo Hmyin and Moung Myo. It will be in the recollection of a few of our readers that the nucleus of that library was formed, some fourteen years ago, by the purchase of the late Professor Childers' collection of printed books. Since then many and valuable additions have been made to it by gift and otherwise, so that the library can now boast of possessing a collection of palm-leaf MSS. far superior to any in the world. The duty of cataloguing all these MSS. will be assigned to the Pali professor in the High School, Rangoon, a post recently resigned by Dr. Forchhammer on his taking exclusive charge of the Archæological Survey. His successor has not yet been appointed. The ceremony took place on Jan. 8 in the presence of all the members of the Educational Syndicate and many others interested in the cause of education, while the native community was represented by a hundred Hpoongyees, and many Burmans of the better class, with a sprinkling of Burmese ladies. A Burmese gentleman, a trustee of the great pagoda, commenced the proceedings by reading out a formal legal document handing over to the Educational Syndicate for ever all the MSS., which, he said, were valued at Rs. 10,000. This document was then signed by the two donors, witnessed by the Registrar, and formally handed to the President of the Syndicate, who again made over a copy to each of the two donors. As Moung Hpo Hmyin read out the deed, a nobleman of the quarter, according to an old Burmese custom, poured water from a golden cup into a silver bowl, to which was attached a piece of silver muslin, the ends of which were held by the donors and their families. The pouring of the water and the reading of the deed ended simultaneously, when the priest gathered up the muslin and appendages into a roll, and left them in the silver bowl. As this was done, the priest and Burmans exclaimed in a long breath " Tha doo," which is the Burmese pronunciation of the Pali and Sanskrit word " sâdhu," signifying the sacred consummation of a deed of merit. The President of the Syndicate then delivered an appropriate address, pausing from time to time in order that it might be translated to the Burmans present. This ended, the Tsayadawgyi (or Superintendent-general) of the Shway Dagon Pagoda made the following speech in Burmese :—

" Gentlemen : Twenty-four hundred years have rolled away, since our Gaudama Buddha propagated his doctrines over all the East. Previous to this, he had been in his successive existences for many thousands of world-cycles endeavouring to search after knowledge. In his last existence, an existence of complete enlightenment, he, as one of the Tathagatas, preached to all mankind of the mystery of suffering, of the reason of human being, of the path-way leading to eternal freedom from care. Following the Master's precepts and steeped in his doctrines, men throughout the world lived simply and well, and felt no pain of regret when their life ebbed away. We see everywhere before us the various kinds of existence. Some are rich, others poor ; joy smiles on one, sorrow overwhelms another ; a third is doomed to a life which is a living death. Yet the unhappy of to-day may be the thrice-contented of the morrow. For all things change—change without cessation—according to the individual merits or demerits in present or in former existences. What then, but a life of merit, can make a man blessed ? and in what way blessed but by the fullness and tranquillity of knowledge ? You, gentlemen of the Syndicate, are fostering in the people of this country a life of unworldliness by inviting them to the study of the wisdom of their past. These ancient records will promote a higher life and, between the peoples of the West and the East, a kindlier life. They will learn of one another ; for knowledge is knowledge everywhere. Our priesthood rejoices that these records will be for ever preserved here, free of access to all of any race and of any creed. We assure you, gentlemen, of our support in your endeavours to establish a national library worthy of the name. Let the language of wisdom—of truth—be taught amongst nations, and evil will wane and goodness increase, lands will grow prosperous and contented, and peace will brood over mankind. It is, gentlemen, our common wish that our Burma may for ever flourish happily and at peace."

It should be noted that the greater portion of the palm-leaf books presented on this occasion had but recently been rescued with difficulty from the fire in Latter Street when Moung Myo's house was burnt to the ground. While, as we stated above, the value of these latest accessions was estimated at Rs.10,000, the value of the whole collection now owned by the Educational Syndicate is said to amount to Rs.53,000.

-----

## Buddhist Relics in Western India.

### Discovered by Mr. J. M. Campbell.

The following letter is published in the *Times of India* for March 1st, and being of exceptional interest, we have reprinted it in its entirety :—

SIR,—Remembering the kind interest you took nearly ten years ago in the discovery by the late Dr. Bhagwanlal and myself of Buddhist relics in a mound at Sopara near Bassein, I venture to offer you some account of the recent opening of a Buddhist mound in the forest to the south of Girnar Hill, about six miles south-east of the city of Junagadh in Kattywar. Our labour and success at Sopara brightened in Pandit Bhagwanlal's mind the memory of the old brick mound he had seen as a lad among the Girnar Hills. He remembered neither its site nor its name. But he felt if we went there together we might find the mound. Leave difficulties and the Pandit's too early death prevented our carrying out the plan for a Girnar relic hunt. Last Christmas Mr. Ratiram Durgaram, who had been of the greatest service both to the Pandit and to me in preparing the Sopara account, went with me to Girnar. With the kind help of the Junagadh Dewan, Rao Bahadoor Haridas Veharidas, and the special Dewan, Khan Bahadoor Ardeshir Jamsetjee, inquiries as to old brick buildings soon brought news of a mound in the Boria Valley to the south of Girnar Hill. There was one great tower, Lakha Medi, or Lakha's Ruin, called after Lakha, a raiding ruler of Cutch, whose name through not less than a thousand years has remained the local legend-centre. Near Lakha's Tower, the forest people said, were many other brick walls and heaps. The news was tempting. Still as it had been arranged that we should spend the next day on Girnar Hill the visit to Lakha's Tower had to stand over. From the foot of Girnar, the headman of one of the hill-foot villages pointed to the south valley as the site of Lakha's Ruin. The valley was filled with deep leafy forest. But so lofty was the ruin that the trees which crowned it stood out of the sea of leaves as if from an island knoll. As the south face of Girnar is difficult of descent, the expedition to the mound had again to stand over. Next morning (Dec. 28) we started for Lakha's ruin. Leaving the usual Girnar carriage road, perhaps 500 yards east of the unbridged crossing of the Sundrika—that is about a mile and a half east of Junagadh city—we entered the woody plain to the right or south of the main road. The path winds through beautiful woods and hills. On the right stands the lofty, almost overhanging, cleft peak of Datar, its slopes to the skirts of the topmost crags hidden deep in forest; all round spread the woody valley, bounded to the south-east by a flat-topped ridge about 500 feet high; and on the left, perhaps the grandest hill-side in Western India, the sheer west cliff of guardian Girnar rises to its crown of temples and crags. After about a mile the path begins to rise, winding up about 500 feet to the crest of Varai Mata's pass over a flat-topped ridge that, lying north-east and south-west, joins the skirts of Datar and Girnar. From the crest stretches south the lovely forest valley of Boria, girt with woody crag-tipped hills 2000 to 3000 feet high. Datar's crags stretch along the west; the south and east are closed by lofty swelling hills, forest clad almost to their tops; and the whole north is filled by the splendid scarps and pinnacles of the south face of Girnar. Except one hamlet of buffalo rearers and a clearing round Boria Mata's temple, the Boria Valley is unbroken forest, passing through which openings or leafless branches from time to time give lovely peeps of the lofty crags and pinnacles of Datar and Girnar. About the end of the second mile the path reaches the level of the winding Godajili, and again and again crosses its banks, shady with the blue drooping plumes of the water jambul, fresh *kuranj* trees, thick clusters of golden feathery bamboos, green or russet teak, ruddy fading *davre*, and aged banyan and twinkling pale-stemmed *pipals*, perhaps a trace of the time when they were the trees of knowledge to settlements of Buddhist forest hermits. Single loose bricks notable for size and perfect baking now and again gleam ruddy in the pathway, and at one side or other thick with brush-wood or coppice swells a brick-strewn mound, appa-rently a house or a temple plinth. Most of the heaps and lines of bricks are too ruined to tell their tale. Once or twice the ground rises in a brick-strewn mound, ten to fifteen feet high and 30 to 50 feet in diameter, temptingly suggesting worn and brick pil-fered, but unrifled, Buddhist stupas or relic cairns. The third mile brings to the shrine of Boria Mata and the dwelling of her rich *gosai* care-taker in the centre of a tilled clearing of perhaps fifteen acres. Half a mile to the west, hid to the last in the dense forest, stands Lakha's large round-topped tower, from base to crest thick covered with trees. From the path 50 or 60 paces to the right through brushwood lead 15 to 20 feet up a slope of trap rock and boulders to a skirt or fringe of laid boulders. Within this boulder fringe the whole ground is brick. The rough looseness of the surface brickwork, the want of marked outline or architectural feature, the masking of bricks fallen from the cornices and copings on the crown of the dome; and the thickness of the trees and brush-wood round its skirts and on its sides and summit, make Lakha's Tower difficult either to measure or to describe. The tower stands on a knoll or natural plinth which, strewn with trap rocks and boulders, rises fifteen to twenty feet above the level of the path. Careful search has found no traces of a rail or other enclosing wall. But the edge where the trap boulders give place to brick may with care be traced round almost the entire foot of the mound by a row of roughly laid blocks of undressed trap 227 yards in circumference. Before the present digging was begun, the mound rose from this basis a massive conical tower to a height of 60 feet, with a surface slope of about 87 feet and a narrowing to 211 feet, or, roughly, to a little less than one-third of its base. Whether the absence of any marked circling path or of any sudden change of outline at the meeting of the conical base and the hemispheri-cal dome is in accordance with the original design, or whether the path has been washed or the angle flushed by bush growth and fallen bricks, it is not possible to say. Traces of a narrow pathway seemed fairly clear round the north-west shoulder, but round the east and south they either entirely disappeared or were at a higher or lower level. This much seems clear. If the meeting point between the base and the tower was ever marked, it must have been by a very narrow pathway or shallow angle. At sixty feet without any marked

circling path or sudden change of outline, the top of the narrowing cone forms the basis of a hemispherical flat-topped dome, rising from its base circumference of 211 feet in steep, almost bulging, sides, rough with great bricks whose outstanding ends and corners alone make a footing possible. With a surface length of 25 feet the dome rises 20 feet in sheer height to the foot of a loose brick cornice or parapet rough with out-standing brick ends and corners that crowns and encircles the top. This encircling brick cornice or parapet varies in height from five feet along the north and south faces, where it seems but little damaged, to three feet on the east and west crest, where in parts it is much broken. Originally, or at least formerly, the parapet or cornice seems to have been in the form of an eight-rayed star, each ray in about six feet narrowing from a five-foot base to a point. The space which this parapet enclosed was, roughly, circular, the diameter varying in different parts from 25 to 30 feet. The middle of the top, in which stood a large old myraboilam tree, was hollow about five feet below the level of the north and south, and two to three feet below the level of the east and west crests. Such a top was too small for either a fort or a palace: the site was unsuited to a watch tower; beyond doubt, the woody knoll was a Buddhist relic mound. The people persisted Lakha's Tower was no burial mound. Lakha had made a vow that he would build a tower whose toplight would overshine the light of Ambaji's temple on the crest of Girnar. The Mother let the vain king build till his tower was several hundred feet high. Then at the end of each day's building she swept her hand across the tower top, and destroyed the work of the day. The king was at last forced to leave his vow unfulfilled, and the beacon tower was left to moulder into ruin. In thick forest to the west of the great mound wide stretches are covered with bricks piled in long heaps, parked in conical knolls, or laid flat to form a pavement. These stores of bricks seem the remains of a monastery and of hermits' huts. Two of the most promising mounds were dug into down to what seemed the ground level, but nothing was found. On the 28th December, the top of the great mound was cleared of trees. On the 29th digging began by sinking a six feet square shaft into the centre of the mound top. About two feet below the surface were found a broken black clay water-bowl. From the look of the earth and the pieces of the bowl, it seemed not unlikely that in recent times some ascetic or hermit had coaxed his friends to let him have the top of Lakha's Tower as his last resting place. Some bones, apparently of a sheep or deer, suggested that the mound top hollow may have been a panther's or a tiger's lair. About three feet deeper (10 feet from the level of the highest part of the crest) appeared a block of dressed white sandstone set on end (3' 3" long by 1' 8" broad by 6" thick). From the foot of this upright stone stretched a large slab (7' 7" by 3' 10" by 8"—10") lying north-east and south-west with a marked downward tilt to the west, its upper face carved with three cross beams and five uprights in the Buddhist rail pattern. Along the south end of this slab runs a raised rabiting (4" broad and 4" deep) to fit into the slip probably of a corner pillar. The end of the slab that lay to the north was much broken, running into a rough point. On the north-east corner of this slab lay a second block of sandstone (8" thick, 2' 6" long, and from 2' 4" to 1' broad), face down, the face carved in the rail pattern with remains of two uprights and two cross beams. A third fragment of rail (16" long, 11" broad, 9" thick) was found close by. Like the main slab, one end of this third block is rabited to fix into a pillar slit. Nine other small rail fragments were found, too worn and decayed to piece together. About two feet below the main rail (12 feet from the top) were 13 pieces of sandstone slabs, apparently paving flags, two of them 4″ and the rest 2″ thick. At the same level was a massive block of stone, a rough half circle about a foot high. The block would have been about a foot broad had not its heart been hollowed 4″ deep to fit some central pillar. The hope that the large slab might prove the cover of a relic chamber was disappointed. Nothing was found under the slab but earth and stones. Some rows of carefully laid brick on the west face of the shaft suggested a chamber. Still there were no traces of corresponding rows on any of the other three faces of the shaft. The brick work was much spoiled by the soaking in of water and by the passage and working of the roots. On the whole, the tilted position of the slab and the absence of sound brick masonry suggested that the top of the mound had at some time been opened and dug into about eight feet by pilferers or treasure seekers, who were unable to remove the heavy rail slab. After the shaft was sunk about twelve feet to get rid of the earth and bricks, it was found necessary to cut a chasm about three feet wide from the centre to the eastern surface of the mound. Nothing more was found, and there was little change in the rough brick and earth till about thirty feet from the top of the mound a carefully laid face or layer of brick was reached, stretching about fourteen feet east from the centre of the shaft. About a foot below this smooth layer of brick, and about two feet to the east of the centre of the shaft, was a carefully laid slab. This slab proved so large (5′ 9″ by 3′ 5″ by 8″), and the upper part of the inner face of the north side of the shaft and cutting had become so loose by the few days' sunning, that it was necessary to widen the shaft as much as could be done without affecting the outer shape of the mound. The widening of the shaft was completed on the night of the 5th of January. The central slab was raised and found to have its down-turned face carved in the Buddhist rail pattern. The ground under the slab was carefully examined to the depth of three feet. The slab lay on a very even cushion of earth and brick. It had clearly been laid with care and kept its position unchanged. But the hope that this slab was the roof of a relic chamber was an empty hope. Clearly this and the upper rail fragment had been held worshipful by the builders of the mound. Could the mound have been raised solely in honour of these rail fragments? It seemed more likely that the stones were connected with the still unreached relic in whose honour the mound had been built, and that the slab had been laid above the relic, partly to guard the relic and partly because of the rails' mystic scaring influence. In spite of this second disappointment, and notwithstanding the difficulty of the work, as nothing but a few top feet of the mound had ever been opened, it seemed wrong to give it up. Before digging further the bricks above had become so dangerously loose that the overhanging portions of the top of the mound had to be thrown down into the shaft and east cutting. When the fallen earth was cleared in the eastern cutting on the level of the central slab, and from 9 to 27 feet east of the west rim of that slab, several large fragments of stone appeared. The smooth swelling upper face and the hollow under face of certain of the blocks suggested they were fragments of the umbrella canopy which is so favourite an ornament of Buddhist relic mounds and relic tombs. Pieces of the canopy passed so far under the north side of the cutting that in the loose state of the overhanging brickwork no attempt could safely be made to dig them out. To the north of the central slab were also some large blocks of sandstone, which were too deeply bedded to be safely disturbed. On the

evening of the 6th January some of the loose and more overhanging parts both of the north and the south of the shaft and east cutting were removed. But on the 7th the bricks on the north side of the shaft proved so loose that the attempt to dig out the central slab had to be abandoned. I could not stay longer at Junagadh. Before leaving on the 8th January arrangements were made for carrying on the work. It was agreed that to secure the record of its appearance before the digging began, photographs should be taken of the mound whose shell was still untouched. After the photographs were taken, it was arranged that the top of the mound should be removed, and the digging be carried on with a much roomier shaft and eastern cutting. Very fairly successful photographs of the outside of the mould, of the cutting, and of the lovely circle of hill and forest views from the top of the mound, were taken on the 13th January by Mr. Pocha, a skilful Parsee photographer at present living in Junagadh. On the 24th January the work of clearing the top of the mound, which had been unavoidably delayed, was started. The work of removing so great a mass of masonry proved heavy. But by the 5th of February the top of the mound had been levelled to a depth of thirty feet. No stones were found in this upper part or dome of the mound. But in clearing the chasm a little to the south-east of the fragments of the umbrella canopy, the workers came across a large stone with the centre bored for a round pillar about a foot in diameter. This slab seemed to have originally been a square of about 7′ 4″. It appeared to be the top of such a tee as would form the socket of the base of a centre umbrella pillar. The two blocks of stone that lay to the north of the central slab were also taken out and found to be of the same form, though less massive than the stone with the centre ground or hollowed as if to fit a pillar found close under the summit fragment of rail. The interest of the public, which had much abated from its first keenness, was refreshed on the 5th February by the news that a large cobra had been seen stealing out from the hollow under surface of an umbrella fragment. Attempts to secure the cobra, even though aided by the State snake-charmer, were vain, and the hope that the guardian snake-spirit might be caught and to regain his freedom be forced to part with the story of his treasure died away. Still, the sight of the guardian snake placed beyond doubt the existence of treasure. A few days after the disappearance of the guardian cobra, and his refusal to be charmed, the boys' schools in Junagadh town became almost empty. Mothers were keeping their boys at home, as it was rumoured fifty boys were to be sacrificed to the great cobra to coax him into showing the thirty lakhs of treasure of which he was trustee, and which were wanted by the State for railway extension. The attendance at the schools remained low for several days. But the plot had been found out and prevented. The cobra trustee remained unbribed by boys' blood, and the extension of State railways had to be postponed. On the 6th February all the stones unearthed were carried to the foot of the mound and examined by a master mason, who succeeded in piecing together eleven of the larger fragments of the umbrella so as to include about three-quarters of the rim, showing that the umbrella was originally about ten feet in diameter. The position of the stones when found and the character of the surrounding brickwork showed that the umbrella fragments had been laid with care in the places in which they were found, but that the umbrella was broken into fragments before it had been embedded in the mound, relic-tomb, or other structure. To the north of the central slab, close to the grooved pillar-fitting or collar stone, on February 6, were found three fragments of three male standing images nearly life size—one fragment the lower half of a figure, a second the chest and shoulders, and the third a pair of feet. As the whole upper part of the mound was now clear, the sinking of a fresh shaft and eastern cutting about twenty feet broad was begun. In the shaft at a depth of five feet below the central rail slab—that is about 35 feet from the summit—four more fragments of images were found, one of shoulders and chest and three of legs and feet. The images like those of which the fragments had already been found were male standing figures, carved with little skill. The seven pieces were found to belong to five distinct figures, of which four were about life size, and one was smaller. As in the case of the umbrella fragments, the pieces of these figures, though carefully laid in the mound, had clearly been broken before they were buried. The work was steadily carried on till at noon on the 11th February about five feet below the under-figure fragments and nine feet below the second great rail slab—that is, about 39 feet from the summit or half way down the mound—in the heart of the shaft the workmen came across a block of white sandstone. When the bricks were cleared round it, the stone was found to measure about 1′ 2″ square and 5″ thick. It was split in two, apparently the result of a pickaxe blow on one of the overlying bricks. This block proved to be the guard or fender of a second block of stone of the same size (1′ 2″ square) as the fender and 9″ thick. A guard was put over the box, and news was sent to me that the wished-for coffer was found.

I reached Junagadh on the 16th, being joined on the way by Mr. Cousens of the Archæological Survey, with whom the Dewan and I had been in communication, and who was fortunately no further away than Palitana. On the morning of the 17th, with Khan Bahadur Ardeshir, Mr. Cousens and I went to the mound and found it still a notable structure, in spite of the loss of about thirty feet of its height and of almost all of its tees. At the north foot of the mound we found the stones carefully laid, the fragments of the five standing male figures, the three-quarters rim of the ten-foot umbrella, the rails, and the central block of the tee. After looking hastily over the stones we went up the mound and, entering from the east, found the chasm and cutting widened into an opening about 20 feet broad, the floor smoothly laid with lines of great 18in. long bricks, and the side walls and back of the shaft rising near the centre to between 20 and 30 feet. The spot in the centre of the shaft floor where the stone box had been found was covered by an upturned basket. The mark of the stone was still plain on the damp earth. The earth was examined, but nothing was found. About 6in. behind the basket stood the stone box. On the top of the box was the broken guard or fender about 1′ 2″ square and 5″ thick. Lifting the fender showed the relic box or coffer about 1′ 2″ square and 9″ deep. The centre of its top was cut in a circle about 5½″ across. This circular opening was filled with a flat circular lid or stopper flush, with the box like the stopper of a Chinese preserve jar. When picked out the lid was found to be an inch thick and to rest on a narrow ledge or hip that ran round the side of a cup-shaped hollow about 5½″ across and 4½ inches deep. This hole was almost completely filled with a flat-bottomed reddish clay stone casket, with shallow hanging grey lid. The bowl was smooth and grey, much the shape of a small finger glass about 2 1-7 inch high and 4 inches across the rim, and with sides 7-32 of an inch thick. The lid, which is ruddier than the bowl, and overhangs its rim, is 4½ inches in diameter and ⅞ inch deep. Both the lid and the bowl have been shaped by turning them on a lathe. Unlike the smooth bowl the lid is scored by five circular grooves in two

sets, a set of three circles near the rim, and a second set of two circles near the centre. Except for the lip inside of its rim, the lid is shaped like a saucer. The considerable difference between the grey tint of the bowl and the ruddy colour of the lid raised the doubt whether they could belong to each other. Examination showed that the lid did not fix the bowl and was too big for it. A handful of fragments of the same red clay-stone in tint similar to the lid was produced by Mr. Ardeshir. They had been found about four feet to the east of the stone box and at the same level. The fragments had among them segments of the rim of a bowl, which on comparison proved to be slightly larger than the casket bowl, while they exactly fitted the casket lid. Mr. Cousens suggested that the shattered bowl was the bowl first prepared for the relics, and that it had been cracked perhaps in dropping it into the coffer hole, and therefore rejected and afterwards crushed to flakes by the weight of the overlying masonry. The clay-stone casket lid was somewhat firmly stuck by the damp. A little sunning and the gentle persuasion of a penknife blade loosened the lid and showed in the centre of the claystone bowl, and about half its size, a small metal casket or bottle green with verdigris. The bottle was almost round, about 1½ inches high and the same in breadth. In the centre of its top was a flat circular drum-like knob, about ⅜th of an inch high and 7-16th in diameter. The surface of the upper half of the metal casket seemed marked with lines which looked much like letters. Gentle rubbing with a split lemon took off the verdigris and also the marks, which had seemed like scratchings or gravings. The box was shown to be of smooth plain copper. The working of a penknife edge along the band round the middle of the box showed that, like the outer clay-stone cover, the metal casket was in two nearly equal parts lid and bowl. The sides of the copper casket were only 1-32 of an inch thick, and through this slender side in the lower part of the casket verdigris had eaten a small hole. The raising of the lid of the copper casket showed a bright smooth slightly tarnished silver casket, a smaller edition of the copper casket, and with the same central drum-shaped knob or lifter. The inside surface of the lid of the copper casket had a smooth purplish sheen. Over the silver casket and between the sides of the silver and the copper casket were damp remains, judging by the traces of texture, apparently of leaves. Excluding the knob, the silver casket is 1 3-16ths of an inch high and 1 7-16th across at the broadest. The central drum-like knob, which in shape is the same as the copper casket knob, is 5-16 of an inch high and 13-32 across. The sides are very thin, thinner even than the sides of the copper casket. The raising of the silver casket lid showed a small round spike-topped gold casket, bright and untarnished, in size and shape like a small chestnut. Between the sides of the silver and the gold caskets were small dark pill-like balls apparently of some decayed vegetable substance. Including its blunt spike, the gold casket is 13-16th of an inch high and ⅞ across. Like its envelopes, the gold casket is in two nearly equal parts, a lid half an inch and a bowl a 21-32ds of an inch high. In the bowl of the golden casket, with a thin sprinkling of black gritty charcoal, were seven tiny articles. Four of them were precious stones—a slightly oval flat cone of ruby, 3-16ths of an inch at longest as if out of a ring; a tiny pebble of sapphire, little more than ⅛th of an inch in diameter; a slightly oval spark of emerald, with a longest diameter of about ⅛th of an inch; and a roughly three-cornered bead of drilled crystal aquamarine or beryl. There were two small pieces of wood, one a dry barkless greenish grey fragment of twig, perhaps of sandalwood, 7-16th of an inch long by 3-16ths in diameter, and a smaller roughly three-cornered fragment of twig of the same grain as the last, and ¼ of an inch in longest measurement. The item in whose honour and for whose protection against evil these six precious things had been placed in the gold casket, for which the gold, silver, copper and stone covers had been laid in the stone box, and for which the eighty feet high and 100 yards broad mound had been raised round the coffer, was a fragment about the size of the little finger nail (⅜ of an inch long, ¼ of an inch broad, and ⅛ at the thickest), in colour streaked brown and drab as if by fire, in fibre not easy to tell for bone, stone or clay. On the whole, the relic seems most like bone, but without special microscopic testing the material cannot be ascertained. It is clear that the relic, whether it is of stone or of bone, must have belonged to some one held in the very highest reverence by the builders of the mound. As in the case of the Sopara relics the extreme minuteness of this Girnar fragment raises a strong presumption that the relic does not belong to any local saint. The building into the mound of fragments of dressed stone suggests that the relic was formerly placed in some older structure which became ruined, and whose fragments, or some of whose fragments, were for honour and safety embedded in the new mound. No writing, not even a letter, has been found either near the mound or on any of the articles the mound enclosed. No coin has come to light. Except the shape and material, there is nothing to fix the date of the mound. Though nearly three times as large as the Sopara mound, between 80 and 90 feet high instead of 27, and about 230 yards round instead of 65, the sameness of the huge bricks and of the style of building with brick and earth without cement, and the close resemblance in the position and in the character and details of the relics and their envelopes would suggest that the two mounds are of the same age, namely, about B.C. 150 or more than 2000 years old. At the same time, following General Cunningham's directions for fixing the age of a mound by its shape, the two-thirds cone and one-third dome, not separated by any circling path or marked angle of the Girnar mound, is from 150 to 200 years later than the well-marked and nearly equal division of the Sopara mound into base and dome. This later date agrees with the remains of the enclosed earlier building. The structure to which the fragments belong is not likely to be older than B.C. 250 —the time of Asoka—and would probably have lasted unharmed for more than 100 years. The copy of the Asoka edicts, carved both at Girnar and Sopara, and the extreme minuteness and costly housing of the relics in both cases, support the view that both treasures belong to the original relics of Gautama Buddha, which, about B.C. 250, the Emperor Asoka presented to the leading cities near which copies of the Asoka edicts were carved. Besides in being without the coin which served to fix the date of the Sopara mound, the Girnar relics are wanting in Sopara's choice crystal casket, and still more in the charming circle of the eight Buddhas seated inside of the coffer guarding the copper casket. On the other hand, the much larger size of the Girnar mound gives it greater importance, which the nature of the relic, if it proves to be a bone, deserves ; and the carefully arranged fragments of the older structure which the Girnar mound encloses add greatly to the value and interest of the find. The presence of these fragments of stone in the Girnar mound, surrounding and resting over the central relic coffer, point to the fact that, before they were enclosed in the present mound, the relics had a home in some older structure. This consideration is of importance in strengthening the claims, both of the Sopara and of the Girnar treasures, to be actual relics of the divine pessimist

Gautama Buddha (B.C. 640). On the 18th and 19th, after the examination of the relics was over, a study of the different fragments of stones, thanks to Mr. Cousens's special knowledge, secured most interesting results. Examination of the umbrella showed that both in the upper and in the under surface of its rim were four sockets, the upper set 5″ by 5″ by 2″ deep, the under set about 4″ square and 2″ deep ; and that, in each case, the socket in the upper face was immediately above the socket in the under face. Through the lip of the rim between each pair of sockets a hole, about a finger thick, was drilled, probably to hold flags or streamers. An examination of the seven-figure fragments showed that they belong to five distinct figures, all of standing men, four of about life size and the fifth somewhat smaller. No trace of any of the heads has yet been found, but in two instances the hands clasped in front of the breast show them to be devotional figures. The base of each of the statues ends in a tenon or knob. As Mr. Ardeshir had already noticed, the tenon of the fifth or smaller figure was found to fit into one of the four sockets on the upper rim of the umbrella. The appearance of this figure standing on the edge of the umbrella rim, leaning slightly forward, re-called to Mr. Cousens a rock-carved relic tomb or daghoba in No. XIX. of the Ajanta Caves in Khandeish, where over the daghoba rises a triple umbrella, the weight of the umbrellas being borne partly by the central pillar, partly by a ring of figures standing on the lower umbrella rim and holding up the rim of the upper umbrella. This suggested the reason for the difference in the size of the figures. Four figures belong to the lower larger group which held up the main umbrella ; the fifth is one of the four smaller figures that helped to support the lighter upper umbrella. This again suggested that the massive square block of stone found near the central rail, pierced by a large round hole, is the tee or base, which served as a socket to the central pillar, the main support of the umbrella. The fact that the tenons on the larger figures fitted into the sockets on the surface of this great block supported, if it did not prove, the correctness of this view. The question remained. Were there more than two umbrellas ? To this the heavy rounded stones grooved on one side to hold a pillar supplied the answer. Of these three blocks, of which details have already been given, the block found at the top of the mound was much the most massive ; and of the two others, one was considerably heavier and stronger than the other. An examination of these blocks satisfied Mr. Cousens that they were brackets or collars designed to rest on an outstanding rim or shoulder round the pillar, and serving to spread the weight of the upper umbrellas. He was satisfied that each of these three blocks formed part of three different collars which supported three distinct stone umbrellas. From these stones Mr. Cousens was able to re-construct the three umbrellas, each hung with flags through the rim holes, each upheld by a ring of four figures, and the topmost surmounted by some wheel or other Buddhist finial. In Mr. Cousens's opinion the whole structure, the tee basis, and the triple umbrella, originally stood on the top of some daghoba or built relic tomb in form like those domed cairns of which examples occur in almost every set of Buddhist caves. According to Mr. Cousens's calculations, which are based on the ten feet breadth of the chief umbrella, the height of the daghoba or relic tomb was about 20 feet, and the height of the tee and triple umbrella about 20 feet more. The whole original structure would thus be 40 to 50 feet high. Mr. Cousens came to the conclusion that the umbrella on the daghoba originally built to receive the relics had from faulty construction and top heaviness fallen and been shattered, and that the authorities of the time, anxious to secure the safety of the relic and prevent any risk of its being carried away, had enclosed the daghoba in a mound, laid the relics in a box in the centre of the mound, and filled in the pieces of the ruined umbrella and rails, partly honouring them, partly holding them lucky and evil scaring, partly calculating that the weight of the embedded slabs would block the progress of any chance relic-rifler. The pleasure of this theory is that, if it is correct, further digging is likely to disclose fresh fragments of umbrellas and other parts of the original structure. As there is still a depth of about 50 feet and a base of about 70 yards to dig through, there seems a fair chance that Mr. Cousens's theory may prove true and that the enterprise and liberality of the Junagadh Durbar in carrying out the work of excavation may be rewarded by the recovery of a building which in age and interest will rival even Junagadh's glory, the venerable Edict Stone. The figure fragments have disappointed the hope that they might show traces of Greek influence. All five images are the woodenest, most club-footed figure heads, with no trace of Greek or any other artistic skill. Mr. Cousens's diagrams and patient explainings have enabled the authorities at the mound, and the clever enthusiastic master mason who pieced together the fragments of the umbrella, thoroughly to understand the form of the monument, further portions of which may be looked for. The care and skill hitherto shown in the excavation give confidence that nothing will be put aside as either too commonplace or too minute to be worth preserving. The opening of so great a mass of brick is a long, heavy, and costly task. But the chance of adding a fresh interest and pride to Junagadh is fully appreciated by all in authority, by no means least by H. H. the liberal Nawab Saheb. The Vizier Bahudinbhai, and other leading officials, including the learned Acharya Walabji Haridat, the curator of the Rajkote Museum, have more than once visited the mound and shown an interest in, and a desire to help, the work. The success of the operations is mainly due to the complete arrangements provided by the Dewan, Rao Bahadur Huridas Vehâridas, and to the labours of the special Dewan, Khan Bahadur Ardeshir Jamsetjee. Than Mr. Ardeshir no more intelligent, careful, or devoted master of works could be found. The relics have been photographed by Mr. Pocha under Mr. Cousens's supervision. Since the coffer was found, the central well has been carried down ten feet further, that is close on 50 feet from the top of the mound. The central shaft and the eastern cut will be cleared to the foundation of the mound. If no more stones are found either in the shaft or in the cross section, it may be neither necessary nor desirable further to injure the mound, which, though domeless, is still an object of much interest and curiosity. If stones are found either in the shaft or in the eastern cut, still more if diggers touch an enclosed daghoba, it may be necessary to remove almost the whole of the encasing mound. It is understood that H. H. the Nawab is likely to present the original relics to the Rajkote Provincial Museum. If further fragments of the earlier building are recovered, it is hoped that the original daghoba or relic tomb may be restored, furnished with facsimiles of the relics, and set up on or close to the site of Lakha's Tower.—Yours &c.

J. M. CAMPBELL.

*Ahmedabad, February 20.*

# Dr. Leitner on Muhammadanism.

A lecture on "Muhammadanism" was delivered on Sunday afternoon, 6 Nov., at South Place Chapel, Finsbury Square. Dr. G. W. Leitner, lecturing on the Islamic religion, said his experiences of Muhammadanism began in 1848. He had studied Arabic in a Mosque School at Constantinople, where he had learnt large portions of the Koran by heart. He had also studied the Muhammadans in India and elsewhere, whether Sunnis, Shiahs, or Wahabis, and had endeavoured to learn their sacred literature. Without a knowledge of Arabic, it was impossible to exercise any influence over the Muhammadan mind. But there was something better than knowledge, and that was sympathy. There were instances of great scholars who, for want of sympathy, went far astray as regards their judgment on this religion. He hoped to promote that "fellow-feeling" which ought to exist between various religions. "In proportion as we love truth more and victory less," says Herbert Spencer, "we shall become anxious to know what it is which leads our opponents to think as they do." Even more profound is the Tibetan Lamas' vow never to *think*, much less to say, that their own religion is better than that of others.

Muhammadanism was not a religion invented by Muhammad, because he only professed to preach the religion of his predecessors. "To walk with God," to have God with them in their daily life, with the object of obtaining the "*peace* that passeth all understanding," to *submit* to the Divine will—this is Muhammadanism, or, more correctly, "Islám." In one sense this faith was like, and in another sense unlike, both Judaism and Christianity. To walk with God was what the prophets of the latter religions taught, and in that sense they were all Muhammadan. But the system founded by Muhammad was partly eclectic and partly directly inspired—if we admit inspiration—from the Source of all Goodness. The Judaism known to Muhammad was chiefly the traditional oral form as distinct from Greek or Buddhistic importations. Muhammad thought the Jews would accept him as their Messiah, but the "exclusiveness" of the Jews prevented this. The idea of Muhammad was not to limit the benefits of his religion to his own people, but to extend them to the world. The religion he taught was Judaism plus proselytism; it was Christianity *minus* the teaching of St. Paul.

The Muhammadans *practise* what we *preach*, e.g., if the Sermon on the Mount be translated into actual life, it appears to be more translated into Muhammadan than into the ordinary Christian's life. The bulk of Muhammadans belong to the *Sunni* denomination, which is guided by the "consensus fidelium." Sometimes their preachers follow other vocations, but there are others who are ministers by profession. No such thing as a pope exists among them. An ordinary Muhammadan would say, "By resigning myself to the Divine Will I am myself the representative of the faith of which Muhammad was the exponent." The *Shiah* denomination represents the hereditary principle as regards the successors of the Prophet, and considers them infallible; Muhammad made no such claim himself, for on one occasion he had a revelation censuring himself for having turned away from a beggar to an illustrious man, and he *published* the revelation. (Applause.) Dr. Leitner then read out and greatly praised the letter of the eminent Sheikh-ul-Islám, of Turkey, to a convert, Mr. Schumann, published in the *Diplomatic Flysheets* of the 16th October, 1888, to which Dr. Leitner referred as a treasury of little known or forgotten facts. In that letter the Sheikh-ul-Islám had said, "On the day when you were converted to Islám your sins were annulled, and only from that day your good or evil actions will be taken into account." This was not so literally, for the Muhammadans consider that the sins of *all* are taken account of; "the objection of one who is learned is better than the consent of a thousand who are ignorant." The Koran also says to all, "Avoid sin, and apply yourself to righteousness."

Their religious books contain instructions for ablutions, and thus lay down that "cleanliness is next to Godliness." Muhammadan rites may be learnt "from the first Mussulman that you meet," which is more than can be said of every Christian. Their alms, which are only a pecuniary prayer, consist in giving not less than one-fortieth part of their goods to the poor, to the redemption of slaves, etc. They are only allowed to give what they are in lawful possession of; it would not do to rob a till to build a chapel. (Applause.) The pilgrimage to Mecca was of great importance as a bond of union, and as a stimulus for the diffusion of culture, largely by the means of the sacred language of all the pilgrims, Arabic, which holds the same position that Latin did when it was the language of the learned in all Europe. Fasting was, of course, a discipline. The fulfilment of the duties of purity and cleanliness also meets hygienic requirements; these duties were certainly not imposed to worry the worshippers.

The rich man is considered the natural protector of the poor, and the poor takes his place at the table of the rich. A morsel of bread is given to any one who needs it, and Muslim charity is administered direct, not by the circuitous means of a Poor Law system. Were similar customs observed elsewhere, there would be no Nihilists and no Socialists. From every Oriental religion's point of view, it is the duty of the *giver* to be obliged to the receiver, since it enables the former to exercise the privilege of benevolence. (Cheers.) Servants have the same fare as their masters. In a Mosque there is perfect equality among the worshippers, no pews being found there.

The marriage contract requires attestation by two witnesses. The husband is to enjoy his wife's company, but cannot force her to accompany him to another country; he is, however, in the latter case, bound to continue to maintain her. When a connubial quarrel takes place, arbitrators may be chosen, and divorce is allowed if the parties cannot remain together otherwise than in a state of enmity. Divorce could not be obtained very easily, as some made out. At marriage a certain dowry is named, which is paid to the wife in the event of divorce. The Christian and Hindu view of marriage, that it is spiritual, is, in theory, higher than the Muhammadan; but, in practice, the family life of Muhammadans is generally the perfection of tenderness, purity, and peace. Whether the *sacramental* or the *contract* view of marriage be taken, the union is, in the vast majority of cases, of a permanent nature, and a most excellent thing it is so. Having lived with Muhammadans from 1848 to a short time ago, he had heard of far more cases of divorce among Europeans than among them. The lives of most Muhammadans afford a pattern to us. Most of them have only one wife, and, like ourselves, they find that quite enough! Muhammad came into a society where *unlimited* polygamy existed, and where female children were often killed. He tried to check this. He directed that they should marry more than one wife only if they could deal with equal justice and equal love to them all. Thus he effected a great reform for the state in which he lived.

The above allegation had been made by nearly all European writers, and he (the lecturer) would examine it. The fact was that, to the very great credit of Muhammad, in spite of many temptations, he preserved the utmost chastity. Living among heathen Arabs, he, at the age of twenty-five, married a woman of forty (equivalent to one of fifty in Europe); and he married her because she was extremely good to him, and was his first disciple. During the whole period of this marriage (twenty years) he remained absolutely true to her. When fifty-five he took wife after wife. In the case of a man who had shown such self-control till that age there must be reasons, other than those assigned, for his many marriages. The women he married, chiefly widows of his persecuted followers, would have perished had the Prophet not taken them into his frugal household. The lecturer scouted the idea that the Prophet had any notion of lust in so doing, and said that if Christians cultivated true charity they would have a different view of other religions, and would endeavour to learn about them from original sources.

Celibacy is rare among Muhammadans. Adultery is punished equally both in man and woman, the culprit being publicly flogged with a hundred stripes. In cities or villages where there are only Muhammadans there are no taverns, gaming-houses, or brothels, nor have they any idea of legalising prostitution. Consequently there are some evils, physical and moral, which are unknown among them. He had seen young Muhammadan fellows at school or college, and their conversation was far purer than that of most English young men. The married woman is in a better position than the married English woman, and why does the latter try to convert her? Liberty, justice, and equality with discipline—these things are held in high repute. There is latitude in interpreting the Koran, which is suited to all countries and all ages. There was a law laid down for its interpretation, that a conditional sentence was to take precedence of an absolute one. Muhammad would include Unitarians among true worshippers; for those who believe in God and the last day "shall have no fear upon them, neither shall they grieve." The object even of their religious wars, the much-misunderstood Jihád, was the *protection* of mosques, synagogues, and churches. War was only to be engaged in for self-defence. Many Muhammadans subscribe to churches, but how many Christians subscribe to mosques? The Jewish, Christian, and Muhammadan religions are sister faiths, having a common origin; and the day will come when Christians will honour Christ more by also honouring Muhammad. (Great and continued applause.)

# Prof. Lanman on Oriental Studies in America.

At the monthly meeting of the Bombay Branch of the Royal Asiatic Society, on the 16th January, upon the conclusion of Mr. Modi's paper, Dr. Peterson said that the Society had present that evening as a visitor in the person of Dr. Charles Lanman, Professor of Sanskrit, Harvard College, Cambridge, Massachusetts, U.S.A., one whose name was not only well known to all Sanskritists, but who had also this special interest for them in that room, that he was the first representative of the flourishing school of American Orientalists who had visited them. It had long been the privilege of the Society to give a hearty welcome to scholars of Europe coming to India. They could say of Europe and America now, Dr. Lanman was sure beforehand of a hearty welcome. He would confer a favour on the Society if he would tell them something of the progress of the studies in America to which he was himself contributing so much. Mr. Lanman replied: I assure you that it is with no small degree of pleasure that I have been received so cordially by the European scholars of Bombay and by the Royal Asiatic Society. I come from the youngest of all the great nations of the world to the oldest seat of Indo-European civilization. But it may interest you to hear that even in my distant land the study of the beginnings of that civilization is not neglected. Many years ago Mr. Salisbury took up Sanskrit and became Professor in Yale College. He had two pupils—James Hadley, who was cut off in his best years ; and William Dwight Whitney, who became Salisbury's successor. To Whitney's efforts and indomitable persistence are in great measure due the prosperity and achievements of the American Oriental Society, which was founded in 1842, and hopes soon to celebrate its semi-centennial. Professor Whitney has done more than any one else for the progress of Oriental studies in America. With Professor Roth in 1852 he published the first edition of the Atharva Veda. Since then he has published, with more marvellous thoroughness, the Pratishakyas of the Atharva Veda and of the Taittiriya Samhita ; and, in addition, a complete index to the Atharva Veda, and a work upon the roots of the Sanskrit language, with their derivatives assembled in groups under each root. His grammar of the Sanskrit language is quite different from the native Hindu treatment of the subject, and aims to present all the facts of the language in a vigorously logical and systematic manner. The late Professor Avery devoted himself to grammatical studies, and towards the end of his life to the languages of the hill-tribes of Assam. Professor Bloomfield is now editing the Kaushika Sutra. Dr. Perry has made a recast of Professor Bühler's Sanskrit Primer. And Professor Hopkins, after completing and publishing the late Dr. Burnell's version of Manu, is now devoting himself with extraordinary zeal and success to the Mahabharata. Dr. Williams Jackson has just closed a course of study with my old friend and fellow-student, Professor Goldner, of Halle, in Germany, and is preparing an Avestan Reader, which will be of the greatest service in opening up the field of Iranian antiquities in general and the religion of Zoroaster in particular to the younger students of America. But not only the literature and antiquities of India are being prosecuted in the West, the antiquities of the great Mesopotamian empires are eagerly studied. The Wolfe Babylonian expedition brought to New York many objects of interest several years ago, and the inscriptions are now being translated by Prof. Lyon, of Harvard. Hebrew, Syriac, and Arabic all find able and enthusiastic devotees. I trust that many of my colleagues will come to the East and get upon the ground what it is well nigh impossible to get from books—the general impression of the land, the people, the customs, and ways of life. And I can only hope that they may receive as kind a welcome and find as helpful friends as I have done.—(*Times of India* for Jan. 25, 1889.)

---

## The Coins of the Early Gupta Kings.

Mr. Vincent A. Smith, of the Bengal Civil Service, has published in the January Number of the Royal Asiatic Society's Journal an elaborate monograph of nearly 160 pages on *The Coinage of the Early or Imperial Gupta Dynasty of Northern India.* Mr. Smith is well known as a specialist, or, perhaps we should rather say, *the* specialist, on this branch of Indian numismatics ; and his article on the gold Gupta coins, which was published five years ago in the Journal of the Asiatic Society of Bengal, has hitherto been the standard authority. It was, in fact, the first attempt at a complete and scientific treatment of the subject.

It must now give way to the present work, which embodies all the results of its predecessor corrected and amplified, and in addition treats of the silver and copper coinage. Mr. Smith has neglected no means of obtaining information of coins existing in public and private collections, and the result is that he has been able to give a description of nearly all the important or interesting Gupta coins in the world. His examination of the series preserved in the Bodleian was especially satisfactory, as it was the means of making known a collection, the importance of which was scarcely appreciated before, and which is worthy of being much better known. Mr. Smith appropriately takes as his motto the aphorism of Saint-Hilaire : " La Numismatique est patiente, et elle amasse les faits spéciaux qui la concernent, jusqu'à ce que l'histoire vienne plus tard en donner la véritable clef, si jamais elle le peut." How much the study of numismatics, aided by such history as may be gleaned from inscriptions, has already been able to achieve, may be seen from the Historical Introduction which constitutes Chapter I. The article is illustrated by four well-executed autotype plates of coins, and one of monogrammatic emblems.     E. J. Rapson.

---

## New Books.

---

*Buddhism.* By Sir Monier Monier-Williams, K.C.I.E. (pp. xxxii. and 563.)

The substance of this latest work on Buddhism originally consisted of six lectures delivered in Edinburgh in March, 1888. They are here presented in a much expanded form and exhibit that religion in its connexion with Brahmanism and Hinduism, and even with Jainism, on the one hand, and in its contrast with Christianity on the other. This design made it perhaps incumbent on the lecturer to treat Buddhism as a whole, instead of sketching out its two great phases, each with its subdivisions, in parallel tableaux. The latter course, however, would have led him into tedious details foreign to his purpose, though it could not have failed to bring out in strong relief the lamentable picture of moral collapse which, as contrasted with the southern forms, religious practice in the present state of the so-called Northern Buddhism exhibits. Ample proof of this is contained in the latter part of Sarat Chandra Das's " Narrative," from which Sir Monier has made various pertinent quotations on other matters, and is given also by recent travellers (such as Professor Garbe) who have had opportunities for observing both forms of Buddhism on the spot. Further contrasts are supplied by the mode of prayer in vogue in both systems; for, while in the Southern Buddhist countries the three-refuge formulary is held to be the only legitimate form of prayer, a mystical sentence—Om mani padme hûm, " om ! the jewel in the lotus ! hûm !"—has sprung up in Tibet, " the constant repetition of which is one of the most amazing instances of the tyranny of superstition to be found in any part of the world." The descriptions of the senseless rapidity aimed at in uttering and repeating this formulary lead one to suppose that in the event of the Tibetans ever becoming familiarized with the uses of steam power, they will apply it in the first place to prayer-machines. Concerning the origin of this formula the author makes the following suggestive remark :

"Doubtless the prayer really owes its origin to the close connexion which sprang up between Northern Buddhism and Śaivism. The worshippers of Śiva have always used similar mystical sentences and syllables called Dhâranis, to which a kind of miraculous efficacy is attributed. In all probability an occult meaning underlies the 'Jewel-lotus' formula, and my own belief is that the majority of those who repeat it are ignorantly doing homage to the self-generative power supposed to inhere in the universe—a power pointed at by the popular Sânkhya theory of the union of Prakriti and Purusha, and by the universal worship of the Linga and Yoni throughout India."

To which he appends the following note :

"I had formed this opinion long before I saw the same view hinted at in one of Koeppen's notes (see my 'Brâhmanism and Hindûism,' p. 33). It is certainly remarkable that the name mani is applied to the male organ, and the female is compared to a lotus-blossom in the Kâma-śâstras. I fully believe the formula to have a phallic meaning, because Tibetan Buddhism is undoubtedly connected with Śaivism."

We meet with even a greater contrast when confronting the ancient teaching with the present practice generally. But this great change could not have come about if, as the author is careful to remark (p. xv), Buddhism had not "contained within itself, from the earliest times, the germs of disease, decay, and death" and were not "its present condition one of rapidly increasing disintegration and decline." This is especially to be borne in mind at a time like the present when some enthusiastic students of that ancient religion are labouring to throw a halo of sanctity round the life and teaching of its founder, and, by clothing its dogmas and ceremonial in a terminology borrowed from the Christian Scriptures and practice, are seeking to place it on a level with Christianity. But Buddhism will never look like Christianity for all that, in spite of the Tamulian saying, 'Water mingled with milk will become milk, and its colour will not be known as that of water.'

A sober and dispassionate disquisition on Buddhism, on the lines sketched out by Sir Monier, will therefore be doubly welcome. He says on this point :

"It is, indeed, one of the strange phenomena of the present day, that even educated people who call themselves Christians are apt to fall into raptures over the precepts of Buddhism, attracted by the bright gems which its admirers delight in culling out of its moral code, and in displaying ostentatiously, while keeping out of sight all its dark spots, all its trivialities and senseless repetitions; not to speak of all those evidences of deep corruption beneath a whited surface, all those significant precepts and prohibitions in its books of discipline, which indeed no Christian could soil his lips by uttering."—p. 541.

"Buddhism has in its moral code much common ground with Christianity, and in its medieval and modern developments presents examples of forms, ceremonies, litanies, monastic communities, and hierarchical organizations, scarcely distinguishable from those of Roman Catholicism; and yet a greater contrast than that presented by the essential doctrines of Buddhism and of Christianity can scarcely be imagined."—p. 14.

The author holds that Gautama did not aim at becoming a great social reformer in opposition to orthodox Brâhmanism, but that he was only the first to establish a universal brotherhood (Sangha) of cœnobite monks, open to all persons of all ranks.

"In other words, he was the first founder of what may be called a kind of universal monastic communism (the Buddhist monks never, as a rule, lived alone), and the first to affirm that true enlightenment—the knowledge of the highest path leading to saintship—was not confined to the Brâhmans, but open to all the members of all castes. This was the only sense in which he abolished caste. His true followers, however, constituted a caste of their own, distinguished from the laity. From the want of a more suitable term we are forced to call them 'monks.'

"This Order of monks was not a hierarchy. It had no ecclesiastical organization under any centralized authority. Its first Head, Gautama, appointed no successor. It was not the depository of theological learning. Nor was it a mediatorial caste of priests, claiming to mediate between earth and heaven. It ought not to be called a church, and it had no rite of ordination in the true sense. It was a brotherhood, in which all were under certain obligations of celibacy, moral restraint, fasting, poverty, itineration, and confession to each other—all were dominated by one idea, and pledged to the propagation of the one doctrine, that all life was in itself misery, and to be got rid of by a long course of discipline, as not worth living, whether on earth or in heaven, whether in present or future bodies. The founding of a monastic brotherhood of this kind, which made personal extinction its final aim, and might be co-extensive with the whole world, was the Buddha's principal object."—p. 72.

"In brief, a carefully-regulated monastic brotherhood, which opened its arms to all comers of all ranks, and enforced on its members the duty of extending its boundaries by itinerancy, and by constantly rolling onward the wheel of the true doctrine (Law), constituted in its earliest days the very essence, the very backbone of Buddhism, without which it could never have been propagated, nor even have held its own."—p. 73.

On the origin and development of image-worship, so prevalent in all Buddhist countries, we make the following interesting quotation :—

"It was indeed by a strange irony of fate that the man who denied any god or any being higher than himself, and told his followers to look to themselves alone for salvation, should have been not only deified and worshipped, but represented by more images than any other being ever idolized in any part of the world. In fact, images, statues, statuettes, carvings in bas-relief, paintings, and representations of him in all attitudes are absolutely innumerable. In caves, monasteries, and temples, on Dâgabas, votive Stûpas, monuments, and rocks, they are multiplied infinitely and in endless variety, and not only are isolated images manufactured out of all kinds of materials, but rows on rows are sculptured in relief, and the greater the number the greater religious merit accrues to the sculptor, and—if they are dedicated at sacred places—to the dedicator also.

"And not only images of the Buddha, but representations of every object that could possibly be connected with him, became multiplied to an indefinite extent.

"The gradual growth of what may be called objective Buddhism, and the steps which led to every kind of extravagance in the idolatrous use of images, may be described in the following manner.

"It was only natural that the disciples of an ideally perfect man, who had taught them that in passing away at death he would become absolutely extinct, should have devised some method of perpetuating his memory and stimulating a desire to conform to his example. Their first method was to preserve the relics of his burnt body, and to honour every object associated with his earthly career. Then, in process of time, they began to worship not only his relics but the receptacles under which they were buried, and around these they placed sculptures commemorative of his life and teaching. Thence they passed on to the carving or moulding of smaller statuettes of his person in wood, stone, metal, terra-cotta, or clay, and on these they often inscribed the well-known Buddhistic formulæ mentioned before (see p. 104). Eventually, too, painting was pressed into the service, and frescoes on walls became common. Indeed in some temples paintings take the place of images, as objects of adoration. It seems likely that the use of images and paintings was at first confined to the brotherhood, and it is alleged that they were only honoured and not worshipped. But the more the circle of uncultured and unthinking Buddhists became enlarged, the more did visible representations of the founder of Buddhism become needed, and the more they became multiplied.

"Nor was this all. The reaction from the original simplicity of Buddhism led to a complete repudiation of its anti-theistic doctrines. It adopted polytheistic superstitions even more rapidly and thoroughly than Brāhmanism did. People were not satisfied with representations of the founder of Buddhism. They craved for other visible and tangible objects of adoration, for images of other Buddhas and Bodhisattvas, of gods many and lords many, insomuch that a Buddhist Pantheon was gradually created which became peopled with a more motley crowd of occupants than that of Brāhmanism and Hindūism."—p. 467.

We should, however, be doing grievous injustice to Buddhism were we to leave out of sight the gorgeous architectural remains and monuments of decorative art,—the marvel of travellers in Hither India, Further India, and Island India,—which owe their origin to those very agencies in the luxuriant growth of that religion in the early centuries of the middle ages down to the end of the twelfth.

The last lecture, which treats of Buddhism as contrasted with Christianity, is the one most thoroughly elaborated, and the one, of all others, intended to serve a practical purpose. To any one who has carefully watched the course of recent events in Buddhist countries over which England now holds sway, it cannot be doubtful that that ancient faith is beginning to lose its hold upon the priesthood and in the second place upon the people at large. The author of this work, as we stated above, fully shares this opinion. We will, in conclusion, give his answer to the all-important question, What is Buddhism?

"What is Buddhism? If it were possible to reply to the inquiry in one word, one might perhaps say that true Buddhism, theoretically stated, is Humanitarianism, meaning by that term something very like the gospel of humanity preached by the Positivist, whose doctrine is the elevation of man through man—that is, through human intellect, human intuitions, human teaching, human experiences, and accumulated human efforts—to the highest ideal of perfection; and yet something very different. For the Buddhist ideal differs toto caelo from the Positivist's and consists in the renunciation of all personal existence, even to the extinction of humanity itself. The Buddhist's perfection is destruction."—p. 11.

*Der Sarpabali, ein altindischer Schlangencult.* Von Dr. Moriz Winternitz. Wien, 1888. (43 pages, 4to.)

The object of this learned and incisive treatise is to revindicate serpent worship to the Aryan Indians, in controversion of the prevailing opinion that such worship was peculiar to the Indian aborigines, but not to the Brahmanic Hindus. The author, after giving an account of the important part which the serpent plays in the myths and religious ceremonial of the Hindus, as well as in Buddhist lore, specifies the various sacrificial rites as detailed in the ancient Hindu ritual, and sums up his argument in the following words: "Many reasons have been brought forward why the cult of the serpent should not be Aryan, not Brahmanic, not indigenous. It is especially Fergusson, the author of the great work on Tree and Serpent Worship, who traces the cult of the serpent to an extraneous, non-Indian influence. He boldly asserts that snake worship was not known in India before the rise of Buddhism. 'We shall, of course,' he says, 'look in vain, in the Vedas or any of the earlier writings in Sanskrit, for any traces of serpent worship. Not only was it repugnant to their own feelings, but they so utterly despised the Dasyus—or by whatever other name they chose to designate the aborigines—that they would not even condescend to notice their superstitions.' I believe I have proved in the preceding pages that we may not look in vain for traces of serpent worship in the earlier literature of India, nay even in that of the Vedic period. For we do not only find a full-grown snake cult in the Grihyasûtras, that is in the manuals of the orthodox ritual of the Brahmans, but also the clearest traces of it in the Atharvaveda, and in the Black and the White Yajurveda, in fact, everywhere but in the Rigveda. And are we justified in ascribing to the Rig-veda, as is generally done, such an exceptional position? Are we justified in considering anything that is not in the Rigveda as simply non-Aryan? As old myths tell everywhere of fiends and demons who had to be subdued by the gods, so the history of religions shows that dreaded demons and evil spirits were worshipped long before prayers and sacrifices were offered up to more benign deities. And whether many of the incantations of the Atharvaveda are not traceable to a more hoary antiquity than the hymns of the Rigveda, whether the mantras of the Atharvaveda were not rather of the mass of the people, and the Rigveda hymns of the priestly caste, these questions will remain undecided till the commentary to the Atharvaveda shall have been made accessible to us, and till the study of the latter shall be pursued on the same lines as that of the Rigveda. At any rate it is certain that the serpent cult was as much as any other, *e.g.* that of the Manes, part and parcel of the Aryan, Brahmanical worship. Indeed, it is as much a fact that we find serpent worship mentioned in ancient Vedic and Brahmanic writings, as it is that we meet with serpents as mythological beings throughout the whole extent of Indian literature."

*Note.*—Mr. S. d'Oldenbourg, who has made a special study of Indian and Persian myths and folk-lore, has kindly furnished us with the following further references and observations :—Page 14, note 3. The Armenian story appears to betray the influence of the Iranian story about Ahrimân and the snakes which grew out of the King's shoulders (Firdausi). —P. 15. The oldest known version of the legend about the snake and the girl is found in Kathâsaritsâgara, vi. 8 ff. where Guṇâdhya is the child. For other versions of the birth of Sâlivâhana see the Siṃhâsanadwâtrimśikâ.—P. 16. In Buddhist books serpents and Nâga tribes are often confounded with one another. Concerning Jîmûtavâhana, compare a number of snake stories in Târanâtha's History of Buddhism, especially pp. 108, 109. For Buddhistic stories about serpents see further the portion of the Meghasûtra edited by Mr. C. Bendall (Jour. R. As. Soc., Apr. 1880) ; Th. Pavie, Quelques observations sur le mythe du serpent chez les Indous (Journal Asiatique, sér. 5, vol. v. 469–529) ; and the Nâgapûjâvidhi, a small Buddhist tract (Paris, Bibl. Nat., D. 117).

*The Paddhati of Śârngadhara, a Sanskrit Anthology.* Edited by P. Peterson. Vol. I. The Text. Bombay, 1888. Pp. 7 and 759. (Bombay Sanskrit Series, No. xxxvii.)

The existence of this valuable anthology, in which verses of upwards of 200 poets are quoted, has been known these forty years. Weber and Aufrecht gave descriptions of the Berlin and Oxford MSS. respectively. Hall, in the learned introduction to his edition of Vâsavadattâ, fixed its date at about the middle of the 14th century. Aufrecht devoted a comprehensive treatise to it in vol. xxvii. of the Zeitschrift d. Deutschen Morgenländischen Gesellschaft, while Boehtlingk incorporated a large number of verses from it in his "Indische Sprüche" (see also vol. vii. of "Mélanges Asiatiques," p. 652). But it has been left to Professor Peterson, of Bombay, to bring out an edition of the whole work, for which he has had the use of a number of good MSS. heretofore inaccessible to European Sanskrit scholars. It will suffice to have called attention to this important publication. When the second volume shall have been brought out, which is to contain "a full critical apparatus, with notes to the book, and an introductory sketch of the literature embraced in it," we propose to return to the subject in detail.

*Sanskrit Grammar*, by W. D. Whitney. Second (revised and extended) edition. Leipzig, 1889. (Pp. xxvi. 552.)

Ten years have elapsed since Professor W. D. Whitney, of Yale College, New-Haven, revolutionized the method of studying Sanskrit by freeing that study from the trammels of the highly artificial systems of the old Hindu teachers, and reconstructing it on a historico-philological basis as the facts of the language presented by the existing literature in its various successive stages seemed to demand. We can well imagine how the late Professor Goldstücker would have chafed had he lived to see that an attempt was made—and with signal success too—by a scholar of established reputation to teach Sanskrit on those new lines. But the new method has not only gained a sure footing in Europe,

it is also generally accepted and further developed by the respectable school of Sanskritists in the United States, who acknowledge Professor Whitney as their *guru.* All these years the latter has been sedulously at work in revising the old, collecting fresh materials, ranging them in the general scheme, and making his book more perfect in every sense. It would be beside the province of the RECORD to enter into a discussion of general principles or an examination of scientific details. Suffice it to say that every page of the new edition bears evidence of the scrupulous care and extensive reading which the author has brought to bear upon his work. We hope to meet him again at no distant date in a field in which he earned his early laurels, viz. the Atharvaveda.

*A Catalogue of the Collections deposited in the Deccan College. With an Index.* Compiled by Shridhar R. Bhandarkar, M.A. Bombay, 1888. (Pages 542.)

This welcome and useful compilation gives in a handy volume, with a general index of 61 closely-printed pages, lists of all the Sanskrit MSS. purchased for the Government of Bombay since 1868, when the search for Sanskrit MSS. in the Bombay Circle was first organized, down to 1884. While heretofore Sanskrit scholars in quest of rare MSS. had to hunt through 18 or 19 un-indexed catalogues, their labour is now reduced to a minimum by this timely publication. The collections themselves were formed, and the original lists drawn up, by Drs. Bühler, Kielhorn, R. G. Bhandarkar, and Peterson : and a descriptive account of certain classes of those MSS. by certain specialists in various parts of Europe has been under preparation at the instance of the Bombay Government for a number of years. As, however, a further number of years is likely to elapse before that detailed account can be issued, it has justly been thought opportune to produce on a uniform plan a new edition, in one volume, of all the lists. The editor has also, with the advice and guidance of his father, Dr. R. G. Bhandarkar, verified or corrected many of the original entries as to the accuracy of which he was in doubt.

*Kittel's Canarese Dictionary.*—In 1879, the Rev. F. Kittel undertook, at the instance of the Secretary of State for India and the Bâle Missionary Society, to compile from all the available sources—printed manuscript and oral—and on the principles of modern philology a dictionary of the Canarese or Kannaḍa language, in its various periods from the ancient literature down to the vernacular of the present day. Mr. Kittel was specially qualified for such a task, not only by long residence in the Canarese country, but also by his valuable publications on the earlier literature of the Canarese people, and his critical researches in reference to Dravidian comparative philology. After 10 years' zealous labour he has recently sent the work to press : and we are able to judge, by the first sheet just to hand, that this dictionary will mark an epoch in the philosophical analysis and intercomparison of the languages of Southern India. The Dravidian elements of the language are made recognizable by somewhat larger type; but great care has also been bestowed on the Sanskrit ingredients: and it may here be noted as an interesting fact that to many of these in their Canarese garb significations are attached which they are not known to possess in Sanskrit literature. The type of the Bâle Mission Press, Mangalore, leaves nothing to be desired, and the printing is as compact as can well be.

Canarese is not a language that has many votaries in Europe. The late Sir Walter Elliot was one of the best Canarese scholars we have known, and he kept up his interest in the language to the very last. The great German poet, Friedrich Rückert, had studied Canarese with the same earnestness and perseverance that he had bestowed on Tamil and many other Oriental tongues; and some 44 years ago he lent to the present writer his MS. Canarese dictionary, a goodly quarto, in which he had copied out, from Reeve's great work, all the purely Canarese words, with their meanings. What may have become of this priceless relic?

*Arabic Dictionaries by Arabs.* — In 1870, the Maronite Butrus el Bistani brought out at Beyrout his great Dictionary Mohit el Mohit, in 2 large volumes. A valuable work containing additions and corrections to it, by Ahmed Faris, was published at Constantinople in 1882, under the title of el-Jâsús 'ala-l-Kámús. In the course of the present year, a comprehensive dictionary, Kámús 'arabi, 1200 pages in lexicon-octavo, three columns, by Sayyid Shartúni, will be issued from the Jesuit press at Beyrout. And last, not least, the celebrated Dictionary Tâj et 'Arús, composed by Muhibeddin Abu'l Faiz es-sayyid Muhammad Murtezâ el Husaini, a little after the middle of last century (see Lane's Thesaurus, Preface), is about to be made accessible to Arabists. It contains, in addition to el-Fírúzabádi's commentary to the great Kámús, 20,000 more words than the latter, and will be issued at the Press of Sheikh Muhammad 'Abdul Wáhid et-Túbi and Sayyid 'Omar Husian el-Khashahâb at Cairo in 10 volumes 4to. at 480 pages each. The text will be carefully revised by Professors of the University of el-Azhar, and the whole publication will be under the superintendence of 'Ali Jevdet Bey, who was Director of the Búlák printing office in its most glorious days. Subscriptions to the whole work (including postage) to the amount of £4 will be received up to September of the current year when, on the publication of the last volume the price will be raised.

The following *works* are either *in progress* or *projected* at the printing press of the Jesuit missionaries at *Beyrout*: Abulfaraj's History of the Dynasties, the Annals of Eutychius, and the Chronicon of Ibn Amid. A work on Arabic synonymous terms, being an anthology from the best authors, to be followed in due course by a volume of philological notes. The Makámát of Badi'az-Zemán, with full commentary. A volume of letters from the Khalifs and the best writers of the first century after the Hijrah. The third volume of Notes to the Majáni el-adab, or Flowers of Arabic Literature, by Father L. Sheikho. (The tables and indices will be published separately.) The first volume of "The Christian Poets of Arabia" is about to appear, and the others will follow soon. The first volume contains several inedited Divans. There is a probability of Father Sheikho preparing for the press from the few available MSS. an edition of the Shafâ of Ibn Siná,—a Herculean task to which few others would be equal.—In *Syriac*, a dictionary (Syriac-Latin) of the classical language is in progress, and the second volume of the Syriac-Arabic dictionary by Father G. Cardahi is finished. Of the poems of Ebedyesu the first 25 Sessions are in type.

The publications of the Jesuit Press at Beyrout are conspicuous for their scrupulous accuracy, which makes them specially adapted as text-books for students. The reasonable price also at which they are sold places them within reach of those with whom economy is law.

*Hindi Grammar, in Hindi and English.* By Âryâ. Benares, 1888. We highly recommend the plan on which this introductory grammar is composed. Each simple Hindi rule is followed by an English translation, by which means the English student is at once familiarized with the Hindi grammatical terms; and one or more examples are given under each rule to illustrate its application. There is a short appendix on the peculiarities of the Braj dialect, with examples chiefly selected from the Rájnîti. The last four pages give a comparative table of words in Sanskrit, Prakrit and Hindi.

---

# Obituary.

---

**Pierre Gustave Garrez**, whose sudden death took place in Paris on the 3rd December last, was the third of the great Sanskrit scholars whom by a strange fatality France has lost in one year. He was less known in this country than Hauvette-Besnault, and Bergaigne; but he had made his mark amongst the savants of France by the depth and range of his Oriental scholarship as evidenced in his modest, but incisive contributions to the *Journal Asiatique* and the *Revue critique*: and it is but right and just that a word of mournful and appreciative regard should be devoted to the memory of this accomplished scholar in the *Oriental Record*, whose literary sympathies are international. While we refer the reader for a full account of his life, character and studies, to two memoirs which his friends Mr. A. Barth and Mr. E. Senart have contributed, the one to the *Revue critique* for the 28th January of the present year, and the other to the November-December number of the *Journal Asiatique* for 1888, we would confine ourselves to a brief record of a fellow-worker, who, for indefatigable industry, strict method of research, and total absence of self-seeking in the liberality with which he placed the brilliant results of his studies at the disposal of others, well deserves to be held up as an example to the rising generation of Oriental students.

Gustave Garrez was born in Rome in 1834, and received his education in Paris. In 1854 he entered the army and took part in the Crimean war. Soon after his return to France he quitted the military service to devote himself exclusively to study. Endowed with an astounding capacity for work and a rare penetration into the spirit and idiom of language, he first set himself to acquire some of the leading languages of Europe. The study of Duncker's History of Antiquity soon opened up before him the vista of Oriental research. He devoted himself to Sanskrit with zeal and perseverance, following the rigorous method of native grammarians, and he succeeded in making himself at home in all departments of its rich and varied literature. The study of the Buddhistic books of Nepal led him on to take up Pali, and an acquaint-ance with the Prakrit of the Jainas facilitated his study of the modern Prakrits, Hindustani, Hindi, Gujarati, Marathi. Of the Dravidian languages, he had acquired a respectable knowledge of Tamil. Zend, Pehlvi, Persian, Armenian, Syriac, Arabic, Hebrew were added in due course. But these extensive linguistical pursuits were only intended as vehicles for profound literary, historical and archæological investigations. And as he neglected none of the other sources of knowledge—travels, statistics, missionary and commercial reports—he was a veritable encyclopædia of information about the East. That information, too, was so systematically stored, so free from uncertainty or confusion, that it could be made available at any moment. But his constant eagerness to add, to improve, to consolidate, his extreme fastidiousness in committing his views to writing, and a certain diffidence as to his own shortcomings—perhaps also his personal independence—made him reluctant to writing books. All we have from his pen are some reviews and treatises, all bristling with novel and brilliant observations, incisive criticism, and pro-found learning. It is some consolation to know that these essays are about to be collected in a volume, the memorial of one who sought his ambition, and found gratification, rather in constantly enlarging his literary horizon by indefatigable, unostentatious study than in publishing books, calculated though they might have been to ensure his name to be enrolled amongst the foremost Oriental scholars of the age.

**Nassau Lees.**—We deeply regret to have to record the death at the age of 64 of Major-General W. Nassau Lees, LL.D., Ph.D., which occurred on March the 9th, at his residence in Grosvenor Street. He was the fourth and youngest son of the Rev. Sir Harcourt Lees (whose father—the Baronet—had won military laurels with the British troops under the Marquis of Granby in Germany), and entering the Bengal army in 1845, he received his commission in the following year. He remained in active service up to 1884, when he was placed on the supernumerary list, and was advanced from the rank of a Colonel to be a Major-General in 1885.

His military qualifications were supplemented by a profound and scholarly knowledge of Oriental subjects, and his is perhaps the most remarkable case of a man distinguishing himself in the army and holding at the same time high civil appointments requiring both time and study and literary attainments. He was at different periods of his service Principal of the Cal-cutta College (Madrashah), Examiner in Persian at the College of Fort William, Calcutta, Examiner of Mahom-medan Law and Persian Translator to the Indian Government, Professor of Law, Logic, Literature and Mathematics, Examiner in Arabic at the Mahommedan Colleges at Calcutta and Hooghly. He was also Ex-aminer of the Military Class in the Medical College, and was called upon, when necessary, to give his opinion on language qualifications of civil and military officers. In London society Lees was well known, and he belonged to the Athenæum, Carlton, Conservative and other Clubs. A Tory in politics, he twice sought election for Parliament, on both occasions, however, suffering defeat.

As an author Lees was perhaps best known through his Commentary of "Az-Zamakhshari," a most valuable exegesis of the Coran, which made his name not only famous among Arabic scholars, but elicited also a handsome acknowledgment from the Shah of Persia. His editions of Persian and Arabic authors were very numerous, and we shall give in our next issue as far as possible a complete list of his works. Most remark-able among his Persian editions are the "Nafa-tátu 'l-Uns" of Jámí and the "Vís u Rámíu" of Fakhru 'd-dín As'ad Jurjáni. He was the author also of a series of Arabic and Persian Elementary School Books which were for a long time universally adopted in India. On every question almost referring to the East Lees has written at different times—on Land and Labour; on the drain of Silver to the East; on Tea, Cinchona; on the Sale of Waste Lands, etc., etc. He received innumerable distinctions at home and abroad, and was esteemed by all who in his various pursuits chanced to meet him. He was a corresponding member of the Imperial Academy of Sciences of Göttingen, and of the German Oriental Society of Berlin.

---

# Oriental Notes.

---

**Sanskrit MSS. in Oudh.**—We have received Pandita Devi Prasáda's Catalogue of Sanskrit MSS. existing in Oudh Province for the year 1887, compiled by order of Government, N.W. Provinces and Oudh. It is printed at the Government press, Alhahabad. It deals with MSS. of hymns, ceremonials, theo-logy, rituals, ancient legends, language, versification, rhetoric, astronomy, astrology, law, philosophy, medicine, Jain religion, etc.

**Vedanta Philosophy.**—The first number of a new periodical devoted entirely to the doctrine of Advaita, and published by the Hindu Union Press, has just reached us from the Saidapet, in the Madras Presidency. It contains, besides an article entitled "Ourselves," in which the aims of this new under-taking are explained, papers on "The Two Ways of Contem-plation," "Mumukshutva," "The Rationale of Prayer," "The Opponents of Vedanta," "The Province of Philosophy," "Questions on Bhagavad Gita," and "Jottings." The follow-ing works on the "Vedanta Philosophy" are also announced as in preparation:—1. "Outlines of Advaita Philosophy," translation of a small text-book, with exhaustive comments, glossary, etc. 2. "The Seven Stages of Vedanta," a trans-lation of a recognized treatise, with notes. 3. "Vedanta Catechism," a translation of a standard text-book, with notes, etc. 4. "Compendium of Advaita Philosophy," translation of a standard work, with notes, glossary, etc.

**Colombo Museum.**—We have received the Administration Report of the Colombo Museum for the year 1887, compiled by Mr. A. Haly, Director, and Mr. V. H. M. Corbet, Librarian, which shows a very prosperous state of affairs in what is one of the most interesting institutions of its kind. There is not only noticeable a considerable increase in the attendance of readers, but outside students have also more extensively availed them-selves of the liberality of the trustees in allowing them to borrow books for their private studies. As far as the library is concerned, the staff seems somewhat hampered by overwork in making satisfactory progress with the necessary task of cataloguing. The librarian gives a list of the accessions during the year, and also comments upon the Ola MSS. acquired by special vote of the Ceylonese Government during the years 1870-82. Incidentally it is mentioned that a translation of Juan Rodriguez de Saa y Menezes' "Rebelion de Ceylan, y les progressos de su conquista en el gobierno de Constantino de Saa y Norona" (printed at Lisbon in 1861), which was com-menced by Mr. Corbet, is in course of being completed by Major St. George.

ASIATIC SOCIETY OF BENGAL.—As an extra number of this Journal, Prof. Grierson will publish "Materials for the Modern Literary History of Hindūstān." The volume will contain notices of over nine hundred authors, dating from about the year 700 A.D. down to the present day, of whom only about seventy have been dealt with by Garcin de Tassy. The Geographical limits of the work are Rājputānā and the Gangetic plain as far East as Bhāgalpur. It deals only with vernacular authors who wrote in a stage of language later than that which is commonly considered as Prākṛit, and excludes from consideration those who only wrote in the exotic Urdū. Many of the nine hundred names mentioned are, of course, little more than entries in a catalogue, but the author has succeeded in collecting particulars hitherto unpublished in any European language concerning a large proportion.

HINDU PANTHEISM. — A revised edition will shortly be published of the *Manual of Hindu Pantheism*, which appeared seven years ago in Trübner's Oriental Series. During the interval that has elapsed, the author has devoted his leisure time to the study of the Upanishad literature in India, and has thereby been enabled to improve the book. The notes have been carefully corrected, and, in many cases, enlarged. The original text, too, which forms the basis of the work, has been collated with several manuscripts, and the translations modified accordingly. English students will probably find this to be one of the most useful aids to a right understanding of Vedantic doctrines.

PALI.—Three native works on Pali Grammar not printed before, we believe, have recently appeared in Ceylon :—

1. Padasādhana, an ancient work by the Monk Piyadassi, Sastradhara Press, Colombo.

2. Cabdabindu, with Sinhalese Commentary.

3. Bālappabodhana, with Pali Commentary.

The last two were published at the Vidyodaya College, Colombo.

———

On the eve of going to press we have received the following *Preliminary Prospectus* of an *International Society for the Scientific Study of the Philippine Islands.* We propose to revert to the subject in detail in our next issue.

## ASSOCIATION INTERNATIONALE DES PHILIPPINISTES.

### I.

Le but de cette Association est l'étude des Philippines sous un point de vue scientifique et historique, avec ce propos l'Association devra

1ᵗᵉʳᵐᵉⁿᵗ Convoquer des Congrès internationaux.

2°. Ouvrir des concours publics sur des théses en rapport avec le but de l'Association.

3°. Travailler à la formation d'une bibliothèque et d'un musée d'objets philippinois.

4°. Publier des ouvrages, mémoires, etc.

### II.

L'Association sera composée de membres fondateurs et de tous ceux que le Comité de Direction voudra bien admettre.

Le Comité Directive qui dirigera l'Association sera formé par un Président, cinq Conseillers et un Secrétaire général, chacun appartenant à une nationalité différente (Autriche, Angleterre, Allemagne, Espagne, France, Hollande, et Philippines).

*Président*—Prof. F. Blumentritt.

*Conseillers*—Dr. R. Rost.     Dr. Planchut.
   „ A. B. Meyer.     „ Riedel,
   „ A. Regidor.

*Secrétaire*—Dr. T. Rizol.

We have also just received the prospectus of the Eighth International Congress of Orientalists which will be held at Stockholm and at Christiania from the 2nd to the 13th of September, 1889, under the patronage of His Majesty the King of Sweden and Norway, Oscar II. Full particulars will be given in our next issue, and we now only mention that it will consist of the following Sections, in which English, French, German, Italian, Latin and the Eastern Languages will be admissible :

1. Semitic and of the Islam.
2. Arian.
3. African, including Egyptology.
4. Central Asia and the Far East.
5. Malay and Polynesia.

———

## American Notes.

———

AN INTERNATIONAL LANGUAGE.—The American Philosophical Society's Committee appointed to consider an International Language have made a Supplementary Report in which they answer Mr. Alexander J. Ellis's strictures on their proposal for a Congress to consider the question. The same Supplementary report also reviews all works that have appeared on the subject since the first report was issued, and reiterates the radical objections to Volapük as a universal language. Up to the present about twenty societies have expressed their willingness to send representatives to a Congress should one be convened.

PROFIT SHARING.—The problem how to bring employers of labour and their employés into relations of harmony and mutual helpfulness is one of the great questions of the day. The favour with which leading economists, at home and abroad, regard the method of a division of profits between the two parties to the labour contract, as a means to this end, is well known. John Stuart Mill, Henry Fawcett, Francis A. Walker, and Carroll D. Wright—to name no others—consider this system of "industrial partnership" worthy of wide and careful trial. Thus far there has been a deficiency of full and exact information for those interested. Mr. Nicholas P. Gilman, editor of the *Literary World* of Boston, has made a thorough examination of the subject, and a book will soon be published by him (Houghton, Mifflin and Co.) entitled "Profit Sharing between Employer and Employé: a Study in the Evolution of the Wages System." The book contains an exhaustive account of the application of the method to a great variety of industries in France, Germany, England and the United States, interesting biographical sketches of Leclaire, Godin, Boucicaut and other noted industrialists who have developed it, an examination of the results actually achieved, and a candid argument in favour of its further extension. The volume will undoubtedly attract wide attention as the first comprehensive work on Profit Sharing in our language. Written in popular style, and giving an impartial statement of all the facts of the matter down to the present year, it should not be confounded with the numerous books on the "labour question" which propose, with no little crudeness, impracticable remedies for the entire regeneration of modern society. The work is a study, on the inductive method, of what has been done on one line of social improvement, and it keeps closely to this line.

BUREAU OF EDUCATION.—A very important "Circular of Information" (No. 5, 1888) has been issued by the Hon. H. R. Dawson, the Commissioner of Education for the U. S. A. It is by the Rev. A. D. Mayo on "Industrial Education in the South." The author of this "Circular" has been engaged for the past eight years in the cause of education through all the Southern States, though not in any official or government capacity. From his connection with and knowledge of the scholastic needs of the Southern States, he was invited by the

Bureau of Education to compile this monograph, which was afterwards ordered by Congress to be printed. The Rev. Mr. Mayo commences by stating the purposes of the essay; he then discusses the conditions of American and Southern life, the Southern resources, rising industries, the disadvantages of the existing labour system, illiteracy, etc., showing general education to be a prime need. He gives a statement of Southern achievements in popular education, industrial schools, manual and industrial training in public schools and private academies, with the means and methods of promoting and improving such training. The Appendixes contain views and descriptions of the leading Southern educational institutions which have adopted industrial training.

THE SOURCES OF THE MISSISSIPPI.—Since our paragraph appeared on Captain Glazier's claims to the discovery of the real source of the Mississippi, we have received a report read before the Minnesota Historical Society, by the Hon. H. James Baker, on the "Sources of the Mississippi; their Discoverers Real and Pretended." In this report Captain Glazier's exploration is stated to have been a mere pleasure excursion, and at the time he made it the Government surveyors of the United States were actually corroborating the discoveries of Schoolcraft and Nicollet. From all reliable data at hand it appears that Captain Glazier re-discovered Elk Lake, a well-known sheet of water, and named it after himself.

TENTH CENSUS OF THE UNITED STATES. — The United States Tenth Census of 1880 is now rapidly approaching completion. Volumes 17 and 19 are now before us. The former consists of Part II. of the Water-Power of the United States, with articles on the Water-Power of the North-West, and of the Mississippi and some of its tributaries, by James L. Greenleaf, C.E., etc. The Water-Power of the region tributary to the Mississippi River on the West below Dubuque, and the Ohio River basin and the Ohio State Canals by Dwight Porter, Ph.B., etc. Mr. W. G. Elliot, C.E., etc., etc., contributes an article on the Water-Supply of certain cities and towns of the United States. The latter volume, compiled by Mr. George E. Waring, jun., contains Part II. of the Social Statistics of Cities divided into two parts; part one being on the New England and Middle States, and part two on the Southern and Western States. The historical sketches in this volume of the District of Columbia are particularly interesting; the ground now occupied by the city of Georgetown was visited in 1608 by Captain John Smith, the famous navigator, who met the Indians in conference. The town was laid out on February 27th, 1752, in eighty lots, with streets and lanes, and was named in honour of King George the Second of England, by his faithful subjects the colonists. The city of Washington (of magnificent distances) was a creation of a later date, an Act being approved by President Washington, July 16th, 1790, and in 1791 Commissions were appointed to superintend the affairs of the new city.

JOSEPH JONES, OF VIRGINIA.—The letters of comparatively unimportant personages often throw considerable light on the history of the times in which they lived, but Joseph Jones, of Virginia, whose letters the Hon. Worthington C. Ford, of the Department of State, Washington, has edited, cannot be said to have been an unimportant person, although, as the editor of his "Letters" says, few details of his life are accessible. He was born in 1727, and became a representative of King George County, Va., in the Colonial House of Burgesses. At the outbreak of the War of Independence he was a member of the Committee of Safety, and in 1776 served in the Virginia Convention. In 1777 he represented his native State in the Continental Congress, but this he resigned to accept the position of Judge of the General Court (January 29, 1778). He served in Congress again from 1780 to 1783. In 1788 he was again a member of the Virginia Convention and in 1789 he again served on the bench. His death took place October 28, 1805. The letters that Mr. Ford has edited cover a period of ten years, being from 1777 to 1787, and are to Washington, Madison, Jefferson. The first letter to Washington relates to a Captain Munroe and recruiting in Virginia. It is of interest to note that this Captain James Munroe was the son of Elizabeth, the sister of Joseph Jones, the writer of the letters, and Spence Munroe, and this Captain Munroe afterwards became President of the United States. The last letter in the volume from Jones to Madison relates to the continued

session of Convention and to the decision of the Legislature of Virginia to accept the payment of the taxes in tobacco in consequence of the scarcity of specie, and the inadvisability of issuing more paper money. Only 250 copies have been printed of this highly interesting collection of letters.

BRITISH GUIANA.—"Timehri," the journal of the Royal Agricultural and Commercial Society of British Guiana, vol. ii. new series, part 2, December, 1888, contains several papers on this interesting colony, which we have no doubt when fully explored will become one of the great gold-producing countries of the world. We believe Governor Schomburg was the first writer who called attention to the resources of this wonderfully fertile portion of South America.

A CODE OF MORALS.—Mr. John S. Hittell, author of several works on California, has brought out with the Bancroft Company, San Francisco, "A Code of Morals," in which he says he has attempted to do for his own age what Epictetus and Marcus Aurelius did for theirs. He divides his "Code" into "Individual Duties," "Social Duties," "Industrial Duties," "Political Duties," and "Religious Duties."

GEOLOGY.—"Shall we Teach Geology?" which is a question that has been lately coming to the front in the systems of modern education, is the title of a small volume by Prof. Alex. Winchell, A.M., F.G.S.A., etc., published by Messrs. S. C. Griggs & Co., of Chicago. We presume geology is a subject which will at some future day form part of the curriculum of the schools; but whilst Geography, the science of the Earth's surface, is so much neglected, we can scarcely expect the interior to be studied. We believe that writing lately from one of the universities some one said: "We have just established a Chair of Geography, but as yet we have no books, no maps, and no lecture-hall." A literary note before us says:—"A contest has long been waged among educators as to which is of greater practical value in education, the Classics or the Sciences. For many years the friends of the Classics had it pretty much their own way, but of late the Scientists have been putting in some strong pleas in behalf of their side of the case. The latest of these, about to be issued in book form by S. C. Griggs & Co., Chicago, is by the well-known author and scientist, Dr. Alexander Winchell, University of Michigan, and is entitled, 'Shall we Teach Geology'? Few, if any, American writers are better qualified for discussing this question than Dr. Winchell. While his treatise is a special plea for teaching Geology in the public schools, it is intended to cover the whole ground of contest between the Sciences and the Classics, and hence promises to be of great interest not only to teachers, but to all who are interested in observing the tendencies of modern education."

CURRENCY OF THE U.S.—The annual Report of the Comptroller of the Currency to the Second Session of the Fiftieth Congress of the United States, December 1, 1888, consists of two volumes, the second—a volume of over eleven hundred pages—is a tabular account of the condition of the National Banks, up to Thursday, October 4th, 1888. From the numerical index of banks which, with an index of towns, will be found in this volume, we learn that 3924 have been registered since the national banking system came into operation.

SHAKESPERIANA.—This Magazine, which is just commencing its sixth volume, will still be published by the Leonard Scott Publication Company, who have now removed back to New York, but it has now become the acknowledged organ of the New York Shakespeare Society.

———

## European Notes.

———

THE PHILOSOPHY OF MYSTICISM (London, George Redway, York Street, Covent Garden.)—Three or four years ago Baron Carl du Prel, Doctor of Philosophy, published a work on Physical Philosophy, treating on dreams, somnambulism, memory, and the doctrine of the soul, which attracted the attention of Edward von Hartmann, who in his work on the "Moderne Probleme" devotes a considerable space to the review of Du Prel's "Philosophy of Mysticism," which is the English title of the above work, and at the same time a literal translation as near as possible of that of the German volume. Mr. C. C. Massey has translated this work in two volumes containing over six hundred pages. It will be a welcome addition to the literature of psychical research, a subject which, since the Psychical Society has been established, has attracted many inquiring students.

PRACTICAL HERALDRY, (London, George Redway, York Street, Covent Garden).—Charles Worthy, Esq., who was for some time principal assistant to the late Somerset Herald, has issued an excellent little work on "Practical Heraldry, or an Epitome of English Armoury," which is a useful manual of the subject. It contains 124 illustrations to the text from designs by the author.

A DICTIONARY OF PHOTOGRAPHY.—Mr. E. J. Wall, who contributed to the "Amateur Photographer" a Dictionary of Photography,' which ran through a series of numbers of that journal, has now revised it, brought it down to the present time, and published it with Messrs. Hazel, Watson, and Viney (Limited), Long Acre. Of course such a book is best tested by practice, but from looking through it we should think it is a very good encyclopædia of the photographic art, and contains matter that to procure in some other forms would cost one hundred times more than the cost of this Dictionary.

PROBLEMS OF THE HIDDEN LIFE.—This is the title of a volume of essays on the ethics of spiritual evolution by "Pilgrim," published by George Redway, Covent Garden. It is dedicated "to all lovers of the perfect." This is one of the occult books now so fashionable, but we really do not see that it brings us any nearer to perfection or to Nirvana, of which it discourses. Some of the matter in it is good, especially the quotations from the poems of Sir Edwin Arnold.

THE GOVERNMENT YEAR BOOK.—Under this title Mr. Fisher Unwin has published a very useful reference annual edited by Mrs. Lewis Sergeant. A record of the forms and methods of government of Great Britain, her colonies and foreign countries. The Government Year Book covers somewhat the same ground as the Statesman's Year Book, is carefully compiled, and costs very little more than half the price of that publication.

AMUSING CHAP-BOOKS.—Mr. Robert Hays Cunningham has made a collection of Amusing Prose Chap-Books, chiefly of the last century (Glasgow, Thos. D. Morrison). The eighteenth century might be called the chap-book era, and the trade employed thousands of producers and distributors and, it appears to have been a profitable trade, as one publisher is known to have retired with a fortune of £30,000 when money was more valuable and its purchasing power much greater than at the present time. In this collection of Chap-books we find some old favourites such as "The King and the Cobbler," "Jack the Giant Killer," "Bamfylde Moore Carew," "Dick Whittington," "Blue Beard," "Robin Hood." etc. Mr. Cunningham contemplates making a collection of Poetical Chap-books. Such collections are the means of preserving the folk-lore of our ancestors which would be unavoidably lost to posterity were it not for such collectors and editors as Mr. Cunningham. Chap-books having been the literature of the lower classes, the future historian has through them an insight into their tastes brought readily to his hand.

THE BOOK LOVERS' LIBRARY (Elliot Stock).—The new volume of this Library is by Mr. Edward Smith, being notes on the books and opinions in the last three centuries of "Foreign Visitors in England, and what they have thought of us." This should certainly not be one of the least interesting volumes of this elegant little series.

## Colonial Notes.

GOLD FIELDS OF VICTORIA.—By the Reports of the Mining Registrars for the quarter ending September, 1888, we find that the gold yield was 157,271 oz. 2 dwt. 14 grs., being an increase of 7077 oz. 19 dwt. 14 grs. on the previous quarter, but 2631 oz. 3 dwt. 17 grs. less than the corresponding quarter of last year. The present Report contains views of the extended Hustler's Freehold Co.'s Mine, Sandhurst; the Loganstone, near Beechworth, and Granit Tors; The Old Man; Pilot Ranges; —three notable views in the gold-mining districts of the colony.

BIBLIOGRAPHY OF CYPRUS.—An attempt at a bibliography of Cyprus was made by Mr. C. Delaval Cobham in 1886, and he now sends us a revised and enlarged second edition, from the prefatory note to which we quote the following: "I have attempted to register in these pages the titles of all books treating of Cyprus, its people, history, numismatics, epigraphy and language, of which I have found any trace. I have included the papers most important to antiquaries and linguists which have appeared in Magazines or in the Transactions of learned Societies; also the few books printed in the Island. I have added a list of local newspapers, of Parliamentary papers, and of the fugitive pieces which record a controversy, not yet extinguished, concerning the "transformations and migrations" of Cypriot antiquities purchased from Signor L. P. di Cesnola by the Metropolitan Museum of Art at New York." We have tested the accuracy and reliability of his entries carefully, and can confidently recommend the little pamphlet as a safe guide to the literature of the Island. Mr. Cobham has certainly performed a very praiseworthy and painstaking piece of work.

## Books Received.

Spelin. A Universal Language by Prof. George Bauer, of Agram, Austria, translated by Chas. T. Strauss, New York. —Dodd, Mead, and Co.'s Catalogue of Books from the presses of William Caxton, Wynken de Worde, and Richard Pynson.— Proceedings of the Canadian Institute, October, 1888.—Annual Report of the Curator of the Museum of Comparative Zoology (Prof. A. Agassiz), 1887-8. — Babylonian and Oriental Record, Vol. III. No. II.—Gold Fields of Victoria. Reports of the Mining Registrars for the quarter ending June, 1888. — Annual Report of the Comptroller of the Currency, U.S.A., December 1, 1888, Volume I.—Algunas Obras Raras Sobre la Lengua Cumanagota.—Volumen I. Arte Bocabulario Doctrina Christiana y Catecismo de la Lengua de Cumana, compuestos por el R. P. Fr. Francisco de Tauste. Publicados de nuevo por Julio Platzmann.—Volumen II. Principios y Reglas de la Lengua Cumanagota compuestos por el R. P. Fr. Manuel de Yangues con un Diccionario. Publicados de nuevo por Julio Platzmann.—Volumen III. Arte y Testoro de la Lengua Cumanagota por Fr. Matias Ruiz Blanco. Publicado de nuevo por Julio Platzmann.—Volumen IV. Confes-onario Mas Lato en Lengua Cumanagota, por Fr. Diego de Tapia. Publicado de nuevo por Julio Platzmann.—Volumen V. Confessonario Mas Breve en Lengua Cumanagota, por Fr. Diego de Tapa. Publicado de nuevo per Julio Platzmann (Teübner, Leipzig).—The Anglo-Indian Codes. Edited by Whitley Stokes, D.C.L. Vol. II. Adjective Law (Clarendon Press, Oxford and London).—La Religion en Chine. A propos du Dernier livre de M. A. Reville. Par M. C. de Harlez (Siffer & Cie., Gand).—'Ilmu hal. A Manual of the Doctrine and Practice of Islam. Translated from the Turkish by Claude Delaval Cobham, B.C.L., etc., Commissioner of Larnaca. (Nicosia).

### NOTICE TO CORRESPONDENTS.

All communications should be addressed to the *Editor of* "*Trübner's Record*," 57 and 59, Ludgate Hill, London, E.C., and they should be accompanied by the sender's name and address (not necessarily for publication). Every care will be taken with MSS., but the Editor cannot hold himself responsible for rejected communications, which—if to be returned to the sender—should be accompanied by postage. MS. should be legibly written, and on one side of the paper only. Books for review should be addressed to the Editor.

## American Literature.

**American Ancestry**; giving the Name and Descent in the Male Line, of Americans whose Ancestors settled in the United States previous to the Declaration of Independence, 1876. V. 3. 8vo. cloth. *Albany (N.Y.)*. £1 10s.

**American Genealogies.** — Supplement to the "Index to American Genealogies" issued in 1886. 8vo. paper, pp. 61. *Albany (N. Y.)*. 6s.

**Andrews (G.)** — Genealogy of the Andrews of Taunton and Stoughton, Mass., Descendants of John and Hannah Andrews, of Boston, Mass., 1656 to 1886. 8vo. cloth, pp. 86. *Washington*. 9s.

**Appleton's Annual Cyclopedia and Register of** Important Events, Index to Volumes for 1876 to 1887 inclusive. 8vo. cloth, pp. 144. *New York*, 18s.

**Bancroft (H. H.)** — History of the Pacific States of North America, v. 18. California, v. 6. 1848–1859. 8vo. cloth, pp. xi. and 787. *San Francisco*. £1 4s.

**Becker (A.)** — Tempted of the Devil; Passages in the Life of a Kabbalist. A Story retold from the German by M. W. Macdowall. 12mo. cloth, pp. 330. *Boston*. 7s. 6d.

**Bliss (W. R.)** — Colonial Times on Buzzard's Bay. 8vo. cloth. *Boston*. 10s.

**Bolton (C. K.)** — Bolton Genealogy. Descendants of William Bolton, of Reading, Mass., 1720. 8vo. paper, pp. 8. *Albany (N.Y.)*. 3s.

**Boyer (J. A.)** — Boyer's Legal Directory of the United States and Canada. Containing a Digest of Collection Laws, Name of one Attorney in each County; also List of Merchants. 8vo. sheep, pp. xi. and 334. *Philadelphia*, 18s.

**Brooks (E. S.)** — The Story of the American Sailor in Active Service on Merchant Vessel and Man-of-War. 8vo. cloth, pp. 336. *Boston*. 12s. 6d.

**Cocker (W. J.)** — The Government of the United States. 12mo. cloth, pp. 274. *New York*. 3s. 6d.

**Davidson (J. W.)** — The Florida of to-day. A Guide for Tourists and Settlers. 12mo. cloth, pp. 254. Illustrated. *New York*. 6s. 6d.

**Digby (W.)** — Digby's Journal. The British Invasion from the North. The Campaigns of Generals Carleton and Burgoyne from Canada, 1776-7, with the Journal of Lieut. W. Digby. Edited with Historical Notes by James Phinney Baxter. 8vo. cloth, pp. 412. *Albany (N.Y.)*. £1 4s.

**Fallows (S., D.D.)** — A Complete Dictionary of Synonyms and Antonyms; with an Appendix embracing a Dictionary of Briticisms, Americanisms, Colloquial Phrases, etc., in Current Use; the Grammatical Uses of Prepositions and Prepositions Discriminated; a List of Homonyms and Homophonous Words; a Collection of Foreign Phrases, and a Complete List of Abbreviations and Contractions Used in Writing and Printing. 12mo. cloth, pp. 512. *New York*. 5s.

**Fay (E. A.)** — Concordance of the Divina Commedia. 8vo. cloth. *Boston*. £2 2s.

**Fisher (H. L.)** — Olden Times; or, Pennsylvania Rural Life some Fifty Years Ago, and other Poems. 8vo. cloth, pp. x. and 472. Illustrated. *York (Pa.)*. 12s.

**Foster (F. P., M.D.)** — Illustrated Encyclopædic Medical Dictionary; being a Dictionary of the Technical Terms used by Writers on Medicine and the Collateral Sciences in the Latin, English, French, and German Languages. 4to. cloth. In 4 Vols. Vol. I. *New York*. £2 5s. (by subscription).

**Frost (J.)** — The Presidents of the United States from Washington to Cleveland; comprising their Personal and Political History; brought down to the present time by Harry W. French. 12mo. cloth, pp. 547. *Boston*. 7s. 6d.

**Harcourt (Helen)** — Home Life in Florida. 12mo. cloth, pp. 433. *Louisville (Ky.)*. 6s. 6d.

**Henshall (J. A., M.D.)** — More about the Black Bass; being a Supplement to "The Book of the Black Bass." 12mo. cloth, pp. 104. *Cincinnati*. 7s. 6d.

**Hill (A. S.)** — Our English. 16mo. cloth, pp. 245. *New York*. 5s.

**Hinman (Russell)** — Eclectic Physical Geography. 12mo. cloth, pp. 382. Illustrated. *Cincinnati*. 7s. 6d.

**Holcomb (Mrs. H. H.)** — Bits about India. 16mo. cloth, pp. 272. Illustrated. *Philadelphia*. 6s.

**House (E. H.)** — Yone Santo; a Child of Japan. 12mo. cloth, pp. 285. *New York*. 5s.

**Lietze (E.)** — Modern Heliographic Processes. A Manual of Instruction in the Art of Reproducing Drawings, Engravings. Manuscripts, etc., by the Action of Light; for the Use of Engineers, Architects, Draughtsmen, Artists, and Scientists. With 32 Illustrations on Wood and 10 Specimen Heliograms. 8vo. cloth, pp. viii. and 143. *New York*. 15s.

**Liggens (Rev. J.)** — The Great Value and Success of Foreign Missions. With an Introduction by Arthur T. Pierson, D.D. 12mo. cloth, pp. xi. and 137. *New York*. 4s.

**Lockwood (S., Ph.D.)** — Readings in Natural History. Animal Memoirs, Part I. Mammals. Crown 8vo. cloth, pp. xviii. and 318. Illustrated. *New York*. 3s.

**Lockwood (S., Ph.D.)** — Readings in Natural History. Animal Memoirs, Part II. Birds. Crown 8vo. cloth, pp. viii. and 397. Illustrated. *New York*. 3s.

**Lowell (P.)** — The Soul of the Far East. 12mo. cloth, pp. 226. *Boston*. 6s. 6d.
A thoughtful review of the individuality, family life, language, art, religion, and imagination of the people of Eastern Asia, Japan, and Corea.

**Lunt (H.)** — Across Lots. 12mo. cloth, pp. 253. *Boston*. 6s. 6d.
The papers of this volume are full of the spirit of outdoors and of tender sympathy with nature.

**McLean (Sally Pratt)** — Lastchance Junction, far far West. A Novel. 12mo. cloth, pp. 258. *Boston*. 6s. 6d.

**Montague (F. C.)** — Arnold Toynbee. 8vo. paper, pp. 70. Johns Hopkins University Studies, 7th Series, No. 1. *Baltimore*.

**Moses (B.)** — The Establishment of Municipal Government in San Francisco. 8vo. paper, pp. 83. *Baltimore*. 2s. 6d.

**Murfree (Miss M. N.)** — The Despot of Broomsedge Cove. 12mo. cloth, pp. 490. *Boston*. 6s. 6d.

**Nestle (E.)** — Syriac Grammar; with Bibliography, Chrestomathy, and Glossary. Second enlarged and improved edition of the "Brevis Linguæ Syriacæ grammatica;" from the German by A. R. S. Kennedy. 12mo. paper, pp. 195. *New York*. 15s.

**Owen (Catherine)** — Progressive Housekeeping. Keeping House Without Knowing How, and Knowing How to Keep House Well. 12mo. cloth, pp. 180. *Boston*. 5s.

**Patten (S. N.)** — The Stability of Prices. 8vo. paper, pp. 72. *Baltimore*. 4s.

**Poole (W. F.) and Fletcher (W. I.)** — Poole's Index to Periodical Literature. The First Supplement, Jan. 1882, to Jan. 1887. Royal 8vo. cloth, pp. 483. *Boston*. £1 16s.

**Pushkin (A.)** — Poems; from the Russian, with Introduction and Notes by Ivan Panin. 16mo. cloth, pp. 179. *Boston*. 10s.

**Reeder (A. P.)** — Around the Golden Deep. A Romance of the Sierras. 12mo. cloth, pp. 500. *Boston*. 7s. 6d.

**Religious Condition of New York City; Addresses** made at a Christian Conference held in Chickering Hall, New York City, Dec. 3, 4, and 5, 1888, by Revs. J. M. King, R. S. MacArthur, C. H. Parkhurst, and others. 12mo. paper, pp. 196. *New York.* 2*s.* 6*d.*

**Richards (W. C.)—The Apostle of Burma. A** Missionary Epic in Commemoration of the Centennial of the Birth of Adoniram Judson. 12mo. cloth, pp. 146. *Boston.* 5*s.*

**Riley (J. W.) — Pipes o' Pan at Zekesbury.** 12mo. cloth, pp. 245. *Indianapolis.* 6*s.* 6*d.*

**Rives (Amélie)—The Quick or the Dead.** 12mo. cloth. *Philadelphia.* 5*s.*

**Salisbury (J. H., M.D.)—The Relation of Ali-**mentation and Disease. 8vo. cloth, pp. xi. and 332. *New York.* £1 5*s.*

**Simonds (W. E.)—A Digest of Patent Cases;** embracing all Patent Cases decided in the Federal and State Courts from 1789 to 1888. 8vo. sheep, pp. 940. *New York.* £3.

**Stark (J. H.) and Green (S. A.)—Antique Views** of ye Towne of Boston. 4to. cloth, pp. 378. Illustrated with Rare Maps, Old Prints, etc. *Boston.* £1 10*s.*

**Stedman (E. C.)—The Star Bearer.** Illustrated by Howard Pyle. 12mo. cloth. *Boston.* 6*s.* 6*d.*

**Stedman (E. C.) and Hutchinson (Ellen M.)—A** Library of American Literature from the Earliest Settlement to the Present Time. In 10 Vols. Vols. 7–10. 8vo. cloth. *New York.* 15*s.* each.

**Thompson (M.)—The Story of Louisiana.** Illustrated by L. J. Bridgman. 8vo. cloth, pp. 337. *Boston.* 7*s.* 6*d.*

**Wilcox (Ella Wheeler) — Poems of Pleasure.** 12mo. cloth. *New York.* 5*s.*

**Wilcox (Ella W.)—Poems of Passion.** *Edition de luxe.* 4to. cloth. Illustrated. *New York.* £1 1*s.*

**Wilkie (F. B.)—Pen and Powder.** 12mo. cloth, 383. *Boston.* 7*s.* 6*d.*

**Young (C. A.)—A Text-book of General Astro-**nomy for Colleges and Scientific Schools. 8vo. cloth, pp. 551. *Boston* and *London.* 10*s.* 6*d.*

---

## European Literature.

**Amélineau (E.)** — Contes et Romans de l'Egypte chrétienne. 2 vols. 12mo. pp. lxxxvii. 193 et 263. *Paris,* 1888. 10*s.*

**Babelon(E.)**—Manuel d'Archéologie orientale. Chaldée-Assyrie-Perse-Syrie-Judée-Phénicie-Carthage. 4to. sewed. *Paris,* 1888. 3*s.* 6*d*

**Bouchard (J.)**—Projet de plantation de tabac à Sumatra (Indes néerlandaises). 8vo. pp. 19. *Angoulême,* 1889.

**Carnoy (E. Henry) et Jean Nicolaïdea.**—Traditions de l'Asie Mineure. 12mo. cloth, pp. 370. *Paris,* 1889. 7*s.* 6*d.*

*** Les littératures populaires de toutes les nations. Tome xxxviii.

**Carnoy (H.) et J. Nicolaïdes**—Traditions populaires de l'Asie Mineure. 8vo. *Paris,* 1889. 7*s.* 6*d.*

**Catalogue (un premier) des manuscrits grecs du car-**dinal Ridolfi. Publié par H. Omont. 8vo. pp. 18. (Extract.) *Paris,* 1888.

**Ciampoli (D.)**—Letterature slave. I. Bulgari, Serbo-croati, Yugo-Russi. 8vo. pp. 4, 144. *Milano,* 1888.

The second volume, Russi-Polacchi-Boemi, in the press.

**Darmesteter (J.)**—Lettres sur l'Inde. A la frontière afghane. 8vo. pp. xxx. 362. *Paris,* 1888. 3*s.* 6*d.*

**Delavay et Franchet.** —Plantae Delavayanae. Plantes de Chine, recueillies au Yunnan par l'Abbé Delavay et décrites par A Franchet, attaché à l' Herbier du Muséum. Livraison I. Royal 8vo. pp. 80. With 15 Plates. *Paris,* 1889. 10*s.*

*** The work will be completed in 20 Fasc. in about five years.

**De-Marchi (F. A.)**—Metodo pratico per lo studio della lingua araba parlata. 2ᵃ ediz. 8vo. *Milano,* 1889. 2*s.* 6*d.*

**Dezobry et Bachelet.**—Dictionnaire général de bio-graphie et d'histoire de mythologie, de géographie ancienne et moderne comparée des antiquités et des institutions grecques, romaines, françaises et étrangères. 10ᵉ édition, entièrement refondue par E. Darsy. 2 vols. 8vo. sewed, pp. 3000 à deux colonnes. *Paris,* 1888. £1 5*s.*

**Directorio general de la ciudad de Mexico.** Con derecho de propiedad literaria concedido por el Supremo Gobierno de la República Mexicana. 4to. pp. 156, 144. *Madrid,* 1888.

**Fujishima (Ryauon)**—Le Bouddhisme japonais. Doc-trines et histoire des douze grandes sectes bouddhiques du Japon. Post 8vo. sewed, pp. xliii. 160. *Paris,* 1889. 5*s.*

**Γέδεων (Μανουηλ Ιω.)**—Κανονικαὶ διαταξεις ἐπίστολαι, λησεις, Θεσπισματα τῶν ἁγίωτατων Πατριαρχῶν Κωνσταντινουπολέων. 8vo. sewed, pp. 418. Εν Κωνσταντινουπόλει, 1888. 12*s.*

**Girenas.**—Le Livre des salutations adressés aux nations orientales et occidentales composé pour le 8ᵐᵉ congrès des Orientalistes, qui se réunira à Stockholm en 1889. *Leipzig,* 1889. 6*s.*

**Groff (W. N.)** — Diverses études. I. Le Pronom égyptien. II. Note sur Jaqob-el et Josep-el. 4to. pp. 10. *Paris,* 1888.

**Guillaume (P.)**—Istorio de sanct Poncz. Mystère en langue provençale du XVᵉ siècle. Publié d'après un manu-scrit de l'époque. Roy. 8vo. pp. xv. 244. (Extract.) *Paris,* 1889.

**Hiao-king.** *Vide* Rosny.

**Histoire de Mar Jab-Alaha, Patriarche et de Raban·** Sauma. Demy 8vo. sewed, pp. xii. 188. *Paris,* 1888. 7*s.*

*** Chaldean text in the characters.

**Houtsma (M. Th.)**—Recueil de textes relatifs à l'histoire de Seldjoucides. Vol. II. Histoire de Seldjoucides de l'Irâq par al-Bondârî, d'après Imâd-ad-din al-Kâtib al Is-fahâni. Texte Arabe. 8vo. pp. l. 324. *Leiden,* 1889. 9*s.*

**Issaverdens (J.)**—Histoire de l'Arménie. Enrichie de nombreuses figures exécutees aux frais de J. Arathoon de de Batavia. Two vols. 16mo. pp. 397 and 493. *Venice,* 1888.

**Kessler (K.)**—Mani. Forschungen über die Manich-äische Religion. Ein Beitrag zur vergleichende Religions-geschichte des Oriénts. Vol. I. Voruntersuchungen und Quellen. Roy. 8vo. sewed, pp. xxvii. 407. *Berlin,* 1889. 14*s.*

**Kiessling (J.)**—Untersuchungen über Dämmerungser-scheinungen. Zur Erklärung der nach dem Krakatau Ausbruch Beobachteten atmosphärisch-optischen Störung. Mit neun Farbendrucktafeln nach Aquarellen von Prof. Dr. Pechnel Loesche. 4to. cloth, pp. viii. 172. *Hamburg,* 1888. £1 16*s.*

**Kohler (J.)**—Rechtsvergleichende Studien über islam-itisches Recht, das Recht der Berbern, das chinesische Recht und das Recht auf Ceylon. 8vo. sewed, pp. 252. *Berlin,* 1889. 6*s.*

**Lanessan (J. L. de)**—L'Indo-Chine française. Etude politique, économique et administrative sur la Cochinchine, le Cambodge, l'Annam et le Tonkin. 8vo. sewed, pp. viii. 760. With 5 coloured maps. *Paris,* 1888. 15*s.*

**Loise (Ferd.)**—Histoire de la poésie en rapport avec la civilisation dans l'antiquité et chez les peuples de race latine. Vols. 1 et 2. 8vo. *Paris,* 1889.

Tome I. L'Antiquité (Monde oriental, monde classique, monde chrétien). 4s.

Tome II. La France depuis les origines jusqu'à la fin du dix-huitième siècle. 5s.

Loret (V.)—Manuel de la langue égyptienne. Grammaire, tableau des hiéroglyphes, textes et glossaire. 2 Livraisons. 4to. Paris, 1888. £1

Mallet (D.)—Le culte de Neit à Saïs. Thèse présentée à l'école du Louvre. Royal 8vo. pp. x. 252. Paris, 1888. 15s.

Mayet (P.)—Japanische Bevölkerungsstatistik. Historisch, mit Hinblick auf China, und kritisch betrachtet. Royal 4to. pp. 20. Extract. Berlin, 1889. 1s. 6d.

Mittheilungen des akademisch-orientalischen Vereins zu Berlin. No. II. Royal 8vo. pp. 29. Berlin, 1889. 1s. 6d.

Moerkerken (P. H. Van)—Over de verbinding der volzinnen in 't gotisch. 8vo. pp. 104. Gent, 1888. 1s. 6d.

Ottino (G.) et Fumagalli (G.)—Bibliotheca bibliographica. 8vo. Rom, 1889. £1.

Parnaso venezolano. Serie I. Tomo V. Don Abigail Lozano, Curaçao. 8vo. pp. 126. Madrid, 1888.

Peiser (F. E.)—Keilinschriftliche Acten-Stücke. Aus babylonischen Städten. Von Steinen und Tafeln der Berliner Museums in Autographie, Transcription und Uebersetzung herausgegeben und commentirt. Roy. 8vo. pp. xii, 124. With 23 Plates. Berlin, 1889. 12s.

Pepe (Lazz.) — Lectiones in sanctam scripturam. Parts I. II. et III. Accedunt lectiones archaeologicae hebraicae. 8vo. sewed. Torino, 1888. 8s.

Petit (Edouard).—Le Tong-kin. Royal 8vo. pp. 239. With Plates. Paris, 1889.

Petit (Ernest)—Chartes de l'abbaye cistercienne de Saint-Serge de Giblet, en Syrie. 8vo. pp. 11. Paris, 1889.

Petit (L. D.)—Bibliographie der middel-Nederlandsche taal en letterkunde. 8vo. pp. 298. Ghent, 1889.

Posewitz (Th.)—Borneo. Entdeckungsreisen und Untersuchungen. Gegenwärtiger Stand der geologischen Kenntnisse. Verbreitung der nutzbaren Mineralien. Roy. 8vo. pp. xxvii. 385. With 4 coloured Maps in Royal folio and 29 Profils and Illustrations. Berlin, 1889. 15s.

Réville (Albert).—La Religion Chinoise. (Histoire des Religions, III.) 8vo. sewed, pp. vii. 699. Paris, 1889. 12s.

Rosenberg (J.)—Das aramaeische Verbum im babylonischen Talmud. Roy. 8vo. pp. 66. Marburg, 1889. 2s.

Rosny (Léon de)—Le Hiao-King. Livre sacré de la Piété filiale. Publié en Chinois avec une traduction française et un commentaire emprunté aux sources originales. Post 8vo. sewed, pp. 176. Paris, 1889. 12s.

Scerbo (Fr.)—Grammatica della lingua ebraica. 8vo. pp. viii. 159. Firenze, 1888. 5s.

Senart (E.)—Notes d'épigraphie indienne. 8vo. pp. 53. With 3 Plates. (Extract Journal Asiatique.) Paris, 1889.

Serrure (C. A.)—Essai de Grammaire gauloise, d'après les monuments épigraphiques, suivi d'une reproduction des principaux textes et d'un coup d'œil sur la langue des Gaules, depuis César jusqu'à Charlemagne. 8vo. pp. viii. 56. Gent, 1889. 4s.

Simon (R.)—Beiträge zur Kenntniss der vedischen Schulen. 8vo. pp. vii. 113. Kiel, 1889. 4s. 6d.

Smith (S. A.) — Die Keilschrifttexte Asurbanipals, Königs von Assyrien (668-626 v. Chr.). Nach dem in London copirten Grundtext mit Transscription, Uebersetzung, Kommentar und vollständigem Glossar. Fasc. III. Unedirte Briefe, Depeschen, Omentexte u.s.w. Royal 8vo. sewed, pp. vii. 129. With 28 Plates. Leipzig, 1889. 18s.

Sommer (H. O.)—Erster Versuch über die englische. Hirtendichtung. Royal 8vo. pp. 131. Marburg, 1889. 3s.

Steenackers (F.) et Uéda Tokunosuke — Cent proverbs japonais. 4to. With many Illustrations. Paris, 1889. £1 5s.

Stoll (Otto)—Die Ethnologie der Indianerstämme von Guatemala. 4to. pp. xii. 112. With 2 Coloured Plates. Leiden, 1889. 5s.

Supplement to Vol. I. Internationales Archiv für Ethnographie.

Weber (W.)—Der Arabische Meerbusen. Vol. I. Historisches und Morphologisches. Mit einer Tiefenkarte. Royal 8vo. pp. 62. Marburg, 1889. 2s.

Westphal (A.)—Les sources du Pentateuque. Etude de critique et d'histoire. I. Le problème littéraire. 8vo. pp. xxx. 326. Paris, 1889.

Wiener (C.)—Chili et Chiliens. Royal 8vo. pp. 388. With Illustrations. Paris, 1889.

Winckler (Dr. Hugo)—Die Keilinschrifttexte Sargons. Nach den Papierabklatschen und Originalen neu herausgegeben. 2 vols. 8vo. With 49 Plates. Leipzig, 1889. £2 8s.

Vol. I. Historisch-sachliche Einleitung; Umschrift und Uebersetzung; Wörterverzeichniss.

Vol. II. Texte. Autographed by Dr. L. Abel.

## Oriental Literature.

### ANGLO-INDIA.

Beck (Th.)—Essays on Indian Topics. Royal 8vo. sewed, pp. 127, iii. Allahabad, 1888. 2s.

Bhandarkar (Shridhar R.)—A Catalogue of the Collections of Manuscripts deposited in the Deccan College. With an Index. Royal 8vo. boards, pp. 542. Bombay, 1888.

Bhoja Champu. Bálakánda. Translated into English by M. C. Shadagopa Chári. 8vo. pp. 29. Trichinopoly, 1888. 1s.

*₊* An English translation of the story of Rama as contained in the Sanskrit poem by Bhoja.

Code (The) of Civil Procedure Act XIV. of 1882. Edited by Srínivásavaradá Chári and Co. 8vo. pp. 308. Madras, 1888. 5s.

Democracy not suited to India. By Oday Pertap Singh, the Raja of Bhinga, Oudh. Royal 8vo. sewed, pp. 104. Allahabad, 1888. 1s.

Digest of Civil Cases reported in the four Series of the Indian Law Reports. Edited by S. Rágavaiengár. 18mo. pp. 276. Madras, 1888. 6s.

*₊* Continuation of the Digest of the Indian Law Reports of Civil cases for 1886 and 1887.

Digest (A) of Criminal Cases for 1887. Edited by T. V. Sámináda Aier. 8vo. pp. 54. Kumbakonam, 1888. 1s. 6d.

Khory (Rustomjee Naserwanjee). — The Bombay Materia Medica and their Therapeutics. 8vo. cloth, pp. 600, xxxix. Bombay, 1887. 18s.

Kraft (Prince).—On Cavalry. Specially translated from the German. 8vo. sewed, pp. 67. Allahabad, 1888. 5s.

Pamphlets issued by the United Indian Patriotic Association. No. 11. Published by Th. Beck. Royal 8vo. sewed, pp. ix. 122 and xliii. Allahabad, 1889. 2s.

*₊* Showing the seditious character of the Indian National Congress and the opinions held by eminent Natives of India, who are opposed to the movement.

Provincial (The) Small Cause Courts Act, No. IX. of 1887. Edited by M. S. Tiruvéngada Chári. 8vo. pp. 217. *Madras*, 1888. 8*s*.

*** The enactments relating to the constitution and powers of Small Cause Courts are edited with Notes of Cases, Government notifications and rulings, etc.

**Sheppard (R. S.)**—English Lessons. A Handbook specially designed for the Use of Candidates for the F.A. and B.A. Examinations. 8vo. pp. 436. *Madras*, 1888. 8*s*.

**Standing Orders (The)** of the Board of Revenue. Edited by T. Kuppusámi Naick. 2nd edition. 8vo. pp. 790. *Madras*, 1888. 10*s*. 6*d*.

**Standing Orders (The)** of the Board of Revenue. Edited by C. Annádurai Aier. 3rd edition. 8vo. pp. 685. *Madras*, 1888. 16*s*.

**Times (The)** of India. Calendar and Directory for 1889. 8vo. bound, pp. xcvii. 1120, 59. With Portrait. *Bombay*, 1889. 18*s*.

**Venkatarámasámi (C.)**—Biographical Sketches of Deccan Poets. Second Edition. 12mo. pp. 157. *Madras*, 1888. 3*s*. 6*d*.

*** This book is a reprint of what appeared in a book of biographical sketches of 149 Deccan poets, published at Calcutta 60 years ago and since long out of print.

**Wilson (Lieut. Col. W. J.)**—History of the Madras Army. 4 vols. 8vo. cloth. *Madras*, 1882-88. £1 4*s*.

*** The Atlas to the work will be published very soon.

### ARABIC.

**Simit-us Sibiau.** By Moulvi Usuf Sahib. New edition. 8vo. pp. 416. Lithographed. *Madras*, 1888. 9*s*.

*** A religious work in Arabic verse with the meaning of the text in a mixture of Arabic and Tamil, and in some parts in pure Arabic without any translation.

روايات الاغاني Rewayât El-Aghani. Selection of Stories taken from the Kitab El-Aghani. 2 vols. 8vo. sewed. *Beirut*, 1888. 6*s*.

الخلاصة الطبية El-kholasat Ettobiyat. Internal Pathology. By H. de Brun. Vol. I. 8vo. sewed. *Beirut*, 1888. 6*s*.

*** This translation in Arabic is done under direction of the author by his scholar Khirallah Farage Sfayr.

الشهاب الثاقب Eshihab Ethahib. Handbook of Letter-Writing. By Saïd El-Khoury El-Chartoumi. New edition. 8vo. sewed. *Beirut*, 1888. 3*s*. 6*d*.

*** One of the most complete works of this kind, containing 260 letters and other pieces. This new edition contains notes to the work.

الف ليلة وليلة Alf Lailat wa Lailat. Arabian Nights. Vol. I. Edited by P. A. Salhani. Royal 8vo. sewed, pp. 451. *Beirut*, 1888. 6*s*.

*** The first volume of a new edition of the Alf Laila, in Arabic, printed without the vowels. In the Preface the editor gives his opinion about the existence of the Arabian Nights. He thinks the book of really Arabic origin.

اللباب Al-Lobab, seu Dictionarium Syro-Arabicum. Auctore P. Gle. Cardahi Libanense. Vol. I. Royal 8vo. sewed, pp. iv. 620. *Beirut*, 1888. £1 12*s*. 6*d*.

*** The first complete Syriac-Dictionary published. This first volume contains the first eleven letters or the half of the Syriac alphabet. The second volume is in the press.

مقالات علم الادب Makalât Ilm Eladab. By Cheikho de la Compagnie de Jésus. 8vo. sewed. *Beirut*, 1889. 4*s*.

*** This work contains the rules of the most known Arabic authors for style and composition.

نهج المراسلة Nahj El-morasalat. Small Handbook for Letter-Writing. By Rachid El-Khoury El-Chartouni. 12mo. sewed, *Beirut*, 1888. 1*s*. 6*d*.

*** Containing about 250 letters on all different matters.

### BURMESE

### (Including Karen and Shan).

**Awwadakata.** By U. Thumana. Demy 8vo. pp. 60. *Rangoon*, 1888. 1*s*.

*** Book of Admonition. In Burmese.

**Conti (Rev. G.)**—Kibícé Alë Ahoé Adédoûdosa Bya Alé. 12mo. pp. 93. *Toungoo*, 1888. 1*s*. 6*d*.

*** Explanation of the Catholic Doctrine in Karen.

**Cushing (Rev. J. N.)**—Elementary Shan Handbook. 8vo. pp. 272. *Rangoon*, 1888. 15*s*.

**Dhammapadagatha.** In Burmese. By Captain T. H. Lewin. Demy 8vo. pp. 52. *Rangoon*, 1889. 1*s*. 6*d*.

**Douglass (Mrs. M. C.)** — Midwifery. In Burmese. 8vo. pp. 160. *Rangoon*, 1888. 6*s*.

**Judson (Rev. A.)**—A Grammar of the Burmese Language. Fourth edition. 8vo. pp. 64. *Rangoon*, 1888. 3*s*.

**Kibícé Alé Ahoé Abísépho Anikhí.** By Rev. G. Conti. 8vo. pp. 183. *Toungoo*, 1888. 3*s*. 6*d*.

*** An abridgment of the Christian Doctrine for children. In Karen.

**Lonsdale (A. W.)**—The First Step in Burmese. Third edition. 8vo. pp. 70. *Rangoon*, 1888. 3*s*.

**Mahosadha Játaka Vatthu.** By U. Awbatha. Two vols. Demy 8vo. pp. 492. *Rangoon*, 1888. 3*s*. 6*d*.

*** One of the books of the Játakattha Vannaná.

**Myittawdakadipani.** By Maung Gyi. In Burmese. Demy 8vo. pp. 59. *Rangoon*, 1888. 3*s*.

*** Compilation of the private correspondence which passed between the Atwin Wun, Maingkaing Myoza and the Myook of Salin.

**Temi Játaka Vatthu.** By U. Awbatha. Second edition. Demy 8vo. pp. 218. *Rangoon*, 1888. 3*s*.

*** One of the books of the Játakattha Vannaná.

### CANARESE.

**Gnána Sindu Vémba Vedánta Sástram.** In Canarese. Second edition. 8vo. pp. 420. *Madras*, 1888. 3*s*. 6*d*.

**Liturgy** of the Basel German Evangelical Mission Churches in South-Western India. In Kanarese. Third edition. 8vo. pp. 220. *Mangalore*, 1888. 2*s*. 6*d*.

**Reader (Fourth)** in Canarese. Part I. Translated by Rev. H. A. Kaundinya. 12mo. pp. 244. *Mangalore*, 1888. 1*s*. 6*d*.

*** The first edition of the Kanarese version of the Government Fourth Reader of the Vernacular Series.

### HINDUSTANI

**Jamaul Achar.** By Rev. E. Sell. 4to. pp. 60. Lithographed. *Madras*, 1888. 2*s*. 6*d*.

*** Poetical selections in Hindustani.

**Khan-i-Lazat Tarjamai Alváni Namat.** Translated by Sayed Abdur Rahimán Sahib. 8vo. pp. 162. Lithographed. *Madras*, 1888. 3*s*.

*** A Hindustani translation of a treatise on cookery.

**Kitab-i-Salis.** By Rev. E. Sell. Second edition. 8vo. pp. 29. *Madras*, 1888. 1*s*.

*** A collection of stories in Hindustani.

**Mahabul-ul-Khutab.** By Moulvi Baker Ajab. 8vo. pp. 156. Lithographed. *Madras*, 1888. 2*s*. 6*d*.

*** A poem in Hindustani. An exposition of the works and words of Mahomed.

**Masnavi.—Bakh-i-Frum.** Masnawi Moulana Reom. By Munshi Mislam Ali Sahib. 8vo. pp. 156. *Madras*, 1888. 2*s*. 6*d*.

*** A metrical translation of the Masnawi of Moulana Reom.

## MALAYALAM.

**Gundert (H.) and L. Garthwaite.** A Catechism of Malayalam Grammar. Sixth edition. 12mo. pp. 157. *Mangalore*, 1888. 1s.

**Ramáyana** and the Santaná Gopálam and Parvati-parinayam. In Malayalam. With Notes. By M. Séshagiri Prabu and P. O. Pothan. In two parts. 8vo. pp. 306. *Calicut*, 1888. 5s.

**Sri Garuda Puránam.** By E. Kunnan Nambiar and V. Kannan Gurukkal. 8vo. pp. 57. *Calicut*, 1888. 2s. 6d.

*** A new metrical translation of the well-known Sanskrit work in Malayalam. In very easy popular metre.

**Travancore (The) Revenue Manual.** Edited by M. R. Krishna Rao. 8vo. pp. 416. *Mangalore*, 1888. 6s.

*** This manual in Malayalam is prepared for official purpose.

## SANSKRIT.

**Amarakosha.** By Dewji Bhunji. Sanskrit in Devanagiri. 12mo. pp. 116. *Cochin Town*, 1888. 1s.

*** This edition of the standard Sanskrit Lexicon contains the text of the first three chapters.

**Ashtánga Hiridayam** or **Bápatam.** With Commentary Sutrástánam. By P. Súrianáráyana Rao. Sanskrit and Telugu text. 4to. pp. 400. *Madras*, 1888. 16s.

*** A part of a standard medical work treating the hygea.

**Bálamanoramai.** By Vasudéva Dikshit. Nos. 1 to 9. 8vo. *Tanjore*, 1888.

*** This standard Sanskrit Grammar, with Commentary, called Bálamanoramai, is now brought out as a serial publication in monthly parts.

**Bhágavata (Churniká).** Or the Bhágavatapurán, by the Reputed Author Vyas. together with its Substance in Sanskrit. Edited by Nathubhái Talakchand. Oblong, pp. 1574. *Bombay*, 1888. £1 1s.

*** The present edition contains a short work in praise of the Purán called Bhágavata Máhátmya, or the Glory of the Bhágavata.

**Bhoja Champu, Bálakánda.** *Vide* Anglo-India.

**Hamsavada Champu Kávyam.** By A. Krishnasámi Aier. Sanskrit in Devanagiri characters. 16mo. pp. 118. *Tinnevelly*, 1888. 1s. 6d.

*** A Sanskrit poem in a new form, based on the legend of the destruction of Kamsa by Krishna.

**Kamalálaya Mahatmiam.** Sanskrit Text in Grandha characters. 8vo. pp. 121. *Tanjore*, 1888. 2s. 6d.

*** An extract from the Skandha Purana; containing the sacred legend of a Saiva shrine at Tiruvárur.

**Krishna Yajurvedasya Taittiriya Sanhitá,** or the Taittiriya Text of the Black Yajurveda. Roy. 8vo. sewed, pp. 534. *Bombay*, 1888. 10s. 6d.

*** Vedic Hymns. Edited by Rájárám Shástri Bodas and Shivrám Shástri Gore.

**Panchadashi;** or a Book on Vedánta Philosophy, consisting of 15 Chapters. By Vidyáranya. With a Commentary by Rámkrishna. Roy. 8vo. pp. 440. *Bombay*, 1888. 8s.

*** The original text is a well-known and authoritative treatise on Vedanta philosophy, by Vidyáranya.

**Sarngadhara.** The Paddhati. A Sanskrit Anthology. Edited by P. Peterson, M.A. Vol. I. 8vo. sewed, pp. 7, 757. *Bombay*, 1888. 12s. 6d.

*** Bombay Sanskrit Series, No. XXXVII. This first volume, containing the Text, will be followed very soon by the second volume, containing a full critical apparatus with notes to the book, and an introductory sketch of the literature embraced in it.

**Sidhánta Saila Sangraham.** By C. R. Sriniván Sástri. 8vo. pp. 117. *Chillambram*, 1888. 2s. 6d.

*** A Sanskrit dissertation on the Advaita philosophy by Appaia Dikshit.

**Sivagána Siddhiar.** First Sútram with Commentary. By A. Sivachári. Tamil and Sanskrit in the Grandha characters. 16mo. pp. 756. *Madras*, 1888. 6s.

*** A well-known religious work about the wisdom attainable by following the Saiva system and the glory of Siva.

**Válmiki Rámáyana.** With Commentary. Edited by T. V. Narasimma Chari. Sanskrit and Telugu Text. Nos. 15 to 18. 8vo. *Madras*, 1888. 1s. each.

**Vrata Chúdámani.** Sanskrit Text in Grandha characters. 12mo. pp. 125. *Madras*, 1888. 2s. 6d.

*** A book of extracts from the Sanskrit Puranas, indicating the various Hindu vows.

## TAMIL.

**Arabian** Nights Entertainments. Edited by P. Mánikka Mudali. Three vols. 8vo. pp. 1568. *Madras*, 1888. 16s.

*** A complete edition of the Arabian Nights in Tamil.

**Sivagána Siddhiar.** *Vide* Sanskrit.

**Sri Bhakti Sílámritam.** By Rájáram Govinda Rao, Suria Vamsi. 8vo. pp. 901. *Tanjore*, 1888. 9s.

*** Tamil lyrics respecting the 82 celebrated votaries of Vishnu known in Upper India.

**Sri Mahá Bhágavatam Dasamaskandam.** By Lakshmammál Nátakam. Vol. I. Numbers 1 to 16. 8vo. *Madras*, 1887-88. 1s. each number.

**Tévára Tirattu.** Edited by A. Rámasámi Aier. 8vo. pp. 214. *Madras*, 1888. 5s.

*** Praise of Siva and appeal to his mercy in verse. Containing selections from the Téváram of Agastya, Tiruvásakam of Manikka Vasakar, and other sacred poetry of the Sivites.

**Unáni Vaidya Dhátu Vriddhi Bodini.** By P. Mahomed Abdulla Sahíb. 12mo. pp. 347. *Madras*, 1888. 3s. 6d.

*** A medical tract in Tamil pointing out the Mahomedan method of improving one's blood.

**Vaidya Chillaraikoral.** By Agastiar. 16mo. pp. 760. *Madras*, 1888. 2s. 6d.

*** A collection of the minor medical works in Tamil ascribed to the Sage Agastya.

## TELUGU.

**Abhinaya Darpanam.** By N. Tiruvéngadá Chári. Second edition. 8vo. pp. 92. *Madras*, 1888. 2s. 6d.

*** "The Mirror of the Ballet," as the title of this book implies, treats of the motions of the hands in dancing, etc., and other matters connected with the native nautch dance.

**Achala Grandham.** By Sivaráma Dikshit. 12mo. sewed, pp. 120. *Madras*, 1888. 2s. 6d.

*** Treats of the Vedanta philosophy in Telugu.

**Ashtánga Hiridayam.** *Vide* Sanskrit.

**Dwádasasa Vidvataharitram.** By Laksharáya Kavi. Part 1. 8vo. pp. 95. *Cocanada*, 1888. 2s. 6d.

*** Stories of some clever Pandits in Telugu.

**Indian Penal Code,** Act XLV. of 1860. In Telugu. Translated by Sitáramaier. 8vo. pp. 467. *Madras*, 1888. 10s. 6d.

*** Contains the rulings of all the High Courts up to 1866.

**Panchatantra.** With Commentary. By Venkatanáda Rájá Kavi. Second edition. 8vo. pp. 206. *Madras*, 1888. 2s. 6d.

*** The story of Panchatantra in verse by Venkatandha, in which a consecutive series of actions are ascribed to irrational beings.

**Sri Hálásya Mahátyam.** Translated by Tirumalai Chetti Jagannádha Kavi. 8vo. pp. 454. *Madras*, 1888. 6s.

*** A Telugu version of the original work on which the local legend of the town of Madura and its temple and the 64 amusements of Siva is founded.

**Sri Sumanobhiranjani.** Edited by D. Krishnamurti Súri. Vol. I. No. 1. 8vo. pp. 19. *Madras*, 1888.

*** The annual subscription price of this serial publication in Telugu is 6s. including postage.

**Valmiki Rámáyana.** *Vide* Sanskrit.

# 𝔍𝔞𝔭𝔞𝔫𝔢𝔰𝔢 𝔒𝔣𝔣𝔦𝔠𝔦𝔞𝔩 𝔓𝔲𝔟𝔩𝔦𝔠𝔞𝔱𝔦𝔬𝔫𝔰.

The following Official Publications issued in different European languages have—it is believed—never before reached Europe, and may be of unique interest to those watching the progress of European civilization in the East.

## EDUCATION.

**History (A Short) of the Department of Education.** Translated and published by the Department of Education. 8vo. sewed, pp. 52. *Tokio*, June, 1887.

**Instruction No. 1 of the Department of Education** for Regulations as to Instruction in the Simpler Elementary School Course. Translated and published by the Department of Education. 8vo. sewed, pp. 2. *Tokio*, December, 1886.

**Instruction No. 3 of the Department of Education** for Regulations as to the Adoption of Books and Charts for Public and Private Elementary Schools. Translated and published by the Department of Education. 8vo. sewed, pp. 5. *Tokio*, July, 1887.

**Instruction No. 4 of the Department of Education** for the principal items as to the Disbursement of the Educational Expenses of Male Pupils in Ordinary Normal Schools. Translated and published by the Department of Education. 8vo. sewed, pp. 4. *Tokio*, the 7th month of the 20th year of Meiji (1887).

**Instruction No. 6 of the Department of Education** for Particulars as to the Military Exercise under "Gymnastics" in ordinary Middle School Course. Translated and published by the Department for Education. 8vo. sewed, pp. 2. *Tokio*, July, 1887.

**Instruction No. 8 of the Department of Education** as to Table showing the Amount of Salaries of Officials in Ordinary Normal Schools. Translated and published by the Department of Education. 8vo. sewed, p. 1. *Tokio*, the 7th month of the 20th year of Meiji (1887).

**Notification No. 3 of the Department of Education** for the Limits within which Higher Middle Schools are to be established. Translated and published by the Department of Education. 8vo. sewed, pp. 2. *Tokio*, December, 1886.

**Ordinance No. 2 of the Department of Education.** Regulations concerning the Examination of School Books and Charts. Translated and published by the Department of Education. 8vo. sewed, pp. 4. *Tokio*, July, 1887.

**Ordinance No. 4 of the Department of Education.** Detailed Rules relating to Degrees. Translated and published by the Department of Education. 8vo. sewed, pp. 6. August, 1887.

**Ordinance No. 7 of the Department of Education.** Regulations concerning the Examination and Approval of School Books and Charts. Translated and published by the Department of Education. 8vo. sewed, pp. 10. *Tokio*, the 20th of the 9th month, 19th year of Meiji.

**Ordinance No. 8 of the Department of Education** relating to Subjects of Study and the Standard to be attained in Elementary Schools. Translated and published by the Department of Education. 8vo. sewed, pp. 8. *Tokio*, the 14th of the 8th month of the 19th year of Meiji.

**Ordinance No. 9 of the Department of Education** relating to Subjects of Study and the Standard to be attained in ordinary Normal Schools. Translated and published by the Department of Education. 8vo. sewed, pp. 8. *Tokio*, the 14th of the 8th month of the 19th year of Meiji.

**Ordinance No. 10 of the Department of Education.** Regulations as to the Admission to ordinary Normal Schools of Pupils from Various Districts of Fu and Ken. Translated and published by the Department of Education. 8vo. sewed, pp. 10. The 14th of the 8th month of the 19th year of Meiji.

**Ordinance No. 11 of the Department of Education.** Regulations relating to the Performance of Duties by the Graduates of Ordinary Normal Schools. Translated and published by the Department of Education. 8vo. sewed, pp. 3. *Tokio*, the 14th of the 8th month of the 19th year of Meiji.

**Ordinance No. 12 of the Department of Education.** Regulations as to the Licensing Elementary School Teachers. Translated and published by the Department of Education. 8vo. sewed, pp. 8. *Tokio*, the 20th of the 9th month of the 19th year of Meiji.

**Ordinance No. 14 of the Department of Education.** Subjects of Study and the Standard to be attained in Ordinary Middle-Schools. Translated and published by the Department of Education. 8vo. sewed, pp. 7. *Tokio*, the 20th of the 9th month of the 19th year of Meiji.

**Ordinance No. 16 of the Department of Education.** Subjects of Study and the Standard to be attained in Higher Middle Schools. Translated and published by the Department of Education. 8vo. sewed, pp. 5. *Tokio*, the 20th of the 9th month of the 19th year of Meiji.

**Ordinance No. 17 of the Department of Education.** Subjects of Study and the Standard to be attained in the Higher Normal School. Translated and published by the Department of Education. 8vo. sewed, pp. 12. *Tokio*, December, 1886.

**Ordinance No. 18 of the Department of Education.** Regulations as to the Admission to the Higher Normal School of Pupils from Various Districts. Translated and published by the Department of Education. 8vo. sewed, pp. 2. *Tokio*, December, 1886.

**Ordinance No. 19 of the Department of Education.** Regulations relating to the Performance of Duties by the Graduates of the Higher Normal School. Translated and published by the Department of Education. 8vo. sewed, pp. 2. *Tokio*, December, 1886.

**Ordinance No. 21 of the Department of Education.** Regulations as to Licensing Instructors for Ordinary Normal Schools, Ordinary Middle Schools and Higher Female Schools. Translated and published by the Department of Education. 8vo. sewed, pp. 8. *Tokio*, the 7th month of the 20th year of Meiji (1887).

**Ordinance No. 25 of the Department of Education.** For Appendix to Subjects of Study and the Standard to be Attained in Elementary Schools. Translated and published by the Department of Education. 8vo. sewed, pp. 2. *Tokio*, the 7th month of the 20th year of Meiji (1887).

**Ordinance (Cabinet) relating to the Titles and the Manner of the Treatment of Public School Officials.** Translated and published by the Department of Education. 8vo. sewed, p. 1. *Tokio*, the 7th month of the 20th year of Meiji (1887).

**Ordinance (Imperial) relating to the Official Regulations for the Higher Normal School, the Higher Middle School, and the Tokio Commercial School.** Translated and published by the Department of Education. 8vo. sewed, pp. 3. *Tokio*, December, 1886.

**Ordinance (Imperial) relating to the Imperial University.** Translated and published by the Department of Education. 8vo. sewed, pp. 5. *Tokio*, the 9th of the 3rd month of the 19th year of Meiji.

**Ordinance (Imperial). General Regulations for Schools.** Translated and published by the Department of Education. 8vo. sewed, pp. 2. *Tokio*, the 12th of the 8th month of the 19th year of Meiji.

**Ordinance (Imperial) relating to Elementary Schools.** Translated and published by the Department of Education. 8vo. sewed, pp. 4. *Tokio*, the 12th of the 8th month of the 19th year of Meiji.

**Ordinance (Imperial) relating to Middle Schools.** Translated and published by the Department of Education. 8vo. sewed, pp. 3. *Tokio*, the 12th of the 8th month of the 19th year of Meiji.

Ordinance (Imperial) relating to Normal Schools. Translated and published by the Department of Education. 8vo. sewed, pp. 3. *Tokio*, the 12th of the 8th month of the 19th year of Meiji.

Ordinance (Imperial) relating to Degrees. Translated and published by the Department of Education. 8vo. sewed, pp. 2. *Tokio*, the 7th month of the 20th year of Meiji (1887).

Ordinance (Imperial) relating to the Ranks of the Officials in the Imperial University. Translated and published by the Department of Education. 8vo. sewed, pp. 2. *Tokio*, the 7th month of the 20th year of Meiji (1887).

Ordinance (Imperial) relating to the Official Regulations for Ordinary Normal Schools. Translated and published by the Department of Education. 8vo. sewed, pp. 4. *Tokio*, the 7th month of the 20th year of Meiji (1887).

Outlines (Descriptive) of the Various Schools in Japan. Translated and published by the Department of Education. 8vo. sewed, pp. 31. *Tokio*, September, 1887.

Outlines of the Modern Education in Japan. Translated and published by the Department of Education. 8vo. sewed, pp. 184. With 32 Tables. *Tokio*, March, 1888.

Report (Twelfth Annual) of the Minister of State for Education for the Seventeenth Year of Meiji (1884). Translated and published by the Department of Education. Royal 8vo. sewed, pp. ii. 129. *Tokio*, 4th month, 21st year of Meiji (1888).

Report (Fourteenth Annual) of the Minister of State for Education for the Nineteenth Year of Meiji (1886). Translated and published by the Department of Education. Royal 8vo. sewed, pp. ii 139. *Tokyo*, 9th month, 21st year of Meiji (September, 1888).

## POST.

Report (Annual) of the Postmaster-General of Japan for the Year ending December 31st, 1874. 8vo. sewed, pp. 10. (*Tokio*), 1875.

Report (Fourth) of the Postmaster-General of Japan for the Half Fiscal Year ending June 30th, 1875. 8vo. sewed, pp. 19. (*Tokio*), 1875.

Report (Fifth) of the Postmaster-General of Japan for the Fiscal Year ended June 30th, 1876. 8vo. sewed, pp. 24. *Tokio*, 1876.

Report (Sixth) of the Postmaster-General of Japan for the Fiscal Year ended June 30th, 1877. 8vo. sewed, pp. 36. *Tokio*, 1877.

Report (Seventh) of the Postmaster-General of Japan for the Fiscal Year ended June 30th, 1878. 8vo. sewed, pp. 37. (*Tokio*), 1878.

Report (Eighth) of the Postmaster-General of Japan for the Fiscal Year ended June 30th, 1879. 8vo. sewed, pp. 39. (*Tokio*), 1879.

Report (Ninth) of the Postmaster-General of Japan for the Fiscal Year ended June 30th, 1880. Translated from the Japanese. 8vo. sewed, pp. 46. (*Tokio*), 1880.

Report (Tenth) of the Postmaster-General of Japan for the Fiscal Year ended June 30th, 1881. Translated from the Japanese. 8vo. sewed, pp. 29. (*Tokio*), 1881.

Report (Eleventh) of the Postmaster-General of Japan for the Fiscal Year ended June 30th, 1882. Translated from the Japanese. 8vo. sewed, pp. 34. (*Tokio*), 1882.

Report (Twelfth) of the Postmaster-General of Japan for the Fiscal Year ended June 30th, 1883. Translated from the Japanese. 8vo. sewed, pp. 16. With 5 Tables. (*Tokio*), 1883.

Report (Thirteenth) of the Postmaster-General of Japan for the Fiscal Year ended June 30th, 1884. Translated from the Japanese. 8vo. sewed, pp. 15. With Appendix of 15 Tables. (*Tokio*), 1884.

Report (Fourteenth) of the Postmaster-General of Japan for the Fiscal Year ended June 30th, 1885. Translated from the Japanese. 8vo. sewed, pp. 13. With Appendix of 19 Tables. (*Tokio*), 1885.

Report (Fifteenth) of the Administration of Posts of Japan for the Fiscal Year ended 31st March, 1886. Translated from the Japanese. 8vo. sewed, pp. 14. With Appendix of 14 Tables. (*Tokio*, 1887.)

## TELEGRAPH.

Imperial Government Telegraph Service Regulations applicable to Telegraph Correspondence, Japan. 8vo. sewed, pp. 45. (*Tokio ?*) the 1st day of the 7th month, 18th year of Meiji.

Telegraph Code. 8vo. sewed, pp. 22. (*Tokio*), the 1st day of the 7th month, 18th year of Meiji.

Report (First) of the Chief Commissioner of Imperial Government Telegraphs, Japan. For the period from the First Projection of the Telegraphs to June 30th, 1875. In English and Japanese. Small 4to. sewed, pp. 33. With 9 Tables. (*Tokio*), 1875.

Report (Second) of the Chief Commissioner of the Imperial Government Telegraphs, Japan. For the Fiscal Year ended June 30th, 1876. In English and Japanese. Small 4to. sewed, pp. 18. With 3 Tables. (*Tokio*), 1876.

Report (Third) of the Director of the Imperial Government Telegraphs, Japan, for the Fiscal Year ended June 30th, 1877. In English and Japanese. Small 4to. sewed, pp. 35. (*Tokio*), 1877.

Report (Fourth) of the Director-General of the Imperial Government Telegraphs, Japan, for the Fiscal Year ended June 30th, 1878. In English and Japanese. Small 4to. sewed, pp. 31 and Appendices A-D, pp. 8. (*Tokio*), 1878.

Report (Fifth) of the Director-General of the Imperial Government Telegraphs for the Fiscal Year ended June 30th, 1879. In English. Small 4to. sewed, pp. 26. With 5 Tables. (*Tokio*), 1879.

Report (Sixth) of the Director-General of the Imperial Government Telegraphs for the Fiscal Year ended June 30th, 1880. Small 4to. sewed, pp. 31. With an Appendix in Japanese, pp. 52. With 1 Table. (*Tokio*), 1880.

Report (Seventh) of the Director-General of the Imperial Government Telegraphs for the Fiscal Year ended June 30th, 1881. Small 4to. sewed, pp. 22. With 5 Tables, 3 in English and 2 in Japanese, and a Japanese Appendix pp. 35. (*Tokio*), 1881.

Report (Eighth) of the Director-General of the Imperial Government Telegraphs for the Fiscal Year ended June 30th, 1882. Small 4to. sewed, pp. 23. With 5 Tables, 4 in English and 1 in Japanese, and a Japanese Appendix, pp. 34. *Tokio*, 1882.

Report (Ninth) of the Director-General of the Imperial Government Telegraphs for the Fiscal Year ended June 30th, 1883. Small 4to. sewed, pp. 24. With 2 Tables. (*Tokio*), 1883.

Report (Tenth) of the Director-General of the Imperial Government Telegraphs for the Fiscal Year ended June 30th, 1884. Small 4to. sewed, pp. 26. With 2 Tables. (*Tokio*), 1884.

Report (Eleventh) of the Director-General of the Imperial Government Telegraphs for the Fiscal Year ended June 30th, 1885. Small 4to. sewed, pp. 20. With 2 Tables. *Tokio*, (1885).

Report (Twelfth) of the Director-General of the Imperial Government Telegraphs for the Fiscal Year ended March 31st, 1886. Small 4to. sewed, pp. 51. With 3 Tables and a Map. (*Tokio*), 1886.

## MISCELLANEOUS.

**Administrative Regulations** promulgated by His Imperial Japanese Majesty's Government, and in Force on the 1st day of the 12th month of the 18th year of the Meiji. Two parts in one. 4to. half-bound, pp. iv. 148 and iv. 140. (*Tokio*, 1885.)

Part I. 1. Regulations relating to public order and security; 2. Regulations relating to public health; 3. Regulations relating to public revenue; 4. Regulations relating to ships and navigation.

Part II. 5. Miscellaneous regulations.

**Cabinet Impérial** Bureau Général de Statistique. Résumé Statistique de l'Empire du Japon. No. II. 4to. boards. pp. vii. xii. 134. With two coloured statistical Plates and a Map. *Tokio*, 1888.

**Journal of the College of Science, Imperial University, Japan.** Published by the University. Tokyo. Vol. I. Part 2. 4to. sewed, pp. 113–209. With 1 Plate. *Tokyo*, 1887.

*** Contents: Beiträge zur Theorie der Bewegung der Erdatmosphare und der Wirbelstürme, von Dr. Phil. Dirô Kitao.

**Journal of the College of Science, Imperial University, Japan.** Published by the University, Tokyo. Vol. I. Part 3. 4to. sewed, pp. 210–336. With 11 Plates. *Tokyo*, 1887.

*** Contents: On the Formation of the Germinal Layers in Chelonia. By K. Mitsukuri and C. Ishikawa.—On the Caudal and Anal Fins of Gold-Fishes. By S. Watase.— Some Notes on the Giant Salamander of Japan (Cryptobranchus Japonicus, Van der Hoeven). By C. Sasaki.—A Pocket Galvanometer. By Aikitu Tanakadate.—Some Occurrences of Piedmontite in Japan. By B. Kotô.—The severe Japan Earthquake of the 15th Jan., 1887. By S. Sekiya.—Electrical Resistance of Nickel at High Temperature.—The Constants of a Lens. By Aikitu Tanakadate.

**Journal of the College of Science, Imperial University, Japan.** Published by the University, Tokyo. Vol. I. Part IV. 4to. sewed, pp. 337-384. With 5 Plates. *Tôkyô*, 1887.

*** Contents: Ueber einige Tricladen Europa's. By F. Ijima. —A Model showing the Motion of an Earth-particle during an Earthquake. By S. Sekiya.—On Aluminium in the Ashes of Flowering Plants. By Hikorokurô Yoshida.—The Effects of Dilution and the Presence of Sodium Salts and Carbonic Acid upon the Titration of Hydroxyamine by Iodine. By Tamemasa Haga.—Notes on a large Crystal Sphere. By C. G. Knott.— The Marine Biological Station of the Imperial University at Misaki. By K. Mitsukuri.

**Journal of the College of Science, Imperial University, Japan.** Published by the University, Tôkyô. Vol. II. Part 1. 4to. sewed, pp. 1–75. With 1 Plate. *Tôkyô*, 1888.

*** Contents: Ueber die Darstellbarkeit willkürlicher Functionen durch Reihen die nach den Wurzeln einer transcendenten Gleichung fortschreiten. By R. Fujisawa.—On the Composition of Bird-lime. By E. Divers and M. Kawakita.— On Anorthite from Miyakejima. By Y. Kikuchi.—The Source of Bothriocephalus latus in Japan. By. I. Ijima. — Earthquake Measurements of Recent Years, especially relating to vertical Motion. By S. Sekiya.

**Report of the Commissioner of the Imperial Mint** for the Year ending 31st March, 1887. Royal 8vo. sewed, pp. 40. With a Table. *Hiogo*, 1887.

**Treaties and Conventions** between the Empire of Japan and other Powers, together with Universal Conventions, Regulations and Communications since March, 1854. Revised edition. In English, French, German, Dutch, etc. 4to. half-calf, pp. ix. v. 1216. With Synoptical Index, pp. 92, 5. *Tokio*, 1884.

---



The following bibliography does not aim by any means at being complete, but it is hoped that few important Armenian works published of late years in Tiflis will be found missing. They are all in the modern Armenian idiom and in Armenian characters.

**Abeliantz (Alex.)**— *Vide* Hugo.

**Aboviantz (Kévork).**—Short Armenian History. 8vo. pp. 18, 265. *Tiflis*, 1884.

**Achoughe Djivani.** Songs. 8vo. pp. 241. *Tiflis*, 1886.

**Achoughe Gharibe.** A Tale with Songs. 8vo. pp. 115. *Tiflis*, 1887.

**Adamian (Petrosse)**—Shakespeare and his Tragedy "Hamlet." A Review. Small 4to. pp. x. 113. *Tiflis*, 1887.

**Aghaïantz (Gazaros).**—The Armenian Sound. 8vo. pp. 50. *Tiflis*, 1874.

**Aghaïantz (Gazaros).**—Anahite (Diane). A Tale. Royal 8vo. pp. 75. *Tiflis*, 1881.

**Aghaïantz (Gazaros).**—Poetry. Small 4to. pp. 32. *Tiflis*, 1882.

**Aghaïantz (Gazaros).**—Arégnazane. A Tale. 8vo. pp. 56. *Tiflis*, 1887.

**Aghaniantz (Guionte).** — George Rolleston. Translated into Armenian. 8vo. pp. 168. *Tiflis*, 1879.

**Aghaniantz (Guionte).**—Lacidé. The Third Gold (?) Translated into Armenian. 8vo. pp. 32. *Tiflis*, 1879.

**Aghaniantz (Guionte).**—Actéa. A Tale. Translated into Armenian. 8vo. pp. 148. *Tiflis*, 1885.

**Aghaniantz (Guionte).** — Eantchoux. Jean Ernste Smolear. Translated into Armenian. 8vo. pp. 39. *Tiflis*, 1885.

**Aghaniantz (Priest Guionte).**— *Vide* Hofmann.

**Aïvazian (Archbishop Gabriel).** — History of the Khalibian School. Royal 8vo. pp. x. 393. *Tiflis*, 1880.

**Akimiantz (Kévork).**—Nala and Damayanti. Translated into Armenian. 8vo. pp. iii. 54. *Tiflis*, 1877.

**Amiriantz (Séiade).**—A Drop of Blood. Translated into Armenian. 8vo. pp. 36. *Tiflis*, 1885.

**Amiriantz (Séiade).**—Hamlet, King of Danemark. Translated into Armenian. 8vo. pp. 48. *Tiflis*, 1886.

**Apiantz (Lazarus).**— *Vide* Francline.

**Arakéliantz (Hratchéa).**—The State and its Principles. 8vo. pp. 2, 54. *Tiflis*, 1883.

**Aramiantz (Misak).**—From Salian to Etchmiadzine. Memoirs of a Pilgrim. 8vo. pp. 5, 165. *Tiflis*, 1887.

**Araratiantz (Alexander).**—Two Hills. 8vo. pp. vi. 30. *Tiflis*, 1876.

**Araratiantz (Alexander).** — The Consequences of Poverty. Poetry. Small 8vo. pp. 66. *Tiflis*, 1877.

**Araratiantz (Alexander).**—Poetry. 8vo. pp. vi. 117. *Tiflis*, 1880.

**Arankhaniantz (Avétik).** — Doctor Bock's Advices. Translated into Armenian. 8vo. pp. 76. *Tiflis*, 1876.

**Artzrouni (Sénékerime).**—The Will of Samuel Mouratian. 12mo. pp. 132. *Tiflis*, 1879.

**Athanassiahtz (Ohannès).**—The Vegetation of Erivan. 8vo. pp. 96. *Tiflis*, 1881.

**Avaliantz (Madathia).**— *Vide* Housset.

Babaïantz (Dr. Avetik).—The Question of the Preservation of Health in Schools. Roy. 8vo. pp. 3, 75. Tiflis, 1879.

Babaïantz (Avetik).—The Passions and their Influences. Roy. 8vo. pp. 46. Tiflis, 1880.

Babaïantz (Avetik). — The Preservation of Health of Children. 8vo. pp. 35. Tiflis, 1882.

Babaïantz (Avetik).—The Present System of the Preservation of Health in Medicine. 8vo. pp. 2, 70. Tiflis, 1886.

Bagratouni (Arsène). — The Ten Commandments. 8vo. pp. 9, 100. Tiflis, 1881.

Bagratouni (Arsène).—The Last Recall. 8vo. pp. 6, 120. Tiflis, 1883.

Bagratouni (Arsène).—Explication of the Armenian Liturgy. 8vo. pp. 5, 253. Tiflis, 1884.

Bahathriantz (Arakel).—The Kindergarten and its Indication. 8vo. pp. 3, 24. Tiflis, 1882.

Barkhoudariantz (Kevork).— Vide Schiller.

Bógnazariantz. Vide Secrets.

Bersié. Caesar and God. Translated into Armenian by A. Hovhannissiantz. 8vo. pp. 46. Tiflis, 1885.

Caurna (Miss Susane).—Children and their Friends. Translated by G. Kafiantz. 8vo. pp. 156. Tiflis, 1887.

Dalógéoziantz (Hacop).— Vide Molière.

Emanuel (Don).—Poetry. 8vo. pp. 24. Tiflis, 1880.

Emin (M.) — Moses of Khoren and the old Armenian Stories. Translated by G. Khalathiantz. 8vo. pp. 84. Tiflis, 1886.

Emin (M.)—Moses of Khoren and the old Armenian Stories. Translated by Khatchatour Hovhannissiantz. 8vo. pp. 71. Tiflis, 1887.

Francline, the Advices of the Learned Richard. Translated into Armenian by Lazarus Apiantz. 12mo. pp. 132. Tiflis, 1879.

Géghamiantz (Hovakime).—The Poll-Tax. A Tale. 8vo. pp. 58. Tiflis.

Géghamiantz (Hovakime).—Ginedeva. A Tale. Part I. Small 8vo. pp. 240. Tiflis, 1883.

Goukassiantz (Haïrapèt).—The Protestantism among the Armenians of the Caucasus. Small 8vo. pp. 173. Tiflis, 1886.

Goulamiriantz (Abgar).— Vide Ilynski.

Goullakiantz (Avétik). — The Water-Bearer of Granada and an Egg of Nurnberg. Translated into Armenian. 8vo. pp. 40. Tiflis, 1881.

Hakhverdiantz (Kévork).—Poetry of Saïath-Nova. Royal 8vo. pp. 172. Tiflis, 1852.

Halladjiantz. Collection of National Songs. 8vo. pp. 183. Tiflis, 1878.

Haïk, Aram, Vahagune, by A. M. E. P. 8vo. pp. 5, 30. Tiflis, 1881.

Haraut. The Armenian Press in Russia and the Caucasus. 8vo. pp. 135. Tiflis, 1878.

Hofmann.—Fidelity conquers all Troubles. Translated by the Priest Guioute Aghaniantz. 8vo. pp. 141. Tiflis, 1877.

Hofmann. — From Darkness to Light. Translated by Guioute Aghaniantz. Small 4to. pp. 144. Tiflis, 1877.

Housset (Araéne).—The Daughters of Eve. Translated into Armenian by Madathia Avaliantz. 8vo. pp. 337. Tiflis, 1884.

Hovhannissiantz (Abgar).—Armenia and the Armenians in the Eyes of other Nations. 8vo. pp. 96. Tiflis, 1881.

Hovhannissiantz (A.)— Vide Bersié.

Hovhannissiantz (Khatchatour).— Vide Emin.

Hugo (Victor). — Claude Gueux. Translated into Armenian by Alex. Abéliantz. Small 4to. pp. 48. Tiflis, 1886.

Hugo (Victor).—The Last Day of the Criminal. Translated by Alex. Abéliantz. 8vo. pp. 152. Tiflis, 1887.

Ilynski (Doctor).—What is the Plague? Translated into Armenian by Abgar Goulamiriantz. 12mo. pp. 11, 56. Tiflis, 1880.

Jeritziantz (Alexander).—Nerses the Fifth. Armenian Catholic. 3 Parts. Roy. 8vo. pp. 28, 65 and 36. Tiflis, 1878.

Jeritziantz (Alexander).—The Mekhitarists of Venice. 8vo. pp. 162. Tiflis, 1883.

Jeziantz (Karapèt).—The Forced Union of the Armenians with the Roman Church. Roy. 8vo. pp. 270. Tiflis, 1884.

Kafiantz (G.)— Vide Caurna.

Khalathiantz (Grikor).—Lazarus de Parbe and his Writings. A Review. Roy. 8vo. pp. 113. Tiflis, 1883.

Khalathiantz (Grikor).—On Armenian Ethnography. 8vo. pp. 115. Tiflis, 1887.

Khalathiantz (Grikor).— Vide Emin.

Khatissiantz (Gabriel). — The Pedagogic Advices. Part I. 8vo. pp. 126. Tiflis, 1882.

Kostaniantz (Karapèt). — The Sighs of Stephan Orbelian. 12mo. pp. 69. Tiflis, 1885.

Kostaniantz (Karapèt).—The Armenian Convents. 8vo. pp. 99. Tiflis, 1886.

Lalaïantz (Jerouande).—The Sack of Ahmed. Translated into Armenian. Small 8vo. pp. 32. Tiflis, 1881.

Lalaïantz (T.)— Vide Sand (G.) ; Molière.

Léréutz. Poetry. 8vo. pp. 48. Tiflis, 1883.

Lessing.—Nathan the Sage. Translated by K. Barkhoudariantz. Royal 8vo. pp. 208. Tiflis, 1878.

Lissitziantz (Stephen)—The Brave Soldiers. Comedy. 8vo. pp. 18. Tiflis, 1885.

Madathiantz (Niazmi). — Krte-Krte. A Comedy. 8vo. pp. 49. Tiflis, 1884.

Mandiniantz (Sédrak).—The Religions. Psychological Researches. 8vo. pp. 107. Tiflis, 1879.

Meliantz (Arame). — The Great Armenian Monk St. Mesrop. 8vo. pp. 7, 47. Tiflis, 1883.

Molière.—The School for Husbands. A Comedy. Translated into Armenian by Hacop Dalegéoziantz. 8vo. pp. 44. Tiflis, 1880.

Molière. — The Imaginary Invalid. A Comedy. Translated into Armenian by F. Lalaïantz. 8vo. pp. 104. Tiflis, 1886.

Nalbandiantz (Michael).— Vide Raubert.

Navassardiantz (Dr. Bagarate). — On Diphtheria. Small 8vo. pp. 25. Tiflis, 1879.

Navassardiantz (Dr. Bagarate).—Some Medical and Sanitary Advices. 8vo. pp. 9, 63. Tiflis, 1886.

Navassardiantz (Tigran).—The Labour and the Rest. Translated into Armenian. Small 8vo. pp. 39. Tiflis, 1877.

Nazariantz (Ohannès). — Anecdotes. Part I. 8vo. pp. 223. Tiflis, 1876.

The Same. Part II. 8vo. pp. 153. Tiflis, 1876.

The Same. Part III. 8vo. pp. 13, 253. Tiflis, 1883.

**Nazariantz (Oh.)**—History of the First Council of the Armenian Masters. 8vo. pp. 8, 169. *Tiflis*, 1883.

**Pellico (Silvio).**—Francisco da Rimini. Translated into Armenian by A. M. E. P. 8vo. pp. 68. *Tiflis*, 1860.

**Raubert (Clemence).**—Duchesse de Chevreuse. Translated into Armenian by Michael Nalbandiantz. Royal 8vo. pp. 50. *Tiflis*, 1858.

**Renan (Ernst).**—Islamism and Science. Translated by Gara. Royal 8vo. pp. 26. *Tiflis*, 1884.

**Sand (George).**—The Naked Rose. Translated into Armenian by J. Lalaïantz. 12mo. pp. 96. *Tiflis*, 1882.

**Schiller.** William Tell. Translated into Armenian by Kévork Barkhoudariantz. 8vo. pp. 205. *Tiflis*, 1873.

**Schiller.** The Maid of Orleans. Translated by K. Barkhoudariantz. Royal 8vo. pp. 168. *Tiflis*, 1878.

**Schiller.** Don Carlos. Translated by K. Barkhoudariantz. Royal 8vo. pp. 278. *Tiflis*, 1878.

**Schiller.** The Song of the Bell. Translated by K. Barkhoudariantz. Small 8vo. pp. 29. *Tiflis*, 1884.

**Secret (The) of Kharabagh.** Taken from Bégnazariantz. 8vo. pp. 15, 406. *Tiflis*, 1886.

**Shakespeare.** *Vide* Adamian.

**Thatéossiantz (A.)**—Kephyr; or, the Useful Drink of the Caucasus. Small 8vo. pp. 5, 10. *Tiflis*, 1887.

**Thokhmakhiantz (Arsène).**—The South Foot of the Mount Masis. Small 8vo. pp. 13, 66. *Tiflis*, 1882.

**Voutchetitch (B.)**—Two Christmas Trees. Translated into Armenian by Oh. Nagariantz. 8vo. pp. 24. *Tiflis*, 1882.

Appendix containing a few useful books for the study of Armenian published in Europe.

**Aucher (P. Paschal) and Lord Byron.**—A Grammar Armenian and English. 8vo. sewed, pp. 144. *Venice*, 1873. 4s.

**Aucher (P. P.) and John Brand.**—Dictionary, English and Armenian. Roy. 8vo. sewed. *Venice*, 1868. £1 1s.

**Bedrossian (Rev. F.)**—New Dictionary, Armenian-English. Roy. 8vo. sewed, pp. xxx. 786. *Venice*, 1875-79. £1.

**Byron (Lord)**—Armenian Exercises and Poetry. In Armenian and English. 12mo. sewed, pp. 172. *Venice*, 1870. 4s. 6d.

**Byron (Lord)**—Childe Harold's Pilgrimage. Italy. 8vo. sewed, pp. 147. *Venice*, 1872. 3s.

**Byzance (Néandre de)** — Dictionnaire français-arménien. 4to. pp. 1298. *Constantinople*, 1884. £3 3s.

**Dictionnaire Arménien-Français.** 12mo. boards, pp. 498. (*Constantinople*), 1887.

**Haïsdan (Le).**—Organe de l'Association patriotique arménienne. (Armenian-French Text.) Published by M. J. Droussali and M. Sévasly. (Fortnightly.) Annual subscription, 10s.

**Issaverdens (Rev. Dr. James).** — The Armenian Church. Its History, Rites, and Ceremonies. 12mo. sewed, pp. 387. *Venice*, 1877. 4s.

**Issaverdenz (Rev. Dr. James)**—Armenia and the Armenians. Being a Sketch of its Geography and Civil and Church History. 2nd edition. 12mo. sewed, pp. 410. *Venice*, 1878. 4s.

**Nercetes.**—Preces Sancti Nersetis Clajensis Armeniorum Patriarchae. 36 linguis edita. With Portrait. 12mo. sewed, pp. 600. *Venetiis*, 1882. £1 1s.

---

## AN IMPORTANT COLLECTION OF BOOKS

RELATING TO

### British India.

ON SALE BY TRÜBNER & Co.

---

### ANGLO-INDIA.

**AGNEW (William Fischer).**—The Law of Trusts in British India. With an Appendix. 8vo. cloth, pp. lxviii. 555. *Calcutta*, 1882. £1 5s.
*** Tagore Law Lectures, 1881.

**AINSLIE (WHITELAW).**—Materia Indica; or some Account of those Articles which are employed by the Hindoos and other Eastern Nations in their Medicine, Arts, and Agriculture. 2 Vols. Royal 8vo. bound, pp. xxiv. 654 and xxxix. 604. *London*, 1826. 18s.

**ANGLO-INDIAN** Ready Reckoner and Vade Mecum. 8vo. cloth, pp. 222. *Bombay*, 1884. 6s.

**ARMY REGULATIONS,** India.—Vol. vii. Dress. Royal 8vo. cloth, pp. 162. *Calcutta*, 1886. 7s. 6d.

**ASIATICK MISCELLANY (The).**—Consisting of Original Productions, Translations, Fugitive Pieces, Imitations and Extracts from Curious Publications. Vol. I. 4to. bound, pp. vi. 514. *Calcutta*, 1785. 18s.

**ASSAM.**—Mills (A. T. Moffatt)—Report on the Province of Assam. Folio, half-bound. *Calcutta*, 1854. 18s.

**ATKINSON (J. E. T.)**—Economic Products of the North Western Provinces. Part I. Gums and Gum-Resins. 4to. sewed, pp. v. 51. *Allahabad*, 1876. 3s. 6d.

**BALFOUR (E.)**—Cyclopaedia of India and of Eastern and Southern Asia, Commercial, Industrial and Scientific. Products of the Mineral, Vegetable and Animal Kingdoms, Useful Arts and Manufactures. With Supplement. Together 3 Vols. Royal 8vo. half-bound, pp. iv. 2054, 730 and viii. 837. *Madras*, 1857-62. £2 10s.

**BALFOUR (E.)**—The Timber Trees, Timber and Fancy Woods, as also the Forests, of India and of Eastern and Southern Asia. 3rd edition. Royal 8vo. cloth, pp. xii. 370. *Madras*, 1870. 18s.

**BANNU.**—Thorburn (S. S.)—Bannú, or our Afghan Frontier. With one Map of Bannu District. 8vo. cloth, pp. x. 480. *London*, 1876. 18s.

**BELL (H. C. P.)**—The Máldive Islands. An Account of the Physical Features, Climate, History, Inhabitants, Productions, and Trade. Folio, sewed, pp. 134. With Maps. *Colombo*, 1883. 10s. 6d.

**BELLARY.**—Kelsall (John)—Manual of the Bellary District. Compiled under the Orders of Government, dated September 9th, 1869. No. 2646. 8vo. cloth, pp. xi. 390, x. With Map. *Madras*, 1872. £1 1s.

**BENGAL.**—Adam's Report on Vernacular Education in Bengal and Behar. Submitted to Government in 1835, 1836, and 1838. With a Brief View of its Past and Present Condition. By the Rev. J. Long. 8vo. sewed, pp. vi. and 342. *Calcutta*, 1868. 7s. 6d.

**BENGAL.**—Beverley (H.)—Report on the Census of Bengal, 1872. Folio, boards, pp. 19, xiv. 210, ccxxxvi. With 4 Coloured Maps. *Calcutta*, 1872. 12s. 6d.

**BENGAL.**—Kerr (J.)—A Review of Public Instruction in the Bengal Presidency, from 1835 to 1851. Part 1. 8vo. pp. v. 200. *Calcutta*, 1852. 3s. 6d.

**BENGAL.**—Coloured Map of Bengal. Scale, 32 British miles = 1 inch. *Calcutta*, 1878. 3s. 6d.

**BENGAL.**—Minute by the Lieut.-Gov. of Bengal on the Mutinies as they affected the Lower Provinces under the Government of Bengal. Folio, sewed, pp. 88. *Calcutta*, 1858. 8s.

**BENGAL.**—Mookerjee (S. C.)—Travels in Bengal. Travels and Voyages between Calcutta and Independent Tipperah. Post 8vo. cloth, pp. xxvi. 223. *Calcutta*, 1887. 15s.

**BENGAL.**—Mouat (F. J.)—Report on the Jails of the Lower Provinces of the Bengal Presidency for the year 1868. Roy. 8vo. pp. vi. 183. *Calcutta*, 1869. 9s.

**BENGAL.**—O'Shaughnessy (W. B.)—The Bengal Dispensatory. Chiefly compiled from the works of Roxburgh, Wallich, Ainslie, Wight and Arnot, Royle, Pereira, Lindley, Richard and Gee. Including the Results of Numerous Special Experiments. Published by order of Government. 8vo. half-bound, pp. xliv. xxiii. 794. With 10 Plates. *Calcutta*, 1841. £1 12s. 6d.

**BENGAL.**—Prinsep (J.)—Strictures and Observations on the Mocurrery System of Landed Property in Bengal. Originally written for the *Morning Chronicle*, under the Signature of Gurreel Doss, with Replies. 8vo. pp. 156. *London*, 1794. 5s.

**BENGAL.**—Public Opinion and Official Communications about the Bengal Music School and its President. 8vo. sewed, pp. 186. *Calcutta*, 1876. 5s.

**BENGAL.**—Annual Report on the Administration of the Bengal Presidency during the year 1863–64. 8vo. sewed, pp. x. 119. With Appendix, pp. lxxx. 5s.

**BENGAL.**—Annual Report on the Administration of the Bengal Presidency for 1865–66. 8vo. sewed, pp. xii. 180, xlviii. *Calcutta*, 1866. 5s.

The same. 1866-67. Sewed, pp. xii. 178, lii. *Calcutta*, 1867. 5s.

**BENGAL.**—Appendix to the Report on the Administration of the Jails of the Lower Provinces, Bengal, for 1868. Vol. II. With Plates. 8vo. sewed, pp. iii. Dcccciii. *Calcutta*, 1869. 12s. 6d.

**BENGAL.**—Report on the Administration of Bengal 1871-72. Part I. The General Report. 4to. boards, pp. ii. 258. *Calcutta*, 1872. 7s. 6d.

**BENGAL.**—Report on the Administration of Bengal 1872-73. With a Statistical Summary. Four Parts in One. Royal 8vo. half-bound, pp. 52, 131, 463 and 127. *Calcutta*, 1873. £1 11s. 6d.

**BENGAL.**—Introduction to the Bengal Administration Report of 1872-73. 8vo. bound, pp. 52. *Calcutta*, 1873. 3s. 6d.

**BENGAL.**—Report (the Fifth) from the Select Committee on the Affairs of the East India Company. Two Vols. (I. Bengal Presidency. II. Madras Presidency.) 8vo. cloth, pp. 841 and 745. (*London*, 1812). *Madras*, 1866. £1 10s. or 18s. each Vol.

**BENGAL.**—Report (Third) on the State of Education in Bengal; including some Account of the State of Education in Bellar, and a Consideration of the Means adapted to the Improvement and Extension of Public Instruction in both Provinces. By W. Adam. Royal 8vo. pp. iv. 239. *Calcutta*, 1838. 5s.

**BENGAL.**—Report (General) on Public Instruction in the North-Western Provinces of the Bengal Presidency, for 1850–51. 8vo. pp. 243. *Agra*, 1852. 4s.

**BENGAL.**—Report (General) on Public Instruction in the Lower Provinces of Bengal for 1869-70. With Appendices. 8vo. pp. vi. 91, 389, 43, 61, 159. *Calcutta*, 1870. 15s.

**BENGAL.**—Reports (with Proceedings and Appendix) of the Committee appointed by Government to Enquire into the State of the River Hooghly. With 7 Maps. Folio, pp. 17, xx. 132, 102, and Appendix xi. *Calcutta*, 1854. 9s.

**BENGAL.**—Rouse (C. W. Boughton)—Dissertation concerning the Landed Property of Bengal. 8vo. pp. xv. 320. *London*, 1791. 9s.

**BENGAL.**—Roy (Parbati Churn) — The Rent Question in Bengal. (Reprinted from Bengal Public Opinion.) 8vo. boards, pp. vi. ii. 269. *Calcutta*, 1883. 5s.

**BENGAL.**—Stewart (Charles)—The History of Bengal from the First Mohammedan Invasion until the Virtual Conquest of that Country by the English A.D. 1757. 8vo. cloth, pp. xvi. 332, xxx. *Calcutta*, 1847. 4s.

**BENGAL-SUGAR.**—An Account of the Method and Expence of Cultivating the Sugar-Cane in Bengal. With Calculations of the First Cost to the Manufacturer and Exporter, and Suggestions for attracting that Article of Eastern Produce exclusively to Great Britain. 8vo. pp. 162. *London*, 1794. 3s. 6d.

**BENGAL-TEA.** — Papers regarding the Tea Industry in Bengal. 8vo. boards, pp. 4, xxviii. 169. *Calcutta*, 1873. 10s. 6d.

**BENGAL.**—Trevelyan (Ernest John)—The Law relating to Minors in the Presidency of Bengal. 8vo. cloth, pp. xxiv. 491. *Calcutta*, 1878. 15s.
*** Tagore Law Lectures, 1877.

**BENGAL.**—Wylie (M.)—Bengal as a Field of Missions. 8vo. cloth, pp. viii. 389. With a Map. *Calcutta*, 1854. 5s.

**BERAR GAZETTEER.** — Gazetteer for the Haidarabad Assigned Districts, commonly called Berár, 1870. Edited by A. C. Lyall. With Two Maps. 8vo. cloth, pp. xii. 282, xxiii. *Bombay*, 1870. 7s. 6d.

**BERAR.**— Kitts (Eustace J.) — Report on the Census of Berar, 1881. Folio, pp. xii. 237, 207. *Bombay*, 1882.

**BHATTACHARYYA** (Krishna Kamal)—Law relating to the Joint Hindu Family. 8vo. cloth, pp. xx. 741. *Calcutta*, 1885. £1 7s. 6d.
*** Tagore Law Lectures, 1884-85.

**BHUT (DEVANNA)**—The Smruti Chandrika on the Hindu Law of Inheritance. Translated from the Original by T. Kristnasawmy Jyer. 2nd edition. 8vo. cloth, pp. x. 272. *Madras*, 1867. 18s.

**BIDDULPH (MAJOR J.)**—Tribes of the Hindoo Koosh. Royal 8vo. cloth, pp. 164, clxix. With Plates, Tables, and 1 Map. *Calcutta*, 1880. 15s.

**BLOCHMANN (H.)**—School Geography of India and British Burmah. 8vo. sewed, pp. iv. 100. *Calcutta*, 1873. 2s.

**BOILEAU (A. H. E.)**—Personal Narrative of a Tour through the Western States of Rajwara, in 1835. 4to. pp. vii. 331. With Plates and Maps. *Calcutta*, 1837. 5s.

**BOMBAY** Army List, 1st August, 1887. Compiled, by Permission of Government, in the Adjutant-General's Office, Head Quarters. 8vo. sewed, pp. 241. *Bombay*, 1887. 3s. 6d.
The Same of 1st October, 1883. pp. 240. *Bombay*, 1883. 2s. 6d.

**BOMBAY** Civil List, corrected to 1st October, 1880. Showing the Names and Designations of the Civil and Military Servants of Government in the General, Revenue, Judicial, etc. 8vo. sewed, pp. xxxvi. 295. *Bombay*, 1880. 7s. 6d.

**BOMBAY** Code (The)—Consisting of the Unrepealed Bombay Regulations, Acts of the Supreme Council relating solely to Bombay, and Acts of the Governor of Bombay in Council. With Chronological Table. 8vo. cloth, pp. xxiv. 774. *Calcutta*, 1880. £1 1s.

**BOMBAY.**—Report (General) on the Administration of the Bombay Presidency for the year 1868-69. 8vo. pp. v. 320. *Bombay*, 1869. 5s.

**BOMBAY.**—Report of the Bombay Chamber of Commerce for the year 1868-69. Presented to the Annual General Meeting held on the 4th October, 1869. 8vo. boards, pp. 10, xxii. 331. *Bombay*, 1870. 7s. 6d.

**BOMBAY.** — Report of the Department of Public Instruction in the Bombay Presidency for the year 1867-68. With Appendices. 8vo. cloth, pp. vi. 488, iv. *Bombay*, 1868. 7s. 6d.
The same, 1868-69. 8vo. cloth, pp. iv. 395. *Bombay*, 1869. 7s. 6d.

**BOMBAY.**—Transactions of the Literary Society, Bombay. 3 vols. 4to. bound. With numerous Plates and Facsimiles. *Bombay*, 1819–23. £1 10s.

**BOSE (SHIB CHUNDER)**—The Hindoos as they are. A Description of the Manners, Customs, and Inner Life of Hindoo Society in Bengal. Second edition, revised and enlarged. 8vo. cloth, pp. xii. 343. *Calcutta*, 1883. 12s. 6d.

**BOWER (H.)**—Essay of Hindu Caste. 8vo. pp. 123. *Calcutta*, 1851. 2s. 6d.

**BROADLEY (A. M.)**—Ruins of the Nalanda Monasteries at Burgáon, Sub-Division Bihár, Zillah Patna. 8vo. pp. 24. With Plates. *Calcutta*, 1872. 3s. 6d.

**BROUGHTON (L. P. DELVES)** — The Code of Civil Procedure. Being Act VIII. of 1859 and the Acts amending and extending it. Fourth edition, revised, corrected and enlarged by C. J. Wilkinson. 8vo. cloth, pp. l. 909. *Calcutta*, 1871. £1 15s.

**BROUGHTON (THOMAS DUER)**—Selections from the Popular Poetry of the Hindoos. (Text and English Translation.) 8vo. leather, pp. 156. *London*, 1814. 3s.

**BROWN (CHARLES PHILIP)**—Wars of the Rajas, being the History of Anantapuram. Written in Telugu in or about the years 1750–1810. English Translation. 8vo. leather, pp. 91. *Madras*, 1853. 3s.

**BUIST (GEO.)**—Outline of the Operations of the British Troops in Scinde and Affghanistan, betwixt Nov. 1838 and Nov. 1841. (With Remarks on the Policy of the War.) 8vo. boards, pp. xv. xi. 314. With 2 Plates. *Bombay*, 1843. 7s. 6d.

**BURGESS (J.)**—The Rock-Temples of Elephanta or Ghárápurí. With Illustrations. Royal 8vo. cloth, pp. 80. *Bombay*, 1871. 6s.

**BURGESS (J.)** — The Rock Temples of Elurá or Verul. 8vo. sewed, pp. 77. *Bombay*, 1877. 4s.

**BURGESS (J.)**—Notes on the Bauddha Rock-Temples of Ajanta, their Paintings and Sculptures, and on the Paintings of the Bagh Caves, Modern Bauddha Mythology, etc. 4to. sewed, pp. 111. With 32 Plates. *Bombay*, 1879.

*** Archæological Survey of Western India, No. 9. Out of Print.

**BURGESS (J.) and Bhagwanlal Indraji Pandit.**—Inscriptions from the Cave-Temples of Western India, with Descriptive Notes, etc. 4to. sewed, pp. 114. With Numerous Plates. *Bombay*, 1881.

*** Archæological Survey of Western India, No. 10. Out of Print.

**BURGESS (J.)**—Notes on the Amarávati Stupa. 4to. sewed, pp. 57. With 17 Plates. *Madras*, 1882. 12s. 6d.

*** Archæological Survey of Southern India, No. 3.

**BUTTER (DONALD)**—Outlines of the Topography and Statistics of the Southern Districts of Oudh and of the Cantonment of Sultanpur-Oudh. Royal 8vo. boards, pp. 183. With 3 Plates. *Calcutta*, 1839. 3s.

**CALCUTTA.**—Administration Report of the Calcutta Municipality for 1868. With 9 Appendices. Folio. *Calcutta*, 1869. 5s.
The same for 1870. Folio. *Calcutta*, 1871. 6s.

**CALCUTTA.**—Administration Report of the Municipality of the Suburbs of Calcutta for the Year 1876–77. With Appendices. Folio, sewed, pp. iv. 75. *Calcutta*, 1877. 3s.

**CALCUTTA.**—Gastrell (J. E.) and H. F. Blanford.—Report on the Calcutta Cyclone of the 5th October, 1864. With 7 Plates. 8vo. cloth, pp. v. 150, xxv. *Calcutta*, 1866. 7s. 6d.

**CALCUTTA.**—Historical Notice concerning Calcutta in the Days of Job Charnock. From the East India and Colonial Magazine, 1837. 8vo. sewed, pp. 22. *Calcutta*, 1871. 1s. 6d.

**CALCUTTA.**—Report on the Census of Calcutta in 1866. Folio, boards, pp. ii. 228. With Tables. *Calcutta*, 1866. 5s.

**CALCUTTA REVIEW (The)**—Vols. 1 to 81, or Numbers 1 to 175. Post 8vo. partly bound. With Index to Vol. 1 to 50. In 2 Parts. *Calcutta*, 1844–89. 72 *Guineas*.

*** A fine clean copy of a complete set. Very rare and scarce. (Nos. 39 and 40 have never been published.)
(Trübner & Co. supply the continuation. Published Quarterly. Price each Number, 8s.)

**CALDWELL (The Right Rev. R.)**—Records of the Early History of the Tinnevelly Mission of the Society for Promoting Christian Knowledge and the Society for the Propagation of the Gospel in Foreign Parts. 8vo. cloth, pp. xii. and 356. *Madras*, 1881. 18s.

**CALDWELL (The Right Rev. R.)**—A Political and General History of the District of Tinnevelly in the Presidency of Madras, from the Earliest Period to its Cession to the English Government in A.D. 1801. Royal 8vo. cloth, pp. x. and 300. *Madras*, 1881. 12s. 6d.

**CAMPBELL (GEORGE)**—The Capital of India. With some Particulars of the Geography and Climate of the Country. 8vo. sewed, pp. 67. *Calcutta*, 1865. 1s.

**CAMPBELL (G.)** — Specimens of Languages of India. Including those of the Aboriginal Tribes of Bengal, the Central Provinces, and the Eastern Frontier. Folio, boards, pp. 6, 303. *Calcutta*, 1874. £1 11s. 6d.

**CAMPBELL (JUSTICE)**—The Ethnology of India. 8vo. sewed, pp. 152. 3s. 6d.

**CARR (CAPTAIN M. W.)** — Descriptive and Historical Papers relating to the Seven Pagodas on the Coromandel Coast. By W. Chambers, J. Goldingham, B. G. Babington, Rev. G. W. Mahon, Lieut. J. Braddock, Rev. W. Taylor, Sir W. Scott, Ch. Gubbins. Edited by Captain M. W. Carr. 8vo. half bound, pp. 245. With a Map and 24 Plates. *Madras*, 1869. 15s.

**CASHMERE.**—Davidge Brothers' Travellers' Companion and Guide to Cashmere. With Diary. 8vo. boards, pp. 91. *Lahore*, 1872. 2s.

**CASHMIR.**—Ince (J.)—The Kashmir Hand-book. A Guide for Visitors. With Maps and Routes. New Edition. Small 4to. cloth, pp. xxi. 271. *Calcutta*, 1872. 12s. 6d.

**CASHMIR Flower,** containing a Short History of Kashmir by Harischandra. In Hindi. 8vo. sewed, pp. 44. *Benares*, 1884. 2s. 6d.

**CASSELS (WALTER R.)**—Cotton. An Account of its Culture in the Bombay Presidency. Prepared from Government Records and other Authentic Sources, in accordance with a Resolution of the Government of India. Royal 8vo. cloth, pp. x. 347. With Maps and Tables. *Bombay*, 1862. 15s.

**CAUTNER (REV. HOBART)**—The Oriental Annual, or Scenes in India. With 22 Engravings from Drawings by W. Daniell. 8vo. leather, pp. 242. *London*. 5s.

**CAYLEY (DR. H.)**—Report on the Route to the Karakash River, via the Changchemnoo Valley and Pass. With a Map. 8vo. sewed, pp. 29. *Lahore*, 1868. 2s. 6d.

*** Selections from the Records of the Government of the Panjab.

**CHINGLEPUT.** — Crole (C. S.) — The Chingleput, late Madras District. A Manual compiled under the Orders of the Madras Government. Royal 8vo. half-bound, pp. iii. 439, xli. With Map. *Madras*, 1879. 10s. 6d.

**CHUCKERBUTTY (S. GOODEVE)**—Popular Lectures on Subjects of Indian Interest. 8vo. cloth, pp. 213. *Calcutta*, 1870. 5s.

**CHUNDER (Bholanauth)** — The Travels of a Hindoo to various parts of Bengal and Upper India. With an Introduction by J. T. Wheeler. Two vols. 8vo. cloth, pp. xxv. 439, viii. 409. With a Map. *London*, 1869. 15s.

**CLARKE (C. B.)**—Commelynaceæ et Cyrtandraceæ Bengalensis (Paucis aliis ex terris adjacentibus additis). Folio, half-cloth, pp. 133. With 93 Plates. *Calcutta*, 1874. £1 8s.

*(To be continued.)*

No. 244.

# TRÜBNER'S RECORD,

## A JOURNAL DEVOTED TO THE LITERATURE OF THE EAST.

### WITH NOTES AND LISTS OF CURRENT

### American, European and Colonial Publications.

MAY, 1889.    THIRD SERIES. VOL. I. NO. 2.    PRICE 2s.

## The Great Khalif's Confession.

[Abd-er-Rahman III. ascended the throne of the Moorish Empire in Spain when a mere youth of twenty. He at once set himself to repair the confusion into which the kingdom had fallen in the hands of weak predecessors. He subdued the recalcitrant Arab usurpers who had fastened on parts of the Empire ; he made the rebellious Christians submit ; fortress after fortress fell ; and in the midst of success he never abused his power. Mr. Stanley Lane-Poole in his " Moors in Spain " thus writes of him :

" The Moorish historians describe this resolute man in colours that seem hardly consistent with his strong imperious policy : nevertheless they describe him faithfully as the mildest and most enlightened sovereign that ever ruled a country. 'His meekness, his generosity, and his love of justice became proverbial. None of his ancestors ever surpassed him in courage in the field and zeal for religion. He was fond of science, and the patron of the learned, with whom he loved to converse. Many anecdotes are told of his strict justice and impartiality."

He made Cordoba, after Byzantium, the most beautiful of cities then existing. The great work of his later years (outside the toils of government, which he never in any sense deputed to others) was the building of the great palace of Ez-Zahará (the Fairest), in honour of the best loved of his wives, and named after her. He was devotedly attached to her, and she once begged him to build her a city, which should be called after her name, which he did ; having all his life had great delight in building.

After his death a paper was found in the Khalif's own handwriting, in which he had carefully noted those days in his long reign, in which he had been free from all sorrow : they numbered only fourteen. " O man of understanding," he added, " wonder and observe how small a portion of unclouded happiness the world can give even to the most fortunate."]

Abd-er-Rahman the Great in his ivory chair
Sat thinking of palaces stately and fair,
From the which he might gather a hint of grace,
That would lead him some worthier line to trace

In the spacious palace he now would design
To honour Ez-Zahará of grace divine—
The first of his wives for beauty, and more—
For sweetness and truth, and the love she bore.
And there rose in his fancy the images fair
Of towers and domes in the clear blue air,
With their crests whereon the Crescent would gleam,
Reflecting the sunlight like faëry dream.
And his mind as he sat, by the strangest law,
Went ranging back, with a sense of awe,
O'er the years that had passed since, young and bold,
He ascended the throne of the Emirs old :
When he grasped the reins of a falling state,
And proved restoration was not too late,—
That the sceptre which weakling hands had swayed,
Unworthy of those who the kingdom made,
With the sense that the Prophet, the Sent of God,
Was with them to lighten their arduous load,
In the hands of a man of might and will
Might blossom and flower, as aforetime, still.

He thought of his labours by sword and pen,
Of the strifes he had waged with rebellious men :
Of the battles and sieges, the sudden surprise,
When the waves of revolt, like a sea, did rise :
Of the hours of thought, the sagacious plan,
The swift attack, himself in the van,
By which he secured the kingdom's peace,
And had fixed the laws that gave rich increase—
Till the Moorish power had once again
For tears given smiles unto sunlit Spain,—
And the wealth that was better than warlike spoil—
Content and abundance of wine and oil :
Till the downtrod Spaniards once more were free
From the lash of the Arab nobility ;
And robber and brigand no more could rove,
And ravish the fruits of the field and grove :
Till even the Christians confessed 'twas good
To honour a king that no foe withstood :
Who had equal justice for sovereign goal,
And built up the fragments to one grand whole.
And the care of his empire so sore had weighed
That he felt for success in his soul he paid.
*His* joy he had yielded that Spain might smile,
And its valleys be rich in their wine and oil —

Where the Mosque and the Temple not far apart
Heard the prayer in each from the fervent heart,
And the " Allah, mashallah," rising clear,
In the Christian awakened no sense of fear.

    And he knelt as the Azan rang overhead,
And when he arose, he mused and said :

    " For the people the King, be he chosen or heir
To the throne, if true, must the burden bear :
His life he gives for the good of all,
If he strive but to follow the nobler call.
There is no rest for the head that guides,
Nor the heart that has room for a world besides
The personal need, and is fain to rise
To the law of the godlike and truly wise.
Of the days of my life how few have been
Untroubled, reposeful, and serene !
From one care forth still another sprang,
And the same sad tune through all there rang
In my ears : nought holds : all yields to change,
Whether still we stand, or more boldly range.
I have ceaseless laboured and sought the good
Of the ever-vagrant multitude,
Who deem that I, in this chair of state,
With the bowing crowds who upon me wait,
Must needs be happy and free from care,
And enjoy old age, with the amplest share
Of love and honour, and cheerful rest,
With nought of trouble to stir the breast.
Alas ! alas ! they but judge by shows :
If I count up my gains to the latest close,
My joys I scarcely can reckon so high
That I need much to boast of my destiny :
Of all the changeful days of my life,
I find but a few unmarred by strife,
Or change, or death, or the sense of loss,
Or the darkening shadow of some cross :
With the Christian's creed I needs must close
That a cross from my blessings hath oft arose.

    " But the palace shall all the fairer be,
For love finds joys in extremity :
In the dangers it knows, and the risks it runs,
And the labours that grow with the lessening suns ;
Ez-Zahará shall shine in the light, and tell
To future times that I loved as well
As fought and conquered, and ruled, and gave
Laws that were fruitful to yield and save.
And perchance in the years when Spain hath ceased
To share in the joys of the well-spread feast
Of a faithful rule, and is forced to bow
To another sceptre than rules it now,
Ez-Zahará will still remain to tell
Abd-er-Rahman's wish was to rule it well ;
And when, with wonder, the travellers gaze
On the golden domes, and the winding ways,

On the pillared courts, and the fountains fair,
And the rich mosaics of colours rare :
On the spires that shine, and the crests that glow,
And the gates with their richly-carven show,
They will say Abd-er-Rahman of lion heart
Found gain in the beauty of love's own art ;
And he spread over Spain his tokens true
Of a love that with time ever waxed and grew ;
And softened his rule and made it great :
For love is the power that upholds a state,
As it holds the soul of a man and makes
Even weak souls strong for other's sakes."

ALEX. H. JAPP.

## The Anthropological Survey of Bengal.

Mr. H. H. Risley, of the Bengal C.S., who has been entrusted with the Anthropological Survey of Bengal, and whose articles on *Widow and Infant Marriage in Bengal* and on *Primitive Marriage in Bengal* (Asiatic Quarterly Review for Oct. 1887, and July, 1888) have attracted a good deal of attention, writes in a letter dated Calcutta, 27 March, as follows to Dr. Rost in reference to the progress of his work :—

"My Anthropological Report stands thus :—I am working up the materials under the title, 'The Tribes and Castes of Bengal,' and four volumes making about 1800 pages are now standing in type. Vols. I. and II. bearing the sub-title 'Anthropometric Data' consist of measurements and the conclusions provisionally drawn from them. Vols. III. and IV. (sub-title 'Ethnographic Data') comprise descriptions, arranged in the form of a dictionary, of every caste, sub-caste, sept, section, etc., that I can hear of in 'Bengal,' *i.e.* in the administrative area under the Lieutenant-Governor of Bengal. This reading of Bengal enables me to deal with the Nepalese and Tibetan races, but the attempt to make the work complete for administrative purposes has added greatly to its bulk."

We supplement this information by an extract in reference to Mr. Risley's work from the Annual Address delivered by the President of the Asiatic Society of Bengal at Calcutta on Feb. 6th of the present year :—

"Mr. Risley has been invited by the Committee of the Paris Exhibition to take part in the Anthropological Section, and a series of life-size models of representative types of the races of Bengal are now being prepared at the School of Art for exhibition at Paris. This experiment is of special interest as being an attempt to combine artistic effect with the accurate delineation of feature required for scientific purposes. A number of measurements of each subject are taken on the French system, and the model is worked up in strict accordance with these dimensions, a list of which will be attached to the final castings. If scientific opinion in Europe approves of these figures, it is hoped that some permanent demand may arise which would lead to an extension of the series, and while offering employment to the indigenous modellers, would at the same time admirably illustrate the marked diversity of type met with within even the limits of a single Province, and would afford the means for systematic study of Indian ethnology in Europe" (p. 64).

## Note on the State of Burma in March, 1889.[*]

The work of pacification and settlement in Upper Burma has necessarily been gradual. For seven years before the annexation a semi-civilized and passionate people had been subjected to mis-government of the worst kind. Tyranny, injustice, and weakness in the administration had thoroughly disorganized the social fabric and reduced every part of the country to a state of anarchy. The whole kingdom was the prey of robber bands who lived by plunder and committed the most atrocious crimes, often under the hardly concealed protection of some Minister of State or local official. The circumstances of the annexation intensified the difficulties with which the new Government had to contend. The capital fell almost without a blow, and the King and his family became prisoners of war. The army, or the armed rabble which supplied its place, had never met British troops in the field and learned the futility of resistance. The failure, which was perhaps under the circumstances unavoidable, to thoroughly disarm the Burmese soldiers allowed numbers of armed and undisciplined men, unaccustomed to labour, to be at large without suitable employment. These men joined one or other of the principal gangs of robbers and became formidable disturbers of the peace. The annexation of the whole of Burma from the Chin hills on the west to the Shan country on the east, and from the sea on the south to the Kachin hills on the north, allowed no outlet for the restless spirits who either preferred a lawless life to settled employment or were induced to join one or other of the Pretenders who made futile efforts to overthrow the new Government. The task before the Administration was not to carry on a Government already existent, but to reintegrate a disorganized community and to restore order in a country which

had for years been in a state of anarchy. It will be the object of this note to indicate briefly what progress has been made in this work.

2. Before proceeding to a detailed review of the several districts into which Upper Burma is divided, it is well to note some general points in which improvement is obvious to all who have followed the progress of events since the occupation of Mandalay in 1885. In the first place there are now scarcely any large bands of dacoits under well-known leaders firmly established in the rich districts of the plains. Bo Swè no longer divides the Minbu district with Ôktama; Hla U is almost forgotten in Sagaing. Where in 1886 dacoit bands numbered their members by scores and hundreds, those which now remain are counted by fives or at most by tens. In the second place, the atrocity of the crimes which are committed has diminished. In the early months of 1886 well authenticated stories were told of the burning and torture of women and of other horrible crimes. Such atrocities are now of rare occurrence. The introduction of order and good government and the enlistment of the people on the side of the Administration have made steady progress. The results are apparent in almost every district. It may be confidently asserted that no part of the country which had been reduced to order at the beginning of 1888 has been suffered to relapse into confusion, while the area under settled government has been steadily extended.

3. To proceed to an examination of the state of the several districts, the first and most important is Mandalay, in which is situated the last seat of Government of the Burmese kings. The town of Mandalay has been singularly free from serious crime since the beginning of 1887. Early in that year a conspiracy, which might have been formidable, was discovered and the conspirators were promptly punished. Since that time the town has been perfectly quiet, and the people of Mandalay have lived as free from danger as the people of Rangoon. The recurrence, in each hot weather, of destructive fires in the town is not in any way the result of criminal acts. In only one case during the last two years has there been any doubt as to the accidental origin of any large fire; and even in that case, a case of recent occurrence, the suspicion that the crime of arson was committed has not been verified. The state of the Mandalay district, the large area stretching north, south, and east of the town, is almost equally satisfactory. In 1887 various leaders, Bo Zeya, Bo To, Bo So, and others of less note, divided the district almost to the gates of Mandalay. Bo Zeya has been driven out and has taken refuge in a remote Shan State; Bo So has surrendered and taken service under the British Government, and now loyally exercises his influence in

[*] This admirable Memorandum on the pacification of Burma, by Mr. Henry T. White, Chief Secretary to the Chief Commissioner, is on account of its great importance reprinted in full.

preserving order in the tract of country in which he formerly lived as a robber chief. Bo To alone remains and causes slight disturbance to the north-west of Mandalay. His power has much diminished; but he still commits occasional dacoities and can at times get together ten or fifteen followers. His haunts are the islands of the Irrawaddy and the borders of the Mandalay, Sagaing, and Shwebo districts. Systematic action is being taken against him and there is every reason to hope that he will be run down before the end of the present open season. The remoter parts of the district on the borders of the Myitngè were thoroughly and effectually examined towards the close of the year 1888 with the most satisfactory result. A good road has been made for 40 miles towards the Shan States to the great convenience of traders and travellers; and along this road, which passes through country where in 1886 strong bands of dacoits and rebels withstood our troops, English and Native travellers can now proceed in safety without escort. Trade with the Shan States continues to increase and many caravans of mules, bullocks, and men on foot constantly pass to and from Mandalay and the States of Thibaw and Theinni. Instances of attacks on any of these caravans are almost unknown. Of the opening of the railway to Mandalay it is scarcely necessary to speak. The value of this important work is too obvious to need exposition. But it may be remarked in connection with the present subject that the work has suffered practically no interruption from dacoits; that for months past the Engineers have been able to move about without escorts; and that the railway from the Toungoo district to Mandalay was adequately guarded during construction by a battalion of 700 men.

4. In the Shwebo district, which lies on the west of the Irrawaddy river, progress almost equally conspicuous has been made. Shwebo was at first a turbulent and troubled district, where large bands of dacoits, favoured by the vast forest tracts which cover a great part of the country, defied the local authorities. The district is not yet entirely free from dacoity, but there are no large and organized bands; and the crimes which occur are of a comparatively unimportant type. The most serious event in recent months has been the surprise of a party of Burmese police which fell into an ambush and lost some of their number and several guns. The administration of the Shwebo district has made steady progress and the district cannot now be considered disturbed. This result is in no small measure due to the influence of Maung Tun, the representative of the most notable local family, who has loyally aided the Government from the beginning and whose personal exertions have been unremittent. This circumstance is noted as one instance among

many in which judicious use has been made of the services of Native officials who have shown readiness to accept appointments under the British Government.

5. Mandalay and Shwebo are the only two districts in the Northern Division which may be described as districts in the plains where it is possible to establish settled administration on ordinary lines without extraordinary difficulty. The circumstances of the remaining districts of the Northern Division are different. The Myadaung district consists of a strip of country on the west of the Irrawaddy river bordering on the Shan State of Wuntho, and widening out towards the south where it adjoins the districts of Shwebo and Ye-u; and of a strip of country on the east of the river bordering on the Shan State of Momeik. The condition of the Myadaung district has not been entirely satisfactory, though even here the only serious occurrence during the past few months was the successful attack by dacoits on a small party of military police which fell into an ambush and lost five or six men. The band which committed this crime consisted of not more than 40 men. The District authorities took steps to prevent the commission of further acts of violence and to punish the villagers which had afforded shelter and support to the dacoits. The rest of the Myadaung district has been free from crime of special importance. It must be noted that during the greater part of the year 1888 paucity of qualified officers rendered it necessary to leave the Myadaung district in charge of an officer recently transferred from India who has not yet acquired a knowledge of the Burmese language. A more experienced officer has been in charge since December last; and the present state of the district is by no means unsatisfactory. On the Wuntho border peace has been preserved and the relations of the local officers with the Sawbwa of Wuntho, though not cordial owing to the persistent refusal of the Sawbwa to meet the British Officers in British territory, are still free from any serious complications.

6. The Bhamo district is essentially a hill district. It consists of the Mogaung subdivision, a large extent of country on the west of the Irrawaddy, peopled largely by Kachins, and of a considerable tract of country bordering on hills inhabited by Kachins on the east of the river. The Kachins are a wild race who were never thoroughly dominated by the Burmese, and who even in recent years gave much trouble to the Burmese Government. It was not to be expected that they would at once settle down and abandon their habit of raiding, which had become traditional with them for many generations. The necessity of punishing the Kachins in the Mogaung subdivision for attacks on traders during the open season of 1887-88 and for harbouring the rebels who attacked Mogaung itself in

May, 1888, has been recognized by the Government of India. These operations are still in progress. On the east of the river the Bhamo district borders on the frontier province of Yunnan as well as on the Kachin hills. The south-east part of the district consists of part of the old Shan State of Mohlaing ; and within sight of Bhamo is the Kachin hill of Pônkan against which an abortive expedition was led in 1886. There have been three events of some gravity in these parts of the Bhamo district during the past few months. In January a band of some 100 outlaws, mostly deserters from the Chinese garrison in Yunnan, assembled on the north-east of Bhamo. They were promptly and judiciously attacked by the District Superintendent of Police under the direction of the Deputy Commissioner and were dispersed with heavy loss. Somewhat later a gathering of dacoits and outlaws assembled in the part of the district which formerly belonged to the State of Mohlaing and which is now known as the Upper Sinkan township. The origin of this gathering is somewhat obscure. But it is believed to have been formed in the interest of Kan Hlaing, a claimant to the Sawbwaship of Mohlaing, who has many friends and adherents in the Upper Sinkan township. This band was attacked in a strong position by an inadequate force of police with the result that the police were compelled to retire with loss and with the sacrifice of their transport and baggage. A strong body of troops was immediately sent against the dacoits, and the position was carried after a stout resistance. Our loss on this occasion was considerable ; but the dacoits had learnt a lesson and the gathering dispersed as suddenly as it had collected. After this one encounter at Malin the troops never succeeded in coming within striking distance of the dacoits. While these events were in progress reports were current that a large band of Chinese deserters and other outlaws were assembled at Pônkan hill. The Sawbwa of Pônkan has yet to be taught a lesson. He is an insignificant person, but he lives in a hill difficult of approach and he has gathered courage by reason of immunity from punishment for former offences. The reported gathering at Pônkan has never appeared in the plains. On one or two occasions dacoits were reported to be present at Mansi, 13 miles from Bhamo, at the foot of Pônkan hill, and more than once troops were sent against them, but on arrival found the place deserted. On the last occasion, within the last few days, a force despatched from Bhamo came upon a body of men near Mansi, in a stockaded position, and drove them out. This band is reported to have consisted of Kachins from Pônkan, and no Chinese are believed to have been present. It seems more than probable that the alleged gathering of Chinese at Pônkan had no real existence. The more southern parts of the Bhamo district have been disturbed by a dacoit leader named Hla Gyaw who takes refuge in the Kachin hills and with whom the police have not yet succeeded in coming to terms. The difficulty of dealing with dacoits in a hill country is much greater than in the plains.

7. The remaining district in the Northern Division is that of the Ruby Mines. This tract formerly was part of the Shan State of Mainglôn. It lies on the borders of the Shan States of Mainglôn, Thibaw, Momeik, and Taungbaing. The State of Momeik has suffered owing to the feeble nature of the native administration. In pursuance of the policy which, with the approval of the Government of India, has been adopted in respect of all the Shan States, Momeik has been allowed to administer itself. It is not possible, with the resources at our command, to place garrisons in every Shan State, and it is not desirable to do so. In return for their autonomy the Sawbwas are expected to maintain order in their States and to guard their borders against attacks from without. Momeik is physically a difficult country to administer ; on the north-east it merges into a mountainous tract occupied by Kachins over whom the Sawbwa has little or no control. Here, in a practically inaccessible hill, has lived for some time a scion of the Burmese Royal House named Yan Naing. This Prince for some time troubled the Ava district and it was on his behalf that in 1887 the conspiracy in Mandalay previously mentioned was concerted. Driven out of the plain country, he has sought refuge in these remote hills, and from time to time his followers have threatened Momeik. The Chief Commissioner had intended that during the present season Lieutenant Daly, the energetic and capable Superintendent of the Northern Shan States, should visit Taungbaing, on the borders of which State Yan Naing is established, and secure either his capture or surrender. Lieutenant Daly's visit to Taungbaing was postponed owing to the unexpected delay in the recruitment of the companies of the Shan levy which were to form his escort. Meanwhile the Deputy Commissioner of the Ruby Mines, anxious to strike a blow at Yan Naing, arranged, without the Chief Commissioner's knowledge, to send troops to Momeik. It seems probable that Yan Naing was in communication with Kan Hlaing and that the disturbances raised by the latter in Bhamo were intended to be movements in support of Yan Naing's action. If the Chief Commissioner had been informed that any considerable body of men were moving down on Momeik under Yan Naing, he would have taken measures in consultation with Sir George White to deal with them. The despatch of a small body of British troops to Momeik without any civil officer to give them

information and to guide them was not a measure which the Chief Commissioner would have adopted, and although the dacoits were ultimately defeated with loss, it was not altogether happy in its results. The Ruby Mines district has been in a more disturbed state during the last few months than since the beginning of 1887, when it was first occupied. But the disturbances are not internal. They are the work of outlaws from the adjacent States which are not under our immediate administration. Steps have been taken to bring these States into order and to disperse any gathering of dacoits which may have collected therein. It may be remarked that in the telegrams sent to the English papers everything has been said to magnify the disturbances in and about the Ruby Mines. The assertion for example that the sanitarium, which is held by a strong body of British troops, was in danger of being seized by the gang of dacoits who were dispersed near Momeik is absurd as well as false.

8. Turning to the Central Division, we deal first with the rich and important district of Kyauksè, which was disturbed by gangs of dacoits, who collected on the hills which border the district on the east under the command of a Pretender known as the Setkya Prince. These gangs committed many dacoities in the Kyauksè district; but they were effectually dealt with and dispersed. The Setkya Prince was forced to fly to the neighbouring Shan State of Yatsauk, where he was arrested and delivered up by the loyal Sawbwa of that State. He was tried and sentenced to death; and the country is thus rid of a person who, though himself of no special note, has been the cause of much trouble during the past three years. Of equal importance has been the surrender of the well-known leader Myat Hmôn, who was formerly a king in the Southern part of the district. It was apprehended that Myat Hmôn and his followers might give trouble during the open season. The apprehension was not realized, as Myat Hmôn and all his followers surrendered with their arms to the Deputy Commissioner of Kyauksè. They received a free pardon and are now living peaceably in their own villages. Since the dispersal of the Setkya Pretender's gang at the beginning of the dry season, the Kyauksè district has been and continues to be perfectly quiet and free from serious crime.

9. The Sagaing district, which includes the old district of Ava, was seriously disturbed in the beginning of 1888. Systematic efforts under the able direction of Colonel W. P. Symons, Mr. G. M. S. Carter, and Lieutenant H. A. Browning were made throughout the past year to thoroughly settle this important district. These efforts were entirely successful. The most notable leader on the Ava side, Shwe Yan, has been killed; on the Sagaing side,

Min O and Nyo Pu have been captured, Nyo U has been killed, and Bo Sawbwagyi has been tried and executed; Bo To alone remains. Not only have the leaders been killed or captured, but the members of their gangs have been individually accounted for, and the villages which formerly harboured and paid tribute to them are now ranged on the side of the authority. Practically the whole of the Sagaing district has been reduced to perfect order, the local officers have obtained a thorough hold of the country, and hundreds of families who had taken refuge in Mandalay and elsewhere have returned to their old homes. There have recently been dacoities on the Ava side, but no serious outbreak of crime has occurred. The excellent results achieved in Sagaing are undeniable, and the present condition of the district compares most favourably with its condition in 1886–87, in 1887–88, or even in the comparatively well-ordered times of Mindôn Min.

10. The rest of the Central Division has been undisturbed by serious outbreaks of crime. In the south of Ye-u there have been sporadic dacoities, such as may be expected to occur in parts of the province for some years to come. But there has been no revival of organized dacoity on a large scale such as that which prevailed in the district during the year 1887. The Upper and Lower Chindwin districts have been and still are remarkably free from crime.

11. The record of events in the Southern Division is less completely satisfactory. This division consists of the Pakôkku, Myingyan, Magwe, and Minbu districts. The Pakôkku district embraces the country between the Lower Chindwin district and the Minbu district. It includes the tract known as the Yaw country, which lies along the borders of the Chin hills, and takes in the valley of the Myittha river, an affluent of the Chindwin, up to the borders of the Shan State of Kalè. This part of the district had not been brought under settled administration before the present season. Early in 1887 Captain Eyre, the Deputy Commissioner, visited the country and made arrangements for administrating it through the local Burman officials. No British officials and no police were stationed there. The people were allowed to retain their arms as a protection against Chin raiders. In accordance with the Chief Commissioner's expectations, the cessation of the heavy rains was the signal for the commission of raids by the Chin tribes on the border of Yaw and Kalè. The natural raiding proclivities of the Chins were fostered by a Pretender known as the Shwegyobyu Prince who had been driven from the plains and forced to take refuge in the hills. The Chief Commissioner had foreseen the occurrence of Chin raids as soon as the season was favourable,

and the fulfilment of his expectations in this respect rendered necessary the despatch of an expedition against the Chins. As soon as these operations were on foot, a rising took place in the Yaw country. Owing to causes which might have been prevented and for which the officers, civil and military, and the troops stationed in Yaw, are responsible, the rising assumed a more formidable appearance than its actual importance justified. The villagers who, as has been explained above, were armed, saw the troops inactive or unsuccessful and joined the dacoits. For some days a British garrison was shut up in Gangaw by a contemptible gang of dacoits. Prompt measures were taken for their relief and troops were sent from all sides into the Yaw country. The result was the almost immediate dispersal of the dacoit gangs. As in the case of the Ruby Mines, exaggerated reports have been spread of the occurrences in Yaw. The Yaw country is now being thoroughly and systematically settled by Colonel Symons and Mr. D. Ross. It may be noted that though several serious raids were committed by Chins at the close of the last rainy season, no raids of such magnitude as those committed on the Chittagong side have yet occurred in Burma. In the rest of the Pakôkku district vigorous and successful action has been taken against such dacoit gangs as still remained. Some time ago the most notable leader, Nga Kwe, was killed; and within the last few days a leader of less note, but still of some importance, named Yan Shin, was killed in fight by a small party of Burmans led by Burmese civil officers. At present the Pakôkku district is undisturbed.

12. Part of the Myingyan district has not yet been thoroughly reduced to order. This is the difficult tract lying to the east on the borders of Meiktila, and to the south on the borders of Magwe. It includes the Popa tract, where good work has been done by Captain Tinley, but which is still not thoroughly in order. As already noted, the physical difficulties of this tract of country are very great, and can scarcely be realized by any one who has not travelled through it. It is a mass of hills and ravines where dacoits have many advantages over troops and police. The administration of the Myingyan and Meiktila districts cannot, however, be entirely absolved from blame for the continuance of serious dacoities in this tract, and especially for the collection of a large and formidable band of dacoits under a leader who styles himself Kywèyaza. In February this gathering was successfully dealt with by a combined movement of troops and police from Meiktila and Myingyan; and systematic operations for the pacification and settlement of the tract under reference are now in progress. The dacoit leaders Yan Nyun and Nga Cho are still at large. But they are being closely pursued, and recently they have been unable to commit any serious crimes. The Chief Commissioner has just learnt that Bo Cho and all his gang have offered to surrender with their arms, and Yan Nyun, it is reported, is anxious to surrender, but his crimes are too great to permit of his being given a free pardon. The rest of the Myingyan district, apart from this tract, is quite quiet.

13. The Magwe district, which includes Yenaugyaung and Taungdwingyi, is the only district in the plains of Upper Burma which is still in an unsatisfactory state. There have been many dacoities of a serious nature in this district; and bands of dacoits have collected and have on more than one occasion been successful in encounters with the military police. The Chief Commissioner attributes the unsettled state of the Magwe district partly to the *personnel* of the district staff. The Myoôk of Magwe was an old Burman official who contrived to retain the confidence of the local officers, although there is much reason to believe that he was working with the dacoits. In the neighbourhood of Yenangyaung the crimes which have been committed are probably connected with the oil industry. The lease of the wells and the monopoly of purchasing oil to a European firm has not been pleasing to the native well-owners and to others formerly connected with the trade. A change has recently been made in the district staff and, if necessary, further changes will be made. In the mean time active operations are in progress and the need of systematic working has been pointed out to the District Officers.

14. The Minbu district was formerly one of the most unsettled in the whole province. During the past few months excellent progress has been made in its settlement. The principal dacoit leaders, Ôktama, Ôktaya, and Byaing Gyi, are still at large; but they are being constantly and persistently hunted and they have no opportunity of collecting any formidable gathering during the present season. In the Salin subdivision and on the borders of the hills to the west conspicuous success has been attained by the Deputy Commissioner, Mr. Hartnoll, and by the Subdivisional Officers acting under his directions. The state of the Minbu district is better now than at any previous time since the annexation. The people have begun to appreciate our administration and the settlement of the district is proceeding in a systematic manner.

15. The Eastern Division, which consists of the Pyinmana, Yamèthin, and Meiktila districts, has continued undisturbed. These districts are as quiet as any districts in Lower Burma. On the borders of Pyinmana dacoit bands have been harboured in the

adjacent Shan hills, and occasionally have descended into the plains of the district as they descend from time to time on villages in the adjacent Lower Burma district of Toungoo. Steps have been taken to deal with the State where these bands are harboured. Meanwhile forest and agricultural work is in full progress throughout the district.

16. The Shan States have for the most part been free from disturbance. Perfect order has been maintained without difficulty in the whole of the Southern and Eastern States. In the north, as already explained, Momeik has been disturbed, and Mainglôn has continued to afford a refuge for dacoits. There was also in January last a disturbance not of a very serious nature in Southern Theinni. The Sawbwa of Southern Theinni, who seems to be scarcely equal to the duties of his position, was driven out by a party of insurgents; but the rising was at once suppressed by the Superintendent of the Northern Shan States with a handful of men, and there has been no recurrence of disorder. In the south, the expedition to Eastern Karenni was successfully carried out and Mr. Hildebrand succeeded in effecting what promises to be an entirely satisfactory settlement in that State. On his return he arranged some boundary disputes, not of a very serious nature, between the Western Karenni Chief Pobya and the Sawbwa of Mobyè.

17. From the preceding paragraphs it will be seen that the greater part of Upper Burma is settling down in a very satisfactory manner. In Sagaing, Kyaukse, and Minbu conspicuously good results have been attained. In other districts less has been done of late because less remained to do. Except in Magwe and part of Myingyan, the only disturbances of any consequence have occurred on the outskirts of the province in places where we had neither troops nor police and have been caused by persons who have been driven out of their former haunts in the plains. The occurrence of these disturbances on the outskirts is an indication of the permanent nature of the settlement which has been effected in the interior of the province.

18. The revenue of Upper Burma has increased from Rs. 22,24,980 in 1886–87 to Rs. 50,16,360 in 1887 and 1888. It is estimated that in 1888–89 the revenue will amount to Rs. 68,60,000 of which Rs. 59,09,512 had been collected up to the end of February. In 1889–90 the revenue is estimated at Rs. 75,92,000. This is exclusive of the estimated gross earnings of the Toungoo-Mandalay Extension Railway and of local revenue. The land revenue has been—

| | Rs. |
|---|---|
| In 1886–87 ... ... | 16,71,730 |
| In 1887–88 ... ... | 37,87,733 |
| In 1888–89 ... ... | 41,16,000 |
| In 1889–90 ... ... | 44,83,000 |

The land revenue for the last two years is estimated only. The actuals to the end of February amount to Rs. 36,29,270. The stamp revenue has increased as follows :—

| | | | | Rs. |
|---|---|---|---|---|
| 1886–87 | ... | ... | ... | 33,940 |
| 1887–88 | ... | ... | ... | 1,07,720 |
| 1888–89 | ... | ... | ... | 1,40,000 estimated. |
| 1889–90 | ... | ... | ... | 1,51,000 estimated. |

The actuals to the end of February are Rs. 1,25,344.

The excise revenue has also increased thus—

| | | | | Rs. |
|---|---|---|---|---|
| 1886–87 | ... | ... | ... | 67,250 |
| 1887–88 | ... | ... | ... | 2,90,660 |
| 1888–89 | ... | ... | ... | 3,80,000 estimated. |
| 1889–90 | ... | ... | ... | 6,11,000 estimated. |

The actuals to the end of February amount to Rs. 3,21,245.

19. The stamp and excise revenue has been affected by the extension of the Stamp, Court-fees, and Opium Acts to Upper Burma; but the land revenue, which consists for the most part of a tax upon households (thathameda), is a sure indicator of the increased tranquility of the country. Thathameda is assessed at an average rate of Rs. 10 per household, so every increase of Rs. 10 in the thathameda means, speaking broadly, that a household has settled down to peaceful pursuits, or that a household which had escaped assessment owing to the Revenue Officers having been occupied in suppressing disturbances has now been assessed because Revenue Officers have had leisure to attend to the assessments. In the Eastern division the increase of land revenue has been most marked. It has risen from Rs. 1,47,070 in 1886–87 to Rs. 4,94,200 in 1887–88 and to Rs. 6,15,000 in 1888–89.

20. Lower Burma may be said to have returned to its normal state. The first two quarters of the year are usually the most fruitful in crime, and therefore the present quarter will probably be found to show a larger number of violent crimes than the preceding quarter; but it will certainly be far more free from crime than the corresponding quarter of last year. The Thayetmyo district in the early months of last year was much disturbed. One part of it, the Myedè division, was effectually settled by Mr. J. S. D. Fraser, and has since remained undisturbed. In the western part it was apprehended that Po Thu Daw, a dacoit leader who with his gang lives in the fastnesses of the Arakan Yomas, might give trouble. He has, however, been kept in check by operations undertaken by the Deputy Commissioner, Mr. Burne. These operations have had no conspicuous results, the country in which they are carried on being unfavourable. But they have at least prevented Po Thu Daw from collecting men and descending on the plains. The number of dacoities in the Thayetmyo district during the past few months has been large ; but there has been a con-

siderable decrease as compared with the number in previous years. In Tharrawaddy excellent results have been attained, and though there have been some cases of dacoity in one part of the district during the past few days, there is no reason to apprehend any serious outbreak of crime in this district, which is in good hands. In Pegu and Hanthawaddy sporadic dacoities have occurred, but there has been nothing of the nature of gang dacoities on a very serious scale. In Sandoway a small gang of dacoits gave some trouble in December and January, but is not likely to assume formidable dimensions. The rest of the lower province is undisturbed.

RANGOON, 18th March, 1889.

---

## The Nicobar Islanders.

### By EDWARD HORACE MAN.

[By the kind permission of the Council of the Anthropological Institute, we print some portions of the Introduction (read as a separate paper before the Institute on June 26, 1888, and printed in the current number of their Journal) of Mr. Man's forthcoming work on the Nicobarese. We hope to be able to give in our next issue a chapter extracted from the body of this work. Mr. Man, who has in an official capacity resided in the Andaman and Nicobar Islands for the better part of twenty years, and has made a scientific study of the inhabitants of both groups of islands as well as of the languages and dialects spoken there, is justly considered the best living authority on everything relating to them. We here append a list of his publications, with a view to showing how much of what we know about the Andamanese and Nicobarese is due to his indefatigable labours in this field of research :—

List of Nicobarese Words (with sentences) in the Nancowry dialect (Journ. Asiatic Soc. Bengal for 1872) ;

The Lord's Prayer in the South Andamanese dialect, —conjointly with Capt. R. C. Temple (Trübner & Co. 1876) ;

The Arts of the Andamanese and Nicobarese,—with observations by General Lane-Fox, F.R.S. (Journal Anthropolog. Institute for 1878) ;

Note on two Maps of the Andaman Islands,—conjointly with Capt. R. C. Temple (Journ. Roy. Geogr. Society for 1880) ;

On the Andaman and Nicobar Objects presented to General Pitt-Rivers, F.R.S. (Journ. Anthropol. Inst. for 1882) ;

Illustrative Catalogue of Nicobarese Objects exhibited in the International Exhibition at Calcutta, 1883 (Trübner & Co.) ;

On the Aboriginal Inhabitants of the Andaman Islands,—with Report of Researches into the Language of the South Andaman Island, by A. J. Ellis, F.R.S. Illustrated (Trübner & Co. 1885) ;

A Brief Account of the Nicobar Islanders (Illustrated, Journ. Anthropol. Institute, 1886) ;

Illustrative Catalogues with Collections of Nicobarese Objects sent to 1, the British Museum, 2, the Oxford University Museum, 3, the Imperial and Royal Court Museum, Vienna ;

Illustrative Catalogues with Collections of Andamanese Objects sent to the Ethnographical Museum, Florence, and the Imperial and Royal Court Museum, Vienna.

*In Course of Publication.*

A Grammar and Dictionary of the Nicobarese (Nancowry dialect) ;

A Monograph on the Nicobarese Islanders (Illustrated) ;

A Grammar and Dictionary of the S. Andaman language.]

There may be said to remain at the present day but few races regarding whom accounts, more or less accurate, have not been published, but year by year the researches of Science reveal in clearer and yet clearer light the great care which is required of those who undertake the task of describing the condition and customs of uncivilized peoples, and it is now a recognized fact that any detailed report which is not based upon a long and intimate acquaintance with the language, as well as with the country and its inhabitants, must be received with extreme caution, so difficult is it for civilized man to appreciate the position and modes of thought of those in a lower scale than himself in the human family, not to mention those wild children of the forest whose wants are for the most part limited to the spontaneous products of the jungles, and whose knowledge of the past, present, and future has a not much wider range.

In 1871, when I was first appointed to the Nicobar Islands, I commenced a study of the dialect spoken by the natives living in the vicinity of the Government Settlement in Nancowry Harbour, with a view to facilitating ethnological researches among them. From that time to the present during my official residences in the group—of terms of varying duration, but amounting in all to nearly seven years—I have prepared a vocabulary estimated to contain between 6000 and 7000 words of the language as spoken in the Central Group, besides collecting several hundred words of the five remaining dialects. The task, though not on untried ground, as in the case of my concurrent efforts in the same direction at the Andamans, was not lightened to any appreciable extent by the labours of others, for the lists prepared by Fontana (1795), Barbe (1846), and the members of the Novara Expedition (1858), all of whom passed but a short time in the islands, were necessarily meagre and inaccurate ; moreover, as they were not based on any recognized system of transliteration, and as the vowels were in no instance accentuated, it will be readily understood that the value of the contributions was considerably lessened.

It has been well said, that to describe any language, "we must view it in relation to man generally, and to the particular race to which it belongs. We must first consider what the objects are which every language must accomplish ; and next, the different degrees and modes in which those objects are accomplished in different classes, before we can appreciate the character of the particular tongue which may form the subject of our investigation." These remarks are especially applicable to races which, like the Nicobarese, manifest in the structure of their language the external and alien influences which have been brought to bear upon them.

Among the many hindrances experienced in endeavouring to acquire a knowledge of the dialects of these islanders is the almost insurmountable one of obtaining the required information from persons whose articulation has not been materially affected by the frightful dental incrustation which is so general among the adult population. This fact, when taken into consideration with the extensive range of sounds contained in the language—a large proportion of which consist of nasal diphthongs—will proclaim the task of transliteration to be one requiring time and much careful study. With the valuable assistance of Mr. A. J. Ellis, F.R.S., the sounds found in use among the Nicobarese have been reduced to a system rendered by an alphabet of 60 letters, comprising 21 oral vowels and diphthongs, 14 nasal vowels and diphthongs, and 25 consonants.

The natural reserve of the natives towards aliens in all matters connected with their religious beliefs, superstitions, and practices adds greatly to the difficulties to be overcome in studying the race and acquiring a fair knowledge of their language, and the result attained has been achieved only by dint of constant gifts and promises of further reward, whereby attendance more or less regular, if not attention, has been partially secured.

But before we proceed to a consideration of the habits and customs of the Nicobarese, it may be well to gain a general idea of the position of the group, and of the main points of interest connected with their past history so far as this is ascertainable from the accounts of early navigators and settlers.

A glance at the map (xviii.) will show the islands to be situated between the sixth and tenth degrees of north latitude and between the meridian of 92° 42′ and 94° E. of Greenwich ; they thus lie midway between Little Andaman and Acheen, and form, with the Andamans, Coco and Preparis Islands, a series, as it were, of stepping-stones of volcanic origin, connecting the province of Burma with the large island of Sumatra.

Regarding the origin of the group, many theories, it is almost needless to say, have been advanced. Mr. S. Kurz considered that they "are, in all probability, remnants of a mountain range that connected Sumatra . . . . and Arakan," while Mr. A. O. Hume, although favouring the same theory, admits that a consideration of the fauna is not in support thereof, "since not only are almost all the most characteristic species of the Arakan Hills as we now find them absent from these islands, but these latter exhibit a great number of distinct and peculiar forms constituting where the ornis is concerned, if we except the cosmopolite waders and swimmers, considerably more than one-third of the whole number known ;" by others, again, it has been argued that evidence is afforded by the flora and fauna that the Nicobars were, at some remote period, connected with Sumatra and the Malayan Peninsula, and that the Andamans at the same time being connected with Burma, the greater part of the entire eastern section of the Bay of Bengal was almost entirely landlocked, the Ten-degree channel and the Straits of Malacca forming the only outlets.

But as none of the above theories can be said to meet satisfactorily all the difficulties which the matter at issue presents, we can only hope that ere long more exact geological or other reliable data will be forthcoming, by the aid of which light will be thrown on the vexed question of the past connection of these islands with the neighbouring continents.

The Nicobar Archipelago comprises twelve inhabited and seven uninhabited islands, viz. :—

| | Square miles. | | Square miles. |
|---|---|---|---|
| Car Nicobar | 49·02 | Merōe | 0·2 |
| Batti Malv. | 0·8 | Trak } Treis } | 0·2 |
| Chowra | 2·8 | | |
| Tillangchong | 6·5 | Menchal | 0·5 |
| Terressa | 34·0 | Pulo Milo } Little Nicobar } | 57·9 |
| Bompoka | 3·8 | | |
| Camorta | 57·91 | Cabra } Condul } Great Nicobar } | 333·9 |
| Trinkut | 6·40 | | |
| Nancowry | 19·32 | | |
| Katchal | 61·7 | | |

It will thus be seen that the aggregate area of the group is about 635 square miles, or little more than one-fourth of that of the Andamans.

For convenience of reference, the Nicobars are in the following pages divided into three groups, viz. the Northern, Central, and Southern ; but it should be explained that this must not be taken arbitrarily, for while *geologically* (as was pointed out by the late Mr. S. Kurz) there are only two divisions characterizing respectively the northern and southern portion of the group, we find, *philologically*, no fewer than six subdivisions or dialects spoken within the same area.

The physical aspect of the Nicobars leaves nothing to be desired to enhance its loveliness, and far surpasses that of the Andamans ; the graceful and lofty Arecas, which are here abundant, are entirely lacking there, and whereas the Andaman jungles present almost one continuous mass of nearly the same colouring, the Nicobar forests exhibit the most varied and luxurious forms of vegetation. Tree ferns, which are not found at the Andamans, grow in wild profusion along the river banks of Great Nicobar, where they frequently attain a height of forty to forty-five feet.

The waters which lave these shores possess that extreme clearness and depth of colouring which is generally observable in the region of extensive coral reefs.

There are several convenient harbours and many good anchorages at the Nicobars ; of the former, the best known are Nancowry and Ganges Harbours, and Campbell and Sawi Bays, the last of which serves, however, only at such seasons of the year when there is no risk of northerly gales.

In some of the larger islands there are navigable channels, and at Great Nicobar rivers which would prove of inestimable value in developing the internal resources of the country.

Several of the Nicobar Islands, especially of the Southern Group, are covered with hills ranging from 600 to 2000 feet in height, and these—with the exception of Terressa and Bompoka—are clothed from the summit to the water's edge, and particularly near the sea-level, with lofty and dense jungle. The northern and central islands are conspicuous for the extensive grass heaths which cover most of the high land, and these, though pleasing when viewed from a distance, are invariably found in connection with the most sterile soil, consisting chiefly of magnesium and poly-cistina clay.

The chief drawback to residence at the Nicobars is the malarial fever which prevails more or less at all seasons, especially in the vicinity of Nancowry Harbour, and which has proved peculiarly fatal to Europeans and other aliens, though the aborigines themselves are by no means free from its ravages. This evil is doubtless to be traced to the presence of numerous brackish-water swamps, to shallow estuaries, which are partially uncovered at low water, to exposed coral reefs, and to the extensive muddy foreshores that abound in various localities, the foul exhalations from which are sufficient to account for the insalubrity of the islands. The comparative immunity enjoyed by the residents in the present British settlement—although still located in Nancowry Harbour—is, of course, due to the adoption of certain sanitary measures which were beyond the reach of the earlier colonists, who, moreover, did not possess the advantage of a sanitarium within easy access such as is now found at the Andamans ; they were likewise ignorant of the benefits to be derived from the use of quinine and other modern prophylactics and were frequently enfeebled through lack of suitable nourishment, and thus were reduced to a condition in which they readily fell victims to the malarial poison.

The improvement which has taken place in late years in the sanitation of the Government station is attributable primarily, it would seem, to the extensive removal of the coral reefs, which surround the promontory on which the colony has been planted, and secondarily to the partial reclamation of the fetid muddy foreshore. No doubt if more labour were available, a further considerable improvement might be effected by reclaiming a vast swamp which exists in the immediate vicinity of the settlement.

With regard to the numerical strength of the aboriginal population, from a census taken in 1884 it would seem that at Car Nicobar—which is the principal island of the group, and contains probably fully half the entire population—a decided increase is taking place; while at Chowra, Terressa, and Bompoka, judging from the number of children to be met with, a like result obtains; but in the central and also in the southern portions of the group the strikingly small ratio of the juvenile element denotes a corresponding diminution of inhabitants. A more just estimate can be formed by the following table of the residents I found at the various villages in 1886 :—

| | Men. | Women. | Male Children. | Female Children. | Total. |
|---|---|---|---|---|---|
| Great Nicobar | 67 | 51 | 29 | 15 | 156 |
| Little Nicobar | 35 | 34 | 9 | 6 | 84 |
| Condul | 19 | 12 | 7 | 4 | 42 |
| Milu | 3 | 3 | ... | ... | 6 |
| Camorta | 162 | 152 | 66 | 60 | 440 |
| Nancowry | 91 | 88 | 23 | 19 | 221 |
| Trinkut | 38 | 39 | 12 | 5 | 94 |
| Katchal | 114 | 103 | 47 | 50 | 314 |
| Terressa | 121 | 119 | 172 | 151 | 563 |
| Bompoka | 18 | 20 | 27 | 26 | 91 |
| Chowra | ... | ... | ... | ... | 700 |
| Car Nicobar | ... | ... | ... | ... | 3500 |

Writing in 1844, the Rev. J. M. Chopard, who passed two years at Terressa, estimated the population of the entire group as about 8000, and stated that the opinion of the natives was significant of the gradual approaching extinction of the race; contrary to the universal experience of modern travellers he feared that, should "Christian civilisation not come to the help of these wretched savages, the time is probably not distant when they will have disappeared entirely." In his estimate, however, he allows 2000 as the probable number of the inhabitants of Car Nicobar, and 600 as that of Terressa, whereas, according to the census given above, the population of the former island was found to be about 3500, and that of the latter about 560, or nearly half the total number of inhabitants in the other islands of the group. These discrepancies may partly be explained by the statement made by some of the oldest residents in the Central Group, who affirm that during the past forty or fifty years they have been visited with epidemics of small-pox and dysentery introduced among them by traders from the Straits and Burma, which have occasioned a terrible increase in the mortality.

In studying the aborigines of the Andamans and those of the Nicobar Archipelago, the most casual observer could hardly fail to be struck with the wide distinctions which exist, not only in their language and physical characteristics, but also in their culture and customs. While the Andamanese, in spite of their many excellent qualities, must be regarded as one of the most degraded and barbarous races in existence, the Nicobarese, especially of the northern islands, prove themselves worthy to be ranked almost on terms of equality with their kinsmen inhabiting the Malayan Peninsula, and evidence is not wanting to show that they are capable of acquiring and *surviving* a higher degree of civilization than that which they have as yet attained.

Before considering the affinities of the Nicobarese with existing races in neighbouring lands, it will be well to explain that the inhabitants of these islands are divided into two groups, viz. the (so-called by way of distinction) coast people, who are found on all the twelve inhabited islands; and the inland tribe, known as Shom Peñ, who are confined to the interior of the one large island called Great Nicobar. The Shom Peñ have been—and I believe with good reason—accepted as the pristine indigenes, and their remote origin and purity of breed is apparently beyond question, while the various sections of the coast tribe, although differing from each other according to external influences and other circumstances, are without doubt descended from a mongrel Malay stock, the crosses being probably in the majority of cases with Burmese, and occasionally with natives of the opposite coast of Siam, and perchance also in remote times with such of the Shom Peñ as may have settled in their midst; the fact that the Shom Peñ present Mongolian affinities would thus to some extent account for the frequent occurrence of the oblique eye in a more or less marked degree throughout the group.

As mentioned in a previous paper read before the Institute in December, 1885, the inference which I have ventured to draw from all the information and facts which have come to my knowledge is, that the circumstance of the presence in modern times of the Shom Peñ in one island only of the group is probably due to the extermination of those of the tribe who held aloof or remained hostile at the other islands, which from their small size and extensive grass heaths, would afford scant shelter or sustenance to fugitives. It may also be that those who chose to cast in their lot with the invaders were spared, a supposition which is seemingly confirmed by the slight measure of kinship which is found to exist at the present day between the sections in the southernmost part of the group.

As some writers have gone so far as to question the existence of any affinity between the Nicobarese and the Indo-Chinese family, it seems desirable to point out certain facts and ethnic characteristics, which, taken into consideration with the *primâ facie* evidence afforded by the general physical resemblance of the inhabitants of the various sections of the group to Malays or Burmese, or to what may be described as a cross between the two, leave no room for further doubt or hesitation on the subject.

I. We find that the Nicobarese invariably erect their dwellings on piles according to the custom which prevails from the frontiers of Tibet to the islands of the South Sea; while even among those natives of India who inhabit a marshy country this practice is never adopted.

II. The wilful staining of the teeth by the constant use of *pán*, without subsequent cleansing, is a habit they share with nearly all the races of Transgangetic India and the Archipelago.

III. The practice of perforating the ear-lobe and carrying wooden cylinders in the aperture for the purpose of ornament is a custom as universal among the Nicobarese as among any of the numerous tribes inhabiting the territories between and inclusive of Assam and Borneo.

IV. The artificial deformation of the head by flattening the occiput and forehead in infancy as practised by the natives of the central and southern coast tribes is described as one of the customs of certain tribes in Borneo and the Malayan Peninsula, while it has no place among the institutions of any of the various races of Hindustan.

V. The Nicobarese entertain the same general aversion to the use of milk as an article of diet which is found to be common to the various races of Indo-China and the Archipelago.

VI. The weakness or "brittleness" of the marriage tie and the facility of divorce have been described as a "feature common to the delineations of most of the tribes of Indo-China and the Indian Archipelago," and as presenting a striking contrast to the respect for the marriage bond shown by natives of India. Among the Nicobarese, as among the Dayaks of Borneo, many husbands have changed their wives three or more times before finding the partner with whom they are willing to pass the remainder of their days.

VII. The singular custom known as "couvade," or paternal lying-in, which is one of the institutions of the Dayak, and inferentially may be taken as existing among other Malay tribes which have as yet been but imperfectly described, is practised by all the communities at the Nicobars, including the inland tribe of Great Nicobar; it is by them regarded as a custom of remote antiquity, and is called "otó" in the dialect of the Central Group.

VIII. Here too, as among the Burmese and Malays, affection towards infants and between lovers is betokened by sniffing the face and not by kissing with the lips.

IX. In their social life and manners the Nicobarese differ from the generality of Asiatics, and resemble the Burmese in being free from caste prejudice; in frankly yielding to the superiority of a European; in not fawning on persons of superior culture or position; in regarding discipline or any continued employment as most irksome; and—in the case of the more advanced natives of the Car Nicobar—in being inquisitive and eager for information and readily fraternizing with strangers. All seek the society of their fellows without restraint, and their social gatherings are enlivened by the presence of their wives, sisters, and sweethearts, with whom they mix on equal terms, like the Burmese. They, moreover, resemble the Burmese and differ from the natives of India in speaking without hesitation of their wives and families.

X. The Nicobarese belief in spirits called iwi (or siya as they are named at Car Nicobar), who cause sickness and death unless propitiated and scared away, corresponds with that of the Burmese in ndts. A like agreement between the Nicobarese and one or other of the various sections of the Burmese race is found in the practice of placing money either in the mouth or against the cheek of a corpse prior to burial in order that it may benefit the spirit on its arrival in Hades, and in the custom of making offerings at the funeral and at the subsequent memorial feasts in order to gratify and propitiate the departed spirit.

XI. Some minor analogies between the customs of the Nicobarese and Burmese might be pointed out, viz. while the Burman observes four days of worship in every month, i.e. the eighth day of the waxing moon, full moon, the eighth day of the waning moon, and the last day of the last quarter, the native of Car Nicobar regards the first three of these days as a holiday (anóila) on which no work may be undertaken; the Burmese and Talein courting customs, as described by Forbes, accord with those in vogue at the Nicobars and more especially at Car Nicobar; the Burmese love of sport and amusement such as canoe-racing, feats of agility and strength, and skill in dancing, singing, etc., is equally shared by the Nicobarese, among whom wrestling, skipping, and stick-fights take the place of the Burmese sparring and football; the eating of dogs' flesh, again, which is so generally associated with certain of the Indo-Chinese races, has been practised by the Nicobarese from remote times, though now-a-days the custom is confined almost entirely to the natives of the single island of Chowra.

XII. Although, in seeking to establish proof of racial affinity, rather than of mere social contact, but little dependence can of itself be placed on the test afforded by linguistic affinities, it is not without interest to point out that the remarkable idiom of speech known to grammarians as numeral affixes or auxiliaries, which is so universally characteristic of the various Indo-Chinese languages, is a striking feature of all the dialects spoken in the Nicobar Islands, while sundry other peculiarities might be enumerated indicating such affinities to the Malay and Burmese languages as cannot but be regarded as possessing some significance when supported by the foregoing evidence, all of which tends to establish the kinship existing between the tribe under consideration and the Indo-Chinese family.

Finally, it may be further urged as arguing a bond of kindred between the Nicobarese and the Malayo-Burman races that while the former entertain no objection to marriages of their women with Malay, Burmese, or Chinese, only one or two instances can be discovered of unions between Nicobarese and Hindoos and others; indeed the very idea of such alliances is almost repugnant to them, as is borne out by the observation more than once made to me when discussing the subject with natives of Car Nicobar, "he 'nother kind man."

[The author thus concludes the prefatory remarks from which these extracts are taken and passes on to a careful consideration of various points of interest to anthropologists in reference to the constitution of these islanders—e.g. form and size, physical powers and senses, motions, development and decay, crosses, abnormality, pathology, colour, odour, teeth, hair—and in subsequent papers proposes to submit to the Council of the Anthropological Institute the results of his further researches on matters connected with the culture of the Nicobarese.]

---

## Precis of Paper on the Funeral Rites and Ceremonies of the Nicobarese.

[Forwarded for the Brit. Assoc. Meeting, 1889.]

Mr. E. H. Man, who, during a residence of many years in the Nicobar Islands, has made a careful study of the aboriginal inhabitants as well as of their language, forwards a paper treating in detail of the Nicobarese funeral rites and ceremonies.

The mortuary customs in the Central and Southern Islands differ in many points from those observed by the tribes inhabiting the northern portion of the Archipelago: all alike appear to indulge in demonstrations of grief which amount to frenzied extravagance, and which are induced in the majority of the mourners less by real sorrow than by the dread entertained of the disembodied spirit, who is credited with peculiar activity and malevolence immediately after its release.

It is incumbent on all friends and relatives to repair

as speedily as possible to the hut where a death has taken place, and those who fail to bring with them the customary offering of white or coloured calico must make a valid excuse to the chief mourner, who would otherwise regard the omission as a slight to be remembered and rendered in kind at the earliest opportunity. These offerings, which vary from a few yards to an entire piece of calico, are, as soon as presented, torn into lengths of about two yards and utilized for shrouding the corpse; they must be of new material, and may be of red, white, blue, striped or checked, but never of black calico.

In all their funeral appointments the Nicobarese have, it appears, an unexplained preference for uneven numbers; the body must be washed *once*, *thrice*, or *five* times; it is laid on a bed of the calico in lengths, 30 being used for a headman and 29 or any less uneven number for persons of minor importance; under the calico are placed 3, 5, or 7 areca spathes, and these again are kept in position by 5, 7, or 9 swathes or bands of calico. Curious v-shaped pegs to the number of 7 or 9 are used to secure the body in the grave, in order to prevent its abstraction by a class of evil spirits whose energies are supposed to be devoted to this end.

A practice analogous to that of barring the ghost by fire prevails also in these islands, and a pyre is ignited with fire-sticks—which are only used on these occasions—at the foot of the hut, for the twofold purpose of keeping the disembodied spirit at a distance and apprizing friends approaching or passing in a canoe of the sad event.

Mourners are required to abstain from food from the time of the death until after the prescribed cleansing of the dwelling and personal ablutions and lustration by the *menluana* or priest-medicineman on the following day; quids of betel and sips of almost boiling water are the only refreshment permitted during the interval.

There are cemeteries attached to every village, in which each family owns a certain area. The natives of the inland and coast tribes in the Southern group leave the dead undisturbed; but at Car Nicobar, Chowra, Teressa, and Bompoka ossuaries are found, whither, after successive exhumations, the remains are deposited. At Car Nicobar mortuary huts are kept exclusively for the reception of the dead prior to their interment. Certain sacrificial acts are also performed at the grave, and on the succeeding days, which are of interest, and throughout the group the memory of the dead is kept alive and their manes propitiated by frequent feasts, which are celebrated in their honour at intervals during the mourning period, which extends sometimes over two or three years.

# Specimens of Tagal Folklore.

By Dr. J. RIZAL.

### I. Proverbial Sayings.

*Malakas ang bulong sa sigaw*, low words are stronger than loud words.

*Ang lakí sa layaw karaniwa 'y hubad*, a petted child is generally naked (*i.e.* poor).

*Humpasíng magulang ay nakatatabá*, Parents' punishment makes one fat.

*Ibang harí ibang ugalí*, new king, new fashion.

*Nagpupútol ang kapus, ang labis ay nagdurugtong*, what is short cuts off a piece from itself, what is long adds another on (the poor gets poorer, the rich richer).

*Ang nagsasabíng tapus ay siyang kinakapus*, He who finishes his words finds himself wanting.

*Nangangakô habang napapakô*, Man promises while in need.

*Ang naglalakad ng maráhan, matinik may mababaw*, He who walks slowly, though he may put his foot on a thorn, will not be hurt very much (Tagals mostly go barefooted).

*Ang maniwalá sa sabi 'y walang bait na sarili*, He who believes in tales has no own mind.

*Ang may inínuksok sa dingding, ay may titíngalain*, He who has put something between the wall may afterwards look on (the saving man may afterwards be cheerful).—The wall of a Tagal house is made of palm-leaves and bamboo, so that it can be used as a cupboard.

*Walang mahirap gisingin na paris nang nagtutulog-tulugan*, The most difficult to rouse from sleep is the man who pretends to be asleep.

*Labis sa salitá, kapus sa gawá*, Too many words, too little work.

*Hipong tulog ay nadadalá ng ánod*, The sleeping shrimp is carried away by the current.

*Sa bibig nahuhuli ang isdá*, The fish is caught through the mouth.

### II. Puzzles.

*Isang butil na palay sikip sa buong bahay*, One rice-corn fills up all the house. = The light. The rice-corn with the husk is yellowish.

*Matupang akó so dalawá, duag akó sa isá*, I am brave against two, coward against one. = The bamboo bridge. When the bridge is made of one bamboo only, it is difficult to pass over; but when it is made of two or more, it is very easy.

*Dalá akó niya, dalá ko siya*, He carries me, I carry him. = The shoes.

*Isang balong malalim punô ng patalim*, A deep well filled with steel blades. = The mouth.

*Bibinká ni kaká di mo mahiwá*, You cannot cut my

brother's pudding. — Water. The water never gets frozen there.

*Walang sanga, walang ugat, humihitik ang bulaklak,*
Without branches, without roots, it is loaded with flowers. — The stars in the sky.

*Dalawang urang naghahagaran,* Two big sticks running after one another. — The legs. Urang is a piece of wood which people put in the ground to mark off orchards, gardens, etc.

*Tinagá ko sa gubat, sa bahay nagiiyak,* I wounded him in the wood, but he only cried at home. — The Tagal guitar. The wood of which the guitar is made is cut in the wood, but it sounds in the house only when it is finished.

### III. Verses.

*Kahoy na likŏ at buktot*
*Hutukin hangang malambot,*
*Kapag tumaas at tumayog*
*Mahirap na ang paghutok.*

Put straight the curved and crooked tree while it is tender; afterwards when it is grown and high you can no longer bend it.

*Kahoy na babad sa tubig*
*Sa apuy ay huag ilápit*
*Kapag nu tiyŏ 't nag init*
*Pilit din ñgang magdirikit.*

Do not put near the fire the tree which has been long in the water; when it gets dry and hot it will surely be burnt.

---

## The Progress of Assyriological Researches during the last Twelve Months.

[The following abbreviations will be used throughout this article: *Ac.* = The (London) Academy; *Berlin RA* = Sitzungs-berichte der Königlich Preussischen Akademie der Wissenschaften zu Berlin; *BOR* = The Babylonian and Oriental Record; *PAOS* = Proceedings of the American Oriental Society; *Proc.* = Proceedings of the Society of Biblical Archæology; *V. Cgr.* = Verhandlungen des VII. Internationalen Orientalisten-Congresses gehalten in Wien im Jahre 1886; *ZDMG* = Zeitschrift der Deutschen Morgenländischen Gesellschaft; *Zeits.* = Zeitschrift für Assyriologie und verwandte Gebiete.]

ASSYRIOLOGY has made a considerable progress in the last year with respect to almost every one of its branches.

There are two J o u r n a l s nearly exclusively devoted to cuneiform researches, *viz.*, the Paris *Revue d'Assyriologie*, conducted by Professor Oppert, of which the first fasciculus of the second Volume has appeared, and the Munich *Zeitschrift für Assyriologie*, of which the second part of the fourth Volume is forthcoming just now. A considerable space for Assyriological papers is reserved also in the *Proceedings* of the London *Society of Biblical Archæology*, of which each

issue of the last year contained such articles. Furthermore, the New-Haven *Hebraica* have opened their pages to treatises on cuneiform subjects, and some of them are met with also in the London *Babylonian and Oriental Record*, under the direction of the Sinologist Professor Terrien de Lacouperie.

There being available to readers at present a quarterly bibliography of the books in question, in the above-mentioned *Zeitschrift* as well as in Professor August Müller's *Orientalische Bibliographie* (Berlin, H. Reuther, 1887 ff.), I may be allowed to confine myself in the following sketch to a brief mention of the chief titles, or even names of authors, in general, referring those who wish to have the bibliographical details at their disposal to the two magazines alluded to.

Indeed, modern Assyriological literature is growing to such an extent that at present it is almost impossible for beginners to have always before their mind what has been done from the very beginnings of Assyriology up to the present date. The announcement of a collective re-edition of Edward Hincks' works, upon which a short account was given by Dr. Adler (*PAOS*), will ;therefore be welcomed by all interested in these studies. From the April number of the Johns Hopkins University *Circulars* we also learn that of Sir Henry Rawlinson's works a new edition by Dr. W. M. Arnolt and Dr. C. Johnston, jun., is on the eve of being prepared.

A very few L i s t s, or N o t i c e s, of recently acquired C o l l e c t i o n s of Babylonian and Assyrian antiquities are as yet at hand. Among recent works in that respect, we can only mention the continuation of Menant's Catalogue of the Paris Collection Le Clercq, Adler's notes on a collection in the National Museum at Washington, and Pinches' description of the tablets in the private possession of Sir Henry Peek. A few remarks on a new collection in the British Museum were given by E. A. Wallis Budge (*Zeits.*), and on three collections, which have lately been acquired for the University of Pennsylvania, two "letters" are about to be published by R. F. Harper, and Dr. Hilprecht (*ibidem*). There has, finally, been given a tentative list of eighty-five of the British Museum Collections, with additional notes on their extension and value, by Bezold (*Berlin RA*.)

Most satisfactory is the enlargement of the horizon as to the editions and interpretations of C u n e i f o r m T e x t s which have been made during that period, and are due to the co-operation of English, French, German, and American writers.

In respect of the O l d e s t I n s c r i p t i o n s, *viz.*, those of Urbau, Gudea, and Khammurabi, we first mention the second part of the second volume of E. de Sarzec's *Découvertes en Chaldée*, in which, in masterly heliogravure reproductions, a considerable part of the lately acquired Louvre Collection is made available to those who study the old-Babylonian inscriptions as well as to those who are interested in the origin and development of the oldest period of art in lower Mesopotamia. Only a few philological treatises on these inscriptions have appeared, however, in addition to that monumental work, viz., A. Amiaud's edition, translation, and commentary of the "Inscription G de Goudea," and of an Assyrian legend of Dungi (*Zeits.*), and an article by the same author on a bilingual inscription of that period (in Oppert's *Revue*). Some general notes on the old-Babylonian inscriptions have been given by Zimmern, who also explained, for the first time, an important passage in one of the Gudea Cylinders, concerning a "vision" of this ancient "ruler" (*Zeits.*).

Of a great number of the D o c u m e n t s belonging to the A s s y r i a n  E m p i r e, a fresh, and of some of them a very comprehensive, study has been made. E. Allen, of the Johns Hopkins University, gave some corrections and additions to the inscriptions of Tiglathpileser I., as published by Professor Lotz, with the assistance of Dr. Delitzsch (*PAOS*). The Rev. P. V. Scheil, a promising pupil of Dr. Oppert and Prof. Amiaud, completed, in a handsome 4to. volume, a new edition of the important inscription of Shamshirammân IV., accompanied by a transliteration, translation, philological, geographical, and historical notes, and a full vocabulary. The most valuable of all such editions appears to be Dr. Winckler's "Inscriptions of Sargon II.," in two vols. The first part of his work contains a long and most important "Historical Introduction" concerning the reign of this mighty Assyrian king, followed by the transcript and translation of most of his inscriptions and, again, by an exhaustive vocabulary. The second part comprises on 49 beautiful 4to. plates, which have been autographed by the skilful hand of Dr. Abel, the whole treasure of Sargon texts in· the Louvre, British Museum, and Berlin Collections, with a very few exceptions (K. 1349, and some brick-legends). We have thus obtained a most careful and reliable reproduction of the texts from Khorsabad which have hitherto been inaccessible to many and extremely difficult to study, in the beautiful, but naturally very inaccurate edition of Botta. And Dr. Winckler's "Introduction" appears to serve as a correct guide for further publications of "historical" texts, which should be accompanied by historical notes, a method which was observed by G. Smith, in his *Asurbanipal*, but was gradually abandoned by the German School.

In respect of the Sennacherib Texts, we owe an addition to the published material to Mr. B. T. A.

Evetts, who gave a passage of the so-called Rassam Cylinders, which considerably differs from Taylor's and Bellino's texts, adding variants, transliteration, translation, and notes (*Zeits.*). Of the texts of Esarhaddon, some emendations, including additions and philological notes, have been published by Prof. R. F. Harper (*Hebraica*). A fresh study has been made also of the well-known inscriptions of Sardanapallos, by S. A. Smith, who published—in several articles (*Proc.*; *V. Cgr.*; Oppert's *Revue*) as well as in a separate work, *die Inschriften Assurbanipals*, three parts of which have already appeared—a full translation of the celebrated "Rassam Cylinder" of this king, and, in addition to it, a large number of letters and despatches which are mostly written under his reign, and partly relate to public affairs. A comprehensive edition of all the principal texts of Sardanapallos' brother, Saosduchinos, is being prepared and, we believe, will shortly appear, by Dr. C. F. Lehmann, in which again a "historical introduction" to the inscriptions will be given. An unknown brick-legend from the temple at Aboo-Habba, referring to both kings, has been published and translated by Bezold (*Zeits.*).

In addition to the historical I n s c r i p t i o n s of the neo-B a b y l o n i a n  E m p i r e, several new texts have been discovered and published. The Rev. C. J. Ball gave the cuneiform text of two inscriptions of Nebuchadnezzar II., in the British Museum (*Proc.*). Mr. E. A. Wallis Budge published a most valuable cylinder of Neriglissar (being the second of this king which is known at present), in private possession, and promised to supply a translation and a commentary to the same (*ibidem*). To the two Cylinders of Nabopolassar discovered by Dr. Winckler, a third has been added and translated, by the Rev. J. N. Strassmaier (*Zeits.*). The valuable document of Nabonidus in · Rawlinson's *W.A.I.* v. plate 65, has been translated, for the first time in full, and explained by Professor Teloni (*ibidem*). And two more cylinders of the same king have been published, with a transliteration and an attempted translation, by Bezold (*Proc.*), on some chronological notes of which recently Dr. Oppert has communicated a few important remarks (*Zeits.*).

We mention here, finally, the first volume of a work which, when completed, will be a useful and trustworthy book of reference, and be welcomed not only by Assyriologists, but also by Historians and Bible students, viz., of Professor Schrader's *Keilinschriftliche Bibliothek*, which contains as careful as possible a transliteration and translation of the principal inscriptions of Rammânnirârî I., II., and III., Shalmaneser I. and II., Tuklatadar I. and II., Ashurrishishi, Tiglathpileser I., Ashurnasirpal, and Shamshirammân, which are given by the Editor, in co-operation with

Drs. Abel, Peiser, Winckler, and others. At the same time, in England, of a New Series of the *Records of the Past*, under the editorship of Professor Sayce, one volume has appeared, which does not supply, however, a transliteration of the texts the versions of which are given.

To these so-called "Historical Inscriptions" we may add here a series of other cuneiform texts, which either have been published for the first time, or have obtained new elucidations from recent researches. First of all, the **Legal Documents**, private contracts, and such similar texts have been enriched by a vast collection, very carefully autographed and published by the Rev. J. N. Strassmaier, who completed, in four parts, his 1134 *Inschriften von Nabonidus*, with five most important *Indices*; began a new series of such texts, by editing the Inscriptions of Nebuchadnezzar II., of which the second part will shortly appear (comprising 460 numbers on 272 pages); and lately gave, in addition to these documents, the contracts of the time of Nabopolassar, of Smerdis, and of the Arsacide Dynasty *(Zeits.)*. A similar edition of 21 texts in the Berlin Museum was brought out by Dr. Peiser, under the title *Keilinschriftliche Aktenstücke*, and accompanied by a transliteration, translation, and glossary. E. A. Wallis Budge published some important legal documents, containing different, and partly very early dates, of a fine collection which he himself had acquired last year in the East for the British Museum *(Zeits.)*. Among those who devoted special papers to the puzzling expressions to be met with in these "contracts," we mention Oppert, Peiser, Meissner *(Zeits.)*, and Revillout *(Proc.)*. A tablet mentioning the 8th year of Cambyses, which was published by Mr. Pinches *(BOR)*, has recently been examined from a chronological point of view, by J. A. Payne *(PAOS)*. Finally, Dr. Brünnow published two contracts containing so-called Phoenician legends, adding photographic reproductions of the tablets themselves *(Zeits.)*.

Of the greatest value appears to be the new accession of fresh materials from Mesopotamia with respect to the cuneiform **Letters** and **Despatches**. First the Berlin, and then the British Museum, acquired a series of very important tablets, covered with cuneiform inscriptions, which are supposed to have been found in Tell-el-Amarna in Egypt, and containing correspondence carried on between the Egyptian rulers of the xviiith Dynasty, principally Amenophis III. and IV., and the Asiatic monarchs of the Kashshû Dynasty, Burnaburiash, and others. The first account of the Berlin Collection has been given by Erman and Schrader *(Berlin RA)*, and specimens of the texts were published by Winckler *(ibidem)* and by Lehmann *(Zeits.)*, while of those of the London Collection the first specimens

were communicated by Budge *(Proc.)*. Also the Bulaq Museum acquired some of the tablets, a few of which were made known by Winckler *(Berlin RA)*, and some others are in the possession of Mr. Bouriant at Cairo, of which a short account has been given by Sayce *(Ac.)*. Besides the above-mentioned scholars, also Brugsch, [Brunengo], Delattre, Jastrow, Pognon, Tiele, Wiedemann, and Bezold have contributed articles upon the important "find."

Of the **Religious Literature** of Mesopotamia, but a few inscriptions were published, or examined last year. Mr. Budge gave a most valuable edition of a beautifully preserved Babylonian tablet of the so-called Creation Series *(Proc.)*. Dr. Brünnow began the autographing, translation, and explanation of a series of very interesting Assyrian hymns *(Zeits.)*. Pater Delattre translated anew some of the oracles purporting to be given to king Esarhaddon *(BOR)*. Furthermore, a somewhat fanciful hypothesis of Mr. Pinches, who thought to have discovered, on one of the clay-tablets from Kouyunjik, the expressions of a "Messianic idea" *(Ac.)*, induced Mr. Evetts to publish the very text in question, adding variants from a duplicate *(Proc.)*. Bezold published a "Hemerology" in the recently acquired "Budge Collection" of the British Museum *(Zeits.)*, and also a "List of Gods" *(Proc.)*, upon which a vivid discussion arose between Evetts, Halévy, Houghton, Oppert, and Pinches *(Ac.; Zeits.)*. On the Deluge text, a few remarks were made by E. (in the *Expositor*) and by M[eissner] *(Zeits.)*; and of a single passage of it, concerning the dimensions of the Babylonian Ark, an explanation has been attempted by Haupt *(PAOS)*.

There are, finally, a few editions of texts to be mentioned with regard to the **Scientific** Babylono-Assyrian **Literature**. Some new Syllabaries have been published by Jastrow *(Zeits.)*, and by Bezold *(Proc.)*. The latter author also attempted to give restorations of, and additions to, the "Babylonian Chronicle" from two duplicates, and published some texts, and extracts from texts concerning the star KAK. SI. DI, on which remarks were added by Francis Brown *(ibidem)*. We are looking forward to a comprehensive treatment of all the questions connected with the last-named inscriptions, by Dr. Jensen, whose *Babylono-Assyrian Kosmology*, we hear, is in the press.

It will be seen from the above list of publications of cuneiform texts that at present Assyriologists are laying the chief stress of their researches on making as many inscriptions as possible available to students, and thus laying a sound foundation for **Grammatical** and **Lexicographical Investigations**. We think that we are not far wrong in designating that very fact as the surest guarantee that Assyriology has really come to a more scientific method of working than it hitherto appeared to do in giving translations without the texts, or trying to stamp the Assyrian grammar which, strictly speaking, does not yet exist, as the leading guide for comparative Semitic philology, and its lexicon as a source of numerous emendations of the Hebrew Bible. There has far more to be done, *critical* editions have to be supplied, the different kinds of texts to be classified, and carefully examined with respect to their mutual relation, before such efforts can be made with any prospect of success. We cannot, therefore, agree with Dr. Adler in regard of his criticism of Nöldeke's article *Semitic Languages* in the *Encyclopædia Britannica* (*Proc. Am. Phil. Assoc.*), nor with the way in which, in one of the "Addresses" on *Semitic Studies in America* (*Hebraica*), our knowledge of Assyrian is spoken of as perfectly equal to that of the other Semitic tongues. Under the title: "What can be done?" it is said there: "1) *Hebrew*, at all events, can be taught. . . . 2) *Assyrian* may be taken up; . . . . experience has shown that Assyrian is far easier to grasp than Arabic. . . . . 3) *Arabic* should not be forgotten in the overwhelming interest now centering in Assyriology. . . . . 4) I shall not speak of Syriac, Aramaic, or Ethiopic, in one or more of which something may also be done. . . ." I fear that, the study of Assyrian being compared in this manner with that of Arabic, and the other languages, none of them will gain from the others. We must never forget that not one chapter of the Assyrian Grammar can at present be worked out in any completeness, and that a work for Assyrian like Dillmann's *Äthiopische Grammatik* for Ethiopic will remain a *desideratum* for decades.

There have also been issued, however, a number of grammatical and lexicographical papers and books during the last months. G. Bertin gave not less than five different "grammars" of cuneiform literature, on 117 pages 8vo.! And Professor Delitzsch succeeded in finishing the German edition of his *Grammar* in Petermann's *Porta*, while Bezold (*V. Cgr.*) and afterwards, treating the subject from a somewhat different standpoint, Dr. Haupt (*PAOS*), contented themselves with publishing *Prolegomena* to a future Assyro-Babylonian grammar. In addition, there have been issued several articles concerning grammatical subjects: by Professor Barth, on the changes of sound among the Assyrian *Liquidae* (*Zeits.*), on biliteral formations of nouns, and on very ancient pluralic analogous formations (*ZDMG*); by Dr. Jensen, on exclamation, interrogation and negation in Semitic (*Zeits. f. Völkerpsych.*); by Prof. D. H. Müller, on the Semitic sibilants (*V. Cgr.*); by Prof. Schrader, on the true pronunciation of the signs

*A.A* and *I.A* (*Zeits.*); and by Dr. Adler, on the verbs ל״ו and ל״י (*PAOS*).

The discussion of the Sumero-Akkadian problem has been as flourishing as ever. In that respect, it is especially to be noticed that Professor Delitzsch entered anew on the controversy, sharing now Dr. Halévy's theory of the Antiakkadism, which has been rejected again by Dr. Oppert. Some remarks by Bezold on the Babylonian "woman's language" (*Proc.*) led to a discussion between him (*ibidem*), a writer E. (in the *Expositor*) and Professor Sayce (*Ac.; Proc.*). The "Kossaean" language has been vigorously attacked as to its existence by Dr. Oppert, who defined the difference between the Κοσσαῖοι and the Κίσσιοι of the classic writers (*Zeits.*). Finally, the Hittite inscriptions were taken up by the Rev. C. J. Ball and explained as containing an Eranian language (*Proc.*), a discovery which appears not to be verified by the new find of a key for these puzzling monuments, of which Dr. Winckler gave a previous short account (*Berlin RA*).

As to palæographical researches, we may mention here, for the sake of completeness, that concerning the question as to the derivation of the cuneiform characters, Professor Sayce met Dr. de Lacouperie's view on their Chinese relationship (*BOR*). Among the most important books, however, we owe to the last year, is a new Sign-List by Dr. Brünnow, the third part of which is just about to issue. This work will comprise, on 596 splendidly autographed quarto pages, the whole treasure of simple and compound Assyrian ideographs, with all their explanations as supplied by the published cuneiform texts, and numerous references to modern Assyriological literature. In addition to the principal list, the author will give there: lists of ideographic signs, of non-Semitic verb prefixes and suffixes, of fragments of groups, of verbal forms with their Assyrian equivalents, of the names of the cuneiform signs, of the signs themselves arranged according to their form, and of the non-Semitic and Semitic values of signs.

The same scholar has laid down, in a brief sketch, the rules of a new order of words for the lexicographical grouping of the Assyrian language, thus opening up a most important question which ought to be settled as soon as possible (*Zeits.*). In America, a new Assyrian Dictionary is announced as "fairly under way" (*PAOS*); and of Prof. Delitzsch's *Wörterbuch zur gesamten bisher veröffentlichten Keilschriftliteratur*, the second part, comprising אמר-אדר, has appeared, but has been criticized again, by E., in the *Expositor*. Prof. Golenischeff published the first part of a glossary, arranged according to the cuneiform signs. Among some further contributions to Babylono-Assyrian lexicography, we may especially mention the following papers: by Dr. Jensen, on

## TRÜBNER'S RECORD.



Delitzsch's *Wörterbuch* (*Wiener Zeits. f. d. K. d. Morg.*), on a passage in a bilingual incantation, *W. A. I.* iv. 8, and on *ḫimu* (*Zeits.*); by Dr. Jastrow, on *kudûru* (*PAOS*); by the Rev. C. J. Ball, on *urkarina* (*Proc.*); by Prof. Barth, on *bîtḫilâni* (*Zeits.*); by Dr. Feuchtwang, on בחל (*ibidem*); by Director Vollers, on מרדה (*ibid.*); by Prof. Fraenkel, on מכותא, פתורא, נמרתא, *madudu*, תבקין, בלש, בותתא, רמפש, משכא, and آلماس (*ib.*); and by Prof. Perruchon, on *annâ-أنّ* (*ibidem*).

In respect of the H i s t o r y of Mesopotamia and the neighbouring lands, we are very glad to mention here, first of all, the completion of Tiele's excellent *Geschichte*, which is certainly one of the indispensable text-books for any Assyriologist. The author has also entered in the work, for the first time, a comprehensive historical criticism of the inscriptions of Babylonian and Assyrian kings, with regard to their compilation and reliability. On a single historical question, concerning the conquest of Samaria, a discussion was opened and settled by Delitzsch, Haupt, Sayce, Schrader, Tiele, and Winckler. Prof. Amiaud gave some communications as to the Second Esarhaddon (*BOR*), and Pater Delattre on the monuments of Cyrus (*le Muséon*), while the classic writers were examined anew, in respect of Assyrian notices, in a *Programm* by Evers. A few g e o g r a p h i c a l points were illustrated by Amiaud, Delattre, Hagen, R. F. Harper, Moritz, and Tomkins. And of the researches on Babylono-Assyrian C u l t u r e, we may call attention to Mr. Budge's remarks upon a Persian weight (*Proc.*), Pater Delattre's article on the hydraulic works in Babylon (*Revue d. ques. scient.*), Prof. Oppert's (*Zeits.*) and Dr. Lehmann's (Berlin Archæol. Soc.) treatises on Assyrian measures and weights, and Dr. Winckler's note on an artificial reservoir of Nebukadnezzar II. (*Hebraica*).

A very significant progress has been made as to C h r o n o l o g y. Dr. Mahler edited two parts of his "chronological Lists." Dr. Oppert made new investigations on *the real Chronology and the true History of the Babylonian Dynasties (BOR)*, and on the time of Khammurabi (*Zeits.*) previously discussed by Bezold (*Proc.; Ac.*). And Prof. Bilfinger published a *Programm* on the Babylonian double-hour. Above all, the Rev. J. Epping, in co-operation with the Rev. J. N. Strassmaier, made a fresh study of the astronomical texts from Mesopotamia, viewed from an astronomical standpoint, in two "letters" (*Zeits.*), and in a systematical pamphlet (additional to the "Voices from Maria-Laach"), with the full calculus concerning the constellations of the planets, and an explanatory list of technical terms, their cuneiform ideographs being put in order, translated, and autographed by Strassmaier.

There have been contributed also several papers on Assyrian and Babylonian R e l i g i o n, partly connected with the Old Testament. The most valuable work in that respect is, no doubt, an enlarged English edition of Schrader's *The Cuneiform Inscriptions and the Old Testament*, by the Rev. C. Owen Whitehouse, the second Volume of which has lately appeared. Another paper by Prof. Schrader (*Zeits.*) relates to the goddess Ishtar, and to the remarks, which have recently been made upon the subject by Prof. Kuenen. Dr. Lyon published some notes on the Assyrian prayers (*PAOS*), and many, and among them very remarkable and valuable contributions to the matter in question, we find in Dr. Halévy's *Recherches bibliques* (in the *Revue des Ét. juives*) and *Notes assyriologiques* (*Zeits.*). The views of Dr. Jeremias on the "life after death" according to the Babylonian mythology were treated again by Dr. Adler and by Prof. Jastrow, and, we believe, were successfully refuted by Dr. Feuchtwang (*ibidem*). Prof. Kohler published some remarks upon the names of the friends of Daniel (*ibidem*), Dr. Neubauer (*ib.*) and Prof. Sayce (*BOR*) some on Jareb-Sargon, and the Rev. C. J. Ball (*ib.*) some on יהוה, To Prof. Edw. Meyer we owe some very interesting *Miscellen* on Nimroud (*Zeits. f. Altt. Wiss.*).

We finally have to mention a few articles on Babylonian and Assyrian A r t. As to the architecture, Dr. Borchardt published a Babylonian ground-plan (*Berlin RA*), and Mr. Koldewey (*Zeits.*) as well as Director Erman (*Wochens. f. class. Phil.*) gave additional remarks upon the Babylonian nekropoles lately discovered by the members of a Prussian Expedition. Mr. Ward continued his articles on the "cylindrical objects" from Mesopotamia (*PAOS*), and Oberhummer and Ohnefalsch-Richter contributed papers on the finds in Cyprus, in the new journal "The Owl," while an article on "Persian art from Susa" was published by Jastrow. Prof. Babelon's instructive *Manuel d'Archéologie*, comprising the antiquities of Chaldæa, Assyria, Persia, Syria, Judæa, Phoenicia, and Carthage, will shortly appear in a revised and enlarged English edition, which has been undertaken by Mr. B. T. A. Evetts.     C. Bezold.

*London, April 28th*, 1889.

The above Report on the progress of Assyrian studies—the first that has appeared in the pages of THE RECORD—gives us some idea of the learning, zeal and perseverance with which this new and important branch of Semitic philology is cultivated among us. The results of the decipherments are also year after year attaining a corresponding measure of certainty and trustworthiness. Though the materials on which the Assyriologist has to work somewhat differ from those which the editor of texts in the ancient classical languages of the East or West has before him, the principles of sound criticism on which cuneiform documents should be prepared for publication cannot but be assumed to be identically the same as those applying to the other ancient languages. If the editorial *canones* generally adhered to by oriental and classical scholars have not always been strictly observed by Assyriologists, a certain plausible excuse may perhaps be found in the fact that occasionally genial sagacity and a large amount of enthusiasm have been allowed to take the place of an exact philological training. The inconveniences which have arisen, and may again arise, from the non-pursuit of a strictly scientific method in editing cuneiform documents have suggested to Dr. C. Bezold the advisability of laying down, in his latest publication ('Proceedings of the Society of Biblical Archæology,' vol. xi. p. 131 ff.), a series of *canones* for the guidance of young Assyriologists. We take leave to transfer these rules to the pages of THE RECORD, in order to insure for them a wider currency than they would otherwise attain.

" . . . . It is, of course, a matter of the first importance to know exactly how cuneiform texts, to which duplicates, or parts or fragments of them, or so-called 'parallel texts' have been found, are to be published; and it appears to be of almost equal importance that Assyrian scholars should be able to criticize fairly the first edition of a cuneiform text, when, after that first edition, duplicates (or parts or fragments of them, or so-called 'parallel texts') have been discovered. As it seems, that several Assyriologists have omitted to form for themselves a clear idea as to these two points, I may be allowed to give here a brief statement of what I have sketched out for myself during the last few years with regard to that question, although I am fully aware that Semitic, and other, scholars might consider it superfluous to repeat here rules of so elementary a character as the following :—

"1. In case of duplicates existing in addition to a principal text, either, (*a*) both, the text and the duplicate(s) might be given in separate editions, without any restorations ; or (*b*) both, the text and the duplicate(s) might be published separately, but restored from each other, the restorations being indicated by *outline* types (or by brackets or by any other mark) ; or (*c*), the principal text might be published alone, the restorations, as taken from the duplicate(s), being indicated by *outline* types, *etc.*

"2. Whatever the method of editing may be, the numbers of both the text and the duplicate(s) should be named, and in the above case 1, *c*, it should be indicated, what is 'text,' and what is derived from the 'duplicate(s),' supplying the variants.

"3. Under no conditions, must the principal text and the duplicate(s) be mixed in an edition.

"4. Under no conditions, must the fact be concealed, when there is, one or more, duplicates of a text, and such characters, as are indistinct in the 'text,' but perfectly clear in the duplicate(s), must not be given as 'clear' in the text, the duplicate(s) being not even mentioned.

"5. When *outline* characters are printed in a text, of which duplicates are not mentioned, and therefore (after No. 4) do not exist, these characters should indicate either, (*a*) that there is no other epigraphic possibility of restoring the sign in question than the one involved in the restoration, or (*b*) that a parallel phrase or word, used more or less often, gives a correct guide for the restoration in question ; or (*c*) that the present state of our knowledge of the Assyrian language enabled the writer to restore the traces of signs which are left in the text.

" The possibility of restoring signs depends, of course, on the more or less extended knowledge of the sum total of epigraphic modifications of the Babylono-Assyrian signs, which can only be obtained by copying carefully, and during a long period, inscriptions from the original tablets, and will never be got from any grammar or '*Schrifttafel*.' Besides the script itself, the copyist can take advantage of the space left on the clay in place of the expected, and therefore restored, signs. The shape and peculiarities of the tablet, the place of its origin, its state of preservation, its contents, and many other things, which cannot be reduced to general rules, may serve as guides in such cases, and according to the motives which induced the copyist to make his restoration, the latter itself acquires different degrees of certainty.

" Restorations of that kind are therefore merely a matter of practice. For, I firmly believe that two pairs of eyes, equally strong and equally trained, do see, under the same conditions (of light, *etc.*), exactly the same traces.

" As to the restorations obtained by the above-mentioned 'knowledge of the language,' very often the combination of indistinct traces into a good Assyrian phrase depends on a l u c k y  g u e s s, which n o b o d y  i s  o b l i g e d  to make at the time of publication. This leads us, finally, to

"6. In criticizing editions, a difference should be made between first and second editions, and between texts without, and texts with, duplicates. It would be unfair to blame a writer for not making use of duplicates, which are either not available or entirely unknown. And the same may be said, of course, of those who condemn the edition of a text without restorations, and correct it from parallels, which they themselves have but lately found. Above all, it must never be forgotten that Assyriology is not a mere philological discipline, but a b r a n c h  o f  A r c h æ o l o g y.

" I should be very glad, if these few rules, which appear to be, as I repeat once more, of quite a rudimentary character, and do not pretend to be anything but the common axioms of text-editions applied to the Assyrian literature, should be either observed, or should be discussed by any Assyriologist, or Philologist, who considers them to be inadmissible. As in Assyriology the publication of texts makes a rapid progress, so important a question should be cleared up at once."

## Honorary Degrees conferred by the University of Edinburgh.

On the 18th of April last the University of Edinburgh celebrated its spring graduation ceremonial in the Synod Hall, Castle Terrace, on which occasion the honorary degree of LL.D. was conferred upon the following distinguished scholars. Prof. Kirkpatrick, in submitting their names, said :—

I have first to ask your Lordship to confer the honorary degree of Doctor of Laws, in absence, on Sir Syed Ahmed Khan, Bahadur, K.C.S.I. Born in 1817, and descended from ancestors of distinction under the old Moghul Empire, Sir Syed was raised to the nobility by the last Emperor of Delhi in 1836. The following year he entered the British Civil Service, and was shortly afterwards appointed to a Judgeship. During the Mutiny of 1857 he behaved with noble heroism, and was instrumental in saving the lives of the twenty European residents at Bijnore, in the North-Western Provinces of India, a signal service for which he was rewarded with a pension and various honours. In 1876 he retired from the judicial service, and in 1878 his honourable official career was fitly crowned by his election as a member of the Viceregal Council. Parallel with his official life runs his still more distinguished career as a man of letters and a benefactor of India. In 1847 appeared his important "Archæological History of Delhi," followed by numerous pamphlets and articles on political and other subjects, essays on the Life of Mohammed, and many admirable and eloquent speeches, and in 1864 he was elected a Fellow of the Royal Asiatic Society. In 1875 he founded the Mohammedan Anglo-Oriental College of Aligarh, an institution unique in character, chiefly destined to benefit his fellow-Mussulmans, but open to students of all races and creeds. In this greatest and most arduous work of his life he was powerfully seconded by the Viceroy, by the Lieutenant-Governor, Sir William Muir, and by other distinguished friends ; and the College, standing in the beautiful Muir Park and attended by several hundred students, is now beneficently promoting the higher education among the Mohammedan and other natives of India, and breaking down the barriers of racial prejudice. Sir Syed is therefore beloved and esteemed by all who share his enlightened views. He is the most illustrious Mohammedan subject of our Empress-Queen, and he is peculiarly worthy of this high academic distinction. (Applause.)

I have now to ask your Lordship to confer the degree, in absence, on William Dwight Whitney, Professor of Sanskrit and Comparative Philology in Yale College. After studying Sanskrit at Berlin and Tübin-
gen for three years, Professor Whitney was appointed to the Chair of Sanskrit and Comparative Philology in Yale College in 1854. In 1856, in conjunction with Professor von Roth, he edited the Sanskrit text of the Atharva-Veda. During the last thirty years he has been one of the master spirits of the American Oriental Society, having been for several years its corresponding secretary, and latterly its president ; and in the journal of that society he has published a translation of an astronomical work termed the Sûrya Siddhânta, the text and a translation of two Vedic grammatical works, an Index Verborum to the Atharva-Veda, and other important works. He is also the author of an excellent Sanskrit grammar, treating of the language in its historical development, and supplemented by an important catalogue of all genuine Sanskrit roots. Among his other works must be mentioned "Language and the Study of Language," the "Life and Growth of Language," the "Essentials of English Grammar," and his collected "Oriental and Linguistic Studies." Nor has he disdained less recondite subjects ; for he has also published a German grammar and a German reader, two admirable works of their kind. It is mainly to Professor Whitney's unwearying labours as a teacher and an author that America is indebted for her flourishing school of Oriental philology, in which he is *facile princeps*, and on these grounds he was invited to become one of our Tercentenary honorary graduates. I have now the honour of of requesting that the degree be conferred upon him in absence. (Applause.)

I have further to ask your Lordship to confer the degree, in absence, on Rudolf von Roth, Ph.D., Professor of Oriental Languages in the University of Tübingen. After completing his studies in Germany, and in London, and in Paris, Professor von Roth was appointed a "Privatdocent" at Tübingen in 1845, and a Professor in 1856. One of his greatest works is the famous St. Petersburg Sanskrit Dictionary, a marvel of erudition, of which he and Dr. von Böhtlingk were the joint authors. With the collaboration of Professor Whitney of Yale College, he has also published a standard edition of the Atharva-Veda, or sacred hymns of the Hindus ; and the learned treatises he has written on this subject have inaugurated a new era in philological research. He is also a high authority on the Zend-Avesta, or ancient Persian books of Zoroaster, and he has attained a European reputation as a lecturer on comparative religion. As one of the greatest of modern Orientalists, Professor von Roth was invited to honour the University with a visit, and to receive the degree of LL.D. on the occasion of the Tercentenary Festival, but has hitherto been unable to undertake so long a journey. The Senatus therefore request that the degree be now conferred upon him in absence. (Applause.)

I have next to present to your Lordship Whitley Stokes, C.S.I., C.I.E., Hon. D.C.L. Oxon., Hon. LL.D. Dublin, Barrister-at-Law, etc. Mr. Stokes was invited to receive the degree on the occasion of the Tercentenary Festival, but was unfortunately unable to honour the University with his presence on that occasion. In the course of his career in India, he has filled several of the most important legal and administrative offices. From 1877 to 1882 he was Law Member of the Governor-General's Council ; in 1879 he presided over the Indian Law Commission ; and he has drafted the Indian Codes of Criminal and Civil Procedure and a number of important statutes. He has also written and edited valuable law-books on Liens, on Powers of Attorney, on Hindu Law, Indian Statutes, and the Anglo-Indian Codes, the last of which are now passing through the Clarendon Press. Such, in outline, has been one of his distinguished careers. The other may be summed up in a single phrase : Mr. Whitley Stokes is the greatest living Celtic scholar. He seems equally at home in the Irish, Breton, and Cornish languages, and he is one of the foremost and most frequent contributors to the *Revue Celtique* and the *Zeitschrift für Vergleichende Sprachforschung.* Outstanding among his numerous works and articles in this department are his " Tripartite Life of St. Patrick," his masterly "Celtic Declensions," and his text and translation of ancient "Irish Glosses." Nor must it be forgotten that he rendered a signal service to another branch of philology in the year 1868, when he framed a scheme for the collection, copying, and cataloguing of the Sanskrit MSS. preserved in India, thus rescuing many priceless treasures from oblivion. It is on these more than doubly ample grounds that the Senatus desire your Lordship to enrol Mr. Stokes among the Honorary Doctors of this University.

---

## The Vedic Schools of India.*

None of the various divisions existing of old among the Brahmans of India deserves so much attention on the part of the Sanskritist as the classification of Brahmans according to the particular branch of the Veda to which they are devoting their studies. The antiquity of this principle of division is distinctly proved by the contents of the Indian inscriptions. Each of the original *śākhās* and *charaṇas* dividing anew, whenever a slight difference of opinion would arise among the adherents of one school, it was but natural that the number of schools should have gone on increasing to a surprising extent, and that the want of

* *Beiträge zur Kenntniss der vedischen Schulen.* Von Dr. Richard Simon. Kiel, 1889. Pp. vi and 114.

collecting and perpetuating their names should have been felt at an early period. One of the lists of Vedic teachers which have come down to our times is the Charaṇavyûha, first edited by Professor Weber ; another is contained in the Introduction to Râmakrishṇa's Commentary of Pâraskara's Gṛihyasûtra. A careful edition of the hitherto unpublished Sanskrit composition of Râmakrishṇa forms the main bulk of the present work, the value of which is enhanced by a series of highly instructive prefatory remarks and a full Index of names.

Dr. Simon has spared no pains to supply from other works the information to be derived from the statements of Râmakrishṇa. As for the Charaṇavyûha, a collation of the Munich MS. (cod. Haug No. 45), and of Dr. Wilson's translation of the Charaṇavyûha, would hardly have yielded any appreciable results besides those obtained by Dr. Simon from the printed editions and several MS. copies of the Charaṇavyûha and its Commentary. Dr. Wilson's translation has appeared in his posthumous work on Indian Castes, and the MS. on which it is founded is designated by him as superior in correctness to most of those in Europe. Yet hardly any one among the readings mentioned as peculiar to this copy—such as, *e.g.* the way in which the 2, 5, 14, and 15 divisions of the Vâjasaneyas are spelt, and the divisions of the Kauthamas into seven Bhedas—is not found in one of the copies consulted by Dr. Simon as well.

The name of the Seṅgara dynasty, by which Râmakrishṇa was patronized, is not quite so unknown as Dr. Simon seems to think. Seṅgara appears to be a Prakritic transformation of the Sanskrit name Śṛiṅgivara, as may be gathered from a passage of Aufrecht's Bodleian Catalogue referred to in the Petersburg Dictionary s.v. Further information regarding the Seṅgara (*alias* Sangara, Segara) princes of Bhareha, a town situated at the confluence of the Chambal (Charmaṇvatí) and Jumna rivers, may be collected from the Introductions to West and Bühler's Digest of Hindu Law and to Mandlik's Hindu Law. It must remain a matter of doubt however whether the Seṅgaras of Bhareha in the N.W. Provinces and those of Madrupattana in Southern India were at all connected with one another, especially as their respective genealogies differ entirely, except perhaps in the well-known epithet Sâhi (derived from the Persian *shâh*), which is common to several princes of both dynasties. The coincidence of the names of these two princely houses may be purely accidental, both apparently deriving the appellation of Seṅgaras from such well-known mythical personage as the sage Rishyaśringa. As regards the date of Râmakrishṇa, Dr. Simon is certainly right in referring it to no earlier period than the last century. He might have strengthened his case by availing himself of the date of Mitramiśra's Vîramitrodaya, which is largely quoted by Râmakrishṇa. The Vîramitrodaya has been shown by Professor Bühler to have been compiled in the first half of the seventeenth century, by the order of King Vîrasimha, the ill-famed murderer of Abul Fazl, the minister and biographer of Akbar. In spite of its modern date, Râmakrishṇa's dissertation on the

Vedic schools is a valuable mine of information, and Dr. Simon has gained a claim to the gratitude of Sanskrit scholars by rendering it generally accessible.

J. JOLLY.

---

# Eighth International Congress of Orientalists

*Which will be held at Stockholm and at Christiania from the 2nd to the 13th September 1889.*

*Patron :* H.M. the King of Sweden and Norway Oscar II.

*General Secretary.*—Count Carlo Landberg, Ph.D. *Committee for Sweden.*—M. E. Tegnér, Ph.D., Professor of Semitic Languages at the University of Lund, one of the 18 members of the Swedish Academy; M. R. Almkvist, Ph.D., Professor of Comparative Philology at the University of Upsala; M. Fr. Fehr, Ph.D., Pastor Primarius of Storkyrkan; The Count Carlo Landberg.

*Committee for Norway.*—M. E. Blix, Ph.D., formerly Minister of Public Instruction in Norway, Professor at the University of Christiania; M. J. Lieblein, Professor of Egyptology at the University of Christiania; M. S. Bugge, Ph.D., Professor of Indo-European Philology at the University of Christiania; M. C. P. Caspari, D.D. & Ph.D., Professor of Theology at the University of Christiania; M. A. Seippel, Ph.D., Professor of Semitic Languages at the University of Christiania.

### GENERAL DIRECTIONS.

I. The Congress will be composed of five sections, the first of which will be divided into two distinct sub-sections:

*Sections.*—1st, Semitic and Islâm: *a.* Languages and literatures of Islâm; *b.* Semitic languages, other than Arabic; text and cuneiform inscriptions. 2nd, Aryan languages. 3rd, African languages, including Egyptology. 4th, Section of Central Asia and the Extreme East. 5th, Section of Malayan and Polynesian languages.

II. The official languages employed at the general meetings will be English, French, German, Italian, Latin and Eastern languages. At the sectional meetings the president will decide if languages other than the above mentioned can be admitted.

III. Beside the opening and closing general meetings, a general meeting of the various sections presided over by His Majesty the King of Sweden and Norway will be held at Stockholm. Papers to be read at this meeting must not extend over twenty minutes.

IV. At Christiania the Congress will be opened and closed in the name of His Majesty by the Minister of Public Instruction.

V. Each section shall elect from among its members a President, two Vice-Presidents and two Secretaries. Should the section contain less than 15 members one Vice-President may be elected, appointing in every case the two Secretaries so as to facilitate the publication of the daily bulletin of the Congress. It is advisable to appoint the Secretaries without distinction of nationality so that the report may be drawn up as speedily as possible.

VI. Each section shall fix for itself the order of the day.

VII. The Secretaries are earnestly requested to forward to the General-Secretary a précis of the papers after each meeting, as well as the order of the day of the following section. The members of the Congress are also requested to forward to the Secretaries of their sections a résumé of the intended communications. The résumés of the papers to be read at the three general meetings are to be forwarded to the General-Secretary.

VIII. The Proceedings of the Congress will be published at the expense of the Congress, but will contain only such papers as are presented during the Congress, and have a scientific value.

IX. To facilitate the despatch of these Proceedings, members are requested to write their addresses in the register opened at the Secretary's office.

X. On arriving at Stockholm, members are requested to inscribe their names, nationality, and Stockholm address, so that the list of members present may be distributed before the opening meeting.

XI. His Majesty has consented to accept the presentation of such works as may be left for that purpose at the President's office. These will be acknowledged in time by His Majesty's private Secretary. Members are advised to inscribe on a register *ad hoc* name, address and works presented to His Majesty.

The General-Secretary would be much obliged by being informed in time of the titles of the works to be presented, so that a printed list may be issued previous to the opening meeting.

### PROGRAMM FOR STOCKHOLM.

The Congress will meet at the Palace of the Swedish Nobility, Riddarhuset, situated in the Riddarhustorget, at the back of the statue of Gustavus Vasa. The opening and closing sittings, as well as the general meeting, will be held in the large Concert-Hall of the Royal Academy of Music. Places will be reserved for delegates.

*Sunday, Sept. 1st.*—At 7 p.m.: Friendly réunion in the state rooms of the Grand Hotel with refreshments.

*Monday, Sept. 2nd.*—At 11 a.m.: Opening session. The delegates of foreign powers will be presented to His Majesty and to the Royal Princes. Opening speech delivered by His Majesty the King. Words of Welcome by the President of the Congress. Report read on the two prizes founded by the King, and presentation of these prizes to the successful competitors. Communications made by the foreign delegates. The subjects of such communications should, before being admitted, be communicated to the General-Secretary on the previous day. The members will then betake themselves to the rooms in the Riddarhuset assigned to the various sections, and will proceed to elect their officers. Official dress. Professors and members of Universities are requested to appear in their robes or gowns.

*Sittings.*—3.5 p.m.: Semitic section 1a. and Aryan section 2; 7 p.m.: Reception at HASSELBACKEN; From 6 p.m. to 7½ p.m. river steamers starting from the piers near the Grand Hotel will convey members across; and from 10 p.m. till midnight they will be taken back to the town by the same boats.

*Tuesday, Sept. 3.*—9½ a.m.—12: Aryan section 2; Semitic section 1b.; African section 3; Section for Central Asia and Extreme East 4; 2 p.m.—4 p.m.: Semitic section 1a.; 9 p.m.: A soirée given by COUNT and COUNTESS LANDBERG to the foreign members of the Congress will take place in the assembly rooms of the Grand Hotel.

*Wednesday, Sept. 4.*—9½ a.m.—12: Semitic section 1b. Aryan section 2. African section 3. Polynesian section 4. 4 p.m.: Excursion by special train to Gamla-Upsala, where the members of the Congress will be received by the students of the University, and where, near the graves of Odin, Thor, and Freya, the mead of the Gods will be served, according to a custom still in use in this locality so rich in memories. The members will here be presented, in the name of the King, with a suitable memorial of the Congress. All the military bands from Stockholm will be in attendance. From there by the same train to Upsala, where a fête will take place, at which the celebrated choir of students will be present. 11 p.m.: Return to Stockholm by special train.

*Thursday, Sept. 5.*—9½ a.m.—12½ p.m. : Aryan section 2. Semitic section 1*a*. Section of Central Asia and Extreme East 4. 2 p.m.—4 p.m.: Semitic section 1*b*. African section 3. Excursion through the town. 7 p.m.: Gala representation at the Royal Opera. Evening dress.

*Friday, Sept. 6th.*—11 a.m. : General meeting of all the sections under the presidency of H. M. the King in the Concert-Hall of the Royal Academy of Music. 7 p.m. : Reception at the palace of Drottningholm. Special steamers starting from the pier at Riddarholmen will convey members to the palace. The delegates of foreign powers will embark on the Royal yacht. Official or evening dress. 11 p.m. : Return to Stockholm.

*Saturday Sept. 7th.*—11 a.m.: Meeting of the Presidents of sections, of the Committee of organization and of delegates. 1 p.m.: Closing of the Congress in the Concert-Hall of the Academy of Music with address delivered by His Majesty. Official or evening dress. 5 p.m. : Banquet given by the Committee of organization to the foreign members of the Congress in the large dining room of the Grand Hotel. 11 p.m. : Departure by special train for Christiania. Sleeping accommodation will be provided.

Luggage may be registered gratis after 9 p.m. in the halls of the Grand Hotel and Hotel Rydberg. It will be delivered at Christiania without further trouble on the part of the members.

### PROGRAMM FOR CHRISTIANIA.

*Sunday, Sept. 8th.*—8 a.m. : Arrival at Charlottenberg. Breakfast at the station. Tickets will be given admitting members free of expense. 12 : Arrival at Christiania. No business. The members will meet at the Secretary's office young scholars, who have undertaken the task of showing the town to those members, who may wish to visit it. 8 p.m. : Réunion in the halls of the Frimurerlogen.

*Monday, Sept. 9th.*—10 a.m. : Opening session in the large hall of the University. Presentation of works. Official or evening dress. 2—4 p.m. : Meetings of the various sections. 4½ p.m. : Excursion to Bygdö. After visiting the palace of Oscarshall and the ancient Norwegian structures collected by His Majesty, a reception in the royal palace of Bygdö will be held, and the members received by M. Holst, chamberlain to H. M. the King of Norway, in the name of his Sovereign. Special steamers will convey the members.

*Tuesday, Sept. 10th.*—9½—11½ a.m. : Sittings of the various sections. 12½ p.m. : Excursion by special train to the falls of Hönefos. 4½ p.m. : Dinner at Hönefos. 6½ p.m. : Return by special train. Arrival at Christiania at 11 p.m. The train will stop at Drammen, where tea will be served by the ladies of the town.

*Wednesday, Sept. 11th.*—10 a.m.—12: Sittings of the various sections. 2 p.m.: Closing Meeting of the Congress in the Hall of the University. 5 p.m.: Banquet given to the foreign members of the Congress in the large hall of the Frimurerlogen. 10 p.m. : Departure by special train for Götheborg. Luggage may be registered at the Victoria and Skandinavia Hotels. It will be delivered at the station at Götheborg.

*Thursday, Sept. 12th.*—9 a.m. : Arrival at Wennersborg. The ladies of the town will serve coffee. 10 a.m. : Departure in special steamers for Götheborg, passing through the locks of the canal and river of Götha. 2 p.m. : Arrival at Götheborg. 8 p.m : Farewell reception. The following morning members may proceed either by train to Malmö, or by steamer to Copenhagen.

### OBSERVATIONS REFERRING TO THE JOURNEY.

1. Members of the Congress will have a right to a reduction of 50 per cent. on the price of tickets on all railways in the United Kingdoms.

2. Thursday and Friday, 30th and 31st August, evening, a special train will leave Malmö for Stockholm, at an hour to be fixed at a later date. The directors of the railway will provide sufficient carriages to enable each member to make himself comfortable for the night. Sleeping cars will also be provided. The ticket of membership shown at the ticket office will suffice to procure an ordinary railway ticket.

3. All members of the Congress are earnestly requested to wear in the buttonhole the small rosette in the national colours of Sweden and Norway, which will be handed to them at Stockholm, Sweden and Norway being at this period overrun by travellers.

### SOJOURN IN STOCKHOLM.

The Grand Hotel being one of the largest and best conducted hotels in Europe, members are advised to patronize it, as they can all find suitable accommodation. Price of rooms, service and lights included : 2nd floor, looking on the port : 5 crowns (Swedish currency); back or other rooms: 3.50 crowns. 3rd floor, looking on the port : 4 crowns; other rooms, 3 crowns. 4th floor, looking on the port : 3 crowns. Lift. Special table d'hôte for members from 12—2 p.m. : 3 crowns, wine not included. Thursday, September 5, the table d'hôte will cost 4 crowns, wine not included; admission till 5½ p.m. Restaurant à la carte at any hour. The gala performance in the theatre will begin on this day at 7 p.m.

The Hotel Rydberg, situated in the principal square of the town, and belonging to the same proprietor, is also recommended. Price of rooms, service and lights included : 1st floor, looking on the square : 5 crowns (Swedish); back rooms : 3.50. 2nd floor, looking on the square : 6 crowns ; back-rooms : 3. 3rd floor : 2.50—5. 4th floor, looking on the square : 4 crowns ; other rooms : 3.50. Lift. Table d'hôte du déjeuner for members, wine not included : 3 crowns. There will be no table d'hôte for the dinner Thursday, September 5.

The Secretary's office of the Congress at Stockholm will be in the Palace of the Nobility, Riddarhuset, to the left in the entrance-hall. Under-Secretaries will be found there, who will furnish all necessary directions, and ready to do the honours of the town to such members as may desire their services.

Ladies will not be admitted to the closing dinner given to the members on Saturday, September 7th, nor to that given at Christiania, Wednesday, September 10th ; but they may take part in all the other fêtes.

To retain rooms both in Stockholm and Christiania, apply to the " Secrétariat du VIIIième Congrès international des Orientalistes, Stockholm," but not previous to July 15th, naming floor, position, number of rooms and beds required. By return of post a card naming No. and price of rooms in both towns will be sent. Previous to that date, all communications may

56 TRÜBNER'S RECORD. [1889.

be addressed to Count Landbérg, whose address till July 15th is Stuttgart.

So that arrangements made may not be upset at the last moment, members are requested to give due notice whether they intend taking part in the Congress at Christiania. Those members who only decide to do so at Stockholm, have only themselves to blame if everything does not correspond to their wishes. The Committee of Organization expresses the hope that all the members of the Congress will also meet together in Christiania, a hospitable town, on which nature has lavished its richest treasures.

### SOJOURN IN CHRISTIANIA.

Before leaving Stockholm, members must apply to the Secretary's office for a card bearing all directions necessary to enable them to find without difficulty their lodgings on arrival at Christiania. The Hotels Victoria and Skandinavia are particularly recommended. Prices are more moderate than at Stockholm, both for rooms and table d'hôte du déjeuner.

### HOW AND WHERE TO OBTAIN CARDS OF MEMBERS.

To secure membership, foreigners will pay a fee of twenty francs=16 shillings=8 rupees. Requests to be enrolled in the list of members should be addressed either to Count Landberg, Stuttgart, or to one of the following gentlemen: France and Colonies: M. E. Leroux, libraire-éditeur, 28, Rue Bonaparte, Paris. England: T. W. Rhys Davids, Esq., Secretary of the Royal Asiatic Society, 22, Albemarle Street, Piccadilly, London. Italy: Cav. Professore Schiaparelli, 22, Via della Lungara, Roma. Syria and Palestine: M. Jules Loytved, Vice-Consul for Sweden and Norway, Beyrouth. East Indies: Professor P. Peterson, Bombay University. Turkey (in Europe): Legation of Sweden and Norway, Constantinople. Belgium, Holland and Dutch Colonies: M. J. E. Brill, Leyden. Spain and Portugal: M. Fr. Codera, University, Madrid. Egypt: M. Vollers, Director of the Khedivial Library, Cairo.

Subscribers are requested to send their fees and full address to one of the above-mentioned gentlemen. They are also requested to state at the same time whether they intend to appear in person at the Congress. Cards of membership will be forwarded by return of post, and will serve as receipt for payment of fees.

Any person who may intend to bring forward a motion during the meeting of the Congress, or who has any communications to make, or wishes for special information, is requested to make such intention known to the General-Secretary previous to August 1.

For Swedes the subscription will be 30 crowns; they may, however, take part in the Congress at Christiania by only paying the amount of a railway ticket with 50 per cent. deduction.

Scandinavians are requested to communicate with some member of the Committee of Organization.

The daily bulletin will furnish all directions which may be necessary.

The Committee of Organization will strain every nerve to render the sojourn in Sweden and Norway pleasant to the savants who may join the Congress. The patriarchal hospitality of the two countries, the innate cordiality of their inhabitants, who have at all times done honour to science, will be the best guarantee of a sincere welcome,—to say nothing of the unique opportunity offered to the members of visiting the most beautiful parts of our countries.

The Committee of Organization has moreover the high honour of working under the patronage of H.M. Oscar II., who has not only shown a special interest in the objects of the Congress, but has accorded them at all times his valuable aid.

The Committee of Organization would be glad if Orientalists from all parts of the globe would seize this opportunity to do homage by their presence to the august monarch of the North, who, himself a *savant*, considers it a glory and a duty to be a protector of the science which teaches us to decipher the most ancient annals of mankind.

THE COMMITTEE OF ORGANIZATION,
Stockholm and Christiania, *January*, 1889.

## New Books.

*Mekka* von Dr. C. Snouck Hurgronje. Herausgegeben von "het Koninklijk Instituut voor de Taal-, Land- en Volkenkunde van Nederlandsch-Indië te 's-Gravenhage." Vol. I. Die Stadt und ihre Herren (xxiii and 228 pages 8vo. with two plates). The Hague, M. Nijhoff, 1888.—Vol. II. Aus dem heutigen Leben (xviii and 397 pages) ib. 1889.—Album of pictures (40 plates fol.).

Well prepared as an Arabic scholar, and also accustomed to speak the vernacular, the Dutch savant Dr. Snouck Hurgronje went to Jeddah, the port of Mecca, in the year 1884 with the intention of studying the nature and action of Islám by personal observation in the holy city which has remained untouched by European influences. He stayed at Jeddah for five months to familiarise himself still better with the language and customs of the country, and to form connections, and then went to Mecca, where he resided for nearly six months among the Muslim theologians as one of themselves. He had planned to join in the great festival of the pilgrims at Mecca and then to visit Medina. But through the intrigue of the French Vice-Consul at Jeddah he was ordered out of the city. He had, however, made such good use of his sojourn there that he brought away with him a far more accurate acquaintance with that city than any of his predecessors had done who visited Mecca only during the pilgrimage season when everything is in an abnormal condition. Mecca, a city of about 60,000 inhabitants, in an absolutely barren locality, and without industry worth mentioning, derives its livelihood solely from the pilgrims. From the time of their gradual appearance till the end of the festival when, after viewing the sacred places and visiting Medina, they return to their several homes, every Meccan tries to derive the utmost gain from those visitors (who number about a hundred thousand, and are most of them in easy circumstances) as guides, letters of lodgings or animals for riding, agents and general advisers, solicited or unsolicited. During that season the inhabitants are agitated by a feverish thirst after gain; it is their harvesting season. But as soon as the pilgrims are gone the natives resume their quiet, normal life of enjoyment and study, they then show their better qualities. It was, therefore, fortunate that Dr. Snouck resided at Mecca during the period of rest.

Dr. Snouck having previously brought out some of

the results of his journey,* now presents us in the comprehensive work before us with the main outcome of his studies and observations. The first volume contains topographical matter, and then gives the political history of Mecca from Muhammed down to the present day. For this he had the advantage of using valuable manuscript chronicles, copies of which he had procured at Mecca. He was also enabled by his intimate acquaintance with the locality and the people to utilize the well-known histories of Mecca to a greater extent than it would otherwise have been possible.

That history has for many centuries been closely connected with that of the exceedingly numerous descendants of Hasan, the son of 'Alī and of Fâtima, the daughter of the Prophet Muhammed. No family of rank in Europe can, as to ancient lineage, even distantly compare with the Hasanides and Husainides of W. Arabia, who since the seventh century A.D. have been acknowledged by all Arabs to be of high nobility. The proudest Beduin chief humbly kisses the hand of the poorest of those descendants of the Prophet. A Sherîf (Hasanide) gives as a rule his daughter in marriage to none but a Sherîf. But in no sense does this noble race of the Prophet's children form a priestly caste or any particularly pious community. They are genuine, unbridled Arabs, not rarely downright robbers. Indeed, that sanctity, so strongly inculcated by the Muhammedan religion, of Mecca and its territory, where it is not even lawful to hunt, has, since the Hasanides have gained the ascendency, unceasingly and often for years in succession, on account of their family feuds, been profaned through bloodshed. A Grand Sherîf of Mecca was never for a moment safe from being attacked or even driven out by a brother, cousin, or distant relative. Those doings, however, were checked, though at times also countenanced, through the influence of the Muhammedan Power whose temporary supremacy was acknowledged in Mecca and therefore invested with the highest authority in the eyes of all the faithful. In most cases that Power was the ruler of Egypt, for hungry Mecca has principally to rely on that country for donations of grain. Dr. Snouck portrays to us the changeful tableaux of frictions between the Egyptian, in later times the Osmanli, highest functionaries and the Grand Sherîfs. The latter could not be completely set aside since it was through the Sherîfs only that an influence could be exerted on the Beduins with whom the Turks of Cairo and Constantinople did not understand how to deal direct. The want of consistency in the administration, the influence of intriguers of every kind, and the consequent frequent change of Governors often allowed the Sherîfs a free hand, even in open rebellion. There is a certain romantic charm attaching to these people

who have uninterrupted feuds against one another and yet possess a strong feeling of reciprocal interest, which e.g. would prevent them from totally annihilating a defeated enemy. It is fortunate, however, that the influence of the foreign governors has gradually gone on increasing, especially since the opening of the Suez Canal and the laying of a telegraphic cable connecting Mecca with Stamboul. According to Meccan standard, Turkish rule upon the whole means, after all, progress, though that rule is not always represented by such capable and energetic men as Osman Nûrî Pascha, who was Governor during Dr. Snouck's residence, but was unfortunately soon recalled.

But while the first volume gives us many a deep insight into the daily life of the holy city, we find a great deal more of this in the second. They are indeed but sketches; still you would rarely meet with such a comprehensive and life-like view of a strange civilization as you do in this volume. With Lane's power of observation which does not lose sight of the minutest detail, Dr. Snouck combines the large views of the historian. He shows us how the population of Mecca, a strange motley of people from all Muhammedan countries, is constantly renewed and yet constantly forms a unit of truly Arabic or rather Meccan character. The people make their living by the sanctuary; they worship the Prophet and the saints in a manner which he himself would have stigmatized as idolatry; they constantly have God and his legate upon their lips—without any hypocrisy, to be sure, for no one is tainted with free-thinking,—but mostly also without any deeper religious feeling. Holding fast to the belief that God is all-merciful, they live and let live, and consciously also commit many a sin. It was just the same 1200 years ago, for Mecca never really was an abode of gloomy asceticism. Dr. Snouck does not gloss over any dark part, but takes equal care to show the bright sides in bold relief. We see then that those people with their mediæval ways of thinking have after all a far greater resemblance to ourselves than we might suppose. Dr. Snouck introduces us into the most recondite mysteries of the house; and we are taught more plainly than ever that the prime evil of Muslim matrimony does not lie in polygamy, but in the ease with which the marriage tie can be cut asunder. In forming a matrimonial alliance the contracting parties have no intention of binding themselves for life or even of blending their mutual interests. Generally speaking, concubinage (sanctioned both by law and custom) with a slave woman, especially an Abyssinian, is of a far closer nature and more akin to our idea of marriage. Such a woman has no property of her own, but her dependence on the man is different to that of a free woman. When she has had a child she may no longer be sold, and on the owner's death she is free. The children of a slave mother, be she or they jet black, are by right and custom on an even footing with those of free mothers. Though apparently standing outside the law, the wife also in Mecca often reigns supreme in the house, she torments and plunders her husband. As Dr. Snouck corrects the current ideas concerning

* We draw special attention to the Dutch treatise "Een Rector der Mekkaansche Universiteit" (in "Bijdragen tot de Taal-, Land- en Volkenkunde van Ned. Indië," vol. xxxvi.), to his collection of Mecca proverbs and phrases (in German, ib. vol. xxxv. also published separately at the Hague in 1886), to which are added valuable philological and explanatory notes; and to the account he gave of his journey at a meeting of the Berlin Geographical Society on March 5, 1887.

the harem, so he does especially those on slavery. Prompted by his own experience and that of other un-biassed Europeans, he pronounces emphatically, nay acrimoniously, against the anti-slavery policy. We highly recommend his exposition to all those, who in the crusade against the slave trade in which at this moment not only England and Germany, but also—of course from pure philanthropy!—the Roman Church are engaged, have preserved their independence of judgment.

The chapter which treats of literary studies pursued at Mecca at the present day is highly instructive. In the spacious halls surrounding the Kaaba (the sanctuary which has had its origin in heathen times), partly also in private buildings, lectures are delivered by a large number of savants to students of various ages and from different countries, from Marocco to Celebes and Kashghar, in all branches of scholastic theology in the widest sense. The author himself attended as a student the lectures of the Rector, the hoary Ahmed Dahlän, on Baidhäwi's commentary on the Korän. These lectures do not indeed contain anything materially new, their main object is merely to prevent the substance of old literary knowledge from falling into disuse. We have here a complete reproduction of mediæval times. The description of the present subjects of instruction and method of teaching, interwoven as it is with lucid delineations of the character and personal habits of some of the most prominent lecturers, is preceded by an excellent historical review of the development of the science of Isläm, from which we again learn that from its very commencement it had a strong tendency to ossification in it. This tendency has also exerted its influence upon mysticism, which, however, still possesses much vitality, though not in literary matters. We wish further to draw the reader's attention to Dr. Snouck's exposition of the highly artificial recitation of the Korän, which is something altogether apart from the understanding of it. We are astounded to learn that the sacred volume is now only used for ritual purposes, that it is of no consequence to understand its meaning, and that it is actually not understood by all those who have not studied exegesis expressly.

Although the pilgrims for several months entirely put their stamp upon Mecca, in many respects those visitors are of by far greater importance who have come to reside there for years or for good. Dr. Snouck as a Dutchman took of course special interest in the thousands of Muslim colonists from the Dutch East Indies, who after the principal island are simply called "Jävä."* Able to converse in Malay and Javanese as well as in Arabic, Dr. Snouck kept up a familiar intercourse with those "Jävä," and he describes their various classes, from the scholar who belongs to Mecca's most illustrious men down to the ignorant pilgrim who quits the place in the same stupidity that he

brought with him. He points out—and this part of the whole work is of the most practical importance—how paramount is the influence of this Jävä Colony, and more especially of their learned men, upon their co-religionists at home, and how thus pan-islamic sentiment and hatred of the rule of the infidel are powerfully fostered. This fact can scarcely be agreeable to a nation of about four millions, more than two-thirds of whose thirty millions of subjects are Muslims, while among the rest Isläm is spreading more and more. As, however, those people, by their national and geographical insulation, are far apart from one another, and as some of them are devoid of energy, we are confident that the Dutch, cool and circumspect as they are, will know how to meet any dangers arising from that cause. Also England has found by "the Great Mutiny" what a danger her immense number of Muslim subjects are. But any one who in blind confidence still imagines that the Indian Muhammedans have by this time found out what they owe to England, can learn from Dr. Snouck by the way that their hatred of England has become more intense since. Let him consider, too, that Russia, a power not near so repellant to the Moslims as are the more cultured European nations, has advanced close to the gates of India !

The Album contains partly views of Mecca, partly portraits of natives of Mecca and Jeddah and of pilgrims of all classes ; all but two from photographs taken by Dr. Snouck himself or by an Arab whom he had instructed in that art. There are, besides, coloured pictures of all sorts of articles peculiar to Mecca. Among the portraits the various kinds of "Jävä" are most numerous. There are not many purely Arab types, for even in the Sherifs and Sayids (Husainides) you can frequently trace the blood of the black mothers. While we admire the stately military figure of the above-named Osman Pascha, the grand Sherif looks downright disfigured by his gold-lace gala uniform.

What we have said about this remarkable book does not claim to give more than a brief outline of its rich contents. May it also in England find attentive readers !                          TH. NÖLDEKE.

*Strassburg, March* 13, 1889.

---

*A Group of Eastern Romances and Stories from the Persian, Tamil, and Urdu.* With Introduction, Notes, and Appendix. By W. A. Clouston. Privately printed, 1889. (xl and 586 pages.)

Mr. Clouston, who has with indefatigable industry and a rare grasp of the folklore literature in all its ramifications, been wont to administer to the wants of lovers of Eastern fictions in prose and poetry, presents to us now, as a sequel to such popular romances as the Book of Sindibad and the Bakhtiyar-nameh, a group of less-known "Eastern Romances and Stories" in a ponderous volume of 629 pages. The History of Nassar, the History of Farrukhruz, and a number of shorter stories, are from the Persian collection entitled Mahbúb ul Kulúb, the English translation of which, by Mr. E. Rehatsek, of Bombay, is now very scarce. The story of the King and his four Ministers was

* A special branch of "Jävä" is formed by the descendants of Malays who had been taken to the Cape Colony years ago. These Cape people (*ahl-käf*), it is supposed, have been strongly blended with Dutch blood, and speak the Dutch of the present Boers. Several also of these Moslims, whose vernacular is Teutonic, visit Mecca annually as pilgrims.

specially translated for the present publication by Pandit S. M. Nateśa Śástrí, of Madras. Apparently, two different recensions of this tale are known in Tamil literature ; see the notices in Taylor's Catalogue of Oriental MSS. vol. iii. pp. 163, 165, and 460. Still, as the statements in this Catalogue have to be taken *cum grano salis*, a more thorough examination of the MSS. in question is required before their relation to one another can be decided. The Rose of Bakâwalî, originally a Persian romance, is here given after two versions made from Nihâl Chand's Urdu translation. Mr. Clouston would have done well if he had for comparison's sake referred also to the Malay recension of the story, a full analysis and partial translation of which was given by Mr. D. Gerth van Wijk in the "Bijdragen voor de taal-, land- en volkenkunde van Nederlandsch-Indië" for 1883, from the lithographed text edition which appeared at Singapore in 1880 (180 pages 4to.). As is the case in most Malay translations of works of fiction (compare, *e.g.* the Panchatantra), the Malay narrator has imparted to his work much matter that is simply the fruit of his own imagination. With that thoroughness that characterizes all his publications, Mr. Clouston has, by the addition of introductory matter, of parallel stories, illustrations, references, and appendices, made his book as complete as possible, and has thus earned a fresh title to the gratitude of all friends of Eastern romance.

*Grammatica elementar do Kimbundu ou lingua de Angola*, por Héli Chatelain. Genebra, 1888—89. (pp. xxiv and 172.)

*Ki-mbundu* is the language of the *A-mbundu* or indigenous inhabitants of the ancient kingdom of Angola, and is mainly represented by two dialects, the one spoken in the Portuguese province of Loanda, and the other in the interior. It belongs to the great Ba-ntu family of African languages, the area of which is comprised within the great triangle between the Kilimanjaro and the Kameroons in the north, and the Cape of Good Hope in the south, some "enclaves" formed by Hottentot tribes being alone excepted. Its closest affinities are with the Kishikongo, spoken in the modern province of Congo, the Umbundu, spoken in Benguella, the Oshindonga S. of the Cunene river, and the Kinyika of Mombasa on the E. Coast. Also the Kioko and Lunda languages on which it borders on the East are mentioned as nearly related. The Kimbundu was the first African language of which some grammatical notices were written. They are to be found in the Catechism of Padre Pacconio, which appeared at Lisbon in 1642 (second edition 1661, third 1784). The first real grammar, by P. Pedra Dias, was published at Lisbon in 1697, and another, by the Italian Capuchin friar B. M. de Cannecattim, was brought out in 1805 (second edition 1859). Neither these books nor the subsequent "Elementos grammaticaes" of Francina have contributed in any way to give a correct idea of the mechanism of the language. Mr. Chatelain, the author of the present grammar, which is introduced to the reader in an English preface by Dr. R. N. Cust, deserves high credit for the lucidity and philological

acumen with which he has placed before the student the somewhat complicated grammatical structure of Ki-mbundu, and for the practical sense which has guided him in not only illustrating his rules with pertinent examples (most of which are accompanied by an English translation besides the one in Portuguese), but in also adding under each head exercises for translation from Ki-mbundu. This book is at once a boon to the student of African languages, while it is pre-eminently calculated to serve practical requirements.

*The Anglo-Indian Codes.* Edited by Whitley Stokes, D.C.L. Vol. II. Oxford, 1888. Pp. 1224.

It is hardly necessary to say that this volume, like its predecessor, is a work of the first order, indispensable to every one connected with the administration of India, and a mine of valuable information for legal questions of every kind. During his long and distinguished career in India, the writer took a leading part in the framing of its recent legislation, and those Acts in the present collection are few if any, regarding which Mr. Stokes might not with justice say, *quorum pars magna fui.* This is especially true with regard to the Codes of Criminal and Civil Procedure which form the main bulk of this volume. As a signal proof of the progress of legislation in India, we may instance the law of debt, in which the term of imprisonment in execution of a decree has been reduced to six months, or six weeks in minor cases, as an important step towards an entire abolition of 'a barbarous expedient of a rude age.' Infinitely greater still is the progress as compared to ancient laws of the country, and the natives of India ought to take the trouble to compare, with the wise provisions of the present Code, the primitive rules of procedure in the Sanskrit law-books, among which the administration of ordeals, sitting in Dharna, confinement of the defendant by the plaintiff, and vague rules about prescription and limitation, play a prominent part. The introductions contain a very valuable resumé of the history and motives of each Act. The Index is very copious.

*Marathi English Primer*, by Ganesh Hari Bhide. Bombay : Education Society's Press, 1889. (pp. 7 and 108.)

This extremely useful book gives far more than one would expect from a mere Primer. In its simple and practical arrangement it treats, in 25 lessons (pp. 1—68) of the different parts of Marathi Accidence. Every rule or grammatical fact is stated briefly and intelligibly, and illustrated with examples. Lists of words follow each Lesson in alphabetical order, and exercises for translating from one language into the other. Thus the student obtains by easy and progressive stages a good stock of words as well as a familiarity with the principal grammatical forms. All paradigms and lists of classified words are relegated for reference to the two Appendices which occupy 40 pages. We trust the author may be encouraged to bring out a second part dealing with complex sentences and the details of Marathi idiom.

*Second Edition of the S'abdakalpadruma.*—The new edition of the great Sanskrit Encyclopædia, the Śabdakalpadruma, now passing through the press in Calcutta, commends itself in the first place to all Sanskrit students outside Bengal by not only being in the Devanagari character, but also by its clear, neat and compact type. All the poetical quotations, besides, are made prominent as such, which is a great improvement upon the original Bengali edition and its reproduction by Messrs. Baradakanta & Co. Altogether the typography and general get up of this second edition are in keeping with the best style of modern Sanskrit publications, and do high credit to the enterprising publishers, the brothers Barada Prasad and Hari Charan Vasu. These have also—and we mark this as the most distinguishing characteristic of this new edition, and one which will specially urge it on the attention of Sanskrit scholars and Learned Societies—made provision for incorporating in a large Appendix a vast deal of additional matter, which further research in all departments of Sanskrit literature has brought to light, so as to make this celebrated Cyclopædia representative of modern scholarship in all branches of Sanskrit literature. This last feature is calculated to make this edition indispensable also to the owners of the previous issues. Perhaps, however, the publishers may see their way to bringing out the Appendix as a separate work.

*Hikáyat-i Yúsuf*. Madras, 1889.—The translation, by Capt. H. Eardley-Wilmot, of Æsop's Fables (313 in number) into idiomatic Persian would be well worth recommending as a text-book for beginners, more especially as in all cases of difficulty the *izáfat* has been marked, if the editor had but taken the trouble to add such a full glossary as a beginner needs. Unless he—the sooner the better—supplies this serious defect, his book will fail to be really serviceable. On the other hand, the fact of the "morals" of most of the Fables being taken from the Dīwân-i Hâfiz, Gulistan, Bostan, and Anwar-i Suhailî, deserves every praise.

*Indische Reiseskizzen.* Von Richard Garbe. Berlin, 1889.

The advantages enjoyed by Sanskritists living in India over their brethren in Europe have been commented upon a great deal. To be cut off entirely from every opportunity of personal intercourse with the natives of India is, no doubt, a material disadvantage to the student of Indian antiquities. The work under notice, together with the learned publications by the same writer in the field of Indian philosophy, furnishes ample proof of the manifold benefits to be derived from a trip to India by the Sanskrit scholar. Professor Garbe having been enabled through the judicious patronage of the Prussian Ministry and the Academy of Sciences to make a protracted sojourn in India, chose the Sâmkhya system of philosophy for the principal subject of his duty. Dr. Thibaut introduced him to the foremost Pandits of Benares, with some of whom he formed a close acquaintance. The sacred city of the Hindus abounds in specialists for every branch of Indian learning, who freely communicate their knowledge to Sanskritists from Europe; but their entire ignorance of European modes of thought, and their fondness of negative propositions, graphically described by Prof. Garbe, are serious drawbacks and very apt to engender a feeling of despair in the heart of the European who wishes to penetrate into their secrets. Armed with patient ardour, and well prepared for his task, Prof. Garbe succeeded in the end in overcoming all these obstacles. Though Benares was the principal scene of his labours, his remarks are not confined to that city; and his vivid description of the sights of Bombay, Rajputana, Agra, Delhi, Allahabad, Calcutta, and Ceylon, and of the life of Europeans in India, makes his book very pleasant reading.

*Indian Music.*—For many years Râjah Saurîndra Mohan Thâkur has been considered as the representative and a very *avatára* of the Indian science of music,—a science little studied, little known and still less appreciated in Europe. We cannot, therefore, but admire the courage with which, in his "Contribution à l'étude de la musique Hindoue" (Paris, 1888), M. J. Grosset, a pupil of Professor P. Regnaud, of the "Faculté des lettres de Lyon," has grappled with the extraordinary difficulties which the editing and tentative translation of the 28th chapter of the Bhâratîyanâtyaśâstra presented to him, while we are not surprised that, so far as we know, no Sanskrit scholar has ventured yet on a critical examination of that learned treatise. Professor P. G. Ghârpure, one of the leading members of the Musical Association at Poona, and himself a well-known musician both in theory and praxis, has quite recently put forth a comprehensive scheme for the publication, in serial form, of the most celebrated works, in Sanskrit and other languages, on Hindu music, together with all the paraphernalia of translations, commentaries, etc., required to insure completeness. The first fasciculus of vol. i. of his "*Studies in Indian Music*" brings, besides introductory matter, the commencement of the Râgavibodha,—Sanskrit text with commentary and English translation, on the completion of which the following important treatises, Nâradî śikshâ, Bharata nâtya, Sangîta ratnâkara, and Sangîta darpana, are to be taken up. We wish the editor and his band of learned pandits every encouragement and success in this noble enterprise. The first number leaves nothing to be desired as to the care bestowed on the Sanskrit text and English translation. May the editing of the more ancient and more difficult treatises prove equally satisfactory!

Another edition is being added to the numerous texts of the *Bhagavadgítâ* which annually like mushrooms spring up in the vernacular presses of India. But the one under notice, by P. D. Goswami, of Srampore, has also Sanskrit and English notes, a new English translation, and "an esoteric exposition in English." The latter gives it its peculiar stamp. The editor would have done better if he had called his exposition Vedantic, for practically it consists of Vedantism carried to extremes. The word 'esoteric' has with sober-minded philosophers acquired of late an unenviable notoriety. Neither the translation, however, nor the notes which accompany it, appear to us—so far as the first fasciculus enables us to judge—to be at all tainted with esoterism, though we prefer the version given in Protap Chandra Roy's English Mahâbhârata. On the other hand, this new exposition of the Gîtâ is not without interest to us as exhibiting a feature of Hindu interpretation of but recent growth, a blending of Vedantism and Sinnettism.

*The Languages of Assam.* — Assam, like Chutia Nagpore, has long attracted the attention of students of the aboriginal tribes of India and of their languages. Indeed, as a glance at the map will show, it forms quite a cluster of tribal divisions consisting of various clans of Nágas, each speaking a different language, Kacharis, Mikirs, Ákas, Singphos, Abors, Miris, and numerous others. Grammatical sketches and vocabularies of many of these tongues and dialects are to be found in the Journal of the Asiatic Society of Bengal. It is, however, only of late years that they have received a further and more scientific treatment at the hands of Government officers and missionaries. We subjoin a list of these later publications, some of which may not yet have fallen under the notice of European glottologists :

S. Endle, Outline Grammar of the Kachári (Bárá) Language as spoken in District Darrang, Assam ; with Illustrative Sentences, Notes, Reading Lessons, and a Short Vocabulary ; Shillong, 1884.—J. D. Anderson, Short List of Words of the Hill Tippera Language ; Shillong, 1885.—C. A. Soppitt, Short Account of the Kachcha Naga (Empéo) Tribe in the North Cachar Hills, with an Outline Grammar, Vocabulary, and Illustrative Sentences ; *ib.*, 1885.—J. F. Needham, Outline Grammar of the Shaiyáng Miri Language ; with Sentences, Phrase-Book, and Vocabulary ; *ib.*, 1886.—C. A. Soppitt, Short Account of the Kuki-Lushai Tribes, with an Outline Grammar of the Rangkhol-Lushai Language ; *ib.*, 1887.—R. B. McCabe, Outline Grammar of the Angámi Nágá Language ; with a Vocabulary and Illustrative Sentences ; Calcutta, 1887.—C. R. Macgregor, Outline Singpho Grammar, [with Singpho and Khámpti Vocabulary ; Shillong, 1888].—A. J. Primrose, Manipuri Grammar, Vocabulary, and Phrase Book ; to which are added some Manipuri Proverbs ; *ib.*, 1888.—W. E. Witter, Outline Grammar of the Lhótá Nágá Language ; with a Vocabulary and Illustrative Sentences ; Calcutta, 1888.—We do not know whether this goodly array of linguistical books is due to any special encouragement on the part of the Chief Commissioner and his Assistants. At any rate, the taste for this kind of literary work appears to have been singularly developed among that band of students, and we heartily congratulate all concerned on the outcome of their labours.

## Oriental Notes.

VERNACULAR LITERATURE OF INDIA.—From a letter from Mr. *George A. Grierson*, B.C.S., dated Gayá, 1 March, 1889, we extract the following :—

"My work on the *Modern Vernacular Literature of India* is nearly all printed off, and will be published very shortly. It will contain all the information I have been able to collect about Hindustani literature since the time of Prithiwí Ráj. I am also trying to translate the Padmávatí of Mallik Muhammad, written in very old Hindí of the sixteenth century. I have done about half in a rough translation already, but it is very difficult, and no native scholar can help me. It is invaluable, as it is written throughout *phonetically* in the Persian character, though it is the purest Hindí."

ASIATIC SOCIETY OF BENGAL.—On February 6th, *Lieut.-Colonel J. Waterhouse*, B.S.C., President of the Asiatic Society of Bengal, delivered the annual address on the Society's work and the progress of Oriental research during the past year. It forms a pamphlet of 78 pages, and is well worth perusal. It gives not only a detailed survey of the Society's operations in all the branches of literature and science within its scope, but passes in review also what has been done by other Oriental Societies in India and out of India, and by order or under the patronage of the Indian Government. The comprehensiveness of this survey may be gathered from the following list of heads under which each subject of inquiry is reviewed : Oriental Literature, History and Philology (pp. 4–16), Numismatics, Archæology and Epigraphy, Geography and Surveys, Geology, Meteorology, Chemistry, Telegraphy and Electrical Science, Photography, Museums, Other Institutions and Societies, Anthropology and Ethnology, Bacteriology, Botany. The good sound sense which pervades the Presidential Address, and the practical suggestions with which it is interspersed, give additional zest and interest to this elaborate and valuable composition.

NOTES FROM HYDERABAD.—Mr. *Syed Ali Bilgrami* writes under date of April 4th :—" My brother, who is now the Director of Public Instruction, is getting a press and set of Arabic types from Beyrouth, and we shall then publish some rare Arabic books. I have also, at the request of Dr. Leitner, undertaken the editorship of an Arabic Quarterly Journal. The material for the first number is quite ready, and I hope to print it this month, although it is to be issued from July. I have at last succeeded in obtaining some sheets of Sáyana's commentary on the Atharva-veda, which is being edited by S. P. Pandit, and I hope to bring out the Hindi translation of the first Kánda, which I began in the India Office Library in October, 1887, within a couple of months. The MS. is very nearly ready, but I have to compare the translation with Sáyana, and fix upon some press to publish it."

STRAITS BRANCH R.A.S.—We have just received No. 19 of the Journal of the Straits Branch of the Royal Asiatic Society, 1887, with the following contents :—Report of a Journey from Tuarau to Kiau and Ascent of Kinabalu Mountain. By R. M. Little.—Pulau Langkawi. By E. W. Maxwell, C.M.G.—The Negri Sembilan : Their Origin and Constitution. By Hon. Martin Lister.—Raja Ambong, a Malay Fairy Tale. By W. E. Maxwell, C.M.G.—Report on the Padi-Borer. By L. Wray, jun.—Summary of the Report on the Pomelow Moth. By L. Wray, jun.—Manangism in Borneo. By Rev. J. Perham.—Exploring Expedition from Selama, Pérak, to Pong, Patani. By Arthur T. Dew.—Birds from Pérak.—Occasional Notes.

SIR EDWIN ARNOLD.—In appreciation of the genius, taste and learning which Sir Edwin Arnold has displayed in his recent illustration of Persian poetry, the Shah has conferred on him the decoration of a Commander of the Imperial Order of the "Lion and Sun."

WORKS OF THE LATE GENERAL W. NASSAU LEES.—

ENGLISH.

Instruction in the Oriental Languages considered. London, 1857.

A Biographical Sketch of the Mystic Philosopher and Poet Jami. Being the Preface to his "Lives of Mystics." 8vo. Calcutta, 1859.

The Cultivation of Tea in India. 8vo. Calcutta, 1863.

The Drain of Silver to the East, and the Currency of India. 8vo. pp. xii. 196. London, 1864.

The Land and Labour of India. A Review. 8vo. London, 1867.

Materials for the History of India for the Six Hundred Years of Mohammadan Rule, previous to the Foundation of the British Indian Empire (Journal Royal Asiatic Society of Great Britain and Ireland, vol. iii. part 2). London, 1868.

*** . . . . Although written more than twenty years ago, it opens with a thoughtful review of the relation of the natives of India to their English superiors which might be studied with advantage at the present day.—*Athenæum.*

Indian Musulmans and Four Articles on Education. London, 1871.

Memorandum written after a Tour through the Districts in Eastern Bengal in 1864-65. Calcutta.

On Chinchona. (London.)

On the Sale of Waste Lands. (Calcutta.)

### ARABIC.

Lees' Arabic Series. No. I. Arabic Inflection. 12mo. Calcutta. No. II. Arabic Syntax. 12mo. Calcutta. No. III. Tushfat-ul Talabin. 12mo. Calcutta.

كتاب اصطلاحات الشيخ محمد علي التهانوي

Dictionary of the Technical Terms used in the Sciences of the Musulmans. By Muhammad 'Ali Al-Tahánawi. Edited by Abd Al-Haqq, Gholam Kadir, W. Nassau Lees. Sprenger and Mohammed Wajyh. 2 vols. (20 parts). With Supplement. 4to. Calcutta, 1853-64.

*₀* Published in the Bibliotheca Indica.

كتاب حكايات وغرائب وعجائب ولطايف ونوادر ونوايد ونفايس The Book of Anecdotes, Wonders, Marvels, Pleasantries, Rarities, and Useful and Precious Extracts. By our Master, the Shaikh, the very Learned Ahmad Shaháb Al-Din Al-Qolyoobi. Edited by W. Nassau Lees and Mawlawi Kabir Al-Din. 8vo. pp. 236. Calcutta, 1856.

Coran. In Arabic. With Commentary of the Imam Aboo Al-Qasim Mahmood bin 'Omar al-Zamakhshari, entitled the Kashshof 'an Haqaiq al-Tanzil. Edited by W. N. Lees and Maulavis Khadim Hosain and 'Abd Al-Hayi. 2 vols. Royal 4to. Calcutta, 1856-61.

*₀* This valuable work, so much esteemed among Sunnis, is very scarce.

Us-Suyuti. The Tarikh Al-Kholfáa; or, History of the Caliphs from the Death of Mohammad to the Year 900 of the Hijrah. By the Celebrated Jalál Al-Din Al-Osyooti. Edited by W. N. Lees and Mawlawi Abd Al-Haqq. 8vo. pp. 543. Calcutta, 1857.

Jam'i Al-Romooz. A Commentary on the Noqnayah (the Abridgment of the Wikaya). By Shams-al-din Mohammad, of Khorasan. Edited by W. N. Lees. Royal 4to. pp. 748. Calcutta, 1858.

Ikhwânu s'-Safá. Edited by W. N. Lees. 8vo. Calcutta, 1886.

فتوح الشام المنسوب الى الواقدي Futúh ul Shám Wáqidi. The Conquest of Syria, commonly ascribed to Aboo 'Abd Allah Mohammad B. 'Omar Al-Wáqidi. Edited, with Notes, by W. N. Lees. 9 Fasc. (Complete.)

*₀* Published in the Bibliotheca Indica.

محبة الفكر مع شرحها نزهة النظر Nokhbat-al Fikr and Nozhat-al Nazr by Shahab al-din Ahmad Ibn Hajar al-'Asqalani. Edited by Capt. W. Nassau Lees and Mawlawies 'Abd-al Haqq and Gholam Qadir. 1 Fasc. (Complete.)

*₀* Published in the Bibliotheca Indica.

فتوح الشام Futúh-ul-Sham. A'zádi. Being an Account of the Moslim Conquests in Syria. By Aboo Asma'il Mohammed bin Abdallah Alazdi Al-Baçri. Edited by Capt. W. N. Lees. 4 Fasc. (Complete.)

*₀* Published in the Bibliotheca Indica.

### PERSIAN.

Lees's Persian Series. No. I. Qawaid-i-Hosainee; or, a Persian Grammar in Oordoo. Prepared under the Superintendence of the Publisher (W. N. Lees) by Saiyid Tafazzol Hosain. 12mo. pp. 76. Calcutta, 1855.

No. II. "The Hidayat Al Sibyan," or, Persian Primer. Prepared under the Superintendence of the Publisher (W. N. Lees) by Saiyid Tafazzol Hosain. 12mo. pp. 44, iv. Calcutta, 1855.

No. III. The Golshan-i-Sibyan; or, Persian Reader. No. I. Prepared under the Superintendence of the Publisher (W. N. Lees) by Saiyid Tafazzol Hosain. 12mo. pp. 72, ii. Calcutta, 1855.

No. IV. Iqd-i-Laálf; or, Persian Poetry Reader. No. I containing the Pand-Nameh or Karimá, commonly ascribed to S'adi, and the Tarji'i Band called Má Maqimán. 12mo. pp. 55. Calcutta, 1855.

No. V. The 'Iqd-i-Marján; or, Persian Poetry Reader No. II., containing the Pand-Nameh of Shaikh Farid Al-Din 'Attár, and the Qiççah-i-Yoosof. Being an Extract from Jámi's celebrated Poem Yoosof and Zolaikhá. 12mo. pp. 168. Calcutta, 1855.

نفحات الانس من حضرات القدس Jami's Nafahat al-Ons. The lives of the Soofis. In Persian. With Life by Lees. Thick 8vo. pp. 740. Calcutta, 1859.

*₀* A notice of celebrated Sufis and Saints modernised from an older chronicle.

اقبال نامه جهانگيري تصنيف معتمد خان Iqbál namah i Jahangiri taçnif Moetamad Khan. Edited by Lees. 8vo. pp. 740. Calcutta, 1859.

تاريخ بيهقي Tárikh-i Baihaki, containing the Life of Masaud, son of Sultan Mahmud, of Ghaznin. Edited by W. H. Morley, and printed under the Supervision of Capt. W. N. Lees. 8vo. pp. 868. Calcutta, 1861-62.

*₀* Published in the Bibliotheca Indica.

تاريخ فيروز شاهي Tárikh-i Firúz-Sháhi of Ziá'al Din Barni, commonly called Zia 'i Barni. Edited by Saiyid Ahmad Khán, Capt. W. N. Lees, and Mawlawi Kabir Al-Din. 8vo. pp. 602. Calcutta, 1862.

*₀* Published in the Bibliotheca Indica.

عقد المنطق منتخب بوستان Selections from Sadi's Bostan. Edited by W. N. Lees. With English Translation and Notes by Adalut Khan. Two vols. 8vo. Calcutta, 1863-68.

طبقات ناصري Tabaqát-i Násiri of Aboo 'Omar Minhaj ad-Din Othman, Ibn Siraj al-Din Al-Jawzjani. Edited by Capt. W. N. Lees, Maulawis Khadim Hosain, and Abd Al-Hai. pp. 453, 9 and 4. Calcutta, 1864-65.

*₀* Published in the Bibliotheca Indica.

ويس و رامين Wis o Rámin. A Romance of Ancient Persia. Translated from the Pahlawi, and rendered into Verse by Fakr al-Din, As'ad Al-Astarabadi, Al Fakhri, Al Gurgani. Edited by Capt. W. N. Lees and Munshi Ahmad Ali. 8vo. pp. 400, vi. Calcutta, 1864-65.

*₀* Published in the Bibliotheca Indica.

عالمكير نامه Álamgir Námah, by Muhammad Kazim Ibn-i-Muhammad Amin Munshi. With Index of Names. Edited by Maulawis Khadim Hussain and Abd-al Hai under the Superintendence of W. N. Lees. 8vo. pp. 1107. Calcutta, 1865-73.

*₀* Published in the Bibliotheca Indica.

منتخب التواريخ Muntakhab Al-Tawárikh of Abd Al-Qadir Bin i Maluk Shah Al-Badaoni. Edited by Capt. W. N. Lees and Maulavi Ahmad 'Ali. 8vo. pp. 407, 7. Calcutta, 1865.

*₀* Published in the Bibliotheca Indica.

بادشاهنامه Bádsháh Námah. By Abd al-Hamid Láhawri. Edited by Mawlawis Kabir-al-din Ahmad and Abdal-Rahim under the Superintendence of W. N. Lees. 2 vols. 8vo. Calcutta, 1867-68.

*₀* Published in the Bibliotheca Indica.

## American Notes.

THE NAME OF AMERICA.—It has long been supposed that the name of the Continent of America was derived from Amerigo Vespucci, though no very good reason has ever been given for the supposition. Recent researches have shown that, so far from having been named after any European, it is very nearly the same as the native name. Amaracapana or Amaraca land was the aboriginal name for Venezuela, where the Spaniards made their first settlement, and it is much more likely that America should be derived from that than from the Christian name of a Florentine explorer. The subject is fully treated in "The Empire of Amaraca," a small book treating of the origin of the national name, published by the "American News Company," New York.

LOCAL CONSTITUTIONAL HISTORY OF THE UNITED STATES.— A new treatise in the series of the Johns Hopkins Studies in Historical and Political Science, edited by Herbert B. Adams, will be issued this year on U.S. Local Constitutional History by George E. Howard, of Nebraska University. Vol. I. will be on the Development of the Township, Hundred, and Shire. Vol. II. on the Development of the City and the Local Magistracies. The history of local institutions has thus far been treated almost entirely in monographs dealing with special topics, or relating to particular phases or periods of development. Moreover, a large and valuable portion of this literature is dispersed through the voluminous publications of learned societies, and therefore inaccessible to the general reader. It is practically impossible for any one but a specialist to obtain a clear understanding of the present state of inquiry on the subject. Besides, much of the material requisite for a comprehensive view has never been explored. There is needed, in short, a book, which shall gather up, sift, and skilfully arrange the results already obtained by the host of writers on Græco-Roman, Germanic, and English institutions, and supplement them by further investigation, particularly for this country. Such is the scope of the present work. It is intended as a contribution towards placing local constitutional history where it deserves to be placed, on a level with the history of the national constitution. Each institution is followed through every stage of evolution, from its ancient prototype under the tribal organization of society, to its existing form in the new states and territories of the West. The author has aimed at presenting a clear and logical statement of constitutional facts— the details of offices, powers, and functions; while bringing into special prominence the process of organic growth, differentiation, and decay. The work is, however, very largely the result of independent study of the original records; and many topics are treated from these sources for the first time. Particular attention has been given to the bibliography, which is brought down to date. The first volume, comprising about 600 pages octavo, will be ready for delivery shortly.

A NEW TEXT BOOK OF ASTRONOMY.—(*A Text Book of General Astronomy for Colleges and Scientific Schools, by Charles A. Young, Ph.D., LL.D., Professor of Astronomy in the College of New Jersey (Princeton), Boston and London, Ginn & Co.*)—American books, especially scientific ones, are so often made by getting together a dozen books on a given subject, and making a thirteenth out of them, that it is a real pleasure to come across an author like Professor Charles A. Young, who writes from his own knowledge and not from that of others. Of course no one can invent scientific facts; they may promulgate theories which may or may not afterwards be proved to be facts; but at the same time a compilation is one thing, and the work of an author who understands his subject and digests all the facts connected with it is another. Professor Young claims that his "Text Book" is not a compilation, and we agree with him on that point. It is an excellent and efficient manual of practical astronomy, not only for the student, but also for the mariner and the general reader, written by one whose astronomical knowledge is "thorough," and who puts his knowledge and experience before the student in a plain, straightforward and practical manner. Our cousins across the water very often produce text-books for students noted for their utility, and we consider this the best text-book of astronomy which has appeared up to the present time.

BIBLIOGRAPHY OF THE NORTH AMERICAN ABORIGINAL LANGUAGES.—The third issue of the series of linguistic bibliographies compiled by Mr. James Constantine Pilling for the Bureau of Ethnology is on the Iroquoian Languages, and contains 214 pages. This family of languages appears to be particularly rich in works treating on it. Mr. Pilling gives facsimiles of several title-pages of scarce books on Iroquoian, but these are more curious than useful. One lithograph illustration, however, is the Cherokee alphabet, with the sounds of

the vowels and consonants, which is practically useful, and as it is from the collections of the American Board of Foreign Missions, it is no doubt correct and reliable.

THE AMERICAN GEOGRAPHICAL SOCIETY.—The Bulletin of this Society (No. 1, Vol. 21) for March 31st, 1889, contains an article by Carl Lumholtz, M.A., of the Academy of Sciences, Christiania, on the natives of Australia, amongst whom he resided four years (1880-1884). For twelve months he lived amongst the cannibals of North-Eastern Queensland, and in parts where no white man had ever been before. The Portuguese in the Track of Columbus is a second article on this subject, by Dr. P. J. J. Valentini, in the same number, on the geographical discoveries made in 1493. Civil Engineer R. E. Peary, of the U.S. Navy, contributes an article on the Rio San Juan de Nicaragua which is the route favoured by the Americans for a canal from the Pacific to the Alantic Oceans; it is a noble river, with splendid scenery along both banks; the thermometer along it in six months from the middle of December, 1887, to the middle of June, 1888, was maximum 92° and minimum 64°; the nights are always cool, and flannel sleeping suits and woollen blankets are necessary when navigating it. An article by Mr. Eugene Schuyler on the Russian traveller, Prjevalsky, with Geographical Notes by Mr. Geo. C. Hurlbut, and a Washington letter on Geographical Events, finish up the number.

THE PHILOSOPHICAL SOCIETY OF WASHINGTON.—The Annual Presidential Address, delivered Dec. 8, 1888, before this Society by Colonel Garrick Mallery, of the U. S. Army, was on "Philosophy and Specialities." In this address Colonel Mallery reviews the discoveries of Science in connection with the existing religious beliefs. He says that last year a sarcastic definition of "Faith" was given as a "belief in what you know is not true." In speaking of the transmission of ideas he says, "Composition means far more than merely writing out ideas, and unless the ideas are properly composited so as to be understood by other minds, it is doubtful if they are clear to the writer. When Jacob Böhme was on his death-bed, a deputation of his disciples came to him begging him to have an obscure passage in his writings explained before it was too late. 'My children,' said the mystic, 'when I wrote this, I understood its meaning, and no doubt the Omniscient God did. He may still remember it, but I have forgotten.' The incredible part of the story is that Böhme ever did understand the passage he had written so obscurely."

## Colonial Notes.

THE TORCH.—In No. 7 of the Torch and Colonial Book Circular, Mr. Petherick gives a select list of the more recent English and American Bibliographical publications useful to booksellers and librarians. Besides the usual useful bibliographies of English and American publications, recent Colonial publications, and books relating to the Colonies, it gives the Bibliography of Australia—New South Wales—1851 to 1860.

PETHERICK'S COLLECTION OF FAVOURITE AND APPROVED AUTHORS.—This is a series of works issued by E. A. Petherick and Co., 33, Paternoster Row, and 3, St. James Street, Melbourne, by arrangement with the proprietors of the copyrights of standard works, by which they can be circulated in the Colonies (*only*) at a reasonable price to meet Colonial wants. Circulating libraries being few and far between, and distances great, if a book is to be read, it has to be bought. The volumes now ready are Thomas Hardy's "Desperate Remedies" and George Meredith's "Rhoda Fleming." These are to be followed shortly by Mrs. Mona Caird's "Wing of Azrael." These volumes are well printed and on good paper, very unlike the miserable reprints so often produced in the United States.

### NOTICE TO CORRESPONDENTS.

All communications should be addressed to the *Editor of "Trübner's Record,"* 57 and 59, Ludgate Hill, London, E.C., and they should be accompanied by the sender's name and address (not necessarily for publication). Every care will be taken with MSS., but the Editor cannot hold himself responsible for rejected communications, which—if to be returned to

the sender—should be accompanied by postage. MS. should
be legibly written, and on one side of the paper only. Books
for review should be addressed to the Editor.

*NOTICE TO ADVERTISERS.*

All communications respecting advertisements should be
addressed to Messrs. F. TALLIS AND SON, 22, Wellington
Street, W.C. *Terms for the insertion of advertisements :*—

| WHOLE PAGE (ordinary position) | ... £5 | 5 | 0 |
| HALF PAGE ,, ,, | ... 2 | 15 | 0 |
| QUARTER PAGE ,, ,, | ... 1 | 10 | 0 |

Special positions per contract.

# American Literature.

**Alcott (Louisa M.)** — A Modern Mephistopheles;
[also] A Whisper in the Dark. 16mo. cloth, pp. 350.
*Boston*. 7s. 6d.

**Baker (W. S.)** — Bibliotheca Washingtoniana; Descriptive List of the Biographies and Biographical Sketches of
George Washington. 4to. cloth, pp. xv. and 179. *Philadelphia*. £1 4s.

**Bancroft (H. H.)** — History of the Pacific States of
North America. Vol. 25. Oregon, Vol. 2, 1848-1888.
8vo. cloth, pp. x. and 808. *San Francisco*. £1 4s.

**Baylor (Frances C.)** — A Shocking Example and other
Sketches. 12mo. cloth, pp 364. *Philadelphia*. 6s. 6d.

**Berg (L. De C.)** — Safe Building. Series I. 8vo. cloth.
*Boston*. £1 5s.

**Bolles (A. S.)** — The Banker's Almanac and Register
and Legal Directory for 1889. 8vo. cloth. *New York*. £1.

**Boston** Legal Directory for 1869. A List of Lawyers
and Banks. 12mo. paper, pp. 68. *Boston*. 6s.

**Brown (Mary E., and W. A.)** — Musical Instruments
and their Homes. With 270 Illustrations in Pen and Ink
by W. Adams Brown. The whole forming a Complete
Catalogue of the Collection of Musical Instruments now in
the Possession of Mrs. J. Crosby Brown, of New York.
4to. cloth. *New York*. £2 10s.

**Brownell (W. C.)** — French Traits. An Essay in Comparative Criticism. 12mo. cloth, pp. 411. *New York*. 7s. 6d.

**Bruce (P. A.)** — The Plantation Negro as a Freeman;
Observations on his Character, Condition, and Prospects in
Virginia. 12mo. cloth, viii. and 262. *New York*. 6s. 6d.

**Bunce (O. B.)** — The Story of Happinolande, and other
Legends. 12mo. cloth, pp. 188. *New York*. 1s. 6d.

**Burge (L.)** — Aryas, Semites and Jews, Jehovah and
the Christ. 12mo. cloth, pp. 308. *Boston*. 7s. 6d.

**Burgwyn (C. P. E.)** — The Huguenot Lovers. A Tale
of the Old Dominion. 12mo. paper, pp. 219. *Richmond
(Va.)*. 3s.

**Calkins (N. A.)** — Ear and Voice Culture by Means of
Elementary Sounds. 16mo. cloth. *New York*. 2s. 6d.

**Carnahan (J. R.)** — Pythian Knighthood; its History
and Literature. 4to. cloth, pp. 600. *Cincinnati*. 15s.

**Carson (H. L.)** — History of the Celebration of the
One Hundredth Anniversary of the Promulgation of the
Constitution of the United States. 2 vols. 4to. cloth.
Illustrated. *Philadelphia*. £2 10s.

**Cooke (Rose T.)** — Steadfast. The Story of a Saint
and a Sinner. 12mo. cloth, pp. 426. *Boston*. 7s. 6d.

**Crosby (Rev. H.)** — The Bible View of the Jewish
Church, in Thirteen Lectures, delivered during January-
April, 1888, in the Fourth Avenue Presbyterian Church,
New York. 12mo. cloth, pp. 211. *New York*. 5s.

**Curry (J. L. M.)** — Constitutional Government in
Spain; a Sketch. 16mo. cloth, pp. 222. *New York*. 5s.

**Cutler (Rev. C.)** — The Beginnings of Ethics. 12mo.
cloth, pp. 324. *New York*. 6s. 6d.

**Dexter (S.)** — A Treatise on Co-öperative Savings and
Loan Associations. Including Building and Loan Associations, Accumulating Fund Associations, Co-operative Banks,
etc. With Appendix, containing Laws, Precedents, and
Forms. 12mo. cloth, pp. 299. *New York*. 6s. 6d.

**Dick (W. B.)** — Log and Lumber Measurer. Tables,
with Instructions for their Use, showing at a Glance the
Cubical Contents of Logs and the Feet of Inch-Boards
they contain, the Measurement of Timber of all Kinds and
Dimensions. 16mo. boards. *New York*. 1s. 6d.

**Dodge (T. A.)** — Great Captains. 8vo. cloth, pp. 219.
Illustrated. *Boston*. 10s.

**Dolaro (Selina)** — Bella-Demonia; A Dramatic Story.
12mo. cloth, pp. 265. *New York*. 5s.

**Doty (A. H., M.D.)** — A Manual of Instruction in the
Principles of Prompt Aid to the Injured; Designed for
Military and Civil Use. 12mo. cloth, pp. 224. *New York*.
6s. 6d.

**Field (Rev. H. M.)** — Gibraltar. 8vo. cloth, pp. vii. and
139. Illustrated. *New York*. 10s.

**Fix (H. G.)** — Manual of Strategy, with Maps and Plans.
From the French by H. Rowan Lemly. 16mo. cloth, pp.
137. *Washington*. 2s. 6d.

**Flinn (F. M.)** — Campaigning with Banks in Louisiana,
'63 and '64, and with Sheridan in the Shenandoah
Valley in '64 and '65. Second Edition. 12mo. cloth,
pp. 239. *Boston*. 4s.

**Ganguillet (E.) and Kutter (W. R.)** — A General
Formula for the Uniform Flow of Water in Rivers and
other Channels. From the German, with Numerous
Additions, including Tables, Diagrams, and the Elements of
over 1200 Gaugings of Rivers, Small Channels, and Pipes,
in English Measure, by Rudolph Hering and J. C. Trautwine, jun. 8vo. cloth, pp. xxi. and 240. *New York*. 18s.

**Gilder (J. L., and J. B.)** — Authors at Home. Personal
and Biographical Sketches of Well-known American
Writers. 12mo. cloth, pp. 354. *New York*. 7s. 6d.

**Granville (A. W.)** — The Legend of Kaara; or, The
Tale of the Five Knights. An Eastern Romance. [A
Poem.] 12mo. cloth. Illustrated. *Chicago*. 3s.

**Green (T. M.)** — Historic Families of Kentucky; with
Special Reference to Stocks immediately derived from the
Valley of Virginia; tracing in detail their various Genealogical Connections and Illustrating from Historic Sources
their Influence upon the Political and Social Development
of Kentucky and the States of the South and West. First
Series. 8vo. cloth, pp. 304. *Cincinnati*. 15s.

**Green (W. H., D.D.)** — A Grammar of the Hebrew
Language. Part I. New Edition, enlarged. 8vo. cloth.
*New York*. 8s. 6d.

**Hall (Rev. J. A.)** — Glimpses of Great Fields. 12mo.
cloth, pp. 239. *Boston*. 6s. 6d.

**Hare (J. I. C.)** — American Constitutional Law. 2 vols.
8vo. sheep, pp. xlix. and 1400. *Boston*. £3.

**Harper (W. R.), and Burgess (I. B.)** — Inductive
Greek Method. 12mo. cloth. *New York*. 6s.

**Harper (W. R.), and Burgess (I. B.)** — Inductive
Latin Method. 12mo. cloth. *New York*. 6s.

**Hayes (H.)** — A Daughter of Eve. 12mo. cloth, pp. 447.
*Boston*. 7s. 6d.

**Heap (D. P.)** — Ancient and Modern Light-houses.
8vo. cloth, pp. x. and 221. Illustrated. *Boston*. £1 5s.

**Holder (C. F.)** — All About Pasedena (Southern
California) and its Vicinity. Its Climate, Missions, Trails
and Cañons, Fruits, Flowers, and Game. 12mo. cloth,
pp. 141. Illustrated. 2s. 6d.

Holst (H. v.)—John Brown. Edited by Frank Preston Stearns. 12mo. cloth, pp. 232. *Boston.* 7s. 6d.

International Medical Annual and Practitioner's Index. A Work of Reference for Medical Practitioners. Edited by A. G. Bateman and others. Seventh year. 8vo. cloth, pp. xviii. and 544. *New York.* 14s.

Irving (Minna)—Songs of a Haunted Heart. 12mo. cloth. *New York.* 5s.

Janvier (T. A.)—The Mexican Guide. New Revised Edition for 1889. 12mo. cloth. Illustrated. *New York.* 12s. 6d.

Johnson (Mrs. H. K.)—Raleigh Westgate ; or, Epimenides in Maine. A Romance. 12mo. cloth, pp. 259. *New York.* 4s.

Johnston (Rev. J.)—A Century of Christian Progress and its Lesson. 8vo. cloth, pp. 214. *New York.* 5s.

Johnson (W. S.), and Humphrey (J. N.)—Word with Words. A Practical Etymology and Word Analysis. Fourth Edition. 8vo. boards, pp. 67. *Milwaukee.* 3s. 6d.

Kirwin (T.)—Modern Electricity. What is Electricity ? Its Relation to Magnetism ; how it is Produced and how Utilised in the Arts. 16mo. cloth. *Boston.* 2s. 6d.

Kounse (N.)—Arius the Libyan. A Romance of the Primitive Church. New Cheap Edition. 12mo. paper. *New York.* 2s. 6d.

Lee (Mary C.)—A Quaker Girl of Nantucket. 12mo. cloth, pp. 320. *Boston.* 6s. 6d.

Malone (J. S.)—The Self. What is It ? 12mo. cloth, pp. 158. *Louisville (Ky.).* 4s.

McLean (J.) — The Indians ; their Manners and Customs. 12mo. cloth, pp. 350. Illustrated. *Toronto.* 6s.

Merriman (M.)—A Treatise on Hydraulics. 8vo. cloth, pp. 381. *New York.* 15s.

Mills (C. De B.)—The Tree of Mythology, its Growth and Fruitage. Genesis of the Nursery Tale, Saws of Folklore, etc. A Study. 8vo. cloth, pp. 288. *Syracuse (New York).* 15s.

Mitchell (J. A.)—The Last American ; a Fragment from the Journal of Khan-Li, Prince of Dimph-Yoo Chur and Admiral in the Persian Navy. 12mo. cloth, pp. 78. *New York.* 6s.

Mixter (W. G.) — An Elementary Text-book of Chemistry. 12mo. cloth, pp. 859. *New York.* 12s. 6d.

Morgan (Anna)—An Hour with Delsarte ; a Study of Expression. Illustrated by Rose Mueller Sprague and Marian Reynolds. 8vo. cloth, pp. 115. *Boston.* 10s.

Needle-Craft ; Artistic and Practical. 4to. cloth, pp. 320. *New York.* 5s.

Odlin (W.)—Curiosities of Matrimony ; being a Compilation of such Marriage Announcements in the last Hundred Years as called forth the most brilliant Wit of the Poets. 12mo. paper, pp. 55. *Concord (N. H.).* 1s. 6d.

Omar Khayyám. The Strophes of Omar Khayyám ; from the Persian by J. Leslie Garner. With an Introduction and Notes. 16mo. cloth, pp. xi. and 75. *Milwaukee.* 4s.

Peck (W.)—The Story of the Puritans. Illustrated by O. Herford and E. W. Kemble. 12mo. cloth. 8s. *Johnsbury (Vt.).* 6s.

Perez (B.) — The First Three Years of Childhood. Edited and translated by Alice M. Christie ; with an Introduction by Ja. Sully. 12mo. cloth, pp. xxviii. and 294. *Syracuse (New York).* 7s. 6d.

Periam (J.)—The National Cyclopedia ; a Dictionary of Useful and Practical Information for the Farm, Home, and School. New Edition Revised and Enlarged. 3 vols. 4to. half morocco, pp. 1000. Illustrated. *Chicago.* £3 3s.

Preyer (W.)—The Mind of the Child. Part 2. The Development of the Intellect. Observations concerning the Mental Development of the Human Being in the First Years of Life. From the German by H. W. Brown. 12mo. cloth, pp. xl. and 317. *New York.* 7s. 6d.

Ringwalt (J. L.)—Development of Transportation Systems in the United States. With Illustrations of Hundreds of Typical Objects. Folio, cloth, pp. 398. Illustrated. *Philadelphia.* £1 10s.

Roche (J. A., D.D.)—The Life of John Price Durbin, D.D. With an Analysis of his Homiletic Skill and Sacred Oratory. With an Introduction by Randolph S. Foster, D.D. 12mo. cloth, pp. xvi. and 369. *New York.* 7s. 6d.

Ross (P.)—Scotland and the Scots. Essays Illustrative of Scottish Life, History, and Character. 8vo. cloth, pp. 256. *New York.* 5s.

Ross (J. D.)—Scottish Poets in America. Being a Collection of Sketches contributed to the New York *Home Journal.* 8vo. cloth, pp. 200. *New York.* 7s. 6d.

Saltus (E.)—A Transaction in Hearts. An Episode. 12mo. cloth, pp. 188. *New York.* 5s.

Savage (T.)—Manual of Industrial and Commercial Intercourse between the United States and Spanish America, for the year 1889. 12mo. cloth, pp. 629. *San Francisco.* 12s. 6d.

Schouler (J.)—History of the United States under the Constitution. Vol. 4. 1831–1847. 12mo. cloth. *Washington.* 10s.

Shinn Commercial Speller. 16mo. cloth, pp. 155 *Cleveland (O.).* 3s.

Shinn (G. W., D.D.)—King's Handbook of Notable Episcopal Churches in the United States. 8vo. cloth, pp. 286. *Boston.* 5s.

Stedman (T. L.) and Lee (K. P.)—A Chinese and English Phrase-Book in the Canton Dialect. 12mo. cloth. *New York.* 7s. 6d.

Thorpe (F. N.)—The Government of the People of the United States. 12mo. cloth, pp. 308. Illustrated. *Philadelphia.* 5s.

Thrum (T. G.)—Hawaiian Almanac and Annual for 1889. A Handbook of Information on Matters relating to the Hawaiian Islands. 15th Year. 8vo. paper, pp. 110. *Honolulu (H. I.).* 5s.

Todd (C. B.)—The Story of Washington, the National Capital. 12mo. cloth, pp. xv. and 416. *New York.* 9s.

United States.—Department of the Interior. Bureau of Education. Report of the Commissioner of Education for 1886–87. 8vo. cloth, pp. 1170. *Washington.*

United States.—Treasury Department. Annual Report and Statements of the Chief of the Bureau of Statistics on the Foreign Commerce and Navigation, Immigration, and Tonnage of the U.S., for the Fiscal Year ending June 30, 1888. 8vo. cloth, pp. cviii. and 1004. *Washington.*

Washington (G.)—The Writings of George Washington, including his Diaries and Correspondence. Edited by Worthington C. Ford. In 14 vols, Vol. I. 8vo. cloth. *New York.* £1 5s.

Welch (A. S.)—The Teacher's Psychology. 12mo. cloth, pp. 300. *New York.* 6s. 6d.

Whiton (J. M.)—The Law of Liberty, with other Discourses. 12mo. cloth. *New York.* 6s. 6d.

Wigmore (J. H.)—The Australian Ballot System as Embodied in the Legislation of Various Countries. With an Historical Introduction. 8vo. cloth, pp. 155. *Boston.* 5s.

Wilson (J. G.) and Fiske (J.)—Appleton's Cyclopædia of American Biography. In 6 vols. Vol. 6. Royal 8vo. cloth. Illustrated. *New York.* £1 4s. per vol.

Winchell (A.)—Shall we Teach Geology ? A Discussion of the Proper Place of Geology in Modern Education. 12mo. cloth, pp. 217. *Chicago.* 5s.

Woodhull (J. F.)—Simple Experiments for the Schoolroom. 16mo. cloth, pp. 80. *New York.* 2s. 6d.

## European Literature.

At-Tabari.—Annales. Auctore Abu Djafar Mohammed Ibn Djarir At-Tabari. Quos ediderunt J. Barth, Th. Nöldeke, P. de Jong, E. Prym, H. Thorbecke, S. Fraenkel, J. Guidi, D. H. Müller, M. Th. Houtsma, S. Guyard, V. Rosen et M. J. de Goeje. II. 6. (Sectionis secundae pars sexta.) Quam ediderunt D. H. Müller et M. J. de Goeje. Royal 8vo. sewed, pp. 1201 to 2017 and xix. *Leiden*, 1889. 11s.

Babelon (E.) — Manuel d'Archéologie orientale. Chaldée—Assyrie—Perse—Syrie—Judée—Phénicie—Carthage. Bibliothèque de l'enseignement des beaux-arts. 8vo. pp. 318. *Paris*, 1888.

Bastian (A.)—Die Culturländer des Alten America. Vol. III. 2. Nachträge und Ergänzungen aus den Sammlungen des Ethnologischen Museums. *Berlin*, 1889. 4s.

Bedjan (le Père) — Histoire de Mar Jab-Alaha, patriarche et de Raban Sauma. (Texte syriaque.) 8vo. *Paris*, 1889. 7s.

Berichte des VII. internationalen Orientalisten Congresses. Gehalten in Wien im Jahre 1886. Royal 8vo. pp. 129. *Wien*, 1889. 4s.

Biblioteca Arabo-Sicula, Raccolta da Michele Amari. (Versione Italiana.) Appendice. 8vo. sewed, pp. xii. 88. *Turin*, 1889. 2s.

*⁎* The "Arabic Texts" of this Collection are contained in the publications of the "Deutsche Morgenländ. Gesellschaft."

Böhtlingk (Otto)—Sanskrit-Wörterbuch in kürzerer Fassung. Vol. VII. Fasc. 2. General-Index zu den 6 Nachträgen und letzte Nachträge. 4to. sewed, pp. 161 to 390. *St. Petersburg*, 1889. 7s. 6d.

*⁎* This part completes the work. Price of the whole work, £3 2s. 6d.

Bourgoin (J.)—Précis de l'art arabe et matériaux pour servir à l'histoire, à la théorie et à la technique des arts de l'Orient musulman. Livraison 1 à 6. 4to. With 60 Plates. *Paris*, 1889. 7s. 6d.

*⁎* The work will be complete in 30 Fasciculi.

Bühler (G.) — Ueber das Leben des Jaina Mönches Hemachandra, des Schülers des Devachandra aus der Vajraśakhâ. 4to. pp. 90. (Reprint.) *Leipzig*, 1889. 4s. 6d.

Chabot (A.)—Grammaire hébraïque élémentaire. 3e édition, viii. 126. With 1 Table. *Freiburg*, 1889. 2s.

Cholet (Cte de).—Excursion en Turkestan et sur la frontière russo-afghane. 12mo. *Paris*, 1889. 4s.

Dalmedico (Moïse M.)—Méthode théorique et pratique pour l'enseignement de la langue turque. Deuxième partie. Langue officielle et littéraire. 8vo. sewed, pp. 352. *Constantinople*, 1888. 9s.

Δελτίον 'Αρχαιολόγικον, τοῦ ἔτους 1888. *Athen*, 1889. 6s. 6d.

Dewitz (H.) — West- und Centralafrikanische Tagschmetterlinge. Royal 8vo. pp. 11. With 2 Plates. (Reprint.) *Berlin*, 1889. 2s.

Gestetner (A.)—Mafteach ha-Pijutim. Index zu Dr. Zuns' Literaturgeschichte der synagogalen Poesie. Royal 8vo. pp. viii. 126. *Frankfurt/a/M.*, 1889. 2s.

Gibara (Gius.) — Grammatica element. del l'arabo volgare. Con la pronunzia figur. e varie annotaz. sull' arabo moderno. 8vo. pp. 36. *Bari*, 1889. 1s. 6d.

Groneman (J.)—In den Kĕdáton te Jogjákártâ. Oepâtjârâ, Ampilan en Tooneeldansen. Met Fotogrammen van Cephas. Text pp. 69, royal 8vo. cloth. Atlas, folio, oblong, cloth. *Leiden*, 1888. £2 2s.

The same, Edition de Luxe, £3 18s.

Heerdt (P. F.)—Routes pour les navires à vapeur entre Aden et les Indes orientales Néerlandaises. 4to. *Amsterdam*, 1889. 1s. 6d.

Heerdt (P. F. van)—Currents and Surface Temperature near Cape Guardafui. Imperial 4to. With 12 Charts. *Amsterdam*, 1889. 4s.

Hélouis (F.)—Mahomet et l'islamisme. Impressions maçonniques. 8vo. pp. 16. *Paris*, 1889.

كتاب سيبويه.—Le Livre de Sîbawaihi. Traité de Grammaire arabe par Sîboûya, dit Sîbawaihi. Texte arabe, publié d'après les manuscrits du Caire, de l'Escurial, d'Oxford, de Paris, de Saint-Pétersbourg et de Vienne par Hartwig Derenbourg. Tome II. 2e Partie. Royal 8vo. pp. 321 to 498, ii. *Paris*, 1889. 12s.

Kroenlein (J. G.) — Wortschatz der Khoi-khoin (Namaqua-Hottentotten). Royal 8vo. pp. vi. 350. (*Berlin*), 1889. 25s.

Lanessan (J. L. de)—L'Empire d'Annam. Son organisation sociale et politique. 8vo. pp. 13. *Paris*, 1889.

Levi (Dr. Sim.)—Vocabolario geroglifico copto-ebraico. Vol. VII. (Supplem.) 4to. pp. 288. *Torino*, 1889. £1 10s.

Martin (J. P. P.)—Les origines de l'église d'Edesse et des églises syriennes. 8vo. sewed, pp. 153. *Paris*, 1889. 3s.

Maspero (G.)—Etudes égyptiennes. Tome II. fasc. 1. *Paris*, 1889. 15s.

Maspéro (G.)—Un Manuel de hiérarchie égyptienne et la culture et les bestiaux dans les tableaux des tombeaux de l'ancien empire. Royal 8vo. sewed pp. 112. With 2 Plates. *Paris*, 1888. 15s.

*⁎* Etudes égyptiennes, Tome II. 1er Fasc.

Maspéro (G.)—Aegyptische Kunstgeschichte. Deutsche Ausgabe von G. Steindorff. Royal 8vo. sewed, pp. ix. 335. With Illustrations. *Leipzig*, 1889. 9s.

Muratorii (C. S.)—Ad rerum italicarum scriptores addimenta quae subtitulo Bibliothecae Arabico-Siculae collegit atque Italice transtulit M. Amari. Appendix. Folio, pp. viii. 24. *Turin*, 1889. 2s. 6d.

*⁎* Vide Biblioteca Arabo-Sicula.

Orientalisten Congress. *Vide* Berichte und Verhandlungen.

Peiser (F. E.)—Keilinschriftliche Acten-Stücke aus Babylonischen Städten. Von Steinen und Tafeln des Berliner Museums in Autographie, Transscription und Uebersetzung herausgegeben und commentiert. Royal 8vo. sewed. With 2 Plates. *Berlin*, 1889. 12s.

Philippson (L.)—Kesher ben Nethaniah, die Enthronten. Trauerspiel. Ins Hebräische uebersetzt von H. L. Teller. 8vo. pp. xxvii. 182. *Wien*, 1889. 3s.

Radloff (W.)—Versuch eines Wörterbuches der Türk-Dialecte. Fasc. I. *St. Petersburg*, 1889. 4s.

Rasmussen (C.) — Grönlandsk Sproglaere. 8vo. *Kopenhagen*, 1889. 4s. 6d.

Reinisch (L.)—Die Saho-Sprache. Vol. I. Texte der Saho-Sprache. 8vo. *Wien*, 1889. 3s.

Riegl (Alois)—Die Aegyptischen Textilfunde im k. k. österreichischen Museum. Allgemeine Characteristik und Katalog. With 13 Plates. *Vienna*, 1889. 9s.

Schell (le P. V.)—Inscription assyrienne archaïque de Šamšî-Rammân IV. Roi d'Assyrie (824–811). Transcrite, traduite et commentée. 4to. pp. vii. 68. *Paris*, 1889. 8s.

Semper (C.)—Reisen im Archipel der Philippinen. 2 Theil. Wissenschaftliche Resultate. 2 Band. Malacologische Untersuchungen v. R. Bergh. 16 Heft. Nudibranchien vom Meere der Insel Mauritius. 2. Hälfte. 4to. sewed, pp. 815 to 872. With 3 Plates. *Wiesbaden*, 1889. 15s.

Silvestre (J.)—L'empire d'Annam et le peuple annamite. 12mo. *Paris*, 1889. 3s. 6d.

Stübel (A.), W. Reiss uud B. Koppel.—Kultur und Industrie südamerikanischer Völker. Nach den im Besitz des Museums für Völkerkunde zu Leipzig befindlichen Sammlungen. Text und Beschreibung der Tafeln von M. Uhle. Vol. I. Alte Zeit. folio, pp. iii. 106. With 28 Plates in Portfolio. *Berlin*, 1889. £4.

Vol. II. Neue Zeit, will be ready next year.

Tabari, *vide* At-Tabari.

Uhle, *vide* Stübel.

Varones ilustres de la Compañia de Jesús. Tomo II. Misiones de la China, Goa, Etiopia, Malabar. Segunda edición. Con licencia de la autoridad eclesiástica. 4to. pp. 666. *Madrid*, 1889.

Verhandlungen des VII. internationalen Orientalisten-Congresses. Gehalten in Wien im Jahre 1886. Semitische Section. Royal 8vo. pp. 265 and 104. With 3 Plates. *Wien*, 1888. 15s.

Verhandlungen des VII. internationalen Orientalisten-Congresses. Gehalten in Wien im Jahre 1886. Aegyptisch-Afrikanische Section. Royal 8vo. pp. 110. *Wien*, 1888. 4s.

Verhandlungen des VII. internationalen Orientalisten-Congresses. Gehalten in Wien im Jahre 1886. Hochasiat-ische und Malayo-polynesische Section. Royal 8vo. pp. 107. *Wien*, 1889. 4s.

Zeitschrift für Assyriologie und verwandte Gebiete. Herausgegeben von C. Bezold. Vol. IV. Royal 8vo. pp. 66. *Leipzig*, 1889. Pro complete, 18s.

---

# Oriental Literature.

## ANGLO-INDIAN.

Bose (Ram Chandra).—Hindu Philosophy popularly explained. The Heterodox Systems. 16mo. pp. 427. *Calcutta*, 1888. 6s.

*** Contains chapters on Buddhism, Jainism, Charbakism, the Doctrines of Ramanuja, etc.

Cranenburgh (D. E.)—The New Code of Civil Procedure. Royal 8vo. pp. 638. *Calcutta*, 1888. 9s.

*** Annotated with rulings of the High Courts in India up to June, 1887, and supplemented by a copious index.

De Monte (Salvador).—Exchange Calculator. Sterling into Rupees, and Rupees into Sterling. From 1s. to 2s. 3d. progressing by 1/32th of a Penny, to which are appended Table of Stamp Duty on Bills of Exchange drawn in India on England, on France, on Germany, Table of Stamp Duty on Bills of Exchange drawn in England, Table of Foreign Coins. New Edition. Royal 8vo. pp. 500. *Bombay*, 1888. 18s.

Doberck (W.)—Observations made at the Hongkong Observatory in the Year 1887. Folio, sewed, pp. 144. With Appendices. *Hongkong*, 1888. 10s. 6d.

Ghosh (Jogendra Chandra).—Brahman The Priest. An Address read before the Fifth Annual Meeting, held in Calcutta. 8vo. sewed, pp. 52. *Calcutta*, 1888. 1s.

Ghosh (Mahima Chandra).—Notes on Green's Readings from English History. Part III. 12mo. pp. 99. *Calcutta*, 1888. 2s. 6d.

Gilbert (Charles F.)—Hints to Travellers in Kashmir. 12mo. pp. 115. *Calcutta*, 1888. 3s. 6d.

Hall (Dr. Geoffry C.)—The Complications of Cataract Operations. Second Edition. 16mo. sewed, pp. 63. *Calcutta*, 1888. 6s.

How will it end?—A Story of Anglo-Indian Life. By M(iss) W(illiams). 8vo. pp. 177. *Calcutta*, 1888. 3s.

Hudson (Captain H. I.)—Indian Articles of War. 8vo. pp. 296. *Calcutta*, 1888. 10s. 6d.

*** An Annotated Edition of Act V. of 1860.

Jones (T. W.)—Rules and Tables for Permanent-Way Inspectors and Inspectors of Works. Being a Collection of Useful Information for Practical Men for 4'-8½", 5'-6", and Metre-Gauge Railways. With Tables and Explanatory Diagrams. Second Edition. Revised and Enlarged. 4to. cloth, pp. vii. 174. With 23 Plates. *Calcutta*, 1888. 18s.

Láhiri (Prasanna Kumár).—Notes on Smiles' Character. 12mo. pp. 282. *Calcutta*, 1888. 3s. 6d.

Lloyd (Major A. C.)—Infantry Outpost Defence. 8vo. pp. 68. *Calcutta*, 1888. 3s. 6d.

Majumdár (Pratap Chandra).—The Treatment of Typhoid Fevers. 12mo. sewed, pp. 124. *Calcutta*, 1888. 6s.

*** On Homœopathic Principles.

Marahman (J. C.)—Outline of the History of Bengal. 12mo. pp. 222. *Calcutta*, 1888. 2s. 6d.

Mitra (A. C.)—Digest of Rulings of the Privy Council. 8vo. pp. 382. *Calcutta*, 1888. 14s.

*** It contains cases decided from 1825 to 1887.

Mukharji (Sambhu Chandra).—Travels and Voyages between Calcutta and Independent Tipperah. 16mo. double crown, sewed, pp. 361. *Calcutta*, 1888. 16s.

*** This book gives a faithful picture of Hill or Independent Tipperah, and points out to young Bengal fond of travelling in Europe that there are many wonderful things nearer home which should engage their attention before they think of undertaking a journey beyond the seas.

Pál (Bholá Náth).—Studies in English Prose and Poetry. Third Edition. 12mo. pp. 260. *Calcutta*, 1888. 2s. 6d.

Prasáda (Pandita Deví).—A Catalogue of Sanskrit Manuscripts existing in Oudh Province for the Year 1887. Compiled by order of Government, N. W. P. and Oudh. 8vo. sewed, pp. 139. *Allahabad*, 1888.

Prinsep (H. T.)—The Code of Criminal Procedure. Royal 8vo. pp. 484. *Calcutta*, 1888. £1 10s.

*** With notes of all judgments and orders thereon.

Pryer (H.)—Rhopalocera Nihonica. A Description of the Butterflies of Japan. Part I. English Text, pp. 11; Japanese Text, pp. 20. With 3 Plates of 35 Coloured Illustrations. Part II. English Text, pp. 26; Japanese Text, pp. 24. With 3 Plates of 69 Coloured Illustrations. 4to. *Yokohama*, November, 1886, and July, 1888. £1 1s. each.

Rámáyan (The Exploits of Ráma). By Bhanubhakt. In Nepali. Royal 8vo. pp. 176. *Benares*, 1888. 5s.

Sádik (Khalil).—India. Demy 8vo. pp. 59. *Calcutta*, 1888. 2s. 6d.

*** Work on Politics. Supports in the main the policy of A. O. Hume, C.B.

Sen (Bankim Chandra).—A Complete Key to Bholá Náth Pál's Studies in English Prose and Poetry, and Láhiri's Select Poems. Part I. 12mo. pp. 96. *Calcutta*, 1888. 6s.

*** Five Shillings is the price for the work complete.

Sen (Keshub Chunder).—Lectures. 16mo. double fcap. sewed, pp. 172. *Calcutta*, 1888. 4s.

Sen (Keshab Chandra).—Diary in Ceylon. 16mo. pp. 83. *Calcutta*, 1888. 1s. 6d.

*** The account of a journey undertaken by the late Babu Keshab Chandra Sen to Ceylon in 1859.

Turnbull (Rev. A.)—A Nepáli Grammar and English-Nepáli and Nepáli-English Vocabulary (about 4000 Words). Designed for the Use of Missionaries, Tea-planters, and Military Officers. (In the Roman Character.) Royal 8vo. cloth, pp. iv. 303. *Darjeeling* (1888). 10s. 6d.

Wilson (J. M.)—Reminiscences of Behar. 8vo. pp. 161. *Calcutta*, 1888. 8s.

*** Contains important information about indigo planting and the indigo planter's life.

## ARABIC.

Ezekiel (A. D.)—Natural History, Matter and Motion (Catechism). Royal 8vo. pp. 81. *Poona*, 1888. 6s.

*** Arabic text in the Hebrew characters.

Káfiya (The Whole).—By Ibn-ul Hájib. Royal 8vo. pp. 140. *Cawnpore*, 1888. 1s.

———— Sharh-i-Mullá Jami. Commentary on Káfiya. By Maulána 'Abd-ur-Rahmán Jámi. Royal 8vo. pp. 414. *Lucknow*, 1888. 2s.

*** Káfiya is a well-known work on Arabic Syntax. Arabic Text in Nastálik character.

Kurán-i-Sharíf.—In Arabic. Edited by Munshi Nawal Kishore. Folio, pp. 654. *Lucknow*, 1888. 5s.

Shamsul Márif, or the Sun of Knowledge. By Shekh Ahmed bin Ali Buni. 8vo. pp. 512. Lithographed. *Bombay*, 1888. 5s.

Sharh-ul-'Akáid ma' Háshiya-i-Nazmul-Faraid. By Maulavi Muhammad Hasan of Sambhal, Moradabad. Folio, pp. 250. *Lucknow*, 1888. 8s.

*。* A Commentary on Articles of Faith in Arabic. With marginal notes (named) Nazm-ul-faraid (a piece of verse).

## BENGALI.

Adhunik Hindu Law.—By Abhaya Chandra Datta. 4to. pp. 108. *Mymensingh*, 1888. 3s. 6d.

*。* The Law of inheritance, adoption, etc., of the Hindus. In Bengali.

Arabya Upanyás.—The Arabian Nights' Entertainments. Translated into Bengali by Hari Charan Basu. Third Edition. 8vo. pp. 508. *Calcutta*, 1888. 6s.

Bángálá Byákaran.—By Jagadbandhu Modaka. Fourth Edition. 12mo. pp. 244. *Calcutta*, 1888. 2s.

*。* A Bengali Grammar in Bengali.

Bétal Panchabinsati.—By Kalidas Gupta. Revised Edition. 12mo. pp. 114. *Calcutta*, 1888. 1s.

*。* Twenty-five tales of the Demon in Bengali.

Bhabanshadh (A Medicine for Worldliness). By Shashadhar Tarka Churamani. 12mo. pp. 246. *Calcutta*, 1888. 2s. 6d.

*。* This work is written in imitation of the Bhagavadgitá, and it attempts to explain certain doctrines inculcated in that work.

Bhuchitrábali.—By Shashi Bhushan Chatterji. New Edition. Roy. 4to. pp. 21. Lithographed. *Calcutta*, 1888. 3s. 6d.

*。* An Atlas in the Bengali Language.

Brahma Baibarta Puran.—I. Brahma Khanda; II. Prakriti Khanda; III. Ganesh Khanda; IV. Srikrishna Jauma Khanda. Translated by Kali Prasanna Bidyaratna. 8vo. pp. 640. *Calcutta*, 1888. 8s.

*。* A Puran describing the Evolution of the World from Brahma. In Bengali.

Draupadir Bastraharan Gitábhinaya.—By Matilál Rayá. Fourth Edition. 8vo. pp. 141. *Calcutta*, 1888. 2s. 6d.

*。* A Melodrama in Bengali describing the Disrobing of Draupadi.

Harish Chandra Natak. A Drama describing the Sufferings of Harish Chandra. By Manomohan Basu. In Bengali. 8vo. pp. 128. *Calcutta*, 1888. 2s. 6d.

Hindu Dharma Sambandhíya.—Chitrábali. Mythological Pictures of the Hindus. In Bengali. Lithographed. 4to. pp. 8. *Calcutta*, 1888. 12s. 6d.

*。* There are six pictures in the work. It is published by the Calcutta Art Studio.

Huglir Imambari.—By Swarna Kumari Devi. 12mo. pp. 256. *Calcutta*, 1888. 3s. 6d.

*。* Based on the story of the princely liberality of Muhammad Moshin and his sister, Munnajan Khanum, in the time of the British Conquest of Bengal.

Mahábhárata. — By Kashirám Das. In Bengali. Second Edition. 8vo. pp. 924. *Calcutta*, 1888. 3s. 6d.

Manu Samhita.—The Institutes of Manu. In Bengali. 8vo. pp. 14. *Calcutta*, 1888. 1s. 6d.

*。* The translation follows the commentary by Kulluka Bhatta.

Narasarira Tattwa.—By Jagadish Chandra Lahiri. 8vo. pp. 246. *Calcutta*, 1888. 10s. 6d.

*。* A homœopathic work on human physiology in Bengali.

Ram Chariter Artha.—By Satish Chandra Maiti. 12mo. pp. 155. *Calcutta*, 1888. 1s. 6d.

*。* A key to Rám Charita.

Ram Chariter Suchru Byákhyá Sahit Artha Pustak. 12mo. pp. 145. *Calcutta*, 1888. 2s.

*。* A key to Rám Charita.

Ramayana.—By Krittibas Pandit. In Bengali. Revised Edition. Roy. 8vo. pp. 508. *Calcutta*, 1888. 3s.

Ratna Jhári (A Fountain of Gems).—By Amritalál Chatterji. 12mo. pp. 321. *Calcutta*, 1888. 14s.

*。* Containing information on a variety of subjects useful to middle-class Hindu families.

Sáhitya Shikshá. By Jogandra Chandra Chatterji. 8vo. pp. 161. *Calcutta*, 1888. 2s. 6d.

*。* Selections from Modern Bengali Literature in Bengali.

Sitaharan. By Matilál Rayá. Third Edition. 8vo. pp. 145. *Calcutta*, 1888. 2s. 6d.

*。* The Abduction of Sitá. In Bengali.

Sonár Saunár.—The Golden Family. In Bengali. 12mo. pp. 228. *Calcutta*, 1888. 3s. 6d.

*。* A faithful picture of the Bengali middle-class life of the present day.

## GUJARATI.

Astrology, or Natural Philosophy. By Mobed Aspandiárji Barjorji Panthaki. Demy 12mo. pp. 100. *Bombay*, 1888. 2s. 6d.

*。* A small tract on popular Hindu Astrology in Gujaráti.

Bháratártha Prakaah, or Substance of the Máhabhárat Puran. Translated into Gujaráti. By Manishankar Mahánand. Demy 8vo. *Ahmedabad*.

*。* This Gujaráti Translation of this Puran is published in small parts, at different prices and still in progress (vol. xii. 1888).

Chámprájhádo ne Sonaráni Nátak Saptánki, or the Drama of King Chámpráj Hádá and his Queen Sonaráni, in seven Acts. By Vaghji Asháprám Ojhá. 12mo. pp. 151. *Morvi*, 1888. 2s. 6d.

Chandraprabhá Charitra, or the Story of Princess Chandraprabhá. Translated into Gujaráti by Vishvanáth Vithalji and Keshaalál Harirám. 16mo. pp. 206. *Bombay*, 1888. 2s. 6d.

*。* A religious tale inculcating that there is no act of religious merit superior to imparting education without any remuneration.

Dankapur (Divya) Maháras Mahátmya; or, the great Glorification of the Glorious Town of Dankapur. By Keshashankar Jayashankar. Royal 4to. pp. 263. Lithographed. *Ahmedabad*, 1888. 2s. 6d.

Gangá Govind Sinh Athavá Váran Hestingsano Jamano Háth; or the Tale of Gangá Govind Sinh, the Right-hand Man of Warren Hastings. Translated into Gujaráti by Narayan Hemchandra. Super-royal 32mo. pp. 350. *Bombay*, 1888. 2s. 6d.

*。* A historical tale in connection with the recovery of land-revenue in Bengal.

Gáyakavádi Fojdári Sangraha, or a Collection of the Criminal Laws of the Gáekwádi State. By Narharilál Chandulal Joshi and Vakil Umiyárám Tuljárám Majmudár. In Gujaráti. Royal 8vo. pp. 974. *Ahmedabad*, 1888. 14s.

Jrávati, or a Tale of that Name. Translated into Gujaráti by Chhaganlál Thákordás Modi. Demy 8vo. pp. 292. *Bombay*, 1888. 5s.

*。* A historical tale of the time of Emperor Akbar of Delhi. The original work is said to be in the Dutch language.

Kalpasutrasya Bálav Bodhah, or Instruction to the Inexperienced in the Work "Kalpasutra." By Bhattárak Shrirájendrasuri. Royal 8vo. pp. 504. *Bombay*, 1888. 8s.

*。* Contains a description of the duties of a Jain, etc.

Madhupaduta Kávya, or Verses on the Bee Messenger. In Gujaráti. By Shrikrishnalál Govindrám Devashrayi. Demy 8vo. pp. 76. *Ahmedabad*, 1888. 2s. 6d.

*。* Lamentations in poetry of a husband at the absence of his beloved wife, etc.

Prakaran Sangraha, or a Collection of different Subjects. Super-royal 12mo. pp. 408. *Bombay*, 1888. 3s. 6d.

*。* Tracts explaining Jain philosophy and different matters of the Jain religion. Gujaráti in Bálbodh characters.

Shivapurán Bháshántar, or the Shiva Purán. Translated into Gujaráti. By Bhat Narottam Amarji. Vol. iii. No. 9–10. Demy 4to. pp. 40. *Bombay*, 1888. 2s. 6d.

*₊* One of the principal 18 Puráns, glorifying the god Shiva.

Sugandhamán Sado Athavá Rangelun Láchhan, or Putrefaction in Perfume of the Gilded Vice. By Jehángir Nasarvánji Patel. Demy 12mo. pp. 273. *Bombay*, 1888. 3s. 6d.

*₊* A Pársi tale in Gujaráti.

Svadharmábhimána, or Consciousness towards one's own Religion or Duty. By Jatáshankar Liládhar Trivedi. Demy 8vo. pp. 183. *Ahmedabad*, 1888. 2s. 6d.

*₊* An advocacy of the Vedic Religion, Indian Aryan Morals, Customs, etc., etc.

Svargá Rohini A'khyán, or the Story of the Ascent to Heaven. Royal 4to. pp. 90. Lithographed. *Ahmedabad*, 1888. 2s. 6d.

*₊* A story taken from the 18th or last chapter of the Mahábhárata Purán.

Vidyá Lakshmi, or a Tale of the Girl named Vidyá Lakshmi. By Anantprasád Trikamlál Vaishnava. Royal 12mo. pp. 170. *Ahmedabad*, 1888. 2s. 6d.

## HINDI.

Biswen Bansa Batiká. By Lal Kharga Bahadur Malla. 8vo. pp. 92. *Bankipore*, 1888. 6s.

*₊* A genealogy and history of the Biswen Family of Majhauli in Hindi.

Kalidasa's Sakuntala, or the Lost Ring. Translated into Hindi by Dube Nandalál Vishvanáth. Demy 12mo. pp. 185. *Bombay*, 1888. 2s.

*₊* This Hindi translation appears to have been made carefully. Explanatory notes are added to it.

Khyál Rana Ratan Sinhaka. By Mungilál Halwai. 12mo. pp. 48. *Calcutta*, 1888. 2s. 6d.

*₊* The songs of Rana Ratan Sinha in Marwari Hindi.

Mahábhárat Uddyog Parb. Translated into Hindi by Pandit Mahesadatta. Roy. 8vo. pp. 596. *Lucknow*, 1888. 6s.

*₊* The Great War, Book of the Uddyoga.

Mahábhárat Virát Parb. Translated into Hindi by Pandit Kunja Bebari. Folio, pp. 174. *Lucknow*, 1888. 2s.

*₊* The Great War, Book of the Viráta.

Panchadashi Bháshá Vártá; or, a Commentary on the Work on Vedánta Philosophy, consisting of fifteen chapters. By Svámi Atmasvarupji. Roy. 8vo. pp. 510. *Bombay*, 1888. 10s. 6d.

*₊* A Hindi translation of the original Sanskrit treatise on Vedánta philosophy, by Vidyáranya.

Pushti Márgiya, Padasangraha; or, a Collection of Pada Songs relating to Pushtimárga, or the Way of Religious Enjoyment. Parts I. to III. Edited by Thákurdás Surdás. Roy. 4to. pp. 1032. *Bombay*, 1888. £1 8s.

*₊* Pada songs in Hindi, classified under the different tunes in which they are to be sung.

Rámáyan (The Exploits of Rám).—By Tulsi Dás. Fourth Edition. In Hindi. Roy. 8vo. pp. 633. *Meerut*, 1888. 3s.

Ramayana.—By Tulsi Dás. New Edition. Royal 8vo. pp. 492. *Calcutta*, 1888. 3s. 6d.

Rám Lílá Sundar Kánda. The fifth Book of the Ramayana in the form of a Drama. By Damodasa Bishnu Sapre. 8vo. pp. 68. *Calcutta*, 1888. 2s. 6d.

Sakuntala, or the Lost Ring. A Sanskrit Drama of Kálidás. Translated into Hindi Prose and Verse. With Notes by Raja Lachman Sinha. 4to. boards, pp. 177. *Benares*, 1888. 7s. 6d.

## HINDUSTANI OR URDU.

'Abkát-ul-Anwár fi Imámat-il-Ayyimmat-il-Athár, jild-i-su'um. The Scent of Blossoms in the Narrative of the Imáms. Vol. III. By Maulvi Sayyid Hámid Husain. Royal 4to. pp. 586. *Lucknow*, 1888. 10s. 6d.

Al Masáib, Jild-i-Duom.—By Mirza Kásim Ali. Royal 8vo. pp. 600. *Lucknow*, 1888. 3s. 6d.

*₊* Selections from Bahru-l-Masaib. In Urdu and Arabic.

Khayálát-i-Azád (Free Thoughts).—By Maulavi Sayyid Muhammad 'Abd-ul-Ghafúr, Shahbár. Royal 8vo. pp. 128. *Bankipur*, 1888. 2s. 6d.

*₊* Humorous and witty letters and meaning of certain words. In Urdu.

Makhzan-ul-mufradát ma'rúf ba Jám'í-ul-adwiya. By Maulavi Muhammad Fazl-ul-lah. Royal 8vo. pp. 282. *Lucknow*, 1888. 3s.

*₊* A magazine of medicines in Urdu.

Mukhtasar Shahábiah, or the Book prepared by Shahábuddin. Translated into Urdu by Kázi Kutbudin Khatib. 8vo. pp. 467. *Bombay*, 1888. 8s.

*₊* Rules for prayers, marriage and divorce. Directions for pilgrimage to Mecca and Medina, etc.

Sauda.—Kulliyát-i-Sauda. The Complete Works of Sauda. Urdu and Persian. Second Edition. Royal 8vo. pp. 644. *Cawnpore*, 1888. 3s.

## MARATHI.

Aindrajálik Kárda Chatushtaya, or Four Packs of a Conjuror's Cards. By Govind Morobá Kárlekar. 12mo. pp. 48. With cards. Lithographed. *Bombay*, 1888. 3s. 6d.

*₊* Card tricks in Maráthi.

Garibánchá Vaidya ashvini kumár; or, the Physicians of Heaven, the Medical Adviser of the Poor. 12mo. pp. 68. Lithographed. *Bombay*, 1888. 3s. 6d.

*₊* A popular tract on Hindu medicine in Maráthi.

Goldsmith's Comedy, The Good-natured Man. Translated into Maráthi by Raghunáth Bálkrishna Rájádhyaksha. New Edition. 12mo. pp. 192. *Poona*, 1888. 3s. 6d.

Hemamuktá Sanváda; or, a Conference between Gold and Pearl. By Chintáman Ganesh Joshi. Demy 12mo. pp. 182. *Bombay*, 1888. 3s. 6d.

*₊* A conversation between gold and the baser metals on the one part and pearl and the precious stones on the other part, each party disputing the other's alleged excellence and superiority.

Manjughoshá; or, the Sweet-Voiced. A Novel in Maráthi. 8vo. pp. 141. *Poona*, 1888. 3s. 6d.

Nibandha Málá Bhág I lá, or a string of Essays. Part I. In Maráthi. By Vishnu Krishna Chiplunkar. 8vo. pp. 400. *Poona*, 1888. 2s. 6d.

*₊* A reprint of literary, historical and social essays.

Pándava Pratáp katháras áni A'machin Puránen Shimagá áhet kin káyat; or, the Eloquent and Charming Account of the Achievements of the Pándava Princes, and are our Purans indecent. Translated into Maráthi by Káshináth Sambháji. Demy 8vo. pp. 216. *Bombay*, 1888. 3s. 6d.

Talekar (Srikrishna Raghunátha Shástri).—A School Dictionary. English and Maráthi. Revised and Enlarged. Seventh Edition. Post 8vo. cloth, pp. viii. 370. *Bombay*, 1889. 3s.

## PERSIAN.

Aesop's Fables.—Translated into Persian. (From the English of the Rev. G. F. Townsend, M.A.) By Capt. H. Eardley Wilmot, Madras Staff-Corps. Roy. 8vo. boards, pp. 138, v. *Madras*, 1889. 5s.

Ikhtiyarát-i-Badi'í.—By Háji, Zain-ul-'Attár. Royal 8vo. pp. 579. *Cawnpore*, 1888. 3s. 6d.

*₊* A medical work in Persian.

Ma'árij-un-Nabúwat fi Madárij-il-Fatúwat. The Steps
to Prophecy, being the Degrees of Liberality. By Múin-ud-
din, Káshifi. Roy. 8vo. pp. 1176. *Cawnpore*, 1888. 8*s*.

Manákib-i-Hafiziyya. The Abilities of Háfiz. By
Maulvi Ghulam Muhammad Hádi 'Ali Khán. Roy. 8vo.
pp. 260. *Calcutta*, 1888. 2*s. 6d*.

Muntakhab-i-Gulistán wa Bostán Musamma ba Ikd-
i-Gul wa Ikd-i-Mauzún. By Maulvi Muhammad Muhyy-
ud-din. Roy. 8vo. pp. 222. *Allahabad*, 1888. 2*s*.
*₊* Selections from Gulistán and Bostán, named the Ikd-i-
Gul and Ikd-i-Mauzun.

Muntakhab-ul-Lughát. The Select Dictionary. By
Maulvi 'Abd-ul-rashid. Roy. 8vo. pp. 700. *Calcutta*,
1888. 2*s. 6d*.

Sad Hikáyat; or, a Hundred Stories. By Khán
Bahádur Maulavi Sayid Abdul Fattah. Demy 8vo. pp. 152.
Lithographed. *Bombay*, 1888. 1*s. 6d*.
*₊* Popular stories in Persian.

Sadi.—The Bostan of Shaikh Sadi. Translated into
English. By Ziauddin Gulam Mobeddin Munshi. Revised
by Rochfort Davies, Esq. 8vo. cloth, pp. 282. *Bombay*,
1889. 6*s*.

## SANSKRIT.

Bhagavadgítá; or, the well-known Philosophical Poem.
Sanskrit and Hindi Text. With Hindi Commentary by Svámi
Anandagiri. Royal 8vo. pp. 610. *Bombay*, 1888. 9*s*.

Brihajjyotishárnavántargata Shastha Mishraakand-
hokta Bráhmanotpatti Márttandákhyo Shodashádhyáyah, or
the 16th chapter, entitled Mártanda, giving the origin of
Bráhmans, being the 6th section of the work, entitled the
Great Ocean of Astrology. By Harikrishna Venkatrám
Shástri. Sanskrit and Hindi Text. Oblong. 237 leaves.
Lithographed. *Bombay*, 1888. 9*s*.

Brihatpáráshara Horá Shástram; or, the large Work
on the Astrological Science by Páráshara. Sanskrit and
Hindi Text. Translated by Shridhar Jatáshankar. Royal
4to. pp. 387. *Bombay*, 1888. 16*s*.
*₊* Indian Astrology. The Commentary on the latter part
of the work is accompanied by a translation in Hindi.

Hitopadesá of Náráyana Pandit. Edited by Káshináth Pandurang Parab. Royal 12mo. pp. 140. *Bombay*,
1888. 1*s. 6d*.
*₊* A well-known class-book for beginners.

Kálidása. Raghuvansha; or, History of the Raghu's
race. With the Commentary of Mallinátha. Edited by
Káshináth Pándurang Parab. Royal 12mo. pp. 326.
*Bombay*, 1888. 2*s. 6d*.

Kalidasa's Vikramorvasiya (Urvashi won by Valour).
With the Commentary of Ranganátha. Edited by Káshináth
Pándurang Parab and Mangesh Rámkrishna Telang. Royal
12mo. pp. 151. *Bombay*, 1888. 2*s*.

Magha's Sisupálavadha. With the Commentary of
Mallinátha; or, the Destruction of Shishupála. Edited by
Pandit Durgá Prasád and Pandit Shivadatta. Royal 8vo.
pp. 658. *Bombay*, 1888. 8*s*.
*₊* This legend of Prince Shishupála is to be found in the
Sabháparva of the Mahábhárata Purán.

Patanjali's Mahábháshya Naváhnikam; or, the great
Commentary by Patanjali. Together with the Commentary
on it, entitled Naváhnikam, by Kaiyata. Edited by Náráyana
Shástri. 8vo. pp. 288. *Poona*, 1888. 8*s*.
*₊* The first part of the Mahábháshya, together with Notes
on it, by Bálashástri.

Pramitáksharákhyatikásahita Muhurtachintámani.
By Dawadnya Ráma. Oblong, 146 leaves. *Bombay*, 1888.
5*s*.
*₊* An astrological work on auspicious days for commencing any work.

Sánkhya Káriká. By Iśwara Krishna. Translated
from the Sanskrit by H. Th. Colebrooke. Together with
Bháshya, or Commentary of Gaudapáda. Translated and
illustrated by an original Comment by H. H. Wilson, M.A.
Edited by Tukáram Tátyá. Demy 8vo. pp. 282. *Bombay*,
1888. 6*s*.
*₊* A collection of memorial verses or stanzas giving a
summary of the Sánkya system of philosophy.

Sankshepa - Sáríraka, Prathama, Divitiya, Tritiya,
Chaturtha Adhyáya. "Inquiry into the Embodied Spirit."
Abridged. Chapter I. to IV. By Sárvajna Muni. With
Commentary by Madhusudan Sarasvati. In Sanskrit.
Royal 8vo. pp. 1024. *Benares*, 1888. 16*s*.
*₊* On the Vedánta or, Brahma-Sutra.

Sanskrit Text-Book. With Introduction, English
Translation and Notes (Grammatical and Explanatory).
Sanskrit and English. Edited by P. K. Padmanábha
Bhástri. Royal 12mo. pp. 36. *Bombay*, 1888. 1*s*.

Sapta-Śati Bháshá Tiká Sahit. The Seven Hundred.
With the Commentary. Sanskrit and Nepáli. Translated
by Pandit Devaráj. Royal 8vo. pp. 108. *Benares*, 1888.
3*s*.

Sárasvatam Vyákaranam; or, the Work on Sanskrit
Grammar, entitled "Sárasvata." By Anubhutisvarupá-
chárya. Royal 16mo. pp. 281. *Bombay*, 1888. 2*s*.

Sárarvatam Vyákaranam, Purvárdham, or the First
Half of the Work on Sanskrit Grammar, entitled, Sárasvata.
By Anubhuti Svarupáchárya. With Commentary by Bhatt
Vásudev. Royal 12mo. pp. 186. *Bombay*, 1888. 2*s*.

Sártha Panchadashi, or the Work on Vedántic Philosophy in Fifteen Chapters, by Vidyáranya, together with its
Meaning. Sanskrit and Maráthi. Translated by Khando
Krishna, alias Bábá Garde. 8vo. pp. 227. *Poona*, 1888.
10*s. 6d*.
*₊* The original text is an authoritative treatise on Vedanta
philosophy.

Shankardigvijaya Mula Sahit; or, Shankará's Victory
over the World. By Mádhava. Sanskrit Text, with
Gujaráti Translation by Shri Krishnalál Govindrám
Deváshrayi and Purushottam Káhánji Ghándi. Royal 8vo.
pp. 388. *Ahmedabad*, 1888. 10*s. 6d*.
*₊* A short account of the controversial exploits of Shankar-
áchárya, the great reformer and teacher [of Vedánta
philosophy.

Sri Harsha. Khandana-khandkádyam. Refuting by
rendering the Beginning ineffectual. Demy 8vo. pp. 784.
*Benares*, 1888. 18*s*.
*₊* A very important work on logic. In Sanskrit.

Suklayajuh Práti Śákhyam Uvvata Kritabháshya-
yutam. Práti Sákhya of the White Yajur-Veda. With
the Commentary of Uvvata. By Katyána. Edited by
Pandit Yugal Kishora Páthaka. Text Sanskrit and Vaidic.
Demy 8vo. pp. 100. *Benares*, 1888. 2*s*.

Taittiriya Sanhita (Krishna) of the Black Yajurveda.
Edited by Rájárám Shástri Bodas and Shivram Shástri Gore.
Roy. 8vo. pp. 534. *Bombay*, 1888. 9*s*.
*₊* Vedic hymns.

Vishnu Sahasranáma; or the Thousand Names of the
God Vishnu. Roy. 32mo. 76 leaves. *Bombay*, 1888. 1*s*.
*₊* An extract from the Mahábhárat.

Yajurvedi Brahma Nitya Karma; or Daily Religious
Duties of a Bráhman of the Yajurveda Sect. Roy. 18mo.
pp. 32. *Ahmedabad*, 1888. 1*s. 6d*.

No. 245.

# TRÜBNER'S RECORD,

## A JOURNAL DEVOTED TO THE LITERATURE OF THE EAST.

WITH NOTES AND LISTS OF CURRENT

### American, European and Colonial Publications.

*Edited by Dr. Rost, of the India Office.*

JULY, 1889.　　　　THIRD SERIES. VOL. I. NO. 3.　　　　PRICE 2s.


## The Study of Oriental Languages.

The Committee of the Imperial Institute have taken a step of undoubted importance in the establishment, in union with University College and King's College, London, of a school for the study of modern Oriental languages. In a communication which he has addressed to us, Sir Frederick Abel solicits our aid in making the scheme known to those to whom its objects may be of service ; and we comply with his request with the utmost readiness. It is, indeed, with no small satisfaction that we see it is at length being recognized that if Great Britain's rapidly increasing commerce with her great Eastern dependencies is to be conducted so that all parties may derive the greatest benefit, the study of Oriental languages on the part of her merchants and traders is imperatively necessary. Insignificant as is the Eastern trade of other nations in comparison with that of England, they have long ago provided facilities for the teaching of Asiatic and African dialects. In France an institution having such an object has existed for nearly a century. It receives from the State the free use of a large building, and a grant of over £6000 a year. It gives gratuitous instruction in the chief Oriental tongues, and the Minister of Public Instruction has recently added a commercial section to it. Vienna possesses a famous Oriental Academy ; while in Berlin the Imperial German School of Living Oriental Languages, although only a year old, is already enjoying an annual subvention of £3600, and giving entirely free tuition. And, at last, in England, too, something is going to be attempted.

Under the scheme above indicated, it is proposed, in one branch, to give instruction in Sanskrit, Bengali, Hindi, Hindustani, Tamil, Telugu, Punjabi, Pali, Marathi, Gujarati, Arabic and Persian ; while, in the second, the languages to be taught comprise colloquial Arabic, modern Greek, colloquial Persian, Russian, Turkish, Chinese, Burmese, Japanese, Malay and Swahili. It must be noted, also, that the tuition to be given is not intended to be of an academic character. It will rather " have particular reference to commercial and official requirements, and to the facilitation of colloquial intercourse with natives of Oriental coun-

tries." That is precisely what is wanted, and the benefits likely to accrue from such a facilitation are simply immeasurable. The only wonder is that they have not been sooner perceived. No educated Englishman goes to France or Germany expecting to find anything else but the languages of those countries generally spoken ; and yet, somehow or other, when he goes, for instance, to India, ten thousand miles further away from his tight little island, he is surprised, and often annoyed, to discover that the inhabitants of Southern Asia speak also the dialects peculiar to their portion of the globe. All who have journeyed in the East will only too regretfully admit that the lack of the means of colloquial intercourse between British traders and Eastern natives forms an irritating barrier to the extension of our commerce, and none the less irritating because it might with a little effort be easily surmounted. No one, too, who has noticed how happily circumstanced is the man who can utter even a few words of the language of the people among whom for the time being fate has placed him will be disposed to dispute the modest claim of Sir F. Abel, that, if it is going a little beyond its original scope in exercising educational functions, the Imperial Institute is, by providing in the United Kingdom the important aid to the official and commercial sections of the community which has long been furnished to Continental nations, at the same time undertaking a work of considerable public utility.—*Newcastle Daily Chronicle*, July 2.

---

## Two Eastern Fables.
### By Dr. J. Rizal.

There are two Fables, the one in Japan and the other in the Philippine Islands, which have many traits in common, and the intercomparison of which may perhaps be of some interest to Ethnologists.

The Philippine children, in their earliest years, learn the *Tale of the Tortoise and the Monkey*; or, as it is called in the Tagal language, *Ang buhay ni pagong at ni matsing*. There is scarcely in Tagal literature another tale more popular and better known than this, although there are many prettier and more interesting. To it are traceable many sayings, phrases, maxims, and comparisons, which have received currency in reference to various conditions of common day life. This tale runs as follows :—

' "The tortoise and the monkey found once a banana tree floating amidst the waves of a river. It was a very fine tree, with large green leaves, and with roots, just as if it had been pulled off by a storm. They took it ashore. 'Let us divide it,' said the tortoise, 'and plant each its portion.' They cut it in the middle, and the monkey, as the stronger, took for himself the upper part of the tree, thinking that it would grow quicker, for it had leaves. The tortoise, as the weaker, had the lower part, that looked ugly, although it had roots. After some days, they met.

'Hallo, Mr. Monkey,' said the tortoise, 'how are you getting on with your banana tree ?'

'Alas,' answered the monkey, 'it has been dead a long time! And yours, Miss Tortoise ?'

'Very nice, indeed ; with leaves and fruits. Only I cannot climb up, to gather them.'

'Never mind,' said the malicious monkey, 'I will climb and pick them for you.'

'Do, Mr. Monkey,' replied the tortoise gratefully.

And so they walked towards the tortoise's house.

As soon as the monkey saw the bright yellow fruits hanging between the large green leaves, he climbed up and began plundering, munching and gobbling, as quick as he could.

'But give me some, too,' said the tortoise, seeing that the monkey did not take the slightest notice of her.

'Not even a bit of the skin, if it is eatable,' rejoined the monkey, both his cheeks crammed with bananas.

The tortoise meditated revenge. She went to the river, picked up some pointed snails,* planted them around the banana tree, and hid himself under a cocoa-nut shell. When the monkey came down, he hurt himself and began to bleed.

After a long search, he found the tortoise.

'You wretched creature, here you are !' said he. 'You must pay now for your wickedness ; you must die. But as I am very generous, I will leave to you the choice of your death. Shall I pound you in a mortar, or shall I throw you into the water? Which do you prefer ?'

'The mortar,—the mortar,' answered the tortoise : 'I am so afraid of getting drowned.'

'O ho !' laughed the monkey ; 'indeed ! You are afraid of getting drowned ! Now I will drown you.'

And, going to the shore, he slung the tortoise and threw it in the water. But soon the tortoise reappeared swimming and laughing at the deceived, artful monkey."

* A kind of spiral periwinkle, called *susū* in Tagal.

This is the Philippine tale of the monkey and the tortoise. The Japanese fable, *Saru Kani Kassen*, or, *Battle of the Monkey and the Crab*, as published by *Kobunsha* at Tokyo, is as follows :—

"A monkey and a crab once met when going round a mountain.

The monkey had picked up a persimmon-seed, and the crab had a piece of toasted rice-cake. The monkey seeing this, and wishing to get something that could be turned to good account at once, said : 'Pray, exchange that rice-cake for this persimmon-seed.' The crab, without a word, gave up his cake, and took the persimmon-seed and planted it. At once it sprung up, and soon became a tree so high, one had to look up at it. The tree was full of persimmons, but the crab had no means of climbing the tree. So he asked the monkey to climb up and get the persimmons for him. The monkey got up on a limb of the tree and began to eat the persimmons. The unripe persimmons he threw at the crab, but all the ripe and good ones he put in his pouch. The crab under the tree thus got his shell badly bruised, and only by good luck escaped into his hole, where he lay distressed with pain and not able to get up. Now, when the relatives and household of the crab heard how matters stood, they were surprised and angry, and declared war and attacked the monkey, who, leading forth a numerous following, bid defiance to the other party. The crabs, finding themselves unable to meet and cope with this force, became still more exasperated and enraged, and retreated into their hole, and held a council of war. Then came a rice mortar, a pounder, a bee, and an egg, and together they devised a deep-laid plot for revenge.

First, they requested that peace be made with the crabs ; and thus they induced the king of the monkeys to enter their hole unattended, and seated him on the earth. The monkey, not suspecting any plot, took the *hibashi*, or poker, to stir up the slumbering fire, when bang ! went the egg, which was lying hidden in the ashes, and burned the monkey's arm. Surprised and alarmed, he plunged his arm into the pickle-tub in the kitchen to relieve the pain of the burn. Then the bee, which was hidden near the tub, stung him sharply in the face, already wet with tears. Without waiting to brush off the bee, and howling bitterly, he rushed for the back door ; but just then some seaweed entangled his legs and made him slip. Then down came the pounder tumbling on him from a shelf, and the mortar, too, came rolling down on him from the roof of the porch, and broke his back and so weakened him that he was unable to rise up. Then out came the crabs in a crowd and brandishing on high their pincers, pinched the monkey to pieces."

There is no doubt that these two tales, although their ends are very different, have both only one origin, or perhaps one is a modification of the other. There the monkey plays the same part—greedy, malicious, wicked, and revengeful; the Japanese persimmon-tree is the Philippine banana, which grows and brings forth fruit quicker than any other tree. There are many points of resemblance between the crab and the tortoise, and there is a mortar mentioned too. Which of both tales is the more ancient? Which is the more original, and where do they come from?

A careful analysis and intercomparison of both tales will show us that the leading idea of both came either from the South, from Sumatra, Java, Borneo, Mindanao, or had its origin from the Philippine Islands, and afterwards migrated northwards with the people or the race which came from the South to inhabit the Japanese and the Riu-Kiu Islands, being modified in its course in conformity with the climates and the customs of the different countries. There is a Japanese tradition of a hero called, I think *Timuotenho*, who is supposed to have come from those Southern Islands. The Malay origin of the Japanese people is worth being treated separately.

The Tagal tale exists in the Bisaya Islands too, with few modifications. We do not know if there is another analogue in the Malay Archipelago, in Sumatra or Java. If there is, a comparison with the Tagal version would throw perhaps more light on its origin. For the moment we shall satisfy our curiosity by making an analysis and drawing some deductions suggested by a strict intercomparison of both tales.

The beginning of both is the same, except that the Japanese has a crab instead of a tortoise. This change is very important. I was told, when I was in Japan, that the tortoise was with the Japanese people a symbol of eternity or of something sacred, holy, etc., which may be suggested by the Chinese civilization. This is not the case with the Tagal, which sees in the tortoise a poor little innocent thing, but artful in its way, rather to be pitied than admired or respected. But there is in the Philippines a superstition also, that if somebody puts his foot on a tortoise, the sole of the foot will burst into many lines. Perhaps it is a pious superstition to prevent naughty children from stepping on poor slow walking tortoises.

The Philippine banana tree is more natural than the persimmon-seed and the rice-cake in the Japanese tale. Perhaps because there is no banana tree in Japan, the people have been obliged to adopt these modifications. It seems too foolish or too wise to exchange a *piece of toasted rice-cake* for a *persimmon-seed*. Besides, *the toasted rice-cake* shows more of a refined civilization than a mere banana tree. Further, the phrases " *At once it (the persimmon-seed) sprung up, and* SOON BECAME A TREE SO HIGH. . . . . *The tree was full of persimmons,*" may more fitly be applied to a banana tree than to a persimmon-seed. Further, people often pull up banana trees, as the heroes of our story do, plant them and get fruits (or the heart which brings the fruits) in three or four days. The case is unnatural for a persimmon-seed. So we think that the Tagal version is more natural.

" *But the crab had no means of climbing the tree.*" This phrase would be correct in the case of a tortoise; we think the crab with its pincers and feet could climb as well as a monkey; at least, the crab climbs very well on any stone, wall, etc. This *impossibility of climbing*, more natural in a tortoise, suggests the supposition that the crab was not in the original tale.

In what follows, the two fables nearly agree till we come to where the crab escapes into his hole.

In the Philippine tale, the revenge of the tortoise, although a little childish, shows a very primitive and peculiar way, " *with pointed periwinkles,*" while in the Japanese there are traces of a more advanced state of society, like the war between crabs and monkeys. The *council of war*, held in the hole of the crabs, is very remarkable. *The rice-mortar, the pounder, the bee and the egg,* helping the exasperated crabs, give us an idea of the free imagination of the Japanese people. Not only the animated beings, but the inanimate things too, speak and give advice, feel and move like the others.

*First, they requested that peace be made with the crabs; and thus they induced the king of the monkeys to enter their hole unattended. . . . .*

It seems to us that all this part is interpolated by some not very clever story-teller, perhaps in order to gratify the natural wish for revenge. Then if the monkeys were the stronger and the crabs the weaker, which desired that peace be made, these could not have induced the king to come unattended, as he is not constrained by a more powerful foe; but the crabs would go to the monkeys to ask for peace and to offer conditions. The same may be said of the egg which burst under the ashes only in order to burn the monkey's arm. This part may have been added long after the wandering people came to Japan; moreover, the *hibashi* only exists in cold climates. The way how the tale ends is rather complicated than natural, while in the Philippine version it is plainer and shows a more delicate observation of character and feeling. The mischievous monkey lays a very wicked *dilemma* before the tortoise, pretending to be generous ; *either to die by being pounded in a mortar or to be drowned.* The artful but not wicked tortoise, knowing the real intention and malignity of the monkey, beats him with the same weapons and chooses the mortar. The monkey, continuing his wickedness till the last, refuses what he promised and throws the tortoise into the water. The interest is maintained till the very conclusion.

In both versions there is a great deal of morality : it is the eternal fight between the weak and the powerful. In the Philippine version we find more philosophy, more plainness of form, while in the Japanese there is more *civilization*, and so to speak, more diplomatic usage.

After this short analysis we may give it as our opinion that this Japanese tale had its origin from some South country from where would come also the Philippine version. This last is evidently nearer to the primitive form (if not the primitive form itself), than the Japanese. The Japanese version is much changed and added to, perhaps by other peoples and other civilizations it has met with. This tale may perhaps be considered as one of the oldest tales in the Far East. The differences between both versions show that one is not a copy of the other, and that they must have existed in both countries long before the Europeans came to that part of the world. The fact that this tale is known everywhere in the Philippines, in every island, province, village and dialect, proves that it must be the inheritance of an extinct civilization, common to all the races which ever lived in that region.

In conclusion we would give expression to a wish that Oriental scholars who make a study of the Malay Archipelago may tell us if there are tales of this kind known there in connexion with the versions we have been placing before our readers.

------

## An Uráṇw or Kuṇr'kh Folk Tale.

The following tale was related to me by a Christian Uráṇw or Kuṇr'kh named Elias Bochcho. He belonged to a small village called Chipra, about six miles west of Ránchí, the chief town in the wild, hilly district of Chutia Nagpur, which lies on the Western side of Bengal, bordering on the Central Provinces of India.

He was educated in the S. P. G. Mission at Ránchí, and was able to read, write, and speak English very fairly.

He said that the tale was told him by his mother. His mother was entirely uneducated, and could only understand the Uráṇw or Kuṇr'kh language.

There are internal evidences of matter, idioms and words in the tale itself, which prove it to be a genuine Uráṇw tale, and not made up by the Christian narrator.

My mother has called my attention to the likeness between this tale and the Greek myth of Chronos eating his children.

Biṛi darû chanddo gahi khíṛi<br>
Sun and moon of tale.

Oṇghon enne manjâ chanddo taṇghai khaddârin oṇtâ<br>
One   thus happened moon   her   children one

bajâ   tule kulliyâ chichchâ darâ tân   kandan<br>
leaf-basket with covered gave and she-herself sweet-potato

pûkhâ darâ mokhâ- ge ukkiyâ<br>
steamed and eating for eat.

Â birim biṛi adi gusan barchâkî âniyâ "An dhiyâ,<br>
That time very sun her   to   came having told "Oh sister,

nîn endaran mokhdî ? En-gâ hoṇ tanikan chî ?"<br>
thou what   eat ? Me for also little give ?"

Chanddo chichchâ<br>
Moon   gave.

Biṛi mokh îriyâ darâ adin menjâkî "Dhiyâ, id<br>
Sun eat saw and her asked having "Sister, this

endarâ talî ?"<br>
what is ?"

Chanddo âniyâ "En oṇghai khaddain kûl kîrâ turu<br>
Moon answered I   my   children belly hunger from

pû'khan darâ mokhâ laggen.<br>
steamed and eating am at.

Biṛi astle chhachhem taṇghai eṛpâ kerâ darâ taṇghai<br>
Sun thence silently its   house went and its

khaddârin oṇtâ   kuṇdâ   nû pûkhâ darâ mokkhâ.<br>
children one earthen-pot in steamed and ate.

Antle   chanddo taṇghai khaddârin chalkhâ chichchâ<br>
Afterwards moon her   children opened gave.

Biṛi idin îriyâ darâ chanddon piṭâ-ge oṇtâ eṛet dharchâ<br>
Sun this saw and   moon   kill for one bow seized

darâ khechchâ.<br>
and drove away.

Chanddo oṇtâ baṛâ mann nû nûkharâ kerâ.<br>
Moon   one banyan tree in   hid   went.

Biṛi aṇṛsiyâ darâ chanddon khottâ darâ taṛâ khechâ<br>
Sun arrived and   moon   cut   and half piece

otthaṛâ.<br>
took out.

Kuṇr'khar ânar kî â baṛâ maundim chanddo nû innâ<br>
Kuṇr'khar tell that that banyan tree very moon in to-day

gûṭî otharî.<br>
till is seen.

Phin ba'anar kî biṛi chanddon khottâ aṇiwge   chanddo<br>
Again they say that sun moon   cut therefore   moon

êkâ êkâ biri sannî kohâ manî.<br>
what what time small large becomes.

Phin Anar   kî biṛi gahi boṇ khadd gutṭhî rahchâ—<br>
Again they tell that sun of also child many remained—

Abṛâ   gutṭhî rahchâ hole ormâ âlar biṛnâ tule kheor<br>
Those all many remained then all   men sun-heat from die will

paheṇ.<br>
perhaps.

## Variant Readings and Notes.

*Derd*, a particle, sometimes meaning 'and' and sometimes 'then.'

*Khiri*, is generally used by Urāṅws for 'tale.' The Hindi word barankā, however, was used by the narrator.

*Onghon*, derived from on = 'one' + gahi = 'of' + on = 'one.'

*Bajd*, a very large basket used for collecting leaves in.

*Tule*, a postposition signifying instrumentality. *Tulein* is an emphatic form of *tule*. There are two other postpositions, *ti* and *turu*, used in nearly the same sense as *tule*.

*Kulliyā*, from kullnā = 'to cover.' Not to be confounded with *kulnā* 'to open, to untie.'

*Chichchā*, a verb added to other verbs in an intensive sense.

*Tān*, according to Flex (Introduction to Urāṅw Language, Calcutta, 1874) = 'self.' Indeed it is strictly a reflexive pronoun. Hence at first sight it seems as if *ād* would be more suitable here, but *ād* is really a demonstrative pronoun and literally means 'that one yonder.' It is used of others or when a new person is introduced, whereas *tān* has two uses. 1. The reflexive use. 2. It refers back to the original nominative case in a sentence as here.

*Pākhā* is the proper Urāṅw word. The word used by the narrator was *bhapchā*, a word belonging to the Chuṭia Nagpur dialect of the Bihāri language, but conjugated after the Urāṅw fashion.

*Barchākī*, conjunctive participle. See Flex, p. 21.

*An*, 'Oh,' Interjection. See Flex. p. 28.

*Dhiyā*, not often used. This word is used by Tulsi Dās in his Old Hindi translation of the Ramāyana. The Hindi word 'bahin' was used by the narrator.

*Mokhā*. The narrator also used the form 'mūkhdī.' These are dialectic differences.

*Tanikan*, a Nagpuri word used by the Urāṅws, but the proper Urāṅw word would be 'jokk.' There is a tendency amongst the Urāṅws to use words belonging to the Nagpuri dialect of the Bihāri language, and I have no doubt that in course of time the Urāṅw language will die out, and the Bihāri take its place amongst them.

*Chī.* The shorter or root form of the imperative. This form is indefinite as to gender. The longer forms are *chid* (masc.) and *chiai* (fem.).

*Mokh*, qy. should be 'eat' or 'ate.'

*Āniyā*. This verb seems to have two senses. The root idea is *tell*. 1. To *tell* a person *directly* without reference to any former subject or conversation. 2. To *tell* a person *in reply* to something said, *to answer*. Mr. Hahn, in his Urāṅw translations of Old and New Testament History, has wrongly used the phrase *jawāh chichchas*, lit. = 'answer gave' for 'answered,' but I believe it would be more in accordance with Urāṅw usage to write *āniyas*.

*Khaddain*. Note that in the first line of this tale the form *khaddārin* is used. In the Urāṅw language there are two sets of forms. 1. One set are used by *men or women* talking with *men*. 2. The other by *women* talking with *women*. "Khaddain" is used when women talk with women. The sun and moon are both feminine in the Urāṅw language, so the moon would rightly use "khaddain" in replying to the sun's question. "Khaddārin" is used in the first line by the man Elias Bochcho, who was narrating the tale to me, as I was a man. If this tale were being told by a woman to another woman, it would be khaddain also in the first line.

*Turu*, vide 'tule' above.

*Pākh'an* is the proper Urāṅw word, but the narrator used 'bhapch'an,' a Nagpuria Bihāri word conjugated after the Urāṅw fashion. *Pākhch'an* and *Pokhch'an* are dialectic differences.

*Astile* = 'from that place.' *Astile* is another form of this word.

*Kundā*. A very large *ghaṛā* or water-pot

*Antle*. The original word used was 'table,' a mixture of Nagpuri and Urāṅw.

*Idin*. This pronoun refers to the action of the moon and not to the moon herself.

*Piṭāge*. Infinitive of purpose, cf. Latin subjunctive with ut.

*Eret* = 'a bow' and not the 'arrow,' which would be 'chār,' cf. Sanskrit shar.

*Dharchā* = 3. sing. fem. past tense from dharnā—1. = to take hold of, to catch hold of. 2. = to catch. 3. = to hold fast.

*Khechchā* = 3. sing. fem. past tense, from Khednā = to drive away, to pursue. Not to be confounded with kechchā + khe'enā = to die.

*Barāmann*. The Banyan tree (Ficus Bengalensis). A kind of fig tree. Barā must not be confounded with the Hindi word 'barā,' signifying 'big, great, large.'

*Tara Khechā*. Both of these words seem to mean 'piece.' *Tarā* is used with the Urāṅw word for 'bread,' *Tarā asmā* = 'a piece of bread.' Qy. Does *Tarā* mean 'half, the piece broken off'? *Khechā* according to my wife is a Bihāri word, cf. the Nagpuriā sentence 'dehak ho ek khechā' = 'Give lad one piece.' This is the usual word for 'piece.'

*Ghṭl* = 'till, up to, during.'

*Manndim*. dim is an emphatic suffix and = 'same.'

*Hon* = Hindi *bhī* = 'also.'

*Guṭhī*. Used, according to Flex, to form the plural of feminine nouns. But according to Flex *khadd* is masculine, so his rule does not hold good here. See further his Introduction, page 4, where he states, "If the plurality of relatives or children is to be denoted, the words 'baggar,' and 'kharrā' are added to the indefinite nominative singular, e.g. 'dadā baggar = brothers, khadd kharrā = children.'" Also note that 'guṭhī' is used with the pronoun *abrā* a little further on, and so it is used with pronouns also, and Mr. Flex's rule requires to be altered or further explained.

*Abrā*, vide Flex, p. 9. "By adding 'brā' to the indefinite form *i* and *ā*, another demonstrative pronoun is obtained, which is generally used to denote a plurality of things near or remote, thus:—'Ibrā endra rai' = 'What is all this?' 'Abṛan itra ondra' = 'Bring all that here.'"

*Abrā guṭhī*. Note the construction and cf. Flex's remarks in his Introduction, p. 4. "The nominative plural of feminine nouns is formed by adding 'guṭhī' to the nominative singular, e.g. sing. *erpā* = 'a house'; plural *erpā guṭhī* = 'houses.' However, it seems that *guṭhī* is used here with 'abrā,' a pronoun, and also with *ibrā* and with other pronouns, so his rule would seem to require alteration. See also note on *khadd guṭhī* above.

*Hole . . . . pahen*, vide Flex's Introduction p. 22. The conditional of the past tense. The literal translation of this passage seems to be as follows:—"All these remained then all people from the heat will die but," i.e. "If all these remained, then all men would die from the heat."

*Birnā*. My wife pronounces this word 'biḍna,' and says there is another form 'biḍai' or 'biṛi.' These last two forms are used mostly of the 'sun,' whilst the former are used of the 'heat of the sun.'

*Pahen* is used here as the sign of the past conditional, but it is really a conjunction and means 'but.'

---

### Free Translation.
#### Tale of the Sun and the Moon.

Once upon a time the Moon covered up her children with a large leaf-basket and having boiled sweet-potatoes, sat down to eat them.

At that time the Sun came to her and said, "Sister! What are you eating? Give me also a little."

The Moon gave.

The Sun tasted it and asked her, "Sister, what is this?"

The Moon said, "I have boiled my children through hunger, and I am eating them."

The Sun went quietly away to his home and boiled his children in a very large pot and ate them.

Then the Moon uncovered her children.

The Sun saw this and took a bow to kill the Moon and drove her away.

The Moon went and hid in a banyan tree.

The Sun came up and cut the Moon and took out a small piece.

The Kuṇr'khars say that the same banyan tree is seen in the Moon to this day.

Again they say that the Sun cut the Moon in two; therefore the Moon is sometimes small and sometimes large.

They say there were also many children of the Sun, but if they had remained all men would have died from the heat.

*Urâṇw Folk Tales in general.*

As a rule they are very simple and generally have to do with country life,—objects of nature such as the Sun, Moon, stars, trees, rivers, etc., are referred to,—animals, birds, fishes, and insects are often represented as acting and talking as if they were human beings.

The Urâṇws are a down-trodden race, and many of their tales relate how some clever tenant or servant has outwitted his oppressive landlord or unjust master.

There are some very pathetic tales about the ill-treatment of younger brothers by their older brothers; sisters by their brothers,—the youngest brother, however, usually takes the part of his sister—nephews by uncles, etc.

---

It is my intention to publish from time to time translations of Urâṇw Folklore, such as tales, songs and riddles, in the RECORD.

I have also ready for publication an Ethnological sketch of these people, a collection of their tales, songs and riddles in the original, with translations, a full grammar and vocabulary, and colloquial phrases, in fact an Urâṇw Chrestomathy. If the means are forthcoming, they can be brought out almost directly; as it is, I have exhausted my resources in collecting the materials. If they are to be made known to the literary world, I am compelled to appeal for assistance to those wealthier than I am.

I have materials, too, relating to the *Bihârî dialect* as spoken by the Urâṇws. They are bilingual in Chuṭiá Nagpur; and I intend to bring these out as soon as I have finished working up the Urâṇw papers.

I have also materials relating to the Ethnology and Philology of the *Kolarian* tribes of Central India. These are not quite so forward as my Urâṇw and Bihârî studies, but I hope in the course of another year or two to prepare these also for the press.

My object in going so far afield has been to endeavour to trace out the Non-Aryan elements in the Aryan languages of India. Sanskrit scholars have approached this question from a Sanskrit point of view. Dravidian, or rather Scythian scholars, have looked at it from a Dravidian or Scythian point of view, and there may be those who would approach it from a Thibetan or Kolarian.

For I cannot help thinking that just as there are traces of Welsh in our English language and English dialects, so there must be some traces of Non-Aryan words and idioms in the Sanskritic and Prakritic dialects of their Aryan conquerors. These traces may be slight, and may not be found in Vedic Sanskrit, but surely some of the words of every-day life and some of the turns of speech that are common to the Brahmin and the Sudra which are found in the Prakrits and Neo-Aryan Vernaculars may have been taken from Non-Aryan sources.

In conclusion I should like to mention that in studying these languages and in taking notes on the traditions, habits, customs, and characteristics of these people, I have had extraordinary opportunities and facilities, for I have lived during the past nine years in the closest daily personal and home intercourse with them. I shall be glad to receive help and advice from those who are in a position to give them, and in return I would give them any information I may be able with regard to the Ethnology and Philology of the Northern Dravidian and Kolarian races.

HUGH RAYNBIRD.

*Hackwood, Basingstoke.*

---

## Ferishta in Bijapur.

Genius belongs to no country, and Bijapur may fairly claim Ferishta as the greatest of her sons. For though he was a Persian from the shores of the Caspian, he and his work are essentially creations of the Deccan. Born at Astrabad, he was twelve years of age when he reached Ahmednagar. His father was Persian tutor to the young Prince, and died there. He was in his twentieth year when he arrived at Bijapur.

> " Thebes did his green unknowing youth engage.
> He chooses Athens for his riper age."

It was in Bijapur that he wrote his history and spent the remainder of his days. Here for the first time on the palmy plains of India the Muse of History sat down, pen in hand, and the everlasting tablet on her knee. There had been histories before in these parts, but we may say of them—

> " Ships were drifting with dead
> To shores where all was dumb."

Ferishta wrote his history during the most flourishing period of Bijapur, and it was fortunate that Ibrahim Adil Shah II., he who sleeps under the majestic mausoleum of the Roza, was his patron. He told him to write without fear or flattery, and he has done so:

which cannot be said of our own great writers during either Elizabeth or James I. Witness their sycophantic dedications.

He was engaged twenty years on the work, and General Briggs a similar period on the English translation, which was published in 1829. During these sixty years enormous advances have been made in the science of Indian history. Moreover, there are many names of places in Ferishta that require verification, others are little known, and of some the locality is vague, and not seldom incapable of identification by the reader. Let him turn up Hunter. He will do so, often without the least assistance, and sometimes with names of considerable importance. What we now want (the book being now scarce and costly) is an annotated edition abreast of the age. If Dr. Burgess in his learned leisure could now be persuaded to do this, his knowledge of Indian topography and Indian mediæval history would supply the desideratum : and we believe that he could be persuaded.

When Ferishta left Ahmednagar in 1589, he was a very young man ; but he had seen a great deal more than most men see in a lifetime. They had in fact been making history for him in that capital, and he had ample opportunity of seeing everything, as he was Captain of the Palace Guard. For some years the gigantic shadow of Akbar had fallen on the Deccan kingdoms, and sooner or later (the sooner the better) they were all to go to the wall. Nagar's turn came first. But long before this came about the ground was ploughed up by intestine divisions. One claimant to the throne sought protection under Akbar, two lay captives in the Fort of Loghur, while a madman known in history as *Diwana* was put to death by his own son—the son, *i.e.* the next King, in his turn was executed by the people, the youth having already extinguished most of the aspirants to the throne by murdering fifteen Princes of the blood in one day.

These are some of the tableaux in this Witches' Dance of Ahmednagar, the gates of which were burned down and the ashes once so red-hot that people could not go out or in ; with of course the usual revolutionary cordon of bluelights and fireworks —heads hoisted on poles—ditch filled with dead bodies —prime minister on an ass with his face to the tail. This was the work that was going on in Nagar (1588) when Ferishta was there, but he does not speak much about it—merely dovetails those events with which he had the deepest concern into a few pages of his history, and, like a man who has been in the horrors of shipwreck or the carnage of battle, does not care to speak about it. John Knox does very much the same in his History of the Reformation. When Ferishta

therefore left Ahmednagar for Bijapur in 1589, you may believe it was not with a heavy heart, but rather with a feeling of relief, when he turned round and saw the last of the capital of the Bahmanis and Nizam Shaha.

He had no doubt had his amusements there like other young men. There was chess in the Garden of Eden, the so-called eighth Paradise. There were single stick and wrestling in the palace courtyard, and duels in galore in these palmy days of single combat. Often he had watched nobles, princes, philosophers and divines measuring their strength and dexterity, and seen some of them carried dead from the maidan. Chowgan may have been played —polo, though Poona was non-existent. One of the early Kings of Delhi lost his life by a fall in the game of chowgan. And some Tora Bibi (ah! these Tora Bibis somehow come to influence a man in the turning point of his existence) who knows, maid of Chand Sultana, perhaps her whose tomb we see to-day, or otherwise, may have made an inroad on his affections. He must, however, bid good-bye to them all : so past the Black Mosque, past the Farah Bag Palace with its lakes and singing-birds, across the Sina where he remembers, for he has noted it, the great flood (1562) which rolled away to destruction 25,000 men from the camp of the Bijapur General. With one last look at Salabat Khan's tomb, perched on its lofty eminence, he bids a final adieu to Ahmednagar and all its interests, and hurries his steed to the new world that lies before him. A day or two would bring him to Bijapur.

The Bijapur which we see to-day is not the Bijapur which Ferishta saw in 1589, exactly three hundred years ago. We now see its ghost. But from the Palace of the Seven Stories we can see the ground he often travelled over and the place he made his home. That great street nearly three miles in length, which bisects the city now crowded on either side with the ruins of tomb, mosque or mahal, was then alive with thousands of people. We are not left in doubt on this point, for we have an exact description (Assad Beg, 1604) by one whom Ferishta knew, for he travelled with him that year to Berhampore. The bazaar which lined this great street was filled with shops, brimful of every commodity that the East and the then West could furnish. Cairo or Damascus to-day may exhibit its counterpart, but not its extent. All the luxuries and necessities which the ingenuity of man could devise—crystal goblets, porcelain vases, gold and silver ornaments, rare essences and perfumes, double-distilled spirits from Dabul or Goa, tobacco also and the finest wines from Portugal, with groups of pleasure-seekers, fair-faced choristers and dancing-girls : everything to fill with wonder the stranger from distant provinces. As he passed the great suburbs of Sahapur and Torvi, now a white heap of ruins, he saw indications of what awaited him in the palaces of the nobles and the garden houses of the rich, embowered in greenery, flowers of every hue and creepers trailing up to lattice and jalousie, with bubbling springs of water, fountains and streams which transported his mind to the Koran Paradise and the Garden of God.

The Ibrahim Roza which we see to-day, battered with age, the elements and Aurungzebe's cannon, had then the appearance of a forest of bamboos, covered here and there by tattered screens to hide the workman from the heat and his mason craft from the public gaze. Amid piles of timber and masses of stone, hewn and unhewn, the design of the architect was dimly creeping out, and through the network the skeletons of a half-finished minaret, or bulbous dome that was to be, projected their outlines. But the din was overpowering from hammer, anvil and bellows, and the work was never to cease day or night for the next twenty years ; 5000 men were engaged on it when Ferishta entered the city of Bijapur. He saw the Jama Mosque, and was doubtless at the earliest opportunity among its 5000 worshippers who bent the knee to the one God ; and he was in Bijapur when the two hairs of the Prophet (he does not say of his beard) arrived from Mecca. He saw the lovely Mehtar Mehal spick and span, not one cornice or frieze abraded, not one line blurred or effaced, a perfect gem of exquisite purity and grace. The moat in the picture in Ogilby's Atlas (1680) is full of open-mouthed crocodiles ; but he does not mention them. One building he did not and could not see, and that was the Dome of Mahmud. Mahmud succeeded Ibrahim. He could walk around Nagar in half an hour. He found half a day was too little for the circumference of Bijapur.

Ferishta in his history never falls into the extravaganza of Greeks and Indians in tracing the genealogy of his dynasties up to the gods ; a very fine thing no doubt on paper, but Moses and Mahomed herded cattle, so the progenitors of his kings are mostly mean men. The Empire of Delhi was founded by a slave, so runs the proverb, and Yoosuf Adil Shah, reputed son of Amurath II. of Constantinople, was sold as a Georgian slave before he clambered up the steps of the throne of Bijapur. Ahmed Nizam Shah, *primo huomo* of Ahmednagar, was a slave. So was Bedir. Golconda Turki in the service of Mahomed Shah Bahmaue, Goolburga's first sovereign, turned up a heap of antique golden coins (bright and shining as that treasure trove, the hoard of Indo-Scythian Kings, unearthed beyond Peshawur the other day) and is forthwith invested with the shadowy ensigns of royalty. Sometimes he tacks

on a legend as Buchanan does with his *Rex Scotorum.* " Who will buy the Kingdom of Delhi for Rs. 2000 ? (I am afraid rupees were not invented then, but never mind) shouts a Dervish from his dung-heap (1350). " I have only Rs. 1600," replied a passer-by, Bheilile Lodi, Afghan. " Shabash ! " said the Dervish. The bargain is concluded and the House of Lodi commences business. The buyer argues, if he loses the Kingdom of Delhi, he can't be far wrong, for he has secured the blessing of a holy man.

One more legend. It happened once on a time that the father of Mahmud of Ghuznee was engaged in the amusement of the chase, and he saw a doe grazing with her fawn. Spurring his horse he seized the fawn, which he could do without losing his seat, and having tied up its legs proceeded homewards. Happening to look back he observed that the doe was following him exhibiting every demonstration of affection. His soul melted within him, and he unbound the fawn and set it at liberty. The happy mother turned her face to the wilderness, but looked back again and again on the face of her benefactor. That night he had a dream, when lo, the Prophet of God, on whom be peace, appeared unto him, and spoke these words to the sleeper :—

" That generosity which you have this day shown to a distressed animal has been appreciated by God, and the Kingdom of Ghuznee is assigned to you as your reward. Let not thy power, however, undermine thy virtue, but thus continue to exercise thy benevolence towards mankind."

Europe itself has not furnished a legend more beautiful, and it will commend itself to every race and creed under the sun as long as there are hearts to beat in unison with that great Creator of whom it is said that mercy is His prevailing attribute. A legend and lesson in one.

I have read somewhere that the Deocani kings governed their subjects wisely and well. I have serious doubts about this. I don't think that the history of the world, the Twelve Cæsars excepted, furnishes so much bloodshed in the same time. Nagar, Bedir, Golconda, Bijapur had all armies disproportionate to their size. Each of them could bring out almost as many men as the British force in India (1889). Bizianagar's 800,000 men are mythical, and not bearing on the point one way or another.

No amount of reasoning will ever convince us that nations with such armaments can be either happy or comfortable. All productive labour, that is, labour to cultivate the soil or manufacture its products, was swept away, and none left but the lame, the halt and the blind, those who were under age and over age.      .

" I have come to hunt men not beasts." Goolburga

was invested with banditti, and the Shah Bahmani (1368) cleared the country of 8000 of them, and piled their heads in a ghastly pyramid outside the gates of the city. What boots it that the throne of Golconda cost four millions sterling, that Bedir had 100 dishes of gold, each to hold a roasted lamb, and 100 vessels of the superb porcelain of China; that Bijapur's Prime Minister had 250 servants, 400 horses and 200 elephants; and that the streets of Nagar on a gala day were adorned with gold and silver tissue, velvets, brocades, with other rich cloths and costly ornaments.

> "Ill fares the land to hast'ning ills a prey,
> Where wealth accumulates and men decay."

Trite but true.

Some things Ferishta knew and some things he did not and could not know. Talikoti (1565) was nearer to him than we are to the Crimean War, and when Bizianagar, that great bulwark of the Hindu world, went down with the roar of artillery, which now for the first time reverberated among the fastnesses of the Krishna, he only saw Islam triumphant. Triumphant and intolerant! Was not the power of the sword the history of Mahomedanism? But he could not know that this intolerance would subvert every kingdom in the Deccan, arm Sivaji with unconquerable strength, and create the new nation of the Mahrattas who were to water their horses in the Ganges. He was an enemy of duels, and had seen six respectable persons who had no real animosity to each other lose their lives in a few hours. The Duke under the walls of Nagar had to preach the same sermon over the bodies of two of his officers in 1803. He was a Free Trader, and were we not assured of the veracity of the translator, we might fancy that some of his sentences were written by that sturdy old radical General Briggs himself for some Anti-Corn Law Catechism. He was the declared enemy of strong drink, for the reason that when men form themselves into societies for drinking, they unbosom their secret thoughts to each other and often hazard desperate undertakings. "Shah Bahmani II. (1443) held conversation with neither Nazarenes nor Brahmins." Ferishta must have done so, or where did he get the following sentences? "Baber rendered good for evil." "There is a gratification in having it in one's power to pardon far superior to that of indulging in revenge." And again, "Clemency is a virtue that descends from God." He speaks of conduct unworthy even of Franks and Kurds. In other words:

> "For Turkish force and Latin fraud
> Will break your shield however broad."

Most notable is Ferishta's respect for women. In this he vindicates our higher human nature and gives India a place in the history of chivalry. Over all his 2000 pages there is not a single type of cruelty taken from the fair sex. None of his women are Jezebels, Messalinas or Lady Macbeths. Amid a weltering sea of blood the Deccani woman stands forth as she did in the Mutiny, a refuge for the oppressed and a consolation in the hour of need. He has only two Sultanas. Of the one, Rozeea (1236), he says, you can find no fault in her except that she was a woman, for she had every good quality of the ablest of princes. Chand Sultana (1599) he has placed on a pedestal among the "immortals" side by side with Joan of Arc. He describes her "in armour, a veil on her face and a naked sword in her hand." That veil has now been gently removed and reveals to us blue or grey eyes, and a thin aquiline nose. Her face was fair, but her character was fairer; her form was light and graceful, but she was of womanly resolution and had the soul of a heroine: and the pedestal on which she stands is a bastion of Ahmednagar. A fell woman is this "Noble Queen."

In the year 1601 the Emperor Akbar set his heart on a great marriage, no less than that of Prince Dauiyal, his youngest son, Viceroy of Birar, to Zohra Begum Sultana, daughter of Ibrahim Adil Shah II., he of Roza celebrity. The Prince was dissipated. Of Zohra little is known, but I shall always believe, until I am corrected, that the suburb of Zohrapore, outside the Fatke Gate and near the tomb of her father, preserves her name. Her body lies in the vault of Ibrahim Roza. (*Cousens' Bijapur*, 1889.) The first overtures must have come from Akbar. The political reasons are obvious, and so the betrothal took place and Mir Jamal-ud-din Hosein was sent from Agra to bring the bride home. But Zohra did not like the man—positively disliked him, though he was an Emperor's son. He was a drunkard, and no woman in her right senses will marry a drunkard.

So Zohra took to her devotions and embroidery, resolved not to marry the man, or to have anything to do with him. Every art was no doubt plied, but all was of no avail. Jamal, who had £100,000 a year from their Majesties of Golconda and Bijapur, kicked his heels, and her father beseeched, but she was as hard as the nether millstone. They then thought that time would come to their aid and mitigate the dislike. Time did nothing of the sort. But Burns for the nonce:—

> "Time but the impression deeper makes,
> As streams their channels deeper wear."

And the impression, as I have said, was most unfavourable. So 1601-2-3 and 4 passed. Akbar at first fretted and fumed and laid the blame on Jamal. It was all very well for him with his ten lakhs a year. He would stay as long as he could. He sent for Assad Beg and swore a great oath, the exact words of which were that "By God's will I will send some one to bring him back with dishonour, and he will see what will become of himself and his children." So he sent Assad. "Bring the bride and don't remain in Bijapur more than one day." The decree was inviolable, for who can stand before the wrath of the King? and if he hadn't, I have no doubt his head would have answered for it.

So Assad went and—I can scarcely bear to write it—brought away the bride of Bijapur. Their first halting-place was on the Bhima. I dare say you know the place, the ferry on the old road to Sholapore: it was the frontier of the kingdom to which Zohra was now to bid adieu. Ferishta was in the cavalcade—what part he played in the episode I am about to relate I know not. He is a dark horse, for it is not to him that we are indebted for this account, but to Assad Beg. I wish that Ferishta had told us all about it, for it would have been ten times more interesting than these wretched Bahmani Kings. They halted, as I have said before, on the Bhima, and I am sure the bride wished herself sewn in a sack and thrown into the Bhima anywhere—anywhere out of the world rather than proceed to the dismal Daniyal at Burhanpore. Here she was, however, on the threshold of the unknown, with a dark and stormy water before her. What strong crying and tears came from that curtained couch and scarlet palanquin I know not; but I know that there were black and lurid clouds when the sun went down that night, and the wind began to rise and catch up the sand in eddying columns, spinning them away to the dusky horizon, and little waves began to plash and moan through the seething reeds which quivered in the wind like her own forlorn hopes on the margin of the Bhima. A great storm arose: it blew down the tents and scattered the bride's trousseau to the winds; and when the morning dawned, the bird had flown. What did she care about the throne of the Great Moghuls?

But she was brought back, I am sorry to write it, "in great shame." The story is soon told—on to Nagar and Prince Daniyal: on to Mungi Peyton, on the Godavery, which you may see on the map, where the marriage took place: on to Burhanpore, the seat of the Prince's Government (still accompanied by Farishta), to drink and doom.

"Tak awa your bluidy bridegroom," was the bitter cry of Lucy Ashton, the Bride of Lammermoor—which Death did to Zohra's infinite relief, April, 1605. Akbar died in October: and you now know the reason why.　　　　　　　　　　　　　J. D.

[From the Pioneer.]

---

# Archaeological Discoveries in Madras.

Mr. A. Rea, M.R.A.S., First Assistant to the Director-General, Archæological Survey of India, has submitted a report concerning his Archæological discoveries in the Kistna District in December and January. A few of his more interesting remarks are given below:—

## A TRADITIONAL DUTCH COLONY.

About a mile south by east of Juvaladinne, a quarter of a mile distant from the coast line, and on the south of a salt marsh once traditionally a natural harbour, or arm of the sea, is an extensive mound. It rises with a somewhat steep slope to a height of about 15 feet direct from the edge of the waterline of the marsh. The top of the mound is nearly level; and forms almost a square, with sides of about 69 yards in length. The angles are rounded off and stand north and south, east and west, with the sides on the intermediate points of the compass. Broken bricks are strewn over the surface of the north-west side, which has less drift sand than the others. Beyond this mound to the south, the ground is broken by a number of smaller ones now covered by sand. The large mound is supposed to be the site of a fort, and is named Gudikurtikota; it is also known after the European settlers whom local tradition states to have built it, as Uland or Wallandula kota, that is, the "Fort of the Hollanders." The Dutch had early settlements at various parts of the coast—at Pulicat, for example, where the remains of a fort and numbers of tombs still exist to testify to their presence. There they had a mint where gold was coined. They are also said to have founded the first fort at Masulipatam under the kings of Golconda in the beginning of the 17th century. Numbers of inscribed tombstones of that date still exist there. These seem to resemble those of Pulicat, for they have each a coat-of-arms and inscriptions, all executed with considerable skill. I find, too, that the site in Masulipatam, where the Dutch had their villa residences, is still known as Vallandupalem. If a European Dutch colony has really existed near Juvaladinne, which seems probable, it may have been in conjunction with an earlier native one. It would be a convenient site for carrying on an inland trade with the town of Nellore. At Franguladinne, Buddhist stupas and other interesting remains of the same period were lately discovered on ground adjacent to the mound on which had been the European colony. The tradition, therefore, as to the Dutch fort near Juvaladinne, there is reason to believe, may be trustworthy. It is another discovered example of these numerous and hitherto unknown sites of ancient cities or seaports which in early times flourished all along this part of the coast. They show that a very extensive trade must have been carried on, but through the civil wars which desolated the country, they had fallen to mere fishing villages. The recession of the sea left them further and further inland, leaving their natural harbours but mere marshes : their *raison d'être* had thus gone. The trade never revived, and all that remains to prove what has been, is only shown by the ruins now covered by mounds.

### DISCOVERY OF STUPA, NO. 3, PEDDA GANJAM.

The discovery of these remains was first announced in December, 1888. It forms the third of this class of Buddhist relics found at the Franguladinne mounds. If not extensive, and with but little of it remaining, it shows some interesting features, and is important in helping to prove the previous existence of a large Buddhist settlement at the place. The two former stupas stand at the south-west extremity of the site, and on the west side of the canal. This is on the extreme north, or about a mile distant, and on the east bank of the canal. It is hardly to be expected that any remains will be found in this locality in a very complete condition : the mounds are all low, and the walls are easily got at. In addition, they seem to have suffered at the hands of some former iconoclasts, or through some great catastrophe, or inundation. A small mound about 50 feet in diameter by 4 feet high, surrounded by others, to all appearances the same, had bricks and some chips of white marble strewn over its surface. A close examination showed at one point four or five bricks, lately uncovered by the rain, evidently laid so as to form part of a circular wall. A trench dug in front of these showed at least eight courses of brickwork standing on a foundation of blocks of stones. This was traced out for over a quarter of a circle with an exterior diameter of 32 feet ; it also exposed two projecting facets, each of a length of 9 feet 6 inches, on the north and east faces of the circle. The most interesting feature was revealed by the shaft sunk in the centre. It showed a rectangular pit, 10 feet 6 inches by 8 feet, with vertical sides, which had originally been dug in the clay and closely packed with stones and earth. On the removal of the stones, and at a depth of 2 feet 6 inches from the surface, was a series of large bricks. Below was a large svastika formed of eight bricks ; four radiate at right angles from the centre, while other four lie at right angles to their extremities. On the top of the east arm of this figure was a smaller one of four bricks, each pointing to the right and laid with its end against the side of another. All the bricks fitted together in the centre ; it had no arms at the extremities. On the top of this was a square of four bricks. The large under bricks measure 19in. by 9in. by 3½in. Curiously, the objects lay facing different points of the compass ; the lower one at one point west of

north and the two upper at one point east of north. It will be remembered that in stupa No. 1, at Pedda Ganjam (Bogandanidibha), two large svastikas were found in the centre, but the one not lying directly on the top of the other, a packing of stones being between the two. In that case they also lay with two points of difference, so the coincidence can scarcely be said to be accidental. In the present case a few bricks lie in a line along the north, east, and south sides of the pit at a level with the lower svastika. It would be interesting to know whether this feature is peculiar to this locality only. It is unlikely that it would be so, and it may occur elsewhere ; though it probably was only used in certain classes of stupas, else we might have heard of it before. No relic casket was found, and none could have existed, and been subsequently removed, for the topstone-packing appeared as if it had never been disturbed. In one of the bricks of the small central square a bone—evidently human—is embedded in the material. It was in a crumbling condition. This bone may have been the sarira or relic of the holy man deposited in its proper place, but without an enclosing box.

### NOTES ON THE SCULPTURED SLABS.

The following are the white marble sculptures now found :—This panel is in two pieces, with the top broken off and lost. The principal figure is a seated Buddha ; the head has been broken, but the rest of the figure is complete. His right hand is raised in benediction, and he sits with the left folded across the body, the folds of his robe hanging over his elbow. He is seated on a cushioned throne, with two attendant fan-bearers standing on his left. Similar figures would be on the right, but this is broken away. Directly under his seat are four grotesque bhutas or dwarfs ; two below support other two who climb up the front of the throne. The left under one has what appears to be a torch in his hand, and holds it up to the two others above. His breasts are made so as to form two eyes, and a nose is represented as a projection extending from the middle of his chest down to his navel. The whole front of his body thus has the appearance of a large face supported on two short legs, giving it a most grotesque appearance. The right dwarf looks up shading his eyes with his left hand, while his right holds a ball. The right upper dwarf has a club in his hands, and attempts to climb up the front of Buddha's throne. The other dwarf, again, crawls upon the other's back, and supports himself by grasping his neck-band with the right hand, and seizing the back lock of hair in his teeth. It would be interesting to learn to what race these pigmies belonged ; they cannot have been Buddhists, from the hostile attitude they are always shown as bearing towards the author of the religion. They may possibly be fanciful representations of the demons of darkness. But the offering-bearing attendants are also usually dwarfs of a somewhat negro type; they may be a race who, without adopting the religion, were brought into subjection by the Buddhists. Or is it possible that the idea may have been taken from the Greeks, who represented similar large-headed, short-legged, fighting dwarfs on their vases? This may have been so, as the Buddhists undoubtedly owe the origin of some of their finest art, if not to Greek sculptors themselves, at least to their direct influence. On each outer side of these dwarfs are two jewelled women, standing with their arms around each other's necks. The peculiarities of dress worn by the different figures merit attention. The two on each side of Buddha are males; one carrying a long-bow. They wear a waist-cloth with robes flowing down, and partly covering the lower limbs; they have bangles on the wrists and over the elbows. The two women standing on each side of the throne are in each case differently dressed. On both sides, the female standing on the right has a long robe, girt at the waist with a belt, and flowing down and covering the limbs to the ankles. They wear a peculiar high head-dress. A number of thin bangles encircle the wrists and the arm above the elbow; a double bracelet is round the neck; and a long thread passes over the left shoulder, behind the waist belt and down round the right ankle. The two wearing this form of dress probably represent married ladies. The other two females standing on the left of the others may represent

AN ANCIENT SACRED TREE (ADANSONIA DIGITATA).

At Chezala, standing in a line with, and south from the chaitya, inside the outer court, is a large tree which, having a hollow core, is popularly stated to grow from out of a subterranean cave. It is known as Peruleni pedda manu, the nameless great tree. Around the base is a platform 25 feet by 22 feet 6 inches and 3 feet high. The circumference of the trunk at that height is 58 feet 6 inches. The first branches are 9 feet 6 inches from the ground, and there the girth is 56 feet. The spread of the foliage is 78 feet across, and the height of the tree is about 87 feet. It has large five to seven-lobed leaves: large flowers; and seed in a hard woolly pad. It must be of great age.

TRACES OF THE ANCIENT MANUFACTURE OF STEEL.

At Chezala, between the Kapoteswara temple and the west tank, are some large and ancient heaps of *débris* from the smelting of iron ore. No such industry is carried on in the village nowadays, nor even has been in recent times; but a local tradition states that in ancient days an extensive manufacture of steel was

carried on here, the ore being brought from the hill of Guttikonda in the Dachipalie taluk. India was anciently famous for its steel, blades of high temper and quality being in great repute. The manufacture reached a high state of perfection before the Christian era. Though this industry has undoubtedly been carried on here, it would be hazardous to assert that it might have flourished at so early a date as that: there are no visible proofs present to fix even its approximate date.

BURIAL CUSTOMS.

In the burial-grounds on the east side of the village of Chezala are some modern kistvaens which have been erected by certain of the castes to cover the remains of the dead. Though these differ considerably from the megaliths—of the pre-historic tribes—which exist all over the country, they are nevertheless interesting in showing that the custom is not yet extinct, but is still practised by some and probably always has been from pre-historic times. The custom had at one time been a general one in use by all the tribes scattered over the country, and though it had fallen into disuse by other sections of the people, it has survived here, probably through the facility with which the people can procure suitable slabs of pavement from the adjoining quarries. This would seem to have been the case, for even here, members of the castes—which use these kistvaens—when they cannot afford them, dispense with their use altogether. It does not, therefore, seem to be a matter of caste necessity, though they have a preference for its use when possible, and were stone unavailable, it would probably fall into disuse completely, even the tradition of its having been so used would disappear, as it has done elsewhere. A consideration of this circumstance might go to prove that at different periods in early times a considerable migration of the original people, who used this mode of burial, had taken place; and that they must have come from hilly tracts where stone was plentiful and easily obtained. When they settled in their new habitation on the plains, they would take their customs with them, and this special one they would, for a time, continue to practise, even in spite of the difficulties attendant on procuring stone slabs of suitable size. These difficulties would in time gradually force themselves upon the people, till the custom fell into disuse: and this neglect would in time permeate even the tribes who dwelt nearer the hills; till it disappeared altogether. The custom which supplanted the use of megaliths was probably that of placing the remains in earthenware sarcophagi. The intermediate or transition stage would be shown when these two occur simultaneously, or when the earthen sarcophagus was placed inside a kistvaen. The latter stage would be reached when the earthenware grave stood apart and free of any such enclosure. Even this latterly fell into desuetude, probably through some sufficient cause, though we cannot at present say what it may have been. The remains were then simply placed in the earth without any enclosure whatever, as is that in general modern use. In the custom which prevails here, the body is laid horizontally in a shallow grave, the earth is heaped over it in a long narrow mound, and these kistvaens are then placed over it. They do not approach a square, as in the ancient examples, but bear a proportion to the size of the body. At the head and feet are small upright slabs about two feet broad. Long slabs are placed upright at the sides, and another of sufficient length and breadth to cover these four upright stones is laid on the top. In some instances a separate stone is placed upright at the head of the grave. Their use thus seems primarily to be to protect the mound, and prevent its being washed down by the weather. Another important purpose these kistvaens would serve, and probably one of the first considerations which influenced their adoption would be—in a time when they were more numerous than they even are now—to protect the remains from the ravages of wild beasts. Those who still practise this mode of burial are Vaishnavas of the following castes : the Gentuous or Balingallu, here known as Telakallu (cultivators) ; Sukalavallu (dhobies or washermen ; by the Sathani) (or Sudra priest for the Vaishnavas) ; Salavallu (weavers or workers in cloth) ; and the Pariahs, Saivites of the same castes, burn their dead. This is curiously the reverse of the custom peculiar to the sects further south, where the Saivites bury and the Vaishnavas burn. With the Saivites here, a shallow grave is also dug, and after the remains are placed therein, bushes are cut on the spot, and heaped over the body. Large stones are then thrown over this and the pile is lighted in the evening. When everything is consumed the earth is heaped over. The absence of Kistvaens in these cases seems to be simply that no purpose would be served by their use. With the others, of course, the case is different. In the casting of stones over the layer of bushes, we probably have a simple explanation of the presence of such in some of the pre-historic graves at Pallavaram and other places lately examined. In these particular cases, cremation may have been practised, and the small holes which were seen in some of the pyriform tombs may have been to facilitate the burning. In the village, all Brahmins, both Vaishnava and Saivite, practise cremation. Some years ago a carpenter fell over the rocks on the west side of the Devarakonda hill, and was killed. He was buried where he fell, and a cairn of stones heaped over the grave. An upright stone post with a nandi on the

top, and an inscription recording his name and the year of his death, was placed to mark the spot. The fact of his remains not being removed to the ordinary burial-place in the village seems to have been through a superstition held regarding the nature of the fatality, and the sacredness of the hill, the scene of the sacrifice, as related in the Sthala Purana, of two devotees of Siva.

LEGEND OF THE STHALA PURANA.

(An adapted Buddhist Jataka.)

The legend of the origin of the temples at Chezala, as narrated by a Brahmin of the village, is as follows. The story is a version of one of the Buddhist Jatakas :— In Cashmere, one of the largest and richest of the 56 kingdoms of India, a king named Sivichakravarti, son of Mandata, and grandson of Yayatimaharaja (see the Aranyaparva of the Mahabharata), reigned peacefully and justly during his long period of years. He had two brothers—named Mahadambara and Jimutavahana. One day Mahadambara asked his brother Sivi to permit his going on a pilgrimage to all the sacred shrines and rivers in Southern India. The king was much pleased with the request, and ordered his prime minister to make all the necessary arrangements for his brother's journey, and at the same time directed 1500 people to accompany him. The prime minister did accordingly, and Mahadambara started immediately with the escort given by his brother the king. He visited a number of holy shrines and rivers, and at last came to a place named Cherum Cherla, where many Yogis were doing penance in the caves of Devarakonda (a hill now also named Mehalamallayakonda). He went and conversed with the Yogis for some days. By so doing, he suddenly lost all interest in worldly affairs, joined the Rishis, and began penance along with the others. Some days after he died, and his body was buried on the summit of the hill. Through the power of his penance, it assumed the form of a Linga. The people who saw this built a temple over the Linga, and named it Mahadambareswara. The followers of the prince, who had been ordered to return to Cashmere, went their way and told everything to king Sivi, who, up to this, had been expecting his brother's return. After hearing these things the king grieved for his brother Mahadambara, and after consulting with his younger brother Jimutavahana, that prince promised to bring the missing brother, and started with an escort of the same number of followers. After spending many days on the way, he reached Cherla, where he made inquiry for his brother. When he came to understand that Mahadambara had lost his life, and had been transformed into a Linga, he determined to do the same ; he dismissed his escort and sat as a Yogi on the same hill. His penance exceeded in severity that of his brother, for which his body soon attained Kailasa. On the return of the followers to Cashmere, they informed King Sivi what Jimutavahana had done, and that they had not seen the other brother Mahadambara there. The king, who had grieved about the first brother, now fell into deep sorrow over the fate of the other, and calling his Prime Minister, handed him his ring. The Prime Minister received it, and was instructed that he should carefully govern the kingdom for some months, as the king wished to visit the place where his two brothers had gone. So the king immediately started with 1,000,001 people, and making some haltings by the way, at last reached Cherum Cherla. On learning of the deification of his two brothers, and seeing the Linga of the former, Sivi determined to perform 100 yahas because of the holiness of the place. He made all ready and selected a place for yahasala by the side of a water-channel, near to the great tree. He completed 99 yahas, and began the performance of the last. On completing 100 yahas, the merit would be the attaining of the realm of Brahma. But this deity and other devas conferred with Siva and Vishnu to interrupt the last yaha of Sivi, so that it might be rendered ineffectual, if he did not stand the test they proposed to impose. The three therefore—Brahma, Rudra and Vishnu—descended to Buloka, at a spot now named Rupanaguntla (rupu, sight). The place was thus named through the Trimurti here making themselves visible to the sight of mortals. They then stepped over to Kandlagunta, from whence they looked for Sivi (kandlu, looking). After leaving this place, they halted at Vipparlanagari, and there transformed themselves,—Siva as a hunter, Brahma as an arrow, and Vishnu as a bird (kapota-pakshi). The hunter with his arrow then ran and jumped about, affecting a desire to shoot the bird at a place named Kunkulagunta (kunkal, jumping about). Then the hunter followed the bird to where Sivi was engaged in his yaha. The bird flew rapidly and alighted on Sivi's hand, making signs that it wished protection. Shortly after, the hunter appeared before Sivi, who had the bird in his bosom, and spoke thus : "My Lord, I am a hunter who live on the flesh of birds and animals ; this bird that you now hold in your bosom I have pursued from early morning, but it escaped me. I am hungry and thirsty, so in justice give it to me, so that I may kill and eat it." Sivi replied that it was not justice to deliver over the bird when it had fled to him for protection, but promised instead to give whatever the hunter wished, land, gold or wealth, anything but the bird. The hunter would have none of these, but only demanded the bird's flesh to appease hunger. Then Sivi said he would give of his own

flesh a weight equal to that of the bird's. To this the hunter agreed, and Sivi placed the bird on one scale. With his own hands he tore of portions of his body, and placed them in the other scale ; but by the power of the Trimurti, they did not balance the weight of the bird. On seeing this, King Sivi procured a Gandakattari (long shears) and cut his body in two pieces, and had one-half placed on the scales. Immediately the Trimurti—Brahma, Rudra, and Vishnu —assumed their real shapes and appeared before Sivi ; and Siva addressed him thus : "My dear believer, I am much pleased with your yahas, and sacrifice for the sake of the bird, ask whatever you wish, I will make your body more beautiful than before, and you may be a king of kings." King Sivi, overjoyed, replied thus : "O Paramesvara, Parvatisameda, Annadarat-shaka, O Patbunta, Sri Mahadeva, I want nothing but this which you might vouchsafe me. I want no kingdom such as I enjoyed in my worldliness. I desire only the bliss of Kailasa for myself and the 1,000,001 people who followed me here ; and that all our bodies should be transformed into Lingas to remain for ever in the boundaries of Cherum Cherla." Siva immediately granted these requests. Sivi and his followers attained Kailasa, and their bodies were transformed into Lingas. The Brahmans at once erected a temple over and named Sivi's linga Kapotas-vara, as he gave up his life for a Kapotapakshi.

In support of the legend the Brahmans point to the white marble linga which has two large holes on the top, and small marks round the sides. One of the holes is said to hold but one pot of water ; while the other, which represents Sivi's throat, can receive numberless pots. The small marks on the sides are the scratches made by Sivi's nails when he tore the flesh from his body. The story not only occurs in the Mahabharata, but also in the Buddhist Jatakas, where the king's sacrifice was made to save the life of a hunted pigeon. The connection of the legend with the place may be very ancient, and probably originated during the Buddhist occupation. The Hindoos having a similar story, adopted it, using their own version with their own deities as the principal actors to the exclusion of the Buddhist characters who had figured in the tale. It is doubly interesting when we consider that it was also a Buddhist legend, and, taken in conjunction with the ' discovery of Buddhist remains, may be looked on as additional proof of the identity of the shrine. The legend, as related, has, therefore, been given in full.—From the *Times of India*, June 11.

---

## A Coincident Idiom.

Ibn Batuta notes a peculiar conversational idiom of the people of Kalhát in Oman, the Calaiate of the old Portuguese writers on the Indies.

"Although they are Arabs," says the Moor, " they

don't speak correctly. After every phrase they have a habit of adding the particle *no*. Thus they will say: 'You are eating,—no?' 'You are walking,—no?' 'You are doing this or that,—no?'" (*Ibn Batuta.* French ed. II. 226).

This idiom is partially represented by the French '*n'est-ce pas ?*' or the German '*Nicht wahr ?*' But we find it re-appear much more closely in some parts of Scotland. Thus in a very clever volume of sketches of Scotch rustic life in Ayrshire, lately published by Mr. D. Douglas, of Edinburgh,* the idiom recurs precisely in the Kalhát form, though it may be doubted, from the mode of printing, whether the author himself quite sees the nature of the said idiom.

So, one of the characters, speaking of a deceased person believed to have left wealth, says : "'I'm supposing there'll be three, or maybe four thousand, when a's dune.'

'I would na be surprised,' remarked Robert dryly.

'Eh, but that's a large sum na'." (This should be printed 'a large sum,—na ?').—p. 74.

Again, speaking of the death of a neighbour, Peter Shule the *betheral* (i.e. sexton) says :

"'What would be the matter, na ?'" And then referring to an alleged omen afforded by a cock crowing unseasonably, the same person says : "'It's by ordinar' (i.e. quite extraordinary) 'what's revealed to bruit beasts. That cock would ken fine, na (?)' said Peter meditatively."—pp. 228, 229.

20, 6, 89.                    H. YULE, Col.

---

## The "Krakatoa Eruption" and the Javanese Chronicles.

At page 7 of that magnificent book, "The Eruption of Krakatoa," published for the Royal Society last year by Messrs. Trübner and Co., Professor Judd—one of the authorities on "Volcanoes"—says :

"At some unknown period this volcano became the scene of an eruption, or series of eruptions, which, judging from the effects they have produced, must have been on even a far grander scale than that which four years ago attracted so much interest."

In a Javanese book called "Pustaka Raja," the "Book of Kings," containing the Chronicles of the Island, 'kept secret during centuries in the Royal Archives, and only recently made public, we find the following interesting and curious account of an eruption of the mountain Kapi :

"In the year 338 Saka [i.e. A.D. 416], a thundering noise was heard from the mountain Batuwara,† which

was answered by a similar noise coming from the mountain Kapi, lying westward of the modern Bantam. A great glaring fire, which reached to the sky, came out of the last-named mountain ; the whole world was greatly shaken, and violent thundering, accompanied by heavy rains and storms, took place ; but not only did not this heavy rain extinguish the eruption of fire of the mountain Kapi, but it augmented the fire ; the noise was fearful, at last the mountain Kapi with a tremendous roar burst into pieces and sunk into the deepest of the earth. The water of the sea rose and inundated the land. The country to the east of the mountain Batuwara, to the mountain Kamula,* and westward to the mountain Raja Basa,† was inundated by the sea; the inhabitants of the northern part of the Sunda country to the mountain Raja Basa were drowned and swept away with all their property.

"After the water subsided the mountain Kapi and the surrounding land became sea and the Island of Java‡ divided into two parts.

"The city of Samaskuta, which was situate in the interior of Sumatra, became sea, the water of which was very clear, and which was afterwards called the lake Sinkara.§ This is the origin of the separation of Sumatra and Java."

---

## New Books.

*A Chinese Manual,* containing a Condensed Grammar with Idiomatic Phrases and Dialogues. By R. K. Douglas. (W. H. Allen.)

Professor Douglas has by this publication supplied a real want, and he has done his work in a masterly manner and to the purpose. This country having, through the annexation of Upper Burma, been brought into neighbourly contact with China, the necessity for the study of Chinese on the part of civilians and military men employed in the frontier districts was brought nearer home than it had been heretofore. Messrs. Allen & Co. have been first in the field in arranging for, and bringing out, a good practical manual for the use of students of Chinese, and they have earned the thanks of the public for their spirited enterprise. The author has judiciously chosen the Mandarin form of Chinese, which is the medium of intercommunication of educated natives throughout the empire, and is also spoken in its Western and South-Western provinces : and he has adopted, with a few slight modifications, Sir T. Wade's mode of transcription, who is the recognized authority in this country

---

* Chronicles of Glenbuckie, by Henry Johnston.

† Now called Pulosari, one of the extinct volcanoes in Bantam, and the nearest to the Straits of Sunda.

* Now called the "Gedé" mountain.

† The most southern volcano of Sumatra, and situate in the "Lampung" country.

‡ The Sanskrit *Yawa-dwipa*.

§ The well-known Lake of the "Menang-Kebo" country.

on Chinese orthography. But he has wisely broken with the tradition in making the polysyllabic nature of modern Chinese also visible to the eye in his mode of transcription, giving, *e.g.*, the word hiaughiajên, 'villager,' as one word, though it consists of three separate Chinese words. For practical purposes especially, for which this manual is mainly intended, this method is invaluable. The arrangement of the book itself leaves nothing to be desired, the so-called grammatical part taking up the smaller, the idiomatic phrases and dialogues the larger half, which is as it should be. The table of contents exhibits the natural sequence in which the various grammatical questions are treated. We cannot close this brief notice without a word of recognition of the beautiful Chinese type employed, and of the handsome style in which the book has been got up, much to the credit of the old-established printing firm of Stephen Austin and Sons, Hertford.

*Anglicised Colloquial Burmese*, or, How to Speak the Language in Three Months. By Lieut. F. A. L. Davidson. (W. H. Allen & Co.)

A good Burmese grammar has long been one of the chief *desiderata* of the candidates for the Indian Civil Service, and the demand has increased since, in consequence of the annexation of Upper Burma, an additional staff of civilians and military officers has been required. There have been reprints, and a French translation, of Judson's somewhat meagre outline of Burmese grammar, and two improved editions of his dictionary have appeared as a stop-gap for a more comprehensive work which is much needed. Latter's and Chase's useful manuals are out of print; the latter especially, pre-eminently practical, would have been well worth a somewhat improved re-issue. In the mean time a scientific grammar of the language was promised us from Burma, but the promise has not yet been made good. Under these circumstances, we were justified in the eager expectation with which we opened the book under notice. As it lays no claim to scientific treatment, being intended only for non-commissioned officers and soldiers, our task is limited to the investigation of how far the little manual fulfils its modest promise. Its arrangement—a skeleton grammar preceding a skeleton vocabulary and colloquial sentences—quite suits its purpose. It is also perfectly intelligible that the Burmese words should appear in an Anglicised, as contradistinguished to a Romanized, form. Burmese is one of those unfortunate Eastern tongues on which (as in the case of Turkish, Persian, Malay, Siamese and Tamil) an alphabet has been foisted utterly unsuited for the representation of their phonetic elements, while on the other hand it is a written and a literary language, with a spelling settled by centuries of usage. Hence, the word as spelt appears in many cases to have undergone a complete transformation when pronounced even by an educated native. The authors of previous grammars adopted a modified form of Romanisation, a sort of compromise between Romanising and Anglicising. The author of the present manual appears to have given the words simply as he heard them pronounced. So far as this agrees with the general scheme

of his book, no fault will be found with him for having done this. But then he should have been more consistent. There is, in the first place, no complete or trustworthy table of the phonetic elements of the language. Further, a word we find written one way in one place, another way in another place (*lo, low; tsai, say, say; yay, yey*). *Ai* and *ay*, etymologically quite distinct, are frequently confounded, as are also *ou* and *au*. The same word is written now *byee*, now *byĕ*, while *ĕ* now represents *t*, now *f*. Also the Burmese words are not always trustworthy; a war-boat, *e.g.* is not *hlai-yai*, but *yai-hlay*; a waterman is not *yai-thai*, but *yay-tha*. In taking down vocables from the lips of natives, one is exposed to constant pitfalls, as the slightest variation of utterance may cause a change in the spelling; and much vigilance and constant inter-comparison are required to secure uniformity, which even in a book of such modest aims is a most desirable qualification. We have no doubt, however, that in spite of the slight imperfections we have mentioned, this little manual will be found to answer its purpose, though it has but whetted our appetite for a scientific grammar. There is one other point which we would refer to before we have done. In the section on the Alphabet (pp. 97-102) we have a reproduction of the same antediluvian type which appears to have done duty since the early part of the present century. As Burmese is coming to the fore, and its language and literature are taking their places side by side with the other Indian vernaculars in the curriculum of the selected candidates, would not one of our great Oriental printers consider it worth his while to purchase a fount of representative Burmese type? or do they hope or expect that the India Council will go to that expense for them?

*K. F. H. van Langen, Handleiding voor de beoefening der Atjehsche taal.* 's Gravenhage, 1889 (xii. and 158 pages); and *Woordenboek der Atjehsche taal.* 's Gravenhage, 1889 (vi. and 238 pages).

No one who has attentively watched the stubborn resistance which the Achinese have opposed to the Dutch forces these fifteen years since Achin was occupied by the latter, can be in the least surprised at the slow progress which these have made in acquiring the vernacular of that warlike race. It is true, a few meagre vocabularies have appeared, and but last year a volume of conversations—in Dutch, Malay, and Achinese—with a brief grammatical introduction, was brought out by Major H. A. N. Catenius, by which practical requirements were served. We owe, however, to Mr. K. F. H. van Langen, a Dutch civilian for many years stationed at Oleh-Oleh, the first grammar and dictionary of the language, which, if not fulfilling all conditions as to completeness and precision, furnish at least a trustworthy foundation for more incisive grammatical studies and a more comprehensive incorporation of the lexical materials. As early as in 1882, the author contributed a brief article on the subject, entitled "Atjehsche taalstudiën," to the "Tijdschrift voor Indische taal-, land- en volkenkunde," vol. xxviii. p. 176 ff. If he has allowed seven more years to elapse before publishing the results of his linguistical researches he can certainly not be reproached with producing what was not properly matured. From the existence of a number of Sanskrit inscriptions in Achinese territory he rightly concludes that the Hindu immigration in Sumatra must have proceeded from the North-East coast of Achin. The early traces of Hindu influence in the vocabulary of the native race were subsequently more or less obliterated by the ascendency which the Islam gained. The results, however, of these extraneous influences were so different in different parts of the territory, that at present four main dialects of the language may be distinguished, of which the one spoken in the twenty-five and the twenty-six Mukims (or parishes) takes the lead. In the "Tijdschrift" of the Geographical Society of the Hague for 1888, there is a valuable article by the same author on the West Coast of Achin, in which details are given concerning the four languages spoken there in addition to the Achinese dialects, and the districts are specified in which each language prevails. (See "Afdeeling: meer uitgebreide artikelen," pp. 508-14).

The language itself, though Malayan in its whole conformation and possessing a large ingredient of Malay words, occupies an independent place of its own; it would appear to be nearer akin to the Batak than to the Malay proper. The Arabic character with which it is written seems even less adapted to it than it is to Malay. We fail to see, e.g. what force or function the purely Arabic letter 'ain has in such native words as 'óh, as far as (= Malay sampei), and 'oi, to creep. We beg leave to refer for a number of valuable philological observations on this language to a review of the two works under notice in "De Indische Gids" for June, pp. 1055-63, and would only add, with regard to the literature, that even when the Achinese power was at its height early in the seventeenth century, the Sultans caused the laws and chronicles of the country to be written in Malay, and that, if subsequently many books were written in the vernacular, most manuscripts have perished since in the fierce war with the Dutch, so that Achinese MSS. are of extremely rare occurrence. However, in the article previously referred to on the West Coast of Achin, no fewer than ten works written in Achinese are specified. The author has therefore laid the student under all the greater obligations by the selection of extracts from these Achinese works, which form the second part of his grammar. They are all (pp. 95-158) in the Arabic character, the first three also romanized, and the first five accompanied by a Dutch translation. It should also be mentioned that on Mr. van Langen's return to India, the task of carrying the grammar and dictionary through the press devolved on Dr. Wijnmalen, the learned Secretary of the Asiatic Society of The Hague, who has acquitted himself of it with his wonted scrupulous care and conscientiousness, and that both that Society and the Dutch Colonial Office deserve much credit for having subsidized both works, the production of which, at the hands of the well-known publishers Messrs. M. Nijhoff & Co., leaves nothing to be desired.

*Epigraphia Indica and Record of the Archæological Survey of India.* Edited by Jas. Burgess, Director-General of the Archæological Survey of India. Parts I.—III.

Hitherto the student of Indian inscriptions had to search for the records as yet published in the pages of various learned Periodicals of India and Europe, besides the volumes of the Archæological Survey and other independent works. The foundation of a new Quarterly exclusively devoted to Epigraphy is sure to meet with a very warm reception, therefore, on the part of all students of Indian History.

Dr. Burgess has succeeded in securing the assistance of the most competent scholars in every branch of Indian Epigraphy, and the majority of the records published in the first three parts possess an exceptional value and interest. Thus Prof. Bühler has edited and translated, among other noteworthy inscriptions, the recently discovered twelfth Edict of King Asoka according to the Shâhbâzgarhi version, and the equally new copper plate of king Harsha, which was obtained by Dr. Führer from the Collector of Azamgarh. This grant of king Harsha, together with the Sonpat seal deciphered by Mr. Fleet, is the only authentic record of one of the most eminent personages in the ancient history of India, and extremely important both as confirming the statements of Harsha's biographer Bâna, and of Hiouen Thsang, and for correcting and enlarging them. The genealogical portion of the grant under notice refers to three more predecessors of Harsha, besides those mentioned by Bâna and the Chinese traveller. The latter authority tries to make a Buddhist of Harsha; but in the grant, Harsha describes himself as a worshipper of Maheśvara or Śiva. The foot-note signed A. F. undoubtedly comes from Dr. A. Führer, who has long been engaged on a new edition of the Śrîharshacharita. It is satisfactory to know that the best MSS. of Bâna's work agree with the grant in giving Yaśomatî as the name of Prabhâkaravardhana's queen. The Central Provinces inscriptions, which have been deciphered by Prof. Kielhorn, belong to the twelfth century, and throw a great deal of new light on the history of the Chedi dynasty of Ratnapur, and of neighbouring dynasties. The Badaun inscription, edited by the same scholar, contains a list of the early rulers of that town, none of whom had been known hitherto. Prof. Kielhorn has published, moreover, no less than eight old inscriptions from Khajurâho (Kharjûravâhaka), another ancient town in the North-West Provinces, in which the rise and history of the Chandellas of Bundelkhand is recorded; and we are looking forward very much to his promised edition of the important Siyadoni inscription, to be published in Part IV. Dr. Hultzsch, of the Madras Archæological Survey, has contributed a number of difficult grants and other inscriptions from different parts of India. We are glad to learn that the same scholar's work on the inscriptions of Southern India, which is likely to prove an excellent starting-point for all future inquiries into South Indian history, is on the eve of publication. Prof. Eggeling's careful edition and translation of the interesting inscription found in a

7

well near Delhi, in which a brief abridgment of the history of that city is given, is highly welcome, although that inscription had been twice edited before. The correctness of Prof. Eggeling's proposed identification of the term pratigana with the modern parganâ 'a district,' is borne out by the fact that the same result has been arrived at, independently, by Dr. Hultzsch in his edition of that inscription (Journ. of the Germ. O. S. xl. p. 58). If possible, the number of facsimiles should be increased in the future issues of this most valuable and promising new Quarterly.

J. JOLLY.

*A Progressive Grammar of the Malayalam Language for Europeans*, by L. J. Frohnmeyer. Mangalore, 1889. (xvi. and 307 pages.)

The Malayâlma—or, as it was formerly called, the Malabar—language, which is spoken by about four millions of the inhabitants of the Malabar coast and in Travancore, is so near akin to Tamil that doubts have been expressed whether it stands to the latter in the relation of a daughter to the mother, or whether both are traceable to one common source. The former opinion was held by F. W. Ellis both in his learned "Dissertation on the Malayâlma Language" and in his "Kural" upwards of three-quarters of a century ago. The latter is the opinion of Dr. Gundert, the highest modern authority among natives as well as Europeans on the subject of Malayâlma philology. High Tamil and Malayâlma would appear to have begun differenciating at least eight or nine hundred years ago, when the pronominal verb-terminations, still traceable in the earliest Malayâlma poetry and in the old inscriptions, were gradually dropped, since which time the dialectical peculiarities have independently developed into a distinct language. It is interesting to pursue this intercomparison of the two languages in detail. In the common Malayâlma vernacular we observe that not only the characteristics of personality, number and gender have been abandoned, but that also many Old-Tamil forms, obsolete in modern Tamil, have been retained. On the other hand, the proportion of Sanskrit ingredients in Malayâlma is far greater, while in Tamil it is considerably less, than in any other Dravidian tongue. The author of the excellent manual, the title of which stands at the head of this notice, has paid special attention to this subject, and he gives numerous instances even of Sanskrit nominal and verbal inflexions which are part and parcel of the language. It was probably the frequent occurrence of such ready-made Sanskrit words in Malayâlma poetry which induced Mr. F. W. Ellis to remark that "the language of Malayâlma poetry is a mixture of Sanskrit, generally pure, with Sen and Kodun Tamil. . . . . Declined or conjugated forms from the Sanskrit are not admissible into Tamil. They are not admissible, also, in Malayâlma prose, but in verse they are often used with such profusion as to give it the appearance of that fanciful species of composition called in Sanskrit Manipravâlam, and in English 'maccaronic verse,' rather than the sober dress of grammatical language"

(Dissertation on the Malayâlma Language, pp. 21, 22). The popular songs or romances of the Malayâlees are altogether free from those excrescences of epic poetry, being composed in the ordinary dialect. There are also considerable differences between the vernacular speech of the North and that of the South. But the dialect spoken by the Mâpillas, or Muhammadans of Malabar, who have achieved a certain notoriety in the modern history of India, has been made the subject of a separate treatise by the late Dr. Burnell (Specimens of South Indian Dialects, No. 2). They have successfully adapted the Arabic character to their dialect; and a number of well-lithographed books are annually produced at their presses. It should also be mentioned that, as Dr. Burnell has shown (*l.l.* p. 11), the earliest known specimen of spoken Malayâlma, found in Varthema's travels (1506), already exhibits the language devoid of personal verb terminations as it is now. The philological treatment of the language dates from Dr. Gundert's works, whose own literary compositions in the language itself take a high rank for purity of style. His big grammar is in every way a pattern; but, being written in the vernacular, can only be of service to those already acquainted with the language. Mr. Frohnmeyer has, therefore, rendered a signal service to European students by elaborating a practical manual in which, according to a skilfully devised analytical method, all the facts of the language are stated, explained and richly illustrated by examples. These examples are chosen with a view to the practical acquisition of the vernacular and to the imparting of much useful knowledge concerning the literature, customs, habits, household occupations, etc., of the people, and the natural history and government of the country. It is one of the most practically useful grammars we have seen. Full and ample indices facilitate reference to its rich and varied contents. As for beauty of type and general correctness the book leaves nothing to be desired and reflects, as indeed do all its publications in Dravidian philology and literature, the highest credit on the Basel Mission Press, Mangalore.

*Alberuni's India. An English Edition, with Notes and Indices*, by Dr. Edward C. Sachau. London, 1888. (Vol. I. 1. and 408 pages; Vol. II. 427 pages.)

Professor Sachau's translation of Alberuni's Indica is now before us. Whoever glances, even superficially, at the contents of these two handsome volumes, cannot but feel impressed with the vast amount of honest, painstaking and unflinching labour which is represented in this translation. With a single exception— need we name Gildemeister?—there is, we are convinced, not another living Orientalist possessed of such a command of the Arabic and Sanskrit languages and literatures, as is indispensable to any one who would attempt this task, and, if there were, we doubt whether he could have accomplished it more satisfactorily. Professor Sachau gratefully acknowledges the aid afforded him by Sanskritists such as Kielhorn and

Jacobi, and he expresses himself deeply obliged to Dr. Schram, the astronomer of Vienna ; but in the main the work is his own, and so is the merit. Nobody can pay a readier homage to his scholarship and his assiduity than we do ; and we expressly disclaim any disposition of finding fault with the splendid results of his *labor improbus*, if we take the liberty of offering some observations confined to the narrower compass of our own studies, viz. the questions of Arabic language and literature connected with the matter. Nor would there seem to be any need for a more comprehensive notice of a work generally known and deservedly appreciated * in its bearing on large topics of Indian letters and history.

Professor Sachau complains, not without reason, of "the concise style of the author, so sorely fraught with ambiguity," where, in hundreds of examples, "every single word is perfectly clear and certain, and still the sentence may be understood in entirely different ways" (II. 259 ; cp. i. xlviii ; cp. Text, xxxiii sq.). "Under these circumstances," he says (I. xlix), "I do not flatter myself that I have caught the sense of the author everywhere, and I warn the reader not to take a translation, in particular a first translation, from Arabic for more than it is." We may state, at once, that, generally speaking, the reader would not do well to derive a motive of distrust from these modest words. We have collated carefully pages 3-26 of Vol. I. with the Arabic text, and we have not found, in this pretty difficult piece, many passages calculated to induce us to doubt the justness of the translator's view, but only a few, respecting which we felt ourselves compelled to think him wrong. This is the case in some places where a train of ideas has been expressed by Beruni in those concise sentences, which mark, if we may say so, simply the stepping-stones of his thought, the connexion between them being but rarely suggested by some particle or other. Such a hint seems to be intended, in the very first sentence of the book (٣, 4) ‡ by the particle اذ : which we should, in consequence, in the place of *for* I. 3, 5, have preferred to render by *only because*. I. 6, 7 sqq. (٣, 17), the rendering, it seems, should have run thus : "*The same tendency prevails throughout our whole literature on philosophical and religious denominations. He, therefore, who does not know the true state of things regarding those* (books), *derives therefrom statements* (or *data*) *which gain for him with their* (i.e. the denominations') *adherents and those knowing the state of things nothing but shame, if he is an honest character, or* (the necessity of) *persisting*

in *litigious wrangling, if baseness* (of nature) *rules him ; while he, who knows the true state of things, can, at the utmost, but rank them* (i.e. those books) *with the number of fables and legends, to which one listens for the sake of pastime and amusement, not in order to take them for true or credible.*" The purport of this rendering will be found, we trust, more in accordance with the general bearing of the text ; and, moreover, it dispenses with the alteration of the manuscript's reading proposed in ٣, 20 (يجيب for يحسب).* I. 7, 9, *however* : the meaning of the author will become more perspicuous, if we put instead of this *on the other hand*. No contrast is intended ; also the direct information of Eranshahri is worthless, because it is drawn from unclean sources. I. 18, 32 : It is perfectly clear—nor are we willing to impute to the translator that he did not see this—that the example proposed refers to line 19 above, not to the sentences immediately preceding it (l. 24 sqq.). The latter, apparently, are a sort of parenthesis : and this might have been indicated by a different breaking of the paragraphs. Another example of a similar parenthesis is found in I. 19, 9 : *The books . . . are composed in metres, by which they intend, considering that the books soon become corrupted by additions or omissions, to preserve them exactly as they are, in order to facilitate their being learned by heart.* Read instead of this : *The books are composed in metres* (by which they intend to preserve them exactly as they are and [i.e. or at least] to make apparent instantly every corruption caused by additions and omissions) *to facilitate*, etc. We cannot conceive a doubt about the connexion between the phrases *are composed in metres* and *to facilitate* ; and we confess ourselves unable to construe the Arabic words ٩, 21, to ١٠, 1, with به in the nominative, with any expression compatible with rule. The word ظهر, of course, is ambiguous, but perfectly justified in the meaning attributed to it in our rendering. In ١٢, 2, considering the diplomatic accuracy of Professor Sachau's editorship, we are inclined to assume that the ؏ denoting the end of the clause is in the manuscript. But if so, we suspect a mistake of the scribe, because we deem it impossible not to conclude the sentence حمد ١٢, 2, and connect the وليكتب الى with the following الكتاب الى. We cannot see any reason for the quoting of the anecdote told ١٢, 2 to 7, except as an illustration to the preceding theme. The writer means : "Now, what a conceited fellow that man is, you may guess from the fact, that his pandits, whom he extols even above the much-praised Greeks, felt themselves con-

---

* Cp. *e.g.* the latest reviews in the *Academy* of April 20, 1889, and in the *Saturday Review*, same date.

‡ We quote by the Oriental figures the text, by the ordinary ones the translation ; in both, the numbers denote, besides the volume of translation, the pages and lines.

---

* The ambiguity, which leads astray for once the acute scholar, is the same unlucky carelessness in the use of pronouns, common to Arab writers, which he himself has noticed in the Preface to his Edition, p. xxxiv.

strained to confess their utter inability to cope even with an inferior pupil of the Greeks like me." The correction implied by this in I. 23, 19 sq. needs no further explanation.

In some passages of the same part of the book we venture to propose alterations of single words. I. 4, 5, (٣, 13), for *cupidity* read *partiality*. I. 8, 2 (٣, 16), for *customary exoteric expressions* r. *myths* (μῦθος is translated generally by رمز or مثل). This is a singular coincidence with II. 256, 37. I. 24, 29, for *to correct them*, r. *to corroborate them*, or *to testify to their truth*; and accordingly, l. 31, for *does not admit of any correction* r. *is erroneous* (باطل ١٢, 13, i.e. it cannot be asserted or justified by any parallel from another creed). I. 25. 21 (١٢, 1 read خرف instead of خزف) for *sour dates* r, *potsherds*. I. 25, 30, for *original* r. *derived*, and l. 35, for *derived* r. *original* (١٢, 3, 5).

The *Annotations* which fill the second half of the other volume, "do not pretend to be a running commentary on the book, for that cannot be written except by a professed Indianist. They contain some information as to the sources used by Alberuni, and as to those materials which guided me in translating." We cannot pretend to any judgment in Indian matters; but we may safely express our warm admiration as to the extent of illustrative extracts from Sanskrit authors, and to the great number of striking elucidations on Indian subjects condensed in the notes. As for the remarks dealing with Mohammedan and Arabic topics, we confess we are in a rather awkward situation. It is not, of course, the principal interest of the book which rests in these, and, moreover, any seeming disparity in the treatment might be fairly covered by the editor's words just quoted. Besides this, criticism on that point is rendered especially difficult to us by the fact, that in more than one case, we could hardly do without referring to some publications of our own, which, it would seem, have escaped the attention of the commentator when collecting the substance of his notes. This might perhaps produce an unfavourable impression to the impartiality of the judgment passed; we refrain, therefore, from any such criticism, simply offering some stray suggestions, in the hope that they may not be found quite superfluous.

II. 252, 262, 274. There can be no doubt about the use Oriental writers made of Porphyry's Φιλόσοφος Ἱστορία. "Porphyry" is cited by the author of the Fihrist, more frequently by Ibn Abi Uṣeibi'a, and the latter has some extracts from the life of Pythagoras, which show the identity of the quoted work with the "history of philosophy." The note of Wenrich referred to II. 274, 11 (where we have to read 281 instead of 287) is from Qifṭi (MS. Berol. Or. Fol. 493, fo. 104v.), who has transcribed it literally from the Fihrist (253, 18). Its

purport, therefore, is only that the author of the Fihrist once had seen a copy of the fourth book in Syriac; but the existence of more complete copies in Arabic is vouched for simply by I. A. Uṣ.'s quotations from the first book. There is much interesting matter about Greco-Syrian literary history in I. A. Uṣ., but Professor Sachau is right in complaining that all this has not yet been investigated. Only let us observe, that *e.g.* more than one valuable hint in this direction has been given by Dr. Steinschneider. As to Socrates (II. 262) we take the liberty of referring to our pamphlet *Die griechischen Philosophen in der arabischen Ueberlieferung* (Halle, 1873), p. 36 sqq. The Greek form of the dictum sought for by Prof. S. II. 313, ult. is in Diog. Laert. vi. 5 (Antisthenes) or 48 (Diogenes)—quoted by Zeller, ii. 1, p. 208 (2nd ed.)—probably in the latter place, cf. on the frequent confusion between Socrates and Diogenes p. 36 sq. of the pamphlet, and ZDMG. xxxi. 514.

II. 246, 14 sq. On Abu-l-Khair Ibn-el-Khammâr see Ibn Abi Uṣeibi'a I. 322 sq., whence the notices given by Prof. S. from the MSS. of Shahrazûrî and Baihaqi may be supplemented, perhaps also, in a few points, corrected. There is some doubt about the time of his death, but this and other items cannot fully be discussed here.

II. 260, 23. We do not think Alberuni alludes to any other "hidden vowel" than that known in Arabic grammar as الاختلاس, which is practically the same as the رمز in pausal forms. For this kind of slurred vowel is called by Ibn 'Aqîl in his commentary to the Alfîya (p. 351, 11 ed. Dieterici) an اشارة الى الحركة بصوت خفى, which is only a more elaborate expression of Beruni's term حركة خفية. We should propose, therefore, to understand the word "our companions" اصحابنا ١, 19 as an allusion to no others than the Arab grammarians, for which we have, at any rate, Prof. Sachau's own permission, II. 260, 8. Cf. the Arabic pausal forms like هُو (Mufaṣṣal, 162, 10).

II. 270, 31. The Greek original of Galen's "commentary on the aphorisms of Hippocrates" will never be identified, because Beruni's quotations—probably second-hand ones—are referred by him erroneously to a commentary on the aphorisms, whereas they are really taken from the—Greek or Arabic, but certainly spurious—commentary on the ὅρκος, on which may be consulted Sanguinetti, Journ. As. 5th ser. vol. iii. (1854) p. 242 note. The passages in question occur in Sanguinetti's extracts from I. A. Uṣ. 1, 1, vol. iv viz. Beruni i. 35, 12 = Sang. p. 205 (I. A. Uṣ. Text I. (p. 20, 4); i. 222, 9 = Sang. p. 205 (Uṣ. 20, 2); i. 222, 18 = Sang. p. 196 (Uṣ. 18, 6); ii. 168, 11 = Sang. p. 198 f. (Uṣ. 18, 20). The quotation i. 36, 17, is virtually identical with ii. 168, 11, but does not occur in the same wording in Uṣ.; he, on the other hand, adduces the verses i. 36, 21 (identified by Prof. S. in the notes ii. 271, 21 from the προτρεπτικός) in his text i. 15, 32. From all this it results that Beruni has taken his information about Galenus (or Pseudo-Galenus) from no very reliable sources.

II. 270, 36. The كتاب البرهان of Galenus is the ἀποδείξεως πραγματεία (de libr. propr. c. xi. vol. xix. 41 ed. Kühn); see I. A. Uṣ. i. 100, 12; Fihrist 291, 5, and comp. Fabricius, Bibl. gr. (ed. Hamb. 1708) iii. 552.

II. 270, 38. The identity of the كتاب اعمال الطب with Galenus' περὶ ἤθῶν cannot be doubted; see Gal. de libr. propr. c. xiii.; Fabricius, iii. 554; Uṣ. i. 100, 29 (omitted by Klamroth ZDMG. xl. 636); Fihrist 291, 7 (do.). By a remarkable coincidence, also, Beruni's quotation I. 123, 32 contains an allusion to the Emperor Commodus, different from the other one commented upon in the Berlin Hermes, xviii. 623.

II. 343, 14. There is, exactly to the point, a note on Abu Ma'shar's relation to his teacher Al-Kindi, and their common relation to India, in Loth's paper "Al-Kindî als Astrolog" (Morgenlandische Forschungen, Leipzig, 1875), p. 265, 267.

The *Preface* of Professor Sachau represents his fourth Memoir on Beruni and his works—the former three accompanying his edition and version of the *Chronology*, and the edition of the *Indica*. There was indeed a difficulty of ˙saying something new on the matter; but the Professor has succeeded also in this with remarkable tact and perfect success. His *pièce de résistance* this time is the relation between Beruni and the Ghaznevides on the one side, and of Mohammedan and Indian literature on the other. We cannot prolong this notice by discussing some points on which we disagree with him; nor shall we—for reasons stated above—criticize his notice (p. xxx-xxxv) of the translations of Indian works into Arabic. We confine ourselves to the simple remark, that there is no true authority for assuming the existence of an Indian *physician* of the name of *Kanka*; see a paper of our own, in ZDMG. xxxiv. 495, and which contains some further information about Indo-Arabic medicine, with indications of other publications on the subject not mentioned by Professor Sachau. Here, as in some other passages, we are at a loss to understand the principles which guide him in his choice of things to be mentioned or to be omitted;* but this is no cause why we should shrink from freely acknowledging the great services rendered by him to Oriental learning. Among these services the book before us ranks in the very first order.

* Cp. Kautzsch, Grammatik des Biblisch-Aramäischen, Leipzig, 1884, p. 16, l. 27.

It might not, perhaps, appear appropriate to praise, in the Publishers' own Record, the elegant get-up of the volumes. But we may state, that the book has come out of Messrs. Ballantyne's press remarkably free from misprints. Those few we have noticed every careful reader may correct for himself, as, e.g. *Harpocrates* (I. xxviii, 26) for *Hippocrates*, or A.H. (II. 256, 15), instead of A.D.; II. 271, 5 for 189 read 614; I. 33, 15-16 read *But for this*—at least *But this* does not seem adequately to render the evident meaning of the sentence.

A. MÜLLER.

KÖNIGSBERG, 11*th May*, 1879.

---

*New Grammars of African Languages.* — Major Henrique Auguste Dias de Carvalho, of the Infantry Staff of the Portuguese Army, has published this year (1889) at the National Press at Lisbon, a Grammar of the Lunda language, spoken in the Central Region of South Africa, north of the Zambesi, lying between the colonies of Portugal on the East and West coast: it is called "Methodo Pratico para fallar a lingua da Lunda," and is in the Portuguese language. The author was the chief of the Portuguese Exploring Expedition to the Kingdom of Lunda, and its mysterious Sovereign, the Muátiânvua, or, as commonly called, the "Muáta Janvo." Only a portion has reached this country, but it is a meritorious work, and a clear addition to the stock of human knowledge, as nothing was known previously. It is only to be hoped that compiling a grammar does not become the first step to political annexation.

The Roman Catholic Congregation of St. Esprit at Loango, on the West Coast of Africa South of the Equator, published last year a short Grammar of the Language spoken in the Basin of the Kongo between Stanley Pool and the Sea: it is called the "Fiote" Language, and describes itself as the Dialect of Loango. The compiler is a Roman Catholic Missionary named Ussel, and it is in the French language, and is printed at the Mission Press at Loango. He was assisted by a brother missionary named Schmidt, who died in 1882, and by his Bishop, Mgr. Carré, and the children educated at the Mission School greatly helped him. It is a very meritorious little work, and is carefully compiled and nicely printed. The author makes no allusion to the grammatical works which preceded his, notably Mr. Holman Bentley's Dictionary and Grammatical Preface of the Kongo Language, with a copy of which the author supplied Bishop Carré three years ago. No doubt this work is conscientiously prepared from original sources by a capable man. It belongs to the Bantu Family.          R. N. C.

---

*The Journal of the Straits Branch of the Royal Asiatic Society*, No. 19, Singapore, 1887, contains the following papers: 1. Report on a Journey from Tuaran to Kian, and ascent of Kinabalu mountain, by R. M. Little. The height of this mountain in the north-east hook of Borneo Mr. Little has found to be only 11,562 feet, as against the usually accepted height of 13,698 feet. 2. Pulau Langkawi, by the Hon. W. E. Maxwell. This is an important contribution to our knowledge of that beautiful group of islands, about 70 miles north of Pinang, the interior of which, however, has still to be explored. 3. The Negri Sembilan, their origin and constitution, by Martin Lister. This paper, elaborated from native records, gives the political history of the " Nine Territories " or petty states near Malacca, a brief account of which may be found in Newbold's Malacca, ii. 76 ff. 4. Raja Ambong, a Malay Fairy Tale, by the Hon. W. E. Maxwell (57 pages Malay text, and 17 pages English analysis). This is the third of Mír Hassan's stories, and, like the two previously printed, a fine specimen of modern Malay prose. 5. Report on the Padi-borer, and 6. Summary of the Report on the Pamelow Moth, by L. Wray, jun. The former treats of a maggot which commits great ravages amongst the rice crops ; the latter gives a description of a small moth, the caterpillars of which attack the pomeloe fruit. 7. Manangism in Borneo, by the Rev. J. Perham. The important part played by male and female manings (medicine men, sorcerers) amongst the Dayak tribes in north-west Borneo has been adverted to by the author in previous papers, and is now here treated in greater detail. Among other Malayan tribes they go by the names Pawang Payang, Bailan, Balian, Walian, Dato and Si Bago. See on the general question Professor Wilken's essay, " Het Schamanisme bij de volken van den indischen archipel," in "Bijdragen tot de taal-, land- en Volkenkunde van Nederlandsch-Indië," vol. xxxvi. 8. Exploring Expedition from Selam, Perak, over the mountains to Pong, Patani, in November, 1883, by A. T. Dew. This expedition was undertaken with the object of trying to discover whether a road could be made calculated to tap this disputed territory in the event of the pending negotiations with Siam leading to its restoration to Perak. 9. On Birds from Perak, by R. B. Sharpe.—The "Occasional Notes" contain a valuable biographical memoir of Captain T. J. Newbold, by the Hon. W. E. Maxwell.

*Persian Portraits: A Sketch of Persian History, Literature, and Politics.* By F. F. Arbuthnot. (Quaritch.)

If we had not an account of Persian literature in the Encyclopœdia Britannica,—extremely condensed, it is true, but by a master hand,—we should be obliged to go to foreign countries for information on this interesting topic ; for none of the few English books bearing on the subject treats of the literature as a whole, and Dr. Rieu's Descriptive Catalogue of the Persian MSS. in the British Museum, as well as Dr. Ethé's forthcoming Catalogues of similar collections in the libraries of the Bodleian and the India Office, are obviously not histories of Persian literature, though they are calculated to supply most valuable materials towards such a work. In the meanwhile Mr. Arbuthnot has brought out, to interest the general reader in those matters, a very readable book called ' Persian Portraits,' which, besides giving a brief summary of Persian history, politics, and domestic manners and customs, treats mainly of poets and poetry, and of those Oriental tales the origin or development of which has generally been assigned to Persia. The volume may safely be commended as giving a judicious selection of what is likely to prove most attractive. We would, however, venture to express a hope that the elaboration of a scholarly and comprehensive History of Persian Literature, at the hands of one or more of the gifted Persian scholars of whom this country has every reason to be proud, may soon become a reality.

---

# Obituary.

Ánandarám Borooah (Vaduyá).—I have been asked to contribute a notice of the life of Anandaráma Vaduyá (' Borooah '). His death is announced in the *Indian Magazine* for March as having been caused by fever and paralysis, but I cannot hear of any obituary notices by his friends, such as might have been expected to appear in the Indian press. I understand that he died as long ago as the beginning of January last. Pending fuller information from such quarters, I venture to subjoin the few facts of his life that I have been able to ascertain, together with some notice of the useful works by which his name will be long remembered among Sanskritists.

The deceased scholar was born in 1850, being the second son of Gargaráma Vaduyá and his wife Durlabheçvari, of Gauhati (Gowhatty) in Assam. Of his family and caste I have no means at hand of ascertaining any further facts, though I think that his caste-name is not uncommon in Assam. I may here note, in passing, that my transcription of his name is taken from the Nagari title-page of his edition of the *Mahávirachurita*, where the name appears as वडुवा. I have never heard the name pronounced by an Asámí, but probably ' Borooah ' is about as misleading as ' Oude ' and the other ' popular ' spellings to which the average resident in India clings with such tenacity. He was educated at Presidency College, Calcutta, and graduated B.A. at the Calcutta University in 1869.

Proceeding to England as a candidate for the Civil Service, for which he was selected in 1870, he matriculated at the London University in the same year, and entered as a student of the Middle Temple, and in 1872 was called to the bar. He revisited England at least once ; for I met him in London about 1884. His manner, with strangers at least, was very reserved and retiring.

Of his career as a civilian, which he commenced in Bengal in 1872, I have little or nothing to say. At the time of his death he was Joint-Magistrate and Deputy-Collector at Jessore. But I cannot forbear to remark that his life gives us all an example, whether in government service or out of it, to show that a mass of routine work need not crush out literary activity when a man is really in earnest. As a rule the Civil Service of India has done little for the literature and science of the country, the exceptions to this being chiefly men in the Educational Department. But certainly Anandaráma Vaduyá's twelve well-spent years of service show him to have been a kindred spirit with administrators like Colebrooke and Burnell among the illustrious dead, and the small band of living workers like Grierson, Fleet, and R. C. Temple. Vaduyá's first work appeared in May, 1877, and from its preface we find that it was commenced about 1873 and announced in March, 1876. This was his

"Practical English-Sanskrit Dictionary," a most original and truly practical work. Not content with commencing with such a *magnum opus* as a dictionary, he added to its second and third volumes two new and original works, viz. his "Higher Sanskrit Grammar," and a List of Sanskrit Geographical Names, illustrated by a valuable prefatory essay. Both are thoroughly original works, and rather suffer by being united with the Dictionary ; the latter is I believe still a unique contribution to Indian research, though only a small one : the great value of the former (now published separately) may be seen from the frequent references to it in Dr. J. S. Speijer's recent work on the same subject.

In the same year, 1877, appeared the edition of Bhavabhūti's Mahāvīracharita, already referred to in passing, which was followed in 1878 by the essay on Bhavabhūti intended to have formed a part of the same book. A third work was completed by Vaduyā in 1877, and appeared in 1878, viz. his "Companion to the Sanskrit-reading Undergraduates of the Calcutta University." This consists of criticisms on the Commentaries of the two set portions of *Kāvyas* in the University curriculum for 1878 ; and forms, with the works last mentioned, Vaduyā's sole contribution to the criticism of the *Kāvya*-literature. But small in bulk though it is, I cannot but consider it an important contribution to Sanskrit scholarship. European editions of Sanskrit classics generally consist of texts with, occasionally, a few original explanatory notes, and at best more or less meagre extracts from the great native commentators. Indian editors, on the other hand, do not really *elucidate* either text or commentary, but compose a learned super-commentary, which is often, as in the case of Tāranātha on the Siddhanta-Kaumudī, obscurer than the work professed to be explained, Vaduyā takes a most useful middle course, and without being carried away by the authority of Mallinātha or even by that of Amarasiṃha or Pāṇini, explains both commentary and text. This is most useful to the European student. There are plenty of helps for Kālidāsa and Manu *themselves* ; but for the due understanding of Mallinātha, Govindarāja or Kullūka, to what work can one refer a pupil ? My own acquaintance, such as it is, with these important scholiasts, was first derived, in orthodox fashion, from the mouth of my '*āchārya*' (Vaduyā's teacher, too, at Presidency College, by-the-by), who himself was instructed by duly qualified Brahmans : but I question whether the average European student is in a position to study these writers as they deserve.

Here, then, was a good and new departure worthy of imitation by Sanskritists in all lands, and especially in India.

Vaduyā's remaining works are devoted to the sides of Sanskrit study in which he evidently felt most interest, lexicography, grammar, and *ars poetica*. To the first-mentioned class belongs the work which he was publishing at the time of his death, a new edition of the Amara-Kosha, with several unpublished commentaries, while with the second and third we may rank his Dhātu-vṛitti-sāra,* published in 1886, his

collection of *Alaṅkāra*-writers and the extensive work on Prosody which he published in 1882, under the somewhat eccentric title of Volume the *Tenth* of a projected Comprehensive Sanskrit Grammar. These substantial volumes, each carefully planned and worked out, might well have occupied the leisure of even a far less busy man for a good twenty years.

But it is not only on the extent of this good scholar's work that I would insist. There is something also in its method and spirit that demand our attention. We often hear complaints of the effect of Western education on India ; that the old learning is passing away and giving place to an ungodly and bastard veneer of European instruction (I fear I must hardly call it education), tending to replace the grand old figure of the pandit of old, by that terrible production of the nineteenth century known as 'the Bābū,'* the butt of satire both European and native as well. Yet Ānandarāma Vaduyā, born near, and educated in, Bengal, the hot-bed of 'Bābū-dom,' a seeker and a successful seeker of Government employ, the chief prize of this curious educational compromise, never lost his interest in the problems of Sanskrit scholarship.

Evidently well grounded in Pāṇini (and where, I would ask the advocates of English education for India, can we find a finer educational instrument than the great Indian grammars studied in the light of modern research ?) Vaduyā brought to bear on the criticism of Sanskrit texts something of the spirit of what we understand by classical *scholarship*. He neither discusses the old scholiasts and grammarians with the slavish obsequiousness of a mere follower of tradition, nor yet ignores them like the uninitiated foreign critic, but rather weighs one with another and adjusts the results by the standard of modern research.

Such seems to me the character of Vaduyā's work, and it is because I so strongly feel the value of his example to all of us Oriental students, whether European or native, that I have ventured to draw out this notice to a greater length than I had at first intended.

CECIL BENDALL.

*British Museum, July,* 1889.

**W. Wright.**—By the death of Dr. W. Wright, Sir Thomas Adams' Professor of Arabic in the University of Cambridge, which took place on the 22nd May last, his university has lost one of its most eminent professors, and Semitic scholarship one of its most devoted and most illustrious representatives. A long and wearying illness, borne with patience and quiet resignation, had long been preparing his friends for the worst ; but the intelligence of his death was received as an irreparable calamity all over the learned world.

William Wright was born in India, in the Presidency of Bengal, on the 17th January, 1830. His father was the late Alexander Wright, a military officer in the service of the East India Company. His mother was a daughter of D. A. Overbeck, the last Dutch Governor of Chinsurah. On his father's quitting the service with his pension, Wright came home with his parents,

---

* The title-page of this work is somewhat obscure. It runs thus : Dhātuvṛttisāra . . . With extracts from Ramanatha's Manorama.—From the Dhātu Kosa of Anundoram Borooah. What is this Dhātu Koça ? A projected work of Ānandarāma's ? It is curious that neither the Sanskrit title-page nor the colophon of the book mention it. I should be obliged if any friend of the deceased scholar would inform me on this point in order that the work may be properly catalogued in the Supplementary Sanskrit Catalogue which I am preparing for the British Museum. A post card sent to me at the British Museum, London, or to the Editor of this Journal, would be of service. Cannot Ānandarāma's friends also let us know in what condition his unfinished works and other papers have been left ?

* European readers, who do not know what a 'Bābū' is, (and I have been often asked), should read the exquisitely humorous description of him in Aberigh-MacKay's "Twenty-one Days in India," or Çivacandra Vasu's "The Hindus as they are." How little other Hindus covet the title may be seen from a postscript to a business letter coming from a Bombay correspondent, whom I had wrongly addressed as 'Bābū' : "Please do not address me as Bābū. I am not a Bengali."

and resided from 1840 onwards at St. Andrew's in Fife, where he received his education at the Madras College and the University till the end of 1848. In the following year he went to Germany for the purpose of continuing his general and classical education.

A few notes concerning the two leaders of Semitic, more especially Arabic, studies on the continent since the early years of the present century may not be out of place here; for we hold it to be mainly due to their paramount influence that Arabic scholarship has, with a few notable exceptions, kept itself singularly free from those petty jealousies which have been rife in other fields of Oriental research. S. de Sacy and after him Fleischer were on all hands, not excluding even the learned Sheikhs of the Levant, acknowledged to be the embodiments of Arabic learning, and from their verdict there was no further appeal. The spirit and method of De Sacy's teaching during a period of thirty years had knit together the select band of his pupils (of these, to the best of our knowledge, but one survives, Professor Stickel), and had guided and directed their subsequent literary work. On his death his mantle descended on Prof. Fleischer, who himself had sat at De Sacy's feet. Thenceforward, students of Arabic flocked to Leipzig from all parts of Europe, and from the United States, to profit by Fleischer's lectures. And as Fleischer occupied his chair in the University over half a century, almost all the best Arabic scholars of his time have either been his pupils or have at least been subject to his literary influence and inspiration: and their consensus may be taken as the standard by which all matters relating to Arabic scholarship are judged. Wright was not a pupil of Fleischer, but he was in constant touch and correspondence with him for upwards of 30 years: and Fleischer always entertained the very highest opinion of his critical Arabic scholarship, and thought him second to none as an Arabic grammarian.

Early in 1849, Wright went to Halle, where Roediger, at whose house he was staying, inspired him with such enthusiasm for Semitic studies that Wright plunged into them heart and soul. Indeed, the lectures of Roediger, Arnold and Haarbrücker held out to him a wider scope for the study of all the branches of Semitic philology and literature than he would at that time have found at Leipzig, where Fleischer, though *principum princeps* in Arabic, taught scarcely anything besides but Persian and Turkish. After two years' assiduous study at Halle, Wright betook himself to Leiden to work among the Arabic manuscripts in the University Library. The first fruit of his labours—The Travels of Ibn Jobair, Leiden, 1852—gave such promise of future excellence that the Senate of that University, at the instance of Dozy, conferred on him the honorary degree of Ph.D. Of his further literary projects, a statement of which he sent to Prof. Fleischer in November, 1852, we mention here the text edition of El-Makkari's Literary History of the Arabs of Spain, the first volume of which had fallen to his share and was published in 1855. In the same year he was appointed Professor of Arabic in University College, London, and in the following year he accepted a similar Professorship in Trinity College, Dublin, where he remained till 1861. During this period he brought out the Book of Jonah in Chaldee, Syriac, Aethiopic and Arabic, with glossaries; Opuscula Arabica, from MSS. in the University Library of Leiden; and the first volume of an Arabic Grammar, which, though purporting to be "translated from the German of Caspari," contained so many additions and corrections as to be almost an independent work. The second edition (1874-75) of this Grammar, improved and enlarged throughout, deserves this name in a still

higher degree. A third edition is imperatively called for.

With his appointment, in 1861, as Assistant in the Department of Manuscripts, British Museum,—he became Assistant Keeper in 1869,—Wright entered upon a new sphere of activity, for it fell to his lot to catalogue the newly acquired collection of Syriac MSS. The three magnificent quartos which this catalogue comprises (1870-72) are a monument of patient scholarship and form together with his elaborate and exhaustive article on Syriac Literature (in the Encyclopædia Britannica) a treasury of information on this branch of Semitic studies. His catalogue of the Ethiopic MSS. of the British Museum (1877) followed in due sequence. He compiled these catalogues in the course of his official duties, not, as has wrongly been asserted, because he had a predilection for that dry kind of work. Anyhow, no one could have brought higher qualifications to the task, no one could have accomplished it better. His long occupation with the Syriac MSS. further produced a number of other publications in that language, such as his Contributions to the Apocryphal Literature of the New Testament, the Apocryphal Acts of the Apostles (2 vols.), the Homilies of Aphraates, the Chronicle of Joshua Stylites, the full text of the Kalīlah wa Dimnah, and a great many minor articles, all replete with learning, in the Journal of Sacred Literature and other serials.

In the winter of 1870 he was appointed Sir Thomas Adams' Professor of Arabic at Cambridge, and was elected at the same time to a Fellowship at Queens' College. For 19 years he discharged his professorial duties with scrupulous care, lecturing to one student with the same painstaking attention as to a dozen. One of his favourite subjects was the Comparative Grammar of the Semitic languages. He worked at the same time at his edition of the Kámil of el-Mubarrad, which he completed, with the exception of the Introduction, at the decipherment of inscriptions, and at old Arabic poetry. He was also an active member of the Old Testament Company on the Bible Revision. And, further, he was entrusted with the editorial control of the Oriental Series of the Palæographical Society, and took a leading part in its production. Lastly, his help, in many cases at a vast expenditure of time, was ungrudgingly given towards the publication of important works in Semitic philology and literature. Thus, the late Professor Dozy has acknowledged Wright's valuable contributions to his "Supplément aux Dictionnaires Arabes"; Dr. Payne Smith has done the same in reference to the careful revision which his Syriac Thesaurus has undergone at Wright's hands; Dr. Neubauer, in a recent number of the *Athenæum*, has expressed his unbounded gratitude for similar help received. Of the numerous other scholars who have been beholden to him in this way we will but mention the late Professor Palmer, some time his colleague at Cambridge, who in the Preface to his Arabic Grammar expresses his gratitude to him "not only for carefully revising the proofs, but for kindly giving many valuable suggestions and criticisms,"—aid which he never could have solicited or accepted if, as his biographer asserts, he never "forgot or forgave" that Wright had beaten him in the contest for the Professorship of Arabic in the University of Cambridge. And all that aid, be it remembered, was given to others with the same scrupulous and painstaking care as if he had been working at publications of his own. Surely, if we divide the workers in the wide field of Eastern research into two camps,—the one consisting of those who make the promotion of Oriental learning their paramount aim, uninfluenced by considerations of ambition, gain, or self-assertion, and the second made up of those with whom the advancement of science and literature is subordinated to egotistical objects and designs.—Wright certainly belonged in the fullest sense to the former. His time and vast learning were ever at the service of his pupils and friends, and his hospitable house was the resort of many foreign savants (and those not of the Syriac and Arabic persuasion only) who were visiting England for the purposes of pleasure or research, and with whom a trip to Cambridge was a literary feast. There was no Semitic scholar of any note who did not know Wright personally or at least by correspondence. His extremely rich album containing the photographs of most of them would be well worth preserving as an heir-loom in the Library of his College.

Looking back upon Wright's Cambridge career, we are satisfied that those who were mainly instrumental in securing his election were but consulting the best interests of the University, inasmuch as he was already then enjoying a European reputation not as an Arabist only, but as a Semitic scholar generally. The excellence of their judgment has borne good fruit to the University ever since. By the general consensus of the foremost Arabists and Semitic philologists all over the civilized world, Wright was considered as one of themselves: and the deep and genuine sorrow with which the intelligence of his death was received on the continent told volumes of the place of honour and affection he had held in their hearts. For with all his deep and extensive learning, he was a kindly, warm-hearted, unpretending scholar whose sterling worth none but kindred spirits could fully grasp and appreciate.

That foreign Universities and Academies should have vied with one another in doing honour to him, is but natural. He held the honorary degrees of D.D. of Jena, LL.D. of Cambridge, Dublin, Edinburgh and St. Andrew's; he was a Corresponding Member of the Institut de France, the Royal Societies of Berlin, St. Petersburg, Amsterdam and Göttingen, and of the Reale Istituto Lombardo; and Honorary Member of the German Oriental Society, the Asiatic Society of Bengal, and the American Oriental Society. He also had the high and rare distinction of being a Knight of the Prussian order "Pour le mérite."

His Lectures on Comparative Semitic Grammar are being printed by the Cambridge University Press, and provision is being made for the publication of several of his projected Syriac and Arabic texts.

### Works of the late Dr. William Wright.

The Travels of Ibn Jubair, edited from a MS. in the University Library of Leyden. 8vo. Leiden, 1852.

Al-Makkari. Analectes sur l'histoire et la littérature des Arabes d'Espagne. Publiés par R. Dozy, G. Dugat, L. Krehl et W. Wright. 4 volumes. 4to. Leiden, 1855-61.

Opuscula arabica. Collected and edited from MSS. in the University Library of Leyden. 8vo. Leiden, 1859.

Cureton (D. W.)—Ancient Syriac Documents relative to the Earliest Establishment of Christianity in Edessa. Syriac and English Edited with Preface by Dr. Wright. 4to. London, 1864.

Kamil (The) of El-Mubarrad. Edited for the German Oriental Society from the Manuscripts of Leyden, St. Petersburg, Cambridge, and Berlin, by W. Wright. 11 Parts. 4to. Leipzig, 1864-82.

Contributions to the Apocryphal Literature of the New Testament. Collected and Edited from Syriac Manuscripts in the British Museum. 8vo. London, 1865.

Aphraates, the Persian Sage. Homilies. Edited from Syriac MSS. of the Fifth and Sixth Centuries in the British Museum, by W. Wright. Vol. I. The Syriac Text. 4to. London, 1869.

Arabic Reading Book. Part I. 8vo. London, 1870.

Catalogue of Syriac Manuscripts in the British Museum. Acquired since the year 1838. 3 Parts. With Appendices and Indices. 4to. London, 1870-73.

The Apocryphal Acts of the Apostles from Syriac MSS. Syriac and English 2 volumes. 8vo. London, 1871.

Grammar of the Arabic Language. Second edition. 2 vols. 8vo. London, 1874-75.

Catalogue of Ethiopic Manuscripts in the British Museum. Acquired since the year 1847. 4to. With 13 Facsimiles. London, 1877.

The Chronicle of Joshua the Stylite. Composed in Syriac A.D. 507. With an English Translation and Notes by W. Wright. Demy 8vo. Cambridge, 1882.

Kalilah wa Dimnah; or, the Fables of Bidpai, translated from Arabic into Syriac. Edited by W. Wright. 8vo. London, 1884.

Arabic Reading Book. With complete Glossary. Vol. I. The Text. 8vo. London, 1870.

Jonah Tetraglott. The Book of Jonah, in four Semitic Versions, viz. Chaldee, Syriac, Aethiopic, and Arabic. With corresponding Glossaries. 8vo. London, 1867.

On Syriac Literature (contained in the last edition of the Encyclopædia Britannica).

**Rao Saheb V. N. Mandlik.**—By the death of the late Rao Saheb Vishwanath Narayen Mandlik, C.S.I., the whole Hindoo community of Bombay lose, as Dr. Blaney said, their intellectual leader, and it will be difficult, if not impossible, to find any one to take his place. He represented a class, always rare, that now seems to have disappeared. A Hindoo of the Hindoos, he was still steeped in all the learning and culture of the West. He owed his eminence to the impartial way in which native talent is encouraged and rewarded by the British Raj, yet he never forgot that he was descended on the female side from the family of the last Peshwa. He rose to be Government Pleader and head of the Native Bar, and, had he been spared, he would probably have attained a seat in the High Court. In legal matters he had an unusually clear and subtle intellect, and yet he performed an act of piety that would have been more proper to his ancestors by having himself weighed in silver, the Rs. 10,000, or thereabouts, that turned the scales going to the poor in charity. He spent half his scanty leisure in advocating political and educational reforms, and the other half in deprecating any attempts at social reform, which so many of his educated countrymen deem far more important. His fine library was full of the masterpieces in English literature, and these he studied closely, but he was at the same time known all over India as one of the very first Sanskrit scholars of the day. He was a man of defined purpose, strong will, quick apprehension, vigorous intelligence, and wonderful versatility. He was perhaps the most distinguished of the first batch of talented Elphinstonians; he never forgot how much he owed to his *alma mater*, and almost to the day of his death he continued to take the liveliest and warmest interest in the progress and prosperity of the Bombay University. An acting professorship led him to a minor political appointment in Sind, afterwards to a Deputy Educational Inspectorship, and then to the post of Personal Assistant to the late Mr. James Gibbs. He found time privately to read law, and at the age of thirty he passed the pleader's examination. Henceforward he devoted his business hours to the active prosecution of his profession, and ultimately succeeded Mr. Nanabhai Haridas as Government Pleader. He was always a leader in municipal matters, whether as a member of the Bench of Justices, or as a member of the Corporation or Town Council; and finally as Chairman of the Corporation. He was the first native Fellow of the Bombay University. For the unexampled period of eight years he was a member of the Bombay Legislative Council, and this led in its turn to his appointment and re-appointment as a member of the Vice-regal Council, where again he was the first native of Bombay to enjoy that honour. In both Councils he always took an independent line, looking upon himself very properly as the representative of native interests. If he sometimes carried this principle to an extreme, he never lost the regard of his colleagues ; and, however much he differed from them in the discussion of public affairs, he never carried his partizan feelings into his private personal relations with his opponents ; and perhaps the most sincere tribute paid to his memory in the Corporation on the 9th inst. was paid by Mr. Ollivant when he said they had often had considerable differences of opinion, and had taken different views ; but he could say that amongst his native friends in Bombay he was quite sure he had no more sincere well-wisher than the late Rao Saheb. On Hindoo law he was at once an accurate and prolific writer and a recognized authority. His large edition of the "Institutes of Manu" in Sanskrit is well known to all students, but his most important effort in Sanskrit literature, the work of his later years, was not completed at the time of his death. He wrote much in English, and at his own expense he reprinted in three volumes all that was of value in the Transactions of the old Bombay Literary Society, and it was probably for these and other reasons that Sir Raymond West paid the Rao Saheb a very high but not unmerited compliment, when in honour of his name a Sanskrit scholarship was founded last year in the University. "His services," said Sir Raymond, "have been constant and unremitting, and nothing can give us greater pleasure than to find that he is so highly appreciated, and that his name is to remain for ever in the golden book of this institution. He will be enshrined amongst the best and most deserving men of our institution, uniting within himself the attributes of a Sulpicius, a Varro, and a Mæcenas, and the fame of them all." But how did a busy lawyer manage to achieve distinction in so many different ways? We will borrow our answer from Dr. Blaney. "From my personal knowlege," testifies Dr. Blaney, "I can say that he was employed from four o'clock every morning until he retired to bed at night." And according to the same authority, this incessant and unremitting labour hastened his death, and he "succumbed at last to the influence of overwork." At all events, he died in harness. The brilliant success of the Rao Saheb's career is from first to last a telling answer to those new-fangled India *fainéants* who profess to believe that natives of parts have no chance of rising under the English régime ; and we only hope that some well-qualified person will write the story of the Rao Saheb Mandlik's life from the days when he was a schoolboy at Ratnagherry to the time he was a member of the Viceroy's Council at Simla.

At the moment of our going to press the melancholy intelligence of the death of Professor **M. Amari** reaches us. We shall give a full obituary notice of him in our next issue.


# Oriental Notes.

THE BOPP FUND, established on the 16th May, 1866—the day on which, fifty years before, Bopp had dated the preface to his first publication, "Das Conjugationssystem der Sanskrit-Sprache in Vergleichung mit jenem der griechischen, lateinischen, persischen und germanischen Sprache,"—has the two-fold object (1) of supplying to a young scholar, of whatever nationality, who has completed his university course, the means for continuing his studies wherever he may choose, and (2) of giving prizes for literary work done, or in support of literary investigations, those studies being in each case limited to Sanskrit philology and the comparative grammar of the Indo-Germanic languages. All applications and proposals should be addressed to the Royal Society of Berlin (die königliche Akademie der Wissenschaften) by the 1st of February in each year : they are entrusted to a committee consisting of five members chosen by the ' Akademie," three of whom must be Academicians, while two may be outsiders. The awards, which are not necessarily restricted to the applications sent in, are made on the 16th May. The present members of the Committee are the Professors Dillmann, J. Schmidt, Steinthal, Weber and Zupitza. In the current year an award of 900 marks (£45) has been made to Professor Th. Zachariæ, of Greifswald, to enable him to bring out his edition of Hemachandra's Anekârthasangraha, and one of 450 marks (£22 10s.) to Dr. W. Prellwitz, of Königsberg, as a subvention towards his researches in comparative grammar. The interest of the funded property amounts at present to 1638½ marks ; but only 1350 are annually spent, the balance being added to the capital until the latter shall yield 1800 marks annual interest. But, as is the case with all foundations of this kind which receive no fresh accessions, it is feared that when that object shall have been attained, the rate of interest will again have gone down, and the Penelopeian work of accumulating interest will have to be recommenced. The Bopp Fund had once before (in 1878, 1879) an annual income of upwards of 1800 marks ; but in consequence of the lowering of the rate of interest and other causes of this nature, its income has since considerably decreased. Might not, in consideration of the aid which philological research owes to the Fund, Bopp's centenary (14 Sept. 1891) be made the occasion for opening a fresh list of subscriptions ?—(From the *National-Zeitung* of 17th May, 1889.)

SOUTH INDIAN INSCRIPTIONS.—We are able to report that rapid progress is being made with the printing of the first volume of Dr. Hultzsch's "*South Indian Inscriptions*." The advance sheets which have reached us comprise—I. Sanskrit Inscriptions of the Pallava and Eastern Châlukya Dynasties, and II. Tamil and Grantha Inscriptions. With these we enter upon a new and hitherto untrodden field of epigraphical research, which is sure to yield an invaluable harvest to the future historian of South India. We trust the advisers to the Government of India will see and urge the necessity of illustrating this valuable work with a rich supply of facsimiles.

HISTORY OF ARMENIA.—We have received from the Mekhitarist press of S. Lazzaro, Venice, a profusely illustrated History of Armenia, in three volumes, oblong folio, by the well-known historian, Dr. J. Issaverdens. This great work will be found of special interest at the present time when the Armenian question is again coming to the fore, and the pictorial representation of the chief events in the history of that nation, and of the localities in which they were enacted, may be particularly welcome. The price of the three volumes is Four Guineas.

VAJIRAÑAN LIBRARY.—In an interesting communication from Bangkok bearing the well-known signature "O.F.," in the "Athenæum" of July 13th, an account is given of the Vajirañan Library of the Siamese capital. This is a subscription library under the presidency of the King, and its members issue a weekly literary paper in Siamese, to which also the King contributes. On the recent occasion of the opening of a new building for its accommodation, a volume of verses by the members, with a preface by the King, was brought out, all of an ethical character, which are said to show much natural ability and to possess some value as works of art.

ORIENTALISTS' CONGRESS.—From an article on the forthcoming *Eighth International Congress of Orientalists*, in the June number of the "Oesterreichische Monatsschrift für den Orient," we learn that in addition to the presence of Oriental scholars from all parts of Europe, there will not only be representatives from North and South America, but also delegates from Turkey, Egypt, Persia and Arabia, who, it is anticipated, will impart a truly Oriental colouring to that brilliant assemblage.

THE CONSTITUTION OF JAPAN.—An edition of the New Constitution of the Empire of Japan, with the addresses delivered at a meeting held in commemoration of its Promulgation on April 17th, 1889, has been printed by the Publication Agency of the Johns Hopkins University, Baltimore. As only a limited edition has been printed of this interesting document, we anticipate it will soon be exhausted.

---

## American Notes.

THE INTRODUCTION OF PRINTING INTO NEW YORK.—Antiquaries, book collectors, and bibliographers generally have for a long time accepted it as an incontrovertible fact that the volume known as "Bradford's Laws, 1694," was the first book printed in New York, being partly printed in 1693. The following Pennsylvania Act is also supposed to have been printed in that year, as well as two or three separate New York Acts usually bound in that volume:

Anno Regni Gulielmi & Mariæ, | Regis & Reginæ | Angliæ, Scotiæ, Franciæ & Hiberniæ, | QUINTO. *An ACT for granting to King William and Queen | Mary the Rate of One Penny per Pound upon the | clear Value of all the Real and Personal estates, | and Six Shillings per Head upon such as are not | otherwise rated by this Act. To be imployed by the | Governour of this Province of Pennsylvania and | Territories thereof, for the Time being, towards | the Support of this Government.* | Folio, pp. (4).

William Bradford, it will be remembered, was the first printer not only of New York but of Pennsylvania as well. He was born in Leicester, England, May 20, 1660. Being a Quaker, he emigrated in 1682, and landed on the spot where Philadelphia was afterwards built. In 1685 he began printing under the patronage of the Friends. In 1692 he incurred the displeasure of the dominant party in Philadelphia through his sympathy with George Keith, and was imprisoned for libel. After his release, he accepted the offer of the New York Council to set up a press in that colony, and on April 10, 1693, was duly appointed "Printer to the Majesty King William and Queen Mary"; establishing himself in the present city of New York, and his salary in that office commenced on that day.

It has been commonly accepted, as we remarked, that the book quoted above, or either of three other Acts, were the first fruits of Bradford's press in New York, which have been preserved and are still extant in one or more specimens of each. To these George H. Moore, LL.D., the Superintendent of Lenox Library, now adds the record of a publication hitherto unrecognized, but which he thinks may prove to be the earliest of them all.[*]

Upon news of the French invasion of New York in the winter of 1692–3, Dr. Moore says: "Governor Fletcher displayed great energy and activity, taking the field in person, proceeding with uncommon celerity to the scene of action and providing by every means in his power for the security and protection of the frontier. His services were cordially recognized by all, and by none more emphatically than the friendly Indians in alliance with the English, who bestowed on him the name of *Cayenquirago, the Great Swift Arrow*, to commemorate the rapidity of his movement from the city of New York to the scattered settlements in the wilderness above Albany. The journal of this expedition and other documents, official and semi-official, illustrating the transactions connected with it, were brought together and printed in New York by authority of the Governor himself. The exact date of appearance of the work cannot be readily fixed; but it is certain that before the summer of 1693 was fairly forward, that valiant soldier was enabled to read the flattering record of his achievements from the types of William Bradford, the poor printer whom he had just rescued from Quaker persecution in Philadelphia. It is not difficult to understand with what zeal and alacrity the grateful protégé would hasten to perform his part in the work of ' booming his benefactor.' It would be unreasonable to doubt either that Fletcher was desirous to give the publicity of print to the record of his successful expedition or that the printer was eager to gratify his friend and patron. The thanks of the popular branch of the legislature were formally voted to the Governor for his promptness and zeal in appearing against the French on the frontier, by a resolution of the 22nd March, 1693, the very day before the ' encouragement to the printer' passed the Council : and a copy of this resolution duly authenticated is the last article in the book. The work thus produced in New York was reprinted a few weeks later in London, and we are indebted to that republication for the greater part of our present knowledge of its existence. It was licensed in London, September 11, 1693, and in one of the London journals of the 16th September, 1693, the following advertisement announced the fact that

"' On *Tuesday* next, the 19th Instant, will be publish'd.
' A Perfect Journal of the late Actions of the *French* at *Canada*, with the Manner of their being Repulsed by His Excellency *Benjamin Fletcher*, their Majesties Governour of *New-York*. Impartially related by Collonel *Nicholas Reyard* and Lieutenant Collonel *Charles Lodowick* : To which is added the Present State and Strength of *Canada* given by 3 Dutchmen, late Prisoners there.
' Price stitch'd 6d.
' Printed for *Richard Baldwin*. 1693.'

"It is not improbable that this was part of the title of the original publication in New York, excepting the imprint—and that the variation in the English edition belongs to that alone. The title of that edition is as follows:

"A | Journal | of the | Late Actions | of the | French at Canada. | With | The Manner of their being Repuls'd, by | His Excellency, Benjamin Fletcher, Their | Majesties Governour of New-York. | Impartially Related by Coll. Nicholas Reyard, | and Lieu-| tenant Coll. Charles Lodowick, who attended His | Excellency, during the whole Expedition. | To which is added, | I. An Account of the present State and Strength of Canada, | given by Two Dutch Men, who have been a long Time Pri-| soners there | and now made their Escape. | II. The Examination of a French Prisoner. | III. His Excellency Benjamin Fletcher's Speech to the Indians. | IV. An Address from the Corporation of Albany, to His Excellen-| cy, Returning Thanks for His Excellency's early Assistance for | their Relief. | Licensed, Sept. 11th, 1693, Edward Cooke. | London, Printed for Richard Baldwin, in Warwick-Lane, 1693. | 4to. Title and Preface, 2 leaves. Text, 22 pages.

"The English edition is introduced by a spirited preface to the reader, who is assured by the editor that ' we have this Credit to the Truth of our Narration, That 'tis no more than what has been already Printed at New-York by his Excellency's (the Commander in chief in the Expedition) particular Authority there,' etc. Governor Fletcher's successor and bitter enemy, Lord Bellomont, furnished, a few years later, an account of this publication, which is very entertaining, though by no means complimentary to his predecessor or the people whom they governed, whether lay or clerical. Writing to the Lords of Trade, Nov. 12, 1698, he says : ' The printed accounts of his great exploits against the French which he published and sent into England I cannot possibly get one of them for love nor money, and I am told he made it his businesse to get up all the printed copies, which is an argument with me of his consciousnesse that he had imposed a romance instead of a true narrative,' etc.—*N. Y. Col. MSS.* iv. 426. It is not difficult to understand the reason why a publication which had disappeared within five years after it was printed in New York in 1693, should be well-nigh unknown two centuries later. The facts now stated seem to warrant the suggestion that ' The Perfect Journal,' etc , may have been ' the first-born of the press in New York.' They certainly deprive the first edition of the Laws of the honor- hitherto commonly assigned to that interesting and valuable volume, which still remains the most considerable monument of typography in New York before 1700."—From the "*Publishers' Weekly*," New York.

LOCAL CONSTITUTIONAL HISTORY OF THE UNITED STATES.—A very valuable series of papers has been commenced by Professor George E. Howard of Nebraska University, on the Local Constitutional History of the United States. These appear as extra volumes in the "Johns Hopkins University Studies in Historical and Political Science." The first volume containing the development of the township, hundred, and shire, is now ready, and the second volume on the development of the city and local magistracies is in preparation. The history of local

---

[*] This information is quoted from a most interesting pamphlet entitled "*Typographia Neo-Eboracensis Primitiæ—Historical Notes on the Introduction of Printing into New York 1693*, by George H. Moore, LL.D., Superintendent of the Lenox Library. New York : Printed for the Author, 1888. 16 p. O. pap.

institutions has thus far been treated almost entirely in monographs dealing with special topics, or relating to particular phases or periods of development. Moreover a large and valuable portion of this literature is dispersed through the voluminous publications of learned societies, and therefore inaccessible to the general reader. It is practically impossible for any one but a specialist to obtain a clear understanding of the present state of inquiry on the subject. Besides much of the material requisite for a comprehensive view has never been explored. There is needed, in short, a book which shall gather up, sift, and skilfully arrange the results already obtained by the host of writers on Græco-Roman, Germanic, and English institutions, and supplement them by further investigation, particularly for this country. Such is the scope of the present work. It is intended as a contribution towards placing local constitutional history, where it deserves to be placed, on a level with the history of the national constitution. Each institution is followed through every stage of evolution, from its ancient prototype under the tribal organization of society, to its existing form in the new states and territories of the West. The author has aimed at presenting a clear and logical statement of constitutional facts—the details of offices, powers, and functions; while bringing into special prominence the process of organic growth, differentiation, and decay. The work is, however, very largely the result of independent study of the original records; and many topics are treated from the sources for the first time. Particular attention has been given to the bibliography, which is brought down to date.

ANNUAL REPORT OF THE CHIEF OF ENGINEERS OF THE UNITED STATES ARMY.—Brigadier-General Thomas Lincoln Casey, in his report to the Hon. C. Endicott (U.S.), Secretary of War for the year 1888, in four parts, estimates that his department will require an appropriation of $50,000 for this year's expenditure, $5000 each for the eight military divisions and departments west of the Mississippi River. and $10,000 for the publication of maps for the use of the War Department. No one who has not examined this Report, which is in four bulky 8vo. volumes, would credit the amount of work that falls to the lot of the United States Corps of Engineers, or the economical and expeditious way in which it is carried out.

THE DEVELOPMENT OF LANGUAGE.—In a paper read before the Canadian Institute, Toronto, April, 1888, Mr. Horatio Hale elaborates some of his remarks in a former paper on the language of children, and on their aptness in finding out how to communicate with one another even to creating a language which they mutually understand. We need scarcely say that Mr. Hale's researches and suggestions are always interesting and suggestive, even to those who do not entirely agree with them.

---

## NOTICE TO CORRESPONDENTS.

All communications should be addressed to the *Editor of "Trübner's Record,"* 57 and 59, Ludgate Hill, London, E.C., and they should be accompanied by the sender's name and address (not necessarily for publication). Every care will be taken with MSS., but the Editor cannot hold himself responsible for rejected communications, which—if to be returned to the sender—should be accompanied by postage. MS. should be legibly written, and on one side of the paper only. Books for review should be addressed to the Editor.

---

## NOTICE TO ADVERTISERS.

All communications respecting advertisements should be addressed to Messrs. F. TALLIS AND SON, 22, Wellington Street, W.C. *Terms for the insertion of advertisements :—*

| | | | £ s. d. |
|---|---|---|---|
| WHOLE PAGE (ordinary position) | ... | | £5 5 0 |
| HALF PAGE | ,, | ,, | ... 2 15 0 |
| QUARTER PAGE | ,, | ,, | ... 1 10 0 |

Special positions per contract.

---

# Four Curious Korean Books, etc.

東國文獻備考. 102 vols. "A Collection of Miscellaneous Historical Events and Laws pertaining to the East Country (The Kingdom of Chosun, or Korea)." Compiled and written by *Kim Chi In* (Korean name), a Member of the Council of State, Prime Minister of the Realm, who had held offices of Astronomer Royal, Preceptor of the Sovereign, etc. Written in 1771.

This work is in MS.—in 101 vols. of subject matter with an index volume; total pp. about 12800; size of page, 8½in. by 14in. The volumes are time-stained, backs worm eaten in places; all written matter is perfectly and clearly legible, and volumes are well bound and strong. The writing and composition are Chinese of the ancient, high literary style; characters are modern square or printed form. This work is rare; is not obtainable in the Korean capital; is not, and probably has never been, in print, a limited number of copies for the use of the Royal family and Government only having been prepared. This copy was only obtained by the direct aid of the Palace officials of Korea, for the use of an official (foreign) resident in Seoul during the first year of the treaties with Korea. The work is official in character and authentic in Korea. It includes a great variety of subjects—not clearly indicated by the title—among which are Government, observations upon men, animals, physical changes, astronomical phenomena of high antiquity, chronological data pertaining to dynasties of Kings of Korea and of China, etc.

大典會通. 5 vols. "Compendium of Great Laws." The official printed collection of Constitutional Laws of the Government of Korea — consisting of the original laws of Kin-cha (Kitsse), founder of the State of Chosön (B.C. 1122), with their modifications by the Kings of Korea to the present time. In 5 vols.—pages 8in. by 12in.—a total of about 600 pages. A rare book. In good condition, strongly bound, printed from large wood and small iron type.

易言. 4 vols. This title may be translated "*Easy Lessons.*" The *original* is a work in pure Chinese, written by the Chinese General *Ma*, for translation into the Korean phonetic alphabet, the object being to acquaint the Korean people with Chinese ideas and experience of Western Governments and peoples. It is perhaps the only high-class work which has ever been translated and printed in the Korean alphabet.[*] The work is in four volumes, size of page 8½in. by 14in. (appendix), total pages, about 350; is beautifully printed in the characters of the Korean alphabet. The value of the book lies in its being the only *standard* available for use in rendering the official, or high-class language of Korea in the native alphabet; also in its political significance, as regards Chinese relations to Korea and her confessed attitude *vis-à-vis* nations of the West. The work has been suppressed entirely.

大東輿地圖. This, an Official Map of Korea, issued by the Government about 40 years ago, for use in its own offices, is made up of 22 sub-maps of latitudinal sections of Korea; scale, about three miles (geographical) to one inch. Total size of map (sections placed together) about 22ft. by 11ft. Includes separate maps of Seoul (capital of Korea), on a large scale. This map is no longer made—is extremely rare; it is a very remarkable map in construction, fullness and accuracy; shows fortifications, ancient strongholds, grades of local government, fire signal towers, etc., throughout the kingdom. Is well printed and bound, folds up complete in book shape—one volume, 10in. by 14in. by 4in.—cloth board binding. The map is well coloured.

---

[*] The official written language of Korea is *Chinese*, and the *native* characters are only used (with the remarkable exception of this volume) by women and the illiterate public generally.

# American Literature.

**Abbot (Ezra).**—The Authorship of the Fourth Gospel and other Critical Essays; selected from the Unpublished Papers of the late Ezra Abbot. 8vo. cloth, pp. 501. *Boston.* 18*s.*

**Andrews (C. M.)**—The River Towns of Connecticut. A Study of Wethersfield, Hartford, and Windsor. 8vo. paper, pp. 126. *Baltimore.* 5*s.*

**Andrews (E., M.D.), and (E. W., M.D.)**—Rectal and Anal Surgery, with Description of the Secret Methods of the Itinerant Specialists. Second edition, revised and enlarged, with Illustrations and Formulary. 8vo. cloth, pp. xiv. and 140. *Chicago.* 7*s.* 6*d.*

**Angel (Rosa E.)**—This Side and That. Poems. 12mo. cloth, pp. 160. *Cincinnati.* 5*s.*

**Angerstein (E., M.D.), and Eckler (G.)**— Home Gymnastics for the Well and the Sick, adapted to all Ages and both Sexes; with Directions how to Preserve and Increase Health; also how to Overcome Conditions of Ill Health, by Simple Movements of the Body; translated from the eighth German edition. 8vo. cloth, pp. 94. Illustrated. *Boston.* 7*s.* 6*d.*

**Annual American Catalogue, 1888.** Being the Full Titles, with descriptive Notes, of all Books recorded in the "Publishers' Weekly," 1888; with Author, Title, and Subject Index, Publishers' Annual Lists, and Directory of Publishers. 8vo. half leather. *New York.* 18*s.*

**Baird (W. R.), and Babcock (F. S.)**—A Guide to the Principles of the Law. Third Edition. 12mo. cloth, pp. xxiv. and 321. *New York.* 12*s.*

**Bamford (Mary E.)**—Up and Down the Brooks. 16mo. cloth, pp. 222. Illustrated. *Boston.* 4*s.*

**Bastin (E. S.)**—College Botany; including Organography, Vegetable Histology, Vegetable Physiology, and Vegetable Taxonomy; with a Brief Account of the Succession of Plants in Geologic Time, and a Glossary of Botanical Terms; being a Revised and Enlarged Edition of the "Elements of Botany." 8vo. cloth, pp. xv. and 451. Illustrated. *Chicago.* 15*s.*

**Bateman (C.)**—Somerville Latrobe. The First Ascent of the Kasai; being some Records of Service under the Lone Star. 8vo. cloth. Illustrated. *New York.* £1 10*s.*

**Billington (C. E., M.D.)**—Diphtheria: its Nature and Treatment. 8vo. cloth, pp. 326. Illustrated. *New York.* 12*s.* 6*d.*

**Bowden (T. R.)**—Blunders in Educated Circles Corrected. 32mo. cloth, pp. 76. *New York.* 4*s.*

**Boylston (P.)**—John Charáxes. A Tale of the Civil War in America. 12mo. cloth, pp. 289. *Philadelphia.* 6*s.* 6*d.*

**Buck (A. H., M.D.)**—A Manual of Diseases of the Ear, for the Use of Students and Practitioners of Medicine. 8vo. cloth, pp. 420. Illustrated. *New York.* 12*s.* 6*d.*

**Burroughs (J.)**—Indoor Studies. 16mo. cloth, pp. 256. *Boston.* 6*s.* 6*d.*

**Century Dictionary (The).** An Encyclopedic Lexicon of the English Language; prepared under the Superintendence of W. Dwight Whitney. In 24 parts. Part I. 4to. paper. pp. 272. *New York.* By subscription only, 12*s.* 6*d.* per part.

**Campbell (Mrs. H.)**—Prisoners of Poverty Abroad. 12mo. cloth, pp. 248. *Boston.* 5*s.*

**Canfield (W. B., M.D.)**—Practical Notes on Urinary Analysis. Reprinted from the "Maryland Medical Journal." 16mo. paper, pp. 38. *Baltimore.* 1*s.* 6*d.*

**Cartheny (J. de).**—The Wandering Knight. His Adventurous Journey; or, a Mediæval Pilgrim's Progress. 12mo. cloth, pp. xiv. and 346. *New York.* 5*s.*

**Chamberlain (Rev. N. H.)**—The Sphinx in Aubrey Parish. A Novel. 12mo. cloth, pp. 481. *Boston.* 7*s.* 6*d.*

**Chapin (J. H.)**—From Japan to Granada. Sketches of Observation and Inquiry in a Tour Round the World in 1887–88. 12mo. cloth, pp. xi. and 325. Illustrated. *New York.* 7*s.* 6*d.*

**Cicero, Marcus Tullius.** Brutus de claris oratoribus. Edited with an Introduction and Notes by Martin Kellogg. 12mo. cloth, pp. xxviii. and 196. *Boston.* 4*s.*

**Convers (D.)**—Marriage and Divorce in the United States; as they are and as they ought to be. 16mo. cloth, pp. 266. *Philadelphia.* 6*s.* 6*d.*

**Cooke (F. E.)**—Story of Theodore Parker. To which is added an Introduction and a Bibliography of Books and Articles by and pertaining to him. 12mo. cloth, pp. 175. *Boston.* 5*s.*

**Crocker (G. G.)**—Principles of Procedure in Deliberative Bodies. 18mo. cloth, pp. 169. *New York.* 4*s.*

**Crull (E. S.)**—Crull's Time and Speed Chart for the Use of Superintendents, Train-masters, Train-dispatchers, Conductors, Engineers, and all interested in Constructing New and Special Time-tables and the Running of Trains. 12mo. cloth, pp. 71. *New York.* 5*s.*

**Cummings (A.)**—The Fall of Kilman Kon. 12mo. cloth, pp. 348. *New York.* 7*s.* 6*d.*

**Curry (Rev. D.)**—Christian Education. Five Lectures delivered before the Ohio Wesleyan University on the Merrick Foundation, 1st series. 12mo. cloth, pp. 131. *New York.* 4*s.*

**Denton (S. F.)**—Incidents of a Collector's Rambles in Australia, New Zealand, and New Guinea; illustrated by the Author. 8vo. cloth, pp. 272. *Boston.* 12*s.* 6*d.*

**Derrécagaix (V.)**—Modern War: Translated by C. W. Foster. Part I. Strategy. With Plates. 8vo. cloth, pp. xv. and 710. *Washington.* £1 16*s.*

**Dewey (M.)**—Rules for Author and Classed Catalogues as used in Columbia College Library; with 52 Facsimiles of Sample Cards; Bibliography of Catalogue Rules by Mary Salome Cutler. 8vo. paper, pp. 48. *Boston.* 6*s.*

**Dixon (B. H.)**—Homer Genealogy; Brief Account of the Family of Homer or de Homere of Ettingshall, Co. Stafford, England, and Boston, Mass.; the Ancestors and Descendants of Captain John Homer, who came to Boston, Mass., about 1690. 4to. cloth, pp. 27. *Albany (N.Y.).* 12*s.*

**Drake (S. A.)**—Burgoyne's Invasion of 1777. With an Outline Sketch of the American Invasion of Canada, 1775–76. 16mo. cloth, pp. 146. Illustrated. *Boston.* 2*s.* 6*d.*

**Draper (L. C.)**—An Essay on the Autographic Collections of the Signers of the Declaration of Independence and of the Constitution. From Vol. 10, Wisconsin Historical Collection. Revised and Enlarged. 8vo. cloth, pp. 117. *New York.* 12*s.*

**Durand (J.)**—New Materials for the History of the American Revolution; translated from Documents in the French Archives and edited by J. Durand. 12mo. cloth, pp. 311. *New York.* 9*s.*

**Ebers (G.)**—Margery ('Gred): A Tale of Old Nuremberg; from the German by Clara Bell. Revised and Corrected in U.S. Authorized edition. 2 vols. 16mo. pp. 279 and 300. *New York.* cloth, 8*s.*; paper, 5*s.*

**Edwards (W. H.)**—The Butterflies of North America. 3rd series, part 7. 4to. paper. *Boston.* 12*s.*

**Egleston (J.)**—Catalogue of Minerals and Synonyms Alphabetically Arranged for the Use of Museums. 8vo. paper, pp. 198. *Washington.*

**Emerson (R. W.)**—Fortune of the Republic. [*Also*] American Civilization. The Emancipation Proclamation. 16mo. paper. *Boston.* 1*s.*

**Endlich (G. A.) and Richards (L.)**—The Rights and Liabilities of Married Women, concerning Property, Contracts and Torts, under the Common and Statute Law of Pennsylvania. 8vo. sheep, pp. xxxii. and 493. *Philadelphia.* £1 10*s.*

**Esperanto (Dr.)**—An Attempt towards an International Language ; translated by H. Phillips, jun. ; with an English International Vocabulary compiled by the Translator. 8vo. paper, pp. 56. *New York.* 1*s.* 6*d.*

**Examination and Education** : the American Supplement to the "Nineteenth Century," for March, 1889. 8vo. paper, pp. 36. *New York.* 1*s.* 6*d.*

**Fiske (J.)**—The War of Independence. 16mo. cloth, pp. 200. *Boston.* 4*s.*

**Fiske (J.)**—The Beginnings of New England ; or, the Puritan Theocracy in its Relations to Civil and Religious Liberty. 12mo. cloth, pp. 296. *Boston.* 10*s.*

**Fox (W., M.D.)**—Atlas of the Pathological Anatomy of the Lungs; with 45 Lithographic Plates and other Illustrations. 8vo. half cloth. *Philadelphia.* £6 6*s.*

**Fullerton (G. S.)** — A Plain Argument for God. 12mo. cloth, pp. 110. *Philadelphia.* 6*s.*

**Gemmill (J. A.)**—The Canadian Parliamentary Companion, 1889. 16mo. cloth, pp. 444. *Ottawa.* 12*s.*

**Geyer (M. S.)**—Reference Directory of the Booksellers and Stationers of the United States and Canada ; including all Dealers in the Book, Stationery, Paper, Toy, Fancy Goods, Notions, Picture, and Picture Frame Trades, with a list of Wholesale Druggists, and the purchasing Agents (Stationery) for Railroads ; [also] Book Publishers, Bookbinders, Lithographers, and Manufacturers of Stationers' Specialities; corrected to January 1st, 1889 ; [also] a List of all Paper-Mills in the United States and Canada, giving Daily Capacity and Kinds of Goods Manufactured, 1889. 8vo. cloth, pp. 471. *New York.* £2 10*s.*

**Gilchrist (F. B.)**—The True Story of Hamlet and Ophelia. 12mo. cloth, pp. 339. *Boston.* 7*s.* 6*d.*

**Graham (D., M.D.)**—Massage ; its History, Mode of Application and Effects, Indication and Contra-Indication. 8vo. cloth, pp. 300. *New York.* 12*s.* 6*d.*

**Grotius (Hugo).**—A Defence of the Catholic Faith concerning the Satisfaction of Christ against Faustus Socinus ; translated with Notes and an Historical Introduction by Frank Hugh Foster. 12mo. cloth, pp. lv. and 314. *Andover (Mass.).* 7*s.* 6*d.*

**Haines (E. M.)**—The American Indian. 8vo. cloth, pp. 800. Illustrated. *Chicago.* £1 10*s.*

**Harris (S. S., D.D.)**—The Dignity of Man : Select Sermons. With a Memorial Address by Rt. Rev. H. C. Potter, D.D., Bishop of New York. 12mo. cloth, pp. 266. *Chicago.* 7*s.* 6*d.*

**Hathaway (W.)** — Living Questions : Studies in Nature and Grace. 12mo. cloth, pp. 365. *New York.* 6*s.* 6*d.*

**Hayes (P. S., M.D.)**—Electricity and the Methods of its Employment in removing Superfluous Hair and other Facial Blemishes. 16mo. cloth, pp. 128. *Chicago.* 5*s.*

**Haygood (A. G.)** — Pleas for Progress. 12mo. cloth, pp. 320. *New York.* 5*s.*

**Hazard (R. G.)**—Works. 4 vols. Vol. I. Essays on Language, New Edition. 2. Freedom of Mind in Willing, New Edition. 3. Two Letters on Causation and Freedom of Mind in Willing, New Edition. 4. Economics and Politics. 8vo. cloth. *Boston.* 10*s.* each vol.

**Heaton (J. L.)**—The Story of Vermont. Illustrated by L. J. Bridgman. 8vo. cloth, pp. 319. Illustrated. *Boston.* 7*s.* 6*d.*

**Hofmann (K. B.), and Ultzmann (R.)** — Analysis of the Urine, with Special Reference to Diseases of the Genito-Urinary Organs. Translated by T. Barton Brune, M.D., and H. Holbrook Curtis, M.D. Third Edition, Revised and Enlarged. 8vo. cloth. Illustrated. *New York.* 10*s.*

**Howard (O.)**—The Life of the Law ; or, Universal Principles of Law. 8vo. cloth, pp. 114. *Richmond (Va.).* 4*s.*

**Howard (G. E.)**—An Introduction to the Local Constitutional History of the United States. Vol. 1. Development of the Township, Hundred, and Shire. 8vo. cloth, pp. xii. and 526. *Baltimore.* 18*s.*

**Howe (W. W.)**—Municipal History of New Orleans. 8vo. paper, pp. 33. *Baltimore.* 1*s.* 6*d.*

**Jackson (A. W.)**—The Immanent God and other Sermons. 12mo. cloth, pp. 159. *Boston.* 5*s.*

**James (B. W., M.D.)**—American Health Resorts. With Notes upon their Climate. 12mo. cloth. *Philadelphia.* 10*s.*

**Jamieson (A.)**—Electrical Rules, Tables, Tests, and Formulæ. 12mo. cloth, pp. 84. *New York.* 4*s.*

**Japan.**—Constitution of the Empire of Japan. With the Addresses at a Meeting delivered in Commemoration of its Promulgation at the Johns Hopkins University. 12mo. cloth. *Baltimore.* 2*s.* 6*d.*

**Jenks (J. W.)**—Road Legislation for the American State. 8vo. paper, pp. 83. *New York.* 4*s.*

**King (C.)**—Laramie ; or, The Queen of Bedlam. A Story of the Sioux War of 1876. 12mo. cloth, pp. 277. *Philadelphia.* 5*s.*

**Landon (J. S.)**—Constitutional History and Government of the United States ; a Series of Lectures. 8vo. cloth, pp. 389. *Boston.* 15*s.*

**Lee (W., M.D.)**—Lee Genealogy. John Lee, of Agawam (Ipswich), Mass., 1634-1671, and his Descendants of the name of Lee, with Genealogical Notes and Biographical Sketches of all his Descendants as far as can be obtained; including Notes on Collateral Branches. 8vo. cloth. Illustrated. *Albany.* £1 10*s.*

**Letchworth (W. P.)**—The Insane in Foreign Countries. Notes of an Examination of European Methods of Caring for the Insane. 8vo. cloth. Illustrated. *New York.* 15*s.*

**Leffmann (H., M.D.) and Beam (W.)**—Examination of Water for Sanitary and Technical Purposes. 12mo. cloth, pp. 106. *Philadelphia.* 6*s.* 6*d.*

**Leonard (C. H., M D.)**—The Vest-Pocket Anatomist. Fourteenth rev. edition. 12mo. cloth, pp. 297. *Detroit.* 5*s.*

**Lindsey (C.)**—Rome in Canada. The Ultramontane Struggle for Supremacy over the Civil Power. 8vo. cloth, pp. xlvii. and 398. *Toronto.* 12*s.*

**Lossing (B. J.)**—Hours with the Living Men and Women of the Revolution. A Pilgrimage. Illustrated by Facsimiles of Pen-and-Ink Drawings by H. Rosa. 12mo. cloth, pp. 239. Illustrated. *New York.* 10*s.*

**MacCoun (T.)**—An Historical Geography of the United States. 12mo. cloth, pp. 46. With 44 Maps. *New York.* 5*s.*

**Meriwether (L.)**—The Tramp at Home. 12mo. cloth, pp. x. and 296. *New York.* 6*s.* 6*d.*

**Mitchell (S. W., M.D.)**—The Cup of Youth, and other Poems. 8vo. half-bound, pp. 76. *Boston.* 7*s.* 6*d.*

**Montgomery (D. H.)**—The Leading Facts of French History. 12mo. cloth, pp. 321. *Boston.* 3*s.* 6*d.*

**Murray (W. H. H.)**—The Story that the Keg Told Me; [also,] The Story of the Man who Didn't Know Much. 12mo. cloth, pp. xvi. and 454. *Boston.* 7s. 6d.

**Murrell (W., M.D.)**—Masso-Therapeutics; or, Massage as a Mode of Treatment. Fourth edition, revised and enlarged. 12mo. cloth, pp. 236. *Philadelphia.* 7s. 6d.

**Nehrling (H.)**—North American Birds. With 36 Coloured Plates after Water-Colour Paintings by Robert Ridgway, A. Goering, and Gustav Muetzel. In 12 Parts. Part 1. 4to. paper, pp. 48. With 3 Plates. *Milwaukee (Wis.).* 6s.

**Queiros (Eça de).**—Dragon's Teeth: A Novel from the Portuguese by Mary J. Serrano. 12mo. cloth, pp. 516. *Boston.* 7s. 6d.

**Raue (C. G., M.D.)**—Psychology as a Natural Science Applied to the Solution of Occult Psychic Phenomena. 8vo. cloth, pp. 541. *Philadelphia.* 18s.

**Raymond (R. W.)**—Evolution of Animal Life. 12mo. paper, pp. 20. *Boston.* 1s.

**Roe (E. P.)**—The Home Acre. 12mo. cloth, pp. 252. *New York.* 7s. 6d.

**Rollins (Alice W.)**—From Snow to Sunshine: with Facsimiles of Water-Colour Drawings of Butterflies by Susie Barstow Skelding. 16mo. paper. *New York.* 7s. 6d.

**Safford (O. F., D.D.)**—Hosea Ballou: a Marvellous Life-Story (of a Universalist Minister). 12mo. cloth, pp. 290. *Boston.* 5s.

**St. John (E.)**—A Postal Dictionary: Being an Alphabetical Handbook of Postal Rates, Laws, and Regulations for all who use the Mails. Compiled from Official Sources. 18mo. paper, pp. 94. *New York.* 1s.

**Sanborn (J. W.)**—Go to the Ant and Learn many Wonderful Things; a Book for the Young. 12mo. cloth, pp. 119. *Cincinnati.* 3s.

**Sawyer (H. C., M.D.)**—Nerve Waste. Practical Information concerning Nervous Impairment in Modern Life; its Causes, Phases, and Remedies, with Advice on the Hygiene of the Nervous Constitution. Second edition. 8vo. cloth, pp. 160. *San Francisco.* 5s.

**Schaack (M. J.)**—Anarchy and Anarchists. A History of the Red Terror and the Social Revolution in America and Europe. 8vo. cloth, pp. 698. *Chicago.* 18s.

**Schaff (P., D.D.)**—The Progress of Religious Freedom as shown in the History of Toleration Acts. Reprinted from the papers of "The American Society of Church History." Vol. I. 8vo. cloth, pp. 126. *N. York.* 7s. 6d.

**Schnée (E.)**—Diabetes: Its Cause and Permanent Cure; from the Standpoint of Experience and Scientific Investigation; from the German by R. L. Tafel. Revised and Enlarged by the Author. 8vo. cloth, pp. 215 *Philadelphia.* 10s.

**Scudder (H. E.)**—George Washington. An Historical Biography. 16mo. cloth, pp. 248. *Boston.* 4s.

**Senn (N., M.D.)**—Surgical Bacteriology. 8vo. cloth, pp. 270. With 13 Plates. *Philadelphia.* 9s.

**Senn (N., M.D.)**—Experimental Surgery. 8vo. cloth, pp. 522. *Chicago.* £1 6s.

**Senn (N., M.D.)**—Intestinal Surgery. 8vo. cloth, pp. 269. *Chicago.* 12s. 6d.

**Seymour (T. D.)**—A Concise Vocabulary to the First Six Books of Homer's Iliad. Square 8vo. cloth, pp. 105. *Boston.* 3s.

**Sharp and Alleman.**—Lawyers' and Bankers' Directory for 1889. Containing the Names of over Six Thousand Attorneys and Bankers. Collection Laws, with Forms, etc. 8vo. sheep, pp. 1124. *Philadelphia.* £1 10s.

**Shields (C. W., D.D.)**—Philosophia ultima; or, Science of the Sciences. Vol. 2. The History of the Sciences and the Logic of the Sciences. 8vo. cloth, pp. 482. *New York.* 16s.

**Smart (C.)**—Handbook for the Hospital Corps of the United States Army and State Military Forces. 16mo. cloth, pp. 577. Illustrated. *New York.* 12s. 6d.

**Snyder (W. L.)**—The Geography of Marriage; or, Legal Perplexities of Wedlock in the United States. 12mo. cloth, pp. 334. *New York.* 7s. 6d.

**Solomon.**—Pükeds de Salomon. Being a Translation of the Proverbs of Solomon from the Original Text into the Universal Language Volapük, by S. Huebsch. 16mo. paper, pp. 45. *New York.* 2s. 6d.

**Starr (L., M.D.)**—Hygiene of the Nursery. Including the General Regimen and Feeding of Infants and Children, and the Domestic Management of the Ordinary Emergencies of Early Life. Second edition. 12mo. cloth, pp. 280. *Philadelphia.* 5s.

**Steele (J. D.)** — Hygienic Physiology, with special reference to the use of Alcoholic Drinks and Narcotics; being a Revised Edition of "Fourteen Weeks in Human Physiology"; Enlarged Edition, with Selected Readings, edited for the use of Schools, in accordance with the recent Legislation upon Temperance Instruction. 12mo. cloth, pp. xii. and 401. *New York.* 5s.

**Strahan (J., M.D.)**—The Diagnosis and Treatment of Extra-uterine Pregnancy. Being the Jenks Prize Essay of the College of Physicians of Philadelphia for 1888; with Bibliography. 8vo. cloth, pp. 134. *Philadelphia.* 7s. 6d.

**Sunderland (J. T.)**—The Liberal Christian Ministry. 16mo. cloth, pp. 96. *Boston.* 2s. 6d.

**Thompson (J., D.D.)**—Christian Manliness and other Sermons. 12mo. cloth, pp. 303. *New York.* 5s.

**Trent (W. P.)**—English Culture in Virginia. A Study of the Gilmer Letters and an Account of the English Professors obtained by Jefferson for the University of Virginia. 8vo. paper, pp. 141. *Baltimore.* 5s.

**Tuckerman (B.)**—Life of General Lafayette; with a Critical Estimate of his Character and Public Acts. 2 vols. 12mo. cloth, pp. 275 and 266. *New York.* 15s.

**Turchin (J. B.)**—Noted Battles for the Union during the Civil War in the United States of America, 1861–5: Chickamauga. 8vo. cloth, pp. 295. *Chicago.* 15s.

**Tuttle (H.)**—Studies in the Outlying Fields of Psychic Science. 12mo. cloth, pp. 250. *New York.* 6s. 6d.

**United States.**—Tenth Census. (Vol. 21.) Report on the Defective, Dependent, and Delinquent Classes of the Population of the United States, as returned at the Tenth Census (June 1, 1880). By F. Howard Wines. 4to. cloth, pp. 581. *Washington.*

**United States.**—Tenth Census (Vol. 22.) Report on Power and Machinery employed in Manufactures, Embracing Statistics of Steam and Water Power used in the Manufacturing of Iron and Steel, Machine Tools and Wood-working Machinery, Wool and Silk Machinery, and Monographs on Pumps and Pumping Engines, Manufacture of Engines and Boilers, Marine Engines and Steam Vessels, by W. P. Trowbridge. Report on the Ice Industry of the United States by H. Hall. 4to. cloth, pp. 642. Illustrated. *Washington.*

**United States.**—Index-Catalogue of the Library of the Surgeon-General's Office. Authors and Subjects. Vol. 9. Medicine (Popular)–Nywelt. 4to. cloth, pp. 1054. *Washington.*

**Valentine (F. C., M.D.)**—600 Medical Don'ts; or, The Physician's Utility Enhanced. 18mo. paper, pp. 144. *New York.* 1s. 6d.

**Valk (F., M.D.)**—Lectures on the Errors of Refraction, and Their Correction with Glasses. Delivered at the New York Post-Graduate Medical School, with Illustrative Cases from Practice, both Private and Clinical. 8vo. cloth. *New York.* 15s.

**Van Harlingen (A., M.D.)**—Handbook of the Diagnosis and Treatment of Skin Diseases. Second Edition, Revised and Enlarged. 8vo. cloth, pp. 427. *Philadelphia.* 12s. 6d.

**Van Hoosear (D. H.)**—Fillow, Philo, and Philleo Genealogy. A Record of the Descendants of John Fillow, of Norwalk, Connecticut, a Huguenot Refugee from France. 8vo. cloth, pp. 272. *Albany.* £1 4s.

**Van Nüys (J. C.)**—Chemical Analysis of Healthy and Diseased Urine, Qualitative and Quantitative. 8vo. cloth, pp. 204. *Philadelphia.* 10s.

**Van Pelt (Rev. D.)**—A Church and Her Martyrs. (Holland). 16mo. cloth, pp. 336. *Philadelphia.* 6s.

**Vincent (M. R., D.D.)**—Word Studies in the New Testament. Vol. II. The Writings of John The Gospel, The Epistles, The Apocalypse. 8vo. cloth, pp. 607. *New York.* £1.

**Virginia.**—A Synopsis of the Geology, Geography Climate, and Soil of the State; together with its Resources of Mines, Forests, and Fields, its Flocks and its Herds. 8vo. paper, pp. 116. *Richmond (Va.).* 2s. 6d.

**Waring (G. E., jun.)**—Sewerage and Land Drainage. 4to. cloth, pp. 200. Illustrated. *New York.* £1 10s.

**Webb (S.)**—Socialism in England. 8vo. paper, pp. 73. *Baltimore.* 4s.

**Wentworth (G. A.), McLellan (J. A.) and Glashan (J. C.)** — Algebraic Analysis: Solutions and Exercises illustrating the Fundamental Theorems and the most Important Processes of Pure Algebra. Part I. 12mo. cloth, pp. 418. *Boston.* 4s. 6d.

**Werner (E.)**—The Alpine Fay: a Romance from the German by Mrs. A. L. Wister. 12mo. cloth, pp. 356. *Philadelphia.* 6s. 6d.

**Wernse (W. F.)**—American Banker's Manual. Containing a Summary of all the Important Laws, Forms and Usages of and concerning Banks, Bankers, and Bank Officers; also a brief and complete Statement of the Law of Notes, Bills of Exchange, and Cheques; also Laws relating to National Banks, etc. with a Digest of Cases and a complete Synopsis of the most important Branches of Commercial Law of the Several States. 8vo. sheep. *New York.* £1 10s.

**Wheeler (W. A.)**—An Explanatory and Pronouncing Dictionary of the noted Names of Fiction; including also Familiar Pseudonyms, Surnames bestowed on Eminent Men, etc. Nineteenth edition, with Appendix by C. G. Wheeler. 12mo. cloth, pp. xxxiv. and 440. *Boston.* 10s.

**Whitney (J. D.)**—The United States. Facts and Figures Illustrating the Physical Geography of the Country and its Material Resources. 8vo. cloth, pp. 484. *Boston.* 15s.

**Wiggin (J. B.)**—The Wild Artist in Boston: a Story of Love and Art in the Actual. 12mo. cloth, pp. 407. *Boston.* 6s. 6d.

**Woerner (J. G.)**—A Treatise on the American Law of Administration. 2 vols. 8vo. sheep. *Boston.* £3.

**Wood (H. C., M.D.)**—Therapeutics: its Principles and Practice. Seventh Edition, Re-arranged, Re-written, and Enlarged. 8vo. cloth, pp. xvi. and 905. *Philadelphia.* £1 10s.

**Woodman (A. J.)**—Picturesque Alaska. A Journal of a Tour among the Mountains, Seas, and Islands of the Northwest, from San Francisco to Sitka. 12mo. cloth, pp. 212. *Boston.* 6s.

**Woolley (Celia P.)**—A Girl Graduate. 12mo. cloth, pp. 439. *Boston.* 7s. 6d.

---

## European Literature.

**Alker (E.)**—Die Chronologie der Bücher der Könige und Paralipomenön im Einklang mit der Chronologie der Aegypter, Assyrer, Babylonier, Phönizier, Meder und Lyder. Royal 8vo. pp. v. 160. *Leobschütz,* 1889. 3s.

**Amiaud (A.)**—La légende syriaque de Saint Alexis, l'homme de Dieu. 8vo. *Paris,* 1889. 7s. 6d.

**Annales** du musée Guimet. Bibliothèque de vulgarisation. Tome 1. Les moines égyptiens. 18mo. *Paris,* 1889. 3s. 6d.

**Annuaire (Grand)** commercial, industriel, agricole et vinicole de l'Algérie et de la Tunisie. 6e année, 1889. *Paris,* 1889. 10s.

**Baillet (A.)**—Le décret de Memphis et les inscriptions de Rosette et de Damanhour. 8vo. *Paris,* 1889. 6s.

**Bastian (A.)**—Einiges aus Samoa und anderen Inseln der Südsee. *Berlin,* 1889. 2s.

**Becker (H.)**—Die Brahmanen in der Alexandersage. 4to. pp. 34. *Leipzig,* 1889. 1s.

**Bourgoin.**—Précis de l'art arabe. Livr. 1–6. 8vo. *Paris,* 1889. 7s. 6d.

**Brandt (A. J. H. W.)**—Die mandäische Religion. Ihre Entwickelung und geschichtliche Bedeutung erforscht, dargestellt und beleuchtet. Roy. 8vo. pp. xii. 236. *Leipzig,* 1889. 8s.

**Brugsch-Bey (E.)**—La tente funéraire de la Princesse Tsimkheb, provenant de la trouvaille de Deir El-Bahari. With 1 Map and Plates. Royal 4to. *Cairo,* 1889. 15s.

**Crawford (F. Marion)**—Zoroastre. Préface par E. Chesneau. 16mo. *Paris,* 1889. 3s. 6d.

**Derenbourg (Hartwig)**—Ousâma ibn Mounkidh. Un émir syrien au premier siècle des croisades (1095–1188). 1re Partie. Vie d'Ousâma (Chap. i–v.). Royal 8vo. pp. x. 202. *Paris,* 1889.

**Franck (A.)**—La Kabbale ou la philosophie religieuse des Hébreux. Royal 8vo. *Paris,* 1889. 7s. 6d.

**Gopcevic (Spiridion)**—Makedonien und Alt-Serbien. With numerous Illustrations, Plates and a Map. 4to. *Vienna,* 1889. 20s.

**Groneman (J.)** — In den Kĕdáton te Jogjâkártâ. (Depâtjârâ, Ampilan en Tounecldansen. Met Fotogrammen van Cephas. Text, pp. 69, royal 8vo. cloth. Atlas, Folio oblong, cloth. *Leiden,* 1888. £2 2s.

The same, Edition de Luxe, £3 18s.

**Harlez (M. C. de)**—La religion en Chine. A propos du dernier livre de M. A. Réville. (Extrait du "Magasin littéraire et scientifique"). 8vo. pp. 33. *Gand,* 1889.

**Harlez (C. de)**—Kia-li. Livre des rites domestiques Chinois. 8vo. *Paris,* 1889. 2s. 6d.

**Hoffmann (O.)**—Das Praesens der indo-germanischen Grundsprache in seiner Flexion und Stammbildung. Royal 8vo. pp. iv. 145. *Göttingen,* 1889. 4s.

**Imbault-Huart (C.)**—Manuel de la langue coréenne parlée, à l'usage des Français. I. Introduction grammaticale. II. Phrases et dialogues faciles. III. Recueil des mots les plus usités. 8vo. pp. 114. *Paris,* 1889.

**Joannis** Episcopi Ephesi Syri Monophysitae commentarii de beatis Orientalibus et historiae ecclesiasticae fragmenta. Latine verterunt W. J. van Douwen et J. P. N. Land. 4to. *Amsterdam,* 1889. 5s.

**Kahan (J.)**—Ueber die verbalnominale Doppelnatur der hebräischen Participien und Infinitive und ihre darauf beruhende verschiedene Konstruktion. 8vo. pp. 43. *Leipzig,* 1889. 1s. 6d.

**Kawczynski (Max)**—Essai comparatif sur l'origine et l'histoire des Rythmes. 8vo. *Paris,* 1889. 5s.

**Kia-li.** Livre des rites domestiques chinois. Traduit par C. de Harlez. 18mo. *Paris,* 1889. 2s. 6d.

**Langen (K. F. H. van).** —Handleiding voor de Atjehsche Taal. Royal 8vo. *The Hague,* 1889. 5s.

**Langen (K. F. H. van).**—Woordenboek der Atjehsche Taal. 8vo. *The Hague,* 1889. 9s.

Levy (J.)—Neuhebräisches und chaldäisches Wörterbuch über die Talmudin und Midraschim. Nebst Beiträgen von H. L. Fleischer. 22 (Schluss) Lieferung. Royal 8vo. pp. 180. *Leipzig*, 1889. 10s.

*₊* The Dictionary is now complete in 4 vols. Price complete 7 guineas.

Morayta (M.)—Alt-Aegypten. Essay. Deutsch von A. Schwarz. Royal 8vo. pp. 76. *Berlin*, 1889. 1s. 6d.

Nallvkine (V. P.)—Histoire du Khanat de Khokand. Traduit par A. Dozon. 8vo. *Paris*, 1889. 10s.

Néroutsov Bey (le Dr.)—L'Ancienne Alexandrie. Etude archéologique et topographique. *Paris*, 1889.

Recueil de textes relatifs à l'histoire des Seldjoucides par M. J. Houtsma. Vol. II. 8vo. *Leiden*, 1889. 9s.

Reinisch (Leo).—Die Saho-Sprache. Vol. I. Texte der Saho Sprache. 8vo. pp. vi. 315. *Wien*, 1889. 8s.

Saineanu (Lazăr).—Dicţionar Romăno-German. Continênd nomenclatura completă a Vocabularului romăn, etc. 8vo. pp. xii. 429. *Bucureştĭ*, 1889. 5s.

Schrader (F.)—Der Karmapradîpa. I. Prapăthaka. Mit Auszügen aus dem Kommentar des Açărka. Herausgegeben und übersetzt. 8vo. *Halle*, 1889. 2s.

Snouck-Hurgronje (C.)—Mekka. II. 8vo. *The Hague*, 1889. 17s. 6d.

Stübel (A.), W. Reiss, und B. Koppel.—Kultur und Industrie südamerikanischer Völker. Nach den im Besitz des Museums für Voelkerkunde zu Leipzig befindlichen Sammlungen. Text und Beschreibung der Tafeln von M. Uhle. Vol. I. Alte Zeit. Folio, pp. iii. 106. With 28 Plates in Portfolio. *Berlin*, 1889. £4.

Thyret (H.)—Ueber Umbildung und Einschränkung des gothischen und angelsächsischen Wortbegriffs im Neuenglischen und Neuhochdeutschen. I. 8vo. *Leipzig*, 1889. 1s.

Weber (A.)—Ueber den zweiten, grammatischen, Pârasîprâkaça der Krishnadâsa. 4to. pp. 91. Reprint. *Berlin*, 1889. 6s.

Zeys (E.)—Essai d'un traité méthodique de droit musulman (école malékite). Tome I. Fasc. I. Royal 8vo. pp. 104. *Alger*, 1889.

---

# 𝔒riental 𝔏iterature.

---

## ANGLO-INDIA.

### (Miscellaneous.)

Baroda State.—Report on the Administration of the Baroda State for the Official Year ending 31st July, 1886. Royal 8vo. pp. 341. *Bombay*, 1888. 12s. 6d.

*₊* The Report is framed on the model of Administration Reports of the British Territories.

Bhándárkar (Rámkrishna Gopál)—The Critical, Comparative, and Historical Method of Inquiry as applied to Sanskrit Scholarship and Philology and Indian Archæology. 8vo. pp. 26. *Bombay*, 1888. 1s. 6d.

Carter Digby (J. H.)—Faithful; or, a Story of Love and Adventure. 8vo. pp. 168. *Lahore*, 1888. 18s.

*₊* Only 50 copies have been printed.

Court (Major H.)—Translation of Sikkhán de Ráj di Vikhia, or History of the Sikhs. 8vo. pp. 326. *Lahore*, 1888. £1 4s.

*₊* A short Gurmukhi Grammar and a Vocabulary of Technical Terms are appended.

Dillon (J. Emil von)—The Home and Age of the Avesta. Translated from the German by T. A. Walsh. Roy. 8vo. pp. 94. *Bombay*, 1888. 3s.

Dutt (R. Chunder)—A History of Civilization in Ancient India based on Sanskrit Literature. Vol. I. Vedic and Epic Ages. Demy 8vo. cloth, pp. xvi. 302. With a Map. *Calcutta*, 1889.

*₊* The work will be completed in 3 volumes.

Ghose (J. N.)—Illusions and Hallucinations. 8vo. pp. 34. *Lahore*, 1888. 6s.

*₊* Only 100 copies have been printed.

Kraft (Prince)—On Infantry. Specially translated from the German. (Reprinted from the "Pioneer.") 8vo. sewed, pp. 88. *Allahabad*, 1889. 6s.

Malcolm's History of Persia (Modern). By Lieut.-Colonel M. H. Court. Foolscap, pp. 290. *Lahore*, 1888. £3 3s.

Marston (E. W.)—Lessons in the Makráni-Baloochee Dialect. 8vo. pp. 23. *Kardchi*, 1868. 1s.

*₊* A few colloquial sentences in Makráni-Baluchi with their translation into English.

Melvill—A Short Sketch of the Life of the Late Lamented Sir Maxwell Melvill, K.C.I.E., C.S.I. By Phirozshá Dhanjibhái. 8vo. pp. 46. *Surat*, 1888. £1 8s.

*₊* Only 100 copies have been printed.

Paul (N. C.)—A Treatise on the Yoga Philosophy. 3rd edition. Demy 8vo. pp. 60. *Bombay*, 1888. 1s. 6d.

Reirson (D. P. J.)—The Practical Guide. 2 vols. With Illustrations. 8vo. pp. 50 and 55. *Lahore*, 1888. 12s. 6d.

*₊* Contains the most approved systems of excavating cuttings, embanking, drainage, etc.

Wilson (Mrs. Fr. H.)—The Shevaroya. A Story of their Past, Present, and Prospective Future. 8vo. pp. 96. *Madras*, 1888. 3s. 6d.

*₊* Guide to visitors to Yercand, with a graphic description of the Shevaroy Mountains.

## ARABIC.

Kitab-i-Hujaj. — Compiled by Maulavi Muhammad 'Abd-ul-láh. Royal 8vo. pp. 3012. *Lucknow*, 1888. 9s.

*₊* A book of claims on law and religion in Arabic.

Machuel (L.)—Grammaire élémentaire d'Arabe regulier. Deuxième édition. Post 8vo. cloth, pp. 239. *Alger*, 1889. 6s.

Maváhib ul Makkiyah; or, the Gifts received at Mecca. In Arabic and 'Arvi. Translated by Mahomed Gaus Labai A'lim. 8vo. pp. 84. Lithographed. *Dhárdvi*, 1888. 12s. 6d.

*₊* Extracts from the sayings of the Prophet Mahomet called the Traditions.

Sedira (Belkassem Ben).—Dialogues Français-Arabes. 3e édition. 12mo. cloth, pp. viii. 370. *Alger*, 1889. 3s.

Thomson-Wortabet (W.)—Arabic-English Dictionary. Post 8vo. half-bound, pp. 706, 15. *Cairo*, 1888. £1 2s. 6d.

## BRIJ.

Rámáyana.—Shriyuta Gosvámi. Tulsidáskrit Rámáyana; or, The Epic Poem of the Ramayana, by Tulsidás. In the Brij Dialect. Royal 4to. pp. 662. *Bombay*, 1888. 14s.

Rámáyana. — Tulsidáskrit Rámáyana; or, the Epic Poem of the Rámáyana, by Tulsidás. In the Brij Dialect. Demy 4to. pp. 605. *Bombay*, 1888. 9s.

## GUJARATI.

Krishna Janma Khanda Purvárddha; or, the First Half of the Section about the Birth of the God Krishna. Translated into Gujaráti by Purohit Somá Válji. Royal 8vo. pp. 362. *Bombay*, 1888. 9s.

Marzbán (Jehángir Behrámji)—Mumbáithi Káshmir ;
or, from Bombay to Cashmere. In Gujarati. Royal 12mo.
pp. 300. *Bombay*, 1888. 7*s.* 6*d.*

Parshian Tells athvá 1001 Divasni Vártá ; or, the
Persian Tales, or 1001 Days. Translated into Gujaráti by
Jijibhái Kharshedji Kápadyá. Second edition. Demy 8vo.
pp. 348. *Bombay*, 1888. 12*s.* 6*d.*

*.* A well-known Collection of Oriental Tales.

Prabodha Kávya Dohana ; or, a Select Collection of
Instructive Verses. In Gujarati. Compiled by Bálábhái
Nagindás and Harilál Chhotálál. Royal 8vo. pp. 412.
*Ahmedabad*, 1888. 7*s.* 6*d.*

*.* Extracts from the works of popular poets of Gujarát.

Shankar Sanhitá ; or, a Book Describing the Greatness
of Shankar. In Gujarati. Royal 8vo. pp. 234. *Bombay,*
1888. 6*s.*

Vakil (Govindlál Báláji)—Hindu Law. In Gujaráti.
12mo. pp. 686. *Ahmedabad*, 1888. 7*s.* 6*d.*

*.* A Tract on Hindu law of inheritance, marriage, divorce,
etc.

## HINDI.

Bhágavat Purán.—Ekádashaskanda Bháshá ; or, a
free vernacular rendering of the 11th Book of the Bhágavat
Purán. In Hindi. By Chaturdás. 8vo. pp. 192. *Bombay,*
1888. 3*s.*

Premaságar ; or, the Sea of Devotional Love. By
Lallu Pandit. In Hindi. Royal 4to. pp. 368. Lithographed. *Bombay*, 1888. 6*s.*

Prithvíráj Rasan. By Chandra Vardái. Royal 8vo.
pp. 36. *Benares*, 1888. 3*s.*

Rámásvamedh.—The Sacrifice of the Horse. By
Rama. Super Royal 8vo. pp. 438. *Agra*, 1888. 3*s.*

Rámáyan.—The Exploits of Ráma. By Tulsídás.
In Hindi. Third edition. Royal 8vo. pp. 616. *Lucknow,*
1888.

## HINDUSTANI.

Bible.—First Book of Genesis. With Urdu Translation by Bishambar Náth. 8vo. pp. 241. *Delhi*, 1888. 3*s.*

Fallon (S. W.)—A Romanized English - Hindustáni
Law and Commercial Dictionary of Words and Phrases.
English and Urdu. Edited and revised by Lála Fhakír Chand
Vaidya of Delhi. Roy. 8vo. pp. 815. *Benares*, 1888. 7*s.* 6*d.*

Fasl-ul-Khitáb li Muqaddamat-i-ahl il kitáb bissa-i-
awwal wa duwum. By Núr-ud-dín. 8vo. pp. 468. Lithographed. *Delhi*, 1888. 9*s.*
*.* Remover of the religious quarrels which exist among
Mohammadans, Jews and Christians.

Map of India.—In Urdu. By Janárdan Vásudev
Godbole. Folio. Lithographed. *Bombay*, 1888. 14*s.*

Naqsha-i-Zil'-i-Karnal. Folio. *Lahore*, 1888. 9*s.*
*.* Map of the Karnál District in Urdu.

Naqsha-i-Zil'-i-Delhi. Folio. *Lahore*, 1888. 9*s.*
*.* Map of the Delhi District in Urdu.

Naqsha-i-Zil'-i-Jhang. Folio. *Lahore*, 1888. 9*s.*
*.* Map of the Jhang District in Urdu.

Jámí-i-'Abbási. By Muhammad Bahá-ud-dín Amílí.
8vo. pp. 324. *Delhi*, 1888. 7*s.* 6*d.*
*.* A Book on Muhammadan Religion in Hindustani.

## MARATHI.

Bhágavat Puran by Ecknáth. In Marathi. Royal
8vo. pp. 1512. Lithographed. *Poona*, 1888. 16*s.*

Bhaktisár Navanáth ; or, a Book consisting of the
Legends of Nine Saints of the Náth Panth or Sect. It is
also called Bhaktisár, or the Essence of Devotion. In
Marathi. By Malu Dhundi Narhari. Royal 8vo. pp. 874.
*Bombay*, 1888. 10*s.* 6*d.*

Indian Penal Code (The).—Being Act No. 45 of 1860
(amended by Acts 27 of 1870, 19 of 1872, 10 of 1873,
8 of 1882, and 10 of 1886). With Explanatory Notes and
Abstracts of Decisions of the High Courts of Calcutta,
Bombay, Madras, and Allahabad. In Marathi. By Trim-
bakrás Náráyan Rájamáchikar and Shivrám Hari Sáthe.
New edition. Royal 8vo. pp. 596. *Poona*, 1888. £1 1*s.*

Kathásárámrita Grantha ; or, the Nectar of the
Puránic Stories. In Marathi. By Mahipati. Edited and
Annotated by Krishna Shástri Pitre. Oblong. 194 leaves.
*Bombay*, 1888. 12*s.* 6*d.*
*.* This work is an abstract of portions of the Padma, Váyu,
Skanda, and some other Puráns.

Ramá Nátak ; or, the Drama of Ramá. In Marathi.
By Trimbak Áppáji Bhonjále, alias Tátyábá Punenkar.
12mo. pp. 76. *Poona*, 1888. 2*s.* 6*d.*

Rámavijaya Kathárása ; or, the Eloquent and Charming Account of the Achievements of the God Ráma. Translated into Marathi by Murkar Mandali. 12mo. pp. 240.
*Bombay*, 1888. 4*s.*
*.* This book is a short substance of Válmiki's Rámáyana.

Ramayana.—Eknáthi Bhávártha Rámáyana ; or Substance of Rámáyana by Eknáth. Oblong, 1325 leaves.
*Bombay*, 1888. £3 18*s.*
*.* Reproduction of Valmiki's epic poem in Marathi. Eknáth
is one of the popular saints and poets. He composed several
works in the irregular but popular Ovi metre.

Sangita Ratnaprabhá Natak ; or, the Musical Drama
of Princess Ratnaprabhá. By Shivrám Vinayak Gogte.
12mo. pp. 141. *Poona*, 1888. 4*s.*
*.* A love tale in Marathi.

Yashavantráya Mahákávya ; or, the Great Poem
about Yashavantráya. In Márathi. By Vásudev Váman
Shástri Khare. 12mo. pp. 244. *Poona*, 1888. 3*s.*
*.* An historical tale of Marátha rule. The story is
well related and earned a reward from the Dakshina Prize
Committee.

Yurop ; or, a Map of the Continent of Europe. In
Marathi. By Janárdan Vásudev Godbole. In one sheet.
Lithographed. *Bombay*, 1888. 9*s.*

## PERSIAN.

Ahmad Munshi (Ghulám).—Anglo-Persian Grammar,
in Catechism Form. Demy 8vo. pp. 130. *Bombay*, 1888.
4*s.*

Desátir (The) ; or, Sacred Writings of the Ancient
Persian Prophets, together with the Commentary of the
Fifth Sasan, translated from the Ancient Persian Version.
Translated by Mulla Firus Bin Káus. Demy 8vo. pp. 210.
*Bombay*, 1888. 6*s.*

Sahiár (E. R.)—A Complete and Copious Glossary of
Difficult Words and Phrases occurring in the Second Book,
Panjáb Series, with their Pronunciation in Gujaráti and
Meanings in English, together with Adjective, Noun, and
Infinitive Forms, and Arabic Singulars and Plurals. Persian
and English. Royal 16mo. pp. 88. *Bombay*, 1888. 1*s.* 6*d.*

Takmila-i-Hamla-i-Haidari.—The Completion of the
Attack of Haidari. In Persian. Versified by Sayyid Pasand
'Ali, Bilgirámi. Haidari. Folio, pp. 342. Lithographed.
*Agra*, 1888. 9*s.*

Táskar (Sohrábji Kuvarji)—A Persian Poem in Praise
of the Intrinsic Merits, Bravery and Benevolence of Khán
Bahádur Cursetji Rustomji, Chief Justice, Baroda. In
Persian and English. Demy 4to. pp. 8. *Surat*, 1888.
£3 15*s.*
*.* Brief description of the successful official career of
the Chief Justice of the Baroda State. Only 8 copies have
been published.

Táskar (Sohrábji Kuvarji)—In Praise of the Bene-
volence and the Bravery of Khán Bahádur Sheth Padamji
Pestonjee, First-Class Sirdár of the Deccan. Persian and
English. Demy 4to. pp. 7. *Bombay*, 1888. £3 15*s.*
*.* Only 6 copies have been printed.

Táskar (Sohrabji Kuvarji)—A Persian Poem in Commemoration of the Jubilee Year of Her Most Gracious Majesty the Queen-Empress of India. In Persian, English, and Gujaráti. Demy 4to. pp. 12. *Surat*, 1888. £3 15s.

*₊* Persian verses with their translation in English and Gujaráti. Only 6 copies have been printed.

## SANSKRIT.

**Bramhavaibartta Purana.**—By Maharshi Vedavyasa. Edited by Pandit Jibananda Vidyasagara. 2 vols. 8vo. *Calcutta*, 1889. £1 10s.

**Chakradatta.**—A Treatise on Hindu Medicine by Chakrapani Datta. Edited by Pandit Jibananda Vidyasagara. 8vo. pp. 471. *Calcutta*, 1888. 6s.

**Champuramayana.**—A Poem in Prose and Verse by Bhoja Raja. Edited and published with a full commentary. By Pandit Jibananda Vidyasagara. Second edition. 8vo. pp. 370. *Calcutta*, 1889. 3s. 6d.

**Dharma Sindhu**; or, The Ocean of Religious Duties. With Notes. By Káshináth Upádhyáya. Roy. 8vo. pp. 386. *Bombay*, 1888. 9s.

**Kavyasangraha.**—In Three Volumes. Edited and Published with a Full Commentary. By Pandit Jibananda Vidyasagara. Vols. II. and III. pp. 412 and 530. *Calcutta*, 1888. 6s. each vol.

**Manu Smriti**; or, The Institutes of Manu, together with the Bhaktámara Stotra or Hymn. Sanskrit and Mágadhi. Translated by K. Venkratraman Shástri Suri and Krishnáji Bishto Bhágvat. Royal 8vo. pp. 487. *Bombay*, 1888. 18s.

**Manu Smriti Bháshá Tiká**, or the Institutes of Manu. With a Translation in Hindi, by Pandit Gangádhar Pushkarlál. Royal 4to. pp. 836. *Bombay*, 1888. 16s.

**Mohamudgara**; or, Panacea for Distraction by Paramahansa Sankaráchárya. Edited and Published with Bengali, Hindi, and English Translations. By Durga Das Ray. 12mo. pp. 16. *Darjeeling*, 1888. 1s.

**Rajaprashasti.** A Poem. By Prof. Taranatha Tarkavachaspati. Edited with a Commentary by Pandit Jibananda Vidyasagara. Fourth edition, 8vo. pp. 32. *Calcutta*, 1888. 1s.

**Ramayana.**—Vedánt Rámáyana; or, the Rámáyana explained by the Vedántic Philosophy. By Pandit Shivasaháya Shivasampat Upádhyá. Royal 4to. pp. 226. *Bombay*, 1888. 6s.

*₊* An explanation of the great epic the Ramayana, as an allegory of Vedántism. In Sanskrit and Hindi.

**Shrutabodha.**—A Poem by Kalidasa. Edited with a Commentary by Pandit Jibananda Vidyasagara. Second edition. 8vo. pp. 12. *Calcutta*, 1888. 6d.

**Susruta**; or, System of Medicine. Taught by Dhanwantari, and composed by his disciple Susruta. In six divisions, Sutra, Nidana, Sharira, Chikitsa, Kalpa, and Uttaratantra. Edited by Pandit Jibananda Vidyasagara. Third edition. 8vo. pp. 915. *Calcutta*, 1889. 12s. 6d.

**Tattva Bodhini.**—The Essence of Knowledge. A Commentary by Jnanendra Sarasvati. In Sanskrit. Roy. 8vo. pp. 698. *Benares*, 1888. 12s. 6d.

*₊* A commentary on Siddhanta Kaumudi.

**Uttararamacharita.**—A Drama in Seven Acts. By Bhavabhuti. Edited and published with a full commentary. By Pandit Jibananda Vidyasagara. Second edition. 8vo. pp. 268. *Calcutta*, 1889. 3s. 6d.

**Vetala Pancha Vinshati**; or, Twenty-five Tales Related by a Vampire to Rajah Vikramaditya. Second edition. 8vo. pp. 148. *Calcutta*, 1888. 2s. 6d.

---

# AN IMPORTANT COLLECTION OF BOOKS

### RELATING TO

## 𝕭ritish 𝕴ndia.

### ON SALE BY TRÜBNER & Co.

*(Continued from page 32.)*

**CLARKE (C. B.)**—Compositæ Indicæ descriptæ et secus Genera Benthamii ordinatæ. 8vo. boards, pp. xxiv. 347, xlv. *Calcutta*, 1876. 15s.

*₊* Out of print.

**CONNELL (C. J.)**—Our Land Revenue Policy in Northern India. 8vo. cloth, pp. viii. 203. *Calcutta*, 1876. 12s. 6d.

**COLEBROOKE (H. T.)**—A Digest of Hindu Law on Contracts and Successions. With a Commentary. By Jagannátha Tercepanchánana. In three vols. 8vo. bound in half-leather, pp. xxxv. 515, x. 587, and vii. 639. *Calcutta*, 1801. £2 2s.

**COLEBROOKE (H. T.)**—Two Treatises on the Hindu Law of Inheritance. 4to. half-bound, pp. xv. 377. *Calcutta*, 1810. 15s.

**COLEBROOKE (H. T.)**—Two Treatises on the Hindu Law of Inheritance. Dáya-Bhága and Mitácshara. Third Edition. With Index. Royal 8vo. cloth, pp. xix. 377, ix. *Madras*, 1867. £2 2s.

**COORG.**—Rice (L.)—Coorg Inscriptions. Translated for Government. 4to. boards, pp. 16, 28. With Plates. With Index. *Bangalore*, 1886. 9s.

**COORG.**—Richter (C. G.)—Manual of Coorg. A Gazetteer of the Natural Features of the Country and the Social and Political Condition of its Inhabitants. With 1 Map and 4 Illustrations. 8vo. boards, pp. xi. 474. *Mangalore*, 1870. 16s.

**COTY.**—Geofry.—Coty and her Sisters, or Our Hill Stations in South India. 12mo. cloth, pp. vi. 158. *Madras*, 1881. 2s. 6d.

**COWELL (HERBERT)**—The Hindu Law. Being a Treatise on the Law administered exclusively to Hindus by the British Courts in India. 2 vols. in One. 8vo. cloth, pp. xix. 373, xviii. 333. *Calcutta*, 1870–71. £1 16s.

*₊* Tagore Law Lectures, 1870–71.

**CUNNINGHAM'S** Reports of Operations and Proceedings of the Archæological Surveyor to the Government of India during the Seasons 1861 to 1865. 5 Parts in 1. Small folio, cloth, pp. 48, 50, 50, 94 and 88. With 8 Plates. *Calcutta*, 1862–66. £1 1s.

**CUNNINGHAM (ALEXANDER)**—Coins of Alexander's Successors in the East. The Greeks and Indo-Scythians. Parts 1–3. With Plates. 8vo. sewed, pp. 105. *London*, 1868. 5s.

**DACCA.**—Taylor (James)—A Sketch of the Topography and Statistics of Dacca. With 1 Map. 8vo. pp. vi. 371. *Calcutta*, 1840. 6s.

**DA CUNHA (J. GERSON)**—Notes on the History and Antiquities of Chaul and Bassein. With 17 Photographs, 9 Lithographed Plates, and a Map. 8vo. cloth, pp. xvi. 262. *Bombay*, 1876. £1 5s.

**DA CUNHA (J. G.)**—Contributions to the Study of Indo-Portuguese Numismatics. 4 Fasc. 8vo. sewed, pp. 125. With 9 Plates. *Bombay*, 1883. (2s. 6d. each Fasc.) 10s.

**DAS (ABHAY CHARAN)**—The Indian Ryot, Land Tax, Permanent Settlement, and the Famine. 8vo. cloth, pp. 661. *Howrah*, 1881. 12s.

**DASS (REV. ISHUREE)**—Domestic Manners and Customs of the Hindoos of Northern India, or more strictly speaking, of the North-West Provinces of India. Second Edition. 12mo. cloth, pp. xi. and 280. *Benares*, 1866. 7s. 6d.

**DEROZARIO (M.)**—The Complete Monumental Register, containing all the Epitaphs, Inscriptions, etc., in the different Churches and Burial Grounds in and about Calcutta. 8vo. pp. 230. *Calcutta*, 1815. 5*s.*

**DEY (KANNY LOLL)**—The Indigenous Drugs of India; or, Short Descriptive Notices on the Medicines, both Vegetable and Mineral, in Common Use among the Natives of India. 8vo. cloth, pp. iv. 130. *Calcutta*, 1867. 3*s.* 6*d.*

**DOMESTIC** (Indian) Economy and Receipt Book. By the Author of "Manual of Gardening for Western India." Fifth edition, revised. 8vo. cloth, pp. viii. 677. *Madras*, 1860. 6*s.*

**DORJE-LING.** With 3 Maps. 8vo. sewed, pp. ii. 57; x. xxxi. xiv. iii. v. *Calcutta*, 1838. 3*s.* 6*d.*

**DUBOIS (J. A.)**—Mœurs, Institutions et Cérémonies des Peuples de l'Inde. 2 vols. 8vo. boards, pp. xxxii. 491, 955. *Paris*, 1825. 10*s.* 6*d.*

**DU PERRON (M. Anquetil)**—Recherches Historiques et Geographiques sur l'Inde. 2 Parts in 1. With Maps and 10 Plates. 4to. half-bound, pp. lxii. 598. *Berlin*, 1786. 9*s.*

**DUSRE (Munshi Kali Prasad, Scrivashava)**—The Kayastha Ethnology; being an Inquiry into the Origin of the Chitraguptavansi and Chandrasenavansi Kayasthas. 8vo. cloth, pp. 9, ix. 30, 4. *Lucknow*, 1877. 5*s.*

**DUTHIE (J. F.)**—Illustrations of the Indigenous Fodder Grasses of the Plains of North-Western India. 2 Parts. 80 Plates. 4to. *Roorkee*, 1886–87. £2 2*s.*

The same. Letterpress. 8vo. pp. xxiv. 90, vii. With 6 Plates. *Roorkee*, 1888. 10*s.* 6*d.*

**DUTT (H. C.)**—Short Discourses on Scripture Subjects. (Second Series.) 8vo. cloth, pp. 109. *Calcutta*, 1871. 3*s.* 6*d.*

**DUTT (H. C.)**—Three Years in Europe, being Extracts from Letters sent from Europe by a Hindu. Second edition. 8vo. sewed, pp. 120, vi. *Calcutta*, 1873. 2*s.* 6*d.*

**DUTT (J. CH.)**—Kings of Kashmira. Being a Translation of the Sanskrit Work Rájataranggini of Kahlana Pandita. Two vols. Small 8vo. sewed, pp. v. 303, xxiii. xliv. 320. *Calcutta*, 1879–87. 10*s.*

**DYMOCK (W.)**—The Vegetable Materia Medica of Western India. Five Parts. 8vo. pp. xiv. 786. *Bombay*, 1883. £1 2*s.* 6*d.*

**EDGAR,** or the New Pygmalion and the Judgment of Tithonus. 8vo. cloth, pp. 151. *Madras*, 1883. 3*s.* 6*d.*

**ELLIOT (H. M.)**—Memoirs of the History, Folk-lore, and Distribution of the Races of the North-Western Provinces of India. Being an amplified edition of the Original Supplementary Glossary of Indian Terms. Edited and revised by John Beames. Two vols. 8vo. cloth, pp. xx. 369, 396. With Maps. *London*, 1869. £1 16*s.*

**ESSAYS** by the Students of the College of Fort William in Bengal. To which are added the Theses pronounced at the Public Disputations in the Oriental Languages on the 6th February, 1802. 8vo. bound, pp. xvi. 228. *Calcutta*, 1802. 10*s.* 6*d.*

**FAULKNER (A.)**—Dictionary of Commercial Terms with the Synonyms in Various Languages. 8vo. half-bound, pp. 158. With Appendix. *Bombay*, 1856. 5*s.*

**FERGUSSON (J.)**—Tree and Serpent Worship; or Illustrations of Mythology and Art in India in the first and fourth Centuries after Christ. From the Sculptures of the Buddhist Topes at Sanchi and Amravati. 4to. half-mor. pp. x. 274. With 100 Plates. *London*, 1873.

*** Out of print and valuable.

**FERGUSSON (J.)** and James Burgess —The Cave Temples of India. With Map, numerous Illustrations, and 98 Plates. Royal 8vo. half-bound, pp. xx. 536. *London*, 1880. £2 2*s.*

**FIREBRACE (F.)** — Papers prepared for the Use of the Thomason Civil Engineering College, Roorkee. No. VII. Surveying. Fourth edition. With numerous Plates and Illustrations. 8vo. sewed, pp. xv. 293, vi. *Roorkee*, 1883. 12*s.* 6*d.*

**FLEET (J. F.)**—The Dynasties of the Kanarese Districts of the Bombay Presidency from the earliest Historical Times to the Muhammadan Conquest of A.D. 1318. With Plates. 8vo. sewed, pp. 106. *Bombay*, 1882. 5*s.*

**FORREST (G. W.)**—Selections from the Letters, Despatches, and other State Papers preserved in the Bombay Secretariat. Edited by G. W. Forrest.

Maratha Series. Vol. I. 4to. half-bound, pp. xxxiv. 730, iv. *Bombay*, 1885. £1 10*s.* 6*d.*

Home Series. 2 vols. 4to. half-bound, pp. lii. 450 and 450. *Bombay*, 1887. £2 2*s.*

**GAZETTEER** of the Central Provinces of India. Edited by C. Grant. Second edition. With 1 Map. 8vo. cloth, pp. 4, clvii. 582. *Nagpur*, 1870. £1 1*s.*

**GELL (F.)** — A Handbook of Common Plants in Eastern India; being a Catalogue of Native Names of Trees and Plants. Small 8vo. half-bound, pp. xiii. 111. *Bombay*, 1863. 5*s.*

**GEOGHEGAN (J.)**—Some Account of Silk in India, especially of the various attempts to encourage and extend Sericulture in that Country. Small folio, pp. xv. 126 and 15. *Calcutta*, 1872. 7*s.* 6*d.*

**GHOSE (LOKE NATH)**—Music's Appeal to India. An Original, Instructive and Interesting Story. 8vo. sewed, pp. 24. *Calcutta*, 1873. 1*s.*

**GHOSE (L. N.)**—The Music and Musical Notation of Various Countries. 8vo. sewed, pp. 55. *Calcutta*, 1874. 2*s.*

**GHOSE (L. N.)**—The Modern History of the Indian Chiefs, Rajas, Zamindars, etc. Part I. The Native States, etc., etc. Part II. The Native Aristocracy and Gentry, etc., etc. 2 vols. 8vo. cloth, pp. vii. 217 and ix. 611. *Calcutta*, 1879–81. 15*s.*

**GHOSE (NAGENDRA NATH)**—The Effects of Observation of England upon Indian Ideas and Institutions. 8vo. sewed, pp. 47. *Calcutta*, 1877. 2*s.* 6*d.*

**GHOSE (N. N.)**—Kristo Das Pal. A Study. 8vo. cloth, pp. 202. *Calcutta*, 1887. 6*s.*

**GHOSE (RASHBEHARY)**—The Law of Mortgage in India. 8vo. cloth, pp. vii. 362. *Calcutta*, 1877. 10*s.*

*** Tagore Law Lecturer, 1875-6.

**GHOSHA (PRATA PACHANDRA)**—Durga Puja. With Notes and Illustrations. 8vo. boards, pp. xxii. 83, lxx. *Calcutta*, 1871. 7*s.* 6*d.*

*** A very interesting book on this national festival of the Hindus of Bengal.

**GOA.** — Da Fonseca (José Nicolau) — An Historical and Archæological Sketch of the City of Goa. Preceded by a short Statistical Account of the Territory of Goa. With Map, Plan, and Lithographic Plates. 8vo. cloth, pp. xi. 332. *Bombay*, 1878. 10*s.* 6*d.*

**GOODEVE (L. A.)** and J. V. Woddman. — Full Bench Rulings of the High Court at Fort William. From its Institution in 1862 to the Commencement of the Bengal Law Reports. 8vo. cloth, pp. xxviii. 1025, 44, lxii. *Calcutta*, 1874. £3.

**GOPINATH (Sadashirji Hate)**—Regeneration of India. 8vo. cloth, pp. iv. 79. *Bombay*, 1883. 2*s.*

**GRAY (J. E.)**—Illustrations of Indian Zoology. Consisting of Coloured Plates of New and hitherto unfigured Indian Animals, from the collection of Major-General Hardwicke. Parts 1 to 5. 50 Plates. Folio. *London*, 1830. £1 10*s.* or each part 7*s.* 6*d.*

**GREENLAW (ALEX. JOHN)**—Masonic Lectures. Delivered in Open Lodge, Chapter, etc. 8vo. cloth, pp. viii. 241. *Madras*, 1870. 18*s.*

**GRIBBLE (J. D. B.)**—Two Native States. Being Letters from Hyderabad and Mysore. (Reprinted from the Madras Christ College Magazine.) 8vo. cloth, pp. 120. *Madras*, 1886. 3*s*.

**GRIFFITH (WILLIAM)**— Notulae ad Plantas Asiaticas. Part I. Development of Organs in Phanœrogamous Plants, arranged by J. McClelland. 8vo. boards, pp. viii. 255. *Calcutta*, 1847. 15*s*.

**GRIGG (H. B.)**—Manual of the Nilagiri District in the Madras Presidency. With numerous Maps and Illustrations. 8vo. cloth, pp. xiv. 578. With Appendix, pp. 127. *Madras*, 1880. £1 10*s*.

**HAMILTON (E.)**—Translation of the Letters of a Hindoo Rajah, written previous to, and during the Period of his Residence in England. To which is prefixed a Preliminary Dissertation on the History, Religion, and Manners of the Hindoos. Fifth edition. 2 vols. in 1. 8vo. cloth, pp. lii. 270, and 342. *London*, 1811. 12*s*. 6*d*.

**HASTINGS (WARREN)** — Narrative of the Insurrection which Happened in the Zemeedary of Banaris in the Month of August, 1781, and of the Transactions of the Governor-General in that District. With an Appendix. 4to. boards, pp. 70, 213. *Calcutta*, 1782. 15*s*.

**HEDAYA (The)** or Guide. A Commentary on the Mussulman Laws. Translated by Order of the Governor-General and Council of Bengal, by Ch. Hamilton. 4 vols. 4to. leather. *London*, 1791. £5 5*s*.

<sub></sub>*** The great law-book of the most orthodox sect of Islam. By Burhánée d'Din Ali.

**HICKEY (WILLIAM)**—The Tanjore Mahratta Principality in Southern India ; the Land of the Chola, the Eden of the South. Second edition. With 2 Maps. 8vo. cloth, pp. xxxii. 225, clxvi. *Madras*, 1874. 7*s*. 6*d*.

**HINDU MUSIC.**—Reprinted from the "Hindoo Patriot" (Sept. 7, 1874). 8vo. sewed, pp. 52. *Calcutta*, 1874. 1*s*. 6*d*.

**HOGG (FRANCIS R.)**—Practical Remarks chiefly concerning the Health and Ailments of European Families in India, with especial reference to Maternal Management and Domestic Economy. 8vo. sewed, pp. vi. 230. *Benares*, 1877. 5*s*.

**HORMUSJEE (DORABJEE)**—The Oriental Calculator, or Tables for the Calculation of Interest, Exchange, and Commission, etc. Third edition. *Bombay*, 1860. 3*s*. 6*d*.

**JOLLY (JULIUS)**—Outlines of a History of the Hindu Law of Partition, Inheritance and Adoption, as contained in the Original Sanskrit Treatises. 8vo. cloth, pp. xi. 347. *Calcutta*, 1885. £1 5*s*.

**JONES (WILLIAM)** — Hindu Gesetzbuch oder Menu's Verordnungen nach Culluca's Erläuterung. Ein Inbegriff des Indischen Systems religiöser und bürgerlicher Pflichten. 8vo. sewed, pp. xlviii. 528. *Weimar*, 1797. 6*s*.

**KALYPADA** Mukhopadhya.—Bahoolina Tatwa, or a Treatise on Violin. Royal 8vo. sewed. 5*s*.

**KHETRA** Mohana Goswámi.—Kantha Kaumudi ; or a Guide to Vocal Music. Royal 8vo. sewed, pp. 403. *Calcutta*, 1875. 8*s*.

**KHORY (RUST. NASERW.)**—The Bombay Materia Medica and their Therapeutics. 8vo. cloth, pp. 600, xxxix. *Bombay*, 1887. 18*s*.

**KING (G.)**—A Manual of Cinchona Cultivation in India. Folio, boards, pp. 80. With 1 Plate. *Calcutta*, 1876. 6*s*.

**KITTS (EUSTACE J.)**—Serious Crime in an Indian Province. Post 8vo. boards, pp. viii. 97. *Bombay*, 1889. 2*s*. 6*d*.

**LABORIE.**—An Abridgment of the Coffee Planter of St. Domingo. Also Notes on the Propagation and Cultivation of the Medicinal Chinchonas or Peruvian Bark Trees. By W. Gr. McIvor. With 6 Plates. 8vo. sewed, pp. 82. *Madras*, 1863. 7*s*. 6*d*.

**LEGENDS** of the Shrine of Harihara in the Province of Mysore. Translated from the Sanskrit by Rev. Th. Foulkes. 8vo. cloth, pp. 99. *Madras*, 1876. 3*s*. 6*d*.

**LEITNER (DR. G. W.)**—The Theory and Practice of Education. With special Reference to Education in India. (Reprinted from the "Panjab Educational Magazine.") 8vo. sewed, pp. 32. *Lahore*. 2*s*. 6*d*.

**LEITNER (G. W.)** — The Languages and Races of Dardistan. 3 Parts. 4to. With several Maps and Plates. *Lahore*, 1874. £1 5*s*.

**LEITNER (G. W.)**—The Languages and Races of Dardistan. Part III. Legends, Riddles, Proverbs, etc., of the Shina Race. 4to. sewed, pp. iii. 109. *Lahore*, 1873. 12*s*. 6*d*.

**LEITNER (G. W.)**—A Sketch of the Changars and of their Dialect. Folio, sewed, pp. 21. *Lahore*, 1880. 9*s*.

**LEITNER (G. W.)**—A Detailed Analysis of Abdul Ghafur's Dictionary of the Terms used by the Criminal Tribes in the Panjab. Folio, sewed, pp. 28. *Lahore*, 1880. 15*s*.

**LEITNER (G. W.)**—Linguistic Fragments discovered in 1870, 1872 and 1879, relating to the Dialect of the Magadds and other Wandering Tribes, etc., etc. With an Account of Shawl-weaving, etc. Folio, sewed, pp. 28, 14. With Drawings and Specimens of Colour. *Lahore*, 1882. 8*s*.

**LETHBRIDGE (E.)**—The Topography of the Mogul Empire as known to the Dutch in 1631. Translated from the Latin of Joannes de Laet. 8vo. sewed, pp. 63. *Calcutta*, 1871. 3*s*. 6*d*.

**LEWIN (CAPT. T. H.)**—The Hill Tracts of Chittagong and the Dwellers therein, with Comparative Vocabularies of the Hill Dialects. Royal 8vo. sewed, pp. 151. Out of print. *Calcutta*, 1869. 9*s*.

**LITURGY** of the Basel German Evangelical Mission Churches in South-Western India. 8vo. boards, pp. viii. 172. *Mangalore*, 1875. 7*s*. 6*d*.

**LOBB (S.)**—A Modern Version of Milton's Areopagitica. With Notes, Appendix, and Tables. 8vo. sewed, pp. 14, xx. 391. *Calcutta*, 1872. 7*s*. 6*d*.

**LONG (REV. J.)**—Scripture Truth in Oriental Dress; or Emblems explanatory of Biblical Doctrines and Morals. With Parallel or Illustrative References to Proverbs and Proverbial Sayings in the Arabic, Bengali, Canarese, Persian, Russian, Sanskrit, Tamil, Telugu, and Urdu Languages. 8vo. cloth, pp. viii. 269. *Calcutta*, 1871. 5*s*.

**LUCKNOW.**—Murray's Lucknow Guide. Including Notes on Cawnpore, Agra, and Delhi. With a Map of Lucknow, 8vo. sewed, pp. xii. 67. *Lucknow*, 1882. 3*s*.

**MC CRINDLE (J. W.)**—Ancient India as described by Megasthenes and Arrian. Being a Translation of Fragments of the Indika of Megasthenes and Arrian. 8vo. cloth, pp. xi. 223. With a Map. *Calcutta*, 1877. 7*s*. 6*d*.

**MC IVOR (W. G.)** — Our Mountain Ranges. How their Resources may be turned to account and India converted into the Garden and Grain Store of the World. 8vo. sewed, pp. 31. With 4 Plates. *Madras*, 1867. 7*s*. 6*d*.

**MACNAGHTEN (W. H.)** — Principles and Precedents of Hindu Law ; being a Compilation of Primary Rules relative to the Doctrine of Inheritance, Contracts and Miscellaneous Subjects. Together with Notes, Illustrative and Explanatory and Preliminary Remarks. Second edition. 8vo. cloth, pp. xx. 366. *Madras*, 1865. £1 11*s*. 6*d*.

**MADANAKAMARAJANKADAI.**— The Dravidian Nights, etc. *Vide* Sastri.

**MADRAS.** Its Army and Commerce viewed in Connection with Bengal Policy. By a Tax Payer. 8vo. sewed, pp. 43. *Madras*, 1872. 1*s*.

**MADRAS.**—Carmichael (D. F.)—A Manual of the District of Vizagapatam, in the Presidency of Madras. 8vo. cloth, pp. vi. 398. With Portraits of the Wild Races and a Map of the Vizagapatam District. *Madras*, 1869. 12*s*. 6*d*.

**MADRAS** Civil Engineering College Papers. III. Earthwork. Practical Methods of setting out Slopes for Excavations and Embankments, Calculation of and the Equalization of Cuttings and Embankments, with Hints on the Execution of the Work, best Form of Tools, Turfing, etc. 8vo. pp. 41. With 5 Plates. *Madras*, 1861. 4*s*.

(*To be continued.*)

# PERIODICAL PUBLICATIONS.

## ANALES DEL MUSEO NACIONAL DE MEXICO.

Tomo IV. Entrega 3ª. Sumario. El Tonalamatl, por el Sr. Lic. Manuel Orozco y Berra (páginas 33-44, y láminas 7-10).—Los trabajos lingüísticos de D. Miguel Trinidad Palma, por F. P. T.—Lista de los pueblos princi-pales que perteneciam antiguamenta á Tetzcoco, con una advertencia, por F. P. T.—Arte Mexicana, por el P. Antonio del Rincon (1595). With 4 Plates.

Price of each Number, 8s. 6d.

## THE CALCUTTA REVIEW.
### EDITED BY H. A. D. PHILLIPS, C.S.

No. CLXXVI. April, 1889. *Contents* : Cameos of Indian Districts. I. Purneah Bengal. By H. G. Cooke, C. S.—The Relations of Missionaries to Great European and Asiatic Governments. By Robert Cust.—Some Agrarian Questions in the Punjab.—Social Improvements. Past and Future. By Esmé.—The Apportionment of Compensation in Land Acquisition Proceedings. By F. E. Pargeter, C. S.—Tax-ation in India, Parts III. and IV. By Mohiny Mohun Roy. —Trial of Questions of Fact in British India. By Romesh Chunder Bose.—The Novels of Emile Zola.—Indian Codifi-cation. By the Editor.—Malarial Fever in Bengal. By W. H. Gregg, Surg. Major.—The Indian National Congress (Independent Section). 1. By K. S. Ganapati Ayyar, B.A. and B.L. ; 2. By a Mahomedan.—Early British Administra-tion in India. By the Editor.—The Sacrifice of Rath. By W. L. G.—The Quarter. By the Editor.—Summary of Annual Reports.—Critical Notices.—General Literature.—Vernacular Literature.

Single Parts, 6s.     Annual Subscription, £1 4s.

## CHINESE RECORDER AND MISSIONARY JOURNAL.

Vol. XX. No. 4. April, 1889. The New Testament in Chinese. Paper III. Translation of the Nü Len Nü. By Mrs. A. S. Parker.—In what Lines of Action can our three Missions most effectively Prosecute their Work in Union ? By Rev. N. J. Plumb.—The Missionaries and the Mandarins.—Remember the Sabbath Day to keep it Holy.—Another Phonography.—Chinese Methodist Episcopal Mission of California Conference. By Mrs. S. L. Baldwin.—Historical Landmarks of Macao. By Rev. J. G. Thomson, M.D.—Correspondence.—Our Book Table.—Diary of Events in the Far East.—Missionary Journal.

Monthly.     Annual Subscription, 15s.

## THE CHINA REVIEW;
### OR, NOTES AND QUERIES ON THE FAR EAST.

Vol. XVII. No. 4. *Contents* : The Life of Lao-Tse. By G. von der Gabelentz.—Samuel Wells Williams. By Thomas W. Pearce.—Budget of Historical Tales. By R. W. Hurst. —A Trip from Kiukiang to the Lushan Hills. By J. Leu-mann.—Metrical Translations from the Shi King. The " Shang Min," Decade of Part III. By W. Jennings, M.A. Muh-T'ien-Tsze Chuen. By E. J. Eitel, Ph.D.—Notes and Queries.—Curious Names. By G. M. H. Playfair.—Bad Language. By G. M. H. Playfair.—The Tartarian Lamb. By E. H. Parker.—Ancient Books. By E. H. Parker.—Pasquinade from Formosa. By G. M. H. Playfair.—Notices of New Books.—Collectanea Bibliographica.—Books Wanted, Exchanges, etc.—To Contributors.

Bi-monthly.     Annual Subscription, £1 10s.

## INTERNATIONALES ARCHIV FÜR ETHNOGRAPHIE.

Band II. Heft I. and II. *Inhalt* : Dr. F. von Luschan. Das Türkische Schattenspiel. Mit Tafel I.-IV.—Dr. Heinr. Schurtz. Das Wurfmesser der Neger. Mit Tafel V. und Abbildungen im Text.—R. Parkinson. Beiträge zur Ethnologie der Gilbert-Insulaner. Mit Abbildungen im Text.—Nou-velles et Correspondance.—Questions et Réponses. Musées et Collections.—Dr. G. J. Dozy.—Revue Bibliographique.—Explorations et Explorateurs.—Nominations, Nécrologie. Band II. Heft III. *Inhalt* : Dr. F. Von Luschan. Das Türkische Schattenspiel (Fortsetzung).—R. Parkinson. Beiträge zur Ethnologie der Gilbert-Insulaner (Schluss).—Felix Driessen. Tie and Dye Work manufactured at Semarang Island, Java, with Plate VI. and Illustration.—Nouvelles et Correspondance.—Questions et Réponses.—Musées et Collections.—Dr. G. J. Dozy. Revue Bibliogra-phique.—Explorations et Explorateurs, Nominations, Nécro-logie.

Each Part, 3s. 6d.     Annual Subscription, £1.

## THE JOURNAL OF THE ANTHROPOLOGICAL SOCIETY OF BOMBAY.

Vol. I. No. 6. *Contents* : Statistics of Suicides in the City of Bombay in the year 1886. Compiled by E. Rehatsek.—Note on the Statistics of Suicides. By J. De Cunha.—On Anthropology in India. By H. H. Risley.—On the Pitars or Tánks. By K. Raghunathjee.—On Popular Superstitions in Bengal. By Kedarnath Basu.—On the Gondhalis, a Class of Maratha Bards. By Purshotam Balkrishna Joshi.—On Amulets. By Dr. Gerson da Cunha.

Price 5s. per Number.

LONDON : TRÜBNER & CO., 57 AND 59, LUDGATE HILL.

# TRÜBNER'S RECORD,

## A JOURNAL DEVOTED TO THE LITERATURE OF THE EAST.

### WITH NOTES AND LISTS OF CURRENT

#### American, European and Colonial Publications.

*Edited by Dr. Rost, of the India Office.*

SEPTEMBER, 1889.  THIRD SERIES. VOL. I. NO. 4.  PRICE 2*s.*

A POETICAL TRANSLATION OF CHAPTER I. OF

## The Dhammapada

By SIR EDWIN ARNOLD, K.C.I.E., C.S.I.*
*Author of " The Light of Asia," &c.*

Thought in the mind hath made us.  What we are
 By thought was wrought and built.  If a man's mind
Hath evil thoughts, pain comes on him as comes
 The wheel the ox behind.

All that we are is what we thought and willed ;
 Our thoughts shape us and frame.  If one endure
In purity of thought, joy follows him
 As his own shadow—sure.

' He hath defamed me, wronged me, injured me,
 Abased me, beaten me !"  If one should keep
Thoughts like these angry words within his breast
 Hatreds will never sleep.

 He hath defamed me, wronged me, injured me,
 Abased me, beaten me !"  If one should send
Such angry words away for pardoning thoughts
 Hatreds will have an end.

For never anywhere at any time
 Did hatred cease by hatred.  Always 'tis
By love that hatred ceases—only Love,
 The ancient Law is this.

The many, who are foolish, have forgot—
 Or never knew—how mortal wrongs pass by :
But they who know and who remember, let
 Transient quarrels die.

Whoso abides, looking for joy, unschooled,
 Gluttonous, weak, in idle luxuries,
Mâra will overthrow him, as fierce winds
 Level short-rooted trees.

Whoso abides, disowning joys, controlled,
 Temperate, faithful, strong, shunning all ill,
Mâra shall no more overthrow that man
 Than the wind doth a hill.

Whoso *Kâshya* wears—the yellow robe—
 Being *anishkashya* †—not sin-free,

---

* From " The Buddhist," published in Colombo.
† There is a play here upon the words *Kâshya*, " the yellow
robe of the Buddhist Priest," and *Kashya*, " impurity."

Nor heeding truth and governance—unfit
 To wear that dress is he.

But whoso, being *nishkashya*, pure,
 Clean from offence, doth still in virtues dwell,
Regarding temperance and truth—that man
 Weareth *Kâshya* well.

Whoso imagines truth in the untrue,
 And in the true finds untruth—he expires
Never attaining knowledge : life is waste ;
 He follows vain desires.

Whoso discerns in truth the true, and sees
 The false in falseness with unblinded eye,
He shall attain to knowledge ; life with such
 Aims well before it die.

As rain breaks through an ill-thatched roof, so break
 Passions through minds that holy thought despise ;
As rain runs from a perfect thatch, so run
 Passions from off the wise.

The evil-doer mourneth in this world,
 And mourneth in the world to come ; in both
He grieveth.  When he sees fruits of his deeds
 To see he will be loath ;

The righteous man rejoiceth in this world
 And in the world to come : in both he takes
Pleasure.  When he shall see fruit of his works
 The good sight gladness makes.

Glad is he living, glad in dying, glad
 Having once died ; glad always, glad to know
What good deeds he hath done, glad to foresee
 More good where he shall go.

The lawless man, who, not obeying LAW,
 Leaf after leaf recites, and line by line,
No Buddhist is he, but a foolish herd
 Who counts another's kine.

The law-obeying, loving one, who knows
 Only one verse of DHARMA, but hath ceased
From envy, hatred, malice, foolishness—
 *He* is the Buddhist Priest.

London, *May 14th*, 1889.  EDWIN ARNOLD.

The *Dhammapada* is a compilation of verses,[*] principally from the Sutrapitaka, made at the first great council of the Buddhist Church (which was held in the year after the passing away of our Lord Buddha, at the Sattapanni cave near Rajagriha, under the presidency of the great Mahakasyapa), and confirmed at the two succeeding councils. The selection was made as a sort of manual for the student of the spirit of true Buddhism, and almost all the purely moral sayings of our Lord are included in it. It is not to be supposed that there is any chronological order to be observed in its compilation; in many cases where two or three verses are to be found upon the same subject they were delivered by the Lord Buddha on entirely different occasions. The word *Dhammapada* is usually translated "Verses of the Law"; perhaps "Portions of the Law" would be more correct, as there is a reference here to the *Sattatimsa-bodhipakkhiya-dhamma*, or "The Thirty-seven Portions or Parts of the Law"[†] (or thirty-seven steps of the Path to Nirvana) laid down by our Lord. But Buddhist terminology in the English language is at present so unsettled and unsatisfactory that it is very difficult to give a translation which shall at once convey the whole meaning of the original as understood by an Eastern student. The *Dhammapada* is said to have three meanings, one within the other : first, its obvious meaning; second, that contained in what is called "the abridged or contracted explanation"; and third, that contained in the complete or perfect explanation. As known to the Southern Church, it consists of twenty-six sections, which are named as follows :—

1. *Yamakavagga*[‡] (the section of the pairs of opposites), containing a series of verses arranged in

pairs, the second of which praises some particular virtue, while the first shows the evil of its opposite.

2. *Appamádavagga* (the section on hastening to do good), which shows the evils of delay and the necessity of hastening to perform good works.

3. *Chittavagga* (the section of the mind or of thought), which speaks of the corruption and the cleansing of the mind, and the attainment of purity of heart.

4. *Pupphavagga* (the section of flowers), which shows the exaltation of the way to Nirvana, and compares the life of a man who follows the thirty-seven Portions of the Doctrine to a carefully-woven garland of beautiful flowers—each virtue being a blossom fitted in the exact place where it can show to the best advantage, and most add to the beauty of the whole.

5. *Bálavagga* (the section of the fool), explaining the nature of the foolish man.

6. *Panditavagga* (the section of the wise man), showing the nature and customs of the truly wise man.

7. *Arahatavagga* (the section of the Arahats), which speaks of the qualifications and powers of the Arahat or fully-developed man.

8. *Sáhassavagga* (the section of thousands), so called because it states that one good word is better than a thousand foolish ones; that one verse well understood is better than a thousand repeated without understanding, etc.

9. *Pápavagga* (the section of sin), explaining the action of sin and the method of escaping from it and attaining salvation.

10. *Dandavagga* (the section of injuries or punishments), which condemns the infliction of injury on any one.

11. *Jardvagga* (the section of decay), which explains the nature of decay of the body, and the coming of old age.

12. *Attavagga* (the section of self—*i.e.* self-protection), explaining how to protect one self from all spiritual harm.

13. *Lokavagga* (the section of the world), speaking of this world and the future worlds, and pointing out the Good Path.

14. *Buddhavagga* (the section of the Buddhas), in which the qualities of a Buddha are mentioned.

15. *Sukhavagga* (the section of happiness), showing in what true happiness consists.

16. *Piyavagga* (section of affection), showing the good and evil of the affections, and on what objects they should be fixed, and bidding us beware of sin.

17. *Kodhavagga* (the section of anger), warning us against the evil effects of anger.

18. *Malavagga* (the section of impurity), adverting to the evils of impurity either of mind or body.

19. *Dhammatthavagga* (the section of morality), ex-

---

[*] In the Chinese preface to the *Dhammapada* it is written:—"The verses called *Dhammapada* are selections from all Sutras. These are the words of Buddha Himself, spoken as occasion suggested, not at any one time, but at various times, and the cause and end of their being spoken is also related in the different Sutras. After Buddha left the world, Ananda collected a certain number of volumes, in each of which the words of Buddha are quoted, whether the Sutra be large or small, with this introductory phrase :—'Thus I have heard.' It was from these works that the Shamans (monks) in after years copied out the various *Gathas*, some of four lines, some of six lines, and attached to each set a title according to the subject therein explained. But all these verses without exception are taken from one or other of the accepted Scriptures, and therefore they are called 'Law-verses,' or Scripture extracts, because they are found in the canon."

[†] The "Thirty-seven Portions of the Law" are the *Satipatthana*, or Four Earnest Meditations, the *Sammappadhana*, or Four Great Efforts, the *Iddhipada*, or Four Steps to the attainment of wonderful powers, the *Balani*, or Five Superhuman Powers, the *Indriyani*, or Five Superhuman Senses, the *Bodhi-anga*, or Seven Kinds of Wisdom, and the *Arya-ashtangika marga*, or Noble Eight-fold Path. These are explained in the second part of Mr. C. W. Leadbeater's *Introductory Catechism of Buddhism*.

[‡] This is the one translated above by Sir Edwin Arnold.

plaining the nature of the true Doctrine, and the necessity of holding firmly by it.

20. *Maggavagga* (the section of the Path), in which the nature of the Noble Eightfold Path is explained.

21. *Pakinnakavagga* (the miscellaneous section), containing advice on various subjects.

22. *Nirayavagga* (the section of the hells), describing the nature of the men whose *karma* will bring upon them terrible suffering after death.

23. *Nâgavagga* (the section of the great), which explains the nature of the truly great man. This is sometimes called the Elephant section.

24. *Tanhâvagga* (the section of desire), showing what desire or lust is, and its evil effects.

25. *Bhikkhuvagga* (the section of monastic life), describing how a monk should live.

26. *Brahmanavagga* (the section of the Brahman), showing that the true Brahman is the pure-minded man, whether his birth be high or low—not the mere man of high caste.

In conclusion, I may say that I consider the study of the *Dhammapada* of the greatest importance, since it is of itself sufficient, if properly comprehended, to give a perfect understanding of the nature of Buddha's religion. I am 'much pleased to hear that Sir Edwin Arnold, to whom we already owe so much, has commenced a poetical translation of it, and I hope that he will find time to complete it.

H. SUMANGALA,<br>*High Priest.*

Colombo.

## The Bashkir.

### GEOGRAPHICAL POSITION.

The Bashkir, more accurately Bashkurt, are the most important of the tangled group of Turko-Tatar races that lie scattered over the extreme eastern borders of Russia. A line drawn from Orenburg due north through Ufa and Perm bisects Bashkiria into two not unequal portions, and would also mark that part of the territory in which the Bashkir are most compact. East of this line they are scattered over the Urals well across the Siberian frontier, and westward they extend as far as the valley of the Volga. Outside the governmental divisions of Ufa, Orenburg, Perm, Viatka, Kazan, and Samara, the Bashkir are not met with. The town of Ufa is the centre of Bashkiria, both for administrative purposes and geographically.

### POPULATION.

The lowest estimate that I have seen of the number of Bashkir is Castrén's,[*] 150,000, the highest that of Hellwald,[†] whose estimate is 750,000. As is generally

<hr>

[*] Ethnologische Vorlesungen.
[†] Die Erde und ihre Völker.

the case, the truth is a mean between these extremes. Kazantseff,[*] whose figures may be taken as absolutely reliable, states that the Bashkir number 224,331 males and 235,986 females, a total of 460,317.

### RACE AND ORIGIN.

The origin, the early home, and the remoter history of this most interesting people are unknown. As with their neighbours the Tchouwash, so with the Bashkir, historians and ethnologists have offered many plausible hypotheses as to their connection on one side with the Ugro-Finnic races, and on the other with the Turko-Tatar; but it is hardly probable that at the present time we possess sufficient information to generalize on this matter with any degree of assurance. That the Bashkir at one time were spread much further to the south than at present is clear from the accounts of Arabian travellers who found them scattered over the steppes watered by the Lower Ural. It is also quite certain that before the expansion of Muscovite power in the south, the Bashkir wandered with their flocks and herds over the greater part of the plains of the Lower Volga. When they were visited by the Arabian travellers, they were the neighbours of the Magyar. Among the Bashkir themselves exist various traditions as to their origin. One is that they are descended from the Buriät of Irkutsk, a tradition that may have been in Castrén's mind when he suggested that the Bashkir were from Southern Siberia, a mixed race of Tatar and Ostiak. If the Kirgiz name for the Bashkir, *Istiak*, be the same word as Ostiak, there may be something in this theory. But the most prevalent opinion among the Bashkir is that they are remnants of the Nogai, and certain ethnological details, as, for instance, uniformity of face-index, height, colour of hair and skin, etc., bear them out in this. The prevalence of numerous theories as to origin has given rise to a controversy which may be thus stated: Are the Bashkir of Ugro-Finnic or of Turko-Tatar origin? Are the alleged traces of Ugro-Finnic origin due to long vicinage to the Finnic races, the Ostiak and others, whereby their physical appearance has been slightly altered by intermarriage, and phonetic changes introduced into their language? In the space at my disposal I am unable to enter at large into this interesting question. A most succinct and able examination of the whole question is made by Vambéry. With him as guide I would place these considerations before the reader: Nearly a thousand years ago we find Ibn Fozlan describing the Bashkir as a Turkish people, "The worst of all the Turkish peoples," he calls them. As to their being Turks, he is followed by all subsequent Mohammedan writers. So far all is plain. It is only

<hr>

[*] Opisanie Bashkirtsev.

when we begin to examine their physical characteristics that the problem becomes complicated, and that we seem to discover evidence of a mixture in the race. To go into statistics is quite outside the scope of this paper ; it may be sufficient to state that the investigations of anthropologists like Ujfalvy and Baudouin de Courtenay have brought to light distinct traces of Ugric admixture, but not of sufficient importance to affect the preponderating Turkish element in the race. If history and anthropology alike agree in proving that the Bashkir are Turks, the evidence of language is still stronger in this direction. Vambéry shows that in his examination of the modern Bashkir language, he has found traces of grammatical forms which enable him to place this dialect as a link in the long chain of Turki dialects that commences on the Irtish and among the Altai, and stretches to the Middle Volga. The same distinguished Orientalist shows that the Bashkir dialect bears strong resemblance to the dialect of the Tobolsk Tatars on one side, and to that of the Kirgiz on the other, but at the same time he notices such phonetic and grammatical peculiarities as prove it to have been all along an independent language, however much its dialectic simplicity may have been injured by the intellectual influences of the more cultured language of Kazan. The one point on which the Bashkir differs from its cognates is the slight trace of Ugric influences already referred to. This is seen in the first place in phonetics, as for instance in the change of *s* into *h* :—

| *Bashkir.* | *Turkish.* |
| --- | --- |
| hezmek | sezmek, to forebode. |
| höndürmek | söndürmek, to extinguish. |
| höz | söz, a word. |

Secondly, in word-store, where we have elements of unquestionable Ugric origin.* These Ugro-Finnic traces are, however, of so slight a nature considering the geographical position of the Bashkir and their juxtaposition to Finnic tribes for perhaps 2000 years that they ought not to afford grounds for ascribing an Ugric (Vogul or Ostiak) origin to them. It may be taken as proved that this fraction of the Turkish race, although at one time mixing sporadically with Ugric elements, has always retained its direct ethnic connection with the other peoples of the Turko-Tatar race.† Ahlquist's conclusion on this point is worth quoting : "The notion that the Bashkir, a few hundred years ago, might have been some sort of Finns or Hungarians who during their nomadic life became Tatarized, can only be believed by him who has no idea how hard it is for a nation, or even a great body of people, to change both language and nationality."‡

* Vambéry, Das Türkenvolk.
† *Ibid.*
‡ Ahlquist, Unter Wogulen und Ostjaken.

## HISTORY.

The earliest information we possess of the Bashkir is drived from the writings of those Arabic merchants and envoys already alluded to, who visited the Bolgar during the height of their power for the purposes of commerce. We are told that the Bashkir had as their neighbours the Petcheneg and the Bolgar, the latter living in towns on the banks of the Kama and Volga. It is, perhaps, reasonable to suppose that the Bashkir were not altogether uninfluenced by this commerce, and by the comparative civilization of their neighbours, and that they derived considerable profit from trading in skins and honey, and from allowing their extensive territories to be worked for minerals. Be this as it may, whatever degree of prosperity was theirs was suddenly and ruthlessly stopped when in 1236 Tchengis-Khan made his terrible onslaught on Eastern Europe. The Bolgar resisted him and were almost annihilated. The Bashkir, with commendable wisdom, at once gave in their submission to the Mongol conqueror, became his allies, and preserved all their rights and privileges. Indeed, Tchengis seems to have made considerable additions to their territory, at any rate to have given them the seal and banner as tokens of national independence. From this time until 200 years later, when the Golden Horde began to decline, we hear little of the Bashkir. Internal dissensions had so eaten away the strength of the Mongol Khans at Kazan and Astrakhan, that the Moscow princes towards the close of the 15th century were able to inflict serious damage on them. At that time the Bashkir on the Bialaya and Ika rivers were subject to Kazan ; those on the Uzen to Astrakhan ; while their brethren in the hills and on the plains east of the hills owed allegiance to the Siberian Khans. They were thus brought into connection with the Russians, and it is evident enough that they must have suffered crushing defeat, for we soon hear of them petitioning the Moscow princes to receive their allegiance. The journey of their deputies to Moscow and its incidents, and their reception by Ivan the Terrible, are still the theme of Bashkir folk-tales. In 1556 they were formally admitted as subjects of the Czar. The officials sent to govern them were so numerous that Ivan gave orders for founding a city which might serve as the administrative centre of Bashkiria. This was the origin of the town of Ufa, the first Russian colony among the Bashkir. The next 200 years are filled with rebellion, and blood, and confusion. At the beginning of this period we find the Siberian and Kirgiz Khans in alliance with the disaffected Bashkir, attempting the capture of Ufa, and repulsed with heavy loss. But nevertheless we find the work of administration and reconciliation going steadily forward. Large powers of self-government in the election of elders and the control of tribal affairs were delegated to the Bashkir. Every effort was made to conciliate them, yet rebellion follows rebellion. In 1676 they were in league with the Kirgiz-Kasaiak and Kalmyck, under Ayuk-Khan. Thirty years later their allies are the Tcheremiss and Mestcher. In 1735 they are engaged single-handed against Russia, when 30,000 of them were slain. After 20 years the fanatic Mollah Batyraha-Ajin succeeds in exciting them to rebel, a movement having a religious rather than a political significance. In Pugatcheff's rebellion against Katharine II. a small section of the Bashkir took part; but save for the exploits of their young leader Salavat, one of their national heroes, the affair, as far as the Bashkir were concerned, was of little importance. Towards the close of the last century they were formed into an irregular cavalry organization against the Kirgiz, who were at that time rather unruly neighbours of Russia. This organization consisted of 12 cantonal divisions, each canton with its own officers appointed by the crown. This was a military form of government, closely resembling the Cossack organization, and having little in common with the ordinary Russian system of village government by elected elders. Within recent years a dual system combining civil and military government has been established, under which the country has been subdivided into 28 cantons, and in which the Teptiär and Mestcher are included. The central administrative chancery is at Ufa, under the direction of a Russian general, who controls all affairs and receives reports at stated intervals from his subordinates in the villages and yurts.*

### RELIGION.

Our scant knowledge of the early religious life of the Bashkir is derived from the writings of those Arabian travellers to Bolgar of whom mention has been already made. When they visited the Bashkir in the 10th century, they found a most comprehensive list of objects of adoration—serpents, fish, and other living creatures; but, in addition, they had a separate list of twelve gods, and it is interesting to notice how near these wild Bashkir nomads came to Pantheism, Winter, Summer, Rain, Storm, Trees, Cattle, Water, Night, Day, Death, Life, Earth. There was, moreover, one great unknowable deity supreme over all the others. It was not until the years 1313—1326 that the Bashkir embraced Islam. Their great apostle

was Azbek-Khan. The nomadic Bashkir are not strict Musalmans, neglecting as useless and cumbrous many important details of Mohammedan ritual, and mixing together in their worship ancient heathen usages with the purer religion of the Prophet. But as they become settled in towns and villages, it is remarked that they are more precise, more exact in their devotions, in their attention to ablutions and fasts, and more intolerant of unbelief and of their besetting sin, intemperance.* In every village there is a mosque, and adjoining it the *medress*, or elementary school, where the boys are taught to read the Koran. These elementary schools are widely used; I have seldom met a Bashkir altogether illiterate. In the towns and larger villages a few of the well-to-do have even commenced to teach their girls. The clergy are under the control of the Mufti at Ufa, and have three ranks, *Akhun*, *Mollah*, and *Azautchi*. They are paid no salary, but enjoy considerable emolument from free-will offerings.

### PERSONAL APPEARANCE AND COSTUME.

The outward appearance of the Bashkir differs very little from that of the Tatars in the N.W. and W. of Siberia, those viz. on the outposts of Tatardom. We have the slight evidences of Ugric admixture already referred to, an admixture which probably dates from pre-Mongolic times. The head is large and flat, the face round and smug, the forehead flat and narrow, the eyes small, generally grey or dark-brown, nose short and blunt, mouth medium, large and prominent ears, beard and moustache dark brown, nearly always thin, the head shaven in accordance with ordinary Musalman usage, straight legs, gait light and easy, height medium, build graceful and well-proportioned, with a tendency towards obesity in middle-age. Some travellers make a point of distinguishing between the outward appearance of the Bashkir on the steppe and their brethren in the hills and forests. One authority describes the forest Bashkir as having a long face, an oval or rather a convex profile, a round prominent nose, high stature, and other characteristics reminding one of the Asiatics of the Caucasus. I have been able to procure a photograph of one of these forest Bashkir possessing the features here described, but I think I am accurate in stating that these long-faced Bashkir are rare among the hills and forests, and, moreover, that they are not seldom met with as dwellers on the steppe. The principal garment worn by the Bashkir is a long

---

* The chief military duties of the Bashkir are garrisoning the Orenburg and Siberian cordons, and acting as a police Every male Bashkir must take his turn in serving. When on duty he must support himself and his horse, as the government stipend is only one rouble a month.

* I have noticed the same process at work among the nomadic Tekké of the Transcaspian desert. As soon as they become in any degree sedentary, as in the neighbourhoods of Askhabad and Merv, they are better Musalmans, at any rate more formal and fanatical.

*caftan* reaching below the knees, with a broad collar open and thrown back. Rich Bashkir have their *caftans* made of blue cloth, with fancy stitching or embroidery about the shoulders and breast; the poorer have home-made whitish or brown cloth. Trousers are worn very wide and short. The summer head-dress is a cap of white felt, in winter a low broad cap of sheep-skin or other fur is worn pressed down on the ears. The piercing frosts which prevail in Eastern Russia make furs a necessity, and the richer Bashkir display considerable taste and sometimes not a little foppery in arranging them. Their forests produce deer, bears, wolves, foxes, notably the silver fox, badgers, ermine, marten, etc. The variety of

much darker than that of the men, plaited into thin tails, to the end of which are attached small silver coins. Many Bashkir belles blacken their eyebrows and teeth, and stain their finger nails with the red juice of a certain plant. Moreover they are devoted to the use of powder and rouge. I speak of the wealthy. Their poorer sisters eschew all and every elaborateness of toilet arrangement, their simplicity in many cases being more primitive than charming. The garments worn by the women are a shirt embroidered round the neck and breast, and a long outside garment resembling the men's *caftan*, except that in summer it is worn without sleeves, and that it is ornamented with embroidery and innumerable little metal discs or silver coins sewn on

FOREST-BASHKIR.

STEPPE-BASHKIR.

skins gives every scope to the Bashkir dandy, who is often most elaborately befurred. Sheepskins worn with the woolly side next the body are the winter covering of the poorer classes. Long boots, blue or yellow, of soft leather, in accordance with the directions in the Koran, adorn the feet of the well-to-do; the poor wear commoner and plainer materials, and leather or bark sandals often very skilfully made. The underclothing is a shirt of cotton or linen, the front in most cases embroidered in various designs with red thread. Among the Bashkir one meets many rather pleasant-looking women. A handsome woman, as we understand the term, does not exist in all Bashkiria. Their hair is either dark brown or black,

round the breast and neck. The girls have their heads uncovered, the married women wear the *kashbav*, a sort of ornamental hood. In their ears are heavy silver earrings of simple workmanship. But their most splendid adornment is the *kalyabash*, an elaborate head-dress overloaded with silver and gold ornaments and coins, and often costing as much as one thousand roubles. Like the Kirgiz and Turkoman the Bashkir women are not veiled.

### MARRIAGE.

The primitive nature of Bashkir society is well exemplified by reference to their marriages. The consent of the bride, and her wishes one way or the other, are not considered, and have nothing to do with the matter. It frequently happens that a girl of ten is married to a wealthy old beau of sixty who has previously arranged all particulars of the *kalym*, the number of cattle, the sum of money, the minor presents of clothes, etc., which he is to bestow *on her father* as her equivalent.* The Bashkir have no desire for sons ; daughters, especially if they are at all presentable, are preferred as more valuable merchandise. A Bashkir with a large family of good-looking young girls is either actually or prospectively a wealthy man. Among the Bashkir polygamy is rapidly becoming extinct. Not so very long ago the officials and other wealthy Bashkir often possessed four wives. But it was quite as frequently the case that their circumstances though easy did not allow of this. As a consequence quarrels and divorce suits were perpetually before the Mufti, and were a source of grave scandal in the community. So the Mufti enacted (1864) that those who could not bring evidence to prove that they were in a position to support a plurality of wives were to rest satisfied with one. Since that time monogamy has been more and more the rule. The social position of the women is wretched : they are despised, beaten, treated like dogs. Not only do the ordinary household duties, such as preparing the food and making the clothes, fall upon them ; in addition they shear the sheep, tend and milk the cattle, and take the larger share in the cultivation of the ground.

### CHARACTER.

The Bashkir are pleasant-mannered, peaceful, obedient, patient, and hospitable, in no way resembling the "thieving wolves" whose characteristics they were said to possess in former times. But on the other hand many travellers with considerable truth have noted their cunning, their extreme selfishness, their laziness, and dirt, their astounding inquisitiveness, and a lingering desire to possess themselves of other people's horses by unlawful means.

### SEMI-NOMAD AND SETTLED.

The pure nomadic state of life as we find it among the Turkoman and Kara-Kirgiz no longer exists in Bashkiria. Although the process is a slow one, we find the settled life gradually taking the place of the nomadic. The Bashkir may therefore be divided into sedentary and half-nomadic. The sedentary Bashkir engage in trade in the towns with fair success, in the country in agriculture, cattle raising, bee-culture, hunting, and timber felling. They are very indifferent agriculturists.†

With the better classes one will always find a tolerably clean and comfortable whitewashed room, often with the addition of a Dutch stove. A long bench serves as chairs, tables and bed. Often a handsome rug from Central Asia or a soft felt of home manufacture adds colour and an air of luxury to the room, and the Russian *samovar* or tea-urn is found in every decent house. The Tangaur-Bashkir* of the South Ural district afford a good example of the semi-nomad. Although compelled in recent years by the force of circumstances to resort in some measure to agriculture, their old nomadic forms of life retain fast hold of them. In the neighbourhood of Verkhny-Uralsk we find semi-nomadic Bashkir settled for many generations, but their agriculture is still wretched, worse even than that of their Tchouwash neighbours, and their poverty and misery are extreme. Although the process of assimilation to the settled population around them is gradually going on, they have always a hankering after the roaming life on the steppe. In winter the semi-nomad lives in a low felt or rough wooden hut. These huts are wretched erections, unfinished, ruinous, and filthy. Their interiors closely resemble the Kirgiz *kibitka*, the same fittings and furniture. An assemblage of these huts is called an *uzbe*. In summer his home is somewhat similar, but lighter, more easily moved from place to place. The summer *kibitka* are often very tastefully decorated, a wealthy nomad sometimes spending one or two hundred roubles on external ornaments of different kinds.

### FOOD.

The most common dish is dried cheese made of sheeps' milk crushed between stones, mixed with flour, and either baked into cakes or soaked in sour milk. This is a tasty enough article of food, and is said to be very nutritious. They have a great variety of food made from milk, the most important are *kalyk*, sour milk, and *kaimak*, thick clotted cream. A favourite dish is boiled meat minced finely and again boiled with cheese and served up in a semi-liquid state with bread. There is also a less savoury dish known as *bish-barmak*, a hotch-potch of fat or oil, with meat. But their choicest morsel is *tchutch-paria*, small cakes filled with finely-cut meat, boiled in butter or water. Their drinks are numerous and good. Cows' milk, the famous *koumys* or fermented mares' milk, a sort of butter-milk called *airan* prepared from cows' and goats' milk, but judging from the method employed in preparing it not very inviting. As the Bashkir are most proficient bee-farmers, we find among them several wholesome drinks derived from honey. The

---

* A rich Bashkir will sometimes pay as much as R.3000 ready money, in addition to cattle, etc., for the girl of his choice. The poorer pay with cattle and horses, and I have heard of one poor fellow whose *kalym* was a black astrakhan cap and some tobacco.

† Including mountain and forest they occupy some 33 millions of acres, or about 51,600 square miles of territory.

* The Bashkir were originally divided into three tribes or clans—the Tangaur, Karagai-Kaptchak, and Burzian, the first-named most to the South.

best is *buza*, enjoying a great reputation. This *buza* if kept two years becomes exceedingly potent.

### FESTIVALS.

A pleasure-loving people, the Bashkir have numerous amusements and festivals. The most important of these is the great vernal *feast of the plough—saban* or *sabandoi*, an inheritance from pagan times. When the ground is free of snow and begins to wear its fresh spring garment of green, a day is appointed for the *sabandoi*. The elders go together to the mosque to pray for a bounteous harvest; the young men in their finest attire and seated on their swiftest horses assemble at a well-known spot some three or four miles from the village. At a given signal all race home at full speed. As they arrive in the village, the street is lined with spectators to congratulate the first rider who arrives. Afterwards those who have taken part in the race together visit every homestead to congratulate the owner on the approach of spring, and to wish him a good harvest with abundance of calves and innumerable swarms of bees. The owner then feasts his youthful guests, to one a piece of bread, to another meat; they finish with *airan* and *buza*. In their festivals music and dancing play a prominent part; this is the case even with their minor gatherings known as *riin* or *djin*, ordinary merry-meetings in the fields in summer time. The songs of the Bashkir, *ir*, are very poor. Although mostly of an erotic character, they are sung to the saddest of improvised minor airs. The music-man or *kuraigi* (kurai, a flute) is an institution in Bashkiria. The musical instrument most in use is the *kobyz*, a small metal pipe held in the teeth and played with the aid of the tongue, the fingers opening and shutting the keys. Many of the women are most proficient players of the *kobyz*. According to Vambéry their dance resembles the national Hungarian dance in many particulars, commencing with a slow measured movement, and increasing in swiftness as the passion of the theme intensifies. Literature they have none, except the songs already alluded to. In this respect they are far behind their neighbours of Kazan, whose literary activity makes itself felt over all the Mohammedan portions of the Russian Empire.

### LIVE STOCK.

The chief wealth of the Bashkir consists of course in cattle, a small breed like that seen in Northern Russia. Their horses are also of small growth, of no beauty, but swift and durable. Goats and sheep they possess in enormous flocks. Camels are raised in large numbers, but the intense frosts of winter are not favourable to them, and in consequence the Bashkirs' camel is rather a weakly animal. Geese, ducks, turkeys, and hens are possessed by the settled Bashkir, seldom if ever by the nomads.

### SPORT.

Lakes and streams are numerous and abound in fish. —shad, pike, bream, roach, perch, carp, tench, sterlet, grayling and trout. In the forests as already mentioned deer abound, also bears, wolves, foxes. The bears are of two kinds, a small brown animal and a larger grey sort weighing eight or nine hundredweight. These forests are very extensive, and contain a great variety of timber—oak, birch, elm, maple, black poplar, willow, lime, aspen, spruce, silver fir and larch.

MICHAEL A. MORRISON.

COMPARISON OF CARDINAL NUMBERS 1-20 OSMANLI AND BASHKIR.

| | OSMANLI. | | | BASHKIR. | |
|---|---|---|---|---|---|
| 1 | مِر | bir | | براو | bräv |
| 2 | ایکی | iki | | ایکاو | ikäf |
| 3 | اوچ | utch | | اوساو | üsäv |
| 4 | دوررت (درد) | dörd dört | | دوررناو | dörtäv |
| 5 | بش | besh | | بیشاو | bishäv |
| 6 | آلتی | alty | | الناو | altav |
| 7 | یدی | yeddi | | جهداو | ǧedäv (ǧ = ɡ) |
| 8 | سکز | sekkiz | | سهنز | sigiz (iz = u Fr.) |
| 9 | طقوز | dogguz | | دوفنز | dogiz (iz = u Fr.) |
| 10 | اون | ohn | | اون | on |
| 11 | اون بِر | on-bir | | اون بهر | on-bĭr |
| 12 | اون ایکی | on-iki | | اون ایکی | on-iki |
| 13 | اون اوچ | on-utch | | اون اوش | on-üsh |
| 14 | اون دوررت | on-dört | | اون دوررت | on-dört |
| 15 | اون بش | on-besh | | اون بش | on-bish |
| 16 | اون آلتی | on-alty | | اون آلتی | on-alty |
| 17 | اون یدی | on-yeddi | | اون جهدی | on-ǧedy |
| 18 | اون سکز | on-sekkiz | | اون سهنز | on-segiz |
| 19 | اون طقوز | on-dogguz | | اون دوفنز | on-dogiz |
| 20 | یکرمی | ikirmi | | جکرمی | ǧegirmi |

## Syed Ali Mohamed Shad of Patna.

Among the modern Urdū poets who have attained to a recognized position among their own countrymen, Syed Ali Mohamed Shad of Patna is one of the most noteworthy. In the style and subject-matter of his writings he rises considerably above the level of the ordinary Oriental poet and story-teller, and exhibits a favourable specimen of the influence of Western culture on the Oriental mode of thought and representation. He deserves, therefore, to be made more widely known to lovers of Urdū literature in Europe. The Syed comes of an ancient family, which still holds a good position in Bihar. On his father's side he traces his line through some thirty-two generations back to the Prophet Muhammad, through the Imám Husain and the Prophet's daughter Fātimah, and among his ancestors he counts a King of Shirāz, Husain Fīrūzī. On his mother's side he is descended from several Nawābs and Vazīrs. As is now the case with most Muhammadan families of ancient lineage in Bihār, the Syed's family has lost much of its former greatness, and he retains but a small portion of the landed property that once belonged to his ancestors. He commenced his literary career about thirty years ago. But the work by which he first established his position as an Urdū writer of originality and versatility was a novel called Sūratu-l-Khayāl, or "A Product of the Imagination," the first volume of which the Syed published in 1880. It at once attracted wide attention and met with a very favourable reception, both among native and European readers of the current Urdū literature. The first volume was followed, in short intervals, by two others which completed the story. The main object of the Syed in writing this novel, as he explains in his preface, was the instruction and entertainment of his countrywomen; and he briefly aims to show that a good wife can manage to remain virtuous even in circumstances of the greatest temptation, and become a source of strength and guidance to her husband. The moral tone of the book is perfectly healthy, and the situations of peril to the virtue of the unprotected heroine are presented with great delicacy. The following is a very brief outline of the story. " It opens with the marriage of Wilayatī, the daughter of a wealthy Muhammadan gentleman of Patna, to a wealthy but dissipated young man of Gayā, who neglects his wife and wastes his property in riotous living. Brought to the verge of ruin, he reforms and sends for his wife from Patna. On her way to join him, she is set upon by robbers and carried off to their village. One of their women, out of jealousy, helps her to escape into the jungle, where she wanders about in utter destitution, till she is found by some faqīrs and taken to a neighbouring police station. The dāroghah, or native officer in charge of the station, is captivated by her beauty; but with the help of a kindly old woman she contrives to escape unhurt from his clutches, and to flee to Calcutta. Having by a misadventure become separated from her companion on the way, she finds herself utterly helpless in that large and unknown city. After nearly falling a victim to the evil designs of a scoundrel who offers her his help, she finds a safe refuge in the house of a Persian merchant's lady. Here she lives in peace for some time, till on the return of the merchant from a journey, she is pestered by his advances, to escape which she transfers herself to the house of a good old Muhammadan lawyer and his wife. While she is living with them, her husband comes down to Calcutta to consult the lawyer in a suit pending in one of the Calcutta courts. Husband and wife, as usual in Muhammadan marriages, had never seen each other; however, Wilayatī recognizes her husband by his name, but refrains from making herself known to him, lest, owing to her adventures, he should suspect her innocence. Karīm Hūsain, the husband, who is unaware of the identity of his wife, soon falls deeply in love with her, and proposes to marry her. Wilayatī accepts the proposal, on condition that he should first safely escort her back to her home in Patna. Karīm Hūsain consents; but at the very moment of starting, Wilayatī is arrested by the police on two separate false charges of theft and desertion, preferred by the Dāroghah and the Persian merchant respectively. With some difficulty she succeeds in establishing her innocence, but in the course of the trial she cannot avoid disclosing her identity, and Karīm Hūsain becoming aware of the fact that she is his wife. He is equally surprised and delighted with the unexpected revelation. Unfortunately they now resolve to stay a few days in Calcutta to see the sights of the place. The baffled Dāroghah and Persian merchant profit by the delay to trump up a false charge of opium smuggling against the husband, in order to get him out of the way and possess themselves of the person of his wife. They succeed in getting Karīm Hūsain arrested, and Wilayatī removed, with the aid of a faithless servant, to a lonely house belonging to the merchant. The conspirators, however, fall out about the spoils, and in the course of a violent altercation the merchant stabs the servant, and is arrested by the police for murder. This saves Wilayatī; during the night she contrives to make her escape from the merchant's house, but is immediately arrested by the police on suspicion of being a loitering thief. On the following day she is placed before an English magistrate, and after a patient and careful investigation, the innocence of both herself and her husband is fully proved, and they are permitted to depart. But they are now quite penniless; in the course of their misadventures, they had been robbed of everything. They drive for help to their old friend, the lawyer, but find that he had left the town, and get into a quarrel with the cabman whom they are unable to pay. Out of this predicament they are delivered by a kind Muhammadan stranger, who not only pays the cabman but advances them sufficient to proceed by countryboat up the river to Patna. The river journey takes some weeks. After some days, they are joined by another passenger, who, observing some valuable pearls in the possession of Karīm Hūsain, one night, mistaking his victim, throws Wilayatī overboard. No one notices the deed, and the boat proceeds on its journey. Wilayatī, however, luckily clutching a floating bamboo, is carried by the current to the shore, where she tries to proceed on her journey on foot along the bank. During her wearisome journey, she meets with various adventures ; but at last, one night, she is attacked by a hyena and severely wounded. Some people, however, deliver her and carry her to the hospital in Mungīr, where she is carefully treated and healed by the English doctor. He afterwards also assists her in returning to her home in Patna. In the meantime her father had died, and her family affairs had fallen into great disorder ; of her husband too she could obtain no tidings. So she sets out on a pilgrimage to Mekka, accompanied by a friend and two servants. On the way from Jeddah to Medinah, her servants are intercepted by Bedawin robbers, and on her way from Medinah to Mekka, the same fate overtakes herself and her friend. After several months of slavery among the Bedawin, she is rescued by Turkish troops and carried to Mekka, where by a lucky chance she finds her two servants, who had been similarly rescued. They now perform all the ceremonies of the Hajj, and, as a crowning act of devotion, Wilayatī consents to defray the expense of the return of a poor Indian pilgrim. It so happens, that this pilgrim returns in the same ship with her, and when they meet on board, she discovers that the pilgrim whom she had befriended was her long-lost husband. Both now return home without any further mishap."

The novel has considerable literary merits. The subject is taken from the every day life among Muhammadans of India, and has nothing of the childishly fantastic and grotesque with which most Urdū stories abound. There is nothing exaggerated or improbable in most of the incidents of the story ; though a succession of misfortunes like those presented in it are not likely to occur in real life. The whole is very cleverly constructed so as to keep the reader's interest fully sustained throughout to the end of the book. The two principal characters are thoroughly well maintained : Wilayatī, the well-born lady of the purdah, simple and innocent, yet withal shrewd and plucky ; on the other hand, Karīm Husain, the husband, good-natured but dull. The minor characters, too,—the native police officer, the English Magistrate, the Persian merchant, the Musalman gentleman and lawyer, the Bangālī Baboo, the English and native ladies,—they are all drawn very life-like, and are all made to speak their own peculiar Hindustānī. The whole story is put in the mouth of Wilayatī, who is represented as relating her experiences to her lady friends. This accounts for most of the peculiarity, irregularity and occasional unrefinedness of the diction ; and one cannot help regretting that the author should have chosen a

setting for his story that allowed him but little scope for the employment of choice and standard Urdū. The literature of that language can hardly yet be said to have attained a stage that admits of no further improvement of the language, and permits authors to turn to the cultivation of its bye-ways.

The Syed has published many other works : the *Fughān-i-Dilkush*, a controversial pamphlet in defence of himself ; the *Samarah-i-Zindagī*, a short poem in commemoration of the day on which his son was first sent to school ; the *Nawā-i-Waṭan*, a history of the Urdū language in Bihār ; the *Qadr-Kamāl*, a pamphlet in defence of the old poets ; the *Yomiyyah 'Aqāïdi-l-Imāmiyyah*, an Arabic tract on the principles of the Shīā religion ; the *Maṣnawī-i-Chashma-i-Kauṣar*, a comparison of the condition of the Muhammadans of the present day with that of their forefathers at the time of the conquest. But the best of all, both in poetic feeling and felicity of expression, is his *Nawīd-i-Hind*, a poem written in commemoration of the Jubilee of Her Majesty. The subject is an allegory on the vicissitudes of Indian history. Mother India, a wealthy lady, has two sons—the Hindū and the Musalmān. At first she entrusts the management of her house and property to her elder son, the Hindū. He neglects his work, and brings the family into sore difficulties. The mother now transfers the management to her younger son, the Musalmān. He is a headstrong man and mismanages the property, and creates discord in the house. He not only quarrels with his elder brother, but his two sons—the Sunnī and the Shī'ā—begin to quarrel among themselves. The mother remonstrates and rebukes ; but the undutiful son turns her out of the house, and leaves her at the mercy of wicked men and wild animals (an allusion to the desolation of India during the Marātha and French wars). At length she is rescued by a noble-hearted passer-by, the English. He takes her under his protection, and undertakes to manage her property. After a time she falls seriously ill, and doctors are sent for from England, who succeed in not only restoring her, but raising her to a more flourishing condition than she ever enjoyed before. This is an allusion to the mutiny, the re-conquest of India and its transfer to the Crown of England. The latter part of the poem is devoted to a glowing description of the prosperity of India under the rule of Her gracious Majesty, and the joyful event of her Jubilee.

## The Vernacular Examinations.

It is almost universally admitted that the present system of examinations in the native languages, especially for military officers, is by no means satisfactory. Although something has been done of late years to make the lower examinations more of a test, and less of a farce, than they formerly were, yet great changes will have to be made before these examinations will fulfil the object for which they are, or ought to be, intended. One meets every day young officers who have recently passed the Higher Standard, but are unable to speak two sentences correctly, or to understand the simplest report made by a sepoy. They have had to learn up a lot of semi-Persian words and phrases from Munshis and books, in order to get through the examination, and have not yet become acquainted with the ordinary terms used in conversation by the classes with whom they have to deal. The officers themselves are not to blame; having passed the examination, they have done all that is required of them, and a few months in a native regiment will enable them to pick up a smattering of a dialect that is more intelligible to the sepoys than that of the "Bagh-o-Bahar" and "Prem-Sagar." It may be useful to know what is generally termed "Munshi bát" in order to be able to converse with educated Mussulmans and others, but it would be utterly useless, as all Bombay officers know, to address the ordinary Bombay sepoy in the high-flown language of the "Bagh-o-Bahar." The first question that presents itself is, "What is the object of the Higher Standard Examination?" Probationers for the Staff Corps would probably reply that the Higher Standard Examination was instituted in order that they should not get into mischief when they first join a native regiment, and to enable them to get six months' leave to Bombay or Poona when they happen to be serving in an unpleasant station. There is no doubt, however, that it is really intended to insure officers possessing a good colloquial knowledge of the language, together with sufficient acquaintance with the written and printed characters to enable them to read a fairly easy letter in the Urdu and Hindi characters. Under the present system, however, the greatest stress is laid on the least important parts of the examination. In every regiment there are plenty of sepoys and non-commissioned officers capable of translating well from English into Hindustani, and after once passing the examination, an officer is never required to write a letter in the latter language with his own hand. Yet the translation from English into Hindustani is the part of the examination which is considered of the greatest importance, and which is the stumbling-block of the great majority of unsuccessful candidates. On the other hand, there are few natives in any regiment that are able to make an intelligible translation into English, and an officer may often be called upon to translate a paper read by a native from Hindustani into English. In the Higher Standard Examination,

however, this is entirely ignored. By all means let an officer be able to dictate a letter in Hindustani, and any one knowing the language well colloquially should be competent to do this. The test books laid down for the Hindustani Higher Standard are quite unsuitable, especially for the Bombay Presidency. Years ago the Bombay Civil and Military Examination Committee recommended the substitution of some more modern book for the "Prem-Sagar," and even advocated that the exercise in the Devanagari character should be entirely dispensed with. No notice, however, was taken of the Board's recommendation. Are there so few books in the language that none more suitable than the "Bagh-o-Bahar" and "Prem-Sagar" could be selected for the test books, if test books are required? Even the "Bagh-o-Bahar" is by no means wildly exciting, and the translation of the Indian Articles of War would be at least as interesting, and certainly more useful. The examinations in modern languages recently instituted by the War Office for officers of the Army are very good examples of what examinations should be to be of any practical value. No test books are laid down, and the paragraphs for translation are selected by the examiner from modern books and newspapers. Besides translation to and from the language, candidates have to write from dictation (which is itself no mean test), to write an essay, and to copy two or three pages of manuscript in a given time. The above constitutes the literary part of the examination. For the colloquial, besides conversing for fully half an hour with the examiner, a short paragraph, dictated slowly in English, has to be written at once into the language, and a paragraph read by the examiner in the language, rendered into English. Of a maximum of 800 marks, 640 must be obtained to qualify as interpreter, and 400 to pass. An examination drawn up on similar lines for Hindustani, with slight modifications, if substituted for the present Higher Standard and Higher Pass tests, would meet all requirements. So much stress need not be laid on written translations into the language, while, on the other hand, more attention should be paid to translation into English and to the colloquial. The lower standard might be abolished, as being of no practical value, even as an inducement to study the language; and the degree of honour, if considered necessary to retain it, might be left as it now stands. By this means a better practical knowledge of the language would be secured, and young officers would not be obliged to waste so much time in learning phrases and expressions, which on this side of India are only used by Munshis and in books, and which they invariably forget a few months after having passed the examination.

## Commemoration Day at Oxford.

Among the honorary degrees conferred by the University of Oxford on June 26 last, there was one which may be recorded as almost unique when we contrast the importance of the literary services of the recipient with the length of time that has been allowed to intervene between the period within which they were rendered and their actual recognition by the University. The name of *Mr. B. H. Hodgson* as the great pioneer of European research into the Buddhistic literature of Nepal and Tibet has been a household word with Oriental students these sixty years. He began as early as in 1824 to utilize his rare opportunities for collecting materials bearing on those studies. From the time of his discovery of a Sanskrit, by the side of a Tibetan, Buddhistic literature, he worked incessantly for thirty-four years in making that literature accessible to European research, not only by his own summaries of its contents, but by liberally placing copies of the voluminous original documents in the great Oriental libraries in Calcutta, London and Paris. And his contributions to our knowledge of the languages, ethnology, and zoology of those border-lands of India are as valuable as his works on Buddhism, and many of them have up to this day remained the only sources of information on those branches of investigation. Mr. Hodgson is now close upon ninety: and while the Indian Government has passed over in silence his distinguished and disinterested labours, it is at least a gratification to see that the University of Oxford has bestowed in the year of Grace 1889 what would not have been a premature tribute to eminent scholarship thirty years ago. All honour to those who have been instrumental in wiping out this blot on the English sense of justice !

We now proceed to give the text of the Latin address delivered by Prof. Bryce in introducing the candidate :—

Insignissime Vice Cancellarie Vosque, Egregii Procuratores !

Si in hac aetate nostra nihil magis admiratione dignum quam quod populorum Asiae res antiquissimas et caligine longa demersas in lucem protulerint doctorum virorum studium atque labor infinitus, nulli magis gloria ista tribuenda quam huic seni quem mihi adstare videtis. Quum enim juvenis admodum legati munere apud regulum Nepalensem fungeretur, primus omnium libros vetustos, alios Tibeticis, alios sacris Indorum literis exaratos, qui Sakyamunii illius vitam, praecepta, disciplinorum ejus res gestas, totam denique fidei atque cultus Buddhici rationem delineant, e latebris eruit, magna mercede quaesitos doctorum coetui donavit, ipse scriptis adcuratissime enucleavit ; qui gentium quoque quae Emodos montes adcolunt, libros antea plane

incognitos, pervestigandos sibi sumpsit, tantaque est sollertia, tanta cura usus, ut hodie etiam post annos triginta, si quis ad linguas earum, mores, ritus cognoscendos accederit, e fontibus ab hoc viro reclusis haurire soleat. Praesento vobis Brianum Houghton Hodgson, societatis regiae socium, ut admittatur ad gradum doctoris in jure civili, honoris causa.

Ante diem VIum Kal. Iul. 1889.

---

## Letter from Mr. W. W. Rockhill to the Editor.

Lusa (Kumbum), *March 19th*, 1889.

Thinking you might like to hear how I am getting along in my journey through the Chinese Empire, I avail myself of an opportunity which presents itself of sending letters to Shanghai to let you know of my whereabouts.

I reached Kumbum—or rather the village of Lusa which is a few hundred yards from the Lamasery—in the early part of February, and have been off and on here ever since. The famous butter bas reliefs which Huc first made known to the world were extremely curious. They were exhibited on the night of the 15th of the first month (the Chinese feast of lanterns). They did not, however, come up to what I had expected from Huc's account. The famous tree (there are four by the way at Kumbum, all equally genuine) is a failure, at least at this season of the year. The country has proved especially interesting ethnologically, as it is peopled by tribes of various nationalities, languages, and customs.

A curious people four days south-east of here are the Salar who speak Turki. They say they came from Turkestan, but when and how I cannot learn. Prjwalsky appears to me to have uselessly complicated the ethnology of the country by calling the Eastern Tibetans Tangutans, which is only the Mongol name of the Banaka or Tent Tibetans inhabiting Amdo and the southern Kokonor region. They call themselves Bopa (the same as the Tibetans further west where the word is pronounced Penba), and the Chinese call them Sifan. They are as thoroughly Tibetan as possible, their language being entirely Tibetan, with but slight dialectic variations. In fact, as far as pronunciation goes, it is less corrupt by far than the language of Lhasa or Western Tibet.

I hope in two or three days to leave here for the Kokonor and the Tsaidam. When I reach the latter place, I will see which way I can go. If I cannot get men to accompany me to Lhasa,—for that is the only difficulty I have encountered, the cowardice of the people of those parts who fear the nomadic Tibetans

worse than all the demons and fiends of Buddhism,—
I will try and go south from Barang Tsaidam to
Chamdo, and thence to Batang, Litang, Ta-chien-lu
to Chung King, and then down the Yang-tze-kiang to
Shanghai. I still hope to be able to get to Lhasa, as
I expect in a day or two to receive a pass from the
Kantsa lama Arabtan, who is the chief of the Banaka,
which I have got a friend to go and ask for me. If I
get it, it will prove of great value, and, I think, greatly
facilitate travelling in Tibet. Things are made a little
difficult just now, as the people hereabout have just
heard of the Sikkim troubles, and as they thiuk Sikkim
is somewhere between here and Lhasa, they fancy
the road to the latter place is exceptionally difficult.
There are many other things of which I would like to
tell you ; but time is lacking, and I must stop. Since
leaving Lanchau I have sketched the route with pris-
matic compass and aneroid, and I believe I have already
been able to correct some errors in existing maps.

[With some of the above statements may be compared
Prejevalsky's "Mongolia," English trans., 1876, vol. ii.
pp. 149, 301—5, as pointed out to us by Sir H. Yule.
—Edit.]

## New Books.

*The Social and Military Position of the Ruling Caste
in Ancient India, as Represented by the Sanskrit
Epic.* By E. W. Hopkins. [From the Journal of
the American Orient. Soc. vol. xiii. 1888.]

This is a very careful and systematic attempt at
collecting historical data from the Mahâbhârata, not
only as regards the position of the ruling caste, but on
a variety of other subjects as well, such as the status
and rights of woman, the nature of the Sabhâ or
Council, the position of priests, warriors, slaves, farmers,
traders, and other classes of society, taxation, agriculture, dress, amusements, courts of law, the whole social
and political organization of ancient India in short.
It is surprising to find that the great Epic should yield
so much information on all these heads, but it should
be borne in mind that the Sanskrit law-books, which
represent the principal source for all inquiries into the
constitutional history of India, are closely connected
with the Mahâbhârata in many ways. Thus the recent
researches of Professor Bühler have shown that upwards
of two hundred and sixty verses, i.e. one-tenth of the
Code of Manu, may bo identified with texts from the
Mahâbhârata, without being attributed to Manu in
the latter work. Nor does the notion that the plot of
the Epic was unknown to the compiler of Manu's Laws
withstand a close examination of the facts. Duncker
has used that erroneous notion as a starting-point in
his attempts at fixing the age of the Code of Manu, but
the legends quoted iu chapters vii.—x. are mostly taken
from the Mahâbhârata. The remark, for instance, that
the vice of gambling has caused great enmity in a former

age (Manu, ix. 227) contains a distinct allusion to
the match played between the two kingly cousins, the
principal incident of the Epic.

Professor Hopkins, the editor and continuator of
Burnell's Manu, has also been careful to collect parallels
from the law-books to the passages adduced by him
from the Mahâbhârata. This feature of his work
becomes specially noticeable in the interesting chapter
on women, the perfect agreement between the law-
books and the Epic rendering it possible to supply and
elucidate the statements of the latter by means of the
former, and *vice versâ.* The question as to the existence
of polyandry in ancient India may serve as an instance
of this. Prof. Hopkins is certainly right in supposing
that the rule quoted by Âpastamba regarding the
delivery of a bride to a whole family corresponds to
the instances of a match between one maiden and a
number of brothers, which are recorded in the Mahâbhârata. One might go further than this and suggest
that the well-known match between Draupadî and the
Pâṇḍu brothers actually caused the framing of the legal
rule referred to. In support of his theory regarding
the limitation of polyandry to un-Aryan tribes, Prof.
Hopkins might have adduced the text of Bṛihaspati,
in which "the delivery of a bride to a whole family"
is censured as a wicked custom confined to the Dekhan.

It is impossible, within the compass of a brief notice,
to do justice to the details of Professor Hopkins's
elaborate investigations. The Introduction contains
a very able discussion of the origin of the Epic, in which
the "inversion theory" of Holtzmann is supplanted
by what might be called the ethical theory, the ethical
sense of a subsequent age being made responsible for
the discrepancies visible in the text of the Epic as it
now stands. The discussion of the military institutious
and art of war of the ancient Indians is specially
copious. The origin of Sir W. Jones's poem, "What
coustitutes a state ? Not high-walled battlements or
laboured mound, Thick wall or moated gate, but men,"
is incidentally traced to a sentiment from the Epic,
"Wherever learned priests are, that is a city." While
agreeing with Professor Hopkins as to the Indian
origin of the poem, I should consider it more probable
that the renowned translator of Manu derived the
leading idea of his poem from that curious distinction
of the various sorts of a fortress in Manu, a fortress
consisting of a desert, of earth, of water or trees, of
mountains, or *of men.*　　　　　J. Jolly.

A. Sydenstricker : *An Exposition of the Construction
and Idioms of Chinese Sentences, as found in Colloquial Mandarin.* Shanghai, 1889.

The little volume before us deserves better than
many more ambitious works the name of "Grammar"
which its author modestly disclaims. It is written on
the "synthetic" plan, that is to say, it does not analyze
the Chinese sentence but shows how to construct it.
This plan recommends itself particularly for works
treating of the modern dialects and intended for
practical use.

Considering the limited space which the author
allows himself, his "exposition" is remarkably complete

and contains none but very familiar examples. This has the advantage that a comparative beginner, who has just only collected a small vocabulary, can with its aid arrange and sift his stock of phraseology so that it becomes of real practical use to him.

It is necessary that a grammar of modern Chinese confine itself to one dialect only and leave out all such elements as are, though frequently met with in colloquial, derived from literary sources. Otherwise the rules will not fit and practice will not obey.

M. Bazin was, I think, the first to have adapted the synthetic method to colloquial Mandarin, and this method has been recently applied to the old style by Prof. von der Gabelentz.

M. Bazin has pointed out that the name of a "monosyllabic" language is misapplied in the case of modern Chinese. His view is, I should think, pretty generally accepted at present, though it has never since, if I mistake not, been properly formulated. A glance into any dictionary, say Stent's Vocabulary, or into Mr. Sydenstricker's book, will convince any one, who is deceived into the contrary belief by the syllabic system of writing. From the first chapter of the volume before us, treating of the analysis and formation of words, it will be seen that all words of more than one syllable are formed either by composition or by suffixes. The difference is that while in the former each element contributes its quotum to the meaning of the compound, the signification of the suffix, if it has one, is lost or not appreciable in the compound. Now, with regard to composition it may be said that, where two words belonging to different categories (substantives, verbs, etc.), combine in such manner that one determines the other, becoming its attribute or adverb, each word preserves its independence. If, on the other hand, two words, belonging to the same category, combine to form either a synonym or an abstract, then they become one—a real compound. As to suffixes, the most conservative must admit that they lose in combination everything that constitutes the individuality of a word meaning tone and even phonetic value.

The construction of the sentence in Modern Chinese is extremely simple. The parts of speech are recognized by position and context; the grammatical relations capable of expression are very few. Prepositions and suffixes render the modern languages at once more intelligible and less pliant than the old and book style. In the absence of a verb the copula is more frequently used and the subject and predicate (resp. object) are determined by their relative positions before and after the copula (resp. verb). The attribute and adverb are treated alike and correspond to the genitive case. The dative is an indirect object and the instrumental a genitive "oriundi." The verb has a præterit or aorist tense, formed by a suffix, but the perfect and future tenses are formed by the aid of auxiliaries. There is no real passive form in Chinese, it is rendered by certain verba recipiendi followed by the root of the verb, which may be interpreted as an infinitive or as a noun. It will have been seen that the idiom under review is extremely poor as far as grammatical forms are concerned. But something is done by means of

final particles which express the interrogative, imperative, optative, etc., and more still by the accent and the living intonation to which no grammarian can do entire justice.

The system of transcription adopted in Mr. Sydenstricker's book cannot be found fault with except that, where no attention is paid to the tones, the final *h* seems superfluous.

I can see no reason why compound words should not be written in one, but it would be well in that case, to mark, as our own dictionaries do, the syllable on which the accent rests.

It would be so much labour lost to note the tone of each word, for it can be found in any dictionary, and to pronounce each word of a sentence in its own proper tone would be not only pedantic but incorrect. As a general rule, words carrying the accent retain their proper tones, while the remaining words fit themselves in according to certain rules such as that a third tone before another third becomes a second tone, a fourth tone before another fourth also a second and so on. But it would be very useful indeed if once a complete scale of the *natural* tones, first pointed out by Dr. Edkins, were furnished, and a table drawn up showing to which of these natural tones the traditional tones recognized by each dialect correspond.　　A. R.

*Western China : A Journey to the Great Buddhist Centre of Mount Omei.* By Rev. Virgil C. Hart, B.D. Boston, Ticknor & Co., 1888, pp. 302.

We trust the time has gone by when those who felt called upon to add to the long list of books about China, also conceived it to be their duty to begin upon the assumption that China was like *x* in an algebraic equation—a quantity wholly unknown, and to be ascertained by the work in hand. On this plan the physical features, the general history, the laws, customs and language of the Chinese all passed in review, every time a new writer took his pen in hand, and the result was to produce a series of works, which, whatever their excellences, stood to each other much in the relation of different stanzas of the celebrated poem known as "The House that Jack built." The day for books of this description has, we say, definitely passed, having closed with the second and comparatively recent edition of the "Middle Kingdom," a work not likely to be supplanted, however much it may—and doubtless does—need to be supplemented. What we want now is a series of volumes presenting separate parts of China, written by those who have had some special opportunities of observation, and who have what the theologians term an "effectual call" to put the product of their observations into print. The present volume is one of this general description. It is written by a missionary of the American Methodist Episcopal Church (North) who has been in China for more than twenty years, and who has been for a part of that time superintendent of an important mission in Central China. Mr. Hart indulges in no preface, although he dedicates his book to his fellow travellers, one of whom was Mr. Faber, so well known as a Chinese scholar and a Chinese author. The special occasion for the long, laborious and expensive journey which Mr. Hart undertook in the spring and summer of 1887, was to endeavour to repair the injury which was done to the new mission begun in Szechuan, by the riot at Chungking in the summer of 1886. As the work is intended for general readers, no more prominence is given to the special affairs of the Methodist Mission than is necessary to make the narrative intelligible. The details of the riot are given at the end of the book, and the comments upon the circumstances in the earlier portion, an arrangement which tends to the confusion of the reader.

The work is illustrated with a map sufficiently precise for the need, and by thirteen engravings, most of them very good, and apparently taken from drawings. The map purports to be that of "Szechuan," although it is labelled "Western China," after the title of the book. It is not quite clear, however, why the author should confine the use of this phrase to the single province of Szechuan, when Shensi, Kansu, and Shansi, none of which were entered on this journey, are equally entitled to the term. Four chapters are devoted to the voyage to Chungking, one to that city, one to the great brine and gas wells, two more to travel from Chungking to the capital of the province and thence to Mount Omei, three more to that famous mountain, and the concluding one to the province in general. There is very little in Mr. Hart's book which has not been already described by former travellers, but this does not detract from the value of the work, which is a real addition to the books on China. It is a most welcome relief to those whose life in China is spent in the relatively uninteresting parts of the Empire—of which there are vast tracts—to read of this beautiful land, which is so favoured in climate, in scenery, and in productions. The catalogue of fruits reads like that of the sub-tropical regions, and however indifferent they may be to sublime scenery, few will hear without surprise of Chinese who buy milk fresh from the cow at the somewhat vague rate of "about one cent" for "a fair sized tea-cup two thirds full," or of wild strawberries on Mount Omei for which the Chinese care nothing. The cheapness of oranges is mentioned, but not the custom of which we have heard of selling them at a merely nominal rate, if the skin is returned to be used as a medicine. No adequate notice is taken of the variation between the dialect of Szechuan and that of other parts of China, but this may be due to the fact that the book is written for American readers, to whom such distinctions would be of little value. But if the readers are other than residents of China, what could they possibly understand by the information (p. 34) that "we have a mammoth *yulo* on each side of the boat"? In the same manner must the person to whom Chinese terms are unfamiliar be mystified on being told (p. 107) that stones around a compound indicated it "to be the property of the *pa-hsien*." On the next page the Loh family are apparently epitomised in the phrase "white horse with black mane," an appellation which must remain wholly enigmatical to every American reader.

And why, we must enquire, should the Chinese language be referred to by one who is a member of the China Branch of the Royal Asiatic Society (p. 115) as "the Mongolian tongue"? Several references occur (*e.g.* p. 62) to "cities of refuge," by which are apparently meant fortifications into which the people retreat in the time of insurrections. But to readers who know nothing of such Chinese structures, and the reasons for their use, the technical term 'city of refuge,' would suggest the wholly misleading idea of the 'avenger of blood.' We read (p. 179) of a Buddhist priest, who was "a sort of *cicisbeo*," but we confess that not having recently travelled in Italy we are not much enlightened. On page 162 we meet our old friend "the *Blue* river," which we had supposed had retired with the Abbé Huc, whom we have always understood to be its inventor—but perhaps we are all astray on this point. On page 61 "*Mayer*" is quoted, which reminds us of an Indiana justice of the peace, who based his decision of a case on "the first *claw* of the statute." On p. 149 the opinion is expressed with what seems to us a very extravagant comparison, that the Taoist priesthood, "not unlike the men who stood before Moses in the presence of Pharaoh, has doubtless as great an influence in China, as the Nile sorcerers had in Egypt."

It is a matter of courtesy to allow every latest traveller to adjust the population of interior provinces in China to suit himself. Accordingly we shall not try to beat Mr. Hart down to asking "the usual discount," when he gives (p. 208) the enormous total of 45,000,000 people for Szechuan. But we must mildly though firmly beg him not to increase it (p. 289) to "fifty millions." Few occurrences are more depressing when one has arranged for a fixed number of persons than to have them suddenly (and without explanation) increased by about eleven per cent. It is an ungrateful task to seem to be 'blowing fur to find flaws,' yet we never read a new book on China without being reminded of the second of the remarks, by means of which the nephew of the Vicar of Wakefield established himself in Paris as an art connoisseur. Why should not a writer's meaning be so conveyed that the reader not merely *can* get it, but *must* get it? On page 274 we have a description of a dangerous passage in the Wind-box gorge, followed by a paragraph beginning, "*While here* we had an episode which came near proving fatal to one of our party. Dr. Morley took books and went to the upper part of the suburbs, where we had made heavy sales on our way up river." What are the "suburbs" of the "Wind-box gorge"? Nothing which follows throws any light on the place at which the trouble in question took place.

In books which are made up from a running journal, there is a special liability to repetition of the same fact. This often annoys a reader like a grain of dust in the eye, for it is a subtle intimation that the author has forgotten what he said, and supposes that his readers have done the same. Our author is not free from such blemishes on his pages. For example the great Yü passed his own door three times on p. 68, and three more times on p. 90. Twice the Szechuan people came from Kuangtung, twice the houses are of one story, with mud walls and whitewashed (pp. 118

and 148), and twice Chang Fei, Kuan Yü and Liu Pei are described in their historical setting.

We hope Mr. Hart's example in writing a readable volume will be followed by some of the many foreigners, mostly missionaries, who are living in the provinces of Yünnan, Kueichou, Shensi and Kansu. The province of Shensi, too, is not yet thoroughly exploited, and it contains almost sixty Protestant missionaries besides many Roman Catholics. The greater part of these provinces must prove a rich territory for intelligent observers and accurate writers.

[*From the North China Daily News* of June 11, 1889.]

# Obituary.

**Shripad Babaji Thakur.** — Telegraphic news has been received of the sad and untimely death of Mr. Shripad Babaji Thakur, of the Bombay Civil Service. Mr. Thakur was struck down with paralysis at Shikarpur on the morning of the 22nd July, and died the same evening at nine o'clock. In his untimely death the native community of Western India has been deprived of another important member. He was, says a correspondent who knew him well, a profound linguistic scholar. His intellect was so powerful that he was able to master several Western and Eastern languages, Latin, Greek, French, German, Italian, Spanish, Sanskrit, Pali, Zend, Arabic, Persian, Kanarese, Guzerattee (Marathi being his vernacular) and Hebrew. A thorough knowledge of all these languages he acquired by his own exertions. He graduated a Bachelor of Arts in the Bombay University in Greek in 1868, and proceeded to England to compete for the Bombay Civil Service Examination, which he passed with credit, not only to himself, but to the community to which he belonged. He was always unassuming, genial as a friend, and full of humour, as fond of making a joke as he was keen in appreciating it in any of the languages he so cleverly mastered. He was specially engaged, as leisure from official duty permitted, in collecting materials for an Encyclopædic dictionary in Sanskrit. This work, for which as a philologist he was particularly fitted, must now ever remain unfinished, and the educated natives will have ever to mourn the loss of a scholar of gigantic intellect cut off in the prime of life at the early age of forty-two. He was a barrister-at-law and Sessions Judge, Shikarpur, at the time of his death. He had, perhaps, the largest library that any native or English scholar possessed in India. —[*Times of India* for July 30.]

**Michele Amari,** whose death took place at Florence, on the 21st of July, was one of those rare men who make their scholarship entirely subservient to political ends. Born at Palermo on the 7th of July, 1806, he inherited from his father that revolutionary spirit which stamped and characterized his whole political and literary career, while his learned compatriot Domenico Scinà inspired him with a love for the study of the history of his native island. The first fruits of his researches in this direction appeared in 1834 in a work entitled '*La Fondazione della Monarchia dei Normanni in Sicilia,*' which laid the foundation of his fame as a historian. In 1841 he brought out in Palermo the first edition of his celebrated '*Storia dei Vespri Siciliani,*'

a subject at which he had been working for a number of years. That edition bore the title, '*Un Periodo della Storia Siciliana nel Secolo XIII.,*' and pervaded as it was by a glowing hatred of the Bourbon dynasty, it attracted at once the notice of the King of Naples and his minister Del Carretto, who sent the publisher to prison. Amari would have shared his fate had he not evaded persecution by flight to Paris, where he continued his studies amid the greatest privations, and published a much enlarged edition of his work under its more comprehensive title, in 1843. It has not only many times been reprinted since, but has also been translated into German and English. It was here that Amari, convinced that the history of Sicily could not be adequately gone into without an acquaintance with the Arabic sources, took up the study of that language under Professor Reinaud, and with the aid and encouragement of the Baron Mac-Guckin de Slane : and he devoted himself to it with such zeal and perseverance that he was able to contribute to the *Journal Asiatique* in 1845 a translation of Ibn Haukal's description of Palermo, and in the following year the Arabic text, with translation and notes, of Ibn Jobeir's Travels in Sicily. These peaceful occupations suffered a temporary interruption when, on the outbreak of the revolution in Sicily in 1848, he was invited to return to Palermo, and was made a member of the Sicilian Parliament. When he was subsequently offered the portfolio as Minister of Finance, he accepted the charge only on condition that his services were to be gratuitous, while he threw himself on the hospitality of his brother. Soon after his return from London, where he had gone on a political mission in the following year, the reaction set in, and he had again to seek safety in flight. For the next ten years we see him again in Paris, where he continued to collect materials for his great History of the Arabs in Sicily. Concerning this project, he says in a letter to Professor Fleischer under date of 11th April, 1853 : "I myself have explored for my purposes the libraries of Paris, London and Oxford ; disinterested friends have done the same for me at Leyden and Gotha. I have copied a St. Petersburg MS., and procured the transcript of one belonging to the Escurial, as well as valuable extracts from Tunisian MSS., and have brought together everything written by Arabs about Sicily and about the Arabs of Sicily, as well as the works of the latter both in prose and poetry. When my materials had thus attained the greatest possible completeness, I set to work to elaborate from them a history of the Arabs in Sicily, which is now passing through the press in Florence. It remains for me to edit the text of those materials for the study of the original sources. This *Bibliotheca Arabico-Sicula* should, strictly speaking, consist of two divisions, viz. Arabic works on Sicily, and writings of Sicilian Arabs. But I intend to confine myself to the first division only, which will fill an octavo volume of about 650 pages" (Zeitschrift des Deutschen Morgenländ. Ges., vol. vii. 415). The *Bibliotheca Arabico-Sicula* was published at Leipzig at the expense of the German Oriental Society in 1855–57, and three appendices appeared, one with Fleischer's emendations in 1875, the second in 1887, and the third in 1889. The '*Storia dei Musulmani di Sicilia*' came out in three volumes at Florence, 1852–72. Two other monumental works on this subject should here be mentioned, *Diplomi arabi dal R. Archivio fiorentino* (Florence, 1863–67), and *Le Epigrafi arabiche di Sicilia trascritte, tradotte e illustrate* (Palermo, 1875). The only publication of his that belongs to the category of writings by Sicilian Arabs is his translation of *Solwan el mota' ossiano Conforti politici di Ibn Zafer, arabo siciliano del xii. secolo* (Florence, 1852). Further, he wrote *Abbozzo di un catalogo dei manoscritti arabici della Lucchesiana di Girgenti* (1869), *Nuovi ricordi arabici su la storia di Genova* (Genoa, 1873), and, in 1858, a memoir, in French, on the chronology of the Koran, for which he received the prize of the Institute, but which has not yet been printed. He furnished, besides, many valuable contributions to the Transactions of learned Societies in Italy and to literary serials.

In 1859, Amari was appointed professor of Arabic in the University of Pisa, and was subsequently called to Florence in the same quality. He filled the post of Minister of Public Instruction from 1862 to 64 ; but he soon retired from public life and also resigned his professorship in 1866, to spend the rest of his days in literary work.

As a noble and disinterested patriot his name will ever remain associated with the regeneration of the Italian kingdom. He was one of the foremost Arabic scholars of his time, and a kind and ever helpful friend to younger scholars who sought his aid and counsel.

**Professor S. Beal.**—It is with much regret that we have to record the death of Dr. Samuel Beal, Professor of Chinese at University College, London, which took place on Tuesday, August 20, at the Rectory of Greens Norton, near Towcester, in Northamptonshire. For some years past he had been in weak health.

Professor Beal was born in 1825, and educated at Trinity College, Cambridge, where he graduated B.A. in 1847. He never proceeded to a higher degree, though the University of Durham conferred upon him the honorary degree of D.C.L. in 1885. After holding several curacies, he was appointed to a chaplaincy in the Royal Navy in 1852. The accident of his serving upon the Sybille during the Chinese War of 1856-58 gave the impulse to the course of his studies for the remainder of his life. He must already have made progress in the knowledge of Chinese, for we learn from the Navy List, that he was especially mentioned in despatches for his services as Chinese interpreter on the occasion of the destruction of forty war junks up Escape Creek in the Canton River. On retiring from the Navy in 1877, he was appointed by the Admiralty to the Greenwich Hospital living of Falstone, in Northumberland ; and in the same year he was elected to the chair of Chinese in University College, London. In 1880, he was transferred to another Greenwich Hospital living, that of Wark, also in Northumberland ; and only last year the Crown presented him to the more valuable preferment of Greens Norton.

Professor Beal's name will always hold a high place in Oriental scholarship as being the first Englishman (following in the steps of Rémusat and Julien) to translate direct from the Chinese the early records of Buddhism in that country, which throw such a flood of light upon the dark period of Indian History. So far as we know, his first publication was a paper on "The History of the Temples of Hakodate," read before the Chinese Branch of the Royal Asiatic Society in 1857. In the same year he printed for private circulation a pamphlet aiming to prove, that the Shogun or Tycoon was not the real Emperor of Japan. At the second Oriental Congress, held in London 1874, he presented a report upon the Chinese Buddhist books in the India Office Library ; and at the Berlin Congress (1883) he read a paper upon "The Buddhist Councils."

But the work by which Prof. Beal's fame was established is the series of books in which he traced the travels of the Chinese Buddhist pilgrims in India from the fifth to the seventh century A.D. The first of this series was *The Travels of Sung-Yun and Fa-Hien*, translated from the Chinese, with notes and prolegomena

(Trübner, 1869). Next followed *The Si-yu-ki ; or Buddhist Records of the Western World*, translated from the Chinese of Hiuen Tsiang, which forms two volumes of "Trübner's Oriental Series" (1884). And finally the series was completed only last year by the publication of *The Life of Hiuen Tsiang, by the Shamans Hwui Li and Yen Tsung*, with a preface containing an account of the works of I-Tsing. We believe that he has left in MS. some further contributions to the same subject.

Among Prof. Beal's other works may be mentioned, *The Catena of Buddhist Scriptures from the Chinese* (1872), *The Romantic Legend of Buddha* (1876) ; *Text from the Buddhist Canon commonly known as the Dhammapada*, translated from the Chinese, with accompanying narratives (1878) ; the *Fo-sho-hing-tsan-king* ; a Life of Buddha translated from the Chinese version of a Sanskrit original, forming vol. xix. of "The Sacred Books of the East" ; and *Buddhism in China*, in the series of "Non-Christian Religious Systems" of the S.P.C.K. Such, in brief, is the record of an active life which was by no means entirely devoted to the pursuit of Oriental studies. Chinese scholars as good—nay, better—may survive, but none more laborious and single-minded. J. S. C.—(*Academy*.)

---

## American Notes.

**Blackfoot Language, North America.**—The compiler of the Grammar and Dictionary of the Language of the Blackfoot Indians, published by the Society for Promoting Christian Knowledge, is the Rev. John William Tims, trained at the Church Missionary College, Islington, and sent out in 1883 to the North-West American Mission of that Society. His station is at "Blackfoot Crossing," on the Canadian and Pacific Railway, in the Province of Alberta, and the Diocese of Calgary, which, for the present, is united to Saskatchewan, about 50° N. Lat., and 110° W. Long., on the east side of the Rocky Mountains.

The Blackfoot (called by the French Pieds Noirs, and by the Germans Schwarzfüsse) are so called from their black mocassins : they are, or were, a powerful tribe, and were divided into four bands : 1. The Blackfoot proper ; 2. The Pe-e-gun ; 3. The Blood ; 4. The Small Rover. Under the arrangement of the Canadian Government, Reserves have been set apart for these tribes, and the Reserve of the Blackfoot proper, where Mr. Tims resides, is actually upon the railway. The Reserve for the Blood band is to the South, not far from the frontier of the United States : it is stated with confidence that the same language is spoken by the Blackfoot proper, the Pe-e-gun, and the Blood ; this Philological work is of considerable importance. No portion of the Scriptures has as yet passed through the Press, but a portion exists in MS.

The Tribe belongs to the great Algonquin Family and, like all the languages of North America, it is Polysynthetic. The Written character is the Roman. Vocabularies existed previously, but this is the first Grammar, and we have to thank Mr. Tims for this important contribution to knowledge.

**The Kwa-Gutl Language, Vancouver's Island.**—The Royal Society of Canada has published in its Transactions, vol. vi. sec. ii. 1888, a capital Grammar of this Language, compiled by the Rev. Alfred Hall, of the Church Missionary Society, who has resided ten years at Alert Bay amidst this tribe. Translations of two Gospels in this Language have been published by the British and Foreign Bible Society. This is an entirely fresh contribution to existing knowledge, and reflects great credit on the compiler. The Roman character is used. The language is Polysynthetic.

THE PACIFIC STATES HISTORIES—How it came about that they were written, and how the work was done.—The *Academy* (London) says, "The history of this work, as well as its contents, is of public interest." Why it is of public interest is because nothing of the kind was ever before attempted; nothing of the kind was ever before accomplished. The old way of writing history, and not at all a bad way, was for a person to take up some small field, or epoch, which had already, as a rule, been pretty well worked over, and about which were several tolerably fair works extant. These, with some further facts which he could gather, were his material, over which he would devote the leisure of years, and produce a volume or two. Some would accomplish more than this, but many more would accomplish less.

At the outset of his historical undertakings, Mr. Bancroft was faced by the stubborn fact that his plans could not be carried out by one person within the period of his natural life. Twenty or thirty persons would be required to complete them within the time he might reasonably expect to live. Consequently he must have assistance, and that of the highest order—trained help and plenty of it, or else give up the undertaking, or modify his plan.

Why not modify the plan, and undertake less? For two reasons: First, there was a natural unity or oneness in it which he did not like to break—which could not be broken without disadvantage to any one of the several parts; and secondly, he felt that if he neglected to do this work that it never would be done, which was very true.

For example, in the work of collecting, gathering in the material—which alone, if he had gone no further, would have been more than ever one man had ever achieved in this direction, for any country in any age—he began in California. But California being at one time held by Spain and a province of Mexico, to obtain her early annals he was obliged to go to Mexico and to Spain. Then he found that in writing the history of California he must of necessity, to make it thoroughly understood, give so much of the Mexican affairs, government, law, commerce, mines, manufactures, routine of legislation and society, and current of events, that it seemed more satisfactory to him to do the whole than a part of this necessary work. Besides there was nothing extant that could properly be called a history either of Mexico or Central America in any language. Hence these Republics were brought within his field.

Toward the north and east the unity of the subject obtained in a still greater degree. The territory bordering what is now the Mexican republic had all of it not long since belonged to Mexico. Texas achieved her independence from Mexico and then joined the northern confederation. The vast region west of the Rocky Mountains and south of latitude 42°, Oregon's southern boundary, came into the possession of the United States with California. Oregon, Washington, Idaho, and Montana were once one territory with British Columbia under the name of the Northwest Coast under the domination of the Hudson's Bay Company; and when the Oregon region and the California country fell under the same general government, and gold was found, and population flocked in, it seemed of the same vital importance that the history of both should be preserved.

Consequently the work of collecting, Mr. Bancroft having entertained no idea of writing history up to this time, gradually extended itself over the entire western portion of North America, from Alaska to Panamá, including all of Mexico and Central America. This area once determined upon as the field of his labours, he confined himself to it, though frequently urged by Dr. Draper and others to enlarge it, particularly in regard to the native races of South America. And under this arrangement, the library gradually grew, the world being ransacked for its increase, until the collection in books, manuscripts, and maps numbered fifty thousand, all of which found

safety and convenience of arrangement in a building erected especially for the purpose on Valencia Street, in San Francisco.

The collection was formed on the basis of restricting it entirely to works relating to the territory covered, that is, books written or printed within the territory covered, or written or printed elsewhere but in some particular relating to it. One feature of the library, of inestimable value, is the thousands of manuscripts it contains in which are related the experiences of pioneers, of those who came early to the country and helped to make it what it is. This library is in fact the largest collection of books, maps, and manuscripts relating to a single subject or territory in the world.

The point of time when Mr. Bancroft entered upon his vast and remarkable labours was most opportune. Had he begun earlier the country would not have been old enough to have had its history sufficiently matured. Had his work been put off until ten years later, much valuable material would have been lost which he has saved.

But when ready to write his history, how was he to get at the facts he required mingled as they were with such a mass of matter which he did not require. This for some time was a serious question, until the plan was finally adopted of indexing the whole library as we would index a single volume. This work occupied six men for ten years, and cost $80,000. It was the only way whereby any subject could be immediately traced to what all the authors had said of it. The information required was then extracted by one set of assistants, and handed to Mr. Bancroft, who examined the extracts, arranged the information in the proper order for presenting it in the most natural and interesting way. He then placed it in the hands of yet more competent assistants, who winnowed it of the chaff, and threw out whatever irrelevant matter had crept in and returned it in as perfected a manner as possible to Mr. Bancroft, who wrote the history from the material thus prepared, referring to the original authorities as occasion demanded.

Then there were maps to be drawn and engraved, new matter to be inserted, dates and statements to be verified, several revisions to be made, both before and after the work had been put into type, which with the indexing and a hundred like labours, the work and responsibility regarding which it is difficult to convey any adequate idea of.

But the work being done and well done, the public now can have the benefit of it, and at a very small cost as compared with the time and money the author and publishers have bestowed upon it. In fact, a book is the cheapest thing in the world.

You may obtain the labour of a lifetime for a few shillings. If but one copy of Mr. Bancroft's books had been published, the actual cost of that one copy would have been over £100,000.

The work is well condensed. It was no small thing to do to compress the vast amount of information contained in 60,000 volumes in so small a compass. To make every one of Mr. Bancroft's volumes, on an average over 3000 volumes have been used, and some of them have drawn from no less than 10,000 volumes.

The reception of these books by the press, by reviewers, and by scholars and learned men in both America and Europe has been something marvellous. And as one volume after another was put into print they grew more and more in public favour. There never was anything like it. It seemed that the more people learned of the wonderful development which had taken place in America during the past twenty-five to fifty years, the more they wanted to know. No historical works in the world sustain a higher reputation to-day than these.

In glancing through the several series of histories, one is astounded with the amount of labour performed by Mr. Bancroft, even with his large library at hand and his corps of able assistants. And one is more and more impressed with the importance and value of these works to future generations. As the process of empire-building goes on these volumes will settle more firmly into the foundations of history, and millions yet unborn will read and profit by them.

Up to the present time the History Company of San Francisco only sold Mr. Bancroft's History as a complete work by subscription, but they have now decided to sell any complete State or subject separately, which is a valuable concession to the wants of the public and ought to bring a reciprocative amount of patronage.

THE MERIDEN SCIENTIFIC ASSOCIATION.—Meriden, Conn., which cannot be a very large district, is luckier than many larger ones in having a Scientific Association that takes note of and publishes from time to time records of the biology or physiography of the place. Volume three, now before us, contains the following Meridenial articles: The Ash Bed at Meriden; The Trap Ridges of Meriden; A Supplementary List of Birds of Meriden; The Butterflies of Meriden; and The Forest Trees and Shrubs found in Meriden. The association now numbers one hundred and fifty members, who sometimes indulge in papers further afield than Meriden. Amongst those of 1867 may be mentioned, Some Dictionary Errors; New Theories in regard to Water; Language of India; Japan; Oceanic Islands; Talk on Electricity, etc.

SOME AMERICAN PERIODICALS.—"Poet Lore," Philadelphia, a monthly magazine published on the 15th of every month, is a journal devoted to Shakespeare, Browning, and the comparative study of literature, and edited by Charlotte Porter, the late editor of "Shakespeariana," and Helen A. Clarke. "Table Talk," Philadelphia, now in its fourth volume, edited by Mrs. S. T. Rover, Tillie May Torney, and Mrs. Joseph Whitton, has a literal title as it is devoted to culinary matter and housekeeping. Mrs. S. T. Rover edits the culinary department and answers housekeepers' enquiries. The " Office Men's Record," Kansas City, Mo., which commenced in January this year, is a monthly magazine of practical knowledge. devoted to improvements in office work and the interests of office men. The topics of its articles seem well selected and to the purpose, if we may judge by the number before us.

REPORTS OF THE CONSULS OF THE UNITED STATES.—We have received these valuable budgets of information, numbers 99 to 105, with the index for volume 29. They contain some notable articles, numbers 99 and 100, which is on Systems of Taxation, and is a volume of over 500 pages, containing a series of reports by American Consuls in various parts of the world on the system of taxation prevailing in the district in which they reside. In submitting these to the President, Mr. Secretary Bayard said that he was led to order the preparation of these reports by the consideration that fiscal questions were of continually increasing importance, both in national and local administration, and that, although the reports would necessarily be imperfect from a purely scientific point of view, they would nevertheless afford a basis for interesting comparisons of the methods employed in other countries. "The reports," continues Mr. Bayard, "are intended to show merely what is the actual condition of taxation in different countries, without regard to the reasons of such condition, or the theories that have been applied in leading to it. To examine the subject as its importance demands would require the knowledge of highly trained economists and practical financiers; but the following reports will be sufficient to awaken a spirit of inquiry that cannot but be productive of good results." The countries reported on are Austria, Bohemia, Belgium, Denmark, France, Germany, Greece, Italy, Netherlands, Russia, Poland, Spain. Sweden, Switzerland, and Great Britain. The manner in which taxation in England is treated in the reports will perhaps give an idea how the whole is done. The Consul-General in London describes the local taxation of the metropolis; the Consul at Bristol discusses taxation, local and national, with the Parliamentary returns of revenue; the Consul at Leeds deals mainly with the powers and duties of Local Boards in regard to rates and borrowing; and similarly the reports from Liverpool, Newcastle, Sheffield, Cork, Edinburgh, Dunfermline, and Cardiff deal first with Imperial taxation, and then with the incidence of local taxation in their respective districts. This method, or lack of method, is the cause of much repetition, especially in regard to Imperial taxation, which might have been avoided by more careful editing in Washington. But of the value and interest of the mass of facts and figures relating to Imperial and local taxation in the various European countries brought together in this volume there can be no question whatever.—No. 101 contains an article by Consul Brown on the present state of Nicaragua Canal Construction. The past, present, and future of the Republic of Columbia (formerly known as New Granada, and also as a member of the United States of Columbia, which included Venezuela, and Equador, and expired in 1830) is given by the Consul residing there. This is now a region of interest from the claims it makes to certain gold mines said to be in the area of British Guiana, in fact, the gold mining area seems to be where the boundaries of Columbia and British Guiana meet.—In No. 102 Consul E. L. Baker gives particulars of the navigation, commerce, and industries of the Argentine Republic. — No. 103 contains, amongst other articles, an account of the famine in China, by Consul-General Kennedy, of Shanghai, and also one by the same gentleman, on the trade of Shanghai in 1888.—In No. 104 Consul F. D. Hill contributes an article on Paraguay, its history, geography, resources. peoples, products, government, commerce, etc. Consul Griffin, of Sydney, makes a report in No. 106, on the Bismark Archipelago, consisting of the island of New Britain, New Hanover, and a group of smaller islands in the eighth degree of south latitude, between meridians 148° and 154° east longitude. And in the same number Consul Herring, of Honduras, reports on the lands and land-laws of that republic.

THE BUREAU OF EDUCATION.—We have received Circulars of Information, Nos. 3, 4 and 7 (1888), and No. 7 (1889), issued under the supervision of the late Commissioner of Education, the Hon. N. H. R. Dawson. These circulars are as follows: History of the Higher Education in South Carolina, by Collyer Meriwether, A.B.; Education in Georgia, by Charles Edgworth Jones, late of Johns Hopkins University; History of Education in Florida, by George Gary Bush, Ph.D.; and Higher Education in Wisconsin, by William F. Allen and David E. Spencer, of the University of Wisconsin. The foregoing form Nos. 4, 5, 6 and 7 of Contributions to American Educational History, edited by Herbert B. Adams. Prof. W. T. Harris, editor of the Journal of Speculative Philosophy and Professor of the late School of Philosophy at Concord, has just been appointed Commissioner of Education by the present administration. Although editor of a "speculative," journal this gentleman is a practical educationalist, and is the compiler of Appleton & Co.'s "Readers," which are second to none in the United States. We are quite sure the interests of the Bureau of Education will be well looked after under his régime.

---

# European Notes.

OCCULT BOOKS.—Mr. Geo. Redway, of York Street, Covent Garden, has recently published two books, which carry us back to the times of Lilly, and as one of the authors has it "Old World Lore." One is a foolscap 8vo. volume, entitled "A Handbook of Cartomancy, Fortune Telling and Occult Divination," by "Grand Orient," which professes to bring together "the genuine remains of the ancient and traditional science of the sublime kings of the East," but what they had to do with the method of fortune telling by cards, which is one of the chapters, the author does not tell us. The other volume, an 8vo. by Rosa Baughan, is "On the Influence of the Stars," in three parts, Astrology, Chiromancy, and Physiognomy. This author laments that we have so long been oppressed with realism, and it is to satisfy an interest growing out of this oppression that this book of "Old World Lore" is written. We always considered that what was real was true, or founded on fact. Is it to get away from this influence the book was written? We are afraid the authoress has not studied the meaning of phrases so much as she has the stars, as she certainly does not wish her readers to understand that there is no truth in what she expounds.

MARRIAGE AND KINSHIP.—Mr. C. Staniland Wake, the author of the "Evolution of Morality," has issued (George Redway, York Street, Covent Garden, London) a bulky 8vo. volume on the Development of Marriage and Kinship. Mr. Wake's researches on this subject are interesting when they reach the domain of history, and he has collected matter together which places the subject in a new light, and shows the deductions of some former students of the subject to have been erroneous. He has, however, discovered nothing new on the pre-historic relation of the sexes, which, as far as we can see, must remain a matter of speculation.

PAUL OF TARSUS.—The author of the "Rabbi Jeshua" (George Redway, York Street, Covent Garden) has attempted in this book to depict the life of Paul divested of the miraculous, and we must say that the author has produced an account which, although adhering to history, reads like a novel.

THE PERIODICAL PRESS INDEX—the first annual volume of which is to be published by Messrs. Trübner & Co. in January next—is now in active preparation. This reference work, as our readers are aware, is intended as an index to subjects treated in the principal periodical publications of England and America, the more important of the continental magazines and reviews also being included. The scheme of arrangement comprises (1) a subject index, supplemented (2) by a catch word index, and this combination it is believed will render reference to any given subject both easy and expeditious. So useful a work has rarely been projected, and we cannot doubt that it will prove an indispensable adjunct to the library-table and the desk. Full prospectuses of the first volume, which will deal with the publications of the current year, will be issued in October; meanwhile the publishers will forward specimen pages on application.

## Oriental Notes.

SINHALESE DICTIONARIES. — Clough's Sinhalese-English Dictionary, published in 1830, having long been out of print, the Ceylon Branch of the Royal Asiatic Society prepared a scheme, in 1884 (see the *Proceedings* for that year, p. xlix), for the elaboration of a scientific dictionary which should "deal with the language in historical sequence from the earliest inscriptions downwards." There would appear, however, to have been great difficulties in preparing a work of such dimensions, and the carrying out of that plan was abandoned, at any rate for the time being. In the meanwhile a work of a more practical character, viz. a new edition of Clough, greatly revised and enlarged, was undertaken by the Rev. G. Baugh, and the Rev. F. Tebb, and after they left the island, was finally prepared for the press by Pandit B. Gunasekara, Mudaliyar, who bestowed great care upon its scientific correctness, especially in reference to terms bearing on the different departments of natural history. Of this valuable dictionary, the printing of which was commenced in 1887, four parts have appeared, and the fifth, completing the work, and intended to contain also a list of more characteristic Sinhalese names of families and places, will probably be issued early next year. We are glad to be able to state that its counterpart, a new English and Sinhalese Dictionary, is now also passing through the press. This is not an improved edition of the one by Clough which appeared 68 years ago, but an entirely new work. The author is the Rev. C. Carter, one of the best Sinhalese scholars living, who by previous publications—Sinhalese Lesson Book, 1860; Sinhalese Verbs reduced to Conjugations, 1883—has done much to simplify and facilitate the acquisition of the Sinhalese language by Europeans. The work will appear in five parts and be completed by the end of 1891. The price is fixed at 6s. per part, or 25s. in advance for the entire work.

NOTICES OF SANSKRIT MSS.—Dr. Rájendralála Mitra has issued his twenty-third part of Notices of MSS. or volume ix. part 2, published under the orders of the Government of Bengal. Some of the custodians of the collections of MSS. visited by Dr. Rájendralála Mitra's Pandits "cannot understand why a foreign government should wish to know the contents of works which, it openly declares, treat of a false religion," and there is also a feeling, "that it would be impious to let foreigners have access to what is most sacred, and that of itself is a serious deterrent." This feeling is intensified in the case of Jains, as the Hindus have a proverb that "One should rather run the risk of being eaten up by a tiger than enter a Jain temple, even if it be the only shelter available." In the letter from Dr. Rájendralála Mitra conveying this Report to the Hon. Secretary of the Asiatic Society of Bengal, is an interesting account of the progress of this search for MSS., and a summary of the work that has so far been accomplished.

THE ORDEAL BY BOILING OIL IN CEYLON. — Recently the district Judge at Kalutara, in Ceylon, had before him three persons, including a village headman, charged with causing grievous hurt to four others by requiring them to plunge their right hands into a cauldron of boiling oil. The medical evidence described the hands as being in "a sodden, suppurating condition," the fingers being in some cases deformed. In all cases the injured persons were unable to follow their ordinary avocations for about a month. The facts of the case, as stated in the judgment, were these:—A woman in the village had some plumbago and rice stolen from her; a headman made inquiry, and, failing to obtain a clue to the theft, announced that it would be necessary on the third day to hold an ordeal by boiling oil. This appears to be a not uncommon custom in remote parts of the country, and the formalities are as follows:—Some oil from newly-gathered king cocoanuts is manufactured by one of the friends of the complainant; this is poured into a cauldron and heated to boiling point. Each of the suspected parties is supposed to dip his hand into the vessel of boiling oil, and is at liberty to sprinkle as much of the hot oil as he brings up with his fingers on the person of the complainant, who stands close at hand. Any exclamation of pain on the part of the suspected person is construed into an admission of guilt. If no such exclamation is made the innocence of the party is supposed to be established. In the present case the evidence established that the pressure on the accused was not merely moral; they were forced to dip their hands into the burning oil. No force appears to have been used in bringing them to the scene of the ordeal; they collected there in response to the orders of the headman, who, seated on a platform opposite the vessel of oil, appears to have acted as the presiding judge. Each of the complainants deposed to the fact that they were reluctant to submit to the ordeal, but were forcibly dragged up to the cauldron by the other two accused, and their hands plunged into the boiling oil. They had sufficient self-control to abstain from calling out, except a boy of 17, who cried out lustily, and was thereupon pronounced the guilty one. The judge took the fact that it was a custom into account, but refused to dismiss the prisoners with a warning as suggested by their counsel. He fined them 100 rupees each, with the alternative of rigorous imprisonment for ten months.— *The Times*, of 14 August.

SPECIAL LECTURES ON ORIENTAL SUBJECTS. — Writing from Berlin, a correspondent in that city says: "Special lectures are to be given in the winter term at the Berlin Oriental Seminary—'On the Treaties China has concluded with Foreign Nations'; 'On the Religion and Habits of the Japanese'; 'On the Geography and Modern History of Northern Africa' (not including Egypt); and 'On the Geography of Southern Africa and History of the Discoveries there.' With regard to the practical utility of the Seminary, which has only existed for two years, I may mention that the authorities seem thoroughly satisfied. They are paying a great deal of attention to the acquirement of Suaheli for the purpose of German intercourse with East Africa. On Aug. 18 the German Society of Friends of Photography will open a Photography Jubilee Exhibition, the main object of which is to show the manifold advantages afforded by photography to science, art, commercial industry, and military purposes. The Ministry of Commerce has promised to award State medals to successful exhibitors who are specialists, not amateurs."

THE PADMA-PURÁNA, on a critical edition of which the late Rao Saheb V. N. Mandlik, of Bombay, had been engaged, is ready for the Press.

DR. M. A. STEIN has recently had the good fortune to have access to the codex archetypus of the *Rájatarangiṇí* and to several other old S'áradá MSS. of that work, all of which he has carefully collated. He is ably assisted in this, and in the compilation of indices, and identification of names of localities, by Pandit Govind Kaul, already mentioned by Prof. Bühler in his Kashmir Report.

SENHOR AGOSTINO SISENANDO MARQUES, the second in command of the Portuguese Expedition to the capital of the Muata Yanvo in Central Africa, South of the Equator, has published in the Portuguese language, at the National Press, Lisbon, a most interesting account of the progress of his exploration, *Os Climas eas Producções das terras de Malange a Lunda*; it is accompanied by illustrations of the Flora of the Region. The matter is entirely new.

DICTIONARY OF WESTERN TIBET.—Captain H. Ramsay, British Joint Commissioner, Ladakh, has prepared for the press *A Practical Dictionary of the Language and Customs of Ladakh or Western Tibet*. The existing dictionaries and other helps for the acquisition of Tibetan either regard the classical language only or any dialects but the Western, whereas Capt. Ramsay's English-Ladakh Vocabulary—in which also the habits, rites and customs of the people are incidentally dealt with —is intended as a practical introduction to the living language of Western Tibet, gathered from the mouths of the people exclusively. Messrs. Trübner and Co. will be the publishers.

CHINESE-JAPANESE DICTIONARY.—We have received copies of *A Dictionary of Chinese-Japanese Words in the Japanese Language*, by J. H. Gubbins, Japanese Secretary of H.B.M.'s Legation in Japan. It is a well-known fact that the greatest obstacle to the mastering of the Japanese written language consists in the so-called *Kan-go* or Chinese words (chiefly dissyllabic) which have received currency in Japan, and which are pronounced by the Japanese in a manner which would not be intelligible to a Chinese. So far from these words being gradually eliminated with a view to the simplification of the written language, this Chinese-Japanese ingredient has, according to Mr. Gubbins, a tendency towards constant expansion. "Being adapted to the various necessities of every-day life, it has lost its former purely literary and classical character, and is now fast becoming the common property of all classes of the people. There is moreover in this growth of the language a vigour which appears to gather fresh impetus as it proceeds." The necessity for a separate dictionary of these words for the use of European students having arisen,—for the Japanese have long had their own Kan-go dictionaries—Mr. Gubbins is supplying a pressing want. He has adopted the European alphabetical arrangement, grouping the words under the first of the two characters with which they are written,—the initial Chinese-Japanese character being in each case treated separately, and its meanings given without reference to the compounds in which it occurs. Where these initial characters have the same sound, and where, in the case of two or more words coming under the same initial character, the sound of the second of the two characters of which the words are composed is in each case the same, the arrangement is determined by the number of strokes in the respective characters. We beg leave, in conclusion, to transcribe from the author's preface two passages of general interest on the impersonality of Chinese-Japanese words: "A study of *Kan-go* discloses the fact that these compound words cannot be judged according to the syntax which governs most European languages, and that consequently it is not possible to classify them arbitrarily as nouns, adjectives, verbs, etc., to the exclusion, in each case, of their use as other parts of speech. The impersonality of the Chinese and Japanese languages creates a gulf of distinction between them and Western languages. We may bridge over this gulf in a measure by applying the syntactical methods of the West,—and indeed this course is forced upon us if we would render the ideas of those languages in terms of our own so as to harmonize meaning with idiomatic construction. But scientifically this mode of treatment is inadmissible, being foreign to the genius of both languages." "Comparing Chinese-Japanese with English we find that the dissimilarity between the two is heightened by the contrast between vagueness of meaning on the one hand and precision on the other. This vagueness of the former is redeemed to a great extent by the comprehensiveness which is its natural complement, and the peculiar excellences of the one language begin exactly where the merits of the other, if extended beyond certain limits, become by exaggeration faults of over-precision, and therefore narrowness and insufficiency of meaning."

### NOTICE TO CORRESPONDENTS.

All communications should be addressed to the *Editor of* "*Trübner's Record*," 57 and 59, Ludgate Hill, London, E.C., and they should be accompanied by the sender's name and address (not necessarily for publication). Every care will be taken with MSS., but the Editor cannot hold himself responsible for rejected communications, which—if to be returned to the sender—should be accompanied by postage. MS. should be legibly written, and on one side of the paper only. Books for review should be addressed to the Editor.



# American Literature.

**Abbott (C. C.)**—Days Out of Doors. 12mo. cloth. *New York.* 7s. 6d.

**Abbott (L.)**—Signs of Promise. Sermons Preached in Plymouth Pulpit, Brooklyn, 1887-9. 12mo. cloth. *New York.* 7s. 6d.

**Allen (N., M.D.)**—Physical Development ; or, The Laws Governing the Human System, 8vo. cloth. *Boston.* 12s. 6d.

**Allen (W. B.)**—Cloud and Cliff : or, Summer Days at the White Mountains. 12mo. cloth, pp. 227. *Boston.* 5s.

**American Coin.** A Novel. By the Author of "Aristocracy." 12mo. cloth. *New York.* 4s.

**Austin (J. O.)** — Ancestry of Thirty-three Rhode Islanders, born in the 18th Century; [also,] 27 Charts of Roger Williams' Descendants to the Fifth Generation, and an Account of Lewis Latham, Falconer to Charles I., with a Chart of his American Descendants to the Fourth Generation ; [also,] a List of 180 existing Portraits of Rhode Island Governors, Chief Justices, Senators, etc. 4to. cloth, *Albany (N. Y.).* £1 10s.

**Avery (Adeline B.) and Finch (Julie E.)**—The King's Daughter's Diary : a Journal of Religious Themes, Meditations, and Incidents. 12mo. cloth. *Philadelphia.* 9s.

**Bancroft (H. H.)**—History of the Pacific States of North America. V. 11. Texas, v. 2, 1801-1809. 8vo. cloth. With Map. *San Francisco.* £1 4s.

**Bancroft (H. H.)**—History of the Pacific States of North America. Vol. 12: Arizona and New Mexico, 1530-1888. 8vo. cloth. *San Francisco.* £1 4s.

**Barns (C. E.)**—A Disillusioned Oculist : a Drama-Novel. 12mo. paper. *New York.* 2s. 6d.

**Barns (C. E.)**—A Venetian Study in Black and White. 12mo. paper. *New York.* 2s. 6d.

**Barns (C. E.)**—Digby, Chess Professor. 12mo. paper. *New York.* 2s. 6d.

**Barns (C. E.)**—Solitarius to his Dœmon : Three Papers. 12mo. paper. *New York.* 2s. 6d.

**Bartlett (T.)** — Heart Stories. 12mo. cloth. *New York.* 4s.

**Bishop (H. G.)**—The Practical Printer. Information for Printers, suitable for the Boy, the Journeyman, the Foreman, the Manager, and the Proprietor. 16mo. cloth, pp. 200. *New York.* 6s.

**Bixby (J. T.)**—Religion and Science Allies ; or, Similarities of Physical and Religious Knowledge. 12mo. paper. *Chicago.* 2s.

**Boone (R. G.)**—Education in the United States : its History from the Earliest Settlements. 12mo. cloth. *New York.* 7s. 6d.

**Brandes (G.)**—Impressions of Russia. From the Danish by S. C. Eastman. 12mo. cloth. *New York.* 6s. 6d.

**Briggs (S. R.)**—New Notes for Bible Readings ; with Selections from D. L. Moody, J. H. Brookes, and others; also, Brief Memoir of the late S. R. Briggs by the Rev. J. H. Brookes. 8vo. cloth. *New York.* 5s.

**Brush (Christine C.)**—Inside our Gate. 12mo. cloth. *Boston.* 5s.

**Burnham (B. F.)**—Elsmere Elsewhere ; or, Shifts and Makeshifts, Logical and Theological, by a Disciple of J. Freeman Clarke, D.D. 18mo. paper. *Boston.* 2s. 6d.

**Burnham (S. W.)**—Truths that I have Studied ; or, Studies of Health on a Psychic Basis. 12mo. paper. *Chicago.* 2s. 6d.

**Carus (P.)**—Fundamental Problems : the Method of Philosophy as a Systematic Arrangement of Knowledge. 12mo. cloth. *Chicago.* 5s.

**Caspar (C. N.)**—Directory of the American Book, News, and Stationery Trade, Wholesale and Retail. 8vo. half-leather. *Milwaukee (Wis.).* £3 3s.

**Cathrein (Rev. V.)** — The Champions of Agrarian Socialism : a Refutation of Emile de Laveleye and H. George ; translated, revised, and enlarged by Rev. J. U. Heinzle. 16mo. cloth. *New York.* 2s. 6d.

**Chapman (Rev. J.)**—Weeks' Genealogy. Leonard Weeks, of Greenland. New Haven, and Descendants, 1639–1888. 8vo. cloth. *New York.* £1.

**Chenery (E., M.D.)**—Alcohol Inside and Out from Bottom Principles. 12mo. cloth. *Boston.* 7s. 6d.

**Church (I. P.)**—A Treatise on Hydraulics and Pneumatics for Use in Technical Schools. 8vo. cloth. Illustrated. *New York.* 12s. 6d.

**Clarke (Mrs. A.)**, and others.—The Ideal Cookery Book—Economy, Wealth, and Comfort in the Household. 1349 new, useful, and unique Recipes in Cookery and all Departments of Housekeeping. 12mo. cloth. *Chicago.* 7s. 6d.

**Clark (F. E.)**—The Mossback Correspondence, together with Mr. Mossback's Views on Certain Subjects, with a Short Account of his Visit to Utopia. 12mo. cloth, pp. 194. *Boston.* 6s. 6d.

**Conn (R. R.)** — The Human Moral Problem : An Inquiry into some of the Dark Points connected with the Human Necessities for a Supernatural Saviour. 12mo. cloth. *New York.* 4s.

**Corning (J. L., M.D.)**—Treatise on Hysteria and Epilepsy, with some concluding Observations on Epileptic Insomnia. 12mo. cloth. *Detroit (Mich.).* 2s. 6d.

**Current Discussions in Theology** ; by the Professors of Chicago Theological Seminary. Vol. 6. 12mo. cloth. *Boston.* 7s. 6d.

**Cushing (W.)**—Anonyms : a Dictionary of Revealed Authorship. 8vo. paper. Part I. *Cambridge (Mass.).* £1 5s.

**Deems (Rev. C. F.)**—Christian Thought ; Lectures and Papers on Philosophy, Christian Evidence, Biblical Elucidation. Sixth series. 8vo. cloth. *New York.* 15s.

**Donahoe (D. J.)**—Idyls of Israel and other Poems. 16mo. cloth. *New York.* 5s.

**Edwards (W. H.)**—The Butterflies of North America. Third series, part 8. With Three Coloured Plates and Descriptive Text. 4to. paper. *Boston.* (By subscription only.) 12s.

**Egypt, The Light of** ; or, the Science of the Soul and the Stars. By Swastika. 8vo. cloth. *Chicago.* 15s.

**Ellwanger (G. H.)**—The Garden's Story ; or, Pleasures and Trials of an Amateur Gardener. 16mo. cloth. *New York.* 6s. 6d.

**Evans (W. L.)**—Memory Training. 12mo. cloth. *New York.* 6s. 6d.

**Foote (A. R.)**—Economic Value of Electric Light and Power. 12mo. cloth. *Cincinnati.* 5s.

**Fowler (J. A.)**—History of Insurance in Philadelphia for Two Centuries, (1683–1882.) 8vo. sheep. *Philadelphia.* £2 10s.

**Goodloe (D. R.)**—The Birth of the Republic. Compiled from the National and Colonial Histories and Historical Collections, from the American Archives, and from Memoirs, and from the Journals and Proceedings of the British Parliament. 12mo. cloth. *New York.* 10s.

**Gould (E. W.)**—Fifty Years on the Mississippi ; or, Gould's History of River Navigation. 8vo. cloth. *St. Louis (Mo.).* 18s.

**Grimes (J. S.)**—Geonomy : Creation of the Continents by the Ocean Currents ; [also,] Kosmonomia ; the Growth of Worlds and the Cause of Gravitation. New edition. 16mo. cloth. *Philadelphia.* 2s. 6d.

**Griswold (W. M.)**—The Annual Index to Periodicals for 1888, [brought down to July, 1889.] 8th annual issue. 8vo. boards. *Bangor (Me.).* 6s.

An Index to the following periodicals : Academy, American Magazine, Andover Review, Atlantic, Baptist Quarterly, Belford's, Canadian Methodist, Century, Chautauquan, Chicago Law Times, Church Review, Cosmopolitan, Education, Forum, Harper's, Harvard Magazine, Lippincott's Magazine of American History, New England Magazine, New Englander, New Princeton, North American Review, Overland, Political Science Quarterly, Popular Science, Quarterly Journal of Economics, Reformed Quarterly, Revue de Belgique, Revue Historique, Scribner's Magazine, Unitarian Review, Universalist Review, and Woman.

**Grumbine (J. C. F.)**—An Old Religion. A Study. 16mo. paper. *Chicago.* 2s. 6d.

**Haferkorn (H. E.) and Heise (P.)**—Handy Lists of Technical Literature ; Reference Catalogue of Books printed in English from 1880–1888, with a Select List of Books printed before 1880. Part 1, Useful Arts in General, Products, and Processes used in Manufacture, Technology and Trades, with Key containing a List of Publishers, etc., and their Addresses. 8vo. paper. *Milwaukee (Wis.).* 7s. 6d.

**Hale (E. E.)**—Sunday-school Stories on the Golden Texts of the International Lessons of 1889. Second part. 16mo. cloth. *Boston.* 5s.

**Hale (Miss L. P.) and Whitman, (Mrs. B.)**—Sunday-school Stories for Little Children on the Golden Texts of the International Lessons of 1889. 16mo. cloth. *Boston.* 5s.

**Haw (M. J.)**—The Beechwood Tragedy. A Tale of the Chickahominy. 8vo. cloth, pp. 241. *Richmond, (Va.)* 4s.

**Haygood (A. G.)**—The Man of Galilee. 12mo. cloth. *New York.* 4s.

**Hereford (Elizabeth J.)**—Rebel Rhymes, and Other Poems. 12mo. cloth. *New York.* 5s.

**Herndon (W. H.) and Weik (J. W.)**—Herndon's Lincoln : The True Story of a Great Life : The History and Personal Recollections of Abraham Lincoln. 3 vols. 12mo. cloth. Illustrated. *New York.* £1 2s. 6d.

**Hildreth (G. L.)**—The Masque of Death and other Poems. 12mo. cloth. *New York.* 5s.

**Hill (M. B.)**—The Laws of the United States relating to Patents and Trade-Marks, with Forms. 8vo. cloth. *Peoria (Ill.).* 12s.

**Holland (J. W., M.D.)**—The Urine, the Common Poisons, and the Milk. Memoranda, Chemical and Microscopical, for Laboratory Use. Third edition, Revised and Enlarged. Illustrated. 12mo. cloth. *Philadelphia.* 6s.

**Hurlbut (H. H.)**—The Hurlbut Genealogy; or, Record of the Descendants of Thomas Hurlbut, of Saybrook and Wethersfield, Conn., who came to America as early as the year 1637; with Notices of Others not identified as his Descendants. 8vo. cloth. *New York.* £1 10s.

**Hutchinson (W. F.)**—Practical Electro-Therapeutics. 12mo. cloth. *Philadelphia.* 7s. 6d.

**Jessop (G. H.)**—Judge Lynch. A Romance of the California Vineyards. 12mo. paper. *New York.* 2s. 6d.

**Johnson (W. W.)**—A Treatise on Ordinary and Partial Differential Equations. 8vo. cloth. *New York.* 15s.

**Jones (R. M.)**—Eli and Sibyl Jones; their Life and Work. 12mo. cloth. *Philadelphia.* 7s. 6d.

**Kalakaua (King).**—The Legends and Myths of Hawaii; the Fables and Folk-lore of a Strange People; by his Hawaiian Majesty Kalakaua. Edited with an introduction by Hon. R. M. Daggett. 8vo. cloth. Illustrated. *New York.* 15s.

**King (C.)**—Between the Lines. A Story of the War. 12mo. cloth. Illustrated. *New York.* 6s. 6d.

**Knott (E. E., Compiler)**—Ready Reference Manual of the Statute Laws of the States and Territories in the United States and the Provinces of Canada, with National, International Laws, and Miscellaneous Information, etc. 8vo. cloth. *Burlington (Vt.).* 10s.

**Lanier (J.)**—Zalo and Zimee. A Story in Rhyme. 16mo. paper. *Middletown.* 2s.

**Leahy (D. F.)**—The American Law Primer, for Public and Private Schools, Families, and the Unprofessional Generally. 12mo. cloth. *San Francisco.* 5s.

**Lodge (H. C.)** — George Washington. (American Statesmen Series.) Two vols. Crown 8vo. cloth, pp. 341 and 399. *Boston.* 12s. 6d.

**Loomis (A. L., M.D.)**—Modern Treatment of Bright's Disease of the Kidney. 16mo. cloth. 2s. 6d.

**Loomis (L. C., M.D.)**—The Index Guide to Travel and Art Study in Europe. Revised edition for 1889. 16mo. leather. Illustrated. *New York.* 15s.

**Massachusetts** Historical Society Collections, Vol. II. 6th Series. Letter-book of Samuel Sewall. Vol. II. 1712–1720. 8vo. cloth, pp. 377. *Boston.* 15s.

**Mayer (J.)** — German for Americans. A Practical Guide for Self-instruction and for Colleges and Schools. 12mo. cloth. *Philadelphia.* 6s.

**McCarty (L. P.)**—Annual Statistician and Economist for 1889. 8vo. cloth, pp. 672. *San Francisco.* 21s.

**McMaster (J. B.), and Stone (F. D.), Editors.**—Pennsylvania and the Federal Constitution. 8vo. cloth. *Philadelphia.* £1 10s.

**McNaughton (J. H.)**—Onnalinda. A Romance. 4to. cloth. *Caledonia (N. Y.).* 15s.

**McPherson (Rev. J. G.)**—Tales of Science; being Popular Scientific Papers. 12mo. cloth, pp. 277. *New York.* 6s. 6d.

**Michael (J.)**—The Formation of the Singing-Registers, for Musicians and Physicians; from the German by G. B. Cornell. 12mo. cloth. *New York.* 2s. 6d.

**Mills (C. K., M.D.)**—Cerebral Localization, in its Practical Relations. A Paper read before the Congress of American Physicians and Surgeons, Wash., D.C., Sept. 1888. 8vo. cloth. *Philadelphia.* 3s.

**Moses (J.)**—Illinois; Historical and Statistical. Comprising the Essential Facts of its Planting and Growth as a Province, County, Territory, and State; derived from Authentic Sources, including Original Documents and Papers; with Statistical Tables relating to Population, Financial Administration, Industrial Progress, Internal Growth, Political and Military Events. In Two Vols. Vol. I. 8vo. cloth. *Chicago.* £1 1s.

**Mundt (Mrs. C. M.)**—The Merchant of Berlin. A Historical Novel. New cheap edition. 12mo. paper. *New York.* 2s.

**Murray (Rev. A.)**—The Spirit of Christ : Thoughts on the Indwelling of the Holy Spirit in the Believer and the Church. 12mo. cloth. *New York.* 6s. 6d.

**Norman (L.)**—A Popular History of California from the Earliest Period of its Discovery to the Present Time. Second edition, revised and enlarged by T. E. 16mo. cloth. *San Francisco.* 6s.

**O'Brine (D., M.D.)**—A Laboratory Guide in Chemical Analysis. Second edition. 8vo. cloth. *New York.* 8s. 6d.

**Osler (W., M.D.)**—The Cerebral Palsies of Children. A Clinical Study from the Infirmary for Nervous Diseases, Philadelphia. 8vo. cloth. *Philadelphia.* 10s.

**Parreidt (J.)**—A Compendium of Dentistry for the Use of Students and Practitioners. Authorized Translation by L. Ottofy. With Notes and Additions by G. V. Black. 8vo. cloth. *Chicago.* 12s. 6d.

**Parsons (F.), Crawford (F. E.), and Richardson.**—The World's Best Books. A Key to the Treasures of Literature. 12mo. cloth. *Boston.* 6s. 6d.

**Peabody (C. H.)**—Thermo-Dynamics of the Steam-Engine and other Heat Engines. 8vo. cloth. *New York.* £1 1s.

**Pepper (G. W.)**—The Border Land of Federal and State Decisions; being the Sharswood Prize Essay for 1889, in the Department of Law, University of Pennsylvania. 8vo. half-sheep. *Philadelphia.* 6s.

**Peters (H.)**—Pictorial History of Ancient Pharmacy. With Sketches of Early Medical Practice. Translated from the German, and revised, with additions, by Dr. W. Netter. 8vo. cloth. *Chicago.* 10s.

**Philipson (Rabbi D.)**—The Jew in English Fiction. A Course of Lectures. 12mo. cloth, pp. 166. *Cincinnati.* 6s.

**Plato.**—Protagoras; with the Commentary of Hermann Sauppe. Translated, with Additions, by J. A. Towle. 12mo. cloth. *Boston.* 4s.

**Porter (D. D.)**—Naval History of the Civil War, including all the Operations in Conjunction with the Navy. 4to. cloth. *New York.* £1 7s. 6d.

**Porter (D. D.)**—Pictorial Battles of the Civil War. 4to. cloth. *New York.* £3 10s.

**Pritchard (W. B., M.D.)**—Manual of Dietetics for Physicians, Mothers, and Nurses. 12mo. cloth. *New York.* 2s. 6d.

**Ranney (A. L., M.D.)**—Lectures on Nervous Diseases. 8vo. cloth. *Philadelphia.* £1 7s. 6d.

**Raymond (Grace)**—How they Kept the Faith. A Tale of the Huguenots of Languedoc. 12mo. cloth. *New York.* 7s. 6d.

**Reich (E.)**—History of Civilization. Lectures on the Origin and Development of the Main Institutions of Mankind. 12mo. cloth. *Cincinnati.* 15s.

**Reisig (F. W.)**—The Guide to Piece Dyeing. Containing 100 Samples of the Author's own Colouring; each Sample accompanied with a Recipe. 8vo. cloth. *New York.* £5 5s.

**Ripper (W.)** — Machine Drawing and Design for Technical Schools, Science Schools and Classes, and Engineer Students. 4to. cloth, 52 Plates. *New York.* £1 18s.

**Roosa (D. B. St. J., M.D.)**—The Old Hospital and other Papers. Being the Second Revised Enlarged Edition of "A Doctor's Suggestions." 8vo. cloth. *New York.* 15s.

**Roosevelt (Th.)**—The Winning of the West. Two vols. 8vo. cloth. *New York.* £1 5s.

**Salter (W. M.)** — Ethical Religion. 12mo. cloth. *Boston.* 7s. 6d.

**Schenck (Mrs. E. H.)** — The History of Fairfield, Fairfield County, Conn., from the Settlement of the Town in 1639 to 1818. Vol. I. 8vo. cloth. *New York.* £1 5s.

**Schultze (A.)**—The Books of the Bible briefly Analyzed for Use in Bible Instruction and for Bible Students in General. 16mo. paper. *Boston (Pa.).* 1s. 6d.

**Shapley (R. E.)**—Solid for Mulhooly. A Political Satire. New edition, with original Illustrations by T. Nast. 16mo. cloth. *Philadelphia.* 4s.

**Shuey (E. L.)**—A Handbook of the United Brethren in Christ. New edition, revised and enlarged. 18mo. cloth. *Dayton (O.).* 1s.

**Spofford (A. R.)**—American Almanac and Treasury of Facts, Statistical, Financial, and Political, for 1889; Compiled from Official Sources. 12mo. cloth. *New York.* 7s. 6d. Abridged Edition, paper, 2s.

**Steward (J. S., M.D.)**—Obstetrics Synopsis. 12mo. cloth. *Philadelphia.* 6s.

**Stewart (Mrs. E. D.)**—Memories of the Crusade. A Thrilling Account of the Great Uprising of the Women of Ohio in 1873 against the Liquor Crime. By Mother Stewart, the Leader. 12mo. cloth, pp. 550. Illustrated. *Columbus.* 12s.

**Tompkins (C. R.)**—A History of the Planing-Mill; with Practical Suggestions for the Construction, Care, and Management of Wood-working Machinery. 12mo. cloth. *New York.* 6s. 6d.

**Valdés (Don A. P.)**—Maximina. From the Spanish by Nathan Haskell Dole. 12mo. pap. *New York.* 2s. 6d.

**Valdés (Don A. P.)**—The Marquis of Peñalta (Marta Y. Maria); A Realistic Social Novel; from the Spanish by Nathan Haskell Dole. 12mo. paper. (New Cheap Edition.) *New York.* 2s. 6d.

**Warner (C. Dudley)**—Studies in the South and West. With Comments on Canada. 12mo. half leather. *New York.* 9s.

**Washington (G.)**—The Writings of George Washington. Including his Diaries and Correspondence. Edited by Worthington C. Ford. In 14 vols. Vol. 2, 8vo. cloth. *New York.* £1 5s.

**Weaver (J., D.D.)**—Christian Doctrine. A Comprehensive Treatise on Systematic and Practical Theology, by 37 different writers. 12mo. cloth. *Dayton (Ohio.)* 12s.

**Whitham (J. M.)**—Steam Engine Design for the Use of Mechanical Engineers, Students, and Draughtsmen. 8vo. cloth. *New York.* £1 6s.

**Wicks (W. S.)**—Log Cabins; How to Build and Furnish them. 18mo. half-cloth. *New York.* 7s. 6d.

**Wilson (A.)**—Historic and Picturesque Savannah. Illustrated by Georgia Weymouth. 8vo. cloth. *Boston.* £1 5s.

**Wilson (G. H.)**—The Musical Year-book of the United States. Vol. 6. Season of 1888–1889. 16mo. paper. *Boston.* 6s.

**Winter (W.)**—The Press and the Stage. Oration Delivered before the Goethe Society, in Answer to Dion Boucicault. 8vo. paper. *New York.* 7s. 6d.

**Wright (G. F., D.D)**—The Ice Age in North America and its Bearings upon the Antiquity of Man; with an Appendix on "The Probable Cause of Glaciation" by Warren Upham. 8vo. cloth. Illustrated. *New York.* £1 5s.

---

# European Literature.

**Album von Celebes-Typen.**—Circa 250 Abbildungen auf 37 Tafeln in Lichtdruck. Herausgegeben von Dr. A. B. Meyer. 4to. In Portfolio. *Dresden*, 1889. £2.

**Alker (E.)**—Die Chronologie der Bücher der Könige und Paralipomenon im Einklang mit der Chronologie der Aegypter, Assyrer, Babylonier, Phœnizier, Meder und Lyder. 8vo. *Leobschütz*, 1889. 3s.

**Allmer (A.) et P. Dissard.**—Musée de Lyon. Inscriptions antiques. 8vo. *Paris*, 1889. £1 10s.

**Aphrahat's** des persischen Weisen Homilian. Aus dem Syrischen uebersetzt und erläutert von Georg Bert. Vol. III. 3/4. Die Akten des Karpus, des Papylus und der Agathonike. Eine Urkunde aus der Zeit Mark Aurel's untersucht von A. Hornack.

**Appert (G.) et H. Kinoshita.**—Ancien Japon. 8vo. *Paris*, 1889. 15s.

**Audibert (G.)**—La femme persane jugée et critiquée par un Persan. Traduction annotée du Téédib-el-Nisvan. 12mo. pp. v. 95. *Paris*, 1889. 2s. 6d.

**** Bibliothèque orientale elzévirienne. LXII.

**Bastian (A.)**—Indonesien oder die Inseln des Malayischen Archipel. Fasc. IV. Borneo und Celebes. Royal 8vo. pp. 184. With Three Plates. *Berlin*, 1889. 7s.

**Boué (A.)**—Die europäische Türkei. Deutsch von der Boué-Stiftung-Commission der kais. Akademie der Wissenschaften in Wien. Two vols. Royal 8vo. pp. x. 674 and 564. With Portrait. *Wien*, 1889. 19s.

**** A German Translation of "La Turquie d'Europe" par A. S. Boué, *Paris*, 1840.

**Brandt (A. J. H. W.)**—Die mandaeische Religion, ihre Entwicklung und geschichtliche Bedeutung. 8vo. *Leipzig*, 1889. 8s.

**Brünnow (R. E.)**—A Classified List of all simple and compound Cuneiform Ideographs occurring in the Texts hitherto published. With their Assyro-Babylonian Equivalents, Phonetic Values, etc. Three vols. *Leiden*, 1888-89. £2 8*s.*

**Buehler (G.)**—Ueber das Leben des Jaina Mönches Hemachandra des Schülers der Devachandra aus der Vajrasâkhâ. 8vo. *Leipzig*, 1889. 4*s.* 6*d.*

**Catalogue des Manuscrits orientaux de la Bibliothèque Nationale.** IV. Manuscrits arabes. 2e fasc. *Paris*, 1889. 16*s.*

**Catéchisme bouddhique,** ou Introduction à la doctrine du Bouddha Gotama. Extrait à l'usage der Européens, des livres Saints des bouddhistes du Sud et annoté par Soubhadra Bhikshou. 12mo. pp. iv. 125. *Paris*, 1889. 2*s.* 6*d.*

*** Bibliothèque orientale elzévirienne. LXI.

**Colonies (les) françaises.** Notices illustrées. Publiées par ordre du sous-secrétaire d'état des Colonies. Sous la direction de M. Louis Henrique. Vol. I. Colonies et protectorats de l'océan indien, la Réunion, Mayotte, les Comores, Nossi-Bé, Diego-Suarez, Sainte-Marie de Madagascar, L'Inde française. Suivie d'une notice sur Madagascar. 8vo. pp. 435. *Paris*, 1889. 3*s.* 6*d.*

Le même. Vol. II. Fasc. 1 to 4. Notice sur Madagascar ; L'Inde française ; La Réunion ; Mayotte, les Comores, Nossi-Bé, Diego-Suarez, Sainte-Marie de Madagascar. 8vo. *Paris*, 1889. 1*s.* each.

**Ende (L. v.)**—Die Baduwis auf Java. (Reprint.) 4to. pp. 7. *Wien*, 1889. 1*s.* 6*d.*

**Franke (Dr. R. Otto)**—Die indischen Geschlechtslehren mit einem Excurs über das Doppel-Geschlecht im Sanskrit. 8vo. *Kiel*, 1889. 9*s.*

**Gazella (la) di Berzu.** Traduzione dal persiano di Vitt. Rugarli e versi di G. Albini. 4to. pp. 34. *Bologna*, 1889.

**Glaser (Dr. Karl).**—Altnordisch. 8vo. *Triest*, 1889. 1*s.* 6*d.*

**Golénisheff (S. W.)**—Opit Graphicheski Raspoloyhennago Assiariiskago Slovarya. 8vo. *St. Petersburg*, 1889.

*** An attempt at an Assyrian Dictionary, arranged graphically.

**Gopčević (S.)**—Makedonien und Alt-Serbien. 8vo. *Wien*, 1889. 20*s.*

**Gondareau (G.)**—Excursions au Japon. 8vo. *Paris*, 1889. 7*s.*

**Hanusz (J.)**—Lautlehre der polnisch-armenischen Mundart von Kuty in Galizien. 8vo. pp. iv. 94. *Wien*, 1889. 5*s.*

**Huart (Clément).**—La religion de Bab Réformateur persan du XIXe siècle. 12mo. pp. 64. *Paris*, 1889. 2*s.* 6*d.*

*** Bibliothèque orientale elzévérienne. LXIV.

**Justi.**—Storia della Persia antica. Prima versione italiana. 8vo. pp. 346. With 42 Woodcuts and 2 Maps. *Milano*, 1889. 6*s.*

**Kayser (Gabriel).** — Bibliographie d'ouvrages ayant trait à l'Afrique en général dans ses rapports avec l'exploration et la civilisation de ces contrées depuis la commencement de l'imprimerie jusqu'à nos jours, précédé d'un indicateur. 8vo. *Paris*, 1889. 8*s.*

**Lagarde (P. de)**—Uebersicht über die im Aramäischen, Arabischen und Hebraeischen übliche Bildung der Nomina. (Extract.) Roy. 4to. pp. 240. *Göttingen*, 1889. 20*s.*

**Landau (W.)** — Reisen in Asien, Australien und Amerika. 8vo. *Berlin*, 1889. 6*s.*

**Landberg (le Comte de).**—Primeurs Arabes. Fascicule II. Diwân de Zoheyr avec le commentaire d'El-A'Lam. Post 8vo. pp. 36, 243. *Leyde*, 1889. 6*s.*

**Lequeux (A.)**—Le Théâtre japonais. 12mo. pp. 84. *Paris*, 1889. 2*s.* 6*d.*

*** Bibliothèque orientale elzévirienne. LXIII.

**Maspero.**—Les Momies royales do Deir el Bahari. 8vo. *Paris*, 1889. £2 10*s.*

**Meyer (A. B.)** Lung Ch'üan-Yao oder altes Seladon-Porzellan. Nebst einem Anhange über damit in Verbindung stehende Fragen. (Abhandlungen und Berichte des k. Zoologischen und Anthropologisch-ethnographischen Museums zu Dresden, 1888, 1889. No. 3.) 4to. pp. 41. With 3 Plates. *Berlin*, 1889.

**Meyer (Dr. A. B.)**—*Vide* Album.

**Morgan (Camillo) und Burger (Fritz).**—Nassr-Eddin Schah und das Moderne Persien. With Portrait and Illustrations. 8vo. *Dresden*, 1889. 4*s.* 6*d.*

**Ollivier-Beauregard.**—En Orient. Etudes ethnologiques et linguistiques à travers les âges et les peuples. 8vo. pp. viii. 252. *Paris*, 1889.

**Osman-Bey.**—Kibrizli-Zadé. Les Russes en 1877-78. Guerre d'Orient. 8vo. pp. iii. 229. *Berlin*, 1889. 5*s.*

**Piehl (Karl).**—Inscriptions hiéroglyphiques recueillies en Europe et en Egypte. Publiés, traduites et commentées. Two l'arts. 1re l'artie, l'lanches (1 to 194); 2e Partie, Commentaire (pp. 139). 4to. *Leipzig*, 1886-88. £3 8*s.*

**Quatrefages (A. de).** — Histoire générale des races humaines. Introduction à l'étude des races humaines. 1re et 2me partie. Two vols. . Royal 8vo. With Maps, Plates and Illustrations. *Paris*, 1887-89.

*** Bibliothèque ethnologique. 1re Partie. Questions générales, 12*s.* 2me Partie : Classification des races humaines. 15*s.*

**Raboisson (l'abbé).**—En orient Récits et notes d'un voyage en Palestine et en Syrie par l'Egypte et le Sinai. Two vols. 4to. *Paris*, 1889.

*** Contents : 1re Partie, Comprenant l'Egypte et le Sinai, pp. 323. With 75 Photographs and 9 Maps. 2e Partie, Comprenant la Palestine et la Syrie. pp. 359. With Photographs and Maps.

**Rinn (Louis).**—Les origines berbères. Etudes linguistiques et ethnologiques. 8vo. *Paris*, 1889. 10*s.*

**Simonsen (D.)**—Sculptures et Inscriptions de Palmyre à la Glyptothèque de Ny Carlsberg, décrites et expliquées. Post 8vo. boards, pp. 63. With Zincographic Plates and 18 Photogravures. *Copenhagus*, 1889.

**Svoronos (J. N.)**—Etudes archéologiques et Numismatiques. 1er Fasc. 8vo. *Paris*, 1889. 4*s.* 6*d.*

**Tcheng-Ki-Tong.**—Les Chinois peints par eux-mêmes. Contes chinois. 12mo. pp. viii. 344. *Paris*, 1889. 3*s.* 6*d.*

**Tchou-Hi.**—Kia-li. Livre des rites domestiques chinois. Traduit pour la première fois, avec commentaires, par C. de Harlez. 12mo. pp. 171. *Paris*, 1889. 2*s.* 6*d.*

*** Bibliothèque orientale elzévirienne. LX.

Van Bruyssel (Ernest).—La république orientale de l'Uruguay. 8vo. pp. 247. *Brüssel*, 1889. 5s.

Vernes (M.)—Précis d'histoire juive depuis les origines jusqu'à l'époque persane. 8vo. With Two Maps. *Paris*, 1889. 6s.

Verrier (Dr. E.)—Sur la déformation des pieds chez la chinoise, au point de vue ethnographique. Avec Figures. 8vo. pp. 10. (Bulletin de la Société d'Ethnographie, Août, 1889). *Paris*, 1889.

Vitale (avv. E.)—Vocabulario di tutte le parole che esistono nella storia di Scems-Ed-Dju e Nur-Ed-Djn estratta dalle Mille e una notte. Trascrizione in caratteri europei. 16mo. pp. 27. *Napoli*, 1889. 2s.

Winckler (H.)—Untersuchungen zur altorientalischen Geschichte. 8vo. pp. 157. *Leipzig*, 1889. 12s.

Wunderer (C.)—Bruchstücke einer afrikanischen Bibelübersetzung in der pseudocyprianischen Schrift Exhortatio de poenitentia, neu bearbeitet. 8vo. *Erlangen*, 1889. 1s. 6d.

Youssouf (R.)—Dictionnaire Turc-français. En caractères latins et turcs, à la portée de tout le monde. Two vols. demy 8vo. pp. 1336. *Constantinople*, 1888. 15s.

---

# Oriental Literature.

## ANGLO-INDIA.

### (Miscellaneous.)

Burma.—Pocket Almanac and Directory for 1889. Edited by G. W. D'Vaux. Royal 16mo. pp. 600. *Rangoon*, 1889. 8s.

Kipling (Rudyard).—Soldiers Three. Demy 8vo. pp. 97. *Allahabad*, 1889.

Kipling (Rudyard).—In Black and White. Demy 8vo. pp. 186. *Allahabad*, 1889.
*.* Stories of Native Life.

Kipling (Rudyard).—The Phantom Rickshaw and other Eerie Tales. Demy 8vo. pp. 114. *Allahabad*, 1889.

Kipling (Rudyard).—The Story of the Gadsbys. Demy 8vo. pp. 100. *Allahabad*, 1889.

Kipling (Rudyard).—Under the Deodars. Demy 8vo. pp. 186. *Allahabad*, 1889.

Malabari.—The Life and Life-Work of Behramji M. Malabari. By Dayaram Gidumal. Post 8vo. cloth, pp. vi. cxx. 329. *Bombay*, 1888. 10s. 6d.

Rao (M. Srinivása).—A Manual of Hindu Law. 8vo. pp. 133. *Kumbakonam*, 1889. 8s.
*.* A compilation chiefly based on the decisions of the High Courts and the Privy Council.

Shortt (Dr. John).—A Manual of Indian Agriculture. 8vo. pp. 336. With Illustrations. *Madras*, 1889. 10s. 6d.

Sleeman (Lieut.-Col. W. H.)—Rambles and Recollections of an Indian Official. 8vo. pp. 234. *Lahore*, 1888. 8s.

Subha Row (T.)—Discourses on the Bhagavat Gítá. 8vo. pp. 103. *Bombay*, 1889. 2s. 6d.

Turnovers from the Civil and Military Gazette. July to September, 1888. 8vo. pp. 104. *Lahore*, 1888. 6s.

Woodrow (E. Marshall).—Hints on Gardening in India. New edition. 8vo. pp. 644. *Bombay*, 1888. 15s.
*.* Useful work for amateur gardeners in India.

## ARABIC.

الف ليلة و ليلة   Alf Lailat wa Laila. Arabian Nights. Vol. II. Edited by P. A. Salhani. Post 8vo. sewed, pp. 455. *Beirut*, 1889. 5s.
*.* Vol. I. *Vide* Trübner's Record, No. 243, p. 24.

Beaussier (M.)—Dictionnaire pratique Arabe-français. Contenant les mots employés dans l'arabe parlé en Algérie et en Tunisie, ainsi que dans le style épistolaire, les pièces nouvelles et les actes judiciaires. 4to. pp. xii. 764, 8. *Alger*, 1867. £2 2s.

Karaháf-ul-'uyún.—The Opener of Eyes. Arabic and Persian. By Hakim Muhammad Salím Khan. Royal 8vo. pp. 156. Lithographed. *Lucknow*, 1888. 2s. 6d.

Muntakhbát-ul-'Arabía.—Arabic Selections. New edition. 16mo. pp. 72. *Lahore*, 1888. 1s. 6d.

Yoga Philosophy of Vashisht.—Jog Bashisht (In Arabic). 4to. pp. 664. *Lahore*, 1888. 10s. 6d.

## BURMESE.

Attika Kammatan. By Shwogyin Sadaw. Third edition. Demy 8vo. pp. 183. *Rangoon*, 1889. 2s. 6d.

Danadivisodhavi Kyan. By Maung Saing. Burmese. Pali Text. Demy 8vo. pp. 106. *Rangoon*, 1889. 2s.

Kayanupathana Kyan. By Shwe Pyi Mingyi. Second edition. Royal 8vo. pp. 334. *Rangoon*, 1889. 6s.

Maung Po Kyaw.—A Book of Botany for Burmese People. In Burmese. Crown 8vo. pp. 98. *Rangoon*, 1889. 15s.

Pakeinnaka Meggakata Kyan. By U Pan Tha. Demy 8vo. pp. 56. *Rangoon*, 1889. 1s.

Tareiksaanmya Pyazat. Part I. By Maung Taing. Demy 8vo. pp. 33. *Rangoon*, 1889. 1s.

## CHINESE AND JAPANESE.

Ball (J. Dyer).—How to speak Cantonese. Fifty Conversations in Cantonese Colloquial. With the Chinese Character, Free and Literal English Translations, Romanised Spelling, and Tonic and Diacritical Marks, etc. Preceded by five short lessons of one, two, and three words. Royal 8vo. pp. 179. *Hong Kong*, 1889. 15s.

Ball (J. Dyer).—How to write Chinese. Part I. Royal 8vo. pp. 25, 76, 4, viii. *Hong Kong*, 1888. 10s. 6d.
*.* Containing General Rules for Writing Chinese, and particular Directions for Writing the Radicals.

Ball (J. Dyer).—How to write the Radicals. 8vo. pp. 40, 7. *Hong Kong*, 1888. 3s. 6d.

Giles (Herbert A.)—Chinese without a Teacher ; being a Collection of Easy and Useful Sentences in the Mandarin Dialect, with a Vocabulary. Second and enlarged edition. 8vo. boards, pp. ii. 65. *Shanghai*, 1887. 7s. 6d.

Imbrie (W.)—Handbook of English-Japanese Etymology. Second edition. Post 8vo. cloth, pp. viii. 287, xv. *Tokyo*, 1889. 6s.

Smith (A. H.)—The Proverbs and Common Sayings of the Chinese. Royal 8vo. half-bound, pp. 364. *Shanghai*, 1888. £1 10s.

**Stedman (T. L.) and K. P. Lee**—A Chinese and English Phrase Book. In the Canton Dialect, or Dialogues on Ordinary and Familiar Subjects for the Use of the Chinese Resident in America, and of Americans desirous of learning the Chinese Language. With the Pronunciation of each Word indicated in Chinese and Roman Characters. 8vo. boards, pp. iv. 177. *New York*, 1888. *7s. 6d.*

**Whitney (W. N.)**—A Concise Dictionary of the Principal Roads, Chief Towns and Villages of Japan, with Populations, Post Offices, etc. Together with Lists of Kan, Kuni, Kori, and Railways. Compiled from Official Documents. Demy 8vo. boards, pp. v. 248. With Map. *Tōkyō*, 1889. *6s.*

## GUJARATI

**Apakritya Shástra ; or the Law of Torts.** By Keshavlál Motilál Vakil. 8vo. pp. 301. *Ahmedabad*, 1889. *10s. 6d.*

**Cervantes' Don Quichot.** Translated into Gujaráti by Púrni. Edited and Revised by Bejanji Karáni. New edition. Royal 8vo. pp. 746. With 128 Pictures. *Bombay*, 1888. *12s. 6d.*

**Musalmáni Káyado ; or Mahomedan Law.** Translated into Gujarati by Vrijavalavdás Jethábhái. Royal 8vo. pp. 421. *Ahmedabad*, 1888. *4s.*
*°* An Annotated edition of Mahomedan Law of Inheritance, Contract, etc.

**Sindbád Vahánvantini Sáta Safar.** Translated by Pánde Jesang Ratanchand. 12mo. pp. 80. *Ahmedabad*, 1888. *1s. 6d.*
*°* The seven voyages of Sindbád the Sailor in Gujaráti.

## HINDI.

**Bhágavat Ekádashaskandha Bháshá ; or a free Vernacular Rendering of the 11th Book of the Bhágavat Purán in Hindi.** By Chaturdás. Royal 8vo. 138 leaves. *Bombay*, 1888. *3s.*
*°* This 11th book is chiefly a dialogue between Krishna and his friend Uddhava.

**Bhágavat Gítá ba zabán Bhákhá**—The Bhagavat Gítá in Hindi. Translated by Lála Achal Prasád. Royal 8vo. pp. 95. Lithographed. *Mirzapur*, 1889.

**Bhágavata Shankánivárana**, *vide* Sanskrit.

**Bháwa Parkásha Satik**, *vide* Sanskrit.

**Hátim Tái ; the Story of Hátim Tái.** Edited by Lála Rama Sarup. Royal 8vo. pp. 264. *Meerut*, 1888. *2s.*

**London Yáttra pratham bhág.** By Shrí Matí Har Devi. Part I. In Hindi. 8vo. pp. 128. *Lahore*, 1888. *3s.*
*°* An account of a Voyage to London by the daughter of the late Rái Kanhya Lál of Lahore.

**Mahábhárat Anusásan Parb.**—The Great War-Book the Anusásan. Translated into Hindi by Pandit Kali Charan. Super royal 8vo. pp. 670. *Lucknow*, 1888. *7s. 6d.*

**Mahábhárat Dron Parb.**—The Great War-Book the Dron. Translated into Hindi by Pandit Kali Charan. Super royal 8vo. pp. 708. *Lucknow*, 1888. *8s.*

**Mahábhárat Karn Parb.**—The Great War-Book the Karn. Translated into Hindi by Pandit Kali Charan. Super royal 8vo. pp. 376. *Lucknow*, 1888. *4s.*

**Rámáyana**, *vide* Sanskrit.

**Rús ki Tárikh.**—History of Russia. Edited by Munshi Nawal Kishor. Super royal 8vo. pp. 576. *Lucknow*, 1888. *£1 10s.*
*°* Hindi Translation of Sir D. Mackenzie, M.A.

**Vídnyánamoksha**, *vide* Sanskrit.

## HINDUSTANI.

**Aftáb-i-Dágh.**—The Sun of Dágh. By Nawáb Mirzá Khán Dágh. Royal 8vo. pp. 136. Lithographed. *Lucknow*, 1888. *4s.*

**Aína-i-Zozgár.**—Mirror of Time. By Ahmad Husain Khán. In Urdu. 8vo. pp. 132. *Lahore*, 1888. *2s.*

**Bostan-i-Satwat.**—The Garden of Satwat. In Urdu. By Nawáb Muhammad Nakí 'Alí Khán, *alias* Nawab Majíd-ud-daulá Satwat. Royal 8vo. pp. 172. *Lucknow*, 1888. *2s. 6d.*

**Bostán-i-Hikmat.**—The Rose Garden of Advice. Translated by Fakir Muhammad Khán. Sixth edition. Royal 8vo. pp. 510. Lithographed. *Lucknow*, 1888. *3s. 6d.*
*°* An Urdu Translation of the Persian Anwár-i-Suhaili.

**Buláqí-Dás-Táríkh-i-Jubilee.**—In English and Urdu. 8vo. pp. 208. Lithographed. *Delhi*, 1888. *£2 16s.*
*°* History of H.M.'s Jubilee.

**Díwán-i-Mushkil.**—The Difficult Love-Poem. By Sayyid Amín-ud-din. Royal 8vo. pp. 130. Lithographed. *Agra*, 1888. *2s. 6d.*

**Gulistáne Panjatan ; or, the Garden of the five Personages.** By Aládin Gulám Husen. In Urdu. Demy 4to. pp. 221. *Bombay*, 1888. *16s.*
*°* A Collection of various Mahomedan Religious Songs.

**Gulshan-i-Farhat.**—The Garden of Farhat. By Munshí Ambásahái Farhat. Royal 8vo. pp. 216. Lithographed. *Lucknow*, 1888. *3s.*

**Map of Africa (Naqsha-i-Africa).**—In Urdu. *Lahore*, 1888. *9s.*

**Map of the Punjab (Naqsha-i-Punjab).**—In Urdu. *Lahore*, 1888. *9s.*

**Mikyás-ul-Ash'ar.**—Measure of Verses. In Urdu. By Mirza Muhammad Ja'far Auj. Royal 8vo. pp. 328. *Lucknow*, 1888. *8s.*

**Najm-ul-Amsál.**—(A Collection of Proverbs. Vol. V.) By Najm-ud-Dín. In Urdu. 8vo. pp. 320. Lithographed. *Delhi*, 1888. *3s. 6d.*

**Ram (Rái Bahádur Ganga).**—Pocket Book of Engineering. In English and Urdu. 16mo. pp. 515. Lithographed. *Lahore*, 1888. *6s.*

**Regulations (Musketry) for the Native Army, 1888.** Translated into Urdu by Lieut. G. F. H. Dillon. Royal 8vo. pp. 134. Lithographed. *Meerut*, 1888. *3s.*

**Shiblí Nu'mani (Muhammad).**—Royal Heroes of Islám. In Urdu. Royal 8vo. pp. 278. Lithographed. *Agra*, 1888. *3s.*
*°* This Part contains the Life and History of the Reign of Mámím Rashid, King of Persia.

**Tambíh-ul-I'lám wa Hidayát-ul-Awámm.** By Maulavi Sayyid Muhammad 'Alí Hasan. Super royal 8vo. pp. 120. Lithographed. *Lucknow*, 1888. *9s.*
*°* Publishing the (Religious) Proclamation and Guidance for the People.

**Totá Kahání.**—Tales of a Parrot. By Haidar Husain. In Urdu. 8vo. pp. 64. Lithographed. *Lahore*, 1888. *1s.*

**Wakái'-i-Sair wa Siyáhat, Doctor Bernier ba Ahd-i-Shábjahan wa Aurang-i-Zeb, Jild-i-Awwal.** Translated into Urdu by Khalifa Sayyid Muhammad Husain Khán. Royal 8vo. pp. 494. Lithographed. *Meerut*, 1888. *6s.*
*°* Events of the Travels and Voyage of Bernier to India, during the time of Shábjahán and Aurangzeb.

Zulfagár-i-Haidari. By F. S. Shahábud-din Husain. In Urdu. 8vo. pp. 178. Lithographed. *Ferozopore City, 1888. 4s.*

## MARATHI.

Bhagavadgitá, *vide* Sanskrit.

Bhaktavijaya Kathárasa; or, the Embellished Narration of the Account of the Triumph of Devotion. By Murkar & Co. In Marathi. 8vo. pp. 247. *Bombay, 1888. 3s. 6d.*

Bhaktisár Navanáth Grantha; or, a Book consisting of the Legends of Nine Saints of the Náth Panth or Sect. By Málu Dhundi Narhari. In Marathi. Royal 8vo. 319 leaves. *Poona, 1888. 16s.*

*** The book is written in the old Purán style, and relates the Legendary Stories of the Saints of the Náth Sect.

Bháratetihásar; or, Substance of the Bhárata Purán by Vyása. By Antun Dhonduji. 8vo. pp. 224. *Bombay, 1888. 3s.*

*** Short substance in prose of the Mahábhárata Purán, in Marathi.

Bombay District Municipal Acts (The) of 1873 and 1884. With Explanatory Notes and Election Rules. In Marathi. By Trimbakráv Náráyan Ráj Máchikar and Shivrám Hari Sáthe. 8vo. pp. 124. *Poona, 1888. 3s.*

Káshikhand Grantha; or, the Glory of Káshi or Benares. By Shivdás Gomá. Edited, with Notes, by Krishna Shástri I'tre. In Marathi. Royal 8vo. pp. 624. *Bombay, 1888. 14s.*

*** Mythological Tales from the Skand Purán.

Lias (Prof.)—Commentary on the First Epistle to the Corinthians. Translated into Maráthi by Rev. J. Taylor. 8vo. pp. 261. *Bombay, 1888. 6s.*

Rámavijaya; or, the Glory of King Ráma. By Shridhar. In Marathi. Royal 4to. pp. 604. *Bombay, 1888. 12s. 6d.*

*** The theme of this poem is the same as that of the Rámáyana.

Vetál Panchavishi; or, the Twenty-five Stories, related to King Vikram by Vetál, the King of the Demons. In Marathi. Demy 4to. pp. 79. Lithographed. *Poona, 1889. 1s. 6d.*

## PERSIAN.

Gudastai-Dánish.—Bouquet of Learning. In Persian. By Maulvi Muhammad Muhayyud din. Royal 8vo. pp. 174. Lithographed. *Allahabad, 1888. 4s.*

Gulistán ba tasáwír. By Shaikh Muslih-ud-din Sa'dí of Shiraz. Second edition. Super royal 8vo. pp. 260. With Illustrations. Lithographed. *Lucknow, 1889. '3s.*

Gulistán-i-Hind.—The Rose Garden of India. By Kunwar Durgáprasád, Talúkadár of Hardvi, Oudh. Royal 4to. pp. 384. *Lucknow, 1889. 6s.*

*** A History of India, in Persian, written in commemoration of the Queen's Jubilee, 1887.

Kashaháf, *vide* Arabic.

Muntakhbát-i-Fársí. — Selections in Persian. By Maulavi Muhammad Amjad Alí, Professor Muir, Central College, Allahabad. Demy 8vo. pp. 180. Lithographed. *Allahabad, 1889. 3s. 6d.*

## SANSKRIT.

Adhyátmarámáyana. By Vyás. With a Commentary in Sanscrit, by Shrirám Himmati. Royal 8vo. pp. 444. *Bombay, 1888. 7s. 6d.*

*** A Purán relating the same story as in Válmiki's Epic, and therefore called after this. It supports the Doctrines of the Advaita School of the Vedánta Philosophy.

Æsop's Fables and Morals in Sanskrit Verse. With Parallel Passages drawn from various Sanskrit Authors to illustrate the Morals. By Vidyádhar Váman Bhide. Demy 12mo. pp. 60. *Bombay, 1888. 2s.*

Ashtánga Sangraha; or, a Compendium of the Hindu System of Medicine, containing eight Divisions, with Notes. By Vágbhata. In Sanskrit. Royal 8vo. pp. 872. *Bombay, 1888. £1 16s.*

*** An authoritative work on Hindu Medicine studied in Western India.

Bhagavadgitá. With a Maráthi Translation. By Rámchandra Bhikáji Gunjikar. Royal 32mo. pp. 316. *Bombay, 1888. 2s. 6d.*

Bhagavadgitá. With Sanskrit and English Notes, Translation and an Esoteric Exposition in English. By P. D. Goswani. Small 8vo. In Parts. *Calcutta, 1889. 6s.*

*** Parts I. and II. (pp. 1-94) have already been published.

Bhágavata Shankánivárana Manjari. By Shivasaháya Shivasampati Upádhyáyaji. In Sanskrit and Hindi. Oblong, 130 leaves, lithographed. *Bombay, 1888. 10s. 6d.*

*** A Work removing the doubts raised in regard to the Authenticity of the Bhágavata Purán.

Bháwa Parkásha Satik. By Bháw Mishra. Sanskrit Text with Hindi Translation by Ráo Shri Krishan Chandra. Four vols. 8vo. *Delhi, 1888. £1 18s.*

Laghuyogavásishtham; or, an Abridgment of the Work "Yogavanishtha." By Abhinand Pandit. In Sanskrit. Oblong, pp. 650. *Bombay, 1888. 18s.*

*** An Abstract of Yogavásishtha, one of the Vedánta Treatises, and considered as an Appendage to Válmiki's Rámáyana.

Mahábhárat; or, the Mahábhárat Purán. By Vyas. With a Commentary in Sanskrit. By Nilkantha Govind. Five vols. Oblong. 2461 leaves. *Bombay, 1888. £7 7s.*

*** This edition is accompanied by a short Alphabetical Index and an elaborate Index to each Parva. A Re-publication of the well-known edition.

Rámáyana. By Tulsidás. With a Commentary by Mahant Rámacharan. Hindi and Sanskrit Text. Second edition. Royal 4to. pp. 1472. *Lucknow, 1888. £1 1s.*

Rámáyana. By Tulsidás. With Commentary by Pandit Sukadevlál. Hindi and Sanskrit text. Royal 4to. pp. 666. *Lucknow, 1888. 7s. 6d.*

Vaidya (Lakshman Ramchandra).—The Standard Sanskrit-English Dictionary. Containing Appendices on Sanskrit Prosody and Names of Noted Mythological Persons, etc. (For the Use of Schools and Colleges.) Small 4to. half-bound, pp. xv. 889. *Bombay, 1889. 10s. 6d.*

Vidnyánamoksha. By Rámánandagiriji Paramahansa. In Sanskrit and Hindi. Royal 8vo. pp. 234. *Bombay, 1888. 5s.*

*** Work on Popular Vedántism, Eternal Happiness, etc.

## TAMIL.

Bhagavad-Gíta (The). —A Sanskrit Philosophical Poem, in the Form of Dialogues between Krishna and Arjuna. Translated into English and Tamil by the late Rev. H. Bower. Post 8vo. boards, pp. lvi. 137. *Madras, 1889. 8s.*

Pillai (P. Sundaram).—An Introduction to Science in Tamil. 8vo. pp. 100. *Madras, 1889. 2s. 6d.*

Punya Sángopánga Muyarchi. Translated into Tamil by Rev. Father Bangaru. 12mo. pp. 353. *Trichinopoly, 1888. 9s.*

Tamil-English Dictionary. Revised and enlarged. Published by the Government of Madras. 8vo. pp. 738. *Madras, 1889. 8s.*

# OSCAR II.

## KING OF SWEDEN AND NORWAY.

An account of the Eighth International Congress of Orientalists would be incomplete unless it were ushered in by a brief sketch of the life and literary work of its Royal Patron and Protector, Oscar II, King of Sweden and Norway, who, by the boundless hospitality extended to its members, and by the leading personal interest he took in its proceedings, mainly ensured its unparalleled success.

Oscar Frederik was born at the Castle of Stockholm on the 21st January, 1829, as the third son of Prince Oscar (subsequently King Oscar I.), and received from his royal grandfather the title of Duke of East Gothland. His early education was entrusted to Mr. F. F. Carlson, the historian, who instilled in the young prince that love for historical research which was to bear such good fruit in later years. In 1845 the prince received his officer's patent both in the army and navy, but he then and ever after evinced a predilection for the latter branch of the service. He took part in the naval evolutions in the summer of 1846, and in subsequent expeditions under S. von Krusenstjerna. His poetical genius derived from these its noblest subjects and its happiest imagery. At the University of Upsala (1846-49) Prince Oscar devoted himself mainly to historical and literary studies. Under the reign of his father, and subsequently under that of his elder brother Charles XV., he was the chief protector of the military and musical institutions of the two kingdoms. He took a warm interest in literature, arts, and manufactures, and was one of the great promoters of the Arctic expeditions, and of the voyage of the "Vega" round the world. In 1857, on the 6th June, he married Sophia, Princess of Nassau. Four Princes have issued from this happy union. On the 18th September, 1872, he succeeded his elder brother on the throne. Under his reign literature, art, and industries are flourishing as they never did before.

It would be impossible to give within a brief space a sketch of his many literary productions. A complete list of them is to be found in a monograph entitled, "*Hans Majestät Koning Oscar II.'s Bibliografi*, 1849–1887. *Utgifven af C. M. C.*" Stockholm, 1888 (19 pages). In 1857 he gained the prize of the Swedish Academy for his cyclus of poems *Ur Svenska Flottans Minnen* (Mementos of the Swedish Fleet). From 1859 to 1863 there appeared his "Contributions to the History of Sweden during the Years 1711, 12, 13." Five editions of his volume of poems called *Nytt och Gammalt* (Things New and Old) betoken the high appreciation in which his poetry is held by the public. He translated Herder's *Cid* and Göthe's *Torquato Tasso*. Many of his poetical and historical works, and of his addresses, have been translated into German, French, and English. A collective edition of his works has been in progress since 1885. The members of the last Oriental Congress will ever remember the ease, elegance, and terseness with which His Majesty handled not only the current languages of Europe, but also Latin, a language not generally kept up by crowned heads. Well says Professor Louis de Geer, in an address printed in the Transactions of the Swedish Academy for 1874, and quoted as motto in the above-mentioned Bibliography: "On the horizon of Swedish oratory we observe at least one star of first magnitude shine out in ever increasing brilliancy. Who is that speaker with the lofty thoughts and the noble words who kindles patriotism in every breast, and weaves fresh garlands of the fairest flowers of reminiscence and hope in every region? Round his shoulders hangs the purple: it is the King himself!"

*Drinking Horn presented by H. M. KING OSCAR II. as a Memorial to be used at all subsequent Congresses.*

# TRÜBNER'S RECORD,

## A JOURNAL DEVOTED TO THE LITERATURE OF THE EAST.

### WITH NOTES AND LISTS OF CURRENT

### American, European and Colonial Publications.

*Edited by Dr. Rost, of the India Office.*

| NOVEMBER, 1889. | THIRD SERIES. VOL. I. No. 5. | PRICE 2s. |


## THE EIGHT

# International Congress of Orientalists,

### HELD AT

## STOCKHOLM AND CHRISTIANIA.

### SEPTEMBER, 1889.

Ever since at the conclusion of the Seventh International Oriental Congress, held at Vienna towards the end of September, 1886, the invitation from the King of Sweden to hold the next Congress at Stockholm was conveyed by Count Landberg to the assembled members, and accepted by them with acclamation, preparations for making the forthcoming Congress a festive gathering on a grand and unprecedented scale appear to have been set on foot. Not only were invitations sent out at an unusually early date, but the printed programme containing information about even the most minute details calculated to insure the comfort of the members and to make the Congress as a social *réunion* generally attractive, proved beyond doubt the forethought of the organizers as well as the solidity and liberality of all the arrangements ; and from the time that the foreign visitors set foot on Swedish soil they became aware that the reception which awaited them was not of yesterday's planning. The newspaper press in this country and abroad has been lavish in its praise of the boundless hospitality accorded by King and country to their foreign guests, no less than of the circumspection and untiring exertions of the General Secretary, Count Carlo Landberg.

We name especially the *Academy*, the *Athenæum*, the *London and China Telegraph*, the *Times*, the *Schwäbische Merkur*, the *National-Zeitung*, and the *Freie Presse*, from whose columns we have culled here and there a passage that appeared to us noteworthy for embodiment in a general sketch of the Congress. The abstracts of papers read, for which we are indebted to the individual authors,—we much regret our inability to give a résumé of *all* the papers,—will, we venture to hope, be the more welcome to our readers as a few years generally elapse before the "Transactions" of these Congresses become accessible to the public.

In the evening of the 1st September a sort of informal réunion was held in the reception rooms of the Grand Hotel at Stockholm, at which about 300 members attended and were hospitably entertained to a cold collation. These preliminary gatherings are very enjoyable. Many savants shake hands again who never meet except at these triennial congresses, while others are brought face to face for the first time who had till then known one another only by photograph or correspondence.

The solemn inauguration of the Congress took place

on the following day at noon, when His Majesty King Oscar II. opened the proceedings in person in the Salle des Blasons of the Riddarhuset, or Palace of the Nobility, which presented both without and within a festive appearance quite unusual at such scientific meetings. The members assembled were in *grande tenue*, the *Corps diplomatique* being seated on the right of the throne, and the Delegates on the left ; many of these wore their academical dress, while the scene was further enlivened by the presence of natives of Eastern countries in their national costumes and of a large number of ladies. His Majesty addressed in a clear, sonorous voice a speech of welcome (in French) to the assembled members. Count d'Ehrenheim, the President of the Committee of Organization, replied briefly, whereupon Count Landberg delivered the opening discourse, referring in conclusion to the two prizes—one on the history of the Semitic languages, and another on the civilization of the history of the Arabs before Muhammad—which the King had offered for competition in 1886. No European savants having come forward as competitors, and none of the Orientals having entirely complied with the conditions of the awards, Sheikh Mahmúd Shukri el-Alúsí, of Baghdad, who had competed for the second prize, was considered worthy of honourable mention, and received a gold medal and the order of Wasa. His Majesty at the same time seized the opportunity to show his appreciation of the distinguished services in the Semitic branch of Oriental research of Professors Nöldeke, of Strasburg, and Goldziher, of Buda-Pest, by bestowing a gold medal on each. The one intended for the former, who was not present at the Congress, was handed to the German Ambassador for transmission. Also Professor J. M. de Goeje, of Leiden, received on this occasion from the Khedive a high decoration in recognition of his valuable publications on Arabic history and geography, while the representative of the publishing firm of Brill & Co., of Leiden, was similarly honoured. Baron von Kremer and other delegates from different European countries then addressed His Majesty briefly and tersely, an example which was not followed by the Oriental guests in their lengthy, often tediously lengthy, effusions. After the meeting the various sections constituted themselves, and two of them, the modern Semitic and the Aryan, began their work in the afternoon. Even more brilliant than the opening ceremony was the *fête* which the King had prepared for his guests at the *château* of Drottningholm (Queen's Island). Three large steamers and a smaller one conveyed His Majesty with his suite, a number of distinguished guests specially invited, and the members of the Congress, six hundred in all, from the landing stage of Riddarholm up the Mälar Lake, a distance of about

six miles, between islands and islets, all beautifully wooded, and, as are also both banks, studded with villas and hamlets. The sun had set when Drottningholm was reached, where a military band was playing in the park. After arrival at the Palace, the vestibule and grand staircase of which were lined with Swedish Life Guards, the members passed through a suite of reception rooms to the throne room, where the King and Crown Prince chatted affably with their guests. Later on a sumptuous supper was served in five rooms on the ground floor. The progress back to Stockholm took more than double the time occupied in the outward journey. But that tardiness was welcome to all. For the sight that presented itself baffled all description. Not only were the palace grounds illuminated with Bengal fire, while the opposite shore was lined with variegated lights, but the whole distance to Stockholm was ablaze. Every villa, every rock, every cluster of trees exhibited illuminations of every kind and of almost every colour and device. The firing of cannons, the rising of rockets, the changeful play of fireworks, added to the fairy-like character of the scene, and when Stockholm was reached long after eleven o'clock, an electrical refractor had made the large church of Riddarholm, with its steeple of cast iron, stand out as in daylight. In spite of the lateness of the hour, the number of sight-seers who were lining the road from the landing stage to the Grand Hotel, a distance of a mile, was so great that police and military had some difficulty in keeping it clear for the carriages and preventing accidents. Indeed, the warm interest which the population not of Stockholm and Christiania only, but of every town and village evinced, along which the members of the Congress were conveyed by steamer, carriage or train, was one of the most charming features of this festive gathering.

The real literary work was done at the meetings of the various sections which were held on five mornings during the whole Congress, discussions being excluded from the general meetings which likewise took up five mornings. It was at those general meetings that addresses of a more varied character and calculated to interest a dilettante audience were delivered. Several of these had perhaps no more immediate concern with the objects of the Oriental Congress than had the many dilettanti whose admittance to the membership was so severely, though by no means unjustly, animadverted upon. Our task of giving an ever so brief account of the subjects treated at the special meetings will be light, as the abstracts which follow, so far as they have been received up to the date of our going to press, will speak for themselves.

Before the commencement of the proceedings in the Muhammadan fraction of the Semitic Section on the

3rd of September, a tribute of mournful regard was paid to the memory of the three great Arabists deceased since the last Congress, Fleischer, Wright, and Amari.

Of the papers read on that day we mention here the following : on the eschatology of Musa bin Maimún, by Dr. Wolff ; on the Muhammadan tradition, by Dr. Goldziher, in which the author proved that the so-called Sunna was not orally handed down, but was from the very beginning recorded in writing ; on a projected edition of the greatest Turkish lyrical poet Bâki, by Dr. Dworak ; on the Diwan of Muhammad's court poet Hasan bin Thabit, by Abdalla Fikri Pascha ; and a paper by Sheikh Hamza Fathullah "on the rights of women according to the Law of Islam " ; the two last-mentioned addresses were delivered in Arabic. In the non-Muhammadan Section Professor Guidi, of Rome, spoke on the Syriac sources of the history of the Sassanides, and Dr. Strassmaier on certain Cuneiform inscriptions from the reign of Xerxes and Artaxerxes, the remainder of the time being taken up with discussions on the so-called Sumerian question, in which Drs. Jensen, Haupt, Halévy, Hommel and D. H. Müller took part. At the conclusion of the meeting, on the proposal of Professor Oppert, the members honoured the memory of their deceased *collaborateur*, M. Amiaud, by rising from their seats. In the Aryan Section papers were read by H. H. Dhruva on the Sanskrit translation of Euclid, by Jolly on the law code of Hârîta, by Oldenberg on the Upanishads, and by the Parsee priest Jivan Jamsetji Modi "on the Haoma in the Avesta." In the Egyptian Section communications were made by O. Beauregard on the pronunciation of Old-Egyptian, and by Piehl on the proper arrangement of a Hieroglyphical Dictionary, while in the Section on Central Asia and the Far East a paper on " Pidgin-English in China" was read by Mr. Leland ; one by Dr. Inouyé " on the Dissidence of Chinese Philosophers on Human Nature," in which the lecturer traced through all the well-known Chinese writers the effects their philosophy has had generally on human nature, a question where the ground was not always very secure. There were, besides, papers by Dr. Cust on the geographical distribution of the Turk languages, and by A. Amirchanjanz on the development of the Jaghatai language within the last 500 years.

In the afternoon an entertainment of a novel character was given to the members of the Congress in the Swimming School, where, in the presence of the King and Crown Prince, the most wonderful swimming feats and aquatic gymnastic exercises were exhibited by men, boys, and girls. Count and Countess Landberg gave in the evening a grand reception and sumptuous repast to the members of the Congress, which His Majesty and the Crown Prince again graced with their presence.

Among the surprises prepared for their guests was the tasteful imitation of the dancing of a Bayadère, followed by that of Derwishes.

According to the programme the papers read in the morning of the 4th September included the following : on the hereditary Kingdom of Cyrus according to the Cuneiform inscriptions and the Bible, by J. Halévy, who endeavoured to prove that Cyrus was not an Aryan, but an Elamite ; on Palmyrenian sculptures and inscriptions, by Dr. Simonsen ; on a projected edition of the Masoretic Old Testament, by Dr. Ginsburg, and on chronological data from the Cuneiform inscriptions, by Professor Oppert. During the reading of the last two papers King Oscar was present. In the other Sections we note : on the origin and signification of the oldest Sâmans, by Professor Hillebrandt ; on a conception of a later Hindu deity intermediate between Indra and Ganeśa, by Count de Gubernatis ; on the Shâhbâzgarhi version of Aśoka's edicts, by Mr. Johansson ; on the Mansehra version of the 13th edict of Aśoka, by Professor Bühler ; on the Avaśyaka commentaries of Jain literature, by Professor Leumann ; on the Nyâya-vindu-ṭîkâ, an ancient Buddhistic work on logic, by Professor Peterson ; on the system of measures among the ancient Egyptians as compared with those of the other nations of antiquity, by Brugsch-Pascha ; on the inscriptions found on tombstones on the Upper Yenisei, by Professor Donner ; on the linguistical position of the Australian languages, by Dr. Schnorr von Carolsfeld ; on the Malayo-Japanese fable of the monkey and the tortoise, by Professor Kern. Professor van der Lith communicated some further proofs of the truthfulness of the author of the Kitâb 'ajá'ib al Hind ; and Mr. Hj. Stolpe discoursed on the ideographic script discovered in Easter Island.

The afternoon was devoted to a visit to Upsala, and in the first place to Gamla (Old) Upsala, a small hamlet famous for its ancient historical and mythological associations, where three hills are supposed to contain the tombs of Odin, Thor, and Freyr. There the members of the Congress were met by the students, some 900 in number, who in their white caps presented a striking appearance. By direction of His Majesty Count Landberg presented to the Congress, as a memorial to be used at all subsequent Congresses, a drinking horn elaborately wrought of precious metals and enamelled, while students handed round similar horns containing hydromel or the mead of the gods. Speeches were made in honour of the occasion and of the time-hallowed locality, whereupon two trains conducted the students and visitors to New Upsala. A procession headed by the students and a military band having been formed at the Railway Station, some twenty minutes' walk brought the members to the University building, perhaps the handsomest of its kind in all Europe. The streets were thronged with people, and every window was crowded with eager faces. The structure, only recently built, stands on an eminence overlooking the city, and on the base of the hill the Gothic Cathedral raises its lofty towers. The fine Aula and vestibule of the University, and its solidly finished lecture and committee rooms, fully corresponded with the beauty of its exterior appearance. Some addresses were delivered in the Aula, and the students' choir delighted the audience by their splendid singing, the band playing in the intervals. A liberal and sumptuous supper was served in different parts of the spacious vestibule. Those few who were fortunate enough to be present when the famous *Codex Argenteus*—the Ka'ba of all Teutonic philology—was exhibited in the rector's room will have carried away with them the impression that the sight of this treasure alone outweighed all other literary treats which were offered to the members of the Congress. Though it was long after midnight when the return train steamed into Stockholm, the Railway Station and streets in its vicinity were crowded with sight-seers watching the excursionists as they were making their way to the various hotels.

At the meetings of Sections on the 5th Sept. papers were read by Lagus on the opinions held by the Arabs concerning the Arctic Ocean; by Grünert on compound words in the Arabic; by Dr. Klein on the date and import of the Book of Judith; by Professor Chwolson on certain Syro-Nestorian tomb-inscriptions in the District of Semiryetchie (Kuldja) on the frontiers of China; by Dr. Ginsburg on the new series of publications of the London Palæographical Society, the series to consist of specimens of Biblical (O. T.) MSS., the chief editorship of which Dr. Ginsburg himself had been asked to undertake. On the conclusion of his address, Professor Merx moved that in memory of Professor Weil, recently deceased, the members of the Section rise from their seats. In the Egyptian Section a memoir by Miss A. Edwards was read concerning Mr. Flinders Petrie's recent discoveries in the Fayum; Mr. Marucchi gave an account of his Egyptological studies in the Vatican, and stated that Pope Leo XIII. proposed to have all the Egyptian monuments in the Vatican published; M. de Cara spoke on the identity of the goddesses Iris and Iktar; Mr. Hyvernat on Coptic palæography. For a résumé of Professor Johannes Schmidt's lecture on the original seats of the Indo-germanic tribes we refer to the Appendix. By special invitation from His Majesty, all the foreign members attended a gala performance of Verdi's Aïda at the Opera in the evening.

A general meeting of all the Sections was held on Sept. 6, under the presidency of the King, at which the following addresses were delivered : Brugsch-Pascha gave an account of a Mummy which had recently arrived from Egypt, and of the funeral ceremonies of the ancient Egyptians; Professor Max Müller placed a volume of his new edition of the Rig-veda and Sâyaṇa's commentary on the table and gave a history of his labours on that work; Professor Oppert discoursed on Babylonian astronomy; Professor de Goeje read a dissertation on the legend of St. Brandan in its relation to Eastern legends; Professor Dillmann moved for an address to Archduke Rainer to thank His Highness for his eminent services to Oriental literature by the acquisition of the Fayûm manuscript treasures; Professor Haupt gave a description, from Cuneiform records, of the violent death of Sargon II.; Dr. Hildebrand explained a series of drawings which were made of the ruins of Palmyra by Swedish officers in 1710 and exhibit many more of the wonderful remains of that city than can now be traced; Professor Karabacek drew attention to certain unique gold coins of Muhammad and his opponent Museilima, and to the important historical inferences to be deduced from them; and lastly M. Halévy sketched, from documents recently discovered, the state of Palestine before the immigration of the Israelites.

In the evening a grand fête was given to the foreign members of the Congress by the City of Stockholm at a commodious and spacious resort called Hasselbacken, which was reached by little *bâteaux mouches* in about ten minutes. The entertainment, which was of the most lavish character, was joined in by many of the citizens, and was enhanced by fireworks and illuminations of every description.

Before the closing ceremony took place on the following day at noon, two papers were read which had remained over from the previous day, viz. on the history of the Parsis, by the priest Jivanji Modi, and on rude attempts at ornament and writing found in Oceania, by Dr. Stolpe. Various natives of Eastern countries then addressed to His Majesty words of gratitude in their own languages. The King, in a happily worded extempore Latin speech, thanked the various donors of books for their gifts, and declared the Stockholm part of the Congress closed, whereupon Professor Dillmann replied in the same language. In the evening a final banquet was given to the foreign members by the Committee of Organization at the Grand Hotel, which was on the same grand scale as all the previous entertainments : and between 10 and 11 o'clock by far the greater number of the members departed by two special trains for Christiania not only free of expense, but also free from the annoyance of having to pass through the customs at the Norwegian frontier. At

Charlottenberg the two trains were to halt, to allow the passengers ample time for breakfast at 8.55 and 9.38 respectively, a wise arrangement evidently made with the view of preventing the usual rush and crowding at a not very large station. Through an accident which happened to the engine of the second train between the Wäse and Skasokörr Stations, 300 kilometers from Stockholm, the train did not reach Charlottenberg till about noon. But no one appeared to be disconcerted by the delay, and as the weather was lovely, the utmost good humour prevailed ; and when the two trains, now combined in one of great length, steamed out of Charlottenberg station at about half-past twelve, their passengers were cheered by a very large concourse of people. A few hours' journey through the most picturesque scenery brought the train to Christiania, each station seeming to be more and more crowded until the capital was reached. The station at Christiania was beautifully decorated with flags and evergreens, and the students' choir welcomed the guests with glees. The streets leading to the principal hotels were lined with many thousands of eager spectators ; and the learned men from America and all parts of Europe came in, here as elsewhere, for much of the curiosity with which the Orientals in their several picturesque costumes were gazed at. At the social gathering in the evening which was held in the Frimurerlogen it was refreshing to the foreign savants to see the Norwegian professorial element so largely represented.

The opening meeting on the 9th September at 10 a.m. was held in the Aula of the University ; it was graced by the presence of Prince Eugen and presided over by Mr. Bonnevie, the Minister of Education and Public Worship, who delivered an appropriate address. He was followed by the celebrated Egyptologist Professor Lieblein, who gave a sketch of the various Oriental scholars whom Norway had produced—Lasson, Holmboe, Broch, Schreuder among the dead, Caspari, Bugge, Blix, Seippel, Friis, Skrefsrud, Dahle among the living. After him the Parsee priest, Jivan Jamsetji Modi, made a speech on the monotheistic character and tendency of his religion. Then Professor Max Müller, after some preliminary remarks on the " Sacred Books of the East," gave a discourse on the influence which the contact with Christianity has exerted on the Hindu Religion. Mr. Harilal Dhruva, of Baroda, having chanted a hymn from the Rigveda, Professor Deussen gave a philosophical exposition of that hymn, whereupon the proceedings were brought to a close, as they had been opened, by the academical choir.

The excursion to Oscarshall and Bygdö, for which the members embarked at four, was another of those delightful pleasure trips which had been arranged with so much forethought, and were carried out with royal splendour. While the view from the former on Christiania and the intervening fjord rivalled anything in grandeur and loveliness that the guests had yet seen in Scandinavia, the inspection of the wooden structures which King Oscar II. had had erected in close imitation of ancient Norwegian buildings was an instructive sight which was greatly appreciated by all. The evening was spent at the Royal domain of Bygdö, where Prince Eugen and Privy Councillor Holst did the honours as the King's representatives at a sumptuous *souper dînatoire*, after which the celebrated composers Herr and Fru Gründahl, assisted by a choir of 30 singers, gave a series of recitals. The pleasures of the return journey were much enhanced by displays of Bengal lights and fireworks at various vantage points. It was indeed a lovely sight. The journey to Hönofos, or the falls of the Höna, and back, which took up the better part of the following day, was, in addition to the picturesqueness of the sight, remarkable for the popular character of the *fête*, the inhabitants of the place, including the school-children, adding much to the general enjoyment. The members were here photographed in a group. At the Drammen Station on the return journey tea and light refreshments were offered by the ladies of the town.

At the sectional meetings on Monday afternoon and Tuesday morning the following papers were read : in the Semitic Sections,—Von Mehren, on a mystic treatise in Arabic entitled " The Bird " by Avicenna ; Almqvist, contributions to the lexicography of Modern Arabic ; Merx, on the Messianic doctrine among the Samaritans ; Halévy, on the Semitic article ; Hommel, on the Sumerian question ; Sayce, on the so-called Kappadokian Cuneiform inscriptions ; Tegnér, on Assyrian metrics ; Glaser, on the numerous Sabæan inscriptions collected by him ; Euting, on the Nabatæan inscriptions found by him in the Sinaitic peninsula ; Jäger, on Assyrian riddles and proverbs ; Ball, on an inscription on a Babylonian mace-head ; Caspari, on Hieronymus' translation of the Alexandrian version of the Book of Job ; Hildebrand, on the Oriental coins found in Sweden. In the Aryan Section, J. Burgess read a paper on archæological researches in India, which led to a motion, proposed by Dr. Bühler, duly seconded and carried, that the Government of India should be memorialized as to the importance of carrying on its archæological surveys with the assistance, where obtainable, of the native princes. A proposition, formulated by E. Kuhn, in favour of a scientific investigation of the languages spoken on the North-Western frontier of India, was likewise adopted. Dhruva gave a history of the Gujerati language, which he traced back to the early part of the ninth century. De Esoff drew a sketch of the history of the Armenian language in Europe; Tsagarelli treated of the Georgian monuments in the Holy Land and Sinai; Bugge made some remarks on Armenian etymology; Teguér spoke on the letters *l* and *r* in the Aryan languages; Ludwig on Rigveda textual criticism; and Vasconcellos-Abreu on the Sanskrit inscription of Cintra. In the other Sections we note a memoir, by Miss A. Edwards, on Mr. Flinders Petrie's discoveries in the Fayum (read by Dr. Cust); a paper by E. Schiaparelli on an inedited inscription from the time of Amenophis I.; one by Amélineau on Coptic poetry; Cordier, on the history of the Swedish Company in the East in the eighteenth century; Boell, on the Chinese word Shang-ti, and on the transliteration of Chinese words; and Daae, on the Land Tax in China.

On Wednesday, the 11th of September, only the first division of the Semitic section had a short meeting, at which De Goeje made some observations on a passage of Ibn Khordâdbeh concerning the commercial intercourse held in olden times between Slaves and Normans and the Levant. Further, Seippel read a paper on a hitherto unknown name of the Normans (Urmân); Kresmarik communicated some remarks on the *waqf*; Schiaparelli on Tha'lab's Qawâ'id al-shîr; Bashîr ibn Rustân spoke in Arabic on "el ajab fî lughat el 'arab," and Shu'aib ibn 'Abdallah on "el bayân wel tahsîl."

Many valuable and interesting papers were for want of time laid on the table as read, and will in due course appear in the printed Transactions of the Congress. After all, the social intercourse between the savants,— many of whom had not perhaps met for years, while others met here for the first time,—formed one of the chief attractions and advantages of the Congress, which greatly tended to strengthen existing bonds of friendship, to smooth down differences, and altogether to promote a kindly spirit. It is certainly a matter for regret that the all-absorbing gorgeous entertainments left too little room for such quiet communing. May at future Congresses judicious provision be made also in this direction! Such a wise concession would be greatly appreciated and be productive of much good.

At the final general session held in the afternoon of the 11th September, under the presidency of M. Bonnevie, Mr. Dhruva chanted a Sanskrit hymn he had composed in honour of Norwegian hospitality. Dr. Inouyé gave his impressions to the same effect in a German address, and Count de Gubernatis read a paper on the origin of the cosmographical beliefs embodied in Dante's *Purgatorio*. In conclusion, Brugsch-Pascha gave a discourse on recent discoveries in Egypt in connexion with the Exodus. After a valedictory address by Professor Lieblein, Mr. Bonnevie, in the name of the King, declared the Congress closed.

In the morning a meeting of the Delegates and Committee of Organization had been convened to take into consideration the question as to where the next Congress was to be held. As, however, no invitation had been received to that effect, a permanent Committee was appointed to take this matter in hand. This Committee was to consist of the Presidents of the three previous Congresses, with Count Landberg as General Secretary of the last Congress, and to be empowered each to appoint another scholar of recognized standing for consultation. At the banquet at which the members were entertained in the Frimurerlogen in the evening 430 covers were laid, and roast bear was one of the dainties of the *menu*. Two trains starting at 10 and 11 p.m. respectively conveyed the foreign members to Göteborg. At Trollhätta, in Sweden, which was reached about 9 the next morning, a halt of five hours was made to allow ample time for breakfast and for a visit to the celebrated falls and the locks on the Göta Canal. The grandeur and beauty of the sight, enhanced by splendid weather, were greatly enjoyed at the best points. This last day of the Congress festivities will long live in the memories of those who followed them up to the end. It was closed by a sumptuous entertainment provided by the citizens of Göteborg to the members of the Congress, every one of whom carried the impression away with him from Scandinavia that nothing could have exceeded the right Royal splendour and the lavish hospitality with which King Oscar II. had entertained his guests, and that the people of Sweden and Norway at large had betokened their interest in the foreign savants with a heartiness, kindness and tact that left nothing to be desired. Nor should it be forgotten that the members owe a heavy debt of gratitude to Count Landberg, who, with His Majesty's approbation, had devised all the arrangements, and at great sacrifice had assisted in providing for the comfort and hospitable entertainment of a large concourse of guests from many lands, and to whose energy and talent of organization the success of this Congress is mainly due.

# Abstract of Papers read at the Congress.

## On the Nabataean Inscriptions in the Sinaitic Peninsula.

### By Prof. J. Euting.

Whereas the number of Nabataean inscriptions copied by previous travellers scarcely comes up to 300, Prof. Euting succeeded last spring in adding 700 to the collection. He achieved this success simply because he travelled as an Arab, and climbed barefooted along the rocks in places overlooked by other collectors. Also of many inscriptions previously known he brought home better copies and squeezes yielding the novel and important result that some of the inscriptions were found to be dated. Thus, one showing the year 126, "being the year of the three emperors," agrees according to the æra of Bosra, which commences in the year 111 A.D., with 237 of our æra. The other bears the date 85 (= A.D. 196). As compared with Glaser's S. Arabian inscriptions,* these Nabataean inscriptions are not important on account of their age any more than by their contents, for they mostly convey only greetings and names. But they furnish valuable material for tracing the history of the origin of Arabic writing. The writers of those stone records were, in his opinion, neither shepherds nor pilgrims, but merchants who, while returning from a caravan journey (perhaps from S. Arabia to Petra), found a temporary resting-place for their camels in these valleys so rich in pasturage. These merchants, well acquainted with writing, would while away their time by inscribing their names upon the rocks, with greetings to those who might follow in their wake.

---

## So-called Kappadokian Cuneiform Tablets.

### By the Rev. A. H. Sayce, M.A.

In 1881 Mr. Pinches drew attention to two Cuneiform tablets, said to come from Kappadokia, one of which was in the British Museum, the other in the Louvre. They were written in a peculiar form of Cuneiform script, and did not seem to be in the Assyrian language; Mr. Pinches concluded therefore that they represented the ancient language of Kappadokia. The following year Prof. Ramsay was starting on a tour of exploration in eastern Asia Minor, and I asked him to inquire for Cuneiform tablets. His inquiries proved fruitless, however; but just before he left Kaisariyeh he noticed some tablets in a shop which he bought for a small sum of money. On his return to England, he handed them over to me. I found that they were similar to the two tablets published by Mr. Pinches, and published transliterations of them in the "Proceedings of the Society of Biblical Archæology," November, 1883. The tablets are now in the British Museum.

Since then I have myself purchased some Kappadokian texts, others have been obtained by Dr. Peters for the University of Pennsylvania, while more than twenty are in the collection of M. Golénisheff at St. Petersburg. The latter are mostly in a very perfect condition, and as some of them are written in the more ordinary type of Cuneiform, a comparison of the latter with what may be termed the Kappadokian script has enabled M. Golénisheff and myself to identify the Kappadokian characters to which a false value or no value at all had previously been assigned. As soon as the true values of the characters were ascertained, I found that the language of the tablets was an Assyrian dialect, which presented several phonetic peculiarities and contained words which are probably of foreign origin. The phonetic peculiarities agreed with those of certain of the Tel el-Amarna texts from Northern Syria, as, for instance, the substitution of *gimel* for *kaph*. Moreover, the forms of the characters resemble those of the Syrian tablets from Tel el-Amarna, and since the Kappadokian tablets contain phrases which are common in the Tel el-Amarna texts, but are unknown in Assyrian of later date, we may conclude that the library from which they are derived was founded in the same age as that of the Tel el-Amarna collection. It was probably situated in the country called "Khanu the greater" by the Assyrians, mention of which is made in a letter of Assur-yuballidh of Assyria to the Egyptian king.

A large proportion of the proper names occurring in the Kappadokian texts are compounded with the name of Assur, and so imply that the library belonged to an Assyrian colony. Some of the foreign names found in them are said to be those of *gari* or "strangers." The title of *limmu* is also met with. All the tablets I have examined relate to commercial transactions, principally to the lending of money. One of them is a quittance for the receipt of a large amount of lead.

---

## On Some Later Babylonian Inscriptions.

### By the Rev. J. N. Strassmaier.

The Rev. J. N. Strassmaier, S.J., laid before the meeting a small collection of Babylonian inscriptions and made a few remarks on them. The collection contained one inscription of *Marduk-aplu-iddin* (722-710 B.C.), one of *Sargon* (710-705 B.C.), three of

---

* Professor Euting's communication was preceded by one from Dr. Ed. Glaser on the results of his journey in S. Arabia. He stated that whereas previously only two to three hundred inscriptions from those parts had been known, he had brought home copies of 900, some of which are of the highest historical value, and probably go back 2500 years. It is much to be regretted that the speaker saw himself compelled by constant interruptions to cut short an account which would have been of the highest interest.

*Esarhaddon* (681-667 B.C.), three of *Samaš-šum-ukin* (667-647 B.C.), four of *Kandalanu* (Kineladanos of the Canon of Ptolemæus, 647-625 B.C.), four of *Labâši-Marduk*, the son of Neriglissar (556 B.C.), six of *Xerxes* (485-464 B.C.), ten of *Artaxerxes* (464-423 B.C.), a letter of Nûr to his brother Iddin-Bel from the year 164 of the Seleucide era (= 148 B.C.), and a small inscription in Babylonian characters, but apparently in a new language, hitherto unknown. The texts with a transliteration will appear in the Transactions of the Congress.*

### On Two Recent Publications on Semitic Epigraphy.

#### By Professor D. H. MÜLLER.

Professor D. H. Müller placed on the table of the Semitic Section his two recent publications, viz. 1, a Glossary to the Corpus Inscriptionum Semiticarum, and 2, Epigraphic Monuments from Arabia, from Euting's copies and squeezes, and gave a brief account of each.

No. 1 is a criticism of part iv. fasc. 1 of the Corpus Inscriptionum Semiticarum recently edited by MM. J. and H. Derenbourg, and containing 69 Sabœan and Himyaritic inscriptions. The author, while giving due praise to the Institute de France (Académie des Inscriptions et Belles Letters) for the great services it has rendered to Semitic epigraphy and Semitic studies generally,† sees himself compelled to pass a severe criticism on this part of the Corpus. Although of the 69 inscriptions here brought together there are only 18 not yet previously published, the reviewer charges the editors with a large number of wrong readings and interpretations and with a want of that epigraphical tact and philological criticism which are the main bases of every successful decipherment. He concludes with these words : "The Corpus Inscriptionum Semiticarum will for a long time continue to be the work by which

Semitic studies will be gauged and directed. Such an important publication has therefore to be judged by a different standard to that which would apply to an individual attempt at decipherment. In such a work reliability and solid methodical criticism, together with a complete command of all the known material and the literature, are indispensable postulates."

No. 2 contains 150 newly-published inscriptions from el-Ōra (N. Arabia) which were collected by Prof. Euting, of Strassburg, and committed to the editor for publication. One-half of them were found to be attributable to a Minœan colony who had their commercial factories in this neighbourhood throughout at least 200 years. The remaining 75 inscriptions are written in a character and in a North Arabian dialect which had already produced a literary language about ten or twelve centuries before Muhammad. In the grammatical sketch which the author gives of this dialect he defines exactly its position within the range of the Semitic languages. Palœographically the writing proves to be a transition alphabet between the Phœnician and the Sabœan. The inscriptions derive from Thamûd, who is mentioned in the cuneiform writings and the Korân. The graphic representations laid before the Section specially interested the members. The author gives the name of Lihyânî to this new language and writing, and shows that already on a Babylonian cylinder (of the year 1000 A.C.) in the British Museum this character is found engraved. In conclusion he speaks in glowing terms of Euting's immortal services in making these remarkable documents available, and pays a tribute of gratitude to what we owe to Doughty, Huber and Glaser.

### On the Origin and the Date of Composition of the Navigatio Sancti Brandani.

#### By Professor J. M. DE GOEJE.

It has been more than once remarked that there exists a striking resemblance between the well-known tale of Sindbad's adventure on the back of the whale-island, and that of the Navigatio. Dr. Schröder endeavoured to prove in the introduction to his edition of the Navigatio that the Orient owes this tale to the Occident, but his argument cannot be accepted. On the contrary, all tends to show that the author of the Navigatio borrowed this tale from Sindbad.* A careful examination of all the passages of the Navigatio in which the whale occurs leads to the conclusion that two different tales have been combined, one, that

---

* Prof. J. Oppert drew attention to the importance of these inscriptions with some laudatory remarks, and Prof. Haupt suggested that henceforth new texts communicated to the Congress should be written on a black board.

† On this subject Prof. Müller spoke as follows: "The 26th January, 1867,—the day on which E. Renan, together with de Saulcy, Longperier, and Waddington, placed before the 'Académie des Inscriptions et Belles Lettres' the proposition that they should undertake the publication of a *Corpus Inscriptionum Semiticarum*,—will ever remain memorable in the history of Semitic epigraphy and philology. The *Institut de France* has not only given a new and powerful impulse for the sifting and investigation of the existing epigraphical material, but has constantly directed its attention towards the exploration of new fields of research, and the collection of numerous inscriptions. In reviewing at the present time, after the lapse of 22 years, what has been done in Semitic epigraphy, and how rich, and in part how trustworthy, the materials are, we may justly say that not the least part of the merit is due to the publication of the *Corpus Inscriptionum* undertaken by the Institute."

---

* In the Dutch periodical "de Gids" (August, 1889) Prof. de G. proved that the romance of Sindbad the Mariner has been composed in the end of the ninth or the beginning of the tenth century.

of the Sindbad adventure, the other that of the whale, wholly subjected to St. Brandan, which transfers on its back the Saint and his monks to the Birds' Paradise. This latter, the old Brandan legend, has been preserved from a now lost Life of St. Brandan by Rodolphus Glaber in the Historia sui temporis, written in 1047. To this old legend must also be traced the statement that the peregrination lasted seven years. Besides the episode of the whale-island, the author of the Navigatio borrowed several other tales from Sindbad, even the description of the Paradise itself. It is probable that, whilst being in the East, he assisted at a recital of the tale of Sindbad, and, misled by the resemblance in sound between the names of Sindbād and St. Brandan (as the English sailors made St. John from Sindan), he took the hero of that tale to be his saint. He could the less doubt of their identity, as the tale had in common with the old Brandan legend an adventure on the back of a whale, and as the seven voyages of Sindbad seemed to correspond with the seven years of the peregrination of the saint. That the author must have been in the East is clear from his description of the miraculous lighting of the lamps of the altar, which took place every year on the eve before Easter in the Church of the Holy Sepulchre at Jerusalem.

The author of the Navigatio borrowed also, but indirectly, from the tale of the adventurers of Lisbon, who, in the tenth century, made a voyage of discovery in the Atlantic. Edrisi, who wrote in 1154, gave some extracts from this tale.

The particulars about the birthplace and the monastery of St. Brandan, given in the beginning of the Navigatio, seem to belong to the old legend. From the circumstance that one or two Irish names have been falsely translated, we may conclude that the author was not a born Irishman.

The second part (which could not be read) contains the proofs that the Navigatio has been composed in the 11th century, and shows that neither the known passage of the Martyrologium of Tallaght, nor Bili's life of St. Machutus (St. Malou) are in opposition with that conclusion. Both furnish us with valuable information about the growth of the Brandan legend. It gives further an ample discussion of the relation existing between the Navigatio and the Imram Maelduin, and ends by showing that the Navigatio had never in Ireland the popularity which it enjoyed on the continent of Western Europe.

## On the Works of el-Ḳifti.

### By Professor A. MÜLLER.

Jamāl uddin Abu'l-Hasan 'Alí Ibn el-Qifti was born at Qift in Upper Egypt in 568 A.H. (1172–3 A.D.). His family had held various high offices of State in the service of the Ayyabides, and he also was employed in various branches of the administration. About 611 (1214) he was appointed Wazír at Aleppo, which post he filled at longer intervals until his death in 646 (1248). As by reason of his position he had access to official sources of information, his numerous historical works on the earlier and contemporaneous history of various Muhammadan States and dynasties would be of the utmost importance to us if they had not been lost soon after his death, probably on the occasion of the sacking of Aleppo by the Mongols in 658 (1260). All that remains to us consists, besides some passages quoted by contemporaneous writers, of an abstract of a grammatical work, and further an abstract of the كتاب إخبار العلماء بأخبار الحكماء. a comprehensive collection of biographico-bibliographical notices of philosophers and authorities on exact sciences amongst the Greeks and Eastern nations. This abstract is the work of a certain Zauzani, in all probability a native of Aleppo, who composed it only two years after the author's death. Its full title appears to have been طبقات الحكماء واصحاب العلوم والطبائع, but it is generally quoted as the تاريخ الحكماء. In spite of the existence of a great number of MSS. of this work in various libraries, it has not been handed down to us in good condition, because all the MSS. are based on one and the same and in many respects faulty Archetypus. Nevertheless the work is of great importance as a valuable supplement to the Fihrist, Ibn Abi Uçeibi'a, etc., as well as for the control of contemporaneous literature on the same subject, and contains even after the extracts given by Amari, Wenrich, Flügel, Steinschneider, and others, a great deal that would make a complete edition desirable.

## On a hitherto unknown work of Yakut.

### By Dr. H. ETHÉ.

Dr. Ethé called the attention of the Islamitic section to a hitherto unknown but highly important work of the famous Yâkût (author of the Mu'jam-albuldân and the Mushtarik, 1179—1230) which he found whilst cataloguing the new stock of Arabic MSS. in the Bodleian Library. The work in question is the Mu'jam-aludabâ, a biographical and bibliographical dictionary of the most renowned grammarians, philologists and rhetoricians of the first five centuries of the Hijrah, arranged alphabetically according to the first letter. The Bodleian copy (Bodl. Or. 753), written in splendid Naskhí, but undated (formerly belonging to Archdeacon Barnes in Calcutta and bought by the library 1880 of Mr. Gee in Oxford), contains only the *first volume* from Alif to the middle of Ḥâ, altogether 335 biographies, full of the most valuable and interesting details. Dr. Ethé proposes to publish shortly a complete list of the extant biographies.

## On the State of Islam under the Umayyades.

### By Professor Dr. GOLDZIHER.

Professor Goldziher stated that in a chapter of the forthcoming second volume of his " Muhammadan Studies " he had treated of the religious life of the Moslems under the Umayyade dynasty and of the relative position of the religious communities. He had shown in it that the party of the Murǵites, who are generally supposed to be a *dogmatic* fraction, were originally a *political* party representing the opposition to the intransigent religious enemies of the Umayyade dynasty. He had also sketched out the fact of all those conflicting parties making their appearance already in the oldest *ḥadîth*, and had illustrated that statement by examples.

## On the History of the Development of the Madhab el Ash'arîyeh.

### By Dr. M. SCHREINER.

Dr. Schreiner submits an inquiry, from the original sources, into the internal development of the Ash'aritic doctrines and their influence on the course taken by Muhammadan divinity. He shows how the Ash'aritic dogmatic system passed, from its beginnings until the sixth century, through successive stages of development by Ibn Fûrak, al-Bâḳillânî, al G'uwainî, al-Isfarâîni, when it reached its zenith in al-G'azâlî.

## On the Knowledge which the Arabs possessed of the Polar Sea.

### By Professor W. LAGUS.

The lecturer stated that he had for some time been engaged on investigations concerning the above subject. He referred to what Reinaud and Mehren had said about it as long as thirty years ago, and to subsequent publications. Some of the latter, however, required correction, and he instanced a passage in Istakhri in which Mordtmann understood the word ـ to mean Britain, whereas it is really (see de Goeje's edition) the dual of ـ which means ' a desert.'

## On Ibn Sina's Treatise entitled ' The Bird.'

### By Professor A. F. VAN MEHREN.

" The Bird " is one of the mystic treatises of the celebrated Arabic philosopher Ibn Sina or Avicenna, probably written after his Hay b. Yaqzân during his sojourn at the court of Alâ-ed-Daulah at Ispahan. Its style, especially at the commencement, is full of enigmatical expressions, and presents many difficulties; these are lessened, however, by the commentary and Persian translation, the work of a certain Omar b. Sabhan, a copy of which is in the British Museum (Cat. Cod. MSS. Or. II. 450, No. 26).

The following is an account of this allegorical composition, which resembles in many points one of the didactic poems of Aurelius Prudentius, a Christian poet of the fourth century (*cf.* Aur. Prudentii Clementis carmina, ed. Dressel, Lips. 1860, p. 162).

After a preface addressed to his friends, in which he speaks of the qualities of real friendship, he proceeds : A party of hunters go out to catch birds. After laying their nets, they caught a good number, and among them was the author of this story. Shut up in their cages, they at first were suffering from their captivity ; but they gradually became accustomed to it till a small number of them succeeded in escaping, while the rest, still in captivity, seeing them rise in the air, asked them to show them the means of obtaining their freedom and to aid their escape. These after some hesitation offered to assist their unfortunate companions, and showed them the way to escape safely from their captivity. When they had in their flight arrived in sight of eight high mountains, they made great efforts to pass over their summits, and after crossing the last they gained access to the palace of the Great King. Admitted to his presence, they began to describe to him their wretched condition as caused by the ends of the chains still attached to their feet. Then he promised to furnish them with a messenger who should convey to their oppressors the order to detach those chains. That messenger of deliverance is the angel of Death.

Professor v. Mehren has the intention of including this treatise, together with extracts from the Persian commentary, in his forthcoming edition of all the mystic treatises of Avicenna, the first fasciculus of which, dedicated to the Congress, contains the above-mentioned Hay b. Yaqzân.

## On the oldest form of the Upanishads.

### By Professor H. OLDENBERG.

There is no doubt that *upa-ni-shad* literally means the (reverential) sitting down by somebody or something. But the correct interpretation that by this term the sitting down of the pupil by the master is intended who proposes to hand down to him the mysterious doctrine of the Upanishad appears to be untenable, for the reason that the Upanishad texts constantly and customarily speak of a "reverential sitting down" in a very different connection, that is to say, of that reverential sitting down in which the pious and wise concentrate their thoughts upon the highest objects of all pondering, viz. the Âtman or Brahman. Although in all cases in which a verb is required in speaking of a sitting down in that sense *upa-ās* is used rather than a compound of the root *sad*, usage at once reverts from *upa-ās* to *upa-ni-shad* as soon as a substantive is required to convey that meaning. The oldest Upanishads (also called *ādes'a*, *nāmadheya*) consisted in brief instructions as to in what form or under what definite name the pious had to conceive of the Brahman. Round this nucleus those further prose and metrical elements which followed the diction used in the Brāhmaṇa texts gathered themselves that we find combined in such texts as the Bṛhad Āraṇyaka or in the Chāndogya Upanishad.

## On the Origin and Import of the oldest Samans.

### By Professor A. HILLEBRANDT.

Professor Hillebrandt states that the two oldest melodies used in the Hindu ritual, Bṛhad and Rathantara, were connected with the solstice festivals, and that originally the former belonged to the summer solstice, and the latter to the winter solstice. This fact explains the strange comparisons drawn in reference to them ; Bṛhadrathantara, *e.g.* are the two breasts of the year, or Rathantara is what is short, Bṛhad what is long, inasmuch as Rathantara was originally sung on the shortest, Bṛhad on the longest day of the year. Thus some curious customs, hitherto left unnoticed, gain greater significance. It is said, *e.g.* in one of the ritual manuals that Prajāpati created the thunder after the Bṛhad. Actually, at the Mahāvratīya festival on the day of the summer solstice drums are used, and with the beating of drums the thunder is imitated. The rite connected with the Rathantara is still more remarkable. Prajāpati, it is said, created Rathantara, and in its wake the sound of the chariot is created. In correspondence with this, the Rathantara is to be introduced on a certain day by the noise of chariots. The author recognizes in this an old Aryan rite of the winter-Solstice festival and compares with it the custom prevalent (according to Grimm) in some parts of Schleswig of rolling a wheel through the village at the Christmas season. He further endeavours to show that Sāmans had their original cult in popular practice, and thence became elements of Brahmanic sacrifice. This would explain the reason why in several law-codes the chanting of the Sāmans is mentioned in a sneering manner. The melodies were originally based on worldly texts which were perhaps something like the ditties and saws customary with us at the summer-Solstice festivals. When those tunes were received into the Brahmanic cult, religious texts were chosen for them to replace the lay ones, and texts from the Ṛksaṃhitā were selected for the purpose.

## Archæological Researches in India.

### By Dr. J. BURGESS, C.I.E.

The absence of any historical literature in India renders the scientific survey and delineation of its monuments indispensable to the proper study of the national history, as well as of the development of its art and architecture, which bear the clearest records of the growth of religions, of manners and customs, of the taste, civilization, and prosperity of its peoples. The collection of sufficient and accurate data for such a study, and the careful preservation of the monuments themselves, are surely manifest duties of an enlightened Government.

Archæology, as a department of scientific research, based on a groundwork of precise knowledge, with fixed principles, and excluding everything of a merely speculative nature, is a science of recent growth, concerned with the logical deduction of the history of man and his arts from the monuments and other works he has left. This strictly scientific method the author would have applied to the Indian surveys. Like all other branches of research, however, its methods have grown from materials collected by pioneers who had not the opportunity of applying or developing these methods, and the paper was largely concerned with the history of these workers,—the rise of the Asiatic Societies of Bengal, Madras, and Great Britain, the services of Jones, the Daniells, Dr. Francis BuchananHamilton, Col. Colin MacKenzie, Colebrooke, Sir W. Elliot, J. Prinsep, Kittoe, Lassen, H. H. Wilson, and others. The great exponent of scientific Archæology as applied to Indian monuments, however, was the late James Fergusson, D.C.L., F.R.S., whose journeys, between 1834 and 1839, were undertaken with the one object in view of ascertaining the age and objects of the rock-cut monuments of India and those of later date. "Nowhere," he remarked, "are the styles of architecture so various as in India, and nowhere are the changes so rapid, or follow laws of so fixed a nature," and a chronological arrangement thus becomes palpable to the trained student. Fergusson's principles reduce the multifarious details to order, and the details confirm the principles ; and it is to him the students of Indian antiquities owe the means of checking traditions by easy reference to the substantial records to which, in his works and in others owing much to his influence, access is now possible. His works in this department were noticed, and the impulse given to research by the translations of Fahian and Hiuen Tsiang, and then the author passed on to the origin, history, and work of the recent Surveys in Northern and in Western and Southern India, and the publication of the results so far as they have yet been issued ; the materials on hand, however, are very considerable and most important. A volume by Dr. Führer, edited by Dr. Burgess, has just appeared at Calcutta, but he stated that about four volumes from each of the surveys might be produced as rapidly as he could carry them through the press, if only Government would sanction the very moderate outlay required : this it is hoped will be done.

The author glanced at the work done in Epigraphy and the advances made since he started the *Indian Antiquary*, through its agency, the work of Mr. Fleet, and his latest attempt to continue the *Corpus Inscriptionum Indicarum* by the periodical publication of the *Epigraphia Indica* (a copy of which was presented at the Congress), and which has been so favourably hailed by Continental scholars.

In 1885 Dr. Burgess succeeded General Sir A. Cunningham, Director-General of the Archæological Surveys in Northern India, and set himself the task of the accurate and complete delineation of the monuments ; more careful and scientific methods of excavation ; and the most perfect possible reproductions of inscriptions, to be deciphered and edited by the best qualified scholars. Some of the assistants nominated before he took charge were inefficient and the want of funds have disappointed otherwise well-founded expectations. Dr. Burgess retires and the three Surveys in Upper India can be reduced to one, or rather the five circles for all India can be reduced to three, under properly-qualified surveyors, with one or two specialists for epigraphy—each with a small staff of native assistants —those in epigraphy being trained to scientific work in that branch.

Native princes may also come to give valuable help in this Survey, and the wise and munificent patronage of the Maharajas of Baroda and Jaypur was specially noticed.

---

## Asoka's Thirteenth and Fourteenth Edicts in the Mansehra Version.

### By Professor Dr. G. BÜHLER.

Shortly after my arrival at Stockholm on the occasion of the late International Oriental Congress, Dr. J. Burgess handed to me a paper-impression of a large inscription in North-Indian characters which he had received a few days before from Mr. Rodgers, the Archæological Surveyor of the Panjab. After a cursory inspection I was able to announce to him that it contained Aśoka's thirteenth rock edict and possibly the fourteenth. My communication in no way surprised him, and he informed me that the impression was the result of a search instituted by his orders for the missing portions of the Mansehra version. With his permission I made the discovery known at the second meeting of the Aryan Section of the Congress (see Bulletin No. 8), and gave there readings of some of the most important passages of the thirteenth edict. As every addition to our knowledge of the Aśoka inscriptions possesses a considerable interest, I now reproduce the remarks made at the meeting, and add some others on points which have come out during a more leisurely examination of the document.

The impression measures 4 ft. 6 in. in height. Its breadth is in the upper part, down to line 8, about 8 ft. 7 in. and in the lower 6 ft. 2 in. It contains thirteen lines, slanting upwards from the right to the left. All of them are more or less mutilated at the end. In the upper ones about sixty letters or even more are missing, in the lower ones about forty. The first eleven lines and a half contain portions of the thirteenth edict, the latter part of the twelfth line and the thirteenth, fragments of the fourteenth. The first legible words of line 1 are *pacha adhuna ladheshu Kalimgeshu*, which correspond with the beginning of line 2 of the Shâhbâzgarhî version. It is thus evident that the inscription is mutilated also at the top and that its real first line is missing. In the preserved portions there are a good many illegible or disfigured letters, and the appearance of the impression shows that the stone has not been polished, but is full of natural fissures and flaws.

This state of things no doubt diminishes the value of the document. Nevertheless it is by no means useless. It confirms a number of readings found hitherto only in single versions, and furnishes in some passages interesting variæ lectiones. Thus in the sentence where the Shâhbâzgarhî version (l. 6) reads *pratikhagam cha etam savram manus'anam* (not *manushanam*, as my transcript gives erroneously) etc., and alone has fully preserved the last word, the Mansehra version offers, (l. 5) *pra . . . [e]she savram manus'anam*, and thus confirms the correctness of the important word. In the next following sentence, which is considerably shortened in the Shâhbâzgarhî text, the Mansehra version sides, as is frequently the case in the other edicts, with that of Kâlsî and has (line 5, end) : *nasti cha se janapade yatra nasti ime [nika]ya a[namta] yenesha [bra]ma[ṇa] . . .* The highly interesting passage of the Shâhbâzgarhî version which I first explained in the *Academy* of February 23, 1889, is unfortunately not complete. What remains (l. 7) is : *. . . cha aṭavi . . na priyasa rijitari hoti ta pi anuṇayati anunijhapṇye ti. Anutape pi cha prabhave devana priyasa. Vuchati teshu : Kiti !* Here we have a general agreement with the readings which I have given of the Shâhbâzgarhî text and the interesting fuller forms *anuṇayati* for *anuneti* and *anunijhapaye* for *anunijhape*. It deserves also to be mentioned that the *jha* of the latter word is perfectly distinct, which is not the case in the other text. In the preamble to the enumeration of the Greek kings influenced by As'oka's teaching of the law, where the distance of the dominions of the Yona king Antiochus from India is given, the words *a shashu pi yojana[s'a]teshu* are distinct at the end of line 8 with the exception of the syllable *s'a*. The Mansehra text thus furnishes additional proof that the second word is really *shashu*, i.e. *shaṭsu*, and that the passage must be translated, as I have done, "even at (*the distance of*) six hundred Yojanas [where Antiochus the king of the Yonas rules]." Among the names of the Greek kings only that of Alexander, *Alikasudare nama*, has been preserved. In the immediately following list of converted nations the first word of the compound *Visha-Vaji-Yona-Kaṁ[boje]shu* agrees with the Shâhbâzgarhî text, the others with that of Kâlsî. The next compound [*Nabha*]*ka-Nabhapaṁtishu* comes likewise close to the Kâlsî reading *Nâbhake Nabhapaṁtishu*, from which it differs only by the absence of the locative termination in the first word. In the last sentence but one, where the Shâhbâzgarhî version has *savra cha nirati bhotu ya sramarati*, and that of Kâlsî, *shavâ cha nilati hotu uyâmalati*, Mansehra closely agrees with the former, reading (line 2) *savra cha [pi niʼrati hotu ya sramarati*. The fragments of the fourteenth edict are very indistinct. As far as I can make out, the beginning (line 12, end) is *iyaṁ dhramalipi devanaṁ priyena li*, and thus agrees with the text of Kâlsî and the other eastern and western versions. These details show that even in its present mutilated state the new inscription possesses a not inconsiderable value. But from Dr. Burgess's statement regarding the circumstances under which it was discovered and the impression was taken, I conclude that the find may eventually prove to be still more important, and that we may hope to obtain complete copies of the two edicts. The account which Dr. Burgess has given me is as follows.

At a late visit to Mansehra, during which he took the impressions of edicts I.-VIII. and IX.-XII. used for my article in vol. xliii. of the "Zeitschrift der deutschen morgenländischen Gesellschaft" (p. 273 ff.), he noticed that the two inscribed rocks are surrounded by a very large number of big loose boulders, full of natural rents and fissures. It then struck him that the two missing edicts might possibly be incised on one of these. For, owing to the roughness of the stones, the existence of letters might be easily overlooked. As the time of his stay was too limited for a careful examination of each single boulder, he asked the Archæological Surveyor of the Panjab to undertake the task. Thereupon Mr. Rodgers sent, in the beginning of the last rains, a native clerk to Mansehra, with orders to institute a strict search. The latter found, after a great deal of trouble, a third inscribed stone, which had been removed from its original position and had rolled down to a *nulla* or torrent, overhanging its bank. This yielded the impression under notice. As the stone is not in its original position, and as the discoverer is not an archæological expert, it is not at all unlikely that there are more letters on it than the impression contains. It may be that a portion of the inscription is hidden under the stone or has been overlooked in consequence of the bad condition of the surface. It seems to me also very probable, that an impression, taken in sections during a more favourable season by a competent archæologist, will be much more readable than the present one. Under these circumstances I believe it advisable to wait with an attempt at editing the text, until the stone has been examined once more and a fresh impression has been taken. But I should be ungrateful towards Dr. Burgess and Mr. Rodgers, if I concluded this communication without adding that they have laid all students of Indian history under a great obligation by what they have already done.

---

## The Âvasyaka Literature of the Jainas.

A SERIES OF TEXTS BASED ON SOME OLD PRAYERS AND FORMULAS.

By Professor E. LEUMANN.

The original texts (prayers and formulas) from which the whole bulk of Âvasyaka literature derives its origin are six in number; they are named *Âvasyaka-sûtras* from their being 'avasya,' *i.e.* 'necessary' or obligatory to any one adhering to the Jaina creed. On these *Sûtras* (1), which for the greater part are in prose, there exists a metrical *Niryukti* (2), and this again is treated on by a huge prose composition called *Cûrṇi* (3). The fourth state of literary development is represented by a *Bhâshya* (4), written like the Niryukti in the Âryâ metre. Fifthly the Cûrṇi is turned into Sanskrit by Haribhadra (died 906 A.D.) in his Âvasyaka-*Tîkâ* (5). The succession of texts goes on, but in the whole does not exhibit any new features.

In some way the five stages of development described are typical as they are also found with other branches of Jain literature; but what is peculiar to the Âvasyaka branch may be stated under the following heads:

1. The *Sûtras* as texts of their own are lost with one exception and must be reconstructed from Cûrṇi and Tîkâ; a later recension however has been saved.

2. The *Niryukti* is a conglomerate of two chief texts (by Bhadrabâhu and by Siddhasena) and of a great many additions inserted successively.

The *contents of the Niryukti* are partly dogmatic, partly historical or legendary and parabolic. Among the several hundred tales we mention as particularly interesting : 1. The story of princess Vāsavadattā and minister Jogandharāyaṇa ; 2. The story of the apes and the birds (also found in the Pancatantra and the Hitopadeśa) ; 3. The judgment of King Salomo ; 4. The frame story of 1001 night ; 5. The parable of the pounds intrusted ; this is known as yet only from the New Testament, but is found (besides in the Āvaś-yaka-niryukti) also in the sixth Anga of the Jainas, which may have been composed in the second or first century before Christ.

----

### On the Phonology and the Vocabulary of the Baluci Language.

#### By Professor W. Geiger.

Lassen already recognized Balūči as an Iranian language. Subsequently F. Müller and Hübschmann gave a general sketch of its phonology. The material, however, available to them was so limited and meagre that much remains yet to be done. Within the last ten years more abundant materials for the study of Balūči have become accessible by which we have been enabled to draw a distinction between the dialects within the Balūči language (*Geiger*, Sitzungsberichte der K. Bayer. Akad. d. Wissenschaften, Philol.-histor. Classe, 1889, 5, 68 ff.) and to deal with greater precision with its phonology and its position with regard to the other Iranian dialects.

As regards the phonology, it is an important fact that the *z* of the Avestā language is never represented by *d*, as is the case in Old-Persian, Pahlavi and Modern-Persian, but always by *z*. Hübschmann still maintained that there was a twofold representation, viz. by *d* and *z*. It was proved, however, that all the words in which *d* occurs are loan-words from Modern-Persian. Thus *dil*, heart, is the Mod.-Pers. دل, while the genuine Balūči form is *zirdē*. One might, therefore, assume that Balūči belongs to the group which has hitherto been called the Eastern Iranian. When one considers, however, that the Osset, Kurdish, and the dialects of Kashan (according to Shukowsky) likewise have the *z*, it becomes evident that the separation into an eastern and a western Iranian group by reason of this phonetic phenomenon is altogether wrong : *d* is by no means peculiar to all the western dialects, and in fact its area is exceedingly limited.

Another important factor in Balūči phonology is the representation of an old initial *v* by *gw* before *a*, and by *g* before *i*-vowels. By the aid of this law it can strictly be proved that in the Modern-Persian preposi-

tion بر two very different words are represented, viz. 1, the old preposition *upairi*, and 2, the substantive بر = Av. *varaĝh*, breast. The former is in Balūči *awar*, the latter *gwar*. Both expressions are used also in Balūči with the significations of " above," " on" and " near to."

Certain phonetic peculiarities and coincidences in the vocabulary show Balūči to be closely related to the Kurdish. But the question still requires more searching investigation. The Balūči vocabulary is very original. Take *e.g.* the curious word *gwabz* or *gwamz*, wasp; *gwarm*, breakers, derives from the root *var*, to roll, and compares with the Sanskrit *ūrmi*, wave ; *gwask*, a calf, corresponds to the Sanskrit *vatsa(ka)*, while the Modern-Persian دژ was taken as a loan-word with the signification of " boy" ; *kapinjar*, partridge, belongs to Sanskrit *kapinjala*, and is not found in any other Iranian dialect ; the same applies to *kambur*, variegated = Sanskrit *kambara* ; *bōg*, a joint, = Sanskrit *bhōga*, and others.

It is highly desirable that further linguistical material should be made available ; more especially is it an urgent desideratum that in the province of Makrān vernacular texts should be collected. Hitherto more has been done for Northern Balūči than for the group of Southern dialects.

----

### On a Specimen of Mythological Arabism.

#### By Count A. de Gubernatis.

The lecturer began by drawing attention to various points of resemblance between Indra, who was represented as mounted on an elephant, and Ganeśa with an elephant's head. The future historian of India, he said, would find in the series of Pauranic legends, traditions, and usages concerning Ganeśa a last evolution of the Indra myth. The lecturer went through many of those legends in detail, comparing also the double face of Ganeśa with the fact that in many Vedic hymns Indra's name is coupled with that of some other deity, and endeavoured to show that all the various points in Ganeśa's functions went far to prove his descent or development from Indra.

----

### A Testimony for the pre-Historic Migrations of the Indo-Germanic Tribes.

#### By Professor Johannes Schmidt.

When it once became generally recognized that all the peoples who are now comprised under the name of Indo-Germanic have sprung from one common original stock, it was in the first place assumed that that stock had its primordial habitat in inner Asia.

But since the publication of Benfey's preface to the first edition of Fick's "Wörterbuch der indogermanischen Grundsprache" (1868) scholars have more and more adopted the view that Europe was the original home of the Indogermans. It is true that few valid arguments have been brought forward in favour of Asia; but it is equally true that still fewer have been urged in favour of Europe. At any rate, it can be proved from the numerals of the European peoples of our race that middle or northern Europe, recently assumed to have been the primitive habitat of all the Indogermans, inclusive of Iranians and Indians, can on no account lay claim to that honour.

In the Germanic languages the Indo-Germanic decimal system is traversed by a duodecimal system. In the former the numerals "eleven" and "twelve" are conceived of in their relation to "ten" as different to the following numerals up to "nineteen"; got. *ainlif, tvalif*, but *fidvôr-taihun, fimftaihun*. As in the case of "twelve," so "sixty" forms a break. "Twenty" to "sixty" are in Gothic plurals of a stem *tigu-* (*e.g.* dat. *saihs tigum*), whereas the decads from "seventy" onwards exhibit the singular stem *têhunda-* (*e.g. sibuntêhund*), which is carried on to "hundred and twenty." In consequence of this a big hundred of 120 took its stand by the side of the common hundred in the Germanic languages, and by means of this the counting was carried on to sixty big hundreds. Those three new divisions of the numeral system—at 12, 60 and 120—which are unknown in the Indogermanic mother-tongue, are in mutual relation to one another. The one at 60 is the oldest of them, for it is also found amongst the Greeks and Celts. These form the decads to 60 from the cardinal number, from 70 upwards from the ordinal number (ἑξήκοντα, but ἑβδομήκοντα). In all probability the same distinction was originally also made in Latin. Similarly, the Finnic Syrjanes in the northern regions of Europe and Asia make a break after 60. A decimal system cannot work out a division at this stage, it becomes intelligible only as due to the influence of the Babylonian sexagesimal system. The imperfect duodecimal system of the Germanic tribes has arisen from a traversing of the sexagesimal and the decimal systems. Though also in India Babylonian influences can be proved to have exerted themselves in the oldest Vedic time, no disturbance of the old Indo-Germanic numeral system by the sexagesimal one has here taken place. Hence it follows that the Europeans, exposed as they were to a much more thorough influence of the sexagesimal system, must have accepted it in a locality within easier reach of the Babylonian range of civilization than the districts on the Indus, which one would therefore rather look for in Asia than in Europe. At any rate, these facts would forbid us to place the original home of the Indo-Germanic peoples in central or northern Europe.*

## On the Ancient Aryan Languages of Asia Minor.

### By Professor P. Karolidis.

After giving a general sketch of the Asia Minor branch of the Aryan family of languages, the lecturer drew attention to the meagreness of the existing linguistic material and the scantiness of ancient monuments. He then shows that Jablonski, Heeren and Adelung were in error in considering the river Halys as the boundary between the Somitic and Aryan languages, and the Kappadokian as a Syrian or Assyrian tongue. Also later researches (Lassen, de Lagarde, Gosche, and others) have suffered from the meagreness of material and a certain want of comprehensiveness. The author's own investigations are based on the following principles: after reviewing, sifting and comparing all the statements in the ancient writers regarding the descent and affinities of the peoples of Asia Minor, he applies the rules of modern linguistics to the definite results thus gained, and then draws his final conclusions. There are two questions to be considered,—first, what conclusion can with tolerable certainty be drawn from an intercomparison of the old traditions concerning the origin of the people and languages of Asia Minor? and secondly, what materials does modern research offer to us by which to test that question? how far can those materials be used for scientific investigations? and what final conclusions can be drawn from a combination of these various points? As regards the first question, the one point that stands out prominent from the meagre statements of Greek authors is the relationship of Phrygians and Armenians, and of the Phrygian and the Armenian language. He further states that the Phrygians were closely connected with the Greeks on one side and various nations of Asia Minor on the other, and formed as it were a rallying-point between Greeks and Armenians. He attributes far greater significance to the relationship of the Greek and Armenian languages than to the Greek accounts of affinity between Armenians and Greeks. The main difficulty of the inquiry centres in the second part of

---

* It should be noted that in the discussion which followed Prof. A. Weber drew attention to two facts, in proof that the Germanic tribes must in their original seats have been in close and neighbourly relation with the Semites, viz. (1) that the words for *six* and *seven* (only these) are common both to Indogermanic and Semitic languages: and (2) that the Indogermanic tribes reckoned time originally by the *moon* (the measurer). The "twelfth days" (Rigveda iv. 33, 7) representing a compensation between the solar and lunar year seemed likewise, he said, to point to that relation (Ind. Stud. x. 242; xvii. 223).

the inquiry. Here he establishes in the first instance the fact that Greek stands in such close relationship with the Aryan elements of Armenian (more in vocabulary than in grammatical structure) that many points in the etymology and phonology of the former can only be explained from the latter. To prove that old Phrygian was a sister language of both, (1) all words and proper names recorded as Phrygian or Asia Minor by the old authors, (2) Phrygian or Lycian inscriptions, and (3) all traces, still extant in some Greek dialects of Asia Minor, of the old indigenous languages, have to be examined. Many mythological, ethnological and geographical names enter into this inquiry; he treats of them in great detail, and arrives at the conclusion that throughout Asia Minor, from the western coasts where the Greek element commences to the Highlands of Armenia, purely Aryan tongues are to be found, in some of which a greater affinity with Greek must be recognized, while in others there is a preponderating leaning towards Armenian. The languages, therefore, spoken in Asia Minor, especially in Phrygia, formed a connecting link between the Helleno-Pelasgic and the Armeno-Iranian family of languages.

In an Appendix the author treats of the original meaning of the tribal names Χαλδαῖοι and Σύροι in Pontus. The former, he says, has nothing to do with the Kaldi of the Cuneiform inscriptions and the Χαλδαῖοι of Babylonia. On the contrary, he connects this and similar names with the Armenian *halem* " to smelt." The name of the Σύριοι of Asia Minor is referred by him to the name of the sun god Σύρος (identical with Αὐτόλυκος or self-lucescent, the mythical founder of Synope).

---

## On Mr. Flinders Petrie's Discoveries in the Fayum.

### By Miss A. Edwards.

In the general and final meeting of all the Sections under the Presidency of the King at Stockholm, Dr. Cust was permitted to state verbally the purport of a communication made to the Egyptian Section by the celebrated Egyptologist, Miss Amelia Edwards, who, though a member of the Congress, was unable to attend personally, as she had to embark for New York to deliver a course of lectures on Egyptian Exploration in all the chief cities of the United States during the next few months.

The paper related to the discovery, in the neighbourhood of Fayúm, in Central Egypt, by Mr. Flinders Petrie, agent of the Egyptian Exploration Fund, of collections of broken pottery with alphabetic inscriptions. The date of this pottery is attributed approximately on certain independent evidence to the time of

Menepthah, King of Egypt at the time of the Exodus, and Osertisin II. of a much older date. When the alphabetic signs are examined, they are found to be identical in character with the signs of that famous Græco-Phœnician alphabet, which is the mother of all the alphabets of the world, but in less highly developed and therefore more antique forms. Now the oldest previously existing specimens of the Græco-Phœnician alphabet are the Moabite Stone, about 900 B.C., and the scratchings of their names upon the legs of the great statues at Abu Simbul in Upper Egypt by the soldiers of Psammetichus about 600 B.C. It will be at once perceived how important is a discovery that carries back the use of these alphabetic signs to the time of the Exodus, 1490 B.C., and far beyond. We may well hold our breath for the time, and wait till this bold theory is accepted by the competent authorities of Palæography. It has always been a question as to the alphabet, in which the two tables of stone were written by Moses, as there was no independent evidence of the existence of the Græco-Phœnician alphabet at an earlier date than 900 B.C. This evidence has now been supplied.

---

## On the Geographical Distribution of the different Languages of the Turki Branch of the Ural-Altaic Family of Languages.

### By Dr. R. Cust.

The lecturer stated that his paper was printed both in the English and German languages, and widely circulated among scholars, in order that some certainty might be attained for the practical purposes of the translation of the Holy Scriptures. He went over in detail the different languages already known, (1) the Osmanli of the Turkish Empire, (2) the Azerbijani or Trans-Caucasian of the Province of Trans-Caucasia in Russia and Azerbiján in Persia, (3) the Kazáni spoken in the Basin of the Volga, (4) the Chuváeh spoken in the European Provinces of Kazán and Nijni Novgoród, and the Asiatic Province of Orenburg by half a million, (5) the Kumuk spoken on the North-west shore of the Caspian Sea, (6) the Trans-Caspian, (7) the Central Asian or Khiva, (8) the Kirghiz, (9) the Yarkandi, (10) the Nogai, (11) the Yakut. Until the same exhaustive process was undertaken in Central Asia by Russian scholars, that has been completed in British India and the Indo-Chinese Peninsula by British scholars, no finality could be obtained. Dr. Cust called on the Russian scholars to proceed on the task, which they had so well commenced. He mentioned the names of the Academician Radloff, Professor Salemann, Librarian of the Russian Academy, Professor Ilminsky of Kazan, and Professor Ostramoff. He alluded to the meritorious labours of the Rev. Abraham Amirkhanians of the British and Foreign Bible Society, stationed at Orenburg.

Dr. Cust finally insisted on no attempt being made by the State, or by a dominant Religion, to rob a tribe of their ancestral language : the change of a people's vernacular must be the result of the involuntary tendencies of dawning civilization.

---

## On the Watersheep in Chinese Accounts from W. Asia.

### By Professor A. G. SCHLEGEL.

Professor G. Schlegel, of the Leyden University, read a paper on the *Shui-yang* or Watersheep in Chinese accounts from Western Asia and the *Agnus Scythicus* or vegetable lamb of the European mediaeval travellers; both having been a great puzzle to Chinese and European botanists and zoologists. Two years ago Mr. Henry Lee wrote a very interesting book in order to prove that by the vegetable lamb nothing else was meant but the cotton plant. Mr. Schlegel, however, showed that although the watersheep of the Chinese accounts presented the greatest analogy with the vegetable lamb, the former still exhibited many features incompatible with the growth of the cotton plant. He therefore suggested that the legend of sheep growing out of the ground like plants took its origin in miscellaneous notices of the way of training camels in Persia, combined with the way of growing the cotton plant and butchering the living sheep in order to get the wool of the unborn lamb, of which the so-called Astrakan wool is prepared.

In Persia the young camels are kept during a long period after their birth in a kneeling position, with the legs tied down under the belly, in order to accustom them afterwards to kneel before being loaded. They are guarded against the wolves and other rapacious animals by a circular or square enclosure or wall, presenting to the looker-on at a distance the aspect of a field in which sheep grow out of the ground.

As is well known, the finest stuffs in Persia are woven from the hair of the camel ; and it is these stuffs which were imported at a very early period into China, under the name of Hai-si-pu, "cloth of the Western countries," or "cloth of the down of the watersheep."

Dr. Schlegel advanced many other proofs for the general accuracy of the Chinese reports on the productions of Western Asia, and stated as his belief that if the savants who occupy themselves with the study of the languages and ethnography of Western Asia would combine their studies with those of Sinologues, many important results for our knowledge of ancient

Western Asia could be gleaned from the notices to be found in Chinese historical works ; in fact, the only ones we possess concerning these remote ages.*

---

## On the Language and Customs of the People of Hunza.

### By Dr. LEITNER.

The Hunza language, Dr. Leitner pointed out, is one of a class in which nouns can only be conceived of in connection with a possessive pronoun. There is, *e.g.* no abstract word for "head," "wife," "house," but there are separate words for "my head," "his wife," "our house," etc. He drew attention to the important results to be derived from a philological analysis of this language, for which ample materials will shortly be available. The Hunzas are Muhammadans only by name ; witches and fairies play a prominent part in their social and administrative arrangements. Most Hunzas are Mulais, and their head is Prince Aga Khan, of Bombay. They are connected with the Druses of the Lebanon. Their sacred book is the Kalâm-i-pîr, of the contents of which the lecturer gave some interesting specimens.

---

## The Tomb Inscriptions on the Upper Yenisei.

### By Professor O. DONNER.

The first who directed the attention of savants to certain peculiar inscriptions on ancient tombs on the banks of the river Yenisei was the Swedish officer Strahlenberg, who was taken prisoner at Poltava in 1709 and transported to Siberia. There he made himself acquainted with the country and its population, and after his return from captivity elaborated a valu-

---

* Dr. Hirth, while congratulating the learned author of the paper on having succeeded in suggesting so palpable a solution of this problem, said that the chief value of the discovery consisted in the light it threw on the material used by Syrian manufacturers in certain textile fabrics mentioned in old Chinese records as the produce of the country of Ta-tsin. In his own researches regarding the ancient relations between China and the Roman Orient he had endeavoured to show that all the Chinese say about this industry referred to the dyeing, weaving, re-weaving, and embroidering works of the cities of Tyre, Sydon, and Berytos on the Phœnician coast, a district which in ancient commerce furnished a class of articles of equal renown to Manchester goods of our own day. Since the Chinese records, in the face of the fact that about twenty different varieties of cloth were distinguished, must be regarded as an authority supplementing the accounts of classical authors in many important respects, every clue as to the materials used must be highly welcome. Of the principal texture reaching China from the market of Ta-tsin we learn that it consisted of silk, some kind of vegetable fibre, and "the down of the watersheep." The identification of the latter with camels' wool was of great interest, and it would be a good subject to be taken in hand by a connoisseur of Syrian antiquities to find out how far the information preserved in Chinese records could be supported by classical or Western Asiatic research.

able description of the northern and eastern portions of Europe and Asia, which was published in 1730, and contained inter alia the pictures of two tombstones with inscriptions in a language and alphabet altogether unknown. Later on several others of the same kind were published by Pallas and Klaproth and some Russian savants, without, however, a sufficient clue to that interesting script having been discovered. In 1877 the chemist Martinow founded a natural history museum at Minusinsk, and from that date several more tombstones covered with that kind of writing were collected, so that at present the number of them is eight.

On the banks of the Yenisei numerous bronze objects have been found in tombs; they differ in form from those found in other parts, and prove the existence of an Altaic bronze age. In many respects a connection is traceable between these and the bronze objects found in the neighbourhood of Perm, by means of which the Finnic tribes are brought into contact with the Altaic bronze age. The Finnish Archæological Society at Helsingfors thereupon resolved to send, during the last three summers, expeditions to Siberia under the State Archæologist, Professor Aspelin, to take trustworthy copies of the inscriptions, those previously published not being sufficiently accurate. In two summers the expedition took 32 copies, and these have now been published for the Congress.

Even in the last century people were struck with the European appearance of the inscriptions, as well as with the resemblance of some of the letters to the runes, and they gave them this very name. In the opinion of the learned Tychsen (1786) this script had to be connected with the old Greek form four or five hundred years before Christ, when it was still written from right to left. A. Rémusat attributed it to the people called U-sun by the Chinese, Klaproth and Castren to the Kirgiz, while Yadrintsev, Klements and Radloff consider the inscriptions to be older than the Hakases, and as consequently belonging to pre-Christian times. Last summer a Chinese coin of the Emperor Vou-tsoung (841–6 A.D.) of the Tang Dynasty was found, on the smooth side of which two words in Siberian characters were engraved. Similar coins, but without those characters, have been discovered in great numbers, most of them belonging to the same century, several of the seventh, and one of the year 118 B.C. This proves that the Yenisei alphabet must still have been in use about the middle of the ninth century. The bronze age, however, represented by it reaches far back into the preceding time for many centuries.

The writing presents some eighty different shapes or characters, some of which, however, at first sight are recognizable as mere variants. As far as can be gathered at present, there are more than forty characters.

The writing goes from right to left, sometimes turning to the right, as is the case in ancient heathen and Christian tomb inscriptions. Only in No. 17, which contains ten inscriptions, some of the lines show a decided direction towards the right and an arrangement of the letters the very opposite to the usual one. The words are generally separated by two dots placed one over the other or by two short vertical or slanting lines. In its exterior arrangement the script therefore agrees with that in vogue among the non-Semitic tribes in Asia Minor and Greece about four or five centuries before Christ. An examination of the characters leads up to the same result, there being corresponding forms to most of them in the alphabets of Asia Minor derived from the Greek system of writing. It is more especially the Lycian and Karian alphabets which present most analogies. Among the characters which differ from these we note several which agree with similar ones in the Egyptian syllabary. There occurs also a form which to all outward appearance has its exact counterpart only in the Açoka alphabet. Taking all these circumstances together, we can well understand how this script has come to be compared to the northern runes or the Iberian writing. Among the words an interpretation of which I believe I have found is *abagha*, which occurs several times in five inscriptions. But this word happens to occur, not only in Mongol, but also in Yakut, with the meaning of 'uncle,' 'father's brother.' It will, therefore, be necessary for us to await further attempts at decipherments as to language and script. The revision of the inscriptions on the basis of the new impressions taken by the members of the expedition last summer will no doubt greatly contribute to facilitate this work.

---

## On the Linguistic Position of the Languages of Australia.

By Dr. H. Schnorr von Carolsfeld.

The languages of the Australian continent have hitherto been either considered as isolated, or they have been classed with certain African, with the Dravidian, and recently also with the Kolarian languages. It is not our present purpose to discuss these various hypotheses, as they do not rest on a firm basis, and are not affected by the following exposition. The plausible assumption of a connexion between the Australian languages and those of New Guinea and the Melanesian dialects has hitherto been considered as erroneous on account of the contrast subsisting between both groups as to the formation of words, the former generally using suffixes for that purpose, while the latter use prefixes. That contrast, however, need by no means have been an original one, but may in both groups have been evolved in the course of their historical development. The greater, therefore, is the significance that must be attributed to the numerous coincidences in the vocabulary which can be proved in both groups: and in these coincidences nearly all the dialects of New Guinea and Melanesia partake, more especially those of New Caledonia, but also those of the Salomons Islands, the New Hebrides, and Loyalty Islands. Thus *one* in the language of Eddystone (Salomons Islands) is *kamee*, which is evidently related to the South Australian expressions *kooma*, *kouman*. The New South Wales form *mal* has its corresponding forms *mele* in New Guinea, *moli* in the New Hebrides, *mola* in the Salomons Islands. In addition to the numerals, the words expressive of parts of the body—ear, eye, hand, arm, leg, finger, tongue, tooth, head—exhibit a widely spread consanguinity. Thus, when we compare *mana*, mouth, and its congeners of the Salomons Islands, New Hebrides, Maclay Coast (New Guinea) with *muri* (Arimoa), the Australian form *murna* shows that *r* and *n* have both sprung from an older *rn*. Compare the Australian verb *theara*, *terre*, to stand, with the New Caledonian *tur*, New Britain *na-tur*, Salomons Islands *toru*, New Zealand *tur*, New Guinea *toriti*. The group hitherto treated of (Australia, Melanesia, New Guinea) may be further extended to the languages of Ombay, Mangerai, Timbora. Compare for "head" the Australian *kurria*, *korea*, New Guinea *koara*, *garu*, Timbora *kokora*. Lastly, we have to bring within our range the group of the Andaman Islands. The connexion is most strikingly exhibited in one of the terms for "head," which in the Australian language appears as *katta*, *kutta*, *kada*, etc., on the Maclay coast of New Guinea as *gaten*, in the Melanesian languages as *qatu*, *qotu*, and lastly in three Andaman dialects as *chetta*, *kita*, *kude*. A doubtful point here is whether all the Andaman dialects are of one and the same descent; at least the language spoken in Little Andaman, the southernmost of the islands, shows an evident affinity with Dravidian words. Thus *quagé*, ear, may be compared to Dravidian *kouk*, *kchulu*, body, with Drav. *kûl*.

At present it is impossible to define on what ethnographical basis those linguistical affinities may rest. The question is the more difficult to answer as many Australian words appear to belong to a still wider range than the one here referred to. Thus the Australian *tulla*, tongue, can scarcely be disconnected from the Batak, etc., *dila* (compare Malay *lidah*). At all events we would recommend a complete separation of the anthropologico - ethnographical and the linguistical question.

## Helsning till Österlandet.

### VID

ORIENTALISTKONGRESSENS BESÖK I UPSALA,
DEN 4 SEPTEMBER, 1889.

O Österland! Slå dina portar opp,
De strålande, till dina unders rike!
Träd fram i ljus! Bort alla skuggor vike,
Som länge dolt dig under seklers lopp.
Än blott vi sett en strimma af dig gry
Likt sol, som röjs af morgonrodnans sky.

Likt himlafamerande Himalaja,
Som i ditt land sin gletscherpanna höjer,
För vandrarns häpna blick din storhet röjer,
Din älder tusenåra cedrarna,
Din fägring floderna, som slå
Kring dina dalars prakt en gördel blå;

Så ock för forskarns syn, då vördnadsfull
Han sig i dina häfders blad fördjupar,
En visdom hög, hvarvid hans tanke stupar,
En skönhet ädel som det ren6ta gull,
Hvars like ej han någonsin förnam,
I outtömligt flöde qväller fram.

Han lyssnar rörd till Vedas helga sång,
Som väldigt likt en jätteharpa klingar;
Och långt i tiden bort hans tanke svingar
Sig vid Firdusis ljufva toners gång;
Och hänförd af Valmikis höga psalmer
Han tror sig drömma under dina palmer.

Han ser en pelargång af sällsam prakt,
Som trolsk och skymningsfull sin riktning sträcker
Så långt, att ej hans blick dess ända räcker,
Och aningsfullt han drages dit med makt:
Längst bort en ljusning tror han sig förnimma
Och se århundradenas morgon glimma.

O morgonland! Sänd ut af ljus en flod!
Wi helsa dig med tusen varma röster!
Wi helsa Er, I vise ifrån öster,
Der mensklighetens vagga stod!
Gån, sägen, att Europa icke glömmer
Det land, som hennes forntids öden gömmer!

D. S. HECTOR.

## Greeting to the East.

ON THE OCCASION OF THE VISIT OF THE EIGHTH INTERNATIONAL CONGRESS OF ORIENTALISTS TO UPSALA,
ON THE 4TH SEPTEMBER, 1889.

*[Translated from the Swedish of D. S. Hector by Herbert Baynes.]*

Land of the East! throw open now thy gates
Which, shining, guard thy realms of mystery!
Step forth into the light! Bid darkness flee,
In which, long ages, hidden by the fates
Thou languishedst: one gleam, one glimmer grey
We see, e'en as, at dawn, the sun's clear ray.

And, like the heaven-kissing Himalay
Which in thy land its glacier-brow doth raise,
Thy greatness looms before our 'stonished gaze ;
Thy cedars of a thousand years, thy day
Of hoary splendour, and thy beauty true
Which round thy valleys throw a girdle blue !

So is it with the seeker's soul, when oft
With reverence filled he loses self in thee,
Thy past and present, and what is to be :
A wisdom high, a beauty noble, soft
And pure, a spring with waters ever bright,
A well of inexhaustible delight !

He listens rapt, to Véda's sacred song,
Whose high harmonies cling about his ear ;
His thoughts into the past from far and near
Do swing, and round Firdusi's stanzas throng ;
And, wafted by Valmiki's lofty psalms,
Imagines that he dreams beneath thy palms !

He sees a pillared hall of beauty strange,
That stretches, gleam- and gloomful, far and high,
So far, his look can scarce the end descry,
But, full of hope, is borne along its range
Until at length a light upon him beam,
And lo ! the morn of centuries doth gleam !

O Morning-land ! Of light send forth a flood !
We greet thee with a thousand welcomes true ;
Ye wise men from the East, we welcome you.
'Tis there the cradle of our race has stood.
Go, say that we remember to the last
The land that keeps the annals of our past !

---

## The Eighth International Congress of Orientalists at Stockholm and Christiania, and the Sanskrit Idylls about it.

### By H. H. Dhruva, B.A., LL.B., L.A.

The Eighth Congress of Orientalists has come and
gone, and many and better heads have spoken and
written about it. It is here proposed to give the
Sanskrit Idylls that convey an Indian Brahmin's view on
the subject. The first of them was recited at the closing
meeting of the Congress at Stockholm on the 7th of
September, while the second was recited at the closing
meeting at Christiania on the 11th of that month.
They congratulate the Congress and its Patron King,
and thank the King of Norway and Sweden and his
people for the reception accorded to the Congress. The
third and the fourth are descriptive of the feasting
and rejoicings, at the Congress and the Falls at
Trolhätta, the last place the Congress visited. In them
will be found a curious weaving of Oriental imagery
with Western thought.

### Idyll I.

*Congratulatory verses addressed to the Eighth International Congress of Orientalists and its Patron King Oscar II.*

(Sanskrit Text.)

स्वभावसौरस्यविशालिनी सिता
प्रभैषिणी प्रोज्ज्वलहंसवाहनी ।
निशान्धकारं भरते विलोक्य सा
दिशां नु चक्रे भ्रमति स्म भारती ॥ १ ॥
ध्वनिमुखरी दिवमे मंदे मंदे-
दुदितं पश्चिमदेशमंडलं ।
सन्ध्यार्धं त्रा रधिरं परिप्लुतं
तमालनीलं तिमिरं सुविश्रुतं ॥ २ ॥
मिश्रं तमिस्रावृतमघ न श्रुतिः
श्रुतिः समन्तादध मीश्वरीलमे ।
चक्रावले वृष्टिमुखे घने ऽम्बुदे
मृद्वाकलिखा किमुदेति शारदी ॥ ३ ॥
घनं एवं भाव्य सुदुर्लभं क्षणं
दिने दिने मूर्च्छित सुमूर्च्छती ।
दिशः पपाताच तथा यदृच्छया
घ उत्तराले कुरवः समाश्रिताः ॥ ४ ॥
सन्ततवता श्रीः सकला जला वर्ष
क्षमेव तस्याः समुपागतं सर्वं ।
निशा प्रभाता गलितं तमो ऽच्छ-
श्रुतिः प्रसन्ना निखिलाश्च बान्धवः ॥ ५ ॥
प्रतिभियर्षे मुनिमंडले शिव
समाश्रयस्त्वाश्रममाश्रमात्सती ।
सच्चोद्यता धर्मति चक्रवर्तिनी
विराजते विश्वमुखी सरस्वती ॥ ६ ॥
सरस्वतीश्री सद्मप्रसाद उर्वीपतिः कविः सुमतिः
सुयमा जयतादाक्षर नृपतिः शारदा घनं अमति ॥ ७ ॥
जयत्यरीन्नत तेजः शारदार्धभवं भवं ।
आचक्रार्धगिरिरक्तब्रह्मावर्तश्रीसिन्धु-भारतं ॥ ८ ॥

(Romanized Transcript.)

1.* Sva-bhâva-saurasya-viśâlinî sitâ
Prabhaishiṇî projjvala-haṃsa-vâhanî
Niśândhakâraṃ Bharate vilokya sâ
Diśâṃ nu chakre bhramati sma Bhâratî.

2.† S'akais Turushkair Yavanair navair navai-
rudvejitaṃ Paśchima-deśa-maṇḍalam
Sandhyârunaṃ bâ rudhiraṃ pariplutaṃ
Tamâla-nîlaṃ timiraṃ suvistṛitaṃ.

3.† Misraṃ tamisrâhatam atra na dyutiḥ
    Chyutis samantâd atha Grisa-Romake
    Chalâchale vrishṭimukhe ghane · mbude
    Mṛigânka-lekhâ kim udeti S'âradî ?

4.‡ S'amaṃ rasaṃ bhâvya su-durlabhaṃ klamaṃ
    Dine dine vṛiddhimitam.  Sumûrchchhatî
    Divaḥ papâtâtra.  Tayâ yadṛichchhayâ
    Ya Uttarâs te Kuravas samâs'ritâḥ.

5.‡ Svatantratâ s'rîs sakalâḥ kalâ balaṃ
    Krameṇa tasyâs samupâgataṃ svakaṃ
    Nis'â prabhâtâ.  Galitaṃ tamo · ruṇa-
    Dyutiḥ prasannâ.  Militâs'cha bandhavaḥ.

6.† Prati-tri-varshaṃ muni-maṇḍalaṃ nijaṃ
    Samâhvayantyâsramam-âs'ramât satî
    Sattrodyatâ samprati chakravarttinî
    Virâjate vis'va-mukhî Sarasvatî.

7.§ Sarasvatî-s'rî-labdha-prasâda urvîpatiḥ kavis sumatiḥ
    Suyas'â jayatâd Âskara-nṛipatis' s'aradâṃ s'ataṃ jagati.

8.‖ Jayatv atrodgataṃ tejas' S'âradâsambhavaṃ navaṃ
    Â-chandrârka-giri-Skandâvartta-s'rî-Sindhu-Bhâratam.

  * The metre is Vaṃs'astha :
$$\cup-\cup-,\ --\cup-,\ \cup-\cup-,\ --\cup-.$$
  † The metre of verses 2, 3, and 6 may be termed Upajâti' because of the irregularity of the syllables in one of the feet.
  ‡ The metres of verses 4 and 5 are again Vaṃs'astha described above.
  § The metre of verse 7 is an *Âryâ* with 12 *mâtrâs* in the first and third feet, 18 in the second, and 15 in the fourth.
  ‖ The metre of verse 8 is the well-known Anushṭubh S'loka of the Râmâyaṇa, Mahâbhârata, Purâṇas, etc.

(ENGLISH TRANSLATION.)

1. Bhâratî or the Goddess of Learning, white and naturally remarkable for sweetness, seeing Darkness in the (land of) Bharata (i.e. India) of night, desirous of Light wandered in all directions, riding (her) shining swan.

2. The western countries were harassed by the Śakas (Scythians), Turushkas (Turks), and every new succession of Yavanas (Barbarians).  Alas! blood red as the evening sky spread all round!  Darkness as black as the Tamâla trees extended far and wide.

3. Misra (Egypt) was smitten with Darkness.  Here there was no Light but a fall all round in Greece and Rome.  What (then) will the Autumnal Moon shine out of dense clouds constantly fleeting (about her face) big with rain ? (Never.)

4. Seeing that quiet and pleasure were unattainable (there), (and that) trouble was increasing day after day, (she) fainting away fell here from from the sky.  (And) she repaired by chance to what are called the Uttara Kurus or the Northern Kurus.

5. Here Freedom, Fortune, all arts and sciences (and) strength—all that was hers came gradually to her.  The night passed away.  Darkness melted away. The morning Light smiled (and) she met her friends.

6. Now the virtuous (Bhâratî) inviting every three years her Munis from one Âs'rama or hermitage to another is now Chakravarttinî (Universal Empress or going in a circle) engaged (as she is) in a Satra (or long session of Sacrifices) (and she who was Bhâratî, i.e. of India now) shines as universal Sarasvatî (*lit.* moving about the whole World).

7. May His illustrious Majesty King Oscar favoured of Learning and Fortune—a Poet, Prince, and Philosopher—may He glory for a hundred years in (this) World !

8. May this new Light borne of Learning, manifested here, glory as long as the Sun and the Moon, the Hills and the Seas, Scandinavia and India last !

(METRICAL TRANSLATION.)

On swan astride, in search of Light,
The Goddess Bhâratî, pure and white,
From clime to clime, from land to land,
Her course unwitting she did bend ;
When she observed the darksome night
Drop on the Land of Bharat as blight.

The Scythian swarm, the Turkish troop
Each new Barbarian boldly swoop,—
On lands extending westward far,
She saw, all bathed in blood and war,—
Blood crimson as the evening sky
Thick gloom set shrouding low and high.

It smote the Land of Egypt wise.
In Greece and Rome there was no rise,
But fall all round.  How from the cloud,
Big with the rain, that would flit, shroud
Her face, can shine and smile serene
The lovely Dian's dainty mien ?

Her Peace and Bliss for ever gone !
And misery daily growing, alone,
Was left to her ! ha ! Bhâratî feels,
She falls from sky, she faints, she reels !
She here by chance alighted sheer,
On Lands as Northern Kurus we hear.

Her wealth, her freedom, arts, her strength,
To her returned, all all at length
The Darkness melted.  Night was set.
Sweet smiled Aurora.  Friends she met.
From hermitage to hermitage,
Every three years, invites her sage,

Devoted votaries, faultless She,
In sacrificial seasions' glee.
And She, that was up to this time,
The Goddess of old Bharata's clime,
Moves in her right imperial sway,
Sarasvatî that all obey.

Favoured of Fortune and of Her,
The Poet, Prince, Philosopher,
For many a winter, many a spring,
May glorious Oscar rule as King !
And may the Light of Bhâratî now
That's glorious borne as here you view

Shine ever and ever, may ever shine,
So long as Sun and Moon do shine,
So long as proudly stand the Hills,
So long as rolling Ocean reels,
So long as Scandinavia stands,
So long as are true India's Lands.

### IDYLL II.

*Thanking the People of Norway and Sweden for their
hospitable reception of the Congress.*

अथैकदा शैलसुता प्रसन्ना
प्रदक्षिणां सा जगतः सुताभ्यां ।
दिदेश कन्यामणियुग्ममत्र
सिद्धिं च बुद्धिं च पणं चकार ॥ १ ॥
स बर्हिवाहो दिशि संप्रतस्थे
गणाधिपो मूषकवाहनश्च ।
प्रदक्षिणीकृत्य शिवं शिवां च
स आप्तवांस्ते शशिसुन्दरास्ये ॥ २ ॥
प्राप्ते पुनः स्कन्द उमानुतापं
सौहार्द्दहृदया भृशमीयुषी हा ।
सा लज्जमाना पुरुषानभिज्ञ-
मिलाभिधं खण्डमियं प्रपेदे ॥ ३ ॥
विरतिमुपगतो ऽयं देवसेनाधिनाथः
प्रतिभुवममराणामीशिवां स्वर्गमत्र ।
प्रकृतिमनुपमां तां सुस्मितां वीक्ष्य लक्ष्मीं
सुहृदयजनतां गां वासमङ्गीचकार ॥ ४ ॥
स्वर्गोत्तरापथोपाख्याः स्कन्दावर्त्ताः सुहृत्तराः
प्राप्तस्वतन्त्र्यैषो ऽयं भारत्यापि समीप्सितः ॥ ५ ॥
जना जगति मोदन्तामातिथ्योल्लासमानसाः
स्कन्दिनो ऽद्वन्द्विनः प्राचीविद्याध्ययनलालसाः ॥ ६ ॥

1.* Athaikadā S'aila-sutā prasannā
　Pradakshiṇāṃ sā jagataḥ sutābhyāṃ
　Dideśa.　Kanyāmaṇi-yugmam atra
　Siddhiṃ cha Buddhiṃ cha paṇam chakāra.

2.† Sa Barhivāho diśi sampratasthe
　Gaṇādhipo mūshaka-vāhanaś cha
　Pradakshiṇīkritya S'ivaṃ S'ivāṃ cha
　Sa āptavāṃs te s'aśi-sundarāsye.

3.* Prāpte punaḥ Skanda Umā-nutāpam
　Sauhārddahṛidyā bhṛiśam īyushī hā
　Sā lajjamānā purushānabhijñam
　Ilābhidhaṃ Khaṇḍam iyam prapede.

4.‡ Viratim upagato ʼyaṃ Deva-senā-dhināthaḥ
　Prati-bhuvam amarāṇāṃ eshivām svargam atra
　Prakṛitim anupamāṃ tāṃ susmitāṃ vīkshya lakshmīṃ
　Subhridaya-jana-tāṃ gāṃ vāsam aṅgīchakāra.

5.§ Svargottarāpathopākhyas Skandāvarttas suhṛittaraḥ
　Prāptas svatantryaisho ʼyaṃ　Bhāratyāpi samīpsitaḥ.

6.§ Janā jagati modantāṃ Atithyollāsamānasāḥ
　Skandino ʼdvandvinaḥ Prāchī-vidyā-dhyayana-lālasāḥ.

* Verses 1 and 3 are Upajāti—the first of Upendravajrā and
Indravajrā metres.
† Verse 2 is Upendravajrā with its metre :
ᴗ — ᴗ, — — ᴗ ᴗ — ᴗ, — —,
‡ The metre of verse 4 is Mālinī :
ᴗ ᴗ ᴗ, ᴗ ᴗ ᴗ, — — —, — ᴗ —, — ᴗ —, —.
§ The metre of verses 5 and 6 is the well-known Anush-
ṭubh S'loka.

1. Once upon a time Pârvatî (*lit.* the daughter of
the Mountain), well-pleased, directed her two sons to
perform a voyage round the world ; and offered as
prize two beautiful damsels, viz. Siddhi (accomplishment) and Buddhi (intelligence).

2. He (*i.e.* the God of War), riding his peacock, set
out on his journey. (And) here Ganeśa (the God of
Wisdom), riding his mouse, obtained the two sweet
damsels with their faces as beautiful as the moon,
having gone round (his parents) Śiva and Śivā (*i.e.*
Pârvatî).

• 3. Now when Skanda (the God of War) returned,
the affectionate Umâ (Pârvatî) became very sorry.
(And she) being abashed removed herself to the Continent known as Ilâvartta, unknown to men.

4. The General of the Army of the Gods was greatly
dejected. He desired a land that would rival the
Svarga (or Paradise) of the Gods. Here, having seen
Nature incomparable, and Beauty sweet-smiling, and
a Land full of people of good heart, he fixed his
residence.

5. That is that Skandâvartta, or the Continent of
Skanda, known as Svarga (Sverige, Sweden), and
Uttarâpatha (or the North, Norge, Norway), very
friendly. That has been found by Freedom (also as her
home). Even Bhâratî (the God of Learning of Bharata,
India) likes to repair to it.

6. May the Scandinavian People, free from evils,
rejoice in this world, with their hearts delighting in
hospitality, and with their minds bent on learning the
lores of the East !

　　　　The Goddess mountain-born did once
　　　　A voyage round the World her sons,
　　　　The fiery God of War Skanda,
　　　　Ganeśa of Wisdom God, command ;

　　　　She offered prize for marriage meet
　　　　Accomplishment, Intelligence sweet,
　　　　Siddhi and Buddhi, beauties rare,
　　　　To him that home doth first repair.

　　　　Mounting his peacock Skanda flies,
　　　　To get the start, to win the prize.
　　　　Ganeśa cunning still, he schemes,
　　　　His parents Heaven and Earth both deems.

He mounts his mouse, he goes them round,
The much-coveted prize he found.
When Skanda from his voyage is back,
No prize! fond mother is taken aback.

In sorrow Pârvatî hides her face,
Ashamed, she suddenly leaves the place,
To Ila's continent she flies,
Where of the harder sex none hies.

The God of War, full of disgust,
His heavenly home he left, in quest
Of lands that would be Paradise
To him, and more than that likewise.

And here unrivalled Nature found
He, Beauty smiling sweet around,
And Peoples of good heart possesst,
He made it home, his heaven, his rest.

His North Way Norge was yclept,
His Svarga, Sverge, true and apt.
From Skanda, Scandinavia named,
Throughout the world those countries famed.

May Peace, Prosperity, ever bless
The Scandians! May they ever address
To studies of the Orient Light,
To whom guests foreign are delight!

### Idyll III.

*Descriptive of the reception accorded to the Congress.*

कुसुममुपहृतं मे सर्वदाहं वहिष्ये
सहृदयमरविंदाक्ष्या शशांकास्यया तत् ।
सरलललितभावं कोमलत्वं रसाढ्यं
प्रतिमितमिदमस्मिन् पुष्प एतत्प्रसन्नं ॥ १ ॥
कदापि नहि विस्मृतेः पथमथेष्यति स्वागतं
महोदधितरंगिणी प्रणयरंगिणी प्रोज्ज्वला ।
ध्वजैर्नु करपल्लवैरधरनेत्रमुग्धाम्बुजैः
स्मितै रसिकरश्मिभिर्विलसितैस्सुहर्षान्वितैः ॥ २ ॥
प्रदीपमधुराक्षरैः किसलयादिकैस्तोरणैः
प्रसूनचयवर्षणैरनलतारकोद्धर्षणैः ।
स्वभावललिताप्सरोरसिककिन्नरैर्गायनैः
अलौकिकसुनर्त्तनैर्दृङ्मनोहरैर्लास्यकैः ॥ ३ ॥
सुधासवमहोत्सवैरथ रसाकरैर्भोजनैः
सरिन्नगसरोवरप्रथमहर्म्यसंदर्शनैः
निरंतरमहो दिने दिन इहाभिसंमोदिताः
सुराः किमु गृहागता अतिथयो नु प्राचीरताः ॥ ४ ॥
अदृष्टपूर्वं वृत्तेषु काव्येष्वश्रुतपूर्वकं
स्कन्दिनामिदमातिथ्यमानन्दिनां नु नन्दतात् ॥ ५ ॥

1.* Kusumam upahṛitam me sarvadâham vahishye
Sahṛidayam aravindâkshyâ s'as'âṅkâsyayâ tat
Sarala-lalita-bhâvam komalatvam rasâḍhyam
Pratimitam idam asmin pushpa etat prasannam.

2.† Kadâpi na hi vismṛiteḥ patham atheshyati svâgatam
Mahodadhi-taraṅgiṇî praṇaya-raṅgiṇî projjvalâ
Dhvajair nu kara-pallavair adhara-nettra-mugdhâm-
bujaiḥ
Smitai rasika-ras'mibhir vilasitais suharshânvitaiḥ.

3.† Pradîpa-madhurâ-ksharaiḥ kisalayâdikais toraṇaiḥ
Prasûna-chayo-varshaṇair anala-târakoddharshaṇaiḥ
Svabhâva-lalitapsaro-rasika-kinnarair gâyanaiḥ
Alaukika-su-narttanair dṛiṅmanoharair lâsyakaiḥ.

4.† Sudhâsavamahotsavair atha rasâkarair bhojanaiḥ
Sarin-naga-sarovara-prathama-harmya-sandars'anaiḥ
Nirantaram aho dine dina ihâbhisammoditâḥ.
Suraḥ kimu gṛihâgatâ atithayo nu prâchîratâḥ.

5.‡ A-dṛishṭa-pûrvam vṛitteshu kâvyeshva s'ruta-pûrvakam
Skandinâm idam âtithyam ânandinâm nu nandatât.

* Verse 1 is Mâlinî described before.
† Verses 2, 3, and 4 are Pṛithvî:
⏑ — ⏑, ⏑ ⏑ —, ⏑ — ⏑, ⏑ ⏑ —, ⏑ — — , ⏑ —.
‡ The metre of verse 5 is the well-known Anushṭubh S'loka.

1. The flower that has been presented to me by the Lady with her eyes like the Lotus and the face like the Moon, I shall ever bear with my heart. (For) there is imaged, smiling, in this flower, her simplicity and sweetness, and her tenderness full of sentiment.

2. Never, never will that welcome be forgotten like the shining river of regard, surging like the great Sea, What with bannerets, the hands (like tender leaves), the lips and eyes like the sweet lotus, with smiles of sweet rays, and with amusements mixed with intense delight!

3. With sweet words (of welcome) inscribed in illuminations, with evergreens and festoons of leaves, with the showering of flowers, with the breaking forth of clusters of Stars of Fire (in fire works), with music as of the divine choristers and of the naturally sweet fairies, and with opera dances unusual, delightful to the eye and to the mind,

4. With the serving of the mead of Gods and of the festivals flowing with wines and viands of all deliciousness, with the showing to us the Lights of the Rivers (waterfalls), Mountains, Lakes and best of places, O the Orientalists have been entertained here from day to day without stop and cessation as if they were the Gods that had repaired to their houses as guests.

5. What was not seen in life, what was never heard in the songs of Poets, was this hospitality of the Scandinavians—may it resound (throughout the world)!

### IDYLL IV.

*Descriptive of some touches of the Trolhätta Falls last visited by the Congress.*

नृत्यति गायति कूजति मधुरं सुंदरतरं हसति फेनिः
रमते कमते किरणं रमयं तरणेस्तरंगिणी रमयी ॥१॥
हरिरपि निशि निशि दिशि दिशि पिपासति रसं नु
चुंबति सुवदनं
अमृतकरैरालिंगति हृदयं प्रणयी स्फुटं विशति
सरलं ॥२॥
समुच्छलति कम्पते मधुरनीलदुग्धस्मितां
शशांककरवेष्टितां निशि दिनेशभावणितां
दिने क्वचिदियं पुनर्नवनवां मनोहारिणीं
बिभर्ति सरिदद्भुतां श्रियमहो नु वेणिच्छलात् ॥३॥

1.* Nṛityati gâyati kûjati madhuraṃ sundarataraṃ hasati phenaiḥ
   Ramate kamate kiraṇam ramapaṃ taraṇes taraṅgiṇî ramaṇî.

2.* Harir api niśi niśi diśi diśi pipasati rasaṃ nu chumbati suvadanaṃ
   Amṛita-karair âliṅgati hṛidayaṃ praṇayî sphuṭaṃ viśati saralaṃ.

3.† Samuchchhalati kampate madhura-nîla-dugdha-smitâṃ
   S'aśâṅka-kara-veshṭitâṃ niśi dineśa-bhâ-vaṇitâṃ
   Dine Kvachid iyaṃ punaṛ nava-navâṃ mano-hâriṇîm
   Bibharti sarid adbhutâṃ s'riyam aho nu veṇichchhalât.

* The metre of verses 1 and 2 is Gîti with 12 mâtrâs in the first and third feet, and 18 in the second and fourth.
† The metre of verse 3 is Prithvî already described.

1. This beautiful River dances, sings, coos sweetly and smiles beautifully with her (white) foam. She plays about, and she woos the sweet ray of the Sun.

2. Night after night, and from place to place, even the moon desires to drink her nectar, and kisses her beautiful face. She embraces her with her ambrosial rays. And she, full of love, enters her open plain heart.

3. O, she bounds forth, she shakes her sweet greenish (waters smiling) milk-white (with the foam), entwined in the rays of the moon at night, and burnished with the light of the sun sometimes. She bears her ever-renewing wonderful beauty charming to the mind in the form of her tresses as it were. How lovely!

## A further Note on the late Ânandarama Borooah (Vaduya).

As some interest seems to have been excited both in Europe and in India by my attempt at an obituary of Ânandarâma Vaduyâ, I subjoin an extract from a letter received by me from one of the leading Sanskritists of Bengal, or, let me say, of India, Pandit Maheçacandra Nyâyaratna :—

"I read your short sketch of the life of Mr. Borooah which you sent . . . . . Indeed he was a most extraordinary and keen student. One of my students was employed by him as his Pandit, and he said that such were Mr. Borooah's capabilities that, though he was himself short-sighted, and had therefore to seek the assistance of somebody to read to him, he used to make such nice and keen observations on the subjects of his study, that he often astonished his Pandita, and he was able to retain all these in his memory. He died suddenly of paralysis in Calcutta in the midst of a very useful and active career, and has left behind a mass of MSS., the result of several years of patient study and research, and also a good Sanskrit library. He never married, and has no successor, and neither father, mother, nor any near relative ; he was एकमेवाद्वितीयम्. His MSS. and works are with Mr. T. Palit, Barrister-at-Law ; they will not be utilized till Government decides as to the right of publishing them. As you wanted to know his caste, . . . give the following information : He was an inhabitant . . . am ; the King of Assam used to give the title of Borooah to all classes of people, whether Brahmin, Kshatriya, or any other caste. He was a Káyastha."

By the next mail the Pandit was kind enough to forward to me a letter sent from the Mr. Palit referred to, from which it appears that Ânandarâma lost the power of speech for some time before his death and was unable to make a will. His heirs are his step-brothers, Âtmarâma and Keçavarâma, who are in possession of his estate. His library was kept in his house at Berhampur, Murshidabad. It is much to be hoped that his books and papers will fall into good hands. It is lamentable to note the way in which such collections sometimes disappear, especially in the East. CECIL BENDALL.

*British Museum, London, October,* 1889.

## American Literature.

Adams (W. T.)—Within the Enemy's Lines. 12mo. cloth. *Boston.* 7s. 6d.

Aldrich (Anne R.)—The Rose of Flame, and other Poems of Love. Second Edition with added Poems. Sq. 16mo. cloth. *New York.* 4s.

Aldridge (A. F.)—Brawn and Brain,' considered by noted Athletes and Thinkers. 12mo. cloth. *New York.* 2s. 6d.

Allen (A. V. G., D.D.)—Jonathan Edwards. 12mo. cloth. *Boston.* 6s. 6d.
   *⁎* American Religious Leaders.

American Historical Association.  Report of the Proceedings in Washington, D.C., Dec. 26–28, 1888.  By Herbert B. Adams.  8vo. paper.  *New York.*  7s. 6d.
*Contents.*—Report of proceedings; The early north-west, by W. F. Poole; The influence of Governor Cass on the development of the northwest, by Prof. A. C. McLaughlin; The place of the northwest in general history, by Prof. W. F. Allen; Internal improvements in Ohio, 1825–1850, by C. N. Morris; The old federal court of appeals by Prof. J. Franklin Jameson; Canadian archives, by Douglas Brymner; The states-rights conflict over the public lands, by James C. Welling; The martyrdom of San Pedro Arbués, by H. C. Lea; A reply to Dr. Stillé upon religious liberty in Virginia, by Hon. W. Wirt Henry; American trade regulations before 1789, by Willard Clark Fisher; Museum-history and museums of history, by G. Brown Goode.  Index.

Andrews (E. B., D.D.)—Institutes of Economics.  A Succinct Text-book of Political Economy for the Use of Classes in Colleges, High Schools, and Academies.  12mo. cloth.  *Boston.*  6s. 6d.

Arnold (A. N., D.D.) and Ford (Rev. D. B.)—Commentary on the Epistle to the Romans.  8vo. cloth.  *Philadelphia.*  10s.

Baker (I. O.)—A Treatise on Masonry Construction.  8vo. cloth.  *New York.*  £1 1s.

Beale (A. M. A.)—Calisthenics and Light Gymnastics for Young Folks; including Exhibition Marches, Drills, etc., adapted to Home, School, and Self-Instruction.  16mo. boards.  *New York.*  4s.

Binet (A.)—The Psychic Life of Micro-Organisms.  A Study in Experimental Psychology.  From the French by T. McCormack.  With a Preface by Author written for the American Edition.  12mo. cloth, illustrated.  *Chicago.*  4s.

Briggs (S. R.)—New Notes for Bible Readings.  With Selections from D. L. Moody and others, and a brief memoir by Rev. J. H. Brookes.  8vo. cloth.  *New York.*  5s.

Brown (W. L.)—Manual of Assaying Gold, Silver, Copper, and Lead Ores.  With One Coloured Plate and 94 Illustrations on Wood.  Third edition (Third Thousand).  Crown 8vo. cloth, pp. 487.  *Chicago.*  12s. 6d.

Bucknill (J. T.)—Submarine Mines and Torpedoes as applied to Harbour Defence.  8vo. cloth.  *New York.*  18s.

Campbell (W. W.)—Lake Lyrics, and other Poems.  12mo. cloth.  *St. John (N.B.).*  6s.

Craig (T.)—A Treatise on Linear Differential Equations.  Vol. I. Equations with Uniform Co-efficients.  8vo. cloth.  *New York.*  £1 1s.

Curtis (G. T.)—John Charaxes.  A Tale of the Civil War in America.  12mo. cloth.  *Philadelphia.*  5s. 6d.

Cushing (W.)—Anonyms.  A Dictionary of Revealed Authorship.  Part 2—Enquiry to Main.  8vo. paper.  *Cambridge.*

Cynewulf's Elene.  An Old English Poem.  Edited, with Introduction, Latin Original, Notes and complete Glossary, by C. W. Kent.  12mo. cloth.  *Boston.*  3s. 6d.

Davie (O.)—Nests and Eggs of North American Birds.  Third Edition Revised and Enlarged.  Introduction by J. Parker Norris.  Illustrated by Theodore Jasper, M.D., and W. Otto Emerson.  8vo. cloth.  *Columbus (O.).*  10s.

Davis (R.)—Recollections of Mississippi and Mississippians.  8vo. cloth.  *Boston.*  16s.

Day (H. N.)—Elements of Mental Science : Comprehensive Exposition of the Phenomena of the Human Mind, considered in its General Characteristics, in its Particular Functional Activities, and as an Organic Whole.  12mo. cloth.  *New York.*  5s.

Delmar (E. H.)—Trades Directory and Mercantile Manual of Mexico, Central America, and the West India Islands.  Third Biennial Edition.  8vo. cloth.  *New York.*  £3 13s. 6d.

Deems (C. F., D.D.)—The Gospel of Common Sense as Contained in the Canonical Epistle of James.  12mo. cloth.  *New York.*  7s. 6d.

Dixey (W.)—The Trade of Authorship.  12mo. cloth.  *Brooklyn (N.Y.).*  6s.

Donovan (J. W.)—Tact in Court.  Containing Sketches of Cases Won by Skill, Wit, Art, Tact, Courage, and Eloquence, with Practical Illustrations in Letters of Lawyers giving their best Rules for Winning Cases.  Fourth revised and enlarged edition.  12mo. sheep.  *Rochester (N.Y.).*  6s.

Drinker (Elizabeth).—Extracts from the Journal of Elizabeth Drinker, from 1759 to 1807.  Edited by H. D. Biddle.  8vo. cloth.  *Philadelphia.*  10s.

Dumas (A.)—Les trois mousquetaires.  Edited and Annotated, for Use in Colleges and Schools, by F. C. Sumichrast.  12mo. cloth.  *Boston* and *London.*  3s. 6d.

Eckstein (E.)—Nero : a Romance.  From the German by Clara Bell and Mary J. Safford.  Authorized edition.  Two vols. 16mo. cloth.  *New York.*  8s.

Edwards (H.)—Bibliographical Catalogue of the Described Transformations of North American Lepidoptera.  8vo. paper.  *Washington.*

Eggleston (E.)—A First Book in American History, with Special Reference to the Lives and Deeds of Great Americans.  12mo. cloth.  *New York.*  4s.

Elson (L. C.)—History of German Song.  Account of the Progress of Vocal Composition in Germany from the time of the Minnesingers to the present age, with Sketches of the Lives of leading German Composers.  12mo. cloth.  *Boston.*  6s. 6d.

Ely (R. T.)—An Introduction to Political Economy.  8vo. cloth.  *New York.*  6s.
*** Chautauqua Text-books.

Euripides.—Iphigenia among the Taurians.  Edited by I. Flagg.  Crown 8vo. cloth.  *Boston* and *London.*  5s.

Farmer (Lydia H.)—A Short History of the French Revolution for Young People; Pictures of the Reign of Terror.  12mo. cloth.  *New York.*  7s. 6d.

Fay (T. S.)—The Three Germanys : Glimpses into their History.  Two vols. 8vo. cloth.  *New York.*  £1 16s.

Ferguson (Kate L.)—Cliquot.  12mo. paper.  *Philadelphia.*  1s. 6d.

Ferrell (W.)—A Popular Treatise on the Winds.  Comprising the General Motions of the Atmosphere, Monsoons, Cyclones, Tornadoes, Waterspouts, Hail-storms, etc., etc.  By William Ferrell, M.A., Ph.D., late Professor and Assistant in the Signal Service, Member of the National Academy of Sciences, and of other Home and Foreign Scientific Societies.  8vo. cloth.  Illustrated.  *New York.*

Flippin (J. R.)—Sketches from the Mountains of Mexico.  12mo. cloth.  *Cincinnati.*  7s. 6d.

Foster (R. V.)—A Brief Introduction to the Study of Theology.  12mo. cloth.  *New York.*  6s.

Fowler (N. C.)—About Advertising and Printing.  8vo. cloth.  *Boston.*  10s.

**Goss (W. L.)**—Jed : a Boy's Adventures in the Army of '61-'65 ; a Story of Battle and Prison, of Peril and Escape. 12mo. cloth. *New York.* 7*s.* 6*d.*

**Grimshaw (R.)**—Hints on House Building. Some Desultory Notes, in Popular Form, mostly Reprinted from the *Mechanical News.* Second Enlarged Edition. 16mo. cloth. *New York.* 2*s.* 6*d.*

**Gudrun** : a Mediæval Epic. Translated from the Middle High German by Mary Pickering Nichols. 8vo. cloth. *Boston.* 12*s.* 6*d.*

**Hartley (J. S., D.D.)**—Sundays in the Adirondacks. 12mo. cloth. *Utica (N. Y.).* 6*s.*

**Hawthorne (N.)**—The Grey Champion, and other Stories and Sketches. 16mo. cloth. *Boston.* 6*s.*

*** The Riverside Aldine Series.

**Hearn (L.)**—Chita : a Memory of Last Island. 12mo. cloth. *New York.* 6*s.*

**Heaven (Louise P.)** Chata and Chinita. A Novel. 12mo. cloth. *Boston.* 7*s.* 6*d.*

**Hogue (A.)**—The Irregular Verbs of Attic Prose. their Forms, Prominent Meanings, and Important Compounds. Together with Lists of Related Words and English Derivatives. 12mo. cloth. *Boston.* 6*s.*

**Howells (W. D.)**—Character and Comment. Selected from the Novels of W. D. Howells by Minnie Macoun. 16mo. cloth. *Boston.* 6*s.*

**Hunter (T.) and Patten (J.)**—Port Charges and Requirements on Vessels in the Various Ports of the World. New revised and enlarged edition. 8vo. cloth. *New York.* £2 10*s.*

**Klemm (L. R.)**—European Schools ; or, What I Saw in the Schools of Germany, France, Austria, and Switzerland. 12mo. cloth. *New York.* 10*s.*

**Knox (T. W.)**—The Boy Travellers in Mexico. Adventures of Two Youths in a Journey to Northern and Central Mexico, Campeachy, and Yucatan ; with a Description of the Republics of Central America and of the Nicaragua Canal. 8vo. cloth. Illustrated. *New York.* 15*s.*

**Lindsay (Margaret I.)**—The Lindsays of America. A Genealogical Narrative and Family Record ; beginning with the Family of the Earliest Settler in the Mother State, Virginia, and including in an Appendix all the Lindsays of America. 8vo. cloth. *Albany (N. Y.).* £1 10*s.*

**Longfellow (H. W.)**—Ballads, Lyrics and Sonnets from the Poetic Works of H. W. Longfellow. 16mo. cloth. *Boston.* 6*s.*

**McGuire (Mrs. J. W.)**—Diary of a Southern Refugee During the War. By a Lady of Virginia. Third Edition, with Corrections and Additions. 12mo. cloth. *Richmond (Va.).* 9*s.*

**Man.** A Philosophical Treatise on the Human Race. In Three Books. 12mo. cloth. *St. Louis.* 9*s.*

**Miles (M.)**—Silos Ensilage and Silage. A Practical Treatise on the Ensilage of Fodder Corn. Crown 8vo. cloth. Illustrated. *New York.* 2*s.* 6*d.*

**Morgan (H. H.)**—English and American Literature for Schools and Colleges. 12mo. cloth. *New York* and *Boston.* 6*s.*

**Morris (H., M.D.)**—Essentials of Materia Medica, Therapeutics, and Prescription Writing ; arranged in the Form of Questions and Answers. Prepared especially for Students of Medicine. 12mo. cloth. *Philadelphia.* 6*s.*

**Morse (J. T., jun.)**—Benjamin Franklin. 12mo. cloth. *Boston.* 6*s.* 6*d.*

**Moses (B.)**—The Federal Government of Switzerland. An Essay on the Constitution. 12mo. cloth. *Oakland, (California).* 9*s.*

**New York.**—Annotated Code of Civil Procedure of the State of New York, as in force July 1, 1889, with Copious Notes, containing Full Abstracts of the Adjudications ; and Copies of, or References to, all other Statutes relating to the subject of Civil Procedure, to the Close of the Legislative Session of 1889 ; also numerous useful Tables and Appendices. 8vo. sheep. *New York.* £2 5*s.*

**New York.**—Annotated Code of Criminal Procedure and Penal Code, as amended, 1882-9. Eighth Edition Revised (etc.) with Index and Supplement of Notes and Decisions down to June 1, 1889. Edited by G. R. Donnan. 8vo. sheep. *Albany.* £1 10*s.*

**New York.**—Code of Civil Procedure as Amended to, and Including, 1889. Fifth Edition, with References to Code Decisions to July 1, 1889. By C. D. Rust. 12mo. sheep. *New York.* £1 1*s.*

**New York.**—Code of Criminal Procedure as Amended to, and Including, 1889. Fourth Edition, with Reference to Decisions. By C. D. Rust. 12mo. sheep. *New York.* 9*s.*

**New York.**—The Code of Civil Procedure, with Notes by Montgomery H. Throop, containing all the Amendments to and including the year 1889. 8vo. sheep. *Albany.* £1 16*s.*

**New York.**—The Code of Criminal Procedure as Amended, including 1889 ; with Notes of Decisions, a Table of Sources, complete Set of Forms, and a full Index. Ninth Revised Edition. 18mo. cloth. *New York.* 9*s.*

**New York.**—The Penal Code of the State of New York in Force Dec. 1, 1882, as Amended by Laws of 1882-1889, with Notes of Decisions, a Table of Sources, and Index. Ninth Revised Edition. 18mo. cloth. *N. York.* 9*s.*

**New York.**—Parsons' Complete Annotated Pocket Code. The New York Code of Civil Procedure. Complete in One Volume, Chapters 1-22, with Notes and References to June 1, 1889. Fourteenth Edition. 18mo. leatherette. *Albany.* £1 1*s.*

**Needle and Brush,** Useful and Decorative. 8vo. cloth. *New York.* 6*s.*

**Oregon.**—The Laws of Oregon and the Resolutions and Memorials of the Fifteenth Regular Session of the Legislative Assembly thereof, 1889. 8vo. half sheep. *Salem.* 18*s.*

**Parvin (T., M.D.)** — Obstetric Nursing. Lectures delivered at the Training-School for Nurses of the Philadelphia Hospital. New Edition, Revised and Enlarged. 12mo. cloth. *Philadelphia.* 4*s.*

**Peattie (Mrs. E. W.)** — The Story of America. Romantic Incidents of History from the Discovery of America to the Present Time. 8vo. cloth. Illustrated. *Chicago.* £1 8*s.*

**Phyfe (W. H. P.)**—Seven Thousand Words often Mispronounced. A Complete Handbook of Difficulties in English Pronunciation ; including an unusually large number of Proper Names and Words and Phrases from Foreign Languages. 16mo. cloth. *New York.* 6*s.* 6*d.*

**Pittenger (Rev. W.)**—The Interwoven Gospels. The Four Histories of Jesus Christ blended into a Complete and Continuous Narrative in the Words of the Gospels according to the American Revised Version 1881. 12mo. cloth. *New York.* 6*s.*

Platt (Rev. W. H.)—Is Religion Dying? A Symposium; an Hour with the Philosophers. 12mo. cloth. *Washington.* 6*s.*

Publishers' Trade List Annual, 1889. The Latest Catalogues of American Book Publishers; preceded by a Complete List, by Authors, Titles. and Subjects, of Books recorded in *The Publishers' Weekly*, January-June, 1889, and by the American Educational Catalogue for 1889. Seventeenth Year. Royal 8vo. cloth. *New York.* 10*s.*

Putnam (D.) — Elementary Psychology; or, First Principles of Mental and Moral Science: for High Schools, Normal and other Secondary Schools, and for Private Study. 12mo. cloth. *New York.* 5*s.*

Richards (J.)—A Manual of Machine Construction for Engineers, Draughtsmen, and Mechanics, Embracing Examples, Rules. Tables, and References. 16mo. leather. *Philadelphia.* £1 5*s.*

Saltus (E.) — The Pace That Kills : a Chronicle. 12mo. cloth. *Chicago.* 5*s.*

Scudder (S. H.)—The Butterflies of the Eastern United States and Canada; with Special Reference to New England. 3 vols. 4to. hf. levant. *Cambridge (Mass.).* £15 15*s.*

Seilhamer (G. O.)—History of the American Theatre during the Revolution and after. 4to. cloth. *Philadelphia.* £1 5*s.*
The first volume of this work was published last year under the title "History of the American Theatre before the Revolution." The present volume comprises the period between 1774 and 1792. another one being promised to bring the narrative down to the present day. The work is a most comprehensive and minute account of the various American companies, actors, etc., and the plays in which they appeared in the principal cities of the United States. Interesting play-bills, casts of plays, epilogues, etc., are included in the narrative.

Smith (H.) — A Century of American Literature. Benjamin Franklin to James Russell Lowell. Selections from a Hundred Authors. 12mo. cloth. *New York.* 6*s.*

Steele (J. D.)—The Chautauqua Course in Physics. 12mo. cloth. *New York.* 6*s.*
*₀* Chautauqua Text-books.

Sutherland (E.) — The Destiny of America. The Inevitable Political Union of the United States and Canada. 8vo. paper. *Washington.* 1*s.* 6*d.*

Thayer (E.)—A History of the Kansas Crusade : Its Friends and its Foes. Introduction by Rev. E. Everett Hale. 12mo. cloth. *New York.* 7*s.* 6*d.*

Thompson (A. C.)—Foreign Missions. Their Place in the Pastorate, in Prayer, in Conferences. Ten Lectures. 12mo. cloth. *New York.* 9*s.*

Thoreau (H. D.)—Walden. 2 vols. 16mo. cloth. *Boston.* 10*s.*
*₀* Riverside Aldine Series.

Tillman (S. E.)—Elementary Lessons in Heat. 8vo. cloth. *Philadelphia.* 9*s.*

Tincker (Mary A.) — Two Coronets. 12mo. cloth. *Boston.* 7*s.* 6*d.*

Townsend (L. T., D.D.)—The Bible and other Ancient Literature in the Nineteenth Century. 16mo. cloth. *New York.* 2*s.* 6*d.*
*₀* Chautauqua Text-books.

True (F. W.)—Contributions to the Natural History of the Cetaceans. A Review of the Family Delphinidæ. 8vo. paper. *Washington.*

United States Commission of Fish and Fisheries. Spencer F. Baird, Commissioner. The Fisheries and Fishery Industries of the United States. Prepared through the Co-operation of the Commissioner of Fisheries and the Superintendent of the Tenth Census. By George Brown Goode, Assistant Secretary of the Smithsonian Institution, and a Staff of Assistants. Section I. Natural History of Useful Aquatic Animals. With an Atlas of Two Hundred and Seventy-seven Plates. Two. vols. 4to. cloth, pp. xxxiv. and 895. *Washington.* £4 4*s.*

Section II. A Geographical Review of the Fisheries Industries and Fishing Communities for the Year 1880. 4to. cloth, pp. ix. and 787. *Washington.*

Sections III. and IV. The Fishing Grounds of North America. With Forty-nine Charts. Edited by Richard Rathbun. (And) The Fishermen of the United States. By G. B. Goode and Joseph W. Collins. With 19 Plates. 4to. cloth, pp. xviii. 238 and 178. *Washington.*

Section V. History and Method of the Fisheries. In Two Volumes. With an Atlas of Two Hundred and Fifty Plates. Three vols. 4to. cloth, pp. xxii. and 808, xx. and 881. *Washington.*

United States.—Index Catalogue of the Library of the Surgeon-General's Office. Authors and Subjects. Vol. 10. O-Pfutsch. 4to. cloth. pp. 1059. *Washington.*

United States.—Interstate Commerce Commission. First Annual Report on the Statistics of Railways in the United States to the Interstate Commerce Commission for the Year ending June 30, 1888. 8vo. cloth. *Washington.*

Van Dyke (J. C.)—How to Judge of a Picture. Familiar Talks in the Gallery with Uncritical Lovers of Art. 16mo. cloth. *New York.* 5*s.*
*₀* Chautauqua Text-books.

Van Rensselaer (Mrs. S.)—Six Portraits: Della Robbia, Correggio, Blake, Corot, George Fuller, Winslow Homer. 12mo. cloth. *Boston.* 6*s.* 6*d.*

Vincent (J. H.) and Joy (J. R.)—An Outline History of Rome. 16mo. cloth. *New York.* 6*s.* 6*d.*
*₀* Chautauqua Text-books.

Wallack (J. L.)—Memories of Fifty Years. With an Introduction by Laurence Hutton. 12mo. cloth. *New York.* 7*s.* 6*d.*

Watson (P. B.)—The Swedish Revolution under Gustavus Vasa. 8vo. cloth. *Boston.* 12*s.* 6*d.*

West (N., D.D.)—Studies in Eschatology ; or, The Thousand Years in both Testaments, with Supplementary Discussions upon Symbolical Numbers, the Development of Prophecy and its Interpretation concerning Israel, the Nations, the Church, and the Kingdom, as seen in the Apocalypses of Isaiah, Ezekiel, Daniel, Christ, and John. 12mo. cloth. *New York.* 10*s.*

Wickson (E. J.)—The California Fruits and How to Grow Them. A Manual of Methods which have Yielded Greatest Success ; with Lists of Varieties best adapted to the different Districts of the State. 8vo. cloth. pp. viii. and 575. With Numerous Plates and Illustrations in the Text. *San Francisco.* 18*s.*

Wilkinson (W. C.)—Preparatory and College Latin Courses in English. Condensed and Consolidated. 8vo. cloth. *New York.* 8*s.* 6*d.*
*₀* Chautauqua Text-books.

Witthaus (R. A., M.D.)—A Laboratory Guide in Urinalysis and Toxicology. Second Edition. Revised, with Additions, including a Plate illustrating the Colours of Urine. 12mo. cloth. *New York.* 5*s.*

---

# European Literature.

Abel (Prof. Carl).—Ueber Wechselbeziehungen der aegyptischen, indoeuropäischen und semitischen Etymologie. Vol. I. (3 Parts.) 8vo. *Leipsig,* 1889. 20*s.*

Part I. Pott (A. Fr.) Allgemeine Sprachwissenschaft. 3 M. —II. Spiegel (F. von) Die arische Periode und ihre Zustände. 12 M.—III. Bruchmann (K.) Psychologische Studien zur Sprachgeschichte. 9 M.

Abel (Carl).—Einleitung in ein ägyptisch-semitisch-indoeuropäisches Wurzelwörterbuch. 4to. pp. 524. *Leipzig*, 1887. £5 6s.

Abou'l-Walid Merwan Ibn Djanah.—Le Livre des parterres fleuris, d'Abou'l-Walid Merwan Ibn Djanah. Traduit en français sur les manuscrits arabes par le rabbin Moïse Metzger. Royal 8vo. pp. xv. 435. *Angers*, 1889. 15s.
*₊* Bibliothèque de l'Ecole des hautes études, Fasc. 81.

Amélineau (E.)—Monuments pour servir à l'histoire de l'Egypte chrétienne au IVᵉ siècle. Histoire de Saint Pakhôme et de ses communautés. Documents coptes et arabes inédits, publiés et traduits. 4to. pp. cxii. 712. *Paris*, 1889. £3.
*₊* Annales du Musée Guimet, vol. xvii.

Annales (les) impériales de l'Annam. Traduites en entier pour la première fois du texte chinois par Abel Des Michels. Fasc. I. Royal 8vo. pp. xi. 60. *Paris*, 1889.

Annales du Musée Guimet, *vide* Amélineau and Lefébure.

Arrivet (A.)—Dictionnaire Français-Japonais. Des mots usuels de la langue française. Revu avec soin par S. Omayada. 8vo. *Paris*, 1889. 6s.

Aubry (J. B.)—Les Chinois chez eux. Royal 8vo. pp. 300. *Lille*, 1889.

Bacher (W.)—Aus der Schrifterklärung der Abulwalid Merwân Ibn Ganah (R. Jona). 8vo. pp. vi. 104. *Leipzig*, 1889. 4s.

Bargès (J. J. L.)—Inscriptions arabes qui se voyaient autrefois dans la ville de Marseille. Nouvelle interprétation et commentaire. 8vo. pp. 83. With Facsimiles. *Paris*, 1889.

Beiträge zur Assyriologie und vergleichenden semitischen Sprachwissenschaft. Herausg. von F. Delitzsch und P. Haupt. Vol. I. Fasc. 1. Royal 8vo. pp. 368. With Portrait. *Leipzig*, 1889. £1 3s.

Boetticher (E.) — La Troie de Schliemann. Une Nécropole à incinération à la manière assyro-babylonienne. 8vo. *Leipzig*, 1889. 6s.

Brugsch (Prof. H.)—Die Aegyptologie. Ein Grundriss der ägyptischen Wissenschaft. Fasc. I. Royal 8vo. *Leipzig*, 1889. 10s.

Brun (J.) et J. Tempère. — Diatomées fossiles du Japon. Espèces marines et nouvelles des calcaires argilleux de Sendaï et de Yedo. Royal 4to. pp. 75. With 9 Plates. (Reprint.) *Bassel*, 1889. 12s.

Brunnhofer (H.)—Iran und Turan. Historisch-geographische und ethnologische Untersuchungen über den ältesten Schauplatz der indischen Urgeschichte. 8vo. pp. xxvii. 250. *Leipzig*, 1889. 9s.

Bugge (Sophus).—Beiträge zur etymologischen Erläuterung der Armenischen Sprache. 8vo. *Christiania*, 1889. 1s. 6d.

Casey (D.)—Colonies françaises Guyane. Notes de Voyage. 8vo. pp. 32. *Paris*, 1889.

Chine (la) et ses provinces. I. Yun-Nan. II. Thibet. III. Le Su-Tchuen. IV. Kouy-Tchéou. V. Kouang-Si. VI. Kouang Tong. VII. Macao. VIII. Hong-Kong. IX. Amoy, Fo-Kien et Formose. X. Tché-Kian et Kiang-Si. XI. Missions Franciscaines. XII. Kiang-Nan. XIII. Ho-Nan. XIV. Pé-Tché-Ly. XV. Missions belges. XVI. Mandchourie. XVII. Corée. 8vo. pp. 104. *Lille*, 1889.

Collections scientifiques de l'Institut des langues orientales du Ministère des affaires étrangères, V. 8vo. pp. xxxvii. 136. With a Plate. *Leipzig*, 1889. 7s.
*₊* Containing Catalogue des monnaies Arsacides, Subarsacides, Sassanides, etc., par A. de Markoff.

Colonies (les) françaises. Notices illustrées. Publiées par ordre du sous-secrétaire d'Etat des colonies sous la direction de M. I. Henrique. II. Colonies d'Amérique, Martinique, Guadeloupe, Saint Pierre et Miquelon, Guyane. 8vo. pp. 432. Avec gravures et carte. *Paris*, 1889. 3s. 6d.

Colonies (les) françaises. Notices illustrées. Publiées par ordre du sous-secrétaire d'Etat des colonies. III. Colonies et protectorats d'Indo-Chine, Cochinchine, Cambodge, Annam, Tonkin. 8vo. pp. 430. With Illustrations and 3 Maps. *Paris*, 1889. 3s. 6d.

Des Michels. — Quelques observations au sujet des sens des mots chinois *giao chi*, nom des ancêtres du peuple Annamite. 8vo. pp. 19. *Paris*, 1889.

Dieulafoy (M.)—L'art antique de la Perse. Part V. Monuments Parthes, Sassanides. Royal 4to. pp. 244. With 22 Plates and 122 Illustrations. *Paris*, 1889. £1 15s.
*₊* The work will be completed in those five parts. The price of the complete work is £9.

Dupont (E.)—Lettres sur le Congo. Récit d'un voyage scientifique entre l'embouchure du fleuve et le confluent du Kassaï. 8vo. *Paris*, 1889. 15s.

Dvořák (R.)—Husn u dil (Beauty and Heart). Persiache Allegorie von Fattâhi aus Nisâpûr. Herausgegeben, übersetzt, erklärt und mit Lámi'i's türkischer Bearbeitung verglichen. Royal 8vo. pp. 160. (Reprint.) *Leipzig*, 1889. 2s. 6d.

Ebers (G.)—Papyrus Ebers. Die Maasse und das Kapitel über die Augenkrankheiten. Royal 8vo. pp. 204. *Leipzig*, 1889. 10s.
*₊* Abhandlungen der philol.-histor. Classe der königl. sächsischen Gesellschaft der Wissenschaften XI. 2 und 3.

Edlinger (A. von)—Ueber die Bildung der Begriffe eines etymologisch-vergleichenden Wörterbuches aller Sprachgebiete. Fasc. I. *München*, 1889. 2s.

Enemann (M.)—Resa i Orienten, 1711-1712. Utg. af k. U. Nylander. 8vo. *Upsala*, 1889.

Errington de la Croix (J.)—Vocabulaire français-malais et malais-français. Précédé d'un Précis de grammaire malaise par le Dr. J. Montano. 8vo. pp. xlviii. 266. *Laval*, 1889.

Feige (H.)—Die Geschichte des Mâr 'Abhdîšôr und seines Jüngers Mâr Qardagh. Aus den Handschriften textkritisch herausgegeben, übersetzt und erlautert. 8vo. *Kiel*, 1889. 6s.

Franke (R. Otto).—Die indischen Genuslehren. Mit dem Text der Liṅgânuçâsana's des Çâkaṭâyana, Harṣavardhana, Vararuci. Nebst Auszügen aus den Commentaren des Yakṣavarman (zu Ç.) und des Çabarasvâmin (zu H.), und mit einem Anhang über die indischen Namen. Roy. 8vo. pp. 155. *Kiel*, 1890. 9s.

Groff (W. N.)—Quelques observations sur mon étude sur le papyrus d'Orbiney. 4to. pp. 8. *Paris*, 1889. 6s.

Hetley (Mdme. Ch.) et E. Raoul.—Fleurs sauvages et bois précieux de la Nouvelle-Zélande. *Paris*, 1889. £4 10s.

Hovelacque (A.)—Les Nègres de l'Afrique suséquatoriale (Sénégambie, Guinée, Soudan, Haut-nil). 8vo. pp. xiv. 468. With Illustrations. *Paris*, 1889.

Jolly (J.)—Der Vyavahârâdhyâya aus Hârita's Dharmaśâstra nach Citaten zusammengestellt. 4to. *München*, 1889. 1s.

Khândogjopanishad. — Kritisch herausgegeben und übersetzt von O. Böhtlingk. 8vo. *Leipzig*, 1889. 12s.

Kirste (J.)—The Grihyasutra of Hiranyakeśin. With Extracts from the Commentary of Matridatta. Edited by J. K. Roy. 8vo. pp. xi. 177, 42. *Wien*, 1889. 10s.

Kubary (J. S.) — Ethnographische Beiträge zur Kenntniss des Karolinen Archipels. Veröffentlicht im Auftrage der Direction des Kgl. Museums für Völkerkunde zu Berlin. Unter Mitwirkung von J. D. E. Schmeltz. *Leiden*, 1889. £1 7*s.* 6*d.*

Laillet (L.) et L. Suberbie.—Carte de Madagascar. D'après leurs documents personnels complétés à l'aide des cartes de la marine et les itinéraires suivis par divers voyageurs. Scale, 1 to 1,000,000. *Paris*, 1889. 15*s.*

Lefébure (M. E.)—Les Hypogées royaux de Thèbes. Seconde Division. Notices des Hypogées. Publiée par E. Naville et E. Schiaparelli. 4to. *Paris*, 1889. £2.
*₊* Annales du Musée Guimet, vol. xvi. 1.

Lefébure (M. E.)—Les Hypogées royaux de Thèbes. Troisième division : Tombeau de Ramsès IV. 4to. pp. viii. With 41 Plates and Appendices. *Paris*, 1889. £1
*₊* Annales du Musée Guimet, vol. xvi. 2.

Manuel du Sinologue. Publié par la Société sinico-japonaise. Part I. 8vo. *Paris*, 1889. 6*s.*

Markoff (A. de)—Catalogue des monnaies Arsacides, Subarscides, Sassanides, etc. (Institut des langues orientales.) *Leipzig*, 1889. 7*s.*

Martius (C. F. Ph. v.), A. W. Eichler und J. Urban.— Flora brasiliensis. Enumeratio plantarum in Brasilia hactenus detectarum. Fasc. CVI. Folio, pp. 60. With 9 Plates. *Leipzig*, 1889. 12*s.*

Maspéro (M. G.)—La Mythologie égyptienne. Les travaux de MM. Brugsch et Lanzone. 8vo. pp. 70. *Paris*, 1889. 3*s.* 6*d.*
*₊* Extrait de la Revue de l'histoire des religions.

Matthes (R. F.)—Supplement op het Boegineesch-Hollandsch Woordenboek. 8vo. *The Hague*, 1889. 6*s.*

Merx (A.)—Historia artis grammaticae apud Syros. Composuit et edidit. Royal 8vo. pp. x. 291. With Fac-similes. *Leipzig*, 1889. 16*s.*
*₊* Abhandlungen für die Kunde des Morgenlandes, vol. ix. 2.

Metall-Gefässe (Altindische).—Aus der Sammlung des Bayerischen Gewerbemuseums. Herausg. v. Bayer. Gewerbemuseum in Nürnberg. Roy. 4to. pp. iv. 68. With Illustrations. *Nürnberg*, 1889. 10*s.*

Metzger (M.)—Le Livre des Parterres fleuris d'Abou'l-Walid Merwan ibn Djanah. Traduit en français. 8vo. pp. xv. 435. *Paris*, 1889. 15*s.*

Meyer (W.)—Grammaire des langues romanes. Traduction française par E. Rabiet. Tome I. : Phonétique. 1re Partie : Les voyelles. Royal 8vo. pp. 256. *Paris*, 1889. 20*s.*

Miklosich (F.)—Die slavischen, Magyarischen und rumunischen Elemente im türkischen Sprachschatze. 8vo. pp. 26. (Reprint.) *Leipzig*, 1889.

Müller (D. H.)—Epigraphische Denkmäler aus Arabien. Roy. 4to. pp. 96. With 12 Plates. (Reprint.) *Leipzig*, 1889. 10*s.*

Ollivier-Beauregard. — En Orient. Etudes ethnologiques et linguistiques à travers les ages et les peuples. 8vo. pp. vii. 252. *Paris*, 1889. 10*s.*

Oriental Congress. — Tafelkarte zum VIII. internationalen Orientalisten-Kongress zu Stockholm. Pp. 46. *Stockholm*, 1889. 18*s.*

Qaradagʼi (M. G.)—Neupersische Schauspiele. Fasc. I. Monsieur Jourdan, der Pariser Botaniker, im Qarabâgʼ. Neupersisches Lustspiel. Persischer Text, mit wörtlicher deutscher Uebersetzung, Anmerkungen und vollständigem Wörterverzeichniss, zum Gebrauche der k. k. öffentlichen Lehranstalt für orientalische Sprachen, herausgegeben von A. Wahrmund. Royal 8vo. pp. viii. 36, 34, 30. *Wien*, 1889. 4*s.*

Raoul (E.)—Javanais et Javanieses an Kampong de l'Exposition universelle. 8vo. pp. 32. With Illustrations. *Paris*, 1889.

Raoul (E.)—Annamites et Tonkinois. 8vo. pp. 23. With Illustrations. *Paris*, 1889.

Revillout (E.)—Catalogue de sculpture égyptienne. 8vo. pp. 72. *Paris*, 1889.

Saadeddin et Hassan Edigué. — Alphabet turc. Expliqué en français et suivi de nombreux exercises de lecture et d'orthographie. 8vo. pp. 38. *Constantinople*, 1889. 1*s.*

Schefer (C.) — Quelques chapitres de l'abrégé du Seldjouq Nameh, composé par l'émir Nassir Eddin Yahia. 8vo. pp. 104. With Facsimiles. *Paris*, 1889.
*₊* Extrait du Recueil de textes et de traductions, publié par les professeurs de l'Ecole des langues orientales vivantes.

Schlagintweit (E.)—Indien in Wort und Bild. Eine Schilderung des indischen Kaiserreiches. 2. Aufl. With 417 Illustrations. Fasc. 1. 4to. pp. 12. *Leipzig*, 1889.
*₊* The work will be complete in 45 Fasc. Price of each Fasc. 6*d.*

Schuré (E.)—Les Grands Initiés. Esquisse de l'histoire secrète des religions (Rama, Krishna, Hermès, Moïse, Orphée, Pythagore, Platon, Jésus). 8vo. pp. xxxii. 554. *Lagny*, 1889.

Sprenger (A.)—Mohammed und der Koran. Eine psychologische Studie. 8vo. *Hamburg*, 1889. 1*s.* 6*d.*

Strebel (H.)—Alt-Mexiko. Archaeologische Beiträge zur Kulturgeschichte seiner Bewohner. Vol. II. Roy. 4to. pp. iii. 169. With 34 Plates and 24 Illustrations. In cover. *Hamburg*, 1889. £5.

Tausend und Eine Nacht. Neue illustrirte Pracht-Ausgabe. Uebersetzt von Dr. G. Weil. Four vols. 4to. With 718 Illustrations. *Stuttgart*, 1889. 14*s.*
*₊* A complete translation from the original Arabic. Copies in original binding are to be had at 20*s.*

De Villaret (E.)—Dai Nippon. (Le Japon.) 8vo. With 3 Maps. *Paris*, 1889.

Vitale (Ed.)—Grammatica cinese. Con temi, letture e piccolo vocabolario, non chè tavola delle 214 chiavi. Parte I. 8vo. pp. 114. *Napoli*, 1888. 16*s.* 6*d.*

Wahrmund (A.)—Praktisches Handbuch der neupersischen Sprache. 2. Aufl. Mit Schlüssel. Royal 8vo. pp. xxiii. 324 ; 28 ; vii. 99 and vii. 84. *Giessen*, 1889. 14*s.*

Winckler (H.)—Der Thontafelfund von El Amarna I. herausgegeben. Nach den Originalen autographiert von L. Abel. 33 Metallographic Plates. With Preface and Index by H. Winckler. Folio. *Berlin*, 1889. 20*s.*
*₊* Mittheilungen aus den orientalischen Sammlungen königl. Museen zu Berlin, Fasc. I.

Zaeslin (E.)—Indien und Indier. Reiseblätter. 8vo. *Basel*, 1889. 2*s.*

Zein-el-Asnam. —Conte des Mille et une Nuits. Extrait des manuscrits de la Bibliothèque nationale. Texte arabe, entièrement vocalisé, et vocabulaire arabe, anglais et français des mots contenus dans le texte par Florenco Groff. 8vo. pp. 98. *Paris*, 1889. 6*s.*

Zeitschrift für afrikanische Sprachen. Herausgegeben von C. G. Büttner. Jahrgang II. 1889–90. Fasc. 1. Royal 8vo. pp. 80. Annual Subscription, 12*s.* *Berlin*, 1889.

Zobou (G.)—Correspondance et terminologie commerciales. Français et Turc. Comprenant 1° Vingt sections où sont consignées toutes sortes de lettres commerciales, modèles et formulaires. 2° Un vocabulaire des termes de commerce les plus importants. 8vo. pp. 400, 76. *Constantinople*, 1889. 7*s.* 6*d.*

# Oriental Literature.

## ANGLO-INDIA.

### (Miscellaneous.)

**Beverley (H.)**—The Land Acquisition Acts. Second Edition. 4to. pp. 165. *Calcutta*, 1888. 18s.

*₊* Act X. of 1870 and Act XVIII. of 1885. With introduction and notes.

**Bignold (T. F.)**—Leviora. Poetry. 8vo. pp. 207. *Calcutta*, 1888. 18s.

*₊* A collection of poetical pieces illustrating the miseries of official life of Englishmen in India.

**Blennerhassett (B. M.)**—Notes on First Aid to the Sick and Injured. 12mo. pp. 78. *Lahore*, 1889. 6s.

**Brown (T. E. B.)**—Punjab Poisons. New Edition. 8vo. pp. 220. *Lahore*, 1888. 12s. 6d.

**Cranenburgh (D. E.)**—The New Criminal Court Manual. 8vo. pp. 1298. *Calcutta*, 1888. £1 4s.

**Daji (Bhau)**.—Ram Chandra Ghosh. Preface to the Literary Remains of Dr. Bhau Daji. 8vo. pp. 64. *Calcutta*, 1888. 8s.

**Daji (Bhau)**.—The Literary Remains of Dr. Bhau Daji. Published by Rám Chandra Ghosh. 8vo. pp. 264. *Calcutta*, 1888. £1 10s.

*₊* Collected from various sources.

**Ghose (J. N.)**—Illusions and Hallucinations. New Edition. 8vo. pp. 36. *Lahore*, 1888. 7s. 6d.

**Gossain (H. M.)** and B. B. Bhattacharyya.—Notes on the History of England. 12mo. pp. 180. *Calcutta*, 1888. 2s. 6d.

**Ince's Kashmir Handbook.** Fourth Edition. By Joshua Duke. 8vo. pp. 337. With Maps. *Calcutta*, 1888. 18s.

**Indian (The) Contract Act.** No. IX. of 1872. Edited by H. S. Cunningham and H. Shephard. Fifth Edition. 8vo. pp. 605. *Calcutta*, 1888. £2 2s.

*₊* With an introduction and explanatory notes, table of contents, appendix, index, etc.

**Indian (The) Evidence Act.** No. I. of 1872. Edited by D. E. Cranenburgh. 8vo. pp. 99. *Calcutta*, 1888. 4s. 6d.

*₊* With notes of criminal cases decided by the several High Courts in India.

**Kipling (Rudyard)**.—Plain Tales from the Hills. 12mo. pp. 283. *Calcutta*, 1888.

**Kipling (Rudyard)**—Wee Willie Winkie and other Child Stories. 8vo. pp. 104. *Allahabad*, 1889. 3s. 6d.

**Leitner (G. W. von)**—The Hunza and Nagyr Handbook. Being an Introduction to a Knowledge of the Language, Race, and Countries of Hunza, Nagyr and a part of Yasin. Part I. Folio, pp. 247. *Calcutta*, 1889.

**Maude (C. N.)**—The Invasion and Defence of England. 12mo. pp. 69. *Calcutta*, 1888. 4s. 6d.

**Mehtá (Fateh Lál)**.—Handbook of Meywár, and Guide to its Principal Objects of Interest. 8vo. pp. 55. *Bombay*, 1889. 4s. 6d.

**Mitra (A. C.)**—The Hindu Law of Inheritance, Partition, Stridhan, and Wills. 8vo. pp. 177. *Calcutta*, 1888. 15s.

*₊* With leading cases from 1825 to 1888.

**Mukharji (T. N.)**—A Visit to Europe. With a Preface by N. N. Ghose. 8vo. cloth, pp. xii. 404. *Calcutta*, 1889. 8s.

**Saraswati (Pandit Prán Nath)**.—The Student's Indian Law Code. 8vo. pp. 1191. *Calcutta*, 1888. 18s.

*₊* All the Regulations and Acts of the Indian and Local Legislature included in the University B.L. Course.

**Sen (Keshab Chandra)**.—Diary in Madras and Bombay. 18mo. pp. 88. *Calcutta*, 1888. 2s.

**Sullivan (T. J.)**—The British and Indian Officer's Guide in Leave and Account Matters. 8vo. pp. 398. *Calcutta*, 1888. 18s.

**Thirty Years in the Harem.** 8vo. pp. 200. *Calcutta*, 1888. 14s.

*₊* A story of Turkish life.

**Thompson (Claude)**.—Notes on Tea in Darjeeling. 8vo. pp. 102. *Darjeeling*, 1888. 6s.

**Turnovers from the Civil and Military Gazette.** October to December, 1888. Published by the Editor. 8vo. pp. 109. *Lahore*, 1889. 6s.

## ARABIC.

انيس الجلساء في ديوان الخنساء **Diwân d'al-Hansâ.** Précédé d'une étude sur les femmes poètes de l'ancienne Arabie. 8vo. pp. 247. *Beirut*, 1888. 6s.

انيس الجلساء في ديوان الخنسا **Diwan (Le) d'al-Hansa.** Précédé d'une Etude sur les femmes poète des l'ancienne Arabie. Traduit par le P. de Coppier, S.J. 8vo. pp. cxiii. 228. *Beirut*, 1889. 6s. 6d.

فرائد اللغة . لجزء الاوّل : في الغر وني **Lammens** (le Père).—Philologie arabe. 1re Partie. Synonymes arabes. Texte arabe. 8vo. pp. 528. *Beirut*, 1889.

اقرب الموارد **Saïd El-Choury El-Chartouni.** Arabic Dictionary. Vol. I. Royal 8vo. pp. xvi. 729. *Beirut*, 1889. 17s. 6d.

*₊* The second volume is in the press.

مقامات بديع الزمان الهمذاني **Séances de Badi Uz-Zaman Il-Hamadani.** Commentées par le Cheïkh Mohammad 'Abdo. Royal 8vo. pp. viii. 206. *Beirut*, 1889. 10s. 6d.

**Lessan el Arab.** (Arabic Thesaurus.) Twenty Vols. *Boulaq (Le Caire)*.

*₊* Cet ouvrage comporte 20 volumes dont 14 sont finis. Il faudra de 18 mois à deux ans pour términer les autres.

**Qurán.**—In Arabic and Urdu. Lithographed. 12mo. pp. 740. *Delhi*, 1889. 14s.

**Qurán Majíd Mutarjam ma'i Tafsir-i-Husaini.** Lithographed. 4to. pp. 680. *Delhi*, 1889. 10s. 6d.

*₊* The Qurán in Arabic, Urdú and Persian. With Commentary by Husain.

**Qurán Majíd Mutarjam ma'i Múzih-ul-Quran.** 4to. pp. 900. *Delhi*, 1889. 6s.

*₊* The Qurán with translation and commentary in Arabic and Hindustani by Sháh 'Abdul Qádir.

Qurán.—Tafsír-i-Fath-ul-Mannán Mashhúr ba Tafsír-i-Haqqáni ka chauthá hissa. By Abu Muhammad 'Abdul Haq. 4to. pp. 228. *Delhi*, 1889. 12*s.* 6*d.*

**** A commentary of the Qurán in Arabic and Urdu.

Sunan Ibn-i-Májah. With Commentary by Fakhr-ul-Hasan. In Arabic. New Edition. 4to. pp. 332. *Delhi*, 1889. 7*s.* 6*d.*

**** Sayings of Muhammad. A collection of traditions.

Tafsír-i-Yasir Afghání. By Murád 'Ali. Arabic and Pushto. 8vo. pp. 808. *Delhi*, 1889. 12*s.* 6*d.*

**** An easy commentary in Afghani language.

'Uddat-ul-Hisn-ul-Hasín. By Shaikh Muhammad Jazri. In Arabic. 4to. pp. 44. *Delhi*, 1889. 1*s.* 6*d.*

**** Sayings of Muhammad. A book of traditions.


## CHINESE AND JAPANESE.

Hirth (F.)—Ancient Porcelain. A Study in Chinese Mediaeval Industry and Trade. 8vo. pp. 88. *Shanghai*, 1888. 3*s.* 6*d.*

Hirth (F.) — Wôn-Chien, Tzŭ-Chii Ju-Mén. Notes on the Chinese Documentary Style. 8vo. pp. vi. 150. *Shanghai*, 1888. 3*s.* 6*d.*

Journal (The) of the College of Science, Imperial University, Japan. Vol. III. Part. I. 4to. pp. 89. With 15 Plates. *Tôkyô*, 1889. 7*s.* 6*d.*

**** Contents : Jurassic Plants from Kaga, Hida, and Echizen. By Matajirō Yokoyama. With 14 plates.—On Pyroxenic Components in certain Volcanic Rocks from Bonin Island. By Yasushi Kikuchi. With 1 plate.

Journal (The) of the College of Science, Imperial University, Japan. Vol. III. Part 2. 4to. pp. 90 to 172. With 10 Plates. *Tôkyô*, 1889. 7*s.* 6*d.*

**** Contents: The Eruption of Bandai-San. By S. Sekiya and Y. Kikuchi. With 10 plates.

List (New) of Missionaries in China, Korea, and Siam. Corrected to March, 1889. 8vo. *Shanghai*, 1889. 1*s.* 6*d.*

Sydenstricker (Rev. A.)—A New Work for the Use of Learners of the Language. Being an Exposition of the Construction and Idioms of Chinese Sentences as found in the Colloquial Mandarin. 8vo. pp. 88. *Shanghai*, 1889. 6*s.*

Whitney (W. N.)—A Concise Dictionary of the Principal Roads, Chief Towns and Villages of Japan, with Populations, Post-Offices, etc. Together with Lists of Ken, Kuni, Kori, and Railways. Compiled from Official Documents. With Appendix. Demy 8vo. boards, pp. v. 248 and 167. With Map. *Tôkyô*, 1889. 8*s.*

Whitney (W. N.)—Appendix to a Concise Dictionary of the Principal Roads, Chief Towns and Villages of Japan. Demy 8vo. boards, pp. ii. 167. *Tokyo*, 1889. 3*s.*

**** Contents : The Constitution of Japan, and Laws Relating thereto, the Law for the Organization of Cities, Towns, and Villages, together with Statistical Information respecting Territory, Population, Agriculture, Industry, etc.

Williams (F. Wells).—The Life and Letters of S. Wells Williams, LL.D. By his Son. 8vo. pp. 490. *Shanghai*, 1889. £1 2*s.* 6*d.*


## GUJARATI.

Basalá (Behrámji Dosábhá).—A Travel in the World Within. In Gujaráti. 8vo. pp. 228. *Goora*, 1889. 6*s.*

**** A collection of the Eastern and Western moral and mental philosophy.

Dalál (D. D.)—Exhaustive Notes on Robinson Crusoe. English and Gujaráti. 12mo. pp. 136. *Surat*, 1889. 2*s.* 6*d.*

Desái (Barjorji Palanji).—History of the Achaemenides. In Gujaráti. Royal 8vo. pp. 516. *Bombay*, 1889. 12*s.* 6*d.*

**** Being a chronicle of the Pársi monarchs of the Achaemenian dynasty of ancient Persia.

Gargasanhitá.—Translated into Gujaráti by Baldevrám Krishnarám Bhatta. Royal 8vo. pp. 590. *Bombay*, 1889. 14*s.*

**** Adventures and exploits of the God Krishna.

Glossary (A Complete) of Words, Principal Parts of Grammar, together with a free Translation of 40 Lessons occurring in Howard's Second Book, Part II. By Moti Magan, Magan Zaver, etc. 8vo. pp. 128. *Ahmedabad*, 1888. 1*s.* 6*d.*

Howard's English Primer. Translated into Gujaráti. With Pronunciation of Words. By Bháidás Dámodardás. 8vo. pp. 48. *Bombay*, 1889. 1*s.*

Jáni (Bhagubhái Ramshankar).—Life of His Highness Mahárájá Sir Sayájiráo Gáikwár, G.C.S.I. 8vo. pp. 58. *Bombay*, 1889. 10*s.*

**** A short sketch of the life of the present Gáikwár Maharaja Sayajirao in Gujaráti.

Kávya Sudhákara, Pratham Bhág. By Mehetá Nathushankar Udayashankar Dholkiyá. In Gujarati. Part I. 8vo. pp. 188. *Ahmedabad*, 1889. 3*s.* 6*d.*

Moos (Ardeseer Frámji) and Nánábhai Rastamji Rániná. A Dictionary, English and Gujaráti. Part IX. Demy 4to. pp. 100. *Bombay*, 1889. 7*s.* 6*d.*

**** A useful work executed with much care and labour.

Mukti Malá, Jivarájajivana Mukti A'khyán, Bhág Pehelo. By Pránlál Shambhulál Desái. Part I. Roy. 8vo. pp. 98. *Broach*, 1888. 3*s.*

**** A drama in Gujaráti inculcating the doctrines of popular Vedántism.


## HINDI.

Bhárata Sára Bháshá.—Translated into Hindi by Pandit Gangádhar Pushkarlál. 4to. pp. 530. Lithographed. *Bombay*, 1889. 7*s.* 6*s.*

**** A Hindi translation of the abridgment of the Mahábhárata Purán by Vyása.

Premságar ; or, The Sea of Devotional Love. In Hindi. By Lallu Pandit. 4to. pp. 377. *Bombay*, 1889. 4*s.* 6*d.*

Sadi's Gulistan. In Hindi and Persian. 8vo. pp. 352. *Delhi*, 1889. 3*s.* 6*d.*

Satyá Mrita Praváh.—The Nectar Stream of Truth. By P. Sharadhá Rám. In Hindi. 8vo. pp. 264. *Delhi*, 1888. 15*s.*

## HINDUSTANI.

**Bahár-i-adad.**—The Spring of Morality. By Muhammad 'Umar and Muhammad 'Abdulla. In Urdú. 8vo. pp. 118. *Lahore*, 1888. 2*s.*

**Hayát-i-Sa'di.** By Altáf Husain. New Edition. 8vo. pp. 256. *Lahore*, 1889. 3*s. 6d.*

*₊* Life of the well-known Persian poet Sadi in Urdu.

**Ibn-ul-waqt.**—Son of Time. By Muhammad Nazír Ahmad. In Urdu. Lithographed. 8vo. pp. 224. *Delhi*, 1889. 3*s. 6d.*

**Injíl-i-Yúhanna kí tafsír.** By Rev. R. Clarke and Imám-ud-din. 4to. pp. 452. Lithographed. *Ludhiána*, 1889. 7*s. 6d.*

*₊* A commentary on the Gospel of St. John in Urdu.

**Majmú'a-i-Ta'zirát-i-Hind.** By 'Abd-ul-ahd. Lithographed. 8vo. pp. 238. 1889. 3*s. 6d.*

*₊* The Indian Penal Code in Hindustani.

**Mu'ín-i-tarjama 'Amoz.** By Saiyid 'Alí Sher. 8vo. pp. 112. *Ludhiána*, 1888. 1*s. 6d.*

*₊* A help to English translation in Urdu and English.

**Qurán.**—In Urdu and Arabic. Lithographed. 12mo. pp. 740. *Delhi*, 1889. 14*s.*

**Qurán Majíd, etc.** *Vide* Arabic.

**Tashíl-ut-tarjama.** By Mádho Náráyan. 8vo. pp. 64. *Delhi*, 1889. 1*s.*

*₊* Translation made easy in Hindustani and English.

## JAPANESE (*vide* CHINESE).

## PERSIAN.

**Báriá (Shápurjí Bhikháji).** — Manual of Persian Grammar. Compiled from various sources. New Edition. 12mo. pp. 175. *Bombay*, 1888. 2*s. 6d.*

**Karimá.** Persian. With Gujaráti and English Transliteration and Meanings of Every Word and Sentence. By Jijíbhái Kharsetji Kápadyá. 12mo. pp. 142. *Bombay*, 1889. 1*s. 6d.*

**Munshi (Ghulám Ahmad).**—Anglo-Persian Grammar in Catechism Form. Containing: 1. The Orthography. 2. The Accidence. 3. The Syntax and the Etymology. Second Edition Revised. Post 8vo. pp. viii. 120. *Bombay*, 1888. 3*s. 6d.*

**Sadi's Gulistan.** *Vide* Hindi.

**Sikander Náma.** With Commentary. In Persian. By Muhammad Ghufrán. Vol. II. 8vo. pp. 492. Lithographed. *Lahore*, 1889. 3*s. 6d.*

## SANSKRIT.

**Bhaktitatvámrita Grantha;** or, the Work on Substance of Devotion. Sanskrit Text with Maráthi Commentary. By Bálábová Dnyáneshvari. Oblong, 423 leaves. *Bombay*, 1889. 18*s.*

**Rámáyana of Valmiki.** With the Commentary of Rama. Parts I. and II. Royal 8vo. pp. 1482. *Bombay*, 1889. £1 4*s.*

*₊* A republication of the celebrated Indian epic.

**Ratanjankar (N. G.).**—A Guide to Sanskrit Sandhi. Demy 12mo. pp. 20. *Bombay*, 1888.

**Riksanhita Sáyanácharya Virachitá Bháshya Sahitá** Padapátha Yutácha Prathama Shtakah Dvitiyoshtakah. Edited by Rájárám Shástri Bodas and Shivrám Shástri Gore. Royal 8vo. pp. 1646. *Bombay*, 1889. £1 10*s.*

*₊* A republication of the most ancient sacred book of the Hindus.

**Sanskrit Text (The).**—With Full Notes and Translation. By F. R. Krishnacháriar. 8vo. pp. 32. *Bombay*, 1889. 1*s. 6d.*

**Shántikamalákarah.** By Kamalákar Bhatta Rámkrishna. Oblong, 228 leaves. *Poona*, 1889. 9*s.*

*₊* A republication of a learned treatise on Shantis or Pacificatory Ceremonies, which form an important branch of the ceremonial Hindu laws.

**Smriti Sár Sangraha.** By Rághu Nandan Bhattácháryya. Part I. 8vo. pp. 819. *Calcutta*, 1888. £1 10*s.*

*₊* A collection of Smriti compilations called the Nibandhas.

**Tantrasárah.**—The Substance of the Tantras. Bengali and Sanskrit. Translated by Kali Prasanna Bidayáratna. 8vo. pp. 402. *Calcutta*, 1888. 9*s.*

**Uttarámacharita.** By Bhavabhuti. Edited with English Notes by Shrinivás Govind Bhánap. 8vo. pp. 216. *Bombay*, 1888. 4*s.*

*₊* A Sanskrit drama describing the events in the Uttara Kánda of the Rámáyana.

**Vaiaheshik darshan.** By Kanád. Edited with Commentary by Gautam and Lekhráj. 8vo. pp. 46. *Lahore*, 1889. 3*s. 6d.*

*₊* A book on philosophy in Sanskrit.

**Yogakalpadrumah.** By Brahmánand Svámi. Sanskrit-Hindi Text. 12mo. pp. 286. *Bombay*, 1889. 2*s. 6d.*

*₊* A fabulous tree of Indra's Heaven yielding all information about spiritual devotion.

**Yogaratnákarah.** In Sanskrit. With a Preface by Dr. A'nná Moreshvarkunte. Royal 8vo. pp. 508. *Poona*, 1889. 15*s.*

*₊* Treatise on Hindu medicine published by several pandits.

---

### NOTICE TO CORRESPONDENTS.

All communications should be addressed to the *Editor of* "*Trübner's Record*," 57 and 59, Ludgate Hill, London, E.C., and they should be accompanied by the sender's name and address (not necessarily for publication). Every care will be taken with MSS., but the Editor cannot hold himself responsible for rejected communications, which—if to be returned to the sender—should be accompanied by postage. MS. should be legibly written, and on one side of the paper only. Books for review should be addressed to the Editor.

### NOTICE TO ADVERTISERS.

All communications respecting advertisements should be addressed to Messrs. F. TALLIS AND SON, 22, Wellington Street, W.C. *Terms for the insertion of advertisements:*—

| | | | |
|---|---|---|---|
| WHOLE PAGE (ordinary position) | ... | £5 | 5 0 |
| HALF PAGE | ,, | ,, ... | 2 15 0 |
| QUARTER PAGE | ,, | ,, ... | 1 10 0 |

Special positions per contract.

No. 248.

# TRÜBNER'S RECORD,

## A JOURNAL DEVOTED TO THE LITERATURE OF THE EAST.

WITH NOTES AND LISTS OF CURRENT

### American, European and Colonial Publications.

*Edited by Dr. Rost, of the India Office.*

FEBRUARY, 1890.  THIRD SERIES. VOL. I. NO. 6.  PRICE 2s.

## The Salt of Charity.

[This story is told in the Talmud of Rabbi Joohanan ben Zacchai and the daughter of Nicodemus ben Gorion.]

The Rabbi in the Holy City's streets
Met, clothed in the garments of the poor,
The child of one whose wealth was known to all.
And as she picked the scanty scattered grain
From off the dusty pathway of the street
He said to her, "Daughter, why this trade
For one whose playthings once were made of gold ?
Where are thy father's boasted riches now ?"
Then said the maiden with a saddened heart,
"Amidst my father's store of corn and oil
(Alas, that I who loved him have to say)
The salt was wanting that would keep it sweet.
For things unsalted haste to putrify,
And charity keeps riches from decay.
This did my father lack, and therefore I
Pick from the street the scattered grain for food.
'Tis salt of charity keeps riches pure ;
So from my sorrow may a proverb rise,
And rich men be the stewards of the poor."

WILLIAM E. A. AXON.

## A Siamese Version of "The House that Jack Built."

### By Dr. O. FRANKFURTER, Bangkok.

1. *Jăng mi jai kăb ta pluk thŭa nga xǫi hăi lăn făo. Lăn măi făo. Ka kin thŭa kin nga khóng jai khóng ta chĕt nĕt chĕt thŭnan. Jai ma jai dă ta ma ta ti.*

2. *"Păi păi há phì phran." "Phì phran khá phì phran xùai jĭng ka. Ka kin thŭa kin nga chĕt met chĕt thănan khóng jai khóng ta, iai ma jai dă ta ma ta ti."*

*"Kŏng kan ărăi khóng ku ? Măi rụ măi xị."*

3. *"Păi păi há phì nú." "Phì nú khá phì nú xùai kăt sái thănu phì phran. Phì phran măi jĭng ka." Ka kin—la—*

*"Kŏng kan ărăi khóng ku ? Măi rụ măi xị."*

4. *"Păi păi há phì mëo." "Phì mëo khá phì mëo xùai kăt nú. Nú măi kăt sái thănu phì phran." Phì phran—la—*

*"Kŏng kan ărăi khóng ku ? Măi rụ măi xị."*

5. *"Păi păi há phì má." "Phì má khá phì má xùai kăt mëo. Mëo măi kăt nú." Phì nú—la—*

*"Kŏng kan ărăi khóng ku ? Măi rụ măi xị."*

6. *"Păi păi há phì mǫi khọn." "Phì mǫi khọn khá phì mǫi khọn xùai jon hú má. Má măi kat mëo." Phì mëo—la—*

*"Kŏng kan ărăi khóng ku ? Măi rụ măi xị."*

7. *"Păi păi há phì făi." "Phì făi khá phì făi xùai măi mǫi khọn. Mǫi khọn măi jon hú má." Phì má—la—*

*"Kŏng kan ărăi khóng ku ? Măi rụ măi xị."*

8. *Păi păi há phì nạm." "Phì nạm khá phì nạm xùai dăb făi. Făi măi măi mǫi khọn." Phì măi khọn—la—*

*"Kŏng kan ărăi khóng ku ? Măi rụ măi xị."*

9. *"Păi păi há phì tălĭng." "Phì tălĭng khá phì tălĭng xùai thăb nạm. Nạm măi thăb făi." Phì făi—la—*

*"Kŏng kan ărăi khóng ku ? Măi rụ măi xị."*

10. *Păi păi há phì xạng." "Phì xạng khá phì xạng xùai thëng tălĭng. Tălĭng măi thăb nạm." Phì nạm—la—*

*"Kŏng kan ărăi khóng ku ? Măi rụ mă xị."*

11. *" Păi păi há phì mëng ฐ̃."　" Phì mëng
ฐ̃ khú phì mëng ฐ̃ xùai tom la xฺang. Xฺang
măi thëng tăลĩng tăลĩng măi thăb nฺam, nฺam
măi dăb făi, făi măi măi mฺai khฺon, mฺai khฺon
măi jon hú má, má măi kăt mëo, mëo măi kăt
nú, nú măi kăt sai thănu phì phran, phì phran
măi jĩng ka, ka kĭn thũa kĭn nga khóng jai
khòng ta chĕt mĕt chĕt thănan, jai ma jai dă,
la ma la ti."*

*" O' păi kŏ păi si."*

12. *Mëng ฐ̃ kŏ păi cha ฿ tom la xฺang. Phì
xฺang kŏ ฿d "jă tom xắn lòi kha ฿" xăn cha ฿
văl pai thëng tăลĩng; tăลĩng kŏ ฿d "jă thëng
xắn lòi kha ฿ xăn cha ฿ thăb nฺam" păi nฺam
kŏ răb dăb făi, făi kĭ răb măi mฺai khฺon, mฺai
khฺon răb jon hú má, má kăt mëo, mëo kăt nú,
nú kĭ rab kăt sai thănu phran, phran kŏ rab
jing ka, ka kĭ ฿d "jă jĩng xắn lòi kha ฿" ka
kŏ răb xฺai thũa khùn nga hăi sĕn thăo phan
thăvi lăn nฺoi kĭ khòi dăi di chŏb kăn thăo ni.*

*Translation.*

1. Once grandmother and grandfather planted beans
and teelseed and made the grandchild keep watch.
The grandchild did not keep watch, then the crow
came and ate seven grains and seven measures of
grandmother and grandfather's beans and teelseed.
Grandmother came, grandmother scolded, grandfather
came, grandfather beat.

2. "Go, go visit Brother Hunter."　"Oh, Brother
Hunter, please Brother Hunter, help to shoot the
crow ; the crow ate seven grains and seven measures
of grandmother and grandfather's beans and teelseed.
Grandmother came, grandmother scolded, grandfather
came, grandfather beat."

"What is that to me ?　Don't know, don't care. "

3. "Go, go visit Brother Mouse."　"Oh, Brother
Mouse, please Brother Mouse, help to bite the bowstring of Brother Hunter.　Brother Hunter does not
shoot the crow."　The crow, etc.

"What is that to me ?　Don't know, don't care. "

4. "Go, go visit Brother Cat."　"Oh, Brother Cat,
please Brother Cat, help to bite the mouse.　The
mouse does not bite the bowstring of Brother Hunter."
Brother Hunter, etc.

"What is that to me ?　Don't know, don't care. "

5. "Go, go visit Brother Dog."　"Oh, Brother Dog,
please Brother Dog, help to bite the cat.　The cat
does not bite the mouse."　The mouse, etc.

"What is that to me ?　Don't know, don't care. "

6. "Go, go visit Brother Earpick."　"Oh, Brother
Earpick, please Brother Earpick, please help to clean
the ear of the dog.　The dog does not bite the cat."
Brother Cat, etc.

"What is that to me ?　Don't know, don't care. "

7. "Go, go visit Brother Fire."　"Oh, Brother Fire,
please Brother Fire, help to burn the earpick.　The
earpick does not clear the ear of the dog."　Brother
Dog does, etc.

"What is that to me ?　Don't know, don't care. "

8. "Go, go visit Brother Water."　"Oh, Brother
Water, please Brother Water, help to extinguish the
fire.　The fire does not burn the earpick."　Brother
Earpick, etc.

"What is that to me ?　Don't know, don't care."

9. "Go, go visit Brother Strand."　"Oh, Brother
Strand, please Brother Strand, help to hem in the
water.　The water does not extinguish the fire.　Brother
Fire, etc.

"What is that to me ?　Don't know, don't care."

10. "Go, go visit Brother Elephant."　"Oh, Brother
Elephant, please Brother Elephant, help to put down
the strand.　The strand does not hem in the water."
Brother Water, etc.

"What is that to me ?　Don't know, don't care."

11. "Go, go visit Brother Gnat."　"Oh, Brother Gnat,
please Brother Gnat, help to sting the elephant's eye,
the elephant will not put down the strand, the strand
will not hem in the water, the water will not extinguish
the fire, the fire will not burn the earpick, the earpick
will not clean the ear of the dog, the dog will not bite
the cat, the cat will not bite the mouse, the mouse
will not bite the bowstring of brother hunter, brother
hunter will not shoot the crow, the crow ate seven
grains and seven measures of grandfather and grandmother's beans and teelseed, grandmother came, grandmother scolded, grandfather came, grandfather beat."

"All right, Ugh ! come on."

12. The gnat went to sting the eye of the elephant.
Then Brother Elephant said : "Don't sting me, please.
Your servant (I) will go and put down the strand."
The Strand then said : "Don't put me down, please.
Your servant will hem in the water, when the water
will extinguish the fire, and the fire will burn the
earpick, and the earpick clean the ear of the dog, and
the dog will bite the cat, and the cat will bite the
mouse, and the mouse will bite the bowstring of the
hunter, and the hunter will shoot the crow."　The

Crow said : "Don't shoot me, please. The crow will undertake to give back the beans and teelseed one hundred thousand fold and more." Little grandchild at last did its work well, and then the story comes to an end.

I have few remarks to add. The story is known all over Siam, and is as great a favourite here among children as *The House that Jack Built* is in Europe.

A gentleman who has been in Europe pretends that the story is not complete, that the gnat also refused to help the child, and that it then went to the Sun. The Sun-myth would be complete; but it must not be forgotten that the Sun must never be mentioned in such stories unless it is under a disguise, and what could be a better disguise than the sting of the gnat, *i.e.* the Sun's rays?

I prefer to leave the Sun elaboration to others.

With regard to the language. I will only mention that 'ku' 'I' is a contemptible term, whilst Xặn, which I translated with 'Your servant,' is a polite term. Phī means elder brother. It is a polite form of address.

I have used Pallegoix's transcription. This transcription has its great faults : letters historically different, which have now the same sound, are not distinguished : no heed is taken of final consonants, and thus the origin of words is still more obscured. A few examples will suffice : 'kan' is Sanskrit 'kāsa'; thānu 'bow,' is Sanskrit dhanus ; mǎi 'not,' is not distinguished from mǎi 'to burn.'

The difficulties which beset a uniform system of transliteration are very great, especially in languages which, like Siamese and Burmese, had to adopt a foreign alphabet. Pallegoix's system is a good working one. It is even now in use among the Roman Catholic converts themselves, of whom many only a few years ago did not even know the Siamese letters.

---

At the very same time that the above reached us from Siam, "The Critic" for November 23rd, 1889, was placed in our hands, which contains the English translation of another version of that Nursery Rhyme, the Aramaic original of which is found in the Haggadah, fol. 23.* We are enabled by the courtesy of Dr. Hoerning, of the Manuscript Department of the British Museum, to print along with the English version the Aramaic text.

---

* Nearly half a century ago Mr. J. O. Halliwell printed this version in "The Nursery Rhymes of England," and states in the introductory note : "The original of ' The House that Jack built' is presumed to be a hymn in *Sepher Haggadah*, fol. 23, a translation of which is here given. The historical interpretation was first given by P. N. Leberecht, at Leipsic in 1731, and is printed in the ' Christian Reformer,' vol. xvii. p. 28." See also his additional note, and Clouston's *Popular Tales*, I. 229.

*Translation of a Hymn from the Sepher Haggadah.*

1. A kid, a kid my father bought
   For two pieces of money.

2. Then came the cat and ate the kid
   That my father bought
   For two pieces of money.

3. Then came the dog and bit the cat
   That ate the kid, etc.

4. Then came the staff and beat the dog
   That bit the cat, etc.

5. Then came the fire and burnt the staff
   That beat the dog, etc.

6. Then came the water and quenched the fire
   That burned the staff, etc.

7. Then came the ox and drank the water
   That quenched the fire, etc.

8. Then came the butcher and slew the ox
   That drank the water, etc.

9. Then came the Angel of Death and killed the
   That slew the ox, etc.　　　　　　[butcher

10. Then came the Holy One, blessed be He,
    And killed the Angel of Death,
    That killed the butcher,
    That killed the ox,
    That drank the water,
    That quenched the fire,
    That burned the staff,
    That beat the dog,
    That bit the cat,
    That ate the kid,
    That my father bought,
    For two pieces of money.　A kid, a kid.

1. חד גדיא . חד גדיא . דזבין אבא בתרי זוזי . חד גדיא . הד גדיא.

2. ואתא שונרא ואכלה לגדיא דזבין אבא בתרי זוזי . חד גדיא . חד גדיא.

3. ואתא כלבא ונשך לשונרא דאכלה לגדיא דזבין אבא בתרי זוזי . חד גדיא . חד גדיא.

4. ואתא חוטרא והכה לכלבא דנשך לשונרא דאכלה לגדיא דזבין אבא בתרי זוזי . חד גדיא . חד גדיא.

5. ואתא נורא ושרף לחוטרא דהכה לכלבא דנשך לשונרא דאכלה לגדיא דזבין אבא בתרי זוזי . חד גדיא . חד גדיא.

174        TRÜBNER'S RECORD.        [1890.

6. ואתא מיא וכבא לנורא דשרף לחוטרא
דהכה לכלבא דנשך לשונרא דאכלה לגדיא
דזבין אבא בתרי זחי . חד גדיא . חד גדיא.

7. ואתא תורא ושתא למיא דכבא לנורא
דשרף לחוטרא דהכה לכלבא דנשך לשונרא
דאכלה לגדיא דזבין אבא בתרי זחי . חד גדיא .
חד גדיא.

8. ואתא השוחט ושחט לתורא דשתא למיא
דכבא לנורא דשרף לחוטרא דהכה לכלבא
דנשך לשונרא דאכלה לגדיא דזבין אבא בתרי
זחי . חד גדיא . חד גדיא.

9. ואתא מלאך המות ושחט לשוחט דשחט
לתורא דשתא למיא דכבא לנורא דשרף
לחוטרא דהכא לכלבא דנשך לשונרא דאכלה
לגדיא דזבין אבא בתרי זחי . חד גדיא . חד
גדיא.

10. ואתא הקדוש ברוך הוא ושחט למלאך
המות דשחט לשוחט דשחט לתורא דשתא
למיא דכבא לנורא דשרף לחוטרא דהכה
לכלבא דנשך לשונרא דאכלה לגדיא דזבין
אבא בתרי זחי . חד גדיא . חד גדיא.

---

## A Contribution to the History of Literary Work in Cairo.

### By Dr. Vollers.

Some three - and - twenty years ago a literary association (gam'iyat el ma'árif) was formed at Cairo, which had the object of propagating in good editions important works of Arabic antiquity. The Association submitted to the Hereditary Prince (the present Khedīv) Taufīk Pascha as a complimentary gift a political treatise (sulūk el málik) splendidly printed, but of inferior value. Another work, unfortunately left unfinished, appeared far better calculated to hand the name of the Association to posterity. This was the Tág el 'arûs, composed a century ago, a work in which Arabic philology, mindful of its grand past, takes a last glorious flight. The printing had proceeded nearly two years (1286—87 H.), and about half of the work had been issued when the undertaking was lamentably cut

short. The Pascha who had been entrusted with the proceeds of the subscriptions fled with the money to Stambul, the Association was dissolved, and all the sheets of the Tág that had been struck off are lying to this day in the printing office of the Wehbi. Urged on by the disappointed subscribers, the Egyptian Minister of Education made repeated attempts at inducing the printer by the grant of a subvention to complete that noble enterprise, but they all failed in consequence of the greediness of the printer, whose name has also in Europe been unfavourably known for the bad faith shown by him to a German savant (see Ibn Abi Usaibia, ed. A. Müller, Introduction). A similar lexicographical undertaking, the printing of the Lisân el 'arab, which was commenced seven years ago on a much slenderer basis than that of the Tág el 'arûs, came likewise to grief, after dragging on a precarious existence for five years. All the more agreeable was the surprise of the small band of Arabic scholars in Europe when a year ago a circular in the columns of the German Oriental Society's Journal announced that the Tág, which was supposed to be irrecoverably lost, was about to be reprinted. At the head of this undertaking stands a gentleman widely known in military, political and literary circles, Ghâzî Mukhtár Pascha, the Sultan's High Commissioner in Egypt. After bringing together at great trouble half of the author's autograph, the Association commenced printing early in 1889, and completed in the middle of September the first half of the work, which corresponds to what had been produced in the earlier edition. We may, therefore, safely predict, without being over-sanguine, that by the middle of the present year the subscribers will have the whole work in their hands. Also the party interested in the printing of the Lisân were stimulated to similar renewed exertion, which, thanks to the leading part taken by Riâz Pascha, the Prime Minister, resulted in financially securing the continuation of that noblest work of the Bulak Press in September of last year. It was a question of vital importance for the new edition of the Tág that in carrying this work through the press the numerous lexicographical works belonging to the Khedivial library should be utilized. These works, on which also Lane's Thesaurus is based, had been lent to the Lisân Society: and petty jealousy hoped to prejudice the printing of the Tág by retaining possession of those works. Here too Riâz Pascha, with that love of justice and fair play which places him so far above other Eastern politicians, has decided that both Associations are to make use of those works in a room of the Bulak printing office specially reserved for that purpose.

Apart from the two great works above described, the

book-market in Egypt is, as appears from the lists of A. Müller's Oriental Bibliography, poor in productions of interest to European students of Arabic. The object is simply to provide for the requirements of the pupils at the Azhar, and to satisfy the aspirations of the educated middle class. We hope to recur to this subject in a future communication.

---

## A Buddhist Jataka.

### By R. F. St. Andrew St. John.

Mr. Rhys Davids, in the introduction to his first volume of "Buddhist Birth Stories," says, "Unfortunately this orthodox Buddhist belief as to the history of the book of Birth Stories (*i.e.* the 550 Játakas) rests on a foundation of quicksand . . . ; but in order to estimate the value we ourselves should give it, it will be necessary by critical and more roundabout methods to endeavour to arrive at some more reliable conclusion. Such an investigation cannot, it is true, be completed until the whole series shall have become accessible in the original Páli text, etc." I do not wish to forestall Mr. Rhys Davids' work in any way, but am of opinion that if these stories are to be thoroughly understood, versions of them must be collected from every source, not only from the Sinhalese, but Burma, Cambodia, or any other Buddhist country. Mr. Ralston has given us some from Tibet. Being acquainted with Burmese, and to some extent with the Burmese form of the Pali, I propose to give from time to time translations of the Burmese Játaka. The present one is given at the end of the Mahájanaka Játaka published in Rangoon, 1884. The Mahájanaka was translated by me in the "Indian Magazine" in 1887.

### Láludáyi Játaka.

A monk of the name of Láludáyi, who was a member of the confraternity of Sávathti, did not always behave himself properly, but gave great cause for scandal owing to his habit of speaking irreverently when called upon to recite the law.

As the people reviled him the matter was brought before Buddha by the elders. He told them that Láludáyi was not to blame, for it was the result of ignorance in a former state of existence, and then related as follows :

Once upon a time there was in a country called Benáres (Báránasi) a Brahman named Aggidatta, who gained his livelihood by tilling the soil. He had a son named Somadatta, who, as soon as he was grown up, was sent to attend upon the Rájá, and the Rájá took a great liking to him. The old Brahman, being very poor, had only one pair of oxen. One of these died, and Aggidatta said to his son, "My dear, one of the oxen is dead, and I am unable to plough, ask the Rájá for an ox and give it to me." When Somadatta heard this, he was, like most young men, shy, and said, "Dear father, it is not easy to make a request of this kind, ask for something which is not so difficult." Aggidatta answered, "In that case, if you do not like to go, I will go myself and ask the Rájá." Somadatta thought, "My father is a slow-witted old fellow, and does not understand the ways of a court, if he goes to the Rájá and makes his request offhand, I shall be put to great shame; it will be better for me to instruct him how to address the Rájá."

So he said, "Dear father, people find great difficulty in addressing a Rájá; I will show you the proper way of remaining in the presence, how to make your obeisance, and how to present your petition." He then took his father to the burial-ground (the most retired spot), and having cut some grass, tied it in bundles and said, "Father, this bundle is the Rájá, and this the Crown-Prince, this the Commander-in-Chief, and this the Prime Minister." He then showed him the proper mode of making obeisance and the manner of retiring, and how he was to stand in a certain spot and invoke blessings on the Rájá.

He then told him that he was to make another obeisance and recite the following stanzas :—

> Mahárájá mé dvé goñá santi,
> Téhi khéttam kasámasé,*
> Déva tésu éko mato,
> Khattiya dutiyam déhi.
>
> Great king, to me two oxen were,
> With them the field we tilled,
> Bright One, of these one's dead,
> O Lord, a second give.

So Aggidatta having practised what his son taught him, said he was ready to go to the Rájá, and Somadatta said, "Very good, I will go in first and then you can follow with a suitable present."

After he had entered, his father came in with the present, and having made his bow stood in a respectful attitude. The Rájá inquired after his health and told him to sit down. Aggidatta then blurted out his verses thus :—

> Dvé mé goñá Mahárájá,
> Yéhi khéttam kasámasé;
> Tésu eko mato Déva,
> Dutiyam gahni Khattiya.
>
> To me two oxen Mahárájá,
> With them the field we tilled,
> Of these one's dead, O bright one,
> The second take, O Lord.

---

* Kasámasé is given by Childers as the 1st Per. Plur. Imperative Átm., but it is certainly not so here.

On hearing this odd request, the Rájá at once saw the mistake, and smiling turned to Somadatta and said in joke, "It seems you have a large number of cattle at home, you had better give him one." Somadatta answered, "Your Majesty, how can I find one at home, there are none but the one which has just been presented to you." The Rájá, being very fond of Somadatta, gave his father the revenues of a village, a change of garments, and sixteen oxen.

Having brought this tale of old times to a conclusion, the Buddha said, " O Monks, that Rájá is now Ánanda, Aggidatta is now Láludáyi, and Somadatta is myself, the Buddha :—verily

> Appasutáyam púriso
> Balibaddho va jírati,
> Mamsáni tassa· vaddhanti,
> Panyá tassa na vaddhati.

> The man who is ignorant
> Like an ox grows old,
> His fleshes increase,
> The wisdom of that one increases not.

---

### Letter from Monsignor Felix Birt, Bishop of Diana and Vicar Apostolic of Tibet, to Mr. W. W. Rockhill.

TATSIENLU, *Sept.* 8, 1889.

I have received the letter which you sent me from Tchong Kin on the 31st July, the eve of your departure for Shanghai. I wrote to you on the 24th July to inform you of the arrival and despatch of your goods and servants, enclosing at the same time a statement of your accounts. Considering the quickness of your journey, my letter will find you neither at Tchong Kin nor at Shanghai, and will only reach you in America. Your servants have twice for three days been put in chains by the Lamas at Tchegundo, and during their captivity two of your horses perished. When on your arrival at Tchegundo the Lamas went to Derge to ask for instructions as to the way in which they were to treat you, you did wisely in taking your departure at once, leaving your goods and servants to follow you at short stages. Had you waited for the return of the Lamas from Derge, it is certain that they would have killed you, or that you would have been compelled to turn off your road towards the north frontier. For the Lamas brought back the order that they were to prevent you at all hazards from exploring between Silinfu and Tatsienlu through the province of Derge. Thanks to your prudence and firmness, to your acquaintance with Tibetan and Chinese, and to your extraordinary self-possession, aided by a robust constitution which has allowed you to brave all hardships, you have been enabled to accomplish this important exploration of an interesting part of Tibet to which no European has hitherto been able to penetrate. Less successful than yourself, Colonel Prejvalsky, in spite of his escort of Cossaks from the Trans-Baikal, deceived by his Tibetan guides, and secretly betrayed by Tso tsung tang, viceroy of Canton, was obliged to return to Silinfu after two days' march. Later on Count Bela Szechenyi, in spite of the flatteries of the Tsong li yamen, and likewise deceived by the Chinese mandarins, was not even able to go beyond Silinfu, and had to reach Tataienlu by the so little interesting Chinese route of Tchenton. Since Messrs. Huc and Gabet's journey to Lhasa in 1845, your exploring expedition, I do not hesitate to say, has been the most difficult and the most important executed in Asia in the course of this century :—the most difficult and the most dangerous, I say, considering that you have traversed these immense steppes, that land of grass, without an escort, only accompanied by a few servants, living on tsamba, the meal of roasted barley and rancid butter, sleeping in the open air, unable to lay in a fresh stock of provisions in those desert regions, and dreading the habitations of man more than the solitude ; for in the centres which are somewhat fertile and inhabited one is sure to find Lamaserais; but the Lamas are the sworn enemies of explorers. You have opened up the road, you have mapped out the route, a route of prime importance for commerce, and of political and civilizing influence for Tibet. I hope this route will henceforward be followed, so that the great Chinaman will no longer be able to say, as he has had the hardihood to affirm in the teeth of all explorers who have preceded you, that there is no route through Derge to reach Tataienlu, Bathang, and Tchamuto, the heart of Tibet. Your successful exploration is a practical answer to that Mandarine trickery which flatly denies the existence of that important route in order to keep it secret. For, in fact, it is open and much frequented by Tibetan caravans. Only they wished to keep it closed to Europeans. Let us hope that the powers will not allow it to be closed again now that you have once made it known and opened it up at the expense of such hardships and dangers. Not only civilization, but also trade will profit by it, inasmuch as a splendid export is here opened up to European products such as red, green, yellow, and brown linen cloths, Indian flowered calicos, and bazaar curiosities so much liked by the Tibetans. Silin is in fact the staple for the trade from the North with Tibet, just as Tataienlu is the staple for the Eastern trade from China with Tibet. These are the two extreme points of your exploration, both very important. But the centre of Derge, Tchegundo, so near to the capital of Derge, has a particular importance which your visit will make known, because Tchegundo and Derge form as it were the centre of a radius by which to reach without the long circuits of the official Chinese route Tchamonto (Tsiamdo), the centre of Tibet, and Bathang, which itself is the key of Sudiya. Since you have travelled through the regions of the Kuku Nor and of Derge with all the attention of a learned and practical explorer, you will have noticed what riches they contain for export. Here one could procure at very low prices musk, gold, wool, hides, rhubarb. Your successful journey has opened up this fine country teeming with natural riches which are lying forgotten and unutilized. May commercial associations and learned societies turn their attention to the people of Tibet, who have so long been forgotten and so vigorously been excluded from civilization by the tyrannical yoke of the Lamas !

---

## Additional Abstracts of Papers read at the Eighth International Oriental Congress.

*On the Language of the so-called Shahbazgarhi Version of King Asoka's Fourteen Edicts.* By Dr. K. F. Johansson, Lecturer in the University of Upsala.

The paper consisted of some introductory remarks to a grammatical treatise with the above title which the speaker had written and sent in for insertion in the Proceedings of the Congress. He began by giving an account of the different versions of these edicts, grouping them in accordance with their mutual inter-connexion :—1) with respect to their contents and sequence of words; 2) with regard to the characters employed; 3) with regard to their language from a philological point of view. He next gave a short account of the discovery and scientific investigation of these extremely interesting memorials with especial reference to the works of Burgess, Cunningham, Bühler, Oldenberg, Pischel, Kern, Senart, and others. After some suggestions as to the position which the language of ‚these inscriptions holds with respect to, or rather within, the group of Indian languages generally and particularly in connexion with periodic arrangement and chronological sequence (i.e. Sanskrit—Prākrits in the widest signification, as Pāli, etc.—Prākrit in its literary form—modern Indian dialects), Dr. Johansson drew attention to the great importance of a synopsis on modern linguistic methods for the investigation of the language of the Prākrit inscriptions. Senart had in his great work, *Les inscriptions de Piyadasi*, certainly given us a sketch of the most important grammatical phenomena, but it had only

been his intention "de resumer . . . dans un inventaire aussi condensé que possible tous les phénomènes grammaticaux dignes d'intérêt," and besides, since he wrote, such important additions had been made to our knowledge and so many contributions, supplementary and corrective, had been gathered together, that a fresh scientific and complete treatment of the language of these inscriptions and the other Prākrit inscriptions was absolutely necessary. The speaker said it was his intention sooner or later to publish a work of this kind.

Meanwhile he had considered it advisable to draw up provisionally a grammatical sketch of the Shāhbāz-garhi dialect. His standpoint was as follows. The dialects of the other inscriptions must be held to have been settled in their main features by the work of Senart and the contemporary writings of Bühler. As to the Shāhbāz-garhi version, this was anything but the case, and till quite recently also the 12th edict had been wanting. For this reason, too, Senart's "inventaire grammatical" proved especially incomplete and unsatisfactory in the case of the Shāhbāz-garhi dialect. As, therefore, Senart himself, and particularly Bühler, have recently published works of extreme importance and apparently decisive in the main with regard to the deciphering of the version, the speaker felt himself justified in making a preliminary attempt at a treatment of the dialect in question.

Dr. Johansson next described the Shāhbāz-garhi inscription, and gave a brief description of its discovery and scientific investigation. Most important, he said, was the reading of Bühler, which was based on Burgess' rubbings, and published in the "Zeitschrift der deutschen morgenländischen Gesellschaft," vol. xliii. p. 128, sqq.

Finally, after some general remarks upon the treatment necessary for a grammatical work, and upon a generally linguistic method, the speaker gave some specimens of sound-changes, which he believed he had reduced to five laws :—

1. The ṛ-vowel has become *a*, *i* or *u* according to the adjacent sounds.

2. -*aya*-, -*ayi*- (but only these combinations) have by phonetic laws become *e*, when the first *a* had the main accent (e.g. *vadheti*, *aradheti*, etc., but *aṇapemi* instead of *aṇapayami* from *aṇapti*, etc.). In the same manner and under the same circumstances -*ava*- became -*o*-.

3. -*ia*-, -*ua*- have become *i*, *u* only when *i* and *u* had originally or secondarily the main or a strong subordinate accent (e.g. *istridhiyachamahamata* from *striadhi-akṣamahāmātrās*).

4. In the Prākrit inscriptions, as well as the Prākrit dialects, it is a general rule that a *long vowel* is succeeded by a *short consonant*. If therefore the

combination *long vowel* + *long consonant* occurred in Sanskrit, that in Prâkrit either the *consonant* or more commonly the *vowel* necessarily became short (cf. Pâli *dîgha-*, *digghikâ* = Sanskr. *dîrgha-*, *dîrghikâ*). The speaker believed, though he was not yet able to prove his theory indisputably, that the following rule held good for all the Prâkrit dialects : *if the sonantic element had the "gestossenen" accent, the vowel remained or became short, while the consonant became or remained long ; if the sonantic element had the "geschliffenen" or "schleifenden" accent, the vowel remained or became long, while the consonant became or remained short* (e.g. Sanskr. *râjñas* = Sh. *raño*, i.e. *rañño*, but *aṇa-* in *aṇapeti* probably = *âñâ-*, Sanskr. *âjñâ-*).

5. In Shâhbâz-garhi assimilations do not occur to the same extent as in the other Prâkrit dialects. Time did not allow of a fuller treatment of this point or the discussion of further questions.

---

*On the Nyâyabinduṭîkâ.* By Professor P. Peterson.

Professor Peterson gave the following account of his forthcoming edition of the Nyâyabinduṭîkâ :—

The first to make known to us so much as the name of the author, the Áchárya Dharmottara, was the Russian scholar W. Wassiljew. During a ten years' residence at Pekin (1840–1850) Wassiljew devoted himself to the study at first hand of Buddhism, fired, as he tells us, with the hope of affording proof that the "Russians too could do something for learning." Wassiljew did much. He would appear to have already mastered both the Chinese and the Tibetan languages ; and with these keys he unlocked the vast stores of Buddhist tradition in Northern Asia. That tradition is not indigenous, and the books in which it is preserved are for the most part translations from Sanskrit. If we can conceive a state of things in which the whole of the New Testament, lost for ages, and perhaps for ever, in the original Greek, should have been suddenly recovered, in the form of a translation into old Gothic, we shall appreciate the service Wassiljew did to the study of Buddhism.

In his first publication, 'Buddhism, its Dogmas, History, and Literature,' Wassiljew had a good deal to tell us of the Buddhist áchárya or teacher, Dharmottara. The Dharmottaríya school, so called after its founder Dharmottara or Uttaradharma, was one of eleven schools into which the great Sthavira sect of Buddhists was ultimately subdivided. Along with three of these schools the followers of Dharmottara asserted that "it was possible for those who had been saved again to fall." Lastly, in a very important passage, which can only be generally referred to here, Wassiljew brings together the names Dignága, Dhar-

makírti, S'ántideva, and Dharmottara in a way which has special significance for our book.

One of the Tibetan works used by Wassiljew, and of which he had already in 1860 prepared a translation into Russian, was Táranátha's history of Buddhism. Schiefner, the translator into German of Wassiljew's first work, published the Tibetan text of Táranátha in 1868 : and independent translations into Russian and German, by Wassiljew and Schiefner respectively, appeared in 1869. In his book Schiefner was able to use the greater part of Wassiljew's notes ; and at page 330 of the German work it will be found that Schiefner corrects from Wassiljew his own translation of a passage in which, according to Wassiljew, Dharmottara is referred to. Schiefner adds the information that the Tibetan Tandjur contains, among other works by Dharmottara, one entitled the Nyáyavinduṭîká.

Now this Nyáya-bindu-ṭîkâ of Dharmottaráchárya is the book which I have the good fortune to offer here to scholars in its lost Sanskrit original form. For the circumstances under which the then unique MS. of the work (written Samvat 1229 = A.D. 1173) was discovered among the palm-leaf MSS. preserved in the Jain temple of Sántinátha, Cambay, I may be permitted to refer to my Third Report. The publication of the book is due to the liberality of the Asiatic Society of Bengal. Observing from the Annual Address of the President of that Society that it was intended to publish some of the Tibetan texts collected by Csoma Körösi and Hodgson, side by side with their Sanskrit originals, I offered to edit in that way Dharmottara's book. This has unfortunately not been found practicable ; but the search for Dharmottara's work in its Tibetan form has at least revealed the fact that the Society possesses a work of the same name by the better known author, Dharmakírti. Both books are, of course, commentaries (ṭîkás) on a work entitled the Nyáyabindu, and it is to be hoped that Dharmakírti's books will ultimately be made available, if not in Sanskrit, at least in a translation from the Tibetan.

The first of the three chapters into which this book is divided had already been printed from the Cambay palm-leaf MS. (A), when I was very unexpectedly put in possession of a second MS. For this find I was indebted to Mr. Bhagvandas Kevaldas, the well-known agent for the search for Sanskrit MSS. in the Bombay Presidency. Mr. Bhagvandas noticed that the Bhao Daji collection of MSS. belonging to the Bombay Branch of the Royal Asiatic Society contained a work styled, in the Catalogue, Laghu-Dharmottara-Sútra. We sent for that book and found to our delight that it contained a second copy of Dharmottara's commentary on the Nyáya-bindu, and a copy of the text of the Nyáyabindu itself (B). This discovery has very greatly lightened the task of editing the book. I have also, through it, been able to present at the end of the commentary the work to which it refers.

In reviewing my Third Report Dr. Bühler was disposed to think that the Nyáyabinduṭíká of my Cambay MS. must be identical with a Dharmottara-vṛitti which he saw in Jesalmir, and of which he had a copy made for the Bombay Government collection. This has not turned out to be the case, but the Jesalmir MS. is nevertheless of great importance to us. It is not Dharmottara's book, but a commentary upon that by a writer whose name is not given. Unfortunately it is a mere fragment, extending only to p. 20 of this edition of the Nyáyabinduṭíká. In a paper, read before the Bombay Branch of the Royal Asiatic Society, I have put together the information contained in the Jesalmir fragment, and have shown in particular that, according to the anonymous commentator, Dharmottara had three predecessors in his task of commenting on these old sûtras, Vinîtadeva, Śántabhadra and Dharmakîrti. As this last writer is known to have written a commentary on a work by Dignága, who is supposed to have been a contemporary of Kálidása's, we obtain from this statement something in the nature of a clue to Dharmottara's date. But for this, and some speculations as to the authorship of sûtras held in such high honour by a succession of famous Buddhist writers, I must take leave here to refer to my paper, which will appear in the forthcoming number of the Society's Journal.

The two MSS. on which this edition is thus based have been very carefully collated by me in collaboration with my Shástri, Mr. Syamji Valji, whose assistance I desire cordially to acknowledge. We cannot hope that our text is absolutely correct. But we have spared no pains to make it as correct as we could.

I had intended to furnish this edition with full notes, but I soon found that the only satisfactory way of explaining a text, which is in places very obscure, would be to attempt a complete translation. I had made considerable progress with a translation when an unexpected opportunity of attending the Stockholm Orientalist Congress rendered it advisable to lay that undertaking aside for the time. The book itself will, I am confident, have great interest for students of Buddhism and of Hindu Philosophy ; and I have ventured to solicit permission, which has been kindly given, to dedicate it to the august and learned Patron of the Assembly. I cannot refrain from adding that to me, the son of a Shetlander, it is as great a pleasure as it is an honour, to present this venerable relic of old-world thought to the Sovereign of Norway and Sweden.

---

*On the Origin of the Cogmographical Beliefs embodied in Dante's 'Purgatorio.'*  By Count A. de Gubernatis.

The lecturer stated that on reading again since his return from India Dante's 'Purgatorio,' he had been vividly reminded of that country by the descriptions of Indian scenery, and its marvellous trees and products. Purgatory was placed by Dante at the antipodes of Jerusalem on a desert island whence the South Star could be seen, and where on a high mountain the earthly paradise extended. That island the lecturer identified with Ceylon, the Taprobane of the ancients : and he pointed out that the indigenous races, Hindus, Buddhists, Muhammadans, and Thomas Christians alike placed Paradise on Adam's Peak. He also referred to traditions regarding the early inaccessibility of the island. All those traditions would appear to have come down to Dante's time. There are also many mediæval maps on which Taprobane figures at the extremities of the earth somewhere about Japan. Another remarkable coincidence consists in the observation made by the Ambassadors from the King of Taprobane to the Roman Emperor Claudius as to their shadow falling on a different side at Rome to what it used to do in their own island. This coincides with Dante's observation about the miscreant Pelasguo's shadow. All these data combined point to Ceylon as the site of the Paradise as conceived by Dante.

---

*Sketch of the History of the Armenian Language in Europe.*  By Dr. G. de Esoff.

The Armenian Language began to be studied in Western Europe, more especially in France and at Rome, about the time of the Crusades. The motives were purely theological, viz. to effect a union between the Armenian and the Roman Catholic Churches. To this circumstance alone Europe owes the publication of its first Armenian primers, grammars, dictionaries, and theologico-polemical works. Since the time of the French Revolution the Armenian language and literature began to be studied for purely literary purposes. The lecturer then proceeded to give a survey of the most prominent savants who have cultivated this language in France, Germany, England, and other European countries. To the Swede, H. Brenner, the merit is due of having brought out in Latin an epitome of the History of Moses of Khorene in the early part of the eighteenth century, thirteen years before the appearance of the edition of that History by the brothers Whiston in 1736.

---

## The New Gupta Inscription found at Bithari.

In one of the *Pioneer Mails* of May reference was made to an "Archæological Find," believed then to be of some importance, but which has since proved to be even more valuable than was first supposed. This find, at first described as a silver inscribed plate, has since proved to be a seal composed of a mixture of copper and silver with a slight admixture of gold, of the class affixed to the copperplate grants of land issued by the reigning powers in days gone by.

The seal was presented to Mr. G. J. Nicholls, C.S., Judge of Cawnpore, by a member of an old Mahomedan family residing at Bithari, near Sayyidpur in the Ghazipur District, and accepted by Mr. Nicholls on behalf of the Government for presentation to the Lucknow Museum, where we believe it now is. The seal was found in 1886 when digging for foundations at Bithari, famous for its stone pillar with the Gupta inscription of the King Skanda Gupta. The seal has now been fully described in the *Journal of the Asiatic Society* for 1889, vol. lviii., by Mr. Vincent Smith, C.S., Dr. Hœrnle, the Secretary of the Society, having added a further paper on this interesting discovery from which the following details are extracted :—

The upper portion of the seal bears in tolerably high relief a device representing Garuda, and this, with a former seal of Samudra Gupta with a like device found attached to a copperplate grant and described by Mr. Thet, has, it is believed, settled the question that the human-faced bird-monster, the vehicle of Vishnu, was the emblem of the early Gupta dynasty. This emblem is found as the bird-headed standard on the gold Gupta coins and on the copper coins of the same dynasty as figured in the plates accompanying the interesting article on this subject, published by Mr. Vincent Smith, C.S., in the *Journal of the Royal Asiatic Society of Great Britain.*

The inscription beneath the Garuda emblem is in eight lines, and the characters are those used by the Gupta kings, and known as peculiar to their coin-legends and copperplate grants and also to the pillars at Bithari and elsewhere.

The importance of this seal lies in the fact that it contains a genealogical list of the early Gupta kings, and that, instead of seven generations, as hitherto deduced from the imperfect records on the Bithari and Bihar stone pillars, nine generations are enumerated, the seal itself being that of Kumara Gupta II., the ninth in succession.

The list of monarchs as given by the seal tallies with those of the Bithari and Bihar pillars up to the sixth, each king being described as the son of his predecessor, as follows :—

1. Gupta.
2. Ghatotkacha.
3. Chandra Gupta I.
4. Samudra Gupta.
5. Chandra Gupta II.
6. Kumara Gupta I.

On the Bithari and Bihar pillars the seventh in suc-

cession is named Skanda Gupta. On the seal now discovered the seventh in succession is entered as Pura Gupta, Skanda being entirely omitted. The eighth name is Narasimha Gupta, the ninth Kumara Gupta II. This introduces into the genealogy of the Guptas three new monarchs, Pura Gupta, Narasimha Gupta and Kumara Gupta II. That Skanda Gupta reigned and bore the Imperial titles is attested by the number of gold coins bearing his name and by the Bithari and Bihar inscriptions. It is suggested that he may have been a brother of Pura Gupta, and having had no son to succeed him, the list being one of succession, his name has been omitted. The seal also gives the names of six queen-wives of the different monarchs. Skanda Gupta's Bithari and Bihar inscriptions include the names of three queens only : but these three, Kumara-devi, Dattadevi, and Dhruvadevi, correspond with the three first queens of the seal list. This seal therefore proves that the early Gupta dynasty did not end, as has been believed, with Skanda Gupta, but that it was carried on for two generations to about A.D. 550 ; and that a second Kumara Gupta reigned and was the last of the Imperial line of early Guptas.

But yet another riddle has been solved by the list on this seal. Coins of a certain Nara or Nara Gupta with the title of Baladitya have been long assigned to the Gupta coinage, but it has been impossible until now to find for them a place. These coins. Dr. Hœrnle now points out are those of Narasimha Gupta, the eighth on the new list. From the testimony of Hiouen Thsang it has been proved that during the reign of a certain Baladitya of Magadha, Mihirakula the Hun was defeated by Yasodharman and retired to Kashmir. This defeat occurred therefore about A.D. 530, seventy years after the great defeat of the Huns in Europe, A.D. 451. From inferences too lengthy to be detailed in this short notice, but which are fully given in Dr. Hœrnle's most interesting paper, there is every reason to assume that Nara Baladitya of the coins, Nara-simha Gupta of the seal list, and Baladitya of Magadha of Hiouen Thsang fame, are one and the same monarch, and that in Narasimha Gupta's reign the final over-throw of the Huns in India took place.

The fortunate unearthing of this seal, therefore, has greatly added to the information previously available regarding the early Gupta rulers of Magadha, whose coins are so constantly procured from the neighbour-hood of Bithari, where near the junction of the Ganges and Goomtee must have been one of their great cities, and where even now, though centuries must have changed the face of the country somewhat, a lovely reach of the Ganges and the swift inflowing of the Goomtee with long lines of high mounds still point to a scene of former greatness, and where, as at Bithari, every step through the fields brings to light relics of the past in the shape of large bricks of the old Buddhist structures.

It is to be hoped that the mystery of the relation-ship of Skanda Gupta and Pura Gupta may yet be solved by some future find which, like this seal, may shed more light into the darkness of early Indian history. M.—[From *The Pioneer Mail* of Jan. 1, 1890.]

# New Books.

*A Concise Dictionary of the Principal Roads, Chief Towns and Villages of Japan* (pp. v. and 248). Appendix to the above, containing the Constitution of Japan, etc., etc. (pp. 167). By W. N. Whitney, M.D., Interpreter of the U.S. Legation, Tôkyô.

The work now before us, taken in connection with its Appendix, is a handbook of speedy reference to the present condition of Japan. It is described as a Concise Dictionary of the Principal Roads, Chief Towns and Villages of that country; and in compliance with its title, it furnishes accurate and official information as to the 852 Principal Roads of the Empire, their starting-points and termini, the various Towns and Villages situated upon them, together with their respective distances from one another. This list is arranged after the order of the English alphabet, followed by Sinico-Japanese characters so far as the roads are concerned. Next follows a list of more than 4500 Towns and Villages arranged as above (i.e. in English and Japanese characters), and in which list we find that due care has been taken to mark out the respective distances of such Towns and Villages from some one or other well-known centre as well as from surrounding Towns and Villages, to show the routes by which they are severally to be reached, and also to afford other minor information such as may be best illustrated by a quotation taken at random :—

"Age-o 上尾 Musashi (Saitama); Nakasendô, Tôkyô-Maebashi ry; po. Pop. 1777."

From which we gather that Age-o is situated in the ancient Province (Kuni) of Musashi, in the modern Prefecture (Ken) of Saitama; is upon the road known as the Nakasendô; is a station upon the Tôkyô-Maebashi Railway, and further that it possesses a Post Office, and has a Population consisting of some 1777 persons according to the Census taken December 31st, 1886. Had Age-o possessed either a Money Order or Telegraph Office, such particulars would have been supplied.

Information of the above character, be it observed, is to be obtained at a single glance. For further particulars we turn to the list of Principal Roads (already alluded to) for Nakasendô and to the list of 37 Railways with their respective stations, for Tôkyô-Maebashi. Under the former we ascertain the exact position of Age-o and its actual distance from numerous other Towns and Villages, and under the latter its position as a station on the Railway, viz. that it is 21½ miles from Tôkyô and at such and such distances from other stations upon the same line. But beyond such particulars already referred to, this Concise Dictionary supplies a list of 123 Towns and Villages whose population at the Census of December, 1887, exceeded 10,000 (one town of 9254, Kanaishi, has, perhaps, crept inadvertently into this list), a list of the Fu (the three Imperial Cities Tôkyô, Ôzaka, and

Kyôto), of Ken (the 42 Modern Prefectures), and of one Chô (comprising the island of Ezo and neighbouring islands), which Fu, Ken, and Chô form the 46 geographical and political districts into which Japan is now divided, a list of Kuni (Ancient Provinces known as such through all history and until recent times), and finally the modern subdivision of the Ken or Prefectures into Kôri or Gun (counties), over 800 in number, and lastly a List of Railways and Stations, with mileage, including those in course of construction as well as those for which charters have been granted. These several lists are followed by tables of mileage, weights, measures, and money reduced into corresponding English equivalents, together with remarks on Japanese syllabary, orthography, syllables in combination, dialects, and accent, drawn up according to the latest and most approved Official authorities.

Whilst the information thus afforded will in particular prove indispensable to all future merchants, travellers, and historians, the Appendix must of necessity interest a far larger class of people, for not only will it be serviceable to all who are brought into immediate connection with Japan, but in its pages will be found many facts worthy of notice by the lawyer, the politician, and the general reader.

This Appendix opens with the text of the new Constitution granted to Japan by the Emperor or Mikado on February 11, 1889—a Constitution which comes into force in January, 1890.

In order that the terms of such Constitution may be understood aright, it is absolutely necessary for us to take a brief glance at the position which Japan claims to occupy among the nations in this nineteenth century. In the first place, she asserts that she is (with the one only exception of China) the most ancient Empire in the world. In the second place, whilst yielding the palm to China in point of antiquity as to Empire, she claims priority in point of antiquity as to Dynasty, surpassing China in this respect by many centuries. In the third place, she claims that her position in the present day as defined in the terms of the Constitution is but the outcome and expression of the "grand precepts" for government laid down by the founder of the Empire 660 B.C.

The earliest known inhabitants* of Japan are usually spoken of as Ainos, whose descendants are now to be met with in the island of Ezo. They once covered the whole surface of Japan. According to Japanese traditions, they were conquered by the Yamatos, who are first heard of as occupying the island of Kiu-shiu. Amongst this latter people an heir-apparent succeeded to the throne in the first half of the seventh century B.C. He, Jimmu by name, conceived the idea of conquering and annexing the whole Japanese group. After many difficulties, he subsequently, 660 B.C., became first Mikado or Emperor. The present Mikado, in his newly-promulgated Constitution, claims to be the lineal descendant of Jimmu the Conqueror, and to be the 121st Emperor of a country which since Jimmu's

---

* There are traces of previous inhabitants, to whom reference is often made by modern writers.

days has never surrendered to the arms of any foreign power. In other words, Japan claims to possess a history of 2500 years, during which she has been ruled over by one unbroken line of Emperors—a claim unequalled in the history of the world.

The Official text of the Constitution (as given in this Appendix) not only claims the conquest of Jimmu as the historical base upon which such Constitution has been granted, but, further, that this latter is in itself but an "Exposition" of his method of government. Thus in the Imperial Oath made at the Sanctuary of the Imperial Palace at the time of the promulgation :—

"We shall maintain and secure from decline the ancient form of Government. . . . . We deem it expedient, in order to give clearness and distinctness to the instructions bequeathed by the Imperial Founder of Our House, and by Our other Imperial Ancestors, to establish fundamental laws formulated into express provisions of law. . . . . These laws come to only an exposition of the grand precepts for the government bequeathed by the Imperial Founder of Our House and by Our other Imperial Ancestors."

In the Imperial speech made on the like occasion we find again :—

"The Imperial Founder of Our House and Our other Imperial Ancestors, by the help and support of the forefathers of Our subjects, laid the Foundation of Our Empire upon a basis which is to last for ever."

That Mitsu Hito, the present Mikado, claims to be the direct descendant and representative of a dynasty founded 2500 years ago, and of a line of Emperors unbroken during that period, is further impressed upon us in the opening clause of the Constitution :—

"Having by virtue of the glories of Our Ancestors ascended the throne of a lineal succession unbroken for ages eternal." . . . .

Accompanying this statement we have information concerning the purport of the new *régime*, which is—"to exhibit the principles by which We are to be guided in Our conduct, and to point out in what Our descendants and Our subjects and their descendants are for ever to conform."

A statement then follows to the effect that the rights of sovereignty in future are to be wielded only in accordance with the provisions now laid down. The rights and property of the people are to be respected and protected. An Imperial Diet is to be convoked for the 23rd year of Meiji (1890), when the present Constitution comes in force. Amendments to the provisions now laid down are only to be made at the initiative of the Sovereign, who will submit a project for the same to the Imperial Diet. Such Diet is to make its vote according to provisions now laid down. In no other way may Sovereign or people be permitted to make any alteration. Ministers of State are made responsible for carrying out, and all subjects are required to yield allegiance to the New Constitution. This declaration was signed by the Mikado and by His Ministers of State, of whom eight are Counts and two are Viscounts, and Presidents of the following Departments : State, Privy Council, Foreign Office, Navy, Agriculture and Commerce,

Justice, Finance and Home Affairs, War, Education, Communication.*

The Constitution consists of 76 Articles, of which 1 to 17 relate to the Emperor ; 18–32 to the rights of Subjects ; 33–54, The Imperial Diet ; 55–56, Ministers of State and Privy Council ; 57–61, Judicature ; 62–72, Finance ; 73–76, Supplementary Rules. These Articles are followed by Ordinances concerning the regulation of both Houses, Peers and Representatives. Then follows the whole text of the Law for the organization of Cities, Towns, and Villages.

This extremely interesting and valuable *vade mecum* to Japan, as it is, concludes with official statistical information respecting Territory, Population, Agriculture and Industry, Domestic and Foreign Commerce, Transport and Navigation, Banking, Insurance, Public Instruction, Religion, Public Hygiene, Public Charities, Police, Prisons, Justice, Army and Navy, Finance and Political Administration.

The only drawback to this Concise Dictionary and Appendix is the omission of a list of the Fu, Ken, Chô, Roads, Cities, Towns, etc., arranged according to the order of their Chinese characters. Inasmuch as such list appears amongst the list of contents of the Appendix, this drawback is a very serious one to students. It is to be hoped that this list will appear in due course, and that the slight error in page 243 of the Dictionary, of speaking of the gold and of the silver *yen* coin, and calling the same *en*, and without specifying whether gold or silver, throughout the Appendix, may be rectified in a later edition.

S. Coode Hore.

*December*, 30, 1889.

---

*Essays on the Chinese Language.*     By T. Watters. Shanghai, 1889.

The author of these Essays, who has been a resident in various parts of China for upwards of twenty-five years, holds a high position among Sinologists as one of the soundest and most solid scholars in their ranks. In his biographical notices of worthies and scholars of Confucianism, which appeared ten years ago under the title "A Guide to the Tablets in a Temple of Confucius," he gave an earnest of his familiarity with Chinese literary compositions ; and that he has not been idle since, the pages of "The China Review" and "The Chinese Recorder" amply testify. The present publication encompasses a large field of mature research:

---

* The oath made by the Mikado at the promulgation of this remarkably enlightened Constitution apprises us, incidentally, of the fact that Japan as a nation has made no actual advance in religion. Thus, whilst Article 28 reads, "Japanese subjects shall within limits not prejudicial to peace and order, and not antagonistic to their duties as subjects, enjoy freedom of religious belief,"—the Mikado retains, as it were for Himself and His people, the worship of Ancestors and of Celestial Spirits :—"We now reverently make our Prayer to Them [*i.e.* Our other Imperial Ancestors] and to Our Illustrious Father [*i.e.* Jimmu] and implore the help of Their Sacred Spirits, and make to Them solemn oath never at this time nor in the future to fail to be an example to Our subjects in the observance of the Law hereby established. May the Heavenly Spirits witness this Our solemn oath !"

it will commend itself not only to students of Chinese, but also generally to lovers of Eastern lore, philosophy, and philology. The range of the contents of this goodly volume may best be seen from the following list of the Essays : I. *Some Western Opinions.* After passing in review the views held by some well-known European writers on language concerning the nature and position of Chinese, he concludes with the following pertinent remarks : " The information necessary to enable us to form correct general judgments on the Chinese language as an instrument of expression and communication, cannot be said even now to be all forthcoming. Nor are we yet in a position to give a final opinion on its rank and value when compared with other languages, or on its descent and kindred. We have among us at present students who are from time to time adding new and interesting facts, which will greatly help the future philosopher to form conclusions wide and general and at the same time accurate. But much still remains to be done before the genius and constitution of the Chinese language are thoroughly understood, and before its rank and value in the world's speech-tribes can be definitely settled." II. *The Cultivation of their Language by the Chinese.* In this valuable treatise— the result, we doubt not, of many years' toil—Mr. Watters notices only those books, or parts of books, " which are specially devoted to philology, and which show us the progress made by the Chinese in the intelligent use and cultivation of their language, written and spoken." But he comprises in his review also what he found recorded concerning the early study of Sanskrit in China. III. *Chinese Opinions about the Origin and Early History of the Language.* This chapter treats also of the native view of the origin of writing. IV. *On the Interjectional and Imitative Elements in the Chinese Language.* In this chapter the author draws attention to the importance, in Chinese, of this large class of emotional words, and of imitative expressions such as the crying of animals, coughing, sneezing, halting, etc. A long treatise is devoted to V. *The Word Tao,* which has been selected to illustrate the variety of meanings with which a single term can be burdened, whereas in chapter VI. *Terms relating to Death and Burial,* the partial richness of the language is exemplified in a review of the vocabulary for year, the various phases of human life, and for death and everything connected with it. This chapter is full of interesting details concerning the burial customs prevalent among the Chinese. VII. *Foreign Words in Chinese.* To a philologist this chapter and the two following are perhaps the most attractive and suggestive in this book. The author modestly calls the examples adduced " only occasional specimens picked up by the way," " merely findings in the desultory reading of an indolent amateur," and disclaims them as " discoveries reached by patient study and critical research." But these specimens show that even such a highly conservative language as Chinese has not been able to lock its doors against the foreigner. Among such intruders we mention *pa-li* (padre), *hia-erh min* (carmin), *ko-ko* (cacao), *chih-ku-la* (chocolate), *k'o-lu-pu* (Krupp), *mi-t'u* (mètre), *fo-lang* (franc). Mr.

Watters gives a number of other words derived from Malay, Persian, Arabic, Turkish, Manchu, Mongolian, and Tibetan. But we refer the reader specially to his notes on the history of the Chinese equivalents for " company," " consul," " pound," " protest." VIII. and IX. *The Influence of Buddhism on the Chinese Language.* On this subject the author speaks with a competency to which but few other Sinologists can lay claim. Since A.D. 67, he says, " the Indian mission-aries taught their brethren in China the Sanskrit language and grammar, and the Chinese have never been attracted to any other foreign language as they were to Sanskrit." But they also taught the Chinese scholars to examine and study their own language and appreciate it properly. They further instructed them in astronomy, arithmetic and medicine. The following are the heads under which he treats of this wide subject. " We first take examples of Sanskrit words introduced into and made current in various degrees in Chinese. We are next to take examples of new Chinese words and phrases due to translations from Sanskrit ; and then of new phrases which though derived from Buddhist sources are not translations. Next we are to consider some instances of new meanings and applications given to old words and phrases ; and lastly we are to notice examples of Proverbs and Common Sayings among the Chinese which are connected with Buddhism." In conclusion, we would ask the author of this instructive book to set to work on a complete translation, with copious notes, of the Travels of I-tsing, a work of great difficulty, but one well worthy of his steel.

---

### *Dr. F. Hirth's Sinological Researches.*

Dr. K. Himly, the well-known Sinologist, gives in the "Münchner Neueste Nachrichten" of 26th and 29th Oct. 1889, an elaborate account of the works of his brother Sinologist, Dr. F. Hirth. This account deserves a special notice, not only by reason of the competency of its author, but also on the ground of the importance of the subject treated of. Friedrich Hirth was born at Gräfentonna near Gotha, studied classical philology at the University of Leipzig, and after taking his degree in 1869, proceeded to China to accept a post in the Imperial Customs Service. To be able to discharge efficiently the official duties assigned to him, he devoted all his youthful energies to the study of the Chinese language and of the country, its inhabitants, geography, products, manufactures, arts and history. One of the first fruits of his industry was a map of the province of Kuangtung, which, with explanatory letterpress, appeared in Petermann's "Mittheilungen" for 1872. It was subsequently supplemented by a valuable essay "on the Chinese sources of the geography of Kuangtung, with special reference to the peninsula of Leichou." His numerous contributions to English serials in China, and to the periodical press in Germany and Austria, are mainly philological and historico-geographical, while a few deal with the history of Chinese art. We will mention only his most prominent publications. Of these, his *Text-book of Documentary Chinese,* in two volumes (with vocabulary and selected translations), and *Notes on the Chinese Documentary Style*, serve pre-eminently a practical purpose. Though the spirit of Chinese grammar, the laws of sequence, and the building up of sentences, have been the same from time immemorial, there is a difference in detail between the style of business or official documents and the *Ku-wen* or ancient style on the one hand, and the conversational style on the other. To guide the student into the intricacies of this documentary style, an acquaintance with which is so important for all purposes of diplomacy and business, Dr. Hirth has framed a number of rules and communicated observations with a view to inducing the reader gradually to make his own grammatical observations and acquiring the habit of deducing for himself rules where rules exist. His wider reputation rests on his " *China and the Roman Orient,*" a work showing the combined results of his early classical studies and of his familiarity with the ancient historical literature of China. Whereas European writers for upwards of 200 years have understood the Chinese term *Ta-ts'in* to apply to the whole of the old Roman empire, Dr. Hirth has proved by a number of convincing arguments that it can only have designated its Asiatic provinces, and that the Chinese description of its capital, An-tu, corresponds as nearly as can be with the account of ancient Antiochia by classical writers. A further contribution from his pen to the history of ancient Chinese trade is contained in the Journal of the Berlin Geographical Society for 1889. He has also ready for the press a translation of Chao-Yu-Kua's account of foreign countries which was composed at the beginning of the 13th century at the Emporium of Thsüan-chou (Marco Polo's Zaitun), chiefly from the reports of Arab traders. Last, not least, we mention his valuable treatise on *Ancient Porcelain: a Study in Chinese Mediæval Industry and Trade* (in vol. xxii. of the Journal of the Shanghai Asiatic Society, and published at Leipzig in 1888). In this treatise he shows—against Stan. Julien's assertion that porcelain was invented between 185 B.C. and 87 A.D.—that it was not invented till about 600 A.D., that it was originally manufactured in the city of Lung-thsüan, and that it found its way from the port of Zaitun to Ceylon, India and Arabia as far as Zanzibar.

During a residence of 20 years in various parts of China, Dr. Hirth has made the best of his opportunities to collect an extensive and most valuable library of Chinese books. One of his latest acquisitions is a manuscript in 24 volumes consisting of vocabularies and official documents in the ten eastern languages which were taught in the Oriental College as established (or rather re-established) at Peking in 1407. Among these are represented two Shan dialects and the Niu-chi (Ju-chi, Jur-chin) language, long since extinct (see Professor T. de Lacouperie's article in Journal of Royal Asiatic Society, vol. xxi. p. 433). May Chinese research long continue to count him amongst its most earnest and most solid cultivators!

---

*Khari Boli ka Padya. The Poetical Reader of Khari Boli.* Compiled by Ayodhya Prasâd, Khatri. Edited by F. Pincott. (W. H. Allen, 1889.)

This anthology of gems composed in the most refined style of modern Hindi may be commended to students of that language. The pieces have been selected from the writings of Râjâ Siva Prasâd, Râi Mohan Lâl, Babu Harischandr, Babu Mahesh Nârâyan, Maulvî Iltâf Husain, Babu Lakshmî Prasâd, and Srî Satyânand Agnihotri, and the editing and printing leave nothing to be desired.

---

*The Mahâjanaka Jâtaka.* Translated into English, with notes, by Taw Sein Ko. Rangoon, 1889.

This birth-story, generally known by the name of Zanekka in Burmese, is one of the ten great (i.e. amplified) Jâtakas which are found at the end of the Jâtaka Book, and translations of which into the vernaculars are favourite reading books in Burma, Ceylon, and Siam. On account of their easy and idiomatic style some of them have been chosen as text books for the examinations. The present translator does not appear to have been aware that he has not been the first in the field ; for there is a good previous translation, by Mr. R. F. St. Andrew St. John, in the second volume (1887) of the " Indian Magazine." We take this oportunity of mentioning that a list of the 550 Jâtakas, compiled from Pali MSS. in various Temple libraries in Ceylon by N. D. M. de Zilva Wikremasingha, is to be found in vol. x. no. 35, of the Journal of the Ceylon Asiatic Society. It generally agrees with the arrangement of the Copenhagen copy.

---

*The Standard Sanskrit-English Dictionary.* By Lakshman Ramchandra Vaidya. Bombay, 1889.

This handy and portable dictionary, filling 842 closely-printed pages of three columns each, not counting an appendix on prosody and an alphabetical list of noted mythological persons, supplies a real want which schools and colleges in India must have inconveniently felt for years, and commends itself to a wide range of students by its cheapness. Its great usefulness even for more advanced students is enhanced by the quotations it gives where necessary, and by its references to standard works. It is sure to obtain a deservedly large sale wherever Sanskrit is studied.

---

*The Age of Patanjali.* By Pandit N. Bhâshyâchârya. Madras, 1889.

In this pamphlet of 17 pages, which originally appeared in " The Theosophist," a Madras Pandit resuscitates the controversy as to the age of Patanjali (whom he assigns to the 10th century B.C.), and the question of his being the author of the Mahâbhâshya as well as of the Yoga Sûtras, which he answers in the affirmative. The weapons with which he defends his position have become somewhat rusty since Goldstücker brought them to the combat some 28 years ago ; nor is the way in which he handles them at all calculated to bring conviction home to his readers. While there can be no question that Western Sanskrit scholars have much to learn from their Indian brethren, the foremost of the latter do not refuse to admit their indebtedness to the former, nor do they set courtesy aside or at defiance.

---

*The Syntax and Idioms of Hindustani.* By M. Kempson. (W. H. Allen.)

This Manual, containing progressive exercises in translation, with notes and directions and vocabularies, aims at explaining and illustrating step by step the various points of *Usage* by the application of the ordinary principles of clause-analysis to the diction of Hindustani. The model sentences are taken from the best modern writers, and the corresponding English phrases have been framed with a view to the rendering of the Urdu idioms, so that the student may gradually be led to clothe his thoughts in proper Urdu dress. The book would be infinitely more useful if all the Urdu Exercises had been lithographed in progressive order of difficulty, so as to accustom the learner to a class of graphic idioms which cannot be mastered except after long and tedious practice. The author hopes to make good this deficiency at some future time. We may add that the rules and explanatory notes are very valuable, and will amply repay a careful study.

---

*The Modern Vernacular Literature of Hindustan.* By G. A. Grierson. Calcutta, 1889. (xxx. 171, xxxv. pp.)

It should be understood at the outset that throughout this valuable and interesting book—a collection of *materials*, Mr. Grierson modestly calls it—by Hindustan is meant Rajputana and the valleys of the Jamuna and of the Ganges as far East as the river Kosi, and that under that term neither the Panjab nor Lower Bengal are included. "The vernacular languages dealt with may roughly be considered as three in number, Marwari, Hindi, and Bihari, each with its various dialects and sub-dialects." In this sense also the term "Hindustani" as applied to language has to be taken; it is used synonymously with Neo-Indian and Neo-Gaudian, and has nothing to do with Urdu. The author has excluded from his work all mention of the numerous anonymous folk-epics and folk-songs current throughout Northern India, many of which, gathered from the mouths of the people in the province of Bihar, he has himself been the first to make accessible. Imbued with a keen appreciation of the beauty of that popular poetry, he would have been its fittest interpreter if the subject had at all entered into the plan of the present work. Perhaps Mr. Grierson may portray for us some day this class of popular literature in a separate work when all the materials for it shall have been gathered and systematically arranged throughout the area with which we are here concerned.

In the introduction the author gives an account of the anthologies and other sources of information which he has utilized for his work, and of the principles on which he has arranged it, and draws a summary sketch of the Vernacular Literature of Hindustan, from the bardic chronicles of Rajputana towards the end of the twelfth century down to the present day, the Augustan Age (16th and 17th centuries) receiving special attention. This sketch is traced with a master's hand within the brief space of seven pages. Following in the wake of Tod, he speaks with enthusiasm of the value of those early chronicles, some of which are derived from older works dating as far back as the ninth century A.D., and asks, "Is it unreasonable to hope that some enlightened prince of Rajputana will rescue these documents from the undeserved obscurity in which they lie, and publish the texts of all of them, with English translations?" After drawing a comparison between the two phases of the Vaishnava branch of Brahmanism that originated early in the 15th century, viz. the religious and literary movement initiated by Rámánand, and that mystic worship which culminated in the Krishna cult, Mr. Grierson presents to us a glowing picture of a phenomenal work which stands at the very threshold of the Augustan age. This is the philosophic epic *Padmáwat* by Malik Muhammad, which, in beauty of poetical sentiment, purity of language, and as a noble specimen of the speech of those days, is of inestimable value. In his opinion, it is well worth hard study and any amount of trouble both for its originality and for its poetical beauty. Mr. Grierson devotes a whole chapter to Tulsi Dás (+ 1624), "the greatest star in the firmament of mediæval Indian poetry," whose Rámáyan, according to Hindu ideas, competes in authority with the Sanskrit work of Válmíki. A work of stern morality, it has been interwoven into the life, character and speech of the Hindu population for more than three hundred years, and being read or heard by all classes alike, it has exerted an incalculable influence for good. "When we reflect," Mr. Grierson continues, "on the fate of Tantra-ridden Bengal or on the wanton orgies which are carried out under the name of Krishna-worship, we can justly appreciate the work of the man who first in India since Buddha's time taught man's duty to his neighbour and succeeded in getting his teaching accepted. His great work is at the present day the one Bible of a hundred millions of people."

We further draw attention to valuable notes on Súrdás, Bírbal, Ballabháchárj, Bihárí Lál Chaube, Harishchandr, Lallújí Lál, and on our contemporary Rájá Śiva Prasád, while we refer Sanskrit scholars to such well-known names as Śárngadhara and Bidyápati. In conclusion, we advert to Mr. Grierson's view of the literary Hindi of the present day as the *lingua franca* of Hindus (p. 107), and on the Hindi and Bihari Drama (p. 154).

Mr. Grierson has by the ability and critical acumen with which he has fixed and sketched out the grammatical peculiarities of the various Hindi dialects of Bihar already earned the thanks of all students of modern Indian philology. In the present work he imparts to those studies a fresh and powerful stimulus by showing what an important factor an earnest investigation of the mediæval poetry of Hindustan is likely to prove in researches on the history and civilisation of that country.

---

*Bilder aus Mekka.*—Mit Kurzem Erläuternden Texte. Von C. Snouck Hurgronje. Leiden, E. J. Brill, 1889. (18 phototypes in folio.)

This is a welcome supplement to Dr. Snouck's "Mekka," a notice of which we gave in No. 2, p. 56. A native of Mecca who had been taught photography by Dr. Snouck sent him a series of impressions which are here reproduced, consisting mostly of views of the sacred city and the sacred territory. Among other interesting sights we have a view of the great mosque at the time of service (*çaldt*), and several scenes from the progress of the pilgrims, and we receive an instructive picture of the situation of the city, the sacred localities, and the busy life which then reigns in those otherwise desolate parts. One picture which is particularly well executed represents a Sherif of high rank with his companions and his richly caparisoned camel, two others portray the bridal throne. The explanatory text is brief, all details being given in the larger work. This album of photographs may, however, prove attractive also as an independent publication. We recommend it to all who would form a correct idea of the centre of Islam.　　　　　　　　　　　　　　Th. N.

———

*Untersuchungen zur altorientalischen Geschichte.* Von H. Winckler. Leipzig, E. Pfeiffer, 1889. 8vo. pp. x. and 157.

The considerable and rapid progress lately made in Cuneiform research, which, among other fresh discoveries, has furnished the student of Eastern antiquities with a large material of historical texts, suggested to various scholars the task of writing a separate and exhaustive history of Babylonia and Assyria from the beginnings of the Mesopotamian kingdoms down to the Persian dominion. The first such sketch, brought out in 1874 and 1875, by the late George Smith, was, though naturally very imperfect, a good attempt at carrying out this idea. But fourteen more years of study and collecting were wanted until the Dutch scholar, Professor C. P. Tiele, succeeded in completing his well-known *Babylonisch-assyrische Geschichte* (Gotha, 1886-8), which is the first history of ancient Mesopotamia, resulting from a careful and objective examination of the original Cuneiform documents.

The last few years have brought us again, however, a considerable enlargement of the historical sources, and have made us modify our views as to the origin and development of the various states of Babylonia in the oldest times.

Dr. Winckler, who during that period was engaged upon preparing a new edition of the inscriptions of Sargon II., and was copying at both the Louvre and the British Museum the monuments relating to that period of Assyrian history, made himself at the same time acquainted with as many Cuneiform texts of historical contents as possible, illustrating the various epochs of the history of Babylonia and Assyria. In collating a good many of the early published inscriptions with the originals, and adding some new ones to the stock of them, which have since arrived in the

British Museum, he soon found that some of these are of the greatest importance for a better understanding of that history. He therefore published, in the *Zeitschrift für Assyriologie*, a series of historiographical articles, including the first edition of two texts of Nabopolassar, the father of Nebukadnezzar II., of several texts of Nebukadnezzar himself, of Khammurabi, and also of the celebrated *Babylonian Chronicle* relating the history of Babylonia and Assyria from about B.C. 750 to about 650. He also treated in these articles an ancient List of Babylonian Kings; on Tiglathpileser III. (hitherto called II.) and the earliest Assyrian rulers; on the Assyrian dynasties; on the murderer of Sennacherib, and on the capture of Samaria by the Assyrians.

The preparation of these papers as well as of the valuable historical *Introduction* to his *Sargon* made Dr. Winckler well acquainted with the still doubtful questions as to Assyrian history, comprising almost every one of its stages of development.

A series of further contributions towards the solution of such problems is the scope of the present book, which chiefly consists in five historical sketches, adding the explanation of some details (*Einzelnes,* pp. 133, ff.) and, on 13 autographed plates, the first, or re-edition of various valuable historical documents in the British Museum, among which we mention especially two lists of Babylonian kings, the so-called *Synchronous History* of Babylonia and Assyria, a chronicle of the time of Nabonidus, and one of the time of Cyrus.

In the first part, "On Babylonian-Assyrian Chronology," the author gives a careful enumeration of the sources comprising the Cuneiform as well as the Latin and Greek documents, adding a most elaborate criticism of their value, when compared with each other. He arrives at the conclusion that the names of the Babylonian dynasties and their duration as furnished in the Cuneiform inscriptions are not to be identified with those given by Berossos, a useless attempt at such an identification having been made by several Assyriologists.

In the second part, concerning "the position of the Chaldaeans in history," the author anew challenges the erroneous statement, hitherto almost unanimously accepted by the historians, that the "Chaldaeans" are identical with the "Babylonians." He shows in a series of specimens, and confirms by some new arguments, that throughout the Cuneiform documents the Babylonians are said to be a different population from that of the Chaldaeans (*Kaldi*), a distinction which is also kept to by Berossos; he further proves that the dynasty of Nabopolassar was a "Chaldaean" one, and finally gives a plausible explanation of the confusion of the two terms in the late classic writers, from whom it crept into modern books.

The solution of some of the most difficult problems in Oriental history is attempted in the third part, which is entitled "The old-Mesopotamian Kingdoms" (*die altmesopotamischen reiche*). As little is known to the general reader about the beginnings of Babylonia and Assyria, we beg leave to insert here Winckler's views on them. According to his investigations the development of the Babylonian-Assyrian Empire was as follows: In the oldest times, we find various centres of cult under the supremacy of one city, the offices of the "king" and the highest "priest" being united in one personage. One important such centre out of the few which are known at present is that of *Sir-pur-la*. The first formation of a larger kingdom in Southern Babylonia, probably a combination of various of those smaller ones (in the cities of *Sir-pur-la*, *Uruk*, *Larsam*, *Nippur*, etc.) is the Empire of "*Shumir* (or *Kingi*) and *Akkadi*," with the capital city of *Ur*, under king *Ur-gur*, succeeded by his son *Dungi*. A later dynasty seems to have been that of the kings of *Nisin* (or *Isin*? ; *Zeits. f. Assyr.*, 1889, p. 430), and again later, the so-called "second Dynasty of *Ur*." The last independent dynasty of Southern Babylonia was that of *Larsam*, and its last king is known under the name of *Rim-sin*, son of the Elamite king *Kudur-mabuk*.

With respect to the development of the empire in Northern Babylonia (with the cities of *Kuta*, *Kharsag-kalamma*, *Babylon*, etc.), we are not yet acquainted with any detailed accounts. Both parts of the land were united under the sceptre of *Khammurabi*, the founder and ruler of the cult-centre in Babylon—most probably living in the third millennium B.C.

It is apparently from one of those Northern Babylonian Kingdoms that the Empire of *Ashshur* (Assyria) is to be derived, though its beginnings are as yet perfectly unknown to us. As soon as both States appear to be united, their vicissitudes, forming the so-called Babylonian-Assyrian history, are to be studied in their mutual connection.

The fourth part, "The Sargonides and Egypt according to Assyrian sources," forms partly an addition, and to some extent also corrections to the *Introduction* in Winckler's edition of the inscriptions of Sargon II., while the fifth contains some valuable contributions "towards the Medic and old-Persian history," relating the origin of the Persian Empire, the order of the succession of the Akhaemenian kings, their nationality, and various points of Medo-Persian geography, as illustrated by the Cuneiform sources.

The above is but a very brief summary of the contents of this useful and interesting book, which includes, besides a number of remarkable details, many and very carefully compiled extracts from the historical Assyrian texts in Roman transcript, accompanied by a literal German translation. We highly recommend it to English readers also as not only most instructive, but at the same time readable and attractive.

C. BEZOLD.

*London, January 9th, 1890.*

---

*An Arabic Reading Book.* By Alan R. Birdwood. (W. H. Allen and Co.)

This useful little Manual is intended as a stepping-stone between the elementary grammars and the more difficult text-books to aid the student in his efforts to obtain a thorough mastery of modern Arabic as spoken in Egypt. Its object, therefore, is to teach idiom, and to initiate the learner into the business and official style of composition. To attain this object the work is divided into four sections, viz. 1, sentences and dialogues ; 2, exercises for translating into English ; 3, extracts from Arabic newspapers and official documents ; and 4, manuscript letters. Ample notes—many of them supplied by Dr. Steingass—occasional translations, and other helps are added to assist the student. We can conscientiously commend this unpretending book to the careful attention of those who, after mastering the elements of grammar, are desirous of further improving their knowledge of the Egyptian dialect of modern Arabic.

---

# Obituary.

---

**Sir Henry Yule.**—We regret to announce the death yesterday of Colonel Sir Henry Yule, whose health had caused grave anxiety to his friends for many months past. Although he had received the well-deserved honour of knighthood, he will be best known to fame and remembered by his friends as plain Colonel Yule, the editor of the "Travels of Marco Polo," and of many other standard books of mediæval adventure in the continent of Asia. The authority which he had acquired as a geographical expert far exceeded that of other Englishmen, and at the same time his care as an editor and the great stores of information he had laid up from diligent inquiry in out-of-the-way places had given him a literary reputation to which perhaps no other writer on Asiatic subjects could lay claim. It is probable that he owed much of this reputation to the care with which he kept aloof from politics and the political side of the Central Asian question ; and so well did he preserve this neutral attitude during the heat of the controversy relating to the last Afghan war that, although it was known that he held strong opinions of his own, no one could say with any degree of certainty whether he belonged to the forward school or that of masterly inactivity. In the character of a master of the geographical and historical sides of the question, without being a partisan, Colonel Yule stood alone. No one attacked him personally, because he was careful to screen his own views behind a cloud of science and research, and also because it was always hoped that his name might be used as a champion by the one side or the other.

Henry Yule was the youngest son of the late Major William Yule, of the Bengal Army. He was born on the 1st May, 1820, at Inveresk, a residence of his family, near Edinburgh. He was educated in Scotland, and, being destined for an Indian military career, entered Addiscombe in February, 1837. He passed out in December, 1838, for the Bengal Engineers, and reached India early in 1840. Although the first Afghan war was then in progress, he was not sent to the front, his earliest employment being in connexion with the canals in the North-west Provinces. His first experiences of real warfare were gained in the Sutlej and Punjab campaigns. On the outbreak of war with Burma, he was sent to the Arracan frontier, and ordered to make a full survey of the borders between that province and Upper Burma. During this work he attracted the attention of the late Sir Arthur Phayre, and when that officer was sent, in 1855, on a special mission to Ava,

Colonel Yule accompanied him as his private secretary, and afterwards wrote an account of the embassy. After his return to India the Mutiny broke out, and during 1857 he was employed on defensive works at Allahabad, Benares, and Mirzapore. In 1858 he was attached to the Railway Department, having previously acted as Under-Secretary in the Public Works Department, and from 1857 to 1862 he held the appointment of Secretary to the same office. In 1862, partly on account of ill-health, he retired from the service with the honorary rank of colonel. After an interval of 13 years he returned to official life as member for the India Council, to which he was appointed in 1875 as a life member. The state of his health compelled his retirement from that post six months ago, and Lord Cross paid a handsome, but well-deserved, compliment to the excellent work he had done during his fourteen years' stay in the India Office. His influence on the many literary and geographical matters submitted to the Library Committee of the India Office was always discriminating and beneficial, and on public work questions he spoke with the experience of one who had treated them in a practical form.

But it is not as an official, however respected and efficient, that Colonel Yule will be best remembered. The engineer officer and member of the India Council sinks in comparison with the geographer and writer. In the earlier years of his career his literary feats were confined to technical subjects connected with his profession. His narrative of the mission to Ava, already referred to, and published in 1858, was his first attempt in the wider field of letters. The most active period of his literary career began after his return from India. In 1866 he published, under the title of "Cathay and the Way Thither," a masterly account of the attempts to reach China overland in the middle ages. The work was marked by great powers of comparison as well as by a research which placed the author in the front rank of geographical experts. It was the first connected narrative of the attempts of Italian priests and merchants to reach the semi-mythical land of Cathay during the period of the Mongol domination from the Danube to the Pacific, and it reopened a chapter of European enterprise that had been closed. "Cathay and the Way Thither" at once became a text-book on the subject of land-intercourse between Europe and China. Excellent as was this work, it was in turn eclipsed by the edition he brought out in 1871 of the "Book of Ser Marco Polo." The journal of the gossiping Venetian had been published several times before both in English and in French, but it was at once admitted that Colonel Yule's edition superseded every other. The merit of his workmanship was not so much in the care with which the text was transcribed, or in the accuracy of the translation (although in both points commendation was fully earned), but in the remarkable wealth of the notes which embraced every branch of the subject, whether it related to China itself or the countries visited *en route* by Marco Polo. Although it was an act of high treason in the eyes of Colonel Yule to say anything disparaging of the Venetian merchant, there could not be any doubt that the marked value of his edition lay in the original matter contributed by the editor, rather than in the old tale of the Italian traveller. Such was the success of the work that a second and enlarged edition made its appearance in 1875, and the work must be described as scarce at the present time. Colonel Yule's next task was in conjunction with the late Mr. Burnell to make a collection of curious and out-of-the-way words and terms—an operation which naturally extended over many years, and at last resulted in the appearance of "Hobson-Jobson, or a Glossary of Anglo-Indian

Terms," in 1886. This work is as remarkable in its way as either of its predecessors. There is hardly a term mentioned in the seventeenth and eighteenth centuries, not merely in published works, but in the factory diaries and the Court-letter books, that does not find a place in this glossary, with a full explanation of its meaning and etymology. The value of this book of reference must increase with time, for while more frequent reference is likely to be made to the manuscript records of the India Office, there is no probability of any one's having the knowledge, the patience, and the leisure to emulate Colonel Yule's Anglo-Indian repertory. Before "Hobson-Jobson" had issued from the Press Colonel Yule was busily engaged editing the "Diary of William Hedges," which made its full appearance last year in three volumes under the auspices of the Hakluyt Society. This work showed all the old qualities of intimate acquaintance with every branch of his subject and the indefatigable research which had characterized the other works we have mentioned. The volumes really give an excellent history of the English in Bengal in the seventeenth century, and with his usual thoroughness Colonel Yule added a biographical account of the principal persons mentioned. In addition to these important works Colonel Yule was the author of several longer articles in the *Encycl. Britannica*, and a large number of fugitive writings in the journals of the learned societies, and in works in which he took a friendly interest, as, for instance, in the late Captain Gill's "River of Golden Sand" [Wood's "Journey to the Sources of the Oxus," second edition, and in Mr. Morgan's translation of Prejevalsky's "Mongolia"]. He was also considered particularly happy in drafting epitaphs, and among others he composed those for the monument over the Well at Cawnpore, and on the statue to Sir James Outram, the Bayard of India, at Calcutta. He had been President of the Royal Asiatic, the Hakluyt, and other societies, and had been nominated a member of most of the leading foreign institutions. [A telegram announcing his election as a corresponding member of the French Institute reached him on Christmas Day, five days before his death. His reply was couched in the following Latin telegram : "Reddo gratiis, illustrissimi domini, ob honores tanto nimios quanto immeritos. Mihi robora deficiunt, vita collabitur. Accipiatis voluntatem pro facto. Cum corde pleno et gratissimo moriturus vos, illustrissimi domini, saluto. — Yule."] Among English honours he long possessed only the Companionship of the Bath, but less than twelve months ago he received, somewhat tardily, the Knight Commandership of the Star of India.

It will thus be seen that Colonel Yule's merit and title to fame lay in the extent of his acquaintance with the facts of Asiatic exploration of all periods, in the precision with which he recorded those facts, and in the editorial care and zeal with which he placed before the reader the works of the men he selected for his special attention. In fact, he was a model editor, and no one could select a better guide than he was in the intricate and frequently little interesting paths of Asiatic research.

The character of the man as much as the nature of his work made him a severe and unsparing critic, but even in this respect he did solid work towards elucidating the problems of his subject, and the light which he threw upon them is both clear and trustworthy. His main purpose was to get at and to record the truth, and in accepting Colonel Yule's facts a subsequent writer will find himself on firmer ground than will be the case with regard to most other authorities on Asiatic subjects.—[From the *Times* of 31st Dec. 1889.]

In addition to the publications mentioned in the

above Obituary Notice, we append a list of Sir H. Yule's contributions to the Transactions of learned Societies and other Serials:—

*Journal Asiatic Society of Bengal.*

Vol. xi. (1842), 853. Notes on the Iron of the Kasia Hills.
 ,, xiii. (1844), 612. Notes on the Kasia Hills and People.
 ,, xv. (1846), 213. A Canal Act of the Emperor Akbar, with some Notes and Remarks on the History of the Western Jumna Canals.
 ,, xxvi. (1857), 1. Account of the Ancient Buddhist Remains at Pagán.
 ,, xxx. (1861), 211. A Few Notes on Antiquities near Jabalpur.
 ,, xxxi. (1862), 16. Notes of a Brief Visit to some of the Indian Remains in Java.

*Journal Royal Asiatic Society, n.s.*

Vol. iv. 340. An Endeavour to Elucidate Rashiduddin's Geographical Notices of India.
 ,, 406. Remarks on the Senbyú Pagoda at Mengún.
 ,, vi. 92. Notes on Hwen Thsang's Account of Tokharistan.
 ,, 275. Note on Northern Buddhism.
 ,, xviii. 323. Remarks on Captain Talbot's Letter on the Rock-cut Caves and Statues at Bamian.

*Journal Royal Geographical Society.*

Vol. xlii. (1872), 438. Papers connected with the Upper Oxus Regions.
 ,, xliv. (1874), 103. Remarks on "Phillips' Notices of South Mangi."

*Proceedings Royal Geographical Society.*

Vol. x. (1865–66), 270. Notices of Cathay.
 ,, iv. n.s. (1882), 649. Notes on the Oldest Records of the Sea Route to China from Western Asia.
 ,, viii. (1886), 103. Obituary Notice of Lieut.-Gen. Sir A. Phayre.

*Asiatic Quarterly Review.*

Vol. i. pp. 119–140. Hobson-Jobsoniana.
 ,, v. pp. 312–35. Concerning some little-known Travellers in the East. No. I. George Strachan.
 ,, vi. pp. 382–98. No. II. William, Earl of Denbigh; Sir H. Skipwith; and others.

Sketches of Java. A Lecture delivered at the Meeting of the Bethune Society, Calcutta, February 13, 1862, by Lieut.-Col. Henry Yule. (Calcutta, 1862.) Pp. 39.

---

**August Engelbrecht Ahlqvist.**—Finno-Ugric philology has sustained an irreparable loss through the death of A. E. Ahlqvist, Professor Emeritus of the Finnish Language and Literature at the University of Helsingfors, which took place at that city on Wednesday, November 20th, 1889.

August Engelbrecht Ahlqvist was born in 1826 in Kuopio, a little town in the very heart of Finland, where the Finnish language, saved from the destructing influence of neighbouring tongues, such as Swedish and Russian, was developing in genuine pristine purity. He acquired Finnish as his mother-tongue and a rare facility in expressing himself tersely and elegantly, which is the more remarkable, as the language at that time was very little adapted for literary use, Swedish still being the language of higher education in Finland. But Ahlqvist devoted all his life to the study of his native tongue, and its rapid progress, culture, and development during the last decennia are in a considerable degree due to Ahlqvist's literary activity not only as a scholar, but also as an original poet and translator of foreign poetical and educational literature. Many ideas and terms, for which there had been no corresponding expressions in Finnish, were by him introduced into the language by means of ingeniously coined original words—a task in which Ahlqvist was greatly assisted by the marvellous elasticity of the language.

Of no less importance than his labours in the popular and national field is Ahlqvist's activity as a scholar. The chair for Finnish philology was founded in 1851, and Ahlqvist was its third incumbent, his two predecessors being M. A. Castrén, the celebrated founder of Ural-Altaic comparative philology, and Elias Lönnrot, the eminent collector and arranger of the Finnish national Epos, the *Kalevala*. It was no easy task for Ahlqvist to show himself worthy of such predecessors; but every one must admit that he fulfilled all expectations.

Ahlqvist was enrolled as a student at the University of Helsingfors in 1844, took the degree of Philosophiæ Magister in 1853, and that of Ph.D. in 1859. In the same year he was a "Docent" at the University, and in 1863 he was appointed Professor. He acted as academical teacher till 1888, when he retired. He held the office of Rector Magnificus of the University from 1884 to 1887.

The Ural-Altaic languages are almost entirely destitute of a history, as no old texts or records exist; the comparative philologist has therefore to collect his materials from the living and spoken languages, and by way of inter-comparison is able to define what is common to the different dialects and what is characteristic in each. This method, initiated by Castrén, Ahlqvist had to follow. As early as in the year 1846, he travelled in several provinces of Finland, studying the patois and collecting Runic songs; many of these were incorporated in Lönnrot's second edition of Kalevala.

In the year 1854 Ahlqvist studied the *Votic* language in the Government of St. Petersburg, and in the following year, in the province of Olonetz, the *Vepsic* language. A few months after his return he started for his long expedition to Siberia. He left Finland in 1856, and went first to Kasan, where he studied the *Tshuvash* language, which he found wholly to be of the Turco-Tataric type. At the same time he acquired considerable knowledge of *Tataric*. From Kasan Ahlqvist rode on towards the south with the object of studying the *Mordvin* language in its varying dialects. Towards the end of 1858 he crossed the frontier between Europe and Asia, and came to Tobolsk in Siberia, and then went on to a little place called Pelym, where he studied the *Vogulic* dialects spoken there, viz. those of Pelym and Konda. Having acquired a sufficient knowledge of these, he travelled through the tracts inhabited by these tribes to take notes of their manners and lore, and finally made a halt on the northern border of the river Sosva, where he studied the so-called *Sosva* dialect. At the end of September he went to Beresov, situate in the province of Tobolsk, to study *Ostjak*, whence he returned home by way of Tobolsk, Perm, Moscow, and St. Petersburg, in 1859.

During the years 1861–62, Ahlqvist sojourned in Germany, Bohemia, and Hungary, where he made himself acquainted with the methods of Indo-European Comparative Philology, which he subsequently, with the necessary modifications, so successfully applied to the Finno-Ugrian languages, more especially to Hungarian.

In 1877 Ahlqvist started on his second Siberian expedition. He stayed chiefly in Beresov, studying the *North-Ostjak* dialect, and a few years later, in 1880, he went for the third time to Siberia in order to investigate more closely the dialect of the *Konda-Vogulic* tribe.

Prof. Ahlqvist has been a very productive scholar. Among his more important works may be mentioned his *Votic Grammar* (in Swedish), published in the 'Acta Societatis Scientiarum Fenniæ' in 1856; *On the Verb in the Moksha-dialect of the Mordvin language* (in Swedish), 1859; *Versuch einer Moksha-Mordvinischen*

*Grammatik*, nebst Texten und Wörterverzeichniss, 1862; *Ueber die Sprache der Nord-Ostjaken*, 1880; *Unter Vogulen und Ostjaken*, Reisebriefe und ethnographische Mittheilungen, 1883 (Acta Soc. Sc. Fenn.).

The works above mentioned are of more or less monographical character, but Ahlqvist has also published a great many comparative essays, of varying extent, among which may be mentioned his paper *On the Relation between the Magyar and Finnish Languages* (in Finnish; in the Journal "Suomi"). On a comparative base stands also one of his chief works, *The Structure of the Finnish Language*, I. (in Finnish), Helsingfors, 1877.

He has also written a few essays on the subject of Kalevala, treating especially of the origin of this important Epos. Ahlqvist's opinion is that it originated among the inhabitants of Eastern Finland and neighbouring parishes of Russia, the so-called Carelians, and belongs exclusively to them. Upon this question he stands in a sharp contrast with the late Prof. J. Krohn, who maintains the probability that even the Tavastians and Western Finns had a share of this, in his opinion wholly national, Epos, although it is only among the less cultivated Carelians that a record of it has been preserved.

Of paramount interest even to other scholars, besides the Ural-Altai philologists, is Ahlqvist's book *Die Kulturwörter der West-Finnischen Sprachen* (Helsingfors, 1875), being an enlarged translation of the original Swedish edition, which was published in 1871.

We owe to Ahlqvist, in addition to the important works just specified, many minor essays dispersed over various serials, and also a considerable mass of manuals. On vacating his chair he found more leisure for working out the rich materials collected by him in his many journeys, but death took him away from amidst his labours. Among the papers he was preparing for publication we may specially mention those on *Tshuvash* grammar and lexicology, with specimens of texts (nearly ready); a *Tsheremiss* vocabulary (containing over 2000 words); a *Tataric* vocabulary; further materials on the *Ersa-mordvin* dialect; and a very important collection in *Vogulic* and *Ostjak* philology and folklore; the sketch of a *Vogul* and a *North-Ostjak* grammar; a *Vogulisches Wörterverzeichniss*, ready for the press. His *Ersa-mordvin* grammar, vocabulary, and specimens of texts is in a sufficiently forward state for being sent to press. The concluding portion of his very interesting *Structure of the Finnish Language* has been left unwritten. However, it is to be hoped that younger scholars will be able to make accessible the results of a life's work which was zealously and conscientiously devoted to investigations on the Finnish language in all its branches.

J. N. REUTER.

The death is announced of Dr. *Gustav Weil*, a distinguished Orientalist and German historian. He was born at Salzburg in 1808, and began his studies in the Talmud under his grandfather, the Rabbi of Metz. It was intended that he should become a theologian, but he preferred the study of History, Philology, and Oriental Literature. In 1830 Dr. Weil went to Paris, where his favourite studies took a wide extension, under the direction of Sylvestre de Sacy. He subsequently visited the East, dwelling for five years at Cairo, where he studied Persian, Turkish, and Arabic. He was at the same time engaged at the public schools of Cairo as French professor and interpreter. Returning to Germany in 1836, deceased occupied various provisional appointments in the University at Heidelberg until 1845, when he was named Professor of Oriental Languages, which appointment he held until his death. This was the first occasion on which an Israelite was admitted to the honour, and Dr. Weil's formal recognition as professor in 1861 caused considerable sensation. He was elected correspondent of the Academy of Inscriptions and Belles Lettres in 1860. Dr. Weil was the author of a large number of original works, essays, translations, etc. Among the former may be cited "The Poetic Literature of the Arabs," 1837; "Mohammed the Prophet: his Life and Teaching," 1843; "History of the Caliphs," 1846–1862; "Historical and Critical Introduction to the Koran," 1844; "Mussulman Legends," 1845; and "History of the Mussulman Peoples, from Mahomet to Selim," 1866. His chief translation was one of the "Arabian Nights," in four volumes, 1837–41.—[From *The Times* of September 10, 1889.]

---

*Alfred von Kremer*, whose death was announced as having taken place in his native city on the 27th December last, was born at Vienna on the 13th May, 1828. After absolving his university studies, he received from the Imperial Academy a travelling allowance for two years to report on the libraries in Syria. On his return to Vienna in the summer of 1851, he was entrusted with the chair for Modern Arabic at the Polytechnic Institute. In the following year he was appointed First Dragoman to the Austrian Consulate in Egypt; he became Vice-Consul at Cairo in 1858, and held the full appointment from 1859 to 1862. He was next transferred to Galacz as Austrian Delegate to the International European Danube Commission, and continued to reside there as Austrian Consul. In 1870 he received the post as Austrian Consul-General for Syria at Beyrout. He had not held that post many years when he was made referee on the Consular service in the Ministry for Foreign Affairs at Vienna. In 1876 he was called to Egypt as a member of the Commission for regulating the national debt. It was in this capacity that he took the initiative for having the spendthrift Khedive removed. In the summer of 1880 he received the portfolio as Minister of Commerce, which he, however, resigned in the following February, as he could not reconcile the prevailing ministerial policy with the strong opinions he held in an opposite direction. We have from the pen of his friend, Professor D. H. Müller, of Vienna, an admirable estimate of his character as a historiographer (*Neue Freie Presse* for Jan. 14 and 15), on which the following sketch is mainly based.

Two immortal works stand out in high relief as the crowning results of a life of literary research,—his History of the Leading Ideas of Islam (*Geschichte der herrschenden Ideen des Islams*, Leipzig, 1864), and his History of Eastern Civilization under the Khalifs (*Kulturgeschichte des Orients unter den Khalifen*, Wien, 1875–77). Many years of arduous reading in all branches of Arabic literature had to be devoted to the collecting, sifting, arranging and working up of the materials for those works. A long residence in the Levant where Islam had gained its triumphs, and a close familiarity with the physical conditions of those parts, and the habits and customs of the people, came to his aid in gauging his judgment on historical questions. The mass of those materials, which would have confused and bewildered a less clear thinker, gained light and life in his hands. But it was the contrast between the present gloomy state of the Muhammadan world and its glorious past that stimulated him to trace the causes of its rise and decay. In all the phases of its changeful history he would seize the most characteristic and essential traits, and investigate the moving principles underlying the great historical dramas that he was engaged in portraying : and by excluding everything immaterial he was able to compass within comparatively narrow limits a comprehensive and perspicuous pragmatical history of the Muhammadan power. His numerous smaller treatises which either (since 1850) preceded or followed the publication of those two great works, were intended to lead up to them or to illustrate and comment upon them. The second part of his last work, "Researches towards a comparative history of civilization," has just been sent to press. By far the most important of his minor essays is the one entitled "*Ueber das Einnahmebudget des Abbasidenreiches.*" In it he describes the revenue budget of the Muhammadan Power under the Abbasides in A.H. 306 (A.D. 918-19) from data in a rare MS. belonging to the library of Gotha and entitled كتاب الوزراء والكتّاب by Hilâl al-Sâby, to which his friend Professor M. J. de Goeje, of Leiden, had drawn his attention. He subsequently copied the whole of this MS. and was preparing the work for publication when death overtook him. The high principles which pervade and characterize all his writings guided him also in his public career both in Egypt and in his native country. What had been laid down as right and good by such of his favourite authors as Ibn Khaldûn, Mavardy, Ma'ǎry, was exemplified by his own unblemished life. None but a man of such grand conceptions and such nobility of character could so successfully have solved those perplexing historical problems as Alfred von Kremer has done.

---

Another great Arabic scholar, *Andreas Heinrich Thorbecke*, has passed away. He was born at Meiningen on the 14th March, 1837, but on his father's death the family settled at Mannheim. At an early age, while at school at Schnepfenthal, still more when he was a pupil at the College at Mannheim, Thorbecke evinced extraordinary philological talents. He studied classical philology at several German universities from 1854 to 1858, but began to devote himself in the following year to Semitic languages, chiefly Arabic, first under Professor Joseph Müller at Münich, and from 1864 to 1868 under Fleischer at Leipzig. In the last-named year he obtained leave to lecture in the University of Heidelberg, and was five years later appointed *professor extraordinarius*. In 1885 he was invited to fill the chair for Semitic languages at Halle, and was nominated *professor ordinarius* in 1888. On Weil's death he was recalled to Heidelberg ; but while staying at Mannheim in the Christmas vacation with the view of arranging for the change of abode, malignant typhus carried him off on the 3rd of January last in the fifty-third year of his age. Thorbecke was undoubtedly one of the foremost Arabists of the day, though he was the very last man to raise any pretensions to that effect. Quite apart from the high standard of his general culture and of his Arabic scholarship in particular, his authority on questions regarding classical Arabic poetry was without a rival. It is much to be regretted that from his extensive collections in this domain he should, owing to his extreme fastidiousness, have published comparatively little. We have only his dissertation on "Antarah as a pre-islamite poet" (Leipzig, 1862), and the first fasciculus of the great collection of poems called the Mufaddaliyát (Leipzig, 1885). In the great edition of the Annals of Tabari he prepared pp. 1-295 of the second part for publication. Researches on the history of the Arabic language were among his favourite studies, witness his edition of Harîrî's work on faulty expressions (1871), and of Sabbâg's grammar of modern Arabic (1886). Whatever proceeded from his pen showed an astounding philological acumen as well as an extensive acquaintance with Arabic literature. His rich lexical collectanea were ever at the service of his fellow-students, to all of whom he had endeared himself by his rare unselfishness and his singleness of purpose.

*We append another notice just to hand.*

The band of German Arabists has been under an evil star these ten years : one after another, its most prominent members have been snatched away by a premature death. In 1881 Loth was taken from us, in 1883 Spitta, in 1884 Teufel, and the early days of 1890 recorded a fresh loss, perhaps the bitterest of all. On the 3rd January Thorbecke died of typhus after a few days' illness. Of the fast decreasing number of Fleischer's pupils he was perhaps the one in whom the master's three chief qualities—acumen, learning, and exactness—were most harmoniously combined. By a strange fatality this death coincided with that of Baron von Kremer, who was not only a loyal Austrian, but also a good German : the greatest historian and the best philologist of Islam have departed this life at one and the same time. Standing on Fleischer's shoulders, Thorbecke could dare to aim at a higher flight than the master himself. The school of modern classical philology which he had passed through before turning his attention to the East, had taught him to take for the basis of all research the principle of constituting a philological text on the most complete attainable manuscript material. He was not the first to adopt this course : Wright and de Goeje had followed it before him. But ever since his first Oriental publication he has taken his stand beside them and as one of them. Having been born on the 14th March, 1837, he was indeed already of mature age, when in 1867, on the occasion of his being admitted a lecturer in the University of Heidelberg, he brought out his "Antarah, ein vorislamischer Dichter," a treatise in which the scholarly excellencies just mentioned are already fully apparent. The number of publications which followed this treatise is not large. In addition to some papers in the Journal of the German Oriental Society, he brought out an edition of 'Hariri's Durrat al-ghawwâss' (1871), 'Al-A'sha's poem in praise of Mohammed' (1875), a portion of the 'Annals of Tabari' (Ser. II. p. 1-295, 1881), 'Ibn Duraid's Kitáb al-malâhin' (1882), and the first fasciculus of his long-expected edition of the 'Mufaddhalíyát,' the most difficult of all collections of Arabic poems (1885).

There are two reasons which account for the sparseness of his publications. In the first he followed the example of Fleischer his great master also in this that he was ever ready to assist others with his superior learning and from the rich materials he had collected—assistance which has been publicly acknowledged by many, though not by all. In the second place he had made it a rule to procure and read through all Arabic texts which had any bearing whatever on his special study of Arabic poetry. It resulted from this method that he had brought together collectanea in which every rare word, every verse quoted somewhere or other was entered, collectanea of a colossal extent such as certainly no other Oriental scholar can boast of. It was owing to this laborious and self-denying method that he had acquired in that special subject a surety which bordered on infallibity, and through which his edition of the Mufaddhalíyát, now a torso, would have become a classical work in its best sense. The best years of his life and an untold amount of labour had been expended by the sower in cultivating his field in the most careful manner ; when the corn began to ripen, he himself was cut down by the sickle of the reaper.

Limited as is the range of Thorbecke's writings, his

high qualifications, not only in Arabic philology and poetry, but also in other branches of Arabic as well as in Persian and Turkish literature, have long been generally recognized. In the Universities of Breslau, Munich, Tübingen, and Vienna, he was nominated for an Oriental chair, and in each case missed the appointment through some untoward chance. It is the merit of the Prussian Government to have redressed this undeserved neglect. In 1885 he was appointed Professor at Halle where he lectured with great success for upwards of four years. Last summer, after Weil's death, the Government of his own native principality offered him the vacant chair at Heidelberg. He loved that beautiful spot above everything—*ille terrarum mihi praeter omnes angulus ridet* he might have said with Horace. All who saw him in those days tell of the joy with which he was looking forward to a return to his native province. In the fulness of it he went shortly before Christmas on a holiday visit to stay with his relatives at Mannheim. There, within three days, the malignant disease carried him off. Also in this case it was one of the best who died. He was a man in the noblest sense of the word, genuine and openhearted, firm and trustworthy, faithful and benevolent. It will be impossible to replace him, not only in the circle of his friends, but also in the domain of Oriental scholarship, which mourns the loss of the greater part of the results of his life's work. A. MÜLLER.

———

We cannot close this heavy list of obituaries without giving expression to our sorrow at the early death of *Georges Guieysse*, a young French savant of rare literary attainments and high promise, who had endeared himself to many of his fellow-students also in this country by the earnestness and solidity with which he devoted himself to his studies, and by his winning and unobtrusive manners. He had from an early period conceived an unconquerable desire for linguistical and philological research, and eagerly availed himself since his fourteenth year of the opportunities which the 'Collège de France,' the 'Sorbonne,' and the 'E'cole des hautes études' offered him to gratify his tastes. In Sanskrit, which he studied under A. Bergaigne and S. Lévi, he made such rapid progress that he was soon entrusted with an Assistant Lecturership. At the time of his last visit in England he was planning an index of all proper names occurring in the ancient Indian inscriptions. It was his intention, after accomplishing this preliminary work, to proceed to Indo-China for the purpose of tracing from its palæographic remains the history of its early civilization, a task for which he appeared to be specially qualified. It was in the midst of this project, at the very threshold of a glorious literary career, that this gifted and enthusiastic youth of little more than twenty was added to the rich harvest of Oriental scholars which death had reaped in Paris within one year. He died on the 17th May last. The addresses delivered in his memory by MM. Bréal, Dietz, Darmesteter, de Saussure, and Lévi bear testimony to the high estimate for genius, character, and scholarship in which he was held in professorial circles and among his fellow-students.

———

## Notes and News.

———


THE ÂNANDÂŚRAMA, an institution founded at Poona by Mr. M. Ch. Âpṭe, a Pleader in the High Court, Bombay, for the propagation and encouragement of Sanskrit learning, is flourishing. The number of Sanskrit manuscripts brought together by purchase, gift or loan already exceeds 12,000, and a number of Pandits living on the premises are constantly engaged in preparing correct editions of valuable works for publication and seeing them through the press. According to the prospectus, "The works printed at the Ânandâśrama press are to be issued when completed, and not in monthly parts, and are to be sold to subscribers at the rate of Rs. 1–8–0 per 200 pages royal octavo, and to non-subscribers at the rate of Rs. 2 inclusive of postage charges. The subscribers are not to pay anything in advance; they have only to send in their names and each work, as it is completed, will be sent to them by value payable post without any extra charge. Refusal to receive any work thus sent will be deemed to be a refusal to continue as subscriber, and no work will be sent afterwards at subscriber's rate. Subscribers will have intimation given them a few days beforehand of any work being posted and its price. It is hoped that the publication will be on an average at the rate of 200 pages per month. The subscribers will at the most have to pay Rs. 18 during the year." The following twelve works have been published to date:—No. I. The Gaṇeśa Atharva S'irsha, with Bhâshya of an unknown author. Edited by Pandit Vâman S'astri Islâmpurkar. No. II. The Rudrâdhyâya, with the Bhâshyas of Sâyaṇa Mâdhavâchârya and Bhaṭṭa Bhâskar. Edited with the assistance of several Pandits. No. III. The Purusha Sûkta, with the Bhâshya of Sâyaṇa Mâdhavâchârya. Edited with the assistance of several Pandits. No. IV. The Yogaratnâkara, by an unknown author. Edited with the assistance of several Pandits. No. V. The Îśavâsyopanishad, with a Vârtika called its Rahasya by Brambhânanda Sarasvati, and the Bhâshya of S'rimat S'ankarâchârya and commentary by S'rimat Ananda Jnâna. No. VI. The Kenopanishad, with two Bhâshyas, the Pada Bhâshya and Vâkya Bhâshya, by S'rimat S'ankarâchârya, and commentary by S'rimat Ânanda Jnâna. No. VII. The Kaṭhopanishad, with the Bhâshya of S'rimat S'ankarâchârya, and commentary by S'rimat Ânanda Jnâna. No. VIII. The Praśnopanishad, with the Bhâshya and commentary as above. No. IX. The Muṇḍakopanishad, with the Bhâshya and commentary as above. No. X. The Mâṇḍûkyopanishad, with the Kârikâs of S'rimat Gauḍapadâchârya, with the Bhâshya and commentary as above. No. XI. The Taittirîyopanishad, with the Bhâshyas of S'rimat Sâyaṇa Madhavâchârya and of S'rimat S'ankarâchârya and commentary on the latter by S'rimat Ananda Jnâna. No. XII. The Aitareyopanishad, with the Bhâshya and commentary as Nos IX. and X. We wish this noble, and in the highest sense patriotic, enterprise every support and success.

WE have received from Mr. C. Baumgarten, of Batavia, the following communication:—In Sir T. Stamford Raffles' History of Java, vol. ii, p. 84 (1st ed.), we find the following extract from a Javanese History. "From this period [525 A.D.] Java was known and celebrated as a kingdom; an extensive commerce was carried on with Gujrat and other countries, and the Day of Mataram, then a safe place, was filled with adventurers from all parts." The Javanese of the present time divide their history into epochs, to which they give different names; so this epoch of their history—the age of their intercourse with foreign peoples—had also a special name. When we ask them for the names of the countries with which they had intercourse, they give us no answer, as no mention is made of them in their annals or old legends. It is, however, a matter of historical importance to know the names of those foreign countries. Luckily, the Javanese of those remote ages have left unimpeachable testimony in their copper and stone inscriptions. Thus, in a large copper plate inscription, dated in the Çaka year 762, in the month Çrawana, the 15th day of the white half of the moon, we find the following names: Chêmpa, Kling, Haryya, Singhâ, Gola, Chwalikâ, Malyala, Karnnaké, Rêman, K'mir. "Chêmpa" might mean the "Champa" of Bengal or of Cochin-China, most probably the latter, as the Javanese had intimate relations with that country. "Kling" is Kalinga. "Singha" the people of Ceylon. "Gola" the people of Golanagara of Burma, mentioned by Professor Forchhammer. "Chwalikâ" probably the Châlukyas of Western India. "Malyala" the Malayalam people of Southern India. "Karnnaké" Karnataka according to Mr. Burnell. "Rêman" the Javanese form of Aramana of the Mahâwansa; also Professor Bastian in his 'Remarks on the Indo-Chinese Alphabets' mentions the Talaings "or Ramans." "K'mir" the Khmer of Cambodia. The only difficulty lies in the name of "Haryya." While we see South India represented by five different names, North India is not mentioned at all. But as there is no doubt that the people of North India had also intercourse with Java, might not "Haryya" mean the people of that extensive country? Perhaps contemporary Burmese or Ceylonese sources may enlighten us.

The following works of *The Catholic Press, Beyrout*, are announced as forthcoming:—The second volume of the Arabic Dictionary (Kâmûs 'Arabi); the second volume of 'Ilm ul adab; Rasâil Badi'iz-Zamân il-Hamadâni; the History of the Dynasties by Abû'l Faraj: a historical study of the last two Emperors of Constantinople; the Diwân of Mgr. Germanos Farhât, Maronite Bishop of Aleppo; the Christian poets of the Arabs (the first volume of about 800 pages will appear in five fasciculi); History of the Maronites; French-Arabic Dictionary (more than 1500 pages of two columns each; Treatise on the French words derived from Arabic; the second volume of P. G. Cardahi's Syriac-Arabic Dictionary; and a Dictionary of classical Syriac and Latin.

ARABIC CHRESTOMATHY IN HEBREW CHARACTERS.—PROSPECTUS.—Arabic literature in Hebrew characters has gradually developed a certain independence. For many years it was necessary to employ translations in the study of the same, until some authors, following the example set by *S. Munk*, published a number of the most important works in the Arabic original. Many of these writings, however, lie still unprinted in the great libraries. To publish them all, or part of them, would entail great difficulty. Munk had intended publishing a *Chrestomathie arabe-rabbinique*. But instead of this he edited the Dalâlat al-Hâirin (More Nebuchim) of Maimonides, without carrying out his original project. Messrs. Kegan Paul, Trench, Trübner & Co. hope to meet a long-felt want by the publication of an

*Arabic Chrestomathy in Hebrew Characters, with a Glossary*. Edited by Hartwig Hirschfeld, Ph.D.

### Contents:

#### First Part.

1. Megillath Antiochus in Arabic (copied from the codd. Berol. Or. fol. 627, Brit. Mus. 2212, 2377, 2673).
2. Extracts from the Yemen Prayerbook (codd. Berol. 576, Brit. Mus. Or. 1480, Add. 2227).
3. Extracts from a collection of Homilies entitled Nûr al-Zulm "Light of Darkness" (cod. Berol. Or. fol. 628, Brit. Mus. 2356).
4. Extracts from an Arabic Midrasch on Leviticus (Collection of MSS. of late Dr. L. Loewe in London).
5. Extracts from Jehuda b. Nissim b. Malkah's Arabic Commentary on the "Sefer Yezirah" (the same collection).
6. Extracts from a "Dictionary of Difficult Words of Bible and Midrasch" (cod. Brit. Mus. Or. 2593).

#### Second Part.

1. Specimen of Sa'adyah's "Kitâb al-Imânât wa'l-itiqâdât ed. Landauer.
2. Extracts of Jehuda Hayyûg's grammatical work "Kitâb al-Lamad wal'layn (cod. Bodl. Poc. 99).
3. Specimen of Ibn Jannâh's grammatical work "Kitâb al-Lum'a" (Sefer Hariqmâh), ed. J. Derenbourg and W. Bacher.
4. Specimen of Mose b. Ezra's Treatise on poetry "Kitâb al-Muhâdara wal'mudzakarah" (cod. Bodl. Hunt. 599).
5. Specimen of Jehuda Hallewi's "Book al-Chazari," ed. Hirschfeld.
6. Specimen of Maimonides Dalâlat al-Hâirin, ed. Munk.

#### Third Part.

1. Treatise on the differences between Rabbanites and Karaïtes attributed to Sa'd b. Mansûr (cod. Berol. Oct. 256 Unicum).

#### Fourth Part: Karaïte Texts.

1. Extracts from Yefet's Commentary on the Pentateuch (cod. Brit. Mus. Or. 2399).
2. Extracts from Jacob Qirqisâni's "Sefer Hammizwôth" (cod. Brit. Mus. Or. 2524).
3. Extracts from Samuel Hârôfê's "Sefer Hammizwôth," called *al-Murschid*, "the Guide" (cod. Brit. Mus. Or. 2405-6).

Dr. Hugo Schuchardt, Professor in the University of Graz, has made for many years a close investigation and analysis of those mixed languages known as *Indo-Portuguese*, *Negro-Portuguese*, and their numerous local subdivisions. The papers which he has brought out from time to time under the title of "Kreole Researches" (*Kreolische Studien*) bristle with valuable observations, and would be highly interesting to the general philologist if they were not scattered in serials not sufficiently known or accessible in this country, where very few savants besides the authors of "Hobson-Jobson" have paid any attention to this class of languages. It has not even been adverted to in any part of the Encyclopædia Britannica. Wherever the Portuguese were brought by their early voyages and settlements in contact with indigenous races, their vernacular became the recipient of local vocables, or became otherwise tainted with a local colouring, while the natives, too, borrowed words from the Portuguese which may still be traced. The best-known of these local variations is the Ceylon Portuguese. But Dr. Schuchardt has extended his studies also to Spanish, which, as were Dutch and English in their turn, was likewise subjected to local vernacular influences at the various outlying settlements. Aided by many correspondents, he has brought, in addition to an astounding linguistical acumen, a very extensive material, procured at great trouble and expense, to bear upon a subject which he has made his special domain. His most recent contribution to these researches deals with the forms of Portuguese in the Ilha do Principe, at Mahé and Cannanore, and other parts of India. Nothing would be better calculated to bring more labourers to this wide and attractive field of philological inquiry than if the author could be induced to republish in book form his various language papers so as to make them widely available.

The TOKIO LIBRARY.—Mr. Tegima, the librarian of the "Tokio Library," has contributed a very interesting article on his library to the columns of the September number of the "Library," published by Mr. Elliot Stock, Paternoster Row.

ROYAL INSTITUTION.—The Christmas Lectures (adapted to a juvenile auditory) will this year be given by Professor A. W. Rücker, F.R.S. (Professor of Physics in the Normal School of Science and Royal School of Mines) on Electricity; they began on Saturday, December 28th.

We welcome with much gratification the announcement that the well-known Oriental publishers, Messrs. Brill & Co., of Leiden, are about to issue an Eastern Asiatic Review under the title of *T'oung pao*, intended to deal with the history, languages, geography and ethnography of Eastern Asia. under the editorship of Professors G. Schlegel and H. Cordier. Five fasciculi forming a volume of about 600 pages will be published per annum, and the papers may be written in French, English, or German. The annual subscription will be 20s. We hope this new review will, under its able editors, fulfil its mission of being a depositary of solid literary research on Central Asia, Malaisia, and the Far East.

In commemoration of the approaching millenary of the birth of Sa'dyah Gaon el-Fayyâmi (892-942), M. Joseph Derenbourg proposes to publish all the existing Arabic versions of the books of the Old Testament by this great Jewish philosopher and interpreter of the Bible. He is at present engaged on a new and critical edition of the prophet Isaiah. M. Derenbourg's undertaking deserves the sympathy of both Jewish and Christian scholars.

## American Notes.

The CALIFORNIA FRUITS.—Under this title Messrs. Dewey & Co., of San Francisco, have published a handsome octavo volume by Edward J. Wickson, A.M., showing how to grow them, and the methods which have yielded the greatest success; with lists of varieties, etc. This is the first manual that has been published on fruit growing in California; hitherto this industry has only been touched upon in State Reports. To Mr. Wickson, therefore, belongs the credit of inaugurating a literature on what is becoming a most important and remunerative industry in California. The illustrations to this work are made by a photographic process, and are portraits of the fruits themselves.

AMERICAN AGRICULTURE.—Iu the Report of the Honourable Commissioner of Agriculture of the U.S.A. for 1888 (published this year) will be found amongst other valuable articles one on Ostrich farming in America. At present the Ostrich farms are situated in the districts of Los Angeles and San Diego, Southern California; but other parts of the United States will no doubt be found suitable as the industry spreads.

VITUS BERING.—The life of the discoverer of Bering's (or Behring's) Straits should be of particular interest to the American public. Messrs. S. C. Griggs & Co., of Chicago, have placed before them Peter Laurisden's account of the great Dano-Russian explorer in an excellent translation by Professor Julius E. Olson; and Lieut. Frederick Schwatka, of Alaskan fame, has contributed an introduction in which he congratulates his countrymen that the work has been published in America, and has not emanated from the Hakluyt Society or any other British source.

INDEX CATALOGUE OF THE LIBRARY OF THE SURGEON-GENERAL'S OFFICE, UNITED STATES ARMY.—Volume X. of this valuable Catalogue is just issued. It contains letter O, and P, to Pfutsch. It contains 7658 author-titles, representing 2905 volumes and 7282 pamphlets. It also includes 14,265 subject-titles of separate books and pamphlets and 29,421 titles of articles in periodicals. Up to the present there have been registered in the ten volumes under Authors, 107,788 titles, 54,298 volumes, 93,002 pamphlets; under Subjects 107,419 book-titles, 336,772 journal articles, and also 4335 portraits.

LABOUR STATISTICS OF THE U.S.A.—The Fourth Annual Report of the Commissioner of Labour, the Hon. Carroll D. Wright, Commissioner of the Federal Government to the Secretary of the Interior, is wholly on Working Women in large cities. Three hundred and forty-three distinct industries are represented in this Report, as found in twenty-two cities. The information has been mainly collected together by women who have interviewed 17,427 of their sex to gather together the facts required. The introduction to the Report, consisting of 67 pages, is exceedingly interesting reading, and shows that the working women are as respectable, as moral, and as virtuous as any class of women in the country, and that prostitutes are recruited to a very limited extent from their ranks.—The Fifth Biennial Report of the Bureau of Labour Statistics of Illinois, as prepared by the Hon. John S. Lord, the Secretary, is the fifth of the series, and consists of three parts, one on mortgage indebtedness; one on the statistics of strikes; and the other on the Coal production of Illinois. With 833 mines the Coal mining of the State must be a very important industry.

CHECK LIST OF BIBLIOGRAPHIES, ETC., ON AMERICAN SUBJECTS.—Mr. Paul Leicester Ford, of Brooklyn, New York, has compiled a Check List of Bibliographies, Catalogues, Reference Lists, and Lists of Authorities of American Books and Subjects. The work is printed with one column on the front page of each leaf, leaving the other column for additions. It has a classified table of contents at the beginning of the book, and an authors' index at the end. Mr. Ford has done much good work in literature, and this he has now presented us with is a very useful one.

THE MUSKHOGEAN LANGUAGES.—This is the fourth series of Mr. James Constantine Pilling's Bibliographies of the North American Indian Languages, published under the auspices of the Bureau of Ethnology (Prof. J. W. Powell, Director). The Muskhogean class of languages comprise the Muskoki, the Creek, Choctaw, Chickasaw, Seminole, Apalachian, and Hitchiti. The fifth bibliography will be the Algonquinian.

THE CONGO STATE.—Mr. Henry Phillips, jun., one of the Secretaries of the American Philosophical Society, read before that Society, November 2, 1888, and February 1, 1889, a very interesting account of the Congo Independent State, which, as he says, is "one of the most curious and most characteristic episodes of the nineteenth century. It was not even upon the soil of Africa that the Congo Independent State took its origin; its birthplace was at Bruxelles, in the palace of a monarch."

AMERICAN LOCAL HISTORY.—Mr. Justin Winsor, the Librarian of the Boston Public Library, gives from time to time bibliographies of special subjects in the "Bulletins" of [Lib]rary. These bibliographies are eventually republished

in a separate form, and the third, which is before us, by Mr. Appleton Prentiss Clark Griffin, also of the Boston Public Library, is an index of articles upon American Local History in the Historical Collections of the Boston Public Library. This Index was commenced in the "Bulletin" of the Boston Public Library in April, 1883, and besides the titles contained in successive numbers of that periodical, the present volume has an "Appendix" or second alphabet embracing titles of articles in publications received too late for insertion in their proper order in the "Bulletin." If we may judge from the bulk of this "Bibliography," which contains 225 pages in double columns, the "Boston Public Library" must contain a very complete collection on American Local History, and our thanks are due to Mr. Griffin for introducing us to these treasures. Some estimate may be formed of the magnitude of his labours when we consider that the titles of articles out of over 300 sets or series of historical publications are to be found in its columns.

## American Literature.

**Abbott (Willis J.)**—Battlefields of '61. A Narrative of the Military Operations of the War for the Union up to the End of the Peninsular Campaign. Illustrated by W. C. Jackson. Illustrations and Map. 8vo. cloth, pp. 10 and 356. *New York.* 15s.

**Adams (H.)**—History of the United States of America during the first administration of Thomas Jefferson. 2 vols. 12mo. cloth. With Map. *New York.* £1.

**Adams (Rev. Myron)**—The Continuous Creation. An Application of the Evolutionary Philosophy to the Christian Religion. 12mo. cloth, pp. 6 and 259. *Boston.* 7s. 6d.

**Aldrich (Herbert L.)**—Arctic Alaska and Siberia; or, Eight Months with the Arctic Whalemen. Map and Illustrations. 12mo. cloth, pp. 6 and 234. *New York* and *Chicago.* Reduced, 7s. 6d.

**Allen (W. B.)**—The Red Mountain of Alaska. 8vo. cloth. Illustrated. *Boston.* 12s. 6d.

**American Railway (The)**: Its Construction, Development, Management, and Appliances. By T. C. Clarke, J. Bogart, M. N. Forney, Horace Porter, and others; with an Introduction by T. M. Cooley. Illustrated. 8vo. cloth, pp. 25 and 456. *New York.* £1 16s.

**Andrews (E. B.)**—An Honest Dollar. American Economic Association. 8vo. paper, pp. 4 and 113. *Baltimore.* 4s.

**Appeal (An) to Pharaoh**; the Negro Problem and its Radical Solution. 12mo. cloth. *New York.* 5s.

**Armstrong (K. L.)**—Little Giant Cyclopedia and Treasury of Ready Reference for 1890. 16mo. sheep, pp. 448. *Chicago.* 6s.

**Atkinson (E.)**—The Industrial Progress of the Nation; Consumption Limited, Production Unlimited. 8vo. cloth, pp. 7 and 395. *New York.* 12s. 6d.

**Atwater (J.)**—American Farmer's Figurer; Tables on: Butter, Broom Corn, Beans, Boards, Car Corn, Shelled Corn, Crib Corn, Cattle, Creamery, Coal, Compound Interest, etc. 12mo. cloth. *Milwaukee (Wis.).* 5s.

**Bancroft (G.)**—Martin Van Buren; to the End of his Public Career. 8vo. cloth. *New York.* 7s. 6d.

**Bancroft (Hubert Howe)**—History of the Pacific States of North America. Vol. XXI. Utah, 1540–1886. Roy. 8vo. cloth, pp. 45 and 808. *San Francisco.* £1 4s.

**Bechtel (J. H.)**—Handbook of Pronunciation and Phonetic Analysis: Designed for Use in Schools and Colleges. 24mo. cloth, pp. 143. *Philadelphia.* 2s. 6d.

**Bell (Alex. Melville)**—Popular Manual of Vocal Physiology and Visible Speech. 16mo. boards, pp. 59. *New York.* 2s. 6d.

Bellamy (E.)—Looking Backward, 2000–1887. New Edition. 12mo. cloth. *Boston.* Cloth, 5*s.*; paper, 2*s.* 6*d.*

Bigelow (H. R., M.D.)—Gynæcological Electro-Therapeutics; with an Introduction by Dr. Georges Apostole. 8vo. cloth. Illustrated. *Philadelphia.* 15*s.*

Björnström (F., M.D.)—Hypnotism; its History and Present Development; Authorized Translation from the Second Swedish Edition, by Baron Nils Posse. 8vo. paper. *New York.* 2*s.* 6*d.*

Blackstock (E. F.)—The Land of the Viking and the Empire of the Tsar. 16mo. cloth. Illustr. *New York.* 6*s.*

Blakelee (G. E.)—Blakelee's Industrial Cyclopedia. A Simple, Practical Guide for the Mechanic, Farmer, Housewife, and Children of every Thrifty Household in Town or Country. Illustrated. 8vo. cloth, pp. 2 and 720. *New York.* 15*s.*

Bosworth (Francke Huntington, M.D.)—Treatise on Diseases of the Nose and Throat. In Two Vols. Vol. I. Diseases of the Nose and Naso-Pharynx. Illustrated. 8vo. cloth, pp. 670. *New York.* £1 10*s.*

Bourinot (J. G.)—Federal Government in Canada. 8vo. paper. *Baltimore.* 5*s.*

Brackett (J. R.)—The Negro in Maryland. A Study of the Institution of Slavery. 8vo. cloth. *Baltimore.* 10*s.* 6*d.*

Brookes (E. S.)—The Story of the American Soldier in War and Peace. Illustrated. 8vo. cloth, pp. 4 and 350. *Boston.* 12*s.* 6*d.*

Brown (Alex., ed.)—The Genesis of the United States. A Narrative of the Movement in England, 1605–1616, which resulted in the Plantation of North America by Englishmen, disclosing the Contest between England and Spain for the Possession of the Soil now occupied by the United States of America; the whole set forth through a Series of Historical Manuscripts now first printed, together with a Re-issue of Rare Contemporaneous Tracts, accompanied by Bibliographical Memoranda, Notes, Plans, and Portraits, and a Biographical Index. Map. Two Vols. 8vo. cloth. *Boston.* £6 6*s.*

Butterworth (H.)—Zigzag Journeys in the British Isles; or Vacation Rambles in Historic Lands. 8vo. boards. Illustrated. *Boston.* 9*s.*

Cable (G. W.)—Strange True Stories of Louisiana. Portrait and Illustration. 12mo. cloth, pp. 8 and 350. *New York.* 10*s.*

Cable (G. W.)—The Silent South; [also] The Freedman's Case in Equity and the Convict Lease System. New Edition. Portrait. 12mo. cloth, pp. 7 and 213. *New York.* 5*s.*

Campbell (J. M.)—Unto the Uttermost. 12mo. cloth. *New York.* 6*s.* 6*d.*

Champney (Elizabeth W.)—Three Vassar Girls in Russia and Turkey. Illustrated by "Champ" and others. 8vo. cloth. *Boston.* 7*s.* 6*d.*

Champney (Elizabeth W.)—Witch Winnie; the Story of a "King's Daughter." 12mo. cloth. Illustrated. *New York.* 7*s.* 6*d.*

Cheney (G. L.)—Belief. 16mo. cloth. *Boston.* 5*s.*

Coffin (C. C.)—Redeeming the Republic. The Third Period of the War of the Rebellion in the Year 1864. 8vo. cloth. Illustrated. *New York.* 15*s.*

Cook (J.)—An Eastern Tour at Home. 12mo. cloth. *Philadelphia.* 5*s.*

Cone (Ada)—Perspective. A Series of Elementary Lectures. 12mo. cloth. Illustrated. *New York.* 5*s.*

Cone (Orello, D.D., ed.)—Essays Doctrinal and Practical, by Fifteen Clergymen; with an Introduction by H. W. Thomas, D.D. 12mo. cloth, pp. 6 and 328. *Boston.* 5*s.*

Conkling (Alfred R.)—Appleton's Guide to Mexico. Third Edition Revised. Illustrations and Map. 12mo. cloth. *New York.* 10*s.*

Constitutional History of the United States; as seen in the Development of American Law; a Course of Lectures before the Political Science Association of the University of Michigan. 12mo. cloth. *New York.* 12*s.* 6*d.*

*Contents*: Introduction by Prof. W. H. Rogers. Lecture 1, The Federal Supreme Court—its place in the American Constitution System, by T. M. Cooley; 2, Constitutional Development of the United States as influenced by Chief Justice Marshall, by H. Hitchcock; 3, Constitutional Development in the United States as influenced by Chief Justice Taney, by G. W. Biddle; 4, Constitutional Development in the United States as influenced by the decisions of the Supreme Court since 1865, by C. A. Kent; 5 The State Judiciary—its place in the American Constitutional System, by D. H. Chamberlain.

Cooley (W. Forbes)—Emmanuel. The Story of the Messiah. 12mo. cloth, pp. 8 and 546. *New York.* 7*s.* 6*d.*

Cosmic Law (The) of Thermal Repulsion. An Essay suggested by the Projection of a Comet's Tail. 12mo. cloth, pp. 3 and 60. *New York.* 4*s.*

Crooker (Jos. H.)—Problems in American Society. Some Social Studies. 16mo. cloth, pp. 3 and 293. *Boston.* 6*s.* 6*d.*

Curtin (Jeremiah).—Myths and Folk-Lore of Ireland. Illustrated. 8vo. cloth. *Boston.* 10*s.*

Curtis (G. T.)—Constitutional History of the United States from the Declaration of Independence to the Close of the Civil War. In two vols. Vol. I. 8vo. cloth. *New York.* 15*s.*

Curtis (W. E.)—Trade and Transportation between the United States and Spanish America. 8vo. paper. *Washington.* 2*s.* 6*d.*

Cushing (Luther S.)—Cushing's Manual of Parliamentary Practice. Revised Enlarged Edition. 16mo. cloth, pp. 200. *New York.* 2*s.* 6*d.*

Dall (W. H.)—A Preliminary Catalogue of the Shell-bearing Marine Mollusks and Brachiopods of the South-eastern Coast of the United States, with Illustrations of many of the Species. 8vo. paper. Illustrated. *Washington.*

De Costa (B. F., D.D.)—Pre-Columbian Discovery of America by the Northmen. New Revised Enlarged Edition. 8vo. cloth. *Albany (N.Y.).* 15*s.*

Drew (B.)—Pens and Types; or, Hints and Helps for those who Write, Print, Read, Teach, or Learn. New improved edition. 12mo. cloth. *Boston.* 6*s.*

Eddy (R., D.D., ed.)—The Universalist Register; giving Statistics of the Universalist Church, and other Denominational Information, etc., for 1890. 12mo. paper, pp. 112. *Boston.* 1*s.* 6*d.*

Ellwanger (G. H.)—The Garden's Story; or, Pleasures and Trials of an Amateur Gardener. Second Edition Revised and Enlarged. 12mo. cloth. Illustrated. *New York.* 7*s.* 6*d.*

Ely (R. T.)—Social Aspects of Christianity; and other Essays. Crown 8vo. cloth. *New York.* 4*s.* 6*d.*

Emerson (G. H., D.D.)—The Bible and Modern Thought. 12mo. cloth, pp. 165. *Boston.* 2*s.* 6*d.*

Emerson (Ralph Waldo)—Essays. First and Second Series. 12mo. paper, pp. 3 and 270. *Boston.* 2*s.* 6*d.* Riverside Paper Series.

Fletcher (Moore Russell, M.D.)—Our Home Doctor. Domestic Remedies Simplified and Explained for Family Treatment; with a Treatise on Suspended Animation and the Danger of Burying Alive, and Directions for Restoration. Portrait. 8vo. cloth, pp. 332 and 70. *Boston.* 9*s.*

Fowler (Nathaniel C., jun.)—About Advertising and Printing. A Concise, Practical, and Original Manual on the Art of Local Advertising. 8vo. cloth, pp. 160. *Boston.* 10*s.*

Frye (G. V.)—The Housewife's Practical Candy Maker. 12mo. cloth. *Chicago.* 5s.

Garretson (J. E.) ["John Darby," *pseud.*]—Man and his World; or, the Oneness of Now and Eternity. A Series of Imaginary Discourses between Socrates and Protagoras. 16mo. cloth, pp. 2 and 259. *Philadelphia.* 5s.

Gibbons (J., Cardinal)—Our Christian Heritage. 12mo. cloth. With Portrait. *Baltimore.* 6s.

Gilman (A.)—The Story of Boston; a Study of Independency. 12mo. cloth. With Map and Illustrations. *New York.* 9s.

Goodholme (T. D., ed.) — Domestic Cyclopedia of Practical Information. New issue. 8vo. cloth, pp. 650. Illustrated. *New York.* £1 5s.

Grier (J. A.)—Our Silver Coinage, and its Relation to Debts and the World-wide Depression in Prices; with an Appendix noting events to August, 1889. Fifth edition. 12mo. paper. *New York.* 1s. 6d.

Grinnell (G. Bird)—Pawnee Hero Stories and Folk Tales; with Notes on the Origin, Customs, and Character of the Pawnee People. Illustrated. 12mo. pp. 417. *New York.* 10s.

Hall (G. F.)—Some American Evils and their Remedies. 12mo. flexible cloth, pp. 2 and 70. *Cincinnati.* 3s.

Harris (W. S.)—The Potter's Wheel, and How it Goes Around; a Complete Description of the Manufacture of Pottery in America. 8vo. paper. Illustrated. *Trenton (New Jersey).* 1s. 6d.

Harris (W. T.) — Introduction to the Study of Philosophy; comprising Passages from W. T. Harris' Writings, selected and arranged with Commentary and Illustrations by Margaret Kiec. 12mo. cloth, pp. 287. *New York.* 7s. 6d.

Hauff (Wilhelm)—The Wine-Ghosts of Bremen. Illustrated by Frank M. Gregory. Translated by E. Sadler and C. R. L. Fletcher. 12mo. half vellum, pp. 26 and 64. *New York.* 7s. 6d.

Heilprin (A.)—The Bermuda Islands; the Scenery, Physical History, and Zoology of the Somers Archipelago; with an Examination of the Structure of Coral Reefs. 8vo. cloth. Illustrated. *Philadelphia.* 18s.

Herrick (Christine T.)—Cradle and Nursery. 16mo. cloth. *New York.* 5s.

Hill (Joshua). — Thought and Thrift. Subjects in Every Letter of the Alphabet for All who Labour and Need Rest. 12mo. cloth, pp. 4 and 358. *Cincinnati.* 6s. 6d.

Hints and Points for Sportsmen, by "Seneca." 16mo. cloth. *New York.* 7s. 6d.

Hitchcock (R.)—Fac-similes of Aquarelles, by American Artists; new works by P. Moran, W. H. Gibson, Maud Humphrey, and others; with Portraits of the Artists and half-tone Engravings of black and white Sketches by them; with text by Ripley Hitchcock. Folio, half cloth. *New York.* £3 3s.

Hitchcock (R.), De Kay (C.) and others.—Modern American Art; text by Ripley Hitchcock, C. De Kay, and others. Folio, cloth. *Troy (New York).* £1 18s.
Contains thirty full-page photogravures of pictures and statuary.

Holmes (O. W.)—The Autocrat of the Breakfast Table. New edition, in two vols. 12mo. cloth. *Boston.* 12s. 6d.

Home Making and Housekeeping. 12mo. cloth. *New York.* 5s.

Inventor's Manual; how to Work a Patent to make it Pay; by an Experienced and Successful Inventor. 16mo. cloth. *New York.* 5s.

Johnson (R.)—A Short History of the War of Secession 1861–1865. New edition. 8vo. cloth. With Maps, etc. *Boston.* 12s. 6d.

Lauridsen (P.)—Vitus Bering; the Discoverer of Bering Strait; revised by the Author, and translated from the Danish by Julius E. Olsen; with an Introduction to the American edition by F. Schwatka. 12mo. cloth. With Maps. *Chicago.* 6s. 6d.

Loti (Pierre).—An Iceland Fisherman. From the French by Anna Farwell de Koven. 12mo. cloth, pp. 252. *Chicago.* 5s.

Lothrop's Annual, by the best American Authors and the best American Artists. 4to. cloth. *Boston.* 10s.

Lowell (A. L.)—Essays on Government. 12mo. cloth. *Boston.* 6s.

Lumholtz (C.)—Among Cannibals. An Account of Four Years' Travels in Australia, and of Camp Life with Aborigines of Queensland. Translated by Rasmus B. Anderson. 8vo. cloth, pp. 18 and 375. *New York.* £1 5s.

Maclay (A. C.)—Mito Yashiki; a Tale of Old Japan; being a Feudal Romance descriptive of the Decline of the Shogunate and of the Downfall of the Power of the Tokugawa Family. 12mo. cloth. *New York.* 7s. 6d.

McFarlane (Rev. S.)—Among the Cannibals of New Guinea; being the Story of the New Guinea Mission of the London Missionary Society. Portrait, Map, and Illustration. 12mo. cloth, pp. 192. *Philadelphia.* 5s.

MacMunn (C. A.)—Outlines of the Clinical Chemistry of Urine. Illustrated. 8vo. cloth. *Philadelphia.* 15s.

Manson (G. J.)—Ready for Business; or, Choosing an Occupation; a Series of Practical Papers for Boys. 12mo. cloth. *New York.* 4s.

Marah (C. L.)—Opening the Oyster. A Story of Adventure. Illustrated. 8vo. cloth, pp. 4 and 361. *Chicago.* 9s.

Mead (C. M., D.D.)—Supernatural Revelation. An Essay Concerning the Basis of the Christian Faith. 8vo. cloth, pp. 13 and 469. *New York.* 12s. 6d.

Melio (G. S.)—Manual of Swedish Drill. Based on Ling's System, as Used in the London Board Schools, the Schools of Leeds, Manchester. etc. Illustrated. 16mo. boards. *New York.* 2s. 6d.

Munson (J. E.)—The Phrase Book of Practical Phonography. 12mo. cloth. *New York.* 10s.

Nast (T.)—Thomas Nast's Christmas Drawings for the Human Race. 4to. cloth. Illustrated. *New York.* 10s.

Nelson (Wolfred, M.D.)—Five Years in Panama. Illustrated. 12mo. cloth. *New York.* 7s. 6d.

Ober (F. A.)—The Knockabout Club in Spain. 8vo. cloth. Illustrated. *Boston.* 10s.

Page (W. M.)—New Light from Old Eclipses; or, Chronology Corrected and the Four Gospels Harmonized, by the Rectification of Errors in the Received Astronomical Tables; with Introduction by Rev. Jas. H. Brookes, D.D. Illustrated. 8vo. cloth, pp. 15 and 590. *St. Louis.* 12s. 6d.

Patten (S. N.)—Malthus and Ricardo; also, the Study of Statistics. By Davis R. Dewey. Also Analysis in Political Economy, by W. W. Folwell. 8vo. paper. *Baltimore.* 4s.

Peter (P. A.)—History of the Reformation. 16mo. cloth. *Columbus (Ohio).* 4s.

Phelps (Harry)—Practical Marine Surveying. Illustrated. 8vo. cloth, pp. 6 and 217. *New York.* 10s. 6d.

Pickings from Puck.—Being a Choice Collection of Pieces, Poems, and Pictures from "Puck"; Pieces and Poems by Munkittrick, Fish, Henderson, and others. Fifth Crop. Folio, paper, pp. 56. *New York.* 1s. 6d.

Pierce (B. K., D.D.)—Audubon's Adventures; or, Life in the Woods. Illustrated. 16mo. cloth, pp. 252. *New York.* 3s.

Richards (J.)—A Manual of Machine Construction; for Engineers, Draughtsmen, and Mechanics; embracing Examples, Rules, Tables, etc. Illustrated. 4to. morocco, pp. 300. *Philadelphia.* £1 10s.

Sanford (F. R.)—The Bursting of a Boom. 12mo. cloth, pp. 250. *Philadelphia.* 6s. 6d.

Schuck (Oscar T.) — Bench and Bar in California. History, Anecdotes, Reminiscences. 8vo. cloth, pp. 16, 13–543, 14, and 5. *San Francisco.* £1 10s.

Seiler (C., M.D.)—Handbook of the Diagnosis and Treatment of Diseases of the Throat, Nose, and Nasopharynx. New Edition, Revised and Enlarged. 8vo. cloth. Illustrated. *Philadelphia.* 12s. 6d.

Shaler (N. S.)—Aspects of the Earth; a Popular Account of some Familiar Geological Phenomena. 8vo. cloth. Illustrated. *New York.* £1.

Sill (E. Rowland)—The Hermitage and Later Poems. 16mo. paper, pp. 3 and 109. *Boston.* 5s.

Smith (B. G.)—From over the Border; or, Light on the Normal Life of Man. 12mo. cloth, pp. 2 and 238. *Chicago.* 6s.

Smyth (Albert H.) — American Literature. 12mo. cloth, pp. 304. *Philadelphia.* 4s. 6d.

Spencer (Guilford L.)—A Handbook for Sugar Manufacturers and their Chemists. 16mo. *New York.* 8s. 6d.

Stickney (A.)—The Political Problem. 12mo. cloth. *New York.* 6s.

"The Song of Songs." 12mo. cloth, pp. 2 and 274. *Boston.* 7s. 6d.

Thomas (Jos., M.D.) — A Complete Pronouncing Medical Dictionary, embracing the Terminology of Medicine and the Kindred Sciences. 8vo. cloth, pp. 844. *Philadelphia.* £1 5s.

Thorburn (W., M.D.)—A Contribution to the Study of Surgery of the Spinal Cord. Illustrated. 8vo. cloth. *Philadelphia.* £1 2s. 6d.

Thurston (Robert H.) — The Development of the Philosophy of the Steam-Engine. An Historical Sketch. 12mo. cloth, pp. 5 and 48. *New York.* 3s. 6d.

Townsend (T. S.)—The Honours of the Empire State, in the War of the Rebellion. 8vo. cloth, pp. 3 and 416. *New York.* 15s.

Trumbull (H. C.)—Principles and Practice; a Series of Brief Essays. 6 vols. 16mo. cloth. *Philadelphia.* 12s. 6d.

Unitarianism; Its Origin and History. A Course of Sixteen Lectures delivered in Channing Hall. 12mo. cloth, pp. 27 and 394. *Boston.* 5s.

Ward (C. O.)—A History of the Ancient Working People from the Earliest Known Period to the Adoption of Christianity by Constantine. 12mo. cloth. *Washington.* 10s. 6d.

Wait (Frona Eunice)—Wines and Vines of California. A Treatise on the Ethics of Wine-drinking. Illustrated. 8vo. cloth, pp. 215. *San Francisco.* 5s.

Walker (Francis A.)—First Lessons in Political Economy. Cloth, pp. 5 and 323. *New York.* 6s. 6d.

Washington.—Constitution, with Marginal Notes and Full Index. Prepared by Andrew Woods. 8vo. paper, 37 leaves. *Washington.* 4s.

Wells (D. A.)—Recent Economic Changes and their Effect on the Production and Distribution of Wealth and the Well-being of Society. 12mo. cloth. *New York.* 10s.

Whittaker's Churchman's Almanac. The Protestant Episcopal Almanac and Parochial List for 1890. Thirty-Sixth Year. 16mo. paper, pp. 314. *New York.* 1s. 6d.

Wiggin (Kate Douglas)—A Summer in a Cañon. A California Story. 12mo. cloth, pp. 5 and 272. Illustrated. *Boston.* 7s. 6d.

Winthrop (A. T.)—Wilfred. A Story with a Happy Ending. 12mo. cloth, pp. 298. *New York.* 5s.

Wood (De V.)—Thermodynamics, Heat Motors, and Refrigerating Machines. 8vo. cloth. *New York.* 18s.

Woolsey (S. C.)—A few more Verses. 18mo. cloth. *Boston.* 5s.

Wright (Carroll D.)—A Report on Marriage and Divorce in the United States, 1867 to 1886; including an Appendix relating to Marriage and Divorce in certain Countries in Europe. 8vo. cloth, pp. 4 and 1074. *Washington.* 12s. 6d.

Young (Julia Ditto) — Adrift. A Story of Niagara. 12mo. cloth, pp. 1 and 275. *Philadelphia.* 6s. 6d.

---

# European Literature.

---

Amiaud (A.)—Les nombres ordinaux en Assyrien. 8vo. pp. 16. (Reprint.) *Paris,* 1888.

Armenian Proverbs and Sayings. With English Translation by the Rev. G. Bayan. 12mo. pp. 58. *Venice,* 1889. 1s. 6d.

Baethgen (Fr.)—Beiträge zur semitischen Religionsgeschichte. (Der Gott Israel's und die Götter der Heiden.) 8vo. pp. 316. *Berlin,* 1888. 10s.

Barth (J.)—Die Nominalbildung in den semitischen Sprache. Vol. I. 1. Die Schlichten Nomina. 8vo. *Leipzig,* 1889. 10s.

Bartholomae (Ch.)—Studien zur indo-germanischen Sprachgeschichte. I. Royal 8vo. pp. x. 148. *Halle a/S.,* 1889. 5s.

*.* Contents: Indogermanisch as mit 4 Exkursen; Zur n-deklination; zur Bildung d. gen. sing.; der abhinitasandhi im rgveda, etc.

Beauregard (O.)—En Orient. Etudes ethnologiques et linguistiques à travers les âges et les peuples. 8vo. *Paris,* 1889. 10s.

Benfey (Th.)—Kleinere Schriften. Ausgewählt und herausgegeben von A. Bezzenberger. Vol. I. Fasc. 1 and 2. 8vo. *Berlin,* 1889. £1 2s.

Berger (P.)—L'Histoire d'une inscription. Une rectification au Corpus inscriptionum semiticarum. 1re partie, No. 122. 8vo. pp. 7. *Paris,* 1889.

Bilguer (von)—Macedonisch-türkische Wörtersammlung mit kulturhistorischen Erläuterungen. 12mo. pp. viii. 42. *Schwerin,* 1889. 1s. 6d.

Bopp (F.)—Grammaire comparée des langues indo-européennes, comprenant le sanscrit, le zend, l'arménien, le grec, le latin, le lithuanien, l'ancien slave, le gothique et l'allemand. Traduite sur la 2e édition et précédée d'introductions par M. Michel Bréal. 3e édition. Tome IV. 8vo. pp. xxxii. 431. *Paris,* 1889.

*.* L'ouvrage forme 5 vols. se vendant 36 frs., Le tome V. se vend séparément 6 francs.

Brandt (A. J. H. W.)—Die Mandaeische Religion. 8vo. *Leipzig,* 1889.

Brhadâranjakopanishad in der Mâdhjamdina-Recension. Herausgegeben und übersetzt von O. Böhtlingk. Roy. 8vo. pp. iv. 72 and 100. *Leipzig,* 1889. 5s.

Bühler (G.)—Das Sukritasamkirtana der Arisimha. Roy. 8vo pp. 58. (Extract.) *Leipzig,* 1889. 1s.

Bugge (S.)—Beiträge zur etymologischen Erläuterung der armenischen Sprache. 8vo. *Christiania,* 1889. 1s. 6d.

**Charvériat (Fr.)**—A travers la Kabylie et les questions kabyles. 12mo. *Paris*, 1889. 3s. 6d.

**Crawford (F. Marion).**—Zoroastre. Avec préface par F. Chesneau. 8vo. *Paris*, 1889. 3s. 6d.

**De Baye (J.)**—Le congrès des Orientalistes. Tenu à Stockholm en 1889. 8vo. *Paris*, 1889. 2s.

**De Cara (p. Ces).**—Gli Hyksôs o re pastori di Egitto. Ricerche di archeologia egizio-biblica. 8vo. pp. 385. *Roma*, 1889. 15s.

**De Gaudalupe (Nuestra Señora).**—Informacion que El Arzobispo de Mexico D. Fray Alonso de Montufar mandó practicar con motivo de un sermón que en la fiesta de la Natividad de Nuestra Señora (8 de Setiembre 1556) predicó en la capilla de S. José de Naturales del Convento de S. Francisco de Méjico, su Provincial Fray Francisco de Bustamante Acerca de la Devoción y culto de Nuestra Señora de Gaudalupe. 8vo. pp. ix. and 102. *Madrid*, 1888. 2s.

**De Harlez (C.)**—La Siao Hio ou Morale de la jeunesse. Avec le commentaire de Tchen-Siuen. Traduite du Chinois. 4to. pp. 368. *Paris*, 1889. 15s.
*₊* Annales du Musée Guimet, vol. xv.

**Delbrück (B.)**—Die indogermanischen Verwandtschaftsnamen. Ein Beitrag zur vergleichenden Alterthumskunde. Royal 8vo. pp. 228. (Reprint.) *Leipzig*, 1889. 8s.

**Dupont (E.)**—Lettres sur le Congo. Récit d'un voyage scientifique entre l'embouchure du fleuve et le confluent du Kassaï. Royal 8vo. pp. viii. and 724. With Plates and Maps. *Paris*, 1889. 15s.

**Duval (R.)**—Le Patriarche Mar Jabalaha II. et les princes mongols de l'Adherbaidjan. 8vo. pp. 44. (Reprint.) *Paris*, 1889.

**Edlinger (Aug. v.)**—Ueber die Bildung der Begriffe. Ein etymologisch-vergleichendes Wörterbuch aus allen Sprachgebieten. Fasc. 1 (A.) Mit einem Anhang. 1. Beiträge zur deutschen Etymologie. 2. Zur Frage über den Ursprung der Sprache. 8vo. pp. iv. and 72. *München*, 1889. 2s.

**Exner (A. H.)**—China, Skizzen von Land und Leuten. Mit besonderer Berücksichtigung Kommerzieller Verhältnisse. Royal 8vo. cloth, pp. viii. and 298. With Portrait, Plates, and Illustrations. *Leipzig*, 1889. £1.

**Frederiks (J. G.) und F. J. Van den Branden.**—Biographisch Woordenboek der Noord- en Zuid-nederlandsche Letterkunde. Nieuwe uitgave. Fasc. 1. Royal 8vo. *Amsterdam*, 1888. per fasc. 2s.
*₊* Will be complete in about 15 fasc.

**Gayet (Al.)**—Les monuments Coptes du Musée de Boulaq. With 100 Plates. *Paris*, 1889. £2.
*₊* Mission archéologique française au Caire, Tome III. Fasc. 3.

**Gestes (les) des Chiprois.** Recueil de Chroniques françaises écrites en Orient aux XIIIe et XIVe siècles (Philippe de Navarre et Gérard de Monréal). Publié pour la première fois pour la Société de l'Orient latin par G. Raynaud. 8vo. pp. xxviii. and 393. *Leipzig*, 1889. 12s.

**Grihyasûtra (The) of Hiranyakeśin.** With Extracts from the Commentary of Mâtridatta. Edited by J. Kirste. Roy. 8vo. pp. x. 177 and 41. *Vienna*, 1889. 10s.

**Guérin (V.)**—Jérusalem. Son histoire. Sa description. Les établissements religieux. 8vo. *Paris*, 1889. 7s. 6d.

**Gutschmid (A.)**—Kleine Schriften. Herausg. von F. Rühl. Vol. I. Schriften zur Geschichte der griechischen Chronographie. 8vo. *Leipzig*, 1889. 14s.

**Guttmann (J.)**—Die Philosophie des Salomon ibn Gabirol (Avicebron) dargestellt und erläutert. 8vo. pp. iv. and 272. *Göttingen*, 1889. 6s.

**Histoire du Roi Djemchid et des Diva.** Traduite du persan par M. Serge Larimoff. 8vo. pp. 27. (Extract.) *Paris*, 1890.

**Huart (C.)**—Bibliographie ottomane. Notice des livres turcs, arabes et persans imprimés à Constantinople durant la période 1304-1305 de l'hégire (1887-1888). 8vo. pp. 66. (Extract.) *Paris*, 1889.

**Itinéraires russes en Orient.** Traduits pour la Société de l'Orient latin par Mme. B. Khitrowo. I. 1. 8vo. pp. 334. *Leipzig*, 1889. 12s.

**Kirste (J.)**—The Grihyasûtra of Hiranyakeśin. With Extracts from the Commentary of Matridatta. 8vo. *Wien*, 1889. 10s.

**Krebs (F.)**—De Chnemothis (humhtp) Nomarchi inscriptione aegyptiaca commentatio. Roy. 8vo. pp. 51. *Berlin*, 1889. 6s.

**Kubary (J. S.)**—Ethnographische Beiträge zur Kenntniss des Karolinen Archipels. Veröffentlicht im Auftrage der Direction des Kgl. Museums für Völkerkunde zu Berlin Unter Mitwirkung von J. D. E. Schmeltz. Heft I. Roy. 8vo. pp. iv. and 114. With 15 Plates. *Leiden*, 1889. £1 2s. 6d.
*₊* The work will be completed in three parts.

**La Grasserie (Raoul de)**—Etudes de grammaire comparée: Des relations grammaticales considérées dans leur Concept et dans leur Expression ou de la catégorie des cas. 8vo. pp. 357. *Paris*, 1890.

**Lallemand (Charles)**—Tunis et ses environs. Texte et dessins d'après nature. Avec 150 Aquarelles tirées en couleurs. 4to. pp. 245. *Paris*, 1890. £1 15s.

**Lamba (H.)**—Dictionnaire des codes égyptiens mixtes. Manuel destiné à rendre les recherches faciles aux personnes même les plus étrangères à l'étude des lois. 8vo. pp. viii. 717. *Paris*, 1889.

**Legrand (E.)**—Notice biographique sur Jean et Théodore Zygomalas. 8vo. pp. 214. *Paris*, 1889.
*₊* Contents: Vie de Staurace Malaxos, par Jean Zygomalas; Catalogues de la Bibliothèque du monastère de la Trinité et de celle de Georges Cantacuzène; le Copiste André Darmarius à Tübingue en 1584, etc.

**Ludwig (A.)**—Ueber die Kritik des Rgveda-Textes. 4to. pp. 66. (Reprint.) *Prag*, 1889. 2s.

**Maimonides' Kiddusch Hachodesch.** Uebersetzt und erläutert von E. Mahler. 8vo. pp. iv. and 115. *Wien*, 1889. 2s.

**Manuel du sinologue ou recueil de renseignements utiles.** A l'usage des personnes qui s'occupent de la Chine et de la littérature chinoise. Publié par la société sinico-japonaise. Part I. 8vo. pp. 64. *Paris*, 1889.
*₊* Bibliothèque sinico-japonaise, vi.

**Maspero (G.)**—Monuments divers recueillis en Egypte et en Nubie par A. Mariette-Pacha. Texte par G. Maspéro. Livr. I. et II. Folio, pp. 1 to 30. Chalon-sur-Saône, 1889.

——— Catalogue du musée égyptien de Marseille. 8vo. pp. viii. and 208. *Paris*, 1889.

**Massaja (G.)**—Miei trentacinque anni di missione nell' Alta Etiopia. Vol. VII. 4to. *Mailand*, 1889. 12s.

**Merx (A.)**—Historia artis grammaticae apud Syros. Composuit et edidit A. Merx. Roy. 8vo. pp. x. and 291. With Facsimiles. *Leipzig*, 1889. 15s.
*₊* Abhandlungen f. d. Kunde des Morgenlandes, etc., Vol. IX. No. 2.

**Meyer-Lübke (W.)**—Grammatik der romanischen Sprachen. Volume I.: Lautlehre. 8vo. *Leipzig*, 1889. 16s.

**Mittheilungen, etc.** *Vide* Winckler.

**Mohammed Esseghir ben Elhadj ben Abdallah Eloufrani.**—Nozhet-Elhâdi. Histoire de la dynastie saadienne au Maroc (1511-1670). Traduction française par O. Houdas. Tome II. 3e série, Volume III. Roy. 8vo. pp. vii. and 568. *Paris*, 1889.
*₊* Publication de l'Ecole des langues orientales vivantes.

Mouzaffer-Pacha et Talaat-Bey.—Guerre d'Orient 1877-1878. Défense de Plevna, d'après les documents officiels et privés réunis sous la direction du muchir Ghazi Osman-Pacha. 8vo. pp.'xvi. and 287. With Atlas in folio. *Paris*, 1889. 15s.

Müller (D. H.)—Epigraphische Denkmäler aus Arabien. 8vo. *Leipzig*, 1889. 10s.

Nestle (E.)—De Sancta Cruce. Ein Beitrag zur christlichen Legendengeschichte. Syriac and English Text. 8vo. pp. viii. and 128. *Berlin*, 1889.

Normand (Ch.)—Histoire ancienne des peuples de l'Orient, depuis les origines jusqu'aux guerres médiques. 12mo. pp. 371. With Illustrations and Maps. *Paris*, 1889.

Pischel (R.) und K. F. Geldner.—Vedische Studien. Vol. I. Fasc. II. 8vo. *Stuttgart*, 1889. 7s.

Plato (H.)—Habla'ath Haddám. Iu Hebrew. 8vo. pp. 20 and 368. *Frankfurt a/M.* 1889. 3s.

Qaragadagi (Muhaemmaed Gaefaer).—Monsieur Jourdan, der Pariser Botaniker, im Qarabeg'. Neupersisches Lustspiel. Persischer Text mit wörtlicher deutscher Uebersetzung, Anmerkungen und vollständigem Wörterverzeichniss. Herausgegeben von A. Wahrmund. Roy. 8vo. pp. viii. 36, 34, 30. *Wien*, 1889. 4s.

Recueil de textes et de traductions publié par les professeurs de l'école des langues orientales vivantes à l'occasion du VIIIe Congrès international des orientalisten tenu à Stockholm en 1889. Two Vols. 8vo. *Paris*, 1889. £1 10s.

Reynaud (P.)—Esquisse du véritable système primitif des voyelles dans les langues d'origine indoeuropéenne. 8vo. pp. 43. *Paris*, 1889.

Sachau (E.)—Arabische Volkslieder aus Mesopotamien. 8vo. *Berlin*, 1889. 6s.

Sámkhya-pravacana-bhâshya, Vijñâuabhikshu's Commentar zu den Sâmkhyasûtras. Aus dem Sanskrit übersetzt und mit Anmerkungen versehen von Richard Garbe. Royal 8vo. pp. viii. and 376. *Leipzig*, 1889. 10s.
*.* Abhandlungen für die kunde der Morgenlandes, Vol. IX. No. 3.

Sayous (E.)—Etudes sur la religion romaine et le moyen age oriental. 8vo. *Paris*, 1889. 3s. 6d.

Schwab (M.)—Magré Dardegé. Dictionnaire hébreu-italien de la fin du 14e siècle reconstitué selon l'ordre alphabétique italien. 8vo. *Paris*, 1889. 6s.

Senart (E.)—Notes d'épigraphie indienne, II. 8vo. pp. 16. Reprint. *Paris*, 1889.

Seyppel (C. M.)—Rajadar und Hellmischu. Altägyptischer Gesang. With 80 Plates. 4to. *Berlin*, 1889. 3s.

Snouck Hurgronje (C.)—Bilder aus Mekka. Royal 4to. 18 photo-lithographic Plates, in Portfolio. With Text. *Leiden*, 1889. £1 1s. 6d.

Sprenger (G.)—Darlegung der Grundsätze, nach denen die syrische Uebertragung der griechischen Geoponika gearbeitet worden ist. 8vo. *Göttingen*, 1889. 2s. 6d.

Strack (H. L.)—Die Sprüche der Väter. Ein ethischer Mishna-Traktat. Herausgegeben und erklärt. 2e wesentlich verbesserte Auflage. 8vo. pp. 66. *Berlin*, 1888. 1s. 6d.

—— Schabbâth. Der Mishnatraktat "Sabbath" herausgegeben und erklärt. 8vo. pp. 78. *Leipzig*, 1889, 1s. 6d.

Sutta Nipâta (das).—Eine Sammlung von Gesprächen, welche zu den Kanon. Büchern der Buddhisten gehört. Aus der englischen Uebersetzung von V. Fausböll ins Deutsche übertragen von A. Pfungst. Fasc I. Royal 8vo. pp. x. and 80. *Strassburg*, 1889. 1s. 6d.

Van Berchem (M.)—Conte arabe en dialecte égyptien. 8vo. pp. 31. (Extract.) *Paris*, 1890.

Vasselot de Régné (de) et de Montmort.—La culture du houblon dans l'Afrique australe. 8vo. pp. 48. *Paris*, 1889.

Villaret (E. de).—Dai Nippon (le Japon). 8vo. pp. x. and 389. With 3 Maps. *Paris*, 1889.

Virey (P.)—Quelques observations sur l'épisode d'Aristée, à propos d'un monument égyptien. 8vo. pp. 50. With Illustrations. *Paris*, 1889. 3s.

Vitale (Ed.)—Vocabolario di tutte le parole che esistono nella storia di Scems-ed-Djn e Nur-ed-Djn estratta dalle Mille e una Notte. Trascrizione in caratteri europei. 8vo. pp. 27. *Napoli*, 1889. 2s.

Wellhausen (J.)—Skizzen und Vorarbeiten. Heft IV. Royal 8vo. pp. 194 and 78. *Berlin*, 1889. 9s.
*.* Contents: Medina vor dem Islam.—Muhammads Gemeindeordnung von Medina. — Seine Schreiben, und die Gesandtschaften an ihn.

Wessely (C.)—Die Pariser Papyri des Fundes von El-Faijûm. Royal 4to. pp. 162. (Extract.) *Leipzig*, 1889. 8s.

Wiedemann (A.)—Aegyptologische Studien. Die Praeposition $\chi$eft. Die Augenschminke mestem. Royal 8vo. 44 autographic pages. *Bonn*, 1889. 2s. 6d.

Wünsche (Aug.)—Der Babylonische Talmud in seinen haggadischen Bestandtheilen Wortgetreu übersetzt und durch Noten erlautert. 2 vols. 8vo. *Leipzig*, 1889. £2 3s.

Zimmern (H.)—Die Assyriologie als Hülfswissenschaft für das Studium des Alten Testaments und des klassischen Altertums. Royal 8vo. pp. 22. *Königsberg*, 1889.

# Oriental Literature.

## ANGLO-INDIA.
### (Miscellaneous.)

Anderson (J. D.)—Short List of Words of the Hill Tippera Language. With their English Equivalents. Also of Words of the Language spoken by Lushais of the Sylhet Frontier. Royal 8vo. pp. 13. *Shillong*, 1885. 3s. 6d.

Barrett (F.)—Tables of Daily Rates of Pay, etc., of British Regimental Warrant and Non-Commissioned Officers and Soldiers in India. Royal 8vo. pp. 32. *Bombay*, 1889. 3s.

Bartley (Mrs. Joanna).—Indian Cookery "Local," for young House-keepers. Second Edition. 8vo. pp. 155. *Bombay*, 1888. 6s.

Bombay University Calendar for the year 1889-90. Royal 12mo. pp. xlii. 532, and cccxxx. *Bombay*, 1889.

Brewin (Mrs. Eliza).—The Jubilee Cookery Book, with various other Useful Receipts. Demy 16mo. pp. 49. *Bombay*, 1887. 3s.

Captain's Daughter (The).—Translated by Stuart H. Godfrey. 12mo. pp. 170. *Calcutta*, 1888. 6s.
*.* A novel translated from the Russian.

Casartelli (L. L.)—The Philosophy of the Mazdayasnian Religion under the Sassanids. Translated from the French, with Prefatory Remarks, Notes, and a Brief Biographical Sketch of the Author, by Firoz Jamaspji Dastur Jamasp Asa. Royal 8vo. cloth, pp. xxvii. and 234. *Bombay*, 1889.

Chaudhuri (A.)—The Student's English Companion. 8vo. pp. 318. *Calcutta*, 1889. 7s. 6d.

Cousens (Henry).—Bijápur, the Old Capital of the Adil Sháhi Kings. A Guide to its Ruins, with Historical Outline. 8vo. pp. 160. *Poona*, 1889. 6s.
*.* Bijápur, once the Capital of the Dekhan, 240 miles South-east of Bombay, is famous for its beautiful architectural works of the Muhammadan Period.

Dharma Sindhu ; or, the Ocean of Religious Duties. By Kashinath Upadhyâya. Edited by Krishnâjee Râmachandra Shâstri Navare. Published by Janârdan Mahâdev Gurjar. Royal 8vo. pp. 386. *Bombay*, 1888. 9s.

**Dvivedi (Manilál Nabhubhái).**—Monism or Advaitism. 8vo. pp. 116. *Bombay*, 1889. 6s.

*** An introduction to the Advaita Philosophy read by the light of modern science.

**Endle (Rev. S.)**—Outline Grammar of the Kachári (Bárá) Language as spoken in District Darrang, Assam. With Illustrative Sentences, Notes, Reading Lessons, and a short Vocabulary. Royal 8vo. pp. xxxi. and 99. *Shillong*, 1884. 7s. 6d.

**Ghose (J. N.)**—Goethe. His Genius, his Theories, and his Works. With a short Notice of his Life. 8vo. pp. 26. *Lahore*, 1889. 3s.

**Ghosh (J. K.)**—The Indian Stamp Act. (Act I. of 1879.) 8vo. pp. 96. *Bhawanipore*, 1888. 6s.

*** Containing Notes, Rules, Notifications, etc.

**Ghosh (Umesh Chandra).**—The Bengal Local Self-Government Manual. 8vo. pp. 171. *Jessore*, 1889. 6s.

*** A very useful hand-book for those who take an interest in local self-government.

**Indian Penal Code (The).**—Edited by D. E. Crauenburgh. Fourth Edition. 8vo. pp. 468. *Calcutta*, 1889. 10s. 6d.

**Kehimkar (Hasem Samuel).**—A Sketch of the History of Beni-Israel, and an Appeal for their Education. Demy 8vo. pp. 38. *Bombay*, 1889. 3s.

**Kelleher (J.)**—Possession in the Civil Law. Abridged from the Treatise of Von Savigny. 8vo. pp. 264. *Calcutta*, 1888. £1 4s.

*** With the text of the title on possession from the digest with notes.

**Lahiri (P. K.)**—Notes on the Entrance Course, 1890. Part I. and II. 12mo. pp. 180 and 226. *Calcutta*, 1889.

*** With hints, model questions, and answers. Price of each part, 6s.

**Lál Ráya (Amrita).**—Reminiscences. English and American. Part I. 8vo. pp. 118. *Calcutta*, 1889. 3s.

**Leitner (G. W.)**—On the Sciences of Language and of Ethnography. With General Reference to the Language and Customs of the People of Hunza. (A Report of an Extempore Address.) 8vo. pp. 16. 1889.

**Linton (James H.)**—The Burman as he is. 8vo. pp. 45. *Calcutta*, 1888. 3s.

*** Gives a favourable account of the Burmese character.

**Macaulay's** Lord Clive. With Introduction and Notes Edited by P. K. Lahiri. 12mo. pp. 192. *Calcutta*, 1889. 3s.

**Macgregor (C. R.)**—Outline Singpho Grammar. Royal 8vo. pp. 24. *Shillong*, 1886. 3s.

**Massa (L. A.)**—Princess Cherry Blossom ; or, Harlequin Yellow Dwarf and the King of the Gold-Mine Shares. Demy 8vo. pp. 34. *Alipur*, 1889. 1s. 6d.

**Mittra (P.)**—Notes on the Entrance Course, 1889. Parts I. to III. 12mo. pp. 476. *Calcutta*, 1888. p.c. 7s. 6d.

**Needham (J. F.)**—Outline Grammar of the Shai 'Yáng Miri Language. As spoken by the Miris of that Clan residing in the neighbourhood of Sadiya. With Illustrative Sentences, Phrase-Book and Vocabulary. Royal 8vo. pp. ii. and 157. *Shillong*, 1886. 6s.

**O'Beirne (Ivan).** — Colonel's Crime. 8vo. pp. 111. *Allahabad*, 1889. 3s.

**O'Kinealy (J.)**—The Code of Civil Procedure. With Notes and Appendix. Third Edition. 8vo. pp. 749. *Calcutta*, 1889. £2 10s.

**Pál (Bholá Nath).**—Studies in English Prose and Poetry. 8vo. pp. 152. *Calcutta*, 1888. 3s.

**Primrose (A. J.)**—A Manipuri Grammar, Vocabulary, and Phrase Book. To which are added some Manipuri Proverbs and Specimens of Manipuri Correspondence. Royal 8vo. pp. 100. *Shillong*, 1888. 7s. 6d.

**Raya (Surendra Nath).**—A History of the Native States of India. Vol. I. Gwalior. 8vo. pp. 129. *Calcutta*, 1888. £1 7s. 6d.

*** Gives a history of the Gwalior State from Ranoji Scindiah, the founder of the family, down to the present day.

**Rivaz (H. T.)**—The Punjab Record. Part I. 8vo. pp. 65. *Lahore*, 1889. 9s.

*** This first Part is the "Judicial" part of the Record.

———— Indices to the Panjab Record, 1888. 8vo. pp. 176. *Lahore*, 1889. 9s.

**Sen (B. K.)**—Modern India and its Future. 12mo. pp. 98. *Calcutta*, 1889. 1s. 6d.

*** Gives a highly optimistic view of the future of India.

**Sherring (H.)** — Light and Shade. 8vo. pp. 185. *Calcutta*, 1889. 9s.

*** Short tales reprinted from various newspapers and short poetical pieces.

**Singh (Bává Naráin).**—Digest of Indian Law Reports, Allahabad Series. Volumes I. to X. From 1876 to 1888. With an Index of Names, Acts, and Contents. 8vo. pp. 750. *Lahore*, 1889. 14s.

**Soppitt (C. A.)**—Short Account of the Kachcha Naga (Empéo) Tribe in the North Cachar Hills. With an Outline Grammar, Vocabulary, and Illustrative Sentences. Royal 8vo. pp. 22 and 47. *Shillong*, 1885. 6s.

———— A Short Account of the Kuki-Lushai Tribes on the North-East Frontier. (Districts Cachar, Sylhet, Nága Hills, etc., and the North Cachar Hills.) With an Outline Grammar of the Rangkhol-Lushai Language and a comparison of Lushai with other Dialects. Royal 8vo. pp. ix. and 88. *Shillong*, 1887. 6s.

**Steel (Mrs.), Mrs. Gardner, Miss Deams.**—The Indian Cook's Guide. 8vo. pp. 135. *Bombay*, 1889. 6s.

**Tiwári (Pandit Jagesvar Prasád).**—Juvenile History of Charkhári. 8vo. pp. 223. *Benares*, 1888. 6s.

**Tkalcic (J. B.)** — Monumenta historica lib. regiae civitatis Zagrabiae. Volume I. 1093-1399. 8vo. *Agram*, 1889. 12s.

**Vágale (Ráo Sáheb Shivrám Sitárám).**—A Manual of the Law of Mortgage. 8vo. pp. 92. *Bombay*, 1889. 7s. 6d.

*** This work has been derived from standard English works on the subject and from Indian Law Reports.

**Williams (Miss Jane).**—Lilian. 8vo. pp. 196. *Calcutta*, 1889. 4s. 6d.

*** A racy Indian novel.

### BENGALI.

**Banerji (Sarat Chandra).**—Srikrishna Charitra. An Account of Krishna. In Bengali. 8vo. pp. 156. *Calcutta*, 1888. 3s.

**Bharatágeman (The Arrival of Bhagat).** By Matilál Raya. In Bengali. 8vo. pp. 109. *Calcutta*, 1888. 3s.

*** Based on the Second Book of the Ramayana.

**Bhattácháryya (Brajanath).**—Pranaya Kánan. (The Grove of Love.) 12mo. pp. 312. *Calcutta*, 1888. 6s.

*** A love story in Bengali.

**Biláti Gupta Kathá (Mysteries of England).**—Translated into Bengali by Bhuban Chandra Mukharji. Vol. I. 8vo. pp. 746. *Calcutta*, 1888. 9s.

*** A Bengali translation of Reynolds's Joseph Wilmot.

**Chakrabarti (Priya Nath).** — Jiban Kumár. 8vo. pp. 156. *Calcutta*, 1888. 3s.

*** An old-fashioned story-book written in Bengali.

**Dádá o Ami (Brother and Myself).** A Drama. In Bengali. 8vo. pp. 104. *Calcutta*, 1888. 3s. 6d.

*** An adaptation in Bengali of the plot of Goldsmith's "She Stoops to Conquer."

Ghosh (Girish Chandra). — Púrna Chandra Nátak. In Bengali. 12mo. pp. 128. *Calcutta*, 1888. 2*s*.

*** A drama taken from Kánchan Málá, a novel published in the Bangadarshan, once a well-known magazine, now defunct.

Hitopadesa. — Translated into Bengali by Jogendra Chandra Chatterji. 8vo. pp. 112. *Calcutta*, 1889.

*** A translation in Bengali verse of Bishnu Sharma's well-known work.

Sánkhya Kárika. — *Vide* Sanskrit.

## GUJARATI.

Bhatt (Purnánand Mahánand). — A Handbook of Gujaráti Grammar. For the use of Officers and Students for the Bombay University Examination. 12mo. pp. 286. *Bombay*, 1889. 6*s*.

Navákhyán Vyákhyá. — *Vide* Sanskrit.

Pesikáká (Hormasji D.) — Madhupán ; or, the Drink Question. In Gujaráti. Royal 8vo. pp. 372. *Bombay*, 1889. £1 1*s*.

Shashikalá Nátak ; or, the Drama of Princess Shashikalá. By Lalubhái Nanabhái Bhatt. 12mo. pp. 270. *Ahmedabad*, 1889. 4*s*. 6*d*.

## HINDI.

Badrikáshrama Darpana. — By Svámi Dudhadsá. In Hindi. Royal 8vo. pp. 28. *Bombay*, 1889. 3*s*.

*** A sketch of the sacred place of Badri, situated on one of the peaks of the Himálaya Mountains.

Hanumán. — A Drama. By Hridayarám. In Hindi. 8vo. pp. 436. *Benares*, 1889. 6*s*.

Ramlílá Uttarkánda. — The Last Book of the Rámayan dramatised. By Dámodar Shástri. In Hindi. 8vo. pp. 78. *Bankipore*, 1889. 3*s*.

*** The seventh book of the Ramayan in the form of a drama.

Upanishad Sárodhár Vedánt Bháshya. — By Ajudhiyá Parshád. 8vo. pp. 364. *Delhi*, 1889. 7*s*. 6*d*.

*** The true essence of the Upanishads in connection with the Vedánt Philosophy. In Hindi.

Yogavásistha Vairágya Prakaran an Mumukshu Prakaran, Prákrat Bhashántar. In Hindi. Royal 8vo. pp. 232. *Bombay*, 1889. 3*s*.

*** A free Hindi translation of the well-known Sanskrit work Yogaváshishta.

## HINDUSTANI.

Abstract (An) of the Indian Law Reports. Allahabad Series, Vol. I. to XIV. From 1876 to 1887. By Sheikh Ghulám Nabi. In Urdu. 8vo. pp. 1018. Lithographed. *Amritsar*, 1889. 16*s*.

Act No. 14 of 1882. With Notes. In Urdu. 8vo. pp. 708. Lithographed. *Lahore*, 1889. 9*s*.

Act No. 17 of 1887. With Notes. In Urdu. 8vo. pp. 90. Lithographed. *Lahore*, 1889. 2*s*.

Bagh Bahár. (The Garden and Spring.) Translated into Urdu by Mir Amman. 8vo. pp. 156. Lithographed. *Lahore*, 1889. 1*s*. 6*d*.

Bruti (J. W.) — Jauhar-i-Farhang (Merits of an Englishman). In Urdu. 8vo. pp. 96. *Peshawar*, 1889. 2*s*.
*** A collection of love verses in the fashion of Urdú poets.

Jagat Simriti. 8vo. pp. 148. *Lahore*, 1889. 2*s*. 6*d*.
*** An Urdu translation of " Manú Simriti."

Janam Sákhí Urdú kalán ma'i taswirát. — Translated into Urdu by Jagan Náth. 8vo. pp. 264. Lithographed. *Lahore*, 1889. 3*s*.

*** Life of Bába Nának. Illustrated edition.

Khuwan-i-Ni'mat. — Translated into Urdú by Ghulám Muhy-ud-din Beg. 16mo. pp. 324. Lithographed. *Lahore*, 1889.

*** This is a Hindustani translation of the English book " Sweet Dishes."

Lal (Sangam). — Lectures on Hindú Law. Part I. In Urdu. 8vo. pp. 138. *Lahore*, 1889. 4*s*. 6*d*.

Law (The) of Torts. Translated into Urdu by Shib Naráyan. 8vo. pp. 257. *Lahore*, 1889. 6*s*.

Mujib-ul-láh (Maulavi Muhammad). — Al Ifádat-fi-Bábish-Shahádat, Hissa-i-Awwal. Vol. I. and II. Royal 8vo. pp. 394 and 264. Lithographed. *Lucknow*, 1889. £1 4*s*.

*** Advantages of the Law of Evidence. Part I. and II. In Urdu.

Sáng-i-Rúpbasant. — By Muhammad Khalil. Royal 8vo. pp. 28. *Meerut*, 1889. 3*s*.

*** Rupbasant, an opera in Urdu.

Surgujasti Hajar. — By Prince Mirza Muhammad Jalal Bahadur. 8vo. pp. 78. Lithographed. *Calcutta*, 1889. 2*s*. 6*d*.

*** The pain of separation, a love poem in Urdu.

Tarjuma-i-Dastúr-ul-Iláj. — Translated by Hakim Muhammad Hadi Husain Khán. 4to. pp. 772. Lithographed. *Lucknow*, 1889. 4*s*. 6*d*.

*** Translated from Persian into Urdu.

## MARATHI.

Dámle (Hari Krishna). — Exercises for Translation into English (Standard IV.). With a Glossary of Difficult Words and Phrases. New edition. 12mo. pp. 54. *Poona*, 1889. 1*s*.

Joshi (Rámchandra Bhikáji). — A Higher Maráthi Grammar. In Marathi. 8vo. pp. 316. *Poona*, 1889. 3*s*. 6*d*.

*** This book on Maráthi grammar is written on the same plan as Dáboda Pándurang's grammar.

Munro. — Vináyak Kondadev Oka. The Life of Sir Thomas Munro. In Marathi. 8vo. pp. 118. *Bombay*, 1888. 2*s*. 6*d*.

Padmanji (Bábá). — A Manual of Hinduism. In Marathi. Two Parts in One. 8vo. cloth. pp. 279, 6, and 6, 435, 8. *Bombay*, 1886–87.

——— Comprehensive Dictionary. English and Marathi. Third Edition. 8vo. pp. 668. *Bombay*, 1889. 14*s*.

Pandurang (Daboda). — A Grammar of the Maráthí Language. In Marathi. Ninth edition. 8vo. cloth, pp. 396. *Bombay*, 1889. 4*s*.

*** A new edition of this grammar used by senior students.

Ratnamálá A'ni Pratápachandra. By Mahádev Vináyak Kelkar. 8vo. pp. 166. *Málvan*, 1889. 4*s*.

*** A novel in Maratti.

Vedánta Dnyána Prakásha, Bhág I lá ; or, the Light of Vedántism. Part I. Translated into Marathi by Váman Bhái Khatri. 8vo. pp. 48. *Bombay*, 1889. 2*s*. 6*d*.

*** A monthly magazine containing translations of the Bhágavata Purán, and some other works on Vedántism.

## SANSKRIT.

**Advaita Brahma Sudhákárika** ; or, The Nectar of the Vedánt Philosophy. With a Commentary in Sanskrit by Govindánanda Sarasvati. Oblong pp. 102. *Bombay,* 1889. 5s.

**Brahma Baibarta Puráṇa.** In Sanskrit. 8vo. pp. 902 and 1029. *Calcutta,* 1888.

*<sub>*</sub>* The Puran describing evolution from Brahma. Volumes I. and II. have been published. The price of the complete work will be £1 10s.

**Dasakumár Charita.** With an English Translation by Jánaki Náth Bhattácháryya. 12mo. pp. 168. *Calcutta,* 1889. 3s.

**Indian Penal Code.** Edited by Vyamhatsar Ramchandra. In Sanskrit. Royal 8vo. pp. 192. *Bombay,* 1888. 6s.

**Isádidasopanishad-Sangraha.** Edited by Pandit Kripa Rám Sarma. 8vo. pp. 36. *Benares,* 1889. 4s.

*<sub>*</sub>* A collection of the ten Upanishads (Isa, Kena, Katha, Prachna, Mundaka, Mándúkya, Taittiriya, Aitreya, Chhandogya, and Vrihadáranya Svetasvato Upanishads).

**Kávyaprakásha** ; or, The Light of Poems. By Mammutbhatt. With a Commentary in Sanskrit by Vámanáchárya. Royal 8vo. pp. 914. *Bombay,* 1889. 14s.

*<sub>*</sub>* Text-book on rhetoric. Treating of the numerous figures of speech used in Sanskrit works.

**Málavikagnimitra.—**A Sanskrit Play. By Kalidása. With the Commentary of Kátayavema. Edited with Notes by Pandit Shankar Pándurang. Demy 8vo. *Bombay,* 1889. 6s.

**Mugdhabodham Byákaranam.—**A Sanskrit Grammar. Edited by Rajani Kánta Gupta. 12mo. pp. 1061. *Calcutta,* 1888. 9s.

*<sub>*</sub>* A well-known Sanskrit grammar by Vopadeva. With commentaries of Durgádás and Rám Tarkabágisha.

**Navákhyán Vyákhya** ; or, an Exposition of the Parable in Nine Parts. Sanskrit and Gujarati Text. By Gosvámi Shri Vrajaráyaji Máháráj and Gopáldás. Royal 4to. pp. 443. *Bombay,* 1889. 10s. 6d.

**Sánkhya Kárika.—**In Bengali, English and Sanskrit. Translated by Debendra Nath Goswámi. 8vo. pp. 268. *Calcutta,* 1889. 14s.

*<sub>*</sub>* Memorial verses on the Sankhya Philosophy.

**Vishvagunádarsha.** — By Venkatádhvari. With the Commentary of Madhura Subbá Shástri. Edited by Shámrás Vithal. 8vo. pp. 239. *Bombay,* 1889. 5s.


## MISCELLANEOUS.

### (Polyglots, etc.)

**BURMESE.—**Selections from the Records of the Hlutdau. Compiled by Taw Sein Ko, Government Translator, and published by authority. In Burmese. Royal 8vo. pp. viii. 25, 159. *Rangoon,* 1888. 7s. 6d.

*<sub>*</sub>* The work has been compiled with a view to the preservation of the official style of writing in Upper Burma and for use as a textbook by candidates for the India Civil Service.

**CANARESE.** — Bhagavadgita. — Kanarese Oriental Bhagvadgita. By Kánale Puttappá. Demy 8vo. pp. 160. *Bombay,* 1889. 4s. 6d.

**Turanga Bhárata.—**By Paramadeva. In Kanarese. Royal 8vo. pp. 520. *Bombay,* 1889. 14s.

*<sub>*</sub>* Substance of the Mahábhárata Purán (in the metre popularly called Turanga) in Kanarese Poetry.

**PANJABI.—Gurú Granth prárthanik Shabad ratnáwal.** (Necklace of Devotional Verses.) In Panjábi. 8vo. pp. 72. *Amritsar,* 1889. 3s.

**Janam Sákhi Bhagat Kabír.** Life of Bhagat Kabír. 8vo. pp. 404. Lithographed. *Lahore,* 1889. 3s.

**PERSIAN.—Muktuhat i Sadiqui.** Sadik's Letters. By Shah Ali Karim. 8vo. pp. 288. *Bankipore,* 1889. 5s.

*<sub>*</sub>* A Persian letter writer.

**POLYGLOT.—Qurán Majíd sed tarjama.** By Wali Ullá. 4to. pp. 799. Lithographed. *Delhi,* 1889. 10s. 6d.

*<sub>*</sub>* Qurán with three translations, Arabic, Persian and Urdú.

**Surhe Dewan Ali.—**By Moulavi Muhammad Abdul Udud. In Arabic and Persian. 8vo. pp. 264. Lithographed. *Calcutta,* 1888. 9s.

*<sub>*</sub>* An explanation of a collection of Ali's poems.

**SINDHI.—Mizan-i-Tibb.—**The Balance of Medicine. By Ayal Rám. In Sindhi. 8vo. pp. 306. Lithographed. *Lahore,* 1888. 14s.

*<sub>*</sub>* Translation of the original work in Persian on Greco-Arabic system of medicine.

**SINGHALESE.—Carter (Charles).** A New English-Sinhalese Dictionary. Part I. (A to Contorted.) Post 8vo. pp. xi. 160. *Colombo,* 1889. 6s.

*<sub>*</sub>* The work will be completed in 5 parts. The subscription price for the whole work is £1 1s.

**TULU.—Manner (Rev. E.)** English-Tulu Dictionary. 8vo. pp. 657. *Mangalore,* 1889.

---

### *NOTICE TO CORRESPONDENTS.*

All communications should be addressed to the *Editor of* "*Trübner's Record,*" 57 and 59, Ludgate Hill, London, E.C., and they should be accompanied by the sender's name and address (not necessarily for publication). Every care will be taken with MSS., but the Editor cannot hold himself responsible for rejected communications, which—if to be returned to the sender—should be accompanied by postage. MS. should be legibly written, and on one side of the paper only. Books for review should be addressed to the Editor.

### *NOTICE TO ADVERTISERS.*

All communications respecting advertisements should be addressed to Messrs. F. TALLIS AND SON, 22, Wellington Street, W.C. *Terms for the insertion of advertisements:—*

| | | | | |
|---|---|---|---|---|
| WHOLE PAGE (ordinary position) | ... | £5 | 5 | 0 |
| HALF PAGE | ,, ,, | ... | 2 15 | 0 |
| QUARTER PAGE | ,, ,, | ... | 1 10 | 0 |

Special positions per contract.

# TRÜBNER'S RECORD,

## A JOURNAL DEVOTED TO THE LITERATURE OF THE EAST.

WITH NOTES AND LISTS OF CURRENT

**American, European and Colonial Publications.**

*Edited by Dr. Rost, of the India Office.*

MAY, 1890.    THIRD SERIES. VOL. II. No. I.

## THE TEMPTATION OF ZOROASTER.

[In the long 19th fargard or chapter of the *Vendidad*, the first book contained in the *Avesta*, occurs this remarkable temptation of the great Eranian prophet, which reminds one of the temptation of Buddha by the fiend Mâra, poetically rendered by Sir Edwin Arnold in the sixth book of his *Light of Asia*. The present attempt at a not too literal metrical rendering is based on the Zend text (xix. 1–35), partly eked out by the Pehlevi version.]

Now from the North, from regions of the North,
Forth Auro-Mainyus rushed, the murderous one,
Demon of demons : then he, evil-minded
And slayer of many men, thus spake aloud :

"Hence, fiend, and slay the holy Zarathust !"
And But the fiend, the murderous, who deceives
The souls of men, came rushing down upon him.
But Zarathustra prayed the sacred prayer,*
The praises of the good Creation and the Law.
And lo ! the fiend, the murderous, who deceives
The souls of men, in terror fled away,          [me !
And screamed : "O Auro-Mainyus, thou tormentest
I see no sign of death upon the Holy One !"

But Zarathustra in his spirit saw
How wicked demons plotted for his death.
Then fearless and unmoved he rose, and stepped
Forth 'gainst their enmity, whilst in his hands
He bare a sling of mighty stones, which God
Had given to him; and o'er this broad, round earth,
Where runs the river with its lofty banks,
He carried them, and thus aloud proclaimed :

"Cruel Auro-Mainyus ! lo ! I come to smite
Thy ill-creation, thy demons, and the fiend,
The spirit of Idolatry ! to combat till such time
As Saoshyant shall come, the Saviour,
The Victor, from the great Sea to the East." †

But evil-minded Auro-Mainyus cried :
"O smite not my creation, Zarathust !

Thou art King Pourushaspa's son, and thou
Art born of human mother : lo ! renounce
The Law of Mazda, and thou shalt receive
Reward as great as Vadaghno the Chief."
But Zarathustra : "I will not renounce
The holy Law of Mazda ! Sooner may
Body and soul and intellect dissolve !"
Quoth Auro-Mainyus : "By what weapon, say,
Wilt thou then smite ? or how wilt thou destroy
My creatures and creation ?"
                               Answer made
The holy Zarathust : "Sacred vessels ‡
And holy prayers, these are my trusty arms.
With these words will I smite and every way
Destroy thee, baneful-minded Auro-Mainyus !
The Holy Spirit made these sacred words,
And the Immortal Saints,§ the strong, the wise,
Have them proclaimed !"
                          And thereupon he prayed
The sacred prayer. The demons yelled aloud,—
The wicked, Evil-minded Ones,—and fled,—
Fled to the lowest depths of murky hell ! ‖

                               L. C. CASARTELLI.

## THE LUSHAIS AT HOME.

Marriage is entirely a civil contract among the Lushais, and can be dissolved by either party. A woman on leaving her husband takes with her only what she brought originally from her father's house. If a young man takes a fancy to a girl and wishes to marry, he informs his father, who sets about negociations with the girl's parents, aided by two old counsellors, who are called *pillai*, and who do all the talking and fix the amount demanded. The parents of the girl generally commence by asking a great deal but eventually a settlement is made, the price being in ordinary cases a gun, valued at Rs. 25 to Rs. 30 and a pig or fowls. On the price being paid the pig

---

* The Ahuna-Vairya prayer.
† The mythological Lake Kauçoya.

‡ The mortar and cup for the haoma sacrifice.
§ The Ameshoçpentas.
‖ This last verse is taken from the very end (§ 147) of the Fargard. It appears to have been misplaced and to belong here.

is killed, and several big jars of rice-beer are brewed and feasting and dancing take place. On the second day the bride goes to her husband's house and they are man and wife. It may happen that a father, tempted by a high offer, gives his daughter in marriage to some one she does not like. In this case she runs away from her husband and is not thought wrong for doing so, but her father has to return the price paid for his daughter, and she is free to marry again. Very lengthened periods elapse sometimes before the price of the bride is paid by the husband, and I mention as an instance an old friend of mine, Shyaltonga by name, who is the father of eight children, and who only paid the remainder of his wife's purchase a very short time ago on receiving a large reward from me for services rendered as a guide.

Women are held in much consideration among the Lushais, and they have much influence and are consulted on all matters. Yet upon them falls all the heavy bodily burden of fetching water, hewing wood, bringing food from the *jhooms*, cooking, brewing liquor and spinning. The Lushais are not prolific as a race, and seldom have more than three or four children. They suckle their children for a great length of time—up to three and four years of age. One peculiarity I have noticed, *viz.* that a mother gives her child rice two or three days after birth, a thing I have never known among any other natives of India. She chews the rice in her mouth and puts it into the child's mouth with her tongue.

Just before entering every Lushai village one sees groups of *machans* made of hewed logs, and alongside them upright poles covered with heads of pigs, deer, gyal and other animals. These are the burial-grounds. When any one falls ill and seems likely to die, the Pui-thiem, literally the great knower (we should call him sorcerer ; *N.B.*—The Lushais call all our doctors pui-thiem), is called in, and as he may direct, a gyal, pig, goat, or dog is killed and feasted on, a slight portion being given to the sick man who may or may not recover. In the event of a goat being the animal killed, a small portion of its skin with hair attached is tied round the sick person's neck. If the sick person dies all the relatives are called in, and according to the family's means pigs, &c., are killed, and all friends and relatives are feasted. Quantities of liquor are drunk, and the next day the body is buried in the ground. If a male, with the corpse is placed his pipe, his knife, dagger or spear, and in all cases cooked rice and a small quantity of rice-beer are placed by the side of the body. In some cases, such as when the father of a family dies, the corpse is dressed in a fine cloth and propped up in the presence of all the friends and relatives, food is placed in front of him and a pipe is placed between his teeth, and he is addressed thus : "Eat and drink. You have a long journey before you.'

When a chief or his son dies, the ceremony is, of course, more imposing. When a large and powerful Syloo chief died some years ago, 60 gyals were slaughtered by his relatives and friends, and the feasting and drinking lasted for several months. On one occasion I myself, when visiting the Howlong Chief Sayipuia, witnessed the funeral rites of his son, a boy about ten years of age, who had been dead for more than a month, going on. I was invited into his house as I had known the boy well, and this is what I saw :—In the centre of the room was a coffin roughly hewed out of a tree in which the corpse lay. The top had been plastered with mud to make it air-tight, and from the bottom of the coffin, through the floor of the house, ran a large bamboo tube, which was buried deep in the ground. By the coffin was a gun, and close to it sat the poor mother weeping and calling on her son by name. At times she would turn to me and say : "Brother, you knew my son and he called you father, and now he is dead." I was much affected, and according to custom I purchased a goat and killed it in honour of the dead. To continue, however. The corpse was kept in this coffin in the house for five months, during which time Sayipuia never left his house, never ate rice or meat. At the end of five months the bones were taken out and removed to the family burial-ground. The Shendus, from what little we saw of their country during the last expedition, have more elaborate burial-grounds. The graves are lined with huge slabs of stone, and slabs are also erected over the tomb ; and on one occasion, in addition to the skulls of animals, two human skulls were seen fastened on poles over the tomb. When Howaata's tomb was opened out by us after burning his village during the late expedition, by his side was Lieutenant's Stewart's gun, the chief's pipe, knife, a bottle of liquor, and a small head-dress made of the tail feathers of the chemraj bird.

The Lushais as a race may be said to be free from any infectious diseases. They suffer from remittent fever, boils, and inflammation of the bowels, brought on from over-eating and over-drinking. They, in the year 1861, brought back cholera, with them from a raid they made in British territory, and thus spread the greatest terror among them, many of them, I am told, blowing out their brains on the first appearance of the disease showing itself. They named cholera vay-dam-loh (foreign sickness). In the same way they once caught small-pox in the Kassalong bazaar in 1860.

A very curious fact is that the Lushais have absolutely no knowledge of any drug or medicine in any form whatever. This I look upon as most extraordinary, and I have never heard of any tribe, however savage it may be, without any knowledge of such. The Chakmas, Mughs, and Tipperahs, who, though to a certain extent civilized, still have the same mode of life as the Lushais, all have their drugs. A great many of the Lushais have, of course, heard of our medicines, and the result is that, when visiting their villages, old men and maidens, young men and old women and children with various ailments are brought to me to be doctored. I restrict myself to cases of fever, and the effect of a few grains of quinine on them is simply marvellous. I have effected a few simple cures with the aid of quinine, chlorodyne, and essence of ginger, but the climax in my doctoring capabilities was reached when a husband brought his wife to me and solemnly assured me that her accouchement was already two months overdue, and could I give any drug that would make up for lost time? I saw at a glance that the poor woman was suffering from dropsy, but looked very wise and suggested that perhaps the cares of his family, coupled with the scarcity of rice, had interfered with his powers of calculation. As I am writing this I have with some difficulty persuaded an old Lushai friend of mine to bring in his daughter to be operated on by our medical officer here. The woman is suffering from a cancerous tumour on the back of the head, which is necessarily very painful, and she has with great courage given herself entirely into my hands, though I told her she would suffer pain and have to be lanced. I am glad to say the operation has been most successful.

The Lushais have in every village one or more blacksmiths, the thir-deng, who is a man of some importance; he receives certain tribute of rice and other produce for his work. Close to the zalbuk a small shed is generally found, and this is the forge, which is very simple but at the same time effective. It consists of two upright hollow bamboos about six inches in diameter, which are placed in the ground; into these two rammers made of birds' feathers, with handles attached, when pulled up and down act as bellows on the channel made at the foot of the bamboos. The Lushais have learnt all they know of blacksmiths' work from Bengal captives, and the trade has been handed down. They can repair the locks of guns, can make spears, daos and knives, and I have heard, though I cannot vouch for the accuracy of it, that they have been known to turn a Snider rifle into a flint lock. Brass they can also work slightly in, the stems of all the women's pipes being made of an ornamental pattern in brass, also the handles of knives. Then, again, the bowls of the men's bamboo pipes are often lined with copper made from pice procured in the bazaar.

The Lushai's knowledge of pottery is confined to making cooking pots and huge big vessels for making rice-beer. They are made of a blackish clay and are very strong and rarely break. The liquor vessels are made nearly an inch thick and about two feet in height. They have wooden platters for their food and wooden or bamboo spoons. They make all kinds of very fine basket-work with split cane and bamboo, and are very ingenious in making devices. It is astonishing what a complete feature in the life of all the Chittagong Hill tribes the bamboo is as well as the cane. I may mention here a few of their uses. First, the houses are nearly all bamboo, the roof being of cane leaves; the water is fetched by the women from their springs in hollow bamboos; from bamboo they make spoons, rice-sifting baskets, baskets to carry loads, baskets to hold their household goods, baskets to hold fowls; they use bamboo root to make handles for their daos; when in the jungle they even cook their rice in green bamboos; and last, but not least, they eat the bamboo shoots, and very delicious they are.

The Lushais give to the name of the Creator the word Pathien, who is supreme. After him comes Khua-Vang, who carries out the Pathien's orders and appears on earth at certain times. I give a story of the appearance of Khua-Vang as it was told me by a Lushai. He was sitting drinking in the chief's house and found he could not get drunk, which perplexed him. On returning to his house he saw a man whom he knew to be Khua-Vang by his enormous stature. He addressed him in fear and trembling, but received no answer, and as he watched him Khua-Vang became smaller and smaller till he dwindled into space. Soon after this his village was raided and an enormous number of captives taken, men and women slaughtered, and the chief's power completely broken. The Lushais further believe that besides the deity the sun and moon are gods, and that the worship of them is agreeable to the deity. Their ideas of an after-world are very quaint. There are two abodes, the Piel-Ral abode and the Mi-thi-Khua (people-dead-village). These two are separated by the big river Piel, from which Piel Ral takes its name. Piel Ral answers to our heaven, and no one from either abode can cross the river. Mighty hunters and great warriors only go to Piel Ral, where they live at ease and have no labour of any kind; they hunt and enjoy themselves. No woman can go to Piel Ral, but small children of both sexes who died before they had left their mothers' breasts are exceptions to this. To the Mi-thi-Khua go all men who have in no way distinguished themselves and all women. Life here is much the same as on earth: they have their daily labour and household duties, etc. In both abodes all live and die three times. After the third death the spirit becomes mist, falls to the ground, and with it is extinguished for ever. The idea is that when people on earth become sick and die, Khua-Vang is slowly but surely eating all the flesh from off their bodies and death is the result, the spirit going to one of the two mentioned abodes.

Every chief has one or two, or in case of big chiefs three or four, old men who act as his councillors and ambassadors : these are called by them *koubal* and by us *karbaris*. On entering a chief's village, the custom is to go to the karbari's, and there wait until the chief demands your presence. These karbaris are held in great estimation, and receive a yearly tribute of rice from the village. I have heard of a custom, answering much to the fiery cross of the old days : when a chief wishes to collect any of his clan or give emphasis to any order, he gives his spear to the messenger. If a hostile message be intended a fighting sword is sent with the messenger. Another form of expressing orders is a small cross made of split bamboo wands, which can signify various things. If the tips of the cross be broken, a demand for blackmail is intended ; if the tips be charred, it implies an urgent assemblage at the chief's house; if a green chilli be fixed on the tip, it implies disobedience to obey orders will be re- warded by punishment as hot as the chilli.

The whole art of war among the Lushais may be described in one word—"surprise." They always send forward spies to see if their foes can be taken un- awares : if the foes be on the alert, they are left in peace. As an instance of this I know of a village in the south of the Hill Tracts whose inhabitants only numbered, men, women and children, about 100. The villagers, owing to a recent raid on a neighbouring village, had a night patrol. Two hundred Shendu warriors crept up to the village at early dawn. One of the sentries saw them and threw a stone at them, whereupon they all disappeared. The village, I may add, was stockaded to a certain extent.

A raid being decided on, the preliminary step is a sacrifice and a big drink. On starting off for the raid the old men and women of the village accompany the raiders for an hour or two on their journey and then leave them with such expressed wishes as these : "May you bring home many heads and come back unhurt!" On arriving at some distance from the village to be raided they make their preparations, and creep up to the village just before dawn. They generally com- mence by firing several shots at the village and rush on the surprised inhabitants. I have never heard of a village thus attacked attempting to defend itself. At the first shot every man, woman and child bolts into the jungle. The women are seized, and if old and unmarriageable killed on the spot. All children too small to travel are killed and frequently torn from their mothers' breasts and murdered before their eyes. After two or three hours' bloodshed, unless the raiders feel no danger of a surprise, in which case they pro- long their stay, they move out of the village, taking the women and girls captives with them, all tied together. They never take a full-grown male captive, it saves them trouble to kill him on the spot. As a rule the heads of all slain are carried off, though some- times only the scalps. On their return journey the captives endure many hardships : if any one through weakness or ill-treatment cannot keep up, instant death is the result. When nearing their village the raiders are again met, if successful, by all the women and old men, who bring them down cooked food and liquor and accompany them in triumph to their houses. On entering the village one or more captives are always sacrificed as a thanksgiving offering, the booty is divided and the captives are set to work as slaves. As a rule after they have been a short time in the village they are well treated. The women invariably marry one from among their captors, and have been known when offered release years after to cling to them and refuse to go back to their own relatives.

One extraordinary custom among the Lushais which I would not have believed had I not had personal knowledge of the fact is that men and women change their sex in all outward appearances and customs. I give as an instance a woman who has twice accom- panied a chief to see me and who is dressed as a man, smokes a man's pipe, goes out hunting with men, lives with them and has in every way adapted herself to the habits of men. She actually married a young girl who lived with her for one year. I myself asked in the presence of several chiefs and other Lushais why she had, being a woman, become a man. She at first denied being a woman, but when I suggested that we should change coats she demurred and finally confessed she was a woman, but that her *khua-vang* was not good and so she became a man. I have heard of other cases in which men have adopted the dress and customs of women.

Constant disputes arise among the chiefs, regarding their necklaces of amber and other stones, which arise through intermarriages of different clans, and I have found it a hard task sometimes to settle these disputes satisfactorily when I have been appointed arbitrator by them. Differences arise owing to sisters, brothers, wives, sons and daughters claiming portions on the death of a chief, and often ended in the old days in bloody feuds.

The Lushais are great at songs and dancing. I give a few typical songs, translated literally :—

1.—"The long day song" runs thus :

> I do not aspire for the day,
> Evening dusk I want not,
> Sweet girls ! their speech I solicit,
> Then I wish for the day again.

2.—An ode to Thluk-Pui, a famous gallant, and his mistress Dil-Thangi, a great beauty :

> Walk on, walk on, Oh Big Thluk-Pui,
> Walking on the cloudy plain
> Far over the vault of the sky,
> Go and embrace Dil-Thangi.

Powerful chiefs have their songs dedicated to them and the various clans have their songs, all of which are sung on the occasion of big feasts.

One of the great difficulties in gathering genealogical tables, etc., is the extraordinary way in which the relatives of two chiefs, who may be at distinct enmity with one another, intermarry, and also the migrations of chiefs and their followers from one clan to another distinct clan. Broadly speaking, I would classify these tribes as follows :—All west of the Koladyne I would call Lushais, and east of it or across it Shendus. These, again, can be classified. The Lushais consist of Syloos and Howlongs and Tanglowas, but have living in their territory Punkhos and Bunjogis, who are distinct off-shoots of the Shendus. The Shendus consist of Molien-Puis, Thlang-Thangs, Lakhers, Halkas, etc., under the general designation of Pois. The main difference in the appearance of the Lushais and the Shendus can be seen at a glance. The Lushai men and women wear their hair tied in a knot at the back of the head, while the Shendus or Pois, as they are called, wear the hair tied in a huge knot right over the forehead : the latter in the case of men only. The languages are totally distinct also, but the Lushai language is, I believe, understood as far as the west border of the Chin country in Burma. One thing has struck me as being most extraordinary, and that is how rarely one meets a really old man amongst these people. Old women I have seen in abundance, but, from what I can judge of their ages, I should say that a man of over 65 years is most uncommon.

Taking the Lushais as I have found them in their own villages, they are far superior to many savages one reads about. They are most hospitable, and I rarely enter a house in any village without being offered food and drink, even when I have known myself at times the person offering it has barely enough for his day's food. They are extremely intelligent and quickly master the meaning of anything said to them or shown them. In fact it is most difficult to reconcile their apparent mildness with the well-known instances of the atrocities committed by them when raiding. One of my old friends and guides, who is now the father of a grown-up family of eight children and who is apparently an exceedingly mild and benevolent old

gentleman, astonished me very much the other day when I questioned him about the feats of his youth. I led him on gradually, and eventually he told me he had with his own hands speared and killed six persons. I asked him if they were men or women, and he then told me three were men and three were women. I got an account of the death of each one from him, his features becoming gradually more ferocious as he continued his narrative, till, finally, when he described how his last victim had been a woman whom he had speared in cold blood, he became quite excited and with a piece of stick in his hand enacted the whole performance over again. He gradually subsided, but no amount of expostulation on my part would convince him that he had behaved in a way not to boast of.

Notwithstanding it being most unpleasant at times, still I have always tried as the most effectual way of thoroughly understanding these people to adopt the policy of "when you are at Rome," etc., and by this means only can one get a thorough insight into the character of the people. Another good old saying I have found most effective, namely, "*In vino veritas*," and many a time by a judicious application of rum at the right moment I have wormed out information which was being kept back.

I have given a fair outline, I think, of the Lushais and their habits and customs, and I will now content myself with giving a few anecdotes in connection with the people generally by way of illustrating their character, etc. I paid my first visit into the heart of the Lushai country in February, 1887, when I went with a guard of ten men to Sayipuia's village, a chief I had heard a great deal of. I trusted to the fact of Sayipuia having previously known Captain Lewin, who interviewed him in · 1872 (from which time he had never seen a European), and to a certain knowledge of the language and of the Lushais' customs and habits which I had acquired in villages within our frontier, to getting, if not a welcome, at any rate an interview. When within a few hours' of the chief's village I left my men behind to cook and proceeded with a friendly chief to show me the way and my interpreter. On reaching the village, I marched boldly in and made for the Karbari's house, and he informed the chief I had arrived. I waited most patiently, according to custom, till the chief sent for me, and as this was not till 9 p.m. I became somewhat anxious. All this time I was surrounded by the men, women and children of the village, who clustered round me in hundreds exclaiming in wonder at my white skin. On the chief sending for me I went to his house, and though at first he was inclined to be grumpy we soon became chatty over several bottles of rum which I produced. I spent the next day with him and gave him more rum and a small present of rupees, he giving me a handsome cloth. The third day I went away well satisfied with my visit and returned to Demagiri, my starting-point, through three other Howlong chiefs' villages, in all of which I was well received. In one village, where Lallura was the chief's name, I as usual produced rum and made merry with the chief and his friends. Unfortunately I found the rum running short, and in an evil moment I had it watered on the quiet to make the supply last longer. But the chief spotted it at once, and was loud in his wrath at my giving him, as he said, "water" and not spirit. I was at my wits' end and in desperation produced my only bottle of whisky: he tasted it, and, with his eyes up-raised, exclaimed: "Words are not available to express how delicious it is!"—and he very soon got drunk. In his cups he boasted of his power and strength, etc., while his old warriors sitting alongside of him commenced chaffing him (he was lame I must mention from an accident to his hip when a boy), saying: "You a warrior and a chief! Why, you can't walk from one village to another," and so on. This little story shows what I have said previously, that no outward respect is paid to a chief, and that they have a great craving for strong drinks.

My next visit to Sayipuia was in December, 1887: on this occasion I knew my ground better, was provided with more authority to deal with him, and last but not least, had a supply of rupees. Accordingly I asked him to swear an oath of friendship with me according to Lushai customs, and he at once agreed, and the following morning was fixed for the ceremony, which took place as follows. A gyal was tied in the open space facing the chief's house. Sayipuia came out dressed in his best, which was a very handsome check cloth, with an enormous plume made of the tail feathers of the bhim-raj, or mocking bird, in his hair, and a spear in his right hand. He called me to him close to the gyal, and both of us, holding the spear in our right hands, simultaneously plunged it into the brute's ribs. Sayipuia drew out the spear and taking the warm blood in his hand smeared his and my hands, face and legs with its blood, and then holding up the spear called out in a loud voice that all might hear as follows:—"When the big streams and little streams shall dry up in these hills, then and not before shall this white man be mine enemy: what is mine is his, and by this oath you all know him to be my friend!"

The ceremony over, we adjourned to the chief's house and ratified the oath in numerous flagons of home-brewed rice-beer. Now I luckily happen to possess a strong head and this has stood me in good stead, as one must drink with these people if one wishes to thoroughly adapt oneself to their customs. The drink is passed round in horns (generally a tame gyal's) and their principle is "no heel taps," each person reversing his horn to show he has emptied it. I was much amused on one occasion at one of these drinking bouts by Sayipuia exclaiming: "This is indeed a chief: why, we can't even make him drunk." The Lushais carry this drinking to such an extent that it is a common thing for the rice of last year's crop to be exhausted before the new crop is ripe, owing to the vast quantities consumed in manufacturing their drink. As a rule the Lushais are not quarrelsome in their cups, but when they have had as much as they can stand they quietly lie down on the floor and sleep off their drunkenness. Instances of quarrelling do of course occur, and I remember once, when sitting in a chief's house, one of his young warriors kept coming up to where I was sitting by the chief and bothering me to give him tobacco, to look at my arms, legs, etc., till I lost patience and told him to desist. The chief, too, seeing I was getting angry, remarked: "Amro! he vay-lall-zong-a thun-ur-in sakei-aug-bok"—"Be quiet, these foreign chiefs when angry are like tigers." I took this as a gentle hint and landed my young friend one straight between the eyes, much to his discomfiture. To my astonishment, instead of there being a row, I was applauded for what I had done, and the next day this same young fellow and I became quite friendly!—[From the *Pioneer Mail*.]

---

## DR. STEIN'S DISCOVERY OF A JAINA TEMPLE DESCRIBED BY HIUEN TSIANG.

### By GEORG BÜHLER.

In his account of the Panjab the Chinese pilgrim Hiuen Tsiang narrates (Beal, *Siyuki*, vol. i. p. 144) that he saw 40 or 50 *li* to the south-east of the hill-town of Siṅghapura by the side of ten sacred tanks, a Stûpa built by Aśoka, a deserted Buddhist monastery and a temple of the White-robed heretics. He adds that in that spot "the original teacher of the White-robed ascetics arrived at the knowledge of the principles he sought, and first preached the law," as well as "that there was an inscription to that effect." Some further remarks on the laws and the images of this teacher leave no doubt that the sectarians, settled near Siṅghapura,* were Śvetâmbara Jainas. The latter point was first noticed by Professor Lassen, *Indische Alterthumskunde*, vol. iv. p. 670, and his identification has been accepted unhesitatingly by all other Orientalists.

The geographical position of Siṅghapura and of the sacred spot near it has been repeatedly discussed by Sir A. Cunningham. In the *Archæological Survey*

* I use throughout the form *Siṅghapura* instead of *Siṃhapura*, because Hiuen Tsiang's transcription points to it, and because it occurs in the Lakkâ Maṇḍal Praśasti.

*Reports*, vol. ii. p. 191 f., he states that Hiuen Tsiang's description of Siṅghapura would fit either Ketâs or Malot in the Salt Range, but gives the preference to the latter town. In his *Ancient Geography*, p. 124 ff., he decides for Ketâs. But, after another tour in the Panjab, he returns (*Archæological Survey Reports*, vol. v. p. 90) to his first opinion. He again identifies Siṅghapura with Malot, and further expresses his belief that Ketâs is identical with the site of the Buddhist and Jaina sanctuaries, because it still possesses a large pool of great sanctity, as well as a number of smaller ponds which presumably represent the ten tanks mentioned by Hiuen Tsiang. This view he declares to be further confirmed by the existence of a ruined monastery on a mound 400 feet to the west of the pools, which would correspond to the deserted monastery of Hiuen Tsiang. But in none of the three accounts of Ketâs occurs any mention of Jaina ruins.

The latter circumstance made me suspect long ago that there must be something wrong or wanting in Sir A. Cunningham's identifications, and I urged at various times friends who resided in the Panjab or visited it on archæological expeditions, to examine carefully the ancient sites in the Salt Range, and especially the neighbourhood of Ketâs, in order to discover Hiuen Tsiang's Jaina temple, and, if possible, the highly important inscription which he mentions. My appeals had, however, no result, until I addressed myself to the present energetic Principal of the Oriental College at Lahore, Dr. Stein, of whose excellent work some account has been given in the pages of this Journal, vol. ii. p. 271. Dr. Stein made a trip to Ketâs during the last Christmas holidays, which resulted in the discovery of the temple, and moreover made it possible to fix with accuracy the site of Siṅghapura, which, since the publication of the Lakkâ Maṇḍal Praśasti in the *Epigraphia Indica*, has become a place of considerable interest. I give his own account of the journey, translating it from a German letter dated December 28, 1889. He says there:

"I left Lahore on Christmas Eve, and arrived next morning in Khewra, the terminus of the branch line of the Sindh Sâgar Railway, which leads to the salt works. From Khewra I intended to start for Ketâs, where Sir A. Cunningham tried to find Hiuen Tsiang's Jaina temple and tanks. The officials in charge of the salt works were not able to give me much information. So I left Khewra, where, in spite of the great age of the mines, neither inscriptions nor any other antiquities are found, by the Ketâs road, which runs up the steep south-eastern scarp of the hills. The first village on the plateau of the Salt Range which I reached was Rotucha, where the old inhabitants whom I questioned regarding ancient ruins pointed without hesitation to

the other side of a hill-chain situated in a westerly direction. They asserted that a place, called Mûrti was found there in the Gamdhala valley, which yielded stone images and beautifully cut blocks, such as had been taken away a few years ago for the erection of the new bridge at Choya Saidan Shah. As the latter town lies on the road to Ketâs, I rode on, and soon convinced myself by ocular inspection that the materials for the bridge just mentioned, which partly were adorned with relievos, must have been taken from an old temple. I further found similar fine slabs of red sandstone in the gateway of the Ziarat at Saidan Shah, which building seems to date from the times of the Moghuls. On account of these discoveries, I resolved to stop for the night in the bungalow at Choya Saidan Shah and to visit Mûrti on the following day. Yesterday, in the morning, I followed the rivulet which flows from Ketâs down the Gamdhala valley, and was not a little surprised when, after a march of about two English miles, my guide showed me the place where all the sculptures had been found in a spot which seems to agree most remarkably with Hiuen Tsiang's description. The bed of the Ketâs brook forms in the narrow and very picturesque Gamdhala valley a number of small tanks, and at a bend, where there are two larger basins, stands the hill of Mûrti. It rises on a basis of solid sandstone to about one hundred feet above the level of the water, and its top expands into a small plateau, about 225 feet long and 190 broad. On this plateau lies a small mound about 40 feet high, and on its west side an enormous mass of rubbish, marking the site of an ancient temple. Two trenches, about 70 feet long, which run north and west, show where the walls stood, the fundaments of which were excavated eight years ago by order of the Assistant Commissioners, in order to furnish materials for the bridge near Saidan Shah. Small fragments of richly ornamented capitals and of friezes can be picked up without trouble from the heap of ruins. From the top of the hill I heard distinctly the murmuring of the brook, which, on leaving the chief tank, forces its way between a number of boulders. Dense groups of trees, such as Hiuen Tsiang describes, are reflected in the limpid waters of the tanks, which still swarm with fish, and frequently attract the sport-loving officers of the Jhelam cantonment. On the whole, I have not seen in the neighbourhood any place to which Hiuen Tsiang's description, 'altogether it is a lovely spot for wandering forth,' would more justly apply. But I anticipate the results of my further excursions of yesterday and of to-day.

"In order to ascertain as quickly as possible if the situation of Mûrti agreed with the distances given by Hiuen Tsiang, I started for Ketâs after a cursory inspection of the plateau and of its surroundings. As I suspected that the small mound on the plateau enclosed Aśoka's Stûpa, which Hiuen Tsiang mentions in the immediate neighbourhood of the Jaina temple, I set, previous to my departure, twenty Kulis to remove the rubbish which covers it. Ketâs, which lies about four miles north-west from the Gamdhala valley, I reached about noon. I at once examined the Tîrtha, already described by Sir A. Cunningham, and the group of ancient temples called Sat-Ghara. I was soon convinced that there is at Ketâs no group of tanks such as that described by Hiuen Tsiang. For the brook, after leaving the *one* large tank, flows downwards in a narrow stony bed. The five tolerably well-preserved temples of Sat-Ghara show the Kaśmîrian style, no trace of Jaina architecture. On further inquiries after ancient sculptures, I was conducted to a modern temple which one of the Purohitas of Ketâs built during the Sikh period with stones brought from Mûrti. It really showed the same square blocks and delicately chiselled ornaments which I had found in Mûrti. To my still greater joy I was shown in the courtyard of the temple of Mahant Sarjû Dâs two richly-ornamented stone pillars which were stated to have come likewise from Mûrti. They have been cut out of the same red sandstone which furnished all the sculptures in the latter place, and they have on two sides deep holes which look as if they were intended for fitting in wooden railings. The sculptures on their capitals differ, but are decidedly in the Jaina style, showing seated, naked male figures with garlands in their hands. You will understand that they forcibly reminded me of Hiuen Tsiang's ' balustrades of different shapes and of strange character.' In the large Stûpa, situated before the east front of the Sat-Ghara temples, I believe I recognize the Stûpa of Aśoka, which, as Hiuen Tsiang says, lay to the south of the town of Siṅghapura. The completely ruinous state of this monument, which rises to the height of nearly fifty feet, would agree well with Hiuen Tsiang's remark, ' the decorations are much injured.' From this last remark you will see that I consider Ketâs, or rather the field of ruins, lying 1—2 miles further north, to be the site of the ancient town, which according to the Chinese pilgrim stood 40—50 *li* (perhaps 6—7 miles) north-west from the Jaina temple. That Ketâs possessed a greater importance than that derived from its ' Nâga ' (sacred tank) is proved by the ruins of ancient forts on the surrounding hills, which would not be necessary for a mere place of pilgrimage.

" I slept last night at Dalwal, a large village without any ancient ruins, and rode this morning south-west to Shib Gangâ and Malot, where I inspected the well-preserved temples in the Kaśmîrian style. These two places are too distant (10 and 14 miles respectively) from Mûrti, and cannot have been the sites of Siṅgha-pura. Besides, the direction to Mûrti (and Ketâs) would not agree. It would be north-east, not south-east, as Hiuen Tsiang says.

" When I returned in the afternoon to Mûrti, I found that one side of the mound had been laid free, and the rough walls of white sandstone, covered with a layer of mortar, two feet thick, convinced me that the mound was not a natural hillock, but a real Stûpa. I then put the Kulis to work on the south front of the temple. At a depth of not more than one foot, beautiful capitals and fragments of pillars turned up, and somewhat later a relievo, three feet high, which apparently had adorned the top of a niche or of a Toraṇ. All in all, we found to-day twenty fragments of sculptures."

In a postscript from Lahore Dr. Stein states that he obtained by further excavations on December 29 fifty more fragments of sculptures, " which were deposited in the bungalow at Saidan Shah pending their transference to the Lahore Museum.' Some pieces, which he brought with him to Lahore, he showed to Mr. Kipling, the Director of the Museum, who fully agreed with him in considering them to be Jaina sculptures.

It seems to me impossible to deny that Dr. Stein has found Hiuen Tsiang's long-looked-for Jaina temple, and that he has shown Sir A. Cunningham's second opinion regarding the site of Siṅghapura to be the correct one. These discoveries possess a very great interest. Whether they will become still more important by the recovery of the curious inscription which Hiuen Tsiang saw, will depend on the result of an application to the Government of the Panjab for the means to fully excavate the site of Mûrti. I trust that it will be successful ; for ancient Jaina sculptures are not very common in Northern India, and the inscription or inscriptions which will certainly come to light will be invaluable for the history of the Jaina sect.    G. BÜHLER.

[From the " Vienna Oriental Journal."]

## ARCHÆOLOGY IN BURMA.

We are in receipt of an advanced copy of Dr. Forch-hammer's Report on *Arakan*, from which we propose to make some extracts, to enable our readers to form an idea of the singular character of the temple ruins in that province. His far more interesting Report on Pagan is now passing through the press. Both are richly illustrated with photographs.

The description of the Mahâmuni Pagoda in Dhaññavatî, the ancient capital, forms the first part of the Report. With its history that of the province is intimately associated. It is traced from the time when legend and history shook hands down to the year A.D. 1784, when the Burmese King Bodawpaya conquered Arakan, sent the brazen image of Buddha preserved in this ancient shrine across the mountains, and had it set up in Amarapura. "Until the removal of the image the Mahâmuni pagoda was the most sacred shrine in Indo-China; the entire religious history of Buddhistic Arakan centres round this 'younger brother' of Gotama; the loss of this relic sank deeper into the hearts of the people than the loss of their liberty and the extinction of their royal house. "It will one day be brought back again," the Arakanese fondly hope. The abolishment of this stronghold of Buddhism has been followed by a general decline of this religion throughout Arakan. The natives totally neglected the shrine; wild jungle overgrew the precincts; in due time the place became haunted and shunned."

While, however, the Mahâmuni Pagoda and similar structures in its vicinity afford few instances of decorative art and few examples of constructive skill, the splendid temples of *Mrohaung*, built by the kings of the Myauk-û dynasty, bespeak the power, resources, and culture of their former rulers. "The architectural style of the Shitthanny and Dukkanthein Pagodas is probably unique in India, and the two shrines are undoubtedly the finest ruins in Lower Burma. They were not constructed by the Arakanese, but by 'Kulas' [strangers] from India; the natives were forced to burn the bricks and bring the stones from distant quarries; Hindu architects and Hindu sculptors raised and embellished the structures; to the Arakanese, compelled to years of unpaid labour, these pagodas are an unpleasant reminiscence of the tyrannic and arbitrary rule of several Myauk-û kings." The Shitthaungpara, or shrine of 80,000 images, erected by King Minbin (1531-53), is the work of Hindu architects and Hindu workmen; "it is more a fortress than a pagoda; its obvious purpose was to serve as a place of refuge to the royal family and retainers. The main temple is built on a promontory half way up the west side of the hill; the side facing the valley rests upon massive stone walls carried up from the base of the ridge to the height of the promontory (about 40 feet); laterally the shrine is protected by walls which branch off from its north and south sides, and connect them with the common basis of the entire structure, the hill. In old Arakanese forts and fortified pagodas (such as the Mahâmuni), it is always the north and east sides which are rendered the strongest; the Mros, Saks, Shans, Burmans, and Talaings usually attacked from these quarters. But when Minbin erected the Shitthaungpara, the cannons of the Dutch and Portuguese had already been heard and felt in the capital of the Myauk-û dynasty, being, in the words of the Viceroy of Goa, "both rich and weak and therefore desirable." The inner passages in the pagoda lead through well-cemented stone-walls of 6 to 15 feet thickness and open toward the hill; the vaulted stone roof and all parts of the pagoda facing the west are in addition covered with layers of bricks 6 to 10 feet high; the outer wall forms a rampart overlooking and commanding the valley. The temple premises can hold a large garrison."

Similarly, of the Dukkhantein Pagoda, or shrine of misery, Dr. Forchhammer says: "The interior of this gloomy temple is throughout in good order. Nothing save a terrible earthquake or a continued bombardment can disturb the compactness of such masses of well-fitted and cemented stones, mantled with thick strata of bricks. No use whatever is made of this temple fortress; the natives do not venture to enter the labyrinth; a superstitious awe impels them to avoid even approaching it. Its peculiar features are the absence of decorative designs, the intricate construction of the interior, and the means employed to render the shrine indestructible. I know of no prototype of this probably unique structure."

Dr. Forchhammer's description of the Mahâti Pagoda, further on, and of the Kado shrine, in the Launggyet circle, that "gem of the art of stone sculpture in Arakan," are well worth careful study. In conclusion, he gives a list, from the Sabbatthânappakaraṇam, of 198 cities which in ancient and more recent times were situated along both banks of the Kaladan river.

To draw attention to his forthcoming work on the Archæological Survey of Pagan, we reprint from the *Rangoon Times* the following brief account of his operations, reserving ourselves the pleasure of giving copious extracts from that work as soon as an advanced copy of it should have reached us.

The staff of the Government Archæologist in Burma, we learn from the last Administration Report, was usefully employed last year in copying, under his supervision, a large number of rare palm-leaf manuscripts which are important alike for the purposes of archæology and of history. The following are the names of the works which were copied during 1887-88:—

(i) The Pagan Yazawin Haung, or Ancient History of Pagan. (ii) The Mazomadetha Yazawin, or History of the Middle Country, *i.e.* the region of the Ganges. (iii) The Thayakithaya Yazawin, or History of Sriksetra, *i.e.* ancient Prome. (iv) The Pagan Yazawin Thit, or History of Pagan. (v) The Myinzaing Yazawin; History of Myinzaing. (vi) The Pinya Yazawin; History of Pinya. (vii) The Sagaing Yazawin; History of Sagaing. (viii) The Inwa Yazawin (3 volumes); History of Ava. (ix) The Talok Yazawin; History of China. (x) The Taungngu Yazawin; History of Toungoo. (xi) The Garuhan Ason Apyat; The Garuhan Decisions. Copies of the following extensive inscriptions were prepared by the Government Archæologist's Burmese Assistant:—(i) The Rajamaniculaceti inscription. (ii) The Mahavijayaramsiceti inscription. (iii) The Mahalokaramsiceti inscription.

For several months of the year Dr. Forchhammer was himself engaged in cataloguing the Nyaungyan Prince's library, which now forms part of the Manuscript Department, Bernard Free Library. The most important work of archæological interest carried out during the past year was the examination of the archæological remains of Pagan, the ancient capital of the Tagaung dynasty, in the Pakoku district of Upper Burma.

The outdoor work at Pagan was greatly facilitated by the Government Archæologist's manuscript researches of the previous year. The survey of these extensive ruins was begun in December, 1888. From clues furnished by the Kalyani inscriptions, which were found in Pegu, and from the Burmese histories, it was conjectured that the most ancient remains of Pagan would probably be met with in the hills to the east of the Shwezigon and Ananda pagodas. These two temples were built in imitation of the Nagazon and Lokananda shrine, which once stood in the ancient Talaing town Thayavate (from the Pali Saravati), but later on formed the southernmost portion of Anawratha's capital. The Pagan of the hills, as distinguished from the town on the river bank, consists of a number of curiously constructed shrines, built against the steep sides of ravines, and an almost interminable labyrinth of artificial caves, perforating the low hills for miles in all directions, and even extending to the bank of the Irrawaddy. These caves were at one time the abode of Buddhist monks. Six weeks were devoted to the exploration and survey of the caves alone. Many contain images of Buddhas, inscriptions, and wall-paintings. These caves and cave temples are older, and in many cases, from an architectural standpoint, more interesting than the shrines erected by Anawratha, Kyanzittha, and Narapatisithu; they are fully described in the report of the Government Archæologist. Attention was at first directed chiefly to the stone and bell inscriptions. Direct duplicate and triplicate ink impressions (estampages) were prepared from 152 inscribed stone slabs, most of them four to six feet high. Many, and probably the most important, lithic monuments were at the close of last century removed from Pagan to Amarapura by order of King Bodawpaya; they are still there, a collection of close on 500 stone inscriptions from all parts of the Burmese empire. Many of these have already been copied by the staff of the Government Archæologist. The language of the inscriptions is generally Burmese, but there is occasionally an inscription in Talaing, and many are in Pali. The square stone pillars in the Myasceti pagoda have on one side a Pali inscription, on the second an inscrip-

tion in Burmese, on the third in Talaing, and on the fourth a long legend in an unrecorded alphabet and language. The dates given on the inscriptions so far deciphered range from B.E. 420 (A.D. 1059) to the close of the last century. The stone pillars which stand near the entrance of the Shwezigon pagoda may be older because they stood originally in Thaton, the capital of the conquered Talaing king Manuha. Anawratha had them brought to Pagan. A number of clay tablets were found with legends of unknown date in Cambojan, Talaing, Burmese, and Nagari characters. All important inscriptions and the tablets are being carefully photographed. With the exception of the palace of Manuha, the last Talaing king, who was brought captive to Pagan by Anawratha, the walls around the central portion of the town and a Hindu temple erected by the Indian masons who built the Ananda and other shrines, all the structures in Pagan are of a religious character. The temples and monasteries are all built of bricks; the Nagazon, Dhammayon, and Kubyaukgyi pagodas show stone slabs inserted at regular intervals above the radiant or pointed arches of the entrances, to give more stability to them. Only Manuha's palace and the Kyaukku temple are constructed of sandstone. In the former the interior pillars exhibit in relief the effigy of Trimurti. The huge pagodas of the 11th and 12th centuries, such as the Thatpinya, Ananda, Dhammayou and Cula Mani appear to be gigantic expansions of the older but smaller temples to the east of Pagan. The latter show far more condensed architectural and ornamental details. The structures of Pagan may be broadly divided into the following groups :—

(i) A pyramid, octagonal, square, or circular at the base; solid brick-work throughout, no interior; often with lateral flight of stairs up to the garbha or bell. The Lokananda and Shwezigon pagoda are typical examples of this class;

(ii) Temples with well-developed interiors, with a central chamber, over which rises the spire, which is either a circular pyramid or a quadrangular mitre. Of this class the many-storied Thatpinyu and the Gubyaukgyi pagodas are examples;

(iii) Temples with interior galleries and antechambers on the four sides, with corresponding entrances from without. The centre is a massive square, usually with an image of Buddha on each side rising from the base to the ceiling and supporting the culminating circular or square spire above;

(iv) Massive circular bells standing on a low quadrangular base; they are built in imitation of similar shrines in Anuradha in Ceylon; in Pagan they are still called "Singhalese pagodas";

(v) The Rahan kyaungs or monasteries are square, clumsy, top-heavy buildings; a chamber for the Prior occupies the centre ; a spacious gallery leads round ; the monastery is usually one-storied, but has passages through the thick exterior walls often two or three, one above the other, with perforated stone slabs as windows; their prototype is the next, namely,—

(vi) the Subterranean monastery—the intermediate stage between the original cave labyrinths in the hills to the east and the monasteries just described. A square hole was dug in the ground, 40 to 60 feet long and 30 to 40 feet deep. The sides were walled with bricks ; at the bottom of the excavation are entrances to intricate subterranean passages and caves. The opening of the hole is on a level with the surrounding ground.

The images at Pagan are for the most part representations of Buddha, and they form a very curious subject of inquiry. In Manuha's palace Trimurti reigns supreme ; altars of Vishnu and Shiva are also met with not only in the temple of the Hindu masons west of the Thatpinyu pagoda, but also on the Buddhist Shwezigon, Nagayon, and the smaller temples of Chaukpalla. A knowledge of the occult art of old Indian chiromancy would be necessary to interpret the curious signs engraven on the tips of the fingers and the palm of Buddha's hand in old Talaing stone images. Brick statues a hundred feet high are often met with. Some of the clay tablets exhibit very neatly impressed representations of Buddha and interesting events of his life. The wooden carved images of Pagan kings in the Kyaukku temple are of particular interest. The pantheon of the 37 Nats of the pre-Buddhistic period represented on the Shwezigon pagoda is the only one of its kind in Burma. Specimens of rich ornamental carving in stone and wood, especially on the perforated stone windows, are numerous in Pagan. The Ananda, Shwezigon, Shwekugyi, and many other temples exhibit series of beautiful variegated tiles, often with figures or legends in low or high relief. The Government Archæologist reports that there is hardly a single object of archæological and historic interest which cannot be found in greater variety and perfection in Pagan than in any other place in Burma, with the exception perhaps of Mrohaung, the ancient capital of the Arakanese kings. Over 250 photographs were taken of the temples and other monuments of the old capital. The painting on the walls of the Kupyaukgyi, Kusaik and other older shrines disclose an art now lost by the Burmese. A report on his researches at Pagan, illustrated with numerous photographs, plans, and sketches, has been prepared by the Government Archæologist.

---

## "MÀYÀ," AS DESCRIBED BY AN INDIAN SCHOOLMASTER OF THE FOURTEENTH CENTURY.

The unreality of the world as the central idea of Hindu philosophy has so far familiarized itself in Europe that the original word Mâyâ has passed from the pages of Schopenhauer into the realm of lighter literature ; and yet it cannot be doubted that many who use the term are still at the mercy of their own preconceptions, that their familiarity does not extend beyond the term to the thought signified.

A striking illustration of this (recently noted in these columns) is afforded by Sir Edwin Arnold in his exposition of Mâyâ as the anticipation of modern science ! To the genuine student, however, of ancient Indian thought, anxious to judge for himself and unable to read the Sanskrit original, the following close translation of an extract from the *Panchadasî*, attributed to the renowned scholiast Mâdhavâchârya, is offered, with the assurance that the traditional explanation of the text after Râmakrishna's gloss has been followed :—

"That which cannot be explained and yet is evident is Mâyâ. This is what ordinary men know about jugglery and the like. This world of phenomena is manifest and an explanation of it is impossible. Regard it, therefore, impartially as the work of Mâyâ. When even all the wise start to explain this world, Nescience (Mâyâ) appears before them in some one quarter or another. How are the body, the organs of sense and of action, and the rest, produced from a germ : in these how comes intelligence ? To such questions what reply have you ? This is the very nature of a germ, you say. Pray tell me then how you discovered this nature ? Inductive methods fail you here, for some germs are known to be sterile. Your final resting-place is in *I know nothing indeed :* wherefore truly do the wise ascribe a magical character to this world. Than this what magic could be greater, that a germ taking up its abode in a womb should become conscious, and gifted with the many offshoots that spring from it—head, hand and foot—should pass in order through the stages of childhood, youth and old age, and see, hear, smell, and come and go ! Turning from our bodies, ponder well the seed and tree. Look now at the tiny seed and now at the majestic banyan tree ! And from such reflection rest assured that this is Mâyâ."

Doubtless we are here presented with but one phase in the conception of Mâyâ, and of this phase we might speak as a foreshadowing of Herbert Spencer; but then only by insisting on verbal similarities to the neglect of that realism which is an essential part of his system. The truth is our heritage of philosophical notions makes it easy for us of Europe to identify Mâyâ with our own notion of the world as unreal in a certain sense ; but in so doing we are apt to forget that the doctrine of Mâyâ, rigorously interpreted, is the negation of all philosophy. For the modern thinker the deduction of the world from reason is the problem of philosophy; for the Vedantin, to whom the world is Mâyâ, inexplicable, false, that problem simply does not exist.

[The author of this paper, which is here reproduced from the *Pioneer*, is Mr. Arthur Venis, an old Balliol man and former Boden Sanskrit scholar, at present Principal of the Benares Sankarit College. He is a rising Sanskrit scholar, best known by his translation of the *Panchadaśi*, from which the above extract is taken.]

## New Books.

*Sculptures et Inscriptions de Palmyre à la Glyptothèque de Ny Carlsberg, décrites et expliquées par D. Simonsen, Rabbin.* Avec 6 planches zincographiées, dessinées par M. le Dr. J. Euting, prof. à l'Univ. de Strassbourg, et 18 photogravures. Copenhague, Th. Lind, 1889. 6 and 63 pp. 8vo.

The publication in question is devoted to the collection of Palmyrean sculptures and inscriptions, several of which were published before they were added to the Glyptothèque of Ny Carlsberg. The collection contains reliefs of groups and single persons, male and female busts, votive tablets, divers fragments of figures, heads, separate inscriptions, terra-cotta medallions and one mummy. Remarkably good photographs are given of all these with the exception of the mummy—which has already been reproduced in the Revue archéologique, 1886, pl. xvi.—while the inscriptions are zincographed from Euting's excellent drawings. We have therefore to deal with a complete collection, of which the book is a scientific illustrated catalogue, being so arranged that every one, even those unacquainted with Palmyrean antiquities, can learn both the age and character of the figures and the contents of the inscriptions.

In the introduction the author treats of the condition and age of the monuments and inscriptions. The preliminary remarks concerning the latter are, perhaps, a little too brief, and might with advantage have been supplemented by a summary of the hitherto unpublished inscriptions. Even if the author considers the inscriptions less important, half the collection being entirely without them, they have nevertheless their undoubted philological interest. Considering the great scarcity of available script in the Palmyrean dialect, even the smallest contribution is of importance.

Of the above-mentioned inscriptions two are bilingual, the rest contain besides the usual "habal" mostly names of persons and deities already known. Several names, however, are quite new. Most of the inscriptions have been published and explained by Clermont-Ganneau, Euting, Sachau and Schröder. Those not yet published are A 5, B 2, C 19-22, D 10, 12, 20-1, 25-6, F 1. The author, who appears well versed in the literature of Palmyrean archæology, has in almost every case found the right explanation. In No. 24 (C 1) indeed צ appears to be represented according to the drawing, whilst on the photograph this line is indistinct. No. 27 (C 7) seems better to be read with Cl. G. עתרן (see the ן in l. 2 and 4), whereby the list Z D M G 35, 740 would be lengthened. No. 6 (C 10) is evidently right in opposition to Z D M G 39, 354,5, No. 4 (C 16) אחיתור very distinctly in opposition to Z D M G *ibid.* 353. In No. 13 (D 13) we would rather incline to the explanation of the new name עתשא given Z M G 35, 739, than to the Persian Atossa. No. 39a (D 6) can with certainty be read שלמת l. 1 and חבל l. 4; perhaps also קלבא with almost equal correctness, the rest being too doubtful to be explained. We cannot assume that the artist destroyed the inscription on account of some mistake made by himself, and substituted 39b, because the latter shows quite a different style, but he seems to have taken the former as a model. Yet what is legible in 39a l. 2, seems rather to be בת than ברת. That No. 36 (D 8) belonged to a double bust is supported by the analogous cases A 5 and Z D M G 35, 735. That יען in No. 21 (D 9) has the same signification as חבל, is possible, but it is striking that both occur together in No. 5 (A 1). No. 25 (D 10) is hitherto unpublished, but much therein is questionable. No. 15 (D 12) is likewise new. The completion of [ברת תימר(צו is according to the space and the whole contents of the inscription probably correct. No. 48 (D 20) brings the new name שביבל. Of great interest is the votive tablet No. 25 (E 2), already published by Cl. G. Rev. Arch. 1886, ii. p. 10-8. Of the bilinguis No. 8 (H 1) the Palmyrean part, which indeed forms only one-sixth of the Greek, is badly mutilated. The rest is correctly read. Without placing before us much that is new, the author has yet treated his subject with learning and discernment, and deserves an honourable place in Palmyrean epigraphy.          H. HIRSCHFELD, Ph.D.

---

### "Fleet's Gupta Volume."

It must in the ordinary course of things usually happen that really great scientific works come into the world without any fuss and without attracting any special public notice. The reason is not far to seek. The subject is necessarily new to the general public, and the treatment thereof usually necessarily abstruse and difficult to follow except to experts. There is no cheap reputation for learning to be made out of a perusal of it. Its contents cannot be aired at places where brilliancy of conversation is at a premium. It cannot be used to point a moral or adorn a tale. It can never in fact be popular. So the "bagmen of science" carefully avoid it, and the public waits patiently, very properly no doubt, for the time when the results arrived at by its author can become a recognized portion of that general knowledge which it has either the capacity to comprehend or the leisure to acquire.

It is no wonder, therefore, that the appearance in 1888 from the Government Press at Calcutta of perhaps the greatest fundamental historical work of our day in India, and certainly one of the most important of historical works that has come from the pen of any Anglo-Indian of any time, has been practically passed over in silence by the public press. In the future, of course, *Fleet's Gupta Volume*, as it is already affectionately styled by the experts who are his contemporaries, and long after both he and they and all who may read these notes are gathered to the majority, will be used both by popular and learned writers on the ancient history of India as the basis on which to frame their works, and will be the well from which sound knowledge on this subject will be drawn. Indeed, it has already proved a fresh starting-point for speculation, affording new grounds for argument and new data for deductions. It is in fact in every way a great work, and as such perhaps the more thoughtful of the reading public may wish to be put in possession of its objects, its methods and its results. Hence this article.

The importance of the inscriptions to be found all about India for the purpose of determining historical facts has long been seen, and the reason why so much time and trouble have been spent upon the volume under discussion and similar works is indicated in the sentence quoted by Mr. Fleet on his title-page from Colebrooke's *Essays:*—" In the scarcity of authentic materials for the ancient, and even for the modern, history of the Hindu race, importance is justly attached to all genuine monuments, and especially inscriptions on stone and metal." Prinsep, the founder of all sound Indian archæology, fifty years ago and more, pointed out the necessity for systematically arranging the epigraphical material at hand, and suggested the title of the work : *Corpus Inscriptionum Indicarum*. The subject has proved a most difficult one, and nothing came of the suggestion till Cunningham, a name also famous in archæological research, took it up, and in 1877 produced Volume I. on the inscriptions of Asoka. Volume II. was to contain those of the Indo-Scythians and the Satraps of Saurashtra, and Volume III. those of the early Guptas, the next dynasty in point of time. But Indo-Scythic chronology is not even yet settled, so Volume II. has not been issued, and it has therefore happened that because the dates of the Guptas have now been independently placed beyond cavil, Volume III. has followed Volume I.

In this same Volume III. the genealogy and chronology of the Gupta Kings and their contemporaries have been decided, and materials have been placed before us for a full account of their history—*i.e.* their doings, their mutual relations, the extent of their dominions—so far as is now possible. Its immediate scope is wide and the subsidiary results are far-reaching in character. The period covered by the records of the Asoka inscriptions may be taken to be from about 300 B.C. to 57 B.C. ; that covered by the Satraps of Saurashtra and the Indo-Scythians may be taken approximately to be from the latter date to about 320 A.D. ; and the present volume takes up the history at that point which ascertained dates commencing in 401 A.D., and ending, as far as definite dates are concerned, with 766 A.D. After this there are many epigraphical remains which defi-

nitely fix dates, and with 1000 A.D. we have Alberuni and many other Mahomedan writers. Indeed with the advent of the Mahomedans chronology begins to lose its characteristic of uncertainty. The importance then of the records of the Guptas and their contemporaries and successors in filling up a long gap in Indian history becomes apparent, to say nothing of the value of data supplied for reference in research on kindred lines.

The records with which Mr. Fleet has concerned himself are those of the early Gupta dynasty, with actual dates extending from 401 A.D. to 466 A.D. ; two inscriptions of the Rulers of Malava, A.D. 424 and A.D. 474, referable to the same dynasty ; two more bearing the names of Budhagupta and Bhanugupta, dated 484 A.D. and 510 A.D., of early Gupta lineage ; records of the feudatory family known as the Parivrajaka Maharajas, A.D. 475 to 528, which prove that the early Guptas were a power at any rate down to 528 ; of the feudatory Maharajas of Uchchakalpa, A.D. 493 to 533–34, or possibly thirty years later ; of Mihirakula, the great Indo-Scythian King of Kashmir and the Punjab, who overthrew the Guptas, and Toramana, his father; of a " mysterious " Emperor Chandra of the same period ; of the powerful North Indian King Yasodharman, who overthrew Mihirakula in 533-34 A.D. ; and of the Kings of Valabhi, A.D. 426 to 766, who used the Gupta era in reckoning. Records are also included in this volume of the connected families of Guptas of Magadha, A.D. *circâ* 475 to 672-73 ; of the very ancient connected family of the Maukharis, whose records extend from the days of Asoka to those of Adityasena (672-3 A.D.) of Magadha ; of the Kings of Kanauj ; and of the Vakataka Maharajas.

The geographical range of these various kings is wide enough to make their records extremely interesting. Skandagupta, the last of the early Guptas of the direct line, held all Northern India, except the Punjab, from Kathiawar to Nepal; Mihirakula fought all over North India from Kashmir to Behar ; his father, Toramana of the Punjab, we find in Kathiawar and in Central India ; the kings of Malava ruled in Central India ; of Valabhi in Kathiawar ; of Kanauj in Oudh and the Panjab ; and the Guptas of Magadha in Behar : while we shall see presently that the Guptas were intimately connected with the ancient Lichhavi family of Nepal.

The mention of the above dates in terms of the Christian era brings us to what Mr. Fleet calls his " leading subject," and which he evidently felt to be by far the most difficult part of his work—" the determination of the exact chronological point to which we must refer the commencement of the era that was used for the purpose of dating the records and coins by the early Gupta Kings and some of their successors." This era has been for convenience called " the Gupta era," the " Valabhi era," or " the Gupta-Valabhi era." In future it will probably be universally called by the first of these titles, not because the Guptas established it, for they did not, but because of this book. At great length Mr. Fleet shows that the epoch of this era was 319-20 A.D., and has thus established a clear certain starting-point for Indian chronology : no mean achievement, as all scholars must allow.

As to the origin of the era, it must have arisen from some historical event in A.D. 320 or close on thereabouts, and that event cannot have occurred in the Gupta family, as at that time it had not risen to supreme power at all : or, in other words, it had not been founded as royal. It must therefore be assumed that the Guptas merely adopted some already recognized era, and Mr. Fleet argues with much force that it was borrowed from Nepal, from the ancient ruling family of the Lichhavi, with whose territories the Gupta dominions at any rate marched, and with whom they were in close friendly and matrimonial alliance, Samudragupta being " the daughter's son of a Lichhavi."

Who were those Guptas ? We first hear of them as *Maharajas*, or feudatory kings, and then in the person of Chandragupta I., the third of the family, as independent kings or *Maharajadhirajas* and *Paramabhattarakas;* and, as will have been above seen, they and their connections ruled over what is now Northern, as distinguished from Southern and Western, India. By caste they were no doubt what are in the present day called Rajputs.

Such briefly is an account of the results achieved by infinite patience and the labours of a first-rate scholar extending over many years, and now recorded in the minutest detail. The available material has been carefully digested, every known argument discussed, and for the examination of experts, all hitherto discussed epigraphical records reproduced by mechanical processes in 45 plates, representing no less than 81 original plates.

A word as to the extreme difficulty of arriving at the results achieved by Mr. Fleet. His success is mainly due to the study of epigraphy—the science that teaches us how to read correctly the inscribed records of the distant past as cut on stones, on metal plates, and on coins, medals, seals, and gems. But everything about an inscription of a new class is a difficult matter. The writing itself is an immense difficulty. It has to be learnt and accurately ascertained before anything definite can result from the reading, and as so much depends on the numerical symbols, these have to be studied with special care. In addition to the character, the language in which the inscription is written has to be mastered in the form it assumed at the time when the record happened to be made, and here the question of orthography is often a perplexing puzzle. When the names and dates, as given in the inscription, have been clearly ascertained, before it can be made available for historical purposes the most difficult point of all arises —the reference of the dates to the corresponding dates A.D. or B.C. This at once opens up a subject of extreme difficulty, for the method of computing time employed by the author of the inscription, and the epoch of the era from which he reckoned, must be ascertained with accuracy. This accomplished, there remains the geography and history disclosed to be considered and explained. It will be readily seen, therefore, how difficult such a task as that Mr. Fleet has been set always is, and why it is that his successful performance thereof has raised him to the high place amongst Orientalists which he now so deservedly occupies.—R. C. T.—[From the *Pioneer Mail* of Feb. 12, 1890.]

*A History of Civilisation in Ancient India, based on Sanskrit Literature.* By Romesh Chunder Dutt. In three volumes. Vol. I. : Vedic and Epic Ages. (Calcutta, Thacker, Spink and Co.; London, Trübner.)

This is not the first time that Mr. Dutt, a Member of the Bengal Civil Service, has shown his deep interest in the education of his countrymen. Ten years ago he wrote a little school-book which has since been accepted as a text-book in many schools in Bengal. Three years ago he presented his countrymen with a complete Bengali translation of the Rigveda ; and now again he places before the public the first volume of a short account of the civilization of ancient India.

The author is well fitted for his task. He possesses a thorough knowledge of Sanskrit literature, is well versed in the works of European scholars, and though saturated with Western ideas, is filled with a genuine love for his country and with a real enthusiasm for his subject. Nor can we doubt that this little book will serve its purpose and help to spread a knowledge of Ancient India among the Hindus of to-day. But though chiefly written for Hindus, a perusal of it will be found useful and interesting to English readers also. And though the author professes to write for the general reader only without "any intention to make any new discoveries," yet it will be no waste of time even for the special scholar to go over the pages of this book.

Mr. Dutt divides the History of India into five epochs, which he calls the Vedic, Epic, Philosophical, Buddhist and Pauranic Periods. Two of these are treated in the present volume. The first part is devoted to the Vedic period, that of the first Aryan settlements in the Punjab, the story of which is told in the hymns of the Rigveda. Mr. Dutt fixes as the date of this period 2000 to 1400 B.C. In the second part of the volume he treats of what he terms the Epic period, "when the nations described in the national epics of India lived and fought ; when the Kurus and the Panchâlas, the Kosalas, and the Videhas held sway along the valley of the Ganges," the period also when the Caste system began to form itself, and lastly the period when the Rigveda and the three other Vedas were finally compiled and arranged, when the Brâhmanas, Âranyakas, and Upanishads were composed. For this so-called Epic period Mr. Dutt allows about five centuries, dating it from 1400 to 1000 B.C. Considering the enormous literature which grew up in this epoch and the great political and social changes which must have taken place at the same time, these limits may seem too narrow rather than too wide. The author, indeed, admits that these dates "are only supposed to be correct within two or three centuries." When we avail ourselves of this admission, the figures 1400 to 1000 are after all not so very different from those assigned by Prof. Max Müller to the Mantra and Brâhmana Periods, which together correspond to Mr. Dutt's Epic Period. But it is, at all events, a good illustration of what the dates of Indian chronology really are when we are told that for one and the same period either 1400 to 1000, or 1000 to 600, may be assigned as a date. What can be the use of giving, especially in a popular book, a chronology which can only serve to impress doubtful opinions upon minds which are unable to follow all the controversies of specialists on the subject, and lead the general reader to accept mere hypotheses as facts? Why, then, not simply state the fact—the only real truth—that we do not know?

But while Mr. Dutt hardly succeeds—and there was no chance of his succeeding—in mapping out the chronological outlines of the History of Ancient India, he has been much more successful in drawing his pictures of ancient Hindu life, in sketching the development of Hindu civilization, the rise of intellectual and the decline of political and social life. It is indeed to be wished that the Hindus may learn that lesson which, our author tells them, they have to learn from the Veda :—

"For the Rigveda gives us a picture of society when there were no caste distinctions, when widows were married, and women had their legitimate influence in the society in which they lived and moved."

It is a real pleasure to read such a chapter as that on the Social and Domestic Life and the Position of Women in the Vedic Age, to hear the author's praises of that age when wives joined their husbands in the performance of sacrifices, and when women "were themselves Rishis, and composed hymns and performed sacrifices like men."

"For there were no unhealthy restrictions against women in those days, no attempt to keep them secluded or uneducated, or debarred from their legitimate place in society."

And a pleasure also it is to read the chapter on the Vedic Rishis, where Mr. Dutt proves, and dwells upon, the fact that those ancient poets of the Vedic hymns were members of an undivided society, a society without caste.

"The Vedic Rishis composed their hymns, fought their wars, and ploughed their fields; but were neither Bráhmans, nor Kshatriyas, nor Vaiśyas. The great Rishi houses of the Vedic age furnished priests and soldiers, but were no more Bráhmans or Kshatriyas than the Percies or Douglases of mediæval Europe were Bráhmans or Kshatriyas."

And again when the author describes the changes which took place in the second phase of Hindu civilization, he succeeds in explaining how it came about that a great nation submitted to the supremacy of priests and became split up into castes. He shows us how the Hindus in that period "unconsciously surrendered all social freedom, and were gradually bound down by priest-imposed laws and restrictions which made further progress on the part of the *people* impossible."

"This is the dark side of Hindu civilization," he adds, with a pathos which sounds the more melancholy because coming from the mouth of a patriotic Hindu. "Priestly supremacy threw its coils round and round the nation from its early youth, and the *nation* never attained that political and social freedom and strength which marked the ancient nations of Europe."

On another occasion, when speaking of the useless speculations contained in the Bráhmanas, he bursts out into the words :

"Such are the inevitable results when priests are made the custodians of the conscience of a nation."

But Mr. Dutt also points out that there is a gulf between the caste system of the Epic Period and the modern caste system. We learn that in that age Bráhmans, Kshatriyas, and Vaiśyas still formed one body, that they were Aryas as opposed to the conquered aborigines, and that there were no caste distinctions among the Vaiśyas themselves. Moreover, the caste system was far from being as rigorous as in later times. Satyakáma, we are are told in one of the Upanishads, the son of a slave-girl, who did not know his father, became a Brahman simply through his love of truth.

"The subjection of women" also was not so far advanced in that period as it became in later days, especially under Muhammadan influences. In the Upanishads we meet with learned ladies like Maitreyí or Gárgí, discoursing on philosophical problems with the great sages, and not to be silenced by a harsh *Mulier taceat in ecclesia*. Women had still a share in sacrifices and religious duties, and frequented public festivities and sights, free from restraint. Mr. Dutt's statement, however, that women "had their rights to property and to inheritance," given without reference, requires some limitation, for we read in the Maitrá-yaneyí-samhitá (4, 6, 7) that man is entitled to heir-ship, but not a woman. And in the Śatapatha Bráhmana (IV. 4, 2, 13) we are told, "They (women) neither own any self, nor do they own any hermitage." (See also Schroeder, *Indiens Literatur und Cultur*, p. 159.) "That women," as Mr. Dutt puts it, "were honoured in ancient India, more perhaps than among any other ancient nation on the face of the globe," may seem an exaggerated statement. But it does not mean so very much when we remember that there never was "on the face of the globe" a nation which had a true respect for women as individuals. However, it would not be very difficult to point out a good many passages in the ancient literature of India where women are spoken of with great contempt. In one of the later portions of the Epic, a woman-hater tells us—with that logic which is peculiar to all woman-haters down to Schopenhauer.—

"A lawgiver says that women are all liars; *it stands so in the Veda*; do you say you are independent? There is not such a thing as women's independence, because women are not independent; it is the opinion of the lord of creation that a woman is not fit for independence."

This predecessor of Mr. Goldwin Smith and Mrs. Lynn Linton might refer to such Vedic sayings as "Woman is Untruth," or to a passage in the Yajurveda where it is explained why women are called "unmanned, excluded from hermitage, and much inferior even to a wicked man."

Sometimes our author is led astray by a kind of patriotism—we should rather say "patriotic weakness" —not rarely found even among European scholars. Thus, he cannot bear the thought that polyandry should have existed at any period in any part of India, and he there-fore declares the five heroes together with the heroine of the Mahábhárata to be "myths pure and simple"! Mr. Dutt gets quite excited about this point :

"Draupadí the daughter of the King of the Panchálas, marries the Pándavas in the modern (*sic*) epic—yes, marries all five of them! And yet polyandry was not only unknown to the Hindus at the time of the Kurus and the Panchálas, but that barborous custom was not known to the Indo-Aryans in any age or period within the four thousand years of their history."

And while we read on page 188, "Draupadî is only a myth, or perhaps an allegory (*sic*) representing the alliance of the Panchâla King with a party to the war,"—we are told on page 194: "It is needless to say that the story of Draupadî herself and of the five Pândavas is an allegory!"

In another passage, again, Mr. Dutt protests strongly against the idea that human sacrifices ever prevailed in India, and he demurs to the conclusions arrived at by Prof. Max Müller and Dr. Râjendra Lala Mitra on that point. We might, indeed, be inclined to admit that *some* of the allusions, but certainly not "that *all* the allusions to human sacrifice in the later (?) compositions of the Epic Period are the speculations of priests." I doubt, however, whether Mr. Dutt will induce many people to see speculations of priests in the simple legend of Śunahśepa, as told in the Brâhmaṇa. And is it, after all, so very unfair to postulate the existence of human sacrifices for a *very remote past* in a country where—not in so very remote a past—thousands of poor women were immolated on the funeral piles of their lords and masters? But we must not be too hard upon the author in this respect. How many statements and denials made in the controversies of European scholars can be traced back to the same psychological motives which seem to have influenced our author!

Though conciseness forms a chief virtue of the present work, yet copious extracts from the Sanskrit works are given, which enable the reader to form his own judgment. These extracts are carefully selected, and may enable many a Hindu reader to acquire a more intimate knowledge of his own ancient literature. Whoever takes an interest in the progress of India will share our wish that Mr. Dutt may soon complete his task—for the benefit of his countrymen.   M. W.

---

*The Hymns of the Rigveda translated. With a Popular Commentary.* By R. T. H. Griffith. Vol. I. (Benares, 1889.)

Accustomed as we have been for years to hear the changes rung on the translation of the Rigveda announced as forthcoming in the new series of the "Sacred Books of the East," we confess that the first goodly instalment of an English translation, just received from a quarter from which we were certainly not prepared to look for such a work, has come upon us as an agreeable surprise. The translator, Mr. Griffith, late Principal of the Benares College, has long made his mark as an able and gifted expositor of Indian poetry of all ages. While his earlier renderings—*Specimens of Old Indian Poetry* (1852), *The Birth of the War God* (1853), and *The Râmâyaṇa* (1870-74)—aim more at a general poetical reproduction of the Sanskrit texts, the present work is characterized by its closer fidelity both to the letter and the spirit of the original, and is intended *to* be "as readable and intelligible as the nature of the subject and other circumstances permit." There are few Sanskrit

scholars, we may readily admit, besides Mr. Griffith, who combine the qualifications for such an exceptionally difficult task. But it would require a detailed examination of his work, and an abler critic than the present writer, to give an estimate of how far that task has been accomplished in it. Our avowed object is only to advert to the paramount importance of this publication, to its presumptive trustworthiness, and to the cordial welcome which is just as sure to be accorded to it by Sanskrit scholars generally as if its appearance had been heralded by successive flourishes of trumpets.

The principles of interpretation by which Mr. Griffith has been guided are stated in these words: "My translation is partly based on the commentary of Sâyaṇa, corrected and regulated by rational probability, context and intercomparison of similar words and passages." From Sâyaṇa, however, he avowedly deviates "both widely and frequently."

The first volume, now before us, contains Ashṭakas I. and II.: three more volumes will bring the remaining six Ashṭakas in due course. As an example of the style in which the translator has adapted his version to the original, we transcribe Hymn CLIV. of the first Book:—

I will declare the mighty deeds of Vishṇu,
    of him who measured out the earthly regions,
Who propped the highest place of congregation,
    thrice setting down his footstep, widely striding.
For this his mighty deed is Vishṇu lauded,
    like some wild beast, dread, prowling, mountain-
      roaming;
He within whose three wide-extended paces
    all living creatures have their habitation.
Let the hymn lift itself as strength to Vishṇu,
    the Bull far-striding, dwelling on the mountains,
Him who alone with triple step hath measured
    this common dwelling-place, long, far-extended.
Him whose three places that are filled with sweetness
    imperishable, joy as it may list them,
Who verily alone upholds the threefold,
    the earth, the heaven, and all living creatures.
May I attain to that his well-loved mansion
    where men devoted to the god are happy.
Fast joined to that, the seat supreme of Vishṇu,
    the mighty strider, is the well of nectar.
Fain would we go unto your dwelling-places,
    where there are many-horned and nimble oxen;
For mightily there shineth down upon us
    the widely-striding Bull's sublimest mansion.

---

*Buddhism and Christianity: a Parallel and a Contrast.* Being the Croall Lecture for 1889-90. By Archibald Scott, D.D. (Edinburgh, 1890).

There can be no question that the more thorough study of Buddhism, facilitated as it has been in recent years by text editions and good translations of many of its sacred books, has mainly resulted in enabling us to form a more independent and more dispassionate estimate of its position as one of the great world-religions, and in reducing the number of its uncompromising admirers to an ever smaller minority. Books like

Kellogg's "The Light of Asia and the Light of the World," and Sir M. Monier-Williams' "Buddhism," which have been written on these lines, have tended to bring about a more impartial view of its teaching and religious praxis, while Dr. Scott, in the course of his six lectures, endeavours "by a fair exposition of what is best and highest in Buddhism to discover its feeling after something better and higher still, and to suggest rather than indicate the place which it occupies in the religious education of humanity." By treating successively of the salient features of both religions in their historical development, the author does not aim at setting off the excellencies of Christianity at the expense of Buddhism, nor does he profess to add any original information on the latter to the stock already available. His object is only to place before an intelligent and well-educated public a trustworthy guide through a labyrinth of conflicting, or at any rate not yet finally settled, opinions on a phase in the religious history of the East which will ever maintain a high claim on the sympathetic interest of the inquirer.

———

Under the unpretending title "*Original Notes on the Book of Proverbs, according to the Authorized Version*," the venerable Dr. S. C. Malan has brought out with Messrs. Williams and Norgate the first instalment of a remarkable work, the materials for which he began to store up in his undergraduate days at Oxford. It consists of a collection of kindred passages culled from Eastern Non-Christian writings, with a few quotations from the Ethiopic Didascalia, and occasional passages "from Greek and Latin favourites." The book, it will at once be seen, while supplying to the practical expositor of the text quite a galaxy of apposite parallels and illustrations, appeals also to the much wider circle of students of proverb lore by reason of the marvellous variety of sources from which the author has drawn. Every literary language of the East—Chinese, Japanese, Mongol, Manchu, Tibetan, Tartar, Sanskrit, Bengali, Tamil, Telugu, Pali, Sinhalese, Kawi, Javanese, Malay, Armenian, Zend, Persian, Pashto, Magyar, Georgian, Russian, Egyptian, and all the Semitic tongues—has supplied its quota, taken not from translations but from the original texts, accessible in many cases only in manuscript copies. No one in Greater Britain, we may safely assert, has that ready command of such a range of Asiatic tongues (and many of them of exceptional difficulty) as Dr. Malan. But how few people ever heard of him, though he has been living among us for nearly half a century? The work under notice shows him to be a scholar of the right type. There is no parade of Oriental characters nor mention of the particular language in each case, the briefest references in foot-notes indicating the original sources from which the parallel passages have been translated, and these indications are only intended for the scholar who is supposed to know in what language each book referred to is written. Thus the arrangement of the work does not convey to the general reader even a distant idea of the vast amount of that linguistical learning deposited in it which in none of Dr. Malan's previous publications has had a chance of being allowed such full play as in

the present one. As a specimen of the wide range over which the illustrations extend, we refer the reader to the notes on VI. 6-8, "go to the ant, thou sluggard," etc. After citing the passages in the Fathers and the various versions of the Apostolic Constitutions in which these verses are commented on, Dr. Malan translates some paragraphs from the Ethiopic recension of the last-named work; he then discusses what the old Greek, Roman and Rabbinic writers relate on the habits of the ant, and winds up with a long array of passages translated from various authorities in Manchu, Arabic, Persian, Ethiopic, Georgian, Sinhalese, Syriac, Zend, Pehlevi, Armenian, Sanskrit, Turkish, Burmese, Pali, Tibetan, Chinese, Mongol, Japanese, Tamil, Hindi,—chapter and verse being given in each case. The compiler, we must add in conclusion, has been rather hard upon his readers who turn to the Indices for information about the sources from which he has drawn. In many cases he omits to mention the language in which a book is written, in others not even the title of the book itself is inserted in the Index. Altogether the information vouchsafed in the Indices is much too meagre and inadequate. We can only account for this extreme and fastidious brevity by assuming that the author, desirous of avoiding all parade of learning, committed the opposite error of crediting his readers with more knowledge of Eastern literature than scarcely any of them would possess. All honour to him, however, for having exercised a kind of self-denial which in this special field of literary research is of the rarest occurrence. May he be spared to bring out the remaining two volumes of this great work while his waning eye-sight still enables him to carry them through the press!

———

*Dictionnaire Français-Arabe.* Par le Père J.-B. Belot, S.J. Première Partie. (Beyrouth, 1890).

This dictionary, the second moiety of which will appear at midsummer of the present year, comprises upwards of 1500 pages of small print in double columns. The vowel points are added throughout. It forestalls in a great measure the dictionary of Gasselin, which comes out in fasciculi, and is not likely to be completed for some years; it has also the advantage of cheapness over the larger work, while in completeness it leaves nothing to be desired. While it gives the Arabic equivalents for each acceptation of a French word, it adds phrases where necessary to show the construction in cases in which the two languages differ. And since Eastern languages differ in their phraseology far more from those of Europe than do the latter from one another, the introduction of idiomatic expressions in the dictionary of an Oriental language appears to us an indispensable desideratum, and in fact far more useful than a long string of synonymous words. In this respect the present work is a pattern of a good dictionary. The only fault we find with it is the smallness of the Arabic type; this drawback, however, was unavoidable, as, on account of the Arabic vowel signs and other diacritical marks, the size of the letters had to be reduced so as to make them fit in with the French type.

———

*De Sancta Cruce. Ein Beitrag zur Christlichen Legenden-
geschichte.* Von Eberhard Nestle. (Berlin, 1889.)

In conformity with a promise given in the preface to
the first edition of his Syriac Grammar (1880), Dr.
Nestle gives here thirty pages of Syriac text containing
fragments of the legendary history of the finding of
the Cross, together with critical apparatus, German
translation and dissertations. This valuable monograph will be especially useful to those students of
Syriac—a small band in this country, we are afraid,—
who possess the second edition of that grammar either
in the original or in the English translation; for the
greater part of the *Chrestomathia*, which forms part of
the grammar, consists of the same texts, and has besides
the advantage of a full glossary, so that the two books
supplement one another. The care which has been
bestowed on this monograph to make it as nearly as
possible exhaustive of the subject of which it treats
deserves high commendation.

------

*The Philosophy of the Mazdayasnian Religion under the
Sassanids.* Translated from the French of L. C.
Casartelli, by Firoz Jamaspji Dastur Jamasp Asa.
(Bombay, 1889.)

There has been noticeable for a considerable number
of years a remarkable revival among the Parsee communities of India, more especially in Bombay, in the
zeal and interest which they have bestowed on all
investigations concerning their ancient religion and
institutions. They have not only at great expense
brought out many important sacred texts, and valuable
aids to the study of Zend and Pehlevi, but have also
liberally assisted Zoroastrian scholars in Europe by the
loan of their own priceless old manuscripts, by sub-
scribing to their publications, and otherwise encouraging
them in their researches. But what we specially appreciate is the thoroughly liberal spirit with which
they make the labours of Western Oriental scholars in
the field of Zend and Pehlevi literature, conflicting
though they often be both as to their methods and in
their results, available to their co-religionists by English
or Gujerati translations, thus placing at their service
whatever has been written in Europe on the subject, and
enabling them to judge for themselves. In this way
they have not only brought out a translation of Prof. W.
Geiger's great work on "The Civilization of the Eastern
Iranians in Ancient Times," but also a criticism upon
it entitled "The Home and Age of the Avesta," by
Dr. E. J. von Dillon. The work under notice may be
designated as one of the most carefully executed translations that have appeared under the auspices of the
Jamshedji Jijibhai Translation Fund. We are indebted
for it to the late Firoz Jamaspji Dastur Jamasp
Asa, son of the High Priest Dastur Dr. Jamaspji
Minocheherji, whose munificent donation of an old
codex of the Zendavesta to the Bodleian Library has
recently been recorded in the literary papers. Concerning Dr. Casartelli's original work, we need not
enlarge on the able notices of it by Barbier de Meynard
and Van den Gheyn. The English translation has the
great advantage of additional notes, compiled with
scrupulous care and containing the views of other Zend

scholars on points open to controversy. We especially
advert to the notes on the age of the Avesta (Introduction, p. II), the distinction of Magism from Mazdeism
(p. 2), the two eternal principles of Mazdeism (p. 4),
the influence of the Jewish and Christian religions
upon Mazdeism, or vice versâ (p. 47), the Homa plant
(p. 123), marriage between near relations (pp. 157, 159),
the seven sisters of Virâf (p. 187), and the final resur-
rection of the world (p. 200). Two Indices enhance the
value of a book which is creditable alike to its author,
its annotator, and the Trustees of the Society under
whose patronage it has appeared.

------

*Sĕrat Kantjil: het Beok van den Kanijil, Javaansch
Dierenepos.* Herziene uitgave. 's Gravenhage, Mar-
tinus Nijhoff, 1889.

The first edition of this collection of Javanese fables
was made from four manuscript copies by the late Dr.
W. Palmer van den Broek, and appeared under the
auspices of the Dutch Asiatic Society in 1878. Some
four years later Professor Kern published some criticisms upon the Javanese text, and expressed a hope
that this interesting book might meet with a translator.
This hope, we regret to say, has not yet been verified,
much as those fables or *dongengs* deserve to be made
generally accessible; for they are neither of Indian nor
Arabic parentage, but of indigenous growth, and the
animals which are represented in them are all, with the
exception of the elephant, natives of the soil. The
*Kanchil* which acts the most prominent part is the
*Moschus Javanicus*, a kind of dwarf gazelle, only 20 to
24 inches in length. In Malay fable its place is taken
by the *Pĕlandok*, which is a somewhat larger kind. Mr.
Klinkert, the editor of the Malay *Hikâyat Pĕlandok*,
rightly compares this popular book to our Reynard the
Fox. There is another Javanese story-book which also
bears the title of *Sĕrat Kanchil*, and was published at
Samarang in 1871, but bears only in its first part some
resemblance to the work under notice. In addition to
the above and similar collections of indigenous fables,
the Dutch have also provided adaptations of other
stories suitable for the young in Java. Thus the story
of Aladdin has appeared both in Javanese and Malay,
both versions being furnished with gorgeously illuminated pictures by Chinese artists. There is also a
considerably amplified recension, in Batavian Malay, of
the story about the monkey and the tortoise, the subject
of a paper by Dr. Rizal in No. 3 of *The Record.*

------

*The Travellers' Malay Pronouncing Hand-Book.* Second
Edition. (Singapore, 1889.)

This handy manual is intended for travellers and
new-comers in the Straits Settlements, to enable them
to converse with native servants and the lower classes
generally. This object should not be lost sight of by
those who use this book; for it does not teach, or
pretend to teach, the colloquial language in vogue
amongst the Malays themselves, especially among educated Malays. The pronunciation given in the third
column is fairly correct; it certainly compares favourably with that given by Hüttenbach in his very meagre
'Anleitung zur Erlernung des Malayischen,' which we

consider to be utterly useless and misleading, as every page literally swarms with blunders. It must have required a great deal of assurance to put forth such an imposture for sale. Indeed, of the thousands of linguistical helps that have passed through our hands, we know of none other that so well deserves being placed in the pillory.

———

*The Prâchîna Gujerâti Sâhityâ Ratnamâlâ* ; or, the Garland of Gems of old Gujerâti Literature. First Gem, the Magdhâvabodha Auktika, or a Grammar for Beginners of the Gujerâti Language. Edited by H. H. Dhruva. (Bombay, 1889.)

The well-known Pandit H. H. Dhruva initiates in this volume a series of ancient Gujerâti texts : the specimen here printed for the first time dates from the end of the 14th century. Besides an English introduction, he reproduces by way of appendix, eight letters (originally addressed to "the Advocate of India") on the unpublished literature of the Gujerâti language. Following in the wake of Tod, A. K. Forbes, Beames, Trumpp, Hoernle, Grierson, and other honoured names, who have endeavoured to draw attention to the remains of early vernacular literature in their importance both for historical and philological research, Mr. Dhruva has the object in this publication of creating an interest in the history and development of his own mother tongue, Gujerâti. We recommend the book to the earnest study of all who consider—and, in our opinion, rightly consider—the older vernacular literature of modern India to be an important factor in the history of Indian lore, thought, religion and civilization.

———

### African Philology.

*Swahili.*—Tales as told by Natives of Zanzibar, with English Translation by the Right Rev. Edward Steere. Crown 8vo. S.P.C.K. 5s.

This useful book consists of tales taken down vivâ voce by intelligent Africans, and on the opposite page is an English translation. Thus the actual conversational, or rather narrative style of the people is faithfully recorded, and the danger of the foreigner using a formal stilted style is avoided. The Swahili is the lingua franca of Eastern Equatorial Africa, and is to a certain extent influenced by Arabic loan-words.

*Yao.*—Introductory Handbook and Vocabulary by the Rev. A. Hetherwick, Missionary of the Scotch Church. S.P.C.K. 5s.

This language belongs, like the preceding one, to the Bantu Family of South Africa, but is much less known. It is spoken over a vast region between the narrow slip of coast occupied by the Portuguese Colony of Mozambîk and the Lake Nyassa. The Mission for the use of which this handbook is composed is stationed at Blantyre, south of the lake. This is a very able and useful compilation.

*February,* 1890.    R. N. C.

———

*Essays on the Chinese Language.* By T. Watters. (Shanghai, Presbyterian Mission Press, 1889.)

We hope that the work under review has received the attention which it deserves at the hands of every student, and we warrant that it has given much satisfaction to all interested in the language.

We had, perhaps, expected to find in it more philology and less history ; but we feel reconciled in finding a great amount of new and interesting matter collected in the attractive volume.

The following are the headings of the eight chapters which make up the book :—

1. Some Western Opinions.
2. Cultivation of their Language by the Chinese.
3. Chinese Opinions about the Origin and Early History of the Language.
4. On the Interjectional and Imitative Elements in the Chinese Language.
5. The word *Tao.*
6. Terms relating to Death and Burial.
7. Foreign Words in Chinese.
8. The Influence of Buddhism on the Chinese Language.

The last four chapters, and more particularly chapters 5, 6, and 8, seem to us, from a philological point of view, the most valuable part of the book ; but chapters 2 and 3 also will be read with much pleasure and to some advantage, not only by Chinese students, but by the more general reader.

We would say, in connection with chapter 1, which is almost entirely made up of quotations, that, while we admit the impossibility of rendering a complete and exhaustive account of Western opinions, it seems to us that the old quarrels about the origin of Chinese, the barren discussions about root similarities, have proportionately too long, the more modern and more scientific views too short a space allotted to them. Thus, while the question whether Shem or Ham was the ancestor of the Chinese people cannot at present rouse a genuine interest any more than the comparative vocabularies of Dr. Edkins and Dr. Chalmers can command a serious attention, the discoveries of Professor von der Gabelentz (Chinesische Grammatik : Lautgeschichtliche und Etymologische Probleme) were well worth adverting to, and their critique by as competent a scholar as our author, and by the light of other Indo-Chinese languages would have proved of incontestable value. Is the Chinese Language or is it not derived from a polysyllabic language ? Is its monosyllabic character the result of an unparalleled self-preservation or of an early organic decay ? These are questions which, if they cannot now be decided, must at least be formulated and ought to be capable of giving a fresh impulse, as they open a new vista to comparative philology. The character of the living language, on the other hand, whether it is isolating and monosyllabic or has ceased to be so, though easier to answer, is a question of minor interest. Nor is Dr. Grube, with due deference to his scholarship, the father of the negative theory which has been running side by side with her positive sister almost since the beginning of Chinese studies in Europe.

Chapter 2 contains a history of Chinese philology in China; that is, of the study of their language by the Chinese. It will be seen that the literature of this, like that of any other department of Chinese inquiry, is well stocked and varied. There is any amount of material on the history of the language in its phonetic, graphic, and idiomatic aspects; and it may be said that, while it will be indispensable to work up the entire volume of this literature before we may hope to approach a solution of the problem what the oldest form of Chinese thought, speech, and writing was like, it remains yet doubtful whether the results of the inquiry will be at all in proportion to its labour. To the student this chapter furnishes a valuable bibliography.

The next chapter is highly interesting, and likely to surprise even those not unacquainted with Chinese works on language. We find in it rudimentary notions of all the principles which have since become recognized as facts, or well maintained as theories in Western science. No doubt if our intercourse with China and our knowledge of Chinese literature had commenced a century earlier, we might have learned from them many truths which we have since discovered independently. The manner of reasoning in connection with the Origin and Early History of the Language, as interpreted by Mr. Watters, is certainly most creditable.

"The faculty of speech is inherent in man's constitution," "speech arose when human life began in the world," and such like expressions, which remind one of the writings of Humboldt and Steinthal, prove that the Chinese had long recognized in speech the characteristic attribute of man, "that which makes him man." They have also distinguished between the two elements of language, viz. sound, which is "the audible result of the impact of the formless essence of matter on body of definite shape," and intelligence conveyed from one individual to another through the medium of sound. The one, which man has in common not only with other living beings but also with lifeless matter, is produced by his throat and mouth as with a musical instrument; but the other, intelligence and reason (*li*), is what lifts him far above the rest of creation. True, there is a certain point of touch between the cry of animals, the song of birds, and the squeal of children on one hand and conscious speech on the other; for, as the former are mere reflex actions, spontaneous utterances without design, so was the latter also at first probably an expression of emotions stirred and emanating from an instinctive feeling. We see that neither the theory of the emotional origin (Steinthal) nor that of Onomatopoesia (Farrar) further detailed in chapter 4, are foreign to the Chinese mind. But the mere sounds have developed into "symbolical expressions of certain thoughts and feelings," "set forms of language," and these have become to him "the handle of the moral nature, the lord of action, the motive power of the mind," etc.; and they are one of the manifestations of the spiritual principle "which goes through the body, seeing in the eye, hearing in the ear, and speaking in the mouth." This development has been, he thinks, a natural and spontaneous one, and still, like a living organism (Schleicher), the

language changes according to time and locality, without that it can be "altered by any conscious exercise of an individual's power," but influenced by and influencing the moral constitution of the entire community. With the Chinese, we observe, philology is a natural science.

There follows a brief history of Chinese writing. Knotted cords are said to have been the first "visible and lasting record and evidence of events and transactions." But they were soon replaced by rude engravings of a pictorial or indicative kind made on bamboo or wood, and these became the elements of the hieroglyphic system of Chinese writing. As with an increased necessity for records the implements improved and the number of characters augmented, the form of the latter was gradually altered and simplified, they ceased to be pictorial representations and became symbols. Deprived of their pictorial character and rapidly multiplying in number by combining on a system of permutation, the desire was felt to have some sort of key to the sound and thus the phonetic value became the leading principle in the formation of new characters. At present, by far the greatest part of Chinese characters exhibits this principle. The history of Chinese writing has yet to be told, and an interesting tale it will be.

The latter part of the book under review, though perhaps the most valuable, we will not attempt to discuss; firstly, because it addresses itself more especially to the initiated student; and secondly, because it could not be done without introducing Chinese characters.

ICHANG, 1*st March*, 1890.          A. R.

---

## Obituary.

---

**Johann Gustav Gildemeister**, whose death took place at Bonn on the 11th of March, was born at Klein-Siemen, a domain in Mecklenburg owned by his father, on the 20th of July, 1812. Both his parents were natives of Bremen, to which city they returned to live when their son was but five years old. He himself was wont to look upon and speak of Bremen as his native place. After passing through the usual course of preliminary education, he went to the University of Göttingen in 1832 to devote himself to the study of divinity and eastern languages. Here the genial lectures of Ewald, which he attended for two years, supplied a solid foundation and gave a powerful stimulus to his labours in this branch of research. In 1834 Gildemeister enrolled himself as a student at Bonn, where the lectures of A. W. von Schlegel and Fr. Lassen on Sanskrit literature were attracting young scholars from all parts of Europe. At the same time he continued his Semitic studies under Freytag, and attended the divinity and philosophy schools. From 1836 to 1838 he studied Oriental manuscripts in Paris and Leiden, and was busy collecting materials towards his well-known work "Scriptorum Arabum de rebus Indicis loci et opuscula inedita" (Bonn, 1838), the introduction to which had previously been issued separately as a specimen, under the title "De rebus Indiæ quomodo in Arabum notitiam venerint," when he took his doctor's degree on the 8th of September, 1838. In this work we trace a happy combination of the twofold direction which he had given to his Oriental researches. In 1839 he was admitted as lecturer for eastern languages in the university, and was made professor extraordinarius in 1844. During an accidental sojourn at Treves he happened to witness the adoration paid to the so-called Sacred Coat. His pronounced critical sense urged him to examine the genuineness of that famous relic, with the result that of the large number of Sacred Coats, the one of Treves was of that class which possessed the very last claim to genuineness. The book in which Gildemeister, in conjunction with Professor von Sybel, had propounded his investigations appeared at Düsseldorf in 1845, and provoked quite a storm of indignation on the part of the Roman Catholics. Gildemeister became impossible in a good Catholic town like Bonn, and at the instance of the Elector of Hesse, with whom the Prussian Government had negotiated for the purpose, he accepted an invitation to Marburg as Professor of Old Testament exegesis,—the first miracle ever wrought by the Sacred Coat. From 1848 till his return to Bonn in 1859 he combined with his professoriate the post of University Librarian, the duties of which he discharged with exemplary conscientiousness. In Bonn, where he now filled Freytag's chair, he was most unselfish and most indefatigable in his literary activity. Up to the time of Lassen's death his lectures extended also over Sanskrit literature and Comparative Grammar; after the appointment of Lassen's successor he confined himself to Semitic languages and Persian. He was an excellent teacher: all his lectures were up to date, his exposition was clear, incisive, and compressed, though exhaustive of its subject. While in the earlier part of his career as an Oriental scholar he gave preponderance to Sanskrit, he later on confined his studies to Semitic literature in all its branches. During the last period of his life he occupied himself almost exclusively with Palestine: and a number of valuable notices, dissertations and reviews on the subject were contributed by him to the Journal of the German Oriental Society and the Transactions of the German Palestine Association.

We add a list of his chief publications:—

I. Kalidasae Meghaduta et Çringaratilaka. Bonn, 1841.

Die falsche Sanskritphilologie. *Ib.* 1840.

Bibliothecae Sanskritae specimen. *Ib.* 1847.

Anthologia Sauscritica, ed. Lassen. Denuo adornavit J. G. *Ib.* 1868.

II. De Evangeliis in Arabicum e Simplici Syriaca translatis. *Ib.* 1865.

Catalogus librorum manuscriptorum Orientalium in Bibliotheca Academica Bonnensi. *Ib.* 1864-76.

Sexti Sententiae. *Ib.* 1874.

Esdrae liber quartus Arabice e codice Vaticano nunc primum editus. *Ib.* 1877.

Acta S. Pelagiae Syriace edita. *Ib.* 1879.

Der Schulchan aruch und was darau hängt. *Ib.* 1884.

Theodosius de situ terrae sanctae. *Ib.* 1882.

Idrisii Palaestina et Syria arabica. *Ib.* 1885.

Antonini Placentini Itinerarium. Berlin, 1889.

---

The death of Professor *Peter de Jong*, of the University of Utrecht, following so closely in the wake of Alfred von Kremer's and Thorbecke's, marks the third great loss which Arabic scholarship has sustained on the continent within the brief space of one month. He was born at Nieuwveen in Holland in 1832, received the greater part of his education at Leiden, was enrolled in that university as a student of divinity and Semitic languages in September, 1851, and took his doctor's degree in June, 1857, on which occasion he brought out his dissertation entitled " Disquisitio de psalmis Maccabaicis." In the previous year he had succeeded Kuenen, on the recommendation of Professor Juynboll, as Adjutor Interpretis legati Warneriani, a sort of fellowship, founded upwards of 200 years ago, for editing and interpreting Oriental texts, and became ten years later sole incumbent of that post. He continued the catalogue, commenced by Weijers, of the Oriental MSS. of the Royal Society of Amsterdam—it appeared in 1862—and at the same time was associated with Professor M. J. de Goeje in working at the catalogue of the Eastern MSS. in the Leiden University Library. In 1866 he was appointed Lector for Persian and Turkish, and in 1870, on the death of Millies, he followed an invitation to Utrecht to fill the chair of Semitic languages in that University. The science of Moslem tradition was the field of research which de Jong had cultivated with greater predilection and more signal success than any other. Everything he published on this subject bears the stamp of the highest accuracy and trustworthiness. On the premature death of Loth, to whom, in the preparation of the international edition of the Annals of *Tabari*, the division treating of the Prophet had been assigned, de Jong took charge of this part. He was also entrusted with an appendix concerning Tabari's authorities from an ancient and unique MS. that had been lent by Baron von Kremer. This text was nearly ready for the press when death overtook him. Of his other text editions of Arabic works we mention that on the Homonyma by Ibn ol Kaisarání (Leiden, 1865); that of Tha'álíbí's Latáif (*ib.* 1867); and that of Ad-Dhahabi's Moshtabih (*ib.* 1881). The oration which he delivered at the anniversary of the Literary Society of Utrecht on the 28th of June, 1887, on the life of Mohammed and the various phases of his doctrine, shows in its terse and clear exposition the master's hand.

---

The circle of Oriental scholars in France, which in the course of last year death deprived of some of its most brilliant gems, sustained a final heavy loss on the 13th December in the decease of *M. Pavet de Courteille*, specially mourned by the French Institute and the Société Asiatique, of both of which learned bodies he was a distinguished member. Born in Paris on the 21st June, 1821, he inherited through his mother, who was a daughter of the great Silvestre de Sacy, the love and rigid method of Oriental research. He received his early education at the Lycée at Versailles, and his first instruction in Hebrew and Syriac from the learned Abbé Fillon, who became subsequently Bishop of Mans. In Paris he attended the lectures of Quatremère, Reinaud, and Caussin de Perceval, on whom the mantle of S. de Sacy had descended, and devoted himself with zeal and perseverance to the study of the languages of the Moslem world. Of these he soon made Turkish his speciality, and adhered to his choice to the end of his life. In 1854, after his appointment to the chair of the Turkish language and literature at the *Collège de France*, he brought out a translation of the poetical work of *Nabi*, and in 1861 a translation of the History of the Campaign of Mohacz, and at the same time turned his attention to the study of the Eastern Turkish dialects. His *Dictionnaire Turc-Oriental* was one of the results of his labours, his edition and translation of *the Memoirs of Baber* was another. In 1882 he brought out, from an Ouigour MS., the *Mi'ráj-námah*, or the legend of the ascension of Muhammad, and at the time of his death he was preparing for publication another Ouigour work, the *Teskere-i-evliá*, or Memorial of the Saints. The funeral orations delivered by M. Renan and M. Barbier de Meynard bear affectionate testimony of the sterling character of the deceased as a friend and colleague.

# Notes and News.

The Government of the Straits Settlements has issued a tentative list of *Geographical Names in the Singapore and Malacca Territories*—one for Penang is in preparation—with a view to the introduction of a uniform spelling, thus adopting the wise course which, projected by the Supreme Government in British India, has been working its way slowly and surely in that vast empire. The system that has been devised appears to us judicious and practical, aiming at a compromise, not so difficult of attainment in Malay names as in the numerous languages of British India, between philological accuracy and the form which those names assume in the utterance of the natives. Accented vowels are sparingly used, since they cannot well be dispensed with altogether. Still a further reduction might perhaps be recommended without prejudice to the practicability of the system.

The Catholic Press at Beyrout, well known for its activity, its excellent type, and the correctness of its productions, is bringing out shortly an edition of *the Diwán of el-Akhtal*, one of the most famous ante-Islamic poets of Arabia, together with an ancient commentary, and grammatical and historical notes by the editor, Father A. Salhani, S.J. The late M. Caussin de Perceval gave an account, from the Kitáb el aghúni, of this early Christian poet which appeared in the Journal Asiatique for 1834. It was one of the projects of the late Professor W. Wright to prepare for the press, from the St. Petersburg MS., then considered unique, an edition of this poet and of the contemporary Jarir. His death prevented the accomplishment of this project, and there existed some uncertainty whether one of the few Arabic scholars competent to undertake the task would volunteer to edit the work from the materials collected and prepared by Wright. The forthcoming Beyrout edition will therefore be doubly welcome, and we would venture to hope that the same learned editor may see his way to bring out likewise a similar edition of Jarir.

A TIBETAN DICTIONARY.—Abbé Desgodins, Vicar Apostolic of Tibet, who has been a missionary on the Chinese borders of that country for 35 years, and whose name occurs in every modern book of travels in that region, has lately returned to France with the manuscript of a dictionary of the Tibetan language, on which he has laboured for a quarter of a century, and which he is desirous of having published in Europe. It will be in Latin, French, and English.—*The Times*, April 2, 1890.

CEYLON ANCIENT LITERATURE. — The Council of the Ceylon Asiatic Society, in its last report, urges on the Government the importance of systematically collecting, transcribing, and publishing the manuscripts of the ancient literature of the island which are scattered about in the libraries of temples, as well as in private houses. The researches which have already been made by individuals, or on behalf of the Government, show that manuscripts of great value may be found. During the last three years private exertions have secured sixty-nine of these; but what is needed is that the work should be undertaken as carefully and systematically as in India, where the duty of preserving the ancient literature of the country has been recognized by the Government, and where the collection of ancient manuscripts has for years past been conducted by a large staff of officers.—*The Pioneer*.

COREAN POPULAR LITERATURE.—At a recent meeting of the Asiatic Society of Japan a paper was read on the popular literature of Corea by Mr. W. G. Aston, formerly Consul-General at Seoul. This literature, he said, has received little attention from European scholars, nor is it much honoured in its own country. It is conspicuously absent from the shelves of a Corean gentleman's library, and is excluded even from the two book-shops of which Seoul boasts, where nothing is sold but works written in the Chinese language. For the volumes in which the native Corean literature is contained, we must search the temporary stalls which line the main thoroughfares of the capital or the little shops where they are set out for sale with paper, pipes, oil-paper, covers for hats, tobacco pouches, shoes, inkstones, crockery—the *omnium gatherum* in short of a Corean general store. Little has been done to present them to the public in an attractive form. They are usually limp

quartos, bound with coarse red thread in dirty yellow paper covers. Each volume contains some twenty or thirty sheets of a flimsy greyish paper, blotched in places with patches of other colours, and sometimes containing bits of straw or other extraneous substances which cause grave difficulties in the decipherment of the text. It is not infrequently a question whether a black mark is part of a letter or only a bit of dirt. One volume generally constitutes an entire work. There are no fly-leaves, no title-page, no printer's or publisher's name, and no date or place of publication. Even the author's name is not given. The printer's errors are numerous, and the perplexity they occasion is increased by the confusion of the spelling. Every writer spells as seems good in his own eyes. There is no punctuation, and nothing to show where one word ends and another begins. A new chapter or paragraph is indicated, not by any break in the printing, but by a circle or by the very primitive device of inserting the words "change of subject." The character used is an alphabetical form of writing which has been in use in Corea for several hundred years. There are numerous contractions, some almost indistinguishable from each other, and the letters run into one another, so that it is hard to know where one ends and another begins. When to these difficulties are added printer's mistakes, erratic spelling, or *lacunæ* produced by holes in the paper, the most enthusiastic student may sometimes be tempted to pass on in despair, leaving a *hiatus valde deflendus* in the story. The language is in the primitive condition of all languages before great writers have arisen. We hardly expect to find epic poetry, and there is none. There is nothing even which corresponds to our own ballads; there is no drama, and apparently no poetry. There are numerous tales, a little history abundantly spiced with fiction, a very few translations of Chinese standard works, and some moral treatises, which are also more or less Chinese. Mr. Aston has also seen a book of useful receipts, an interpreter of dreams, a book on the etiquette of mourning, and a letter-writer. Hardly anything has a distinctively Corean character. The trail of the Chinese serpent is over it all. The books have not even the merit of antiquity, few, if any, being more than 300 years old. Corea, in fact, appears to be as poor in literature as it is in all other respects.—*The Times* of April 1, 1890.

THE ARCHÆOLOGICAL SURVEY OF SOUTHERN INDIA is progressing apace. The latest Government Report to hand, submitted by Dr. E. Hultzsch, epigraphist, is dated the 4th February, and covers his operations from October, 1889, to January, 1890. It gives in the first place an account of the most important Tamil inscriptions in the ancient S'iva temple at Tiruvallam in the North Arcot district, and of the two temples at Melpadi, a neighbouring village. These record a number of political events from A.D. 1010 downwards which partly corroborate data mentioned in other inscriptions, partly supply gaps in chronicles found elsewhere; they deal chiefly with the Chola, Ganga, and Bana dynasties. One important paragraph contains a disquisition about geographical names of that period. The report gives also a table of all the inscriptions copied, together with the names of the kings and dynasties to which they refer. We propose in our next issue to give a full notice of the first volume of the Tamil and Sanskrit inscriptions copied and deciphered by Hultzsch since the date of his appointment as epigraphist in November, 1886. In connexion with this subject, we may mention that while Part V. of the "Epigraphia Indica" is already in type, even Part IV. has not yet reached us. There appears to be something radically wrong in the Calcutta Government despatch department which requires to be seen to. The staff of the Archæological Survey throughout India both for surveying and advice in conservation and for epigraphy is thoroughly efficient, and is doing excellent work. To this, however, we fear the Supreme Government is not sufficiently alive. The whole arrangement would, we imagine, work better if each survey were under its own provincial government.

Dr. M. A. STEIN, Registrar of the University of Lahore, informs us that the Catalogue of the *Jammu Collection of Sanskrit MSS.* is in progress, and that about 1000 MSS.—less than a quarter of the whole number—have been described. Pandit Govind Kaul, who is assisting him in this work, finds Dr. Eggeling's Catalogue raisonné of the India Office collection to be of invaluable service to him. Dr. Stein has finished the collation of the Codex archetypus of the Rájataranginí.

We propose in our next issue to review Dr. Leitner's "*Hunza and Nagyr Handbook*" (Calcutta, 1889), to a highly appreciative notice of which *The Times* of April 9 has given two columns. Meanwhile we refer those to whom the volume itself is not accessible to the various interesting details to be found in *The Times* article concerning the languages and races treated of in that work.

## American Literature.

**Abbot (Francis Ellingwood).**—The Way Out of Agnosticism; or, the Philosophy of Free Religion. 12mo. cloth, pp. 10—83. *Boston. 5s.*

**Adams (Oscar Fay).**—Dear Old Story-Tellers. 12mo. cloth, pp. 4—209. Portrait. *Boston. 6s.*

**Agassiz (Elizabeth C.).**—Louis Agassiz, his Life and Correspondence. New Cheaper Edition. Portrait and Illustrations. 8vo. cloth. *Boston. 12s. 6d.*

**Arey (Albert L.)**—Laboratory Manual of Experimental Physics. A Brief Course of Quantitative Experiments intended for Beginners. 16mo. cloth, pp. 2–200. *Syracuse (N.Y.). 4s.*

**Athletic Sports** in England, America, and Australia; comprises the History, Characteristics, Organization, Famous Players, and Great Contests of Base-ball, Cricket, Tennis, Foot-ball, La Crosse, Polo, Rowing, and Bicycling. Illustr. 8vo. cloth, pp. 600. *Philadelphia. £1 1s.*

**Ayer's (N. W. & Son)** American Newspaper Annual for 1889. 8vo. cloth, pp. 1100. *Philadelphia. £1 10s.*

**Baas (Jos. Hermann, M.D.)**—Outlines of the History of Medicine and the Medical Profession; translated, revised, and enlarged by H. E. Handerson, M.D. 8vo. cloth, pp. 1175. *New York. £1 10s.*

**Balzac (Honoré de).**—Sons of the Soil. Translated by Katharine Prescott Wormeley. 12mo. half russia, pp. 8—419. *Boston. 7s. 6d.*

**Bancroft (Hubert Howe).**— History of the Pacific States of North America. Vol. 20. Nevada, Colorado, and Wyoming, 1540—1888. Royal 8vo. cloth, pp. 37–828. *San Francisco. £1 4s.*

**Barton (W. E.)**—Life in the Hills of Kentucky. 8vo. cloth, pp. 3–295. *Oberlin (O.). 5s.*

**Barrows (Anna, comp.)**—Eggs: Facts and Fancies about Them. 16mo. cloth, pp. 4—159. *Boston. 5s.*

**Bates (Arlo).**—Albrecht. 12mo. cloth, pp. 4–265. *Boston. 5s.*

**Beale (D. J., D.D.)**—Through the Johnstown Flood. By a Survivor. 12mo. cloth, pp. 422. *Philadelphia. 12s.*

**Bentley (M. L.)**—Practical Hints on the Art of Wood-carving. 8vo. paper, pp. 2–43. *Cincinnati. 5s.*

**Beringer (J. J., and S. C.)**—A Text-book of Assaying; for the Use of Students, Mine Managers, Assayers, etc. Diagrams. 12mo. cloth, pp. 400. *Philadelphia. 18s.*

**Bigelow (J.)**—William Cullen Bryant. 12mo. cloth, pp. 6–355. *6s. 6d. Boston.*
*₊* American Men of Letters, No. 11.

**Birney (W.)**—James G. Birney and his Times; the Genesis of the Republican Party, with some Account of Abolition Movements in the South before 1828. 12mo. cloth, pp. 11—443. *New York. 10s.*

**Blackall (Clarence H.)** — Builders' Hardware; a Manual for Architects, Builders, and House Furnishers. Illustrated. 8vo. cloth. *Boston. £1 10s.*

**Blair (L. H.)**—The Prosperity of the South Dependent upon the Elevation of the Negro. 12mo. cloth, pp. 8—147. *Richmond (Va.). 6s.*

**Blavatsky (Mme. H. H.)**—The Voice of the Silence. 12mo. cloth, pp. 79. *New York. 4s.*

**Blunt (Edmund, comp.)**—Mercantile Speller; containing the Correct Ways of Spelling Words used in Correspondence and their Prefixes and Suffixes: for Bankers, Merchants, Lawyers, Author, Typewriters. 8vo. pp. 3–444. *New York. 10s. 6d.*

**Bolles (Albert S., ed.)**—The Banker's Almanac and Register, and Legal Directory for 1890. 8vo. cloth. *New York. £1.*

**Bonham (J. M.)**—Railway Secrecy and Trusts. 12mo. cloth, pp. 3–138. *New York. 6s. 6d.*

**Brace (C. Loring).**—The Unknown God; or, Inspiration among pre-Christian Races. 8vo. cloth, pp. 9–336. *New York.*

**Brennan (Rev. M.)**—Astronomy, New and Old. Illustrated. 16mo. cloth. *New York. 5s.*

**Brewster (F. Carroll).**—Molière in Outline. Translation of all Important Parts of Molière's Works. With Introduction, Notes, etc. 8vo. half morocco. *Philadelphia. 15s.*

**Brewster (F. Carroll).**—Disraeli in Outline. Being a Biography of the Right Honourable Benjamin Disraeli, Earl of Beaconsfield: and an Abridgment of all his Novels; containing Lists of Principal Characters, Plots, Remarkable Passages, Criticisms, etc., with Full Index. 8vo. cloth, pp. 1—304. *Philadelphia. 15s.*

**Brinton (Dan. G., M.D.)**—Essays of an Americanist. Part I., Ethnologic and Archæologic; Part II., Mythology and Folk-lore; Part III., Graphic Systems and Literature; Part IV., Linguistic. 8vo. cloth, pp. 6—498. *Philadelphia. 12s.*

**Brown (W. Hardcastle).**—A Commentary on the Law of Divorce and Alimony. 8vo. law calf, pp. 461. *Philadelphia. £1 4s.*

**Buel (S., D.D.)**—A Treatise of Dogmatic Theology. 2 vols. 8vo. cloth. *New York. £1 10s.*

**Burge (Lorenzo).** — Origin and Formation of the Hebrew Scriptures. 12mo. cloth, pp. 5–132. *Boston. 5s.*

**Burnz (Eliza Boardman).**—Help for Young Reporters. Giving Directions for Reporting in all its Branches. Also containing an Explanation of the Proposed Revision of English Spelling. 16mo. cloth, pp. 2—47. *New York. 5s.*

**Cable (G. W.)**—The Negro Question. 12mo. cloth, pp. 6—173. *New York. 4s.*

**Calvo (Joaquin Bernardo).**—The Republic of Costa Rica, from the Spanish; edited by L. de T., with Introduction and Additions. 12mo. cloth, pp. 2—392. *Chicago and New York. 10s.*

**Catherwood (Mrs. Mary Hartwell).**—The Story of Tonty. 12mo. cloth, pp. 3–227. *Chicago. 6s. 6d.*

**Catholic Congress of 1889.**—The Souvenir Volume of the Centennial Celebration and Catholic Congress of 1889. 4to. cloth, pp. 140. *New York.*

**Chapin (F. H.)**—Mountaineering in Colorado: the Peaks about Estes Park. 12mo. cloth, pp. 168. *Boston. 10s. 6d.*

**Chellis (Mary Dwinell).**—The Attic Tenant. 12mo. cloth, pp. 306. *New York. 6s. 6d.*

**Clark (Kate Elizabeth).**—The Dominant Seventh: A Musical Story. 12mo. half-cloth, pp. 2–164. *New York. 2s. 6d.*

**Clarke (Hugh A.)**—The Scratch Club. 16mo. paper, pp. 2—140. *Philadelphia. 4s.*

**Cleveland (Cynthia E.)** — His Honour; or, Fate's Mysteries: a Realistic Story of the United States Army. 12mo. cloth, pp. 2-258. *New York. 7s. 6d.*

Conard (Howard L.)—Uncle Dick Wootton ; Fifty-three Years a Hunter, Trapper, Trader, Indian Fighter, and Government Scout. With an Introduction by Jos. Kirkland. 8vo. cloth, pp. 473. *Chicago.* 18s.

Conkling (Alfred R.)—Life and Letters of Roscoe Conkling, Orator, Statesman, Advocate. 8vo. cloth, pp. 709. *New York.* 18s.

Conway (Rev. James).—The Respective Rights and Duties of Family, State, and Church in regard to Education. Second Edition. 16mo. paper. *New York.* 1s. 6d.

Cosmic Law (The) of Thermal Repulsion ; an Essay suggested by the Projection of a Comet's Tail. 12mo. cloth. *New York.* 3s. 6d.

Crawley (Edwin S.)—Elements of Plane and Spherical Trigonometry. 12mo. cloth, pp. 2—159. *Philadelphia.* 5s.

Curtin (Jeremiah).—Myths and Folklore of Ireland. 12mo. cloth, pp. 345. *Boston.* 10s.

Dana (Ja. D.)—Characteristics of Volcanoes. With Contributions of Facts and Principles from the Hawaiian Islands. 8vo. cloth, pp. 14—399. *New York.* £1 5s.

Daniel (J. W.)—Oration on the Life, Services, and Character of Jefferson Davis, delivered under the Auspices of the General Assembly of Virginia, at Mozart Academy of Music, Jan. 25, 1890. 8vo. paper, pp. 3—51. *Richmond (Va.).* 2s.

Davis (Eben H., ed.)—The Second Reading-Book. 12mo. cloth, pp. 208. *Philadelphia.* 2s.

Davis (Eben H., ed.) — The Third Reading-Book. 12mo. cloth, pp. 336. *Philadelphia.* 3s.

Day (Alfred).—Complete Shorthand Manual for Self-Instruction, and for Use in Schools and Colleges. 12mo. cloth, pp. 179. *Cleveland (Ohio).* 10s.

Dinners, Ceremonious and Unceremonious, and the Method of Serving Them. 16mo. cloth, pp. 3—80. *New York.* 4s.
*₊* Good Form Series.

Dixon (Rev. T., jun.)—Living Problems in Religion and Social Science. 12mo. cloth, pp. 253. *New York.* 7s. 6d.

Doane (T. W.)—Bible Myths and their Parallels in other Religions ; a Comparison of the Old and New Testament Myths and Miracles with those of Heathen Nations of Antiquity, considering also their Origin and Meaning. Fourth edition, enlarged. 8vo. cloth, pp. 23—589. *New York.* 12s. 6d.

Dodge (Theodore Ayrault).—Alexander. A History of the Origin and Growth of the Art of War from the Earliest Times to the Battle of Ipsus, B.C. 301, with a Detailed Account of the Campaigns of the great Macedonian. 8vo. cloth, pp. 25—693. *Boston.* £1 5s.

Dunbar (Newell).—The Elixir of Life ; Dr. Brown-Séquard's Own Account, etc. Sq. 16mo. cloth. *Boston.* 5s.

Dunton (Larkin, ed.)—The World and its People. Books 1 and 2. 12mo. boards, pp. 2—160 ; 2—159. *Boston.* 2s. each.

Earling (P. R.)—Whom to Trust. A Practical Treatise on Mercantile Credits. 12mo. cloth, pp. 5—304. *New York* and *Chicago.* 10s.

Eaton (Arthur Wentworth).—Acadian Legends and Lyrics. 12mo. cloth, pp. 6—148. *New York.* 6s. 6d.

Ebers (G.)—Joshua. A Story of Biblical Times ; from the German by Mary J. Safford. 16mo. cloth, pp. 7—371. *New York.* 4s. ; paper, 2s. 6d.

Elliott (J. R.)—American Farms; their Condition and Future. 12mo. cloth, pp. 6—262. *New York.* 6s. 6d.
*₊* Questions of the Day Series, No. 62.

Evolution.—Popular Lectures and Discussions before the Brooklyn Ethical Association. 12mo. cloth, pp. 400. *Boston.* 10s. 6d.

Filippini (Alessandro).—The Table ; How to Buy Food, How to Cook It, and How to Serve It. 8vo. oil-cloth cover. *New York.* 16s. 6d.

Fitzsimons (Rev. S.)—A Refutation of Agnosticism. 16mo. paper. *New York.* 1s. 6d.

Folsom (M. M.)—Scraps of Song and Southern Scenes ; descriptive of Plantation Life in the Backwoods of Georgia. 8vo. cloth, pp 200. *Atlanta (Ga.).* 4s. 6d.

Fothergill (J. Milner, M.D.)—The Town Dweller, his Needs and his Wants ; with an Introduction by B. W. Richardson, M.D. 12mo. cloth, pp. 8—118. *New York.* 5s.

Friese (Philip C.)—Semitic Philosophy. Showing the Ultimate Social and Scientific Outcome of Original Christianity in its Conflict with Surviving Ancient Heathenism. 12mo. cloth, pp. 16—247. *Chicago.* 5s.

Germany. — The Federal Constitution of Germany, with an Historical Introduction, translated by Edmund J. James. 8vo. paper, pp. 2—43. *Philadelphia.* 2s. 6d.
*₊* Publications of the University of Pennsylvania, No. 7.

Germs (The) and Developments of the Laws of England, embracing the Anglo-Saxon Laws extant from the Sixth Century to A.D. 1066, as Translated into English under the Royal Commission of William IV., with the Introduction of the Common Law by Norman Judges after the Conquest, and its earliest Proferts in Magna Charta ; with Notes and Comments by J. M. Stearns. 12mo. cloth, pp. 370. *New York.* 12s.

Gibb (M.)—Gibb's Route and Reference Book of the United States and Canada ; for the Use of Commercial Travellers, Merchants, and others. 8vo. flexible leather. *New York.* £1 5s.

God in His World. An Interpretation. 12mo. cloth, pp. 42—270. *New York.* 6s. 6d.

Godwin (H. C.)—Railroad Engineers' Field-Book and Explorers' Guide. Especially adapted to the Use of Railroad Engineers on Location and Construction, and to the Needs of the Explorer in making Exploratory Surveys. 16mo. morocco flaps, pp. 13—358. *New York.* 12s. 6d.

Gould (G. M., M.D.)—A New Medical Dictionary. 8vo. leather, pp. 520, 16s. 6d. ; with thumb index, half morocco, £1 1s. *Philadelphia.*

Grant (G. Monro, ed.)—Picturesque Quebec. With a Preface by Julian Hawthorne ; illustrated by J. Moran, F. B. Schell, Gibson, Ogden, and others. 4to. cloth, pp. 141. *New York.* £1 10s.

Haferkorn (H. E.) and Heise (Paul) comps.—Handy Lists of Technical Literature. A Reference Catalogue of Books printed in English from 1880 to 1888 inclusive. Part 2, Military and Naval Science ; Navigation, Rowing. Sailing, Yachting ; Boat, Ship and Yacht Building ; Ammunition, Arms, Tactics, and War ; together with a Supplementary List of Non-Technical Books, illustrating Soldier and Sailor Life, Battles, etc., and a List of Periodicals and Annuals in these Branches. 8vo. cloth, pp. 4—104. *Milwaukee (Wis.).* 6s. 6d. ; paper, 5s.
Key to ditto, paper, 1s. 6d.

Handy Lists of Technical Literature ; a Reference Catalogue. Part 2. Military and Naval Science ; Navigation, Rowing, Sailing, Yachting ; Boat, Ship and Yacht Building ; Ammunition, Arms, Tactics, and War ; together with a Supplementary List of Non-technical Books illustrating Soldier and Sailor Life, Battles, etc., and a List of Periodicals and Annuals in these Branches. 8vo. cloth, pp. 104. *Milwaukee (Wisconsin).* Paper, 6s. 6d. ; cloth, 7s. 6d.

Henderson (J. C.)—Thomas Jefferson's Views on Public Education. 8vo. cloth, pp. 7—387. *New York.* 9s.

Hervey (Hetta M.)—Glimpses of Norseland. 12mo. cloth. *Boston.* 6s. 6d.

Holst (H. v.)—The Political and Constitutional History of the United States of America. From the German by J. J. Lalor and Alfred B. Mason. Vols. 5 and 6. 8vo. cloth, pp. 490 and 352. *Chicago.* 18s. and 12s. 6d.

Hoppin (Ja. M.)—Old England, its Scenery, Art, and People. Tenth edition, enlarged. 8vo. cloth. *Boston.* 9s.

Horsford (Eben Norton). — The Discovery of the Ancient City of Norumbega ; communicated to the President and Council of the American Geographical Society at Watertown, November 21, 1889. 4to. cloth. *Boston.* 15s.

Horsford (Eben Norton).—The Problem of the Northmen : a Letter to Judge Daly, the President of the American Geographical Society. 4to. paper, pp. 23. *Boston.* 6s.

Houston (E. J.) — Dictionary of Electrical Words, Terms, and Phrases. 8vo. cloth, pp. 600. Illustrated. *New York.* 12s. 6d.

Howland (G.)—Practical Hints for the Teachers of Public Schools. 12mo. cloth, pp. 11-198. *New York.* 7s.6d.
*** International Education Series, No. 13.

Hunt (H. M.)—The Crime of the Century ; or, the Assassination of Dr. Patrick Henry Cronin. 12mo. cloth, pp. 676. *Chicago.* 9s.

Hunt (Theodore W.)—Studies in Literature and Style. 12mo. cloth, pp. 7—303. *New York.* 6s.

Illustrated Fraternal Directory ; including Educational Institutions of the Pacific Coast, 1889. 8vo. boards, pp. 342. *San Francisco.* 10s. 6d.

International Commerce of the United States. Treasury Department. Report for the Fiscal Year 1889. Part 2 of Commerce and Navigation. By W. F. Switzler. 8vo. cloth, pp. 32-897. *Washington (D.C.).* 10s.

Isaacs (Jorge).— Maria. A South American Romance. Translated by Rollo Ogden ; an Introduction by T. A. Janvier. 16mo. cloth, pp. 302. *New York.* 6s.

Jacobi (A., M.D.)—A Treatise on Diphtheria. 8vo. cloth, pp. 252. *New York.* 10s. 6d.

Janvier (T. A.)—The Mexican Guide. New Edition for 1890. 16mo. cloth. *New York.* 16s. 6d.

Jelly (Eva Forde).—Book of Beauty and Fascination ; with One Hundred Health and Toilet Secrets. Portrait. 16mo. cloth, pp. 9-131. *Chicago.* 2s. 6d.

Kellogg (Brainerd). — A Text-book on Rhetoric. Supplementing the Development of the Science with Exhaustive Practice in Composition. 12mo. cloth, pp. 276. *New York.* 6s.

King (C. F.)—The Picturesque Geographical Readers. Vol. I. At Home and at School. Supplementary and Regular Reading in the Lower Classes in Grammar Schools, Public Libraries, and the Home. Illustrated. 12mo. cloth, pp. 9-226. *Boston.* 2s. 6d.

King (C.)—Starlight Ranch, and other Stories of Army Life on the Frontier. 12mo. cloth, pp. 4-260. *Philadelphia.* 5s.

Knoflach (Augustin).—Sound-English. A Language for the World. 12mo. paper, pp. 63. *New York.* 1s. 6d.

Laws of the Territory of the United States North-West of the Ohio River, 1798, sometimes called the Freeman Code ; a Fac-simile Reprint of a Book printed in 1798. [Edition of 30 copies.] Small 4to. calf. *Cincinnati (Ohio).* £3 13s. 6d.

Leland (C. G.)—Practical Education ; Treating of the Development of Memory, the Increasing Quickness of Perception and Training the Constructive Faculty. Third Edition. 12mo. cloth, pp. 280. *New York.* 12s.

Machar (Agnes Maule) and Marquis (T. G.)—Stories of New France. Being Tales of Adventure and Heroism from the Early History of Canada. In Two Series. 12mo. cloth, pp. 12-313. *Boston.* 7s. 6d.

MacQueary (Rev. Howard).—The Evolution of Man and Christianity. 12mo. cloth, pp. 3-410. *New York.* 9s.

Macvane (S. M.)—The Working Principles of Political Economy in a New and Practical Form : a Book for Beginners. 12mo. cloth, pp. 3—392. *New York.* 6s.

Magennis (Margaret J.)—The Foe of the Household ; or, Scenes in Temperance Work. 16mo. cloth, pp. 4-126. Portrait. *Boston.* 3s.

Matthews (W.) — Modern Bookbinding Practically Considered. A Lecture read before the Grolier Club of New York, March 25, 1885, with Additions and new Illustrations. New York, The Grolier Club, privately printed, 1889. [Edition limited to 300 copies.] 4to. cloth, pp. 3-96. *New York.* 18s.

McCollester (Sullivan Holman).—Round the Globe in Old and New Paths. 8vo. pp. 6-354. *Boston.* 7s. 6d.

McCosh (Ja., D.D.)—The Religious Aspect of Evolution. Enlarged Improved Edition. 12mo. cloth, pp. 9-119. *New York.* 6s.

McLaurin (J. J.)—The Story of Johnstown ; its Early Settlement, Rise, and Progress, Industrial Growth, and Appalling Flood on May 31, 1889. Prefatory Note by Rev. J. R. Paxton. Illustrated. 8vo. cloth, pp. 100. *Harrisburg (Pa.).* 15s.

Mellick (Andrew D., jun.)—The Story of an Old Farm ; or, Life in New Jersey in the Eighteenth Century ; with a Genealogical Appendix of the Mellick (Melick) Family. 8vo. cloth, pp. 722. *Somerville (N. J.).* £1 5s.

Mélio (G. L., comp.) — Manual of Swedish Drill (based on Ling's System) for Teachers and Students, compiled and arranged by G. L. Mélio. 12mo. boards, pp. 3-51. *New York.* 2s. 6d.

Merriman (Mansfield) and Jacoby (H. S.)—A Text-Book on Roofs and Bridges. Part 2. Graphic Statics. 8vo. cloth, pp. 7-124. *New York.* 10s. 6d.

Meserve (Andrew L.)—The Fireman's Handbook and Drill Manual. 12mo. cloth, pp. 2-129. *Chicago.* 6s.

Miss Breckenridge : a Daughter of Dixie. By a Nashville Pen. 12mo. paper, pp. 203. *Philadelphia.* 2s. 6d.

Montague (C. Howard). — The Countess Muta. A Novel. 12mo. cloth, pp. 244. *New York.* 2s. 6d.

Monteiro (A., M.D.) — War Reminiscences, by the Surgeon of Mosby's Command. 12mo. paper, pp. 208. *Richmond (Va.).* 3s.

Moorehead (Warren K., comp.)—Fort Ancient, the Great Prehistoric Earthwork of Warren County, Ohio ; compiled from a careful Survey, with an Account of its Mounds and Graves ; with Surveying Notes. 8vo. cloth, pp. 10-129. Map and Illustrations. *Cincinnati (Ohio).* 10s. 6d.

Murphy (T., D.D.)— The Presbytery of the Log College ; or, the Cradle of the Presbyterian Church in America. 4to. cloth, pp. 2-526. Portrait. *Philadelphia.* 12s.

Newton (W. Wilberforce, D.D.) — Dr. Muhlenberg. 12mo. cloth, pp. 10-272. *Boston.* 6s. 6d.

Noyes (H. D., M.D.)—A Text-Book on Diseases of the Eye. 8vo. cloth, pp. 670. *New York.* £1 10s.

Painter (F. V. N.)—Luther on Education ; including a Historical Introduction and a Translation of the Reformer's two most important Educational Treatises. 12mo. cloth, pp. 2-282. *Philadelphia.* 5s.

Palfrey (J. Gorham)—History of New England. Five vols. 8vo. cloth. *Boston.* £3 13s. 6d.

Palmer (B. M., D.D.) — Formation of Character ; Twelve Lectures delivered in the First Presbyterian Church, New Orleans, La. 16mo. cloth, pp. 222. *New Orleans (La.).* 6s.

Paton (J. G.)—John G. Paton, Missionary to the New Hebrides ; an Autobiography. Edited by Ja. Paton. 12mo. cloth, pp. 14-382. *New York.* 7s. 6d.

Paton (W. Agnew).—Down the Islands. A Voyage to the Caribbees. New cheaper edition. Square 8vo. cloth. *New York.* 12s. 6d.

**Patten (Simon N.)** — The Principles of Rational Taxation. 8vo. paper, pp. 2-25. *Philadelphia.* 2s. 6d.

**Payne (F. M.)** — Payne's Business Educator. A Complete Encyclopædia of Business Knowledge and Epitome of United States and State Law. 12mo. cloth, pp. 11-596. *New York.* 10s.

**Payne (F. M.)** — The Legal Adviser; an Epitome of the Business and Domestic Laws of the several States of the Union, and those of the General Government of the United States. 12mo. cloth, pp. 317. *New York.* 7s. 6d.

**P. (G. W.)** — American Whist Illustrated. Illustrated. 16mo. bound, pp. 9-367. *Boston.* 9s.

**Phifer (C. L.)** — Annals of the Earth. 12mo. cloth, pp. 5-289. Portrait. *California (Mo.).* 7s. 6d.

*₂* In blank verso. A description of the Creation, the Garden of Eden, Adam and Eve, etc.

**Philadelphia and its Environs.** A Guide to the City and Surroundings. Illustrated. 12mo. cloth, pp. 32-252. *Philadelphia.* 1s. 6d.

**Pictorial Africa;** its Heroes, Missionaries, and Martyrs. Illustrated. 8vo. cloth, pp. 400. *New York* and *Chicago.* 6s. 6d.

**Plymouth.** — Records of the Town of Plymouth. Vol. I. 1636-1705. Published by Order of the Town. 8vo. cloth, pp. 12-346. *Boston.* 9s.

**Posse (Nils, Baron).** — The Swedish System of Educational Gymnastics. 8vo. cloth, pp. 5-275. *Boston.* 12s.

**Potter (V. M.)** — To Europe on a Stretcher. 12mo. cloth, pp. 100. *New York.* 6s.

Relates the experience of a well-known New York lady, Mrs. Clarkson N. Potter, in two trips to Europe, made practically on a stretcher. She was sent abroad by her physicians to certain baths to cure an illness of many years' standing. Her little sketch shows how much one may enjoy even as a helpless invalid. It also offers hope to the sufferer, as her health was benefited by both trips.

**Powell (E. P.)** — Liberty and Life. Discourses. 12mo. cloth, pp. 3-208. *Chicago.* 4s.

**Prescott (W. H.)** — Works. New Library Edition. 12 vols. 8vo. cloth. *Philadelphia.* 12s. 6d. each.

**Pugh (S. S.)** — Rights and Wrongs. 16mo. cloth, pp. 256. *Boston.* 6s.

**Pynchon (T. Ruggles, D.D.)** — Bishop Butler. A Religious Philosopher for all Time. A Sketch of his Life, with an Examination of the "Analogy." 8vo. cloth, pp. 131. *New York.* 6s. 6d.

**Rankin (Francis H., M.D.)** — Hygiene of Childhood. Suggestions for the Care of Children after the Period of Infancy to the Completion of Puberty. 12mo. cloth, pp. 3-140. *New York.* 4s.

**Ribot (Th.)** — The Psychology of Attention. Authorized Translation. 12mo. cloth, pp. 2-121. *Chicago (Ill.).* 4s.

**Richardson (M. T., ed.)** — Practical Blacksmithing. Vols. 1 and 2. 12mo. cloth, pp. 264-270. *New York.* 5s. each.

**Richardson (M. T., ed.)** — The Practical Horse-shoer. 12mo. cloth, pp. 288. *New York.* 5s.

**Russell (A. P.)** — In a Club Corner. The Monologue of a Man who might have been Sociable. 12mo. cloth, pp. 2-328. *Boston.* 6s. 6d.

**Savage (M. J.)** — The Signs of the Time. 12mo. cloth, pp. 5-187. *Boston.* 5s.

*Contents:* Break-up of the old orthodoxy; The Roman church; Liberal orthodoxy; Unitarianism; Free religion and ethical culture; Scientific materialism; Ingersollism; Religious reaction; Mind cure; Spiritualism; Break-ups that mean advance; The new city of God.

**Savage (M. J.)** — Helps for Dainty Living. 12mo. cloth, pp. 3-150. *Boston.* 7s. 6d.

Practical discourses on: Life's aim and meaning; Things that make honesty hard; The self and others; The problem of evil; Life's petty worries; The commonplace; Helping; Conflicts of conscience; Living by the day; How to die.

**Schaff (Philip, D.D.)** — Literature and Poetry. 8vo. cloth, pp. 7-436. Portrait and Illustrations. *N. York.* 15s.

**Schenck (F. S.)** — The Ten Commandments in the Nineteenth Century. 12mo. cloth, pp. 139. *New York.* 5s.

**Schouler (J.)** — History of the United States of America under the Constitution. [New Issue.] Four vols. Vol. 1, 1783-1801; Vol. 2, 1801-1817; Vol. 3, 1817-1831; Vol. 4, 1831-1847. 8vo. cloth, pp. 16—520; 15—471; 14—539; and 15—559. *New York.* £2 5s.

**Shakespeare (W.)** — Works. Variorum Edition. Edited by Horace H. Furness. Vols. 1 to 7. *Philadelphia.* 18s. each. ·

*₂* Vol. 7, All's Well that Ends Well.

**Shakespeare (W.)** — Macbeth. Edited, with Notes, by Homer B. Sprague. Flexible cloth, pp. 5-237. *Chicago (Ill.)*

**Shay (Frank, comp.)** — Cipher Book; for the Use of Merchants, Stock Operators, Stock Brokers, Miners, Mining Men, Railroad Men, Real Estate Dealers, and Business Men generally. 12mo. cloth, pp. 253. *San Francisco.* £1 5s.

**Shepard (Mrs. Isabel S.)** — The Cruise of the U. S. Steamer "Rush" in Behring Sea; Summer of 1889. Map and Illustrations. 12mo. cloth, pp. 3-257. *San Francisco.* 7s. 6d.

**Sickels (Ivin, M.D.)** — Exercises in Wood-working; with a Short Treatise on Wood. Written for Manual Training Classes in Schools and Colleges. 8vo. cloth, pp. 2-158. *New York.* 6s. 6d.

**Sloane (T. O'Conor, Ed.)** — Facts Worth Knowing. Selected mainly from the "Scientific American" for the Household, Workshop, and Farm. 8vo. cloth, pp. 878. *Hartford (Conn.).* 18s.

**Small (Albion W.)** — The Beginnings of American Nationality. The Constitutional Relations between the Continental Congress and the Colonies and States from 1774 to 1789. [Also,] The Needs of Self-supporting Women, by Clare de Graffenried. 8vo. paper, pp. 3-77-9. *Baltimore.* 5s.

**Smith's Interest Tables** at Five, Six, Seven and Three-tenths, Eight, Eight and one-half, Ten and Twelve per Cent. per Annum; showing the Interest on any Sum from $1 to $10,000, from One Day to Five Years; calculated by Duane Doty. 8vo. cloth, pp. 127. *Milwaukee (Wis.).* 6s.

**Starbrough (Rufus M.)** — The Scriptural View of Divine Grace. 12mo. cloth, pp. 292. *New York* and *Chicago.* 6s. 6d.

**Statutory Requirements** relating to Insurance in the United States and Canadas. Comprising all the Requirements necessary for the Admission and Transaction of Business in the States and in Canada, by Fire, Life, and Casualty Insurance Companies of other States and Foreign Countries; corrected to Dec. 1, 1889. 8vo. cloth, pp. 135. *Hartford (Conn.).* 15s.

**Stebbins (N. L.)** — Yacht Portraits of the Leading American Yachts. Oblong 8vo. cloth (no paging). *Boston.* £2 5s.

**Stockton (Frank R.)** — The Stories of the Three Burglars. 12mo. cloth, pp. 159. *New York.* 5s.

**Stockton (Frank R.)** — The Great War Syndicate. 12mo. cloth, pp. 191. *New York.* 5s.

**Story's Legal Digest** and Directory of Lawyers, containing the Laws of the States and Territories of the United States and of Canada, relating to Civil Rights and Liabilities, etc. Fifth Annual Issue, 1890. 8vo. sheep, pp. 1132-156. *New York.* £1 5s.

**Story (W. Wetmore).** — Conversations in a Studio.— 2 vols. cloth, pp. 2 + 307; 307-578. *Boston.* 12s. 6d.

**Suttner (A. G. v.)** — Djambek, the Georgian. A Tale of Modern Turkey, from the German by H. M. Jewett; with an Introduction by Mangasar M. Mangasarian. 12mo. paper, pp. 4—258. *New York.*

Taylor (C. H. J.)—Whites and Blacks; or, the Question Settled. 12mo. paper, pp. 5—52. *Atlanta (Ga.).* 2*s.*

Thorne (Rob., ed.)—Fugitive Facts; an Epitome of General Information. 8vo. cloth, pp. 2-491. *N. York.* 10*s.*

Thrum (T. G., comp.)—Hawaiian Almanac and Annual for 1890. A Handbook of Information on Interesting Matters relating to Hawaiian Islands. 8vo. paper, pp. 126. *Honolulu (H.I.).* 5*s.*

Thurston (R. H.)—A Handbook of Engine and Boiler Trials and of the Indicator and Prony Brake; for Engineers and Technical Schools. 8vo. cloth, pp. 514. *New York.* £1 1*s.*

Thurston (G. A.)—Forty Years a File-closer. A Humorous Sketch pointed at the Difficulties in the Way of Promotion in the United States Army. By Captain Minus Wonbar. 8vo. paper, pp. 2-40. *Washington (D.C.).*

Tiernan (Mary Spear)—Jack Horner. A Novel. 12mo. cloth, pp. 3—347. *Boston.* 6*s.* 6*d.*

Titled Americans. 16mo. paper, pp. 270. *New York.* 2*s.* 6*d.*

*₊* A list of names of American girls who have married noblemen.

Torrey (Bates)—Practical Typewriting; by the All-finger Method which leads to Operation by Touch; arranged for Self-instruction, School Use, and Lessons by Mail. 8vo. cloth, pp. 64. *New York.* 5*s.*

Varney (G. J.)—A Brief History of Maine. Second Edition. 12mo. cloth, pp. 5—336. *Portland (Me.).* 6*s.* 6*d.*

Vincent (Frank).—Around and about South America; Twenty Months of Quest and Query. Illustrations and Portrait. 8vo. cloth, pp. 22-473. *New York.* £1 1*s.*

Wagner (Arthur L.)—The Campaign of Königgrätz. A Study of the Austro-Prussian Conflict in the Light of the American Civil War. 8vo. cloth, pp. 121. *Leavenworth (Kan.).* 5*s.*

Walworth (Jeannette H.)—A Little Radical. A Novel. 12mo. cloth, pp. 235. *New York.* 5*s.*

Warman (E. B.)—The Voice, how to Train it—how to Care for it. 8vo. cloth, pp. 168. *Boston.* 10*s.*

Warman (E. B.)—The Voice: How to Train It; How to Care for it. For Ministers, Lecturers, Readers, Actors, Singers, Teachers, and Public Speakers. Illustrated by Marian Morgan Reynolds. 8vo. cloth, pp. 4-168. Portrait and Illustrations. *Boston.* 10*s.*

Warren (J. Collins, M.D.)—The Healing of Arteries after Ligature in Man and Animals. Illustrated. 8vo. cloth, pp. 184. *New York.* 16*s.* 6*d.*

Webster (Sidney).—Extradition; the Right to Demand it, the Enlargement of its Jurisdiction and the Improvement of its Methods. 8vo. paper, pp. 31. *New York.* 2*s.*

Wedderburn (Alex. J.)—A Popular Treatise on the Extent and Character of Food Adulterations. 8vo. cloth, pp. 4-61. *Washington (D.C.).* 1*s.* 6*d.*

Wells (D. A.)—The Decay of our Ocean Mercantile Marine, its Cause and its Cure; will Subsidizing Ships bring back our Foreign Commerce and afford Markets for the Surplus Products of our Manufacturing Industries? An Address delivered before the Reform Club of New York, October 18, 1889. 12mo. paper, pp. 2-48. *N. York.* 1*s.* 6*d.*

Wernse (W. F., ed.)—The American Law Digest and Legal Directory. Part First contains a Summary of the most important Branches of the Commercial Law of the several States of this Union, and its Territories, Revised to Date of Issue, with References to Authorities where accessible, etc. Part Second, Legal Directory, etc., 1889-1890. 8vo. sheep, pp. 71-952-50. *New York* and *St. Louis.* £1 10*s.*

Wharton (Morton Bryan, D.D.)—Famous Women of the New Testament: a Series of Popular Lectures delivered in the First Baptist Church, Montgomery, Ala. 12mo. cloth, pp. 340. *New York.* 7*s.* 6*d.*

White (Mrs. B. A.) ["Didama," *pseud.*]—Richmond and Way Stations, '61 and '64. The Story of William G. Warren, a Soldier of the 16th Regiment Massachusetts Volunteers, given from his own Letters. 12mo. paper, pp. 54. *Bellingham (Mass.).* 1*s.* 6*d.*

Wise (T. J., ed.)—A Bibliography of the Writings in Prose and Verse of John Ruskin, LL.D. In four parts. Parts 1-2. 4to. paper, pp. 32-33-64. *New York.* 2*s.* 6*d.* each.

Willcox (G. B.)—The Prodigal Son: a Monograph; with an Excursus on Christ as a Public Teacher. 12mo. cloth, pp. 2-112. *New York.* 4*s.*

Winship (Albert E.)—The Shop. 12mo. cloth, pp. 3-80. *Boston.* 3*s.*

Woodberry (G. E.)—The North Shore Watch, and other Poems. 12mo. half cloth, pp. 2-123. *Boston.* 6*s.* 6*d.*

Wolf (Edmund Jacob, D.D.) — The Lutherans in America. A Story of Struggle, Progress, Influence, and Marvellous Growth; with an Introduction by H. E. Jacobs, D.D. 8vo. cloth, pp. 544. Portrait and Illustrations. *New York.* 16*s.* 6*d.*

Woolfolk (L. B.)—Great Red Dragon; or, London Money Power. 12mo. cloth, pp. 2-328. *Cincinnati.* 6*s.*

Wood's Medical and Surgical Monographs. Consisting of Original Treatises and Reproductions in English of Books and Monographs selected from the latest Literature of Foreign Countries. Vol. 5, No. 2. 8vo. paper, pp. 298-585. Illustrations. *New York.* 6*s.*; for 12 Nos. £3.

Wright (Rev. Jos. H.)—The Patience of Hope, and other Sermons, by the late Rev. J. H. Wright; with a Brief Sketch of his Life. Edited by Oliver J. Thatcher. 12mo. cloth, pp. 224. *New York.* 6*s.* 6*d.*

Yeijiro Ono. The Industrial Transition in Japan. 8vo. paper, pp. 4-121. Map. *Baltimore.* 5*s.*
*₊* Publications of the American Economic Association, Vol. v. No. 1.

Young (Lucien)—Simple Elements of Navigation. 16mo. pocket-book form. *New York.* 10*s.*

---

## New European Books.

Abercromby (J.)—A Trip through the Eastern Caucasus, with a Chapter on the Languages of the Country. With Maps and Illustrations. Demy 8vo. cloth, 1890. 14*s.*

Alfārābī's philosophische Abhandlungen aus Londoner, Leidener und Berliner Handschriften. Edited by F. Dieterici. 8vo. pp. 118. *Leiden,* 1890. 6*s.*

Amélineau (E.)—Histoire du patriarche copte Isaac. Coptic Text with French Translation and Critical Notes. 8vo. *Paris,* 1890. 4*s.*
*₊* (Publications de l'Ecole des lettres d'Alger, vol. ii.)

Amélineau (E.) — Les moines égyptiens; vie de Schnoudi. With Portrait. Small 8vo. *Paris,* 1890. 3*s.*
*₊* (Bibliothèque de vulgarisation, vol. i.)

Amiaud et Scheil, Les Inscriptions de Salmanasar II. roi d'Assyrie (860-824), Original Text with Translation, Commentary, Dictionary, and Notes. Large 8vo. *Paris,* 1890. 10*s.*

Anderson (J.)—English Intercourse with Siam. 8vo. cloth. 1890. 15*s.*

Anuario del Comercio de España, Ultramar, Estados Hispano-Americanos y Portugal for 1890. Large 8vo. cloth. £1 2*s.* 6*d.*

**Apollonius von Perga.** Das 5te Buch seiner Ionica in der arabischen Uebersetzung des Thabit Ibn Corrah, edited, with German Translation and Introduction by Nix. 8vo. *Leipzig*, 1890. 2*s.*

**Apologie der orthodoxen griechisch-orientalischen** Kirche der Bukowina. 4to. pp. 60. *Czernowitz*, 1890. 1*s.* 6*d.*

**Archives** pour servir à l'étude de l'histoire, des langues, de la géographie et de l'ethnographie de l'Asie Orientale (Chine, Japon, Corée. Indo-Chine, Asie Centrale et Malaisie) rédigées par G. Schlegel et H. Cordier. Vol. I. Pt. 1. Annual subscription, post free £1.

**Artin Pacha (Y.)**—L'Instruction publique en Egypte. 8vo. *Paris*, 1890. 5*s.*

**Avesta.**—The Sacred Books of the Parsis (English Translation). Edited by K. F. Geldner. Vol. II. Khorda Avesta. Part 6. Large 4to. pp. 161-277. *Stuttgart*, 1890. 18*s.*

**Barth (A.)**—The Religions of India. From the German. By Rev. J. Wood. 2nd edition. 12mo, cloth. 1890. 16*s.*

**Basset (R.)**—Loqmân Berbère, texte berbère et transcription, avec quatre glossaires et une étude sur la légende de Loqmân. 18mo. *Paris*, 1890. 8*s.*

**Bianconi (F).**—Le Mexique à la portée des industriels, des capitalistes, des négocianta et des importateurs. With a Coloured Map. 8vo. *Paris*, 1890. 4*s.*

**Bibliothek.**—Keilinschriftliche. Sammlung von assyrischen und babylonischen Texten in Umschrift und Uebersetzung. by Schrader. Vol. II. 8vo. pp. 291. With Map. 8vo. *Berlin*, 1890. 12*s.* 6*d.*

**Bijdragen tot de Taal-, Land-, en Volkenkunde van** Nederlandsch-Indie. Edited by the Royal Institute. Vol. V. Part 1. 8vo. *The Hague*, 1890. 4*s.*

**Boerlage (J. G.)**—Handleiding tot de kennis der flora van Nederlandsch Indië. Vol. I. part 1. 8vo. *Leiden*, 1890. 6*s.*

**Bonavia (E.).**—The cultivated Oranges and Lemons, etc., of India and Ceylon. 2 vols. 8vo. cloth, 1890. £1 10*s.*

**Brockelmann (K.)**—Das Verhaeltniss von Ibn-El-Atirs Kamil Fit-Ta'Rib zu Tabaris-Abbar Errusul Wal Muluk. 8vo. pp. 68. *Strassburg*, 1890. 2*s.*

**Bulletin de l'Association de l'Afrique du Nord.** 2nd year. 1890. Yearly subscription 8*s.*

**Burggraeve (le Dr.)**—L'Afrique Centrale et le Congo indépendant belge. pp. 119. With Map. *Paris*, 1890. 1*s.*

**Oat (E.)**—Notice sur la carte de l'Ogooué. With Map. 8vo. *Paris*, 1890. 2*s.* 6*d.*

*** Publications de l'Ecole des lettres d'Alger, Vol. I.

**Catalogue méthodique** et raisonné de la Collection de Mr. de Clercq contenants Antiquités Assyriennes (Cylindres orientaux, cachets, briques, bronzes, bas-reliefs, etc.). Vol. 1. with 6 plates. *Paris*, 1890. 8*s.*

**Central-Anzeiger fuer Juedische Litteratur.** Edited by Dr. N. Bruell. Vol. I. *Frankfurt*, 1890 8*s.*

*** A new bi-monthly periodical of the Jewish Literature.

**Clouston (W. A.)**—Flowers from a Persian Garden and other Papers. Crown 8vo. 1890. 6*s.*

**Codex Peresianus.**—Manuscrit hiératique des anciens Indiens de l'Amérique Centrale; a Facsimile Reproduction with a Glossary and an Introduction by Léon de Rosny. Folio, cloth. *Paris*, 1890. £6.

**Commettant (O.)**—Au pays des Kangourous et des mines d'or. 12mo. *Paris*, 1890. 3*s.* 6*d.*

**Darmesteter (J.)**—Chants populaires des Afghans. Collected and Translated. Second Series. 8vo. *Paris*, 1890. 16*s.*

**De Morgan (J.)**—Mission scientifique au Caucase. Etudes archéologiques et historiques. 8vo. *Paris*, 1890. £1 2*s.* 6*d.*

**Driver (S. R.)**—Notes on the Hebrew Text of the Books of Samuel. 8vo. cloth. 1890. 14*s.*

**Dumoutier (G.)**—Les chants et les traditions populaires des Annamites. Collected and Translated into French. With Illustrations and Portraits. 12mo. *Paris*. 4*s.*

*** Collection de contes et de chansons populaires, vol. IV.

**Dutreuil de Rhins (J. L.)**—L'Asie Centrale (Thibet et régions limitrophes). *Paris*, 1890. £2 17*s.* 6*d.*

**Ephraem Syri,** Hymni et Sermones. Syriac Text with Latin Translation, Variants, and Notes. Three vols. 4to. *Malines*, 1890. £3.

**Firdosi's Koenigsbuch** (Schahname). Trans. into German by F. Rueckert. Edited by Bayer. Part 1. 8vo. pp. 1-439. *Berlin*, 1890. 8*s.*

**Fornander (A.)**—An Account of the Polynesian Race; its Origin and Migration. Second edition. Vol. I. 8vo. cloth, pp. 250. 1890. 7*s.* 6*d.*

**Gasselin (E.)**—Dictionnaire français-arabe. Part 40. 4to. *Paris*, 1890. 3*s.*

**Gesenius (W.)**—Hebraeisches und aramaeisches Handwoerterbuch ueber das Alte Testament. Eleventh edition. By Muehlau, Volck and Mueller. Large 8vo. *Leipzig*, 1890. 15*s.*

**Gravière (J. de la)**—Les ouvriers de la onzième heure. Histoires des premières navigations des Anglais et des Hollandais dans les mers polaires et dans la mer des Indes. 8vo. *Paris*, 1890. 7*s.*

**Hamagid.**—Weekly Periodical in Hebrew. Edited by D. Gordon. Folio. Yearly subscription, 16*s.* post free.

**Hirzel (A.)**—Gleichnisse und Metaphern im Rigveda in culturhistorischer Hinsicht zusammengestellt und verglichen mit den Bildern bei Homer, Hesiod, Aeschylos, Sophokles und Euripides. 8vo. pp. 107. *Leipzig*, 1890. 3*s.*

**Humann und Puchstein.**—Reisen in Klein-Asien und Nord-Syrien, by order of the Royal Academy, Berlin. Text, 4to. with atlas (containing 48 plates, 5 plans, and 3 maps, by H. Kiepert). Folio. *Berlin*, 1890. £3.

**Imbault-Huart (O.)**—Cours éclectique, graduel et pratique de la langue chinoise parlée. Four vols. 4to. *Paris*, 1890. £4 10*s.*

**Internationales Archiv fuer Ethnographie.** Edited by J. D. E. Schmeltz. Vol. III. part 1. pp. 48, text, with one tinted and two Coloured Plates. 4to. *Leiden*, 1890. Subscription price for a vol. of four parts, £1.

**Jennings (H.)**—The Indian Religions; or, Results of the Mysterious Buddhism; concerning that also which is to be understood in the Divinity of Fire. Demy 8vo. cloth, 1890. 10*s.* 6*d.*

**Jonge (J. K. J. de)**—De opkomst van het Netherlandsch gezag in Oost-Indie. Second series. Vol. II. 8vo. *The Hague*, 1890. 11*s.*

**Kaye und Malleson.**—History of the Indian Mutiny of 1857-58. Vol. VI. 8vo. cloth. 1890. 6*s.*

**Kayserling (M.)** — Biblioteca Española-Portugueza-Judaica. Dictionnaire bibliographique des auteurs juifs, de leurs ouvrages espagnols et portugais et des œuvres sur et contre les juifs et le judaïsme. Large 8vo. pp. 155. *Strassburg*, 1890. 6*s.*

With a collection of Spanish proverbs.

**Koenigsberger (B.)**—Die Quellen des Halachah. Vol. I. Midrasch. 8vo. pp. 131. *Berlin*, 1890. 2*s.* 6*d.*

**Kremer (A. v.)**—Studien zur vergleichenden Culturgeschichte, vorzueglich nach arabischen Quellen. Parts 1 and 2. 8vo. *Leipzig*, 1890. 1*s.* 6*d.*

**La Chute des Allompra** ou la fin du royaume d'Ava, resumé de l'histoire diplomatique de l'annexion de la Haute Birmanie, 1884-86. With 6 Coloured Maps. 8vo. *Paris*, 1890. 4*s.*

Leclerq (J.)—Du Caucase aux monts Alaï (Transcaspie, Boukharie, Ferganah). With a Map. 12mo. *Paris*, 1890. 3s.

Legrain (G.)—Le livre des transformations. Papyrus démotique 3452 du Louvre. Translated, with Notes and a Glossary. 4to. and 14 plates in portfolio. *Paris*, 1890. 10s.

Liber (Jeremiae).—Textum Masoreticum acuratissime expressit, e fontibus Masore varie illustravit, notis criticis confirmavit S. Baer et Delitzsch. Large 8vo. pp. 147. *Leipzig*, 1890. 1s. 6d.

Manassewitsch (B.)—Die Kunst die arabische Sprache durch Selbstunterricht schnell und leicht zu erlernen. 8vo. *Vienna*, 1890. 2s.

Margoliouth (D. S.)—An Essay on the Place of Ecclesiasticus in Semitic Literature. 16mo. 1890. 2s. 6d.

Milloué (L. de).—Précis de l'histoire des religions ; Védisme, Brahmanisme, Bouddhisme, Indouisme, etc. With 20 plates. Small 8vo. *Paris*, 1890. 3s.
*.* Bibliothèque de vulgarisation, Vol. II.

Mittheilungen aus den orientalischen Sammlungen der Koeniglichen Museen zu Berlin. Vol. II. Folio, 58 Plates, *Berlin*, 1890. £1 4s.
*.* Contents : Thontafelfund von El Amarna. Part 1. Edited by Winkler.

Muir (J.)—Original Sanskrit Texts on the Origin and History of the People of India. Vol. I. 3rd Edition. Post 8vo. cloth, pp. 544. 1890. £1 1s.

Nathan (filius Jechielis).—Aruch completum, sive lexicon, vocabula et res, quae in libris Targumicis, Talmudicis et Midraschicis continentur, explicans. Edited by Kohut. Vol. VI. Large 8vo. pp. 400. *Leipzig*, 1890. £1.

Oates (E. W.)—The Fauna of British India, including Ceylon and Burma. Edited by Blanford. Vol. I. Birds. 8vo. cloth. 1890. £1 1s.

Paris (C.)—Voyage d'exploration de Hué en Cochin-Chine par la route mandarine. 8vo. *Paris*, 1890. 7s.

Pinart (A. L.)—Vocabulario Castellano-Cuna. Square 12mo. *Panama*. 4s.

Pincott (F.)—The Hindi Manual. Comprising a Grammar of the Hindi Language, both Literary and Provincial. a Complete Syntax, Exercises in various styles of Hindi Composition, Dialogues on Several Subjects, and Complete Vocabulary. New Edition. 8vo. cloth. 1890. 6s.

Radloff (W.)—Versuch eines Woerterbuches der Tuerkdialecte. Part 3. 4to. pp. 641–960. *Leipzig*. 3s.

Rawlinson (G.) — Ancient Egypt. Fifth Edition. Post 8vo. cloth, pp. 410. 1890. 5s.

Reinisch (L.) — Die Kunama-Sprache in Nordost-Afrika. Part 2. Large 8vo. pp. 96. *Leipzig*, 1890. 2s.

Rice (H.)—Native Life in Southern India. Illustrated. Crown 8vo. cloth. 1890. 3s. 6d.
*.* Account of the Manners, Customs, Castes and Sects, Religion and Mode of Worship, Education and Mission Progress among the people of Southern India.

Ritchie (J. E.)—An Australian Ramble; or, a Summer in Australia. Crown 8vo. cloth. 1890. 5s.

Scheil (P. V.)—Inscription assyrienne archaïque de Samsi-Rammân IV. roi d'Assyrie (824–811). Text with Translation and Notes. 4to. pp. 68. *Paris*, 1889. 7s.
*.* A. H. Sayce wrote to P. Scheil : "The inscription is geographically so important, that it well deserved the thorough treatment which it has received at your hands, and you have conferred a benefit on Assyriology by the work."

Schlegel (G.)—Nederlandsch-Chineesch Woordenboek. Vol. IV. Part 3. 8vo. *Leiden*. £1 15s.

Schmidt (R.)—Vier Erzaehlungen aus der Çukasaptati. Sanskrit und German. 8vo. pp. 52. *Kiel*, 1890. 2s.

Scott (A.)—Buddhism and Christianity. 8vo. *Edinburgh*, 1890. 7s. 6d.

Seidel (A.) — Praktische Grammatik der persischen Sprache, mit Lesestuecken und Woerterbuch. 8vo. pp. 192. *Vienna*, 1890. 2s.
*.* Forms Bibliothek der Sprachenkunde, Vol. 26.

Selous (F. C.)—A Hunter's Wanderings in Africa. Being a Narrative of Nine Years spent amongst the Game in the Far Interior of South Africa. With 19 Plates. 8vo. pp. 450. 1890. 18s.

Smith (R. P.)—Thesaurus syriacus. A Syriac Lexicon. Part 8. Folio, pp. 2762–3347. *Oxford*, 1890. £1 16s.

Société d'Ethnographie. Mémoires de la section orientale. Vol. IX. Parts 1 and 2. 8vo. *Paris*, 1890. 6s.

Société Océanienne. Mémoires de la Société. Part I. 8vo. Paris, 1890. 2s. 6d.

Stanley's Briefe ueber Emin Pascha's Befreiung. Edited by J. S. Keltie. Translated into German by H. v. Wobeser, with a Map. 10th edition. *Leipzig*, 1890. 1s. 6d.

Strassmaier (J. N.)—Babylonische Texte. Part 7, 250 autographed pages. *Leipzig*, 1890. £1 1s.
*.* Contains the Inscriptions of Cyrus, King of Babylon (538–529), copied from the original tables in the British Museum.

Tavernier (J. B.)—Travels in India. From the Original French Edition of 1676, with a Biographical Sketch of the Author, Notes, Appendices, etc. Two vols. 8vo. cloth. 1890. £1 16s.

Vial (P.)—De la langue et de l'écriture indigènes au Yun-Nan. 8vo. *Paris*, 1890. 2s.

Vienna Oriental Journal.—Edited by the Directors of the Oriental Institute of the University. Vol. IV. Four parts. 8vo. *Vienna*, 1890. 10s. 6d.

Vossion (M.)—Grammaire birmane d'après A. Judson. 18mo. cloth. *Paris*, 1890. 10s.

Young (F.)—A Winter Tour in South Africa. 8vo. cloth. 1890. 7s. 6d.

---

# New Oriental Literature.

## BRITISH INDIA AND BURMA.

Apte (V. S.)—Student's Sanskrit-English Dictionary. Large 8vo. cloth, pp. 1024. *Poona*, 1890. 18s.
*.* Contains Appendices on Sanskrit Prosody and important literary and geographical names in the ancient history of India.

Dave (Harikrishna Lálshankar)—Short History of Gondal (State in Káthiávád, which passed, in 1870, under British Management). Crown 8vo. pp. 202. *Bombay*, 1889. 5s.

Dnyáneshvari. Oblong, pp. 588. *Poona*, 1889. 12s. 6d.
*.* It is a commentary on the Bhagavat Gitá, held in great veneration, and perhaps the oldest Maráthi work in existence. Written in Maráthi.

Dvivedi (Manilál Nabhubhái)—Siddhánta Sára (Substance of the "Established Truth"). Royal 16mo. pp. 436. *Bombay*, 1889. 9s.
*.* A review of religious and philosophic thought in India, advancing the claims of the Advaita system of philosophy or the doctrine of identity of the universal spirit and matter. The work bears evidence of much research on the subject, and of being the result of close thought. Written in Gujaráti.

Gangádhar (Sarasvati)—Guru Charitra. New Edition. Royal 8vo. 372 leaves. *Bombay*, 1889. 10s.
*.* A very popular book, containing mythological stories and descriptions of Bráhmanical duties. The book is held in great veneration by the people, and the reading is regarded as a religious act of great merit and efficacy. In Marathi.

**Grantha Ratna Málá.**—Edited by Uddhav Shástri Ainápure. Vol. II. Royal 12mo. *Bombay*. Yearly subscription price for 12 monthly parts of about 60 pp. 5*s.* each.

*₀* Contains rare, popular, and hitherto unpublished Sanskrit works belonging to the different branches of literature, with commentaries or with critical and explanatory notes.

**Harish Chandra Kalá.**—Complete Works, edited by Ramdin Sinha. Vol. IV. Part II. (Text and Translation of Sadíya Sarvasva). Vol. IV. Part III. (Text and Translation of 100 aphorisms of Shandilya; Sarbottama stotra; Bhaktamálá, part ii.; Utsabábali, and a discourse on Vaishnabism in India). Vol. IV. Part IV. (Introduction to the Puranas). 8vo. *Bankipore*, 1889. 3*s.* each part.

**Kabiratna (Shyámá Charan)**—Sudhákar Byákaran. 12mo. pp. 294. *Calcutta*, 1889. 4*s.* 6*d.*

*₀* A Sanskrit Grammar based on the system of Pandit Iswarachandra Vidyáságara. A list of grammatical roots is appended.

**Kálidasá's Abhijnánashakuntala.** Acts I. to VII. complete. Edited with a Preface, a close English Translation, and Various Readings, Notes, etc. Royal 12mo. pp. 500. *Poona*, 1889. 6*s.*

*₀* With three appendices, containing the construction of the drama, the story of the drama as given in the Máhábhárat Purán and definition of the metres as occurring in the original text.

**Luiz Gomes (F.)**—The Brahmans. Translated from the Portuguese by J. do Silva. 8vo. pp. 189. *Bombay*, 1889. 3*s.* 6*d.*

*₀* A delineation of Anglo-Indian society previous to the Mutiny of 1857.

**Mandali (Murkar)**—Jaimini Ashvamedha Kathárasa, áni Hindunchen Práchin Vaibhao. Demy 8vo. pp. 268. *Bombay*, 1889. 4*s.* 6*d.*

*₀* The story of the Horse-sacrifice said to have been made by the Pándavas. Annexed is a short paper on the ancient glory of the Hindus, asserting that they were much advanced in arts and sciences, social, political, religious and moral life. Written in Maráthi.

**Modi (Jivanji Jamsedji)**—Bhavishyani Jindagi athavá Átmánum Amarpanum. Demy 8vo. pp. 229. *Bombay*, 1889. 10*s.* 6*d.*

*₀* A comprehensive work on the immortality of the soul. Written in Gujaráti.

**Murray.**—Avifauna of British India and its Dependencies. With Index and many Plain and Coloured Plates. Two Vols. 8vo. wrapper, pp. 880. *Bombay*, 1887–90. £4.

**Nilmani Mukherji.**—Subjects of Examination in the Bengali Language, appointed by the Senate of the Calcutta University for the Entrance Examination for 1890. 8vo. pp. 154. *Calcutta*, 1889. 5*s.*

*₀* Selected from a large number of standard Bengali works in prose and poetry.

**Pharmacographia Indica.**—A History of the Principal Drugs of Vegetable Origin met with in British India. By W. Dymock, Warden, and Hooper. Vol. I. Part 1, post 8vo. pp. 1–304, *Bombay*, 1888. 10*s.* Vol. I. Pt. 2, post 8vo. pp. 305 to 599. *Bombay*, 1890. 10*s.*

**Prabhákar (Shástri).**—Mádhyandini shakhi yotsargopákarma. Oblong, 71 leaves. *Bombay*, 1889. 2*s.* 6*d.*

*₀* The ancient Brahmans studied the Vedas only for six months every year, and commenced and ended their studies through religious ceremonies which are here described according to the Mádhyandina Shákhá of the Yajurveda. Written in Sanskrit.

**Raghurája (Sinha).**—Bhaktamálá; or, Lives of Saints. Super-royal 8vo. pp. 926. *Bombay*, 1889. 12*s.* 6*d.*

*₀* Short account of some of the ancient and modern Hindu saints, collected from Puráns or gathered from traditions. Written in Hindi.

**Rámkrishna Vásudev Shástri Talekar.**—Alankára Darpana. 8vo. pp. 60. 1889. 1*s.* 6*d.*

*₀* Defining and illustrating different figures of speech to be frequently met with in Maráthi poetry. Written in Maráthi.

**Selections from the Records of the Hlutdaw.** Burmese Text. Compiled by Taw Sein Ko, Government Translator, and published by Authority. Large 8vo. boards. *Rangoon*, 1889. 7*s.* 6*d.*

*₀* Contents: Royal Orders.—Laws and Regulations.—Civil Proceedings.—Criminal Proceedings.—Correspondence between the Hlutdaw and the Provincial Officials.—Papers relating to the Shan States.—Ecclesiastic Papers.—Memoranda and Instructions.

**Shrimachchhankaráchárya Charitra.**—By Shrikrishna Shástri Áthalye. Demy 12mo. pp. 152. *Bombay*, 1889. 2*s.* 6*d.*

*₀* Life of the celebrated teacher of the Vedánt philosophy, and author of several works on it, who lived 2000 years ago. Written in Maráthi.

**Suryaram Desái (Ichchárám)** — Hind (India) and Britannia. A Political Allegorical Drama. Demy 8vo. pp. 200. 1889. 4*s.* 6*d.*

*₀* The language, tone and sentiments are sometimes severe. The work is dedicated to Lord Ripon. Written in Gujaráti.

### PERIODICALS.

**English Opinion on India.** — Monthly Periodical. Royal 8vo. *Poona*. Yearly subscription, 15*s.*

*₀* Extracts from articles on Indian political and other questions of the day, published by newspapers and periodicals in England. Written in English.

**Journal of the Bombay Natural History Society.** Edited by H. M. Phipson. Vol. IV. No. 1, pp. 82; No. 2, pp. 80. *Calcutta*, 1889. 6*s.* 9*d.* each part.

*₀* Aims at the advancement of the pursuit of Zoology, Botany, and Geology in all its branches. Written in English.

**Quarterly Journal of the Poona Sárvajanik Sabhá.**—Vol. IX. Parts 3 and 4. 8vo. pp. 124. *Bombay*, 1889. 6*s.* 9*d.*

*₀* Contains the Proceedings of the Association and reviews and discussions on political and other important questions of the day. Written in English.

### ARABIC, PERSIAN, AND TURKISH.

**Abdul Karim Munshi.**—Dictionary of Anglo-Persian Homogeneous Words. Demy 8vo. pp. 68. *Bombay*, 1889. 3*s.*

*₀* A large collection of well-selected words having nearly the same sound and the same meaning arranged alphabetically and explained in English with their equivalents in Persian, illustrated with 1001 gems of Persian poetry, such as popular stanzas, couplets, distichs, hemistichs, enigmas, riddles, chronograms, proverbs, etc.

**Abu Abdulla Muhammad.**—Al Musnad o Lel Imam Safái. Folio, pp. 220. Lithographed. *Arrah*, 1889. 6*s.*

*₀* Standard work of Imam Sáfái's school of Sunnism, based on the Hadis.

**Annuaire Egyptien.** Administratif et commercial. First year for 1890. Large 8vo. wrapper, pp. 384. *Le Caire*, 1889. 12*s.*

*₀* It includes Le Caire, Alexandrie, Port Saïd, Suez, Ismaïla, and all smaller towns of Upper and Lower Egypt.

**Bis chatira.** 12mo. *Constantinople*, 1890. 1*s.*

**Faideli Kraat.** 12mo. *Constantinople*, 1890. 1*s.*

**Flaveli Avamil.** 12mo. *Constantinople*, 1889. 1*s.*

**Flaveli bina.** 12mo. *Constantinople*, 1890. 1*s.*

Hafiz Muhammad.—Abad Ul Mufrad. Folio, pp. 196. Lithographed. *Arrah*, 1889. 6*s*.

**** Lessons on morals and manners based on the Hadis.

Hafiz—English Translation and Explanatory Notes of Fifty Odes (Odes 251–300) by Hormasji Temulji Dádáchanji. Demy 8vo. pp. 76. *Bombay*, 1889. 4*s*.

**** The notes give meanings of difficult words, phrases and explanation of references and grammatical construction, name of the metre and mode of scanning each line.

Hedjire. 12mo. *Constantinople*, 1890. 1*s*.

Kendi Keudmé didikl. 12mo. *Constantinople*, 1890. 1*s*.

Kitabkhāna'l Abuzzia. Parts 1 to 82. 12mo. *Constantinople*, 1888–90. 10*d*. each part.

Kuftari Perischar. 12mo. *Constantinople*, 1890. 1*s*.

Leval talim. 12mo. *Constantinople*, 1890. 1*s*.

Medari Mukialemi. 12mo. *Constantinople*, 1889. 4*s*. 6*d*.

Merat ettrack. 12mo. *Constantinople*, 1890. 1*s*.

Nefaal i Osmani. 12mo. *Constantinople*, 1890. 1*s*.

Tepsirat-ul-Insam. 12mo. *Constantinople*, 1890. 1*s*.

Turkmin Kizi. 12mo. *Constantinople*, 1890. 2*s*. 6*d*.

Usul i Maishat. 12mo. *Constantinople*, 1890. 1*s*. 6*d*.

Zerafet. 12mo. *Constantinople*, 1890. 1*s*.

## CHINA, JAPAN, AND PHILIPPINE ISLANDS.

Doolittle's Vocabulary and Handbook of the Chinese Language. Two vols. *Shanghai*, 1890. £1 15*s*.; single vols. £1 1*s*. each.

**** Useful for those interested in Chinese antiquities and other matters of curiosity.

Gubbins (J. H.) — Dictionary of Chinese-Japanese Words in the Japanese Language. Part 1 (A to J). 8vo. *Tokyo*, 1890. 7*s*. 6*d*.

Journal of the College of Science Imperial University, Japan. 4to. in wrapper as published. *Tokyo*.

**** Vol. III. part 1 contains Jurassic plants from Kaga, Hida, and Echizen, by Matajiri Yokoyama; 66 pp. text, with 14 tinted plates. Pyroxenic Components in certain Volcanic Rocks from Bonin Island, by Yasushi Kikuchi; 23 pp. text, with plate. 1889. 7*s*. 6*d*.

Vol. III. part 2 contains the Eruption of Bandai-san, by J. Sekiya. pp. 82. With 10 folded Maps. 1889. 7*s*. 6*d*.

Laktaw (P. S.)—Lexico Tagalog. Vol. I. Hispano-Tagalog. Small 8vo. wrapper, pp. 620. *Manila*, 1889. 8*s*.

**** Vol. II. Tagalog-Castellaño in the press.

Pocket Chinese and English Vocabulary. By the Author of the Wan tzu tien. 12mo. *Shanghai*, 1889. 7*s*. 6*d*.

Pryer (H.)—Rhopalocera Nihonica: A Description of the Butterflies of Japan. Part 3 (end of the work). With three fine Coloured Plates, and text in English and Japanese. Small folio. *Yokohama*. £1 4*s*. Parts 1 and 2 £1 4*s*. each.

Sydenstricker (Rev. A.)—Exposition of the Construction and Idioms of Chinese Sentences as found in Colloquial Mandarin. 8vo. pp. 88. *Shanghai*, 1889. 5*s*.

Williams (S. W.)—Syallabic Dictionary of the Chinese Language. Third edition. *Shanghai*, 1890. £3 15*s*.

**** Arranged according to the Wu-fang Yuen Yin, with the pronunciation of the characters. This new corrected edition is just out.

---



### FOR THE YEAR 1888.

Abigulan (M.)—Turkish Letters. 8vo. *Constantinople*. (Berberian), 1888.

——— Manual of the Ottoman Language. 8vo. *Constantinople*, 1888.

About (E.)—The King of the Mountains. Translated from the French. pp. 300. *Venice*, 1888.

Agaiantz (L.)—Tork Angel; or, the Beautiful Hagkanusch. 8vo. pp. 41. *Tiflis*, 1888.

——— Aruthiun and Manuel. National Novel. Book I. Second edition. 8vo. pp. 128. *Tiflis*, 1888.

——— The Mother Tongue. Vol. II. 8vo. *Tiflis*, 1888.

Agaphirian (G.)—Religious and Moral Considerations. Translated from the German. Vol. I. and II. 8vo. *Valarschapat*, 1888.

"Agbur." Illustrated Monthly Review for Young People. Vol. VI. Edited by T. Nazariantz. *Tiflis*, 1888.

Alaniantz (G.)—The Doctrine of Religion. Vols. II. and III. 8vo. *Tiflis*, 1888.

**** The first volume has been published in Valarschapat.

"Ararat." Monthly Review. Vol. XXI. *Valarschapat*, 1888.

Araratian (A.)—Founding of the Provincial Educational Institutions. *Tiflis*, 1888.

"Arax." Illustrated Review. Vols. 1 and 2. Edited by Gulasniriantz. *St. Petersburg*, 1888.

**** This review is published half-yearly.

"Ardzagank." Weekly Paper. Vol. II. Edited by A. Havannissian. *Tiflis*, 1888.

"Aregak." A Weekly Paper. Vol. I. Edited by H. Ekinian. *New York*, 1888.

"Arevelian Mamul." A Monthly Review. Vol. XVI. Edited by M. Mamurian. *Smyrna*, 1888.

"Arevelk." Daily Paper. Vol. V. *Constantinople*. 1888.

"Armenia." Vols. III. and IV. Edited by M. Portukalian. *Marseilles*, 1888.

**** This paper is published twice a week.

Armenian - Turkish - French Dictionary. Seventh edition. pp. 300. *Constantinople*, 1888.

Aschik Djivani—Stories translated from the Turkish. Second edition. *Tiflis*, 1888.

"Avetaber." Weekly Paper. Vol. XLV. Edited by Barnem. *Constantinople*, 1888.

Ayvazian (A.)—Primer. *Tiflis*, 1888.

Ayvazian (B.)—From Dark Corners. *Tiflis*, 1888.

Bahtuhindir. — The Adventurer; or, The Poor Wanderer. pp. 120. *Tiflis*, 1888.

Barkhudariants (M.)—Review of Reviews. *Tiflis*, 1888.

Baronian (J.)—The Honest Beggar. *Constantinople*, 1888.

"Basmavep." Quarterly Journal. Vol. XLVI. *St. Lazaro*, 1888.

Bernstein. — Chemistry. Translated into Armenian by S. Muschelian. *Tiflis*, 1888.

Beyazian (J.)—Political Geography. Vol. II. *Constantinople*, 1888.

Biberdjian (A.)—Reading Book. Two Parts. *Constantinople*, 1888.

Biberdjian (S.)—A Short Geography. *Constantinople*, 1888.

Boyadjian (J.)—Arithmetic. *Constantinople*, 1888.

Broschiantz (P.) — Sos and Vardither. A Novel. Second edition. pp. 352. *Tiflis*, 1888.

Bülbülian (A.)—Funeral Oration. *Vienna (Mechitarists)*, 1888.

Calendar (Armenian) for the Year 1889. *Vienna*.

Calendar (Armenian) for the Year 1889. *Venice*.

Calendar (Armenian) for the Year 1889. *Constantinople*.

Calendar (Illustrated Armenian) for the Year 1889. By Nazarian. *Tiflis*.

Calendar (Armenian) for the Year 1889. Edited by the Central Library in Tiflis.

Carmen (Silva).—Piastra Arsa. Translated by Raschid. *Tiflis*, 1888.

Davithian (S.)—Guide for Translation. Volume I. *Constantinople*, 1888.

Demirdjibaschian (E.)—French-Armenian Dictionary. *Constantinople*, 1888.

"Diogenes' Lantern." A Weekly Journal. Edited by Aschdjean. *Constantinople*, 1888.

"Djaschak." Quarterly Review. In the Old-Armenian Language. Vol III. *Constantinople*, 1888.

Djedjizian (J.) — History of Alexander the Great. Translated from the English. *Constantinople*, 1888.

Dreams of Youth. *Constantinople*, 1888.

Dumas (Alex.)—The Necklace of the Queen. Translated from the French. Four volumes in one. pp. 122.

Durian (E.)—The Knowledge of Words. *Constantinople*, 1888.

"Dzahik." Half-Monthly Journal. Vol. II. Edited by Sakaian. *Constantinople*, 1888.

"Ekeletzi Hayastaniayz." A Weekly Paper. Vol. I. Edited by T. Djulfaëtzi. *Constantinople*, 1888.

Encyclica Leo. XIII.—In Armenian. *Roma*. 1888.

"Erkragunt." Monthly Journal. Vol. VI. Edited by E. Demirdjibaschian. *Constantinople*, 1888.

Erzenkian (E.) — Schoolbook of Armenian Notes. Third Edition. *Tiflis*, 1888.

Essayan (N.)—Morning and the Judgment of Time. *Constantinople*, 1888.

Ezekian (A.)—Poetry. 8vo. *Tiflis*, 1888.

Gabrielian (S.)—The Past and the Present of the Armenian Evangelical Church. pp. 60. *Constantinople*, 1888.

Garden (The Spiritual).—Prayer-book. *Constantinople*, 1888.

"Grakan Scharjum." Monthly Journal. Vol. VI. Edited by E. Demirdjibaschian. *Constantinople*, 1888.

Gulamiriantz (A. S.)—Pedagogical Enterprise. pp. 80. *Erivan*, 1888.

"Hantess Amsorya." Monthly Journal. Vol. II. *Vienna*, 1888.

"Hantess Grakan." Edited by M. Barkhudariantz. Vol I. pp. 386. *Moskau*, 1888.

 *₊* Published half-yearly.

Haruthiuniantz (S.)—Poetry. *Tiflis*, 1888.

Haykazuni (H.)—The Death and Biography of Raffi. pp. 28. *Tiflis*, 1888.

"Hayrenik." Weekly Paper. *Constantinople*.

Hindlian (J.)—Peculiarities of the French Language. Fasc. 4 to 6. *Constantinople*, 1888.

——— Solid New Method of the French Problem. Vol. II. *Constantinople*, 1888.

"Hntschak." Monthly Paper. *Montpellier*, 1888.

——— Weekly Paper. Vol. II. Edited by G. Papagian. *Constantinople*, 1888.

Hoffmann.—Abraham Lincoln. Translated by Ter. Sargsian. pp. 144. *Schuscha*, 1888.

Hovhandjaniantz (K.) — Abas. Drama. pp. 64. *Venice*, 1888.

Hovhannissian (A.)—Russian-Armenian Dictionary. Vol. I. (A to H). pp. 591. *Tiflis*, 1888.

Hovhannissian (M.)—The Consolation of the Crowd. A Poem. pp. 70. *Constantinople*, 1888.

Hovsepian (S.) — Turkish Songs. Second Series. *Constantinople*, 1888.

Hugo (Victor).—Les Misérables. Vol. VI. Translated by G. Tchilinguirian. *Constantinople*, 1888.

Jubilee (Fifty Years') of the Armenian Institution in Erivan. 8vo. *Tiflis*, 1888.

Kafthanian (P.)—Zoology. 8vo. *Venice*, 1888.

Kalenderian (M.)—Eve. Manual of Lady Tailoring. Vol. II. *Constantinople*, 1888.

Kamalian (B.)—Songs. *Tiflis*, 1888.

Kamaliantz (S.)—Dzovinar. A Tale. *Tiflis*, 1888.

Kamsarakan (T.)—The Teacher's Daughters. 8vo. *Constantinople*, 1888.

Kapamadjian (M.) — New Elementary Book of Armenian History. 8vo. *Constantinople*, 1888.

Kapamadjian (S.)—Extracts from well-known Authors. *Constantinople*, 1888.

Karakaschian (M. A.) — Small Grammar of the Armenian Language. 8vo. Ninth edition. *Constantinople*, 1888.

Kartalian (E.)—New Elementary Book of Arithmetic. *Constantinople*, 1889.

Ketschian (B.)—History of the Armenian Hospital in Constantinople. pp. 300. *Constantinople*, 1888.

---

*NOTICE TO CORRESPONDENTS.*

All communications should be addressed to the *Editor of "Trübner's Record,"* 57 and 59, Ludgate Hill, London, E.C., and they should be accompanied by the sender's name and address (not necessarily for publication). Every care will be taken with MSS., but the Editor cannot hold himself responsible for rejected communications, which—if to be returned to the sender—should be accompanied by postage. MS. should be legibly written, and on one side of the paper only. Books for review should be addressed to the Editor.

*NOTICE TO ADVERTISERS.*

All communications respecting advertisements should be addressed to Messrs. F. TALLIS AND SON, 22, Wellington Street, W.C. *Terms for the insertion of advertisements :—*

|  |  |  |  |
|---|---|---|---|
| WHOLE PAGE (ordinary position) | ... £5 | 5 | 0 |
| HALF PAGE  ,, | ,, | ... 2 15 | 0 |
| QUARTER PAGE  ,, | ,, | ... 1 10 | 0 |

Special positions per contract.

No. 250.

# TRÜBNER'S RECORD,

## A JOURNAL DEVOTED TO THE LITERATURE OF THE EAST.

WITH NOTES AND LISTS OF CURRENT

### American, European and Colonial Publications.

*Edited by Dr. Rost, of the India Office.*

OCTOBER, 1890.      THIRD SERIES. VOL. II. NO. 2.      PRICE 2s.

## MAHÂMAHOPÂDHYÂYA CHANDRAKÂNTA TARKÂLANKÂRA.

The decay of Sanskrit learning in Modern India has often been deplored. As a general observation the complaint is, no doubt, well founded. The number of men who are pandits in the old sense of the word are growing fewer ; and as a rule the pandits are contented to live on the splendid inheritance of their forefathers, and it is but rarely that any one attempts to advance sciences, some of which, like Philosophy, were once the peculiar boast of the learned men of India, a step beyond the point where they were left by his predecessors, it may be, some centuries ago.

There are, however, exceptions ; and it is a notable one among these to whom the present notice is intended to draw the attention of Sanskritists and students of Indian Philosophy in Europe.

Professor Chandrakânta Tarkâlankâra, Mahâmahopâdhyâya, of the Sanskrit College in Calcutta, traces his descent from Bhaṭṭa Nârâyaṇa, one of the five Brâhmans who, as tradition says, came to Bengal to officiate in certain sacrifices for King Âdisûra. He belongs to the Kânṭâdiyâ division of the Bandyopâdhyâyas (Banerjis), and thus his gotra is Sâṇḍilya. Like all the Râḍhî Brâhmans of Bengal, he is of the Kauthumî branch of the Sâma Veda. He comes of a very respectable family settled in Sherpur near Maimansing, where he was born in 1840. At one time the family had seen better days, and were known as the Chakravartis of Sânakala. It was the grandfather of Professor Chandrakânta who migrated from Sânakal to Sherpur. The Professor's father, Râdhâkânta Siddhânta Vâgîśa, was himself a man of learning, well known in his district ; and it was under his careful instruction that Chandrakânta was first introduced to the study of Sanskrit. After the death of his father, he was obliged to seek for tutors elsewhere, and he bent his steps to the famed indigenous University of Navadvîpa (Nadiyâ). There he studied Law (*smṛiti*) under Brajanâth Vidyâratna and Haridâs Śiromaṇi, the Philosophy of the Nyâya School under Srînandana Tarkavâgîśa and Prasanna Ch. Tarkaratna, and that

of the Vedantic School under Kâśinâth Śâstrî. About the age of twenty-four, having completed his studies, he opened a school (*tol*) of his own in his native village of Sherpur, and commenced teaching pupils, who, according to the custom of the country, received in his house not only free instruction, but also free board and lodging. It was after this that he devoted himself to mastering all the abstruser works on Hindû philosophy. In 1883 he was appointed to his Professorship in the Sanskrit College of Calcutta. He still keeps up his practice of entertaining private pupils, many of whom have honourably passed in the Sanskrit Title Examinations, and obtained degrees in the several Hindû Systems of Philosophy, also in Rhetoric, Law and Literature. The title of Mahâmahopâdhyâya, the highest literary distinction in the gift of the Indian Government, was bestowed on him in 1887, in commemoration of the Jubilee of her Majesty the Queen.

It will be seen from the preceding remarks, that Professor Chandrakânta's Sanskrit learning is of the most varied kind. He is also a voluminous writer on a variety of subjects. Some of his works in Literature are the Prabodha Sataka, the Yuvarâja Praśasti, the Satî Pariṇaya, the Kaumudî Sudhâkara, the Ânanda Taranginî, the Bhâva Pushpânjali. In Law, he has written the Gobhila Gṛihyasûtra Bhâshya, the Śrâddhakalpa Bhâshya, the Gṛihyâsangraha Bhâshya. In Grammar there is his Śikshâ and the Satyavatî Champû, both written in Bengali. In the Philosophy of the Vaiśeshika School he has written the Kusumânjali Ṭîkâ, the Tattvâvalî Saṭîkâ, and above all the Vaiśeshika Bhâshya. These are only the names of works that have been actually published. He has composed upwards of a dozen more, which are still awaiting publication. Moreover, the Professor is a distinguished editor in the Bibliotheca Indica, the well-known collection of Sanskrit works published by the Asiatic Society of Bengal. To that series he has contributed excellent editions of the Gobhila Gṛihya Sûtra, the Parâśara Mâdhava, the Kâla Mâdhava, the Nyâya Kusumânjali, and others.

But though the Mahâmahopâdhyâya is a varied

3

scholar and a voluminous writer, his speciality is Hindū Philosophy, and particularly that system which is known as the Vaiśeshika of Kaṇāda. It is this field in which he has shown himself to be a thinker of great ndependence, force, and originality ; and it will be his works in this branch of learning that will henceforth be classed with the standard works of old, and secure to his name undying fame.

The last remarks apply more particularly to his work which bears the name of Bhāshya, or Exposition, of the Vaiśeshika Sūtras. The Sūtras, or aphorisms, of the Vaiśeshika system of Philosophy, as is well known, are attributed to Kaṇāda. There are no early commentaries on these aphorisms extant. The earliest expository work known is a gloss, called Kiraṇāvali, by Udayana Āchārya,—a gloss not on the Sūtras themselves, but on a work called Padārtha Dharma Sangraha, generally, though not quite correctly, looked upon as a Vaiśeshika text-book. It is this gloss of Udayana which is accepted in Bengal as the orthodox and authoritative interpretation of Kaṇāda's aphorisms. The object of the author of the new Bhāshya is to show that Udayana and the prevalent school in some essential matters have misinterpreted and unjustifiably amplified the teaching of Kaṇāda, and that Udayana, being an adherent of the Nyāya system, has in fact, for objects of his own, adulterated the pure Vaiśeshika doctrine. The Bhāshya thus claims to set forth, for the first time, the doctrine of Kaṇāda in its pure and genuine form. This is the outcome of Professor Chandrakānta's mature thought and close study of the Vaiśeshika aphorisms. It marks a gradually accomplished revolution in his own views. For he was not always of this mind ; he commenced with an unquestioning belief in the orthodox interpretation. It was in this state of mind that he published his Tattvāvalī, a metrical work in the style of the old Kārikās, to which he added copious notes. In this work he fully explains and still upholds with every possible argument the Vaiśeshika doctrines as hitherto understood and accepted in Bengal. The work, when it appeared, was received with an eagerness unprecedented in the history of recent Sanskrit publications ; for it supplied the long-felt desideratum of a good text-book on the Vaiśeshika philosophy for beginners as well as more advanced students. Professor Chandrakānta's latest work, the Bhāshya, as will be readily understood, met with a different kind of reception,— with great joy and praise by some, with much doubt and opposition by others. Whether it will win its way, and revolutionize the teaching of the Vaiśeshika philosophy in Bengal and elsewhere, time only will show.

It is on account of this original and, to a certain extent, revolutionary character of his work, that the Professor calls it a Bhāshya. Among Indian Pandits various names are in use for expository works ; we have the *bhāshya*, the *vṛitti*, the *vivṛiti* or *vivaraṇa*, the *ṭīkā*, and so forth. But it is only the compiler of a bhāshya, whom the rules of learning permit, after he has explained every word and part of a word of his text, to put forth original reflections. Compilers of other kinds of commentaries must confine themselves to the accepted meaning.

The main points of difference between Chandrakānta and the prevalent school are the following :—

1. The orthodox view is that the Vaiśeshika system holds seven categories ( *padārthas*), viz. substance (*dravya*), quality (*guṇa*), action (*karma*), genus (*sāmānya*), individuality (*viśesha*), intimate relation (*samavāya*), and non-existence (*abhāva*). Chandrakānta maintains, that Kaṇāda only teaches the six first-named categories, and that the seventh is an unwarrantable addition of Udayana, which necessitates a higher classification into two categories, viz. existence (*bhāva*), inclusive of the six first named, and non-existence (*abhāva*). He holds that Kaṇāda does not ignore 'non-existence,' but that it is included in his category of 'quality'; for 'quality' is that which depends upon 'substance,' but is neither 'qualified' nor 'action'; and these characteristics are all applicable to 'non-existence.'

2. Substance, quality and action are the three primary categories ; the other three categories are included in them. According to Udayana these six categories are equally considered as primary.

3. According to the usual acceptation, 'substance' includes nine items, viz. earth, water, light, air, ether, mind, soul, time and space. Chandrakānta omits the two last named, which, he maintains, fall under 'ether' (*ākāśa*).

4. Chandrakānta, in opposition to the established school, maintains that 'air' (*vāyu*) has a form (*rūpa*).

5. By the prevalent school, gold and silver are classed as substances of 'light' (*tejah-padārtha*), because under any degree of heat they remain bright melted substances, but do not evaporate. But Chandrakānta maintains, that they are 'earth' substances (*prithivī-padārtha*), and differ in no way from such substances as lac, wax, etc.

6. According to him, 'soul' is an object of inference; it cannot be perceived. This is opposed to Udayana's views.

7. By Kaṇāda 'organism' or 'body' (*śarīra*) is divided into two kinds ; viz. those born from a womb (*yonija*) and those not so born (*ayonija*). According to Chandrakānta, *yoni* has a wider meaning and denotes any means of generation. He includes, there-

fore, organisms born from eggs or from filth (*aṇḍaja* and *svedaja*) among the *yonija* ; and the term *ayonija* to beings, who like the word- or mind-produced sons of Brahma, are born in an extra-natural way.

8. According to the established opinion, the 'supreme soul' (*paramâtmâ*) and the 'human soul' (*jîvâtmâ*) are different 'substances' (*padârthas*). But Chandrakânta holds, with the Vedântists, that they are the same substance. They appear to be different in phenomenal existence (*vyavahâra-daś'â*), but in reality they are one.

These are some of the most striking points in dispute between Chandrakânta and his great predecessor Udayana. To us in Europe, probably, the disputes will appear a piece of anachronism, reminding one of the barren wranglings of the by-gone scholastic philosophy. But in India the old Hindu philosophies are still living forces ; and what is especially noteworthy and cannot but appeal to our European sympathies is the sign, furnished by the Professor's Bhâshya, of a re-awakening of the ancient free spirit of keen inquiry into the great problems of existence and truth.

## BUDDHIST JATAKAS FROM THE BURMESE.

### By R. F. St. Andrew St. John.

#### Mahá Kappiṇṇa.

When our Lord was Mahá Kappiṇṇa, the King of the Apes, Devadatta in the form of a Brahman came in search of a lost ox, and losing his way fell into a ravine. Being unable to get out, and there being no one else to assist him, the King of the Apes descended into the ravine, and said, "Brahman, I will save you ; but as the cliffs are very high, I will first see what I can do with a rock the same weight that you are." Having taken up a rock the same size as the Brahman, he again went down into the ravine, and said, "Brahman, I can get you out ; do not be afraid." Then taking him on his back, he leapt up to the top of the cliff. On getting there, the Ape said, "I am very tired with my exertions, let me rest a little on your breast." As soon as the Ape was asleep, the Brahman thought, "I have come in search of a lost ox, and it is now very late ; it will be better for me to kill the Ape and take him home rather than return empty-handed." So he took a stone, and struck the Ape with it on the head, wounding him badly. The Ape sprang up with a start, and climbing into a tree, said, "Ah ! Brahman, you are indeed a villain ; if I had not got you out of the ravine, you would never have returned home alive ; and if I were not to show you the way, you could not get there. I dare not come down and walk with you on the ground, but will leap from tree to tree, and you may follow my blood-stains." Having thus shown him the road to the village, the Ape left him. However, when he was out of the Bodhisat's sight, the earth opened and swallowed the Brahman before he could reach his home.

#### The Wicked Doctor.

In time long past, when Brahmadatta was King in Báránasi, the Bodhisat was born in a certain village, and used to play with his companions under a banyan tree near the gate of the town.

One day a doctor of no great repute, who was unable to make his living, came out at that gate, and seeing a snake in the tree, thought thus, "I can get no employment in the city ; but if I were to cause this snake to bite one of these children and heal him, I should get a footing."

So he said to the Bodhisat, "If you were to see a starling, would you take it ?" On the Bodhisat answering that he would, the doctor said, "Is not that one up there asleep in the fork of the tree ?" The little Bodhisat, not knowing that there was a snake, seized it by the neck ; but as soon as he saw what it was, he gripped it firmly and threw it down quickly. The snake fell on the doctor and bit him so that he died. The people came to see what was the matter, and when they saw the dead doctor, they arrested the boys and took them before the King of Báránasi. Now, on the way, the Bodhisat said to the other boys, "Do not be afraid when you see the King, but be of cheerful countenance ; I will speak to him, and let him know how the matter stands." When the King saw that they were not frightened, but of a cheerful countenance, he asked, "How is it you look so happy ?" The Bodhisat answered : "My Lord King, in fear and weeping there is no advantage. If we weep, those enemies who see our faces rejoice and take courage. Wise men who understand the advantages of decision, though really afraid, do not show their fear and are not cast down ; so that, when their enemies behold their faces unaltered, they are themselves disturbed. O King, wise men when they are in danger endeavour to extricate themselves by one or other of the five 'expedients.' If they see a way by means of charms they use them ; but if not, they take the counsel of others and act on their advice. They effect their purpose with honied words or by giving presents, or by means of family connections. Verily if these five effect not their escape from a violent death, they shall not escape at all. Our future fate, as the result of what we have done, is sure and powerful. We cannot free ourselves from consequences, and therefore we should school ourselves to bear things without bewailing."

When the King heard this, he caused the matter to be examined into, and the Bodhisat related what had actually occurred. On seeing that they were not to blame, he caused the boys to be released from the stocks, bestowed great gifts on the Bodhisat, and promoted him to the post of Prime Minister.

*Note on the Láludáyi Játaka* (Vol. I. p. 175).—On looking through Fausböll's Collection (Vol. II. p. 164, and Five Játakas, pp. 8 and 31), I found this Játaka given as the Somadatta (Nos. 212 & 414 in the Ceylon list), and my friend Mr. E. Sibree, of the Oxford Indian Institute, has kindly favoured me with a translation. In the main the story is the same, but the gátá are different at the end. Instead of Appasutáyam puriso, balibaddo va jírati, etc. (Dhpada, v. 152, and the text of the story, called Láludáyittherassa vatthu, p. 317), Somadatta says :—

> Akási yoggam dhuvam appamatto
> Samvaccharam biraṇatthambhakasmim
> Vyákási maññaṁ parisaṁ viguyha
> Na niyyamo táyati appapaññan ti.

> Steadily attentive, thou didst right,
> For a year in (the cemetery) full of birana grass,
> Thou alteredst the chief word when thou enteredst the assembly,
> No training protects him who has little brains.

The Brahman answers :—

> Dvayam yácanako, táta
> Somadatta, nigacchati :
> Alábhaṁ dhanalábhañca,
> Evaṁ dhammá hi yácaná ti.

> He who asks, dear Somadatta,
> Runs (I say) a double risk,
> Wealth he gets not, or he gets it,
> This the nature is of asking.

---

## NEW JAINA INSCRIPTIONS FROM MATHURÁ.
### By G. Bühler.

A letter from Dr. A. Führer, dated Mathurá, 11th March, 1890, informs me that a liberal grant by the Government N. W. Provinces has enabled him to resume the excavation of the Śvetámbara temple under the Kankálí Tílá, and that the results of the working season of 1890 considerably surpass those of 1889.

In a little more than two months Dr. Führer obtained a large number of inscriptions, seventeen of which, according to the impressions accompanying his letter, undoubtedly belong to the Indo-Scythic period and furnish most important information regarding the history of the Jaina sect. He, moreover, discovered to the east of the Svetámbara temple a brick Stúpa, and to the west another large Jaina temple, which in his opinion belonged to the Digambara sect. The excavations on these sites yielded 80 images, 120 railing pillars and bars, and a considerable number of Toraṇas and other architectural ornaments, all of which are adorned by exquisite sculptures. He was thus enabled to forward to the Museum at Lakhnau 608 maunds or about a ton and a quarter of archaeological specimens.

Dr. Führer will in due time himself describe his archaeological treasures and make them known by illustrations. But the inscriptions, which he has kindly placed at my disposal, are, I think, well worthy of an immediate notice. They all belong to the class of short donative inscriptions, found on statues, pillars, Toraṇas and other sculptures, and closely resemble those discovered at Mathurá in former years by Sir A. Cunningham, Dr. Burgess, Mr. Growse and Dr. Führer himself. Their dates range between the year 5 of Devaputra Kanishka and the year 86 of the Indo-Scythic era, or assuming the latter to be identical with the Śaka era, between A.D. 83 and A.D. 164. The name of the second Indo-Scythic king Huvishka occurs twice. It is both times misspelt, being given in the one case as Huvashka and in the other as Huviksha. The dates of Huvishka are the years 40 and 44.

Eleven inscriptions give names of various subdivisions of the Jaina monks, mentioned in the Kalpasútra. The already known Váraṇa gaṇa or school, erroneously called Châraṇa in the Kalpasútra, is or rather was named (in one case it is mutilated) three times. Among its kulas, or families, the Aryya-Chetikiya or Aryya-Chetiya occurs twice and the Puśyamitrtya once. Both names turn up for the first time in epigraphic documents. They evidently correspond with the Ajja-Chedaya (in Sanskrit Árya-Chetaka) and the Púsamittijja (in Sanskrit Puśyamitrtya) kulas of the Kalpasútra. With the former kula are associated two śákhás or branches, the Vajanágarí and the Harttamálakadhí. The first is clearly identical with the Vajjanágarí śákhá of the Kalpasútra, and the second must be its Háritamálágárí śákhá. The latter name is certainly corrupt, and probably a mistake for Harttamálagadhí, from which the form of the inscription differs only by the not unusual Prakritic substitution of the surd *ka* for the sonant *ga*. Most of the names of the śákhás are derived from towns. If the proposed restoration is accepted, the name of this śákhá will mean " that of the fortress (gadha) of Harttamála, literally the field or site of Haríta."

Much more frequent in the new inscriptions is the name of the Koṭṭiya or Koṭṭikiya gaṇa, which, as I have shown in my former articles, corresponds with the Kotika or Kodiya gaṇa of the Jaina tradition. It occurs eleven times, and thrice it is combined with the well-known names of the Sthániya, Sthánikíya, or Tháṇiya kula (the Váṇija of the Kalpasútra) and of the Vairí or Vairá śákhá. In four inscriptions it is connected with two new names, that of the Brahmadásika kula, and that of the Uchchenágarí or Uchenágarí śákhá. The Uchchánágarí śákhá stands in the

Kalpasûtra first in the list of the sâkhâs of the Kotika gaṇa. But there is no exact equivalent for Brahmadâsika. The Kalpasûtra, however, mentions in connexion with the Kotika gaṇa a Bambhalijja kula (for which the commentators give the impossible Sanskrit equivalent Brahmaliptaka) and this Prakrit form can be shown to be a correct shortening of the longer name of the inscriptions. It is a general rule in Indian languages that so-called " Kosenamen," or names of endearment, may be formed from compound names by adding to their first part an affix like *ka, la* or *ila*, which serves to form diminutives, and by then omitting the second part. Thus we have Devaka, Devala or Devila, for Devadatta or Devagupta, Siyaka for Simhabhata, and Viśvala for Viśvamalla. According to this principle Brahmadâsa may become Brahmala, and its possessive adjective will be Brahmalîya, which latter is the regular Sanskrit representative of the Prakrit Bambhalijja. With this explanation the identity of the Brahmadâsika and the Bambhalijja kulas may be accepted without hesitation. I will add that the names Brahmadâsika and Uchchanâgarî occur too, the latter with a slight difference in spelling, on Sir A. Cunningham's Mathurâ inscription No. II. of the year 5 (Arch. Survey Reports, vol. iv. plate xiii.). The correct reading of line 2 of the second (recte the first) side is [ku]lâto Brahmadâsikâto Uchanâkarito. The *ld* is slightly disfigured on the facsimile, and instead of the last word we have ubhanakârito, which gives no meaning, and has led to a curious misconception regarding the purport of the document. The inscriptions mention also two sambhogas or district-communities, the Sirika and the Srîguha, or as perhaps it must be read, Srîgraha, which are both known from the inscriptions noticed formerly. In one case there is a mutilated name which looks like .ârina saṃbho[ga]. If we omit the latter, the new inscriptions prove the correctness of the Jaina tradition with respect to the early existence of six divisions of monks, not traced before, and they confirm some of the results obtained in former years.

In addition, they settle another very important question. According to the Śvetâmbara scriptures, women are allowed to become ascetics. But we have had hitherto no proof that this doctrine is really ancient. Dr. Führer's new finds leave no doubt that it was. Most of the Mathurâ inscriptions mention in the preamble the name of the donor's spiritual director, at whose request (nirvartana) the donation was made. Usually this person is characterized as an ascetic by the titles gaṇin and vâchaka, or by the epithet aryya 'the venerable.' The complete inscriptions found in former years show in this position invariably male names. Most of the new inscriptions resemble them in this respect, but some mention females, Aryya-Saṅgamikâ, the venerable Saṅgamikâ, Aryya-Śâmâ, the venerable Śyâmâ, and Aryya-Vasulâ, the venerable Vasulâ, as the persons at whose request the images or other sculptures were dedicated. The position in which these female names occur, as well as the epithet aryya, proves that we have to deal with Jaina nuns who were active in the interest of their faith. This discovery makes it very probable that the Jainas, as the Śvetâmbara tradition asserts, from the first allowed women to enter on the road to salvation, and that the supposition of some Orientalists, according to which the Śvetâmbaras imitated the Bauddhas in the practice mentioned, must be rejected as erroneous.

A closer examination of Dr. Führer's new inscription may possibly reveal other points of interest. But what I have been able to bring forward on a first inspection, certainly justifies the assertion that they are really most valuable, and that Dr. Führer has again laid the students of the religious history of India under deep obligation. I may add that, in my opinion, more may yet be expected from the Kankâlî Tîlâ. For the large temples which Dr. Führer has discovered must, I think, have contained longer inscriptions, recording the dates when, and the circumstance under which, they were built. I trust that the Government of the N. W. Provinces will enable Dr. Führer to resume his operations next year and to institute a careful search for these documents. Should the exploration of the Kankâlî Tîlâ, however, be complete, then the Chaubârâ mound ought to be attacked, because it undoubtedly hides the ruins of an ancient Vaishṇava temple and will yield documents elucidating the history of the hitherto much under-rated Bhâgavatas, a sect which is older than that of the Bauddhas and even than that of the Jainas.—Vienna, *5th April*, 1890.—[From the *Vienna Oriental Journal.*]

---

## THE POHIRAS, A NEW OR LITTLE KNOWN TRIBE IN SANTHALIA.

### By W. H. P. Driver.

The Pohiras derive their name from a corrupt pronunciation of the word "paharia" or hill man, and the pronunciation of this word is a good example of the peculiar dialect of Bengali (or Sanskrit), which they by many generations of seclusion have developed among themselves.

Their *Language*, though plainly of Bengali or Sanskritic origin, is as completely unintelligible to their modern Bengali-speaking neighbours of the plains as broad Scotch is to an ordinary Englishman. Many of the Kolarian languages are known to contain words of a purely Sanskritic origin, proving an intimacy between the Aborigines and the earliest Aryan settlers in India; and so a thorough investigation of the language of the Pohiras might go to prove that this language is a debased dialect of the pure Sanskrit spoken by the earliest Aryan settlers in this part of India. The following is a short list of words that I am unable to connect with any of the known languages of this district; also a list of names of both men and women.

| English. | Pohira. | Men's Names. | Women's Names. |
| --- | --- | --- | --- |
| Body | Gondia. | Pachu. | Paru. |
| Cat | Guni. | Aklu. | Ghasso. |
| Evening | Byar. | Potè. | Kandni. |
| Fence | Badar. | Bonu. | Koili. |
| Girl | Sasi pal. | Deba | Akli. |
| Hare | Susa. | Ambra. | Khandi. |
| Lie | Tanku-kahara. | Bijoi. | Gomhi. |
|  |  | Sobud. | Kachon. |
| 'Langoti' | Gojai. | Jhongu. | Sobni. |
| Mouth | Lolo. | Sorai. |  |
| Pestle | Leda. | Gura. |  |
| Squirrel | Gurguinda. | Rusn. |  |
| Star | Torongoin (s) |  |  |
| Tooth | Dar (s) |  |  |
| Tail | Lanj (s) |  |  |

*Origin and Tradition.*—The Pohiras as far as I know have never before been referred to by any European writers, and neither Europeans nor natives in this district (except a few villagers in their immediate neighbourhood) were hitherto aware of their existence.

E. Ball describes a tribe of Paharia Khasias as inhabiting the Dulmi hill in Manbhum. I questioned the Pohiras regarding that tribe, and they admitted a knowledge of their existence, but denied any affinity with them, and they said the Khasias spoke a different language which was as unintelligible to them as that of their present hill neighbours the Birhors. As all the Aboriginal tribes in their neighbourhood are more or less of Kolarian origin, we may presume that the Pohiras come of the same stock.

The only tradition I could get from them was that many generations ago they migrated to their present quarters from the "Dolmai" hill in the neighbouring district of Manbhum, and that they left a portion of their tribe behind.

*Habitat.*—There are only three small settlements of Pohiras, of three or four families each, within the district of Lohardagga, and they are all located amongst the hills and jungles of the extreme south-east corner. These settlements are near the villages of Peakuli, Araranga and Korlonda in the pargana of Tamar.

*Appearance.*—They are a very diminutive race, even when compared with the Birhors of the same district, but they have better features and lighter complexions. Their women are decently clad and

wear a few bead necklaces and brass bangles. The men wear the "kopin" of the country, and when they can afford it, a piece of cloth over their shoulders.

*Houses.*—They live in small rough huts covered with leaves instead of thatch. These are usually situated at foot of jungle-covered hills which they cultivate.

The Birhors, Korongas and Mundas are their nearest neighbours, but have little intercourse with them except when they visit a neighbouring market.

*Occupation.*—The Pohiras have neither cattle nor ploughs, and their cultivation consists of burning the jungle on the hills and planting seeds of Indian-corn, etc., amongst the ashes. Their agricultural implements consist of a small axe, an iron-pointed stick used for planting seeds and grubbing roots, and a small curved knife used for cutting crops, etc.

*Food.*—Such people are naturally dependent, to a great extent, on the products of the jungle, and they are not very particular as to what they eat. As far as I could learn, only snakes, lizards, crows, kites, and monkeys are forbidden them. Tiger's flesh is considered a delicacy, which, however, they are not often able to indulge in; for, as they remarked to me, the tiger generally eats them when they meet, their primitive weapons and puny strength being of little avail against the monarch of the forest.

*Religion.*—Superstition does not seem to have taken a strong hold of the Pohiras; and they have no priests of their own nor sacred places for altars. They, however, offer a few sacrifices themselves when the spirit moves them; and these functions are performed in front of their own houses. The Sun, as 'Dharam,' or 'Bera Deo,' receives a white fowl in October; their ancestors are remembered in March or April; and the spirits of the various hills have to be propitiated, every hill having a spirit of its own.

The Pohiras have no religious *festivals* of their own, but sometimes attend at those of their neighbours.

*Dances.*—They have two dances peculiar to themselves, the "Dand salia" and the "Korom salia"; but these are not so lively as the dances of either Mundas or Birhors. The style, however, is decidedly Kolarian. The women holding each other round the waist dance in a circle, singing at the same time, while the men beat their drums, and sing and gyrate in the centre. The old people sit round at a little distance, imbibing their home-brewed rice-beer, and every now and again give vent to their enjoyment by grunting, laughing, and pinching each other.

*Marriage Customs.*—The Pohiras do not celebrate their marriages with much ceremony. When a man fancies a girl, he sends a male friend to her father, there being already an understanding with the young woman. The mother is propitiated with a piece of cloth. When preliminaries are settled, the girl's father gives a feast, and the bridegroom, attended by his friends, pays the price of his bride (2s.) into the hands of his father-in-law in the presence of the whole company. He then puts "sindur" on the bride's forehead with his left hand little finger, and she marks him in the same manner. This concludes the ceremony, and the happy pair are at liberty to go off as soon as they like, the rest of the company sitting down to dinner.

Pohiras usually marry when both parties are full-grown. Widows and divorcees are allowed to re-marry, and polygamy is permitted, but not polyandry. Divorce is effected without ceremony, and so is a re-marriage. To prevent too much intermarriage, they have the custom of 'gotors'; no two people of the same 'gotor' being allowed to marry; but, owing to the smallness of their numbers, they do not always adhere strictly to this rule, and all first cousins are allowed to marry.

*Septs and totems.*—The following are the 'gotors' in the settlements I refer to, viz :—

Suor-pohira—Can't eat pigs.

Dhora-pohira.

Badur-pohira—Can't eat flying-foxes.

Gant juria.

Noira-soira—Can't eat honey.

Ghora-thira—Can't eat horses.

*Customs Relating to Children.*—Pohiras, although a poorly-fed and poorly-clad people, still have large families; but twins are never heard of. Children adopt the 'gotor' of the father, and property descends to male heirs only. After childbirth the mother is considered unclean for nine days. After that time she bathes, and the child is named—usually after its grand-parents. At this function a feast is provided by the parents, to which all friends and relations are invited. Boys at the age of eight or ten have the 'sika' marks burnt on their fore-arms, and girls at about the same age are tattooed with an arrow mark on the forehead, and a star on the side of the nose; but this is only when their parents are enterprising enough to undertake a journey to Barabhum, a 'parganna' in the adjoining district of Manbhum, where there are female practitioners in the art of tattooing. Otherwise the girls' faces remain unornamented.

*Death Customs.*—After a death the nearest relatives give a feast to which all friends are invited, and one of their own number acts as barber. The Pohiras usually bury their dead, but those who die of fever are burnt. Their graves are covered over with stones to prevent wild animals from digging up the remains. Pohiras have very hazy ideas of a future state and do not seem to care very much what happens then. They say there are 'ojhas' or diviners amongst their tribe in Manbhum.

---

## NOTES ON THE SUPERSTITIOUS BELIEFS CURRENT IN THE *SUNDARBANDS*.

By Pandit Hara Prasāda Shāstrī.

The Sundarbands are peopled by tigers, rhinoceroses, crocodiles, cobras and other ferocious animals. But the rich forest produce of the *Bunds* has attracted the attention of merchants from remote antiquity. The Banias and traders of India are remarkable for their susceptibility to superstitious fears. Unaided by the scientific knowledge and appliances, which the forest department possess at the present day, they ventured into the wilds of the Sundarbands in the hope of gain. As they had no human appliances to keep them safe from the dangers of that terrible wilderness, they conceived of mythical personages, who would protect them. Every part of the Sundarbands has its own peculiar guardian saint or divinity, and my object in this paper is to give an account of some of these mythical beings.

As a matter of course the Hindu deities precede Muhammadan saints and are supplanted and dispossessed by them. The oldest deities are Kaloo Rai and Dakhin Rai. Kaloo Rai is believed to be the person from whom many of the aboriginal tribes claim their descent. Whenever a man has to do a deed of valour or enterprise, he worships Kaloo and sacrifices a goat to him. Kaloo is in many places the presiding deity of brick-kilns, and is propitiated before setting fire to the kiln. Though Kaloo Rai is worshipped in the Sundarbands, also his rival Dakhin Rai, a Brahmin by caste, is considered as peculiarly the guardian of the Sundarbands. In order to attract people to his jungly dominion, he is said to have created wax, honey, *sundri* wood, and other articles of trade, chiefly obtainable in these forests. He had an immense stature, rode on tigers, and was fond of human sacrifices. He is the lord of crocodiles and other wild sea-animals. Before the arrival of Muhammadan saints, he was the lord and master of the entire area from the borders of Backergunje to Diamond Harbour. But Muhammadan Pirs and Kazis established themselves in forest lands at the same time that their co-religionists were occupying the more civilized and inhabited tracts of the neighbouring countries. The Shah of Bhangore appears to be one of the oldest and most respectable of these Pirs. He occupied one of the corners of the forest, but lived in constant dread of Dakhin Rai and his great minister Sanaton. Chand Sha was also a great personage. His dominion extended down to *Andhar Manik.* He also held a definite portion of the forest and lived in peace with Dakhin Rai. But the greatest of these beings, who is regarded by the Mussalman traders as the empress of the *Sundarbands,* and to whom the others acknowledge their fealty, is Bonbibé. Her capital is at Bhoorcoond, and the extent of her demised land is accurately defined. It is called *Atharobhati* or Eighteen days' voyage. It is bounded by Ero Jole on the south. From thence to Bhobanipúr, thence by crossing Balakhal to Rájápúr, thence to Biyali, to Makhangachcha Asari, Mayenadanga, Amlani and Hasnabad. Thence to Patali with the Kala Khali as the final boundary. She governs this portion of the forest and keeps her *Jagirdars* under control with the assistance of her brother and general Sha Jangúli, who also is one of her principal *Jagirdars.* She obtained a lease of all those forests from the Durbar of Allah. She was in fact one of the most famous houris of Behestha, and God sent her to earth with the special object of establishing her sway over the Sundarbands.

In the neighbourhood of Mecca there lived a pious Musulman named Behram. He had a beautiful wife named Fúlbibi. But she bore him no child. He prayed at the *Darga* and came to know that his wife was barren ; but that if he would take another wife, he was sure to be a father in a short time. He acquainted his wife with this piece of divine intelligence and asked her permission to marry again, promising to do anything for her in lieu of this permission. She gave her permission, but on condition that he would grant the request that she might make at some future time. Thus obtaining permission, poor Behram married Gulal Bibi, and his new wife was in a short time in the family way. When she was in an advanced state of pregnancy, Fúlbibi requested her husband to abandon her co-wife in the forest. The poor man was compelled by his own promise to do so. There in the forest Gulal Bibi gave birth to two children, one male and another female, who were known afterwards as Bonbibi and Sha Jangúli. The helpless mother picked up the male child and joined a caravan which was passing by. Bonbibi was left alone. She remembered Allah, who despatched four of his houris to take care of her. They managed to place her in the hands of her mother in a short time. The mother and daughter grew old. They went to Medina and asked for permission to do some work. The priests there ordered them to proceed to Bengal in India and to take possession of their allotted *Jagir* in the *Sundarbands.* Before entering the forests they came across the Shah of Bhangore, who warned them against the great power and influence of Dakhin Rai. Nothing daunted, they

proceeded to the capital of the Rai and challenged him to fight. Dakhin Rai was quite equal to the occasion, and determined to accept the challenge. But his mother Narayani advised him not to do so. Males, she argued, should not fight ladies. If successful, it would bring them no glory ; but if defeated, they would be covered with shame and dishonour. She offered to accept the challenge herself and the fight began. The duel was terrible. They fought for several days with varying success. By the blessing of Allah, however, Bonbibi ultimately prevailed. She graciously accepted Narayani as one of her female friends, and agreed to leave Kandokhali in the possession of her son. This settlement is said to be still in force.

Bonbibi was anxious that her worship should spread. She took a poor fellow named Dooka, of the village of Baridhati, under her special protection. He was one of the crew in the fleet of a rich merchant named Dhona, who by the favour of Dakhin Rai obtained an immense quantity of valuable forest produce on the condition of making over Dooka as a sacrifice to him. Dooka was left in the forest alone, and Dakhin Rai was on the point of devouring him in the form of a tiger, when Dooka cried to Bonbibi for help, and she appeared on the scene. She upbraided Dakhin Rai as a *Rakshas,* and wanted to dispossess him of *Kandokhali.* But Pir Gazi, who has his dominions beyond the deep sea (his name is Barakhan, and his father was Saba Sekandor), interceded in his behalf and reminded her of her vow of friendship with Narayani, Dakhin Rai's mother. She relented, but compelled Dakhin Rai to pay Dooka a vast amount of wealth. Dooka returned to his native land and began to celebrate the worship of Bonbibi with great pomp and splendour. Though made a Chowdhiry, he with an axe hanging from his neck begged milk of seven neighbouring villages, made *Kshira* of it, and distributed it to his neighbours, and this is the mode of worshipping Bonbibi.

---

## THE EXCAVATED TEMPLE AT NÚRPÚR.

By Chas. J. Rodgers, Archæological Survey, Panjab.

During my tour in the beginning of 1886, I discovered a temple hidden under a mound in the fort of Núrpúr. A short description of it, in anticipation of the publication of a fuller report in the Records of the Archæological Survey, may not be without interest.

The temple is 116 feet 10 inches long and 49 feet broad. It lies pretty nearly north and south. It consists of three rooms. The entrance is in the west side and into the central room. The southern room had four cells in it, one in each corner. Two have entirely disappeared. The roof of the third one is gone, and the fourth is still partly roofed. Only the outer walls of the building now remain. The upper part was ruthlessly thrown down. Earth was thrown on the ruins to hide them, and so thoroughly were they hidden, that, when we held the fort from 1849 to 1857, an English officer, finding the site the highest in the fort, built his house on it.

The chief beauty of the temple is its outer walls. Only the plinth of the south room is left. It is ornamented by a band of leaves, both at the top and bottom. This leaf ornament is common on the buildings of the time of Jahāngīr. From the commencement of the wall of the two cells adjoining the central room the outer walls rise several feet, and from this place the sculptures on them commence.

Commencing from the foundations, the plinth consists of two courses of sculptured stones and an ogee moulding on the slope of which were elephants fighting (these are all defaced). Above this was a thick moulding worked with a zigzag pattern. Over this came a band of grotesque winged heads. This was surmounted by a broad band of sculptured figures of animals and men. Above this again are broad plain bands ornamented with elaborate half lotuses. This continues to the entrance to the temple which was over a small arch.

On the outer walls on the west side of the temple, north of the entrance, the grotesque winged heads change into a very ugly head, such as no beast owns. Over the band of sculptured figures, come now two bands ; one, most elaborately carved half lotuses and leaf ornament ; the other, of exquisite diaper work. These two courses are separated by a thin band on which ducks are sculptured in some parts and peacocks in others. Over these again in one part is a thick semicircular moulding on which is a floral pattern deeply cut.

At the north end of the temple from the N.E. the top semicircular moulding is absent. But the sculpture is finer and there is more of it.

The *singhāsan* or god throne to the north of the central room, is most elaborately sculptured and is one piece of fine red sandstone. In front is a carpet of the same kind of stone on which are carved shells and tassels. Looking over this is seen the innermost room with its singhāsan, made after the fashion of the outer walls, only on a smaller scale. The whole of the walls of this room are wainscotted, *i.e.* divided into panels, the frames of which are beautifully sculptured.

There were many idols found in the *débris*, both inside and outside of the temple, but all were more or less defaced. In fact there is not an image the head of which has not been knocked off.

Built on the N.E. wall there is a suite of three rooms. These are plain and are an addition. The sculpture under them is not spoiled. I believe that were these rooms to be taken down the walls of the temple now hidden would come out perfect. I allowed them to remain because I wished the building to remain exactly as when it was first excavated.

So far as I can ascertain the temple was commenced in the reign of Jahāngīr and never finished. In the time of Shāh Jahān, when the fort was taken by Murād Bakhsh, an order was given to leave the buildings in the fort as they were. But in the reign of Aurangzeb an order was issued to destroy all temples in the hills. The temples in Chamba escaped. But this one in Nūrpūr must have been destroyed then, for not one of the oldest inhabitants had ever heard from their forefathers that such a thing as a temple was ever in that part of the fort where it is situated.

The idol worshipped in it was Krishna. The same idol is now in a wooden temple at the far end of the fort.

My reason for thinking it was never finished is this : the fine thick semicircular top moulding is found only on two portions of the walls. No piece was found in the *débris*. So I conclude the builders got no further than this height of wall. The rebellion of Jagat Singh and his subsequent adventures in Kabul and Gazni and Khost and Andarāb must have swallowed up all the means of the Rāja, and of course prevented him attending to the work personally. That it was thrown down carefully is shown by the fact that although the stones were joined together by iron clamps, only a few were found in the *débris*.

---

## A TRADITION OF LOHARDAGGA, CHOTA NAGPORE.

### By W. H. P. DRIVER.

The 'Dit' rajas were descended from 'Vikramaditya,' and they came into Chota Nagpore from the south-east. They used to live in forts, and were accustomed to work in their fields with their own hands, as the Kols would not pay them any rent. They worshipped the 'Khanda' or straight-sword, which was generally placed on the top of a hill. The 'Dit' rajas disappeared in the south-east of Lohardagga about the same time as the 'Nagbansis' appeared in the north-west of that district. The following information was given me by the 'Munda-Pahan' (priest) of 'Pahartoli' village of Belkadi parganna in Lohardagga :—

"I am a Munda by caste and the 'Pahan' of Pahartoli and my ancestors, for many generations, have been the 'Pahans' of this village. My name is 'Karma,' and I am about 70 years of age. I offer sacrifices at the village 'Sarna' (spirit grove), and also at the top of the hill. In Pahartoli, at the foot of the hill, there are the ruins of a fort called Belkadi-Garh. My ancestors have handed down a tradition that this fort belonged to a 'Dit' raja named 'Hatti-Lal.' Now-a-days our 'Konda Naik,' who is a 'Khandit-Paik-Bhunya' by caste, offers every year, in the month of January, a sacrifice of a black he-goat to the 'Belkadi-Paht-Deota,' on the top of the hill. Formerly one 'Bechu,' a 'Baraik' by caste, who is now dead, used to offer this sacrifice.

"'Hatti-Lal' had a brother named 'Majhi-Lal,' who had a fort at Tettragarh village, about one mile and a half to the west of Pahartoli.

"At Tettragarh the priests have for generations been Uraons by caste. Just now 'Jura-Mahto' is priest; previous to him there was 'Tamba-Mahto,' and before 'Tamba' there was one 'Kaila-Mahto.' 'Jura-Mahto' offers his sacrifices on the 'Bisua-Paht,' where there is a 'Mandil.' The sacrifice consists of a buffalo, and it is offered yearly in August at the time of the 'Dassain' festival. At Dimba village in Doisa parganna, about four miles west of Pahartoli, there is a hill on which a yearly sacrifice of a he-goat or ram is offered to the 'Paht-Khanda-Deota.' The present priest there is a 'Khandit-Paik-Bhunya' by caste, and he is the son of 'Jerka Amant.' At the foot of the Dimba hill are the remains of a fort which tradition says belonged to the 'Dit' rajas."

There are no traces, as far as I can learn, of the 'Dit' rajas in this district further north than Belkadi parganna, but there are the remains of forts ascribed to them in the villages of Siri and Saridkel in the south-east of this district (Lohardagga). The Rajas of Siri-Garh and Saridkel-Garh are said to have disappeared in the 'Tajna' river, which is now only a small rivulet, but was in those days a deep river known as the 'Rani-Da.' There were also some 'Dit'-rajas in Icha-garh in Manbhum, and they are said to have drowned themselves in the 'Chatta-Pokhir' tank near the village of 'Dulmi.'

---

## HINDU FOLK-LORE.

According to a transatlantic philosopher, the proper study of mankind is woman. Next to her perhaps we may place man, and especially man in his social aspect. Few themes indeed are more interesting than the home-life of a people—their folk-lore and superstitions, their carefully cherished legends and traditions, and the proverbs and sayings—"the experience of many and the wisdom of one"—which circulate amongst them as the highest expression of truth, abstract and concrete, in a plain, homely, and old-fashioned dress. Such a

study with regard to Hindoo home life has just been made by Rai Bahadur Kaccoo Mal Manucha, chairman of the Fyzabad Municipal Board, and well known in Oudh as a legal practitioner of no small culture. In the preface to a modest little volume just issued from the London Printing Press at Lucknow, he tells us that while he was enjoying the calm repose of a Civil Court vacation by the cool banks of the Ganges at Hardwar, it occurred to him, from what he observed there as an every-day occurrence, that if a few notes on religious beliefs, social customs, superstition and folklore, proverbs and sayings, puns, riddles, aphorisms, and other miscellaneous matters in common vogue among the Hindoo community generally, and among the country people especially, were brought together, they would "aid a great deal in throwing light upon the hitherto partially explored regions of the mode of life led by the common people." This task, an agreeable but by no means an easy one, Mr. Manucha accordingly set himself, and the little volume before us is the outcome of his efforts. So far as we are able to judge, he has done his work excellently well; at any rate, he has succeeded in producing a most interesting book, and one which should enjoy no small meed of popularity. In the compass of something over a hundred pages, he has gathered together a little of everything that his preface promises, and very curious and characteristic some of it is. We learn, for instance, that if a person is drowned, struck by lightning, bitten by a snake, or poisoned, or loses his life by any kind of accident, or by suicide, then he goes usually to hell. If he die naturally on a bed or a roof, he becomes a *Bhut*, or evil spirit, and with this belief care is taken on the approach of death to move the person carefully on to the floor. The earth is believed to be resting on the horn of a cow, and the raised trunks of eight elephants, called *Diggaj*, or "elephants supporting the regions," and each of the cardinal and sub-cardinal points of the compass has its appropriate guardian. An eclipse is produced by the occasional swallowing up of the sun or moon by the severed head of Ráhu, son of a demon family, who was decapitated by Vishnu for disguising himself as a god and drinking *Amrita*, or nectar. To come to more social matters, we learn that to take a leaf of grass in the mouth is to ask forgiveness, after which to inflict any injury is considered very bad form. Great care is taken to fulfil a promise; but when a promise is repeated three times, it becomes irrevocable, and cannot be broken under dire penalties. Ill will also ensue to the man who shaves on a Monday, Tuesday, Thursday, or Saturday; Tuesday is an especially dangerous day, as in all probability death by the dagger will result from shaving then. At the birth of a child iron in some form or other must be tied to the bed for forty days to keep away the evil spirit, while no marriage will prove fortunate unless a string with seven knots, called *kangná*, is tied round the left hand of the bride and the right hand of the bridegroom. All these things are matters rather of religious belief than of social tradition, but the folklore of the Hindoos is equally curious. Ants, for instance, are held to bless a person with wealth and children if sugar mixed with flour be cast into their haunts. A broom must always be laid flat, or it will bring ill-luck; if you shake your cap, you will get headache; dead bodies if kept in the house during the night grow in size and sit up; if a woman throws away the combings of her hair without spitting upon them, her husband will become unfaithful; if you drink milk or carry perfumes at night, nymphs and fairies will smite you with their shadows; if you love a person who has the bad taste not to love you in return, a little owl's flesh administered to the unresponsive one will bring you love in abundance; and so on and on. We shall quote the whole volume before we exhaust the singular wealth of popular superstitions that Mr. Manucha has here collected for us.

It is, however, in its proverbs and sayings that we find the most characteristic side of Hindoo home life. Once within the realm of these familiar aphorisms, it is not difficult to understand and appreciate the people among whom they are household words, for there is no closer indication of national habits of thought and ways of life than the little bits of oracular wisdom which are in everybody's mouth. Naturally much of the proverbial philosophy of the Hindoo finds a parity in Western sayings, as well as in those of still further East. "Adhá títar, ádhá bater," for instance, literally half partridge, half quail, finds its literary corollary in "neither fish, flesh, fowl, nor good red herring," while

Admí batore gharí gharí
Ishwar lejae ek gharí

has its parallel in many countries. "One hatches the eggs, another carries off the offspring," (Ande sewe koi, bachche lewe koi), will match very well with "Fools build houses for wise men to live in." "Ande ke háth bater," however, "A blind man catching a quail," is more racy of the soil; and "Baniye ki gon men nau man ká dhokhá," "Nine maunds short in a Banya's grain sack," is still more so. "Andhou men káne rájá" (One-eyed is a king among the blind), "Apni gali men kutta bhí sher" (A dog is a lion in its own street), "Asharfíyán luten, koelon par muhar," (Gold squandered, coal sealed up), and "Ek panth, do kaj," (One way, two works), are all old friends in an Eastern dress.

" Tan yahí, man yahí, nainan yahí subháo
Are jawání báorí, ek bar phir ao,"

finds something of a parallel in Horace's (and another's) *Eheu fugaces, postume, postume*—"The days of my youth they are lost to me, lost to me!" Nearly literally rendered the lines run, "Body, mind, and eyes are the same; O wild youth, come back to me once more." Perhaps, too, in "Tant bájá, rág bujhá," (No sooner string sounded than tune discovered), we may discover the rudiments of "No sooner did he open his mouth than he put his foot in it." Of religious aphorisms there are many in the collection before us, and some of them are very curious. Here for instance: "Ját pánt púchche ná koe, Har ko bhaje so Har ká hoe"—None should enquire about caste or creed; he who worships God is His servant. And again (though curious in a different sense this time), "Rám jharokhe baith ke sabká mujrá le, jaisí jiskí chákri waisá usko de," God sitting in a window watches all, and according to the work of each gives wages. Here, too, is a metrical aphorism peculiarly characteristic of Hindooism, though somewhat contrary to the ethics of Christianity:

Age ke din píchhe gae
Har se kiyo na het ;
Ab pachhtáe kyá hot hai
Jab cheríyán chug gain khet ?

rendered in almost literal prose by "Past days have gone by: you made no love to God then; what is the good of repenting now when the birds have eaten away the fields?"

Some of these Hindoo sayings have a flavour almost Rochfoucauldian. "Jíw lewe, jiwaká na lewe"—one may deprive one of his life but not of his livelihood; "Jorú na játa, Ishwar se nátá"—no wife and no grindstone, he'd better be friends with God; "Dhol, ganwár, súd, pasu, narí; yih sab tárná ke adhikárí" —a drum, a rustic, a servant, a beast, and a woman —all these go on right when struck; "Daulatwále ka bhút har jotátá hai"—at the rich man's plough a goblin works; "Ek nár jab do se phansí, jaise sattar waise assí"—if a woman flirts with two men she will with seventy or eighty; "Wuh bhalámánas kaisá, jiske pás nahín paisá?"—how can he be a gentleman who has no pice?; and finally: "Samai pare parakhíye chár: dhíraj, dharm, mitra aur nár" —falling in adversity, test four: patience, duty, friend, and wife. The Baniya, as will have been noticed, has rather a rough time of it in these proverbs; no opportunity is lost in aiming an aphoristic blow at him, and the Mussulman fares little better. "Jis ka Baniyá haigá jár, us ko dushman kyá dark ár?" —what need has he of an enemy that has a Baniya for a friend? "Diyá dán, diyá dán; phir mánge to Musalman"—what is given is given; to ask it back is to act like a Mussulman. Nor is the fakir spared: "Kanthí bándhe Har mile, to bandá bándhe kunda"—

if one can find God by wearing wooden beads, I will put a log round my neck. So in the proverbs of social ethics in this Hindoo collection, we have "Learning, king, creeping plant, woman—these reckon upon no caste or creed; whoever keeps near them they always cling to him." We are warned to keep clear of horny, canine, and feline beasts, and of a drunkard, a king and a woman. We are told that "Woman, land, and riches, all three are roots of quarrel," and that "A woman's wiles no one knows —after killing her husband she will herself become *suttee*"—Triyá charitra na jane koe, khasam márke sattí hoe. *Bis dat qui cito dat* finds a parallel in "Turt dán mahá kalyán"—ready gift is a great virtue; "Sab ko ek lakri hánkná," is tarring with the same brush—"all with one stick driven." In another vein, but equally characteristic is the metric :

Prit na jáne pí ki ját,
Nind na jáne túti khát.
Bhukh na jáne bási bhát,
Piyás na jáne dhobi ghát.

"Love enquires not about the beloved's caste,
Sleep cares not if the bed be broken,
Hunger will not refuse stale rice,
Thirst minds not the laundry water."

"Living in huts and dreaming of palaces," and "Never having seen a mat, dreams of a bed," are also curiously characteristic; while "Jaisá doge, waisa paoge," is as near to "As you sow, so you shall reap," as "Jab tak sáns, tab tak ás," is to "Dum spiro, spero"—and that is very near indeed. Borrowing money, picking quarrels, fostering conceit, encouraging hope, fighting against fate, indolence, "bluffing," ambition, covetousness, humility, foolishness, all find here their appropriate aphoristic condemnation, and proverb *con* jostles proverb *pro* with the same delightful inconsequence as in our English sayings. Here is an instance *pro* : Huqqá Har ká ládlá, rakhe sab ká mán ; Bhári Sabha men yún phire jas Gopin men Kánh—"The pipe is the beloved of God and pleases every one ; it moves in the assembly like Krishna among the milkmaids ; " and here is an instance *con* : Huqqá se hurmat gaí, gaí láj sub chhút ; Sab ká jhúthá piyat hain, gaí hiye kí phút —"With the smoking of pipe honour departs and modesty forsakes ; they smoke it defiled by all so blind of mind do they become." But we have quoted too much already ; for the rest we must refer the reader to Mr. Manucha's book itself, which may be studied with no little pleasure as well as profit.—[*Times of India.*]

New Books.

*Archaeological Survey of India. The Sharqi Architecture of Jaunpur ; with Notes on Zafarabad, Sahet-Mahet and other Places in the N. W. Provinces and Oudh.* By A. Führer, Ph.D. With Drawings and Architectural Descriptions by Ed. W. Smith. Edited by Jas. Burgess, Director-General of the Archaeological Survey of India. (Trübner, London.)

Fergusson distinguishes thirteen separate styles of Indian Saracenic Architecture, every one of which would in his opinion deserve a monograph. The Sharqi Architecture of Jaunpur (1394–1486 A.D.) represents one of these styles, and the historian of Indian Architecture adds that the Mohammedan buildings of Jaunpur are hardly surpassed by those of any city in India for magnificence, and by none for a well-marked individuality of treatment. It is this style which Dr. Burgess has chosen for the subject of the first instalment of his new series of Archaeological Reports, and for describing which he has been able to secure the assistance of such able and trained collaborators as Dr. Führer and Mr. Ed. W. Smith. Dr. Burgess, according to his own statement, has contented himself with the modest task of uniting the archaeological and architectural labours of his assistants into one connected account, and of supervising the printing. It will be permitted to conjecture, however, that Dr. Burgess has devised the whole plan of the work under notice, and has throughout directed the labours of his assistants.

Of the 73 plates, which form the most prominent feature of this Report, almost one-half relates to the Jámi Masjid, one-third to the Atala Masjid, and the remaining ones to the Lál Darwáza Masjid and other buildings of minor importance. The plates are extremely well finished, and they do not only convey a very fair general idea of the buildings, but they abound in ground plans, and upper plans, sections, panels, details of pillars, of screen roofs, etc. A future historian of Indian Architecture will find his task very much facilitated by these careful and reliable reproductions of the Jaunpur antiquities. Besides the plates, Mr. E. W. Smith has supplied accurate architectural descriptions, especially of the Atala Masjid. The materials thus furnished for an elucidation of various difficult points connected with the origin and development of the Jaunpur style are highly valuable for the history of Architecture generally.

The bulk of the letterpress is by Dr. Führer, whose detailed and tasteful account of the history of Jaunpur and its buildings is very pleasant reading. Dr. Führer has succeeded in collecting no less than forty-six inscriptions during his tour in 1886, the majority of which belong to Jaunpur. He was naturally obliged to a great extent to go again over ground already trodden, and we are not sufficiently acquainted with everything that has been printed elsewhere on the subject of the Jaunpur antiquities to be able to say precisely how much is new in Dr. Führer's account of Jaunpur. His is certainly the most comprehensive account hitherto published of that remarkable place.

He was quite right too in embodying in his part of the work the inscriptions, including those already printed, especially the Persian and Arabic ones ; and we have to congratulate Dr. Führer on his acquirements in a new field, his first laurels having been gained in the field of Sanskrit and Páli scholarship. In several instances he was able to give better readings of the inscriptions than those published by Sir A. Cunningham. The longer Sanskrit inscriptions only have been reserved for publication in the *Epigraphia Indica*, that well-known storehouse of Indian Epigraphy. The names and dates recorded in the inscriptions afford a reliable starting-point for all the questions of monumental archaeology connected with Jaunpur.

The hostile dynasties of Delhi and Jaunpur, in spite of the short duration of the Sharqi greatness, were rivals in architecture as well as in power. Nothing can be more original, in the Jaunpur style, than the lofty propylon with sloping walls hiding a single dome and supplying the place of a minaret. As for the domes, we quite agree with the joint authors of the work under review that there is very little evidence of the Buddhists having ever built domes anywhere, and that the first employment of domes and their adjuncts as an imposing part of a range of buildings belongs to the Pathán architects of Jaunpur. A careful examination of the pillars in the Atala Masjid has yielded the result that it contains but few pillars of undoubtedly Hindu origin (Plates xxi.-xxiii.), whether they may have previously belonged to a Buddhistic, a Jaina, or a Brahmanical temple. Although, therefore, there is historical evidence to show that the Atala Masjid was erected on the site of an ancient temple of Ataladeví, the result of the present researches tends to corroborate Fergusson's view that nearly the whole of the present building is really Ibráhím's work. If there should have been Buddhist cloisters, it is evident that no part of them was left untouched by Ibráhím. The Lál Darwáza mosque contains a comparatively large number of genuine Hindu pillars, and the important dated Sanskrit inscription found on one of them proves that pillar, and with it probably many others, to have been brought from an old Benares temple ; but the design of the building is decidedly Saracenic. The curious masons' marks, a full collection of which is exhibited on two plates in the work under notice, are evidently due to Hindu workmen, but it is difficult to decide whether the pillars so marked were re-used by the Mohammedan builders of Jaunpur, or made at the time of the construction of the mosques for the places now occupied by them. Judging from analogous cases in Greek architecture, we would suggest that the 'masons' marks' might be due to the owners of the quarries used for erecting the pillars and buildings. No doubt the workmen employed by the princes of the Sharqi dynasty were natives of India, as may be gathered from their Devanágarí inscriptions, and this fact may be taken to account for the use of the old Hindu ornaments in Mohammedan buildings. On the other hand, the present investigations seem to support the view taken by Sir A. Cunningham when he questions the truth of Fergusson's remark that "nine-tenths at least

of the pillars in these mosques" were *not* taken from Hindu shrines, but made for the purpose.

The most important among the various problems concerning the monumental archaeology of Jaunpur, we mean the origin of its curious blending of the Hindu and Saracenic styles, has been finally solved in this handsome and beautifully illustrated volume.

Dr. Führer has not confined his investigations to Jaunpur, but has visited and described several other towns of his district, which is equally rich in Islamitic and in Buddhistic remains, including as it does the original home of Buddhism. His visit to Sáhet-Mahet has enabled him to collect a number of lac and clay seals, inscribed in the Gupta character, and two copper coins, apparently of the Suṅga dynasty. Dr. Hoey's Buddhistic Sanskrit inscription from Sáhet-Mahet is extremely interesting, as it proves the continued existence of Buddhism in Magadha down to the thirteenth century. The original slab is at present in the Lucknow Museum, of which Dr. Führer is the Curator, and he was enabled in consequence to supply a valuable facsimile of it. In other respects, however, his annotated edition and translation of the inscription in question agrees almost word for word with Professor Kielhorn's paper on the same inscription, in the Indian Antiquary for March, 1888, pp. 61—64, and we do not see why Dr. Führer has nowhere referred to the paper of his predecessor. The text, as printed by Dr. Führer, is not faultless ; thus in line 1-2, *read* ashta, niyamya, sákyasimho, sa tvám, gírvánaváṇínám. As regards the name of the locality mentioned in the inscription, Dr. Führer is probably right in spelling it Ajávriṣha rather than Jávriṣha, the former name making better Sanskrit than the latter. But as for his proposed identification of Ajávriṣha with Srávastí, are we to believe that the latter name, which was still in use in the times of Hiouen Thsang, should have been dropped during the Middle Ages and revived again in modern times ?

There is every reason to believe that Sáhet or Sét, the first part of the name, has been derived from Srávastí or Sávatthi, through the various intermediate forms pointed out by Sir A. Cunningham, the discoverer of the place, see Journ. As. S. B. vol. xxxiv. p. 253. Moreover, though the slab containing the inscription has been found at Sáhet-Máhet, the stratum in which it was discovered is said to indicate that it had been placed in a restored building.

Bhuíla Tál would be even more important for the history of Buddhism than Sáhet-Máhet, if it could actually be proved to have been Kapilavastu, the birthplace of its founder. Dr. Führer has inspected all the places supposed to be identical with the sites referred to by Hiouen Thsang, but a careful examination of them has caused him to embrace the opinion of those scholars who have rejected the attempted identification of Bhuíla Tál with Kapilavastu. The true site of Hiouen Thsang's Kapilavastu remains to be sought, but even this negative result is important, especially as it is based on evidence collected on the spot. It may not be out of place to mention here that Dr. Führer, as noted by Prof. Bühler in the Vienna

Oriental Journal, has recently excavated at Mathurâ a number of highly interesting Jaina inscriptions and sculptures.

Whoever cares for the progress of Indian Archaeology must wish that Dr. Burgess may soon be able to go on with this excellent new series of Reports, the first volume of which may indeed be said to be 'exhaustive and final on the subjects treated' in it.

J. J.

[We append to the above notice, which deals with Dr. Führer's work from an epigraphic and philological point of view, an excellent article by an architectural authority, Mr. W. H. White, which we take the liberty of reprinting from "The Journal of Proceedings of the Royal Institute of British Architects," vol. vi. New Series, No. 17, p. 377.]

Dr. Burgess, the Director-General of the Archæological Survey of India, is to be heartily congratulated upon the first volume of the new Series of Reports begun after the reorganization of the Archæological Surveys in Upper India some five years ago. This volume, presented last April, is an eminently business-like production, of practical value to the architect and archæologist—which could not always be said of earlier Reports—and possessed of many attractions from the historical and the artistic points of view, rendering the book instructive and interesting to the educated public in general. To use Dr. Burgess's words :—" The bulk of the letterpress is by Dr. Führer, whose trained and varied scholarship is a sufficient guarantee for its accuracy and research. The architectural descriptions of the buildings were prepared by Mr. Smith. My work has been to unite these into one connected account, to supervise the printing, and pass the drawings through the press." In so uniting the two sets of materials the editor has, no doubt, controlled individual expressions of opinion by his own wider experience as an expert, and so added to the authority of the work. The plates have been produced by various processes at the Survey of India Office, in Calcutta.

The first chapter of this volume is devoted to the history of Jaunpûr from the beginning of the fourteenth century to the close of the sixteenth century, and is mainly an account of the Sharqî dynasty ; its later history is continued in the second chapter. The buildings of Jaunpûr described and illustrated are the great bridge over the Gûmtî, an excellent view of which forms the frontispiece of the volume ; the Atala Mosque, the Khalis Mukhlis and Jhanjhri Mosques, the Lâl Darwâza Mosque, the City Mosque, and some minor mosques and tombs. The plates, seventy-three in number, are no mere sketches, but architectural plans, sections, elevations and details, drawn to scale, and quite fit to put into competent workmen's hands for execution. It is to be regretted that no geometrical drawings are given of the great bridge of Jaunpûr, described as "its most useful if not its most beautiful buildings" ; the smallness of the staff of draughtsmen allowed by the Government probably prevented Mr. Smith from securing these and other desiderata in the time at his disposal. From the inscriptions, cut in Persian upon the grey sandstone of the Bridge, and

translated by Dr. Führer, it appears that "this magnificent building and splendid foundation was successfully completed . . . in the reign of the great king, emperor, high representative of the emblem of Royalty, shadow of God, the great conqueror . . . Akbar"—described as "Bâdshah" in this inscription, and as "Abûl Ghâzi" instead of "Abûl Fath." Again, that "this lofty bridge was completed under the superintendence of the great Shaikh, just to men, Khwâja Shaikh Nizâm-i-Nizâm-ad-dîn . . . and under the guidance of the unparalleled architect Afzal Ãlî Kâbulî." And again, that "Khân Khânân Munim Khân, the generous, built this bridge by the grace of God. He is named Munim ['one who confers benefits'] because he is gracious and merciful to the people. His *Sirât-al-mustaqîm* ['the established path' of the Muhammadan to Paradise, the 'narrow' path of the Christian] leads the thoroughfare towards the gardens of Heaven. You will find its date if you will deduct the word '*bad*' from '*Sirât-al-mustaqîm*' "—the value of the letters of this word is 981, and the value of those of "bad" is six—thus : 981 — 6 = 975 A.H. = 1567-68 A.D. The story of the origin of the great bridge is that Akbar during a boating excursion saw a poor widow on the bank of the river, lamenting loudly she could not be ferried over ; and the Emperor, having taken her over, ordered boats to be stationed at the landing-place for the future, adding some remarks disparaging to local rulers who had preferred to build mosques rather than bridges ; and with such effect that Munim Khân soon after pledged himself to erect a bridge to mark the place of Akbar's adventure with the widow. Munim Khân's munificent gift measures some 330 feet within the inner faces of the abutments ; it has ten arches, the four central arches being of perceptibly wider span than the others, and the piers are 14 feet in thickness. The neighbourhood appears to have been peculiarly fortunate in respect of bridges, for which the unused materials prepared for Munim's great bridge over the Gûmtî, another bridge was built, in 1569, over the Sâî, eight miles west of Jaunpûr, carrying the 'Allâhâbâd road at a height of twenty-five feet above the winter water-level, and reached by embankments of approach on either side. An earlier bridge, 10½ miles south-east of Jaunpûr, was built in 1510, by Jalâl, son of Sikandar [Alexander] Lodî : it has nine pointed arches, and carries the Banâras road over the Sâî to Jalâlpûr.

The Fort of Jaunpûr is an irregular quadrangle on the north bank of the river Gûmtî : its external walls are of considerable height, and an eastern gateway, its main entrance, is described as resembling "one of the great propylons in front of the masjids [mosques]; the walls batter, and the general design is the same." The Jaunpûr propylons are exceptional in India. A "photo-etching" is given of the gateway and its loop-holed bastions, which have many affinities to the mediæval fortifications of Western Europe.

The Mosque of Ibrâhîm Nâib Bârbak in the Fort is also referred to, with a desire principally as I understand it, to correct technical inaccuracies respecting it in previous Reports issued under the direction of General Cunningham, whose post Dr. Burgess has ably filled. A lât or minar, which stands within it, bears an Arabic inscription, of April, 1376, and is stated to be apparently wholly unaltered from the date of its erection. A translation of this inscription was first published by the late Dr. Blochmann in 1875, but in an incomplete form ; the volume under review gives it in full, the original rubbings having been probably defective. The spirit running through this inscription cannot but be interesting to architects, many of whom doubtless wish that the faith of both Christian and Muhammadan was as pure to-day as in the Middle Ages ; so I venture to extract a part of it, with the words recovered by Dr. Führer given in italics :—" In the name of God, the merciful, the clement. 'Surely, he will build the mosques of God who believes in God and the last day.' "And the Prophet—blessings upon him !—says : 'He who builds a mosque for God will receive from God *a house in Paradise in lieu of every stone and beam used in the mosque.' So, according to the holy writ and the word of the Prophet, peace upon him ! which refers to the erection of mosques, in hope of going to Paradise and gaining salvation, the erection of this mosque in the fort was ordered by* the mighty, the high, the king of the kings of the world, the just, the generous, and great ruler, the lord of the necks of nations, the master of the kings of Arabia and Persia, who professes the exalted 'creed and seizes the firm handle *of the sword,* who watches over God's faith, protects God's lands, and defends God's servants, who gives the faithful peace and security, the heir of the kingdom of Solomon *strengthened* by the *grace of God*, Abûl Muzaffar Fîrûz Shâh, the King. . . . ." The remainder also has lacunæ filled up from recent investigation, and the inscription terminates with the date of the completion of the building, namely, "the exalted month Zi'l Qa'dâh in the year 778 of the Flight of the Prophet" [April, 1376 A.D.].

The Atala Mosque is a most interesting structure, if only because it is typical of a style peculiar to, or perhaps peculiarly characteristic of, the best buildings in Jaunpûr, which have "a gate-pyramid or propylon of almost Egyptian manner and outline." * They have also sloping walls, and an arrangement of plan which in Jaunpûr appears to have been an innovation "quickly perfected and hardly imitated elsewhere," to use Dr. Burgess's words. The twenty-one plates illustrating this mosque are valuable geometrical drawings in pen-and-ink ; and the two (Plates XI. and XVII.) executed by Mr. Edmd. W. Smith himself are excellent renderings, to an inch scale, of Indian ornament executed in the latter half of the fourteenth century, and possessing strange affinity to the mediæval work of Western Europe. The description of this building, which Fergusson considered "the most ornate and most beautiful" of the three principal mosques remaining at Jaunpûr, is given principally by Mr. Smith, on pages 32–40 of the volume.

The sixth chapter is devoted to a description of the Lâl [red] Darwâza [gate] Mosque, so called, it is stated, in memory of the "high gate painted with vermilion"

pertaining to a palace built at the same period close by. Fifteen plates are given, two of which are from photographs, the remainder being geometrical drawings of the same character and excellence as those already mentioned. The inscriptions found bear several and remote dates, equivalent in one instance to A.D. 1071 ; in another to Wednesday, 27th March, A.D. 1168 ; and in another to Wednesday, 15th May, A.D. 1296 ; but the column on which the latter appears also bears a date equivalent to A.D. 1447—this being probably, it is assumed, a record of the date of the erection of the cloisters. The stones used in the construction of the Lâl Darwâza Mosque—from the evidence of some fallen blocks lying about—originally formed parts of Hindû or Buddhist buildings, like all the other similar buildings in Jaunpûr—in fact, like all the old Muhammadan buildings in North-Western India and other parts of the Eastern world. Consequently the inscriptions referred to afford no direct clue to the date of the erection of the present building, nor can the inscription (No. XXVII.) recorded on a pillar of the north-west cloister—"Visadru's son, Kamaû, the architect "—be regarded as having been cut in the time of the Muhammadan rule. It is much more likely to be a record of the Hindû architect who erected the building from which the inscribed stone was torn, though there can be no doubt, as stated on page 51 of the volume, that the cause of the admixture of Hindû and Muhammadan styles in the Jaunpûr mosques was the employment of Hindû masons as chief workmen.

A description of the City Mosque—the Jâmi' [chief] Masjid,† as it is called—occupies the seventh chapter. It is a work of the fifteenth century, probably the latter half, and is stated to have been completed during the reign of Mahmûd Shâh Sharqî, though a native historian attributes its completion to Husain Shâh, whose final abandonment of Jaunpûr, after defeat, took place about A.D. 1749. The photographic view of the mosque proper, taken from the courtyard

* Fergusson's *History of Indian and Eastern Architecture*, pp. 520–525. Murray, 1876.

† The varieties of spelling adopted by different authorities on Indian subjects render their study most difficult to those who, like the writer, have a very slight acquaintance with the Hindûstânî alphabet and grammar. Fergusson spelt most of the Indian names he had to refer to as they are pronounced; in describing the City or Chief Mosque of Jaunpûr, he spelt " Jumma Musjid, Jaunpore." though " jumma "·means literally " Friday," the Muhammadan Sunday. The author of Murray's *Handbook of the Bengal Presidency*, 1882, in which the buildings of Jaunpûr are treated, also designates the City Mosque of Jaunpûr as the *Friday Mosque*—that is to say, *Juma'* or *Jûm's* Masjid, which is applicable to any public mosque, great or small, with slight exception. The term Jâmi' (with the long *â*), as the City Mosque of Jaunpûr is properly called. means, I am informed, "universal," "collective"; and Jâmi' Masjid is as nearly equivalent as possible to "high church" or "cathedral." To make matters more complicated, the author of Murray's *Handbook*, above referred to, puts the apostrophe in *Jami'* before the *i* instead of as here printed, which is as Dr. Burgess has passed it in his volume. Indeed, most of the learned or technical Indian publications of the present day are perplexing to persons who do not know that, in Hindûstânî words. the short *a* is pronounced like *u* in " but," and the long *â* like *oo* in " poor" ; or that, among a mass of other modifications, the ancient capital of the empire is now written " Dihlî."
—W. H. W.

(Plate XLIII.), and that which shows its external wall (Plate XLV.), reveal design of very high character, which must be seen to be thoroughly appreciated, for no one can judge properly of the effect, under a brilliant unchanging blue sky, of Indian sandstone both grey and red, without having looked at it on the spot. The propylon, immediately in front of and concealing the dome of the mosque proper from the courtyard, shown in the first-mentioned plate, is most remarkable, even for India, and shows that the great works of the ancient Egyptians could not have been unknown to the Muhammadan designer. Both propylon and dome are shown geometrically in a lateral elevation (Plate L.), and they appear again in the external elevation of the mosque proper (Plate LII.). Thirty illustrations, of which three are from photographs, are given of this mosque, mostly executed, under careful supervision, by native draughtsman, though a few are by Mr. Smith's own hand.

The minor mosques and tombs at Jaunpûr, some of the buildings at Zafarâbâd (which is four miles south-east of Jaunpûr on a bank of the River Gûmtî), and buildings at Ayodhyâ, Bhutla Tâl, and Sahet-Mahet, are described in the three concluding chapters of the volume. Inscriptions are given with all these, both in the original and in translation.

Two plates (XLI. and XLII.) of masons' marks from the Atala Mosque, the Lâl Darwâza Mosque, and the City Mosque, the three principal buildings of Jaunpûr, are also given. To the forerunners of these the editor returns, in one of the final chapters, with a loving regard. "Once more," he says, "it is necessary to express somewhat of wonder at the noble buildings on which the Musulmân invader drew so largely, and whose beauty formed his style. Though we have not the frank acknowledgments of Khair-ad-dîn and his account how Ibrâhîm thought it consecration enough to knock off the head of any image and build it, face inwards, in a wall, the carved ornament discovered when any stone has fallen—whether in the wall of the Dower-house, the Jâmi' Masjid, the Lâl Darwâza, or the Fort—would tell plainly enough the double use of the materials. . . . All the ornament is purely Buddhist ; the construction, the arches and domes only betray the influence of other taste. The arches are floriated with lotus buds, the spandrils relieved with full-blown lotus flowers, the bands of ornamentation are largely made up of lotus blossoms in every stage, and lotus leaves from every point of view more or less conventionalised, and even the name of God in the *qiblas* [*mihrâbs* or niches in the walls towards which the worshipper turns in prayer] is inscribed on the Buddhist bell."

Now will it be believed—and I am quite prepared, even desirous, to be met with a blunt denial—that the Indian Government propose to economise a few shillings (a rupee nowadays is not worth much more than a shilling) per annum by throwing over Mr. Smith at an early date, and retaining only Dr. Führer in the Archæological Survey of North-Western India ? Yet report says so—the history of the arts in India under the British "Râj" quite favouring belief in its accuracy

—and Mr. Smith may now look forward to the con-dolences or congratulations of his friends on having received his dismissal after assisting to produce the first volume of archæological reports on Upper India which is of any distinct use to the practical Englishman, whether architect, historian, or manufacturer. So much for departmental officialism and the truth of the trite old exclamation : "With how little wit the world is governed !"

Dr. Führer is a German, and though an Oriental scholar, he makes no pretension to any knowledge of practical architecture, or even to have devoted much time to the study of its theory. His sphere is antiquarian, and he is retained specially for the purposes of the Laknau (Lucknow) Museum ; but even in his excavation work he should have the aid of a skilled architect to record the results as they are laid bare. Mr. Edmd. W. Smith, who has worked under more than one architect of position in this country, is well spoken of by his former employers; indeed, the volume under review contains proofs of his capacity to fulful the varied duties imposed upon him. Only those who have attempted to sketch the measure in the open in India know the difficulties of the task ; and only those who have seen the natives at work, and appreciated their willingness to learn, can estimate the value of such guidance as Mr. Smith has been able to give his staff—at what an outlay of rupees ! Mr. Smith has received the magnificent wage of 250 to 300 rupees a month (much less than £30), to measure and produce on paper some of the most remarkable architectural productions of North-Western India, and the native staff he has trained costs about 300 rupees a month more. O Viceroy with greater powers, in spite of telegraphs, than any sovereign of the old world !—O Indian legislative councils of every kind, both at home and in the Peninsula, cannot you continue to give only, say, £30 a month to the pursuit of archæological knowledge, at least in the North-Western Provinces (which, unlike the Panjab, have funds to spare), even for the cultivation of the arts ? You spend annually, O sapient rulers ! comparatively large sums of money in measuring innumerable "longitudinal arcs" ; less would suffice to bring home to Englishmen the value of the artistic records to be found by those who know where and how to look for them in that vast Eastern Empire, which after all is British, and likely to be none the worse administered if Englishmen who live at home at ease can be induced to take an intelligent interest in its affairs.

It has been the wish of many to get all the finer architectural remains in India carefully drawn to scale; and for this purpose Mr. Smith was sent first to Jaunpûr, as being not too large a work to begin with. It was one, moreover, which, though excellently sketched in Fergusson's *Indian and Eastern Architecture* (pp. 520–525), required much more detail in order to give an adequate idea of the style peculiar to the buildings. Now this has been done by Mr. Smith, and the volume under review shows how and with what thoroughness he has performed his task,

During the last cold season just closed, Mr. Smith has been engaged at Fathepûr Sikri, and has prepared, I am told, a very valuable mass of material—all in pencil, and of course unfinished—which bids fair to be superior in artistic finish to his first work at Jaunpûr. He ought, in any case, to have still another season at Fathepûr Sikri, and the monuments of Âgra and other cities still await accurate delineation; but if the Government stop his career, as is threatened, he will not be able to finish even the work of the past season. He has also materials from Badaon and elsewhere which are not yet published; and the opportunity of showing how, after continued practice, he and his staff have at length grasped the peculiarities of Indian ornament, and expressed in pencil and ink its true feeling, has not yet been fully afforded him. General Cunningham, who for so many years held the post since ably filled by Dr. Burgess, never pretended to possess any practical acquaintance with architecture, and he did not seem to care for it. His successor, on the contrary, has shown that in his opinion the office of Director-General of the Archæological Survey of India is nothing unless mainly architectural: he has always maintained that the monumental archæology is the central and essential department of his science. Indeed, if all the materials he has collected, partly through the industry and intelligence of Mr. Smith, were published, it would be seen at once that they are more important than many influential people connected with India suppose.

The value of such a book as the *Sharqi Architecture* ought to lie (1) in the materials it presents for the study of the style *as such* by the historian of art; and (2) for the practical architect, in the suggestions it supplies and the examples it affords of structural expedients and the artistic management of details. Every one will have his own opinion as to how far ancient work can be copied; for example, Indian work often supplies excellent ideas for details of ornamentation where one might be disposed to alter or modify the ornament itself; but to others who are ready to adopt more of the form many of the plates in such a work as the volume in question would be specially valuable. Indeed, the Government may properly be urged and expected to continue this Survey in the North-Western Provinces, and to utilize the architectural members of the Survey, moreover, in advising and controlling a reasonable Conservation of Historical Monuments in the Indian Empire—a course which was long advocated by Fergusson, and is still supported by many experts both at home and in India.

WILLIAM H. WHITE.

---

*The Mahávansa*, Part II. containing Chapters XXXIX. to C. Translated from the original Páli into English, for the Government of Ceylon, by L. C. WIJESINHA, Mudaliyár. To which is prefixed the translation of the First Part (published in 1837) by G. Turnour, C.C.S. Colombo (Trübner, London), 1889.

In a remarkable letter which Sir W. H. Gregory, after quitting his post as Governor of Ceylon, addressed to the Earl of Carnarvon on 1st August, 1877, concern-ing the literary and scientific work undertaken during the five years of his government of that colony, we find, among the important recommendations made to his successor, Sir James Longden, the following:—"That the editing of the Mahávanso may be thoroughly completed by the translation into English of all that has been left incomplete by Turnour. That the text of the first part be revised, the variants inserted, and a translation be made of it into Sinhalese to correspond with what has been done in the case of the second part. That the Tîká, or early Commentary, be revised and translated into Sinhalese and English." The edition of the Páli text of the second part, together with a translation into Sinhalese, by the High Priest Sumangala and the Pandit Batuwantudawe, had then already appeared, and that of the first part was passing through the Government Press, while arrangements were in progress with the Mahá-Mudaliyár L. de Zoysa for continuing the translation commenced by Turnour. Unfortunately, the Mahá-Mudaliyár was for a long time unable to make any progress in the translation through failing health and loss of sight, and as he was anxious to complete his Catalogue of MSS. in the Temple Libraries of Ceylon, the task of furnishing the translation of the second part of the Mahávansa was entrusted to the Mudaliyár L. C. Wijesinha, who has acquitted himself of it in a scholarly manner. L. de Zoysa died in March, 1884. The length of time that has elapsed since up to the publication of the work is amply compensated for by the excellence of Mr. Wijesinha's performance. What still remains to be done is a critical edition and English translation of the Tîká, and we trust the Ceylon Government will not lose sight of this important part of Sir W. H. Gregory's programme.

The translator rightly follows the printed text, and gives his reasons whenever he deviates from it; see his note B on ch. xxxix. and his notes on ch. lxvi. 150; ch. lxxvi. 30, 91, 171, 327; ch. lxxvii. 52. He also reproduces Turnour's translation, marking, however, in italics the faulty words and passages, for which he substitutes in foot-notes his own rendering. The changes he has thus proposed are obviously important and numerous, and he deserves high credit for the pains he has taken in this revision. All honour to the Ceylon Government for having initiated, carried on and brought to a successful termination this noble work.

---

*Anglo-Burmese Hand-book, or Guide to a Practical Knowledge of the Burmese Language.* Compiled by D. A. CHASE. Revised by F. D. Phinney. Rangoon (Trübner, London), 1890.

On several occasions attention has been drawn in these columns to the difficulties students of Burmese have had to contend with in this country owing to the want of a good practical hand-book and of a dictionary that should come up to present requirements (see Second Series, Vol. VIII. p. 111, and Third Series, Vol. I. p. 86). We also stated that Chase's Manual pre-eminently useful and long out of print, would be "well worth a somewhat improved re-issue." Such a re-issue has just left the press, and we congratulate all those who have to learn Burmese for practical purposes on its timely appearance. The avowed improvements the reviser has introduced partly concern the style of the work, and partly affect the Romanizing of the Burmese words which has been brought as closely as possible in harmony with the Hunterian system adopted by the Government of Burma. On comparing the old edition of this manual (1852) with the present one, we notice at once that the editor has bestowed the utmost care on the revision of the spelling of the Burmese words and on the rendering of their pronunciation according to the system now in vogue. For practical purposes this system, barring a few modifications, has a good deal in its favour, provided that the words are also given in the native characters. If they are not, a simple transliteration in Roman characters should take their place ; as, *e.g.* lak-thit-san-kwang, *let-hteit-than-gwin* ; sakkaráj, *thekkayit* ; rhwe-praü-wä, *shwe-pyi-wä*. Otherwise the learner will be unable to form an idea of the spelling, and often also of the meaning, of the Burmese word. Thus, krak (a cock) and kyak (to be cooked) are both pronounced *kyet.* Similarly, maü' (to be dark) is pronounced the same as mí' (fire). But the system adopted by the Supreme Government of representing Burmese in Roman characters can at best be taken only as tentative and provisional until a compromise shall have been worked out exhibiting both the transliteration and the pronunciation, that is, a compromise between Romanizing and Anglicizing. We fear, however, that such a combination could hardly be effected without having recourse to a rather irksome accumulation of diacritical marks. A scientific analysis of the morphology of Burmese is after all still an important desideratum. The late Dr. Forch-hammer had brought together ample materials for the elaboration of such a work. It was one of the books he proposed to write during the well-earned furlough he had so long been looking forward to. Who will now take up the thread of his Indo-Chinese researches ?

---

*The Ásurî-Kalpa: a Witchcraft Practice of the Atharva-veda.* With an Introduction, Translation, and Commentary, by H. W. Magoun. (Baltimore, 1889.)

Dr. Magoun, a pupil of Professor Bloomfield, of the Johns Hopkins University, lays down in this, his first opusculum, the first fruits of his studies on the Atharva-veda ritual, closely interwoven as it is with the early practice of witchcraft in India. It is this feature that makes the elucidation of the pariśishtas of that Veda such an important factor in the history of the old ceremonial in its connection with primitive beliefs and rites ; and for this reason any contribution, from original sources, to the existing scanty materials on these questions must be welcome to those who cultivate this field of research.

---

*The Stories of the Bágh o Bahár : being an Abstract made from the Original Text.* By Edith F. Barry. (W. H. Allen and Co.)

The tale of the four Derwishes, generally known by its fanciful Oriental title of the Bágh o Bahár, has for generations been one of the text-books both for the higher and lower standards of proficiency in Hindustani. Those who have worked their way through it must all have experienced the difficulty of following up the various stories through the involved tangle peculiar to Eastern fiction, while the often wearisome imagery in which the original narrative is clothed can in the long run but have proved distasteful to the Western student. Under these circumstances the epitomiser of this otherwise interesting story-book has done well in presenting to us the purport and main incidents of the stories in a clear, simple and graphic synopsis, thereby rendering welcome aid also to those who in trying to master the intricacies of the original would rightly prefer a readable survey of the book to a close literal translation. We cannot help expressing our opinion on this occasion that it is time the Bágh o Bahár, after serving for the greater part of a century as a text-book for examinations, should make room for standard books better calculated in idiom, terseness of style, and the quality of the subject-matter, to represent the Urdu of the present day. We need only refer to the author of 'Mirát el'arús' and 'Taubat en-nasúh,' and to the Syed 'Ali Mohammad Shád's 'Nawíd-i-Hind' and 'Súratu'l-Khayál,' an interesting analysis of which latter work we owe to the pen of Dr. Hoernle (see this RECORD, Vol. I. No. 4, p. 116). But there are other modern Urdu authors, besides those, whose writings betray a happy blending of the style of the best European models with native originality and power of imagination.

---

*Outline Grammar of the Singpho Language as spoken by Singpho, Dowanniya, and others residing in the Neighbourhood of Sadiya (Assam).* By J. F. Needham, Assistant Political Officer, Sadiya. Assam, Secretariat Press, Shillong, 1889.

This is a Grammar, Phrase-book and Vocabulary of about 119 pages, prepared by an officer of Government, and published at the expense of Government, and printed in the official press of the Administrative Division. It is a very creditable performance, and an entirely fresh contribution to knowledge. Sadiya is on the river Brahmaputra at the head of the Assam valley, which is flanked on both sides by high mountains, and these mountains are occupied by barbarous tribes speaking hitherto imperfectly known languages. They dwell entirely within British territory.

The Singpho are classed in Cust's " Modern Languages of the East Indies," in the Tibeto-Burman Family. They have the Patkoi range on their rear, and they are but an advance guard of a much greater horde lying beyond the Patkoi range within British Burma, known as the Kakhyen or Kaku. They are to a certain extent civilized but Pagan, *i.e.* neither Hindu, nor Mahometan, nor Buddhist. Singpho, or Chingpau, means merely " a man." Vocabularies, and Grammatical Notes, have previously existed, but this Outline Grammar relates to a particular portion of a large tribe localized near Sadiya, and has been compiled by the officer in whose civil charge they have been placed.

The author has already published a Grammar of the

Language of another barbarous tribe, the Miri, and has a third, of the Khampti Language, in preparation. This is very creditable to his industry and ability. It is much to be regretted that other officials do not work the virgin soil of this neighbourhood in the same manner.  R. N. C.

---

*Keilschrifttexte zum Gebrauch bei Vorlesungen heraus-gegeben von L. Abel und H. Winckler.* Folio, pp. iv. and 100. (Berlin: W. Spemann, 1890.)

This handsome volume meets a real want. Hitherto a student who wished to make himself acquainted with the principal results of Assyriology concerning grammar and lexicon of the Cuneiform languages, was at a loss with regard to a trustworthy guide. Delitzsch's *Assyrische Lesestücke* appears to be too expensive for the greater number of students, and besides lacks in a vocabulary adapted to the texts contained therein. We therefore heartily welcome the book before us, which does not boast of laying before the reader "new dis-coveries,"—and yet supplies everything which a be-ginner could expect.

Among the "Assyrian texts" there are specimens given of those of Tiglath-Pileser I., Assurnasirpal, Salmaneser II., Rammannirari, Tiglath-Pileser III., Sargon, Sennacherib, Esarhaddon, and Assurbanipal. The "Babylonian texts" comprise complete or partial editions of inscriptions of Assurbanipal, Nabopolassar, Nebuchadnezzar (II.), Neriglissar, Nabonid, Cyrus, and Xerxes. Extracts from the "Babylonian Chronicle" and the Assyrian account of the Deluge are also appended.

Very short are the representatives of Syllabaries, viz. "Sb." "Sc." 82, 8–16, 1 (read thus!), and the so-called dialectic vocabulary. These may be improved, however, in a second edition of the book, when a com-plete and systematic publication of all the vocabularies from Kouyunjik, exceeding the amount of 160, will have been issued. For a new edition, one and another specimen of omen-texts, letters and contracts, and of sacrificial and astrological texts, would also be needed.

Under the title "Bilingual texts" an extract from the 16th tablet of a series of incantations concerning the evil spirits is given, with restorations from a duplicate. Then follow three hymns, viz. one addressed to the Fire-god, *cf. Cat. Cuneif. Tab. in K. Coll.* vol. i. p. 11; one addressed to the Sun-god, Brit. Mus. Sp. III. 586 and 586a, *cf.* PINCHES, *Trans. Soc. Bibl. Arch.* vol. viii. p. 167 f.; BERTIN, *Revue d'Assyriologie,* vol. i. p. 4; and *Rec. of the Past,* n.s. vol. ii. p. 192 f.; and one addressed to the god NIN.IB, in the Berlin Museum, the first account of which was given in the *Proc. Soc. Bibl. Arch.* vol. xi. p. 45 ff.; *cf. Zeits.* 1889, p. 437, note 1.

A good and full vocabulary to pp. 1–50, compiled by Dr. Winckler, and a *Schrifttafel,* partly autographed, conclude this volume, which we warmly recommend to all those scholars who would wish to place in the hands of their pupils an unpretending, and at the same time correct text-book.  C. BEZOLD.

LONDON, *June* 30, 1890.

---

*Arabic Authors. A Manual of Arabian History and Literature.* By F. F. Arbuthnot. (W. Heinemann, 1890.)

The author of this useful little hand-book modestly disclaims all originality of research in composing his work. He does not write, he says, for the Oriental scholar, but for the general reader, and for the student commencing the study of Arabic. In the absence, however, of a more ambitious and more elaborate and comprehensive English book of reference on the sub-ject, this manual will be of service also to those who have no access to J. von Hammer's ponderous tomes. After a brief sketch of the history of Arabia, the author treats of the three periods of Arabic literature, viz.: 1, the time before Mohammed; 2, from Mohammed to the end of the Khalifate of Baghdad; and 3, from the fall of Baghdad to the present time. Rightly judging that a manual of Arabian history and literature would be incomplete without some special mention of Moham-med, he devotes a chapter to the life of the Prophet and a summary of his doctrines, while in the fourth chapter he deals at greater length with his favourite subject, Arabian tales, and their relation to Persian and Indian stories. The concluding chapter brings together a number of anecdotes culled from celebrated collections, some of them of an early date, and of Arabian *bons-mots.* We have no fault to find with the arrangement of the book, the aim of which is evidently to interest the general reader in Arabic literature and attract fresh students to this field of research. But as in all Manuals trustworthiness in details, including accuracy and con-sistency in the spelling of proper names, is of paramount importance, the author would have done well to subject the proofs to a thorough revision before issuing his book. The letter 'ain, *e.g.,* is sometimes marked, some-times marked in the wrong place, but more generally not marked at all. We find constantly Ibn-Haukul; also Sayuti and Suyuti; al-Zaman, but as-Sikkit, etc. Altogether, the misprints and inaccuracies in spelling would fill a pretty long list.

---

*Remarques sur les mots Français dérivés de l'Arabe.* Par H. Lammens. (Beyrouth, 1890.)

On the lines of Dozy, Engelmann, Devic, and de Eguilaz an attempt is here made at tracing to an Arabic source a large number (close upon 800) of French words for which no other safe or probable etymology has as yet been found. In an introductory Essay the author suggests the operation of certain phonetic laws by which the permutation of consonants in the two respective languages is controlled. These laws, the existence of which was doubted by Devic, are well worthy of careful examination. Many words, concerning the parentage of which previous etymolo-gists were uncertain, have here been defined beyond controversy (see *e.g.* felouque, calfater), while on others (*e.g.* hazard, cancan, gamache, auberge) subsequent writers may be in a position to throw fresh light. The book altogether furnishes a complete index of all French words, modern and old, the origin of which has with more or less success been sought in the Arabic language.

Where the compiler sees reason to differ from his predecessors, he supports his opinion by an able exposition of his views.

---

*Das Runa Simi oder die Keshua-Sprache, wie sie gegenwärtig in der Provinz von Cusco gesprochen wird.* Von Dr. E. W. Middendorf. (Leipzig, F. A. Brockhaus.)

The Keshua language, generally known as Quichua, is by far the most important of the three main languages spoken in the civilized parts of Peru : it belongs, as is well known, to the agglutinative or polysynthetic class. The work under notice is based in the first place on a critical examination of all that has been written on the language these three hundred years, and in the second place on a knowledge of the living tongue acquired during many years' intercourse with the people : and as the author has brought a keen power of linguistical discernment and a rare philological acumen to bear upon his task, it is not bestowing too high praise on him when we say that his book marks an epoch in the scientific treatment of the aboriginal languages of America. The introduction (pp. 1-34) will be studied with profit and interest alike by the historian and anthropologist. The present volume, however, is intended only as the first of a series. The second volume is to contain a complete dictionary ; the third the drama Ollanta ; the fourth the remaining literature ; the fifth will treat of the Aimará language, and the sixth of the Chimu, a language now nearly extinct. All honour to the publisher of such an important and comprehensive, but unremunerative work !

# Obituary.

Pali scholarship, Indo-Chinese philology, and the archæology of Burma have suffered an irreparable loss through the death of *Dr. Emmanuel Forchhammer*, which took place on board the Government steamer under way from Mandalay to Rangoon on April 26. It had been arranged that he should take two years' furlough last August to repair in Europe a constitution enfeebled by eleven and a half years' unremitting labour in Burma : and he had gone to visit the ruins of Old Pagán beyond Mandalay, to settle some questions in reference to the origin of the style of architecture of the later and more celebrated city, when he was seized again with that terrible illness, angina pectoris, from which he had since 1888 periodically suffered extreme pain. He died far away from wife and child, and was buried at Myingyan on the following day.

Emmanuel Forchhammer was born on the 12th March, 1851, at St. Antonien, in the valley of Prättigau, in Switzerland, where his father was Protestant pastor. Sprung from an old Sleswig-Holstein family—the celebrated Kiel Professor of Classical Philology was his brother—the father had settled in Switzerland in his youth, and had studied divinity at Bâle, chiefly under Dr. Beck, who subsequently filled one of the chairs of Divinity in the University of Tübingen. Young Emmanuel received his classical education at home, and when only sixteen and a half years old went to New York, furnished with a letter of introduction to Professor Schaff, the well-known theologian, by whose advice he accompanied Pastor Heusser to New Orleans, where he eventually studied medicine, took his degree,

and became Assistant Surgeon at the Hospital, but subsequently reverted to his favourite pursuits, the study of languages. With this object he made extensive travels in Texas, Louisiana, and Arkansas, sojourning among the various Indian tribes and spending years of hard and patient labour in bringing together valuable materials for the history, analysis, and classification of their languages and dialects. On his return to Europe in 1875, he stayed some time at San Lazzaro, near Venice, to study the Armenian language, and then went to the University of Leipzig with a view to acquiring a wider range of linguistic knowledge and the advantages of a proper methodical training in philology. The languages which, under the excellent guidance of Professors Brockhaus, Fleischer, and Von der Gabelentz, he cultivated with special devotion, were Sanskrit, Pali, Tibetan, Chinese, and Arabic. When, in the early part of 1878, the Professorship of Pali in the Government High School, Rangoon, became vacant, he was recommended for that post, not only as an eminent Pali scholar, but also on account of his special qualification for taking up the scientific investigation of the numerous vernaculars spoken in that province : and he gladly accepted an appointment which, though holding out but a meagre emolument, opened up to him a virgin field of literary research thoroughly congenial to his mind. From the date of his appointment, the 9th January, 1879, he was engaged during his first year in Burma in investigating the Sacred and Vernacular Literature of the Province. With the assistance of three native Pali scholars, one of whom had been specially sent down from the King's Library at Mandalay for this purpose, he made an edition of the Buddhist scriptures after collating the various MSS. found in the monasteries : and forty copyists had to transcribe this text as gáthá by gáthá it was handed to them. For several years he explored the records jealously hidden away in towns, villages and monasteries in the Pegu, Irawady, and Arakan divisions : working his way slowly from monastery to monastery on foot, on horseback, or by boat, classifying the monastic libraries for the Phongyees, amassing materials for his life-work on the archæology of Burma, and taking notes of the history and folk-lore of each place visited. By his kindly nature and his sympathetic interest in the natives, he won for himself the respect and admiration of priest and villager wherever he went. No sooner was it known in any place that the great Pali scholar— the *Dhammathat Sayahgyee*, as he was called—was seated in the *zayat*, than the priests came up to converse with him on points of law and doctrine, and the old *pondawgyee* himself would voluntarily bring forward his choicest *pesaungs* to be catalogued or inspected or borrowed. Dr. Forchhammer was fond of repeating how his sonorous recitation of a few texts from the Pali scriptures, or his quotation from an old Pali authority on some point of contention between *mahagandi* and *sulagandi*, made the yellow-robed priests stare in amazement, and caused the *sadeik* to be slowly unlocked and its lid to be slowly raised, and the silk-swathed mouldering manuscripts within to be unfolded to the eye of the wonderful foreigner. When the learned priest of Maubin declined to exhibit a unique manuscript in his possession, and was proof against the charm of a theological dissertation in Pali, he succumbed precipitately when the Professor produced his camera and threatened to photograph him. The classified list of the MSS. that came under his observation during these years was published at the Government Press in 1882. The new and much enlarged edition which he had ready three years later has not yet been printed. He also supplied Mr. J. Jardine, then Judicial Commissioner of British Burma, with valuable translations from the Pali Law Codes for incorporation in his "Notes on Buddhist Law," which appeared in eight fasciculi at Rangoon in 1882 and 1883; and wrote an appendix containing notes and observations to "Maung Tet Pyo's Customary Law of the Chin Tribe," published in Burmese and English in Rangoon in 1884. In the same year he gained the Jardine Prize Essay, "On the Sources and Development of Burmese Law from the Era of the First Introduction of the Indian Law to the Time of the British Occupation of Pegu." This treatise, on which Bishop Bigandet has passed the highest encomium, was printed at the Government Press, Rangoon, together with the text and translation of King Wagaru's "Manu Dhammasattham," in the following year.

Dr. Forchhammer's work in the High School, on the Educational Syndicate, and on the Textbook Committee, the training of translators and vernacular scholars, the amalgamation of higher native with higher English literature, all taxed his energies to the utmost and narrowed his time for literary labours.

Collaterally with the discharge of these various literary functions, he was constantly at work upon the scientific study of the other vernaculars—Talaing (now almost extinct), Shan, Karen, Kachin, Palaung, and others. He had planned a Comparative Dictionary of these languages; but the more important archæological survey work, with which he was entrusted by the Chief Commissioner on February 16th, 1882, made him set aside those purely philological labours. An article by him "On the Indo-Chinese Languages" (in the *Indian Antiquary* for July, 1882) and a printed letter (August 17th, 1882) "On the Languages and Dialects spoken in British Burma," are the only tangible evidence of the progress he had made in that virgin field of research.

His familiarity, however, with Talaing and Burmese stood him in good stead in the decipherment of the ancient inscriptions to which he thenceforth directed his whole attention—so far, at least, as his other heavy official duties permitted him to do so. As an earnest of his archæological investigations he brought out in 1883 and 1884 two treatises, entitled "Notes on the Early History and Geography of British Burma." A third fasciculus, which should have dealt with the Kalyani inscriptions, has, owing to his morbid fastidiousness, remained in manuscript. At the end of June, 1885, he had completed the archæological survey of Arakan, and he returned to Rangoon with vast materials, both epigraphic and linguistic. His health, however, had suffered beyond retrieval from the treacherous climate of that province. That archæological report, accompanied by numerous photographs, plans, and diagrams, has but recently been carried through the press. It comprises accounts of the Mahâmuni pagoda, of the Mrohaung temples, and the Mahâti, Launggyet, Minbya, Urittaung, Akyab, and Sandoway pagodas.

Early in December, 1888, Forchhammer went to Pagan to make a survey of the famous temple ruins of that ancient city, and he stayed there for four months. Some of the results of his survey are recorded in a letter to the late Sir Henry Yule which appeared in TRÜBNER'S RECORD (Third Series, Vol. I. No. 1), and some further details will be found in Vol. II. No. I, of the same serial. In a letter, dated February 28th of the present year, he expresses his regret at not having visited that jewel of Burman architecture at an earlier period.

A vast chaotic mass of papers remains, which, it is hoped, will be entrusted to some well-known Orientalist, either at home or in Burma, to sort, select, and publish. The collection of lithic inscriptions, palm-leaves, photographs, notes and diaries represents the unremitting work of ten years—work that was to have won for Dr. Forchhammer a world-wide reputation as the pioneer of literary investigation in the Further East, had not death intervened to deprive him of the fruit of long years of toil.

The rich field of literary enterprise in Burma, its claims upon the consideration of European scholars, the need of its development for the better appreciation of the people and for the leavening of the native intellect, these were subjects ever uppermost in Dr. Forchhammer's mind. The jurist of the future will remember that Dr. Forchhammer rendered the Buddhist texts available to the courts of Burma; the historian will remember that he shed the light of antiquarian lore on the vague records of the past; the philologist will bear in mind his labours originating a scientific study of the non-Aryan dialects of the Golden Chersonese. But the Burman will reverence Dr. Forchhammer's memory because, amongst other things, he in a great measure brought about the recovery and retention in Burma of the dispersed treasures of the Royal Library at Mandalay, and caused the Nyaungyan Prince's collection of manuscripts to be rescued from oblivion in Calcutta and deposited in the capital of Burma for the free use of every reader. His unselfish disposition, cultured tastes, and singularly attractive power, obtained for him many friends in Burma, all of whom, we are sure, join us in condoling the loss of so zealous and modest an officer and in offering our sincere sympathy to the widow and the little child now sorrowing in Bangalore.

[Some of the details in this notice have been supplied by the family of the deceased scholar, others have been taken from the obituary in the *Athenæum* for 17th May, and a leading article headed "In Memoriam," in the *Rangoon Times* of 29th April.]

---

Our Calcutta Correspondent telegraphs:—"Much regret is felt at Bhamo on account of the death there on the 16th June of *Mr. Edward Colborne Baber.*" By his death Her Majesty's service in the East loses one of its most brilliant and gifted members. Mr. Baber's constitution never was very strong, and he succumbed, no doubt, to the effects of prolonged residence in unhealthy climates, and the hardships of the remarkable journeys by which he is best known to the outside world. Many who saw Mr. Baber on his last visit to this country two years ago, and who perceived the persistence with which ill-health clung to him, felt that the chances of his return from Bhamo were not very great.

Mr. Baber was educated at Magdalene College, Cambridge, and went out to China in 1866 as a student interpreter in the British Consular service. He acquired Chinese with more than the usual rapidity and thoroughness, and for some years went through the usual grades of official promotion. In 1875 his chance of distinction came. In the February of that year Mr. Margary, an officer of the Consular service in China, who was proceeding under Imperial passports to meet Colonel Browne's mission from Burmah into China, was murdered at Manwyne, on the borders of the two countries. The circumstances surrounding this tragedy were so doubtful and suspicious that Sir Thomas Wade, then British Minister in Pekin, despatched, for the purpose of inquiring into the matter, a mission under the late Mr. Grosvenor, and of this Mr. Baber was a member. The mission left Hankow, on the Yangtze, in November, 1875, reaching Tali-Fu in April, 1876, and Bhamo some time later. The route of the mission between Tali and Momein was described by Mr. Baber, and was subsequently published as a Blue-book. To use the words of Lord Aberdare, then President of the Royal Geographical Society, when presenting Mr. Baber with the Society's gold medal in 1883 :—" This narrative, in spite of the disadvantage of making its appearance as a Blue-book, and therefore obtaining but a limited circulation, yet ' a fit audience found, though few,' and made European geographers acquainted with the fact that a geographical observer and narrator of remarkable power had appeared in the far East." Subsequently the Chefoo Convention was signed with the Chinese Government, and under it a British official was permitted to reside in the town of Chungking, on the Upper Yangtze, for the purpose of studying the trade and trade routes of the region. It was in accordance with the fitness of things that Mr. Baber should have been the first officer appointed to this important and peculiar post, and it was while there that he carried out the series of explorations in Eastern Szechuen and the borders of Tibet which have made his name known to geographers all over the world, and which procured for him the gold medal of the Royal Geographical Society. The peculiar value of these explorations to geography was that they connected the travels of the Baron von Richthofen and those of the brilliant but unfortunate Frenchman Francis Garnier. The record of these was subsequently published by the Royal Geographical Society in the first of its series of "Supplementary Papers." Speaking of these journeys on the occasion already referred to, Lord Aberdare, as the official representative of British geographers, said : —" Of these great services to geography I have given only the dry outlines. It is the merest justice to you to add that your journeys have been exceptionally productive, because of the exceptional store of various and accurate knowledge with which you started on your travels. Your mastery of the Chinese language, and of Chinese customs and habits of thought, enabled you to collect a great amount of miscellaneous information, which has been conveyed in narratives full of novelty, vivacity, and sustained interest. Altogether, both in these journeys and the report of their results, you have displayed the qualities of an accomplished traveller in a degree of which we have had few examples, and which fully justify our choice of you for sharing with Sir Joseph Hooker our highest distinction, even although you have, we firmly believe, only given the first fruits of that rich harvest which we expect from your matured powers and enlarged experience." Of the record itself the late Sir Henry Yule speaks as " that admirable and delightful narrative published in the spring of 1882 by the Royal Geographical Society, which the periodical Press has allowed to pass almost absolutely unnoticed, taking it, I suppose, for a Blue-book, because it is blue." The best account of the aboriginal tribes inhabiting the west and south-west of China is contained in this narrative, and the first Lo-lo manuscripts which reached Europe are believed to have come through Mr. Baber. It is to him also that we owe the account of the manufacture and trade in that curious produce, brick tea. In 1879 Mr. Baber was appointed to one of the most important posts in Her Majesty's service in China —namely, Chinese Secretary of the Legation at Pekin, in succession to another remarkable scholar, the late Mr. Mayers. In 1885 he was appointed Consul-General in Corea, and when the delimitation of the frontiers between Burma and China was expected to take place, in pursuance of the Burma Convention of 1885, Mr. Baber was appointed political officer at Bhamo, on the Upper Irrawaddy. The last official paper from his hands that has been published was a somewhat caustic criticism of the arrangements made for opening to trade what is called the "Ambassador's route" from Bhamo through the Shan States into China. His loss to the British service would be great at any time ; it is

specially so now, when the settlement of frontier questions in the region which he understood so well cannot be long deferred. Mr. Baber was about 45 years of age at the time of his death.—[*The Times* for June 23, 1890.]

## Notes and News.

In continuation of the list we printed in Vol. I. No. 6 of our RECORD, of Sanskrit works published under the patronage of Mr. M. Ch. Apte at the Anandâs'rama Press, Poona, we proceed to give further details concerning Sanskrit texts with commentaries thereon in course of, or designed for, publication. They are as follows :—XIII. S'ri Taittiriyopanishadbhâshyavârtika by S'rimat Sures'varâchârya and its Commentary by S'rimat Anandajnâna. Edited by Pandits at the Anandâs'rama. XIV. The Chhândogyopanishad with the Bhâshya of S'rimat S'ankarâchârya and its Commentary by S'rimat A'nandajnâna and Dipikâs by S'rimat Vidyâranya and Nityânanda (in the press). XV. The Brihadâranyakopanishad with the Bhâshya of S'rimat S'ankarâchârya and its Commentary by S'rimat A'nandajnâna, and Dipikâs by Srimat Vidyâranya and Nityânanda (in course of preparation). XVI. The Brihadâranyakopanishadbhâshyavârtika by S'rimat Sures'varâchârya and its Commentary by S'rimat A'nandajnâna (in course of preparation). XVII. The Krishna Yajurvêdiya S'wetâs'wataropanishad with the Bhâshya of S'rimat S'ankarâchârya and Dipikâ of the same by S'rimat S'ankarânanda and Nârâyana and a Vivarana by S'rimat Vijnâna Bhagavat. Edited by Pandits at the A'nandâs'rama. XVIII. The Saura Purâna by S'rimat Vyâsa. Edited by Pandit Kâs'inâth S'astri Lêlê of the A'nandâs'rama. XIX. The Rasaratnasamuchchaya by Vâgbhatta. Edited by Pandit Krishnaraw Bâpat (nearly ready). XX. The Jivanmuktivivêka by S'rimat Vidyâranya Swâmi. Edited by Pandit Vâsudeva S'âstri Panasikar. XXI. The Brahmasûtras with the Bhâshya of S'rimat S'ankarâchârya and its Commentary by S'rimat A'nandajnâna. Edited by Pandit Nârâyana S'âstri Ekasambekar (in the press) XXII. The S'ankaradigvijaya of S'rimat Vidyâranya and its Commentary by Dhanapatisûri (in course of preparation). XXIII. The Sûtasamhitâ being a portion of Skanda Purâna (in course of preparation). Also the Taittiriya Samhitâ Brâhmana and A'ranyaka with their Bhâshya by S'rimat Sâyanâchârya; undertaken by Mahâmahopâdhyâya Râjârâma S'âstri of Elphinstone College. The S'atapatha Brâhmana with its Bhâshyas undertaken by the same gentleman. (This Pandit is a Hiranyakes'i—the S'âkhâ to which Mr. A'pte himself belongs—and as he knows the Samhitâ, Brâhmana, and A'ranyaka by heart, and will be assisted by well-known Vaidikas of the same S'âkhâ, the editions will be found as correct as possible as to svaras, etc.) The proprietor and head of the Institution has up to date upwards of 4000 MSS. in his possession, and as to his having the loan of MSS. in the private collections of others, he says there is hardly an owner in the Presidency and some places beyond who does not wish to lend his MSS. to him. This catalogue of works thus available shows 6900 entries. The buildings are approaching completion ; but he has had to spend more upon them than the estimated amount. The series is still far from self-supporting, and it is hoped that scholars and libraries will become subscribers. Opinions of Sanskrit scholars are also invited as to particular works the publication of which is considered desirable. We may state that the published works of the series which have fallen under our notice leave in point of correctness and scholarship absolutely nothing to be desired.

If a sufficient number of subscribers can be found, the Basel Mission Press, Mangalore, will print a *Kis'imudr* (i.e. classified) *Glossary of Kanarese Words* with explanatory meaning, by Ullal Narasinga Rau. The words will be grouped under separate headings, such as Agriculture, Architecture, Astronomy, Weights and Measures, etc., and will be of great practical usefulness for administrative purposes. It will comprise about 150 pages in 8vo., and will have a general index to facilitate reference. The price to subscribers will be three rupees, exclusive of postage. The work will by no means be superseded by the great Kanarese Dictionary now passing through the same press, which is not likely to be completed for several years, and does not serve a special practical purpose. Such words as anvâdidâra, sdangal, ardhîli, and the compounds of akrama, and the special meaning of ashtabhoga will in vain be looked for in the greater work, while these terms are fully explained in the Glossary. We are great advocates of special glossaries; for they often contain much information which it is not the province of a general dictionary to give. In fact, a general dictionary, may it be ever so comprehensive, makes special glossaries by no means superfluous.

We have received two numbers of the *Ushâ*, a Vedic periodical published in Calcutta in monthly numbers of about 100 pages octavo. The Editor, Satya Vrata Sâmâs'ramî, is already favourably known through another Sanskrit periodical, the Pratna-kamra-nandinî, the eight volumes of which he edited in a masterly manner up to the year when that publication ceased to appear. The publishing price for Europe will be £1 1s. per annum (inclusive of postage) payable in advance; and the editor's address is Satya Press, 16, Ghoshe's Lane, Calcutta. The periodical is intended to publish rare and important Vedic texts, and to devote a portion of its space to the interpretation, criticism and discussion of Vedic subjects. Amongst the contents of fasciculi 1 to 3 we have noticed the Akabaratantram, the Ashtavikritivivriti, and the first in-stalment of the Sâmaprâtis'âkhyam, and of the Mantrabrâh-maṇam. The last mentioned is a new and revised edition of the text and gloss of this Brâhmaṇa, as given by the same editor in the Pratna-kamra-nandinî for S'âka 1794.

Dr. Pope is passing through the Oxford University Press the *Nâladiyâr, or Four Hundred Quotations in Tamil*, with introduction, translation and notes critical, philological and explanatory, to which is added a concordance and lexicon with authorities from the oldest Tamil writers. It is intended as a supplement to his edition, published in 1886, of the Kural, another and more extensive collection of ancient Tamil senten-tious poetry. Those students who possess the latter work will find in the notes and illustrations a number of stanzas of the Nâladiyâr, or Nâladinannûṛu, rendered into English which will serve as specimens of the style of this composition. The late F. W. Ellis, in his commentary on the earlier part of the Kural, gives also numerous quotations from the Nâladiyâr (see pp. 65, 83, 86, 98, 168, 184, 231, 301, 303), as well as parallel passages from other Tamil and from Sanskrit and Telugu poetry which should set the student on the track of investigating to what extent those early High Tamil poets were indebted to Sanskrit models.

We draw attention to this year's *Annual Address* of the President of the *Asiatic Society of Bengal*, which contains a valuable and complete survey not only of the Society's own operations in its various departments of research during the past year, but also of Oriental work done in relation to India and Central Asia by other societies, of the results of the various archæological and trigonometrical surveys, of geo-graphical and anthropological investigations, and of natural history and other scientific discoveries. Many of the items mentioned have been treated of in detail in the Record; but a summary review of the whole wide field of literary and scientific inquiry, such as is presented in this *Address*, is nowhere else to be found in such a compact form, and is likely to be doubly welcome to the friends of Asian progress.

No. 36 of the *Journal of the Ceylon Branch of the Royal Asiatic Society*, just to hand, contains four interesting papers, two of which deal with the "Moors" of Ceylon, that is, with that portion of the inhabitants of the island who speak the Tamil language and are Muhammadans. Mr. Ahamadu Bawa treats of their marriage customs, and Mr. P. Râmanâthan examines in detail the ethnological question. Mr. D. Fer-gusson, who has already done much good work in connection with the history and literature of Ceylon, supplies a valuable critical essay on Ribeiro's work which would have delighted the heart of Sir Henry Yule. We commend this treatise to the attention of the Hakluyt Society in the hope that the Council of that Society may see their way to arranging for a complete English translation of that book. The fourth article, contributed by Mr. J. H. F. Hamilton, is on the antiquities of Mædamahanuwara in the Kandyan district.

The *Journal of the Straits Branch of the Royal Asiatic Society* continues to supply valuable material to the students of the geography, literature, folklore and natural history of the Far East. No. 19, in addition to the usual reports and occasional notes (the latter including a memoir of the life and literary work of the late Captain T. J. Newbold), brings fore-most of its literary papers the third of Mir Hassan's Fairy Tales both in the Malay original (57 pages) as written down by Mr. W. E. Maxwell from the mouth of the narrator, and a full analysis into which translations of telling passages are interwoven. Mr. Maxwell also supplies an account of the Lankawi Islands which have never before been so fully described. Of other papers we note: Report of a Journey, by Mr. R. M. Little, from Tuarau to Kiau in N.E. Borneo, with an account of his ascent of the Kimabalu Mountain; also the Journal of an Exploring Expedition, by Mr. A. T. Dew, from Selama, Perak, to Pong. Patani, in the Malay Peninsula; a valuable paper by Mr. M. Lister on the history and constitu-tion of the confederation of Protected States which go by the name of Negri Sembilan. The Rev. J. Perham, the great authority on Dayak Folklore, has an important contribution on Manangism in Borneo. Lastly, there are three natural history papers: Report on the Padi-Borer, and another on the Pomelow Moth, both by Mr. L. Wray, jun., Curator of the Perak Museum, and an article on Birds from Perak, by Mr. Bowdler Sharpe, from notes supplied by Mr. Wray.

We reprint from *The Straits Times* an article headed "How not to teach English in Perak," which is highly instructive as showing in what senseless way English is taught in many native schools in the East. For we may look upon Perak only as a specimen. But we would recommend to the attention of Eastern educationists the judicious remarks of Mr. Thorold, the Inspector of Schools, and his suggestions (embodied in this article) for bringing about a better state of things.

"Mr. Thorold, the Inspector of Schools in Perak, as to English teaching, has a good word for the Central School only. As regards all the other schools he has no hesitation in saying that the present system is as bad as it can be. It could not possibly be worse. The teachers seem to teach English, not as though it were a living language, but as though it were a dead thing made up of a number of meaningless sounds. It must be confessed that they are much handicapped by the books out of which they teach. He says:—These are Elemen-tary Primers and Royal Readers such as are used in England, and I understand that they are in use in the schools of the Straits Settlements, but I am surprised that nothing better has been devised. They are quite unsuited for native children; for they deal with scenes on which they have never set eyes, and maxims of a school of morality to which they are and will always remain strangers. They therefore begin their study of a strange language by coming into contact with ideas which they cannot possibly grasp. I may illustrate my meaning by transcribing the titles of some of the stories in these books: 'A Week at the Farm.' 'I will not hurt my little Dog,' 'Mary's little Lamb,' 'Spring,' 'Autumn,' 'The Last Cross Words,' 'Washing Day,' 'Tidy Tom,' 'A Willing Boy.'

These things are all very well for little English children, but are hardly the stuff to set before the sons of Tamil cattle-dealers and Chinese shop-keepers, who wish to learn English in order to be able to buy and sell and speculate, and transact the practical business of life in it.

What, again, is an ordinary Eastern boy to make of such effusions as the following?

> I must not throw upon the floor
>   The crust I cannot eat;
> For many a hungry little one
>   Would think it quite a treat.
> 'Tis wilful waste brings woful want,
>   And I may live to say;
> 'Oh, how I wish I had the bread
>   Which once I threw away.'

It is like setting an Englishman to learn Chinese out of a Chinese treatise on metaphysics.

The teachers appear to proceed as follows: Having taught the boys enough simple words to enable them to read these primers, they cause them to do so in a mechanical manner, translating each word, just as it comes, into Malay, without the slightest regard to the meaning of the whole sentence, to context, grammar, or indeed to any rule of reason or common sense. The results are very remarkable. Innumerable examples might be given, but I will confine myself to three.

1. 'He is going to eat.'
   'Dia ada pergi pada makan.'
2. 'He does not fear.'
   'Dia buat tidak takut.'
3. 'It lives on small birds.'
   'Dia diam atas burong kechil.'

This subject will have to engage the early and earnest attention of the visiting teacher when he comes. In the mean time, I have told the teachers how English should not be taught, and given them a few hints as to how it should; and I will try to get some proper books."

ATTACKS ON FOREIGNERS IN JAPAN.—The last mail from Japan brings details of the attack on Mr. Summers, a clergyman in Japan, which has been referred to in telegrams from Yokohama. Mr. Summers is well known in this country as an Oriental scholar, and has resided in Japan for nearly 20 years past. While driving in a pony carriage through the streets of Tokio he met a procession accompanying the Empress Dowager. He drew to the side of the road and stood still, preparing to take off his hat at what he thought the proper moment. A lancer, who was riding in front of the procession, struck off Mr. Summers's hat with the butt of his lance. Subsequently the lancer was punished, an apology was made by his officer, and there the matter might have ended, so far as Mr. Summers was concerned, but that a portion of the native Press began to excite public feeling against him. In consequence of this students and others began to visit his house in bodies and to send deputations to rebuke him for his supposed disrespect, and to warn and threaten him. Letters also came to him demanding explanations and using threats. On one occasion the Secretary to the British Legation, when visiting Mr. Summers, had to eject one insolent youth. At last Mr. Summers, to avoid further molestation and possible danger, had to leave Tokio for Yokohama, and is now on his way home. A few days later an American missionary, Dr. Imbrie, was assaulted and stabbed by the students of the Higher Middle Class School in Tokio because he entered the grounds where a base-ball match was going on between the boys of his own school and the ruffians who assailed him. When the mail left, the foreign residents in Tokio appear to have felt considerable anxiety at the undisguised hostility of an active and turbulent section of the population, which appears to have got beyond the control of the authorities. It is long since the same anti-foreign feeling has been openly evinced in Japan.—[From *The Times* of June 27.]

DR. GEORGE WATT is making good progress with his Dictionary of Indian Economic Products. The third volume is virtually completed, and it is hoped that the fourth, which will include up to the letter N, may be completed about the end of the year. Drs. Watt and Murray and Mr. J. Duthie are engaged upon the work.

MR. R. SIVASANKARA PANDIYAJI, B.A., has just issued from the Madras "Ripon" Press a little volume of Aryan anecdotes, which deserve to be read if only on account of their characteristicness. Trisanker, for instance, a king of the solar race, wanted to go to heaven in his human body. His domestic priest Vasishtha said it could not be done, and accordingly Trisanker, with the impetuousness of an earthly monarch, went to Viswamitra, a rival priest, who at once undertook the matter. The king went up to heaven in his human body, but Indra learning what had happened declined to admit him, and he was ignominiously hurled downwards, and left suspended in mid-air. "This anecdote," says the editor, "teaches us not to neglect the good advice of our preceptors, and that such negligence will lead to our ruin." Again, when Dharma Raja was going to heaven, "a dog followed him from the very beginning of his journey to the Himalayas. Indra, the lord of Swargaloka, or heaven, appeared before him and asked him to enter heaven; but the righteous monarch desired Indra to admit the faithful dog along with him." Indra, of course refused, and the king thereupon declined to enter heaven. A long discussion followed the announcement of this determination, and eventually Indra, touched by the monarch's attachment to the animal, agreed to admit them both, whereupon the dog at once changed into Yama Dharma Raja, the lord of the lower regions, and praised the king for his noble-

heartedness. Another story illustrates "the advantage of deliberation." A young Rishi—called Chirakari on account of his fixed rule never to do anything without careful deliberation —was ordered by his father in a fit of anger to cut off his mother's head. The young man sat down awhile to deliberate on the matter, and after a considerable time had elapsed, his father's anger cooled, and he came to ask him if the order had been carried out. Chirakari observed that he was still thinking over it, and "on this the father became highly pleased and warmly thanked his son for his policy of deliberation." This anecdote, observes the editor, with singular calmness, "teaches us that it is always better not to do a thing in haste, because haste makes waste!" and it is better not to waste one's mother in a rash way without thinking over it.—[*Times of India.*]

[We should have thought that the legends concerning Trisanku, Sárameya, Chirakári, and so forth, were quite familiar to youthful Hindus; but this is apparently not the case.]

IN the "Proceedings of the Royal Society of Göttingen" (No. 6 of 1890), Professor Kielhorn, by ingeniously restoring the reading of a verse in an inscription of the year 472 A.D., which contains obvious reminiscences of passages in Kálidása's Ritusanhára, but had been misread and mistranslated by previous interpreters, has thereby proved conclusively that that poem must have been composed before that date. If that poem can be assigned to Kálidása its date as settled by Prof. Kielhorn will be an important factor in bringing the controversy about the date of that poet to a termination.

THE valuable article under the heading "The Indian Gypsies," which appeared in *The Pioneer* of the 10th Sept., is an indication of the interest which is still taken in this remarkable people. In England that interest has culminated in the institution of the Gypsy-Lore Society, which was founded in May, 1888, for the purpose of investigating the gypsy question in as thorough and many-sided a manner as possible. Its original formation was chiefly due to a suggestion of Mr. W. J. Ibbetson, a young mathematician of great promise, who was cut off at the early age of twenty-eight in October, 1889. Since its foundation the Society has done good work under the guidance of its President, Mr. C. G. Leland, and has obtained the adhesion of the most distinguished gypsy-logues of Europe and America. The origin of the European gypsies is doubtful, and it is not altogether certain that they are descended from the Nats of India, as stated by the writer of the article under reference. Mr. Grierson, one of the best authorities on the subject, is disposed, on philological grounds, to identify them with the Bhojpuri-speaking Doms of Behar. The balance of evidence seems, however, to be in favour of the Nats, who are by no means confined to Bengal, but are largely to be met with in Upper India, where they carry on the callings of acrobats, jugglers and pilferers in general. The identity of the Nats with the Sansias of Bikanir is open to question. A common origin cannot be predicated simply on the ground that they are both nomad races of predatory habits. A short vocabulary of the language spoken by the Nats was contributed to the January part of the Journal of the Gypsy-Lore Society by that distinguished linguist Surgeon-Major G. Ranking, M.D., of the Bengal Medical Service. It appears to be a canting dialect of Hindi varified by an apparently arbitrary system of prefixes and affixes. Of the prefixes the most common are *ku* or *ka*, thus: *ku-darhi*, beard; *ku-hat*, land; *ka-lota*, a lota; *ka-rat*, night. The ordinary affixes are *chus* and *ma*, thus: *kar-chus*, ear; *chand-chus*, moon; *theli-ma*, bag; *chhati-ma*, chest. Sometimes both a prefix and an affix are attached to a word, as *ku-lakri-ma*, a stick.— [From the *Pioneer Mail.*]

WE regret that in the article entitled *The Temptation of Zoroaster* which headed the previous issue of the RECORD (Vol. II. No. 1), a number of *Errata* should have been left uncorrected. They are as follows :—For *Auro* read throughout *Anro*.

line 9, for *The praises of* read *Praising*.
  ,, 11, ,, *away* read *and screamed*.
  ,, 12, ,, dele *And screamed*.
  ,, 13, ,, for *I see no sign of death upon* read *I see no death sign on.*
  ,, 19, ,, *to him* read *him.*
  ,, 24, dele *The spirit of.*
  ,, 33, for *But* read *And.*
Note † for *Kauçoya* read *Kançoya.*

## American Literature.

**Adams (G. Huntington)**—A Handbook of the Tariff on Imports into the United Sates, the Free List, and the Bond and Warehouse System now in Force; with Notes of Judicial Decisions, and Decisions of the Secretary of the Treasury. 8vo. half roan, pp. 6 and 313. *New York.* 15*s.*

**American Historical Association.** — Report of the Proceedings, Washington, D.C., Dec. 1889. (Papers of the American Historical Association, vol. 4, pt. i.) 8vo. paper, pp. 3 and 92. *New York.* 6*s.*

**American Iron and Steel Association.** Annual Statistical Report for 1889. 8vo. paper, pp. 76. *Philadelphia.* 10*s.* 6*d.*

**Anderson (E. L.)**—Modern Horsemanship. Fourth Edition, Revised and Enlarged. 8vo. cloth. Illustrated. *New York.* £1 8*s.*

**Appel, Theodore (D.D.)**—The Life and Work of John Williamson Nevin, D.D. Portrait. 8vo. cloth, pp. 800. *Philadelphia.* 15*s.*

**Appleton's Annual Encyclopedia** and Register of Important Events of the year 1889. New series, vol. xiv. 8vo. cloth. *New York.* £1 5*s.*

**Balzac (Honoré de)**—Fame and Sorrow, and other Stories. Translated by Katharine Prescott Wormeley. 12mo. half russia, pp. 3 and 338. *Boston.* 7*s.* 6*d.*

**Balzac (Honoré de)**—Père Goriot; from the French by Mrs. F. M. Dey. (The Rialto Series, No. 21.) 12mo. cloth, pp. 2 and 212. *New York and Chicago.* 5*s.*

**Bancroft (Hubert Howe)**—History of the Pacific States of North America. Vol. 26. Washington, Idaho, and Montana, 1845–1889. 8vo. cloth, pp. 26–836. *San Francisco.* £1 4*s.*

**Bazán '(Emilia Pardo)**—Russia, its People and its Literature. From the Spanish by Fanny Hale Gardiner. 16mo. cloth, pp. 2–293. *Chicago.* 6*s.* 6*d.*

**Behrends (A. J. F., D.D.)**—The Philosophy of Preaching. 12mo. cloth, pp. 7–234. *New York.* 6*s.*

**Bergen (J. Y., jun., and Fanny D.)**—A Primer of Darwinism and Organic Evolution. Illustrated. 12mo. cloth, pp. 64 and 261. *Boston.* 6*s.* 6*d.*

**Berry (E. Payson)**—Leah of Jerusalem; a Story of the Time of St. Paul. 12mo. cloth, pp. 7—388. *New York.* 6*s.* 6*d.*

**Blackburn (C. H.)**—The Trial of Jesus from a Lawyer's View. 8vo. paper, pp. 2–68. *Cincinnati (Ohio).* 2*s.* 6*d.*

**Blackmar (Frank W.)**—Spanish Colonization in the Southwest. 8vo. paper. *Baltimore.* 2*s.* 6*d.*
*.* Johns Hopkins University Studies, Eighth Series, No. 4.

**Boisgilbert (Edmund, M.D., pseud.)**—Cæsar's Column: A Story of the Twentieth Century. 8vo. cloth, pp. 367. *Chicago.* 6*s.* 6*d.*

**Bowen (J. L.)**—Massachusetts in the War 1861–1865; with an Introduction by H. L. Dawes. Portrait. 8vo. cloth, pp. 1050. *Springfield (Mass.).* £1 2*s.* 6*d.*

**Bowyer (J. T.)**—The Witch of Jamestown; a Story of Colonial Virginia. 12mo. cloth, pp. 151. *Richmond (Va.).* 7*s.* 6*d.*

**Boynton (H.)**—The World's Greatest Conflict; Review of France and America, 1788 to 1800, and History of America and Europe, 1800 to 1804. 12mo. cloth, pp. 325. *Boston.* 6*s.* 6*d.*

**Brackett (Jeffrey R.)**—Notes on the Progress of the Coloured People of Maryland since the War. A Supplement to "The Negro in Maryland;" a Study of the Institution of Slavery. (Johns Hopkins University Studies, 8th series, Nos. 7, 8, 9.) 8vo. paper, pp. 96. *Baltimore.* 2*s.*

**Bradford (E. H., M.D., and Lovett, Rob. W., M.D.)** —A Treatise on Orthopedic Surgery. Illustrated. 8vo. cloth, pp. 790. *New York.* £1 10*s.*

**Brinton (Daniel G., M.D.) and Davidson (T.)**— Giordano Bruno; Philosopher and Martyr: Two Addresses. 8vo. cloth, pp. 4–68. *Philadelphia.* 4*s.*

**Britton (Wiley)**— The Civil War on the Border, 1861–62. 8vo. cloth, pp. 15 and 465. *New York.* 15*s.*

**Broadus (J. A.)**—Jesus of Nazareth. Three Lectures before the Y. M. C. A. of Johns Hopkins University, in Levering Hall. 12mo. cloth, pp. 105. *New York.* 4*s.*

**Brooks (Elbridge S.)**—A Son of Issachar; a Romance of the Days of Messias. 12mo. cloth, pp. 7 and 293. *New York.* 6*s.* 6*d.*

**Brooks (Mrs. Sarah Warner)**—English Poetry and Poets. 8vo. cloth, pp. 3 and 505. *Boston.* 10*s.* 6*d.*

**Brown (J. Mason)**—The Political Beginnings of Kentucky. A Narrative of Public Events bearing on the History of that State up to the Time of its Admission into the American Union. 4to. paper, pp. 3 and 260. *Louisville (Ky.).* 15*s.*

**Bryant (W. M.)**—The World Energy and its Self-conservation. 12mo. cloth, pp. 14–304. *Chicago.* 7*s.* 6*d.*

**Buck (J. D., M.D.)**—The Nature and Aim of Theosophy. New Enlarged Edition. Square 16mo. cloth. *Cincinnati (Ohio).* 4*s.*

**Buel (J. W.)**—Heroes of the Dark Continent. 8vo. cloth, pp. 576. Illustrations and Map. *St. Louis* and *Philadelphia.* 18*s.*

**Burnham (Clara Louise)**—The Mistress of Beech Knoll: a Novel. 12mo. cloth, pp. 4–413. *Boston.* 6*s.* 6*d.*

**Butterfield (Consul Willshire)**—History of the Girtys. 8vo. cloth, pp. 13–426. *Cincinnati (Ohio).* 18*s.*

**Camden Mountains (The)**; the Norway of America. A Handbook of Mountain, Ocean, and Lake Scenery on the Coast of Maine. Illustrated by W. Goodrich Beal. Oblong paper, pp. 48. *Boston.* 1*s.* 6*d.*

**Checkley (Edwin)**—A Natural Method of Physical Training; being a Practical Description of the Checkley System of Physiculture. Illustrated from Photographs taken especially for this Treatise. 12mo. cloth, pp. 152. *Brooklyn.* 7*s.* 6*d.*

**Child (Theodore)**—Delicate Feasting. 12mo. cloth, pp. 1214. *New York.* 6*s.* 6*d.*

**Childs (G. W.)**—Recollections. 12mo. cloth, pp. 3–404. *Philadelphia.* 5*s.*

**Clokey (Jos. Waddell, D.D.)**—Dying at the Top; or, The Moral and Spiritual Condition of the Young Men of America. New Edition, Revised and Enlarged. 12mo. cloth, pp. 3–124. *Chicago (Ill.).* 2*s.* 6*d.*

**Conway (Rev. J.)**—Rational Religion. 12mo. cloth, pp. 176. *Milwaukee (Wis.).* 6*s.*

**Copeland (T. Campbell)**—The Ladder of Journalism, How to Climb it. Paper, pp. 138. *New York.* 2*s.* 6*d.*

**Craig (J. A.)**—Hebrew Word Manual, etymologically Arranged. 12mo. cloth, pp. 120. *Cincinnati.* 7*s.* 6*d.*

**Crooks (G. R., D.D.)**—The Life of Bishop Matthew Simpson, of the Methodist Episcopal Church. 8vo. cloth, pp. 13–512. *New York.* £1 1*s.*

**Cutler (Julia Perkins)**—Life and Times of Ephraim Cutler, prepared from his Journals and Correspondence, by his Daughter, Julia Perkins Cutler. With Biographical Sketches of Jervis Cutler and W. Parker Cutler. 8vo. cloth, pp. 5 and 353. *Cincinnati.* 12*s.* 6*d.*

**Davis (Mrs. Jefferson)**—Jefferson Davis, Ex-President of the Confederate States. A Memoir, by his Wife. Illustrated. 8vo. cloth. *New York.* £1 10*s.*

**Davis (Jefferson)**—A Short History of the Confederate States of America. 4to. cloth. *New York.* 15s.

**De Graff (E. V.)**—The Schoolroom Guide to Methods of Teaching and School Management. 70th Edition, rewritten. 12mo. cloth, pp. 324. *Syracuse (New York).* 7s. 6d.

**De Leon (T. C.)**—Our Creole Carnivals; their Origin, History, Progress, and Results; with Sketches of Outside Carnivals. 8vo. paper, pp. 5-39. *Mobile (Ala.).* 1s. 6d.

**Dick (H. B.)**—Dick's Book of Alphabets, Plain and Ornamental. For use of Architects, Decorators, etc. 4to. cloth. *New York.* 7s. 6d.

**Field (H. M., D.D.)**—Bright Skies and Dark Shadows. 8vo. cloth, pp. 316. *New York.* 7s. 6d.

**Finerty (J. F.)**—War-path and Bivouac; or, The Conquest of the Sioux. Portrait. Illustrations and Map. 8vo. cloth, pp 450. *Chicago.* 12s.

**Fish (Eldridge Eugene)**—The Blessed Birds; or, Highways and Byways. 12mo. cloth, pp. 253. *Buffalo.* 7s. 6d.

**Fisher (G. Park, D.D.)**—The Nature and Method of Revelation. 12mo. cloth, pp 13-291. *New York.* 6s. 6d.

**Fiske (Amos K.)**—Midnight Talks at the Club. 16mo. cloth, pp. 6 and 297. *New York.* 5s.

**Foster (W. E.)**—References to the Constitution of the United States; with an Appendix. A Model Bibliography of the Sources of the Constitution, in Teutonic, British and Colonial Institutions. 12mo. paper, pp. 2-50. *New York.* 1s. 6d.

**Frederic (Harold)**—The Lawton Girl. 12mo. cloth, pp. 9-472. *New York.* 6s. 6d.

**Frédéricq (Paul)**—The Study of History in Germany and France; from the French by Henrietta Leonard. (Johns Hopkins University Studies, 8th Series, Nos. 5-6.) 8vo. paper, pp. 2 and 33. *Baltimore.* 5s.

**Freethought: Is it Destructive or Constructive?** A Symposium. By R. G. Ingersoll, H. O. Pentecost, and others. 12mo. paper, pp. 82. *New York.* 1s. 6d.

**Frothingham (Octavius Brooks)** — Boston Unitarianism 1820-1850; a Study of the Life and Work of Nathaniel Langdon Frothingham. A Sketch. 12mo. cloth, pp 4 and 272. *New York.* 9s.

**Gardner (Celia E.)**—Seraph, or Mortal? A Romance. 12mo. cloth, pp. 430. *New York.* 7s. 6d.

**Gerhard (W. Paul)**—The Disposal of Household Wastes. (Van Nostrand's Science Series, No. 97.) Fcap. 8vo. boards, pp. 195. *New York.* 2s. 6d.

**Gildersleeve (Basil L.)**—Essays and Studies. Small 4to. cloth, pp. 520. *Baltimore.* £1 1s.

**Goode (G. Brown)** — The Origin of the National Scientific and Educational Institutions of the United States. (Papers of the American Historical Association, vol. 4, pt. 2.) 8vo. paper, pp. 2 and 112. *New York.* 5s.

**Grossmann (Rabbi L., D.D.)**—Maimonides. A Paper read before the Philosophical Society of the University of Michigan, January 19th, 1890. 12mo. paper, pp. 2-38. *New York.* 1s. 6d.

**Guernsey (R. S.)**—New York City and Vicinity during the War of 1812-15; being a Military, Civil, and Financial Local History of that Period, with Incidents and Anecdotes thereof, etc. Vol. I. 8vo. cloth, pp. 480. *N. York.* £1 5s.

**H. (D. G.)**—The Polyglot Pronouncing Handbook: a Key to the Correct Pronunciation of Current Geographical and other Proper Names from Foreign Languages. 16mo. cloth, pp. 3-77. *New York and Chicago.* 2s. 6d.

**Hambleton (G. W., M.D.)**—The Suppression of Consumption. (Facts and Theory Papers, No. 1.) 12mo. cloth, pp. 2 and 37. *New York.* 2s.

**Hammerer (J. Daniel)**—An Account of a Plan for Civilizing the North American Indians proposed in the Eighteenth Century. Edited by Paul Leicester Ford. (Indian Tracts, No. 1, of the Brooklyn Historical Printing Club.) 16mo. paper. *Brooklyn.* 3s.

**Harris (W. T.)**—The Spiritual Sense of Dante's "Divina Commedia." Square 16mo. cloth. *N. York.* 4s.

**Hearn (Lafcadio)**—Youma. A Story of a West Indian Slave. 12mo. cloth, pp. 3-193. *New York.* 5s.

**Hemenway (Francis Dana)**—The Life and Selected Writings of Francis Dana Hemenway. 12mo. cloth, pp. 400. *Cincinnati.* 10s. 6d.

**Henley (W. E.)**—Views and Reviews; Essays in Appreciation. 12mo. cloth, pp. 9 and 235. *New York.* 5s.

**Henning (Crawford D., ed.)**—Quiz Cases on Pleading at Common Law. 8vo. paper, pp. 26. *Philadelphia.* 2s. 6d.

**Herbert (Hilary A., Vance, Zebulon B., Hamphill, J. J., and others)**—Why the Solid South? or, Reconstruction and its Results. 12mo. cloth, pp. 15-4-52. *Baltimore.* 7s. 6d.

**Herrick (Christine Terhune)**—Liberal Living upon Narrow Means. 12mo. cloth, pp. 3-275. *Boston.* 5s.

**Herrick (G. F.)**—An Intense Life. A Sketch of the Life and Work of Rev. Andrew T. Pratt, M.D., Missionary of the A. B. C. F. M. in Turkey, 1852-1872. 12mo. cloth, pp. 96. *New York and Chicago.* 2s. 6d.

**Higginson (S. J.)**—Java, the Pearl of the East. The Riverside Library for Young People. Map. 16mo. cloth, pp. 2 and 204. *Boston.* 4s.

**Hittell (J. S.)**—A Code of Morals. Second Edition. Revised. 16mo. cloth, pp. 54. *San Francisco (Cal.).* 2s. 6d.

**Hoff (C. A., M.D.)**—Highways and Byways to Health. 2 vols. 12mo. cloth. *Philadelphia and St. Louis.* £1 8s.

**Howe (H. M.)**—The Metallurgy of Steel. Illust. Imp. 8vo. cloth. *New York.* £2 12s. 6d.

**Hurd (J.)**—The Union—State. A Letter to our State Rights Friend. 8vo. paper, 135. *New York.* 4s.

**Iliowizi (H. Rabbi)**—Jewish Dreams and Realities contrasted with Islamitic and Christian Claims. 8vo. cloth, pp. 3-279. *Philadelphia.* 10s. 6d.

**Janvier (T. A.)**—The Aztec Treasure House. A Romance of Contemporaneous Antiquity. Illust. 12mo. cloth, pp. 446. *New York.* 7s. 6d.

**Johnston (Rev. J.)**—A Century of Christian Progress, showing also the Increase of Protestantism and the Decline of Popery. Second Edition. 12mo. cloth, pp. 108. *New York and Chicago.* 2s. 6d.

**Jones (J. P.)**—Money. Speech of Hon. J. P. Jones, of Nevada, on the Free Coinage of Silver, in the United States Senate, May 12 and 13, 1890. 8vo. paper, pp. 2 and 116. *Washington.* 3s.

**Karr (Mrs. Elizabeth)**—The American Horse-woman. Third Edition. 12mo. cloth, pp. 16 and 324. *Boston.* 6s. 6d.

**Kimball (Arthur L.)**—The Physical Properties of Gases. 12mo. cloth. pp. 6-238. *Boston.* 6s. 6d.
<br>*** Riverside Science Series, No. 2.

**Kobbé (Gustav)**—The New Jersey Coast and Pine. An Illustrated Guide Book, with Road Maps. 16mo. cloth, pp. 11 and 108. *New York.* 1s. 6d.

**Kunz (G. F.)**—Gems and Precious Stones of North America. A Popular Description of their Occurrences, Value, History, Archæology, and of the Collections in which they exist. Also a Chapter on Pearls, and on Remarkable Foreign Gems owned in the United States. Illustrated with eight Coloured Plates and other Engravings. Imp. 8vo. cloth, pp. 336. *New York.* £2 12s. 6d.

Mack (C. S., M.D.)—Philosophy in Homœopathy. Addressed to the Medical Profession and to the General Reader. 12mo. cloth, pp. 3 and 174. *Chicago.* 6*s.*

Mathews (W. S. B., ed.)—A Hundred Years of Music in America. Portrait. 8vo. cloth, pp. 720. *Chicago.* £1 11*s.* 6*d.*

McCook (H. C.)—American Spiders and their Spinning Work. A Natural History of the Orb-weaving Spiders of the United States, with Special Regard to their Industry and Habits. In 3 vols. Vol. 1, 8vo. cloth, pp. 374. *Philadelphia.* £2 12*s.* 6*d.*

McGill (Alex. T.)—Church Government. A Treatise compiled from his Lectures in Theological Seminaries. 12mo. cloth, pp. 560. *Philadelphia.* 7*s.* 6*d.*

McIntyre (G. P.)—The Light of Persia ; or, the Death of Mammon. Poems of Prophecy, Profit, and Peace. 12mo. cloth. *Chicago.* 6*s.* 6*d.*

Meyer (Rev. F. B.)—Elijah, and the Secret of his Power. 12mo. cloth, pp. 187. *New York* and *Chicago.* 6*s.*

Miller (S. A.)—North American Geology and Palæontology for the Use of Amateurs, Students, and Scientists. 8vo. cloth. pp. 664. *Cincinnati.* £1 11*s.* 6*d.*

Miller (W. B. E.), Hazard (Willis P.), and Others— The Diseases of Live Stock and their most Efficient Remedies. A Popular Guide for the Medical and Surgical Treatment of all Domestic Animals, including Horses, Cattle, Cows, Sheep, Swine, Fowls, Dogs, etc. 8vo. cloth, pp. 2–523. *Philadelphia.* 12*s.* 6*d.*

Mitchell (Donald G., "Ik Marvel," *pseud.*)—English Lands, Letters, and Kings ; from Elizabeth to Anne. 12mo. cloth, pp 2–347. *New York.* 7*s.* 6*d.*

Molée (Elias)—Pure Saxon English ; or, Americans to the Front. 12mo. cloth, pp. 2 and 87. *New York* and *Chicago.* 5*s.*

*** A new universal language, to be built up upon English, is described in this volume.

Montgomery (Rev. M. W.)—The Mormon Delusion ; its History, Doctrine, and the Outlook in Utah. 12mo. cloth, pp. 4–354. *Boston.* 4*s.*

Moody (D. L.)—A College of Colleges, No. 3. 12mo. cloth, pp. 301. *New York* and *Chicago.* 7*s.* 6*d.*

Moreland (F. A.)—Practical Decorative Upholstery. Illust. 8vo. cloth, pp. 320. *Boston.* £1.

Morgan (Appleton)—The Society and the "Fad." being an Amplification of an Address delivered before the Shakespeare Club of New York City, Nov. 1, 1889. Fact and Theory, No. 2.) 12mo. flexible cloth, pp. 2 and 20. *New York.* 1*s.* 6*d.*

Murray (W. H. H.)—Lake Champlain and its Shores. Portrait. 12mo. cloth, pp. 4 and 261. *Boston.* 5*s.*

Needham (Mrs. G. C.)—Poetic Paraphrases. 16mo. cloth, pp. 96. *New York* and *Chicago.* 2*s.* 6*d.*

Ninde (W. X. (Bp.), and Others)— The Kansas Methodist Pulpit. A Collection of Twenty-Four Sermons, by Bishop W. X. Ninde, and Various Members of the Four Kansas Conferences of the Methodist Episcopal Church. Compiled by J. W. D. Anderson. 8vo. cloth, pp. 6-297. *Topeka* (*Kan.*). 9*s.*

Noel (Rev. Arthur Howard)—A Short History of Mexico. 16mo. cloth, pp. 4–294. *Chicago.* 5*s.*

Oldenberg (H., Jastrow, Jos., and Cornill, C. H.)— Epitomes of Three Sciences: Comparative Philology, Psychology, and Old Testament History. 12mo. cloth, pp. 6 and 139. *Chicago.* 4*s.*

O'Reilly (J. Boyle)—Athletics and Manly Sports. New Enlarged Edition. 12mo. cloth, pp. 500. *Boston.* 7*s.* 6*d.*

Pastels in Prose.—From the French. Translated by Stuart Merrill. With Illustrations by H. W. McVicar, and an Introduction by W. D. Howells. 12mo. cloth, pp. 10–268. *New York.* 1*s.* 6*d.*

Patten (Simon N.)—The Economic Basis of Protection. 12mo. cloth. pp. 2 and 144. *Philadelphia.* 5*s.*

Peabody (Andrew Preston, D.D.)—Harvard Graduates whom I have Known. 12mo. cloth, pp. 4 and 255. *Boston.* 6*s.* 6*d.*

Pearson (Rev. R. G.) — Truth Applied ; or, Bible Readings. 16mo. cloth, pp. 244. *Nashville* (*Tenn.*). 7*s.* 6*d.*

Pellew (G. John Jay)—American Statesmen Series. 12mo. cloth, pp. 8 and 374. *Boston.* 6*s.* 6*d.*

Poole (Mrs. Hester M.)—Fruits, and How to Use them. A Practical Manual for Housekeepers ; containing nearly Seven Hundred Receipes for Wholesome Preparations of Foreign and Domestic Fruits. 12mo cloth, pp. 242. *New York.* 5*s.*

Peters (C.)—Home Handicrafts. Sq. 8vo. cloth, pp. 160. *Chicago* and *New York.* 6*s.*

Peters (E. D., jun.)—Modern American Methods of Copper Smelting. Illust. 8vo. cloth. *New York.* £1 5*s.*

Practical Mining.—A Field Manual for Mining Engineers. 12mo. tuck. *New York.* 7*s.* 6*d.*

Pratt (Mara L.)—The Fairyland of Flowers. A Popular Illustrated Botany for the Home and School. 8vo. boards, pp. 2 and 154. *Boston.* 5*s.*

Ram (J.)—A Treatise on Facts as Subjects of Inquiry by a Jury. Fourth Edition, with all the Notes to the previous Editions, by J. Townshend, and Additional Notes and References by C. F. Beach, jun ; with an Appendix containing D. Paul Brown's Golden Rules for the Examination of a Witness. etc., etc. 8vo law calf, pp. 18 and 517. *New York.* £1 4*s.*

Richardson (Anna Martin)—Home-made Candies and other Good Things Sweet and Sour. 12mo. cloth, pp. 6 and 94. *Cincinnati.* 6*s.*

Rivers (J. D.)—The Settlers' Guide to the Great Sioux Reservation. A Valuable and Popular Exposition of the Law. and the Decisions of the Land Department of the General Government on the Rights of Homesteaders, and Town-site Settlers. 12mo. paper. *Chicago.* 1*s.* 6*d.*

Robinson (E., D.D.)—Harmony of the Four Gospels ; with Explanatory Notes and References to Parallel and Illustrative Passages. 16mo. cloth, pp. 192. *New York* and *Chicago.* 3*s.*

Runeberg (Johan Ludwig)—Nadeschda. A Poem in Nine Cantos. From the Swedish by Mrs J. Shipley [Marie A. Brown]. 12mo. cloth, pp. 103. *N. York.* 3*s.* 6*d.*

Sadi-Carnot — Reflections on the Motive Power of Heat ; edited by R. H. Thurston. 12mo. cloth. *New York,* 10*s.*

Samuels (E. A.)—With Fly-rod and Camera. Illust. by the Author. 8vo. cloth, pp. 6 and 477. *N. York.* £1 5*s.*

Seeger and Guernsey's Cyclopædia of the Manufactures and Products of the United States ; comprising every Article made in this country. Indexed and Classified, and under each Article the Names and Addresses of the Best Manufacturers. 8vo cloth. pp. 1300. *New York.* £1 11*s.* 6*d.*

Senex (*pseud.*)—The Evolution of Myth as Exemplified in General Grant's History of the Plot of President Polk and Secretary Marcy to sacrifice two American Armies in the Mexican War of 1846–48. 12mo. paper, pp. 54. *Washington* (*D.C.*). 2*s.* 6*d.*

Serrao (Teodoro).—Brushes and Chisels. A Story. 12mo. cloth, pp. 3 and 213. *Boston.* 6*s.*

Sessions (Francis C.)—In Western Levant. Illust. by H. W. Hall. 12mo. cloth, pp. 252 and 12. *New York.* 7*s.* 6*d.*

Shakespeare (W.) — Complete Works. Bankside Edition. In 20 vols. Vols. 7 and 8. Limited edition of 500 copies only by subscription. 8vo. cloth. 12*s.* 6*d.* each. *New York.*

**Shakespeare (W.)**—Works. New Variorum Edition. Edited by Horace H. Furness. Vol. 8, As You Like It. 8vo. cloth, pp. 2–452. *Philadelphia.* 18s.

**Shields (G. O., "Coquina," *pseud.*)**—Camping and Camp Outfits. A Manual of Instruction for Young and Old Sportsmen. Illustrated. 12mo. cloth, pp. 200. *New York* and *Chicago.* 6s. 6d.

**Shinkichi Shigemi.**—A Japanese Boy. 12mo. cloth, pp. 128. *New York.* 5s.

**Sienkiewics (Henryk)**—With Fire and Sword. An Historical Novel; from the Polish by Jeremiah Curtin. 8vo. cloth, pp. 16–779. *Boston.* 10s. 6d.

**Sinclair (August)**—A Practical Treatise on Locomotive Engines, showing their Performance in running different Kinds of Trains with Economy and Despatch. New Enlarged Edition. 12mo. cloth. *New York.* 8s. 6d.

**Slocum (Joshua)**—The Voyage of the *Liberdade.* 16mo. cloth. *East Boston.* 6s.

**Sterrett (J. Macbride, D.D.)** — Studies in Hegel's Philosophy of Religion; with a Chapter on Christian Unity in America. 8vo. cloth, pp. 11–348. *New York.* 10s. 6d.

**Stetefedt (C. A.)**—The Lixiviation of Silvers Ore. Illustrated. 8vo. cloth. *New York.* £1 5s.

**Sweetser (M. F.)**—The Maritime Provinces. A Handbook for Travellers. Seventh Edition, Revised and Enlarged. 16mo. cloth, pp. 11 and 336. *Boston.* 7s. 6d.

**Switzerland.**—The Federal Constitution of Switzerland. Transposed by Edmund J. James. Publications of University of Philadelphia. 8vo. paper, pp. 3–46. *Philadelphia.* 2s. 6d.

**Talmage (T. De Witt, D.D.)**—Trumpet Peals. A Collection of Timely and Eloquent Extracts from the Sermons of the Rev. T. De Witt Talmage, D.D. Collated and Classified by Rev. L. C. Lockwood. Portrait. 8vo. cloth, pp. 10–486. *New York.* 12s.

**Tea.**—Its Origin, Cultivation, Manufacture, and Use. 16mo. paper, pp. 27. *New York* and *Chicago.* 1s. 6d.

**Thayer (W. M.)**—From Farmhouse to White House; the Childhood, Youth, Manhood, Public and Private Life of George Washington. 12mo. cloth, pp. 501. *Boston.* 7s. 6d.

**Thornton (W. W.)**—A Monograph on the Law of Lost Wills. 8vo. sheep, pp. 9–198. *Chicago.* 15s.

**Thurston (R. H.)**—Heat as a Form of Energy. (The Riverside Science Series, vol. 3.) 12mo. cloth, pp. 3 and 261. *Boston.* 6s. 6d.

**Totten (C. A. L.)**—Yale Military Lectures. Selected from the Series of 1890. 8vo. paper, pp. 3 and 113. *New Haven.* 2s. 6d.

**Totten (C. A. L.)**—Our Race: Its Origin and Destiny. A Series of Studies on the Saxon Riddle; with an Introduction by C. Piazzi Smith. 16mo. paper, pp. 20–268. *New Haven (Ct.).* 4s.

**Towle (G. Makepeace)** — Heroes and Martyrs of Invention. 12mo. cloth, pp. 3 and 202. *Boston.* 5s.

**Van Dyke (H.)**—God and Little Children. The Blessed State of all who Die in Childhood Proved and Taught as a Part of the Gospel of Christ. 12mo. cloth, pp. 4–81. *New York.* 5s.

**Vernon (S. M., D.D.)**—Probation and Punishment. A Rational and Scriptural View of the Future State of the Wicked, with Special Reference to the Doctrine of a Second Probation. 12mo. cloth, pp. 2 and 300. *New York.* 7s. 6d.

**Way (S. P.)**—Sears Genealogy. The Descendants of Richard Sares (Sears), of Yarmouth, Mass., 1638–1888. With an Appendix containing some Notices of other Families by the Name of Sears. 8vo. cloth, pp. 677. *Albany.* £1 10s.

**Weidner (Revere Franklin)**—Studies in the Book. First Series. Containing Studies on the New Testament Historical Books, the General Epistles, and the Apocalypse, interleaved. 12mo. cloth, pp. 120. *New York* and *Chicago.* 6s.

**Weidner (R. F.)**—Studies in the Book. First Series. 16mo. cloth, pp. 120. *New York* and *Chicago.* 5s.

**White (Eliza Orne)**—Miss Brooks. A Story. 12mo. cloth, pp. 2 and 283. *Boston.* 5s.

**White (Mrs. Caroline Earle)**—Love in the Tropics: A Romance of the South Seas. 12mo. cloth, pp. 1–150. *Philadelphia.* 5s.

**Willey (H.)**—A Synopsis of the Genus Arthonia. 8vo. paper, pp. 6 and 60. *New Bedford (Mass.).* 9s.

**Willoughby (W. F.)**—Child Labour. (*Also*) Child Labour by Miss Clare de Graffenried. (Publications of the American Economic Association, Vol. v. No. 2.) 8vo. paper, pp. 3 and 149. *New York.* 4s.

**Wilson (G. H., *comp.*)**—The Musical Year Book of the United States. Vol. 7, Season of 1889–1890. 16mo. paper, pp. 131. *Boston.* 5s.

# New Oriental Literature

## PRINTED IN EUROPE.

**Abel und Winckler.**—Keilschrifttexte zum Gebrauch bei Vorlesungen. 4to. pp. 100. *Berlin*, 1890. 15s.
*** Contains Texts, Vocabulary, etc.

**Acta Mar Kardaghi**, Assyriae prefecti, qui sub Sapore II Martyr occubuit. Syriac with Latin Translation. Edited by Abbeloos. 8vo. pp. 106. *Leipzig*, 1890. 3s. 6d.

**Albéca (A. L. de)**—Côte occidentale d'Afrique. Les établissements français du golfe de Bénin. 8vo. pp. 244. Text with Map. *Paris*, 1890. 6s.

**Al-Coran**, with the Commentary of Béidhâwi on the margin. pp. 816, small folio, full calf. *Constantinople*, 1303. £2 2s.
*** This edition is forbidden in Turkey, and most of the copies confiscated by the authorities.

**Amélineau (E.)**—Les actes des martyrs de l'église copte. Etude critique. 8vo. *Paris*, 1890. 8s.

**Annales** auctore Abu-Djafar Mohammed Ibn Djarir At-Tabari, edited by Barth. Goeje, etc. Royal 8vo. First series, vol. vii. part 1, rec. Prym. *Leide*, 1890. 7s.

**Arbuthnot (F. F.)**—Arabic Authors; a Manual of Arabian History and Literature. 8vo. cloth. 1890. 10s.

**Archiv (Internationales) fuer Ethnographie** edited by Dr. J. D. E. Schmelz. Vol. iii. parts 1 and 2, with coloured plates. 4to. *Leiden*, 1890. Subscription price of the vol. in 6 numbers, £1 1s.

**Bacher (W.)**—Die Agada der Jannaiten. Vol. II. 8vo. pp. 578. *Strassburg*, 1890. 8s.
*** From the death of Akiba to the year 220 A.D.

**Baillie (A. F.)**—Kurrachee, Past, Present, and Future. With numerous Illustrations and Maps. Royal 8vo. *Calcutta.* 1890. £1 1s.

**Barbier de Meynard (A. C.)** — Dictionnaire turc-français, vol. ii. part 4 (end). Large 8vo. *Paris*, 1890. 8s.
*** It gives the derivation of all Turkish words,—Arabic and Persian words employed in the Turkish language—and a large phraseology and collection of Proverbs. Price of the complete work, £3 3s.

**Bergaigne & Henry.**—Manuel pour étudier le sanscrit védique. Large 8vo. wrapper, pp. 336. *Paris*, 1890. 10*s.* 6*d.*
Contents :—Précis de grammaire—Chrestomathie—Lexique.

**Bibliotheca rabbinica.**—Eine Sammlung alter Midraschim. zum ersten male ins Deutsche uebertragen, von A. Wuensche, new edition. 8vo. in 31 parts. *Leipzig*, 1890. 1*s.* 6*d.* each part.

**Blanckhorn (M.)**—Beitraege zur Geologie Syriens. 4to. pp. 135, with Plates. *Berlin*, 1890. £1 10*s.*

**Blondeau (G.)**—Grand annuaire tunisien, administratif, commercial, industriel, agricole, vinicole et viticole. 8vo. *Tunis*, 1890. 3*s.* 6*d.*

**Boerlage (J. G.)**—Handleiding tot de kennis des flora van nederlandsch Indie. Vol. i. part 1. 8vo. *Leiden*, 1890. 6*s.*

**Book (The)** of the Dead. Coloured Facsimile of the Papyrus of Ani, 37 large folio plates in portfolio, with English translation. 1890. £1 15*s.*

**Bourgon (J.)**—Précis de l'art arabe et matériaux pour servir à l'histoire, à la théorie et à la technique des arts de l'orient musulman. Parts 7 to 12, just out ; 6*s.* each part.

**Bournichon (J.)**—L'invasion musulman en Afrique suivie du réveil de la foi chrétienne dans ces contrées et de la croisade des noirs entreprise par le Cardinal Lavigerie. Royal 8vo. pp. 352. *Tours*, 1890.

**Brugsch (H.)**—Die Aegyptologie. Abriss der Entzifferungen und Forschungen auf dem Gebiete der aegyptischen Schrift, Sprache und Alterthumskunde. 8vo. 1890. 14*s.*

**Caitness (Lady).**—Théosophie sémitique. Les vrais Israélites. L'identification des dix tribus perdus avec la nation britannique ; les Suffis et la Théosophie mahométane. 8vo. pp. 149. *Paris*, 1890.

**Cat (E.)**—Essai sur la vie et les ouvrages du chroniqueur Gonzalo Ayora suivi de fragments inédits de sa Chronique. 8vo. *Alger*, 1890. 2*s.* 6*d.*
*₊* Publications de l'Ecole des Lettres d'Alger, vol. iii.

**Colonies françaises.**—Notices illustrées pub. par ordre du Sous-Secrétaire d'Etat, des Colonies par L. Henrique, vol. v. Colonies d'Afrique, part 1 (Sénégal et rivières du sud ; Soudan français). 8vo. *Paris*, 1890. 3*s.*

**Corpus Juris Abessinorum.**—Aethiopic and Arabic text with a Latin Translation and a Dissertation by Dr. J. Bachmann. Part 1. Jus connubii. 4to. *Berlin*, 1890. 16*s.*

**Correspondance** des Deys d'Alger avec la cour de France de 1579-1833, collected and edited by E. Plantet. 2 vols. 8vo. *Paris*, 1890. £1 10*s.*

**Dandin's Poetik (Kâvjâdarça).** Sanskrit and German. Edited by O. Boehtlingk. 8vo. pp. vii. and 138. *Leipzig*, 1890. 10*s.* 6*d.*

**Daniell (C. J.)**—The Industrial Competition of Asia. Demy 8vo. 1890. 12*s.*
*₊* An inquiry into the influence of currency on the commerce of the Empire of the East.

**Delitzsch (F.)**—Assyrisches Woerterbuch zur gesammten bisher veroeffentlichen Keilschriftliteratur. Part 3. Large 4to. pp. 329 to 488. *Leipzig*, 1890. Subscription price of the whole work, £1 10*s.*

**Dobson (G.)**—Russia's Railway Advance to Central-Asia. Crown 8vo. 1890. 7*s.*

**Drury (Robert)**—Journal during Fifteen Years' Captivity in Madagascar, and a further Description of that Island by the Abbé Alexis Rochon. edited with Introduction and Notes by Capt. Pasfield Oliver. With many Illustrations and Plates. 8vo. cloth, pp. 399. 1890. 6*s.*
Contains (pp. 319-335) an English-Malagasy vocabulary.

**Du Chaillu (P.)**—Adventures in the Great Forest of Equatorial Africa. With Illustrations and Map. Crown 8vo. cloth. 1890. 7*s.* 6*d.*

**Ehni (J.)**—Der Vedische Mythus der Yama. 8vo. pp. 216. *Strassburg*, 1890. 6*s.*
*₊* A comparison with the Persian, Greek, and Germanic Mythology.

**Exner (A. H.)**—China. Skizzen von Land und Leuten mit besonderer Beruecksichtigung commerzieller Verhaeltnisse. With many Plates and Maps. Text. Large 8vo. half calf, pp. 298. *Leipzig*, 1889. £1 1*s.*

**Featherman (A.)**—Social History of the Races of Mankind. Vol. iii. Chiapo and Guarano-Maranonians. 8vo. pp. 520. 1890. £1 7*s.* 6*d.*

**Geitlin (G.)**—Principia grammatices neopersicae. 8vo. *Helsingfors*, 1890. 6*s.*
*₊* Cum metrorum doctrina et dialogis persicis.

**Gheyn (Rev. Père van den).**—L'origine européenne des Aryas. 8vo. pp. 47. *Paris*, 1889. 2*s.* 6*d.*

**Glaser (E.)**—Skizze der Geschichte und Geographie Asiens von den aeltesten Zeiten bis zum Propheten Muhammed. Vol. ii. 8vo. *Berlin*, 1890. 18*s.*

**Gordiola (J. G. Y.)**—Manual de lengua sanskrita crestomatia y gramatica. 8vo. *Madrid*, 1890. 16*s.*

**Gosset (A.)**—Les coupoles d'orient et d'occident. Etude historique. théorique et pratique. With 110 Illustrations and 25 Plates. 4to. *Paris*, 1890. £2 7*s.* 6*d.*

**Handy Guide Book** to the Japanese Islands, with Maps and Plans. 8vo. 1890. 6*s.* 6*d.*

**Hardy (E.)**—Der Buddhismus nach aeltern Pali-Werken dargestellt, with a Map. 8vo. pp. 168. *Muenster*, 1890. 3*s.*

**Histoire** de guerres d'Amda Syon, roi d'Ethiopie, translated from the Ethiopian into French by Perruchon. 8vo. pp. 209. *Paris*, 1890.

**Huart (C.)**—Notices d'un manuscript pehlevi-musulman de la Bibliothèque de Ste. Sophie à Constantinople. 8vo. pp. 35. *Paris*, 1890. 2*s.*

**Imbault-Huart (C.)**—Manuel de la langue coréenne parlée à l'usage des Français. Large 8vo. pp. 108. *Paris*, 1890. 9*s.*

**Inagaki (M.)**—Japan and the Pacific and a Japanese view of the Eastern Question. 8vo. cloth, pp. 265 with Maps. 1890. 7*s.* 6*d.*

**Jensen (P.)**—Die Kosmologie der Babylonier. Studien und Materialien. 8vo. *Strassburg*, 1890. £2.

**Khandogjopanishad,** with a Critical Commentary and German Translation by O. Boehtlingk. 8vo. pp. 108 and 93. *Leipzig*, 1889. 12*s.*

**Kiepert (H.)**—Specialkarte vom westlichen Kleinasien. Part 1 in 6 leaves with text. *Berlin*, 1890. 10*s.*
*₊* To be completed in 3 parts before the end of the year.

**Kingscote and Sastri.**—Tales of the Sun : Collection of Stories on Southern Indian Folk-Lore. Crown 8vo. cloth. 1890. 6*s.*

**Krauss (F. S.)**—Volksglaube und religioeser Brauch der Suedslaven. 8vo. pp. 176. *Muenster*, 1890. 3*s.*

**Krueger (W.)**—Berichte der Versuchsstation fuer Zuckerrohr in West-Java, Kagok-Tegal. Part 1, pp. 179, with Plates. *Dresden*, 1890. 15*s.*
——— The same, in Dutch. 15*s.*

**Khush Hal Khan Khatak.**—Afghan Poetry of the Seventeenth Century ; being Selections from his Poems (in Afghan). With Translations and Grammatical Introduction. 4to. cloth, pp. xvii. 120 and 73. 1890. 10*s.* 6*d.*

**Lane (E. W.)**—Account of the Manners and Customs of the Modern Egyptians. 12mo. cloth. 1890. 2*s.*

Lefébure (E.)—Rites égyptiens. Constructions et protection des édifices. 8vo. *Alger*, 1890. 4*s*.
*°* Publications de l'Ecole des Lettres d'Alger, vol. iv.

Lelu (Paul).—L'Afrique du Sud; histoire de la colonie anglaise du cap de Bonne-Espérance et de ses annexes, with a Map. 8vo. *Paris*, 1890. 2*s*. 6*d*.

Loqmân Berbère.—Texte berbère et transcription. Edited by R. Basset, with four glossaries. 8vo. *Paris*, 1890. 6*s*.

Loret (V.)—Manuel de la langue égyptienne. Grammaire, spécimens de texte et glossaire. Part 1. 4to. pp. 60. *Paris*, 1890.

Lynch (J.)—Egyptian Sketches. With 16 Plates. Demy 8vo. 1890. 10*s*. 6*d*.

Manuel du Sinologue ou recueil de renseignements utiles, à l'usage de personnes qui s'occupent de la Chine et de la littérature chinoise. Part I. 1889.

Matsudaira (Y. v.)—Voelkerrechtliche Vertraege von Japan in wirthschaftlicher, rechtlicher und politischer Bedeutung. 8vo. pp. 527. *Stuttgart*, 1890. 12*s*.

Middendorf (E. W.)—Das Runa Simi oder die Keshua Sprache, wie sie gegenwaertig in der Provinz von Cusco gesprochen wird. Large 8vo. pp. 339. *Leipzig*, 1890. Bound, 16*s*.
*°* With dialogues and an alphabetical index.

Miklosich (F.) — Die tuerkischen Elemente in den suedost und osteuropaeischen Sprachen (Greek, Albanian, Roumanian, Bulgarian, Serbian, Russian and Polish). Supplement, part 2. Imp. 4to. pp. 194. *Leipzig*, 1890. 10*s*. 6*d*.

Morrison (W. D.)—The Jews under Roman Rule. With Illustrations. Post 8vo. cloth, pp. 426. 1890. 6*s*.
*°* Forms vol. 24 of the well-known series "The Story of the Nations."

Nathorst (A. G.)—Beitraege zur mesozoischen Flora Japans, with 6 Plates and a Map. 4to. *Leipzig*, 1890. 6*s*. 6*d*.

Oliver (P.)—Madagascar; or, Robert Drury's Journey during 15 Years' Captivity on that Island. 8vo. 1890. 6*s*.

Osthoff und Brugmann.—Morphologische Untersuchungen aus dem Gebiete der indogermanischen Sprachen Vol. V. 8vo. *Leipzig*, 1890. 7*s*.

Palestine under the Moslems. A Description of Syria and the Holy Land from 650 to 1500, translated from the Mediaeval Arabic MS., by Guy Le Strange. With Illustrations and Maps. Crown 8vo. cloth, pp. 624. 12*s*. 6*d*.

Paris (C.)—Voyage d'exploration de Hué en Cochinchine par la route Mandarine. 8vo. *Paris*, 1890.

Perrot and Chipiez.—History of Art in Sardinia, Judaea, Syria and Asia Minor. Translated and edited by F. Gonino. 406 Illustrations and 8 Plates. 2 vols. Roy. 8vo. 1890. £1 16*s*.

Rausch v. Traubenberg.—Hauptverkehrswege Persiens. Versuch einer Verkehrsgeographie Persiens. With a Map. 8vo. pp. 128. *Halle*, 1890. 6*s*.

Reinisch (L.)—Saho Sprache. Vol. II.: Woerterbuch der Sahosprache. 8vo. pp. viii. and 492. *Vienna*, 1890. £1 4*s*.

Rhys Davids (T. W.)—The Questions of King Milinda. Translated from the Pâli by Rhys Davids. 8vo. cloth, pp. 320. *Oxford*, 1890. 10*s*. 6*d*.
*°* Forms Sacred Books of the East, vol. xxxv.

Rumsey (A.)—Al Sirajiyyah; or, the Mohammedan Law of Inheritance, with Notes and Appendix. Second Edition, Revised. Crown 8vo. 1890. 6*s*.

Saint Quentin (R. de).—Abrégé de grammaire hindoustanie, with a Phraseology and a Vocabulary. Royal 8vo. pp. 109. *Rouen*, 1890.

Schlegel (G.)—Nederlandsch-Chineesch Woordenboek. Vol. iv. part 3. *Leiden*, 1890.

Schrader (O.)—Prehistoric Antiquities of the Aryan Peoples. Translated from the German by F. B. Jevons. Large 8vo. cloth. 1890. £1 1*s*.

Schrumpf (G. A.)—A First Arian Reader, consisting of Specimens of the Aryan Languages which constitute the Basis of Comparative Philology. Crown 8vo. pp. 212. 1890. 7*s*. 6*d*.

Schulze (L. F. M.)—Fuehrer auf Java. Handbuch fuer Reisende, Handel und Industrie, with a Railway Map. 8vo. cloth. *Leipzig*, 1890. 10*s*. 6*d*.

Schumacher (G.)—Northern 'Ajlun within the Decapolis. Crown 8vo. pp. 214. 1890. 3*s*. 6*d*.

Seidel (A.)—Praktische Grammatik der japanesischen Sprache, fuer den Selbstunterricht mit Lesestuecken, Systematischen Woerterbuch und 10 Schrifttafeln. 8vo. *Wien*, 1890.

Simon (G. E.)—La cité chinoise. 8vo. pp. 399. *Paris*, 1890. 3*s*.

Stizenberger (E.)—Lichenaea Africana. Part 1. 8vo. pp. 144. *St. Gallen*, 1890. 3*s*.

Strassmaier (J. N.)—Babylonische Texte. Part 8. 8vo. pp. 160. *Leipzig*, 1890. 12*s*. 6*d*.
Contents: Inscriptions of Cambyses, King of Babylon (529–521 B.C.), from the clay plates in the British Museum, first part.

Taramelli e Bellio.—Geografia e Geologia dell' Africa. 8vo. *Milan*, 1890. 12*s*.

Tauber (M.)—Ain Maïr. Novellen und Commentare zu den Talmud-Traktaten Gitin, Chulin, Beza und dem Traktat ueber ehegesetzliche Normen des Maimonides (in Hebrew). Folio, pp. xii. 336 and 28. *Wien*, 1890. 6*s*. 6*d*.

Tchou-Chin-Goura ou une vengeance japonaise. A Japanese Novel. Translated into English, with Notes, by F. Dickins, and in French by A. Donsdebes, with many Illustrations. 8vo. pp. 232. *Paris*, 1890. 12*s*.

Trotter (L. J.)—History of India from the Earliest Times to the Present Day. New edition, revised. Post 8vo. 1890. 6*s*.

Villaret (E. de)—Dai Nippon (Le Japon). With 3 Maps. 8vo. *Paris*, 1890. 7*s*. 6*d*.

Vivarez (M.)—Le Soudan algérien. Projet de voie ferrée transsaharienne (d'Alger au Lac Tchad). 12mo. *Paris*, 1890. 3*s*.

Weisbach (F. H.) — Die Achaemeniden-Inschriften zweiter Art. Edited by F. H. W. Large 4to. pp. vii. and 120, with 16 plates. *Leipzig*, 1890. £1 10*s*.

White (J.)—The Ancient History of the Maori. 4 vols. 4to. cloth. 1890. £2 2*s*.

Wilkins (W. J.) — Daily Life and Work in India. Popular edition. 8vo. cloth, pp. 288, with 59 Illustrations. 1890. 3*s*. 6*d*.

Yokoyama (M.)—Versteinerungen aus der Japanesischen Kreide. 4to. pp. 44, with 8 plates. *Stuttgart*, 1890. 16*s*.

Youssouf (R.)—Dictionnaire portatif turc-français de la langue usuelle. In Roman and Turkish Characters. 12mo. half calf, pp. 846. *Constantinople*, 1890. 7*s*. 6*d*.

Zeitschrift fuer aegyptische Sprache und Alterthumskunde. Published by Brugsch and Erman. Vol. 28, Part 1. Large 4to. pp. 64. *Leipzig*, 1890. Subscription price of the vol. 15*s*.

Zeitschrift fuer Assyriologie und verwandte Gebiete. Edited by C. Bezold. Vol. V. Part 1. 8vo. pp. 136. *Leipzig*, 1890. Price of the vol. in 4 parts, 18*s*.

Zeitschrift der deutschen morgenlaendischen Gesellschaft. Edited by E. Windisch. Vol. 44, Part 1. 8vo. pp. 202. *Leipzig*, 1890. Subscription price of the vol. 15*s*.

# New Oriental Literature.

## BRITISH INDIA, BURMA AND THE STRAITS.

Appayadīkshita, Siddhāntaleśa with extracts of Srīkrishṇa Alaṃkāra. Edited by M. G. Śāstrī Mānavallī. Sanskrit Text. 8vo. wrapper. *Benares*, 1890. 4s. 6d.

**** Forms Vol. I. part i of the Vizianagram Sanskrit Series.

Bibliotheca Indica.—A Collection of Oriental Works published by the Asiatic Society of Bengal. New Series, Nos. 716 to 749. 8vo. *Calcutta*, 1889–90. Price 1s. 6d. to 4s. each part.

**** List of contents sent on application.

Chase (D. A.)—Anglo-Burmese Hand-Book; or, Guide to a Practical Knowledge of the Burmese Language. New Edition, revised by F. D. Phinney. 8vo. limp cloth, pp. 209. *Rangoon*, 1890. 7s. 6d.

Craven (T.)—Royal School Dictionary in English and Roman-Urdu, giving the Pronunciation, Derivation. and Idioms, with Illustrations. Small 8vo. cloth, about 400 pp. text. *Lucknow*, 1889. 4s.

———— English and Hindi Dictionary, Etymological and Idiomatic. With Illustrations. Small 8vo. boards, pp. 307. *Lucknow*, 1890. 2s. 6d.

Grierson (G. A.)—The Modern Vernacular Literature of Hindustan. 8vo. wrapper, pp. xxiii. 159, and xxxv. with three Plates. *Calcutta*, 1889. 12s.

**** A compact literary history from the beginning of the seventh century up to 1887, with two bibliographical indices of the authors and the works.

Journal of the American Oriental Society. Vol. XIV. 8vo. pp. lxviii. and 424. *New Haven* (Conn.), 1890.

Contains the "Kauçika-Sutra of the Atharva-Veda," Sanskrit text, with Extracts from the Commentaries of Darila and Keçava.

Journal of the Asiatic Society of Bengal. 8vo. *Calcutta*. Part I. (Philological Division.)

1888. Special Number, containing Grierson, Literary History of the Modern Vernacular Languages of Hindustan. With Plates. 12s.

1889. No. 2, containing. pp. 37–84, Life of Sumpa Khanpo, also styl+d Yesos Dpal-bbyor by Saratchandra Das. Pages 84–88, Inscribed Seal of Kumara-Gupta by A. Smith, etc., with Plates. 2s. 6d.

1890. No. 1, containing, pp. 1–50, Kavyopadhyaya, Grammar of the Dialect of Chhattisgarh in the Central Provinces, translated from the Hindi by Grierson. Pages 50–99, Notes on a Buddhist Monastery at Bhot Bagan, by Gaur Das Bysack, with Plates. 2s. 6d.

———— The same. Part II. (Natural History Division.)

1889. Nos. 1-4, at 2s. 6d. each; Supplement I. 5s.; Supplement II. 6d.

Journal of the Ceylon Branch of the Royal Asiatic Society for 1888 (vol. x. pp. 219—325). 8vo. *Colombo*, 1890. 5s.

List of Contents: Abamudu Bawa, Marriage Customs of the Moors of Ceylon.—Ramanathan, Ethnology of the "Moors" of Ceylon.—D. Ferguson, Capt. João Ribeiro's Work on Ceylon and the French translation thereof, by Abbé le Grand.—Hamilton, Antiquities of Medamahanuwara.

Journal of the Straits Branch of the Royal Asiatic Society. No. 20 (for 1889), pp. 212, with 2 folded Maps. 8vo. *Singapore*. 9s.

Contents: Proceedings and Report of the Society.—Ridley, Destruction of Coconut-Palms by Beetles.—Treacher, Sketches of Brunai, Sarawak, Labuan and North Borneo.—Haughton, Names of Places in the Island of Singapore and its vicinity.—Journal of a trip to Pahang by Davison.—List of Birds of the Bornean Group of Islands, by Everett.

Murray (John A.)—Edible and Game Birds of British India, with Engravings and plain and coloured Plates. 8vo. cloth. *Bombay*, 1890. 15s.

Proceedings of the Asiatic Society of Bengal, 1889, Nos. 5 10 (May to December), 1890. No. 1 (January). About 24 pages each part. *Calcutta*. Price 6d. each part.

## CHINA AND JAPAN.

Appert (G.) and H. Kinoshita. — Ancien Japon. pp. 252, Text (in French). Post 8vo. cloth, with large Map and Plate in Pocket. *Tokio*, 1888. 6s. 6d.

List of Contents: Lecture des dates.—Listes alphabétiques des Empereurs, des Shogun, des nengo, des daimyō, des châteaux.— Liste des peintres.—Dictionnaire des institutions, coutumes et des personnages de l'ancien Japon.

Aymonier (E.) — Grammaire de la langue chame. Large 8vo. pp. 92, with 5 folded Plates. *Saigon*, 1889. 7s.

Batchelor (Rev. John)—Ainu-English-Japanese Dictionary and Grammar. 8vo. half calf, pp. 287. *Tokyo*, 1889. £1 1s.

Bettany (G. T.)—The Teeming Millions of the East. A Popular Account of the Inhabitants of Asia, with many Illustrations. 8vo. pp. 370. *Shanghai*, 1890. 5s.

Chamberlain (Basil Hall)—Things Japanese. Being Notes on Various Subjects connected with Japan. Crown 8vo. pp. 408, with a folded Map, cloth. *Shanghai*, 1890. 7s. 6d.

Corea.—Annual Trade Reports and Returns for 1889. *Shanghai*, 1890. 5s.

Dudgeon (J.)—Statistics and Resolutions of the Evils of the Use of Opium. Demy 8vo. pp. 40. *Shanghai*, 1890. 2s. 6d.

Du Bose (H. C.)—The Dragon, Image and Demon; or, the Three Religions of China: Confucianism, Buddhism, and Taoism. Crown 8vo. pp. 463. *Shanghai*, 1890. 12s. 6d.

Duncan (C.)—Corea and the Powers; a Review of the Far Eastern Question. Demy 8vo. *Shanghai*, 1890. 5s.

Giles (H. A.)—Chuang Tzu: Mystic, Moralist and Social Reformer. Translated from the Chinese. 8vo. pp. 465. 1890. £1 10s.

Henry (B. C.)—Ling Nam; or, Interior Views of Southern China, including Explorations in the hitherto untraversed Island of Hainan. Crown 8vo. pp. 611. *Shanghai*, 1890. 12s. 6d.

———— The Cross and the Dragon; or, Light in the Broad East, with an Introductory Note by J. Cook. Crown 8vo. pp. 507. *Shanghai*, 1890. 12s. 6d.

Hillier (W. C.)—List of the Higher Metropolitan and Provincial Authorities of China and of the Tsung-Li-Yamen, corrected to end of 1888. Royal 4to. *Shanghai*, 1889. 5s.

Hopkins (L. C.)—Guide to Kuan Hua. A Translation of the Kuan Hua Chih Nan, with an Essay on Tone and Accent in Pekinese and a Glossary of Phrases. 8vo. boards, pp. 221. *Shanghai*, 1889. 12s. 6d.

Journal of the China Branch of the Royal Asiatic Society. New Series, Vol. 24, No. 1 (1889–90). 8vo. pp. 139. *Shanghai*, 1890. 10s.

Contents: Moellendorff, Essay on the Manchu Literature.—Macgowan, Metrology of China.—Extracts from North China Herald. 1889.

Journal of the Peking Oriental Society. 8vo. *Peking*. Vol. II. No. 4, containing—Edkins, Poets of China during the Period of the Contending States and the Han Dynasty.—Martin. Diplomacy in Ancient China.- Shioda Saburo, Origin of the Paper Currency. — Bushell, Specimens of Ancient Chinese Paper Currency, pp. 116. 6s. 6d. Vol. II. No. 5, containing—Edkins, On Li T'ai-Po, with examples of his Poetry.— Verhaeghe de Naeyer, Programme d'histoire de Chine, pp. 82. 5s. 6d.

Legge (Rev. J.)—Christianity in China. Nestorianism, Roman Catholicism, Protestantism. Demy 8vo. wrapper, *Shanghai*, 1890. 5*s*.

List of Chinese Medicines. In Two Parts. *Shanghai*, 1890. 15*s*.
I. Port Lists of Chinese Medicines. II. General Alphabetical List of Chinese Medicines.

Macgowan (D. J.)—Papers on Self-Immolation by Fire and Avenging Habits of the Cobra. Royal 8vo. *Shanghai*, 1890. 3*s*.

Maclay (A. C.)—Mito-Yashiki ; a Tale of Old Japan. Crown 8vo. *Shanghai*, 1890. 13*s*. 6*d*.
*** A Feudal Romance descriptive of the decline of the Shogunate and of the downfall of the power of the Tokugawa family.

Maclellan (J. W.)—The Story of Shanghai from the Opening of the Port to Foreign Trade. Demy 8vo. wrapper. *Shanghai*, 1890. 5*s*. 6*d*.

Nippon Seikōkwai Kito Bun (Prayer-Book). Transliterated in Roman Characters. Post 8vo. cloth, pp. 196. *Yokohama*, 1889. 4*s*.

Opium ; Historical Note on the Poppy in China. *Shanghai*, 1890. 1*s*. 6*d*.

Oriental Cook-Book.—A Guide to Marketing in English and Chinese. Royal 8vo. *Shanghai*, 1890. 15*s*.

Peking Gazette.—English Translation in Abstracts for 1889. 8vo. boards, pp. 189. 1890. 10*s*. 6*d*.

Reports and Returns of Trade for 1889 for the following Ports : — Amoy, Canton, Chefoo, Chinkiang, Foochow, Hankow, Ichang, Kiukiang, Kiungchow, Kowloon, Lappa, Lungchow, Mengtzu, Newchwang, Ningpo, Pakhoi, Shanghai, Swatow, Takow, Tamsui, Tientsin, Wenchow and Wuhu. 2*s*. 6*d*. each.

Report on the Trade of China and Abstract of Statistics for 1889. *Shanghai*, 1890. 5*s*.

Tariff Returns, a Set of Tables showing the Bearing of the Chinese Customs Tariff of 1858 on the Trade of 1885. 2 vols. *Shanghai*, 1890. £1 5*s*.

The Art of Tea Blending.—A Guide to Tea Merchants, Brokers, Dealers and Consumers in the Secret of Successful Tea Mixing. 8vo. *Shanghai*, 1890. 4*s*.

The (Chinese) Customs Gazette.—Quarterly Returns of Trade. *Shanghai*. £1 1*s*. yearly.
Supplement to it : Fines and Confiscations. 5*s*.

Tung-Chia, Lays of Far Cathay and others, a Collection of Original Poems, with Illustrations by H. H. Imp. 8vo. *Shanghai*, 1890. 10*s*.

Underwood (H. G.) — Concise Dictionary of the Korean Language in 2 parts (English-Korean and Korean-English). Student edition. Post 8vo. half calf, pp. 293. *Shanghai*, 1890. £1 5*s*.

———— Introduction to the Korean Spoken Language in 2 parts (I. Grammatical Notes ; II. English-Korean Phrasebook). Post 8vo. half calf, pp. 425. *Shanghai*, 1890. £1 5*s*.

Wan tzu tien.—Vocabulary of Ten Thousand (Chinese) Characters. 12mo. *Shanghai*, 1889. 5*s*.

Watters (T.)—Essays on the Chinese Language. 8vo. pp. 496, half calf. *Shanghai*, 1889. 18*s*.

Williams.—Life and Letters of S. Wells Williams, LL. D., Missionary, Diplomatist, Sinologue, Author of the Syllabic Dictionary. Demy 8vo. pp. 481. *Shanghai*, 1890. £1 5*s*.

Yeijiro (Ono).—Industrial Transition in Japan. Published by the American Economic Association. *Baltimore*, 1890.



### NOTICE TO CORRESPONDENTS.

All communications should be addressed to the *Editor of "Trübner's Record,"* 57 and 59, Ludgate Hill, London, E.C., and they should be accompanied by the sender's name and address (not necessarily for publication). Every care will be taken with MSS., but the Editor cannot hold himself responsible for rejected communications, which—if to be returned to the sender—should be accompanied by postage. MS. should be legibly written, and on one side of the paper only. Books for review should be addressed to the Editor.

### NOTICE TO ADVERTISERS.

All communications respecting advertisements should be addressed to Messrs. F. Tallis and Son, 22, Wellington Street, W.C. *Terms for the insertion of advertisements :—*

| | | | |
|---|---|---|---|
| Whole Page (ordinary position) ... | £5 | 5 | 0 |
| Half Page ,, ,, ... | 2 | 15 | 0 |
| Quarter Page ,, ,, ... | 1 | 10 | 0 |

Special positions per contract.

No. 251.

# TRÜBNER'S RECORD,

## A JOURNAL DEVOTED TO THE LITERATURE OF THE EAST.

### WITH NOTES AND LISTS OF CURRENT

### American, European and Colonial Publications.

*Edited by Dr. Rost, of the India Office.*

APRIL, 1891.    THIRD SERIES. VOL. II. No. 3.    PRICE 2s.

## SANSKRIT PLAYS

OF THE KING VIGRAHARÂJADEVA OF SÂKAMBHARÎ,
PARTLY PRESERVED AS INSCRIPTIONS AT AJMERE.

(*Extracts from a paper, shortly to be published in full.*)

By Professor F. KIELHORN, C.I.E., Göttingen.

Among the papers of General Sir A. Cunningham, transmitted to me by Mr. Fleet, I have found rubbings of two unique stone inscriptions, of which even an imperfect account cannot fail to interest my fellow-students. For these inscriptions contain portions of one or, more probably, two unknown plays, by the king *Vigraharâjadeva of Sâkambharî*, whose Delhi Siwâlik pillar inscriptions I have re-edited in vol. xix. of the *Indian Antiquary*. Actual and undoubted proof is here afforded to us of the fact, that powerful Hindu rulers of the past were both eager and able to compete with Kâlidâsa and Bhavabhûti for poetical fame. And it shows the strange vicissitudes of fortune that the stones, on which a royal author, who could boast of having repeatedly exterminated the barbarians and conquered all the land between the Vindhya and the Himâlaya, made known to his people the products of his Muse, should have been used as common building-material for a place of Muhammadan worship by the conquerors of his descendants.

According to a note on the back of the rubbings, the two inscriptions, which I shall call A. and B., are at the Arhai-din-kâ-Jhonpra, a mosque situated on the lower slope of the Târâgadh hill, at Ajmere, the administrative headquarters of the Ajmere-Merwârâ Division, Râjputânâ.

. . . . . . . .

The inscription B. contains the concluding portion of the fifth act, called *Krauñcha-vijaya*, of the *Harakeli-nâṭaka*, which in line 40, as well as in lines 32 and 35, is distinctly called the composition of the poet, the *Mahârâjâdhirâja* and *Parameśvara*, the illustrious *Vigraharâjadeva of Sâkambharî*. It opens with a conversation held by Śiva, his wife Gaurî, the Vidûshaka, and a Pratîhâra, in which, so far as the fragmentary state of the inscription permits me to see, the worship rendered to Śiva by Râvaṇa is spoken of

with approval. Śiva and his attendants then, for reasons which are not apparent, turn into Śabaras or mountaineers. Noticing some fragrant smell, as of some oblation presented to him, the god despatches his attendant Mûka to ascertain the cause of it. Mûka returns and reports that Arjuna is preparing a sacrifice. He is told to assume the form of a Kirâta, to go near Arjuna and there to await Śiva. As soon as he has left, Śiva perceives that Mûka and Arjuna, who were enemies before, begin fighting with one another. He therefore goes himself, as a Kirâta, to assist his attendant ; and behind the scene a terrible battle ensues between the god and Arjuna, the progress of which is related to Gaurî by the Pratîhâra, and which ends with the god's acknowledging the valour of his opponent, and bringing him unto the stage. It is hardly necessary to say that the poet has here imitated the *Kirâtârjuniya* of Bhâravi.

The remainder of the act is given in the original text below. The two deities, Śiva and Gaurî, reveal to Arjuna their real nature ; and Arjuna asks their forgiveness for whatever he may have done to offend them, and praises Śiva as the most supreme divine being. Śiva, pleased with Arjuna's valour and piety presents him with a mystical weapon and dismisses him. After Arjuna's departure, Śiva tells Gaurî that the poet *Vigraharâja* has so delighted him with his *Harakeli-nâṭaka*, that they must see him too. *Vigraharâja* then himself enters, and after a short conversation, in which he pleads in favour of his *Harakeli*, and the god assures him of the pleasure which that play has afforded to him, and tells him that his fame as a poet is to last for ever, he is sent home to rule his kingdom of *Sâkambharî*, while the god with his attendants is proceeding to Kailâsa.

The contents of the inscription A. contain no reference whatever to those of the inscription B.,—and I therefore would for the present assume that A. contains part,—the end of the third act and a large portion of the fourth act,—of another play by the same royal author, the title of which is not apparent. The inscription opens with a conversation between Śaśiprabhâ and the king (*Vigraharâja*), from which we may conclude that the king was in love with the daughter of a prince *Vasantapâla*. The two lovers, one of whom apparently has seen the other in a dream, being separated, Śaśiprabhâ, a confidant of the lady, is sent to ascertain the king's feelings; and having attained her purpose, she is about to depart, to gladden her friend with her tidings, when the king confesses that he cannot bear to part with Śaśiprabhâ, and proposes to send Kalyânavatî to the princess instead. Accordingly Kalyânavatî is despatched with a love-message, in which the king informs the lady that he is himself detained by warlike preparations directed against the king of the *Turushkas*, who has been reported to be marching against him. Suitable preparations having been made for making Śaśiprabhâ's stay with the king comfortable, the latter goes to attend to his mid-day ceremonies. Thus ends the third act.

At the opening of the fourth act two *Turushka* prisoners appear on the scene, which represents the camp of the king (*Vigraharâja*) of *Śâkambharî* or a place close to it, in search of the royal residence. In their perplexity they luckily meet with a countryman, a spy, sent to the camp by the *Turushka* king. This man tells them how he has managed to enter the enemy's camp in the guise of a beggar, together with a crowd of people who went to see the god Someśvara. He also informs them that the army of the *Châhamâna* (*Vigraharâja*) consists of a thousand elephants, a hundred thousand horses, and a million of men; in fact, that by the side of it the ocean would appear dry. And having pointed out the king's residence, he departs. The two prisoners take their places near the royal quarters; they meet with the king, who is thinking of his beloved, address him (in verses which unfortunately are greatly damaged in the text), and are sent away richly rewarded.

*Vigraharâja* now expresses his surprise that his own spy, whom he has sent to the camp of the *Hammîra*, has not returned yet. But just then the spy comes back and informs his master of what he has been able to learn regarding the enemy's forces and his movements. According to his account, the *Hammîra's* army consists of countless elephants, chariots, horses, and men, and his camp is well guarded. On the previous day it was three *yojanas* distant from *Vavveraa*, the place where *Vigraharâja* then is, but it is now located at a distance of only one *yojana*. There is also a rumour that the *Hammîra*, having prepared his forces for battle, is about to send a messenger to the king.

The spy having been dismissed, *Vigraharâja* sends for his maternal uncle, the râja *Simhabala*, and having explained the state of affairs consults with him and his chief minister *Śrîdhara* as to what should be done. The cautious minister advises not to risk a battle.

But the king himself, intimating that it is his duty to protect his friends, is too proud to enter upon peaceful negociations, and is encouraged to act according to his own views by *Simhabala*. While they are still consulting, the arrival of the *Hammîra's* messenger is announced. The stranger is admitted into the royal presence, expresses his wonder at the splendour and the signs of power which surround the king, is struck with *Vigraharâja's* own appearance, and cannot conceal from himself that the task entrusted to him will be a difficult one to perform.

Here the inscription ends. It may be assumed that *Vigraharâja* and the *Hammîra* on the present occasion did not fight after all, and that the king was eventually united with his lady-love. From the Delhi Siwâlik pillar inscription, the date of which is about ten years later than that of the inscription B., we know that in reality *Visaladeva-Vigraharâja* repeatedly and successfully made war against the Muhammadan invaders of India, by whom a descendant of his was utterly defeated and put to death in A.D. 1193.

. . . . . . . . .

Tradition has it that the *Hanuman-nâṭaka* originally was written on rocks. By a piece of good luck I am enabled to put before the reader portions of two plays which undoubtedly were engraved on stone. And I feel sure, that the able officers of the Indian services, to whose disinterested help scholars in Europe never appeal in vain, will endeavour to advise us soon of the existence of many more stones, with similar inscriptions.

---

## PANDIT SATYAVRATA SÂMÂŚRAMÎ.

Bengal enjoys a well-deserved reputation in the matter of the cultivation of the philosophical and other scholastic branches of Sanskrit study. The Nyâya schools of Nadiyâ are known wherever Sanskrit learning is appreciated. But the study and knowledge of the Vedas have, in that part of India, always been neglected. In the middle of the present century, indeed, their cultivation appears to have been totally extinct. It is said that an inquiry set on foot at that time by the father of Pandit Satyavrata brought to light the fact that there was not a single leaf of the Vedas in the possession of any Hindû family in Bengal. Attempts, it is true, were made repeatedly to re-introduce the knowledge of the Vedas from Benares, the nearest centre of Vedic learning. But all these attempts failed of success, owing to the reluctance of the Benares Pandits to communicate their knowledge to Bangalis, whom they consider foreigners. Bâbû Devendra Nâth Tagore, the head of the Âdi Brahmo Samaj, and the Burdwan Râj Darbâr, both sent, at different times, young men to

Benares to study the Vedas ; but though they returned with a knowledge of the Vedânta and the Upanishads, they came back without any instruction in the Vedas. The first successful attempt at reintroducing Vedic learning in Bengal is connected with the name of the Pandit who is the subject of the present notice, and whose eventful life and brilliant attainments have made him a mark even beyond the borders of his immediate native country.

Pandit Satyavrata Sâmâśrami was born in Patna on the 28th of May, 1846. His original name was Kâlî Dâs, regarding the change of which the following incident is related. At the age of four or five years, when once he was walking in the garden with a servant, he plucked a rose which was much valued by his father. When the servant, who was suspected, silently received the father's scolding, the child voluntarily confessed the truth. This so much pleased the father, that he changed his name from Kâlî Dâs, or the "Servant of Kâlî," to Satyavrata or "Devoted to Truth."

The hereditary titles of the Pandit are Chhâtropâdhyâya Âvasatha Bhaṭṭâchârya. They show that he belongs to the Bhattâchârya division of the Chhâtropadhyâya (Chatterji) clan of Bengal Brahmans, whose gotra is Kâśyapa. The Chhâttropâdhyâyas trace their descent from Daksha, one of the five Kanauj Brahmans whom king Âdisura invited to his court in Bengal. A descendant of his, Sadâśiva by name, received the title of Chhâtropâdhyâya, on account of his Vedic learning, and the further distinction of Âvasatha, on account of his keeping up the Agnihotra, or sacred fire, till the end of his life. It was the sixth descendant of this Sadâśiva, named Gopâla, who, on account of his learning, obtained the additional title of Bhaṭṭâchârya ; and Pandit Satyavrata is the seventh descendant of that Gopâla.

The Pandit's father, Râm Dâs, was a person of considerable wealth, who held successively various responsible posts under the British Government in Mungir and Patna. The great ambition of his life was to revive the study of the Vedas in his native country ; and as his circumstances precluded him from doing this himself, he determined that his eldest son should be consecrated to the accomplishment of his cherished object. Accordingly, when Satyavrata had passed seven years of age, his father removed with his family to Benares, with the sole object of having his son taught the Vedas there. At that age Satyavrata had already passed through a three years' course of elementary training in Bengali and Sanskrit. As remarked already, the Vedic Pandits of Benares were not at all inclined to impart their knowledge to natives of Bengal ; but by dint of accommodation in speech and manners to their views and prejudices, Râm Dâs succeeded in placing his son under the instruction of one of the Sâma Vedic Pandits. At the same time he procured his admission to the monastic school of the Sarasvatî Math (*matha*), where Satyavrata received his training in the secular branches of Sanskrit learning.

The Sarasvatî Math, or monastery, of Benares is one of the ten Maths which the celebrated Śankara Âchârya established in different places of India, with the object of reviving Brahmanic monasticism and thus supplanting the decaying monastic orders of the Buddhists and Jains. From these ten Maths the Sannyâsîs, or Monks, resident in them, are popularly known as the Dasanâmîs or "ten-name-ones." Their proper title, however, is Svâmî or "Lord," after the Svâmî title of Śankara Âchârya himself; and in addition each Sannyâsî bears the name of his proper Math ; thus those of the Sarasvatî Math are all called Sarasvatî. Other titles usual to these Sannyâsîs are Paramahamsa and Parivrâjaka. In course of time a division established itself of Maths of stricter and of looser observance. To the latter class belong seven and one half of the monastic orders (viz., the Vana, Aranya, Giri, Parvata, Sâgara, Bhâratî, Purî and half of the Âśrama). The Sannyâsîs of these orders are called Gosvâmîs (vulgarly Gosains, or "ignorant Svâmîs," *go* meaning "a cow"); they admit men of any caste to their orders and are not generally Brâhmans. The monks of the remaining two and one half orders (viz., the Sarasvatî, Tîrtha and half of the Âśrama) are all Brâhmans and are considered the real Svâmîs. They carry a *danda*, or long staff, of peculiar make, to distinguish them from the Gosvâmîs who may not use it.

The most distinguished member of a Math is always entrusted with the highest secular as well as religious authority over all its Sannyâsîs. During the time when Pandit Satyavrata attended the school of the Sarasvatî Math, two Gaur Brâhmans, that is, members of one of the five northern classes of Brâhmans, were successively at the head of it, viz. Tarka Brâhmânanda and Viśvarûpânanda, both, during their presidency, commonly only known as the Gaur Svâmî. They enjoyed in Benares the reputation of being two of its most learned Sanskrit scholars. There were then only three other Pandits considered their equals, viz., Kakâ Râm Pandit, Sakhâ Râm Bhatta, and Kâśî Nâth Sâstrî.

As usual with such Maths, there is a monastic school in connexion with the Sarasvatî Math of Benares, the duty of a Math consisting not only in the regulation of the life and conduct of its own members, but also in the instruction of the young. The system of the school at that time was—and probably is so still—that the Gaur Svâmî himself taught the most advanced students who did not generally exceed twenty or twenty-two in number. These twenty again taught some hundred students, or five each ; and these hundred taught the rest. Altogether there were at times as many as two hundred and fifty students pursuing their studies in the Math. They were divided in some six or seven classes, new admissions being, as a rule, made only in the lowest class. They were not all natives of Benares, but many came from other and distant parts of the country. But none of them lived in the Math. They simply went there for study, and resided in their own houses or lodgings.

The Vedas were not taught in the Math. Those students who wished to study them had to attach themselves as private pupils to one of the many Vedic Pandits that live in Benares. As the young Satyavrata, like most of the Brâhmans of Bengal, belonged to the Sâma Veda, he naturally desired to devote himself principally to the study of that Veda. But although there were, in those days, in Benares many teachers of the Rig and Yajur Vedas, there were no more than three Pandits who were able to teach the Sâma Veda. These were Nanda Râma Trivedî Gujarâtî, one of the court-pandits of the Mahârâja of Benares ; Govinda Râma Trivedî Nâgar, and Ravi Sankara Trivedî Vannagarî. Besides these there were two other Sâma Vedic Pandits, of whom one lived in Mathurâ, a blind man, known as Mâthura, who was the *guru* of the celebrated Dayânanda Sarasvatî Svâmi, the founder of the Ârya Samaj. The other lived in Pittha Serai in Kanauj ; he was, however, as Satyavrata afterwards discovered, a very indifferent scholar. Besides these five Pandits, there was no other teacher of the Sâma Veda in Northern India ; and even among these there were only two, Nanda Râma Trivedî and the blind Mâthura, who were able, to some extent, to interpret the meaning of the Veda. Every one of them had many pupils, but among all of them there were only six who ever actually finished their study of the Veda with them. These are : 1, the late Âditya Râma Trivedî of the Darbhaugâ Râj Darbâr ; 2, the late Durgâ Râma Trivedî of the Bettia Râj Darbâr ; 3, Sûrya Krishna Trivedî, probably now at the Jammû Râj Darbâr ; 4, Ajudhyâ Râma Miśra, now at the Darbhanga Râj Darbâr as Vedic teacher of the Mahârâja's younger brother Rameshwar Singh ; 5, Khûnkhûn, who is probably now at Benares ; and 6, Satyavrata, now resident in Calcutta. There are many pupils of these six Vedic teachers, but it is to be regretted that none of them has ever had the patience to go through his whole course of Vedic study.

This was the state of Sanskrit learning in Benares, at the time, when Satyavrata, in 1854, at the age of eight years, commenced his study of the Śâstras at the Sarasvatî Math, where, on account of his excellent preliminary schooling, he was at once admitted into the third, instead of the last, class. At the same time his father apprenticed him, for his Vedic studies, to Pandit Nanda Râma Trivedî. Both branches of study were prosecuted by him *pari passu* ; and he devoted himself to them with an energy and success, quite unusual in these days. Considering the extremely conservative habits of India, there is good reason to believe that the manner of life of a Sanskrit student, untouched by the influence of the modern European methods and institutions of education, has not materially changed from what it was centuries ago at any of the great centres of Sanskrit learning. It may, therefore, be of interest to describe briefly the daily routine of Satyavrata's life during the years of his more advanced studentship. His day then commenced at three o'clock in the morning, when he rose and spent two hours in revising the lessons of the previous day. From five to six he used to chant hymns from the Vedas. Then, after a slight breakfast of milk (*dhâroshna*) followed by short prayers he went to his Vedic teacher, with whom he read till ten o'clock. He then returned home, bathed, said his prayers and dined. This took up about two hours. At twelve o'clock he sat down to teach other students of the lower classes of the Sarasvatî Math and other Tols (or schools). At two in the afternoon he went to the Math to read, as a particular distinction, the Darśanas and Upanishads, or Hindu philosophy, with the highest class, which was taught by the Gauŗ Svâmî himself. Here he remained till five. He then went to the Ahalyâ Ghât, which used to be a favourite meeting-place of the students of the Math and other Tols, who assembled there for the purpose of discussing and disputing about the subjects of their study. In these meetings Satyavrata used to take a leading part on account of his superior intelligence and attainments. Then having performed his *sandhyâ*, or evening prayer, he went to wrestle and do other bodily exercises on the *Akhâŗâ* or wrestling-ground of Bishun (Vishnu) on the Daśâśvamedha Ghât, after which he went home to take a slight meal consisting chiefly of milk and sweetmeats. At about seven he went once more to the Sarasvatî Math to receive from the Gauŗ Svâmî his own proper lessons in Sanskrit literature. There he remained till ten, when he returned home, and, having revised his lessons for an hour and taken his supper, retired before twelve. He never slept for more than three or four hours, nor made use of a musquito curtain in summer or a blanket in winter, for fear lest he should sleep too much.

With such persevering application to his studies,

it is no wonder that Satyavrata was one of the most distinguished students of his time. Six years after his admission in the school of the Sarasvatî Maṭh, in 1860, when he was only fourteen years of age, he was already put in charge of other students whom he taught. It is said that he was soon considered such a clever teacher that students of other Tols deserted to join his Tol, and that the head masters of those Tols made it a rule not to admit any new pupil except under a contract to stay with them for a definite period. The whole period of his study extended to twelve years. During that time he read with the Vedic Pandit the whole of the Sâma-veda with its Brâhmaṇas and Anubrâhmaṇas, learnt to chant its hymns accompanied with the proper gestures, and was taught the modes of solemnizing sacrifices. On the last point he had the special advantage of witnessing the performance of a *pishṭa paṣ'u*, or symbolic animal sacrifice, which was solemnized according to Vedic rites on the Ashî Ghâṭ in Benares and lasted for a year before the Sepoy mutiny (1857). He also read portions of the other Vedas, the Nirukta, and the Gobhilîya and Lâṭyâyana Sûtras. With the Gauṛ Svâmî in the Sarasvatî Maṭh he read the Sûtras of all the five philosophical systems, the principal Upanishads, the Kumâra Sambhava, Raghuvaṁsa and other great poems, the Sakuntalâ, Mudrâ Rakshasa and other dramas, portions of the Mahâbhârata and Râmâyaṇa, and many other of the celebrated works of Sanskrit literature. On the completion of his studies, in 1866, being then only twenty years of age, he had the title of Sâmâśramî or "scholar of the Sâma Veda" conferred on him by the Mahârâja of Bûndî in the presence and with the consent of a large number of distinguished Pandits who had been assembled for the purpose.

Following ancient precedent, the young Vedic scholar now determined to travel over Northern India. The object of his travel was to make the acquaintance of other great Vedic scholars and, in intercourse with them, to remove doubts and fill up lacunae in such points of his Vedic knowledge as to which he had been unable to receive fully satisfactory information from the Pandits of Benares. At the same time his journey would afford him an opportunity of visiting many of the famous places of Hindû religious tradition. He set out with a following of twenty-eight pupils, with whom he travelled from five to ten miles daily, marching in the early morning hours. When the sun had risen high, they halted under the shade of trees, beyond the limits of some village. The midday hours were spent in teaching his pupils, dining and resting. In the cool of the evening visits were paid to learned men, if any happened to live in the neighbourhood. On tidings of his arrival reaching the villages around,

many people would come out to see him and supply him with the necessaries of life for himself and his disciples ; and when his way took him through the bazaar of any town or village, the people would line the streets to see him pass. It was considered a great marvel to see a finished Vedic scholar of an age at which others were rather in the habit of commencing their education.

In this manner he travelled by way of Ajudhyâ, the famous residence of Râma, and Kanauj, where he visited, though without any profit, the Sâma Vedic scholar previously mentioned, and Kampilla, the birthplace of king Śrî Harsha, the contemporary of his ancestor Daksha, and Kisaurî, where he saw a large banyan tree the like of which he thought he never saw again, and many other intermediate places, to the great place of pilgrimage, Hardwâr. He reached this place just at the time when the celebrated Kumbha Melâ, which only takes place once in twelve years, was being held. Many rich men, Râjas and Pandits were present there, and Ranbîr Singh, the late Mahârâja of Kashmîr, had convoked an assembly of five hundred of the best known pandits of the North Western Provinces and the Panjâb, to adjudicate on the claim of the Gosains to be considered true Saunyâsîs. Pandit Satyavrata was also invited with four of his ablest pupils. Though the majority were at first in favour of the Gosains' claim, the view of the minority, which was supported by Satyavrata, at length prevailed. Our Pandit was now treated with great respect by the Mahârâja ; but in his hope of profiting from his intercourse with such a great assembly of Pandits for the special object of his travels, he was greatly disappointed. Accordingly he resumed his journey, and bent his steps northwards into the Himâlayas, which have always been looked upon as the fountain-head of the most profound knowledge. Only two of his pupils accompanied him ; the other twenty-six preferring to return home. Travelling by way of Saptaśrota, Rambhâ Sangam, Bîrbhadra and other holy places, he reached Rishikeśa, which appeared to him the most charmingly-peaceful spot he had ever seen. Here he discovered a mysterious Sannyâsî of unknown name and nationality, living in the deepest seclusion and only speaking in Sanskrit, but from whom he received all the information he was in search of. After a few days' stay, acting on hints received from that ascetic, he proceeded by way of Lachhman Jhûlâ, a bridge of ropes, which his two companions were afraid to cross, and Dharmakûp, Dhaneśwar and Dhaneśwarî to the Hemakût mountain, where he searched for and found some of the medicinal herbs mentioned in the Vedas. Thence he visited the Bhîma mountain, where he saw a Bengali mendicant and learnt from him how to reduce gold, silver, and other metals to ashes and use them as medicine. He now retraced his steps to the Lachhman Jhûla, where he was rejoined by his two companions, and having visited with them the Chandî mountain, he returned to Rishikeśa where he vainly sought to find again the mysterious Sannyâsî, and thence, by way of Thaneśwar, Mathurâ and Brindaban, back to Benares, which he reached on the 11th of May, 1867.

Not long afterwards Pandit Satyavrata was appointed by the Mahârâja of Benares to the post at his court which had shortly before been rendered vacant by the death of his teacher Nanda Râma Trivedî. It was not of any value from a pecuniary point of view, but carried with it much literary weight and dignity. This was seen in the controversy which took place about this time between the two Hindû sections, the Śaivas and Vaishnavas, regarding the necessity of submitting to the ceremony of the *taptamudrâ*, or branding with a peculiar sign, as a mark of being *śuddha* or ceremonially pure. In this controversy the Sâmâśramî was invited to take a leading part, and the view upheld by him, that the *taptamudrâ* was not necessary, finally gained the victory. As an immediate consequence, the late Mahârâja of Jaipur, Sawâi Râm Singh, who had been present in Benares and taken a personal interest in the controversy, expressed a wish to take him into his employ at a handsome salary. Also at the great temple of Govindjî in Jaipur, men without the *taptamudrâ* were now permitted to officiate at ceremonies, and the high priest of that temple even offered his daughter, an only child and heiress, to him in marriage. In Benares itself a Professorship in the Sanskrit Department of the Government College was offered to him by Mr. Griffith, who was then the Principal of the College. But all these tempting offers of advancement the Pandit felt himself constrained to refuse in deference to his father's wish that his life should be devoted to the resuscitation of the knowledge of the Vedas in Bengal,—a wish the accomplishment of which was hardly compatible with a lengthened residence outside of Bengal.

In another great controversy, which was originated by the renowned Svâmî Dayânanda Sarasvatî, regarding the propriety of idol worship, Pandit Satyavrata was also called to take a leading part. The writer of the present notice well remembers the great stir which the controversy evoked in Benares. He was also present at the final public disputation which took place, in November, 1869, under the presidency of the Mahârâja of Benares, in his Ânanda Bâgh or pleasure garden. Svâmî Dayânanda's main point was that idol worship could not be proved from the Vedas. Pandit Satyavrata was chosen umpire, and his decision was adverse to the Svâmî's contention. Both parties afterwards published what professed to be a full and accurate account of the disputation, in the Pratna Kamra Nandinî and the Ârya Darpana respectively, though it is almost needless to add that neither side admitted the accuracy of the other's account.

Some years later, in 1873, when the Pandit had already removed his residence to Calcutta, he was involved in a third great controversy on the evils of polygamy. This was originated by the well-known Pandit Ishwar Chandra Vidyâsâgar, who attacked that custom as opposed to the Shâstras, and advocated its suppression by legal enactment. Pandit Satyavrata took up a more conservative position; while admitting its evils, he denied that polygamy was forbidden in the Shâstras, and maintained that it was a custom which had grown up in evil times, that it was already falling into disuse, and that, with the progress of social culture, it was certain to die out without any interference from the British Government. In the end the Pandit's view, which had the concurrence of other eminent men such as the late Professor Târâ Nâtha Tarkavachaspati, prevailed.

The prominent part that fell to Pandit Satyavrata's lot in these controversies could not fail to make his name and learning widely known, especially in his native country of Bengal. One result of his growing fame was that in 1868 he was chosen by the renowned Pandit Braja Nâth Vidyâratna of Nadiyâ, who was looked upon as the head of all Brâhmans of Bengal, as the husband of his granddaughter, the daughter of Pandit Mathurâ Nâth Padaratna. Another and more decisive one in shaping the subsequent course of the Pandit's life was that, at the instance of the well-known Râja Dr. Râjendralâla Mitra, he was charged by the Asiatic Society of Bengal, in 1870, with the preparation of an edition of the Sâma Veda Saṁhitâ for the Bibliotheca Indica. As this charge could only be properly carried out in Calcutta, it became the immediate cause of the removal of the Pandit's residence to that place. Here he was also honoured by the Government with the appointment of Examiner in the Vedas and in Hindû philosophy in connexion with the "Sanskrit Titles Examination."

In the mean time, however, the Pandit had applied himself with his accustomed energy to the attainment of the main object of his life, the spread of the knowledge of the Vedas. He opened a school in his house in Benares, in which he taught the Vedas to private pupils who came to study under him from every part of India, even from as far as Gujarât. Moreover, he now commenced the publication of a monthly journal, under the name of Pratna Kamra Nandinî, which was mainly devoted to the publication of Vedic works, and which eventually ran through a series of seven years. It was printed in Calcutta in 250 copies, most of which were sold in Bengal. The first to be published in the journal was the Sāmaveda, the text of which he accompanied with a commentary of his own, as there were then no suitable manuscripts of the two old standard commentaries of Sayaṇa and Mādhava accessible to him. This edition he subsequently stopped when he was enabled by the Asiatic Society of Bengal to publish the Sāmaveda with the commentary of Sayaṇa. Between 1874 and 1877 he brought out as a separate book, an edition of the White Yajurveda with Mahidhara's commentary and a Bengali translation and notes of his own. From 1881 to 1888 he employed himself in bringing out a Bengali edition of the Sāmaveda. This was practically a reprint in Bengali characters of the Asiatic Society's Nāgarī edition of the Sāmaveda, to which were added a Bengali translation and notes. The necessity of this edition arose from the fact that the Brāhmans of Bengal, most of whom are Sāmavedīs, are quite unfamiliar with the Nāgarī characters. The value of it for Bengal, where the Vedas were hitherto almost unknown, cannot be too highly estimated. He also published editions of most of the Brāhmaṇas of the Sāmaveda, the Shadviṃśa, Devatādhyāya, Vaṃsa, Ārsheya, Saṃhitopanishad, Sāmavidhāna and Mantra, generally with Sayaṇa's commentary, but sometimes with a commentary and Bengali translation of his own. Other Vedic and cognate editions of his comprise the Āraṇya Saṃhitā, the Āgneya and Aindra Parva, the Agnishṭoma Paddhati, the Gobhilīya Gṛihya Sūtra, etc. These too are furnished with commentaries and Bengali translations. In view of the Pandit's object of reviving and diffusing a knowledge of the Vedas among his countrymen, the Bengali translations which he added to most of his editions were of particular value. So also was a Vedic compilation made by himself, the Sāma Sūchi, in two volumes, in which he collected almost all the *sāmas*, or hymns, with their Bengali translations, which were requisite for the performance of the religious ceremonies of the Sāmavedī Brāhmans. Besides the edition of the Sāmaveda, above mentioned, Satyavrata contributed to the Bibliotheca Indica a new edition of the Nirukta, one of the so-called Vedāngas or Appendixes to the Vedas. It is a very scholarly work, and is accompanied with a long introduction, discussing such questions as those of the character, the authorship and the date of the Nirukta and the Vedas generally. Whatever the value of the Pandit's observations, by the modern European standard, may be, they are interesting as showing the view taken of such questions by a native scholar of the old school, who approaches them with a thoughtful mind and in an enlightened spirit. Thus he holds Yāska to be the author of the Nirukta commentary, though not of the portion after the twelfth chapter; and his time he places between Pāṇini and Kātyāyana. The Vedas he holds to be composed at different times, by different persons and for different objects. Since 1889 the Pandit has commenced publishing a new Vedic Journal, the *Ushā*, of which four numbers have now appeared. Its object is to make known, in the original text and vernacular translations, minor Vedic texts, essential to the thorough understanding of sacrificial technicalities and other points. These texts he could not well include in his edition of the Sāmaveda, but, being rare and some of them obscure, they well deserve publication and elucidation.

All the above was work more or less directly connected with the Vedas. One might think it a sufficiently large list for one man to accomplish, considering that most of it was by no means of a light nature. But the Sāmāśramī found time to get through a large amount of other literary work, unconnected with the Vedas, some being editions of Sanskrit works of poetry or philosophy, others compositions of his own in the Sanskrit and Bengali languages. A full list of these publications would exceed the scope of the present notice; but it may be mentioned that among others the Pandit published editions of the Kavi Kalpalatā, a work on rhetoric, the Chandra Śekhara Champū, a composition of mixed prose and verse, the Mīmāṃsā Paribhāshā and Pūrṇaprajña Darśana, two works on philosophy. Among his own compositions are the Sanskrit grammatical treatise Lingabodha and the Bengali philosophical treatises Saukhya Darśana and Pātañjala Darśana. As a curiosity it may be further mentioned, both to show the wide range of the Pandit's studies and his singular absence of prejudice, that he edited the Buddhist work Karaṇda Vyūha, with a translation by himself, as well as the well-known Jain Scriptures published at the expense of Rai Dhanpati Singh in Calcutta.

It would have been strange, if a life of such incessant literary activity, preceded by years of such severe and almost ascetic study, had not left its mark on the Pandit's constitution. A tedious illness of three years' duration and harassing domestic difficulties, happily now passed, have somewhat crippled his naturally strong powers. But it may be hoped that he may yet long be spared both to his country and to philological science, which can ill afford to lose men of his stamp, of whom no country possesses too many.

## CHATTAPÁNI.
### (FROM THE BURMESE.)

A certain householder named Chattapáni, in the country of Sávatthi, who was well versed in the three books of the Pitaka, had got to the stage of Anágámi, had gone one day to listen to the preaching of the law in the Jetavana Monastery, and Passenadi the Rájá also came at the same time.

The religious Chattapáni saw the Rájá enter and reflected thus as to whether he ought to make way for him: "This ruler is only the ruler of a province, above him is the Ekarájá, and over him again is the Ruler of the Universe; he, in turn, is governed by the four Mahárájás, and above them are Sakko, Suyáma, Santussita, and Sunimita Vasavatí; higher than them is Brahma, and still higher the assembly of the perfect; over them, again, are the Paccéka Buddhas, and the highest of all is the Aggarájá the most excellent Buddha. As I am now in his presence, if I were to get up, even though the Governor of the District came in, I should insult the Aggarájá; I will therefore remain as I am, and not move, even at the risk of angering him." So he remained in his place, and the Rájá observing him was angry and did not approach the Buddha. When the most excellent lord knew that the Rájá was enraged at Chattapáni, he spake to him thus, "O Rájá, Chattapáni is wise enough to see both present and future advantage." On hearing this the Rájá was appeased, and after listening to the sermon went back to his palace.

One day as he was sitting in a turret of his palace in Kosala the Rájá beheld Chattapáni coming along the road towards the palace in his sandals, whereupon he ordered his servants to bring him before him. Chattapáni, leaving his shoes and umbrella, came into the Rájá's presence and waited in a position of respect. The Rájá said, "My religious friend, why did you leave your shoes and umbrella?" Chattapáni answered; "My lord, I have come into your presence without shoes and umbrella because you sent for me." Then said the Rájá, "Is it only to-day you have learnt that I am the Rájá?" Chattapáni answered; "My lord, I have always known you were the Rájá." "In that case how was it that you did not move from your place the other day when you saw me come into the Monastery?" "My lord, I saw you come in, but did not move because I was sitting at the feet of the most excellent Buddha, who is your lord and master, and I feared to show disrespect to him." The Rájá being one who regarded the three precious things, answered, "O religious man, let us say no more, I am not displeased with you, but having heard that you are well informed as to what is advantageous in the future as well as now, and that you are well versed in

the Pitaka, I desire that you come constantly to my palace to preach the law." Chattapáni answered; "My lord, I dare not." "Why not?" asked the Rájá. "My lord, it is thus in palaces. When it is not proper, that which is bad is easy, and when proper, the good becomes easy also; and this being the case those who are connected with the Prince have reason to be afraid, and the people of the palace will find it difficult to treat with respect a person so insignificant as I am." On hearing this the Rájá said, "O Chattapáni, say not so, I bear no grudge against thee; do not be afraid, for as I respect religion I will respect you." But Chattapáni answered, "Rájá, in palaces is the seat of power and punishments are many; if you desire to hear the law preached constantly, monks who are acquainted with the Pitaka are not scarce: invite one of them to your palace, for a Rahan is fitted to preach the law." So the Rájá sent him away saying, "Very good: I will invite a Rahan" (Araham). Having sent Chattapáni away, Passenadi the Rájá of Kosala went in to the presence of the Buddha and thus addressed him: "Reverend Lord, both my Queens Mallika, and Vásabha Khattiyá, who is a daughter of your race, desire to learn the Pitakas (Pitakattayam) and, at their instigation, I have come to your presence: in order to assist them I pray that you will come daily to my palace with your 500 disciples (Sangho) and preach the law to them." The most excellent Lord answered, "Buddhas cannot go constantly to the same place." Then said the Rájá, "If that be so and you cannot come, send one of your disciples." The Buddha replied, "Very good, O Rájá, I will send A'nandá." So the Rájá returned to his palace. The Lord then sent for A'nandá and directed him to go daily and preach at the palace. A'nandá accordingly went every day and rehearsed the Pitakas to the Queens. Mallika in a short time was able to repeat them, but Vásabhá the Khattiyá, through inattention, only learnt a very little.

One day the Buddha sent for A'nandá and asked what progress they had made, and A'nandá answered that they were still learning. "Do they learn with reverence?" asked Buddha. "O Lord, Queen Mallika pays great attention." Then said Buddha, "A'nandá, my law is, to those who learn it not with reverence, like unto lovely flowers without fragrance; but to those who learn reverently it is like flowers that have both scent and beauty:

Yathá pi ruciram puppham vaṇṇavantam agandhakam
Evam subhásitá váca aphala hoti akubbato:
Yathá pi ruciram puppham vaṇṇavantam sugandhakam
Evam subhásitá váca saphalá hoti kubbato.

Like a lovely flower, full of colour but scentless,
Even so are well spoken words fruitless to him who act not:
But like a lovely flower full of colour and scent too,
Even so are well spoken words fruitless to him who does act.

## THE FEUD BETWEEN THE OWLS AND CROWS.

When the Lord was dwelling in the Jetavana Monastery in the country of Sávatthi, there was a monk who dwelt in a cell at the foot of a palmyra palm in which a number of crows used to roost. At night the owls would come and bite off the heads of the crows, and every morning the monk picked up one or two bushels of crows' heads and threw them away. One day, in the hall of assembly, the monks asked the Lord what was the reason of this and how long the feud had lasted, and he replied, "Dear sons, at the beginning of this cycle men appointed Mahásámata to be king; four-footed beasts appointed the lion, and fish appointed A'nantá; but when the birds were in consultation as to whom they should appoint they elected an owl, who immediately hooted two or three times. Thereupon a crow stepped forth and said, 'In appearance as far as your body is concerned you are like other birds, but you look as if you were ever in a rage and so terrible do you appear no one will dare to approach you, I object to the appointment.' Another owl, however, said, 'Every one else has consented; how dare you object?' Upon this there was a fight between the owls and crows, and from that day forth a feud. After a long time the crows thought to find out the owls' dwelling-places by stratagem; so they plucked all the feathers out of one of their number, as if he had been punished, and sent him to the owls to ask for help against them. The owls, thinking he was speaking the truth, allowed him to remain with them by day, but objected to his roosting with them at night. In the night the crow screamed out that the other crows was setting upon him again. Next night they allowed him to come to their nest and sleep with them. The crow having found out where they slept went back to his companions. They then got fire-brands which they took to the owls' nest and set it on fire. From that day to this there has been war between the owls and crows, and the owls no longer dare to sleep at night."

R. F. St. Andrew St. John.

---

## THE CHINBÓKS.

It is very difficult, even for those who have been a number of years in this country, to fully realize its extent and the great variety of races inhabiting it. Every now and then some fresh light is thrown on some previously unknown corner, and we are astonished to hear of yet more tribes and races, many of them living in the most primitive and barbarous way. We circulate to-day some interesting notes, witten by Lieutenant R. M. Rainey, Commandant of the Chin Frontier Levy, regarding the Chin tribes bordering on the Yaw Country in the Pakokku district. Most of us probably had some vague ideas about the Chins; we knew that they were savages of the most primitive kind; and we had heard that they disfigure their women by tattooing their faces so as to prevent their being attractive to the Burmans, and being carried off to be sold in the matrimonial markets of Burma. But, beyond this, very few of us indeed had any clear ideas about the Chins at all, and the information contributed by Mr. Rainey seems as strange almost as the fresh information recently contributed by Mr. Stanley about savage races inhabiting the heart of Africa.

The first idea we have to get rid of is that the Chins are a single people all speaking one language. On the contrary, they are known by many names, Welaung Chins, Baungshè Chins, Chinbóks, Chinbons, and Yindus; while the curse of Babel is still in full force among them. The village of Welaung has a dialect of its own, and the three other villages of this group speak a different language. Then there are three distinct dialects of Chinbók, and the language spoken by the Chinbons is quite distinct from any of them, or from Yindu. Apparently speech is still in the state of constant flux and change, which must have been its condition among primitive men everywhere when the communities consisted of families or villages, all at deadly enmity with their neighbours, and when there was nothing to crystallize language into a fairly stable form. The Chins have no literature, of course, not even in that most primitive form of sacred songs handed down orally from generation to generation. Strictly speaking, of course, that would not be literature at all, but such songs must have some effect in fixing language and giving it some persistence; whereas, in such communities as those of the Chins, where a language is confined to one or two villages, the tendency to vary must be in full force, indeed the speech of the people probably varies widely from generation to generation.

There is nothing which can properly be called Government, and no religion beyond that of propitiating the nats, which can only be done by the blood of animals. They do not trouble themselves at all, apparently, about what may come after death. It is solely for the sake of help in the affairs of this life that the nats have to be propitiated. They have no priests, no doctors, and their garments are of the scantiest possible kind. Indeed the women's skirts are so short that in the presence of strangers they must either stand or kneel if they have any regard for decency at all. Yet both men and women indulge in ornaments of various kinds, and some of the Chinbók women have discovered that five inches of telegraph wire, bent into an oval-shaped ring, makes a charming ear-ring. That, however, must be a new fashion, as a few years ago telegraph wire was not to be had. The arms of the men are the primitive bow and spear, and agriculture is of the very rudest and most laborious kind possible. Yet the people cannot be altogether so backward as these facts would lead one to suppose. Their houses are stronger and better built than the average bamboo hut of the Burman; and they have some ingenious constructions which Mr. Rainey dignifies by the name of engineering works. He says that they make bridges on the cantilever principle, and that these are wonderful constructions of bamboo and very clever. They also show some ingenuity in contriving aqueducts. The only other points we need mention about these people are that they are very much given to raiding for the sake of carrying off captives and cattle; and that they seize every opportunity and pretext for a drunken carouse, even the small children getting "as drunk as a lord," at every birth, marriage, death, or other occasion for a festival and pretext for a drink.

With such a people as this it is evident that we must be prepared for a good deal of trouble of one kind and another. The first thing we shall have to do, of course, is to stop them raiding and pillaging their neighbours. That step can only be taken in one way, and that rather a harsh one. We can warn them beforehand that raids will be punished, but the warning is certain to be unheeded until some punishments have actually been inflicted. We should not, however, be known to these people solely as the punishers of raids, and the difficulty is how to approach them in any other way. They are not ripe for the schoolmaster, and any administration of justice among them, if we attempt it, must be of the most primitive kind. Possibly the best plan for the present would be to leave them alone as much as possible, merely instructing the officers serving in their neighbourhood to find out as much about them as possible, and to take every opportunity of cultivating friendly relations with them. We cannot of course expect our officers to learn all their languages and dialects; but this is not necessary. These are sure, under the altered conditions of the present rule, to die out, as the Talaing language is dying, and as others of the indigenous languages of Burma bid fair in time to die out and to be supplanted by Burmese or, eventually perhaps, by English. Without actually learning to speak any of the dialects of Chinland, the officers in and near it can do much to bring about an amicable understanding between us and these people, and this, we trust, they will all earnestly strive to do whenever any opportunity offers.—[From the *Rangoon Gazette*.]

## STAGNATION.

Notwithstanding the long intercourse China has had with the more progressive nations, and the many mechanical appliances pertaining to civilization she has of late years adopted, one cannot help remarking with some degree of surprise how little change has been effected in the national life. Her dalliance with the skill and science of the West is rather a species of coquetry than honest wooing. She will and she will not. To-day extensive schemes are sanctioned, and their execution is even commenced in the greatest haste, and to-morrow all is again at a standstill. The ancient dowager has concluded after all not to "change her estate." Fickle to a degree in her attitude toward that minimum of change which even she sees to be inevitable, she remains immovably constant in her dislike and resistance to every reform which is radical, and to every improvement which is substantial. With a persistency which is beginning to weary her best friends she holds to her worn-out traditions, closes her eyes, and refuses to recognize the dangerous maladies which affect her social and political life, and which she has no real wish to see cured, and the cancer eating at her heart has not yet killed that courage of infatuation which bravely sings "All's well!" Some at least of the rulers of the nation appear to accept the mere appurtenances of civilization as a means of resisting its transforming influence. In regard to everything which seriously affects the national life, things remain in the old unvarying condition of absolute stagnation.

This stagnant attitude toward all true progress is probably due to a variety of causes, some of which are beyond our investigation, and no one of which is of such startling prominence as to make itself felt more distinctly than the rest. The constitutional patience of the Chinaman, which is proverbial, has no doubt its share in the matter. There seems no reason to question that racial characteristics, vague as is our knowledge of them, and far set as are their springs beyond the dawn of history, are constant, and though subject to many exceptions, are a ruling factor in social life. And a Chinaman's patience is the most persistent feature of his character. It is wonderful beyond conception, and if the dictum be true that genius is "infinite patience," China has the best claim in the world to be considered "a nation of geniuses." The Celestial's powers of waiting and endurance are never found wanting. He will try everything before a resort to force. He has in a greater degree than any kind of human being of which we have experience the invaluable faculty of adjusting himself to stubborn and untoward circumstances. It must be a distant mountain indeed, especially if there is anything to be got there, to which this Mahomet will not travel. He is tolerant of everything; dirt, vermin, squeezing, lying, debt, and oppression are written in his vocabulary as among the inevitables of life which it is futile to seek to remove, and which, with a wisdom an unsympathetic world mistakes for guile or laziness, he skilfully wriggles through. The present order of things, however bad, and to our thinking a heaped-up mass of intolerabilities piled high as "Pelion on Ossa," he looks upon not as a human arrangement, but as the very constitution of nature, and he no more thinks of seeking a remedy for its discomforts than the traveller would think of levelling the first mountain over which his way might lie.

This quiescent disposition is but a mental counterpart of the political constitution of the country, which is also admirably suited for maintaining things as they stand, and for nothing else. The Chinese system of government, with all its ramifications, recognized and unrecognized, is one of the most intricate pieces of diplomatic machinery the mind of man ever invented. The sole purpose of its existence is to preserve a careful balance of forces, and resist all encroachment and innovation, and so long as it is not violently meddled with, it will do that with the unfailing exactitude of one of Benson's best chronometers. The political constitution of China should be a mine of wealth to the political student. What the Chinese language is to the philologist the Chinese constitution is to the politician. It petrifies with the strong instinct of conservatism the most primitive forms alongside of the most recent, and so affords peculiar facilities for their study. In other nations we trace the gradual transition from the family to the clan, from the clan to the kingdom, and from the kingdom to the empire; in China we see them all subsisting together. The net outcome is that in the complicated movements of wheel within wheel individuality is well-nigh lost, each one is held remorselessly fast to the system by countless ties and barriers he finds it vain to try and escape, and all those who have the power to effect reform are precisely the ones whose strongest interests are against it.

The entire literature of the country, a power which has always ranked high in its practical influence, is a reinforcing agency on the side of conservatism, and to this should be added, as closely connected with it, the mystic forces acting on man's spiritual nature, borrowing unearthly strength from the dark armoury of superstition, which the three great religions of China wield. The secret sects alone, which are numerically insignificant, stand on the other side. The result has been to set China's golden age far back in the past when all that was ever worth knowing or doing was known and done; the best that is left to virtue or heroism is a pale and feeble imitation of the long-faded splendour, and the people are left to face the future without ideals and without hope. All the stereotyped models of antiquity, and all the sage counsels of their long line of buried but unforgotten ancestors, combine to enforce the pious lesson, "Never complain of heaven or lay blame on men," a sentiment unexceptionable in its way, but which too often becomes the equivalent for the English formula, "Be content with that situation in life in which it has pleased God to place you."

The truth is that powers less tangible and material, yet far more potent than railways, telegraphs, balloons, or phonographs, must be evoked before any deep or lasting impression upon this slumbering mass of stagnant life can be expected. Spiritual forces cannot be conquered with material weapons. It is China's ignorance that is her weakness, and only enlightenment can produce change. Not that the Chinese can be called an ignorant people. Many a people far more ignorant has proved itself capable of rapid reform. But China, great as her wisdom is in some things, is densely ignorant of everything that makes for progress. Few may match her in knowledge of the past, but the prophetic spirit that discerns the future is lost to her, and every step she takes forward is taken trembling, for it is a step in the dark. The schoolmaster, or rather many schoolmasters of many kinds must be the reformers. And light once given will insure progress with the inevitableness of mathematical law. She may, with the stubborn vanity of a will that pits itself against destiny, refuse for long to see what has been placed before her with noon-day clearness, but not for ever. China, tardy as she is in taking her place beside the great nations in the line of advancement, will not be able in the long run to resist the pressure of their influence; and the manufactures, the inventions, but still more the agents of education and of religious teaching she has already admitted within her borders, are so many masses of dynamite planted under the stubborn crust of her exclusiveness and reserve; once but let them touch the heart of what is vital in the life of her masses and the spark is struck which will shiver that crust into a thousand atoms and impel whatever living currents may be beneath it into the stream of progress.—[From *the Chinese Times* of Aug. 30th, 1890.]

## New Books.

*The Grihyasûtra of Hiranyakesin, with Extracts from the Commentary of Mâtridatta.* Edited by Dr. J. KIRSTE. (Printed at the expense of the Imperial Academy of Sciences of Vienna.) Vienna (Hölder), 1889. 8vo. pp. xi. 177, 42*.

The Grihyasûtra of Hiranyakesin, like the other Sûtras belonging to the Black Yajur Veda, is of the greatest importance for the history of Vedic schools and of Vedic learning in Southern India. This alone would justify an edition of this work. But like all the other Grihyasûtras, the Hiranyakesi-Grihyasûtra possesses an interest of its own. It is true, in reading the Grihyasûtras we have to tread the same ground over and over again, but it is also true that every new work of this class adds something to our knowledge of ancient Hindoo life. Rites and customs which are omitted in one Sûtra are mentioned in another. And there are not two Grihyasûtras, however near they may stand to each other, that would exactly agree in describing one and the same ceremony. Thus, Hiranyakesin is closely related to Âpastamba. Yet the two differ in many details, especially in the way they connect the Mantras with the ceremonies. Frequently Hiranyakesin proves useful for settling difficulties in Âpastamba. In fact, Hir. often reads like a commentator of Âpastamba. In the expiation-ceremonies prescribed to avert the evil consequences of certain omina and portenta Hiranyakesin shows much originality and is richer than any other Grihyasûtra.

Most interesting is the ceremony called Śûlagava, as described by Hiranyakesin (II. 8, 1 seqq.). The same ceremony is described also by Âśvalâyana (IV. 8, 1 seqq.) and Pâraskara (III. 8, 1 seqq.), but they both deviate from Hiranyakesin. Âpastamba (19, 13 seqq.) on the other hand gives about the same description of the ceremony as Hiranyakesin, but calls it by another name, Îśânabali 'The offering to Îśâna.' Now, what does *śûlagava* mean? It has hitherto been translated by 'spit-ox' ("*Spiess-Rind*"), which, like many other translations of Sanskrit technical terms, can be understood only by those who know Sanskrit. Now, Hiranyakesin II. 8, 2 and II. 9, 9, uses *śûlagava* masc. in the sense of 'Rudra.' (who wears a spear and rides on a bull), and II. 8, 1 *śûlagavam* (neuter) in the sense of *śaulagava* (this is the reading of the commentator) 'the sacrifice in honour of Rudra.' Though Âśv. and Pâr. use *śûlagava* as a masculine, it can only mean the same as *śûlagava* neut., namely 'sacrifice to Rudra.' *Śûlagava* 'Rudra' may be used in the sense of 'Rudra-sacrifice,' just as *darśapûrnamâsu* 'new and full moon' is used in the sense of 'new and full moon sacrifice.'

Dr. Kirste's edition is an excellent piece of workmanship, and does great honour to the Vienna Oriental Institute, from which it proceeded. Having a rich MSS. material at his disposal, Dr. Kirste has given us a reliable text of Hiranyakesin's Sûtra. In the notes a detailed account is given of the various readings of the MSS. And without swelling the book by those useless and endless discussions of which Indian commentators are so fond, Dr. Kirste has extracted from the commentary of Mâtridatta all that can be of any use for the interpretation of the work. A complete Index of Words makes the book very handy and will prove useful for lexicographical purposes.

The proofs have been read most carefully, and very few misprints like गबवागिं for गबवागिं (p. 45, l. 15) have been left uncorrected.

The language of Hiranyakesin, like that of Âpastamba, shows many peculiarities and irregularities. These have been pointed out by Dr. Kirste in the Preface, p. vii. *seq.* But it would have been advisable to separate the peculiarities occurring in the Mantras from those occurring in the Sûtras. For the peculiarites in the language of the Vedic Mantras have an interest of their own and can hardly be adduced as characteristics for *Hiranyakesin's* language.

All Sanskrit scholars who take any interest in the Sûtra literature will feel indebted to Dr. Kirste for his careful edition of a most interesting work.—M. W.

---

*Corpus juris Abessinorum.* Edidit Dr. Joh. Bachmann. Pars I.: Jus Connubii. Quarto, pp. xlii. and 104. (Berlin, F. Schneider & Co., 1890.)

The *Fetha nagast*, or "Law of the Kings," which up to the present day is in force as being the *Codex juris canonici et civilis* of the kingdom of Ethiopia, has not originated in that country. It proves to be a rather modern Geez translation of an Arabic nomocanon, compiled in the 13th century by a monophysit Copte, Abû Ishâq ibn al-'Assâl, one of the most distinguished scholars of his time. Ibn al-'Assâl appears to have adopted for his work a similar plan to other compilations then in existence, as, *e.g.*, the nomocanon of the Nestorian Abû-l-Faraǵ ibn at-Tajjib (in the 11th century), and as sources for his book has used, besides the Old and New Testament :—the Didascalia of the Apostles, the Canons of the first Councils, and the so-called "statutes of the kings," which, according to Guidi,* probably were written in Syria in the 2nd half of the 5th century and may have given the name to the present work.

From this Arabic nomocanon, a translation into Geez was made, which is attributed to the Diacon Peter 'Abd as-Sajjid (Bachmann, p. xi) and at the earliest date would reach as far back as the 15th century, the earliest MSS. dating of the second half of the 17th century. As usual the translator gave his version as closely to the original as the languages would allow; occasional misunderstandings make the sense of this Ethiopic version difficult or obscure, but this regards single words or phrases only. A most precious work was done with respect to the Geez Text, as Guidi has discovered in a London MS. of the 17th (?) century, by a learned Abessinian of that time, who checked the translation with the Arabic original, and accordingly

* In his report to H.E. the Foreign Minister of Italy concerning the *Fetha nagast*, printed in 1890 for private circulation only.

improved the Ethiopic version; unfortunately, however, his labour has not met with general approval in Abessinia.

Although the *Fetha nagast* was known in Europe long ago, next to little has hitherto been done to make the text available to modern scholars. Only one chapter out of 51 (chap. 44) has been published, with a Latin translation and notes, by Fr. A. Arnold (Halle, 1841), and other notices about the book are found in various Catalogues of Ethiopic MSS., among which we may especially mention here Dillmann's valuable description in his *Cat. cod. manuscr. bibl. Bodleianae Ox.* (1848) and an extract from the work in Zotenberg's *Cat. des man. éth. de la Bibl. nat.* (Paris, 1877).

It is therefore to be welcomed that Dr. Bachmann of Berlin undertook to publish a portion of the work. The present vol. comprises a short description, or enumeration, of 21 Ethiopic MSS., five of which have been used, and of 13 Arabic MSS., of which only one has been accessible to the author. Then follows the "Introduction" to the work in Geez and Arabic, accompanied by a partial Latin translation, and the titles of the chapters of the whole book, 22 of which contain the "canonical" law, while the remainder is devoted to the civil law. The principal part of Dr. Bachmann's work is the Geez text and the Latin translation, with extracts from the Arabic version, of chap. 24 of the *Fetha nagast* "concerning the matrimonial law," to which chap. 25, *de interdicto concubinarum*, is added as an "appendix." So far as we can judge, these translations read well, although they cannot be expected to be quite free from inaccuracies or clerical errors. Finally a "juridical and historical dissertation" has been given concerning "jurisprudence in Abessinia," "author and time of the Abessinian Canon of Laws," "its history," and "its parts and contents."

A continuation of both the text, with translation, and the "dissertation" is promised. As there will also be published an edition of the complete text in Geez by order of the Italian Government through such an eminent scholar as Professor Guidi, it is hoped that we shall soon become acquainted with one of the most important profane works of the Ethiopic literature, for which both the Orientalist and the historian will be thankful to all those who are contributing to its completeness and understanding.

C. BEZOLD.

LONDON, *January* 17, 1891.

———

Dr. Karl Vollers, Director of the Khedivial Library, Cairo, has brought out a manual of the Egypto-Arabic language of conversation, with exercises and a glossary (*Lehrbuch der Ägypto-Arabischen Umgangssprache*, mit Uebungen und einem Glossar, Cairo, to be had of the author, 1890. Printed at the 'Imprimerie Catholique,' Beyrouth; xi. and 231 pp. in small 8vo.). The book is intended for all who wish to acquire the Egyptian dialect without having previously studied the literary Arabic. For this purpose it is of a much briefer compass than the celebrated grammar by Spitta (Leipzig, 1880), which in the first instance is meant for scholars only, but at the same time it is more detailed than M. Hartmann's very serviceable Arabic Guide for Travellers (Leipzig, no date). But while it will no doubt admirably fulfil its practical aim, it will be of interest also to the Arabic scholar; for the author distinguishes more precisely than was done by Spitta the forms of exclusively dialectical growth from those which were directly or indirectly influenced by the literary language. An English translation of this book would be a great boon. The same author has in preparation 1, an Introduction to the Egypto-Arabic official language, and 2, a German-Arabic Dictionary of the Egyptian dialect, inclusive of all technical terms. We may mention here incidentally that Dr. Vollers is the compiler of that important section of the Catalogue of the Khedivial Library (vol. v.) which contains the description (all in Arabic) of the historical manuscripts.

TH. N.

To the same active press which has turned out with such creditable correctness the German book which is the subject of the preceding notice, we owe a volume of *Contes Arabes* édités par le P. A. Salhani, S.J. The four tales here given—the sage Haikar, History of the ten Viziers, the Khoja and the Hag, and the Sparrow and the Fowler—are not generally included in the collections that go by the name of the Arabian Nights, but they are well known from the "Supplemental Nights" of the late Sir Richard Burton. The second, more especially, is a version of the Bakhtiar-nameh, which has lately been made the subject of a separate publication by Mr. Clouston. The philological interest attaching to these *Contes Arabes* lies in their being written in the dialect of Syria, the peculiarities of which the editor has been careful to leave undisturbed.

———

*Lectures on the Comparative Grammar of the Semitic Languages.* From the papers of the late William Wright, LL.D. Cambridge (University Press), 1890.

This posthumous work by the greatest of the Semitic scholars whom the United Kingdom has produced in the present century, would probably, had the author been spared eventually to prepare it for the press, have assumed a slightly more amplified form than, as stated in the preface, he had actually given to it at the last revision. There is a certain fastidious brevity throughout these lectures which is irksome to a student eager to obtain at the master's hands all that he can afford to give. To a wish so natural and so justifiable the author would no doubt later on have made certain, if not ample, concessions. However, we are most thankful for this compendium as it is. Dr. Wright's successor in his chair at Cambridge, Professor W. Robertson Smith, who has edited these lectures, has spared no pains not only in reproducing them from the author's last and most careful revision, but also in supplementing from his own reading and from Professor Nöldeke's notes and suggestions what appeared to be wanting to round off the work in agreement with the author's plan and intentions. Its uncontested merit is the absolute trustworthiness which attaches to it in all its principles, its statements and minutest details. This is no small praise, considering that this book has not been preceded by any similar production either in the English or any other language, for Renan's "Histoire générale des langues Sémitiques" (1855) has not advanced, and is now not likely to advance, beyond the introduction. The lectures were first delivered in the Easter term of 1877, and as they were re-delivered at intervals, they were re-touched, in parts re-written, and the results of more recent researches were taken note of. Professor Wright did not consider that the time had come for the production of a complete system of Semitic Comparative Grammar; but he gave what he thought he was warranted in giving. Thus this volume forms the key-stone of a life's honest, unselfish, unremunerative work, and it will maintain its stand by the side of the best books that may yet be produced in this department of philological research.

---

*Translations into Persian.* By Major A. C. Talbot. Two vols. Calcutta, 1890.—As an aid to the acquisition of a correct, elegant and idiomatic Persian style, Major Talbot has brought out a volume of Persian translations of extracts from English standard authors on historical, ethical, and political subjects. The original text is given in one volume, the Persian version in another. In his renderings Major Talbot has had the assistance of Professor Mirza Hairat, of the Elphinstone College, and of Haji Muhammad Muhsin, of Baghdad, whose names alone would be a sufficient guarantee of the work being well done, were it not that Major Talbot himself enjoys a high reputation in India for his Persian scholarship. A careful study of this work will amply reward those who aim at passing in the highest standard in this language.

---

*Spraakleer der Maleische Taal* door D. Gerth van Wijk. Batavia, 1890.—While the many Malay grammars which have appeared in Holland and Java within the last few years are intended more or less to serve a practical purpose, we may describe the Malay grammar by Professor van Wijk as a purely philological work, the outcome and philosophical digest of a long practical familiarity with the language and of a thorough study of its literature in all its stages and branches. We commend it not only to philologists as a safe guide to a critical acquaintance with Malay, but also to those who know and speak that language as a manual of reference on all questions of scholarship. In fact, the work takes the same position in Malay philology that Platts' Hindustani grammar has now occupied for so many years as the standard grammar of Urdu.

---

*Inscriptions at Śravaṇa Belgoḷa, a chief seat of the Jainas.* By B. Lewis Rice. Bangalore, 1889.—This Government publication, consisting of more than 430 quarto pages and many illustrations, deserves a far more detailed notice than we have space to give to it. Its main interest centres in the fact of the whole of the inscriptions—a few are in Sanskrit, the bulk in ancient Canarese—dealing with Jain history and the Jain faith from an early period down to the present century. The history of the Gaṅga and Râshtrakûṭa dynasties receives from these inscriptions much new light, and the editor who has collected and deciphered this long range of records has spared no pains in making the results of his long and arduous work of decipherment available to the student. The Mysore Government has with praiseworthy liberality sent home for distribution a large number of copies of this book, which has thus become widely accessible for the purposes of historical research.

---

*The Emperor Akbar. A Contribution towards the History of India in the 16th Century.* By Frederick Augustus, Count of Noer. Translated, and in part Revised, by Annette S. Beveridge. (Calcutta: Thacker, Spink and Co. London: Kegan Paul, Trench, Trübner and Co., Ludgate Hill, 1890.)

The Count of Noer's "Emperor Akbar" is a thorough and just biography of the greatest of the Moghul Emperors. Although he is evidently full of enthusiastic admiration for the subject of this historical study, he does not allow his admiration to mislead him into unqualified eulogy. Akbar's character as a whole is so noble that the most searching investigation of contemporary historians, some of whom were by religious bigotry strongly prejudiced against him, can only add to his reputation. One excellent feature of the Count of Noer's biography is the extensive use he makes of the original authorities, familiarity with which is essential for the proper comprehension of Akbar's character. These authorities show that the most serious defect with which Akbar can be charged was his rashness. In illustration of this the Count of Noer quotes from the Akbarnamah the story of how one evening, when Akbar and his warriors were feasting in camp, and their brains were heated with wine, some one was lauding Rajput contempt for death, and "stated that the Rajputs of Bhaganah had a game in which they posted two men on one side with naked pikes, and placed two others exactly opposite, who, upon a signal given, would rush upon the spears until the points came out at their backs. 'If that be the case,' said Akbar, 'I too will run upon my sword,' and thrusting the handle into the wall prepared to execute his words. His companions were motionless with consternation. Man Singh only moved and struck the weapon to a distance, but still the thumb and forefinger of his Majesty were slightly cut before the weapon was removed." Man Singh had the honour of being felled by the Emperor's own hand for his timely interposition. This act of suicidal madness and other stories illustrate Akbar's tendency to foolhardiness, which might at an early stage have brought his beneficent career to an untimely conclusion. On another occasion he was willing to risk the issue of a campaign and the fate of the empire on the fortune of a duel between himself and the hostile commander. But this inconsiderate recklessness, although it must be borne in mind by any one who wishes to form a just view of Akbar's character, was based on his personal valour and skill in arms, which turned the tide of the battle in many a hard-fought contest. It is related that once some artillerymen told Wellington that they had a good opportunity of sending a cannon-ball into the middle of the staff of Marshal Soult, who had ventured imprudently near the English lines. Wellington would not give his sanction, remarking, "We commanding officers have something else to do instead of shooting at each other." Akbar had no such scruples. At the siege of Chitore he picked off many of the enemy with his deadly gun Sangram, and he finally ended that difficult siege by sending a bullet through the forehead of Jai Mall, the commander of the Rajput garrison, upon whose death the enemies' powers of resistance suddenly collapsed.

One of the most interesting chapters in the Count of Noer's work is that in which he narrates Akbar's struggle against the Ulamas and his attempt to found a religion of his own. His idea seems to have been to found a kind of universal religion by selecting the points of agreement between all the religions he knew. He was evidently of the opinion of the Greek philosopher, who, in a polytheistic age, declared that religions were many and God one, and he hoped that all his subjects, whether Mahomedan, Hindoo, Zoroastrian, or Christian, might be induced to sink their differences and join in the worship of one God, recognizing Akbar himself as the representative of God upon the earth. He naturally met with the strongest opposition from the Ulamas, the priests of the ruling race, and therefore the greater part of the destructive part of his religious policy was directed to their overthrow. According to Badaoni, "he despised the ordinances of the Koran as opposed to reason and as being modern, and their founder as one of those poor Arabs whom he called malefactors and brigands. This may be exaggeration, but, if all that is written of him by contemporary writers on the subject be accepted, it is not far from the truth. It is said that he doubted the prophesies of Mahomet, and it is certain that he substituted for the usual formula, "There is no God but God and Mahomet is his prophet," another in honour of himself, "There is no God but God and Akbar is his vicegerent." His opposition to Mahomedanism was also evinced by the favour he showed to other religions. He allowed the Jesuits to teach his son, Murad, the Portuguese language and the Christian creed. In order to conciliate the Hindoos, he forbade the slaughter of animals on Sundays, and for two months and a half in the year. He even went so far as to wear in public the Hindoo *tika* on his forehead, and joined in the *homa* sacrifice of his Rajpootani wives. It also appears that he adopted the doctrine of metempsychosis. From the Zoroastrians he accepted the worship of the sun as the visible symbol of the deity. As far as his new religion resembled Mahomedanism, it drew more from the heterodox Sufis and Shias than from the tenets of the orthodox Sunis. On the whole, however, it was so much opposed in spirit

to Mahomedanism that we are surprised to find that, of the ten members of the new religion whose names have come down to us, nine were Mahometans and only one, the Rajah Birbal, a Hindoo. An attempt was made to induce the faithful and valiant Man Sing to become a member of the new religion, but he replied, "If your Majesty means by the term of membership willingness to sacrifice one's life, I have given pretty clear proofs, and your Majesty might dispense with examining me ; but if the term has another meaning and refers to religion, surely I am a Hindoo." Many others were less scrupulous about sacrificing their religious convictions for the imperial favour. Thousands of disciples joined the new faith, but their insincerity is indicated by the fact that after Akbar's death his religion disappeared. Nevertheless, though he failed to establish a new religion, the noble example he set of religious tolerance has borne abundant fruits, and is remembered with gratitude all over India even to the present day.

The work of translation has, on the whole, been done very well by Mrs. Beveridge. The only fault that we have to find with it is that her familiarity with German occasionally affects the purity of her English. "In this he will have been prompted not only by a desire to foster the growth of Arabian science" looks more like German than English, and this use of " will have been" for " would seem to have been" recurs at intervals through the book. The same German influence may account for the use of such rare un-English words as " book-mindedness," " curial," " God-to-ward," " ontogenistic" (which surely, if such words are admissible outside philosophical treatises, ought to be " ontogenetic"), " godlikedness" used more than once, and "niche" as a neuter verb. Nevertheless, with some such exceptions as these, the style of the translation is decidedly good and reads easily. It must also be borne in mind that, owing to the Count's death before his work was quite completed, Mrs. Beveridge had not merely to translate, but also to face the severe labour of collating her translation with the original sources used so abundantly in the narrative. This must have involved a great deal of additional work. It is a pity that such an important contribution to Indian history as the " Emperor Akbar" should appear in an English guise imperfectly printed. The punctuation throughout the two volumes is most irregular. There are also a large number of mis-spelt and misprinted words, such as "Oriental" I. xlv, "disception" I. 307, "harrassed" I. 282, "aniability" II. 404. On p. 310 of the first volume, six Greek words are printed. They only contain sixteen letters, three of which have gone wrong, not to mention accents and aspirates. A little extra care ought surely to have been taken to avoid such slips. Owing to their presence, Mrs. Beveridge's translation of the Emperor Akbar, wherever it is read on either side of the Atlantic, will not only publish to the world the wisdom and glory of the greatest of the Moghuls, but also give all who read it an unfavourable idea of the capacity and intelligence of the Indian printer.—[From the *Times of India.*]

*Across the Border; or, Pathan and Biloch.* By Edward E. Oliver, M.Inst.C.E., M.R.A.S., etc. Illustrated by J. L. Kipling, C.I.E. (London : Chapman and Hall, 1890.)

With the exception of those officers whose duty has brought them into direct communication with the tribes on the North-West Frontier, there are but few servants of Government who profess to understand border politics, while in the case of the general public the ignorance concerning the clans lying between Kashmir and Karachi is necessarily even more pronounced. In gazetteers, in settlement and administration reports, in memoranda compiled by civil and military officers, and in a few books of travel (mostly written years ago) there is abundance of information of course; but it is not easy of access, and only enthusiastic students will be at the pains to unearth it. Mr. E. E. Oliver, therefore, in examining in detail the present condition of the borderland, describing the habits and customs of the tribesmen, contrasting one clan with another, and discoursing upon their social and religious peculiarities, deserves the thanks both of the official world and the general reading public. Moreover, in the book now under review there are certain dissertations on the political situation in connexion with the great Central Asian Question which are of special interest, now that so much attention is being directed to the defence of India. The fact that the volume is made up of articles which have already appeared in the columns of Indian newspapers does not detract from its value. It would, indeed, have been matter for regret if the series of twenty-four essays on the leading border tribes, which originally appeared in the *Civil and Military Gazette*, had been allowed to be forgotten in the files of that paper. In that case, too, we should never have had from the pen of Mr. J. L. Kipling the admirable sketches which illustrate and give point to Mr. Oliver's letter-press. We therefore welcome "Across the Border" as a most valuable contribution to Indian literature, useful as a book of reference, and yet written in such a style as to attract the general reader. It should be in the hands of every officer of the Frontier Force whose life is spent within the shadow of the hills which guard the approach to India from the west; while to the wider circles of students and experts interested in the Central Asian problem it will give material for thoughtful consideration, though the author belongs neither to the political nor the military branch of the service.

The Pathan and the Biloch have for generations past been held to be little better than robbers and murderers—caterans of the Kohistan delighting in bloodshed, and looking upon the dwellers in the plains as placed conveniently within their reach, their villages lying open to attack and their flocks and herds inviting a raid from the hills. Mr. Oliver declines to paint them altogether in such black colours. Yar Mahomed Yasufzai and Killan Khan, the Marri Chief, of whom "R. K." has sung in connection with "Hurree Chunder Mookerjee, pride of Bow Bazar," and the

abrogation of the Arms Act, had their redeeming qualities. True—

> They were unenlightened men, Ballard knew them not:
> They procured their swords and guns chiefly on the spot;
> And the lore of centuries, plus a hundred fights,
> Made them slow to disregard one another's rights.

But there is an obverse side to the bloody shield of the Pathan and Biloch, and it is given us in "Across the Border." "Possibly it may be thought," says the author, "too much has been made of their romantic side: their alternating pillage, murder and sudden death with softer sentiments, and, as Elphinstone somewhere says, desperate forays with strains that might have tuned a shepherd's pipe. But besides being splendid fighting animals, both have undoubtedly qualities taking and excellent; and the supposition that every Biloch is a thief and every Pathan a murderer in his own heart—in the sense those terms are understood by us— is altogether wide of the mark. Both have held their own as free men through centuries of disturbance; both echo the Briton's sentiment that anything is preferable to slavery. That if 'never united they should always be free' is a familiar saying of their own. Both have the warlike instincts and enterprise which brought the Briton to India and have kept him there, that whilom established the Pathan soldier of fortune, or his descendants, from the Punjab to the Deccan; and that, if the British power were withdrawn, would not improbably find him so establishing himself again. To look at a gathering of Biloch chiefs, or Pathan soldiers in one of our regiments, compels a tribute of admiration."

There are black sheep, no doubt, in abundance among these wild hill men; but taken in the mass, those who know them best hold, and perhaps with justice, that they can furnish splendid soldiers to our Army, and that it is well worth while to bring them under our direct control. What Sir Robert Sandeman has done on the south, and Colonel Warburton on the north, can equally well be accomplished in the central tracts between the Gomal and the Khyber, and in years to come we should reckon among our most loyal subjects the descendants of the savage hillmen who maintained their freedom against the Amirs of Kabul on the one hand, and the Moghul Emperors on the other. Their peculiarities must be studied, their tribal relations be understood, and their religious prejudices which foster fanaticism be overcome by the exercise of tact and discrimination. When this has been done the borderland will be as safe and peaceful as our own settled districts, and it will furnish tens of thousands of brave soldiers ready to defend the few passes which can give admission to an enemy advancing on India through Afghanistan.

We do not intend to enter here upon any dissertation regarding this advance. The author shares with us the view that the danger of any attack in force will declare itself in years to come rather by way of Kabul than Kandahar, and that the prime necessity now is to link up our frontier railways so that the concentration of troops, whether for offensive or defensive operations, may be made at any point from Peshawur to

Chaman. The railway will be the most potent factor in determining the scene of conflict in the first phase of the struggle for Afghanistan, and our advance to occupy strategical positions, whence operations can be boldly carried on, will mainly depend upon the completeness or otherwise of the main lines of communication with our reserves of strength in India. If these lines are menaced by hostile tribes our strength will be frittered away in guarding them, and hence the necessity of making Pathan and Biloch co-sharers in the work of defence. "The theory that we should sit down on the left bank of the Indus and wait until an invading host has formed up on the other side, has been for better or worse permanently abandoned. In its place we have accepted the more reasonable one, that it is better to deal with an enemy outside the gate of the fort than to let him in and fight him afterwards inside. There can be no middle course; no meeting him half-way or fighting him with the river at our immediate back, except under the direst necessity. The passes along the border are the gates of India on the north; to hold them properly, we must be perfectly free to come and go on both sides; and having admitted so much, the only logical continuation of the argument necessitates the tribes who now occupy the passes becoming our certain allies, or our loyal subjects, and the latter appears the safer." There is no flaw in this argument to our thinking, and we should like to see Apozais multiplied beyond the Suleimans and every powerful clan brought well under control.

The general reader will find much to interest him in the description of the various trans-frontier tribes, and not least in the legends which are reproduced to illustrate the romantic side of Biloch and Pathan character. These stories are graphically told and the element of love with its inevitable surroundings of jealousy and revenge is not lacking in them. Details of domestic life, the mysteries of blood feuds, the system of administration, the rude code of laws and customary observances, the military strength of the tribes, and their powers for good and evil, are all given; while great care is shown in describing the country which they hold. There are some interesting chapters on the Peshawar Valley of the past, the Peshawar Pathans of the present, Pathan poetry and "A Bit of the Yaghestan;" while the chapter dealing with Swat, Panjkora and Bajawar has special claims to attention, now that the Khan of Dir has just been ousted from his petty State. An excellent map of the borderland showing the tribal divisions should not be forgotten.—[From the *Pioneer*.]

-----

*The Golden Bough; a Study in Comparative Religion.* By J. G. Frazer, M.A., Fellow of Trinity College, Cambridge. In Two Vols. (London, Macmillan and Co., 1890.)

Mr. Frazer's book carries us back to early and prehistoric times. The opening scene is laid among the Alban Hills, at the Arician Grove, the sanctuary of Diana Nemorensis. Here, from immemorial time, a strange and obscure custom had prevailed, and had lasted on to the days of Imperial Rome, long after its origin and meaning had been forgotten. The priesthood of the goddess, a most important office, conferring on its holder the kingly title of Rex Nemorensis, could be held only by a runaway slave. He must be a murderer, too, for he gained his place only when he had killed his predecessor; and he was in constant fear of being deposed and killed in turn by some fresh aspirant to his insecure and dangerous rank. He remained, therefore, always sword in hand, on the watch for his expected assailant. So far all authorities are in agreement. Some add, further, that his appointed place was that of guardian over a sacred tree, from which no bough was to be broken, and that as long as the tree was intact his life was safe. But if some new runaway could succeed in breaking off a bough he gained the right thereby of fighting the priest in single combat, or more probably of setting upon him unawares, and when he had killed him he became priest and king in his stead. It is certain that the shrine of the goddess was in high repute throughout Italy. It was especially frequented by women desirous either of children or of an easy delivery. A perpetual fire seems to have been kept burning in her sanctuary. At her annual festival the entire grove was lit up by torches, and a feast was held, at which a young kid, wine, and cakes were served up on platters of leaves. Fire, vegetation, and the reproductive powers of nature thus stand out prominently in connexion with the worship of the goddess.

At the same place two minor deities were honoured, the nymph Egeria and Virbius, whom tradition reported to have been Hippolytus, restored to life by the skill of Æsculapius, and hidden by Diana in her grove, where he reigned a forest king and the first priest at her shrine. By some authorities Virbius is identified with the sun.

Now in all this there is much that needs to be explained. The Arician custom is at once strange, and in many ways peculiar to the place. The questions which suggest themselves about it are—What was the nature of the priest's office? whom or what did he represent? why was he called a king? why was he a slave? and why must each fresh claimant have plucked a bough from the sacred tree before he could attack the actual holder of the office? On no one of these points can a direct answer be found. Such myths and traditions as there are give no help whatever. There is no reason to suppose that they have so much as a substratum of truth. One and all, they have been invented by an afterthought to explain matters far older than themselves, the real original purpose of which has been forgotten or has been obscured by a change of creed, and has thus lost the importance which at first attached to it. Mr. Frazer's method of procedure is to bring together proofs of early customs and beliefs which may be combined into a consistent whole, and may explain, at least probably, the original meaning of the Arician custom and the later modifications which were made in it. He shows, first, by an almost needless accumulation of evidence, that primitive man had no notion of the fixity of natural laws. He held, on the contrary, that the weather, for instance, and the course and character of the seasons, were very largely within his own control, and he had many fanciful ways of his own for exerting a supposed influence over them. The supreme power over them was frequently thought to reside in some chosen person, who was more or less held responsible for the use he was assumed to have made of it. With the life of this great functionary the growth of the crops, the course of the seasons, and the maintenance of the entire order of things, were held to be bound up. Mr. Frazer further shows that among many races, and certainly among Aryan races, tree-worship was one of the most early and best-established forms of religious observance. The tree was thought to be the dwelling-place of the tree-spirit, and this spirit was very commonly represented by a living man, who was looked upon as its embodiment and as gifted to the full with its vast and all-pervading powers. The sacred tree was often known and addressed as a king, so that it was quite natural that its human representative should have had the same title conferred upon him. Mr. Frazer suggests, accordingly, that the Arician custom arose from such beliefs as the above. The Arician priest was an incarnation of the tree-spirit, and, as such, would have been credited with the miraculous powers of his divine original. He could send rain and sunshine; the growth of the crops, the multiplication of the flocks and herds, the parturition of women—in a word, the beneficent and reproductive forces of nature would be under his control and dependent on his life. All this, strange as it sounds, is confirmed by ample proof of the prevalence of like beliefs in almost every country. They are found in some places as survivals; the belief has been lost, the custom based upon it has been preserved. Our Jack-in-the-Green and our harvest-home festivities are referred to by Mr. Frazer as unsuspected instances of this. Elsewhere they exist in their old form and in full original force, and they make it likely that in early prehistoric Latium the creed and habits of primitive man may have found their natural outcome in the rites of the Arician Grove.

But here a difficulty occurs. Since the life of the Arician priest was of such supreme importance, how came it that his licensed murder was a part of the Arician custom? An explanation must be sought after the same method as before. In this case, as in numerous others like it, it was held to be necessary that the divine priest should preserve in unabated force the energy of full manhood. If he grew old or feeble, the reproductive powers of nature would share his decay, and a general sterility would supervene. Against this danger, therefore, a special safeguard was contrived. The divine man was not suffered to grow old. His spirit and influence were detached from his body by his death, and were transferred in their unabated vigour to some new frame, and were thence passed on in turn to another and yet another. In this way the succession was kept up; the divine man was maintained in perpetual strength, and a fit habitation was always provided for the indwelling deity to occupy. On such terms as these has the joint office of priest and king been held in many regions, and from immemorial time. But the death of the priest-king was not everywhere and always carried out in fact. In course of years, as men's manners became less rude, and as human life was held in more value, the old custom was modified. Sometimes an image was burnt or destroyed when the appointed day came round, and the human life was spared. Sometimes a temporary transfer of office was made to some new and less worthy occupant, and, in place of the royal priest, a stranger or a slave or a criminal was immolated. We may suppose that in the Arician rites a like modification had at some time been made. There was a human victim still, but it was not a freeman, but a slave. Mr. Frazer thinks it probable that, slave or freeman, he was originally put to death at the close of his year's office, burnt, dead or alive, at the Arician Diana's festival. The custom, as we read of it in historical times, had been so modified as to give him a chance of escape. The essential point was safe. As long as the Rex Nemorensis could hold his own against his assailants, he might be credited with retaining his physical force. *Regna tenent fortesque manu, pedibusque fugaces.* But when the Arician priest was neither strong nor fleet of foot, he must accept his doom; and the tree-spirit, dislodged from the person of its representative, must become incarnate immediately in some more vigorous and more worthy frame. How all this may have been in the earliest times of the institution we have no means of knowing; whether the priest was suffered to escape by the substitution of a slave when the day of death came round, or whether, as in Mexico, the doomed victim was carefully watched and not allowed to escape. The strange thing is that a priesthood on the Arician terms should at any time have been attractive even for a slave, and that willing competitors should have been found for it. But it seems certain that in later days, about which alone we have any positive information, the danger of assault was not what it may have formerly been. As we might well expect, the competition had ceased to be keen. In the reign of Caligula, the Arician priest had had so long a term, and had been so long left unattacked, that the Emperor for a freak gave orders for him to be attacked and killed. The need of such a mandate is some proof of the general security by which the office had come to be surrounded.

Of the two minor deities who were worshipped at the Arician Grove, the nymph Egeria seems to have been the creation of a cognate but independent personifying fancy. Virbius, as the first priest, calls for special notice here. The legend that he had been restored to life may have been an expression in legendary terms of the old belief in the continuity of his priestly office, each new priest being possessed by the same spirit as his predecessor, and thus being for all intents and purposes the self-same person. That Virbius was also identified with the sun is explained by the obvious similarity between the sun as the great source of life and growth, and the divine tree to which like functions were attributed. As the sun governs the seasons, so too did the tree-spirit, and so too did the priest in whom the tree-spirit dwelt. On the plucking of the sacred branch, Mr. Frazer gives reasons for supposing that the sacred tree was the oak, the sacred branch the mistletoe growing on it, and, like the priest, a representative or second home of the tree-spirit's life. We have no space for the long and somewhat circuitous train of evidence which he brings in support of his conclusion. His book will be attractive for all readers. The serious student will find in it a comprehensive survey of some of the most obscure and interesting problems in early religious faith. To those who read for amusement, it will offer an ample store of world-wide myths and legends and fairy tales and curious customs. They may begin by being amused, and may be led on from the fable to the moral, from the graphic descriptions to the theories which they are introduced to illustrate.—[*The Times* of Aug. 30, 1890.]

---

*The Eskimo Colour-names.*

There is a large amount of interest in the colour-names of various races, especially in view of the controversies as to the origin of and development of the sense amongst the ancient races. The American Bureau of Education have just issued *English-Eskimo and Eskimo-English Vocabularies*, compiled by Ensign Roger Wells, jun., United States Navy, and Interpreter John W. Kelly. This pamphlet of 72 pages contains a mass of interesting matter, and presents a very dark picture of the moral and social condition of the Arctic Eskimos of Alaska and Siberia. The status of the women—perhaps the most infallible of all the tests of real civilization that can be applied—is exceedingly low, and they are apparently the enforced victims of their male relations in many discreditable ways. Yet the translations of love-songs contained in this book show that the men are not incapable of tender feeling, and not unable to express them in suitable, and even poetical language. Judging from these vocabularies—the only source of information accessible to me at the moment—the Eskimos are not very observant of colour variations. Black is *Tawk toak*, or *Munok'toak*; Blue is *Tawk rek'toak*; Brown is *Kawek'suruk*; Green is *Shung ok'toak*; Purple is *Tung uk'toak*; Red is *Ka rek cho'ak*; and White is *Ka tak'toak*. A few allied phrases may be named :—To blush is *Ka rek pul'uk to*; evidently connected with the colour of red. Red dye, however, is *Enung ne'ak*. Dark is *Tawk to'ak*. Light is *Ikne a'to*. The interest of the inquiry centres on the name for Blue, about which there has been so much controversy since the promulgation of Geiger's theory that the paucity of early references to that shade evidence a comparatively late development of the colour-sense. The weak point of such a theory is that it argues an exact correspondence between colour names and colour-discrimination — a correspondence which notoriously does not exist. In the case of the Gipsies, as I have elsewhere shown (Stray Chapters, p. 28) they appear to have had and to have lost—in England at least—a name for blue, which is now absent from their vocabulary except in borrowed words. The Eskimos, so far as the evidence of this vocabulary extends, are amongst the many peoples who have no distinctive

term for blue. It is evident that *Tawk rek'toak* means a dark colour, possibly a dark red. This will be seen on comparing the words above given for black, red, blue and dark. It is another instance of the fact that the power of perception and the power of distinctive naming are not necessarily identical. The examples given are from the speech of the Alaskan Eskimos, now subjects of the United States.

WILLIAM E. A. AXON.

*Armytage, Bowdon, Cheshire.*

---

*Wörterbuch des Runa Simi oder der Keshua-Sprache.* Von Dr. E. W. Middendorf. x. and 857 pages. (Leipzig, F. A. Brockhaus, 1890.)

This handsome volume forms the second issue of Dr. Middendorf's ponderous serial on the languages of Peru, and is a sequel to his Keshua grammar which was noticed in our previous number. The Dictionary is mainly based on the excellent "Vocabulario" of Diego Gonzalez Holguin (1608), as well as on the works of Domingo de S. Thomas, J. J. v. Tschudi and Honorio Mossi ; words and phrases now antiquated are marked with an asterisk, while there is an accession of a large number which the author himself collected on his travels. The whole material underwent a strict process of sifting at the hands of an intelligent native from the interior of the province of Cusco, and may be considered to represent the language both as it was 300 years ago, and as it is now spoken. It gives in a third column the Spanish for every word and phrase, and apart from its practical usefulness, highly commends itself to the student of the American aboriginal languages by its strictly scientific method, its completeness and critical accuracy. As to typography, and the general get-up, this publication leaves nothing to be desired.

---

*Ollanta, ein Drama der Keshua-Sprache.* Übersetzt und mit Anmerkungen versehen von Dr. E. W. Middendorf. (Leipzig, F. A. Brockhaus, 1890.)

This third volume of Dr. Middendorf's comprehensive work on the indigenous languages of Peru contains not only the drama Ollanta (best known in this country through Mr. Markham's version) in text and annotated translation, but also an introductory treatise on the religious and political institutions of the Inkas. These institutions form the background of the drama. Though, at least in its present form, it cannot have been composed before the Spanish conquest, it reflects the manners and customs of the antecedent period, and of these the first half of the introduction gives in its 76 pages the most lucid survey we have seen anywhere. This part is well worth being issued separately in an English translation. The second part deals with the drama itself and especially discusses the question as to its age. The volume is a monument of historical *précis* and of critical scholarship.

## Obituary.

---

We announce with much regret that *Sir Richard
Burton*, the eminent Eastern traveller and Orientalist,
who has held the post of British Consul at Trieste since
1872, died there yesterday morning at the age of 69.
In him there has passed away one of the most remarkable and cosmopolitan, and at the same time one of
the most scholarly, explorers of our time. Sir Richard
Burton's name is in popular estimation associated with
Africa, and rightly so, for there he did his most valuable and most original work. His discovery of Lake
Tanganyika, especially when combined with that of
the Victoria Nyanza by his companion Speke, deserves
to rank with Stanley's memorable journeys. He and
his companions were lions in their day, and if the
excitement then was less than it has been over Mr.
Stanley's recent expedition, it was not due to the fact
that the geographical work they did was less important
or accomplished with less hazard. The conditions
which fan excitement and nurse enthusiasm had not
reached the development thirty years ago which they
have attained now.

Richard Francis Burton was born on March 19, 1821,
at Barham House, Herts, the son of Colonel Netterville
Burton, of the 36th Regiment, and his wife Martha
Baker. Richard's grandfather was rector of Tuam, in
Ireland, and his grand-uncle Bishop of Killalo. They
were the first of the family to settle in Ireland, and
belonged to the Burtons of Barker Hill, near Shap,
Westmorland, who, again, are connected with some of
the leading Burton families all over the kingdom.
Much of Richard Burton's eccentricity was inherited
both on the father's and mother's side. Most of his
boyhood and youth was spent at Tours and in wandering with his restless father over the Continent, from
one temporary place of residence to another. Burton's
training and education were thus of an irregular and
spasmodic character, ill-fitted to qualify him for the
routine of an official career. It, however, fostered his
powers of observation, and gave him ample opportunity
of exercising his wonderful faculty for the acquisition
of languages. The Burton children were left very
much to themselves, so that Richard's innate wayward
disposition had little check. At last, in 1840, the
family returned to England, and young Burton was
entered at Oxford, going into residence at Trinity
College in the Michaelmas Term of that year. His
previous training was not conducive to compliance
with Oxford ways. He was leader in the wildest pranks
of his time; in Latin and Greek he made little headway, but he quickly mastered Arabic. Burton soon
got disgusted with University life and resolved to quit
it. This he did by deliberately attending a race meeting
against orders, and was of course "sent down." This
was precisely what he wanted. When he arrived
suddenly in London (in 1842), he told his friends
that he had been allowed an extra vacation for taking
a double first-class with the very highest honours.
Of course the truth was soon discovered, and in the
end he obtained a commission in the East India Company's service. He sailed from England on June 18,
1842, his only companion being a bull-terrier of the
Oxford breed. He landed at Bombay on October 28,
and was posted as ensign to the 18th Regiment, Bombay Native Infantry, which he joined at Baroda. He
soon became master of Hindustani and fencing, and
astonished his fellow officers and displeased his superiors
by the eccentricities of his conduct. Nevertheless, in
1843 he was made regimental interpreter, and succeeded
in indulging his wandering propensities by expeditions
to various parts of India. Burton's career as an

explorer, however, may be said to have begun in 1852,
when he undertook, in the disguise of a Pathan, that
journey to Medina and Mecca the description of which
forms one of the most interesting of his many narratives. His life thenceforth, until he settled down as
Consul at Trieste, was an almost uninterrupted series
of exploring expeditions. Before this (1851) he had
published a volume on "Scinde," giving the results of
his observations while resident in the "unhappy valley,"
and in the same year a volume on "Goa and the Blue
Mountains."

Burton's next expedition was to Somaliland, even
now but little known, and then full of dangers. The
expedition was undertaken by the Directors of the
East India Company, and Burton was accompanied by
Lieutenant Speke. The expedition left Aden at the
end of 1854, and Burton alone, again in disguise,
succeeded, amid the greatest risks, in entering the
sacred city of Harrar. Returning again to Berbera in
the beginning of 1855, Burton intended to penetrate
to the Nile, but shortly after landing the expedition
was attacked, Burton and Speke being wounded, and
narrowly escaping with their lives. The narrative of
this hazardous expedition was published in 1856, under
the title of "First Footsteps in East Africa." After
a short run to Constantinople in 1856, in the vain
hope of being employed in the war against Russia,
Burton returned to England still more disgusted with
officialism, and still more determined to distinguish
himself as an African explorer. He now undertook,
after a trial trip to Zanzibar and other coast towns,
the expedition into the heart of Africa on which his
fame will mainly rest. For years rumours had been
reaching the coast of great lakes in the interior; and
Krapf and Rebmann, two missionaries, had actually
seen a snow-covered mountain just under the Equator.
Livingstone had made his great journey across the
continent (he arrived in England in December, 1856),
and had aroused an interest in Africa which has been
increasing in intensity ever since. We have heard
much recently of the great lakes and rivers and
mountains which covered the old maps of Africa, but
which D'Anville rightly swept away. A great lake
was reported to exist in the Zanzibar interior, and it
was to find this that Burton and his companion Speke
left Zanzibar in June, 1857, under the auspices of the
Royal Geographical Society. For the first time the
route which has now become a well-trodden highway,
from Bagamoyo to Ujiji, was traversed by the feet of
white men. After more than the usual trouble, a final
start was made, and through many trials and sufferings
Ujiji was reached on February 14th, 1858, about eight
months from leaving Bagamoyo. Thus the first of
those great lakes of Central Africa, which probably
form its most remarkable feature, found its place
on the map. Moreover, the expedition went over
hundreds of miles of new country, and in addition
Speke made a run to the north to find that other
great lake, Victoria Nyanza, around which English
and German interests have of late been mainly
centred. Altogether this may be regarded as one of
the most notable of African expeditions, and Burton
was rightly hailed on his return to England, in 1859,
as an explorer of the first rank. He well deserved
the gold medal which the Royal Geographical Society
awarded him, and the many other honours which were
showered upon him. He may justly be regarded as
the pioneer in a region where subsequently splendid
work was done by Livingstone, Cameron, and Stanley.
To the unhappy dispute which followed between
Burton and Speke, and which gave rise to so much
bitter feeling, it is not necessary to do more than
allude.

After a run to the United States in 1860, when Burton visited Salt Lake City and the West (about which he wrote in his "City of the Saints"), he was once more back in Africa. Meantime, January 22nd, 1861, he had married the lady who has been his loyal and helpful companion through life. Lady Burton belongs to the Arundells of Wardour. In August, 1861, Burton and his bride sailed for "the Foreign Office Grave," Fernando Po, to which he had been appointed Consul. His three years' stay here was spent in exploring the whole of the coast region round the Bight of Biafra, varied by a special mission to the King of Dahomey, the results of which are recorded in two separate works. Burton's excellent work in this unhealthy region brought him promotion, and in 1865 he went as British Consul to Sao Paulo, in Brazil. As usual, this born explorer could not rest. He traversed all his province, voyaged down the San Francisco, visited the La Plata States, and subsequently crossed the continent to Chili and Peru, returning by the Straits of Magellan. As usual, the result was a big book, "The Highlands of Brazil" (1869).

From Brazil Burton was transferred to Damascus, where he landed in October, 1869. Damascus he made the basis of an exploration of Syria, but on the reduction of the Consulate he returned to England in 1871. A visit to Iceland in 1872 resulted in an elaborate work on the Island, one of the most complete in our language. In the same year Burton was appointed to the Consulship at Trieste, and that post he filled till the day of his death. But even there he could not rest. In 1876 and 1877-78 he made two visits to the Land of Midian to explore the old mines, the result being two works, too full of learning to be quite popular. In 1882, in company with Commander Cameron, Burton made an expedition to the interior of the Gold Coast for the purpose of prospecting the mines in that unhealthy region, but the only result was another book.

This may be regarded as Burton's last expedition. Since then his health began gradually to break down, and no wonder, considering the hardships he had had to endure from his boyhood upwards. But idleness with Burton meant unhappiness, and if he were not exploring, he was engaged on some scholarly investigation or some literary enterprise. His translation of Camoens (1880) is in itself a masterly performance, abounding with the most recondite and learned annotations. His literal translation of the "Arabian Nights" is the work of an accomplished Eastern scholar, who could treat the curious questions suggested by these stories of a comparatively primitive life with the frankness and some of the recklessness of science. Many memoirs and papers, besides the works we have mentioned, have come from Burton's busy hand, all of them marked by that keen research, frank criticism, and scholarly annotation which make his works a mine of knowledge, but which at the same time render them somewhat difficult reading.

Burton, as might have been expected, was never an official favourite, and his numerous friends are of opinion that his many services entitled him long ago to a handsome retiring pension ; but Government was inexorable, and his only reward was a K.C.M.G., bestowed in 1886. Notwithstanding the apparent brusqueness of his manner and the frankness of his talk, Burton had many warm friends. No man ever succeeded better with the natives either of Africa or Asia ; indeed, with barbarism he had almost more sympathy than with civilization. He was a man of real humanity and an unwavering friend. Like Livingstone and Stanley, he was one of those determined men of action who carry out their purpose through every obstacle. As an observer he was keen and accurate and in spite of his perplexingly allusive style, was clear and graphic in his descriptions. In many respects Richard Burton was one of the most remarkable men of his time ; but he will be longest remembered as the first pioneer in Central Africa, the discoverer of Lake Tanganyika.—[*The Times* of 21 Oct. 1890.]

---

*Sir John Francis Davis* died at his residence near Bristol on 13th November, 1890. Sir John Davis had reached the patriarchal age of 96, having been born on July 16, 1795, and the most important portion of his public career terminated forty years ago. But, although his services cannot be described as living fresh in the public mind to-day, the part he took in our early diplomatic intercourse with China was far too important for his name to be forgotten, and, as he was closely connected with the incidents that accompanied the first appearance of our officials on the Chinese coast, his death not only removes an interesting figure, but severs the only remaining link with the earlier and less satisfactory intercourse between England and China. Sir John Davis was the eldest son of a servant of the East India Company who had been attached to the missions sent to Tibet by Warren Hastings, and who at a later date distinguished himself in the defence of Benares. Through his influence Mr. John Davis was appointed a writer to the Canton Factory at the age of 18, and when Lord Amherst was sent in 1816 as envoy to Pekin, he was attached to the mission. After that abortive embassy returned he resumed his duties at Canton, and in 1832 he had risen to the post of president of the East India Company's factory in China. The withdrawal of the company's charter of exclusive trade with China introduced a totally new condition of things, and the presidentship lapsed. An English official, Lord Napier, came out with full powers from the Government to act as superintendent of trade, but on Lord Napier's death in October, 1834, Mr. Davis was nominated to the head of the commission entrusted with his duties. In the following year he returned to England, and he was absent from China during the trying period of the first Chinese war of 1840-2, which closed with the Treaty of Nankin. In June, 1844, he succeeded Sir Henry Pottinger as chief superintendent of trade and Governor of Hongkong, which post he held for four years. The most important event of his Governorship was the so-called Fatshan affair, which arose out of the attack on a party of Englishmen at that place. The Chinese were on this occasion not much to blame, but Sir John, who had received the dignity of a baronetcy in 1845, declared that he would "exact and require that British subjects should be as free from molestation and insult in China as they could be in England," which was in accordance neither with the treaty nor with possibility. In the execution of his intention to obtain redress, he sent a military expedition up the river to Canton. For this, although successful, he received no thanks from his Government, which entirely disapproved and peremptorily forbade any adventure of this kind. The Fatshan incident entailed the departure of Sir John Davis from China, for, taking Lord Grey's reproof very much to heart, he felt bound to resign. His interest in China and the Chinese during the last forty years remained quite as great as when he resided in the East, and he was particularly active in encouraging a study of the Chinese language, taking, among other things, a prominent part in the founding of the scholarships at Oxford, which bear his name. Sir John Davis, in addition to his diplomatic connexion with China, will be permanently remembered as the author of some of the earliest and most interesting works on the literature, customs and history of that country. No one wrote more agreeably or with equal authority on the subject of the old China, with which he had to deal, from Lord Amherst's mission down to the Treaty of Pekin in 1860.—[*Times* of Nov. 14, 1890.]

*Vilhelm Trenckner*, one of the most learned Oriental scholars, died at Copenhagen on the 9th January after nearly four months' illness. Born in 1823 as the son of an immigrant German baker, he was placed for his first education at "Petri Deutsche Realschule." Subsequently he received private instruction to qualify him for the University, and passed his *examen artium* in 1841. As a student he attended Madvig's lectures on classical philology. The study of Rask's works led him to take up philosophy and general philology. He became a good Arabic scholar, and eventually took up Sanskrit and Pali, which latter language he cultivated to the end of his life. The three editions of Pali texts which we owe to him are (next to Fausböll's) unrivalled for critical scholarship. He was 55 years old before he wrote anything for publication. For the last thirty years he belonged to the staff of teachers at the Copenhagen Orphanage, where not a few of his more gifted pupils profited by his linguistic attainments. His vast collections towards a Pali-English Dictionary, the work of forty years, will be of the utmost service when a new Pali Dictionary comes to be compiled. He left to the Orphanage a legacy of 25,000 crowns, and a similar legacy to the Copenhagen Charity Organization Society.

## Notes and News.

The Government of India has decided to discontinue the annual grant hitherto devoted to the search for, and purchase of, rare Sanskrit MSS., but the decision will not take effect until 1892. A regular staff of native searchers have been employed during the past ten years, and these have visited most of the large temples throughout India, examining and cataloguing the vast collections of works hoarded up in those fanes. The private libraries of many native gentlemen have been likewise carefully sifted, and their contents recorded. Out of the MSS. thus examined, no fewer than 2400 have been purchased by the Government, and rendered accessible to the public at Bombay and Calcutta. The most valuable "finds" have included numerous old Jain MSS., now being submitted to the scrutiny of competent scholars in Bombay. Although the search and purchase grants are to cease, the Indian Government has agreed to continue the allowance of Rs. 9000 per annum for the publication of texts and translations of the Sanskrit and Persian works discovered.

Of M. Ch. Âpṭe's *Ânandâsrama Sanskrit Series*, adverted to in previous issues of the ORIENTAL RECORD, the following fresh instalments have been received. No. 10 : The Mâṇḍûkyopanishad, with kârikâs by Gauḍapâda, with their bhâshya by S'ankara and its commentary by Ânandajñâna, also a dîpikâ of the Upanishad by S'ankarânanda, edited by A. V. Kâthavaṭe; No. 14, Part I. : The Chhândogyopanishad, with the bhâshya of S'ankara and its commentary by Ânandajñâna, edited by Pandit Kâs'inâtha S'âstrî Agâse (Part II. will comprise the dîpikâs of Vidyâraṇya and Nityânanda); No. 19: The Rasaratnasamuchchaya, a compendium of the treasures of medical preparations containing mercury, by Vâgbhaṭṭa, edited by Pandit Krishṇarâva Vinâyaka Bâpaṭa; and No. 21, Part I.: The Brahmasûtrâs of Krishṇa Dvaipâyana, with the bhâshya of S'ankara and its commentary by Ânandajñâna, edited by Pandit Nârâyaṇa S'âstrî Eksâmbekara

(this work will be complete in two parts). These publications fully maintain the high character for careful editing which has been accorded to the previous volumes.

Dr. S. von Oldenburg, successor to the late Professor J. Minayeff in the chair for Sanskrit at the University of St. Petersburg, has been entrusted with the editing of the various Oriental texts and literary papers which his predecessor had prepared for publication. Among them are comprised the index to the "Mahâvyutpatti," and editions of the "Rûpasiddhi" (a Pali grammar), the "Pâpaparimocana" (a kind of Grihyasûtra), and the "Sâsanavamsa"; also a History of Nepal, translated from two MSS. representing a recension different from the one followed by Dr. D. Wright, and an account of his last visit to Burma. There are also translations and analyses of about 250 Jâtakas, as well as other materials towards a complete history of Buddhism, which, however, require arranging and revising. Lastly, a Sanskrit-Newari glossary, explained in English. A collected edition of his many minor contributions to a number of serials, not easily accessible, is in contemplation.

Among the *Ceylon Administration Reports* for 1889 there is one by Mr. F. H. M. Corbet, Librarian of the Colombo Museum, to which we specially invite the attention of our readers. The Library of the Asiatic Society, founded in 1845, the Government Oriental Library, founded in 1870, and the Free Public Library, founded in 1876, are now housed in the Colombo Museum, and are under the same administration. Since April 1, 1885, quarterly lists of books printed in Ceylon have been issued, from which it appears that in the last three quarters of that year 100 books were registered; in 1886, 177; in 1887, 221; in 1888, 323; and in 1889, 260. One copy of each of these publications is placed in the Museum Library. The Museum building is now about to be enlarged so as to afford accommodation to the large collection of manuscript records of the Dutch administration of the island, which amount to no less than 6500 folio volumes. Their historical importance cannot be overrated, and it is due to the energetic representation of Mr. H. C. P. Bell, Government Archæologist, that they are now preserved from neglect and eventual ruin. Many of the accessions which the Government Oriental Library has received in the shape of palm-leaf MSS. in Pali, Sanskrit, and Sinhalese are described in detail; and among the last-named attention is drawn to a class of books called Vittipot or village records, which deal with family genealogies and village settlements. The future compiler of a detailed history of Ceylon will derive most material aid from these ancient records, the importance of which has only recently been fully recognized. Though it must in fairness be admitted that the Ceylon Government has done much to promote and stimulate the search for rare MSS. throughout the monasteries and temple libraries of the island, a still larger subvention is needed to bring the search to a successful issue. Nevertheless it compares in this respect most favourably with the Government of Burma, which years ago made a well-meant effort to do something for the archæology and literary history of the country, but has, it would appear, since Dr. Forchhammer's premature death in April, 1890, done nothing further in the noble work initiated by him than entrust—as we learn from the "Rangoon Gazette" of 25 December last—Mr. Taw Sein Ko, Government Translator, with the special duty of arranging Dr. Forchhammer's archæological papers.

Among valuable *Pali texts printed in Ceylon* within the last year, we mention Moggallâyana Vyâkaraṇa, edited by Devamitta Thera; Samantakûṭavaṇṇanâ, with Sinhalese explanation, edited by W. Dhammânanda Sthavira and M. Ñâṇissara; Abhidhamma Aṭṭhasâlinî Atthayojanâ, edited by K. Paññâsekhara Thera; Mahâbodhivaṃso, edited by Pedianoruwe Sobhita; Suttanipâta, Part I., with Sinhalese paraphrase, revised by Paññânanda Thera; Suttasangaho, edited by M. Varâpiṭiya Sugatapâla; Abhidhammatthasangaho, with Sinhalese explanation, edited by Nanadaramatissa Thero. Of the edition of Buddhaghosa's Visuddhimaggo, with Pandit Parakramabahu's commentary, and a new explanation in Sinhalese, commenced in 1887, 16 fasciculi had appeared early last year. We have also seen the first fasciculus of the Dhammapadaṭṭhakathâ, but are unable to say whether this valuable publication is being continued.

THE last police report from the protected State of Perak, in the Malay Peninsula, referring to *Chinese Secret Societies*, says that in 1888, as in the previous year, they caused "endless trouble and anxiety," although in 1887 four members of the Ghee Hin Association were sentenced to 20 years' rigorous imprisonment for conducting an agency for their society in different parts of the State. The report continues that a greater curse to the peace and prosperity of the State could not exist than the presence of these societies, the very rules of which foster criminals, and whose agents are ever ready to come forward to bail the basest of them. "Their organization is so perfect, their power of striking a blow against the Government so easy and swift, that in a new country, where the security of life and property is all-important, their presence cannot be otherwise than a bane." Half the Chinese in Perak are members of secret societies, tickets being found upon them whenever the police have occasion to search them.

Mr. Giles' great *Chinese-English Dictionary* has been in the press at Shanghai some time; but it is not likely to appear for another year or two. A new book of a practical character for learners of Chinese, by Dr. Edkins, is also in the press. Those who have seen it speak of it in very favourable terms.

THE Imperial decree announcing that *the representatives of the foreign Powers resident in Pekin* would be received in audience by the Emperor was issued to the Chinese Ministers on December 12. The following is the text of this historical document: "Since the treaties have been made with the various nations, letters and despatches under the seals of the Governments have passed to and fro, making complimentary inquiries year by year without intermission. The harmony that has existed has become thus from time to time more and more secure. The Ministers of the various Powers residing in Pekin have abundantly shown their loyal desire to maintain peaceful relations and international friendship. This I cordially recognize, and I rejoice in it. In the first and second months of last year (February, 1888), when there were special reasons for expressing national joy, I received a gracious decree (from the Empress Dowager) ordering the Ministers of the Yamên for Foreign Affairs to entertain the Ministers of the foreign nations at a banquet. That occasion was a memorable and happy one. I have now been in charge of the Government for two years. The Ministers of foreign Powers ought to be received by me at an audience, and I hereby decree that the audience to be held be in accordance with that of the 12th year of the reign of Tung Chih (1873). It is also hereby decreed that a day be fixed every year for an audience, in order to show my desire to treat with honour all the Ministers of the foreign Powers resident in Pekin, whether fully empowered or temporarily in charge of the affairs of their Governments. The Ministers of the Yamên for Foreign Affairs are hereby ordered in the first month of the ensuing new year to prepare a memorial asking that a time for the audience may be fixed. On the next day the foreign Ministers are to be received at a banquet at the Foreign Office. The same is to be done every year in the first month, and the rule will be the same on each occasion. New Ministers coming will be received at this annual audience. At all times of national congratulation, when China and the foreign countries give suitable expression to their joy, the Ministers of the Foreign Office are also to offer a memorial asking for the bestowal of a banquet, to show the sincere and increasing desire of the Imperial Government for the maintenance of peace and the best possible relations between China and the foreign States. In regard to the details, the Yamên is hereby ordered to memorialize for instructions on each occasion." It may be added that the recent death of the Emperor's father will not interfere with the orders of this decree, the friendliness and warmth of the tone of which are not a little remarkable. [*The Times.*]

· THERE are probably few countries where the *System of Examination* has attained so complete a development as is the case in *China*. Unrestricted competition pervades the whole country and penetrates down to, and permeates through, the regions of commerce and agriculture. The application of the same principle is brought to bear with equal stringency on mental and intellectual matters, with such success that the product, the great civilian class in China, has for many centuries held its own against all attacks. Great generals, successful invaders, and powerful emperors have had to bend before the resistless assaults, or obdurate resistance, of this powerful hierarchy; while in modern times European diplomacy has not yet been a match for this strong organization. One peculiarity of the examination system in China is the absence of any limit of age for intending competitors. Children of 12 to 15 and dotards of 80 can all equally compete at the same examination. The veterans rarely or never succeed, but nearly every list of successful candidates contains the names of two, three or four youthful prodigies under 20 years of age. To show also how little age is taken into consideration, examiners, often men not much over 30, take rank, during the period of the *chu-jen* examination, with the highest provincial authority of the provincial capital where such examination is held.—[*Journal China Branch of the R. As. Soc.*]

CHINESE NOVELS.—We learn from the *North China Herald* of Shanghai, discussing Chinese notions about novels, that the writing of this class of literature began in the thirteenth century and continued to be a favourite occupation of Chinese writers for about three centuries. After this it was felt that enough had been provided, and the production almost ceased. The authors concealed their names. The moral teaching of the Confucian school was too powerful for those who loved to give rein to their imagination in novel and play writing to be able to venture on publicity. It was never with the consent of the always dominant moral philosophers that novels grew to the position of influence they now possess in China. This hostility has by no means ceased. Quite lately there appeared in a Chinese newspaper a paper written by an anonymous Confucianist against novels. He is deeply impressed with the need of continuing the crusade against licentious literature and romances commenced by one Chien during the last century, when he founded a school in Soochow for the promotion of the healthy study of the classical books. He held that novels are now so prevalent that they amount to a fourth estate in the realm of teaching; the Confucian, Buddhist, and Taoist literatures being the first, second, and third. But instead of inculcating virtue, they lead men into vice. Every one reads them or hears them read, and it may be questioned whether the moral influence for evil of Chinese works of imagination is, he says, not greater than that of the books of the three religions for good. They suggest to young men that they should lead a licentious life, and represent killing a man as a noble action. To read of these things produces disastrous results on public morality. The many cases of crime in the courts and the number of those who adopt a robber's career are due to the effect of Chinese novel-reading. This author was followed by Shih, who set the example of establishing a paper-burning urn in his family court. Into this urn went all novels and every sort of vicious literature on which he could lay hands, and especially the blocks from which they were printed. For these he made wide search, in the hope of extinguishing the evil at its source. In order to find money to buy them up, he first used his spare funds, and then sold clothing, and even his wife's ornaments, in order that the work of destruction might be more complete. Others of influence in Soochow followed these examples; they created a public opinion, and the consequence was that representatives of sixty-five of the most respectable firms went together to the city temple, burnt incense, and made a vow not to engage in the trade in immoral books. An office was opened in the Confucian temple of the magistracy for buying up the blocks of all immoral books, including novels. There was an immense destruction of this class of literature in the city of Soochow, so that it became hard to meet with vicious publications. This was, however, nearly half a century ago and the evil rose again. Twenty-five years ago the then governor of the district issued a new proclamation reiterating the order prohibiting immoral publications. At the present time there is a flood of books with a bad influence. Such reading as they furnish has more effect in leading young minds wrong, says the Confucianist writer, than all the influence on the side of right or the teaching of the sages. "The foreign reader of Chinese books of an imaginative kind cannot condemn them indiscriminately, because they contain beautiful characters, both of men and women, which exhibit an admirable idea of bravery, filial piety, purity of life, loyalty, and other noble qualities. But there can be no doubt of the bad influence of many of the native books which familiarize the minds of the young with scenes of vice, and hold up successful crime to sympathetic admiration. It must also be remembered that whatever evil there may be in the actual life of the Chinese, they have among them the firm friends of a high morality. The national conscience and the national literature alike testify with unfaltering voice to the duty of every one to be moral, just, and humane."

KISWAHELI, the *lingua franca* of the East Coast of Africa and adjacent islands from the Somali country in the North to the Portuguese possessions in the South, is taking a recognized position as one of the most important and most useful languages under the new colonial arrangements in Eastern Africa. The late Dr. Krapf in 1841, and in more recent times the late Bishop Steere (1870), wrote manuals of that language for missionary purposes. The "Handbook" by the latter (second edition 1885) is admitted to be a pattern of a practical grammar: and his "Swahili Exercises" (1878, second edition 1890) appeared in a German translation in 1887. For in the mean time the political and commercial relations of Germany with Zanzibar and the opposite coast had shown the urgency of early provision being made for German traders and others to learn that language. The interest which had sprung up in Germany in African glottology generally, stimulated as it no doubt was by the place which was assigned to Swaheli in the new school for living Oriental languages at Berlin, made it possible for the enterprizing publishing firm of Asher & Co. to bring out a "Zeitschrift für Afrikanische Sprachen," under the able editorship of Dr. C. G. Büttner. This Quarterly, which has just entered upon its fourth year, is of startling philological value and deserves every support. The "Grammaire Kiswahili" by Père Delaunay (1885) is avowedly based on Steere's works, but contains also much original matter. W. von St. Paul Illaire's "Suaheli Handbuch," though ready in manuscript nearly three years ago, has only just been brought out. It is intended for the students of the Berlin Oriental College, and has the great merit of being in the first place the result of personal intercourse with the natives, and only in the second of drawing on the works of his predecessors. Its companion volume, the Suaheli Dictionary by Büttner, marks a great advance on the one by Dr. Krapf. But the price of these two books appears to us preposterously high, especially when we compare it with that of A. Seidel's "Praktische Grammatik der Suaheli-Sprache," which is one of the best books in Hartleben's series, and may be had for two shillings. But while welcoming the many practical aids to the study of East African languages which the last few years have produced, the philologist looks forward to the "Comparative Grammar of the South-African Bantu Languages" by J. Torrend, S.J., which has been announced as in the press. It will suffice for the present to draw attention to this important work.

We invite attention to the following publications, in South African Languages, of the Press of the Trappists at their great Mission of Mariannhill, Natal, South Africa:

### I. WORKS IN ZULU.

1. *Ikatekisma lobufundiso bvoamakristo* ("A Catechism of Christian Doctrine"), the first Catholic book written in this language. by Father David, Ord. Trap.
2. *Incwadi yemikuleko*, a Prayer-book, by the same.
3. *Ikatekisma elincane*, "A Smaller Catechism," by Fr. Gerard, Ord. Trap.
4. *Kancane Kancane*, "Step by Step," a first reading-book, by Fr. Notker, Ord. Trap.
5. *Ivangeli lika' Mateu*, Gospel of St. Matthew, by Fr. David. Illustrated.
6. *Izinndaba ze Baibele*, a Bible History, by Fr. Gerard. Illustrated.

THE FOLLOWING ARE IN THE PRESS.

7. *Incwadi encane yemikuleko*, "A Smaller Prayer-book," by Fr. David.

8. *Y'ilipi ibandhla eliy'ilo lika'kristo?* ("Which is the true Church of Christ?"), by the same.
9. *Kancane Kancane, II*, Second Reading-book, by Fr. Notker.

We may also mention here—
*Zulu-Grammatik*, a Zulu Grammar for the use of Germans, by Fr. Ambros, Ord. Trap.

### II. WORKS IN SECHUANA.

1. *Kategisema ea Kerrks ee halalelan* ("Catechism of Holy Church"), by Fr. Temming, S.J.
2. *Difela* ("Hymns"), by the same.
3. *Polela ea Ditiragale tsa Testamente emaha* ("Stories from the New Testament"), by the same.

### III. IN THE TETE LANGUAGE.

1. *Nk'uebsi mu njira ia Kupurumuka*, a Prayer-book, by Fr. Czimmermann, S.J.
2. *Revuru rakutoma*, Reading-book, by Fr. Courtois, S.J.
3. *Bsidapi ua Bsindzano*, a Combined Arithmetic, Geography, and Portuguese Grammar and Dictionary for the use of the Natives, by the same.

### IV. IN SESUTO.

*Katekisima*, a Catechism, by the Oblate Fathers.

THE printing of the Mudaliyar A. Mendis Gunasekara's Sinhalese grammar—a work which will mark an epoch in the philology of that language—has now reached p. 320, close to the end of the Accidence.

DR. S. J. WARREN, of Dortrecht, has in an English pamphlet (Two Bas-reliefs of the Stûpa of Bharhut, Leiden, 1890) added to the existing translations two fresh ones, viz. the Bhallatiya Jâtaka (No. 504 of Fausböll's edition) and the Dabbhapuppha Jâtaka (400 *ib.*), and has aptly identified the stories narrated therein with two bas-reliefs on the Stûpa of Bharhut.

PROFESSOR G. BÜHLER, of Vienna, has opened up an entirely new vista in the history of ancient Sanskrit literature by showing the close relationship which exists between certain *Sanskrit and Prakrit inscriptions* of the second, fourth and fifth centuries of our era and the *Kâvya literature* of that period. From an examination of the pieces of artificial poetry contained in these inscriptions he was able to prove conclusively the far earlier occurrence in India of that class of poetical composition than has hitherto commonly been assigned to it. His treatise on the subject, in the "Proceedings of the Imperial Academy of Vienna" for last year, is well worth the most careful study.

ANTIQUARIES and scholars all over India will be glad to hear that the little periodical called *Punjab Notes and Queries*, which supplied so useful a medium of communication in their researches, is proposed to be revived. The more systematically a study is pushed, the more important it becomes for each worker to know what is being done by others in the same field: and it is apparently the great impetus that has been taken in late years by the study of Indian ethnology, with its related questions of caste, customs and folklore, that has given rise to the desire for some suitable means of communication between those who are interesting themselves in these subjects. In response to this demand Mr. W. Crooke, C.S., Magistrate of Mirzapore, has consented to undertake the editorship of the magazine, if sufficient assurances of support on the part of probable contributors are forthcoming; and we should have no doubt that they will be. In the hands of Captain Temple and Mr. Grierson the *Notes* assumed perhaps too purely a philological complexion. Philology is the science of the few: whereas any person with ordinary intellectual interests and the power of observation may aspire to add some grain to the heap of ethnological knowledge; and Mr. Crooke, who will still have the support of Captain Temple on the philological side, wisely intends to broaden the basis of the *Notes*. He proposes also a special section for Anglo-Indian antiquities, which will collect odds and ends of information on the lives and customs of the early Indian worthies, and another for bibliography—both of which should be interesting features.—{*The Pioneer*.}

THERE are two Bo trees at Buddha Gayâ. One is a son of the old tree that was blown down some years ago. It is planted some distance from the temple, and is worshipped by Hindus, not by Buddhists. The other is a son of that tree, *i.e.* a grandson of the old tree that was blown down. It is planted at the temple in the proper place, and is worshipped by Buddhists.

## American Literature.

**Abbot (Willis J.)**—Battlefields and Camp-fires. A Narrative of the Principal Military Operations of the Civil War; from the Removal of McClellan to the Accession of Grant (1862-1863). By W. C. Jackson. Illustrated. 8vo. cloth, pp. 9 and 349. *New York.* 15s.

**Abbott (C. C., M.D.)**—Outings at Odd Times. 16mo. cloth, pp. 10-282. *New York.* 7s. 6d.

**Abel (Mrs. Mary Hinman).**—Practical Sanitary and Economic Cooking; Adapted to Persons of Moderate and Small Means. (The Lamb Prize Essay.) Essay Department, American Public Health Association. 12mo. cloth, pp. 10-190. *Rochester (N.Y.).* 2s.

**Adams (C. Francis).**—Richard Henry Dana. A Biography. Portrait. 2 vols. 12mo. cloth, pp. 4-378 and 3-436. *Boston.* £1.

**Adams (H.)**—History of the United States of America. Vols. V. and VI. The First Administration of James Madison, Vols. I. and II. 12mo. cloth, pp. 4-428; 4-488. *New York.* £1.

**Adams (J. Coleman, D.D.)** — Christian Types of Heroism. A Study of the Heroic Spirit under Christianity. 12mo. cloth, pp. 3-208. *Boston.* 4s.

**Alger (Horatio, jun.)**—The Odds Against Him; or, Carl Crawford's Experience. 12mo. cloth, pp. 3-349. *Philadelphia.* 6s. 6d.

**Altgeld (J. P.)**—Live Questions, including Our Penal Machinery and its Victims. 12mo. cl. pp. 320. *Chicago.* 6s.

**Allen (Elizabeth A.)**—Gold Nails to Hang Memories on. A Rhyming Review under their Christian Names of Old Acquaintances in History, Literature, and Friendship. 8vo. cloth, pp. 6-324. *New York.* 12s. 6d.

**Anderson (Winslow, M.D.)**—Mineral Springs and Health Resorts of California; with a Complete Chemical Analysis of every Important Mineral Water in the World. 8vo. cloth, pp. 30 and 384. *San Francisco.* 7s. 6d.

**Andrews (E. B., D.D., ed.)**—History, Prophecy, and Gospel. A Series of Expositions of the International Sunday School Lessons for 1891. Square 8vo. cloth, pp. 500. *Boston.* 9s.

**Anglomaniacs. (The).**—16mo. cloth, pp. 3-206. *New York.* 5s.

**Appleton's** Annual Cyclopædia of the Year 1889, New Series, Vol. 14. 8vo. cloth. *New York.* £1 5s.

**Archibald (Rev. Andrew W.)**—The Bible Verified; with an Introductory Note by Ransom B. Welch, D.D. 12mo. cloth, pp. 2-215. *Philadelphia.* 4s.

**Arnold (A. B., M.D.)**—Manual of Nervous Diseases. Second edition, revised and enlarged. 12mo. cloth, pp. 7-333. *San Francisco.* 12s.

**Atkins (F. A.)**—Moral Muscle, and How to Use It. A Brotherly Chat with Young Men; with an Introduction by Thain Davidson, D.D. 12mo. cloth, pp. 3-82. *New York and Chicago.* 2s. 6d.

**Babcock (W. H.)**—The Two Lost Centuries of Britain. 12mo. cloth, pp. 239. *Philadelphia.* 6s. 6d.

**Badt (F. B.) and Carhart (H. S.)**—Derivation of Practical Electrical Units. 16mo. cloth, pp. 5 & 56. *Chicago.* 4s.

**Baird (W. Raimond)**—American College Fraternities. Fourth Edition. 12mo. cloth. *New York* 10s. 6d.

**Baker (Arthur L.)**—Elliptic Functions. An Elementary Text-book for Students of Mathematics. 8vo. cloth, pp. 5 and 118. *New York.* 6s. 6d.

**Baker (M. N., ed.)**—The Manual of American Water-Works, compiled from Special Returns, 1889-90; containing the History, Details of Construction, Source and Mode of Water Supply, Pumping Machinery, Dams and Reservoirs, Filters, Distribution, etc, of every Waterworks in the United States and Canada; also, Directory of Waterworks Officials, Engineers and Contractors. Illustrated. 8vo. cloth. *New York.* 18s.

**Balch (F. H.)**—The Bridge of the Gods. A Romance of Indian Oregon. 12mo. cloth, pp. 2-280. *Chicago,* 6s. 6d.

**Ballard (Julia P.)**—Among the Moths and Butterflies; a Revised and Enlarged Edition of "Insect Lives; or, Born in Prison." 8vo. cloth, pp. 31-237. *New York.* 7s. 6d.

**Ballou (Maturin M.)**—Aztec Land. 12mo. cloth, pp. 10 and 355. *Boston.* 7s. 6d.

**Ballou (W. H.)**—The Upper Ten. A Novel of the Snobocracy; Illustrated by H. Clay Coultaus. 12mo. paper, pp. 7-225. *New York.* 2s. 6d.

**Bancroft (Hubert Howe)**—History of the Pacific States of North America. Vol. 19. California, Vol. 7, 1860-1890. 8vo. cloth, pp. 12-826. £1 4s.

**Bancroft (Hubert Howe)**—History of the Pacific States of North America. Vol. 33, Essays and Miscellany. 8vo. cloth, pp. 6-764. *San Francisco.* £1 4s.

**Bancroft (Hubert Howe)**—History of the Pacific States of North America. Vol. 34: Literary Industries. 8vo. cloth, pp. 7-808. *San Francisco.* £1 4s.

**Bartley (Elias H., M.D.)** — Text-Book of Medical Chemistry. Second Edition. Illustrated. 12mo. cloth, pp. 423. *Philadelphia.* 12s. 6d.

**Billington (C. E., M.D.)**—Diphtheria, its Nature and Treatment; [also] Intubation in Croup, by Jos. O'Dwyer, M.D. Illustrated. 8vo. cloth, pp. 326. *New York.* 12s. 6d.

**Binet (Alfred)**—On Double Consciousness. Experimental Psychological Studies; with an Introductory Essay on Experimental Psychology in France. 12mo. paper, pp. 2-93. *Chicago.* 2s. 6d.

**Bissell (Mary Taylor, M.D.)**—Household Hygiene. 12mo. cloth, pp. 5-83. *New York.* 4s.

**Blaisdell (Albert F.)**—Stories of the Civil War. Illustrated. 16mo. cloth, pp. 244. 6s.

**Bolton (Mrs. Sarah K.)**—Famous English Authors of the Nineteenth Century. 12mo. cloth, pp. 4-451. *New York.* 7s. 6d.

**Bolton (Sarah K.)**—Famous European Artists. Illustrated. 12mo. cloth, pp. 423. *New York.* 7s. 6d.

**Boston Homilies.** Short Sermons on the International Sunday School Lessons for 1891. By Members of the Alpha Chapter of the Convocation of Boston University. First Series. 12mo. cloth, pp. 6-408. *New York.* 6s. 6d.

**Bowser (E. A.)**—The Elements of Plane and Solid Geometry. 12mo. cloth. *New York.* 9s.

**Boyd (D.)**—A History of Greeley and the Union Colony of Colorado. Illustrated. 12mo. cloth, pp. 448. *Greeley (Colorado).* 10s. 6d.

**Boyesen (Hjalmar Hjorth)**—Against Heavy Odds. A Tale of Norse Heroism. Illustrated by W. L. Taylor. 12mo. cloth, pp. 5-177. *New York.* 5s.

**Bray (Rev. H. Truro)**—The Evolution of Life; or, From the Bondage of Superstition to the Freedom of Reason. 8vo. cloth, pp. 444. *Chicago.* 10s. 6d.

**Breton (Jules)**—The Life of an Artist. An Autobiography; Translated by Mary J. Serrano. 12mo. cloth, pp. 3-350. *New York.* 7s. 6d.

**Brinton (Daniel G., M.D.)**—Races and Peoples. Lectures on the Science of Ethnography. 12mo. cloth, pp. 313. *New York.* 8s.

**Brinton (D. G.)**— Rig Veda Americanus. Edited by D. G. Brinton. 8vo. cloth, pp. 95. *Philadelphia.* 12s.

**Bromfield (E. T., D.D., ed.)**—The Land We Live In; or, America Illustrated; with Vivid Descriptions of the Most Picturesque Scenery in the United States. 4to. cloth, pp 6-216. *New York.* 12s. 6d.

**Brooks (Elbridge S., ed.)**—Great Cities of the World. Illustrated. Folio, cloth, pp. 3-176. *Boston.* 12s. 6d. and 18s.

**Browne (W. Hand)**—George Calvert and Cecilius, Barons Baltimore of Baltimore. 12mo. cloth, pp. 10-181. *New York.* 4s.

*₊* Makers of America Series, No. 2.

**Bruce (H.)**—Life of General Oglethorpe. 12mo. cloth, pp. 15-297. *New York.* 4s.

*₊* Makers of America Series, No. 1.

**Brugière (Sarah Van Buren)**—Good Living. A Practical Cookery Book for Town and Country. 12mo. cloth, pp. 10-580. *New York.* 12s.

**Brush (Christine Chaplin)**—One Summer's Lessons in Practical Perspective. 12mo. cloth, pp. 3 and 71. *New York and Chicago.* 5s. 6d.

**Butterworth (Hezekiah)**—Zigzag Journeys in the Great Northwest; or, A Trip to the American Switzerland. 8vo. pp. 6-319. *Boston.* Cloth, 12s.; boards, 9s.

**Cady (Annie Cole)**—Worthington's History of the United States. Portrait and Illustrations. 12mo. paper, pp. 3-389. *New York.* 2s. 6d.

**Cady (Annie Cole, ed.)**—Worthington's History of the United States. Illustrated. 4to. boards, pp. 3-176. *New York.* 6s. 6d.

Illustrated profusely. In large type and simple language.

**Campbell (Rob. Allen)**—Our Flag; or, The Evolution of the Stars and Stripes; including the Reason of the Design, the Colours and their Position, Mystic Interpretation; with Selections, Eloquent, Patriotic, and Poetical. Illustrated. 12mo. cloth, pp. 2-128. *Chicago.* 5s.

**Carr (W. G.)**—Scriptural Outlines by Books and Themes. 12mo. cloth, pp. 162. *N. York and Chicago.* 4s.

**Carrington (H. B.)**—Absaraka; or, Wyoming Opened. Sixth edition. Illustrations and Maps. 12mo. cloth, pp. 380. *Philadelphia.* 7s. 6d.

**Champlin (J. Denison, jun.) and Apthorp (W. F., eds.)**—Cyclopedia of Music and Musicians. In 3 vols. Vol. 3. Illustrated. 4to. cloth. £2 10s.

**Champlin (J. E., jun.) and Bostwick (Arthur E.)**—The Young Folks' Cyclopædia of Games and Sports. Illustrated. 12mo. cloth, pp. 4-831. *New York.* 12s. 6d.

**Champney (Elizabeth W.)**—Three Vassar Girls in Switzerland. Illustrated by "Champ," and others. 8vo. cloth, pp. 5-239. *Boston.* 10s. 6d.

**Chesterman (W. D.)**—Guide to Richmond and the Battlefields. Illustrated. 16mo. cloth, pp. 77. *Richmond (Va.).* 1s. 6d.

**Chittenden (Rev. E. P.)**—The Pleroma; a Poem of the Christ, in Two Books of Seven Cantos each, written in Semi-dramatic Form. 12mo. cloth, pp. 347. *New York.* 12s. 6d.

**Claflin (Mrs. Mary B.)**—Brampton Sketches; Old-time New England Life. Illustrated. 12mo. cloth, pp. 4-158. *New York.* 6s. 6d.

**Clark (W.)**—Savonarola. His Life and Times. 12mo. cloth, pp. 2-352. *Chicago.* 7s. 6d.

**Clark (J. E., M.D., ed.)**—Physical Diagnosis and Practical Urinalysis. An Epitome of the Physical Signs of the Heart, Lung, Kidney and Spleen in Health and Disease. Illustrated. 12mo. cloth, pp. 200. *Detroit (Mich.).* 5s.

**Clarke (J. Freeman)**—Deacon Herbert's Bible-class. 24mo. cloth, pp. 4-138. *Boston.* 2s. 6d.

**Cleland (E. Davenport)**—The White Kangaroo. A Tale of Colonial Life, founded on fact. 12mo. cloth, pp. 2-177. *New York.* 5s.

**Clendenin (Rev. F. M.)**—Idols by the Sea: Sermons. 16mo. cloth. *New York.* 7s. 6d.

**Coffin (C. Carleton)**—Freedom Triumphant. The Fourth Period of the War of the Rebellion, from September, 1864, to its Close. 8vo. cloth, pp. 11-506. *N. York.* 15s.

**Cohen (A. J., "Alan Dale," pseud.)**—Familiar Chats with the Queens of the Stage. Portrait. 8vo. cloth, pp. 3-399. *New York.* £1 10s.

**Collis (Septima M.)**—A Woman's Trip to Alaska; being an Account of a Voyage through the Inland Seas of the Sitkan Archipelago in 1890. 12mo. cloth, pp. 12-194. *New York.* 12s. 6d.

**Condit (Rev. U. W.)**—History of Eastern Pennsylvania, from Revolutionary Times to the Present. Illustrated. Royal 8vo. cloth, pp. 500. *Easton (Pa.).* £3 3s.

**Cooke (Josiah Parsons)**—Credentials of Science. [New issue.] 12mo. cloth, pp. 14-324. *New York.* 9s.

**Cooley (T. M.)**—A Treatise on the Constitutional Limitations which rest upon the Legislative Power of the States of the American Union. Sixth Edition, with large Additions, giving the results of the Recent Cases, by Alexis C. Angell. 8vo. sheep, pp. 96-885. *Boston.* 36s.

**Cope (Rufus)**—The Distribution of Wealth; or, the Economic Laws by which Wages and Profits are Determined. 8vo. cloth, pp. 364. *Philadelphia.* 10s.

**Cowley (E., D.D.)**—The Writers of Genesis and Related Topics Illustrating Divine Revelation. 12mo. cloth, pp. 184. *New York.* 5s.

**Cox (Annie F.)**—Baby's Kingdom; wherein may be Chronicled, as Memories for Grown-up Days, the Mother's Story of the Progress of the Baby. New Edition. Illustrated. 12mo. cloth. *Boston.* 18s.

**Cox (Annie F.)**—The Guest-book, in which may be Recorded the Coming and the Going of Guests, with pages for Autographs, Incidents, and Sketches pertaining to Pleasant Visits, Social Calls, and other Gatherings. New Edition. 12mo. cloth. *Boston.* 18s.

**Cox (C. F.)**—Protoplasm and Life: Two Biological Essays. 12mo. flexible cloth. *New York.* 4s.

**Cox (Palmer)**—Another Brownie Book. Illustrated. 8vo. boards, pp. 6-144. *New York.* 7s. 6d.

**Cozzens (S. Woodworth)**—The Ancient Cibola: The Marvellous Country; or Three Years in Arizona and New Mexico. New Edition. Illustrated. 8vo. cloth, pp. 3-547. *Boston.* 10s. 6d.

**Cragin (Edwin B., M.D.)**—Essentials of Gynæcology, arranged in the Form of Questions and Answers; prepared especially for Students of Medicine. Illustrated. 8vo. cloth, pp. 192. *Philadelphia.* 6s. (Interleaved, 7s. 6d.)

**Current Discussions in Theology**, by the Professors of Chicago Theological Seminary. Vol. 7. 12mo. cloth, pp. 11 and 410. *Boston.* 7s. 6d.

**Curtiss (F. H.)**—"The Berkshire News" Comic Cook-Book and Dyspeptic's Guide to the Trade. 12mo. paper, pp. 6-70. *Gt. Barrington (Mass.).* 1s. 6d.

**Custer (Mrs. Elizabeth B.)**—Following the Guidon. Illustrated. 12mo. cloth, pp. 16 and 341. *N. York.* 7s. 6d.

**Cuyler (Theo. L., D.D.)**—How to be a Pastor. 16mo. cloth, pp. 3-151. *New York.* 4s.

**Dabney (Rob. L., D.D.)**—Discussions, by Robert L. Dabney, D.D.; edited by C. R. Vaughan. In four vols. Vol. 1. Theological and Evangelical. In 4 vols. Vol. I. 8vo. cloth, pp. 10-728. *Richmond (Va.).* 9s.

**Dana (J. D.)**—Corals and Coral Islands. New Edition enlarged. Illustrated. 8vo. cloth. *New York.* £1 5s.

**Davenport (F. H., M.D.)**—Diseases of Women. A Manual of Non-Surgical Gynæcology. Illustrated. 12mo. cloth, pp. 317. *Philadelphia.* 7s. 6d.

**Davidson (J. Thain, D.D.)**—A Good Start. A Book for Young Men. 12mo. cloth, pp. 4-283. *N. York.* 6s. 6d.

**Davis (Ellery W.)**—An Introduction to the Logic of Algebra; with Illustrative Exercises. 8vo. cloth, pp. 14 and 119. *New York.* 6s. 6d.

De Leon (T. C.)—Four Years in Rebel Capitals. Inside View of Social Life in the Southern Confederacy, from Birth to Death. 8vo. cloth, pp. 380. *Mobile (Alabama).* 7*s.* 6*d.*

Diehl (Mrs. Anna Randall)—A Practical Delsarte Primer. 16mo. cloth, pp. 66. *Syracuse (N.Y.).* 2*s.* 6*d.*

Dock (Lavinia L., *comp.*)—Text-book of Materia Medica for Nurses. 12mo. cloth, pp. 5–201. *New York.* 6*s.* 6*d.*

Doudney (Sarah)—Old Anthony's Scaret. 12mo. cloth, pp. 5–96. *New York* and *Chicago.* 5*s.*

Dragon-Flies *v.* Mosquitoes : can the Mosquito Pest be Mitigated? Studies in the Life History of Irritating Insects, their Natural Enemies and Artificial Checks, by Working Entomologists. With an Introduction by Rob. H. Lamborn. 8vo. cloth, pp. 2–202, 9 plates. *New York.* 7*s.* 6*d.*

Drake (S. Adams)—The Taking of Louisburg, 1745. Illustrated. 16mo. pp. 8–136. *Boston (Mass.).*

Du Bois (Constance Goddard)—Martha Corey. A Tale of Salem Witchcraft. 12mo. cloth, pp. 3–314. *Chicago.* 6*s.* 6*d.*

Fagan (W. L., *comp.*)—Southern War Songs ; Camp-Fire, Patriotic and Sentimental. Illustrated. 8vo. cloth, pp. 389. *New York.* 15*s.*

Ebers (G.)—The Elixir, and other Tales ; from the German, by Mrs. E. Hamilton Bell. 16mo. pp. 3–261. *New York.* Paper, 2*s.* 6*d.* ; cloth, 4*s.*

Edwards (Rev. Rob. A.)—From Joppa to Mount Hermon. A Series of Narrative Discourses on the Holy Land, Delivered in the Church of St. Matthias, Phil., During the Autumn and Winter of 1889–1890. 8vo. cloth, pp. 2–256. *Philadelphia.* 7*s.* 6*d.*

Everett (C. Carroll, D.D.)—The Science of Thought. New Revised Edition. 12mo. cloth, pp. 10–430. *Boston.* 7*s.* 6*d.*

Farrington (Margaret Vere)—Fra Lippo Lippi. A Romance. Illustrated. 8vo. cloth, pp. 9–225. *New York.* 12*s.* 6*d.*

Felts (W. W.)—Principles of Science. A Scientific Treatise on the Absoluteness of Circular Motion and the Evolution of Force, as Applied to all Phenomena. Illust. 12mo. cloth, pp. 2–98. *San Francisco.* 5*s.*

Fernald (James C.)—The Economics of Prohibition. 12mo. cloth, pp. 10–515. *New York.* 7*s.* 6*d.*

Fernow (Berthold)—The Ohio Valley in Colonial Days. 8vo. boards, pp. 4–299. *Albany.* £1 5*s.*

Field (D. Dudley)—Speeches, Arguments, and Miscellaneous Papers. Edited by Titus Munson Coan, M.D. In 3 vols. Vol. 3. 8vo. cloth, pp. 463. *New York.* 15*s.*

Field (Eugene)—A Little Book of Profitable Tales. 12mo. cloth, pp. 5–286. *New York.* 6*s.* 6*d.*

Finck (H. T.)—The Pacific Coast Scenic Tour ; from Southern California to Alaska, the Canadian Pacific Railway, Yellowstone Park and the Grand Cañon. Illustrated. 8vo. cloth, pp. 12–309. *New York.* 12*s.* 6*d.*

Fiske (J.)—Civil Government in the United States, considered with some Reference to its Origins. 12mo. cloth, pp. 28 and 360. *Boston.* 7*s.* 6*d.*

Forney (M. N.)—The New Catechism of the Locomotive. Illustrated. 8vo. cloth. *New York.* 18*s.*

Foster (Randolph S.)—Philosophy of Christian Experience ; Eight Lectures Delivered before the Ohio Wesleyan University on the Merrick Foundation. Third Series. 8vo. cloth, pp. 1–188. *New York.* 5*s.*

Foster (R. V., D.D.)—Old Testament Studies : An Outline of Old Testament Theology. 12mo. cloth, pp. 370. *New York* and *Chicago.* 7*s.* 6*d.*

Gardiner (F.)—Aids to Scripture Study. 12mo. cloth, pp. 10 and 284. *Boston.* 6*s.* 6*d.*

Gibson (W. Hamilton)—Strolls by Starlight and Sunshine. Illustrated by the Author. 8vo. cloth, pp. 194. *New York.* 18*s.*

Gladden (Rev. Washington)—Burning Questions. A Collection of Sermons. 12mo. cloth, pp. 248. *New York.* 7*s.* 6*d.*

Gladden (Washington)—Santa Claus on a Lark : and other Christmas Stories. Illustrated. 8vo. cloth, pp. 3–178. *New York.* 6*s.* 6*d.*

Glover (Elizabeth)—Family Manners. 12mo. cloth, pp. 37. *New York.*

Golden (W. Echard)—A Brief History of the English Drama ; from the Earliest to the Latest Times. 12mo. cloth, pp. 4–227. *New York.* 6*s.* 6*d.*

Good Things (The) of Life. Seventh Series. Illustrated. Oblong 8vo. cloth, pp. 64. *New York.* 10*s.*

Gordon (A. J., D.D.)—The Ministry of Healing ; or, Miracles of Cure in all Ages. Third edition revised. 12mo. cloth, pp. 249. *New York* and *Chicago.* 6*s.* 6*d.*

Gordon (Julien, *pseud.*)—A Diplomat's Diary. 12mo. cloth. *Philadelphia.* 6*s.*

Gregg (D., D.D.) and Mudge (L. W., D.D.)—From Solomon to the Captivity. The Story of Two Hebrew Kingdoms. 12mo. cloth, pp. 2–292. *New York.* 6*s.* 6*d.*

Griffis (W. Eliott, D.D.)—Honda the Samurai. A Story of Modern Japan. Illustrated. 12mo. cloth, pp. 390. *Boston.* 7*s.* 6*d.*

Guyot (Arnold)—The Earth and Man. Lectures on Comparative Physical Geography in its Relation to the History of Mankind ; from the French by C. C. Felton. Maps and Illustrations. 12mo. cloth, pp. 16 and 334. *New York.* 9*s.*

Gypsy (The) Witches' Dream-Book and Fortune-teller. 16mo. paper, pp. 114. *New York.* 1*s.* 6*d.*

Hagood (Rev. L. M.)—The Coloured Man in the Methodist Episcopal Church. 12mo. cloth, pp. 327. *Cincinnati (Ohio).* 6*s.* 6*d.*

Hallock (C.)—The Salmon Fisher. 16mo. cloth, pp. 126. *New York.* 5*s.*

Halsey (F. A.)—Slide Valve Gears. An Explanation of the Action and Construction of Plain and Cut-off Slide Valves. Analysis by the Bilgram Diagram. Second Edition. Illustrated. 12mo. cloth, pp. 7 and 135. *New York.* 7*s.* 6*d.*

Halstead (W. Riley)—Civil and Religious Forces. 12mo. cloth, pp. 3–148. *Cincinnati.* 3*s.* 6*d.*

Hamilton (E. J., D.D.)—Mental Science. New Issue. 12mo. cloth, pp. 8–416. *New York.* 10*s.*

Hamilton (E. J., D.D.)—The Human Mind. New Issue. 8vo. cloth, pp. 8–720. *New York.* 15*s.*

Hammond (S. H.)—In the Adirondacks ; or, Sport in the North Woods. 12mo. cloth, pp. 3–340. *Philadelphia.* 1*s.* 6*d.*

Hancock (Anson Uriel).—The Genius of Galileo. An Historical Novel. 12mo cloth, pp. 2–507. *Chicago.* 7*s.* 6*d.*

Harding (Chester)—A Sketch of Chester Harding drawn by his own Hand. Edited by his Daughter, Margaret E. White. 16mo. cloth. *Boston.* 7*s.* 6*d.*

Hare (Hobart Amory, M.D.) — A Text-Book of Practical Therapeutics ; with Especial Reference to the Application of Remedial Measures to Disease, and their Employment upon a Rational Basis ; with Special Chapters by Drs. G. E. De Schweinitz, E. Martin, J. Howard Reeves, and Barton C. Hirst. 8vo. cloth, pp. 622. *Philadelphia.* 18*s.*

Hart (D. Berry, M.D.) and Barbour (A. H. Freeland, M.D.)—A Manual of Gynecology. Fourth Edition Revised. Illustrated. 8vo. cloth. *New York.* £1 16*s.*

**Haskins (C. W.)**—The Argonauts of California ; being the Reminiscences of Scenes and Incidents that Occurred in California in Early Mining Days. By a Pioneer. Illustrated. 8vo. cloth, pp. 1–501. *New York.* 16s. 6d.

**Haydn (H. C., D.D., ed.)**—American Heroes on Mission Fields. Brief Biographies. Portraits and Illustrations. 12mo. cloth, pp. 2–31. *New York.* 6s. 6d.

**Hazen (H. A.)**—The Tornado. 12mo. cloth, pp. 5–143. *New York.* 5s.

**Hennequin (Alfred)**—The Art of Play-Writing. Being a Practical Treatise on the Elements of Dramatic Construction, intended for the Playwright, the Student, and the Dramatic Critic. 12mo. cloth, pp. 20–187. *Boston.* 6s. 6d.

**Hermetic Philosophy,** including Lessons, General Discourses and Explications of " Fragments " from the Schools of Egypt, Chaldea, Greece, Italy, Scandinavia, etc. ; Designed for Students of the Hermetic, Pythagorean and Platonic Sciences and Western Occultism. Vol. I. 12mo. cloth, pp. 184. *Philadelphia.* 5s.

**Herr (G. W.)**—Episodes of the Civil War. Nine Campaigns in Nine States. Illustrated. 8vo. cloth, pp. 9–461–30. *San Francisco.* £1 5s.

**Herringshaw (T. W., comp.)**—Local and National Poets of America. Sketches and Selections from more than 1000 Living American Poets. pp. 1000. Portraits. 8vo. cloth. *Chicago.* £1 10s.

**Heyse (Paul)**—The Children of the World. Illustrated. 12mo. paper. pp. 11–573. *New York.* 4s.

**Higginson (T. W.) and Bigelow (E. H.)**—American Sonnets. 16mo. cloth, pp. 20–280. *Boston.* 6s. 6d.

**Himmel (Ernst v.)**—Oceanida. A Psychical Novel. 12mo. paper, pp. 418. *Boston.* 2s. 6d.

**Hind (H. Youle)**—The University of King's College, Winsor, Nova Scotia, 1790–1890. 12mo. cloth, pp. 119. *New York.* 7s. 6d.

**Hochschild (Baron)**—Désirée, Queen of Sweden and Norway : a Memoir ; from the French by M. Carey. 16mo. cloth, pp. 96. *New York.* 6s. 6d.

**Holcombe (W. H., M D.)**—A Mystery of New Orleans. Solved by New Methods. 12mo. cloth, pp. 3–332. *Philadelphia.* 5s.

**Holley (Marietta, "Josiah Allen's Wife," *pseud.*)**—Samantha among the Brethren. Illustrated. 8vo. cloth, pp. 10–437. *New York.* 12s. 6d.

**Hopkins (Mrs. Louis P.)**—Observation Lessons in the Primary Schools. A Manual for Teachers. In 1 vol. 12mo. cloth. *Boston.* 5s.

**House and Pet Dogs.** Their Selection, Care, and Training ; with Portraits of Prize Winning Specimens of all Principal Breeds. 16mo. cloth, pp. 4–115. *New York.* 2s. 6d.

**Hovey (Alvah, ed.)**—American Commentary on the New Testament. 7 vols. 8vo. cloth. *Philadelphia.* £4 10s.

**Howard (G. E.)**—On the Development of the King's Peace and the English Local Peace-Magistracy. 8vo. paper, pp. 65. *Lincoln (Nebraska).* 3s.

**Howe (H. Marion)**—Metallurgy of Steel. Illustrated. Royal 4to. cloth, pp. 380. *New York.* £2 12s. 6d.

**Howell (Sarah Biddle, comp.)**—Nine Family Dinners and How to Prepare Them. Square 16m. paper, pp. 62. *Trenton (N.J.).* 2s. 6d.

**Howells (W. D.)**—A Boy's Town Described for " Harper's Young People." Illustrated. 12mo. cloth, pp. 5–247. *New York.* 6s. 6d.

**Howie (Mrs. Adda F.)**—Modern Fairy Lore : for Young and Old : Fairy Tales. 8vo. boards, pp. 150. *Milwaukee, Wis.* 7s. 6d.

**Humphrey (Frances A.)**—How New England was Made. Illustrated. 8vo. boards, pp. 3–267.

**Huntington (W. R., D.D.)**—The Causes of the Soul. A Book of Sermons. 12mo. cloth, pp. 390. *New York.* 9s.

**Hutton (Laurence)**—Curiosities of the American Stage. Portrait. 8vo. cloth, pp. 8–347. *New York.* 12s. 6d.

**Inazo (Ota Nitobe)**—The Intercourse between the United States and Japan. An Historical Sketch. 8vo. pp. 10–198. *Balt. (Md.).* 6s. 6d.
*** Johns Hopkins University Studies in Historical and Political Science.

**Ingalls (J. M.)**—Handbook Problems in Direct Fire. 8vo. cloth. *New York.* 18s.

**Isham (Asa B.), Davidson (H. M.) and Furness (H. B.)** —Prisoners of War and Military Prisons. Personal Narratives of Experience in the Prisons at Richmond, Danville, Macon, Andersonville, Savannah, Millen, Charleston and Columbia. Illustrated. 8vo. cloth, pp. 11–571. *Cincinnati (O.).* 18s.

**Jackson (Frank G.)**—Decorative Design. An Elementary Text-Book of Principles and Practice. Illustrated. 8vo. cloth. *Philadelphia.* 12s. 6d.

**Jackson (E., M.D.)**—Essentials of Refraction and the Diseases of the Eye. [*Also,*] Essentials of Diseases of the Nose and Throat, by E. Baldwin Gleason, M.D. Illustrated. 8vo. cloth, pp. 276. *Philadelphia.* 5s.

**Jastrow (Jos.)**—The Time-Relations of Mental Phenomena. 8vo. cloth, pp. 1–60. *New York.* 2s. 6d.

**Jay (J.)**—The Writings and Correspondence of John Jay, First Chief Justice of the United States ; edited by H. P. Johnston. 8vo. cloth, in 4 vols. Vol. I. *New York.* £1 5s.

**Jefferson (Joseph)**—Autobiography. Illustrated. 8vo. pp. 3–501. *New York.* £1.

**Jew and Gentile,** a Symposium ; being a Report of a Conference of Israelites and Christians regarding their Mutual Relations and Welfare. 12mo. cloth, pp. 57. *New York and Chicago.* 4s.

**Jewett (Sarah Orne)**—Strangers and Wayfarers. 12mo. half silk, pp. 4–279. *Boston.* 6s. 6d.

**Johnston (Alex.)**—A Shorter History of the United States. 12mo. cloth. *New York.* 6s. 6d.

**Johnson (Elizabeth Winthrop)**—Two Loyal Lovers. A Romance. 12mo. cloth, pp. 381. *New York.* 5s.

**Johnson (J.)**—The Defence of Charleston Harbour, including Fort Sumter and the Adjacent Islands, 1863–1865 ; with Appendix containing many Original Papers from both Sides heretofore unpublished. 8vo. cloth. *Charleston (S. C.).* £1 4s.

**Johnston (R. Malcolm)**—Widow Guthrie. A Novel. Illustrated by E. W. Kemble. 12mo. cloth, pp. 1–309. *New York.* 7s. 6d.

**Johnson (S.)**—Theodore Parker. A Lecture. Edited by J. H. Clifford and Horace L. Traubel. 12mo. cloth, pp. 31–78. *Chicago.* 5s.

**Jonas (C.)**—Bohemian Made Easy. A Practical Bohemian Course for English-Speaking People. 16mo. cloth, pp. 294. *Milwaukee (Wis.).* 9s.

**Jones (A. K., comp.)**—Classified Gymnasium Exercises of System of R. J. Roberts, with Notes. Second edition, Revised and Enlarged. Illustrated. 12mo. cloth, pp. 140. *Springfield (Mass.).* 6s.

**Judge (W. L., "Occultus," *pseud.*)**—Echoes from the Orient. A Broad Outline of Theosophical Doctrines. 12mo. cloth, pp. 4–68. *New York.* 2s. 6d.

**Keddie (Miss Henrietta, "Sarah Tytler," *pseud.*)**—A Houseful of Girls. 12mo. cloth, pp. 3–408. *N. York.* 7s. 6d.

**Kelsey (C. B., M.D.)**—Diseases of the Rectum and Anus. Third edition, Rewritten and Enlarged. Illustrated. 8vo. cloth, pp. 483. *New York.* £1.

**Kerbey (J. O.)**—The Boy Spy. A Story of the late War. Illustrated. 12mo. cloth, pp. 557. *Chicago.* 7s. 6d.

Kerbey (J. O.)—On the War Path. A Journey over the Historic Grounds of the Late Civil War. 12mo. cloth, pp. 302. *Chicago*. 5*s*.

Kerr (Rob. Pollock, D.D.)—The Voice of God in History. Illustrated. 12mo. cloth, pp. 2–283. *Richmond (Va.)*. 7*s*. 6*d*.

King (C.)—Campaigning with Crook, and Stories of Army Life. Illustrated. 12mo. cloth, pp. 6 and 295. *New York*. 6*s*. 6*d*.

King (C. T.) — Picturesque Geographical Readers. Book 2. This Continent of Ours. 16mo. cloth. *Boston*. 3*s*. 6*d*.

Kingsley (J. S.)—Popular Natural History. Illustrated. 2 vols. 8vo. cloth. *Boston*. £2 5*s*.

Kitchin (W. C.)—Paoli ; the Last of the Missionaries. A Picture of the Overthrow of the Christians in Japan in the Seventeenth Century. Illustrated by G. A. Traver and H. Bouche. 12mo. cloth, pp. 5–468. *New York*. 3*s*.

Knox (T. W.)—Teetotaler Dick. His Adventures, Temptations and Triumphs. A Temperance Story. Illustrated. 12mo. cloth, pp. 418. *New York*. 7*s*. 6*d*.

Knox (T. W.)—The Boy Travellers in Great Britain and Ireland. Adventures of Two Youths in a Journey through Ireland, Scotland, Wales and England, with Visits to the Hebrides and the Isle of Man. 8vo. cloth, pp. 14–536. *New York*. 15*s*.

Lanza (G.)—Applied Mechanics. Fourth Edition, Revised and Enlarged. 8vo. cloth, pp. 929. *New York*. £1 11*s*. 6*d*.

Lee (Alfred E.)—European Days and Ways. Illustrated. 8vo. cloth, pp. 3–376. *Philadelphia*. 10*s*.

Leitch (Mary and Margaret W.)—Seven Years in Ceylon. Stories of Mission Life. Illustrated. 8vo. boards. pp. 7–170. *New York*. 4*s*.

Lewis (W. Bevan)—A Text-book of Mental Diseases ; with Special Reference to the Pathological Aspects of Insanity. 8vo. cloth, pp. 22–552. *Philadelphia*. £1 10*s*.

Lincoln (Abraham) — Abraham Lincoln's Pen and Voice ; being a Compilation of his Letters, Civil, Political and Military ; also Public Addresses, Messages to Congress, Inaugurals, etc., by G. M. Van Buren. Portrait. 12mo. cloth, pp. 435. *Cincinnati*. 5*s*.

Lloyd (H. D.)—A Strike of Millionaires Against Miners ; or, the Story of Spring Valley. 12mo. cloth, pp. 264. *Chicago*. 2*s*. 6*d*.

Locke (D. Ross, "Petroleum Nasby," *pseud*.)—The Demagogue. A Political Novel. 12mo. cloth, pp. 4–465. *Boston*. 7*s*. 6*d*.

Loti (Pierre, *pseud*. for Jules Viaud)—Rarahu ; or, the Marriage of Loti ; from the French by Clara Bell. Revised and corrected in the United States. 16mo. pp. 4–296. Cloth, 4*s*. ; paper, 2*s*. 6*d*.

Lowery (Woodbury, *ed*.)—Decisions on the Law of Patents for Inventions Rendered by the United States Supreme Court from the Beginning, 109 United States, 1863–114 United States 1864. 8vo. leather, pp. 52–643. *Washington (D.C.)*. £1 18*s*.

MacBallastir (Cad., *pseud*. for T. C. De Leon)—Society as I have Foundered it : or the Microscopic Metropolitan Menu-Manipulator Marvellously Money-Magnetized. Translated from the Anglo-Maniaque Tongue into American. Illustrated by the Author. Original 400 Edition. 12mo. paper, pp. 2–73. *Mobile (Ala.)*. 1*s*. 6*d*.

Maclay (Arthur Collins)—Mito Yashiki. A Tale of Old Japan. Second edition. 12mo. cloth, pp. 7–456. *New York*. 7*s*. 6*d*.

McCartha (C. L.)—The Lost Tribes of Israel ; or, Europe and America in History and Prophecy. 12mo. cloth, pp. 210. *Greensboro (Alabama)*. 6*s*.

McCarthy (L. P.)—The Annual Statistician and Economist. 8vo. cloth. *San Francisco*. £1 1*s*.

McGuzzler (Steward, *pseud*.)—Society as it Found Me Out. 12mo. cloth, pp. 5–115. *New York*. 2*s*. 6*d*.

McKay (F. E., *ed*.)—Vignettes Real and Ideal. Stories by American Authors. 12mo. cloth, pp. 3–288. *Boston*. 5*s*.

McLean (G. N.)—How to do Business ; or, the Secret of Successful Retail Merchandising. 12mo. cloth, pp. 207. *Chicago*. 10*s*. 6*d*.

MacMinn (Rev. Edwin)—Nemorama the Nautchnee. A Story of India. Illustrated. 12mo. cloth, pp. 3 and 291. *New York*. 5*s*.

McPherson (E)—A Handbook of Politics for 1890 ; being a Record of Important Political Action, Legislative, Executive and Judicial, National and State, from August 31, 1888, to July 31, 1890. 8vo. cloth, pp. 6 and 280. *Washington*. 12*s*.

Maisch (J. M.)—A Manual of Organic Materia Medica. New Fourth Edition. Illustrated. 8vo. cloth, pp. 539. *Philadelphia*. 15*s*.

Martin (H. Newell)—The Human Body and the Effect of Narcotics. 12mo. cloth. *New York*. 8*s*.

Martyn (Carlos)—William E. Dodge. The Christian Merchant. 12mo. cloth, pp. 2–349. *New York*. 7*s*. 6*d*.

Masterpieces of German Fiction. 12mo. cloth. *Chicago*. 7*s*. 6*d*.
Contents : Hans the Dreamer ; All in Vain ; First Love, by Rudolph Lindau ; The Aristocratic World ; The Maid of Oyas, by Fanny Lewald ; The Visit to the Lockup ; The Boarding-School Girls, by Ernest Eckstein ; The Pilot Captain, by Adolph Wilbrandt ; L'Arra Vintu ; Beppe the Star Gazer ; Maria Francesca by Paul Heyse ; Trudel's Ball ; The Fortunes and Fate of Little Spangle, by Hans Hopfen ; Against the Stream, by Ernest Eckstein.

Maybell (Stephen)—Land Currency. A Treatise on the Important Subject of No Tax. 8vo. paper, pp. 50. *San Francisco*. 1*s*. 6*d*.

Maylin (Anne W.)—Here a Little and There a Little. Essays, Sketches and Detached Thoughts. 12mo. cloth, pp. 3–184. *Philadelphia*. 7*s*. 6*d*.

Metheney (Mrs. Mary E.)—Philip St. John. Illustrated. 16mo. cloth, pp. 300. *Philadelphia*. 6*s*. 6*d*.

Meyer (Conrad Ferdinand)—The Tempting of Pescara. From the German by Clara Bell. Revised and Corrected in the U.S. 16mo. paper, pp. 2–184. *New York*. 1*s*. 6*d*.

Monday Club.—Sermons on the International Sunday School Lessons for 1891. 16th Series. 12mo. cloth, pp. 412. *Boston*. 6*s*. 6*d*.

Moore (F. Frankfort)—Coral and Cocoanut. The Cruise of the "Firefly" to Samos. Illustrated by W. H. Overend. 12mo. cloth, pp. 4–379. *New York*. 7*s*. 6*d*.

Morgan (T. J.)—Studies in Pedagogy. 12mo. cloth. *Boston*. 9*s*.

Morris (C.)—An Elementary History of the United States. 10 vols. 12mo. cloth, pp. 7 and 361, and 4 and 397. *Boston*. 7*s*. 6*d*. each. Large paper, £1.

Morris (C.)—Civilization. An Historical Review of its Elements. 2 vols. 12mo. cloth, pp. 13–510 and 7–490. *Chicago*. £1.

Morris (W.)—News from Nowhere ; or, an Epoch of Rest. Being some Chapters from a Utopian Romance. 12mo. cloth, pp. 3–278. *Boston*. 5*s*.

Mortimer (J.) — The Chess-Player's Pocket-Book. 24mo. cloth, pp. 74. *New York*. 2*s*. 6*d*.

Mother Goose.—The Original Mother Goose's Melody, as first issued by John Newberry, of London, about A.D. 1760 ; Reproduced in fac simile from the Edition as Reprinted by Isaiah Thomas. Worcester (Mass.), about A.D. 1785. With Introductory Notes by W. H. Whitmore. 8vo. paper, pp. 124. *Albany (N.Y.)*. 10*s*.

Mulertt (Hugo)—The Goldfish and its Systematic Culture with a View to Profit. Illustrated. 8vo. pp. 108. *Cincinnati (Ohio)*. 2*s*. 6*d*.

Munro (J.)—Pioneers of Electricity. Illustrated. 12mo. cloth, pp. 256. *New York and Chicago*. 7*s*.

**Murray (W. H. H.)**—How John Norton the Trapper Kept his Christmas. Illustrated. 8vo. cloth, pp. 109. *Boston.* 7s. 6d.

**Myers (Rev. E. M., comp.)**—The Centurial. A Jewish Calendar for One Hundred Years. 8vo. cloth, pp. 198. *New York.* 5s.

**Newhall (C. S.)**—The Trees of North-Eastern America; with an Introductory Note by Nathaniel L. Britton. 8vo. cloth, pp. 10-249. *New York.* 12s. 6d.

**Newsom (S.)**—Some City and Suburban Homes. Illustrated. 4to. cloth. *San Francisco (Cal.).* 18s.

**Noyes (W. A.)**—Qualitative Analysis. 12mo. cloth. *New York.* 5s.

**Ober (F. A.)**—The Knockabout Club in North Africa. Illustrated. 8vo. cloth, pp. 4-240. *Boston.* 7s. 6d.

**O'Brien (T. V.)**—Sixty Days in Europe. A Brief Comparative Review. 16mo. paper, pp. 63. *San Francisco.* 1s. 6d.

**O'Connor (Barry)**—Turf-Fire Stories and Fairy Tales of Ireland. Illustrated. 12mo. cloth, pp. 405. *New York.* 6s. 6d.

**Ogden (Christol)** — Ogden's Skeleton Essays; or, Authorship in Outline. 16mo. pp. 253, paper, 2s. 6d.; boards, 4s.

**Ogden (Ruth).**—A Loyal Little Red-Coat. A Story of Child Life in New York a Hundred Years Ago. Illustrated by H. A. Ogden. 8vo. cloth, pp. 5-217. *N. York.* 10s. 6d.

**Orpen (Mrs. Goddard)**—Stories about Famous Precious Stones. Illustrated. 12mo. cloth, pp. 4-286. *Boston.* 6s. 6d.

**Page (Eliza J.)**—Only a Waif. The Romance of an Earthquake. Portrait. Illustrated. 12mo. cloth, pp. 7-295. *St. Louis (Mo.).* 7s. 6d.

**Patterson (Howard)**—Handbook to the United States Local Marine Board Examination for Masters and Mates of Ocean-going Steamships. 8vo. cloth, pp. 48. *New York.* 10s. 6d.

**Patterson (Howard)**—The Captain of the Rajah. A Story of the Sea. Illustrated by Warren Sheppard. 12mo. cloth, pp. 3-155 *New York.* 5s.

**Patterson (Howard)** — Yachting under American Statute. United States Laws and Treasury Instructions for the Guidance of Owners and Officers of American Yachts, etc. General Rules and Regulations Prescribed by the Board of Supervising Inspectors of Steam Vessels, etc. Directions for Seamen and Engineers in Quest of Licenses from the United States Local Steamboat Inspectors, etc. Together with other Valuable Information for Yachtsmen. 8vo. cloth, pp. 84. *New York.* 7s. 6d.

**Paulton (E. A.)**—The American Faust. Illustrated by Ekscrgian. 12mo. cloth, pp. 2-256. *New York.* 6s. 6d.

**Payne's (F. M.)** Business Pointers. Chapters on U. S. Customs Regulations, Legal Forms used in Business, Wages Tables, Rules for Writing Correctly, etc. 16mo. paper, pp. 160. *New York.* 1s. 6d.

**Payne (F. M.)**—Business Pointers and Dictionary of Synonyms, with other Information not generally known; valuable to all Business-men. 16mo. paper, pp. 149. *New York.* 1s. 6d.

**Peabody (Andrew, D.D.)**—Christianity and Science. New Issue. 12mo. cloth, pp. 8-287. *New York.* 9s.

**Pendleton (L.)**—King Tom and the Runaways. The Story of what befell Two Boys in a Georgia Swamp. 8vo. cloth, pp. 5-273. *New York.* 7s. 6d.

**Pentecost (G. F., D.D.)** — Bible Studies for 1891. 12mo. cloth. *New York.* 5s.

**Pentecost (G. F., D.D.)**—Israel's Apostacy and Studies from the Gospel of St. John, covering International Sunday School Lessons for 1891. 12mo. cloth, pp. 8-406. *New York.* 5s.

**Pepper (G. Wharton, ed.)**—The Johnson Prize Essays from Various Law Schools. 8vo. sheep, pp. 5-806. *Philadelphia.* 5s.

**Perry (T. Sergeant)**—A History of Greek Literature. Illustrated. 8vo. cloth, pp. 13-877. *New York.* £1 18s.

**Phelps (Austin, D.D.)**—My Note-Book. Fragmentary Studies in Theology and Subjects Adjacent Thereto. 12mo. cloth, pp. 8-324. *New York.* 7s. 6d.

**Phyfe (W. H. P.)**—Seven Thousand Words often Mispronounced. A Complete Handbook of Difficulties in English Pronunciation. Including an Unusually Large Number of Proper Names and Words and Phrases from Foreign Languages. 7th Edition, with Supplement. 16mo. pp. 499. *New York.* 6s. 6d.

**Pickard (J. L.)**—School Supervision. 12mo. cloth, pp. 12-175. *New York.* 5s.

**Plympton (A. G.)**—Dear Daughter Dorothy. Illustrated by the Author. 12mo. cloth, pp. 3-190. *Boston.* 5s.

**Poor's Handbook of Investment Securities.** A Supplement to Poor's "Manual of Railroads," July, 1890. 8vo. cloth, pp. 267. *New York.* 12s. 6d.

**Pratt (Anna M.)**—Friends from my Garden; with Original and Selected Poems. Illustrated by Laura C. Hills. 8vo. boards, pp. 5-128. *New York.* 12s. 6d.

**Prindle (H. B.)**—A Popular Treatise on the Electric Railway. 12mo. paper, pp. 2 and 58. *Boston.* 2s. 6d.

**Prudden (T. Mitchell, M.D.)**—Dust and Its Dangers. Illustrated. 12mo. cloth, pp. 5 and 111. *New York.* 4s.

**Publishers' Trade List Annual, 1890.** The Latest Catalogues of American Book Publishers; preceded by a Complete List, by Authors, Titles and Subjects, of Books recorded in *The Publishers' Weekly*, January—June, 1890, and by the American Educational Catalogue for 1890. 18th Year. Roy. 8vo. cloth, pp. 3364. *New York.* 12s.

**Putnam (G. P., comp.)**—Tabular Views of Universal History. A Series of Chronological Tables Presenting in Parallel Columns a Record of the More Noteworthy Events in the History of the World from the Earliest Times down to 1890. Continued to Date by Lynde E. Jones. 12mo. half leather, pp. 3-211. *New York.* 9s.

**Reade (H. L.)**—The Story of a Heathen and His Transformation. Illustrated. 12mo. cloth, pp. 5-82. *Boston.* 3s.

**Reddall (H. F., comp.)**—A Pocket Handbook of Biography. 16mo. cloth, pp. 5-263. *Syracuse (N.Y.).* 4s. 6d.

**Reed (Elizabeth A.)** — Hindu Literature; or, the Ancient Books of India. 12mo. cloth, pp. 410. *Chicago.* 10s. 6d.

**Richardson (M. T., comp.)**—Practical Blacksmithing. Vol. 3. Illustrated. 12mo. cloth. *New York.* 5s.

**Robinson (W. C.)**—A Treatise on the Law of Patents for Useful Inventions. 3 vols. 8vo. leather. *Boston.* £7 10s.

**Roe (E. R.)**—Belteshazzar. A Romance of Babylon. 12mo. cloth, pp. 270. *Chicago.* 5s.

**Rosengarten (J. G.)**—The German Soldier in the Wars of the United States. 2nd Edition Revised and Enlarged. 12mo. cloth, pp. 2-266. *Philadelphia.* 5s.

**Saltus (Francis S.)**—Shadows and Ideals. Poems. Square 8vo. half morocco, pp. 10-369. *Buffalo.* 16s. 6d.

**Saltus (Francis S.)**—The Witch of En-dor, and other Poems. 8vo. half morocco, pp. 300. *Buffalo (N.Y.).* 16s. 6d.

**Sargent (C. Sprague)**—The Silva of North America. a Description of the Trees which Grow Naturally in North America, exclusive of Mexico. Illustrated with Figures and Analyses Drawn from Nature, by C. E. Faxon. In 12 vols. Vol. 1. 12 plates. 4to. cloth. *Boston.* £6 6s.

**Sargeant (G. E.)**—Sunday Evenings at Northcourt. Illustrated. 12mo. cloth, pp. 383. *N. York and Chicago.* 5s.

**Savage (M. J.)**—Life. 8vo. cloth, pp. 6-237. *Boston.* 6s.

**Savage (T. E., ed.)**—Manual of Industrial and Commercial Intercourse between the United States and Spanish America for the Fiscal Years 1890-91. 12mo. cloth, pp. 9-529. *San Francisco (Cal.).* 12s. 6d.

**Schreber (D. G. R., M.D.)**—Home Exercise for Health and Cure. From the 23rd German Edition by C. Russell Bardeen. 16mo. cloth, pp. 4-91. *Syracuse (N.Y.).* 2s. 6d.

**Schwab (I., Rabbi)**—The Sabbath in History. Two Parts. 8vo. paper, pp. 3-132 and 133-320. *St. Joseph (Mo.).* 6s. 6d.

**Scotch-Irish Congress.**—The Scotch-Irish in America. Proceedings and Addresses of the Second Congress at Pittsburg, May 29-June 1, 1890. 8vo. cloth, pp. 4-305. *Cincinnati.* 7s. 6d.

**Scott (G.)**—New Coast Pilot for the Lakes. Containing a Complete List of all the Lights and Lighthouses, Fog Signals and Buoys on both the American and Canadian Shores. Illustrated. 8vo. boards, pp. 289. *Milwaukee (Wis.).* 10s. 6d.

**Scudder (Horace E.)**—Scudder's Short History of the United States of America for the Use of Beginners. 16mo. cloth, pp. 288. *New York.* 4s.

**Semple (C. E. Armand, M.D.)**—Essentials of Legal Medicine, Toxicology and Hygiene. 8vo. cloth, pp. 194. *Philadelphia.* 6s.

**Shaler (N. S.)**—Aspects of the Earth. A Popular Account of some Familiar Geological Phenomena. New Cheaper Edition. Illustrated. 8vo. cloth. *N. York.* 12s. 6d.

**Shepherd (H. A.)**—The Antiquities of the State of Ohio. Full of Accurate Descriptions of the Works of the Mound Builders ; Defensive and Sacred Inclosures, Mounds, Cemeteries, and Tombs, and their Contents ; Implements, Ornaments, Sculptures, etc. Illustrated. 4to. cloth, pp. 6-139. *Cincinnati (O.).* 10s. 6d.

**Shields (G. O.)**—The Big Game of North America. Illustrated. 8vo. cloth. *New York and Chicago.* £1 1s.

**Slosson (Annie Trumbull)**—Seven Dreamers. Illustrated. 12mo. cloth, pp. 3-281. *New York.* 6s. 6d.

**Smith (Edgar F.)**—Electro-Chemical Analysis. A Practical Handbook. Illustrated. 12mo. cloth. *New York.* 5s.

**Smith (H. B., D.D.)**—System of Christian Theology. Edited by W. S. Karr, D.D. 4th Edition Revised with an Introduction by T. S. Hastings, D.D. 8vo. cloth, pp. 8-641. *New York.* 10s. 6d.

**Snively (W. H.)**—The Ober-Ammergau Passion Play. Illustrated by W. H. Snively. 12mo. cloth, pp. 68. *New York.* 6s. 6d.

**Southern Baptist Theological Seminary.** The First Thirty Years. With Biographical Sketch. 12mo. cloth. *Baltimore (Md.).* 6s.

**Spear (J. W.)**—Rudolph of Rosenfeldt ; or, The Leaven of the Reformation. A Story of the Times of William the Silent. 12mo. cloth, pp. 2-419. *Philadelphia.* 7s. 6d.

**Spencer (Jesse Ames)**—Memorabilia of Sixty-Five Years (1820-1886). 12mo. cloth, pp. 240. *New York.* 7s. 6d.

**Sprague (Rev. Philo W.)**—Christian Socialism, What and Why ? With Appendix Address of the Bishop of Durham on Socialism. 16mo. cloth, pp. 2-204. *New York.* 4s.

**Starr (F.)**—On the Hills. A Series of Geological Talks. Illustrated. 12mo. cloth, pp. 2-249. *Boston.* 6s. 6d.

**Starr (M. Allen, M.D.)**—Familiar Forms of Nervous Disease. 8vo. cloth, pp. 339. *New York.* 15s.

**Stoddard (W. O.)**—Inside the White House in War Times. Illustrated by Dan Beard. 12mo. cloth, pp. 5-244. *New York.* 6s.

**Strowbridge (J. L.)**—The Cider Maker's Handbook. A Complete Guide for Making and Keeping Pure Cider. Illustrated. 12mo. cloth, pp. 120. *New York.* 5s.

**Sultus (Edgar)**—Love and Lore. 16mo. paper, pp. 112. *New York.* 2s. 6d.

**Sutcliffe (J. D.)**—Hand-Craft. An English Exposition of Slojd as Cultivated in Sweden. Illustrated. 8vo. cloth, *New York.* 6s.

**Swett (Lucia Gray)**—New England Breakfast Breads, Luncheon and Tea Biscuits. Illustrated by L. M. P. 16mo. cloth, pp. 4-129. *Boston.* 6s.

**Swinton (R. B.)**—Chess for Beginners, and the Beginnings of Chess. Illustrated. 8vo. cloth. *Boston.* 7s. 6d.

**Szczepanski (F. v. ed.)** — Bibliotheca Polytechnica. Directory of Technical Literature. 1st Annual Issue, 1889. 12mo. flexible cloth, pp. 41. *New York.*

**Talbot (Ella V.)** — The Perseverance of Chryssa Arkwright. A Lesson in Self-Help. 12mo. cloth, pp. 266. *New York.* 6s.

**Tales and Legends from the Land of the Tzar.** A Collection of Russian Stories. From the Russian, by Edith M. S. Hodgetts. 12mo. cloth, pp. 6-324. *New York.* 9s.

**Taylor (W. M., D.D.)**—The Miracles of Our Saviour Expounded and Illustrated. 12mo. cloth, pp. 6-449. *New York.* 9s.

**Thatcher (G.)** — Talks by George Thatcher, the Celebrated Minstrel. Containing His Monologues, Parodies, Songs, Sketches, Poems, Jokes, etc. 12mo. cloth, pp. 4-168. *Philadelphia.* 1s. 6d.

**Thoreau (H. D.)**—Thoreau's Thoughts. Selections from the writings of Henry David Thoreau. Edited by H. G. O. Blake. 16mo. cloth, pp. 5-153. *Boston.* 6s.

**Thornton (J. P.)**—Training for Health, Strength, Speed, and Agility ; for the Instruction of Amateurs and Others. 12mo. cloth, pp. 250. *New York.* 4s.

**Thus Think and Smoke Tobacco.** A Rhyme (xviith Century) with Drawings and Decorations, by G. Wharton Edwards. 4to. cloth, no paging, leather thongs. *New York.* 12s. 6d.

**Tolstoï (Count Lyof N.)** — Count Tolstoï's Gospel Stories. From the Russian by Nathan Haskell Dole. 12mo. cloth, pp. 4-243. *New York.* 6s. 6d.

**Tolstoï (Count Lyof N.)** — Labour. The Divine Command ; Made Known, Augmented, and Edited by Count Tolstoï. Translated by Mary Cruger. 12mo. cloth, pp. 2-160. *Chicago.* 1s. 6d.

**Townsend (Malcolm, comp.)**—United States. An Index to the United States of America, Historical, Geographical and Political. A Handbook of References combining the Curious in United States History. Maps and Illustrations. 12mo. cloth, pp. 3-482. *Boston.* 7s. 6d.

**Toy (C. H.)**—Judaism and Christianity. 8vo. cloth, pp. 474. *Boston.* 15s.

**Trevert (E.)**—Everybody's Handbook of Electricity ; with Glossary of Electrical Terms and Tables for Incandescent Wiring. Fourth Edition. Illustrated. 12mo. paper, pp. 2-120. *Lynn (Mass.).* 1s. 6d.

**Trevert (E.)**—Experimental Electricity. Illustrated. 12mo. cloth, pp. 3-164. *Lynn (Mass.).* 6s.

**Trevert (E.)**—How to Make Electric Batteries at Home. 16mo. paper, pp. 2-42. *Lynn (Mass.).* 1s. 6d.

**Trumbull (W.)**—The Problem of Cain. A Study in the Treatment of Criminals. 8vo. paper, pp. 94. *New Haven.* 3s.

**Tsar (The) and His People ; or, Social Life in Russia.** Illustrated. 8vo. cloth, pp. 4-435. *New York.* 15s.

**Tuttle (Emma Rood)**—From Soul to Soul. Poems. 12mo. cloth, pp. 9-222. *New York.* 7s. 6d.

**Tuttle (Hudson)**—Religion of Man and Ethics of Science. 12mo. cloth, pp. 3-313. *New York.* 7s. 6d.

**Tyng (C. Rockland,** *comp.*)—Record of the Life and Work of the Rev. Stephen H. Tyng, D.D., and History of St. George's Church, New York, to the Close of his Rectorship. Compiled by his Son. 8vo. cloth, pp. 682. *New York.* 18*s.*

**United States and Canada.**—Book of the Game Laws. A Compendium of the Laws of the United States and of Canada relating to Game and Game Fish, containing the Full Text of all Important Sections of the General Laws, and Digests of Local Laws. Published quarterly and revised to date. Composed and Edited by C. R. Reynolds. Vol. I, No 1. 8vo. paper, pp. 2–228. *New York.* 2*s.* 6*d.*

**United States (Official) Hotel Directory and Railroad Indicator.** Hotel Red Book, 1890. 8vo. cloth, pp. 665. *New York.* 18*s.*

**United States—War Department.** Surgeon-General's Office. Index Catalogue of the Library of the Surgeon-General's Office; Authors and Subjects. Vol. 2. Phædromus–Regent. 4to. cloth, pp. 2–1102. *Washington.* £1 10*s.*

**Universalist Register** for 1891 ; giving Statistics of the Universalist Church and other Denominational Information. 12mo. paper, pp. 112. *Boston.* 1*s.* 6*d.*

**Upton (Mrs. Harriet Taylor)**—Our Early Presidents, their Wives and Children, from Washington to Jackson. Illustrations and Portraits. 8vo. cloth, pp. 7–395. *Boston.* £1.

**Van Cleve (B. Frank)**—The English and American Mechanic. An Every-day Handbook for the Workshop and the Factory. New revised enlarged edition. By Emory Edwards. 12mo. cloth, pp. 500. *Philadelphia.* 10*s.* 6*d.*

**Van Dyke (H. J., D.D.)**—The Church : Her Ministry and Sacraments. Lectures delivered on the L. P. Stone Foundation at Princeton Theological Seminary in 1890. 8vo. cloth, pp. 8–265. *New York.* 7*s.* 6*d.*

**Van Dyke (T. S.)**—Millionaires of a Day. An Inside History of the Great Southern California Boom. 12mo. cloth, pp. 3–208. *New York.* 5*s.*

**Vincent (Frank)**—In and Out of Central America, and other Sketches and Studies of Travel. 12mo. cloth, pp. 5 and 246. *New York.* 10*s.*

**Vincent (J. Heyl, Bishop)** — To Old Bethlehem. 16mo. paper, pp. 2–25. *Meadville (Pa.).* 1*s.* 6*d.*

**Vincent (Marvin R., D.D.)**—Word Studies in the New Testament. Vol. 3, The Epistles of Paul; Romans, Corinthians, Ephesians, Philippians, Colossians, Philemon. 8vo. cloth, pp. 40–664. *New York.* £1.

**Wallace (W. De Witt)**—Idle Hours. A Collection of Poems. 16mo. cloth. *New York.* 6*s.* 6*d.*

**Ward (Herbert D.)**—The New Senior at Andover. 12mo. cloth. *Boston.* 6*s.* 6*d.*

**Ward (Julius H.)**—The White Mountains. A Guide to their Interpretation. Maps and Illustrations. 12mo. cloth, pp. 7 and 258. *New York.* 6*s.* 6*d.*

**Washington (G.)**—The Writings of George Washington, including his Diary and Correspondence. Edited by Worthington C. Ford. In 14 vols. Vol. 8. 8vo. cloth. *New York.* £1 5*s.*

**Washington (G.)**—The Writings of George Washington, including His Diary and Correspondence. Edited by Worthington C. Ford. In 14 vols. Vol. 5.

**Weeden (W. B.)**—Economic and Social History of New England, 1620–1789. 2 vols. 12mo. cloth, pp. 15–446 ; 432–964. *Boston.* £1 2*s.* 6*d.*

**Welch (S. M.)**—Home History. Recollections of Buffalo During the Decade from 1830 to 1840 ; or, Fifty Years Since. Descriptive and Illustrative, with Incidents and Anecdotes. Illustrated. 12mo. cloth, pp. 400. *Buffalo (N.Y.).* 18*s.*

**Wells (Roger, jun.) and Kelly (J. W., comps.)**—English-Eskimo and Eskimo-English Vocabularies; preceded by Ethnographical Memoranda concerning the Arctic Eskimos in Alaska and Siberia by J. W. Kelly. 8vo. paper, pp. 4 and 72. *Washington.*

**Welsh (Alfred H.)**—A Digest of English and American Literature. 12mo. cloth, pp. 5–378. *Chicago.* 7*s.* 6*d.*

**Westbrook (Mary)**—Rachel Du Mont : A Brave Little Maid of the Revolution. A True Story of the Burning of Kingston. N.Y., by the British in 1777. For Girls and Boys and Older People. Square 8vo. half calf, pp. 100. *Albany (N.Y.).* 7*s.* 6*d.*

**Wheeler (A. C., "Nym Crinkle,"** *pseud.*)—The Toltec Cup. A Romance of Immediate Life in New York City. 12mo. paper, pp. 2–333. *New York.* 4*s.*

**Willard (Ashton R.)**—A Legislative Handbook Relating to the Preparation of Statutes ; with a Chapter on the Publication of Statutes. 12mo. cloth, pp. 281. *Boston.* 10*s.*

**Williams (G. H.)**—Elements of Crystallography. 12mo. cloth. *New York.* 5*s.* 6*d.*

**Williams (J. L. & Son,** *comp.*)—1890 Manual of Investments. Important Facts and Figures Regarding Southern Investment Securities. 8vo. cloth, pp. 344. *Richmond (Va.).* 12*s.*

**Williams (R. O.)**—Our Dictionaries, and Other English Language Topics. 12mo. cloth. *New York.* 6*s.* 6*d.*

**Wilson (Mrs. E. C.)**—A Royal Hunt. A Story of Huguenot Emigration. Illustrated 12mo. cloth, pp. 7–394. *Boston.* 7*s.* 6*d.*

**Woodhull (Alfred A.)**—Notes on Military Hygiene. 12mo. morocco flap. *New York.* 12*s.* 6*d.*

**Woods (Katherine Pearson)**—Metzerott, Shoemaker. 16mo. paper, pp. 373. *New York.* 2*s.* 6*d.*

**Wright (T. W.)**—A Text-Book of Mechanics for Colleges and Technical Schools. 12mo. cloth. *New York.* 12*s.* 6*d.*

**York (S. A., jun.,** *ed.*)—Yale Humour. A Collection of Humorous Articles and Illustrations from the Undergraduate Publications. Second edition. 8vo. cloth, pp. 90. *New Haven (Conn.).* 7*s.* 6*d.*

**Young (Lucien)**—Simple Elements of Navigation. *New York.* 10*s.*

**Young (Oscar E.)**—Seaside Songs and Woodland Whispers. Poems. 12mo. cloth, pp. 256. *Buffalo (N.Y.).* 6*s.* 6*d.*

---

## New Oriental Books.

**Aitchison (J. E. S.)**—Notes on the Products of Western Afghanistan and of North-Eastern Persia. 8vo. pp. 228. 1890.

**Alexander (G. G.)**—Confucius the Great Teacher. Post 8vo. cloth, pp. 314. 1890. 6*s.*

**Asao (T. H.)**—Pictures of Ancient Japanese History from the Coronation of the Emperor Jimmu to the Rebellion of Masakado and Sumitomo. Revised by Sir Edwin Arnold. Japanese text, with English Translation and Illustrations. 4to. *Tokyo*, 1889.

**Bélot (J. S.)**—Dictionnaire français-arabe. Vols. I. and II. (*just completed*). 8vo. wrapper, pp. 1609. 16*s.* each.

**Bible.**—Gospel according to St. Mark, translated into the Derawal Dialect of the Multani Language by Dr. A. Jukes. 8vo. pp. 72. *Lahore*, 1886. 2*s.*

**Bible.**—Gospel according to St. John, translated into Zimshian. Post 8vo. limp cloth, pp. 47. 1890. 1*s.*

**Book of Common Prayer** according to the use of the Church of England, together with the Psalms of David translated into the Language of the Cree Indians of the Diocese of Moosonee, edited by John Horden. 8vo. cloth, pp. 296 and 168. 1890. 6*s.*

**Botanical Magazine.** Vol. I. No. 2. Text in Japanese, with wood engravings and coloured plate. 4to. *Tokio*, 1890. 1*s*. 6*d*.

*.* The first japanese Journal on systematic and anatomic botany.

**Cantle (J.)** — Leprosy in Hong Kong. Demy 8vo. pp. 99. 1890. 5*s*.

**Ceylon's Handbook** and Directory and Compendium of Useful Information for 1890–91. Edited by A. M. and J. Ferguson. 8vo. £1 1*s*.

*.* Prefixed is a review of the planting enterprise and agriculture of Ceylon. with statistical information referring to the planting enterprise of other colonies.

**Chartouné.** — Arabic Dictionary. Imperial 8vo. wrapper, pp. 727, 1504, forming Vol. II. 15*s*.

**Chavannes (E.)** — Traité sur le sacrifice Fong et Chan de Se Ma T'sien. 8vo. pp. 95. 1890. 4*s*.

**Contes arabes** édités par le père A. Salhani, S.J., Introduction in French, Arabic Text 87 pages, and Autographed Specimen Sheet of the MS. 8vo. wrapper. *Beyrouth*, 1890.

**Dymock (A. O.)** — Pharmacographia Indica. Being a History of the Principal Drugs of Vegetable Origin met with in British India. Vol. II. Part I. 8vo. pp. 1–304. 1890. 10*s*. 6*d*.

**Gerth Van Wijk (G.)** — Spraakleer der Maleische Taal. 8vo. pp. 302. *Batavia*, 1890. 12*s*. 6*d*.

**Grenon.** — Verdant Simple's Views of Japan ; or, the Contents of his Notebook. A Novel. 8vo. *Yokohama*, 1890. 5*s*.

**Grierson (G. A.)** — Modern Vernacular Literature of Hindustan. 8vo. pp. xxiii. 171, and xxxv. with 2 Plates. 1890. 12*s*. 6*d*.

**Harris (G. W.)** — Practical Guide to Algiers, 1890. 12mo. 3*s*. 6*d*.

**Hetherwick (A.)** — Introductory Handbook of the Yao Language. 12mo. cloth, pp. 281.

*.* The first part (pp. 1–81) contains the grammar ; the second part (pp. 82–281) a Yao-English vocabulary.

**Hultzsch (E.)** — South Indian Inscriptions, Tamil and Sanskrit. Edited and translated by E. Hultzsch. Vol. I. Folio, boards, pp. 183. *Madras*, 1890. 12*s*. 6*d*.

*.* From stone and copperplate edicts at Mamallapuram, Kanchipuram, in the North Arcot District, and other parts of the Madras Presidency collected in 1886–87.

**Hymns** in the Tenni or Slavi Language of the Indians of Mackenzie River in the North-West Territory of Canada. Post 8vo. cloth, pp. 118. 1890. 2*s*.

**Journal of the Japanese Horticultural Society** in Tokio. Numbers 1 to 17 are out, price varies from 1*s*. to 2*s*.

*.* Text in Japanese, with wood engravings in the text and coloured plates.

**Journal** of the Peking Oriental Society, Vol. III. No. 1. 8vo. pp. 95. *Peking*, 1890. 4*s*.

*.* Contains : Traité sur les sacrifices Fong et Chan de Sa Ma T'sien par Edouard Chavannes.

**Journal of the Photographic Society of India.** Monthly Periodical, with Plates. 4to. *Calcutta*. Yearly Subscription 15*s*. post free.

**Lammens (H.)** — Remarques sur les mots français derivés de l'arabe. Forming an Etymological Dictionary of all French Words of Arabic Origin. Post 8vo. wrapper, pp. 314. 8*s*. 6*d*.

**Lessons and Prayers** in the Tenni or Slavi Language of the Indians of the Mackenzie River in the North-West Territory of Canada. Post 8vo. cloth, pp. 81. 1890. 2*s*. 6*d*.

**Madan (A. C.)** — English-Swahili Vocabulary. Compiled from the works of the late Bishop Steere, and from other sources. 12mo. cloth, pp. 56. 1890.

**Mémoires** concernant l'histoire naturelle de l'empire chinois par des pères de la Compagnie de Jésus. Vol. I. complete (containing Heude, Mollusques terrestres). Imp. 4to. pp. 188 text, with 43 plates. *Chang-hai*, 1890. £5.

**Memoirs by Medical Officers** of the Army of India. Part 5, with Plates. 4to. boards. *Calcutta*. 7*s*. 6*d*.

**Middendorf (Dr. E. W.)** — Woerterbuch der Runa Simi oder der Keshua Sprache. Unter Beruecksichtigung der frueheren Werke nach eigenen Studien bearbeitet. Large 8vo. pp. 857. 1890.

**Morris (H.)** — Simplified Grammar of the Telugu Language. Post 8vo. cloth, pp. 159 text, with a language map. 1890. 10*s*. 6*d*.

**Murray (J. A.)** — The Avifauna of the Island of Ceylon. 8vo. pp. 382 text, with engravings, plain and coloured plates. £1 1*s*.

**Murray (J. A.)** — The Edible and Game Birds of British India, with its Dependencies, and Ceylon. 8vo. pp. 236 text, with engravings and coloured plates. 15*s*.

**Mycographia Nipponica.** Illustrations of Edible, Poisonous, and Parasitic Fungi of Nippon. Edited by Nobujira Tanaka and Nagane Tanaka. Vol. I. No. 1 in 2 parts. Text in Japanese. Price of each part with four coloured plates each, 3*s*.

**Naiksargikaprayaçcittikadharmas** (Buddhistische Suehnenregeln aus dem Pratimokshasutram). Von dem tibetanischen Texte ins Deutsche uebersetzt, mit kritischen Anmerkungen herausgegeben und mit der Pali- und einer chinesischen Fassung, sowie mit dem Suttavibhanga verglichen von Dr. Georg Huth. 8vo. pp. 51. 1891. 2*s*.

**Néval (J. de)** — Systeme législatif musulman : Le marriage. 8vo. pp. 215. *St. Pétersbourg*, 1890. 8*s*.

**Nishga Version** of Portions of the Book of Common Prayer. Translated by J. B. MacCullagh. Post 8vo. cloth, pp. 79 and 13. 1890. 1*s*.

**Noer (Count T. A.)** — The Emperor Akbar. A Contribution towards the History of India in the 16th Century. Translated into English from the German and in part revised by Annette S. Beveridge. Two vols. 8vo. cloth, pp. 348 and 455. 1890. 17*s*. 6*d*.

**Ollanta.** — Ein Drama der Keshua Sprache. Translated into German with Notes and an Introduction on the Religious and Government Institutions of the Incas by Dr. E. W. Middendorf. Large 8vo. pp. 393. 1890. 18*s*.

**Patanjali.** — Yoga-Sutra. English Translation, with Introduction, Appendix, and Notes based upon several authentic Commentaries. By Manilal Nabhubhai Dvivedi. 8vo. boards, pp. 99, vii. 1890. 4*s*. 6*d*.

**Records of the Past**, being English Translations of the Ancient Monuments of Egypt or Western Asia. Edited by A. H. Sayce. Second Series, Vols. II. and III. Post 8vo. cloth. 1890. 4*s*. 6*d*. each vol.

**Redhouse (Sir J. W.)** — Turkish and English Dictionary, showing in English the Signification of the Turkish Terms. Part VIII. just out, completing the work, over 2300 pages imperial 8vo. 9*s*. each part.

**Rice (B. Lewis)** — Inscriptions at Sravana Belgoda, a Chief Seat of the Jains. Many of the Inscriptions and Monuments are reproduced in facsimile on twenty-six plates, with over 400 pages text, giving the text of the inscriptions in Roman characters, translation, etc. 4to. cloth. *Bangalore*, 1889.

**Salhani.** — Histoire des dynasties de Bar-Hobraeus. 8vo. wrapper, pp. 591. 15*s*.

**Specimens** of 122 various Handwritings, to accustom the Scholar to the Reading of Old and New Arabic Manuscripts. Reproduced in Facsimile. Second Edition. The second part of the book is a key to it, and contains a reprint of the text in Arabic printing types with vowels. 8vo. boards, pp. 130 and 67. 5*s*.

Steere (E.)—Swahili Tales as Told by Natives of Zanzibar, with an English Translation. Post 8vo. cloth, pp. 501. 1890.

Talbot (A. C.)—Persian Translations of Extracts from Standard English Works on History, with English text. Two vols. 8vo. cloth, pp. 655 and 338. *Calcutta*, 1890. 13s. 6d.

The Traveller's Malay Pronouncing Handbook, for the Use of Travellers and New-comers to Singapore. Third Edition just out. 12mo. cloth. 5s.

Vedas: The Sacred Hymns of the Brahmans; together with the Commentary of Sayanacharya. Sanskrit text. Edited by Dr. Max Müller. 2nd Edition, Vol. I. and II. 4to. (to be completed in 4 vols.) Subscription price to the whole work, £6 6s.

Vedas: Rigveda with the Bhashya by Sayanancharya, 8 Ashtakas and copious notes. Sanskrit text. Edited by R. S. Bodas. 8 vols. 4to. 1890. £5 5s.

*₅* Added are the Sutras of Panini, Unadi, and Phit Sutras Bribadrigvidhana and the Parishishtha.

Vedas: The Hymns of the Rig Veda. Translated into English, with a popular Commentary by Ralph T. H. Griffith. Vols. I. and II. complete as far as published. 8vo. in wrapper. *Benares*, 1890. 10s. each vol.

*₅* The continuation can be supplied immediately after publication at 2s. 6d. each part.

Vollers (Dr. K.)—Lehrbuch der aegypto-arabischen Umgangssprache mit Uebungen und einem Glossar. Post 8vo. pp. 231. *Kairo*, 1890. 6s.

*₅* In preparation by the same author are: 1. Einleitung in die aegypto-arabische Kanzleisprache. 2. Deutsch-arabisches Woerterbuch des aegypt. Vulgaerdialects.

Warren (Dr. S. J.)—Two Bas-Reliefs of the Stupa of Bharhut. 8vo. pp. 20. *Leiden*, 1890. 2s.

Williamson (Rev. H. D.) — Gondi Grammar and Vocabulary. 12mo. cloth, pp. 95. 1890.

---

# Armenian Literature.

## (1890.)

A. M. E. P. Poësie (Tzahkounke). 2s.

Abeghiantz Manduk. Davide et Mhŏre, conta. 2s.

Achoughe Djiwani. Kerime et Asli, contes avec chansons. 2s. 6d.

Agaiantz Ghazarosse. Torkhe Augoghe, conte. 2s. 6d.

———— ———— Aroutioun et Manuel, conte, 2 vols. 6s.

———— ———— Poësie. 6s. 6d.

Aghaniantz Ghioute (prêtre). L'héritier de Tchester-tonn (Tchestertoni jarangé). 4s. 6d.

Akimian (Mlle. Marie). La découverte de la quinine. 2s.

Ananoune. Poësie choisie de H. Hoina. 2s. 6d.

Araskhaniantz Avetik. Le nombre des habitants et ses hésitations. 2s.

———— ———— La force productive de la terre et la population. 2s.

Arménake Siouni. La famine en Arménie et Etch-miadzine. 2s.

Artzrouni Senekerime. Hamlet, tragédie en 5 actes par Shakespeare. 5s.

Atormiantz. Trois contes de Christophe Schmidt. 2s.

Atrpetian (S.) Karapite, le fou. 4s.

Baghdakhudir. Un voyageur infortuné, un voyage en Arménie. 2s.

Bahathriantz (A.) Fables. 3s.

Balazetzi. Thassibe. Une conte. 2s.

Barkhoudariantz Makar (archimandrite). Anecdotes de Pelé Poughi. 3s.

———— ———— Critiques. 3s.

Burkhoudarian Kevork. Les hommes pieux, poésie (Barepachte mardik). 2s. 6d.

Chahboudaghiantz Grikor. L'appel et l'éducation de la femme trad. par Louise Buechner. 2s. 6d.

———— ———— L'éducation du caractère, trad. par André Gabrielli. 3s.

Chahire Khatchatour. Poësie nationale. 2s. 6d.

Chavarche. Le chagrin de famille et la confiance. 2s. 6d.

Chirvanzadé. Les espérances inutiles, une conte. 4s. 6d.

Efimerté ou l'explication des songes (Erazahann). 8s.

Ehramdjiantz Khatchatour. Varvaré, une conte. 2s. 6d.

Eritzian, Alexandre. Les matériaux pour l'histoire de l'Arménie I. 2s. 6d.

Gegamiantz Hovakim (Haikouni). Une critique de "Les étincelles de Raffi." 4s. 6d.

Grikor Grikoriantz (prêtre). Lyre de Zargare, recueil de chansons. 2s. 6d.

Hakhoumian Simeon. Manik, une conte. 3s.

Khalatiantz Grikor. Histoire Moïse de Khorène, trad. par l'archimandrite Khorène Stephané. Une critique. 2s.

Kolmaniantz Mkrtitche. L'honneur, drame en un acte. 2s. 6d.

Koussikiantz Hooh. Nos connaissances, une comédie. 4s. 6d.

Lalaiantz Hoohannes. Beaucoup de bruit pour rien . . . , une comédie en 5 actes de Shakespeare. 3s.

Leo. Conte ou histoire ; critique. 3s.

———— Vahane Mamikonian, conte historique. 2s.

———— Les hommes perdus (Koratzner), une conte. 3s.

———— Pandoukhte, une conte. 2s.

Louma. L'église pillée, une conte. 4s. 6d.

Madathiantz Vassak (Niazmi). Le testament de Mado, comédie en un acte. 1s. 6d.

———— ———— Seiad, poësie. 5s. 6d.

Malkhassiantz Stepan. Le roi Lear, tragédie en 5 actes de Shakespeare. 5s.

Maraghian Harouthioun. La famille ruinée, une conte. 2s.

Martyrossiantz Constantin. La croisade des enfants, une conte. 2s.

Mehrabiantz Arschak. Pour les enfants (Erekhairik), poësie. 4 vols. 13s.

Mekrian Hoohannes (prêtre). Biographie de Mesron Dartian Taghiathiantz. 2s. 6d.

Melik Chahnazariantz Constantin. Recueil des feuilletons Imblatchi Khatchane. 2s.

———— ———— Pchrunke, poësie. 1s. 6d.

———— ———— Le tabac et son influence nuisible. 1s. 6d.

———— ———— Influence nuisible des boissons d'alcools. 1s. 6d.

Mouratzan. La famille d'un protestant, une conte. 2s. 0d.

Mouradiantz (M.) Le petit Artawaz, une conte. 2s.

Nazariantz Hoohannes.  Les superstitions.  Vol. I.
2s. 6d.

————— —————— La demi-impériale, comédie en un
acte.  1s. 6d.

Paniantz, Melik.  Une conte.  2s.

Patkanian Rafael.  Le poisson d'or, de Pouchkine,
poësie.  2s.

————— —————— Poësie pour les enfants.  2s

Phiroumiantz Tigran.  Père Khrimian Hairik, une
biographie.  2s. 6d.

Prochiantz Pertche.  Les mites, une conte (Tzetzer).
4s. 6d.

————— —————— Bghdé, une conte.  5s. 6d.

Raffi, David Beck.  Une conte.  12s. 6d.

————— Khente, une conte ; Djalaleddine une conte,
en un vol.  8s.

————— La femme et la jeunesse arménienne.  6s.

————— Les étincelles.  3ᵉ vol. (fin), une conte.  2s. 6d.

Sahákian Daria.  Conte pour les enfants.  1s. 6d.

Sardariantz Adamé.  Les heures agréables.  2 vols.
2s. 6d.

Sarkssaniantz Leoon.  Un voyage en Arménie.  2s. 6d.

————— —————— Le dialecte d'Akoulissa.  8s.

Schamkhoriantz Schouch (Mlle.)  Loussaneinane.
2s. 6d.

Siouliouk, Madame et sa servante, une conte.  2s.

Soulkhaniantz Stepan.  Deux amis de Ottakar
Schouppé.  2s.

————— —————— Otello, une tragédie en 5 actes de
Shakespeare.  3s.

————— —————— René de Fr. Hoffmann.  4s.

Stepané (archimandrite).  Histoire arménienne de
Moïse de Khorène.  2s. 6d.

Taraiantz, Le chef des brigands, une conte.  2s.

Tchoubar Gevork.  Contes.  6s.

Ter Abrahamiantz Hooh.  Biographie de Narsès V.,
Achtaraketsi.  2s.

————— Grikoriantz (F.)  Sans toit et sans parents de
Alex. Daudet.  2s. 6d.

————— Sarksaiantz  Mr. George Stephenson.  2s.

————— —————— Mrs. Rouchane et Hurizade, une
conte.  2s. 6d.

Terkantz Aristakese (archimandrite).  Poësie (Haierg).
2s. 6d.

Thoumaniantz Archak.  L'ivrogne et l'amour brulaut,
une conte.  2s. 6d.

Toumaniantz Horhanes.  Poësie.  2s.

Toussoufian Hoohannés.  St. Grégoire, l'illuminateur
et ses fils.  1s. 6d.

Tunzbuchiantz.  Le scarabée du pain.  2s.

Tzerentz.  Torosse Levoni, une conte.  4s. 6d.

————— Theodorosse Rechtouni, une conte.  4s. 6d.

————— Erkounk, une conte.  4s. 6d.

————— La dignité des Cátholiques et le père
Khrimian.  2s.

Vartanian Philippe.  Le cœur, mémoire d'un écolier,
par Edmonde de Amitchise.  5s.

————— —————— Des Apenins jusqu'aux Andes, par
Edmonde de Amitchise.  1s. 6d.

————— —————— Arcvelian Vipachkhar.  First vol.
1s. 6d.

Vartanian Phillippe.  Les brigands, tragédie en 5 actes
en Schiller.  2s. 6d.

————— —————— Self-help (Inknognoutioune) de S.
Smaylse.  7s.

Warschamiantz Sargiase.  Archévêque Narsès Varja-
petian.  3s.

Zaliniantz.  La mère infortunée, une conte.  2s.

DERNIERS VOLUMES PUB. PAR LA SOCIÉTÉ DE
PUBLICATIONS ARMÉNIENNES DE TIFLIS.

Vol. 23.  Sahakiantz Sahak, Manuel du Nouveau Testament
pour écoliers et écolières.  2s.

Vol. 24.  Le même, édition de maître.  2s.

Vol. 25.  Mlle. Tekghi Stephoiantz, Socrate, une conte.  2s.

Vol. 26.  Palassaniantz Stepan, Histoire arménienne depuis
le commencement jusqu'à nos jours.  6s.

Vol. 27.  Melik Chahnazariantz Constantin, Guide de la
sériculture pratique.  2s. 6d.

Vol. 28.  Haohann Dardel, Chronologie arménienne.  6s.

# Armenian Bibliography.

(Continued from page 32.)

"Khikar."  Monthly Journal.  Vol. V.  Edited by
J. Baronian.  *Constantinople*, 1888.

"Khosnak."  Weekly Paper.  *Constantinople*, 1888.

Khrimian (M.)—The Family in Paradise.  Second
Edition.  8vo.  *Constantinople*, 1888.

————— Sirach and Samul.  Second edition.  8vo.
*Constantinople*, 1888.

————— The Pearl of Heaven.  Second edition.  8vo.
*Constantinople*, 1888.

Kibal.—The Beerhouse of Luka.  8vo.  *Constantinople*,
1888.

"Krtharan."  A Monthly Journal.  Edited by Atruni.
*Constantinople*, 1888.

Laicus (Ph.)—Cabecilla.  Translated.  8vo.  *Vienna.*
1888.

Lazarian (E.)—Who has Invented the Railway ?
pp. 24.  *Tiflis*, 1888.

Leo.—The Points.  12mo.  *Schuscha*, 1888.

————— Vahan Mamikonian.  *Schuscha*, 1888.

————— The Daughters of the Blind Man.  pp. 37.
*Schuscha*, 1888.

————— The Emigrant.  *Baku*, 1888.

Lerman (Jules).—The Son of Monte-Christo.  Translated by Atruni.  Vol. II. to VI. pp. 1960.  *Constantinople*,
1888.

"Lezu."  A Monthly Journal.  Vol. I.  Edited by
Dervischian.  *Constantinople*, 1888.

Library of Armenian Novels.  Vols. VII. to X.
*St. Petersburg*, 1888.

Malukhian (Kh.)—Military Order for the Caucasus.
*Tiflis*, 1888.

Mamikonian (G.)—The Songs of Aschik Fizahoff.
pp. 52.  *Tiflis*, 1888.

Mamurian (M.)—First Reading Book.  *Constantinople*,
1888.

————— The Swan's Song.  Translated from the French.
pp. 5.  *Smyrna*, 1888.

Mandinian (M.)—Arithmetic Problems.  Vol. III.
Second edition.  *Tiflis*, 1888.

**Mandinian (M.)**—Patriarchical and Patriotic World. Fifth edition. *Tiflis*, 1888.

**"Mankavarjanotz."** A Monthly Journal. *St. Petersburg*, 1888.

**Marie (Jul.)**—Therese. Translated by L. Paschalian. Two Vols. *Constantinople*, 1888.

**"Masia."** Monthly Journal. Vol. XXXVII. *Constantinople*, 1888.

**Matathianz (W.)**—Mado's Will. A Comedy. *Tiflis*, 1888.

**Mehrabianz (A.)** — Firstlings. Vols. III. and IV. *Tiflis*, 1888.

**Mekhitharian (K.)**—Universal Garden. *Smyrna*, 1888.

**Melikhazkazian (A.)**—The Regimen of the Military Man. *Tiflis*, 1888.

———— Prayerbook Abridged. *Tiflis*, 1888.

———— The Culture of the Chinese Nettle. *Tiflis*, 1888.

**Melikschahnazarian (K.)** — Brosamen. pp. 70. *Schuscha*, 1888.

**Minassian (G.)**—Guide to Vocal Music. *Constantinople*, 1888.

**Miridjanian (T.)** — Collection of French Proverbs. Vol. II. *Constantinople*, 1888.

**Mirimanian (B.)**—The People's Library. Fasc. V. The Holy Gregory, the Illuminator. *Tiflis*, 1888.

**"Mschak."** Daily Paper. Vol. XVI. Published by G. Arzeruni. *Tiflis*, 1888.

**Muradian (M.)**—Some Words about the Religions and Cultural Situation of the Russian Armenian. *Constantinople*, 1888.

**Nar Bey (K.)**—Catechism. *Constantinople*, 1888.

**Navasardianz (N.)**—Armenian Popular Tales. pp. 111. *Tiflis*, 1888.

**Nazariantz (J.)**—The Armenian Teacher. Volume IV. Third edition. pp. 308. *Tiflis*, 1888.

———— Reading-Book. Volume I. Second edition. *Tiflis*, 1888.

———— Calendar for the Year 1889. pp. 400. *Tiflis*.

**Nazariantz (T.)**—Armenian Popular Tales. Book IV. *Tiflis*, 1888.

**"Nelos."** Weekly Paper. Vol. I. Published by Itschtuni. *Alexandria*, 1888.

**"Nor-Dar."** Daily Paper. Vol. V. Published by S. Spandarian. *Tiflis*, 1888.

**Ormanian (M.)**—The Pulpit of the Armenian Church. 8vo. *Valarschapat*, 1888.

**Oskian (A. K.)**—Armenian-French Dictionary. *Constantinople*, 1888.

**Pakaschian (J.)**—Book for Beginners in Arithmetic. *Constantinople*, 1888.

**Paschalian (L.)**—Philip's Love. *Constantinople*, 1888. *** A translation from the French.

**Petrosian (J.)**—Gorgdji. A Novel. *Tiflis*, 1888.

**Piloyan (S.)**—Tales from Natural History. Vol. I. pp. 76. *Tiflis*, 1888.

———— The Lost Pearl. A Novel. pp. 175. *Tiflis*, 1888.

**Pirkalemian (L.)** — The Armenian Notary. Vol. I. pp. 232. *Constantinople*, 1888.

**Pirumiantz (T.)**—Pictures from Vaspurakar's Life. Vol. I. pp. 116. *Tiflis*, 1888.

**"Puntsch."** A Weekly Paper. Vol. XXIX. Published by H. Aladjadjian. *Constantinople*, 1888.

**Raffi.**—Samuel. A Novel. Vols. I. to III. *Tiflis*, 1888.

**Sahakian (S.)**—Bible History. pp. 182. *Tiflis*, 1888.

———— The Knowledge of Religion. pp. 484. *Tiflis*, 1888.

**Sarkissian (J.)** — Review of M. D. Thahisdiantz's Biography. *Constantinople*, 1888.

**Schavarsch.**— Family Troubles and Family Truth. A Novel. pp. 208. *Schuscha*, 1888.

**Schirvanzadé.** — The Married Woman. A Novel. *Tiflis*, 1888.

**Segur (Countess).** — The Castle "Guardian Angel." Translated by Dilber. *Constantinople*, 1888.

**Sethian (J.)**—Poems. *Constantinople*, 1888.

**Shakespeare.**—King Lear. Translated by Malkhassian. *Petersburg*, 1888.

**"Sohhak."** A Weekly Paper. Published by Ter. Minassian. *Constantinople*, 1888.

**Stephanian (D.)** — Manual of Geography. Second edition. pp. 302. Illustrated. *Venice*, 1888.

**Sundukiantz (G.)**—Another Sacrifice. A Comedy. Second edition. *Tiflis*, 1888.

**Talavarian (N.)** — Short Natural History. Vol. I. pp. 110. With 70 Plates. *Constantinople*, 1888.

**"Tentess."** A Monthly Journal. Vol. II. Published by O. Akobian. *Constantinople*, 1888.

**Ter-Abrahamiantz.**—Calendar for the Year 1889. pp. 208. *Rostov*, 1888.

**Ter-Leontian (N.)**—The Mother Tongue. Vol. IV. Third edition. *Tiflis*, 1888.

**Ter-Vrthanissian.**—School Regulations for Masters and Mistresses. *Constantinople*, 1888.

**Thorgomian (V.)**—The Nursing. 8vo. *Constantinople*, 1888.

**Thorosian (N.)**—Practical Course of the Ottoman Language. Vol. I. 8vo. *Constantinople*, 1888.

**Thucydides.**—History of the Peloponnesian War. Translated by A. Djarian. pp. 700. *Venice*, 1888.

**Thumanian (A.)**—The Fate is not Extinguished. *Schuscha*, 1888.

**Tigransian (N.)**—Transcaucasian Songs. *Tiflis*, 1888.

**Translation Exercises.** — French-Armenian. *Constantinople*, 1888.

**Tulumbadji Khatschan.**—A Novel. *Tiflis*, 1888.

**Uschinaki (K.)**—The Mother Tongue. Translated from K.B. pp. 79. *Ganzak*, 1888.

**Vardanian (Ph.)**—The Character. Translation. 8vo. pp. 490. *Tiflis*, 1888.

**Vardoff (J.)**—The Guard and Ivy of my Soul. Oriental Popular Songs. *Constantinople*, 1888.

**Verne (J.)**—A Journey Round the World in 80 Days. A Comedy. Translated by S. H. *Tiflis*, 1888.

**Vithal (B.)** — Count Mouval. Translated by J. Schahamian. *Constantinople*, 1888.

*Published Quarterly. Price 6s. per Annum (including Postage to any part of the World). Specimen copy 1s.*

# The Torch

## And Colonial Book Circular.

### Containing Classified Lists of New Publications—English, American, and Colonial—in all Departments of Literature,

#### Compiled by EDWARD A. PETHERICK, F.R.G.S.,

*Member of the Library Association, U.K.*

" Knowledge of books is like that sort of lantern which hides him who carries it, and serves only to pass through secret and gloomy paths of his own ; but in the possession of a man of business, it is as a Torch in the hand of one who is willing and able to show those who are bewildered the way which leads to their prosperity and welfare."

—Steele.

**CONTENTS** of Nos. 1 to 7, September, 1887, to March, 1889.

**I.—Recent English and American Publications.**—Dictionaries and Encyclopædias—History and Biography—Economics, Politics, and Topics of the day—Law and Jurisprudence—Trade and Commerce—Religion and Philosophy—Essays, Criticism, and *Belles-Lettres*—Poetry and the Drama—Fine Arts and Illustrated Works—Education, Philology, &c.—Geography, Topography, Voyages, and Travels—Natural and Physical Science—Medicine, Surgery, Anatomy, &c.—Industrial Arts, Handicrafts, Engineering, Chemistry, and Manufactures—Rural and Domestic Economy, Agriculture, Field Sports, &c.—Novels and Works of Fiction—Christmas Annuals and Numbers—Facetiæ—Miscellanies and Serial Volumes—Books for Young People.

**II.—Recent Colonial Publications and Books Relating to the British Colonies**—The Colonies in General—Australia, Tasmania, Polynesia, and New Zealand—Dominion of Canada—South African Colonies—West Africa—Mauritius and Seychelles—West Indies, Barbados, and British Guiana.

" The foundation of future Colonial bibliography is laid in this section."—*Bookworm.*

**III.—Special Colonial Libraries**—Of Cheap Editions of Popular Works of Fiction, &c., for Circulation in the Colonies and India.

**IV.—Select List of English and American Magazines and Reviews.**

**V.—Recent Bibliographical Publications.**

**VI.—Bibliography of Australasia**—New South Wales.

" A work in which the practical importance of bibliography is realised."—*Bookworm.*

" Promises to be a very complete and scholarly performance."—*N.B. Daily Mail.*

" Enriched with abundant notes and extracts."—*Bookseller.*

**VII.—A Bibliography of Matthew Arnold's Writings and Poetry, also of R. A. Proctor's Works**, accompanied by **VIII.—Publishers' Advertisements.** [Portraits.

*** A few copies of Vol. I. (Nos. 1 to 4) in Roxburgh style 7s. 6d. ; parchment 9s.

" The volume is excellently bound and fit for any drawing-room table as a work of the printers' art."—*Birmingham Post.*

#### A SELECTION FROM NUMEROUS PRESS NOTICES OF *"THE TORCH."*

" Extremely useful. . . . A periodical that should be on the table of every public library."—*Time.*

" *The Torch* forms an attractive record of current literature, quite apart from its colonial interest."—*Academy.*

" A useful and well-arranged work, which will form an indispensable part of every bibliographical collection."—*Notes and Queries.*

" Mr. Petherick's new book Circular has made an excellent start on its career. It is admirably printed and well edited, and promises in every way to be a great success."—*Publishers' Circular.*

" We have to thank Mr. Petherick for his valuable contribution to bibliography in his new periodical *The Torch*, on an excellent plan, well executed, and also in size and type just what it should be."—*Athenæum.*

" That very valuable periodical, *The Torch*, which is, in some respects, most decidedly the foremost of periodical contributions to bibliography."—*European Mail.*

" A publication which should be of considerable utility to the large class of readers of books, and the unhappily small class of buyers. . . . . We do not know where what is given under the colonial heading could be found. This catalogue is, as far as we know, unique, and proportionately valuable."—*Spectator.*

" A most valuable, useful, and unique compilation. . . . . It ought to be added that *The Torch* is enriched with quotations of great interest, showing genuine literary taste and research. New books issued in Canada, America, Australia, or elsewhere, may be heard of in *The Torch*. . . . This new publication of universal information about books will be welcome in England as elsewhere."—*Birmingham Post.*

" A very valuable 'tool' for the bookseller."—*Canadian Bookseller.*

" Likely to fill a want and to give to colonial readers an easily accessible body of information as to what is being done in the literary world."—*Sydney Morning Herald.*

" No praise, it may be said, is great enough for this excellent brochure, which is typical of all that a book circular should be. A very full catalogue is given of recent English publications of every kind, with the names of the publishers and the prices. Where the title of the work is not self-explanatory a brief description is appended. The work differs from many others of its kind, not only in respect to its detailed classification, but by reason of the inclusion of an exhaustive list of recent colonial publications. *The Torch* involves an excellent idea well carried out, the typographical features being all that could be desired." . . . . "Already we have noticed the care, accuracy, and unsparing pains with which this publication is compiled, and in all respects its reputation is sustained by the latest number."—*Adelaide Advertiser* (second notice).

" There will be a steady future for so useful and carefully compiled a publication."—*Paper and Printing Trades Journal.*

" Mr. Petherick has collected together in these four numbers a mass of very useful bibliographical matter, and if he progresses as he has commenced he will make *The Torch* a necessary adjunct to the bibliographical tools of all librarians."—*Trübner's Record.*

" A high class publication, containing bibliographical matter of the greatest value to all who are interested in our colonial possessions."—*North British Mail.*

" *The Torch and Colonial Book Circular* seems to improve with each issue. The classification of books is improved, and the information fuller, which makes this a perfectly complete and reliable classified account of all the new books published during the quarter. The bibliography of Colonial publications is invaluable."—*The British Mail.*

" This Circular is issued in connection with an agency which Mr. Petherick is opening in London for booksellers in the Colonies, and for collectors of Colonial literature in Great Britain and America, and on the Continent. . . . We wish Mr. Petherick and his agency all the success that is deserved, for he has hit upon a want felt both on this side and on that, and met it in a manner equally satisfactory to the old country and the Colonies."—*Sunday Times.*

Published by E. A. PETHERICK & Co., at the Colonial Booksellers' Agency, 33, Paternoster Row, London, E.C. ; and 3, St. James Street, Melbourne.

# CAMBRIDGE UNIVERSITY PRESS.

TRAVELS IN NORTHERN ARABIA, from November, 1876, to August, 1878, and in the PERÆA in May and June, 1875. By CHARLES M. DOUGHTY, M.A. of Gonville and Caius College. With Numerous Illustrations and a Map. 2 Vols. Demy 8vo. £3 3s.

KALILAH AND DIMNAH, or, THE FABLES OF BIDPAI; being an Account of their Literary History, together with an English Translation of the same, with Notes, by I. G. N. KEITH-FALCONER, M.A., late Lord Almoner's Professor of Arabic in the University of Cambridge. Demy 8vo. 7s. 6d.

KINSHIP & MARRIAGE in EARLY ARABIA. By W. ROBERTSON SMITH, M.A., LL.D., Fellow of Christ's College and University Librarian. Crown 8vo. 7s. 6d.

THE DIVYÀVADÀNA, a Collection of Early Buddhist Legends, now first edited from the Nepalese Sanskrit MSS. in Cambridge and Paris. By E. B. COWELL, M.A., Professor of Sanskrit in the University of Cambridge, and R. A. NEIL, M.A., Fellow and Lecturer of Pembroke College. Demy 8vo. 18s.

POEMS OF BEHA ED DIN ZOHEIR OF EGYPT. With a Metrical Translation, Notes and Introduc-

---

## 𝔗𝔯ü𝔟𝔫𝔢𝔯'𝔰 ℜ𝔢𝔠𝔬𝔯𝔡,

A JOURNAL DEVOTED TO THE LITERATURE OF THE EAST,

*With Notes & Lists of Current American, European & Colonial Publications.*

### ORDER FORM.

*To the Publishers of "Trübner's Record,"*

*57 & 59, Ludgate Hill, London, E.C.*

Please enter my name as Subscriber to "Trübner's Record," and send me the parts of the current Volume as they appear, for which I enclose Ten Shillings.

*Signed,*

    ————————————————

*Date* ————————    ————————————————

*Contents announced monthly among the Magazine Lists.*

ONE SHILLING MONTHLY OF ALL BOOKSELLERS.

London: WALTER SMITH & INNES, 31 and 32, Bedford Street, Strand, W.C.

---

# THE READER'S SHAKESPEARE.

### COMPLETE IN NINE VOLUMES.

Extra 8vo. cloth.    Price 6s. each Vol.    The set of Nine Vols. £2 14s.

Vols. I.—III. COMEDIES.  |  Vols. IV.—V. HISTORIES.  |  Vols. VI.—VIII. TRAGEDIES.

Vol. IX. POEMS. Each Volume sold separately.

*(This Edition has been printed from a Fount of New Type at the University Press, Oxford).*

**The convenient size and large clear type of these Volumes render them more easy and pleasant to read than any other Edition published.**

*Seventy-five Copies have been printed on large paper, numbered and signed, price One Guinea each Volume. In handsome cloth, extra gilt, or half-morocco.*

### OPINIONS OF THE PRESS:

" Besides being convenient, it is remarkably handsome. For what may be called library use it is the best Shakespeare we know."—*Guardian.*

" The attempt is very successful. The volumes are of a convenient size, and exceptionally well got up."—*Saturday Review.*

" If any one wishes to read, either for himself or aloud, a play of Shakespeare with pure uninterrupted enjoyment of Shakespeare's genius, he will find this edition the very thing for him. Its convenient size for holding in the hand, its tasteful get-up, its large, clear type, its quasi-antique look and uncut edges, the absence of everything to distract attention from the text, and the general excellence of the text itself, make it at once pleasing to the eye and easy and convenient for continuous reading."—*Scotsman.*

" It promises to be a thoroughly good library edition, and it is certainly cheap."—*St. James's Gazette.*

" It is thoroughly well got up, and may be cordially recommended as a not too expensive library edition."—*Literary Churchman.*

" It is one of the choicest and most attractive issues of our great national poet with which we are acquainted, and may be confidently recommended."—*John Bull.*

" It is a real treasure."—*Church Times.*

WALTER SMITH & INNES, 31 & 32, BEDFORD STREET, STRAND, W.C.

# BOOKS WANTED.

BOOKSELLERS AND PRIVATE INDIVIDUALS will find it to their advantage to communicate with me before disposing elsewhere of any FIRST EDITIONS, in good condition, of the Works of DICKENS, THACKERAY, LEVER, AINSWORTH, MARRYAT, GEORGE MEREDITH, ARNOLD, KINGSLEY, SHELLEY, KEATS, LAMB, BROWNING, JESSE, PARDOE, FREER ; also Books Illustrated by G. or R. CRUIKSHANK, T. ROWLANDSON, J. LEECH, R. DOYLE, W. BLAKE, T. SIBSON, R. SEYMOUR, &c.

All Communications answered.    Catalogues solicited.

WALTER T. SPENCER, 27, NEW OXFORD STREET, LONDON, W.C.

# 350, OXFORD STREET, LONDON.

## BOOKS IN ALL CLASSES OF LITERATURE.

Discount allowed 25 per cent. for Cash, or for a Deposit Account.

### SECOND-HAND BOOKS.

A VERY LARGE AND VARIED STOCK.

CATALOGUES, GRATIS, OF NEW, SECOND-HAND, AND SPECIALLY REDUCED BOOKS.

## JOHN BUMPUS,

BOOKSELLER (By Special Appointment to Her Majesty),

350, OXFORD STREET, LONDON.

# PERMANENT PHOTOGRAPHS

OF THE WORKS OF

# EDWARD BURNE JONES,

AND MANY OF THE PORTRAITS BY

# G. F. WATTS, R. A.,

CAN NOW BE OBTAINED FROM

## FREDERICK HOLLYER, 9, Pembroke Square, Kensington.

LISTS OF SUBJECTS AND PRICES WILL BE SENT POST FREE ON APPLICATION.

*IN THE PRESS.*

In One Volume.    Royal 8vo.

# A SANSKRIT-ENGLISH DICTIONARY

BASED UPON THE ST. PETERSBURG LEXICONS.

BY CARL CAPPELLER,

Professor at the University of Jena.

This English edition of CAPPELLER's Sanskrit Dictionary differs from its German original chiefly in the fact that it covers a considerably extended range of texts (the most important of which are : the second edition of BÖHTLINGK's Sanskrit Chresto-mathie, the Rigveda Hymns translated by GELDNER and KAEGI, the Marut Hymns translated by F. MAX MÜLLER, the Kaṭhopanishad ; the Hitopadeça, Nala, Bhagavadgîtâ, Manu, the plays of Kâlidâsa and the Meghadûta, the Mṛcchakatikâ and Mâlatîmâdhava) and in some minor particulars, of which the author gives an account in the preface.  In all essentials the double character of the work has been preserved : it is intended to be not only a handbook for the beginner in Sanskrit, but also to serve the purposes of the linguistic student.

LONDON: TRÜBNER & CO., 57 AND 59, LUDGATE HILL.

# The Lotos Series.

Now Ready.  Vol. I.  Pott 8vo. cloth, pp. 254.  Price 3s. 6d.

THE

## ORIGINAL TRAVELS & SURPRISING ADVENTURES OF BARON MÜNCHAUSEN.

### Illustrated by ALFRED CROWQUILL.

Messrs. TRÜBNER & Co. *have much pleasure in announcing that the First Volume of this Series is now ready.*

*A limited number of Volumes (four to six) will be issued per annum, and the Publishers believe the* LOTOS SERIES *will appeal to a wide class of readers.*

*It will be the aim of the Publishers to make the* LOTOS SERIES *a Pantheon of Literature which shall contain nothing but gems of the finest quality; and in limiting themselves to no period of the world's literature, and to no special branch or country, they will endeavour to select from all that is good the best.*

*Copyright works not hitherto accessible in cheap form, as well as reprints of older works of approved excellence, will be included in the Series.*

*Each Volume will be, as far as possible, complete in itself, with such additions or improvements upon other editions as to make them original in many important features, and distinguish them from any other editions that may be extant.*

*In fixing the price at 3s. 6d. per Volume, the Publishers will be enabled to create and keep up a high standard of excellence in the technical production of the Series. Each Volume will contain about 300 pages, and will be well printed on specially made paper, while, in some instances, illustrations by well-known artists will be added.*

*The Binding will be in two styles—(1) an artistically designed cloth cover in gold and colours, with gilt edges; and (2) half-parchment, cloth sides, with gilt top, uncut.*

*In addition to this ordinary issue,* a limited number of large-paper copies on Dutch hand-made paper *will be printed, which will be numbered and sold at an advanced price.*

*The size of the ordinary Edition will be 4¼ by 6¼ inches; the large-paper edition, 7¼ by 8¼ inches.*

### IN PREPARATION.

| THE BREITMANN BALLADS. | ESSAYS ON MEN AND BOOKS |
|---|---|
| By CHARLES G. LELAND. | SELECTED FROM THE WRITINGS OF LORD MACAULAY. |
| | With Portraits, and Critical Introduction and Notes, |
| Author's Copyright Edition, with a New Preface and | By ALEXANDER H. JAPP, LL.D., F.R.S.E. |
| additional Poems. | Author of "Life and Writings of Thomas de Quincey," "German Life and Literature," &c. |

*₀* The large paper edition of the above Volumes will be limited to **101** Numbered Copies for sale in England, price **12s. 6d.** each net. The Publishers reserve the right of raising the price of the last twenty copies.

*Other Volumes are in preparation and will be announced at an early date. Detailed Prospectus on application.*

LONDON: TRÜBNER & CO., 57 & 59, LUDGATE HILL.

# DAVID NUTT, 270, STRAND, LONDON.

*D. NUTT Publishes the following Periodicals:*

**The Babylonian and Oriental Record,** 12 Numbers a Year. Royal 8vo. double columns. Subscription, 12*s.* 6*d.* Post-free.

***** The *Babylonian and Oriental Record* (now in its third year of issue) publishes inedited texts, Cuneiform, Pahlavi, Cypriote, Hittite, etc., with Translations and Commentaries, besides Articles on all branches of research connected with the early Civilization of the East. The B. & O. Record is edited by Professor TERRIEN DE LACOUPERIE, who has issued in it many of his epoch-making researches on the derivation of Chinese civilization from Babylonia. Vols. I. and II. of the Record bound at 14*s.* each.

**The Archaeological Review,** 12 Numbers a Year. Royal 8vo. Subscription price, 21*s.* Post-free to Europe and the United States.

***** The *Archaeological Review* (now in its second year of issue) pays especial attention to Religious, Social and Economic Archaeology, branches of the study at present comparatively neglected in England and represented by no other Review. It also issues as a Supplement an Index, arranged under Authors' names, of the papers contributed to English Archaeological Periodicals and to the Publications of Archaeological Societies prior to 1886. Two Volumes are issued a year. Vols. I. and II. (each containing upwards of 500 pages) at 11*s.* 6*d.* each in cloth.

**The Classical Review,** 10 Numbers a Year. Royal 8vo. double columns. Subscription price, 13*s.* 6*d.* Post-free.

***** The *Classical Review* (now in its third year of issue) is the only English Periodical devoted to the systematic study of Classic Antiquity. It aims at supplying the Student with a full record and criticism of what is being done by Classical Scholarship in this Country, on the Continent and in America. Messrs. GINN, of Boston, are the American Publishers. Vols. I. and II. of the " Review " may be had bound at 12*s.* each.

**The Jewish Quarterly Review,** 4 Numbers a Year. Demy 8vo. Subscription price, 10*s.* Post-free.

***** The *Jewish Quarterly Review* (No. 1 of which was issued in October, 1888) aims at supplying a medium for the utterance of Jewish thought and Jewish research upon Jewish Literature and Theology, History and Philosophy. It has been most favourably received by organs of all shades of opinion, Jewish and Christian, the scholarly nature of its articles being freely acknowledged.

D. NUTT is the Publisher of **Professor Terrien de Lacouperie's** Works, which have thrown such new and unexpected light upon all questions connected with the Early History of China (The Languages of China before the Chinese. A few copies left at 10*s.* 6*d.* nett).

D. NUTT is the Publisher of the **Oriental Text Series,** edited by MR. E. A. WALLIS BUDGE, of the British Museum. The First Volume, comprising Inedited Coptic Texts relating to the Legend of St. George, with English Translation, 21*s.* nett.

D. NUTT is the Publisher of MR. E. A. WALLIS BUDGE'S **Egyptian Reading Book.** 10*s.* 6*d.* nett.

D. NUTT is the Publisher of the Second Edition of the REV. C. W. KING'S **Gnostics and their Remains,** entirely Rewritten and one-third larger both as regards Text and Illustrations than the Original Edition which used to fetch 36*s.* in sales. Price, handsomely bound in cloth, 21*s.*

D. NUTT is the Publisher of the Series **English History from Contemporary Writers,** in which the facts of the National History are told in the Words of the Men of the Period. Issued in 16mo. volumes, averaging 200 pages, each Volume dealing as a rule with a period of from Twenty to Thirty Years, each, in cloth neat, 1*s.* Four single and one double Volume are out.

D. NUTT imports all the latest Works Published on the Continent, and issues Catalogues of his Stock in French, German, Italian, Spanish, and Portuguese Literature, Theology, Classics, Educational Works, etc. Sent Post-free for Two Penny Stamps.

D. NUTT issues Six or Eight times a year Catalogues of his very rich **Second-Hand Stock** in all Departments of Theology, Philosophy, History, Literature and Philology. Catalogue No. XI., just issued, deals with the Languages and Literatures of the East. Sent Post-free on Application.

## TRÜBNER'S RECORD, No. 243.

### CONTENTS.

# MESSRS. MACMILLAN & CO.'S LIST.

## MACMILLAN'S COLONIAL LIBRARY
### Of Copyright Books for Circulation only in India and the Colonies.

1. BARKER, Lady.—Station Life in New Zealand.
2. BARKER, Lady.—A Year's Housekeeping in South Africa.
3. BLACK, WILLIAM.—A Princess of Thule.
4. CONWAY, HUGH.—A Family Affair.
5. CRAWFORD, F. M.—Mr. Isaacs: a Tale of Modern India.
6. CRAWFORD, F. MARION.—Dr. Claudius: a True Story.
7. CRAWFORD, F. MARION.—A Roman Singer.
8. CRAWFORD, F. MARION.—A Tale of a Lonely Parish.
9. EMERSON, RALPH WALDO.—The Conduct of Life.
10. FARRAR, Archdeacon F. W.—Seekers after God.
11. FORBES, ARCHIBALD, LL.D.—Souvenirs of some Continents.
12. HAMERTON, P. G.—Human Intercourse.
13. KEARY, ANNIE.—Oldbury.
14. JAMES, HENRY.—Tales of Three Cities.
15. MITFORD, A. B.—Tales of Old Japan.
16. OLIPHANT, Mrs.—A Country Gentleman.
17, 18, 19. OLIPHANT, Mrs.—Literary History of England in the end of the Eighteenth and beginning of the Nineteenth Century. 3 vols.
20. ST. JOHNSTON, ALFRED.—Camping among Cannibals.
21. MURRAY, D. CHRISTIE.—Aunt Rachel.
22. YONGE, CHARLOTTE M.—Chantry House.
23. HARRISON, FREDERIC.—The Choice of Books, and other Literary pieces.
24. THE AUTHOR OF "JOHN HALIFAX GENTLEMAN."—Miss Tommy.
25. MALET, LUCAS.—Mrs. Lorimer.
26. CONWAY, HUGH.—Living or Dead.
27. OLIPHANT, Mrs.—Effie Ogilvie.
28. HARRISON, JOANNA.—A Northern Lily.
29. NORRIS, W. E.—My Friend Jim.
30. LAWLESS, Hon. EMILY.—Hurrish: a Study.
31. THE AUTHOR OF "JOHN HALIFAX, GENTLEMAN."—King Arthur: Not a Love Story.
32. HARDY, THOMAS.—The Mayor of Casterbridge.
33. GRAHAM, JOHN W.—Neæra: a Tale of Ancient Rome.
34. MADOC, FAYR.—Margaret Jermine.
35. YONGE, CHARLOTTE M.—A Modern Telemachus.
36. SHORTHOUSE, J. HENRY.—Sir Percival.
37. OLIPHANT, Mrs.—A House Divided against Itself.
38. THE AUTHOR OF "JOHN HALIFAX, GENTLEMAN."—About Money and other Things.
39. BLACK, WILLIAM.—The Strange Adventures of a Phaeton.
40. ARNOLD, MATTHEW.—Essays in Criticism.
41. HUGHES, T.—Tom Brown's Schooldays.
42. YONGE, CHARLOTTE M.—The Dove in the Eagle's Nest.
43. OLIPHANT, Mrs.—A Beleaguered City.
44. MORLEY, JOHN.—Critical Miscellanies.
45. BRET HARTE.—A Millionaire of Rough-and-Ready, &c.
46. CRAWFORD, F. MARION.—Saracinesca.
47. VELEY, MARGARET.—A Garden of Memories, &c.
48. BLACK, WILLIAM.—Sabina Zembra.
49. HARDY, THOMAS.—The Woodlanders.
50. DILLWYN, E. A.—Jack.
51. DILLWYN, E. A.—Jack and Jill.
52. WESTBURY, HUGH.—Frederick Hazzleden.
53, 54. The New Antigone: A Romance. 2 vols.
55. BRET HARTE.—The Crusade of the "Excelsior."
56. CUNNINGHAM, H. S.—The Cœruleans: a Vacation Idyll.
57, 58. AUTHOR OF "HOGAN, M.P."—Ismay's Children. 2 vols.
59. CRAWFORD, F. MARION.—Zoroaster.
60. NOEL, Lady AUGUSTA.—Hithersea Mere.
61, 62. AUTHOR OF "ESTELLE RUSSELL.—Harmonia. 2 vols.
63. OLIPHANT, Mrs.—The Second Son.
64. CRAWFORD, F. MARION.—Marzio's Crucifix.
65. CRAWFORD, F. MARION.—Paul Patoff.
66. MARTINEAU, HARRIET.—Biographical Sketches.
67. AUTHOR OF "FRIENDS IN COUNCIL."—Realmah.
68. LAFARGUE, PHILIP.—The New Judgment of Paris: a Novel.
69. SHORTHOUSE, J. H.—A Teacher of the Violin, &c.
70. NORRIS, W. E.—Chris.
71. OLIPHANT, Mrs.—Joyce.
72. BRET HARTE.—The Argonauts of North Liberty.
73. CORBETT, JULIAN.—For God and Gold.
74. HARDY, THOMAS.—Wessex Tales.
75. FOTHERGILL, JESSIE.—The Lasses of Leverhouse: a Story.
76. CRAWFORD, F. MARION.—With the Immortals.
77. WARD, Mrs. HUMPHRY.—Robert Elsmere.
78. Fraternity: a Romance.
79. BRET HARTE.—Cressy.
80. MINTO, WILLIAM.—The Meditation of Ralph Hardelot.
81. MURRAY, D. CHRISTIE.—The Weaker Vessel.
82. SHORTHOUSE, J. H.—The Countess Eve.
83. YONGE, CHARLOTTE M.—Beechcroft at Rockstone.
84. WARD, Mrs. HUMPHRY, Author of "Robert Elsmere."—Miss Bretherton.
85. CORBETT, JULIAN.—Kophetua the Thirteenth.
86. AMIEL.—The Journal Intime of Henri Frédéric Amiel. Translated with an Introduction and Notes by Mrs. HUMPHRY WARD.
87. LEVY, AMY.—Reuben Sachs.
88. ARNOLD, MATTHEW.—Essays in Criticism. Second Series.
89. CRAWFORD, F. MARION.—Greifenstein.
90. OLIPHANT, Mrs.—Neighbours on the Green.
91. MURRAY, D. CHRISTIE.—Schwartz.
92. HAMERTON, P. G.—French and English: a Comparison.
93. An Author's Love. Being the Unpublished Letters of PROSPER MERIMEE's "Inconnue."

Volumes I., II., and III., with Portraits, now ready, crown 8vo., price 2s. 6d. each.

## ENGLISH MEN OF ACTION.

GENERAL GORDON. By Colonel Sir William Butler.

The *Spectator*:—"This is beyond all question the best of the narratives of the career of General Gordon that have yet been published."

HENRY THE FIFTH. By the Rev. A. J. Church.

LIVINGSTONE. By Mr. Thomas Hughes.

The Volumes to follow are:

LORD LAWRENCE. By Sir Richard Temple. [*In May.*    |    WELLINGTON. By Mr. George Hooper. [*In June.*

*** *Other Volumes are in the press or in preparation.*

Now Publishing. Crown 8vo. Price 2s. 6d. each.

## TWELVE ENGLISH STATESMEN.

The *Times* says:—"We had thought that the cheap issues of uniform volumes on all manner of subjects were being overdone, but the 'Twelve English Statesmen,' published by Messrs. Macmillan, induce us to reconsider that opinion. Without making invidious comparisons, we may say that nothing better of the sort has yet appeared, if we may judge by the five volumes before us. The names of the writers speak for themselves."

WILLIAM THE CONQUEROR. By Edward A. Freeman, D.C.L., LL.D. [*Ready.*  
HENRY II. By Mrs. J. R. Green. [*Ready.*  
EDWARD I. By F. York Powell.  
HENRY VII. By James Gairdner.  
CARDINAL WOLSEY. By Professor M. Creighton, M.A., D.C.L., LL.D.  
ELIZABETH. By E. S. Beesley. [*Ready.*  

OLIVER CROMWELL. By Frederic Harrison. [*Ready.*  
WILLIAM III. By H. D. Traill. [*Ready.*  
WALPOLE. By John Morley. [*Shortly.*  
CHATHAM. By John Morley.  
PITT. By John Morley. [*Shortly.*  
PEEL. By J. R. Thursfield. [*In the Press.*  

## A MAGAZINE FOR EVERY HOUSEHOLD.
"A Magazine which has no rival in England."—*The Times.*

# THE ENGLISH ILLUSTRATED MAGAZINE.

(PROFUSELY ILLUSTRATED). Single Numbers, price 6d.; Double Number, 1s.

THE ENGLISH ILLUSTRATED MAGAZINE is designed for the entertainment of the home, and for the instruction and amusement of young and old, and it is conducted in the belief that every section of its readers, in whatever direction their tastes and interests may tend, are prepared to demand and to appreciate the best that can be offered to them.

*The Volume for 1888 is now ready, price 8s. It consists of 822 pages, and contains nearly 400 Woodcut Illustrations.*

### MACMILLAN AND CO., LONDON

# PUBLICATIONS

OF

# MR. KARL I. TRÜBNER,

## STRASSBURG.

BENFEY, THEODOR, Vedica und Verwandtes. kl. 8vo. 177 S. 1877. M. 6.

———— ———— Vedica u. Linguistica. 1880. kl. 8vo. 278 S. M. 10 50.

BRUGMANN, KARL (ord. Professor der vergl. Sprachwissenschaft in Freiburg i. B.) Grundriss der vergleichenden Grammatik der indogermanischen Sprachen. Kurzgefasste Darstellung der Geschichte des Altindischen, Altiranischen (Avestischen u. Altpersischen), Altarmenischen, Altgriechischen, Lateinischen, Umbrisch-Samnitischen, Altirischen, Gotischen, Althochdeutschen, Litauischen und Altkirchenslavischen.
    Erster Band: Einleitung und Lautlehre. gr. 8vo. XVIII. u. 568 S. M. 14.
    Zweiter Band: Wortbildungslehre (Stammbildungs und Flexionslehre). 1. Hälfte: Vorbemerkungen, Nominalcomposita, Reduplicirte Nominalbildungen, Nomina mit stammbildenden Suffixen, Wurzelnomina. 8vo. XIV. u. 462 S. 1888. M. 12.

CAPPELLER, CARL (Professor der Sanskrit an der Universität Jena). Sanskrit-Wörterbuch. Nach den Petersburger Wörterbüchern bearbeitet. Lex. 8vo. VIII. u. 541 S. 1887. M. 15., geb. M. 17.

CATALOG der kaiserlichen Universitäts- und Landesbibliothek in Strassburg. Arabische Literatur. 4to. VI. 111 S. 1877. Verfasst von Dr. Julius Euting. M. 7 50.
Festschrift zur 400jähr. Jubelfeier der Eberhard-Karls-Universität zu Tübingen.

———— ———— Hebräische, arabische, persische u. türkische Handschriften, bearbeitet von Dr. S. Landauer. 4to. 75 S. 1881. M. 5.

DÜMICHEN, DR. JOHANNES, Baugeschichte des Denderatempels und Beschreibung der einzelnen Teile des Bauwerks nach den an seinen Mauern befindlichen Inschriften. kl. fol. 50 S. und 57 Tafeln Inschriften nebst 2 Plänen. 1877. M. 60.

———— ———— Die Oasen der libyschen Wüste. Ihre alten Namen und ihre Lage, ihre vorzüglichsten Erzeugnisse und die in ihren Tempeln verehrten Gottheiten, nach den Berichten der ägyptischen Denkmäler. 4 mit 19 Tafeln hieroglyphischer Inschriften und bildlicher Darstellungen in Autographie des Verfassers. 8vo. VI. 34 S. 1878. M. 15.

EUTING, JULIUS, Sechs phönikische Inschriften aus Idalion. 4to. 17 S. mit 3 Taf. 1875. M. 4.

———— ———— Sammlung der Carthagischen Inschriften, herausgegeben mit Unterstützung der k. Akademie der Wissenschaften zu Berlin. Band I. Tafeln 1-202 und Anhang, Tafel 1-6. In 4to. 1883. M. 60.

———— ———— Erläuterung einer zweiten Opferverordnung aus Carthago. Herrn Prof. Dr. H. J. Fleischer zur Feier seines fünfzigjährigen Doctorjubiläums als Gruss dargebracht. 8vo. 10 S. Mit 1 Tafel. 1874. M. 1 60.

EVANGELIEN, Die vier, arabisch aus der Wiener Handschrift herausgeg. von Paul de Lagarde. 8vo. XXXII. 143 S. 1864. (M. 5.) M. 3 50.
(Aus dem Verlag von B. G. Teubner in Leipzig in den meinigen übergegangen.)

HOLTZMANN, ADOLF, Agni nach den Vorstellungen des Mahâbhârata. 8vo. 36 S. 1878. M. 1.

HOLTZMANN, ADOLF, Arjuna. Ein Beitrag zur Reconstruction des Mahâbhârata. 8vo. 69 S. 1879. M. 1 60.

HÜBSCHMANN, H., Das indogermanische Vokalsystem. 8vo. 191 S. 1885. M. 4 50.

———— ———— Etymologie und Lautlehre der ossetischen Sprache. 8vo. VIII. 151 S. 1887. (Sammlung indogermanischer Wörterbücher, I.) M. 4.

KAUTZSCH, E. UND A. SOCIN, Die Aechtheit der moabitischen Altertümer, geprüft. Mit 2 Tafeln. 8vo. VIII. 191 S. 1876. M. 4.

KLUGE, FRIED., Etymologisches Wörterbuch der deutschen Sprache. Vierte, umgearbeitete und vermehrte Aufl. Lex. 8vo. XXIV. u. 453 S. 1889. brosch. M. 10. geb. in Hlbfrz. M. 12.

LAUTH, PROF. DR. JOS., Aegyptische Chronologie, basirt auf die vollständige Reihe der Epochen seit Bytes-Menes bis Hadrian-Antonin durch 3 volle Sothisperioden = 4380 Jahre. Autographirt. 8vo. VI. 240 S. 5 Tafeln. 1877. M. 10.

———— ———— Moses-Hosarsyphos Sali' Hus Levites-A'Haron frater Ziphorah-Dabariah conjux Miriam-Bellet soror Elisheba-Elisebat fratria. Ex monumento inferioris Aegypti per ipsum Mose abhinc annos MMMCD dedicato nunc primum in lucem produxit Franc. Jos. Lauth. Cum duabus tabulis et uno photogrammate. 4to. Lithogr. 248 S. 1879. M. 25.

LESKIEN, A., UND BRUGMANN, K., Litauische Volkslieder und Märchen, aus dem preussischen und dem russischen Litauen. 8vo. VIII. 578 S. 1882. M. 10.
    Inhalt: 1. Litauische Volkslieder aus der Gegend von Wilkischken, gesammelt von A. Leskien. 2. Litauische Lieder, Märchen, Hochzeitsbittersprüche aus Godlewa nebst Beiträgen zur Grammatik und zum Wortschatz der godlewischen Mundart herausgegeben von K. Brugmann. 3. Litauische Märchen, übersetzt von K. Brugmann, mit Anmerkungen von W. Wollner.

OSTHOFF, HERM., Zur Geschichte des Perfects im Indogermanischen mit besonderer Rücksicht auf Griechisch und Lateinisch. 8vo. X. u. 653 S. 1884. M. 14.

PRACANDAPANDAVA. Ein Drama des Râjaçekhara. Zum ersten Male herausgegeben von Carl Cappeller. 8vo. 50 S. 1885. M. 3 50.

RAVANAVAHA oder Setubandha, Prâkrit und Deutsch herausgegeben von Siegfried Goldschmidt. Mit einem Wortindex von Paul Goldschmidt und dem Herausgeber. Erste Lieferung. Text und Wortindex enthaltend. 4to. XXIV. u. 194 S. 1880. M. 25.
    Zweite Lieferung: Uebersetzung. 4to. 136 S. 1884. M. 18.

SABBAGH, MICHAIL, Grammatik der arabischen Vulgärdialecte von Syrien und Aegypten. Mit Anmerkungen herausgegeben von H. Thorbecke. 8vo. X. u. 80 S. 1886. M. 4.

VAITANA SUTRA, Das Ritual des Atharvaveda. Aus dem Sanskrit übersetzt und mit Anmerkungen versehen von Dr. phil. Richard Garbe. 8vo. V. 116 S. 1878. M. 4.

VAMANAS STILREGELN, bearbeitet von C. Capeller. Lex. 8vo. XII. u. 38 S. 1880. M. 1 50.

WHEELER, B. J., Der griechische Nominalaccent. Mit Wörterverzeichniss. 8vo. 146 S. 1885. M. 3 50.

## DETAILED CATALOGUES ON APPLICATION.

# SAMOAFAHRTEN.

### REISEN IN KAISER WILHELMS-LAND UND ENGLISCH-NEU-GUINEA

In den Jahren 1884 und 1885.

### AN BORD DES DEUTSCHEN DAMPFERS "SAMOA."

### VON DR. OTTO FINSCH.

Mit 85 Abbildungen nach Originalskizzen von Dr. Finsch, gezeichnet von M. Hoffmann und A. von Rössler,
6 Kartenskizzen und dem Porträt des Verfassers.

Geheftet, 12*s.*; gebunden, 14*s.* 6*d.*

*** Hierzu ist (einzeln käuflich) erschienen ein Wissenschaftlicher "*Ethnologischer Atlas.*" Typen aus
der Steinzeit Neu-Guineas, in 154 Abbildungen auf 24 lithographischen Tafeln, nach Originalen gezeichnet von
*O.* und *E. Finsch.* Mit erklärenden Text. Gebunden, 16*s.*

Verlag von Ferdinand Hirt & Sohn, Leipzig.

---

# *Official and other Authorized Publications.*

#### JUST ISSUED.

## GREAT BRITAIN.

### *Publications of the Royal Society.*

#### SEPARATE PAPERS FROM THE PHILOSOPHICAL TRANSACTIONS.

TITLE, CONTENTS, INDEX, LIST OF ILLUSTRATIONS, ADJUDICATION OF THE MEDALS, ETC. A. and B. Vol. 179, 1888. 4to. paper, pp. 24. Price 6*d.* each.

ON THE MECHANICAL CONDITIONS OF A SWARM OF METEORITES AND ON THEORIES OF COSMOGONY. By G. H. DARWIN, LL.D., F.R.S. 4to. paper, pp. 70. Price 3*s.*

ON THE PRESENT POSITION OF THE QUESTION OF THE SOURCES OF THE NITROGEN OF VEGETATION, WITH SOME NEW RESULTS AND PRELIMINARY NOTICE OF NEW LINES OF INVESTIGATION. By Sir J. B. LAWES, Bart., LL.D., F.R.S., and Prof. J. H. GILBERT, LL.D, F.R.S. 4to. paper, pp. 108. Price 4*s.* 6*d.*

### *Publications of the Trustees of the British Museum.*

CATALOGUE OF THE MARSUPIALIA AND MONOTREMATA IN THE COLLECTION OF THE BRITISH MUSEUM (NATURAL HISTORY). By OLDFIELD THOMAS. Demy 8vo. cloth, pp. xiv. and 402, with Twenty-eight Plates. Price £1 8*s.*

## INDIA.

### *Publications of the Geological Survey of India.*

A BIBLIOGRAPHY OF INDIAN GEOLOGY. Being a list of Books and Papers relating to the Geology of British India and adjoining Countries, published previous to the end of A.D. 1887. Compiled by R. D. Oldham, A.R.S.M., F.G.S. Super-royal 8vo. wrappers, pp. xiv. and 146. Price 3*s.*

### *Publications of the Indian Meteorological Office.*

INDIAN METEOROLOGICAL MEMOIRS. Being Occasional Discussions and Compilations of Meteorological Data relating to India and the Neighbouring Countries. Published by order of His Excellency the Viceroy and Governor-General of India in Council, under the direction of HENRY F. BLANFORD, F.R.S., Meteorological Reporter to the Government of India. Vol. 3, Part III. The Rainfall of India. Super-royal 4to, wrapper, pp. 368. Price 8*s.* Vol. 3, Part IV. The Rainfall of India. Super-royal 4to. wrapper, pp. 40. Price 3*s.* Vol. 4, Part IV. List and Brief Account of the South-west Monsoon Storms Generated in the Bay of Bengal, during the years 1882 to 1886. The Cyclonic Storms of November and December, 1888, in the Bay of Bengal. Super-royal 4to. wrapper, pp. 98, with Fourteen Plates. Price 6*s.* Vol. 4, Part V. The Cyclone of the 25th May to the 2nd June, 1888, in the Arabian Sea. Super-royal 4to. wrapper, pp. 100, with Fourteen Plates. Price 6*s.*

CHARTS OF THE ARABIAN SEA AND THE ADJACENT PORTION OF THE NORTHERN OCEAN. Showing the Mean Pressure, Winds and Currents in each Month of the Year. Published by order of His Excellency the Viceroy and Governor-General of India in Council. By the Meteorological Department of the Government of India. Oblong folio, pp. 28, with Twelve Plates, cloth. Price 10*s.*

## AUSTRALIA.

### *Publications of the Government of Victoria.*

NATURAL HISTORY OF VICTORIA. Prodromus of the Zoology of Victoria; or, Figures and Descriptions of the Living Species of all Classes of the Victorian Indigenous Animals. By FREDERICK McCOY, C.M.G., M.A., Sc.D. Cantab, F.R.S. DECADE XVII. Royal 8vo. wrappers, pp. 42, with Ten Coloured Plates and Descriptive Letterpress. Price 5*s.*

LONDON: TRÜBNER & CO., AGENTS BY APPOINTMENT, 57 AND 59, LUDGATE HILL.

# THE CALCUTTA REVIEW.

Edited by H. A. D. PHILLIPS, C.S.

No. CLXXV. January, 1889. CONTENTS:—The Working of the Arms' Act (XI of 1878) in the Lower Provinces. By G. Toynbee, C.S.—The Police of Calcutta. By A. H. Giles.—The Out-Still Question in Bengal. By the Editor.—The Land Acquisition Act, and the Law of Compensation. By A. Caspersz.—Taxation in India. By Mohiny Mohun Roy.—Moral Education for Young India. By Rev. T. J. Scott.—The Confessions of St. Augustine.—The Tyranny of Law in Bengal. By F. H. Barrow.—Roads in Bengal. By R. Carstairs.—The National Congress Movement. By an Indian Taxpayer.—An Outline Sketch of the Viceroyalty of the Marquis of Dufferin and Ava.—The Public Service Commission and Judicial Reform. By T. D. Beighton.—The Quarter. By the Editor.—Summary of Annual Reports.—Critical Notices.—General Literature.

Single parts, 6s. Annual Subscription, 24s.

# THE CHINA MEDICAL MISSIONARY JOURNAL.

Vol. II. No. 4. December, 1888. CONTENTS:—Medical Missions. By J. G. Kerr, M.D.—The P'ing Tu Mining Accident. By Robert Coltman.—Reminiscences. By Rev. A. W. Douthwaite, M.D., F.R.G.S.—Random Clinical Notes. By Q.—Cases treated in the Medical Missionary Society's Hospital, Canton. By J. G. Kerr, M.D.—Notes on Cholera in North America—Summer of 1888. By A.P. Pech, M.A., M.D.—Notes on Chinese Materia Medica. By A. W. Douthwaite, M.D.—Cases treated in the London Mission "Viceroy's" Hospital, Tientsien. By the late J. K. Mackenzie, M.R.C.S., L.R.C.P.—Rev. Peter Parker, M.D., First Medical Missionary to China, and Dr. Kwan A-to, First Chinese Surgeon. By J. C. Thomson, M.D. (Illustrated).—Correspondence.—Therapeutic Notes.—Editorials.—Valedictory.—Results of Election.—Official Notice.—Hospital Reports.—Items and Notes.

Quarterly. Annual Subscription, 12s.

# CHINESE RECORDER AND MISSIONARY JOURNAL.

Vol. XX. No. 1. January, 1889. Photograph of Rev. Dr. Yates.—The Moravians and their Missions. By Rev. H. Blodget.—Mohammedanism in China. By Rev. H. V. Noyes.—Missionary Organization in China. By Rev. A. Williamson.—The Proposed Missionary Conference of 1890. By Rev. E. Faber.—Self-Immolation by Fire in China.—Errata and Addenda. By D. J. Macgowan.—Correspondence.—Our Book Table.—Editorial Notes and Missionary News.—Diary.—Events in the Far East.—Missionary Journal.

Monthly. Annual Subscription, 15s.

# THE INDIAN ANTIQUARY.

Part CCXV. Vol. XVII. December, 1888. Part I. CONTENTS—The Use of the Twelve-year Cycle of Jupiter in Records of the early Gupta Period. By J. F. Fleet, Bo. C.S.—Weber's Sacred Literature of the Jains, translated by Dr. H. W. Smyth.—Folk-Lore in Southern India. By Pandit S. M. Natesa Sastri, M.F.L.S.—Miscellanea.—Rambles among Ruins in Central India. By W. Kincaid.—Progress of European Scholarship, No. XI. By W. R. Morfill.—Notes and Queries.—Note on the Derivation of Gutta Percha. By W. E. Maxwell.

Part CCXVII. Vol. XVIII. January, 1889. CONTENTS:—The Inscriptions of Piyadasi. By E. Senart. Translated by G. A. Grierson.—Copper-Plate Grants of the Kings of Kanauj. By Prof. F. Kielhorn.—Folk-Lore in Western India. No. XIII. By Putlibai D. H. Wadia.—Miscellanea.—Notes and Queries.—Book Notice.

Part CCXVI. Vol. XVII. December, 1888. Part 2. will be issued later (in about two months), according to the Index and Register published in it.

Monthly. Annual Subscription, 36s.

LONDON: TRÜBNER & CO., 57 AND 59, LUDGATE HILL.

# NEW WORKS OF FICTION.

### NOW READY.

ULLI: THE STORY OF A NEGLECTED GIRL. Translated from the German of Emma Biller. By A. B. DAISY ROST. Crown 8vo. cloth, pp. viii. and 304. Price 5s.

YANKEE GIRLS IN ZULU LAND. By LOUISE VESCELIUS-SHELDON. With One Hundred Photogravure Illustrations by G. E. GRAVES, from Original Sketches by J. AUSTEN. Crown 8vo. cloth, with Portraits of the Sisters, pp. 287. Price 9s.

UNCLE PIPER OF PIPER'S HILL. An Australian Novel. By TASMA. Second Edition, crown 8vo. cloth, pp. viii. and 348. Price 6s.

THE UNFORTUNATE ONE. A Novel. By IVAN TOORGEYNIEFF. Translated from the Russian by A. R. THOMPSON. Crown 8vo. cloth, pp. 134. Price 3s. 6d.

THE AUTOBIOGRAPHY OF MARK RUTHERFORD AND MARK RUTHERFORD'S DELIVERANCE. Edited by his Friend, REUBEN SHAPCOTT. Third Edition, crown 8vo. cloth, pp. x. and 323. Price 7s. 6d.

### IN THE PRESS.

GIRLALDI. A Tale of the Sects. By ROSS DERING. In Two Volumes.

THE WING OF AZRAEL. By MONA CAIRD. In Three Volumes.

LONDON: TRÜBNER & CO., 57 AND 59, LUDGATE HILL.

# NEW ORIENTAL PUBLICATIONS.

Royal 8vo. cloth. Price £4 8s. 6d.

## A GRAMMAR OF THE CLASSICAL ARABIC LANGUAGE.

Translated and Compiled from the Works of
the Most Approved Native or Naturalized Authorities.
By MORTIMER SLOPER HOWELL.
The following Parts are published : Part I. 1. £1 8s.
Part II. 2. £1 1s.
Parts II. and III. (bound together) £1 11s. 6d.

Demy 8vo. sewed, Two Volumes. Price 3s. 6d. each vol.

## A COLLECTION OF STORIES.

(Taken from the KITAB EL-AGHANI.)

روايات الأغانب

Edited by P. A. SALHANI, de la Compagnie de Jésus,
Beirut.

Post 8vo. sewed. Part I. to XLVI. 3s. each part.

## THE MAHABHARATA

OF KRISHNA-DWAIPAYANA VYASA.
Translated into English Prose.
Published by PRATAP CHANDRA ROY.

The work is published bimonthly.
Price of Part I. to XLV., 3s.
The New Parts can now be supplied at 1s. 6d. each.

*Bombay Sanskrit Series.*
VOL. XXXVII.
Post 8vo. sewed, pp. 7, 757. Price 12s. 6d.

## THE PADDHATI OF SARNGADHARA.

A SANSKRIT ANTHOLOGY,
Edited by PETER PETERSON, M.A.
Vol I.—The Text.
Vol. II. containing an Introduction, Various Readings,
and Notes, will be published in the course of this year.

Two Vols. in One. Small 8vo. cloth, pp. 200 and 214.
Price 3s. 6d.

## THE POPULAR DICTIONARY

IN ENGLISH AND HINDUSTANI and HINDUSTANI AND
ENGLISH.
With a Number of Useful Tables.
Compiled by the Rev. T. CRAVEN, M.A.

8vo. sewed, pp. 64. Price 3s.

## A GRAMMAR OF THE BURMESE LANGUAGE.

By A. JUDSON.
Fourth Edition.

## IN PREPARATION.

Royal 4to. Ten Volumes. Price about Six Guineas.
TAJ - AL - ARUS.

تاج العروس

(ARABIC DICTIONARY.) NEW EDITION.

Royal 8vo. cloth. About 1100 pages. Price about 18s.

## THE PRACTICAL SANSKRIT-ENGLISH DICTIONARY,

Etymological, Philological, and Referential.
Being the Cheapest Comprehensive Sanskrit-English
Dictionary yet Published.
By VAMAN SHIVARAM APTE, M.A.,
Principal and Professor of Sanskrit, Fergusson College,
Poona.

Post 8vo. boards, pp. iv. 65. Price 7s. 6d.

## CHINESE WITHOUT A TEACHER.

Being a Collection of Easy and Useful Sentences in the
Mandarin Dialect. With a Vocabulary.
By HERBERT A. GILES.
Second Enlarged Edition.

Post 8vo. half-bound. Price £1 10s.

## THE PROVERBS AND COMMON SAYINGS OF THE CHINESE.

By ARTHUR H. SMITH,
North China Mission of the American Board.

Royal 8vo. paper, pp. 104, price 1s.

## DEMOCRACY NOT SUITED TO INDIA.

By THE RAJA OF BHINGA, Oudh.

Medium 8vo. paper, pp. viii. and 128, price 2s.

## ESSAYS ON INDIAN TOPICS.

By THEODORE BECK,
Principal of the Mahomedan Anglo-Oriental College, Aligarh.

Post 8vo. boards, pp. viii. 97. Price 2s.

## SERIOUS CRIME IN AN INDIAN PROVINCE.

By EUSTACE J. KITTS, B.C.S.
1. Introduction. 2. Murder. 3. Dacoity. 4. Robbery.
5. Cattle-Theft. 6. House-Breaking and Theft. 7. Crime
and Criminals now and Forty Years Ago. 8 & 9. Appendices and Index.

Royal 8vo. pp. ix. 122, xliii. Price 2s.
*Pamphlets issued by the United Indian Patriotic
Association.*

No. 2.
SHOWING THE SEDITIOUS CHARACTER OF THE
### INDIAN NATIONAL CONGRESS
AND THE OPINIONS HELD BY EMINENT NATIVES OF
INDIA WHO ARE OPPOSED TO THE MOVEMENT.

Demy 8vo. sewed, pp. ii. 193. Price 5s.

## IMPERIAL UNIVERSITY OF JAPAN

(TEIKOKU DAIGAKU).
The CALENDAR for the Year 1888—89.
XXI—XXII Year of Meiji.

Demy 8vo. about 350 pages.

## A SINHALESE GRAMMAR FOR EUROPEAN STUDENTS.

By ABRAHAM MENDIS GUNASEKARA,
Of the Land Registration Department, Ceylon.

PHARMACOGRAPHIA INDICA.

## A HISTORY OF THE PRINCIPAL DRUGS

OF VEGETABLE ORIGIN
MET WITH IN BRITISH INDIA.
By WILLIAM DYMOCK, C. J. H. WARDEN,
and DAVID HOOPER.

# TRÜBNER AND CO.'S LIST.

**NOW READY.**

Crown 8vo. cloth, pp. 262. Price 6s.
NAPLES IN 1888. By EUSTACE NEVILLE ROLFE, and HOLCOMBE INGLEBY. With Illustrations by H. J. I.

Crown 8vo. cloth, pp. xii. and 308. Price 7s. 6d.
IMPERIAL GERMANY. A CRITICAL STUDY OF FACT AND CHARACTER. By SIDNEY WHITMAN.

8vo. cloth, pp. xx. and 306. Price 12s.
LETTERS OF FELIX MENDELSSOHN TO IGNAZ and CHARLOTTE MOSCHELES. Translated from the Originals in his possession, and Edited by FELIX MOSCHELES. With numerous Illustrations and Fac-similes.

Crown 8vo. cloth, pp. xiv. and 138. Price 7s. 6d.
INDIA.—A DESCRIPTIVE POEM. By H. B. W. GARRICK, Assistant Archæologist to the Government of India.

Crown 8vo. cloth, pp. viii. and 288. Price 1s. 6d. ; paper covers, 1s.
THE APOSTLES. By ERNEST RENAN. Translated from the Original French. New Cheap Edition. Uniform in size and price with the Popular Edition of the " Life of Jesus."

Crown 8vo. cloth, pp. xvi. and 246. Price 10s.
NUCES ETYMOLOGICÆ. By R. S. CHARNOCK, Ph.D., F.S.A., F.R.G.S.

Crown 8vo. cloth, pp. 191. Price 3s. 6d.
COUNT TOLSTOI AS NOVELIST AND THINKER. Lectures delivered at the Royal Institution by CHARLES EDWARD TURNER.

Second Edition, demy 8vo. cloth, pp. xii. and 400. Price 9s.
THE MORAL IDEAL. A HISTORICAL STUDY. By JULIA WEDGWOOD.

Crown 8vo. boards, pp. ix. and 95. Price 3s. 6d.
IRRESPONSIBILITY AND ITS RECOGNITION. By A GRADUATE OF OXFORD.

Demy 8vo. cloth, pp. xxiii. and 480. Price £1 5s.
SOCIAL HISTORY OF THE RACES OF MANKIND. THIRD DIVISION. *AONEO-MARANONIANS.* By A. FEATHERMAN.

8vo. cloth, pp. xviii. and 677. Illustrated. Price £1 1s.
INDIAN MYTHS ; Or, Legends, Traditions and Symbols of the Aborigines of America compared with those of other Countries, including Hindostan, Egypt, Persia, Assyria, and China. By ELLEN RUSSELL EMERSON.

Demy 8vo. cloth, pp. xiv. and 266. Price 6s.
THE BACON-SHAKSPEARE QUESTION ANSWERED. By C. STOPES. Second Edition, Corrected and Enlarged.

Fcap. 4to. pp. xvi. and 174, cloth. Price 10s. 6d.
THE GOSPEL OF ST. MATTHEW. IN FORMOSAN (SINKANG DIALECT). With Corresponding Versions in Dutch and English. Edited from Gravius's Edition of 1661 by the Rev. WM. CAMPBELL, M.R.A.S.

Demy 8vo. cloth, pp. x. and 150. Price 5s.
THE EVOLUTION OF THE HEBREW LANGUAGE. By JOSEPH EDKINS, D.D.

New Edition. Crown 8vo. cloth, pp. 213. Price 5s.
WATER ANALYSIS. A PRACTICAL TREATISE ON THE EXAMINATION OF POTABLE WATER. By J. ALFRED WANKLYN, M.R.C.S., and E. T. CHAPMAN, M.R.C.S.

Fourth Edition, crown 8vo. cloth, pp. 212. Price 12s.
A GRAMMAR OF THE JAPANESE SPOKEN LANGUAGE. By W. G. ASTON, M.A., H.B.M.'s Legation, Tokio, Japan.

8vo. cloth, pp. xxv. and 551, price 12s.
A SANSKRIT GRAMMAR, including both the Classical Language, and the Older Dialects, of Veda and Brahmana. By WILLIAM DWIGHT WHITNEY. Second Revised and Extended Edition.

8vo. cloth, pp. 486, price 12s. 6d.
HANDBOOK OF COLLOQUIAL JAPANESE. By BASIL HALL CHAMBERLAIN.

Vol. VI. Completing the Work. 8vo. cloth, pp. vii. and 436. Price £1 1s.
THE RIG-VEDA SANHITA. A COLLECTION OF ANCIENT HINDU HYMNS, Constituting Part of the Seventh and Eighth Ashṭaka of the Rig-Veda. Translated from the Original Sanskrit by H. H. WILSON, M.A., F.R.S. Edited by W. F. WEBSTER, M.A.

Part III. Demy 4to. boards, pp. 96. Price 5s.
A DICTIONARY OF THE TARGUMIM, THE TALMUD BABLI AND YERUSHALMI AND THE MIDRASHIC LITERATURE. Compiled by M. JASTROW, Ph.D.

Demy 8vo. cloth, pp. iv. and 104. Price 5s.
TARGUM ON ISAIAH I.—V. *With Commentary.* By HARRY S. LEWIS, B.A.

*Trübner's Oriental Series.*

In Two Vols. post 8vo. cloth, pp. l., 408 and 431. Price £1 16s.
ALBERUNI'S INDIA. An Account of the Religion, Philosophy, Literature, Geography, Chronology, Astronomy, Customs, Laws, and Astrology of India about A.D. 1030. An English Edition, with Notes and Indices. By Dr. EDWARD C. SACHAU, Professor in the Royal University of Berlin, and Principal of the Seminary for Oriental Languages ; etc., etc.

Post 8vo. cloth, pp. xxvii. and 218. Price 10s.
THE LIFE OF HIUEN TSIANG. By the SHAMANS HWUI LI and YEN-TSUNG. With a Preface containing an account of the Works of I-Tsing. By SAMUEL BEAL, B.A. (Trin. Coll. Camb.); Professor of Chinese, University College, London, etc.

*Trübner's Series of Simplified Grammars.*

Edited by Dr. Rost, Librarian of the India Office.

Crown 8vo. cloth, pp. vi. and 136, price 7s. 6d.
A SIMPLIFIED GRAMMAR AND READING BOOK OF THE PANJABI LANGUAGE. By the Rev. WM. ST. CLAIR TISDALL, M.A., C.M.S.

LONDON TRÜBNER & CO., 57 AND 59 LUDGATE HILL.

# TRÜBNER AND CO.'S LIST.

## WORKS IN PREPARATION.

*Crown 8vo.*

DAYS WITH INDUSTRIALS. ADVENTURES AND EXPERIENCES AMONG CURIOUS INDUSTRIES. By ALEXANDER H. JAPP, LL.D., F.R.S.E., Author of "Industrial Curiosities," "Golden Lives," etc.

*Crown 8vo.*

THE FLOWERS OF THE NIGHT AND OTHER POEMS. By Mrs. PFEIFFER.

*Demy 8vo.*

SOUTH AFRICAN BUTTERFLIES. A MONOGRAPH OF THE EXTRA-TROPICAL SPECIES. By ROLAND TRIMEN, F.R.S., F.L.S., F.Z.S., F.Ent.S., etc. Curator of the South African Museum, Cape Town. Assisted by JAMES HENRY BOWKER, F.Z.S., F.R.G.S., etc. Vol. III. completing the Work.

*Demy 8vo.*

THE YEAR BOOK OF AUSTRALIA FOR 1889. Edited by EDWARD GREVILLE, J.P. EIGHTH YEAR OF PUBLICATION.

*With Illustrations, crown 8vo. about 250 pages.*

AN ACCOUNT OF MISSIONARY SUCCESS IN THE ISLAND OF FORMOSA. Published in London in 1650, and now reprinted, with Preface, by the REV. WILLIAM CAMPBELL, F.R.G.S.

*Crown 8vo.*

AIR ANALYSIS. A PRACTICAL TREATISE ON THE EXAMINATION OF AIR. With Appendix on Coal Gas. By J. A. WANKLYN and W. J. COOPER.

*Crown 8vo.*

CHRISTIANITY AND ISLAM. By ERNEST DE BUNSEN.

*8vo.*

AN ARABIC-ENGLISH DICTIONARY. ON A NEW AND UNIQUE SYSTEM. Comprising about 120,000 Arabic Words; with an English Index of about 50,000 Words. By H. A. SALMONÉ, Arabic Lecturer at University College, London.

*8vo.*

ARABIC-ENGLISH READING BOOK. By H. A. SALMONÉ and H. PRIESTLY, B.A., Late Bengal Civil Service.

*8vo.*

THE ITALIC DIALECTS. I. THE TEXT OF THE INSCRIPTIONS. (Oscan, Paelignian, Sabine, etc.; the oldest Latin and Faliscan; Volscian. Picentine and Umbrian). II. AN ITALIC LEXICON. Being a Complete Concordance to Part I., and giving the Meaning of all Words whose Interpretation is certain. With the Italic Glosses of Varro and Festus, and a Dialect Map. Edited and Arranged by R. SEYMOUR CONWAY, M.A., Fellow of Gonville and Caius College, Classical Lecturer at Newnham College, Author of "Verner's Law in Italy."

*A NEW EDITION. 8vo.*

A GRAMMAR OF THE BURMESE LANGUAGE. By A. JUDSON.

## TRÜBNER'S SERIES OF SIMPLIFIED GRAMMARS.

*Edited By Dr. ROST, Librarian to the India Office.*

*Crown 8vo.*

A SIMPLIFIED TELUGU GRAMMAR. By HENRY MORRIS, M.A.

*Crown 8vo.*

A SIMPLIFIED GRAMMAR OF THE SPANISH LANGUAGE. By W. F. HARVEY, M.A.

*Crown 8vo.*

A SIMPLIFIED CHINESE GRAMMAR. By JOSEPH EDKINS, D.D.

*Crown 8vo.*

A SIMPLIFIED GRAMMAR OF THE BULGARIAN LANGUAGE. By W. L. MORFILL, M.A.

*Crown 8vo.*

A SIMPLIFIED GUJARATI GRAMMAR. By the Rev. WM. ST. CLAIR TISDALL, M.A., Late Principal C.M.S. Training College, Amritsar.

## TRÜBNER'S ORIENTAL SERIES.

*Post 8vo.*

A SKETCH OF THE MODERN LANGUAGES OF OCEANIA. By R. N. CUST, LL.D.

*Post 8vo.*

MISCELLANEOUS PAPERS relating to INDO-CHINA and the INDIAN ARCHIPELAGO. Third Series. Reprinted for the Straits Branch of the Royal Asiatic Society, and Edited by R. ROST, Ph.D., etc., etc., Librarian to the India Office.

*Post 8vo.*

DACAKUMARACARITA OF DANDIN. Translated by EDWARD J. RAPSON.

*Post 8vo.*

A MANUAL OF INDIAN PANTHEISM. THE VEDANTASARA. Translated, with Copious Annotations, By MAJOR G. A. JACOB, B.S.C. With Preface by E. B. COWELL, M.A., Professor of Sanskrit in Cambridge University. A New Edition.

## THE ENGLISH & FOREIGN PHILOSOPHICAL LIBRARY.

*In Two Volumes, post 8vo.*

JOHANN GOTTLIEB FICHTE'S POPULAR WORKS. THE NATURE OF THE SCHOLAR; THE VOCATION OF SCHOLAR; THE VOCATION OF MAN; THE DOCTRINE OF RELIGION; CHARACTERISTICS OF THE PRESENT AGE. With a Memoir by WILLIAM SMITH, LL.D.

*Post 8vo.*

THE SCIENCE OF KNOWLEDGE. By J. G. FICHTE. Translated from the German by A. E. KROEGER. With an Introduction by Professor W. T. HARRIS.

*Post 8vo.*

THE SCIENCE OF RIGHTS. By J. G. FICHTE. Translated from the German by A. E. KROEGER. With an Introduction by Professor W. T. HARRIS.

*Post 8vo.*

THE PHILOSOPHY OF LAW. By Professor DIODATO LIOY. Translated by W. HASTIE.

*Post 8vo.*

MORAL ORDER AND PROGRESS: AN ANALYSIS OF ETHICAL CONCEPTIONS. By S. ALEXANDER, Fellow of Lincoln College, Oxford.

# MR. T. FISHER UNWIN'S SELECTED LIST.

## The STORY of the NATIONS.

Crown 8vo. cloth, Illustrated, and furnished with Maps and Indexes.
6s. each.
Presentation Edition, gilt edges, 8s. 6d.

*Vol. XIX. Now Ready.*

### MEDIA.

By ZENAIDE A. RAGOZIN, Author of "Assyria," "Chaldea," etc.

"That useful series."
*The Times.*
"An admirable series."
*Spectator.*
"That excellent series."
*Guardian.*
"The series is likely to be found indispensable in every school library."
*Pall Mall Gazette.*
"This valuable series."
*Nonconformist.*

"Your useful series."
Rev. W. GUNION RUTHERFORD, M.A., Head Master of Westminster.
"Written by such men and illustrated so liberally, they give promise of being both useful and attractive."
Rev. GEORGE C. BELL, M.A., Head Master of Marlborough.

1. ROME. By ARTHUR GILMAN, M.A. 3rd Edition.
"The author succeeds admirably in reproducing the 'Grandeur that was Rome.'"—*Sydney Morning Herald.*

2. THE JEWS. By Prof. J. K. HOSMER. 2nd Edition.
"The book possesses much of the interest, the suggestiveness, and the charm of romance."—*Saturday Review.*

3. GERMANY. By Rev. S. BARING-GOULD. 3rd Edition.
"Mr. Baring-Gould tells his stirring tale, with knowledge and perspicuity. He is a thorough master of his subject."—*Globe.*
"A decided success."—*Athenæum.*

4. CARTHAGE. By Prof. ALFRED J. CHURCH. 3rd Ed.
"Told with admirable lucidity."—*Observer.*
"A masterly outline with vigorous touches in detail here and there.—*Guardian.*

5. ALEXANDER'S EMPIRE. By Prof. J. P. MAHAFFY. 3rd Edition.
"An admirable epitome."—*Melbourne Argus.*

6. THE MOORS IN SPAIN. By STANLEY LANE-POOLE. 3rd Edition.
"The best on the subject that we have in English."—*Athenæum.*
"Well worth reading."—*Times of Morocco.*

7. ANCIENT EGYPT. By Prof. G. RAWLINSON. 3rd Ed.
"The story is told of the land, people, and rulers, with vivid colouring and consummate literary skill."—*New York Critic.*

8. HUNGARY. By Prof. ARMINIUS VAMBERY. 2nd Ed.
"The volume which he has contributed to 'The Story of the Nations' will generally be considered one of the most interesting and picturesque of that useful series."—*Times.*

9. THE SARACENS. By ARTHUR GILMAN, M.A.
"Le livre de M. Gilman est destiné à être lu avidement par un grand nombre de gens pour lesquels l'étude des nombreux ouvrages déjà parus serait impossible."—*Journal des Debats.*

10. IRELAND. By the Hon. EMILY LAWLESS. 2nd Edition.
"This clear and temperate narrative."—*Spectator.*

11. CHALDEA. By ZENAIDE A. RAGOZIN.
"This is an excellent book."—*Academy.*

12. THE GOTHS. By H. BRADLEY.
"Most learned and satisfactory. . . . . Mr. Bradley's account of the Goths in Spain is particularly good."—*Athenæum.*

13. ASSYRIA. By ZENAIDE A. RAGOZIN.
"Assyrian life has become a reality in her hands. Assyriologists, as well as the general public, will find her book a charming one to read."—*Extract from Letter from Prof. Sayce.*

14. TURKEY. By STANLEY LANE-POOLE.
"He has succeeded well, and is decidedly to be congratulated on having presented a succinct, interesting, and fairly full account of the rise of Ottoman power."—*Athenæum.*

15. HOLLAND. By Prof. J. E. THOROLD ROGERS. 2nd Edition.
"A more interesting volume has not hitherto been contributed to the admirable 'Story of the Nations.'"—*Morning Post.*

16. MEDIÆVAL FRANCE. By GUSTAVE MASSON.
"The book is as instructive as it is interesting."—*Schoolmaster.*

17. PERSIA. By G. S. W. BENJAMIN.
"Told with good literary skill and with ample and accurate knowledge."—*Scotsman.*

18. PHŒNICIA. By Prof. G. RAWLINSON.
"Is full of knowledge and thoroughly readable."—*Saturday Review.*

OTHER VOLUMES IN PREPARATION.—PROSPECTUS POST FREE.

SECOND EDITION, with NEW PREFACE, just ready.

## The Life and Times of Savonarola.

By Professor PASQUALE VILLARI.    Translated by LINDA VILLARI.
Many Portraits and Illustrations. 2 vols. demy 8vo. cloth, 32s.
"Thus to the advantages in the mode of presentation are added the author's learning, research, unfailing enthusiasm restrained by scholarly feeling, and an easy style. . . . A book which is not likely to be forgotten."—*Athenæum.*

In preparation, SECOND EDITION. Small demy 8vo. cloth, 12s.

## English Wayfaring Life in the Middle Ages (FOURTEENTH CENTURY).

By J. J. JUSSERAND.    Translated by LUCY TOULMIN SMITH.
"Now the book appears in an English form and with its English title, very much increased in bulk, and one of the best illustrated volumes of the season—dressed, in fact, in purple and fine linen—a pleasure to handle, a joy to read; and bearing with it, when one gets to the end of it, a conviction that one has become a much more learned man than one was a week ago, for that somehow one has absorbed a great deal that the outer world knows little about. Pray do not order this volume at the library. Buy it, if you are wise; and keep it as a joy for ever."—Dr. JESSOPP, in the *Nineteenth Century*, February.

Crown 8vo. cloth, 6s.

## Indian Life: Religious and Social.

By JOHN CAMPBELL OMAN, Professor of Natural Science in the Government College, Lahore.
"We have seldom come across a work more readable, the view of India presented by it is a truthful one conveyed in pleasant form."—*Athenæum.*

SECOND YEAR OF ISSUE. Now ready, crown 8vo. cloth, 6s.

## The Government Year Book, 1889.

A Yearly Record of the Forms and Methods of Government in Great Britain, her Colonies, and Foreign Countries. With an Introduction on the Diffusion of the Popular Government over the Surface of the Globe, and on the Nature and Extent of International Jurisdiction.
Edited by LEWIS SERGEANT.
"As a handy book of reference for members of Parliament and literary men it is invaluable."—*European Mail.*

London : T. FISHER UNWIN, 26, Paternoster Square, E.C.

# SPENCER BLACKETT'S LIST.

**H. RIDER HAGGARD'S NEW WORKS.**
Now ready at all Libraries. Price 6s. each.

**MR. MEESON'S WILL.** Sixteen full-page Plates.

**DAWN.** By Author of "Jess," "Allan Quatermain," etc.

**THE WITCH'S HEAD.** By H. Rider Haggard.

**THE PREMIER AND THE PAINTER.** By John Freeman Bell. Second and Cheaper Edition, at all Booksellers. 3s. 6d. cloth.

**NEW NOVEL BY FRANK DANBY.**
At all Libraries. 6s.

**A BABE IN BOHEMIA.** By Frank Danby, Author of " Dr. Philips," etc.

**IMPORTANT WORK ON INDIA.**
At all Libraries, One Vol., Crown 8vo. 7s. 6d. Illustrated.

**AN INDIAN OLIO.** By Lieut.-Gen. E. F. Burton (of the Madras Staff Corps), Author of " Reminiscences of Sport in India," etc.

At all Libraries. Two Vols. 21s.

**THE BULBUL AND THE BLACK SNAKE.** By Louis D'Aguilar Jackson.

**A STORY OF ENGLISH COUNTRY LIFE.**
At all Libraries. One Vol. 7s. 6d.

**NEWTON DOGVANE.** By Francis Francis, Author of "A Book on Angling," etc. With Original Illustrations by John Leech. Coloured by hand.

**CHEAP EDITIONS OF POPULAR NOVELS.**
2s. boards ; 2s. 6d. cloth.

**A LOMBARD STREET MYSTERY.** By Muirhead Robertson.

**THE GAY WORLD.** By Joseph Hatton.

**NAN.** By L. B. Walford, Author of "Mr. Smith," etc., etc.

**CORINNA.** By " Rita."

Mr. Spencer Blackett has also arranged to issue a cheap and Popular Edition of the whole of Mrs. WALFORD'S Novels in cloth style only at 2s. 6d., tastefully bound, with Plate.

**POPULAR SHILLING NOVELS.**

**A FATAL AFFINITY.** By Stuart Cumberland.

**DOUBT.** By James Stanley Little. Second Edition.

**AGAINST THE GRAIN.** By Charles T. C. James.

**THE QUEEN'S TOKEN.** By Mrs. Hoey.

**A MERE CHILD.** By L. B. Walford.
**THE ABBEY MURDER.** By J. Hatton.
**GABRIEL ALLEN, M.P.** By G. A. Henty.
**THE PRETTY SISTER OF JOSE.** By F. Hodgson Burnett.    [Shortly.

London : SPENCER BLACKETT, 35, St. Bride Street, E.C.
Successor to J. & R. MAXWELL.

# SIR EDWIN ARNOLD'S WORKS.

Crown 8vo. cloth, pp. viii. and 211. Price 7s. 6d.

**WITH SA'DI IN THE GARDEN;**
OR, THE BOOK OF LOVE.

Crown 8vo. cloth, pp. viii.—264. Price 7s. 6d.

**LOTUS AND JEWEL.**

Crown 8vo. cloth, pp. xiv. and 173. Price 5s.

**THE SONG CELESTIAL;**
Or, BHAGAVAD-GITÂ.

Post 8vo. cloth, pp. viii. and 270. Price 7s. 6d.

**INDIAN POETRY.**

Containing "The Indian Song of Songs," &c.

Crown 8vo. cloth, pp. viii. and 406. Price 7s. 6d.

**THE SECRET OF DEATH.**
WITH SOME SELECTED POEMS.

Crown 8vo. cloth, pp. xii. and 282. Price 7s. 6d.

**INDIAN IDYLLS.**

(From the Sanskrit of the Mahâbhârata.)

Crown 8vo. cloth, pp. xiv. and 320, with green borders. Price 7s. 6d.

**PEARLS OF THE FAITH;**
OR, ISLAM'S ROSARY.

12mo. pp. xvi. and 240, parchment. Price 3s. 6d.
Crown 8vo. cloth, pp. xii. and 294. Price 7s. 6d.
Illustrated Edition. 4to. cloth. Price £1 1s.

**THE LIGHT OF ASIA;**
Or, The Great Renunciation.

**UNIFORM EDITION OF SIR EDWIN ARNOLD'S ORIENTAL POEMS.**
The above Eight Volumes may be had *uniformly bound in cloth*, Crown 8vo., in box. Price £2 8s. *Sold only in Sets.*

**SIR EDWIN ARNOLD'S SELECTED POEMS.**

In one Vol. Crown 8vo. cloth, pp. viii. and 375.

Price 7s. 6d.

**POEMS : NATIONAL AND NON-ORIENTAL.**

WITH SOME NEW PIECES.

Crown 8vo. cloth, pp. 324. Price 7s. 6d.

**INDIA REVISITED.**
With Thirty-two Full-page Illustrations.

Crown 8vo. cloth, pp. 62. Price 1s. 6d. ; paper, 1s.

**DEATH—AND AFTERWARDS.**
Reprinted, with Supplementary Comments, from the *Fortnightly Review.*

LONDON : TRÜBNER & CO., 57 AND 59, LUDGATE HILL.

No. 244.　　　THIRD SERIES. VOL. I. PART 2.　　　PRICE 2s.


# TRÜBNER AND CO.'S LIST.

**NOW READY.**

HAWARA, BIAHMU, AND ARSINOE. With Thirty Plates. By W. M. FLINDERS PETRIE. 4to. boards. Price 16s.

A GRAMMAR OF THE JAPANESE SPOKEN LANGUAGE. By W. G. ASTON, M.A., H.B.M.'s Legation, Tokio, Japan. Fourth Edition, crown 8vo. cloth, pp. 212. Price 12s.

A SANSKRIT GRAMMAR, including both the Classical Language, and the Older Dialects, of Veda and Brahmana. By WILLIAM DWIGHT WHITNEY. Second Revised and Extended Edition. 8vo. cloth, pp. xxv. and 551. Price 12s.

HANDBOOK OF COLLOQUIAL JAPANESE. By BASIL HALL CHAMBERLAIN. 8vo. cloth, pp. 486. Price 12s. 6d.

THE RIG-VEDA SANHITA. A COLLECTION OF ANCIENT HINDU HYMNS, Constituting Part of the Seventh and Eighth Ashtaka of the Rig-Veda. Translated from the Original Sanskrit by H. H. WILSON, M.A., F.R.S. Edited by W. F. WEBSTER, M.A. Vol. VI. Completing the Work. 8vo. cloth, pp. vii. and 436. Price £1 1s.

*.* *This monumental work is now complete in Six Volumes, a few sets only remain of the complete work. Price £5 19s.*

SOCIAL HISTORY OF THE RACES OF MANKIND. THIRD DIVISION. *AONEO-MARANONIANS.* By A. FEATHERMAN. Demy 8vo. cloth, pp. xxiii. and 480. Price £1 5s.

THE SCIENCE OF BEAUTY. An Inquiry into the Laws of Beauty, Ugliness, Sublimity and Meanness. By AVARY W. HOLMES-FORBES, M.A. Second Edition. 8vo. cloth, pp. viii. and 200. Price 3s. 6d.

THE SACRED ANTHOLOGY. A Book of Ethnical Scriptures. Collected and Edited by MONCURE DANIEL CONWAY. New Edition. Crown 8vo. cloth, xviii. and 530. Price 5s.

THE YEAR BOOK OF AUSTRALIA for 1889. Edited by EDWARD GREVILLE, J.P., Commissioner of Land Titles, and for 10 years a Member of the Legislative Assembly of New South Wales. Demy 8vo. boards. Price 10s. 6d.

**TRÜBNER'S COLLECTION OF SIMPLIFIED GRAMMARS.**

OF

THE PRINCIPAL ASIATIC AND EUROPEAN LANGUAGES.

Edited by REINHOLD ROST, LL.D., PH.D.

Crown 8vo. cloth, uniformly bound.

I.

HINDUSTANI, PERSIAN, AND ARABIC. By E. H. PALMER, M.A. Second Edition. 1885. 5s.

II.

HUNGARIAN. By I. SINGER. 1882. 4s. 6d.

III.

BASQUE. By W. VAN EYS. 1883. 3s. 6d.

IV.

MALAGASY. By G. W. PARKER. 1883. 5s.

V.

MODERN GREEK. By E. M. GELDART, M.A. 1883. 2s. 6d.

VI.

ROUMANIAN. By R. TORCEANU. 1883. 5s.

VII.

TIBETAN GRAMMAR. By H. A. JASCHKE. 1883. 5s.

VIII.

DANISH. By E. C. OTTÉ. 1884. 2s. 6d.

IX.

TURKISH. By J. W. REDHOUSE, M.R.A.S. 1884. 10s. 6d.

X.

SWEDISH. By E. C. OTTÉ. 1884. 2s. 6d.

XI.

POLISH. By W. R. MORFILL, M.A. 1884. 3s. 6d.

XII.

PALI. By E. MÜLLER. 1884. 7s. 6d.

XIII.

SANSKRIT. By H. EDGREN. 1885. 10s 6d.

XIV.

GRAMMAIRE ALBANAISE. Par P. W. 1887. 7s. 6d.

XV.

JAPANESE. By B. H. CHAMBERLAIN. 1886. 5s.

XVI.

SERBIAN. By W. R. MORFILL, M.A. 1887. 4s. 6d.

XVII.

LANGUAGES OF THE CUNEIFORM INSCRIPTIONS. By GEORGE BERTIN, M.R.A.S. 1888. 5s.

XVIII.

PANJABI. By the Rev. WM. ST. CLAIR TISDALL, M.A., C.M.S. 1889. 7s. 6d.


LONDON: TRÜBNER & CO., 57 AND 59, LUDGATE HILL.

# WALTER SMITH AND INNES' PUBLICATIONS.

## NOW READY.

# AUTOBIOGRAPHY OF GARIBALDI.

Authorized Translation by A. WERNER.   Three Vols. large crown 8vo. cloth, £1 11s. 6d.
With a Supplement by JESSIE WHITE MARIO, including Fac-Similes of some Letters.

Garibaldi's Reminiscences, written at different periods, were published at Florence in January, 1888.  Signora Mario's Supplement contains explanatory matter and additional Biographical Facts for the advantage of English readers.

"These volumes are interesting and important.  Madame Mario, English by birth and training, and Italian by interest and experience, knows more of Italy and its leaders than any other English writer.  The authorized translation by A. Werner can be trusted for its accuracy. But its value is enormously enhanced by the supplementary volume which Madame Mario contributes.  This is the first important life of the famous General which has been published in English."—*Athenæum.*

# THE READER'S SHAKESPEARE.

COMPLETE IN NINE VOLUMES.   Extra 8vo. cloth.   Price 6s. each Vol.   THE SET OF NINE VOLS. £2 14s.

... ... ... Tragedies. | Vol. IX. Poems.

# Trübner's Record,

A JOURNAL DEVOTED TO THE LITERATURE OF THE EAST,

*With Notes & Lists of Current American, European & Colonial Publications.*

## ORDER FORM.

*To the Publishers of " Trübner's Record,"*

*57 & 59, Ludgate Hill, London, E.C.*

Please enter my name as Subscriber to "Trübner's Record," and send me the parts of the current Volume as they appear, for which I enclose Ten Shillings.

*Signed,*

_______________________________

*Date*

_______________________________

<table>
<tr><td>

# SECOND-HAND BOOKS.

A VERY LARGE AND VARIED STOCK.

*Catalogues, gratis, of new, second-hand, and specially reduced Books.*

# JOHN BUMPUS,

BOOKSELLER

(By Special Appointment to Her Majesty),

350, OXFORD STREET, LONDON.

</td><td>

BY CHARLES G. LELAND.
Author's Copyright Edition, with a New Preface and Additional Poems.

III.—ESSAYS ON MEN AND BOOKS SELECTED FROM THE EARLIER WRITINGS OF LORD MACAULAY.

VOL. I., with Five Portraits—INTRODUCTORY—LORD CLIVE —MILTON—EARL CHATHAM—LORD BYRON. With Critical Introduction and Notes by ALEXANDER H. JAPP, LL.D., F.R.S.E.

Large-paper Copies are also ready.  Price 12s. 6d. each.

LONDON: TRÜBNER & Co., LUDGATE HILL.

</td></tr>
</table>

W. Drugulin

10. Königstraße 10.

Leipzig,

(Germany.)

# ORIENTAL PUBLICATIONS
## Of E. J. BRILL, Leyden.

**Actes** du sixième Congrès Internat. d. Orientalistes, tenu en 1883 à Leide. 1re partie: Compte-rendu des séances, fl. 2.50. 2me Section 1. Sémitique, fl. 15. 3me Section 2; Aryenne, fl. 12.50. 4me Section 3: Africaine; Sect. 4: De l'extrême Orient; Sect. 5: Polynésienne, fl. 14. Les sections 3, 4, et 5 se vendent séparément à raison de fl. 9, fl. 5, et fl. 6.

**Annales** auctore Abu-Djafar Mohammed Ibn Djarir At-Tabari quos ediderunt *J. Barth, Th. Nöldeke, O. Loth, E. Prim, H. Thorbecke, S. Fraenkel, I. Guidi, D. H. Müller, M. Th. Houtsma, Stanislas Guyard, V. Rosen et M. J. de Goeje.* 8o. Tome I. pars 1–5; Tome II. pars 1–6; Tome III. pars 1–7; et 1 vol. Titres, Tables de matières; pages réimprimées. (*Texte arabe.*) fl. 92.30.

**Bâsim** le forgeron et Hârûn Er Rachîd.—Texte Arabe en dialecte d'Egypte et de Syrie. Publ. d'après les MSS. de Leide, de Gotha et du Caire par le Comte *Carlo de Landberg.* Tome I: Texte, traduction et proverbes. fl. 3.

**Catalogus** cod. Arab. Bibl. Acad. Lugd. Bat. Ed. 2a. Auctt. *M. J. de Goeje et M. Th. Houtsma.* Vol. I. fl. 9.

**Dozy, R. P. A.**—Supplément aux dictionnaires arabes. 2 vol. demi mar. fl. 75.

**Goeje, M. J. de,** Mémoire sur les Carmathes du Bahraïn et les Fatimides. fl. 3.

**Ibn 'Abd El Kerim 'ali rizâ von Sirâ.** Das Tarîkh-i-Zendtje. Hrsg. von Ernst Beer. fl. 1.75.

**Ibn-Wadhih** qui dicitur Al-Jâqubi historiae. Edid. indicesque adj. *M. Th. Houtsma.* Vol. I.: Historia antetslamica. Vol. II.: Historia islamica. fl. 15.

**Imad ed dîn el-kâtib el-Isfahânî** conquête de la Syrie et de la Palestine par Salâh ed dîn. *Texte Arabe.* Publ. par le Comte *Carlo de Landberg.* Vol. I. fl. 9.

**Kitâb al Aghâni.**—The 21st volume of the Kitâb al-Aghâni, being a collection of biographies not contained in the edition of Bûlâq by *R. Brünnow.* Part I. Text. fl. 6.

**Kitab al Muwassâ** of Abû 't- Tayyib Muhammed ibn Ishâq al Wamâ by *R. Brünnow.* fl. 3.50.

**Landberg, C.,** Proverbes et dictons du peuple arabe. Matériaux pour servir à la connaissance des dialectes vulgaires recueillis, traduits et annotés. Vol. I. Province de Syrie. Section de Saydâ. *Texte arabe.* fl. 7.

**Livres** des merveilles de l'Inde. Texte arabe publié d'après le MS. *de M. Schefer,* collat. s. l. MSS. de Constantinople par *P. A. v. d. Lith.* Traduct. franç. p. *L. Marcel Devic.* Av. 4 pl. col. tirées du MS. arabe de Hariri d. l. collect. de *M. Schefer.* fl. 12.

**Nöldeke, Th.,** Gesch. d. Perser u. Araber zur Zeit der Sasaniden. Aus d. arab. Chronik des Tabari übers. u. m. ausführl. Erläut. u. Ergänz. versehn. fl. 7.

**Recueil** de textes relatifs à l'histoire des Seldjoucides. Publ. p. *M. Th. Houtsma.* Hist. des Seldjoucides de l'Irâq par al-Bondari d'après Imâd ad-dîn al Katîb al-Isfahânî. fl. 5.25.

**Spitta-Bey, G.,** Contes arabes modernes recueillis et traduits. Texte arabe en caract. lat. avec la traduct. franç. fl. 3.75.

**Land, J. P. N.,** Anecdota Syriaca, colleg. edid. et explicavit. Tom. I. Symbolae syriacae. fl. 7; Tom. II. Joannis episcopi Ephesi monophysitae scripta historica quotquot adhuc inedita supereant. Syriace edidit. fl. 8.50; Tom. III. Zachariae episcopi Mitylenes aliorumque script. hist. graece plerumque deperdita, Syr. edid. fl. 8.50; Tom. IV. Otia Syriaca. fl. 10.50.

**Stephen** Bar Sudaili. The Syrian mystic and the Book of Hierotheos, by *A. L. Frothingham,* jr. (*Texte Syrien.*) fl. 2.50.

**Aryabhatiya (The)** A manual of Astronomy, with the commentary Bhatadîpikâ of Paramâdiçvara ed. by *H. Kern.* (*Sanskrit text.*) fl. 4.40.

**Speyer, J. S.,** Sanskrit Syntax. With an introduction by Dr. H. Kern. Bound in cloth. fl. 9.

**Brünnow, R. E.,** A Classified List of all simple and compound cuneiform ideographs occurring in the texts hitherto published, with their assyro-babylonian equivalents, phonetic values, etc. Parts I. and II. Every part fl. 9.

**Firdusii** Schachnahme edid. *J. A. Vullers.* Tome I.—III. fl. 35.25.

**Recueil** de Textes relatifs à l'histoire des Seldjoucides (*Texte persan*) publ. par *M. Th. Houtsma.* Vol. I. Hist. des Seldjouc. du Kermân, par Muhammed Ibrahim. fl. 3.50.

**Pleyte, W.,** Chapitres supplémentaires du Livre des Morts, 162-174. Texte égyptien autographié d'après les Monuments de Leide, du Louvre et du Musée Britannique par *T. Bylel.* Av. traduct. et comment. par *W. Pleyte.* 3 vol. av. 27 pl. fl. 25.

———, Papyrus de Turin facsimilés par Rossy. 2 vols. dem. mar. d. s. t. fl. 160.

**Hoffmann, J. J.**—A Japanese grammar. 2nd ed. bound in cloth. fl. 12.

A complete catalogue of the publications of E. J. BRILL will be sent post-free on application to any purchaser.

# NEW AMERICAN BOOKS.

8vo. cloth, Illustrated, pp. xx. and 234. Price £1 5s.

THE LIXIVIATION OF SILVER-ORES WITH HYPOSULPHITE SOLUTIONS, with Special Reference to the Russell Process. By CARL A. STETEFELDT. The best Book on the Subject. Every Miner of Silver Ores should have it.

In Two Vols. 16mo. Price, cloth, 8s.; paper, 5s.

MARGERY: A Tale of Old Nuremberg. By GEORG EBERS. Translated from the German by CLARA BELL.

12mo. cloth, Illustrated. Price 2s. 6d.

ALL ABOUT PASEDENA AND ITS VICINITY, Its Climate, Missions, Trails, Canons, Fruits, Flowers and Game. By C. F. HOLDER. A Handbook for Tourists or the general reader, giving information regarding this ideal health resort of Southern California.

8vo. paper. Price 2s. 6d.

ARNOLD TOYNBEE. By F. C. MONTAGUE, Fellow of Oriel College, Oxford. With an Account of the Work of Toynbee Hall in East London, by PHILIP LYTTELTON GELL, M.A., also an Account of the Neighbourhood Guild in New York, by C. B. STOVER, A.B.

Second Edition. Crown 8vo. cloth. Price 5s. 6d.

PSYCHOLOGY. By JOHN DEWEY, Ph.D., Assistant Professor of Philosophy in Michigan University.

12mo. cloth, pp. xvi. and 367. Price 9s.

ENTOMOLOGY FOR BEGINNERS. For the Use of Young Folks, Fruit Growers, Farmers and Gardeners. By A. S. PACKARD, M.D., Ph.D. Second Edition, Revised.

In One Volume. 8vo. cloth. Price £5 5s. nett.

THE GUIDE FOR PIECE DYEING. By F. W REISIG, Practical Dyer and Chemist.

8vo. cloth, pp. xxx. and 715. Price 18s.

MARVELS OF THE NEW WEST. A Vivid Portrayal of the Stupendous Marvels in the Vast Wonderland West of the Missouri River. Six Books in One Volume. Comprising Marvels of Nature, Marvels of Race, Marvels of Enterprise, Marvels of Mining, Marvels of Stock-raising and Marvels of Agriculture, Graphically and Truthfully Described. By WILLIAM M. THAYER. Illustrated with over Three Hundred and Fifty fine Engravings and Maps.

Crown 8vo. cloth, pp. 433. Price 6s. 6d.

HOME LIFE IN FLORIDA. By HELEN HARCOURT, Author of "Florida Fruits and How to Raise Them."

## TRÜBNER'S RECORD, No. 245.

### CONTENTS.

TO THE MEMBERS OF THE

# Eighth International Oriental Congress

AT STOCKHOLM AND CHRISTIANIA.

*It was stated in our Prospectus, at the head of the first Number of the present Series, that the RECORD in its expanded form is the only periodical in the English language intended to supply information on current literary topics in reference to the East, embracing in its scope all branches of Asiatic civilization. We invited the co-operation of scholars in the special departments to which their studies are directed, and ventured to express a hope that the literary public generally would accord to the RECORD its continued support. The forthcoming Eighth International Oriental Congress, at which scholars from almost all parts of the civilized world will be assembled, appears to us an opportune season for again calling attention to its objects. We would gladly have the RECORD serve as a medium of intercommunication, in the wide and varied departments of Oriental research, between those who wish to impart, and those who seek for, intelligence or information, for which purpose it might not only be further expanded, but also be made a monthly publication. This must, however, be contingent on a large amount of support. As it is, we have given expression to the idea in the hope that the members of the Congress will accord it their favourable consideration.*

THE PUBLISHERS.

# JOURNAL OF THE CEYLON BRANCH OF THE ROYAL ASIATIC SOCIETY, 1886.

Vol. IX. No. 33. *Contents*: R. Virchow. The Veddás of Ceylon, and their Relation to the Neighbouring Tribes. Translated from the German. With Three Tables. (Contents: The Veddá Land—Number of the Veddás, Wild and Tame.) Demon Worship—Original Population of Ceylon (Yakkú—etc., etc.).

Price 5*s.*

# JOURNAL OF THE CHINA BRANCH OF THE ROYAL ASIATIC SOCIETY.

## NEW SERIES.

Vol. XXII. *Contents*: The Military Organization of China Prior to 1842.—Notes on the Mineral Resources of Eastern Shantung.—Chinese Partnerships: Liability of the Individual Members.—Notes on the Early History of the Salt Monopoly in China.—The Salt Revenue of China.—Remarks on the Production of Salt in China.—Name of the Sovereigns of the Old Corean States, etc.—Notes and Queries.—Notes of New Books and Literary Notes.—Correspondence. — Proceedings.—Ancient Porcelain.—The Chinese Oriental College.—Notes and Queries — Literary Notes.—Chinese Names of Plants.—Proceedings.—Council's Report for the Year 1887.—List of Members.

Price 7*s.* 6*d.*

# JOURNAL OF THE STRAITS BRANCH OF THE ROYAL ASIATIC SOCIETY.

No. 19. (1887.) *Contents*: Council for 1888.—List of Members for 1888.—Proceedings of the General Meeting.—Council's Annual Report for 1887.—Treasurer's Accounts for 1887.—Report of a Journey from Tuaran to Kiau and Ascent of Kinabalu Mountain. By R. M. Little.—Pulau Langkawi. By W. E. Maxwell, C.M.G.—The Negri Sembilan: their Origin and Constitution. By Hon. Martin Lister.—Raja Ambong: A Malay Fairy Tale. By W. E. Maxwell, C.M.G.—Report on the Padi-Borer. By L. Wray, jun.—Summary of the Report on the Pomelow Moth. By L. Wray, jun.—Manangism in Borneo. By Rev. J. Perham. —Exploring Expedition from Selama, Pérak, to Pong, Patani. By Arthur T. Dew.—Birds from Pérak.—Occasional Notes.

Price 9*s.*

# THE TAPROBANIAN;

Vol. III. Part 3. *Contents*: Notes and Queries.—The History of Kovalan (concluded).—The Divisions of Lanka, or Sri Laka Kadayuru.—Sinhalese Folk-Lore.—Nursery Rhymes and Sayings.

Annual Subscription £1 6*s.* post free.

# THE JOURNAL OF AMERICAN FOLK-LORE.

Vol. II. No. 5. April—June, 1889. Price 4*s.*

Noqollpi, the Gambler; A Navajo Myth. By W. Matthews.—Folk-Lore of the Carolina Mountains. By J. Mooney. — Current Superstitions; II. Omens of Death: Beliefs and Customs of Children. By F. D. Bergen and W. W. Newell.—Children's Rhymes and Incantations. By C. G. Leland.—Rhymes from Old Powder-Horns. By William Beauchamp.—Eskimo Tales and Songs. By H. Rink and F. Boas.—Grateful Animals.—Teton Folk-Lore Notes. By J. O. Dorsey.—Tales of the Mississaguas. I. By A. F. Chamberlain.—Superstitions of Childhood on the Hudson River. By M. H. Skeel.—Japonica. By H. Oertel.—Proverbs and Phrases. By W. W. Newell.—Waste-basket of Words.—Folk-Lore Scrap-book—Notes and Queries.—Record of American Folk-Lore.—Bibliographical Notes.

Annual Subscription, including Postage, 14*s.*

# THE PERIODICAL PRESS INDEX.

## A RECORD OF LEADING SUBJECTS IN CURRENT LITERATURE.

The P. P. Index aims at presenting a record of the more important subjects dealt with in periodical literature at home and abroad. The Index is given in two forms: (1) A Subject Index; and (2) A Leading Key Word Index; the value of which is enhanced by reference to the principal divisions and sub-divisions of the Subject Index. The periodical issue has been stopt, but the Annual Volume for 1889 will be issued early in 1890.

LONDON · TRÜBNER & CO., 57 AND 59, LUDGATE HILL.

# NEW ORIENTAL PUBLICATIONS.

Post 8vo. half-bound, pp. 706, 15.　Price £1 2s. 6d.
## ARABIC-ENGLISH DICTIONARY.
By W. THOMSON-WORTABET,
Professor of English in the Egyptian Government School of
Medicine and Pharmacy.

---

Post 8vo. cloth, pp. 239.　Price 5s.
## GRAMMAIRE ELEMENTAIRE D'ARABE
## REGULIER, etc.
Par L. MACHUEL.
SECOND EDITION.

---

Small 8vo. cloth, pp. viii. 370.　Price 3s.
## DIALOGUES FRANCAIS-ARABES.
Recueil des Phrases les plus usuelles de la langue parlée
en Algérie.
Par BELKASSEM BEN SEDIRA.
THIRD EDITION.

---

Post 8vo. sewed.　Part I. to XLIX.
## THE MAHABHARATA OF KRISHNA-
## DWAIPAYNA VYASA.
Translated into English Prose.
Published by Pratap Chandra Roy.
The work is published bi-monthly.　Price of Part I. to
XLV. 3s. each.
The new parts (from part XLVI.) can now be supplied at
1s. 6d. each.

---

Two vols. in one. 8vo. cloth, pp. 211 and 198, xxx.
Price 5s.
## THE POPULAR DICTIONARY,
In two Parts, English and Hindustani, and Hindustani and
English.
Compiled by the Rev. T. CRAVEN, M.A.
REVISED AND ENLARGED EDITION.

Oblong, 3 volumes.　Illustrated.　Price £4 4s.
## HISTOIRE DE L'ARMENIE.
Par le R. P. JACQUES Dr. ISSAVERDENS.
Mékhithariste de Venise.
Enrichie de nombreuses figures.
Exécutées aux frais
de M. Jean Arathoon de Batavia.

---

4to. Part II. (July, 1888).　With 3 coloured plates.　Price 20s.
## RHOPALOCERA NIHONICA.
A Description of the Butterflies of Japan.
By H. PRYER.
*⁎* Part I. has been published, November, 1886.　The
notes on collecting and nomenclature will appear in Part III.
which is ready for printing.

---

Roy. 8vo. boards, pp. ii. 52, 39.　Illustrated.　Price 6s.
## DESCRIPTION OF
## THE PALMYRA PALM OF CEYLON.
By WILLIAM FERGUSON.

---

Post 8vo. cloth, pp. viii 303, ix.　Price 7s. 6d.
## ALL ABOUT TOBACCO.
Including Practical Instructions for Planting, Cultivation,
and Curing of the Leaf.　With other suitable information
from a variety of sources, referring to the Industry
in Ceylon, Sumatra, South India, etc.
Compiled and published by A. M. & J. FERGUSON.

---

Royal 8vo. half-bound.　Price 12s.
## INDIAN AND ENGLISH EXCHANGE TABLES.
From 1s. 3d. to 1s. 6d. per Rupee, advancing by 1/16 of
a Penny.
By F. A. D. MERCES.
NEW EDITION, ENLARGED.

---

## PUBLICATIONS OF THE ORIENTAL INSTITUTE, WOKING.

श्री विबोधय: मासिक-संस्कृत-पत्रम्
## THE "VIDIODHAY,"
## OR, SANSKRIT CRITICAL JOURNAL
## OF THE ORIENTAL INSTITUTE, WOKING.
PUBLISHED MONTHLY.
Annual Subscription, 8s., Post Free.

المقائيق
## AL 'HAQUÂIQ;
## THE ARABIC REVIEW.
Edited by
KHALIL EFFENDI, SYED ALI BILGRAMI, and
MOHAMED ABDUL JUBBAR.
PUBLISHED MONTHLY.
Annual Subscription, 8s., Post Free.

## Official and other Authorized Publications.
### JUST ISSUED.

## GREAT BRITAIN.
### Publications of the Royal Society.

SEPARATE PAPERS FROM THE PHILOSOPHICAL TRANSACTIONS. Vol. 180, 1889.

SOME OBSERVATIONS ON THE AMOUNT OF LIGHT REFLECTED AND TRANSMITTED BY CERTAIN KINDS OF GLASS. By Sir John Conroy, Bart., M.A. 4to. paper, pp. 46, with One Plate. Price 2s. 6d.　　　(A. 44.)

THE ELECTROMOTIVE CHANGES CONNECTED WITH THE BEAT OF THE MAMMALIAN HEART AND OF THE HUMAN HEART IN PARTICULAR. By Augustus D. Waller, M.D. 4to. paper, pp. 26. Price 2s.　　　(B. 44.)

### Publications of the Browning Society.

PAPERS. 1887-8. Part IX. 8vo. pp. 105, wrapper. Price 10s.—On the Performance of "Strafford." By Dr. Todhunter. —On "A Death in the Desert." By Mrs. Glazebrooke.—A Grammatical Analysis of "O, Lyric Love." By Dr. F. J. Furnivall, M.A.—Some Notes on Mr. Browning's Latest Volume (" Parleyings with Certain People "). By Mr. Arthur Symons.—On the Musical Poems of Browning. By Miss Helen Ormerod.—The Monthly Abstract of Proceedings of Meetings, Forty-fourth to Fiftieth—Browning " Notes and Queries," &c.—Sixth Report of the Committee, 1886-7.

PAPERS. 1888-9. Part X. 8vo. pp. 159, wrapper. Price 10s.—On Browning's Views of Life. By Mr. W. F. Revell.— On Browning's Estimate of Life. By Mr. Edward Berdoe, M.R.C.S.—On Browning's Jews and Shakespeare's Jew. By Professor Barnett.—On Abt Vogler, the Man. By Helen J. Ormerod.—On Browning as a Teacher of the Nine-teenth Century. By C. M. Whitehead.—On " Saul." By Hannah M. Stoddart.—The Monthly Abstract of Proceed-ings of Meetings, Fifty-third to Sixtieth—Browning " Notes and Queries," &c.—Seventh Report of the Committee, 1887-8.

### Publications of the Society for Psychical Research.

PROCEEDINGS. Part XIV. June, 1889. Price 3s.—Opening Address at the Thirtieth General Meeting. By Prof. Henry Sidgwick.—On Apparitions Occurring soon after Death. By the late Edmund Gurney. Completed by F. W. H. Myers.—Automatic Writing. IV. The Dæmon of Socrates. By Frederick W. H. Myers. Supplement.—Recent Experiments in Crystal Vision.—On a Series of Experiments at Pesaro. By H. Babington Smith.—Dr. Albert Moll's " Hypnotism." By Max Dessoir.—The Edmund Gurney Library.—List of Members and Associates.

## INDIA.
### Publications of the Archæological Survey of India.

EPIGRAPHIA INDICA AND RECORD OF THE ARCHÆOLOGICAL SURVEY OF INDIA. Edited by James Burgess, LL.D., C.I.E., etc., etc., Director General of the Archæological Survey of India. Part I. October, 1888. Part II. January, 1889. Price 7s. each.

### Publications of the Indian Meteorological Office.

INDIAN METEOROLOGICAL MEMOIRS. Published under the direction of H. F. Blanford, Meteorological Reporter to the Government of India. Vol. 4, part 6. IX. on Temperature and Humidity Observations made at Allahabad at Various Heights above the Ground. Royal 4to. paper, pp. 34, with Five Plates. Price 3s.

REPORT ON THE METEOROLOGY OF INDIA IN 1887. By John Elliot, M.A., Officiating Meteorological Reporter to the Government of India. (Thirteenth Year.) Super-royal 4to. boards, pp. iv. and 604, with One Map and Four Plates. Price 16s.

## AUSTRALIA.
### Publications of the Linnean Society of New South Wales.

PROCEEDINGS. Second Series. Vol. 3, Part IV. pp. xvi. and 500, Two Plates, in Wrappers. Price 18s.—Revision of the Genus Heteronyx, with Descriptions of New Species. Part I. By the Rev. T. Blackburn, B.A.—Diptera of Australia. Part IV. The Simulidæ and Bibionidæ. By F. A. A. Skuse. (Plate XXXIX.)—Further Notes on Australian Coleoptera, with Descriptions of New Genera and Species. By the Rev. T. Blackburn, B.A.—Contributions towards a Knowledge of the Coleoptera of Australia. No. 5. On Certain Species belonging to Unrecorded Genera. By A. Sidney Olliff, F.E.S.—Descriptions of Hitherto Undescribed Australian Lepidoptera (Rhopalocera). By W. H. Miskin, F.E.S.—Notes on Australian Earthworms. Part V. By J. J. Fletcher, M.A., B.Sc.—On Simple Striated Muscular Fibres. By W. A. Haswell, M.A., D.Sc.—Descriptions of Australian Micro-Lepidoptera. Part XV. Œcophoridæ (continued). By E. Meyrick, B.A., F.E.S.—Jottings from the Biological Laboratory of Sydney Univer-sity. By W. A. Haswell, M.A., D.Sc. No. 10. On Sacculina infesting Australian Crabs. No. 11. On a Method of preparing Blastoderms of the Fowl. No. 12. Note on Urolophustestaceus.—Diptera of Australia. Part V. The Culicidæ. By Frederick A. A. Skuse. (Plate XL.)—List of the Australian Palæichthyes, with Notes on their Synonymy and Distribution. Part I. By J. Douglas Ogilby, F.L.S.—A List of the Birds found in the County of Cumberland, N.S.W. By A. J. North, F.L.S.—Elections.—Announcements.—Notes.—Exhibits.—President's Address. —Office Bearers, etc., for 1889.—Title-Page, Index to Vol. III. etc.

LONDON: TRÜBNER & CO., AGENTS BY APPOINTMENT, 57 AND 59, LUDGATE HILL.

## NEW VOLUMES OF VERSE.

**IN MY LADY'S PRAISE.** Being Poems Old and New. Written to the Honour of Fanny, Lady Arnold. And now Collected for Her Memory, by Sir Edwin Arnold, M.A., K.C.I.E., C.S.I. Author of "The Light of Asia," &c., &c. Imperial 16mo. parchment, price 3s. 6d.

**FLOWERS OF THE NIGHT.** By Emily Pfeiffer, Author of "Gerard's Monument," "The Rhyme of the Lady of the Rock," "Under the Aspens," "Sonnets," &c. Crown 8vo. cloth, pp. x. and 138, price 6s.

**THE DAWN OF DEATH.** By Luscombe Searelle, F.R.G.S. Composer of "Tone Poems," the Operas "Estrella," "Bobadil," "Isidora," etc. Crown 8vo. cloth, price 4s. 6d.

**INDIA :** A Descriptive Poem. By H. B. W. Garrick, Assistant Archæologist to the Government of India. Crown 8vo. cloth, pp. xvi. and 138, price 7s. 6d.

"Each stanza is in itself a vivid picture."—*Evening Post.*

LONDON: TRÜBNER & CO., 57 AND 59, LUDGATE HILL.

## NEW WORKS OF FICTION.

**GIRALDI.** A Tale of the Sects. By Ross Dering. In Two Volumes. Crown 8vo. cloth. Price 12s.

**THE WING OF AZRAEL.** By Mona Caird. In Three Volumes. Crown 8vo. cloth. Price 31s. 6d.

**ULLI :** THE STORY OF A NEGLECTED GIRL. Translated from the German of Emma Biller by A. B. Daisy Rost. Crown 8vo. cloth. Price 5s.

**UNCLE PIPER OF PIPER'S HILL.** An Australian Novel. By Tasma. Second Edition, crown 8vo. cloth. Price 6s.

**AN I. D. B. IN SOUTH AFRICA.** By Louise Vescelius-Sheldon, author of "Yankee Girls in Zulu Land." Illustrated by G. E. Graves and Al. Hencke. Crown 8vo. cloth, pp. 206. Price 7s. 6d.

**YANKEE GIRLS IN ZULU LAND.** By Louise Vescelius-Sheldon. With One Hundred Photogravure Illustrations by G. E. Graves, from Original Sketches by J. Austen. Crown 8vo. cloth, with Portraits of the Sisters. Price 9s.

**A MODERN PALADIN.** By Edward Jenkins, Author of "Ginx's Baby," etc. Cheap Edition, crown 8vo. cloth, pp. 392. Price 5s.

**THE UNFORTUNATE ONE.** A Novel. By Ivan Toorgeynieff. Translated from the Russian by A. R. Thompson. Crown 8vo. cloth. Price 3s. 6d.

**THE AUTOBIOGRAPHY OF MARK RUTHERFORD** AND MARK RUTHERFORD'S DELIVERANCE. Edited by his Friend, Reuben Shapcott. Third Edition, crown 8vo. cloth. Price 7s. 6d.

LONDON: TRÜBNER & CO., 57 AND 59, LUDGATE HILL.

## WORKS IN THE PRESS.

Crown 8vo.

### ENGLISH INTERCOURSE WITH SIAM IN THE SEVENTEENTH CENTURY.

By J. ANDERSON, M.D., LL.D., F.R.S.

8vo. Price 21s. net.

### AN ACCOUNT OF THE ABORIGINES OF TASMANIA,

*Their Manners, Customs, Wars, Hunting, Food, Morals, Language, Origin and General Characteristics,*

Collected from all Sources, from the time of their First Contact with Europeans until their Final Extermination.

By H. LING ROTH,

Assisted by E. MARION BUTLER; with a Chapter on the OSTEOLOGY, by J. G. GARSON, M.D., Vice-President Anthropological Institute, and Lecturer on Comparative Anatomy at Charing Cross Hospital; and a Preface by E. B. TYLOR, F.R.S., D.C.L., LL.D., etc., University Museum, Oxford. With numerous Autotype Plates from Original Drawings made by EDITH MAY ROTH.

This Edition will be strictly limited to the Subscribers, and every copy will be numbered.

Demy 8vo.

### SOUTH AFRICAN BUTTERFLIES:

A MONOGRAPH OF THE EXTRA-TROPICAL SPECIES.

By ROLAND TRIMEN, F.R.S., F.L.S., F.Z.S., F.Ent.S., etc.,
Curator of the South African Museum, Cape Town;

Assisted by JAMES HENRY BOWKER, F.Z.S., F.R.G.S., etc.

Vol. III., completing the Work.

Crown 8vo.

### NEW POPULAR HANDBOOK OF COUNTY DIALECTS.

By the Rev. J. L. SAYWELL, F.R.H.S.

In One Volume. Royal 8vo.

### A SANSKRIT-ENGLISH DICTIONARY

BASED UPON THE ST. PETERSBURG LEXICONS.

By CARL CAPPELLER,

Professor at the University of Jena.

LONDON: TRÜBNER & CO., 57 AND 59, LUDGATE HILL.

# TRÜBNER AND CO.'S LIST.

**NOW READY.**

ISLAM; OR, TRUE CHRISTIANITY, including a Chapter on "Mahomed's Place in the Church." By ERNEST DE BUNSEN. Crown 8vo. cloth, pp. xii. and 176. Price 5s.

DAYS WITH INDUSTRIALS. Adventures and Experiences among Curious Industries. By ALEXANDER H. JAPP, LL.D., F.R.S.E., Author of "Industrial Curiosities," "Golden Lives," etc., etc. Crown 8vo. cloth, pp. 308, with Illustrations. Price 6s.

JOHN LOTHROP MOTLEY. A Memoir. By OLIVER WENDELL HOLMES. New Edition. Crown 8vo. cloth, pp. vii. and 278. Price 6s.

MENDELSSOHN'S LETTERS TO IGNAZ AND CHARLOTTE MOSCHELES. Translated from the Originals in his Possession, and Edited by FELIX MOSCHELES. With numerous Illustrations and Facsimiles. 8vo. cloth, pp. xx. and 306. Price 12s.

FORMOSA (AN ACCOUNT OF MISSIONARY SUCCESS IN THE ISLAND OF). Published in London in 1650, and now reprinted with Copious Appendices, including "Notes of Recent Missionary Work in Formosa." By the Rev. WILLIAM CAMPBELL, F.R.G.S., English Presbyterian Mission, Taiwanfoo. In Two Vols. crown 8vo. cloth, pp. 330 and 339, with Six Illustrations and Map of Formosa. Price 10s.

VERNER'S LAW IN ITALY. An Essay in the History of the Indo-European Sibilants. By R. SEYMOUR CONWAY, Gonville and Caius College, Cambridge; Waddington Classical Scholar in the University of Cambridge; Exhibitioner in Latin in the University of London. With a Dialect Map of Italy by E. HEAWOOD, B.A., F.R.G.S. Demy 8vo. cloth, pp. vi. and 120. Price 5s.

TOLSTOÏ (COUNT) As Novelist and Thinker. Lectures Delivered at the Royal Institution by CHARLES EDWARD TURNER, English Lector in the University of St. Petersburg. Crown 8vo. cloth, pp. 191. Price 3s. 6d.

*The English and Foreign Philosophical Library.*

MORAL ORDER AND PROGRESS. An Analysis of Ethical Conceptions. By S. ALEXANDER, Fellow of Lincoln College, Oxford. Post 8vo. cloth, pp. xxvi. and 414. Price 14s.

HAWARA, BIAHMU, AND ARSINOE. With Thirty Plates. By W. M. FLINDERS PETRIE. 4to. boards. Price 16s.

A GRAMMAR OF THE JAPANESE SPOKEN LANGUAGE. By W. G. ASTON, M.A., H.B.M.'s Legation, Tokio, Japan. Fourth Edition, crown 8vo. cloth, pp. 212. Price 12s.

A SANSKRIT GRAMMAR, including both the Classical Language, and the Older Dialects, of Veda and Brahmana. By WILLIAM DWIGHT WHITNEY. Second Revised and Extended Edition. 8vo. cloth, pp. xxv. and 551. Price 12s.

HANDBOOK OF COLLOQUIAL JAPANESE. By BASIL HALL CHAMBERLAIN. 8vo. cloth, pp. 486. Price 12s. 6d.

THE RIG-VEDA SANHITA. A Collection of Ancient Hindu Hymns, Constituting Part of the Seventh and Eighth Ashṭaka of the Rig-Veda. Translated from the Original Sanskrit by H. H. WILSON, M.A., F.R.S. Edited by W. F. WEBSTER, M.A. Vol. VI. Completing the Work. 8vo. cloth, pp. vii. and 436. Price £1 1s.

*** This monumental work is now complete in Six Volumes, a few sets only remain of the complete work. Price £5 19s.*

SOCIAL HISTORY OF THE RACES OF MANKIND. Third Division. *AONEO-MARANONIANS.* By A. FEATHERMAN. Demy 8vo. cloth, pp. xxiii. and 480. Price £1 5s.

THE SCIENCE OF BEAUTY. An Inquiry into the Laws of Beauty, Ugliness, Sublimity and Meanness. By AVARY W. HOLMES-FORBES, M.A. Second Edition. 8vo. cloth, pp. viii. and 200. Price 3s. 6d.

THE SACRED ANTHOLOGY. A Book of Ethnical Scriptures. Collected and Edited by MONCURE DANIEL CONWAY. New Edition. Crown 8vo. cloth, pp. xviii. and 530. Price 5s.

THE YEAR BOOK OF AUSTRALIA for 1889. Edited by EDWARD GREVILLE, J.P., Commissioner of Land Titles, and for 10 years a Member of the Legislative Assembly of New South Wales. Demy 8vo. boards. Price 10s. 6d.

CHESS OPENINGS, Ancient and Modern. Revised and Corrected to the Present Time from the Best Authorities by E. FREEBOROUGH and the Rev. C. E. RANKEN. With numerous Original Variations and Suggestions by Geo. B. FRASER, Dundee; the Rev. W. WAYTE, London, and other Eminent Analysts. Edited and arranged by E. FREEBOROUGH. Large post 8vo. cloth, pp. 256. Price 7s. 6d.; interleaved, 9s.

THE GOSPEL OF ST. MATTHEW. In Formosan (Sinkang Dialect). With Corresponding Versions in Dutch and English. Edited from Gravius's Edition of 1661 by the Rev. WM. CAMPBELL, M.R.A.S. Fcap. 4to. cloth, pp. xvi. and 174. Price 10s. 6d.

THE EVOLUTION OF THE HEBREW LANGUAGE. By JOSEPH EDKINS, D.D. Demy 8vo. cloth, pp. x. and 150. Price 5s.

## TRÜBNER'S ORIENTAL SERIES.
Post 8vo. cloth, uniformly bound.

# PRINTERS

IN

# Œnglish, Oriental & other Foreign Languages,

## HERTFORD.

MEDALS FROM:

HER MAJESTY THE QUEEN.

EMPRESS EUGENIE.

EXPOSITION UNIVERSELLE DE PARIS 1855.

INTERNATIONAL EXHIBITION 1862.

CONGRES INTERNATIONAL DES
ORIENTALISTES.

BUCKINGHAM PALACE.

SIR,—I have the honour to inform you that His Imperial Majesty the Shah, in accepting your Persian publications, has graciously commanded me to express his high satisfaction to acknowledge that the correctness, good taste, and great skill you display in your publications have highly contributed to diffuse among our Eastern peoples a better knowledge and appreciation of what a practical and artistic typography should be. Receive, Sir, the expression of my best sentiments.

MALCOM.

---

## Printers to the following important Societies, etc. :—

BRITISH MUSEUM.

INDIA OFFICE.

MADRAS GOVERNMENT.

CHIEF COMMISSIONER OF BURMA.

ASIATIC SOCIETY OF BENGAL.

LATE EAST INDIA COMPANY'S COLLEGE.

ROYAL ASIATIC SOCIETY.

BRITISH MUSEUM (NATURAL HISTORY).

BRITISH AND FOREIGN BIBLE SOCIETY.

SANSKRIT TEXT SOCIETY.

PALI TEXT SOCIETY.

INTERNATIONAL CONGRESS OF ORIENTALISTS, LONDON.

HAILEYBURY COLLEGE.

PHILOLOGICAL SOCIETY.

CAMBRIDGE PHILOLOGICAL SOCIETY.

CHAUCER SOCIETY.

EARLY ENGLISH TEXT SOCIETY.

BALLAD SOCIETY.

ENGLISH DIALECT SOCIETY.

INDEX SOCIETY.

WYCLIF SOCIETY.

VILLON SOCIETY, ETC.

# PERIODICAL PUBLICATIONS.

## JOURNAL OF THE AMERICAN ORIENTAL SOCIETY.

Vol. XIII. 8vo. paper, pp. v. 376, and cccxxiii. Price 30s. CONTENTS:—Korea in its Relations with China. By W. W. Rockhill.—The Extremity of the Romans, and praise before the Holy Mysteries: Syriac Texts and Translations. By Professor I. H. Hall.—The Social and Military Position of the Ruling Caste in Ancient India, as represented by the Sanskrit Epic. By E. W. Hopkins.—Proceedings of the Society. Principal Contents: On certain Fragments of Syriac Manuscripts. By I. H. Hall.—Note on Eli Smith's Arabic Version of the Bible. By I. H. Hall.—Naville's Identification of Pithom. By L. Dickerman and W. C. Winslow.—The Holy Houses from the Hebrew Scriptures, etc. By T. O. Paine.—The "Thesis" of Mr. Whitehouse affirming Cairo to be the Biblical Zoan and Tanis Magna. By J. A. Paine.—The Canal of Joseph, etc., in Genesis xlix. By F. C. Whitehouse.—Superstitious Customs connected with Sneezing. By H. C. Warren.—Some Manuscripts of Ptolemy's Star-Catalogues. By I. H. Hall.—Greek Stamps on the Handles of Rhodian Amphorae now in New York. By I. H. Hall.—Greek Inscription from Tartosa, in Syria. By I. H. Hall.—Some Recent Assyriological Publications. By D. G. Lyon.—The Garo Language. By J. Avery.—Burnell on the Date of Manu. By E. W. Hopkins.—Remarks on the Origin of the Laws of Manu. By W. D. Whitney.—Numerical Results from Indexes of Sanskrit Text and Conjugation-Stems. By W. D. Whitney.—Multiform Presents and Transfers of Conjugation in Sanskrit. By C. R. Lanman.—Verbs of the Sanskrit tan-class. By A. H. Edgren.—Sanskrit Manuscript of a Treatise on Logic. By C. R. Lanman.—Vedic Derivatives of the Root prac. By M. Bloomfield.—Letter on Tibetan Lamas and Books. By W. W. Rockhill.—Note on the American Arabic Bible. By I. H. Hall.—Inscriptions from the Cesnola Collection. By I. H. Hall.—Syriac Table for finding Easter in Seleucid Years. By I. H. Hall.—An Inscribed Babylonian Weight (with cut). By W. H. Ward.—Two Stone Objects with Archaic Cuneiform Hieroglyphic Writing (with cuts). By W. H. Ward.—Some Avestan Superstitions and their Parallels. By A. V. W. Jackson.—Ludwig's Views as to Total Sun-Eclipses in the Rig-Veda. By W. D. Whitney.—The latest Translation of the Upanishads. By W. D. Whitney.—The Location of Sippara. By W. H. Ward.—The Imperfect yiktob and Kindred Forms in the Hebrew. By F. Brown.—The Lepcha Language. By J. Avery.—Hirth on China and the Roman Orient. By W. A. P. Martin.—A Greek Hagiologic Manuscript in Philadelphia. By I. H. Hall.—The Identification of Avaris at San. By W. C. Winslow.—The Warrior Caste in India. By E. W Hopkins.—The Correlation of v and m in Sanskrit. By M. Bloomfield.—Negative Clauses in the Rig-Veda. By E. Channing.—The Ancient Persians' Abhorrence of Falsehood. By A. V. W. Jackson.—Hindu Eschatology and the Katha-Upanishad. By W. D. Whitney.—The Ao-Naga Language. By. J. Avery.—A Sacrificial Tablet from Sippar. By D. G. Lyon.—Important Recent Assyriological Publications. By D. G. Lyon.—Three Hymns of the Atharva-Veda. By M. Bloomfield.—Study of the Old Indian Sibilants. By M. Bloomfield and R. H. Spieker.—The Syriac Part of the Chinese Nestorian Tablet. By I. H. Hall.—Some Arabic Proverbs. By J. R. Jewett.—Two Hymns of the Atharva-Veda. By M. Bloomfield.—Condition of Hindu Women according to the Mahābhārata. By E. W. Hopkins.—Avestan Similes: I. from Nature. By A. V. W. Jackson.—A Modern Nestorian Ecclesiastical Calendar. By I. H. Hall.—Inscriptions from the Cesnola Collection. By I. H. Hall.—Note on the proper name Bu-du-ilu. By M. Jastrow, jun.—Assyrian and Samaritan. By M. Jastrow, jun.—The Rising Sun on Babylonian Seals. By W. H. Ward.—The Syriac Text of the Book of the Extremity of the Romans. By I. H. Hall.—Transliteration of Sanskrit Names into Tamil. By J. S. Chandler.—Naville's Book of the Dead. By W. C. Winslow.—Relationship of the Kachari and Garo Languages. By J. Avery.—Notice of the First Part of Delitzsch's Assyrian Dictionary. By D. G. Lyon.—Discovery of the Second Wall, and its Bearing on the Site of Calvary. By S. Merrill.—Ikonomatic Writing in Assyrian. By M. Jastrow, jun.—The Lokman Legend. By C. H. Toy.—A Syriac Biblical Legend. By R. J. H. Gottheil.—A Syriac MS. of the New Testament. By R. J. H. Gottheil.—Avestan Similes: II. From the Animal World. By A. V. W. Jackson.—The Afrigān Rapithwin. By A. V. W. Jackson.—The Battle-Order of the Mahābhārata. By E. W. Hopkins.—Alleged Fire-Arms in Ancient India. By E. W. Hopkins.—Bühler's Manu. By E. W. Hopkins.—Significance of the Gāthās; Yasna 55. By A. V. W. Jackson.—Certain Hymns of the Atharva-Veda. By M. Bloomfield.—The So-called Fire-Ordeal Hymn of the Atharva-Veda. By M. Bloomfield.—Schroeder's Māitrāyaṇī-Samhitā, IV. By W. D. Whitney. Proverb-Literature. By E. W. Hopkins.—Tatian's Diatessaron. By A. L. Frothingham, jun.—Syriac MS. of the Order of Obsequies. By I. H. Hall.—Certain Babylonian Objects. By W. H. Ward.—Design of the Stone Tablet of Abu-Habbu. By W. H. Ward.—Babylonian Tablets at Harvard University. By D. G. Lyon.—Assyrian and Babylonian Casts in the National Museum, Washington. By C. Adler.—Death of Sennacherib, and Accession of Esar-haddon. By C. Adler.—Views of the Babylonians concerning Life after Death. By C. Adler.—New System of Semitic Transliteration. By E. P. Allen.—New Assyrian-English Glossary. By E. P. Allen.—Prolegomena to a Comparative Assyrian Grammar. By P. Haupt.—New Periodical for Assyriology and Comparative Semitic Grammar. By P. Haupt.—Animal Worship and Sun-Worship in the East and West. By S. D. Peet.—Korea in its Relations with China. By W. W. Rockhill.—Edition of the Gāthās. By L. H. Mills.—Conditions of Civilization in the Hindu Middle Age. By E. W. Hopkins.—Rhodian Jar in Boston Museum. By I. H. Hall.—The Syriac Ritual of the Departed. By L. H. Hall.—A Nestorian Liturgical MS. By I. H. Hall.—A Syriac Geographical Chart (with Plate). By R. Gottheil.—Grammatical Works of Hayyūg'. By M. Jastrow, jun.—Proposed Complete Edition of the Works of Edward Hincks. By C. Adler.—Oriental Antiquities in the National Museum at Washington. By C. Adler.—Babylonian Cylinders supposed to represent Human Sacrifices. By W. H. Ward. So-called Emphatic Consonants in Semitic Languages. By G. F. Moore. — Additions to the Library and Cabinet, 1885-1889.—List of Members, 1889.

---

## THE MADRAS JOURNAL OF LITERATURE AND SCIENCE.

### EDITED BY CAPTAIN R. H. CAMPBELL TUFNELL, M.S.C.

Session, 1888-89. CONTENTS:—Proceedings of First, Second, and Third Meetings.—The Legend of St. Thomas. By the Rev. George Milne Rae, M.A.—Etymology of some Mythological Names. By M. Seshagiri Sastri.—Ibn Batûtah in Southern India. By Mrs. L. Fletcher.—Pāndavûla Metta. By the Rev. J. R. Hutchinson.—Indo-Danish Coins. By T. M. Ranga Chari, B.A., and T. Desika Chari, B.A.—On the Original Inhabitants of Bharatavarsa or India. (Continued from p. 137 of this Journal for 1887-88.) By Gustav Oppert.

Each Annual Volume, 10s.

## PERIODICAL PUBLICATIONS.

# TRANSACTIONS OF THE ASIATIC SOCIETY OF JAPAN.

Vol. XVI. Part 3. CONTENTS:—Christian Valley. By J. M. Dixon.—A Literary Lady of Old Japan. By the late Dr. T. A. Purcell and W. G. Aston.—A Vocabulary of the Most Ancient Works of the Japanese Language. By B. H. Chamberlain, assisted by M. Ueda.—Minutes of Meetings. —Report of Council.—Life of Members.

Price 5s.

Vol. XVII. Part 1. CONTENTS: Salt Manufacture in Japan. By A. E. Wileman.—Indo-Chinese Tones. By E. H. Parker.—The Particle Nĕ. By W. G. Aston.—A Review of Mr. Satow's Monograph on "The Jesuit Mission Press in Japan, 1591–1610." By B. H. Chamberlain.—The Gobunsho of Ofumi, of Rennyo Shōnin. By James Troup.

Price 7s. 6d.

# THE BABYLONIAN AND ORIENTAL RECORD.

### A MONTHLY MAGAZINE OF THE ANTIQUITIES OF THE EAST.

*Director*: Prof. Terrien De Lacouperie, Ph. and Litt.D. *Consulting Committee*: Theo. G. Pinches, Wm. C. Capper, W. St. Chad Boscawen, and Prof. C. De Harlez, LL.D. (Continental Correspondent). *Assistant Editor*: Rev. H. M. Mackenzie.

Vol. III. No. 9. August, 1889. CONTENTS: Vedic Chips, I. Nasatya; II. Kava-Sku. By Prof. P. H. Colinet. —Pehlevi Notes, V. A Side-Light on the Khvêtûk-Das Controversy. By Dr. L. C. Casartelli.—Babylonian Medicine: I. Leprosy. By W. St. Chad Boscawen.—A Buddhist Repertory (continued). By Prof. Dr. C. De Harlez.— Studies in Avesta and Pahlavi: I. On Farg. IV. 1-2. By W. Bang.

Vol. III. No. 10. September, 1889. CONTENTS: Origin from Babylonia and Elam of the Early Chinese Civilization: a Summary of the Proofs (continued). By Prof. Dr. Terrien De Lacouperie.—Another Discourse of King Chrosröes, the Immortal-Souled. By Dr. L. C. Casartelli.—Notes on Early Semitic Names. By W. St. Chad Boscawen.—A Buddhist Repertory (continued). By Prof. Dr. C. De Harlez.—Contributions to the Old Persian Lexicography. By W. Bang.

# THE JOURNAL OF AMERICAN FOLK-LORE.

Vol. II. No. VI. July—September, 1889. Price 4s. CONTENTS: Notes on the Cosmogony and Theogony of the Mojave Indians of the Rio Colorado, Arizona. By J. G. Bourke.—Omaha Folk-Lore Notes. By J. O. Dorsey.— Folk-Lore of the Pennsylvania Germans: III. Tales and Proverbs. By W. J. Hoffman.—Current Superstitions: III. Weather-Lore. By Fanny D. Bergen and W. W. Newell. —The House that Jack Built. By H. P. Brewster.—

English Folk-Lore Tales in America.—Leaves from my Omaha Note-book. By A. C. Fletcher.—Arab Legend of a Buried Monastery. By H. C. Bolton.—A Mohawk Legend of Adam and Eve. By A. F. Chamberlain.—Waste-Basket of Words.—Folk-Lore Scrap-book.—Notes and Queries.— Notes of the Folk-Lore of Other Continents.—Bibliographical Notes.

LONDON: TRÜBNER & CO., 57 AND 59, LUDGATE HILL.

---

## *Official and other Authorized Publications.*

### GREAT BRITAIN.

#### *Publications of the Royal Society.*

**A MONOGRAPH OF THE HORNY SPONGES,** by Robert Von Lendenfeld. 4to. cloth, pp. iv. and 936, with 50 plates. Price £3.

The work is divided into three parts :—I. An Introduction, containing a brief historical summary and a detailed list of publications relating to sponges, followed by a description of the methods of research which have been followed ; II. An Analytical portion, devoted to the systematic description of all the known horny sponges ; and III. A Synthetical Part, in which the anatomy and physiology of sponges, especially of horny sponges, are treated, and their phylogeny, systematic position and classification discussed.

#### *Publications of the Trustees of the British Museum.*

**CATALOGUE OF THE FOSSIL REPTILIA AND AMPHIBIA IN THE BRITISH MUSEUM (NATURAL HISTORY),** Part II. containing the Orders Ichthyopterygia and Sauropterygia. By Richard Lydekker, B.A., F.G.S., etc. Demy 8vo. cloth, pp. xxii. and 308. Price 7s. 6d.

**LIST OF THE BOOKS OF REFERENCE IN THE READING ROOM OF THE BRITISH MUSEUM.** Third Edition, Revised. Demy 8vo. cloth, pp. xxvi. and 476, with Diagram, 6s.

**LIST OF BIBLIOGRAPHICAL WORKS IN THE READING ROOM OF THE BRITISH MUSEUM.** Second Edition. Revised. 8vo. paper, pp. xi. and 103. Price 2s.

**CATALOGUE OF ADDITIONS TO THE MANUSCRIPTS IN THE BRITISH MUSEUM IN THE YEARS 1882-1887.** Additional Manuscripts—31,897-33,344. Additional Charters and Rolls—27,005-32,899. Detached Seals and Casts—LII. 1-LXXVII. 12. Papyri—cxvii-cxx. Egerton Manuscripts—2601-2678. Egerton Charters and Rolls —486-584. Royal 8vo. cloth, pp. xv. and 1140. Price £1 1s.

#### *Publications of the Society for Psychical Research.*

**PROCEEDINGS,** Vol. 5, 1888-89. Demy 8vo. cloth, pp. viii. and 606 (containing parts XII., XIII. and XIV.) Price 10s.

## Publications of the Early English Text Society and of the Philological Society.

**ON EARLY ENGLISH PRONUNCIATION.** With Especial Reference to Shakspere and Chaucer. Containing an investigation of the correspondence of writing with speech in England from the Anglo-Saxon period to the existing received and dialectal forms, with a systematic notation of spoken sounds by means of the ordinary printing types, including a re-arrangement of Prof. F. J. Childs' memoir on the language of Chaucer and Gower, reprints of the rare tracts by Salesbury on English 1547, and Welsh 1567, and by Barcley on French 1521, abstracts of Schmeller's Treatise on Bavarian Dialects, and Winckler's Low German and Friesian Dialecticon, and Prince L.-L. Bonaparte's Vowel and Consonant Lists. By Alexander J. Ellis, F.R.S., F.S.A., F.C.P.S., F.C.P., Vice-President of the Philological Society, etc., etc., B.A. Part V. Existing Dialectal as compared with West Saxon Pronunciation, with Two Maps of the Dialect Districts. Demy 8vo. paper, pp. xx—88 and 836. Price 25s.

# INDIA.

## Publications of the Government of India.

**SCIENTIFIC MEMOIRS BY MEDICAL OFFICERS OF THE ARMY OF INDIA.** Edited by Sir Benjamin Simpson, M.D., K.C.I.E., Surgeon-General with the Government of India. Part IV. 1889. 4to. boards, pp. 72, with 4 Plates. Price 4s.

**EPIGRAPHIA INDICA AND RECORD OF THE ARCHÆOLOGICAL SURVEY OF INDIA.** Edited by Jas. Burgess, LL.D., C.I.E., &c. &c., Director General. Part III. April, 1889. Price 7s.

## Publications of the Geological Survey of India.

**RECORDS,** Vol. XXII. Part II. 1889. Royal 8vo. wrapper, pp. 98, with 3 Plates. Price 2s.—Note on Indian Steatite. Compiled by F. R. Mallet.—Distorted Pebbles in the Siwalik Conglomerate. By C. S. Middlemiss, B.A. (With One Plate.)—"The Carboniferous Glacial Period." Further Note by Dr. W. Waagen on a letter from Mr. C. Derby concerning Traces of a Carboniferous Glacial Period in South America. Translated by E. C. Cotes.—Notes on Dr. Waagen's "Carboniferous Glacial Period." By A. B. Wynne, F.G.S., and Dr. Ottokar Feistmantel.—Report on the Oil-Fields of Twingoung and Beme, Burma. By Fritz Noetling, Ph.D. (With One Plate and a Map.)—The Gypsum of the Nehal Nadi, Kumaun. By C. S. Middlemiss, B.A. (With One Plate.)—On Some of the Materials for Pottery obtainable in the Neighbourhood of Jabalpur and of Umaria. By F. R. Mallet.—Additions to the Museum.—Additions to the Library.

# AUSTRALIA.

## Publications of the Australian Museum, Sydney.

**MEMOIRS,** No. 2.—**LORD HOWE ISLAND**: Its Zoology, Geology and Physical Characters. Printed by Order of the Trustees, E. P. Ramsay, Curator. With Maps, Diagrams, and Plates. Royal 8vo. boards, pp. viii. and 132. 7s. 6d.

## Publications of the Government of New South Wales.

**THE HISTORY OF NEW SOUTH WALES.—FROM THE RECORDS.** Vol. I. Demy 8vo. cloth, pp. 650. Illustrated with Maps, Portraits and Sketches. By G. B. Barton, of the Middle Temple, Barrister-at-Law. Price 10s. 6d. This Volume will contain the History of New South Wales from 1783 to 1789, founded on the letters and despatches written by Governor Phillip during that time, and many other records of great historical interest never before published, which have recently been obtained from the Public Record Office in London, the Record Office in Sydney, the collections of Sir Joseph Banks and others, etc., etc.       (*Nearly Ready.*)

## Publications of the Royal Society of New South Wales.

**JOURNAL AND PROCEEDINGS,** Vol. XXII. 1888. With 5 Diagrams and 17 Plates. Price 10s. 6d.—Officers for 1888-89.—President's Address. By C. S. Wilkinson, F.G.S.—Forest Destruction in New South Wales and its Effects on the Flow of Water in Watercourses and on the Rainfall. By W. E. Abbott Wingen.—On the Increasing Magnitude of Eta Argus. By H. C. Russell, B.A., F.R.S., &c. Notes on some Minerals and Mineral Localities in the Northern Districts of New South Wales. By D. A. Porter, Tamworth. (One Plate.)—On a simple plan of Easing Railway Curves. By Walter Shellshear, Assoc. M. Inst. C.E. (One Plate.)—An Improvement in Anemometers. By H. C. Russell, B.A., F.R.S.—On the Anatomy and Life History of Mollusca peculiar to Australia. (With Plates.) By the Rev. J. E. Tenison-Woods, F.L.S., F.G.S.—Considerations of Phytographic Expressions and Arrangements. By Baron Ferd. von Mueller, K.C.M.G., M.D., Ph.D., F.R.S.—Indigenous Australian Forage Plants (Non-Grasses), including Plants Injurious to Stock. By J. H. Maiden, F.L.S., &c., Curator of the Technological Museum, Sydney. Census of the Fauna of the Older Tertiary of Australia. By Prof. Ralph Tate, F.G.S., F.L.S., &c.—Description of the Autographic Stress-Strain Apparatus used in connection with the Testing Machine at the University of Sydney and for Recording the Results of Testing the Strength and Elasticity of Materials in Cross-Breaking, Compression and Tension. By Professor Warren, M.I.C.E., W.H., S.C. (Four Plates.)—The Storm of 21st September, 1888. By H. C. Russell, B.A., F.R.S.—Some New South Wales Tan Substances. Part V., including an Account of Löwenthal's Process for the Estimation of Tannic Acid. By J. H. Maiden, F.L.S., &c., Curator of the Technological Museum, Sydney.—Apps' Induction Coil.—Results of Observations of Comets I. and II., 1888, at Windsor, N.S.W. By John Tebbutt, F.R.A.S., &c.—The Desert Sandstone. By the Rev. J. E. Tenison-Woods, F.G.S., F.L.S., &c. (With Plates.)—On a New Self-Recording Thermometer. By H. C. Russell, B.A., F.R.S., &c.—The Thunderstorm of 26th October, 1888. By H. C. Russell, B.A., F.R.S., &c.—The Latin Verb *Jubere*: A Linguistic Study. By John Fraser, B.A., LL.D.—Notes on some New South Wales Minerals (Note No. 5). By A. Liversidge, M.A., F.R.S., Professor of Chemistry in the University of Sidney.—Proceedings, Donations, &c.—Proceedings of the Sections.—Medical Section.—Microscopical Section.—Title Page, Contents, Office-bearers, Additions to the Library, Index to Volume XXII., and Exchanges and Presentations.

# NEW ORIENTAL PUBLICATIONS.

Small 4to. half-bound, pp. xv. 889.   Price 10s. 6d.

## THE STANDARD SANSKRIT-ENGLISH DICTIONARY.

Containing Appendices on Sanskrit Prosody and Names of Noted Mythological Persons, etc.

(For the Use of Schools and Colleges.)

By LASKHMAN RAMCHANDRA VAIDYA, M.A., LL.B., etc.

---

Small 8vo.   In Parts.   Price 5s. complete.

## BHAGABADGITA.

With Sanskrit and English Notes, Translation, and an Esoteric Exposition in English.

By P. D. GOSWAMI.

*.* Parts I. and II. (pp. 1 to 94) are published.

---

4to. pp. xii. 764, 8.   Price 2 Guineas.

## DICTIONNAIRE PRATIQUE ARABE-FRANÇAIS.

Contenant les Mots employés dans l'Arabe parlé en Algérie et en Tunisie, etc.

Par M. BEAUSSIER.

Interprète principal de l'Armée d'Algérie, etc. etc.

---

Post 8vo. sewed, pp. 455.   Price 5s.

الف ليلة وللة

Alf Lailat wa Laila.   Arabian Nights.

Volume II.

Edited by P. A. SALHANI.

*.* Vol. I. vide Trübner's Record, No. 243, p. 24.

---

Royal 8vo. cloth, pp. iv. 303.   Price 10s. 6d.

## A NEPALI GRAMMAR,

And English-Nepálí and Nepálí-English Vocabulary.

(About 4000 Words.)

Designed for the Use of Missionaries, Tea-Planters, and Military Officers.

By Rev. A. TURNBULL, M.A., B.D., Church of Scotland Mission.

---

8vo. boards, pp. iv. 177.   Price 7s. 6d.

## A CHINESE AND ENGLISH PHRASE-BOOK.

In the Canton Dialect.

Or, Dialogues on Ordinary and Familiar Subjects, etc.

By T. L. HEDMAN and K. P. LEE.

---

Royal 8vo. pp. 179.   Price 15s.

## HOW TO SPEAK CANTONESE.

Fifty Conversations in Cantonese Colloquial.

With Chinese Character, English Translations, Romanized Spelling, etc.

By J. DYER BALL, M.R.A.S., etc., Of H.M.'s Civil Service, Hong-Kong.

---

Royal 8vo. pp. 25, 76, 4, viii.   Price 10s. 6d.

## HOW TO WRITE CHINESE.

Part I.

By J. DYER BALL, M.R.A.S., etc., Of H.M.'s Civil Service, Hong-Kong.

*.* This First Part contains: General Rules for Writing Chinese, and Practical Directions for Writing the Radicals.

---

8vo. pp. 40, 7.   Price 3s. 6d.

## HOW TO WRITE THE RADICALS.

By J. DYER BALL, M.R.A.S., etc., Of H.M.'s Civil Service, Hong-Kong.

---

Post 8vo. cloth, pp. viii. 287, xv.   Price 6s.

## HANDBOOK OF ENGLISH-JAPANESE ETYMOLOGY.

By WILLIAM IMBRIE.

Second Edition.

---

Demy 8vo. boards, pp. v. 248.   With Map.   Price 6s.

## A CONCISE DICTIONARY OF THE PRINCIPAL ROADS, CHIEF TOWNS AND VILLAGES OF JAPAN, Etc.

Compiled from Official Documents.

By W. N. WHITNEY, M.D., Interpreter of the U.S. Legation, Tōkyō.

---

Post 8vo. cloth, pp. vi. cxx. 329.   Price 10s. 6d.

## THE LIFE AND LIFE-WORK OF BEHRAMJI M. MALABARI.

By DAYARAM GIDUAML.

# TRÜBNER AND CO.'S LIST.

## WORKS IN PREPARATION.

8vo. cloth.

### THE LIFE OF CARMEN SYLVA

(QUEEN OF ROUMANIA).

By NATALIE, BARONESS STACKELBERG.

Translated from the German.

With View of the Castle of Pelesch and Four Portraits.

Crown 8vo. pp.    . Cloth, price 2s. 6d. ; wrapper, 1s. 6d.

### HENRY RICHARD, THE APOSTLE OF PEACE,

By LEWIS APPLETON.

With Portraits of Henry Richard, Richard Cobden, Joseph Sturge, Edmund Fry, William Stokes, Elihu Burritt, Arthur G. O'Neill, and the Author.

Royal 4to. cloth, price 25s.

### MACHINE DRAWING AND DESIGN,

For Engineering Students and Practical Engineers :

Being a complete Course of Instruction in Mechanical Drawing, with Exercises on the Application of Principles to Engine and Machine Design.

By WILLIAM RIPPER, M. INST. M.E.,

Gold and Bronze Medallist; Author of "Steam, and the Steam Engine"; Assistant Professor of Mechanical Engineering in the Sheffield Technical School.

Illustrated by Fifty-five Plates and numerous Explanatory Engravings.

Crown 8vo. cloth, pp. iv.-209. Price .

### THE MODERN NOVELISTS OF RUSSIA.

Being the Substance of Six Lectures Delivered at Taylor Institution, Oxford.

By CHARLES EDWARD TURNER,

English Lector in the University of St. Petersburg.

Medium 16mo. cloth, pp. vi. and 156. Price 2s.

### THE CHESS PLAYERS' TEXT BOOK.

An Elementary Treatise on the Game of Chess.

Illustrated by numerous Diagrams specially designed for Beginners and Advanced Students.

By G. H. D. GOSSIP.

Author of "The Chess Players' Manual" and "Theory of the Chess Openings."

Crown 8vo. Price 2s. 6d.

### APPEAL TO CONSERVATIVES.

By AUGUSTE COMTE.

Author of "The System of Positive Philosophy," and of "The System of Positive Politics."

Joint Translators, T. C. DONKIN and RICHARD CONGREVE.

Crown 8vo. stiff wrappers, pp. xvi. and 200. Price 1s. 6d.

### SHAKESPEARE'S CYMBELINE.

Edited, with Notes, by C. M. INGLEBY, LL.D.

Revised by HOLCOMBE INGLEBY, M.A.

Adapted for the Use of Schools.

The above Volume is issued by direction of the Royal Society.

Crown 8vo. pp.    . Wrapper, price 1s.

### ESSAYS: IN THREE KINDS.

By THOMAS SINCLAIR, M.A.

Author of " Humanities," "Quest," " Love's Trilogy," etc., etc.

CONTENTS.—Leisure ; The Mediterranean ; Fountains ; Draught Cattle ; Exhibitions ; Cultures ; Eyes ; Dark Days ; Rough Music ; Moonlight ; National Enmities ; Lies ; Furlough, an Idyl ; Chieville, a Comedietta.

Vol. III. Papilionidæ and Hesperidæ, completing the Work.

Demy 8vo.

### SOUTH AFRICAN BUTTERFLIES:

A MONOGRAPH OF THE EXTRA-TROPICAL SPECIES.

By ROLAND TRIMEN, F.R.S., F.L.S., F.Z.S., F.Ent.S., etc.,

Curator of the South African Museum, Cape Town ;

Assisted by JAMES HENRY BOWKER, F.Z.S., F.R.G.S., etc., etc.,

Colonel (Retired) in the Cape Service ; Late Commandant of the Frontier Armed and Mounted Police ; Governor's Agent in Basutoland, and Chief Commissioner at the Diamond Fields of Griqualand West.

8vo.

### SOCIAL HISTORY OF THE RACES OF MANKIND.

CHIAPO AND GUZANO MARANONIANS.

By A. FEATHERMAN.

8vo. about 300 pages, cloth, gilt top. Price 21s. net.

### AN ACCOUNT OF THE ABORIGINES OF TASMANIA.

Their Manners, Customs, Wars, Hunting, Food, Morals, Language, Origin and General Characteristics,

Collected from all Sources, from the time of their First Contact with Europeans until their Final Extermination.

By H. LING ROTH,

Assisted by E. MARION BUTLER ; with a Chapter on the OSTEOLOGY, by J. G. GARSON, M.D., Vice-President Anthropological Institute, and Lecturer on Comparative Anatomy at Charing Cross Hospital ; and a Preface by E. B. TYLOR, F.R.S., D.C.L., LL.D., etc., University Museum, Oxford. With numerous Autotype Plates from Original Drawings made by EDITH MAY ROTH.

This Edition will be strictly limited to the Subscribers, and every copy will be numbered.

8vo. cloth, pp.    . Price 15s.

### THE HISTORY OF CANADA.

By WILLIAM KINGSFORD.

Vol. III.

This Volume narrates the events of the Conquest of Canada, and its cession to Great Britain under the Treaty of Paris, 1762.

# TRÜBNER AND CO.'S LIST.

**INDIA, PAST AND PRESENT,**

HISTORICAL, SOCIAL AND POLITICAL.

By JAMES SAMUELSON,

Of the Middle Temple, Barrister-at-Law; Author of "Roumania, Past and Present," "Bulgaria, Past and Present," etc.

Illustrated with a Map, Explanatory Woodcuts and Collotype Views, Portraits, Archæological and Ethnological Subjects, from Thirty-six Photographs by Bourne and Shepherd, Calcutta, etc.; Lala Deen Dayal, of Indore; S. Hormusjee, Bombay; Madame Scaramanga, Bombay; and other well-known professional and amateur photographers in India, Europe and America.

---

Crown 8vo. cloth, pp. xxiii. and 302, with Map. Price 8s.

**A HISTORY OF CIVILIZATION IN ANCIENT INDIA.**

Based on Sanskrit Literature.

By ROMESH CHUNDER DUTT,

The Bengal Civil Service; and of the Middle Temple, Barrister-at-Law; Author of "A Bengali Translation of the Rig Veda Sanhita," and other works.

In Three Volumes.

Vol. I. VEDIC AND EPIC AGES.

---

Volume II. 8vo. cloth.

**ELEMENTS OF THE COMPARATIVE GRAMMAR OF THE INDO-GERMANIC LANGUAGES.**

A Concise Exposition of the History of Sanskrit, Old Iranian (Avestic and Old Persian), Old Armenian, Old Greek, Latin, Umbrian-Samnitic, Old Irish, Gothic, Old High German, Lithuanian and Old Bulgarian.

By KARL BRUGMANN,

Professor of Comparative Philology in the University of Leipzig.

Translated from the German by JOSEPH WRIGHT, Ph.D.

---

8vo.

**THE ITALIC DIALECTS.**

I. THE TEXT OF THE INSCRIPTIONS

(Oscan, Paelignian, Sabine, etc.; the oldest Latin and Faliscan; Volscian Picentine and Umbrian),

II. AN ARABIC LEXICON.

Being a Complete Concordance to Part I., and giving the Meanings of all Words whose Interpretation is certain.

With the Italic Glosses of Varro and Festus, and a Dialect Map.

Edited and Arranged by R. SEYMOUR CONWAY, M.A.,

Fellow of Gonville and Caius College, Classical Lecturer at Newnham College, Author of "Verner's Law in Italy."

---

In Two Vols. post 8vo. cloth, about 1250 and 250 pages. Price 32s.

**AN ARABIC-ENGLISH DICTIONARY.**

ON A NEW AND UNIQUE SYSTEM.

Comprising about 120,000 Arabic Words; with an English Index of about 50,000 Words.

By H. A. SALMONE,

Arabic Lecturer at University College, London.

---

In One Volume. Royal 8vo.

**A SANSKRIT-ENGLISH DICTIONARY**

BASED UPON THE ST. PETERSBURG LEXICONS.

By CARL CAPPELLER,

Professor at the University of Jena.

This English Edition of Cappeller's Sanskrit Dictionary differs from its German original chiefly in the fact that it covers a considerably extended range of texts (the most important of which are: the second edition of Böhtlingk's Sanskrit Chrestomathie, the Rigveda Hymns translated by Geldner and Kaegi, the Marut Hymns translated by F. Max Müller, the Kathopanishad; the Hitopadeca, Nala, Bhagavadgita, Manu, the Plays of Kalidasa and the Meghaduta, the Mrcchakatika and Malatimadhava) and in some minor particulars, of which the author gives an account in the preface. In all essentials, the double character of the work has been preserved: it is intended to be not only a handbook for the beginner in Sanskrit, but also to serve the purposes of the linguistic student.

---

Fcap. 8vo. cloth, pp.      Price

**HOW TO BE BEAUTIFUL.**

Nature Unmasked.

By TERESA H. DEAN.

A Book for Every Woman. New Copyright Edition.

---

Demy 8vo.

**ON THE IDEALS OF THE EMOTIONS, THE INTELLECT AND THE WILL.**

*APOLOGIA PRO AMORE.*

A New Theory of Idealism.

By Mrs. P. F. FITZGERALD.

Authoress of "An Essay on the Philosophy of Self-Consciousness," and "A Treatise on the Principle of Sufficient Reason."

---

8vo.

**HUMANITISM.**

The Scientific Solution of the Social Problem.

By W. A. MACDONALD.

"Humanitism" is a new school of social science, and embraces every sphere of human activity. Although based upon the physical sciences, it enters into an historical inquiry, and shows that the history of mankind is marked by ebbs and flows of false subjectivity and objectivity.

---

Crown 8vo.

**AIR ANALYSIS:**

A PRACTICAL TREATISE ON THE EXAMINATION OF AIR,

With Appendix on Coal Gas.

By J. A. WANKLYN and W. J. COOPER.

---

Crown 8vo. 350 pp. cloth gilt, price 5s.

**NEW POPULAR HANDBOOK OF COUNTY DIALECTS.**

By the Rev. J. L. SAYWELL, F.R.H.S.

Author of "The Parochial Histories of Northallerton and Ackworth;" and Contributor to "Yorkshire Archæological and Topographical Journal," "Notes and Queries," &c.

---

LONDON: TRÜBNER & Co., 57 AND 59, LUDGATE HILL.

# TRÜBNER'S ORIENTAL SERIES.

### NEW VOLUMES IN PREPARATION.

Post 8vo. cloth.

**ENGLISH INTERCOURSE WITH SIAM IN THE SEVENTEENTH CENTURY.**

By J. ANDERSON, M.D., LL.D., F.R.S.

Post 8vo.

**BIHAR PROVERBS.**

By JOHN CHRISTIAN.

Post 8vo.

**DACAKUMARACARITA OF DANDIN.**

Translated by EDWARD J. RAPSON.

Post 8vo.

**A SKETCH OF THE MODERN LANGUAGES OF OCEANIA.**

By R. N. CUST, LL.D.,

Author of "Modern Languages of the East," "Modern Languages of Africa," etc.

Post 8vo. cloth, pp. xx. and 532. Price 21s.

**ORIGINAL SANSKRIT TEXTS**

ON THE ORIGIN AND HISTORY OF THE PEOPLE OF INDIA: THEIR RELIGION AND INSTITUTIONS.

Collected, Translated and Illustrated

By J. MUIR, C.I.E., D.C.L., LL.D., Ph.D.

Vol. I. Mythical and Legendary Accounts of the Origin of Caste, with an inquiry into its Existence in the Vedic Age.

Third Edition, Re-written and greatly Enlarged.

New Edition. Post 8vo. cloth, pp. 336. Price 16s.

**THE RELIGIONS OF INDIA.**

By A. BARTH, Paris.

Translated by the Rev. J. WOOD.

# THE ENGLISH & FOREIGN PHILOSOPHICAL LIBRARY.

### NEW VOLUMES IN PREPARATION.

Post 8vo.

**THE PHILOSOPHY OF LAW.**

By Professor DIODATO LIOY.

Translated by W. HASTIE.

Post 8vo. pp. xx. and 314, cloth. Price 10s. 6d.

**ENIGMAS OF LIFE.**

By W. R. GREG.

Seventeenth Edition, with a Postscript.

Post 8vo. cloth, pp. xxiii.—377. Price

**THE SCIENCE OF KNOWLEDGE.**

By J. G. FICHTE.

Translated from the German by A. E. KROEGER.

With an Introduction by Professor W. T. HARRIS.

Post 8vo. cloth, pp. x.—505. Price

**THE SCIENCE OF RIGHTS.**

By J. G. FICHTE.

Translated from the German by A. E. KROEGER.

With an Introduction by Professor W. T. HARRIS.

In Two Volumes, post 8vo.

**JOHANN GOTTLIEB FICHTE'S POPULAR WORKS.**

The Nature of the Scholar; The Vocation of the Scholar; The Vocation of Man; The Doctrine of Religion; Characteristics of the Present Age; Outlines of the Doctrine of Knowledge.

With a Memoir by WILLIAM SMITH, LL.D.

Fichte belongs to those great men whose lives are an everlasting possession to mankind, and whose words the world does not willingly let die. His character stands written in his life, a massive but severely simple whole. It has no parts; the depth and earnestness on which it rests speak forth alike in his thoughts, words and actions. No man of his time—few, perhaps, of any time—exercised a more powerful, spirit-stirring influence over the minds of his fellow-countrymen.

# TRÜBNER'S SERIES OF SIMPLIFIED GRAMMARS.

EDITED BY DR. ROST, LIBRARIAN OF THE INDIA OFFICE.

### NEW VOLUMES IN PREPARATION.

Crown 8vo. pp.

**A SIMPLIFIED TELUGU GRAMMAR.**

By HENRY MORRIS, M.A.

Crown 8vo.

**A SIMPLIFIED CHINESE GRAMMAR.**

By JOSEPH EDKINS, D.D.

LONDON TRÜBNER & CO., 57 AND 59 LUDGATE HILL.

# TRÜBNER'S RECORD,

## A JOURNAL

DEVOTED TO THE

## Literature of the East,

WITH NOTES AND LISTS OF CURRENT

## American, European and Colonial Publications.

No. 247.     THIRD SERIES. VOL. I. PART 5.     PRICE 2s.

## NOTICE.

*We beg to inform our Readers and Correspondents that the amalgamation of the three firms which has recently taken place will in no degree affect the working of the business established by the late Mr. Nicholas Trübner in all its special departments of Oriental, European American, Colonial and Scientific Literature; every branch of which will be maintained as heretofore, so that the change is in the name rather than in the establishment.*

*Our Friends, therefore, may rest satisfied that everything will be carried on without the slightest break in the continuity of the business; and it is our hope that with increased attention to their interests, their kind patronage which has hitherto been extended to the firm of* TRÜBNER & CO., *may in future be extended to that of*

## KEGAN PAUL, TRENCH, TRÜBNER & Co. (Limited).

---

### NOW READY.

### DEDICATED BY SPECIAL PERMISSION TO HER MAJESTY THE QUEEN.

In Two Vols. post 8vo. cloth, about 1250 and 250 pages.

# AN ARABIC-ENGLISH DICTIONARY.

### On a New and Unique System.

COMPRISING ABOUT 120,000 ARABIC WORDS; WITH AN ENGLISH INDEX TO THE SAME.

## BY A. H. SALMONÉ,

Arabic Lecturer at University College, London.

---

*MR. SALMONÉ has prepared an Arabic-English Dictionary on an ingeniously-devised system, by means of which a saving of space will be effected though the Arabic part will comprise about 120,000 words with a copious English Index to the same. Instead of specifying under each root-word the various derivations in succession, and the various broken plurals after the singulars to which they belong, MR. SALMONÉ refers by figures for every one of the 70 common derivative forms to a table which is prefixed to the Dictionary, and in which the consonants and vowel points characteristic of each derivative form are printed in red, so as to be readily distinguishable from the radical letters. The table is accompanied by full explanatory notes as to the use to be made of it.*

LONDON: TRÜBNER & CO., 57 AND 59, LUDGATE HILL.

# R. H. PORTER,
# NATURAL HISTORY PUBLISHER & BOOKSELLER,
### 18, PRINCES STREET, CAVENDISH SQUARE, LONDON, W.



# HAKLUYT SOCIETY.
### ESTABLISHED FOR THE PURPOSE OF PRINTING RARE OR UNPUBLISHED VOYAGES AND TRAVELS.

## ORIENTAL PUBLICATIONS
### Of E. J. BRILL, Leyden.

**Actes** du sixième Congrès Internat. d. Orientalistes, tenu en 1883 à Leide. 1re partie: Compte-rendu des séances, fl. 2.50. 2me Section 1. Sémitique, fl. 15. 3me Section 2; Aryenne, fl. 12.50. 4me Section 3: Africaine; Sect. 4: De l'extrême Orient; Sect. 5: Polynésienne. fl. 14. Les sections 3, 4, et 5 se vendent séparément à raison de fl. 9, fl. 5, et fl. 6.

**Annales** auctore Abu-Djafar Mohammed Ibn Djarir At-Tabari quos ediderunt *J. Barth, Tk. Nöldeke, O. Loth, E. Prim, H. Thorbecke, S. Fraenkel, I. Guidi, D. H. Müller, M. Th. Houtsma, Stanislas Guyard, V. Rosen* et *M. J. de Goeje.* 8o. Tome I. pars 1-5; Tome II. pars 1-6; Tome III. pars 1-7; et 1 vol. Titres, Tables de matières; pages réimprimées. (*Texte arabe.*) fl. 92.30.

**Bâsim** le forgeron et Hârûn Er Rachid.—Texte Arabe en dialecte d'Egypt et de Syrie. Publ. d'après les MSS. de Leide, de Gotha et du Caire par le Comte *Carlo de Landberg.* Tome I.: Texte, traduction et proverbes. fl. 3.

**Catalogus** cod. Arab. Bibl. Acad. Lugd. Bat. Ed. 2a. Auctt. *M. J. de Goeje* et *M. Th. Houtsma.* Vol. I. fl. 9.

**Dozy, R. P. A.**—Supplément aux dictionanires arabes. 2 vol. demi mar. fl. 75.

**Goeje, M. J. de,** Mémoire sur les Carmathes du Bahraïn et les Fatimides. fl. 3.

**Ibn 'Abd El Kerim** 'ali rizâ von Sirâ. Das Tarîkh-i-Zendtje. Hrsg. von Ernst Beer. fl. 1.75.

**Ibn-Wadhih** qui dicitur Al-Jàqubi historiae. Edid. indicesque adj. *M. Th. Houtsma.* Vol. I.: Historia anteislamica. Vol. II.: Historia islamica. fl. 15.

**Imad** ed dîn el-kâtib el-Isfahânî conquête de la Syrie et de la Palistine par Salâb ed din. *Texte Arabe.* Publ. par le Comte *Carlo de Landberg.* Vol. I. fl. 9.

**Kitâb al Aghâni.**—The 21st volume of the Kitâb al-Aghâni, being a collection of biographies not contained in the edition of Bûlâq by *R. Brünnow.* Part I. Text. fl. 6.

**Kitab al Muwassâ** of Abû 't- Tayyib Muhammed ibn Ishâq al Wassâ by *R. Brünnow.* fl. 3.50.

**Landberg, C.,** Proverbes et dictons du peuple arabe. Matériaux pour servir à la connaissance des dialectes vulgaires recueillis, traduits et annotés. Vol. I. Province de Syrie. Section da Saydâ. *Texte arabe.* fl. 7.

**Livres** des merveilles de l'Inde. Texte arabe publié d'après le *MS. de M. Schefer,* collat. a. l. *MSS.* de Constantinople par *P. A. v. d. Lith.* Traduct. franç. p. *L. Marcel Devic.* Av. 4 pl. col. tirées du *MS.* arabe de Hariri d. l. collect. de *M. Schefer.* fl. 12.

**Nöldeke, Th.,** Gesch. d. Perser u. Araber zur Zeit der Sasaniden. Aus d. arab. Chronik des Tabari übers. u. m. ausführl. Erläut. u. Ergänz. versehn. fl. 7.

**Recueil** de textes relatifs à l'histoire des Seldjoucides. Publ. p. *M. Th. Houtsma.* Hist. des Seldjoucides de l'Iráq par al-Bondari d'après Imâd ad-din al Katib al-Isfahânî. fl. 5.25.

**Spitta-Bey, C.,** Contes arabes modernes recueillis et traduits. Texte arabe en caract. lat. avec la traduct. franç. fl. 3.75.

**Land, J. P. N.,** Anecdota Syriaca, colleg. edid. et explicavit. Tom. I. Symbolae syriacae. fl. 7; Tom. II. Joannis episcopi Ephesi monophysitae scripta historica quotquot adhuc inedita supereant. Syriace edidit. fl. 8.50: Tom. III. Zachariae episcopi Mitylenes aliorumque script. hist. graece plerumque deperdita, Syr. edid. fl. 8.50; Tom. IV. Otia Syriaca. fl. 10.50.

**Stephen Bar Sudaili.** The Syrian mystic and the Book of Hierotheos, by *A. L. Frothingham,* jr. (*Texte Syrien.*) fl. 2.50.

**Aryabhatiya (The)** A manual of Astronomy, with the commentary Bbatadipikâ of Paramâdiçvara ed. by *H. Kern.* (*Sanskrit text.*) fl. 4.40.

**Speyer, J. S.,** Sanskrit Syntax. With an introduction by Dr. H. Kern. Bound in cloth. fl. 9.

**Brünnow, R. E.,** A Classified List of all simple and compound cuneiform ideographs occurring in the texts hitherto published, with their assyro-babylonian equivalents, phonetic values, etc. Parts I. and II. Every part fl. 9.

**Firdusii** Schachnahme edid. *J. A. Vullers.* Tome I.—III. fl. 35.25.

**Recueil** de Textes relatifs à l'histoire des Seldjoucides (*Texte persan*) publ. par *M. Th. Houtsma.* Vol. I. Hist. des Seldjouc. du Kermân, par Muhammed Ibrahim. fl. 3.50.

**Pleyte, W.,** Chapitres supplémentaires du Livre des Morts, 162-174. Texte égyptien autographié d'après les Monuments de Leide, du Louvre et du Musée Britannique par *T. Bytel.* Av. traduct. et comment. par *W. Pleyte.* 3 vol. av. 27 pl. fl. 25.

————, Papyrus de Turin facsimilés par Rossy. 2 vols. dem. mar. d. s. t. fl. 160.

**Hoffmann, J. J.**—A Japanese grammar. 2nd ed. bound in cloth. fl. 12.

A complete catalogue of the publications of E. J. Brill will be sent post-free on application to any purchaser.

## NEW AMERICAN BOOKS.

8vo. cloth, pp. ix. and 516. Price £1 1s.

A TREATISE ON LINEAR DIFFERENTIAL EQUATIONS. By THOMAS CRAIG, Ph.D. Volume I.: Equations with Uniform Coefficients.

8vo. cloth, pp. viii.-575. Price 18s.

THE CALIFORNIAN FRUITS AND HOW TO GROW THEM. A Manual of Methods which have yielded Greatest Success, with Lists of Varieties best adapted to the different Districts of the State. By EDWARD G. WICKSON, A.M.

8vo. cloth, pp. ix. and 277. Price 10s. 6d.

THE ART OF BREATHING AS THE BASIS OF TONE PRODUCTION. A Book Indispensable to Singers, Elocutionists, Educators, Lawyers, Preachers, and to all desirous of having a pleasant voice and good health. By LEO KOFLER.

Crown 8vo. cloth, pp. xxxii. and 232. Price 5s.

PRACTICAL BLACKSMITHING. A Collection of Articles contributed at different times by Skilled Workmen to the columns of "The Blacksmith and Wheelwright," and covering nearly the whole range of Blacksmithing from the simplest job of work to some of the most complex Forgings. Compiled and Edited by M. T. RICHARDSON. Illustrated. Volume I.

Crown 8vo. cloth. Price 10s. 6d.

THE THEORY AND PRACTICE OF CATTLE BREEDING. By WILLIAM WARFIELD. Author of "A History of Imported Shorthorns," and a Staff Correspondent of *The Breeder's Gazette.*

Crown 8vo. cloth. Price 6s.

A CENTURY OF AMERICAN LITERATURE. Benjamin Franklin to James Russell Lowell. Selections from a Hundred Authors, chosen and arranged by HUNTINGTON SMITH.

New edition, entirely revised and enlarged. 8vo. cloth, pp. iv.-150. Price 3s. 6d.; paper, 2s. 6d.

HOW TO SELECT COWS; or, The Guenon System Simplified, Explained and Practically Applied. By WILLIS P. HAZARD, M.A., Secretary of the Pennsylvania Guenon Commission; President of the Chad's Ford Farmers' Club; a Vice-President of the Pennsylvania Dairymen's Association, etc.; Author of Treatises "On the Jersey, Guernsey and Alderney Cow," and "On Butter and Butter Making," "The Annals of Philadelphia," etc. With the Report of the Pennsylvania Guenon Commission. Thirtieth Thousand. With nearly One Hundred Illustrations Photographed from Guenon's Engravings.

In One Volume, crown 8vo. cloth, Illustrated, pp. 153, price 3s. 6d.

THE FAMILY HORSE; Its Stabling, Care and Feeding. A Practical Manual for Horse-keepers. By GEORGE A. MARTIN.

CONTENTS:—Selecting a Horse—Feeding and Watering—Barns and Stables—Stable Management—Clipping, Singeing and Trimming—On the Road—Riding on Horseback—Harness and Vehicles—Shoeing and Care of the Feet—Ailments and Remedies—Prize Essays: Stabling, Feed and Care; How to select a Horse and Keep it; Views of a Veteran; The Family Horse in the Prairie States.

Crown 8vo. cloth. Price 15s.

THE PRACTICAL DISTILLER: A Complete and Thorough Treatise on the Art of Distilling and Rectifying Alcohol, Liquors, Essences, Liqueurs, etc., by the Latest and most Improved Methods. By LEONARD MONZERT.

# TRÜBNER'S RECORD, No. 247.

## CONTENTS.



# PUBLISHED BY BLACKIE & SON.

NOW READY, VOLS. I. II. and III.   (Vol. IV. on 13th December.)
To be completed in 8 vols., published quarterly, square 8vo. cloth, 6s. each ; or half morocco, 8s. 6d. each.

**BLACKIE'S MODERN CYCLOPEDIA.**  A Handy Book of Reference on all Subjects and for all Readers.  With numerous Engravings and Maps.  Edited by CHARLES ANNANDALE, M.A., LL.D.

From the *Saturday Review.*—"Will be found a boon to the general reader.  Some handy form of encyclopædia has long been wanted.  This is comprehensive, without being bulky.  The information is succinctly given, sufficiently copious, and strictly relevant.  With these good features must be noticed the excellent type and paper, the useful woodcuts and maps, of these neatly-bound octavo volumes."

NOW READY, VOLS. I. to VI.   (Vol. VII. in December.)
To be completed in 8 vols., small 4to. cloth, gilt top, 10s. 6d. each.

**THE HENRY IRVING SHAKESPEARE.**  Edited by HENRY IRVING and FRANK A. MARSHALL, and illustrated by GORDON BROWNE and other Artists.

From the *Athenæum.*—"The general result is so good that we must congratulate all concerned in the work. . . . It is profusely illustrated by Mr. Gordon Browne, whose charming designs, executed in facsimile, give it an artistic value superior in our judgment to any illustrated edition of Shakespeare with which we are acquainted."

In 4 vols., imperial 8vo. cloth, £5 ; or half morocco, £6 6s.

**THE IMPERIAL DICTIONARY OF THE ENGLISH LANGUAGE.**  A Complete Encyclopædic Lexicon, Literary, Etymological, Scientific, Technological, and Pronouncing.  By JOHN OGILVIE, LL.D.  New Edition, carefully Revised and greatly augmented.  Edited by CHARLES ANNANDALE, M.A., LL.D.  Illustrated by above 3000 Engravings on Wood.

From the *Times.*—"So far as vocabulary and treatment are concerned, we should not wish for anything better than the new 'Imperial.'  Few, except specialists, are likely to come across terms not to be found here ; and the definitions are accurate and intelligible, developing into detailed explanations where necessary.  The etymology is clear and concise, and the illustrations are copious, appropriate, and well executed."

LONDON: BLACKIE & SON, 49 AND 50, OLD BAILEY.

# TRÜBNER & CO.'S NEW BOOKS.

8vo. cloth, pp. xvi. and 390.  Price £1 1s.
## INDIA, PAST AND PRESENT,
HISTORICAL, SOCIAL AND POLITICAL.

By JAMES SAMUELSON,

Of the Middle Temple, Barrister-at-Law; Author of "Roumania, Past and Present," "Bulgaria, Past and Present," etc.

Illustrated with a Map, Explanatory Woodcuts and Collotype Views. Portraits, Archæological and Ethnological Subjects, from Thirty-six Photographs by Bourne and Shepherd, Calcutta, etc.; Lala Deen Dayal, of Indore; S. Hormusjee, Bombay; Madame Scaramanga, Bombay; and other well-known professional and amateur photographers in India, Europe and America.

---

8vo. cloth, pp. viii. and 350.  Price 7s. 6d.
## HUMANITISM:
*The Scientific Solution of the Social Problem.*
By W. A. MACDONALD.

"Humanitism" is a new school of social science, and embraces every sphere of human activity. Although based upon the physical sciences, it enters into an historical inquiry, and shows that the history of mankind is marked by ebbs and flows of false subjectivity and objectivity.

---

Fcap. 8vo. cloth, pp.          Price
## HOW TO BE BEAUTIFUL.
NATURE UNMASKED
By TERESA H. DEAN.
A Book for Every Woman.  New Copyright Edition.

---

Crown 8vo. cloth, pp. 192.  Price 6s.
## ARYAN SUN-MYTHS.
THE ORIGIN OF RELIGIONS.
With an Introduction
By CHARLES MORRIS.

Author of "A Manual of Classical Literature," and "The Aryan Race: Its Origin and Its Achievements."

---

Crown 8vo. pp. xi. and 216.  Cloth, price 2s. 6d.;
wrapper, 1s. 6d.
## HENRY RICHARD, THE APOSTLE OF PEACE,
By LEWIS APPLETON.

With Portraits of Henry Richard, Richard Cobden, Joseph Sturge, Edmund Fry, William Stokes, Elihu Burritt, Arthur G. O'Neill, and the Author.

---

Crown 8vo. pp. v. and 152.  Wrapper, price 1s. Cloth, 1s. 6d.
## ESSAYS: IN THREE KINDS.
By THOMAS SINCLAIR, M.A.

Author of "Humanities," "Quest," "Love's Trilogy," etc., etc.

CONTENTS.—Leisure; The Mediterranean; Fountains; Draught Cattle; Exhibitions; Cultures; Eyes; Dark Days; Rough Music; Moonlight; National Enmities; Lies; Furlough, an Idyl; Chieville, a Comedietta.

---

Vol. III. Papilionidæ and Hesperidæ, completing the Work.
Demy 8vo. cloth.  Price £2 12s. 6d. for the complete work.
## SOUTH AFRICAN BUTTERFLIES:
A MONOGRAPH OF THE EXTRA-TROPICAL SPECIES.
By ROLAND TRIMEN, F.R.S., F.L.S., F.Z.S., F.Ent.S., etc.,

Curator of the South African Museum, Cape Town;

Assisted by JAMES HENRY BOWKER, F.Z.S., F.R.G.S., etc., etc.

---

Crown 8vo. cloth, pp. xxii. and 302, with Map.
Price 8s. each.
## A HISTORY OF CIVILIZATION IN ANCIENT INDIA.
BASED ON SANSKRIT LITERATURE.
By ROMESH CHUNDER DUTT,

The Bengal Civil Service; and of the Middle Temple, Barrister-at-Law; Author of "A Bengali Translation of the Rig Veda Sanhita," and other works.

In Three Volumes.

Vol. I.  VEDIC AND EPIC AGES.

Vol. II.  RATIONALISTIC AGE.

---

4to. pp. xviii.—180.  With Forty Chromo-Lithographic Plates, cloth gilt and gilt edges.  Price £3 3s.
## THE ART ALBUM OF NEW ZEALAND FLORA.

Being a Systematic and Popular Description of the Native Flowering Plants of New Zealand and the adjacent Islands.

By Mr. and Mrs. E. H. FEATON.

Volume I.  Author's Edition.

---

Medium 16mo. cloth, pp. vi. and 156.  Price 2s.

## THE CHESS PLAYERS' TEXT BOOK.

An Elementary Treatise on the Game of Chess.

Illustrated by numerous Diagrams specially designed for Beginners and Advanced Students.

By G. H. D. GOSSIP.

Author of "The Chess Players' Manual" and "Theory of the Chess Openings."

---

Crown 8vo.  Price 2s. 6d.

## APPEAL TO CONSERVATIVES.

By AUGUSTE COMTE,

Author of "The System of Positive Philosophy," and of "The System of Positive Politics."

Joint Translators, T. C. DONKIN and RICHARD CONGREVE.

---

# PERIODICAL PUBLICATIONS.

## THE CHINA REVIEW;
### OR, NOTES AND QUERIES ON THE FAR EAST.

Vol. XVII. No. 6. May and June, 1889. CONTENTS: —The Life and Times of Chwang Tsz'. By Thos. W. Kingsmill.—The Willow Lute; a Chinese Drama in Five Acts. By W. Stanton.—Prolegomena to the Shan Hai King. Translated from original Sources by E. J. Eitel, Ph D. (Tubing.), Inspector of Schools, Hong-Kong.—Notes and Queries.—Notices of New Books. By E. J. Eitel.—Collectanea Bibliographica, etc.

Vol. XVIII. No. 1. CONTENTS :—History of the Churches of India, Burma, Siam, the Malay Peninusla, Cambodia, Annam, China, Tibet, Corea, and Japan, entrusted to the Society of the "Missions Etrangères."—Chinese Law; Translations of Leading Cases. By J. W. Jamieson.—Manchu Relations with Annam. By. E. H. Parker. — Chinese Account of the French Attack upon Pagoda Anchorage. — Contributions to the History of Ancient Original Trade; a Lecture Delivered before the Geographical Society at Berlin on 8th December.—Notes and Queries.—Notices of New Books.—Collectanea Bibliographica, etc.

Bi-monthly, Annual Subscription, 30s.

## THE CALCUTTA REVIEW.
### EDITED BY H. A. D. PHILLIPS, C.S.

No. CLXXVIII. October, 1889. CONTENTS :—The Indian Army.— The Ekadasi Festival at Srirungum. By K. S. Ganapati-Ayyra.—Re-Marriage of Hindu Widows. By Tripura Charan Banerjea. —The Worship of the Phallic Emblem at Tarakeshwar. — Cameos of Indian Districts; III. The Sunderbans. By F. E. Pargiter, C.S.—Indian Constitutional Law, II. By the Editor.—The Voyage to India in the Eighteenth Century. By F. H. Skrine, C.S.— Indian Volunteer Organization. — Theolatry and Anthropolatry; or, a Christian's View of Positivism (Independent Section). By Col. H. Grey, C.S.I. — Some Legal and Constitutional Aspects of the Crawford Case. By a Barrister. —The Quarter. By the Editor.—Summary of Annual Reports.—Critical Notices.—General Literature.

Annual Subscription, 24s.; Single Nos. 6s.

## THE CHINESE RECORDER AND MISSIONARY JOURNAL.

Vol. XX. No. 8. August, 1889. CONTENTS:— The New Education in China. By Rev. L. W. Pilcher.—The Proposed Missionary Conference of 1890. — Notes on the Roman Catholic Terminology. By Rev. G. L. Mason.— How may we best foster Self-support in our Native Churches? By Rev. C. Hartwell. — Country Day Schools. — The Religious Festivals of the Cantonese. By Rev. C. Bone. — Is China Democratic?—The New Testament in Chinese. By H. — A Missionary Journey, etc.

Vol. XX. No. 9. CONTENTS :—The Religious Festivals of the Cantonese. By Rev. C. Bone.—The New Education in China. By Rev. L. W. Pilcher.—Life and Writings of the God of Literature. By Rev. D. N. Lyon.—Chinese Law on the Ownership of Church Property in the Interior of China. By Rev. Gilbert Reid, M.A.—A Notable Gathering in Japan. By Harlan P. Beach, etc.

Vol. XX. No. 10. October, 1889. CONTENTS:—Life and Writings of the God of Literature. By Rev. D. N. Lyon.—The Archimandarite Palladius. By W. A. P. M.— Chinese Law on the Ownership of Church Property in the Interior of China. By Rev. Gilbert Reid, M.A.—The Contrast between Buddhism and Christianity. By Sir M. Monier-Williams, K.C.I.E., D.C.L., LL.D. — The English Language in Chinese Educational Work. By C. D. Tenney, M.A.— Conversation of Mr. Li-Hobsana.—Correspondence.—Our Book Table.—Editorial Notes and Missionary News.—Missionary Journal.

Monthly, Annual Subscription, 15s.

## THE INDIAN ANTIQUARY.

Part CCXXI. Vol. XVIII. May, 1889. CONTENTS.— Copperplate Grants of the Kings of Kanauj. By Prof. F. Kielhorn, C.I.E.—Sanskrit and Old-Kanarese Inscriptions, No. 177. By J. F. Fleet, Bo.C.S., M.R.A.S., C.I.E.—Folklore in Western India, No. XIV. By Putlibai D. H. Wadia.—Miscellanea.—Progress of European Scholarship, No. XVI. By W. R. Morfill. —Notes and Queries.—A Variant of the Bloody Cloth. By Sunhuni Wariyar.—Book Notice. The Life of Hiuen-Tsiang. By Samuel Beal.

Part CCXXII. Vol. XVIII. June, 1889. CONTENTS :
—Sanskrit and Old-Kanarese Inscriptions, Nos. 178, 179, and 180. By J. F. Fleet, Bo.C.S., M.R.A.S., C.I.E.— Some Further Contributions to the Ancient Geography of Guzerat. By G. Bühler, Ph.D., LL.D., C.I.E.—Sirpur Stone-Inscriptions of Siva-Gupta. By Prof. F. Kielhorn, C.I.E.—Weber's Sacred Literature of the Jains. Translated by Dr. H. W. Smyth.—Book Notice. Report on the Search for Sanskrit MSS. in the Bombay Presidency during the Year 1883-84. By R. G. Bhandarkar, M.A., Ph.D.

Monthly, Annual Subscription, 36s.

## INTERNATIONALES ARCHIV FÜR ETHNOGRAPHIE.

Band II. Heft 4. Inhalt :—Dr. F. von Luschan. Das Türkische Schattenspiel (Schluss).—Dr. O. Schellong. Das Barlum-fest der Gegend Finschhafens (Kaiser Wilhelmsland). Mit Taf. VII.—Nouvelles et Correspondance. — Questions et Réponses.—Musées et Collections.—Dr. G. J. Dozy. Revue Bibliographique. — Livres et Brochures. — Explorations et Explorateurs. — Nominations. — Nécrologie. — Reisen und Reisende.—Ernennungen. — Nécrologe.

Each Part, 3s. 6d.; Annual Subscription, £1.

## THE BABYLONIAN AND ORIENTAL RECORD.

Vol. III. No. 12. Contents :—A Life of Buddha (Translated from the P'u Yao King). By the late Dr. Beal.—A Buddhist Repertory. By Prof. Dr. C. de Harlez.—Notes on Early Semitic Names. By W. St. C. Boscawen.—Ketchup, Catchup, and Catsup. By T. de L.—The Tel-el-Amarna Tablets. By W. St. C. Boscawen.

Published montly, Price 1s. 6d.

## PERIODICAL PUBLICATIONS.
# JOURNAL OF THE GYPSY-LORE SOCIETY.

October, 1889. CONTENTS :—Origin of Hungarian Music. By Prof. Emil Thewrewk De Ponor.—The Paris Congress of Popular Traditions. By Charles G. Leland.—The Immigration of the Gypsies into Western Europe in the Fifteenth Century (continued). By Paul Bataillard.—The Red King and the Witch ; A Roumanian Gypsy Folk-Tale. Translated from the Romani of Dr. Barbu Constantinescu by Francis Hindes Groome.—A Transylvanian Gypsy Ballad. By Dr. Heinrich von Wlislocki.—Irish Tinkers and their Language. By David MacRitchie.—Venetian Edicts relating to the Gypsies of the Sixteenth, Seventeenth, and Eighteenth Centuries.—Slovah Gypsy Vocabulary, G—J. By Professor Rudolf von Sowa.—Reviews.—Notes and Queries.

LONDON  TRÜBNER & CO.. 57 AND 59  LUDGATE HILL.

---

## *Official and other Authorized Publications.*

### GREAT BRITAIN.
### *Publications of the Royal Society.*

SEPARATE PAPERS FROM THE PHILOSOPHICAL TRANSACTIONS, 4to. stitched in wrapper.

**ON THE TOTAL SOLAR ECLIPSE OF AUGUST 29, 1886, MADE AT THE ISLAND OF CARRIACOU.** By Rev. S. J. Perry, S.J., F.R.S. Pp. 12, with one Plate. Price 1s.                                          (A. 46.)

**ON THE DETERMINATION OF THE PHOTOMETRIC INTENSITY OF THE CORONAL LIGHT DURING THE SOLAR ECLIPSE OF AUGUST 28-29, 1886.** By Captain W. de W. Abney, C.B., R.E., F.R.S. ; and T. E. Thorpe, Ph.D., F.R.S. Pp. 22. Price 1s. 6d.                                          (A. 47.)

**REVISION OF THE ATOMIC WEIGHT OF GOLD.** By J. W. Mallet, F.R.S. Pp. 47. Price 2s. 6d.     (A. 49.)

---

### INDIA.
### *Publications of the Government of India.*

**CORPUS INSCRIPTIONUM INDICARUM.** Vol. III. Inscriptions of the Early Gupta Kings and their Successors. By John Faithfull Fleet, C.I.E., of H.M.'s Bombay Covenanted Civil Service ; Member of the Royal Asiatic Society of Great Britain and Ireland ; Member of the Bombay Branch of the Royal Asiatic Society ; Member of the Asiatic Society of Bengal ; Corresponding Member of the Royal Society of Science, Gottingen ; Fellow of the University of Bombay. 4to. cloth, pp. viii.—p. 544. Price £2 10s.

**SELECTIONS FROM THE LETTERS, DESPATCHES, AND OTHER STATE PAPERS PRESERVED IN THE BOMBAY SECRETARIAT.** Home Series. Two Vols. Royal 4to. half-bound, cloth sides, pp. lii.-v. ; 450–iv. and 450–iv. With Index. Price £2 2s.

---

### *Publications of the Geological Survey of India.*

**RECORDS.** Vol. XXII. Part III. 1889. Royal 8vo. pp. 60, with Two Plans. Price 2s.—Abstract Report on the Coal Outcrops in the Sharigh Valley, Baluchistan. By the Director, Geological Survey of India.—Notes on the Discovery of Trilobites by Dr. H. Warth, in the Neobolus Beds of the Salt Range. By the Director, Geological Survey of India. —Report of the Chevra Poonjee Coal-Field, in the Khasia Hills. By Tom D. la Touche, B.A., Deputy Superintendent, Geological Survey of India. With Plan.—Geological Notes. By C. L. Griesbach, C.I.E., Deputy Superintendent, Geological Survey of India.—Note on a Cobaltiferous Matt from Nepal. By E. J. Jones, A.R.S.M., Deputy Superintendent, Geological Survey of India.—The President of the Geological Society of London on the International Congress of 1888.—Tin-Mining in Mergui District. By T. W. Hughes Hughes, A.R.S.M., F.G.S. (With a Plan.)— Additions to the Museum.—Additions to the Library.

---

### AUSTRALIA.
### *Publications of the Government of New South Wales.*

**THE HISTORY OF NEW SOUTH WALES.—FROM THE RECORDS.** Vol. I. Demy 8vo. cloth, pp. 650. Illustrated with Maps, Portraits and Sketches. Price 10s. 6d. By G. B. Barton, of the Middle Temple, Barrister-at-Law. This Volume will contain the History of New South Wales from 1783 to 1789, founded on the letters and despatches written by Governor Phillip during that time, and many other records of great historical interest never before published, which have recently been obtained from the Public Record Office in London, the Record Office in Sydney, the collections of Sir Joseph Banks and others, etc., etc.                                          (*Nearly Ready.*)

LONDON : TRÜBNER & CO., AGENTS BY APPOINTMENT, 57 AND 59, LUDGATE HILL.

# NEW ORIENTAL PUBLICATIONS.

20 vols. Subscription price 8 Guineas.

## LESSAN EL ARAB.

لسان لعرب

### ARABIC THERAUSUS.

*₀* The Work will be complete in 20 Vols. 14 Vols. have been published, and the publishers hope to be able to publish the other 6 Vols. in the course of the next two years.

Royal 8vo. sewed, pp. xvi. 729.  Price 17s. 6d.

اقرب الموارد

### SAID EL-CHOURY EL-CHARTOUNI.

Arabic Dictionary.  Vol. I.

*₀* The Second Vol. is in the press.

Royal 8vo. sewed, pp. viii. 206.  Price 10s. 6d.

مقامات بديع الزمان الهمذاني

MAQAMAT DE BADI' UZ-ZAMAN IL-HAMADANI.

Commentées par le CHEIKH MOHAMMAD 'ABDO.

8vo. pp. 247.  Price 6s.

انيس الجلسا في ديوان الخنسا

### DIWAN D'AL-HANSA

Précédé d'une étude sur les femmes poètes de l'ancienne Arabe.

Arabic Text.

8vo. pp. cxiii. 228.  Price 6s. 6d.

## LE DIWAN D'AL HANSA.

Précédé d'une étude sur les femmes poètes de l'ancienne Arabie.

Traduit en Français par le P. de COPPIER, S.J.

8vo. pp. 528.  Price 6s. 6d.

فرائد اللغة. للجزء الاول في الغروني

### ARABIC PHILOLOGY.

Part I.  Arabic Synonymes.

Arabic Text.

By le P. LAMMENS.

Post 8vo. sewed, pp. 458.  Price 5s.

الف ليلة وليلة

### ALF LAILAT WA LAILA.

ARABIAN NIGHTS.  Volume III.

Edited by P. A. SALHANI.

Folio, pp. 247.  Price

## THE HUNZA AND NAGYR HANDBOOK.

Being an Introduction to a Knowledge of the Language, Race, and Countries of Hunza, Nagyr and a Part of Yasin.

Part I.

By Dr. G. W. v. LEITNER.

Oriental Institute, Woking.

Post 8vo. pp. iv. 304.  Price 10s.

## PHARMACOGRAPHIA INDICA.

A History of the Principal Drugs of Vegetable Origin met with in British India.

By WILLIAM DYMOCK, C. J. H. WARDEN, and DAVID HOOPER.

Part I.

*₀* The Work will be completed in Four Parts.

Demy 8vo. boards, pp. v. 248.  With Map.  Price 6s.

## A CONCISE DICTIONARY OF THE PRINCIPAL ROADS, CHIEF TOWNS AND VILLAGES OF JAPAN, ETC.

Compiled from Official Documents.

By W. N. WHITNEY, M.D.,

Interpreter of the U.S. Legation, Tōkyō.

*₀* The price of the Dictionary with the Appendix together is 8s., of the Appendix alone 3s.

Demy 8vo. boards, pp. ii. 167.  Price 3s.

## APPENDIX TO A CONCISE DICTIONARY OF THE PRINCIPAL ROADS, CHIEF TOWNS AND VILLAGES OF JAPAN.

By W. N. WHITNEY, M.D.,

Interpreter of the U.S. Legation, Tōkyō.

Contents: The Constitution of Japan, and Laws relating thereto; the Law for the Organization of Cities, Towns, and Villages, together with Statistical Information respecting Territory, Population, Agriculture and Industry, etc.

Post 8vo. cloth, pp. viii. 287, xv.  Price 6s.

## HANDBOOK OF ENGLISH-JAPANESE ETYMOLOGY.

By WILLIAM IMBRIE.

Second Edition.

Royal 8vo. pp. 80.  Price 3s. 6d.

## ANCIENT PORCELAIN.

A Study in Chinese Mediæval Industry and Trade.

By F. HIRTH, Ph.D.,

Deputy Commissioner and Assistant Statistical Secretary, Inspectorate General of Customs, Shanghai.

8vo. pp. vi. 150.  Price 3s. 6d.

## WEN-CHIEN TZU-CHU JU-MEN

Notes on the Chinese Documentary Style.

By F. HIRTH, Ph.D.,

Deputy Commissioner and Assistant Statistical Secretary, Inspectorate General of Customs, Shanghai.

# TRÜBNER'S ORIENTAL SERIES.

**NEW VOLUMES.**

**IN PREPARATION.**

Post 8vo. cloth.

### ENGLISH INTERCOURSE WITH SIAM IN THE SEVENTEENTH CENTURY.

By J. ANDERSON, M.D., LL.D., F.R.S.

Post 8vo.

### BIHAR PROVERBS.

By JOHN CHRISTIAN.

Post 8vo.

### DACAKUMARACARITA OF DANDIN.

Translated by EDWARD J. RAPSON.

Post 8vo.

### A SKETCH OF THE MODERN LANGUAGES OF OCEANIA.

By R. N. CUST, LL.D.,

Author of "Modern Languages of the East," "Modern Languages of Africa," etc.

**NOW READY.**

Post 8vo. cloth, pp. xx. and 532. Price 21s.

### ORIGINAL SANSKRIT TEXTS

ON THE ORIGIN AND HISTORY OF THE PEOPLE OF INDIA: THEIR RELIGION AND INSTITUTIONS.

Collected, Translated and Illustrated

By J. MUIR, C.I.E., D.C.L., LL.D., Ph.D.

Vol. I. Mythical and Legendary Accounts of the Origin of Caste, with an inquiry into its Existence in the Vedic Age.

Third Edition, Re-written and greatly Enlarged.

New Edition. Post 8vo. cloth, pp. 336. Price 16s.

### THE RELIGIONS OF INDIA.

By A. BARTH, Paris.

Translated by the Rev. J. WOOD.

---

# THE ENGLISH & FOREIGN PHILOSOPHICAL LIBRARY.

**NEW VOLUMES.**

Post 8vo. pp. xx. and 314, cloth. Price 10s. 6d.

### ENIGMAS OF LIFE.

By W. R. GREG.

Seventeenth Edition, with a Postscript.

Post 8vo. cloth, pp. xxiii.—377. Price 10s. 6d.

### THE SCIENCE OF KNOWLEDGE.

By J. G. FICHTE.

Translated from the German by A. E. KROEGER.

With an Introduction by Professor W. T. HARRIS.

Post 8vo. cloth, pp. x.—505. Price 12s. 6d.

### THE SCIENCE OF RIGHTS.

By J. G. FICHTE.

Translated from the German by A. E. KROEGER. With an Introduction by Professor W. T. HARRIS.

In Two Volumes, post 8vo. cloth. Price 21s.

### JOHANN GOTTLIEB FICHTE'S POPULAR WORKS.

The Nature of the Scholar; The Vocation of the Scholar; The Vocation of Man; The Doctrine of Religion; Characteristics of the Present Age; Outlines of the Doctrine of Knowledge.

With a Memoir by WILLIAM SMITH, LL.D.

Post 8vo. cloth, pp. xxvi. and 414. Price 14s.

### MORAL ORDER AND PROGRESS.

AN ANALYSIS OF ETHICAL CONCEPTIONS.

By S. ALEXANDER,

Fellow of Lincoln College, Oxford.

**IN THE PRESS.**

Post 8vo.

### THE PHILOSOPHY OF LAW.

By Professor DIODATO LIOY.

Translated by W. HASTIE.

---

# TRÜBNER'S SERIES OF SIMPLIFIED GRAMMARS.

EDITED BY DR. ROST, LIBRARIAN OF THE INDIA OFFICE.

**NEW VOLUMES IN PREPARATION.**

Crown 8vo. pp.

### A SIMPLIFIED TELUGU GRAMMAR.

By HENRY MORRIS, M.A.

Crown 8vo.

### A SIMPLIFIED CHINESE GRAMMAR.

By JOSEPH EDKINS, D.D.

LONDON: TRÜBNER & CO., 57 AND 59, LUDGATE HILL.

# TRÜBNER AND CO.'S LIST.
## WORKS IN PREPARATION.

8vo. cloth.
### THE LIFE OF CARMEN SYLVA
(Queen of Roumania).
By NATALIE, BARONESS STACKELBERG.
Translated from the German.
With View of the Castle of Pelesch and Four Portraits.

---

Royal 4to. cloth, price 25*s*.
### MACHINE DRAWING AND DESIGN,
For Engineering Students and Practical Engineers :
Being a complete Course of Instruction in Mechanical Drawing, with Exercises on the Application of Principles to Engine and Machine Design.
By WILLIAM RIPPER, M. Inst. M.E.,
Gold and Bronze Medallist; Author of "Steam, and the Steam Engine"; Assistant Professor of Mechanical Engineering in the Sheffield Technical School.
Illustrated by Fifty-five Plates and numerous Explanatory Engravings.

---

Crown 8vo. cloth, pp. iv.-209.   Price   .
### THE MODERN NOVELISTS OF RUSSIA.
Being the Substance of Six Lectures Delivered at Taylor Institution, Oxford.
By CHARLES EDWARD TURNER,
English Lector in the University of St. Petersburg.

---

Volume II. 8vo. cloth.
### ELEMENTS OF THE COMPARATIVE GRAMMAR OF THE INDO-GERMANIC LANGUAGES.
A Concise Exposition of the History of Sanskrit, Old Iranian (Avestic and Old Persian), Old Armenian, Old Greek, Latin, Umbrian-Samnitic, Old Irish, Gothic, Old High German, Lithuanian and Old Bulgarian.
By KARL BRUGMANN,
Professor of Comparative Philology in the University of Leipzig.
Translated from the German by JOSEPH WRIGHT, Ph.D.

---

8vo.
### THE ITALIC DIALECTS.
I. The Text of the Inscriptions
(Oscan, Paelignian, Sabine, etc.; the oldest Latin and Faliscan; Volscian Picentine and Umbrian),
II. An Arabic Lexicon.
Being a Complete Concordance to Part I., and giving the Meanings of all Words whose Interpretation is certain.
With the Italic Glosses of Varro and Festus, and a Dialect Map.
Edited and Arranged by R. SEYMOUR CONWAY, M.A.,
Fellow of Gonville and Caius College, Classical Lecturer at Newnham College, Author of "Verner's Law in Italy."

---

Demy 8vo. cloth, about 352 pp., with Portrait.
### THE GIFT OF D. D. HOME.
By MDE. DUNGLAS HOME,
Author of "D. D. Home, His Life and Mission."

---

Three vols. crown 8vo.
### IN HER EARLIEST YOUTH.
By TASMA.
Author of "Uncle Piper of Piper's Hill," etc.

---

Crown 8vo.
### PREPARATION OF DRAWINGS FOR PHOTOGRAPHIC REPRODUCTION.
By Lieut.-Colonel J. WATERHOUSE, B.C.S., Assistant Surveyor-General of India.

---

8vo.
### SOCIAL HISTORY OF THE RACES OF MANKIND.
Chiapo and Guzano Maranonians.
By A. FEATHERMAN.

---

8vo. about 300 pages, cloth, gilt top.   Price 21*s*. net.
### AN ACCOUNT OF THE ABORIGINES OF TASMANIA.
*Their Manners, Customs, Wars, Hunting, Food, Morals, Language, Origin and General Characteristics,*
Collected from all Sources, from the time of their First Contact with Europeans until their Final Extermination.
By H. LING ROTH,
Assisted by E. Marion Butler; with a Chapter on the Osteology, by J. G. Garson, M.D., and a Preface by E. B. Tylor, F.R.S., D.C.L., LL.D., etc.  With numerous Autotype Plates from Original Drawings made by Edith May Roth.

This Edition will be strictly limited to the Subscribers, and every copy will be numbered.

---

8vo. cloth, pp.   .   Price 15*s*.
### THE HISTORY OF CANADA.
By WILLIAM KINGSFORD.
Vol. III.
This Volume narrates the events of the Conquest of Canada, and its cession to Great Britain under the Treaty of Paris, 1762.

---

Crown 8vo. 350 pp. cloth gilt, price 5*s*.
### NEW POPULAR HANDBOOK OF COUNTY DIALECTS.
By the Rev. J. L. SAYWELL, F.R.H.S.
Author of "The Parochial Histories of Northallerton and Ackworth;" and Contributor to "Yorkshire Archæological and Topographical Journal," "Notes and Queries," &c.

---

Demy 8vo.
### ON THE IDEALS OF THE EMOTIONS, THE INTELLECT AND THE WILL.
*APOLOGIA PRO AMORE.*
A New Theory of Idealism.
By Mrs. P. F. FITZGERALD.
Authoress of "An Essay on the Philosophy of Self-Consciousness," and "A Treatise on the Principle of Sufficient Reason."

LONDON: TRÜBNER & CO., 57 AND 59, LUDGATE HILL.

# IMPRIMERIE CATHOLIQUE,

## BEYROUTH (SYRIE).

Le catalogue de 1890, contenant un riche choix d'ouvrages intéressants pour les Orientalistes, vient de paraître; il sera envoyé gratis et francs à qui en fera la demande.

# NEW WORKS OF FICTION.

**A SYDNEY SOVEREIGN, AND OTHER TALES.** By Tasma, Author of "Uncle Piper of Piper's Hill." In One Volume. Crown 8vo. cloth, pp. . Price .

**STEADFAST: The Story of a Saint and a Sinner.** By R. T. Cooke, Author of "Somebody's Neighbours," "The Sphinx's Children," "Happy Dodd," etc. Crown 8vo. cloth, pp. x. and 322. Price 6s.

**THE APOTHECARY'S DAUGHTERS.** By Henrik Pontopiddan. Translated from the Danish by Gordius Nielsen. Crown 8vo. cloth, pp. 160. Price 3s. 6d.

**GIRALDI.** A Tale of the Sects. By Ross Dering. In Two Volumes. Crown 8vo. cloth. Price 12s.

**ULLI: THE STORY OF A NEGLECTED GIRL.** Translated from the German of Emma Biller by A. B. Daisy Rost. Crown 8vo. cloth. Price 5s.

**UNCLE PIPER OF PIPER'S HILL.** An Australian Novel. By Tasma. Second Edition, crown 8vo. cloth. Price 6s.

**AN I. D. B. IN SOUTH AFRICA.** By Louise Vescelius-Sheldon, author of "Yankee Girls in Zulu Land." Illustrated by G. E. Graves and Al. Hencke. Crown 8vo. cloth, pp. 206. Price 7s. 6d.

**YANKEE GIRLS IN ZULU LAND.** By Louise Vescelius-Sheldon. With One Hundred Photogravure Illustrations by G. E. Graves, from Original Sketches by J. Austen. Crown 8vo. cloth, with Portraits of the Sisters. Cheap Edition. Price 5s.

**A MODERN PALADIN.** By Edward Jenkins, Author of "Ginx's Baby," etc. Cheap Edition, crown 8vo. cloth, pp. 392. Price 5s.

**THE UNFORTUNATE ONE.** A Novel. By Ivan Toorgeynieff. Translated from the Russian by A. R. Thompson. Crown 8vo. cloth. Price 3s. 6d.

**THE AUTOBIOGRAPHY OF MARK RUTHERFORD** AND MARK RUTHERFORD'S DELIVERANCE. Edited by his Friend, Reuben Shapcott. Third Edition, crown 8vo. cloth. Price 7s. 6d.

LONDON: TRÜBNER & CO., 57 AND 59, LUDGATE HILL.

---

# WORKS OF DR. LEITNER.

**THE HUNZA AND NAGYR HANDBOOK.** Being an Introduction to a Knowledge of the Language, Race, and Countries of Hunza, Nagyr, and a part of Yasin. Part I. Folio, pp. 247. 1889. £2 2s.

**HISTORY OF INDIGENOUS ORIENTAL EDUCATION ESPECIALLY IN THE PUNJAB** SINCE ANNEXATION AND IN 1882. Folio, pp. 660. 1882. Price £5.

**THE LANGUAGES AND RACES OF DARDISTAN.** 4to. 1877. Price £1 5s.

**LINGUISTIC FRAGMENTS DISCOVERED IN 1870,** 1872, AND 1879, RELATING TO INDIAN TRADE DIALECTS, THE DIALECTS OF THE CRIMINAL AND WANDERING TRIBES, ETC. With an Account of the Shawl-Alphabet and of Shawl-Weaving. 4 fasciculi. Folio. 1882. Price £2 2s.

*Publications of the Oriental Institute, Woking.*

**THE "VIDIODHAY,"** or, a Sanskrit Critical Journal. Published Monthly. Annual Subscription, 6s., post free.

**"AL 'HAQAIQ."** The Arabic Review. Published Quarterly. Annual Subscription, 8s., post free.

**MUHAMMADANISM.** Being the Report of an Extempore Address, with Appendices. Price 1s.

**INTRODUCTION TO A PHILOSOPHICAL GRAMMAR** OF ARABIC. Price 4s.

**THE SCIENCES OF LANGUAGE AND ETHNOGRAPHY.** Price 1s.

---

# 𝕿𝖍𝖊 𝕷𝖔𝖙𝖔𝖘 𝕾𝖊𝖗𝖎𝖊𝖘.

Pott 8vo., uniformly bound in two styles—(1) cloth, gilt back and edges; (2) half-parchment, cloth sides, gilt top, uncut, each 3s. 6d.

The New Volume is a New Edition of
## THE LIGHT OF ASIA.
By SIR EDWIN ARNOLD, M.A., K.C.I.E., C.S.I.

With Illustrations, and a Portrait of the Author.

*** A Limited Edition (60 copies) has also been printed on Japanese Vellum, price 31s. 6d. net. Early Orders for the above are respectfully requested.

*** The 3s. 6d. Edition is also kept, bound by Zaehnsdorf, in whole calf gilt, price 10s. 6d.

Vol. I.
### THE TRAVELS OF BARON MÜNCHAUSEN.
Illustrated by ALFRED CROWQUILL.

Vol. II.
### THE BREITMANN BALLADS.
By CHARLES G. LELAND.
Author's Copyright Edition, with a New Preface and Additional Poems.

Vol. III.
### ESSAYS ON MEN AND BOOKS SELECTED FROM THE EARLIER WRITINGS OF LORD MACAULAY.
VOL. I., with Five Portraits—INTRODUCTORY—LORD CLIVE—MILTON—EARL CHATHAM—LORD BYRON. With Critical Introduction and Notes by ALEXANDER H. JAPP, LL.D., F.R.S.E.

Vol. V. will be ready in a few days.
### THE MARVELLOUS AND RARE CONCEITS OF MASTER TYLL OWLGLASS.
Newly Collected, Chronicled, and Set Forth in an English Tongue.
By KENNETH H. R. MACKENZIE,
Fellow of the Society of Antiquaries.
And Adorned with many most Diverting and Cunning Devices
By ALFRED CROWQUILL.
A NEW EDITION.
*** Large-paper Copies are also ready. Price 12s. 6d. each.

LONDON: TRÜBNER & CO., 57 AND 59, LUDGATE HILL.

# STEPHEN AUSTIN & SONS,

### (ESTABLISHED 1772.)

## PRINTERS

#### IN

## Gnglish, Oriental & other Foreign Languages,

## HERTFORD.

MEDALS FROM:

HER MAJESTY THE QUEEN.
EMPRESS EUGENIE.
EXPOSITION UNIVERSELLE DE PARIS 1855.
INTERNATIONAL EXHIBITION 1862.
CONGRES INTERNATIONAL DES
ORIENTALISTES.

הַזֶּה הַבַּיִת הוּא הַבַּיִת ׃ אֵלֶּה הַבָּתִּים ׃ הַבָּתִּים הָאֵלֶּה הַבָּתִּים

TΡΠΗΣ ΑΥΤΟΚΑΤΟΡΙΚΑΙ ΡΙΑ ΓΩΤΑΡΖΗΣ

آورده‌اند که حاتم از سهر شاه آباد بیرون

اصو ܂ܘܚܚܠܐ ܂ ܠܐܨܗ ܗܨܪ ܂ ܂ ܂ ܂ ܂

وَأَنْتُمْ مُتَأَكِّمُ خُذُوا لِعِظَامِى أَيْنَ مِرْتُمْ وَحِفَّةً وَأَيْنَ

হে আমাদের স্বর্গস্থ পিতঃ, তোমার নাম পবিত্ররূপে

বিশ্বৰি পৰমেস্বৰ নে জগত নূ অসিহ ৰপিআৰ বীঠা,

Πλευρὰ λαβοῦσα τὴν τῆς Καλλιπαρείο

天 萬 父 萬 生 得 面 四 萬 地 物 母 物

পবিত্ৰ মানিলেঁ জাবো. তুম্হেঁ ৰাজ্য যেবো.

## Printers to the following Societies, etc. :—

BRITISH MUSEUM.     INDIA OFFICE.
MADRAS GOVERNMENT,
CHIEF COMMISSIONER OF BURMA.
ASIATIC SOCIETY OF BENGAL.
ROYAL ASIATIC SOCIETY.
BRITISH MUSEUM (NATURAL HISTORY).
BRITISH AND FOREIGN BIBLE SOCIETY.
SANSKRIT TEXT SOCIETY.
PALI TEXT SOCIETY.
THE LATE EAST INDIA COMPANY'S COLLEGE.

HAILEYBURY COLLEGE.
PHILOLOGICAL SOCIETY.
CAMBRIDGE PHILOLOGICAL SOCIETY.
CHAUCER SOCIETY.
EARLY ENGLISH TEXT SOCIETY.
BALLAD SOCIETY.
ENGLISH DIALECT SOCIETY.
INDEX SOCIETY.
WYCLIF SOCIETY.
VILLON SOCIETY, ETC.

# D. NUTT, 270 & 271, STRAND, LONDON.

# TRÜBNER'S RECORD, No. 248.

## CONTENTS.

# TRÜBNER AND CO.'S LIST.

8vo. cloth.

## THE LIFE OF CARMEN SYLVA

(QUEEN OF ROUMANIA).

By NATALIE, BARONESS STACKELBERG.

Translated from the German.

With View of the Castle of Pelesch and Four Portraits.

In Preparation. Volume II. 8vo. cloth.

## ELEMENTS OF THE COMPARATIVE GRAMMAR OF THE INDO-GERMANIC LANGUAGES.

A Concise Exposition of the History of Sanskrit, Old Iranian (Avestic and Old Persian), Old Armenian, Old Greek, Latin, Umbrian-Samnitic, Old Irish, Gothic, Old High German, Lithuanian and Old Bulgarian.

By KARL BRUGMANN,

Professor of Comparative Philology in the University of Leipzig.

Translated from the German by JOSEPH WRIGHT, Ph.D.

8vo. In Preparation.

## THE ITALIC DIALECTS.

I. THE TEXT OF THE INSCRIPTIONS

(Oscan, Paelignian, Sabine, etc.; the oldest Latin and Faliscan; Volscian Picentine and Umbrian),

II. AN ARABIC LEXICON.

Being a Complete Concordance to Part I., and giving the Meanings of all Words whose Interpretation is certain. With the Italic Glosses of Varro and Festus, and a Dialect Map.

Edited and Arranged by R. SEYMOUR CONWAY, M.A.,

Fellow of Gonville and Caius College, Classical Lecturer at Newnham College, Author of "Verner's Law in Italy."

Post 8vo. cloth. Price 9s.

## THE LIFE AND WORKS OF ALEXANDER CSOMA DE KÖRÖS

Between 1819 and 1842.

With a Short Notice of all his Works and Essays, from Original Documents.

By T. DUKA, M.D.

Post 8vo. cloth. Price 24s.

## SI-YU-KI.

## BUDDHIST RECORDS OF THE WESTERN WORLD.

Translated from the Chinese of Hiuen Tsiang (A.D. 629).

By SAMUEL BEAL,

Professor of Chinese, University College, London.

Two vols., with a specially prepared Map.

8vo. cloth, pp. viii. and 350. Price 7s. 6d.

## HUMANITISM:

*The Scientific Solution of the Social Problem.*

By W. A. MACDONALD.

"Humanitism" is a new school of social science, and embraces every sphere of human activity. Although based upon the physical sciences, it enters into an historical inquiry, and shows that the history of mankind is marked by ebbs and flows of false subjectivity and objectivity.

IN PREPARATION.

## PREPARATION OF DRAWINGS FOR PHOTOGRAPHIC REPRODUCTION.

By Lieut.-Colonel J. WATERHOUSE, B.C.S., Assistant Surveyor-General of India.

8vo. cloth. Price 28s.

## SOCIAL HISTORY OF THE RACES OF MANKIND.

CHIAPO AND GUZANO MARANONIANS.

By A. FEATHERMAN.

8vo. about 300 pages, cloth, gilt top. Price 21s. net.

## AN ACCOUNT OF THE ABORIGINES OF TASMANIA.

*Their Manners, Customs, Wars, Hunting, Food, Morals, Language, Origin and General Characteristics,*

Collected from all Sources, from the time of their First Contact with Europeans until their Final Extermination.

By H. LING ROTH,

Assisted by E. MARION BUTLER; with a Chapter on the OSTEOLOGY, by J. G. GARSON, M.D., and a Preface by E. B. TYLOR, F.R.S., D.C.L., LL.D., etc. With numerous Autotype Plates from Original Drawings made by EDITH MAY ROTH.

This Edition will be strictly limited to the Subscribers, and every copy will be numbered.

8vo. cloth. Price 15s.

## THE HISTORY OF CANADA.

By WILLIAM KINGSFORD.

Vol. III.

This Volume narrates the events of the Conquest of Canada, and its cession to Great Britain under the Treaty of Paris, 1763.

Crown 8vo. In Preparation.

## NEW POPULAR HANDBOOK OF COUNTY DIALECTS.

By the Rev. J. L. SAYWELL, F.R.H.S.

Author of "The Parochial Histories of Northallerton and Ackworth;" and Contributor to "Yorkshire Archæological and Topographical Journal," "Notes and Queries," &c.

Post 8vo. cloth. Price 14s.

## A HISTORY OF BURMA,

Including Burma Proper, Pegu, Taungu, Tenasserim, and Arakan. From the Earliest Time to the End of the First War with India.

By Lieut.-General SIR ARTHUR P. PHAYRE.

Post 8vo. cloth. Price 12s.

## THE ORDINANCES OF MANU.

Translated from the Sanskrit.

With an Introduction by the late A. C. BURNELL.

Completed and Edited by EDW. W. HOPKINS, Ph.D.

## Official and other Authorized Publications.

### GREAT BRITAIN.

#### Publications of the Royal Society.

SEPARATE PAPERS FROM THE PHILOSOPHICAL TRANSACTIONS, 4to. stitched in wrapper.

**ON THE DESCENDING DEGENERATIONS WHICH FOLLOW LESIONS OF THE GYRUS MARGINALIS AND GYRUS FORNICATUS IN MONKEYS.** By E. P. France. With an Introduction by Professor Schafer, F.R.S. (from the Physiological Laboratory, University College, London).  With Three Plates.  Price 5s.  (B. 48.)

**THE DIURNAL VARIATIONS OF TERRESTRIAL MAGNETISM.** By Arthur Schuster, F.R.S., Professor of Physics in Owens College.  With an Appendix by H. Lamb, F.R.S., Professor of Mathematics in Owens College.  Price 2s. 6d.  (A. 51.)

**VARIATIONS OF CARDIUM EDULE APPARENTLY CORRELATED TO THE CONDITIONS OF LIFE.** By William Bateson, M.A.  With One Plate.  Price 6s.  (B. 47.)

### INDIA.

#### Publications of the Government of India.

**CORPUS INSCRIPTIONUN INDICARUM.** Vol. III.  Inscriptions of the Early Gupta Kings and their Successors. By John Faithfull Fleet, C.I.E., of H.M.'s Bombay Covenanted Civil Service ; Member of the Royal Asiatic Society of Great Britain and Ireland ; Member of the Bombay Branch of the Royal Asiatic Society ; Member of the Asiatic Society of Bengal ; Corresponding Member of the Royal Society of Science, Gottingen ; Fellow of the University of Bombay.  4to. cloth.  Price £2 10s.

### AUSTRALIA.

#### Publications of the Government of New South Wales.

**THE HISTORY OF NEW SOUTH WALES.—FROM THE RECORDS.** Vol. I. Demy 8vo. cloth.  Illustrated with Maps, Portraits and Sketches.  Price 15s. ; half bound 21s.  By G. B. Barton, of the Middle Temple, Barrister-at-Law. This Volume will contain the History of New South Wales from 1783 to 1789, founded on the letters and despatches written by Governor Phillip during that time, and many other records of great historical interest never before published, which have recently been obtained from the Public Record Office in London, the Record Office in Sydney, the collections of Sir Joseph Banks, and others, etc., etc.

#### Publications of the Government of Victoria.

**NATURAL HISTORY OF VICTORIA.** Prodromus of the Zoology of Victoria ; or Figures and Descriptions of the Living Species of all Classes of the Victorian Indigenous Animals.  By Frederick McCoy, C.M.G., M.A., S:.D. Cantab., F.R.S.  Decade XIX.  Royal 8vo.  With Ten Coloured Plates.  Price 5s.

LONDON: TRÜBNER & CO., AGENTS BY APPOINTMENT, 57 and 59, LUDGATE HILL.

---

*A celebrated Turkish Romance, translated from a printed but undated text procured a few years ago in Constantinople.*

Crown 8vo. pp. xl. and 420, cloth extra, 10s. 6d.

# THE HISTORY OF THE FORTY VEZIRS;

## OR, THE STORY OF THE FORTY MORNS AND EVES.

WRITTEN IN TURKISH BY SHEYKH-ZÁDA ;

DONE INTO ENGLISH BY E. J. W. GIBB, M.R.A.S.

"A delightful addition to the wealth of Oriental stories available to English readers. . . . Mr. Gibb has considerately done everything to help the reader to an intelligent appreciation of THIS CHARMING BOOK."—*Saturday Review.*

SIR RICHARD F. BURTON says :—"In my opinion, the version is definite and final.  The style is light and pleasant, with the absolutely necessary flavour of quaintness : and the notes, though short and few, are sufficient and satisfactory."

**KEGAN PAUL, TRENCH, TRÜBNER & Co.**

## ORIENTAL PERIODICAL PUBLICATIONS.

### THE CALCUTTA REVIEW.

EDITED BY A. C. TUTE, C.S.

No. CLXXIX. January, 1890. *Contents :*—The Study of Comparative Legislation in France. By Leon Aucoc, Member of the Institute, and President of the Committee of Foreign Legislation.—The History of Israel (Independent Section).—Indian Legislation and Legislative Councils. By H. A. D. Phillips, C.S.—Cameos of Indian Districts. IV. Karnal Punjab. By J. R. Drummond, B.A., C.S.—An Ex-Lieutenant-Governor of India.—Some Relics of Bagapur.

By Rev. W. Ellison.—England's Commercial Supremacy. By William Wilson.—Passenger Fares for Long-distance Railway Travelling. By David Gostling, F.R.I.B.A.—Lord Lansdowne on Education. By the Editor.—"Carry Down the Man a Present."—The Quarter. By the Editor.—Summary of Annual Reports.—Critical Notices.—General Literature.

Quarterly, each No. 6s.

### THE CHINA REVIEW;
#### OR, NOTES AND QUERIES ON THE FAR EAST.

Vol. XVIII. No. 1. July and August, 1889.—*Contents :*—History of the Churches of India, Burma, Siam, the Malay Peninsula, Cambodia, Annam, China, Tibet, Corea, and Japan, entrusted to the Society of the Missions Étrangères.—Chinese Law ; Translations of Leading Cases. By J. W. Jamieson.—Manchu Relations with Annam. By E. H. Parker.—Chinese Account of the French Attack upon Pagoda Anchorage. — Contributions to the History of Ancient Original Trade ; a Lecture delivered before the Geographical Society at Berlin on the 8th December. By Dr. Friedrich Hirth.—Notes. By E. H. Parker, D. J. MacGowan, and

J. Edkins. — Queries. — Notices of Books.— Collectanea Bibliographica, etc.
Vol. XVIII. No. 2. September and October, 1889. *Contents :* On the Management of Silkworms ; A Translation from the Chinese Tsou Tsu-t'ang. By Robert Kliene.—The Ancient Relation between the Japanese and Chinese Languages and Peoples. By E. H. Parker.—Chinese Law ; Extracts from Ta Ching Lü Li.—Notes. By J. Edkins, D. J. Macgowan, and W. J. Macgowan.—Notices of New Books.—Collectanea Bibliographica, etc.

Bi-monthly, Annual Subscription, 30s.

### THE CHINESE RECORDER AND MISSIONARY JOURNAL.

[January issue just received from Shanghai.]

### THE INDIAN ANTIQUARY.

Part CCXXVI. October, 1889. *Contents :*—An Ancient Terra-cotta Seal from Bulandshahr. By F. S. Growse.—Tables for Approximate Conversion of Hindu Dates. By Dr. Robert Schram.—The Inscriptions of Piyadasi. By E. Senart. Translated by G. A. Grierson.—Kalbhavi Jain Inscription. By J. F. Fleet.—The Names of the Coins of

Tipu Sultan. By E. Hultzsch.—The Fate of St. Mark according to an Arab Historian of the Tenth Century. By Major J. S. King.—Hindu Dates, No. 30, Mahakuta Inscription of Bappuvarasa, Saka-Samvat 856. By J. F. Fleet. —Venkatachalapati, a Madras Legend. By S. M. Natesa Sastri. Kali Nag, a Kasmir Legend. By J. Hinton Knowles.

Monthly, Annual Subscription, 36s.

### INTERNATIONALES ARCHIV FÜR ETHNOGRAPHIE.

Band II. Heft VI. *Inhalt :*—Prof. G. Schlegel. Chinesische und Chinesisch - Siamesische Münzen.—Adolph. B. Joske. The Nanga of Viti-Levu.—Prof. H. H. Giglioli. On a remarkable Stone Axe and a Stone Chisel in actual use amongst the Chamacocos of S. E. Bolivia.—J. Rhein. Mededeeling omtrent de Chineesche poppenkast.—Nouvelles et Correspondance.—Kleine Notizen und Correspondenz B. P. Jentink. Wandbehangsels met voorstellingen uit de Hanoe-

man-sage.—Musées et Collections—Museen und Sammlungen—Sch. Museum für deutsche Volkstrachten zu Berlin.—Prof. H. Kern. Le Musée d'ethnographie à Moscou.—Dr. G. J. Dozy. Revue Bibliographique. — Bibliographische Uebersicht. Livres et Brochures.—Büchertisch.—Ed. Seler. Hermann Strebel, Alt Mexico, Arch. Beiträge zur Kulturgeschichte seiner Bewohner. II. Theil.

Each Part, 3s. 6d. ; Annual Subscription, £1.

### JOURNAL OF THE CHINA BRANCH OF THE ROYAL ASIATIC SOCIETY.

Vol. XXIII. No. 3. September, 1889. *Contents :*—The Bore of the Tsien-Tang-Kiang (Hang-chau Bay).—Chinese

Chess.—Proceedings.—Council's Report for the year 1888.—List of Officers of the Society for 1889.—List of Members.

Monthly, Annual Subscription, 25s.

### JOURNAL ANTHROPOLOGICAL SOCIETY OF BOMBAY.

Vol. I. No. 8. *Contents :*—Note on a Mahratta with 24 Digits.—On the Minor Vaishnava Sects of Bengal. By Kedarnath Basu. - On Hindu Civilization in the Far East, as represented by Architectural Monuments and Inscriptions. By E. Rehatsek.—On a Mode of Obession which deals with

the Belief in a part of Bangalore in the Possession of Women by the Spirits of Drowned Persons. By Fred. Fawcett.—Note on a Custom of the Mysore "Gollavalu" Shepherd Caste People. By Fred. Fawcett.

Quarterly. Annual Subscription, 18s. Single Nos. 5s. each.

## THE ORIENTALIST.

Vol. III.  Parts 11 and 12.—*Contents* :—Women during the period of catamenia.  By the Editor.—The Life of Karatôta Kírti Srí Dhammarāma, High Priest of Mātara in the Southern Province of the Island of Ceylon.  By John F. Tillekeratne, Mudliar.—The Pratyáhāra "Has." By the Editor.—The Bālāvatāra.  A Pāli Grammar.  By Lionel Lee.—Dubāsh and Tuppahi.  By the Editor.—Folk-Tales of Bengal.  By S. Mitter.—Tamil Folklore, the last of the Yakkus.—Notes and Queries.  By K. James Pohath.

Annual Subscription, 12s.

## TRANSACTIONS OF THE ASIATIC SOCIETY OF JAPAN.

Vol. XVII.  Part II.  *Contents* :—The Theory of Japanese Flower Arrangements.  By Josiah Conder.—A Grave-stone in Batavia to the Memory of a Japanese Christian of the 17th Century.  By Rev. A. F. King.— The Japanese Legal Seal.  By R. Masujima.—Minutes of Meetings.—Report of Council.—Abstract of a Lecture on Sanitation in Japan.  By W. K. Burton.—Abstract of a Lecture on the Hygienic Aspects of Japanese Dwelling Houses.  By Dr. J. N. Seymour.—List of Members.

Price 12s. 6d.

## JOURNAL OF THE AMERICAN ORIENTAL SOCIETY.

Vol. XIII.  CONTENTS :—Korea in its Relations with China.  By William W. Rockhill, Secretary of Legation of the United States at Peking. — The Extremity of the Romans ; and, Praise Before the Holy Mysteries.  Syriac Texts and Translations.  By Prof. Is. H. Hall, of the Metropolitan Museum of Art, New York City.—The Social and Military Position of the Ruling Caste in Ancient India, as represented by the Sanskrit Epic.  By Edward W. Hopkins, Professor in Bryn Mawr College, Bryn Mawr, Pa.—Proceedings of the Society, May, 1885, to May, 1888. — Additions to the Library-Cabinet, 1885 to 1889.—List of Members, May, 1889.  Price 30s.

## THE THEOSOPHIST.

### A MONTHLY MAGAZINE OF ORIENTAL PHILOSOPHY, ART, LITERATURE, AND OCCULTISM.

### CONDUCTED BY H. S. OLCOTT, P.T.S.

Volume XI.  October, 1889, to September, 1890.

Annual Subscription, 20s. ; Single Nos. 2s.

Vol. XI.  No. 125.  February, 1890.  *Contents* :—Tearing off the "Sheep's Clothing." — Sarvasaro - Upanishad of Krishna-Yajur-Veda. — "Infidel Bob."—The Goddess of Wealth.—Elohistic Teachings.—The Visit of Apollonius to the Mahatmas of India.—The Age of Sri Sankaràchàrya.— Aphorisms from Sanskrit.—Persecution by the Free-thinkers. —Reviews, Correspondence, Supplement, etc.

## THE ASIATIC QUARTERLY REVIEW.

### EDITED BY DEMETRIUS BOULGER.

*Contents* :—Native Princes of India.  By Sir Lepel Griffin, K.C.S.I.—The Model Missionary in China.  By Frederic H. Balfour.—The Turkish Army of the Olden Time (*continued*).  By Colonel Tyrrell.—Political Training of Hindoos. By J. Talboys Wheeler.—Ten Days in Mysore.  By J. D. Rees.—Affghan Poetry of the Seventeenth Century.  By C. E. Biddulph.—The Officering of the Indian Army.—Scholars on the Rampage.—Western Buddhism.  By Miss Helen Graham McKerlie.

January, 1890.  Price 5s.

### LONDON : KEGAN PAUL, TRENCH, TRÜBNER & CO., LIMITED.

# BOOKS ON INDIA

## FOR SALE BY TRÜBNER & CO., LUDGATE HILL.

AINSLIE (Whitelaw) Materia Indica ; or some account of those Articles which are employed by the Hindoos, and other Eastern Nations, in their Medicine, Arts, and Agriculture.  2 vols.  Royal 8vo. bound, pp. xxiv. 654, xxxix. 604.  18s.  *London*, 1826.

ANGLO - INDIAN READY-RECKONER and Vade Mecum.  8vo. cloth, pp. 222.  6s.  *Bombay*, 1884.

ARMY REGULATIONS (India).  Vol. VII.  Dress.  Royal 8vo. cloth, pp. 162.  7s. 6d.  *Calcutta*, 1886.

ATKINSON (Th. W.) Travels in the regions of the Upper and Lower Amoor and the Russian Acquisitions on the confines of India and China, with a map and numerous illustrations.  8vo. cloth, pp. 13, 570 (pub. £2 2s.)  12s.6d. *London*, 1860.

AUDSLEY (George A.) and James L. BOWES.  Keramic Art of Japan.  4to. cloth, pp. xii. 304.  *London*, 1881.
Containing 31 plates, some of them being beautifully coloured.

BALFOUR (E.) Cyclopædia of India and of Eastern and Southern Asia, Commercial, Industrial and Scientific ; Products of the Mineral, Vegetable and Animal Kingdoms, Useful Arts and Manufactures, with Supplement, 2 vols. together 3 vols.  Royal 8vo. half bound, pp. iv. 2054, 730, and viii. 837.  £2 10s.  *Madras*, 1857–62.

BHAGAVAD - GITA (The) ; or, a Discourse between Krishna and Arjuna on Divine Matters.  A Sanskrit Philosophical Poem, translated, with copious notes, an Introduction on Sanskrit Philosophy, and other matter, by J. Cockburn Thomson.  Royal 8vo. cloth, pp. cxxxviii. 158. £1 8s.  *Hertford*, 1855.
Large Paper copy of this well-known translation.  Out of print and scarce.

BIDDULPH (Major J.) Tribes of the Hindoo Koosh.  Royal 8vo. cloth, pp. 164, clxix. with Plates, Tables, and one Map.  15s.  *Calcutta*, 1880.

BLANFORD (W. T.) Observations on the Geology and Zoology of Abyssinia, made during the Progress of the British Expedition to that country in 1867–68, with Illustrations and Geological Map.  8vo. cloth, pp. xii. 487. 12s. 6d.  *London*, 1870.

BOWES (James Lord) Japanese Marks and Seals.  4to. cloth, pp. xii. 379, with Map and Illustrations.  £1 4s. *London*, 1882.
Part I. Pottery.  II. Illuminated MSS. and Printed Books. III. Lacquer, Enamels, Metal, Wood, Ivory, etc.

BRAUNS (D., Ph.D., M.D.) Geology of the Environs of Tokio.  Royal 8vo. sewed, pp. vii. 82, with a Map and 6 Plates.  15s.  *Tokio*, 1881.
Memoirs of the Science Department, Tokio Diagaku, No. 4.

## BOOKS ON INDIA.—*continued.*

BROWN (Alex.) Coffee Planter's Manual. 8vo. pp. xvi. 242. 6*s.* *Colombo,* 1880.

BURGESS (T.) Rock Temples of Elephanta or Ghârâpurî, with Illustrations. Royal 8vo. cloth, pp. 80. 6*s.* *Bombay,* 1871.

—— the same, with 13 Photographs. 20*s.*

BURGESS (F.) Notes on the Amarâvati Stupa. 4to. sewed, pp. 57, with 17 Plates (*Archæological Survey of Southern India, No.* 3). 12*s.* 6*d.* *Madras,* 1882.

CHERAGH ALI (Moulavi) Proposed Political, Legal, and Social Reforms in the Ottoman Empire and other Mohammadan States. Royal 8vo. cloth, pp. xiv. xl. 183. 6*s.* *Bombay,* 1883.

CHRYSANTHEMUM. Monthly Magazine for Japan and the Far East. Vol. II. January to December, 1882. 8vo. cloth, pp. 576, with Plates. 12*s.* 6*d.* *Yokohama,* 1882.

CLOUSTON (W. A.) Group of Eastern Romances and Stories, from the Persian, Tamil, and Urdu, with Introduction, Notes, and Appendix. 8vo. pp. xl. 586. 12*s.* 6*d.* 1889.

"COCOANUT PALM" (All about the), including Practical Instructions for Planting and Cultivating. 8vo. cloth, pp. 235. 5*s.* *Colombo,* 1885.

CORDIER (H.) Narrative of the Recent Events in Tong-King. 8vo. pp. 74. 6*s.* *Shanghai,* 1875.

CORDINER (Rev. James) A Description of Ceylon, containing an Account of the Country, Inhabitants, and Natural Productions. 2 vols. 4to. half-bound, with 25 Engravings. £2 2*s.* *London,* 1807.
　　This important work has become very scarce.

DA CUNHA (J. Gerson) Notes on the History and Antiquities of Chaul and Bassein, with 17 Photographs, 9 Lithographic Plates, and a Map. 8vo. cloth, pp. xvi. 262. £1 5*s.* *Bombay,* 1876.

—— Contributions to the Study of Indo-Portuguese Numismatics. 4 fasc. sewed, pp. 125, with 9 Plates. 10*s.* *Bombay,* 1883.

DA FONSECA (José Nicolau) Historical and Archæological Sketch of the City of Goa, preceded by a Short Statistical Account of the Territory of Goa, with Map, Plan, and Lithographic Plates. 8vo. cloth, pp. xi. 332. 10*s.* 6*d.* *Bombay,* 1878.

DAS (Abhay Charan) The Indian Ryot, Land Tax, Permanent Settlement, and the Famine. 8vo. cloth, pp. 661. 12*s.* *Howrah (India),* 1881.

DASS (Rev. Ishuree) Domestic Manners and Customs of the Hindoos of Northern India, or more strictly speaking, of the North-West Provinces of India. Second edition. 12mo. cloth, pp. xi. and 280. 7*s.* 6*d.* *Benares,* 1866.

DOWNING (C. T.) The Fanqui in China in 1836-7. 3 vols. 8vo. cloth, pp. 316, 306, and 327, with 3 plates. 7*s.* 6*d.* *London,* 1838.

DUTHIE (J. F.) Illustrations of the Indigenous Fodder Grasses of the Plains of North-Western India, 2 parts, 80 plates. 4to. £2 2*s.* *Roorkee,* 1886-87.

—— The same, letterpress. 8vo. pp. xxiv. 90, vii. with 6 plates. 10*s.* 6*d.* *Roorkee,* 1888.

DUTT (Râmesh Chunder) Peasantry of Bengal. 8vo. cloth, pp. xi. 237. 6*s.* *Calcutta,* 1864.

FALLON (S. W.) New Hindustani-English Dictionary, with Illustrations from Hindustani Literature and Folk-Lore. Royal 8vo. cloth, pp. xxiv. and 1216. £3 10*s.* *Benares,* 1879.

—— A New English-Hindustani Dictionary, with Illustrations from English Literature and Colloquial English translated into Hindustani. Royal 8vo. pp. 674. £1 10*s.* *Benares,* 1880-83.
　　Fallon's Hindustani Dictionaries are the best in existence. The Hindustani in the Hindustani-English part is printed in the Arabic and Devanagari, and well as in the Roman characters.

FERGUSON (J.) Ceylon in the "Jubilee Year." With an Account of the Progress made since 1803, and of the Present Condition of its Agricultural and Commercial Enterprises, etc., etc. With much useful statistical information, specially prepared maps, and numerous illustrations. Third edition. 8vo. cloth, pp. xiv. 427. 7*s.* 6*d.* *Colombo,* 1887.
　　Very useful book for capitalists and visitors, and all people interested in Ceylon and its cultivation.

FERGUSON (A. M., and J.) All about Tobacco, including practical instructions for planting, cultivation, and curing of the leaf, with other suitable information, from a variety of sources referring to the industry in Ceylon, South India, Sumatra, Virginia and the West Indies. Royal 8vo. cloth, pp. viii. 303, ix. 7*s.* 6*d.* *Colombo,* 1889.

FERGUSON (W.) Description of the Palmyra Palm of Ceylon. Royal 8vo. pp. ii. 39, with Illustrations. 6*s.* *Colombo,* 1888.

FERGUSSON (J.) and JAMES BURGESS. Cave Temples of India. Royal 8vo. with Map, numerous Illustrations, and 98 Plates, pp. xx. 536, half bound. £2 2*s.* *London,* 1880.

FIRDAUSI. THE SHÁH NÁMEH of the Persian poet Firdausi, translated and abridged in prose and verse, with notes and illustrations, by James Atkinson. Royal 8vo. cloth, pp. xxxi. 608. £3 10*s.* *London,* 1832.
　　This best translation of this well-known Persian work is very scarce.

FRITSCHE (Dr. H.) Climate of Eastern Asia (Journal of the North China Branch of the Royal Asiatic Society, New Series, No. XII.). 8vo. with 18 Plates, pp. 108. 10*s.* 6*d.* *Shanghai,* 1878.

GASTRELL (J. E.) and H. F. BLANFORD. Report on the Calcutta Cyclone of the 5th October, 1864, with 7 Plates. 8vo. cloth, pp. v. 150, xxv. 7*s.* 6*d.* *Calcutta,* 1866.

GEOGHEGAN (J.) Some Account of Silk in India, especially of the various attempts to encourage and extend Sericulture in that country. Small folio, pp. xv. 126 and 15. 7*s.* 6*d.* *Calcutta,* 1872.

GHOSE (L. N.) The Modern History of the Indian Chiefs, Rajas, Zamindars, etc. Part I.—The Native States, etc., etc. Part II.—The Native Aristocracy and Gentry, etc., etc. 2 vols. 8vo. cloth, pp. vii. 217—ix. 611. 15*s.* *Calcutta,* 1879-81.

GHOSE (Nagendra Nath) Kristo Das Pal : a Study. 8vo. cloth, pp. 202. 6*s.* *Calcutta,* 1817.

GHOSHA (Prata Pachandra) Durga Puja ; with Notes and Illustrations. 8vo. boards, pp. xxii. 83, lxx. 7*s.* 6*d.* *Calcutta,* 1871.
　　A very interesting book on this national Festival of the Hindus of Bengal.

GINGELL (W. R.) The Ceremonial Usages of the Chinese B.C. 1121 as prescribed in the "Institutes of the Chow Dynasty strung as Pearls," or Chow-Le-Kwan-Choo. Translated from the Chinese, with notes. 4to. cloth, pp. iv. and 116. 6*s.* *London,* 1852.

GREENLAW (Alex. John) Masonic Lectures, delivered in Open Lodge, Chapter, etc. 8vo. cloth, pp. viii. 244. 18*s.* *Madras,* 1870.

GROSIER (Abbé) A General Description of China. Translated from the French. 2 vols. bound. 8vo. pp. xvi. 582, and viii. 524, with Maps and Plates. 7*s.* 6*d.* *London,* 1780.

HAMILTON (E.) Translation of the Letters of a Hindoo Rajah, written previous to and during the Period of his Residence in England, to which is prefixed a Preliminary Dissertation on the History, Religion, and Manners of the Hindoos. Fifth edition. 2 vols. in 1. 8vo. cloth, pp. lii. 270, 342. 12*s.* 6*d.* *London,* 1811.